OXFORD ENGLISH NOVELS

General Editor: JAMES KINSLEY

CAMILLA

FRANCES BURNEY

CAMILLA

OR

A PICTURE OF YOUTH

Edited with an Introduction by

EDWARD A. BLOOM

and

LILLIAN D. BLOOM

LONDON
OXFORD UNIVERSITY PRESS
NEW YORK   TORONTO
1972

Oxford University Press, Ely House, London W.1

GLASGOW NEW YORK TORONTO MELBOURNE WELLINGTON
CAPE TOWN IBADAN NAIROBI DAR ES SALAAM LUSAKA ADDIS ABABA
DELHI BOMBAY CALCUTTA MADRAS KARACHI LAHORE DACCA
KUALA LUMPUR SINGAPORE HONG KONG TOKYO

ISBN 0 19 255327 5

Introduction, Notes, Bibliography, Chronology
© *Oxford University Press 1972*

PHOTOSET BY BAS PRINTERS LIMITED, WALLOP, HAMPSHIRE
PRINTED IN GREAT BRITAIN AT THE UNIVERSITY PRESS, OXFORD
BY VIVIAN RIDLER, PRINTER TO THE UNIVERSITY

CONTENTS

CAMILLA, OR A PICTURE OF YOUTH

VOLUME I

INTRODUCTION

I

ON 17 July 1786 Fanny Burney became second keeper of the robes to Queen Charlotte. For five years thereafter, in the ceremonial surroundings of the royal household, she felt herself isolated from normal human relationships, and especially from the intimacies of family life. But her unhappiness welled up from more than a sense of alienation. She questioned her strength to confront those responsibilities set for her by Madame Schwellenberg, dresser to Her Majesty, and even by the queen, whose indecisiveness was as exacting as the other's jealousy. During these anxious years, when Fanny Burney was often threatened by loss of self-control, she forced herself to write as a source of discipline. Understandably, her creative attention focused on the tragic. In the late autumn of 1788 the blank verse tragedy *Edwy and Elgiva* was begun, and two years later it was carelessly finished, along with three others that differed from their prototype in heightened melodrama and declamation. By 1791 the novelist, whom Dr. Johnson had once urged to 'fly at the eagle', could no longer find release in composition. She capitulated to a prolonged and undefined illness whose symptoms were eased only when she left the queen's service on 7 July 1791.

The results of those five years were not entirely negative. She developed a lasting affection for the queen and the princesses that was reciprocated; she was granted an annual pension of £100 for the rest of her life; and she brought away 'the skeleton' of *Camilla*, which 'was formed [at Windsor], but nothing was completed'.[1] How the skeleton was fleshed must remain speculative. But it may well have been that as Fanny Burney performed her chores at the royal residences, she recollected an idea tenta-

---

[1] To her father Dr. Charles Burney (5–6 July 1796), in *The Journals and Letters of Fanny Burney (Madame D'Arblay), 1791–1840* (Oxford, 1972–), iii. L. 196. For full citation of this multi-volume work, hereafter designated *JL*, see Select Bibliography.

tively expressed in the earlier *Cecilia*. In her second novel she
had written of the eternal disjunction between the generations:
'the young are rash, and the aged are mercenary; their deliberations are never in concert, their views are scarce ever blended; one
vanquishes, and the other submits.'[1]

Whether this idea was part of conscious thought or not, she
began at odd times between 1786 and 1791 to rough out a related
theme, a few episodes, some dialogue, and character sketches for
what might some day become a novel. There was nothing
systematic about her method. On a scrap of paper she wrote, for
example: 'It is a mistake to suppose the intellect weak in youth,
because the judgment is erroneous.' At another time in a more
detached mood, she scribbled that 'Precaution is not natural to
youth, whose greatest [danger] because greatest weakness is
confidence in its first impulse, which is commonly pleasant
because kind. To be just requires more reflexion; to have foresight, demands more experience.'[2] Whatever she would write—if
indeed she wrote at all—the 'work' was to delineate the conflict
between youth and age, between the vacillation of innocence and
the purposefulness of mature conduct.

As she took hold of the concept with progressive interest and
firmness, Fanny Burney advanced from thematic abstraction,
through scenic particularity, to the concreteness of plot. She
would write of a family and of the way its members—young and
old—reacted to crisis. For example:

A Family brought up in a plain oeconomical, industrious way, all happy,
contented, vigorous, & affectionate.
      Sudden affluence comes to them—
      They are exhilarated
      Some exult—some are even—some gallop on to profusion
      A Sermon on equanimity
      Some grow indolent & insolent
      Suddenly all is lost.
      Reduced to poverty.
      Some humbly sad—some outrageously repining:—some haughtily
hardy—some pettishly impatient—one cheerfully submissive

---

[1] *Cecilia*, ed. Annie Raine Ellis (London, 1882), ii. 42.
[2] Marked 37b, 40b, in a portfolio of fifty-nine scraps of paper containing suggestions for dialogue, etc. for *Camilla* in the Berg Collection of the New York Public
Library. Hereafter these papers will be designated as (Berg) *Scraps*.

A sermon on disappointments.

What of shifts & cramping before seemed nothing, now appear hardships and sorrow.[1]

This is not the precise plot of *Camilla*. But it is one which, when enhanced by the imaginative process, animates the Tyrold family, gives realistic substance to their altering circumstances, and even provides the moral centres—as in the two sermons—for their problems.

Any fictional narrative demands characterization. Fanny Burney had to select the people who moved through the pages of her work, especially those who created tension and conflict. Again, on the blank side of a torn and discarded letter, she sketched a type figure who would emerge finally as one of the antagonists in the novel. For the present he is only Mr. Jocoso, of significant name:

A perpetual joker; saying good and amusing things but never waiting for times & seasons: & therefore, though a man of good Intellect, more wearisome than a fool; by always using every occasion to say a good thing, without attending to anxiety, without listening to Facts, without weighing arguments, without consoling affliction, without caring about reason, & without the smallest attention to the human character, or situations of his Hearers, whom, without meaning it he either wounds or offends at every other word.

Mr. Jocoso becomes a split personality, foreshadowing certain traits of Sir Sedley, who cultivates a merry glibness as he does foppishness. But more importantly, Mr. Jocoso sits for the fully realized portrait of Lionel. Like his stereotype, Lionel is irresponsible, driven on by a naïve need for laughter that

seemed not merely the bent of his humour, but the necessity of his existence: he pursued it at all seasons, he indulged it upon all occasions. With excellent natural parts, he trifled away all improvements; without any ill temper, he spared no one's feelings. Yet, though not radically vicious, nor deliberately malevolent, the egotism which urged him to make his own amusement his first pursuit, sacrificed his best friends and first duties, if they stood in its way.[2]

These were some of the scraps that Fanny Burney carried away from Windsor on 7 July 1791. She felt no urgency to begin shaping them into a novel; with little compunction she apparently

[1] Marked 26b, in (Berg) *Scraps.*
[2] Marked 6b, in (Berg) *Scraps; Camilla*, p. 79.

put them out of sight and out of mind. Within two years, on 28 July 1793, she married Alexandre d'Arblay, an emigré who had found temporary refuge at Juniper Hall in Surrey. She was happier now than she had been for a long time. If she worried at all, it was about a scarcity of money. General d'Arblay had none; she had only her pension—and her talent. Yet she must have remembered what her sister Susan advised her even before the marriage took place. 'For my own part I can only say, & solicit, & urge to my Fanny to *print, print, print!*—Here is a ressource—a certainty of removing present difficulties.'[1]

Fanny Burney's was a practical courage that forced her—even against inclination—to take on the Muses, 'the most skittish ladies living'—the one who pursues 'with Bowls & Daggers' and the other who 'escapes' concealed by a mask. By the time her son Alex was born in December 1794, she had not only disinterred the skeleton but had already begun to think of it as a work of fiction, to give it coherent incidents, a variety of characters, and tonal nuances, all those parts that make for a novel's life and vitality. As early as 10 August, she had reported to her father: 'You spirited me on in all ways, for this week past I have taken *tightly* to the *grand ouvrage.*' She wrote quickly and the number of manuscript pages increased so visibly that she could joke: 'If I go on so a little longer, I doubt not but M. d'Arblay will begin settling where to have a new shelf for arranging it.'[2]

Despite devotion to her husband and later to her child, despite bouts of illness, she was from that first week in August once again the committed novelist. She would work late at night, writing as many as fourteen pages at one sitting. She never considered her effort drudgery; on the contrary, she found it 'delicious to stride on', to create that which would contribute to the well-being of her family. When, after the completion of *Camilla*, she was asked by George III how much time she had given to it, she answered: '*All* my time, sir!—from the period I planned publishing it, I devoted myself to it wholly;—I had no Episode—but a little baby!—My subject grew upon me.'[3]

[1] By Susan Phillips, with a postscript by M. d'Arblay, *JL* (9 June 1793), ii. L. 101.

[2] To Dr. Burney, *JL* (17 May 1793), ii. L. 87; (10 August 1794), iii. L. 149.

[3] To M. d'Arblay, *JL* (3 February 1796), iii. L. 187. For FB's comment to the king, see n. 1.

For all her fluency, she wrote too fast as she near-sightedly peered at the scraps of paper laid out before her, those random jottings written when she did not have to attend the queen. She soon turned out a rough draft of which forty-six folio pages are extant today.[1] They reveal the author's tentative movement through her materials. But what she formulated, she ordered, giving book and chapter numbers to her scribble. In a short time, however, she admitted to herself that she had made a false start, or at least had taken many wrong steps. None of the scenes in the extant portion of the early draft, except the play-acting scene, appear in the printed novel. Ruthlessly she cast them out although she kept the characters whole as she moved them from draft to draft and finally to the published text.

In this early version, probably written late in 1794—just before the birth of Alex—her characterizations are fully formed; only their names undergo change in the next year and a half. There is, for instance, the romantic idealist, a Mr. Ginniston, infatuated with a young lady representative of mindless vanity. Like the later Mr. Melmond, he could not in perceptive moments 'still a secret voice that began whispering: "I fear . . . I fear—I have tied myself for life to a mere beautiful machine!" While she, retreating in deep resentment that she had been exposed, disdainfully muttered "I might just as well have engaged myself to a parish clerk".' Another seminal character is an unnamed Ensign as impetuous as Macdersey and as much addicted to childish rant about honour and duels. Comparably a Miss Hasty will be translated into Miss Dennel, laughter-driven Tybalt into Lionel, Mrs. Lintot (with her 'pharoah' table and Grosvenor Square mansion) into Mrs. Berlinton.

The heroine is at times called Clarinda and at others Ariella. She is as loving and rash as Camilla, given to 'faint screams' and to the delirious sighting of a mysterious 'Form'. Devoted to her parents, she is ever loyal to Leontine, occasionally named Edgar. Before him she would willingly efface herself, if to no avail. 'Yet inferior as I was to him, with what patience, what sweetness did he bear with me! With what delicacy instruct, what softness conciliate, what pain remonstrate! And what might he not have done, had he more fully known his power? To what would I not

---

[1] (British Museum), Barrett, Egerton 3696.

have consented that he had recommended & desired? . . . He was all honour, all truth, all nobleness.'

This early draft suffers from an uncertainty obvious in the excessive use of exclamation marks and rhetorical questions, of monologues and asides more expository than dramatic. Nevertheless, it allowed Fanny Burney to test the technical direction of her novel and, as significantly, to estimate its sales potential. Because she was aesthetically pleased with her first two novels and understood their commercial value, she declined innovation for her third. She became, in effect, self-imitative. Unaware of the artistic trap she was manufacturing for herself and contrary to Burke's earlier advice that her fictional people were 'too numerous', she reported that her 'NEW WORK [was to be] of the same species as Evelina & Cecilia: new *modified*, in being more multifarious in the Characters it brings into action,—but all *wove* into *one*, with a one *Heroine* shining conspicuous through the Group, & that in . . . *the prose Epic style*.' Its over-all design was clear to her from the beginning. She always meant it to be, as she once asserted, '*sketches of Characters & morals, put in action*, not a Romance'.[1]

When she created the major figures in *Evelina* and *Cecilia*, she devised a method of portraiture inseparable from a credible poetics of fiction. Her characters, despite their idealized names, had to meet the requirements of a 'natural and probable human existence', had indeed to dramatize 'the lessons of experience'. They had, in short, to be decent or admirable people who were defective in some quality of thought or behaviour. With reference to *Cecilia*, for example, the novelist wrote: 'I meant in Mrs. Delville to draw a great, but not a perfect character; I meant, on the contrary, to blend upon paper, as I have frequently seen blended in life, noble and rare qualities with striking and incurable defects.'[2] The portrait of Mrs. Delville is unusually grim; for she is denied the ultimate redemption towards which Fanny Burney's significant characters worked and presumably attained.

[1] To Dr. Burney, *JL* (6 July 1795), iii. L.175; (18 June 1795), iii. L. 171. For Burke's concern over the number of characters created by FB, see *The Diary and Letters of Madame D'Arblay*, ed. Charlotte Barrett, with Preface and Notes by Austin Dobson (London, 1904), ii. 92 ff.

[2] For her theory of characterization, see the 'Introduction' to *The Wanderer* (1814); for her intention concerning Mrs. Delville, see *Diary and Letters*, ii. 72.

In her third novel she wanted a heroine who through suffering could discipline indiscriminate goodness with 'precaution'. She wanted a hero cast in the mould of a tutor-husband—like Evelina's Orville—but only after he had learned to temper doubt with trust and affection. She wanted her guardian figures, in this case Mr. and Mrs. Tyrold, to achieve the grace of self-awareness and to acknowledge their own flaws: the first one admitting to parental indulgence and the other to hyper-righteousness. So in 1794 she conceived her major characters, all of whom had been tried and proved earlier. But in the same year she attempted a controlled number of new types—the likeable scapegrace, the spiteful spinster-governess, the villain. These figures made her uneasy and she could only despatch them, whether through exile or death, once they played out their roles as antagonists.

For her '*grand ouvrage*' she needed, as she admitted, 'multifarious' characters, a large number of complementary and contrasting personalities. These she hoped to create by perfecting a formula tried first on the Delvilles in *Cecilia*. 'I merely meant to show how differently pride, like every other quality, operates upon different minds, and that, though it is so odious when joined with meanness and incapacity, as in Mr. Delville, it destroys neither respect nor affection when joined with real dignity and generosity of mind, as in Mrs. Delville.'[1] In 1794 she chose not one but a series of specific character traits for contrapuntal development. Whatever the trait, she illustrated its widely ranging manifestations through several types. Long fascinated by that of levity, she had once identified it as a 'hardener of the heart . . . its self-disguises amuse but beguile the fancy till they deaden all sensation.'[2] Eventually this moral quality would define characters as distinctive from one another as quick Lionel, vapid Indiana, exquisite Sedley, and ill-mannered Clermont. And the fictional utility she attached to levity, Fanny Burney intended for other values that controlled personality, those of calculating selfishness, sentiment, innocence, prudence, and even scholarly dedication.

She also saw her third novel as an amalgam of those themes and tones that she had merged so successfully in the first two. Thus she contemplated scenes of high seriousness 'to make pleasant the path of propriety'. She would ring changes upon them: she

[1] *Diary and Letters*, ii. 154.
[2] Marked 25a, in (Berg) *Scraps*.

would create tense drama as in the mother-daughter conflict; provide moral parentheses in which, for example, a 'slavering' idiot gyrated to prove the inadequacy of mere physical beauty; expound arguments for prudential behaviour through paternal sermons. All that was weighty and grave she chose to alternate with what was light and entertaining. Her comedy, too, would be highly varied: witty interludes as a fop discourses on indolence or a sophisticate on marriage as an 'establishment'; intellectual farce in which *Othello* is acted in dialect and the audience serves as critic; belly-laugh humour when the performers are drawn in slangy or country idiom from 'low' or 'middle' life; sentimental laughter when the aged but lovable Sir Hugh struggles to master 'the classics'. As in *Evelina* and *Cecilia*, the comic scenes had to contribute to a satiric intention, their dialogue revealing the often aimless snobbery of the upper classes, the vulgar greed of the middle station, and the cruel ignorance of the poor.

From the very beginning of composition, Fanny Burney meant *Camilla* (or *Ariella* as she initially conceived the title) to exploit the pathos of 'the tender sympathy'. Because it was axiomatic that 'a crying volume' brought its author more money 'in six months than a heavy merry thing', she permitted herself few stops. She would have her readers weep in sympathy over the heroine's mistakes, in wonder over Eugenia's resignation, in anger over Mr. Tyrold's unwarranted imprisonment. If *Cecilia* made Mrs. Thrale cry herself 'blind over the conclusion . . . 'tis so excessively pathetic', then the third novel must provoke sobs only intermittently stifled.[1]

Finally, Fanny Burney in 1794 intended to manipulate still another reaction—terror. Earlier she had frowned upon Gothicism that makes reason 'an outcast' in fiction; this time, however, she would grasp at its artifices as she wrote her '*Udolphish* volumes'. Fully aware of the selling power of Mrs. Radcliffe's novels, she also wanted to capitalize on fashionable craving for the verbal macabre. She therefore would prolong the description of a bier, its corpse unknown, carried through the sinister woods; she would detail the plight of a heroine seized by near-madness and confronted by spectral 'Forms' at her bedside.

---

[1] For the financial value of the 'tender sympathy' (*Camilla*, p. 845), see Joyce Hemlow, *The History of Fanny Burney* (Oxford, 1958), p. 97. For Mrs. Thrale's reaction, see *Diary and Letters*, ii. 53–4.

It is almost as if in accepting such Gothic elements for her own work, Fanny Burney felt free to abandon one other aesthetic rule that she formerly professed. In 1782, for example, she defended the realism of *Cecilia*'s ending wherein 'the hero and heroine are neither plunged in the depths of misery, nor exalted to UN*human* happiness'. Were it otherwise, she said, she might as well borrow 'the last page of any novel in Mr. Noble's circulating library . . . since a marriage, a reconciliation, and some sudden expedient for great riches, concludes them all alike.'[1] For *Camilla* she meant to borrow that 'last page'—and did with gusto.

When she began the second draft of her 'NEW WORK', the tonal variations, the contrapuntal patterns—if not all the details—of plot and characterization were fixed in her mind.[2]   Again she wrote rapidly and enthusiastically, but this time with critical assurance. She knew she would have to revise, as she had in the past—to alter language and to excise radically—but she now enjoyed a sense of control. Having mastered her materials, she let the words flow. In May 1795, less than a year after she began to write, she told her father that the new book 'will be a great work— I mean in bulk—& very long in hand'. Shortly thereafter, in June and July, she confidently began to think of its publication. The manuscript, its pages mounting in number, represented creative effort, but it was also her '*Brain* work as much fair & individual property, as any other possession in either art or nature'. And she was prepared to fight for what was hers, to secure its maximum value in pounds sterling.[3]

In consultation with her husband, she determined to print the novel by subscription, thereby guaranteeing that 'its sale becomes almost instantly as quick as general'. She appointed as 'bookkeepers' three friends—the Honourable Mrs. Boscawen, Mrs. Crewe, and Mrs. Locke—whose task was to solicit subscriptions from well-born patrons and to keep the lists. Almost at the same time, Fanny Burney, reminded by others 'not to be again . . . the dupe of Booksellers', appointed her brother Charles to serve as agent, to handle potential publishers with 'promised Jewish callousness', and to sell the manuscript without scruple to the 'highest bidder'. In his established role of negotiator, he agreed to abide by a

---

[1] *Diary and Letters*, ii. 81.

[2] The second draft is an incomplete *Camilla* (Berg), *c.* 47 ff., in FB's hand.

[3] L. 175; to Charles Burney, Jr., *JL* (7 July 1795), iii. L. 176.

maxim which he coined and repeated often to his sister. 'What Evelina . . . does now for the Son of Lowndes, & what Cecilia does for the Son of Payne, let your third work do for the Son of its Authour.'[1]

The *Morning Chronicle* for 7 July 1795 made the first public announcement: 'PROPOSALS for printing by Subscription a NEW WORK, in Four Volumes, 12 mo. By the AUTHOR of EVELINA and CECILIA: To be delivered on or before the 1st day of July, 1796. The Subscriptions will be one Guinea; to be paid at the time of Subscribing.' Now Fanny Burney was obliged to concede her private commitment was an open avowal that cut off any retreat. She therefore wrote on to meet a self-imposed deadline.

Even prior to the appearance of the advertisement, her task assumed a new complexity as she herself was torn between the demands of artistic integrity and those of profitable bookmaking. On 6 July 1795 she made her father a promise. 'I will make my Work the best I can . . . I will neither be indolent, nor negligent, nor avaricious. I can never half answer the expectations that seem excited! I must try to forget them, or I shall be in a continual quivering.' Yet one day before, after having long insisted that her great work should not be physically restricted by the computations of booksellers, she confessed to Charles: 'I am now going to work, very reluctantly, to *curtail my* plan, & obviate the threats of loss, or small profit.'[2]

If Fanny Burney could not exorcise the spectre of relentless publishers from her mind, her agent pursued them with practical determination. Early in March 1796 he negotiated successfully with Thomas Payne, at the Mews-Gate, and Cadell and Davies, in the Strand, for the sale of the manuscript. By now his sister had probably finished the second draft of her novel in its entirety. Harassed by the pressure of time, she immediately began her revisions. As she polished and pruned her prose, she turned the completed pages over to General d'Arblay who as an adoring

---

[1] On decision to print by subscription and advice on booksellers, to Charles Burney, Jr., *JL* (5 July 1795), iii. L. 174; L. 176; *JL* (15 July 1795), iii. L. 178. For mention of bookkeepers, to Mrs. Georgiana Waddington (19 June 1795), iii. L. 173. For maxim, to Dr. Burney (15 July 1795), iii. L. 179.

[2] Ll. 175, 174.

suitor had once vowed to be her amanuensis, 'le plus determiné copiste'.[1]

Laboriously he transcribed in the hope that this was the fair copy for Strahan the printer. His hope was delusory, his wife unable to resist the chance to scrawl still further alterations over the meticulously written text.[2] Dutifully, then, he started a new transcription. This time his fair copy remained fair and was sent off in batches to the impatient printers, even while she worked away at the troublesome fifth volume. By mid-June 1796 she crowed to her agent that 'the rest of the Copy of Camilla is dispatched to both the Printers.' Within a few days—on 20 June —she was reading and correcting the first proofs, alphabetizing her subscription lists with a keen eye for protocol and title.[3]

She suspended her 'own favourite intention & desire' when she acceded to familial urging and sold the copyright of *Camilla* to Payne, Cadell and Davies for £1,000. On 6 July the booksellers recorded their acquisition in the Stationers Register. Within the week the *Morning Chronicle* advertised the publication of *Camilla* 'in five vols. price one guinea, sewed, dedicated by permission to the Queen'. The first edition of the novel was distributed, set up for display in bookstalls and circulating libraries. This, characteristically, was a time of dread for Fanny Burney. She distrusted her idleness, so unnatural after a long and strenuous effort. More particularly, ever since the publication of *Evelina*, she feared the invasion of privacy that came with public notice and the inevitable reviews in which she might well 'be horribly mauled'.[4]

The reviews came swiftly: the first one appeared in the *English Review* for August 1796 and the last one in the *Monthly Magazine and British Register* for January 1797. Despite Dr. Burney's efforts to 'fix' favourable notices of *Camilla*, the reactions of the critics were as mixed as those of private readers. If Jane Austen found the novel worthy, Horace Walpole was figuratively sickened by it.

---

[1] On novel's sale, written conjointly with M. d'Arblay, to Charles Burney, Jr., *JL* (14 March 1796), iii. L. 190. For M. d'Arblay's vow, to FB (16 June 1793), ii. L. 110.

[2] An incomplete *Camilla* (Berg) *c.* 685 ff., in M. d'Arblay's hand.

[3] To Charles Burney, Jr., *JL* (17 June 1796), iii. L. 193; to Sarah (Rose) Burney (20 June 1796), iii. L. 194.

[4] She acknowledged her decision to sell *Camilla*'s copyright to Dr. Burney, L. 179. For FB's fear of reviewers, see (Berg), Diary MSS. 647.

'I have not', he told Mary Berry on 16 August, 'recovered of it
enough to be loud in its praise. I am glad however to hear that
she has realized about £2000—and the worth (no doubt) of as
much in honours at Windsor, where she was detained three days
and where even Monsieur Darbelay was allowed to dine.'[1]

More typical of critical comment was that by the *Monthly
Review*'s William Enfield and Ralph Griffiths—the latter a close
friend of the novelist's father. In their statement they approved
the novel's 'highly animated scenes of life and manners' by which
the plot was brought forward; 'the rich and varied groups of
characters'; and the general structure or 'succession of painful and
delightful images', all of which 'must deeply interest the feeling
heart'. Not silent about what they found meritorious, the reviewers
also denounced the inordinate length of the novel and un-
charitably illustrated inconsistencies in characterization, flaws in
grammar and diction, redundancies, and even Gallicisms.[2]

When the elder Charles Burney read their remarks, he felt
personally betrayed, suspected their malicious intention, and
allowed his fury to erupt. 'J'enrage! Morbleu! . . . there is praise,
& now & then handsome praise; but it seems given designedly
with a sparing hand; though the strictures are numerous, & often
severe and unfair.' His daughter, however, after 'the panic of a
first survey', could temper her disappointment with a knowledge
of *Camilla*'s financial success. 'I have not', she said to a friend,
'any great philosophy to boast in sustaining heroically partial
censors, while the Public reception is beyond all possible expectation. The sale has been one of the most rapid ever known for a
Guinea Book: it is 4 times that of Evelina, & nearly double that of
Cecilia. Of the First Edition, containing the immense quantity of
4000, 500 only remain: & it has been printed but 3 Months.'
Indeed, the number of *Camilla*'s sales moved the author to
poetize for her father.

> Now heed no more what Critics thought 'em
> Since this you know—All People bought 'em.

[1] *Jane Austen's Letters to her Sister Cassandra and Others*, ed. R. W. Chapman,
2nd ed. (Oxford, 1952), p. 14; *Horace Walpole's Correspondence*, ed. W. S. Lewis
and A. Dayle Wallace (London and New Haven, 1944), xii. 204. For FB's account
of her stay at Windsor, see *Windsoriana*, *JL*, iii. especially Ll. 195–99.
[2] xxi (October 1796), 156–63.

Translating her exultant jingle into prudent action, she used part of the novel's earnings to build Camilla Cottage. This she and the General revered as their home and their 'bambino's' future portion.

II

Warned by the booksellers of a possible new edition of *Camilla* within five months of initial publication, Fanny Burney was prepared to take on a task that demanded disquieting self-examination. For all her insistence that the reviews would not 'mar' her, she obviously smarted from their censure. Yet she had to admit—if only to herself—that the book was sometimes mawkish, its melodramatic passages too many, and its moral dicta prolonged beyond narrative limits. In fact, she was forced to the humiliating confession that its language was often imprecise and ungrammatical. She therefore urged her father to find a tutor able to discipline *Camilla*. He chose a kindly and learned friend, the Reverend Thomas Twining, often referred to admiringly by Fanny Burney as Aristotelian Twining. When she learned the identity of the novel's tutor, she felt relieved. 'Tell dear Mr. Tw[ining]', she wrote to Dr. Burney, 'I shall receive most gratefully his strictures, & beg them with all the speed his leisure will allow. I am proud *HE* thinks the work *worth flaggelating*.' On 1 July 1797 four folio sheets of strictures arrived and the novelist in the following spring could report to her brother Charles 'several corrections for the new Edition & not a little curtailing here & there'. She urged, indeed, that he not allow a second edition to go forward until her 'prepared' copy was incorporated.[2]

The booksellers, however, had plans of their own, and for the time at least were more concerned with disposing of the initial printing than with publishing a new edition, whose history for the author was to be one of frustration and misunderstanding. Not until about 4 April 1799 did the long-awaited invitation

---

[1] For Dr. Burney's angry expostulation, see (Berg), Diary MSS. 4938–40. For FB's reaction, to Mrs. Waddington, *JL* (2 October–11 November 1796), iii. L. 213; and her jingle (14 October 1796), iii. L. 204.

[2] *JL* (26 February 1797), iii. L. 226; for some of Mr. Twining's detailed comments, see 'Fanny Burney's Revisions of *Camilla*'. See also *JL* (18 March 1798), iv. L. 274.

arrive, and then under such circumstances as to preclude completion of the full-scale revision. As she wrote to her sister Susan ten days later: 'I am now just applied to, at last, for my preparations for a 2^d Edition of Camilla: & I am engaged almost day & night in a revision . . . . But the Work is so long, & the people, waiting to the last moment for the application, are now in such haste, that I am obliged to relinquish every thing for proceeding with the business.' Despite annoyance and customary distrust of her booksellers, she began to think with satisfaction not only of '*honour & glory*' but of the settlement of debts—advertisements, extra sets of the novels, proposals, etc.—that were 'to be deducted from the last payment of the Copyright, . . . not due till the 2^d Edition is printed'. To be sure, she had been obliged to put aside the elaborate 'prepared' revisions in favour of copy—probably a marked-up first edition—so hurriedly 'amended' as to be sent off by 20 April; that is, within a grace period of about two weeks.[1]

Only later was she to learn that the booksellers had not been sufficiently pleased with her emendations to undertake a second edition and that, consequently, she was far from having 'done with the revision'. Through the summer and autumn of 1799, in any event, she was able to enjoy her self-delusion, devoting herself to family affairs and to a hopeful concern for the production of her comedy *Love and Fashion*. Delusion gave way to the terrifying reality of Susan's illness; and when this idolized sister died on 6 January 1800, Fanny Burney, inconsolable, entered into a prolonged melancholy which paralyzed her will to write. She could, however, count on Charles to look after her interests, and this he did with characteristic forthrightness when he requested 'the favour of being informed by Messrs Cadell Junr & Davies, what he is to understand by their advertisement in *The Times* of [5 February 1800], which announces *a new Edition* of Camilla for Sale.' Within a day, on the verso of his letter, Cadell and Davies tartly replied: 'After so repeatedly charging us with wilfully omitting to advertise "Camilla" do not now blame us for inserting it in our List of Novels, with a View to getting rid of the Remainder of our Impression. You will not, we trust, think us capable of putting a new Edition to the Press, without previously informing you or M.^{rs} D'Arblay.'[2]

[1] *JL*, iv. L. 314; to Charlotte Broome, *JL* (22 April 1799), iv. L. 316.
[2] Pierpont Morgan Library (MA 1546).

Shortly after this exchange, we surmise, the stock of the deliberately mislabelled edition had been reduced enough to bring agent and booksellers to mutual agreement for a second edition such as Fanny Burney had been planning. But she continued to be gripped by sorrow and depression, far too distraught for even the practical benefits of a new *Camilla*. In March 1800, hence, she had 'not yet begun *Sir Hugh*', and throughout the remainder of the spring and summer she persistently, candidly admitted that she was creatively inert. Even letter-writing provoked associations which were 'anguish' for her 'disordered mind and spirits'. In June, if she mended at all, it was 'SLOWLY! SLOWLY!'. During the autumn, however, she was again in command of herself; so productive had she been that she could anxiously inquire of Charles on 18 November about the disposition of the wholly revised manuscript she had sent him. This, doubtless, was the interrupted 'prepared' text begun in the spring of 1798. She confided to her brother that she had 'laboured very seriously in its preparation, & inserted all the amendments, verbal, of Mr. Twining, & all the Reviews, besides whatever [she] could devise to Abridge & ameliorate the whole.' About one week later Charles reassured her with the information that all was well with the publishers, that financial arrangements had been concluded. And yet the unhappy saga of the 1802 *Camilla* was not ended.[1]

Almost certainly Fanny Burney expected the new edition to appear by the summer of the following year. On 28 October 1801, for example, M. d'Arblay, visiting in London, reported to his wife that he saw a copy of *Camilla* displayed in a bookshop window. Eager to determine whether this was the revised work, he was about to enter the shop, but just then an acquaintance, like Coleridge's man from Porlock, distracted the general from his mission. At best, however, he could only have suffered disappointment, for the second edition did not appear until 1802 and with a fanfare no more resounding than a modest advertisement in *The Times* of 6 February. By then he and his wife and child were in France; within a year they were cut off from easy communication with England because of the resumption of fighting between the two countries.

[1] To Charles Burney, Jr., *JL* (4 March 1800), iv. L. 369; to Esther Burney, *JL* (13 June 1800), iv. L. 379; to Charles Burney, Jr., *JL* (18 November 1800), iv. L. 397 and (27 November 1800), iv. L. 398.

For ten years they heard nothing; but by 1812 word of the second edition had reached Paris. M. d'Arblay became incensed over the alleged malpractice of the booksellers. In a volatile if quaintly expressed letter to his brother-in-law, he insisted that 'as the legitern depositor of the rights of [his] wife', he owned the novel and its copyright. He grew even more specific in his complaint when he accused Payne, Cadell and Davies of having 'since made a second edition of Camilla without even speaking to the author of that 2^d edition, clandestinely printed in such a manner as to be desabled of making use of the pretty numerous corrections given to them for that 2^d edition already done'. What finally convinced him of the publishers' criminal intent was their refusal to offer 'a single copy of that edition to the Author'.[1] The ways of the English had always confused Fanny Burney's husband and were to do so for the rest of his life. But never was he more confused than at this moment.

The actual reasons for his quarrel with the booksellers may well remain a mystery, though it is likely that his strong reaction was generated more by passion than fact. There is a remote possibility that he forgot the copyright was legally out of his hands or that his wife, often secretive about financial transactions, had not made clear to him the meaning of copyright transfer. Moreover, he had never seen the 1802 *Camilla*. If he had, he would have realized that the book had not been 'clandestinely printed'. The booksellers had not only used the title page to announce 'a new edition' but they incorporated into the text all of Fanny Burney's alterations—those suggested by her own critical sense, those recommended by Thomas Twining and even by hostile reviewers. Payne, Cadell and Davies were guilty of nothing more heinous than a failure in polite communication and generosity.

III

Seemingly, M. d'Arblay abandoned hope for *Camilla* after 1812. Not so did his wife. Despite the sale of copyright, the novel was morally and artistically hers. After all, she wrote it, went through the ordeal of printing it by subscription, waited out the demand for a second edition, and revised it so that it was a better book in 1802 than in 1796. This she did so that its profits, whether invested

[1] Written on 20 July 1812: John Comyn Collection.

in Camilla Cottage or in negotiable securities, might become her son's inheritance. When in 1814, she was forced to sell the cottage at a loss, she accused herself of depriving Alex of what was rightly his. More than ever she sought to protect him financially from his own innocence and a 'world of which he so little knew how to combat the ways and arts'.[1]

She therefore bided her time; and shortly before *Camilla*'s copyright ran out for Payne, Cadell and Davies in 1824, she began to think of a third edition. In a letter to Richard Bentley on 4 November 1835, she intimated a tireless dedication to the novel, which fascinated and frightened her, very much like a child unable to fulfill a natural potential. 'I have long since employed myself occasionally in revising Camilla, as it has been out of print for many years, & has been demanded of me; though, as it is not ready, I have hitherto declined entering into any species of negotiation about it.'[2]

From the two hundred and twenty extant scraps of paper on which she made her revisions, it is possible to approximate the way in which she went about preparing this third edition.[3] Open on the table before her was the 1796 *Camilla* as her working copy. But alongside it was the 1802 text, many of whose changes she approved and so borrowed for the projected new edition. Her writing paper consisted of the blank areas of copybook pages covered with Alex's algebraic equations or of letters whose postmarks span the years between 1819 and 1836. On these bits she made her changes, citing from the first edition volume and page numbers and often cue words. The revisions themselves are startling, far more typical of the young Burney who reworked *Cecilia* than the middle-aged Mme. d'Arblay who altered *Camilla* between 1798 and 1800. They show no diminution in power, either intellectual or imaginative. They reveal that she cut with sensitive determination, eliminating much of the sentimental and many of the Gothic details. Because M. d'Arblay was dead and could no longer take offense, she deleted still more of the innumerable Gallicisms to which the *Monthly Review*—and even friends like Hester Chapone—had taken exception.

Sometime in 1836 she finished her revisions. The scraps and

---

[1] (Berg), to Charlotte Broome (31 March–11 April 1837).

[2] In possession of the Houghton Library, Harvard University.

[3] (Berg), Sheets and Slips for a revised *Camilla*.

slips of paper on which she wrote indicate that she had started with the first volume, methodically moved through the next three, and scrupulously edited all of the fifth and final volume. She needed only to transcribe the materials for the printer, an arduous task even if she could find a copyist. Yet she was ready—at the age of eighty-four—to make this last effort for her son, now so morbidly apathetic that he was unmindful of his religious vocation, his mother, and his own survival.

In the last few months of 1836 Fanny Burney knew that no further exertion was required of her. Alex, touched by a premonition, likened himself to 'the bark . . . now launched against wind and tide'. Never again would he fight for anything even as significant as a problem in chess and algebra. On 19 January 1837 he died alone. For his mother, who now suffered only her controlled anguish, all work on a new edition of *Camilla* became a reproach, a reminder that she was unable to protect her most 'darling loved, and most touchingly loving, dear, soul-dear Alex'.[1]

In 1840, indeed, the year of Fanny Burney's death, *Camilla* again made an appearance, under the London imprint of Joseph Thomas. But it was a depressing return for the work of so famous an author, and had she lived to see it she would have enjoyed neither pleasure nor profit. *Camilla* was brought back as a shabby replica of the 1796 edition, cheaply printed in three volumes and indifferent to all the laborious changes which had been contrived over a period of some forty years. By now the novel was in the public domain, the property of any calculating bookseller who chose to turn it to quick advantage. But Fanny Burney was beyond nostalgia and regret. For too long she had watched over this creation of hers with jealous fidelity but—like Alex himself—it had finally slipped beyond her care.

[1] *Diary and Letters*, vi. 415.

ACKNOWLEDGEMENTS

WHILE preparing this edition, we used the printed materials and the manuscript resources of the Brown University Library, the British Museum, the Bodley, the Houghton Library of Harvard University, the Pierpont Morgan Library, and the Henry W. and Albert A. Berg Collection of the New York Public Library, Astor, Lenox, and Tilden Foundations. We are grateful to these institutions and to their courteous and efficient staffs. Particular thanks are due to Mrs. Charles Szladits and the other officials of the New York Public Library for permission to quote from the Burney manuscripts that are part of the Berg Collection.

As always, we are indebted to Professor Joyce Hemlow who has given to us unstintingly of her friendship and vast knowledge of Fanny Burney.

E. A. B.
L. D. B.

NOTE ON THE TEXT

THIS text is a reproduction of the first edition of *Camilla* published on 12 July 1796, and it has been set from the copy in the British Museum. Obvious misprints and spelling errors have been silently changed; the long 's' has been modernized. Grammatical inaccuracies have also been corrected where Fanny Burney herself made the changes for the edition of 1802. These emendations and clearly omitted words have been placed within brackets in the present text. Certain spelling inconsistencies have been left untouched as long as they conform to acceptable eighteenth-century usage. The reason for these inconsistencies is virtually foreshadowed by a sentence in a letter from Fanny Burney to her brother Charles on 17 June 1796: 'The whole Copy we have sent to the two Printers this dear & blessed morning.' The *Camilla* manuscript was in all likelihood not printed in Andrew Strahan's shop but jobbed by him. We conjecture that he assigned portions of the manuscript to two compositors who worked independently of each other and, in the casual manner of the time which made no provision for a house style, satisfied their own notions of spelling. Apparently, then, Strahan did not supervise the actual printing, but saw the sheets only after they had been delivered to him from separate presses. While it is true that Fanny Burney did the proof-reading and took pride in the fact, she was hurried and not unaware that Strahan charged his authors for all changes defined as 'Extraordinary Correction'. If the novelist worried about these alternate spellings of individual words, she was not so perturbed that she wished to do anything about them.

EDITIONS

During Fanny Burney's lifetime there were in England only two editions of *Camilla*, each consisting of five duodecimo volumes. The first edition appeared in 1796; the second, drastically altered, in

1802. Both authorized versions were produced by Andrew Strahan in London for Payne, Cadell and Davies. Before the second edition, however, several unauthorized printings were issued in Ireland, the United States, and on the Continent. The Dublin bookseller G. Burnett produced a three-volume *Camilla* in 1796. The following year marked a period of exceptional American popularity for the novel, if we may accept the evidence of four editions: one, in three volumes, under the Boston imprint of S. Hall, W. Spotswood (etc.); two in New York City—five volumes each—from the presses of S. Campbell and John Bull; and one of three volumes, printed in Philadelphia by Ormond and Conrad for the Baltimore firm of Birdsall and Wynard. A Parisian publishing house, identified as Maradan Libraire, brought out in 1798 two separate editions of a five-volume abridgement, *Camilla, ou la Peinture de la Jeunesse*. In the same year Friedrich Nicholai published in Berlin and Stettin a four-volume, illustrated *Kamilla oder ein Gemälde der Jugend; . . . Mit einer Vorrede von D. Johann Reinhold Forster*. In 1840, the year of the novelist's death, Joseph Thomas in London issued an inexpensive reprint of the 1796 edition, this time in three compressed volumes.

SELECT BIBLIOGRAPHY

Boswell's Life of Johnson, ed. G. B. HILL and L. F. POWELL. Oxford, 1934, 1950.

The Early Diary of Frances Burney, 1768–1778, ed. ANNIE RAINE ELLIS. London, 1907.

The Diary and Letters of Madame d'Arblay, ed. CHARLOTTE BARRETT, with Preface and Notes by Austin Dobson. London, 1904.

The Journals and Letters of Fanny Burney (Madame D'Arblay), 1791–1840. Oxford, 1972–. vol. ii, ed. Joyce Hemlow and Althea Douglas; vol. iii, ed. Joyce Hemlow, with Patricia Boutilier and Althea Douglas; vol. iv, ed. Joyce Hemlow.

MADAME D'ARBLAY, *Memoirs of Doctor Burney*. London, 1832.

LORD DAVID CECIL, 'Fanny Burney's Novels', in *Essays on the Eighteenth Century Presented to D. Nichol Smith*. Oxford, 1945.

JAMES L. CLIFFORD, *Hester Lynch Piozzi*. Oxford, 1941.

JOYCE HEMLOW, *The History of Fanny Burney*. Oxford, 1958.

JOYCE HEMLOW, 'Fanny Burney and the Courtesy Books', *PMLA*, lxv (1950), 732–61.

The Letters of Samuel Johnson, ed. R. W. Chapman. Oxford, 1952.

ROGER LONSDALE, *Dr. Charles Burney: A Literary Biography*. Oxford, 1965.

PERCY A. SCHOLES, *The Great Dr. Burney*. London, 1948.

Thraliana, ed. Katherine C. Balderston. Oxford, 1942.

CHAUNCEY BREWSTER TINKER, *Dr. Johnson and Fanny Burney*. New York, 1911.

A CHRONOLOGY OF
FRANCES BURNEY

CAMILLA:

OR,

A PICTURE OF YOUTH

BY

THE AUTHOR OF

EVELINA AND *CECILIA*

QUEEN[1]

MADAM,

THAT Goodness inspires a confidence, which, by divesting respect of terror, excites attachment to Greatness, the presentation of this little Work to Your Majesty must truly, however humbly, evince; and though a public manifestation of duty and regard from an obscure Individual may betray a proud ambition, it is, I trust, but a venial—I am sure it is a natural one.

In those to whom Your Majesty is known but by exaltation of Rank, it may raise, perhaps, some surprise, that scenes, characters, and incidents, which have reference only to common life, should be brought into so august a presence; but the inhabitant of a retired cottage,[2] who there receives the benign permission which at Your Majesty's feet casts this humble offering, bears in mind recollections which must live there while 'memory holds its seat,'[3] of a benevolence withheld from no condition, and delighting in all ways to speed the progress of Morality, through whatever channel it could flow, to whatever port it might steer. I blush at the inference I seem here to leave open of annexing undue importance to a production of apparently so light a kind— yet if my hope, my view—however fallacious they may eventually prove, extended not beyond whiling away an idle hour, should I dare seek such patronage?

With the deepest gratitude, and most heart-felt respect, I am,

MADAM,

Your MAJESTY'S

Most obedient, most obliged,
And most dutiful servant,

F. d'ARBLAY.

BOOKHAM,
June 28, 1796

ADVERTISEMENT

THE Author of this little Work cannot, in the anxious moment of committing it to its fate, refuse herself the indulgence of expressing some portion of the gratitude with which she is filled, by the highly favourable reception given to her *TWO* former attempts in this species of composition;[1] nor forbear pouring forth her thanks to the many Friends whose kind zeal has forwarded the present undertaking:— from amongst whom she knows not how to resist selecting and gratifying herself by naming the Hon. Mrs. BOSCAWEN, Mrs. CREWE, and Mrs. LOCKE.[2]

VOLUME I

===

THE historian of human life finds less of difficulty and of intricacy to develop, in its accidents and adventures, than the investigator of the human heart in its feelings and its changes. In vain may Fortune wave her many-coloured banner, alternately regaling and dismaying, with hues that seem glowing with all the creation's felicities, or with tints that appear stained with ingredients of unmixt horrors; her most rapid vicissitudes, her most unassimilating eccentricities, are mocked, laughed at, and distanced by the wilder wonders of the Heart of man; that amazing assemblage of all possible contrarieties, in which one thing alone is steady—the perverseness of spirit which grafts desire on what is denied. Its qualities are indefinable, its resources unfathomable, its weaknesses indefensible. In our neighbours we cannot judge, in ourselves we dare not trust it. We lose ere we learn to appreciate, and ere we can comprehend it we must be born again.[1] Its capacity o'er-leaps all limit, while its futility includes every absurdity. It lives its own surprise—it ceases to beat—and the void is inscrutable! In one grand and general view, who can display such a portrait? Fairly, however faintly, to delineate some of its features, is the sole and discriminate province of the pen which would trace nature, yet blot out personality.[2]

CHAPTER I

A Family Scene

REPOSE is not more welcome to the worn and to the aged, to the sick and to the unhappy, than danger, difficulty, and toil to the young and adventurous. Danger they encounter but as the fore-runner of success; difficulty, as the spur of ingenuity; and toil, as the herald of honour. The experience which teaches the lesson of truth, and the blessings of tranquillity, comes not in the shape of warning nor of wisdom; from such they turn aside, defying or disbelieving. 'Tis in the bitterness of personal proof alone, in suffering and in feeling, in erring and in repenting, that experience comes home with conviction, or impresses to any use.

In the bosom of her respectable family resided Camilla.[1] Nature, with a bounty the most profuse, had been lavish to her of attractions; Fortune, with a moderation yet kinder, had placed her between luxury and indigence.[2] Her abode was in the parsonage-house of Etherington, beautifully situated in the unequal county of Hampshire, and in the vicinity of the varied landscapes of the New Forest.[3] Her father, the rector, was the younger son of the house of Tyrold.[4] The living, though not considerable, enabled its incumbent to attain every rational object of his modest and circumscribed wishes; to bestow upon a deserving wife whatever her own forbearance declined not; and to educate a lovely race of one son and three daughters, with that expansive propriety, which unites improvement for the future with present enjoyment.

In goodness of heart, and in principles of piety, this exemplary couple was bound to each other by the most perfect unison of character, though in their tempers there was a contrast which had scarce the gradation of a single shade to smooth off its abrupt dissimilitude. Mr. Tyrold, gentle with wisdom, and benign in virtue, saw with compassion all imperfections but his own, and there doubled the severity which to others he spared. Yet the mildness that urged him to pity blinded him not to approve; his equity was unerring, though his judgment was indulgent. His partner had a firmness of mind which nothing could shake: calamity found her resolute; even prosperity was powerless to lull her duties asleep. The exalted character of her husband was the pride of her existence, and the source of her happiness. He was not merely her standard of excellence, but of endurance, since her sense of his worth was the criterion for her opinion of all others. This instigated a spirit of comparison, which is almost always uncandid, and which here could rarely escape proving injurious. Such, at its very best, is the unskilfulness of our fallible nature, that even the noble principle which impels our love of right, misleads us but into new deviations, when its ambition presumes to point at perfection. In this instance, however, distinctness of disposition stifled not reciprocity of affection—that magnetic concentration of all marriage felicity;—Mr. Tyrold revered while he softened the rigid virtues of his wife, who adored while she fortified the melting humanity of her husband.   .

Thus, in an interchange of happiness the most deserved, and of parental occupations the most promising, passed the first married years of this blest and blessing pair. An event then came to pass extremely interesting at the moment, and yet more important in its consequences. This was the receipt of a letter from the elder brother of Mr. Tyrold, containing information that he meant to remove into Hampshire.

Sir Hugh Tyrold was a baronet,[1] who resided upon the hereditary estate of the family in Yorkshire. He was many years older than Mr. Tyrold, who had never seen him since his marriage; religious duties, prudence, and domestic affairs having from that period detained him at his benefice; while a passion for field sports had, with equal constancy, kept his brother stationary.

The baronet began his letter with kind enquiries after the welfare of Mr. Tyrold and his family, and then entered upon the state of his own affairs, briefly narrating, that he had lost his health, and, not knowing what to do with himself, had resolved to change his habitation, and settle near his relations. The Cleves' estate, which he heard was just by Etherington, being then upon sale, he desired his brother to make the purchase for him out of hand; and then to prepare Mrs. Tyrold, with whom he was yet unacquainted, though he took it for granted she was a woman of great learning, to receive a mere poor country squire, who knew no more of hic, haec, hoc, than the baby unborn. He begged him to provide a proper apartment for their niece Indiana Lynmere, whom he should bring with him, and another for their nephew Clermont, who was to follow at the next holidays; and not to forget Mrs. Margland, Indiana's governess, she being rather the most particular in point of pleasing amongst them.

Mr. Tyrold, extremely gratified by this unexpected renewal of fraternal intercourse, wrote the warmest thanks to his brother, and executed the commission with the utmost alacrity. A noble mansion, with an extensive pleasure-ground, scarce four miles distant from the parsonage-house of Etherington, was bought, fitted up, and made ready for his reception in the course of a few months. The baronet, impatient to take possession of his new territory, arrived speedily after, with his niece Indiana,[1] and was welcomed at the gate of the park by Mr. Tyrold and his whole family.

Sir Hugh Tyrold inherited from his ancestors an unincumbered estate of £.5000 per annum; which he enjoyed with ease and affluence to himself, and disseminated with a good will so generous, that he appeared to think his personal prosperity, and that of all who surrounded him, bestowed but to be shared in common, rather from general right, than through his own dispensing bounty. His temper was unalterably sweet, and every thought of his breast was laid open to the world with an almost infantine artlessness. But his talents bore no proportion to the goodness of his heart, an insuperable want of quickness, and of application in his early days, having left him, at a later period, wholly uncultivated, and singularly self-formed.

A dearth of all sedentary resources became, when his youth passed away, his own constant reproach. Health failed him in the meridian of his life, from the consequences of a wound in his side, occasioned by a fall from his horse; exercise, therefore, and active diversions, were of necessity relinquished, and as these had hitherto occupied all his time, except that portion which he delighted to devote to hospitality and neighbourly offices, now equally beyond his strength, he found himself at once deprived of all employment, and destitute of all comfort. Nor did any plan occur to him to solace his misfortunes, till he accidentally read in the newspapers that the Cleves' estate was upon sale.

Indiana, the niece who accompanied him, a beautiful little girl, was the orphan daughter of a deceased sister, who, at the death of her parents, had, with Clermont,[2] an only brother, been left to the guardianship of Sir Hugh; with the charge of a small estate for the son of scarce £.200 a-year, and the sum of £.1000 for the fortune of the daughter.

The meeting was a source of tender pleasure to Mr. Tyrold; and gave birth in his young family to that eager joy which is so naturally attached, by our happiest early prejudices, to the first sight of near relations. Mrs. Tyrold received Sir Hugh with the complacency[3] due to the brother of her husband; who now rose

higher than ever in her estimation, from a fraternal comparison to
the unavoidable disadvantage of the baronet; though she was not
insensible to the fair future prospects of her children, which
seemed the probable result of his change of abode.

Sir Hugh himself, notwithstanding his best affections were all
opened by the sight of so many claimants to their kindness, was
the only dejected person of the group.

Though too good in his nature for envy, a severe self-upbraiding followed his view of the happiness of his brother; he regretted
he had not married at the same age, that he might have owned as
fine a family, and repined against the unfortunate privileges of his
birth-right, which, by indulging him in his first youth with whatever he could covet, drove from his attention that modest foresight, which prepares for later years the consolation they are sure
to require.

By degrees, however, the satisfaction spread around him found
some place in his own breast, and he acknowledged himself
sensibly revived by so endearing a reception; though he candidly
avowed, that if he had not been at a loss what to do, he should
never have had a thought of taking so long a journey. 'But the
not having made,' cried he, 'the proper proficiency in my youth
for the filling up my time, has put me quite behind-hand.'

He caressed all the children with great fondness, and was much
struck with the beauty of his three nieces, particularly with that of
Camilla, Mr. Tyrold's second daughter; 'yet she is not,' he cried,
'so pretty as her little sister Eugenia, nor much better than t'other
sister Lavina;[1] and not one of the three is half so great a beauty
as my little Indiana; so I can't well make out what it is that's so
catching in her; but there's something in her little mouth that
quite wins me; though she looks as if she was half laughing at me
too: which can't very well be, neither; for I suppose, as yet, at
least, she knows no more of books and studying than her uncle.
And that's little enough, God knows, for I never took to them in
proper season; which I have been sorry enough for, upon coming
to discretion.'

Then addressing himself to the boy, he exhorted him to work
hard while yet in his youth, and related sundry anecdotes of the
the industry and merit of his father when at the same age, though
left quite to himself, as, to his great misfortune, he had been also,
'which brought about,' he continued, 'my being this present

ignoramus that you see me; which would not have happened, if my good forefathers had been pleased to keep a sharper look out upon my education.'

Lionel, the little boy, casting a comic glance at Camilla, begged to know what his uncle meant by a sharper look out?

'Mean, my dear? why correction, to be sure; for all that, they tell me, is to be done by the rod; so there, at least, I might have stood as good a chance as my neighbours.'

'And pray, uncle,' cried Lionel, pursing up his mouth to hide his laughter, 'did you always like the thoughts of it so well?'

'Why no, my dear, I can't pretend to that; at your age I had no more taste for it than you have: but there's a proper season for every thing. However, though I tell you this for a warning, perhaps you may do without it; for, by what I hear, the rising generation's got to a much greater pitch since my time.'

He then added, he must advise him, as a friend, to be upon his guard, as his Cousin, Clermont Lynmere, who was coming home from Eton school next Christmas for the holidays, would turn out the very mirror of scholarship; for he had given directions to have him study both night and day, except what might be taken off for eating and sleeping: 'Because,' he continued, 'having proved the bad of knowing nothing in my own case, I have the more right to intermeddle with others. And he will thank me enough when once he has got over his classics. And I hope, my dear little boy, you see it in the same light too; which, however, is what I can't expect.'

The house was now examined; the fair little Indiana took possession of her apartment; Miss Margland was satisfied with the attention that had been paid her; and Sir Hugh was rejoiced to find a room for Clermont that had no window but a skylight, by which means his studies, he observed, would receive no interruption from gaping and staring about him. And, when the night advanced, Mr. Tyrold had the happiness of leaving him with some prospect of recovering his spirits.

The revival, however, lasted but during the novelty of the scene; depression returned with the feelings of ill health; and the happier lot of his brother, though born to almost nothing, filled him with incessant repentance of his own mismanagement.

In some measure to atone for this, he resolved to collect himself a family in his own house; and the young Camilla, whose dawning archness of expression had instinctively caught him, he now demanded of her parents, to come and reside with him and Indiana at Cleves; 'for certainly,' he said, 'for such a young little thing, she looks full of amusement.'

Mrs. Tyrold objected against reposing a trust so precious where its value could so ill be appreciated. Camilla was, in secret, the fondest hope of her mother, though the rigour of her justice scarce permitted the partiality to beat even in her own breast. Nor did the happy little person need the avowed distinction. The tide of youthful glee flowed jocund from her heart,[1] and the transparency of her fine blue veins almost shewed the velocity of its current. Every look was a smile, every step was a spring, every thought was a hope, every feeling was joy! and the early felicity of her mind was without allay. O blissful state of innocence, purity, and delight, why must it fleet so fast? why scarcely but by retrospection is its happiness known?

Mr. Tyrold, while his tenderest hopes encircled the same object, saw the proposal in a fairer light, from the love he bore to his brother. It seemed certain such a residence would secure her an ample fortune; the governess to whom Indiana was entrusted would take care of his little girl; though removed from the hourly instructions, she would still be within reach of the general superintendance of her mother, into whose power he cast the uncontrolled liberty to reclaim her, if there started any occasion. His children had no provision ascertained, should his life be too short to fulfil his own personal schemes of economy in their favour: and while to an argument so incontrovertible Mrs. Tyrold was silent, he begged her also to reflect, that, persuasive as were the attractions of elegance and refinement, no just parental expectations could be essentially disappointed, where the great moral lessons were practically inculcated, by a uniform view of goodness of heart, and firmness of principle. These his brother possessed in an eminent degree; and if his character had nothing more from which their daughter could derive benefit, it undoubtedly had not a point from which she could receive injury.

Mrs. Tyrold now yielded; she never resisted a remonstrance of her husband; and as her sense of duty impelled her also never to murmur, she retired to her own room, to conceal with how ill a grace she complied.

Had this lady been united to a man whom she despised, she

would yet have obeyed him, and as scrupulously, though not as
happily, as she obeyed her honoured partner. She considered the
vow taken at the altar to her husband, as a voluntary vestal would
have held one taken to her Maker; and no dissent in opinion
exculpated, in her mind, the least deviation from his will.

But here, where an admiration almost adoring was fixt of the
character to which she submitted, she was sure to applaud the
motives which swayed him, however little their consequences met
her sentiments: and even where the contrariety was wholly
repugnant to her judgment, the genuine warmth of her just
affection made every compliance, and every forbearance, not
merely exempt from pain, but if to him any satisfaction, a
sacrifice soothing to her heart.

Mr. Tyrold, whose whole soul was deeply affected by her
excellencies, gratefully felt his power, and religiously studied not
to abuse it: he respected what he owed to her conscience, he
tenderly returned what he was indebted to her affection. To
render her virtues conducive to her happiness, to soften her
duties by the highest sense of their merit, were the first and most
sacred objects of his solicitude in life.

When the lively and lovely little girl, mingling the tears of
separation with all the childish rapture which novelty, to a much
later period inspires, was preparing to change her home, 'Remember,' cried Mr. Tyrold, to her anxious mother, 'that on you, my
Georgiana, devolves the sole charge, the unlimited judgment, to
again bring her under this roof, the first moment she appears to
you in any danger from having quitted it.'

The prompt and thankful acceptance of Mrs. Tyrold did
justice to the sincerity of this offer: and the cheerful acquiescence
of lessened reluctance, raised her higher in that esteem to which
her constant mind invariably looked up, as the summit of her
chosen ambition.

CHAPTER II

Comic Gambols

DELIGHTED with this acquisition to his household, Sir Hugh

again revived. 'My dear brother and sister,' he cried, when next the family visited Cleves, 'this proves the most fortunate step I have ever taken since I was born. Camilla's a little jewel; she jumps and skips about till she makes my eyes ache with looking after her, for fear of her breaking her neck. I must keep a sharp watch, or she'll put poor Indiana's nose quite out of joint, which God forbid. However, she's the life of us all, for I'm sorry to say it, but I think, my dear brother, poor Indiana promises to turn out rather dull.'

The sprightly little girl, thus possessed of the heart, soon guided the will of her uncle. He could refuse nothing to her endearing entreaty, and felt every indulgence repaid by the enchantment of her gaiety. Indiana, his first idol, lost her power to please him, though no essential kindness was abated in his conduct. He still acknowledged that her beauty was the most complete; but he found in Camilla a variety that was captivation. Her form and her mind were of equal elasticity. Her playful countenance rekindled his spirits, the cheerfulness of her animated voice awakened him to its own joy. He doated upon detaining her by his side, or delighted to gratify her if she wished to be absent. She exhilarated him with pleasure, she supplied him with ideas, and from the morning's first dawn to the evening's latest close, his eye followed her lightspringing figure, or his ear vibrated with her sportive sounds; catching, as it listened, in successive rotation, the spontaneous laugh, the unconscious bound, the genuine glee of childhood's fearless happiness, uncurbed by severity, untamed by misfortune.

This ascendance was soon pointed out by the servants to Indiana, who sometimes shewed her resentment in unexplained and pouting sullenness, and at others, let all pass unnoticed, with unreflecting forgetfulness. But her mind was soon empoisoned with a jealousy of more permanent seriousness; in less than a month after the residence of Camilla at Cleves, Sir Hugh took the resolution of making her his heiress.

Even Mr. Tyrold, notwithstanding his fondness for Camilla, remonstrated against a partiality so injurious to his nephew and niece, as well as to the rest of his family. And Mrs. Tyrold, though her secret heart subscribed, without wonder, to a predilection in favour of Camilla, was maternally disturbed for her other children, and felt her justice sensibly shocked at a blight so unmerited to the hopes cherished by Indiana and Clermont Lynmere: for though the fruits of this change of plan would be reaped by her little darling, they were robbed of all their sweetness to a mind so correct, by their undeserved bitterness towards the first expectants.

Sir Hugh, however, was immoveable; he would provide handsomely, he said, for Indiana and Clermont, by settling a thousand pounds a year between them; and he would bequeath capital legacies amongst the rest of his nephews and nieces: but as to the bulk of his fortune, it should all go to Camilla; for how else could he make her amends for having amused him? or how, when he was gone, should he prove to her he loved her the best?

Sir Hugh could keep nothing secret; Camilla was soon informed of the riches she was destined to inherit; and servants, who now with added respect attended her, took frequent opportunities of impressing her with the expectation, by the favours they begged from her in reversion.[1]

The happy young heiress heard them with little concern: interest and ambition could find no room in a mind, which to dance, sing, and play could enliven to rapture. Yet the continued repetition of requests soon made the idea of patronage familiar to her, and though wholly uninfected with one thought of power or consequence, she sometimes regaled her fancy with the presents she should make amongst her friends; designing a coach for her mamma, that she might oftener go abroad; an horse for her brother Lionel, which she knew to be his most passionate wish; a new bureau, with a lock and key, for her eldest sister Lavinia; innumerable trinkets for her cousin Indiana; dolls and toys without end for her little sister Eugenia; and a new library of new books, finely bound and gilt, for her papa. But these munificent donations looked forward to no other date than the anticipation of womanhood. If an hint were surmised of her surviving her uncle, an impetuous shower of tears dampt all her gay schemes, deluged every airy castle, and shewed the instinctive gratitude which kindness can awaken, even in the unthinking period of earliest youth, in those bosoms it has ever the power to animate.

Her ensuing birth-day, upon which she would enter her tenth year, was to announce to the adjoining country her uncle's splendid plan in her favour. Her brother and sisters were invited to keep it with her at Cleves; but Sir Hugh declined asking either

her father or mother, that his own time, without restraint, might be dedicated to the promotion of her festivity; he even requested of Miss Margland, that she would not appear that day, lest her presence should curb the children's spirits.

The gay little party, consisting of Lavinia, who was two years older, and Eugenia, who was two years younger than Camilla, with her beautiful cousin, who was exactly of her own age, her brother Lionel, who counted three years more, and Edgar Mandlebert, a ward of Mr. Tyrold's, all assembled at Cleves upon this important occasion, at eight o'clock in the morning, to breakfast.

Edgar Mandlebert, an uncommonly spirited and manly boy, now thirteen years of age, was heir to one of the finest estates in the county. He was the only son of a bosom friend of Mr. Tyrold, to whose guardianship he had been consigned almost from his infancy, and who superintended the care of his education with as much zeal, though not as much oeconomy, as that of his own son. He placed him under the tuition of Dr. Marchmont, a man of consummate learning, and he sent for him to Etherington twice in every year, where he assiduously kept up his studies by his own personal instructions. 'I leave him rich, my dear friend,' said his father, when on his death-bed he recommended him to Mr. Tyrold, 'and you, I trust, will make him good, and see him happy; and should hereafter a daughter of your own, from frequent intercourse, become mistress of his affections, do not oppose such a union from a disparity of fortune, which a daughter of yours, and of your incomparable partner's, can hardly fail to counterbalance in merit.' Mr. Tyrold, though too noble to avail himself of a declaration so generous, by forming any plan to bring such a connection to bear, felt conscientiously absolved from using any measures of frustration, and determined, as the young people grew up, neither to promote nor impede any rising regard.

The estate of Beech Park was not all that young Mandlebert inherited; the friendship of its late owner for Mr. Tyrold, seemed instinctively transfused into his breast, and he paid back the parental tenderness with which he was watched and cherished, by a fondness and veneration truly filial.

Whatever could indulge or delight the little set was brought forth upon this joyous meeting; fruits, sweetmeats, and cakes; cards, trinkets, and blind fidlers,[1] were all at the unlimited command of the fairy mistress of the ceremonies. But unbounded as were the transports of the jovial little group, they could scarcely keep pace with the enjoyment of Sir Hugh; he entered into all their plays, he forgot all his pains, he laughed because they laughed, and suffered his darling little girl to govern and direct him at her pleasure. She made him whiskers of cork, powdered his brown bob, and covered a thread paper with black ribbon to hang to it for a queue.[1] She metamorphosed him into a female, accoutring him with her fine new cap, while she enveloped her own small head in his wig; and then, tying the maid's apron round his waist, put a rattle into his hand, and Eugenia's doll upon his lap, which she told him was a baby that he must nurse and amuse.

The excess of merriment thus excited spread through the whole house. Lionel called in the servants to see this comical sight, and the servants indulged their numerous guests with a peep at it from the windows. Sir Hugh, meanwhile, resolved to object to nothing, performed every part assigned him, joined in their hearty laughs at the grotesque figure they made of him, and cordially encouraged all their proceedings, assuring them he had not been so much diverted himself since his fall from his horse, and advising them, with great zeal, to be merry while they could: 'For you will never, my dears,' said he, 'be younger, never while you live; no more, for that matter, shall I, neither, for all I am so much older, which, in that point, makes no difference.'

He grew weary, however, first; and stretching himself his full length, with a prodigious yawn, 'Heigh ho!' he cried, 'Camilla, my dear, do take away poor Doll, for fear I should let it slip.'

The little gigglers, almost in convulsions of laughter, entreated him to nurse it some time longer; but he frankly answered, 'No, my dears, no; I can play no more now, if I'd ever so fain, for I'm tired to death, which is really a pity; so you must either go out with me my airing, for a rest to your merry little sides, or stay and play by yourselves till I come back, which I think will put you all into fevers; but, however, nobody shall trouble your little souls with advice to-day; there are days enough in the year for teazing, without this one.'

Camilla instantly decided for the airing, and without a dissentient voice: so entirely had the extreme good humour of Sir Hugh won the hearts of the little party, that they felt as if the whole of their entertainment depended upon his presence. The carriage, therefore, was ordered for the baronet and his four nieces, and Lionel and Edgar Mandlebert, at the request of Camilla, were gratified with horses.

Camilla was desired to fix their route, and while she hesitated from the variety in her choice, Lionel proposed to Edgar that they should take a view of his house, park, and gardens, which were only three miles from Cleves. Edgar referred the matter to Indiana, to whose already exquisite beauty his juvenile admiration paid its most early obeisance. Indiana approved; the little heroine of the day assented with pleasure and they immediately set out upon the happy expedition.

The two boys the whole way came with offerings of wild honeysuckle and sweetbriar, the grateful nosegays of all-diffusing nature, to the coach windows, each carefully presenting the most fragrant to Indiana; for Lionel, even more than sympathising with Edgar, declared his sisters to be mere frights in comparison with his fair cousin. Their partiality, however, struggled vainly against that of Sir Hugh, who still, in every the most trivial particular, gave the preference to Camilla.

The baronet had ordered that his own garden chair[1] should follow him to young Mandlebert's park, that he might take Camilla by his side, and go about the grounds without fatigue; the rest were to walk. Here Indiana received again the homage of her two young beaus; they pointed out to her the most beautiful prospects, they gathered her the fairest flowers, they loaded her with the best and ripest fruits.

This was no sooner observed by Sir Hugh, than hastily stopping his chair, he called after them aloud, 'Holloa! come hither, my boys! here, you Mr. young Mandlebert, what are you all about? Why don't you bring that best bunch of grapes to Camilla?'

'I have already promised it to Miss Lynmere, Sir.'

'O ho, have you so? well, give it her then if you have. I have no right to rob you of your choice. Indiana, my dear, how do you like this place?'

'Very much, indeed, uncle; I never saw any place I liked so much in my life.'

'I am sure else,' said Edgar, 'I should never care for it again myself.'

'O, I could look at it for ever,' cried Indiana, 'and not be tired!'

Sir Hugh gravely paused at these speeches, and regarded them

in turn with much steadiness, as if settling their future destinies;
but ever unable to keep a single thought to himself, he presently
burst forth aloud with his new mental arrangement, saying:
'Well, my dears, well; this is not quite the thing I had taken a
fancy to in my own private brain, but it's all for the best, there's
no doubt; though the estate being just in my neighbourhood,
would have made it more suitable for Camilla; I mean provided
we could have bought, among us, the odd three miles between
the Parks; which how many acres they make, I can't pretend to
say, without the proper calculation; but if it was all joined, it
would be the finest domain in the county, as far as I know to the
contrary: nevertheless, my dear young Mr. Mandlebert, you have
a right to choose for yourself; for as to beauty, 'tis mere fancy; not
but what Indiana has one or other the prettiest face I ever saw,
though I think Camilla's so much prettier; I mean in point of
winningness. However, there's no fear as to my consent, for
nothing can be a greater pleasure to me than having two such good
girls, both being cousins, live so near that they may overlook one
another from park to park, all day long, by the mode of a
telescope.'

Edgar, perfectly understanding him, blushed deeply, and,
forgetting what he had just declared, offered his grapes to
Lavinia. Indiana, conceiving herself already mistress of so fine a
place, smiled with approving complacency; and the rest were
too much occupied with the objects around them, to listen to so
long a speech.

They then all moved on; but, soon after, Lionel, flying up to
his uncle's chair, informed Camilla he had just heard from the
gardener, that only half a mile off, at Northwick, there was a fair,
to which he begged she would ask to go. She found no difficulty in
obliging him; and Sir Hugh was incapable of hesitating at whatever she could desire. The carriage and the horses for the boys
were again ordered, and to the regret of only Edgar and Indiana,
the beautiful plantations of Beech Park were relinquished for the
fair.

They had hardly proceeded twenty yards, when the smiles that
had brightened the face of Lavinia, the eldest daughter of Mr.
Tyrold, were suddenly overcast, giving place to a look of dismay,
which seemed the effect of some abruptly painful recollection; and
the moment Sir Hugh perceived it, and enquired the cause, the

tears rolled fast down her cheeks, and she said she had been guilty of a great sin, and could never forgive herself.

They all eagerly endeavoured to console her, Camilla fondly taking her hand, little Eugenia sympathetically crying over and kissing her, Indiana begging to know what was the matter, and Sir Hugh, holding out to her the finest peach from his stores for Camilla, and saying, 'Don't cry so, my dear, don't cry: take a little bit of peach; I dare say you are not so bad as you think for.'

The weeping young penitent besought leave to get out of the coach with Camilla, to whom alone she could explain herself. Camilla almost opened the door herself, to hasten the discovery; and the moment they had run up a bank by the road side, 'Tell me what it is, my dear Lavinia,' she cried, 'and I am sure my uncle will do anything in the world to help you.'

'O Camilla,' she answered, 'I have disobeyed mamma! and I did not mean it in the least—but I have forgot all her commands! —She charged me not to let Eugenia stir out from Cleves, because of the small pox[1]—and she has been already at Beech Park—and now, how can I tell the poor little thing she must not go to the fair?'

'Don't vex yourself about that,' cried Camilla, kindly kissing the tears off her cheeks, 'for I will stay behind, and play with Eugenia myself, if my uncle will drive us back to Beech Park; and then all the rest may go to the fair, and take us up again in the way home.'

With this expedient she flew to the coach, charging the two boys, who with great curiosity had ridden to the bank side, and listened to all that had passed, to comfort Lavinia.

'Lionel,' cried Edgar, 'do you know, while Camilla was speaking so kindly to Lavinia, I thought she looked almost as pretty as your cousin?' Lionel would by no means subscribe to this opinion, but Edgar would not retract.

Camilla, jumping into the carriage, threw her arms around the neck of her uncle, and whispered to him all that had passed. 'Poor innocent little dear!' cried he, 'is that all?' it's just nothing, considering her young age.'

Then, looking out of the window, 'Lavinia,' he said, 'you have done no more harm than what's quite natural; and so I shall tell your mamma; who is a woman of sense, and won't expect such a young head as yours to be of the same age as hers and mine. But come into the coach, my dear; we'll just drive as far as Northwick, for an airing, and then back again.'

The extreme delicacy of the constitution of Eugenia had hitherto deterred Mrs. Tyrold from innoculating her;[1] she had therefore scrupulously kept her from all miscellaneous intercourse in the neighbourhood: but as the weakness of her infancy was now promising to change into health and strength, she meant to give to that terrible disease its best chance, and the only security it allows from perpetual alarm, immediately after the heats of the present autumn should be over.

Lavinia, unused to disobedience, could not be happy in practising it: she entreated, therefore, to return immediately to Cleves. Sir Hugh complied; premising only that they must none of them expect him to be of their play-party again till after dinner.

The coachman then received fresh orders: but, the moment they were communicated to the two boys, Lionel, protesting he would not lose the fair, said he should soon overtake them, and, regardless of all remonstrances, put spurs to his horse, and galloped off.

Sir Hugh, looking after him with great alarm, exclaimed, 'Now he is going to break all his bones! which is always the case with those young boys, when first they get a horseback.'

Camilla, terrified that she had begged this boon, requested that the servant might directly ride after him.

'Yes, my dear, if you wish it,' answered Sir Hugh; 'only we have but this one man for us all, because of the rest staying to get the ball and supper ready; so that if we should be overturned ourselves, here's never a soul to pick us up.'

Edgar offered to ride on alone, and persuade the truant to return.

'Thank you, my dear, thank you,' answered Sir Hugh, 'you are as good a boy as any I know, but, in point of horsemanship, one's as ignorant as t'other, as far as I can tell; so we may only see both your sculls fractured instead of one, in the midst of your galloping; which God forbid for either.'

'Then let us all go together,' cried Indiana, 'and bring him back.'

'But do not let us get out of the coach, uncle,' said Lavinia; 'pray do not let us get out!'

Sir Hugh agreed; though he added, that as to the small pox, he could by no means see it in the same light, for he had no notion of people's taking diseases upon themselves. 'Besides,' continued he, 'she will be sure to have it when her time comes, whether she is moped up or no;[1] and how did people do before these new modes of making themselves sick of their own accord?'[2]

Pitying, however, the uneasiness of Lavinia, when they came near the town, he called to the footman, and said, 'Hark'ee, Jacob, do you ride on first, and keep a sharp look out that nobody has the small pox.'

The fair being held in the suburbs, they soon arrived at some straggling booths, and the coach, at the instance of Lavinia, was stopt.

Indiana now earnestly solicited leave to alight and see the fair; and Edgar offered to be her esquire. Sir Hugh consented, but desired that Lavinia and Camilla might be also of the party. Lavinia tried vainly to excuse herself; he assured her it would raise her spirits, and bid her be under no apprehension, for he would stay and amuse the little Eugenia himself, and take care that she came to no harm.

They were no sooner gone, however, than the little girl cried to follow; Sir Hugh, compassionately kissing her, owned she had as good a right as any of them, and declared it was a hard thing to have her punished for other people's particularities. This concession served only to make her tears flow the faster; till, unable to bear the sight, he said he could not answer to his conscience the vexing such a young thing, and, promising she should have whatever she liked, if she would cry no more, he ordered the coachman to drive to the first booth where there were any toys to be sold.

Here, having no footman to bring the trinkets to the coach, he alighted, and, suffering the little girl, for whom he had not a fear himself, to accompany him, he entered the booth, and told her to take whatever hit her fancy, for she should have as many playthings as she could carry.

Her grief now gave way to ecstasy, and her little hands could soon scarcely sustain the loaded skirt of her white frock. Sir Hugh, determining to make the rest of the children equally happy, was selecting presents for them all, when the little group, ignorant whom they should encounter, advanced towards the same booth: but he had hardly time to exclaim, 'Oho! have you caught us?' when the innocent voice of Eugenia, calling out, 'Little boy; what's the matter with your face, little boy?' drew his attention another way, and he perceived a child apparently just recovering from the small pox.

Edgar, who at the same instant saw the same dreaded sight, darted forward, seized Eugenia in his arms, and, in defiance of her playthings and her struggles, carried her back to the coach; while Lavinia, in an agony of terror, ran up to the little boy, and, crying out, 'O go away! go away!' dragged him out of the booth, and, perfectly unconscious what she did, covered his head with her frock, and held him fast with both her hands.

Sir Hugh, all aghast, hurried out of the booth, but could scarce support himself from emotion; and, while he leaned upon his stick, ejaculating, 'Lord help us! what poor creatures we are, we poor mortals!' Edgar had the presence of mind to make Indiana and Camilla go directly to the carriage. He then prevailed with Sir Hugh to enter it also, and ran back for Lavinia. But when he perceived the situation into which distress and affright had driven her, and saw her sobbing over the child, whom she still held confined, with an idea of hiding him from Eugenia, he was instantly sensible of the danger of her joining her little sister. Extremely perplexed for them all, and afraid, by going from the sick child, he might himself carry the infection to the coach, he sent a man to Sir Hugh to know what was to be done.

Sir Hugh, totally overset by the unexpected accident, and conscience-struck at his own wilful share in risking it, was utterly helpless, and could only answer, that he wished young Mr. Edgar would give him his advice.

Edgar, thus called upon, now first felt the abilities which his short life had not hitherto brought into use: he begged Sir Hugh would return immediately to Cleves, and keep Eugenia there for a few days with Camilla and her cousin; while he undertook to go himself in search of Lionel, with whose assistance he would convey Lavinia back to Etherington, without seeing her little sister; since she must now be as full of contagion as the poor object who had just had the disease.

Sir Hugh, much relieved, sent him word he had no doubt he would become the first scholar of the age; and desired he would get a chaise for himself and Lavinia, and let the footman take charge of his horse.

He then ordered the coach[1] to Cleves.

Edgar fulfilled the injunctions of Sir Hugh with alacrity; but had a very difficult task to find Lionel, and one far more painful to appease Lavinia, whose apprehensions were so great as they advanced towards Etherington, that, to sooth and comfort her, he ordered the postilion to drive first to a farm-house near Cleves, whence he forwarded a boy to Sir Hugh, with entreaties that he would write a few lines to Mrs. Tyrold, in exculpation of her sorrowing daughter.

Sir Hugh complied, but was so little in the habit of writing, that he sent over a messenger to desire they would dine at the farm-house, in order to give him time to compose his epistle.

Early in the afternoon, he conveyed to them the following letter:

To Mrs. Tyrold *at the Parsonage House, belonging to the Reverend Rector, Mr.* Tyrold, *for the Time being, at* Etherington *in* Hampshire.

DEAR SISTER,

I AM no remarkable good writer, in comparison with my brother, which you will excuse from my deficiencies, as it is my only apology. I beg you will not be angry with little Lavinia, as she did nothing in the whole business, except wanting to do right, only not mentioning it in the beginning, which is very excusable in the light of a fault; the wisest of us having been youths ourselves once, and the most learned being subject to do wrong, but how much so the ignorant? of which I may speak more properly. However, as she would certainly have caught the small pox herself, except from the lucky circumstance of having had it before, I think it best to keep Eugenia a few days at Cleves, for the sake of her infection. Not but what if she should have it, I trust your sense won't fret about it, as it is only in the course of Nature; which, if she had been innoculated, is more than any man could say; even a physician. So the whole being my own fault, without the least meaning to offend, if any thing comes of it, I hope, my dear sister, you won't take it ill, especially of poor little Lavinia, for 'tis hard if such young things may not be happy at their time of life, before having done harm to a human soul. Poor dears! 'tis soon enough to be unhappy after being wicked; which, God knows, we are all liable to be in the proper season. I beg my love to my brother; and remain,

> Dear sister,
> Your affectionate brother,
> HUGH TYROLD.

P.S. It is but justice to my brother to mention that young Master Mandlebert's behaviour has done the greatest honour to the classics; which must be a great satisfaction to a person having the care of his education.

The rest of the day lost all its delights to the young heiress from this unfortunate adventure. The deprivation of three of the party, with the well-grounded fear of Mrs. Tyrold's just blame, were greater mortifications to those that remained, than even the ball and supper could remove. And Sir Hugh, to whom their lowered spirits were sufficiently depressing, had an additional, though hardly to himself acknowledged, weight upon his mind, relative to Eugenia and the small pox.

The contrition of the trembling Lavinia could not but obtain from Mrs. Tyrold the pardon it deserved: but she could make no allowance for the extreme want of consideration in Sir Hugh; and anxiously waited the time when she might call back Eugenia from the management of a person whom she considered as more childish than her children themselves.

CHAPTER III

Consequences

EVERY precaution being taken with regard to Lavinia and her clothes, for warding off infection to Eugenia, if as yet she had escaped it; Mrs. Tyrold fixed a day for fetching her little daughter from Cleves. Sir Hugh, at the earnest entreaty of Camilla, invited the young party to come again early that morning, that some amends might be made them for their recent disappointment of the ball and supper, by a holiday, and a little sport, previous to the arrival of Mrs. Tyrold; to whom he voluntarily pledged his word, that Eugenia should not again be taken abroad, nor suffered to appear before any strangers.

Various gambols were now again enacted by the once more happy group; but all was conducted with as much security as gaiety, till Lionel proposed the amusement of riding upon a plank in the park.

A plank was immediately procured by the gardener, and placed upon the trunk of an old oak, where it parted into two thick branches.

The boys and the three eldest girls balanced one another in turn, with great delight and dexterity; but Sir Hugh feared committing the little Eugenia, for whom he was grown very anxious, amongst them, till the repinings of the child demolished his prudence. The difficulty how to indulge her with safety was, nevertheless, considerable: and, after various experiments, he resolved to trust her to nobody but himself; and, placing her upon his lap, occupied one end of the plank, and desired that as many of the rest as were necessary to make the weight equal, would seat themselves upon the other.

This diversion was short, but its consequences were long. Edgar Mandlebert, who superintended the balance, poised it with great exactness; yet no sooner was Sir Hugh elevated, than, becoming exceedingly giddy, he involuntarily loosened his hold of Eugenia, who fell from his arms to the ground.

In the agitation of his fright, he stooped forward to save her, but lost his equilibrium; and, instead of rescuing, followed her.

The greatest confusion ensued; Edgar, with admirable adroitness, preserved the elder girls from suffering by the accident; and Lionel took care of himself by leaping instantly from the plank: Sir Hugh, extremely bruised, could not get up without pain; but all concern and attention soon centred in the little Eugenia, whose incessant cries raised apprehensions of some more than common mischief.

She was carried to the house in the arms of Edgar, and delivered to the governess. She screamed the whole time she was undressing; and Edgar, convinced she had received some injury, galloped off, unbid, for a surgeon: but what was the horror of Sir Hugh, upon hearing him pronounce, that her left shoulder was put out, and that one of her knees was dislocated!

In an agony of remorse, he shut himself up in his room, without power to issue a command, or listen to a question: nor could he be prevailed upon to open his door, till the arrival of Mrs. Tyrold.

Hastily then rushing out, he hurried to meet her; and, snatching both her hands, and pressing them between his own, he burst into a passionate flood of tears, and sobbed out: 'Hate me, my dear sister, for you can't help it! for I am sorry to tell it you, but I believe I have been the death of poor Eugenia, that never hurt a fly in her life!'

Pale, and struck with dread, yet always possessing her presence of mind, Mrs. Tyrold disengaged herself, and demanded where she might find her? Sir Hugh could make no rational answer; but Edgar, who had run down stairs, purposing to communicate the tidings more gently, briefly stated the misfortune, and conducted her to the poor little sufferer.

Mrs. Tyrold, though nearly overpowered by a sight so affecting, still preserved her faculties for better uses than lamentation. She held the child in her arms while the necessary operations were performing by the surgeon; she put her to bed, and watched by her side the whole night; during which, in defiance of all precautions, a high fever came on, and she grew worse every moment.

The next morning, while still in this alarming state, the unfortunate little innocent exhibited undoubted symptoms of the small pox.

Mr. Tyrold now also established himself at Cleves, to share the parental task of nursing the afflicted child, whose room he never left, except to give consolation to his unhappy brother, who lived wholly in his own apartment, refusing the sight even of Camilla, and calling himself a monster too wicked to look at any thing that was good; though the affectionate little girl, pining at the exclusion, continually presented herself at his door.

The disease bore every prognostic of fatal consequences, and the fond parents soon lost all hope, though they redoubled every attention.

Sir Hugh then gave himself up wholly to despair: he darkened his room, refused all food but bread and water, permitted no one to approach him, and reviled himself invariably with the contrition of a wilful murderer.

In this state of self-punishment he persevered, till the distemper unexpectedly took a sudden and happy turn, and the surgeon made known, that his patient might possibly recover.

The joy of Sir Hugh was now as frantic as his grief had been the moment before: he hastened to his drawing-room, commanded that the whole house should be illuminated; promised a year's wages to all his servants; bid his house-keeper distribute beef and broth throughout the village; and sent directions that the bells of the three nearest parish churches should be rung for a day and a night. But when Mr. Tyrold, to avert the horror of any wholly unprepared disappointment, represented the still precarious state of Eugenia, and the many changes yet to be feared; he desperately reversed all his orders, returned sadly to his dark room, and protested he would never more rejoice, till Mrs. Tyrold herself should come to him with good news.

This anxiously waited æra at length arrived; Eugenia, though seamed and even scarred by the horrible disorder, was declared out of danger; and Mrs. Tyrold, burying her anguish at the alteration, in her joy for the safety of her child, with an heart overflowing from pious gratitude, became the messenger of peace; and, holding out her hand to Sir Hugh, assured him the little Eugenia would soon be well.

Sir Hugh, in an ecstasy which no power could check, forgot every pain and infirmity to hurry up to the apartment of the little girl, that he might kneel, he said, at her feet, and there give thanks for her recovery: but the moment he entered the room, and saw the dreadful havoc grim disease had made on her face; not a trace of her beauty left, no resemblance by which he could have known her; he shrunk back, wrung his hands, called himself the most sinful of all created beings, and in the deepest despondence, sunk into a chair and wept aloud.

Eugenia soon began to cry also, though unconscious for what cause; and Mrs. Tyrold remonstrated to Sir Hugh upon the uselessness of such transports, calmly beseeching him to retire and compose himself.

'Yes, sister,' he answered, 'yes, I'll go away, for I am sure, I do not want to look at her again; but to think of its being all my doing!—O brother! O sister! why don't you both kill me in return? And what amends can I make her? what amends, except a poor little trifle of money?—And as to that, she shall have it, God knows, every penny I am worth, the moment I am gone; ay, that she shall, to a single shilling, if I die tomorrow!'

Starting up with revived courage from this idea, he ventured again to turn his head towards Eugenia, exclaiming: 'O, if she does but get well! does but ease my poor conscience by making me out not to be a murderer, a guinea for every pit in that poor face will I settle on her out of hand; yes, before I so much as breathe again, for fear of dying in the mean time!'

Mrs. Tyrold scarce noticed this declaration; but his brother endeavoured to dissuade him from so sudden and partial a measure: he would not, however, listen; he made what speed he could down stairs, called hastily for his hat and stick, commanded all his servants to attend him, and muttering frequent ejaculations to himself, that he would not trust to changing his mind, he proceeded to the family chapel, and approaching with eager steps to the altar, knelt down, and bidding every one hear and witness what he said, made a solemn vow, 'That if he might be cleared of the crime of murder, by the recovery of Eugenia, he would atone what he could for the ill he had done her, by bequeathing to her every thing he possessed in the world, in estate, cash, and property, without the deduction of a sixpence.'

He told all present to remember and witness this, in case of an apoplexy before his new will could be written down.

Returning then to the house, lightened, he said, from a load of self-reproach, which had rendered the last fortnight insupportable to him, he sent for the attorney of a neighbouring town, and went upstairs, with a firmer mind, to wait his arrival in the sick room.

'O my dear uncle,' cried his long banished Camilla, who hearing him upon the stairs, skipt lightly after him, 'how glad I am to see you again! I almost thought I should see you no more!'

Here ended at once the just acquired tranquility of Sir Hugh; all his satisfaction forsook him at the appearance of his little darling; he considered her as an innocent creature whom he was preparing to injure; he could not bear to look at her; his heart smote him in her favour; his eyes filled with tears; he was unable to go on, and with slow and trembling steps, he moved again towards his own room.

'My dearest uncle!' cried Camilla, holding by his coat, and hanging upon his arm, 'won't you speak to me?'

'Yes, my dear, to be sure I will,' he answered, endeavouring to hide his emotion, 'only not now; so don't follow me Camilla, for I'm going to be remarkably busy!'

'O uncle!' she cried, plaintively, 'and I have not seen you so

long! And I have wished so to see you! and I have been so unhappy about Eugenia! and you have always locked your door;
and I would not rap hard at it, for fear you should be asleep: But
why would you not see me, uncle? and why will you send me
away?'

'My dear Camilla,' he replied, with increased agitation, 'I have
used you very ill; I have been your worst enemy, which is the very
reason I don't care to see you; so go away, I beg, for I am bad
enough without all this. But I give you my thanks for all your little
playful gambols, having nothing better now to offer you; which is
but a poor return from an uncle to a niece!'

He then shut himself into his room, leaving Camilla drowned in
tears at the outside of the door.

Wretched in reflecting upon the shock and disappointment
which the new disposition of his affairs must occasion her, he had
not fortitude to inform her of his intention. He desired to speak
with Edgar Mandlebert, who, with all the Tyrold family, resided,
for the present, at Cleves, and abruptly related to him the new
destination he had just vowed of his wealth; beseeching that he
would break it in the softest manner to his poor little favourite,
assuring her she would be always the first in his love, though a
point of mere conscience had forced him to make choice of
another heiress.

Edgar, whose zeal to serve and oblige had never been put to so
severe a test, hesitated how to obey this injunction; yet he would
not refuse it, as he found that all the servants of the house were
enabled, if they pleased, to anticipate more incautiously the ill
news. He followed her, therefore, into the garden, whither she had
wandered to weep unobserved; but he stopt short at sight of her
distress, conceiving his errand to be already known to her, and
determined to consult with Indiana, to whom he communicated
his terrible embassy, entreating her to devise some consolation for
her poor cousin.

Indiana felt too much chagrined at her own part in this
transaction, to give her attention to Camilla; she murmured
without scruple at the deprivation of what she had once expected
for herself, and at another time for her brother; and expressed
much resentment at the behaviour of her uncle, mingled with
something very near repining, not merely at his late preference of
Camilla, but even at the recovery of the little Eugenia. Edgar

heard her with surprise, and wondered to find how much less her beauty attracted him from the failure of her good nature.

· He now pursued the weeping Camilla, who, dispersing her tears at his approach, pretended to be picking some lavender, and keeping her eyes steadfastly upon the bush, asked him if he would have any? He took a sprig, but spoke to her in a voice of such involuntary compassion, that she soon lost her self-command, and the big drops again rolled fast down her cheeks. Extremely concerned, he strove gently to sooth her; but the expressions of regret at her uncle's avoidance, which then escaped her, soon convinced him his own task was still to be performed. With anxious fear of the consequences of a blow so unlooked for, he executed it with all the speed, yet all the consideration in his power. Camilla, the moment she understood him, passionately clasped her hands, and exclaimed: 'O if that is all! If my uncle indeed loves me as well as before all this; I am sure I can never, never be so wicked, as to envy poor little Eugenia, who has suffered so much, and almost been dying, because she will be richer than I shall be!'

Edgar, delighted and relieved, thought she was grown a thousand times more beautiful than Indiana; and eagerly taking her hand, ran with her to the apartment of the poor disconsolate Sir Hugh; where his own eyes soon overflowed from tenderness and admiration, at the uncommon scene he witnessed, of the generous affection with which Camilla consoled the fond distress of her uncle, though springing from her own disappointment and loss.

They stayed till the arrival of the attorney, who took the directions of Sir Hugh, and drew up, for his immediate satisfaction, a short deed, making over, according to his vow, all he should die possessed of, without any let or qualification whatsoever, to his niece Eugenia. This was properly signed and sealed, and Sir Hugh hastened up stairs with a copy of it to Mr. Tyrold.

All remonstrance was ineffectual; his conscience, he protested, could no other way be appeased; his noble little Camilla had forgiven him her ill usage, and he could now bear to look at the change for the worse in Eugenia, without finding his heart-strings ready to burst at the sight. 'You,' he cried, 'brother, who do not know what it is I have suffered through my conscience, can't tell what it is to get a little ease; for if she had died, you might all have had the comfort to say 'twas I murdered her, which would have given you the satisfaction of having had no hand in it. But then, what would have become of poor me, having it all upon my own head? However, now thank Heaven, I have no need to care about the matter; for as to the mere loss of beauty, pretty as it is to look at, I hope it is no such great injury, as she'll have a splendid fortune, which is certainly a better thing, in point of lasting. For as to beauty, Lord help us! what is it? except just to the eye.'

He then walked up to the child, intending to kiss her, but stopt and sighed involuntarily as he looked at her, saying: 'After all, she's not like the same thing! no more than I am myself. I shall never think I know her again, never as long as I live! I can't so much as believe her to be the same, though I am sure of its being true. However, it shall make no change in my love for her, poor little dear, for it's all my own doing; though innocently enough, as to any meaning, God knows!'

It was still some time before the little girl recovered, and then a new misfortune became daily more palpable, from some latent and incurable mischief, owing to her fall, which made her grow up with one leg shorter than the other, and her whole figure diminutive and deformed: These additional evils reconciled her parents to the partial will of her uncle, which they now, indeed, thought less wanting in equity, since no other reparation could be offered to the innocent sufferer for ills so insurmountable.

CHAPTER IV

Studies of a grown Gentleman

WHEN the tumult of this affair subsided, Mr. Tyrold and his family prepared to re-establish themselves at Etherington; and Mrs. Tyrold, the great inducement for the separation being over, was earnest to take home again the disinherited Camilla. Sir Hugh, whose pleasure in her sight was now embittered by regret and remorse, had not courage to make the smallest opposition; yet he spent the day of her departure in groans and penitence. He thought it right, however, to detain Eugenia, who, as his decided heiress, was left to be brought up at Cleves.

The loss of the amusing society of his favourite; the disappointment he had inflicted upon her, and the sweetness with which she had borne it, preyed incessantly upon his spirits; and he knew not how to employ himself, which way to direct his thoughts, nor in what manner to beguile one moment of his time, after the children were gone to rest.

The view of the constant resources which his brother found in literature, augmented his melancholy at his own imperfections; and the steady industry with which Mr. Tyrold, in early youth, had attained them, and which, while devoted to field sports, he had often observed with wonder and pity, he now looked back to with self-reproach, and recognised in its effect with a reverence almost awful.

His imagination, neither regulated by wisdom, nor disciplined by experience, having once taken this turn, he soon fancied that every earthly misfortune originated in a carelessness of learning, and that all he wished, and all he wanted, upbraided him with his ignorance. If disease and pain afflicted him, he lamented the juvenile inattention that had robbed him of acquirements which might have taught him not to regard them; if the word scholar was named in his presence, he heaved the deepest sigh; if an article in a newspaper, with which he was unacquainted, was discussed, he reviled his early heedlessness of study; and the mention of a common pamphlet, which was unknown to him, gave him a sensation of disgrace: even inevitable calamities he attributed to the negligence of his education, and construed every error, and every evil of his life, to his youthful disrespect of Greek and Latin.

Such was the state of his mind, when his ordinary maladies had the serious aggravation of a violent fit of the gout.

In the midst of the acute anguish, and useless repentance, which now alternately ravaged his happiness, it suddenly occurred to him, that, perhaps, with proper instruction, he might even yet obtain a sufficient portion of this enviable knowledge, to enable him to pass his evenings with some similarity to his brother.

Revived by this suggestion, he sent for Mr. Tyrold, to communicate to him his idea, and to beg he would put him into a way to recover his lost time, by recommending to him a tutor, with whom he might set about a course of studies:—'Not that I want,' cried he, 'to make any particular great figure as a scholar; but if I could only learn just enough to amuse me at odd hours, and make me forget the gout, it's as much as I desire.'

The total impossibility that such a project should answer its given purpose, deterred not Mr. Tyrold from listening to his request. The mild philosophy of his character saw whatever was lenient to human sufferings as eligible, and looked no further for any obstacles to the wishes of another, than to investigate if their gratification would be compatible with innocence. He wrote, therefore, to a college associate of his younger years, whom he knew to be severely embarrassed in his affairs, and made proposals for settling him in the house of his brother. These were not merely gratefully accepted by his old friend, but drew forth a confession that he was daily menaced with a public arrest for debts, which he had incurred without luxury or extravagance, from mere ignorance of the value of money, and of œconomy.

In the award of cool reason, to attend to what is impracticable, appears a folly which no inducement can excuse. Mrs. Tyrold treated this scheme with calm, but complete contempt. She allowed no palliation for a measure of which the abortive end was glaring; to hearken to it displeased her, as a false indulgence of childish vanity; and her understanding felt shocked that Mr. Tyrold would deign to humour his brother in an enterprise which must inevitably terminate in a fruitless consumption of time.

Sir Hugh soon, but without anger, saw her disapprobation of his plan; her opinions, from a high superiority to all deceit, were as unreserved as those of the baronet, from a nature incapable of caution. He told her he was sorry to perceive that she thought he should make no proficiency, but entreated her to take notice there was at least no great presumption in his attempt, as he meant to begin with the very beginning, and to go no farther at the first than any young little school-boy; for he should give himself fair play, by trying his hand with the rudiments, which would no ·sooner be run over, than the rest would become plain sailing: 'And if once,' he added, 'I should conquer the mastery of the classics, I shall make but very short work of all the rest.'

Mr. Tyrold saw, as forcibly as his wife, the utter impossibility that Sir Hugh could now repair the omissions of his youth; but he was willing to console his want of knowledge, and sooth his mortifications; and while he grieved for his bodily infirmities, and

pitied his mental repinings, he considered his idea as not illaud-
able, though injudicious, and in favour of its blamelessness,
forgave its absurdity.

He was gratified, also, in offering an honourable provision to a
man of learning in distress, whose time and attention could not
fail to deserve it, if dedicated to his brother, in whatever way they
might be bestowed.

He took care to be at Cleves on the day Dr. Orkborne,[1] this
gentleman, was expected, and he presented him to Sir Hugh with
every mark of regard, as a companion in whose conversation, he
flattered himself, pain might be lightened, and seclusion from mixt
company cheerfully supported.

Dr. Orkborne expressed his gratitude for the kindness of Mr.
Tyrold, and promised to make it his first study to merit the high
consideration with which he had been called from his retirement.

A scholastic education[2] was all that had been given to Dr.
Orkborne by his friends; and though in that their hopes were
answered, no prosperity followed. His labours had been seconded
by industry, but not enforced by talents; and they soon found how
wide the difference between acquiring stores, and bringing them
into use. Application, operating upon a retentive memory, had
enabled him to lay by the most ample hoards of erudition; but
these, though they rendered him respectable amongst the learned,
proved nearly nugatory in his progress through the world, from a
total want of skill and penetration to know how or where they
might turn to any account. Nevertheless, his character was unexceptionable, his manners were quiet, and his fortune was
ruined. These were the motives which induced rather the benevolence than the selection of Mr. Tyrold to name him to his brother,
in the hope that, while an asylum at Cleves would exonerate him
from all pecuniary hardships, his very deficiency in brilliancy of
parts, and knowledge of mankind, which though differently
modified, was equal to that of Sir Hugh himself, would obviate
regret of more cultivated society, and facilitate their reciprocal
satisfaction.

The introduction over, Mr. Tyrold sought by general topics to
forward their acquaintance, before any allusion should be made to
the professed plan of Sir Hugh; but Sir Hugh was too well pleased
with its ingenuity to be ashamed of its avowal; he began, therefore,
immediately to descant upon the indolence of his early years,

and to impeach the want of timely severity in his instructors: 'For there is an old saying,' he cried, 'but remarkably true, That learning is better than house or land; which I am an instance of myself, for I have house and land plenty, yet don't know what to do with them properly, nor with myself neither, for want of a little notion of things to guide me by.' His brother, he added, had been too partial in thinking him already fitted for such a master as Dr. Orkborne; though he promised, notwithstanding his time of life, to become the most docile of pupils, and he hoped before long to do no discredit to the Doctor as his tutor.

Mr. Tyrold, whose own benign countenance could scarce refrain from a smile at this unqualified opening, endeavoured to divert to some other subject the grave astonishment of Dr. Orkborne, who, previously aware of the age and ill health of the baronet, naturally concluded himself called upon to solace the privacy of his life by reading or discourse, but suggested not the most distant surmise he could be summoned as a preceptor.

Sir Hugh, however, far from palliating any design, disguised not even a feeling; he plunged deeper and deeper in the acknowledgment of his ignorance, and soon set wholly apart the delicate circumspection of his brother, by demanding of Dr. Orkborne what book he thought he had best buy for a beginning?

Receiving from the wondering Doctor no answer, he good humouredly added, 'Come, don't be ashamed to name the easiest, for this reason; you must know my plan is one of my own, which it is right to tell you. As fast as I get on, I intend, for the sake of remembering my lesson, to send for one of my nephews, and teach it all over again to him myself; which will be doing service to us all at once.'

Mr. Tyrold now, though for a few moments he looked down, thought it best to leave the matter to its own course, and Dr. Orkborne to his own observations; fully persuaded, that the smiles Sir Hugh might excite would be transient, and that no serious or lasting ridicule could be attached to his character, in the mind of a worthy man, to whom time and opportunity would be allowed for an acquaintance with its habitual beneficence. He excused himself, therefore, from staying any longer, somewhat to the distress of Dr. Orkborne, but hardly with the notice of the baronet, whose eagerness in his new pursuit completely engrossed him.

His late adventure, and his new heiress, now tormented him no more; Indiana was forgotten, Camilla but little thought of, and his whole mind became exclusively occupied by this fruitful expedient for retrieving his lost time.

Dr. Orkborne, whose life had been spent in any study rather than that of human nature, was so little able to enter into the character of Sir Hugh, that nothing less than the respect he knew to be due to Mr. Tyrold, could have saved him, upon his first reception, from a suspicion that he had been summoned in mere mockery. The situation, however, was peculiarly desirable to him, and the experiment, in the beginning, corresponded with the hopes of Mr. Tyrold. Placed suddenly in ease and affluence, Dr. Orkborne, with the most profound desire to please, sought to sustain so convenient a post, by obliging the patron, whom he soon saw it would be vain to attempt improving; while Sir Hugh, in return, professed himself the most fortunate of men, that he had now met with a scholar who had the good nature not to despise him.

Relief from care thus combining with opportunity, Dr. Orkborne was scarce settled, ere he determined upon the execution of a long, critical, and difficult work in philology, which he had often had in contemplation, but never found leisure to undertake.[1] By this means he had a constant resource for himself; and the baronet, observing that time never hung heavy upon his hands, conceived a yet higher admiration of learning, and felt his spirits proportionably re-animated by the fair prospect of participating in such advantages.

From this dream, however, he was soon awakened; a parcel, by the direction of Dr. Orkborne, arrived from his bookseller, with materials for going to work.

Sir Hugh then sent off a message to the parsonage-house, informing his brother and his family, that they must not be surprised if they did not see or hear of him for some time, as he had got his hands quite full, and should be particularly engaged for a week or two to come.

Dr. Orkborne, still but imperfectly conceiving the extent, either of the plan, or of the simplicity of his new pupil, proposed, as soon as the packet was opened, that they should read together; but Sir Hugh replied, that he would do the whole in order, and by no means skip the rudiments.

The disappointment which followed, may be easily imagined; with neither quickness to learn, nor memory to retain, he aimed at being initiated in the elements of a dead language, for which youth only can find time and application, and even youth but by compulsion. His head soon became confused, his ideas were all perplexed, his attention was vainly strained, and his faculties were totally disordered.

Astonished at his own disturbance, which he attributed solely to not getting yet into the right mode, he laughed off his chagrin, but was steady in his perseverance; and continued wholly shut up from his family and friends, with a zeal worthy better success.

Lesson after lesson, however, only aggravated his difficulties, till his intellects grew so embarrassed he scarce knew if he slept or waked. His nights became infected by the perturbation of the day; his health visibly suffered from the restlessness of both, and all his flattering hopes of new and unknown happiness were ere long exchanged for despair.

He now sent for his brother, and desired to speak with him alone; when, catching him fast by the hand, and looking piteously in his face, 'Do you know, my dear brother,' he cried, 'I find myself turning out as sheer a blockhead as ever, for all I have got so many more years over my head than when I began all this hard jingle jangle before?'

Mr. Tyrold, with greater concern than surprise, endeavoured to re-assure and console him, by pointing out a road more attainable for reaping benefit from the presence of Dr. Orkborne, than the impracticable path into which he had erroneously entered.

'Ah! no, my dear brother,' he answered; 'if I don't succeed this way, I am sure I shall succeed no other; for as to pains, I could not have taken more if I had been afraid to be flogged once a-day: and that gentleman has done all he can, too, as far as I know to the contrary. But I really think whatever's the meaning of it, there's some people can't learn.'

Then, shaking his head, he added, in a low voice: 'To say the truth, I might as well have given it up from the very first, for any great comfort I found in it, if it had not been for fear of hurting that gentleman; however, don't let the poor gentleman know that; for I've no right to turn him off upon nothing, merely for the fault of my having no head, which how can he help?'

Mr. Tyrold agreed in the justice of this reflection, and undertook to deliberate upon some conciliatory expedient.

Sir Hugh heartily thanked him; 'But only in the mean time
that you are thinking,' cried he, 'how shall I bring it about to stop
him from coming to me with all those books for my study? For,
do you know, my dear brother, because I asked him to buy me
one for my beginning, he sent for a full score? And when he
comes to me about my lesson, he brings them all upon me
together: which is one thing, for ought I know, that helps to
confuse me; for I am wondering all the while when I shall get
through with them. However, say nothing of all this before the
poor gentleman, for fear he should take it as a hint; which might
put him out of heart: for which reason I'd rather take another
lesson, Lord help me!—than vex him.'

Mr. Tyrold promised his best consideration, and to see him
again the next morning. But he had hardly left Cleves ten
minutes, when a man and horse came galloping after him, with a
petition that he would return without delay.

The baronet received him with a countenance renovated with
self-complacency. 'I won't trouble you,' he cried, 'to think any
more; for now I have got a plan of my own, which I will tell you.
Not to throw this good gentleman entirely away, I intend having
a sort of a kind of school set up here in my sick room, and so to let
all my nephews come, and say their tasks to him in my hearing;
and then, who knows but I may pick up a little amongst them
myself, without all this hard study?'

Mr. Tyrold stated the obvious objections to so wild a scheme;
but he besought him not to oppose it, as there was no other way for
him to get rid of his tutoring, without sending off Dr. Orkborne.
He desired, therefore, that Lionel might come instantly to Cleves;
saying, 'I shall write myself to Eton, by the means of the Doctor,
to tell the Master I shall take Clermont entirely home after the next
holidays, for the sake of having him study under my own eye.'

He then entreated him to prepare Dr. Orkborne for his new
avocation.

Mr. Tyrold, who saw that in this plan the inventor alone could
be disappointed, made no further remonstrance, and communicated the design to Dr. Orkborne; who, growing now deeply
engaged in his own undertaking, was perfectly indifferent to
whom or to what his occasional attendance might be given.

CHAPTER V

Schooling of a young Gentleman

MRS. TYROLD expressed much astonishment that her husband could afford any countenance to this new plan. 'Your expectations from it,' she cried, 'can be no higher than my own; you have certainly some influence with your brother; why, then, will you suffer him thus egregiously to expose himself?'

'I cannot protect his pride,' answered Mr. Tyrold, 'at the expence of his comfort. His faculties want some object, his thoughts some employment. Inaction bodily and intellectual[1] pervading the same character, cannot but fix disgust upon every stage and every state of life. Vice alone is worse than such double inertion. Where mental vigour can be kept alive without offence to religion and virtue, innocence as well as happiness is promoted; and the starter of difficulties with regard to the means which point to such an end, inadvertently risks both. To save the mind from preying inwardly upon itself, it must be encouraged to some outward pursuit. There is no other way to elude apathy, or escape discontent; none other to guard the temper from that quarrel with itself, which ultimately ends in quarrelling with all mankind.'

'But may you not, by refusing to send him your son, induce him to seek recreation in some more rational way?'

'Recreation, my dear Georgiana, must be spontaneous. Bidden pleasures fly the perversity of our tastes. Let us take care, then, scrupulously, of our duties, but suffer our amusements to take care of themselves. A project, a pastime, such as this, is, at least, as harmless as it is hopeless, since the utmost sport of wit, or acrimony of malice, can only fasten a laugh upon it: and how few are the diversions of the rich and indolent that can so lightly be acquitted!'

Lionel, the new young student, speedily, though but little to her satisfaction, abetted the judgment of his mother. He was no sooner summoned to Cleves, than, enchanted to find himself a fellow-pupil with his uncle, he conceived the highest ideas of his own premature genius: and when this vanity, from the avowed ignorance of the artless baronet, subsided, it was only replaced by a sovereign contempt of his new associate. He made the most pompous display of his own little acquirements; he took every opportunity to ask questions of Sir Hugh which he knew he could not answer; and he would sometimes, with an arch mock solemnity, carry his exercise to him, and beg his assistance.

Sir Hugh bore this juvenile impertinence with unshaken good humour. But the spirits of Lionel were too mutinous for such lenity: he grew bolder in his attacks, and more fearless of consequences; and in a very short time, his uncle seemed to him little more than the butt at which he might level the shafts of his rising triumph; till tired, at length, though not angry, the baronet applied to Dr. Orkborne, and begged he would teach him, out of hand, some small little smattering of Latin sentences, by which he might make the young pedant think better of him.

Dr. Orkborne complied, and wrote him a few brief exercises; but these, after toiling day and night to learn, he pronounced so ill, and so constantly mis-applied, that, far from impressing his fellow-labourer with more respect, the moment he uttered a single word of his new lesson, the boy almost rolled upon the floor with convulsive merriment.

Sir Hugh, with whom these phrases neither lost nor gained by mistaking one word for another, appealed to Dr. Orkborne to remedy what he conceived to be an unaccountable failure. Dr. Orkborne, absorbed in his new personal pursuit, to which he daily grew more devoted, was earnest to be as little as possible interrupted, and therefore only advised him to study his last lesson, before he pressed for any thing new.

Study, however, was unavailing, and he heard this injunction with despair; but finding it constantly repeated upon every application for help, he was seized again with a horror of the whole attempt, and begged to consult with Mr. Tyrold.

'This gentleman you have recommended to me for my tutor,' he cried, 'is certainly a great scholar; I don't mean to doubt that the least in the world, being no judge: and he is complaisant enough too, considering all that; but yet I have rather a suspicion he is afraid I shall make no hand of it;[1] which is a thing so disheartening to a person in the line of improvement, that, to tell you the honest truth, I am thinking of giving the whole up at a blow; for, Lord help me! what shall I be the better for knowing Latin and Greek? It's not worth a man's while to think of it, after being a boy. And so, if you please, I'd rather you'd take Lionel home again.'

Mr. Tyrold agreed; but asked what he meant to do further concerning the Doctor?

'Why that, brother, is the very thing my poor ignorant head wants your advice for: because, as to that plan about our learning all together, I see it won't do; for either the boys will grow up to be no better scholars than their uncle, which is to say, none at all; or else they'll hold everybody cheap, when they meet with a person knowing nothing; so I'll have no more hand in it. And I shall really be glad enough to get such a thing off my mind; for it's been weight enough upon it from the beginning.'

He then desired the opinion of Mr. Tyrold what step he should take to prevent the arrival of Clermont Lynmere, whom, he said, he dreaded to see, being determined to have no more little boys about him for some time to come.

Mr. Tyrold recommended re-settling him at Eton: but Sir Hugh declared he could not possibly do that, because the poor little fellow had written him word he was glad to leave school. 'And I don't doubt,' he added, 'but he'll make the best figure of us all; because I had him put in the right mode from the first; though, I must needs own, I had as lieve see him a mere dunce all his life, supposing I should live so long, which God forbid in regard to his dying, as have him turn out a mere coxcomb of a pedant, laughing and grinning at everybody that can't spell a Greek noun.'

Mr. Tyrold promised to take the matter into consideration; but early the next morning, the baronet again summoned him, and joyfully made known, that a scheme had come into his own head, which answered all purposes. In the first place, he said, he had really taken so prodigious a dislike to learning, that he was determined to send Clermont over the seas, to finish his Greek and Latin; not because he was fond of foreign parts, but for fear, if he should let him come to Cleves, the great distaste he had now conceived against those sort of languages, might disgust the poor boy from his book. And he had most luckily recollected, in the middle of the night, that he had a dear friend, one Mr. Westwyn, who was going the very next month to carry his own son to Leipsic; which was just what had put the thought into his head; because, by that means, Clermont might be removed from one studying place to t'other, without loss of time.

'But for all that,' he continued, 'as this good gentleman here has been doing no harm, I won't have him become a sufferer for my changing my mind: and so, not to affront him by giving him nothing to do, which would be like saying, "You may go your ways," I intend he should try Indiana.'

Observing Mr. Tyrold now look with the extremest surprise, he added; 'To be sure, being a girl, it is rather out of the way; but as there is never another boy, what can I do? Besides I shan't so much mind her getting a little learning, because she's not likely to make much hand of it. And this one thing, I can tell you, which I have learnt of my own accord; I'll never press a person to set about studying at my time of life as long as I live, knowing what a plague it is.'

Lionel returned to Etherington with his father, and the rest of the scheme was put into execution without delay. Mr. Westwyn conveyed Clermont from Eton to Leipsic, where he settled him with the preceptor and masters appointed for his own son; and Dr. Orkborne was desired to become the tutor of Indiana.

At first, quitting his learned residence, the Doctor might indignantly have blushed at the proposition of an employment so much beneath his abilities: but he now heard it without the smallest emotion; sedately revolving in his mind, that his literary work would not be affected by the ignorance or absurdity of his several pupils.

CHAPTER VI

Tuition of a young Lady

THE fair Indiana participated not in the philosophy of her preceptor. The first mention of taking lessons produced an aversion unconquerable to their teacher; and the first question he asked her at the appointed hour for study, was answered by a burst of tears.

To Dr. Orkborne this sorrow would have proved no impediment to their proceeding, as he hardly noticed it; but Sir Hugh, extremely affected, kindly kissed her, and said he would beg her off for this time. The next day, however, gave rise but to a similar scene; and the next which followed would precisely have resembled it, had not the promise of some new finery of attire dispersed the pearly drops that were preparing to fall.

The uncommon beauty of Indiana had made her infancy adored, and her childhood indulged by almost all who had seen her. The brilliant picture she presented to the eye by her smiles and her spirits, rendered the devastation caused by crying, pouting, or fretfulness so striking, and so painful to behold, that not alone her uncle, but every servant in the house, and every stranger who visited it, granted to her lamentations whatever they demanded, to relieve their own impatience at the loss of so pleasing an image. Accustomed, therefore, never to weep without advantage, she was in the constant habit of giving unbridled vent to her tears upon the smallest contradiction, well knowing that not to spoil her pretty eyes by crying, was the current maxim of the whole house.

Unused, by this means, to any trouble or application, the purposed tuition of Dr. Orkborne appeared a burden to her intolerable; yet weeping, her standing resource, was with him utterly vain; her tears were unimportant to one who had taken no notice of her smiles; and intent upon his own learned ruminations, he never even looked at her.

Bribery, day after day, could procure but a few instants' attention, given so unwillingly, and so speedily withdrawn, that trinkets, dress, and excursions were soon exhausted, without the smallest advancement. The general indulgence of the baronet made partial favours of small efficacy; and Indiana was sooner tired of receiving, than he of presenting his offerings.

She applied, therefore, at length, to the governess, whose expostulations, she knew by experience, were precisely what Sir Hugh most sedulously aimed to avoid.

Miss Margland was a woman of family and fashion, but reduced, through the gaming and extravagance of her father, to such indigence, that, after sundry failures in higher attempts, she was compelled to acquiesce in the good offices of her friends, which placed her as a governess in the house of Sir Hugh.

To Indiana, however, she was but nominally a tutress; neglected in her own education, there was nothing she could teach, though, born and bred in the circle of fashion, she imagined she had nothing to learn. And, while a mind proudly shallow kept her unacquainted with her own deficiencies, her former rank in society imposed an equal ignorance of them upon Sir Hugh. But, notwithstanding he implicitly gave her credit for possessing whatever she assumed, he found her of a temper so unpleasant, and so irritable to offence, that he made it a rule never to differ from her. The irksomeness of this restraint induced him to keep as much as possible out of her way; though respect and pity for her birth and her misfortunes, led him to resolve never to part with her till Indiana was married.

The spirit of Miss Margland was as haughty as her intellects were weak; and her disposition was so querulous, that, in her constant suspicion of humiliation, she seemed always looking for an affront, and ready primed for a contest.

She seized with pleasure the opportunity offered her by Indiana, of remonstrating against this new system of education; readily allowing, that any accomplishment beyond what she had herself acquired, would be completely a work of supererogation. She represented dictatorily her objections to the baronet. Miss Lynmere, she said, though both beautiful and well brought up, could never cope with so great a disadvantage as the knowledge of Latin: 'Consider, Sir,' she cried, 'what an obstacle it will prove to her making her way in the great world, when she comes to be of a proper age for thinking of an establishment. What gentleman will you ever find that will bear with a learned wife? except some mere downright fogrum,[1] that no young lady of fashion could endure.'

She then spoke of the danger of injuring her beauty by study; and ran over all the qualifications really necessary for a young lady to attain, which consisted simply of an enumeration of all she had herself attempted; a little music, a little drawing, and a little dancing; which should all, she added, be but slightly pursued, to distinguish a lady of fashion from an artist.

Sir Hugh, a good deal disturbed, because unable to answer her, thought it would be best to interest Dr. Orkborne in his plan, and to beg him to reconcile her to its execution. He sent, therefore, a message to the Doctor, to beg to speak with him immediately.

Dr. Orkborne promised to wait upon him without delay: but he was at that moment hunting for a passage in a Greek author, and presently forgot both the promise and the request.

Sir Hugh, concluding nothing but sickness could detain him, went to his apartment; where, finding him perfectly well, he stared at him a moment; and then, sitting down, begged him to make no apology, for he could tell his business there as well as any where else.

He gave a long and copious relation of the objections of Miss Margland, earnestly begging Dr. Orkborne would save him from such another harangue, it being bad for his health, by undertaking to give her the proper notion of things himself.

The Doctor, who had just found the passage for which he had been seeking, heard not one word that he said.

Sir Hugh, receiving no answer, imagined him to be weighing the substance of his narration; and, therefore, bidding him not worry his brain too much, offered him half an hour to fix upon what should be done; and returned quietly to his own room.

Here he sat, counting the minutes, with his watch in his hand, till the time stipulated arrived: but finding Dr. Orkborne let it pass without any notice, he again took the trouble of going back to his apartment.

He then eagerly asked what plan he had formed?

Dr. Orkborne, much incommoded by this second interruption, coldly begged to know his pleasure.

Sir Hugh, with great patience, though much surprise, repeated the whole, word for word, over again: but the history was far too long for Dr. Orkborne, whose attention, after the first sentence or two, was completely restored to his Greek quotation, which he was in the act of transcribing when Sir Hugh re-entered the room.

The baronet, at length, more categorically said, 'Don't be so shy of speaking out, Doctor; though I am afraid, by your silence, you've rather a notion poor Indiana will never get on; which, perhaps, makes you think it not worth while contradicting Mrs. Margland? Come, speak out!—Is that the case with the poor girl?'

'Yes, sir,' answered Dr. Orkborne, with great composure; though perfectly unconscious of the proposition to which he assented.

'Lack a-day! if I was not always afraid she had rather a turn to being a dunce! So it's your opinion it won't do, then?'

'Yes, sir,' again replied the Doctor; his eye the whole time fastened upon the passage which occupied his thoughts.

'Why then we are all at a stand again! This is worse than I thought for! So the poor dear girl has really no head?—Hay, Doctor?—Do speak, pray?—Don't mind vexing me. Say so at once, if you can't help thinking it.'

Another extorted, 'Yes, sir,' completely overset Sir Hugh; who, imputing the absent and perplexed air with which it was pronounced to an unwillingness to give pain, shook him by the hand, and, quitting the room, ordered his carriage, and set off for Etherington.

'Oh, brother,' he cried; 'Indiana's the best girl in the world, as well as the prettiest; but, do you know, Dr. Orkborne says she has got no brains! So there's an end of that scheme! However, I have now thought of another that will settle all differences.'

Mr. Tyrold hoped it was an entire discontinuance of all pupilage and tutorship; and that Dr. Orkborne might henceforth be considered as a mere family friend.

'No, no, my dear brother, no! 'tis a better thing than that, as you shall hear. You must know I have often been concerned to think how glum poor Clermont will look when he hears of my will in favour of Eugenia; which was my chief reason in my own private mind, for not caring to see him before he went abroad; but I have made myself quite easy about him now, by resolving to set little Eugenia upon learning the classics.'

'Eugenia! and of what benefit will that prove to Clermont?'

'Why, as soon as she grows a little old, that is to say, a young woman, I intend, with your good will and my sister's, to marry her to Clermont.'

Mr. Tyrold smiled, but declared his entire concurrence, if the young people, when they grew up, wished for the alliance.

'As to that,' said he, 'I mean to make sure work, by having them educated exactly to fit one another. I shall order Clermont to think of nothing but his studies till the proper time; and as to Eugenia, I shall make her a wife after his own heart, by the help of this gentleman; for I intend to bid him teach her just like a man, which, as she's so young, may be done from the beginning, the same as if she was a boy.'

He then enumerated the advantages of this project, which would save Clermont from all disappointment, by still making over to him his whole fortune, with a wife ready formed into a complete scholar for him into the bargain. It would also hinder Eugenia from being a prey to some sop for her money, who, being no relation, could not have so good a right to it; and it would prevent any affront to Dr. Orkborne, by keeping him a constant tight task in hand.[1]

Mr. Tyrold forbore to chagrin him with any strong expostulation, and he returned, therefore, to Cleves in full glee. He repaired immediately to the apartment of the Doctor, who, only by what was now said, was apprized of what had passed before. Somewhat, therefore, alarmed, to understand that the studies of Indiana were to be relinquished, he exerted all the alacrity in his power for accepting his new little pupil: not from any idea of preference; for he concluded that incapacity of Indiana to be rather that of her sex than of an individual; but from conceiving that his commodious abode at Cleves depended upon his retaining one scholar in the family. Eugenia therefore was called, and the lessons were begun.

The little girl, who was naturally of a thoughtful turn, and whose state of health deprived her of most childish amusements, was well contented with the arrangement, and soon made a progress so satisfactory to Dr. Orkborne, that Sir Hugh, letting his mind now rest from all other schemes, became fully and happily occupied by the prosecution of his last suggestion.

CHAPTER VII

Lost Labour

FROM this period, the families of Etherington and Cleves lived in the enjoyment of uninterrupted harmony and repose, till Eugenia, the most juvenile of the set, had attained her fifteenth year.

Sir Hugh then wrote to Leipsic, desiring his nephew Lynmere to return home without delay. 'Not that I intend,' he said to Mr. Tyrold, 'marrying them together at this young age, Eugenia being but a child, except in point of Latin; though I assure you, my dear brother, she's the most sensible of the whole, poor Indiana being nothing to her, for all her prettiness; but the thing is, the sooner Clermont comes over, the sooner they may begin forming the proper regard.'

The knowledge of this projected alliance was by no means confined to Sir Hugh and Mr. and Mrs. Tyrold; it was known throughout the family, though never publicly announced, and understood from her childhood by Eugenia herself, though Mrs.

Tyrold had exerted her utmost authority to prevent Sir Hugh from apprizing her of it in form. It was nevertheless, the joy of his heart to prepare the young people for each other: and his scheme received every encouragement he could desire, from the zeal and uncommon progress in her studies made by Eugenia; which most happily corresponded with all his injunctions to Leipsic, for the application and acquirements of Clermont.

Thus circumstanced, it was a blow to him the most unexpected, to receive from the young bridegroom elect, in answer to his summons home, a petition to make the tour of Europe, while yet on the continent.

'What!' cried Sir Hugh, 'and is this all his care for us? after so many years separation from his kin and kind, has he no natural longings to see his native land? no yearnings to know his own relations from strangers?'

Eugenia, notwithstanding her extreme youth, secretly applauded and admired a search of knowledge she would gladly have participated [in]; though she was not incurious to see the youth she considered as her destined partner for life, and to whom all her literary labours had been directed: for the never-failing method of Sir Hugh to stimulate her if she was idle, had been to assure her that, unless she worked harder, her cousin Clermont would eclipse her.

She had now acquired a decided taste for study, which, however unusual for her age, most fortunately rescued from weariness or sadness the sedentary life, which a weak state of health compelled her to lead. This induced her to look with pleasure upon Clermont as the object of her emulation, and to prosecute every plan for her improvement, with that vigour which accompanies a pursuit of our own choice; the only labour that asks no relaxation.

Steady occupations, such as these, kept off all attention to her personal misfortunes, which Sir Hugh had strictly ordered should never be alluded to; first, he said, for fear they should vex her; and next, lest they should make her hate him, for being their cause. Those incidents, therefore, from never being named, glided imperceptibly from her thoughts; and she grew up as unconscious as she was innocent, that, though born with a beauty which surpassed that of her lovely sisters, disease and accident had robbed her of that charm ere she knew she possessed it. But neither disease nor accident had power over her mind; there, in its purest proportions, moral beauty preserved its first energy. The equanimity of her temper made her seem, though a female, born to be a practical philosopher;[1] her abilities and her sentiments were each of the highest class, uniting the best adorned intellects with the best principled virtues.

The dissatisfaction of Sir Hugh with his nephew reached not to prohibition: his consent was painful, but his remittances were generous, and Clermont had three years allowed him for his travels through Europe.

Yet this permission was no sooner granted than the baronet again became dejected. Three years appeared to him to be endless: he could hardly persuade himself to look forward to them with expectation of life; and all the learned labours he had promoted seemed vain and unpromising, ill requiting his toils, and still less answering his hopes. Even the studious turn of Eugenia, hitherto his first delight, he now thought served but to render her unsociable; and the time she devoted to study, he began to regret as lost to himself; nor could he suggest any possible consolation for his drooping spirits, till it occurred to him that Camilla might again enliven him.

This idea, and the order for his carriage, were the birth of the same moment; and, upon entering the study of Mr. Tyrold, he abruptly exclaimed, 'My dear brother, I must have Camilla back! Indiana says nothing to amuse me; and Eugenia is so bookish, I might as well live with an old woman; which God forbid I should object to, only I like Camilla better.'

This request was by no means welcome to Mr. Tyrold, and utterly distasteful to his lady. Camilla was now just seventeen years of age, and attractively lovely; but of a character that called for more attention to its developement than to its formation; though of a disposition so engaging, that affection kept pace with watchfulness, and her fond parents knew as little for their own sakes as for her's how to part with her.

Her qualities had a power which, without consciousness how, or consideration why, governed her whole family. The airy thoughtlessness of her nature was a source of perpetual amusement; and, if sometimes her vivacity raised a fear for her discretion, the innocence of her mind reassured them after every alarm. The interest which she excited served to render her the first object of the house; it was just short of solicitude, yet kept it constantly alive. Her spirits were volatile, but her heart was tender; her gaiety had a fascination; her persuasion was irresistible.

To give her now up to Sir Hugh, seemed to Mrs. Tyrold rather impossible than disagreeable; but he was too urgent with his brother to be wholly refused. She was granted him, therefore, as a guest, for the three ensuing months, to aid him to dissipate his immediate disappointment, from the procrastinated absence of Clermont.

Sir Hugh received back his first favourite with all the fond glee of a ductile imagination, which in every new good sees a refuge from every past or present evil. But, as the extremest distaste of all literature now succeeded those sanguine views which had lately made it his exclusive object, the first words he spoke upon her arrival were, to inform her she must learn no Latin; and the first step which followed her welcome, was a solemn charge to Dr. Okborne, that he must give her no lessons.

The gaiety, the spirit, the playful good humour of Camilla, had lost nothing of their charm by added years, though her understanding had been sedulously cultivated, and her principles modelled by the pure and practical tenets of her exemplary parents. The delight of Sir Hugh in regaining her, consisted not merely of the renovation of his first prejudice in her favour; it was strengthened by the restoration it afforded his own mind to its natural state, and the relief of being disburthened of a task he was so ill calculated to undertake, as superintending, in any sort, intellectual pursuits.

BOOK II

CHAPTER I

New Projects

THE baronet would, at length, have enjoyed perfect contentment, had he not been molested by the teasing spirit of Miss Margland, now daily at work in proposing a journey to London, and in representing as an indispensable duty, that the young ladies should see and be seen, in a manner suitable to their situation in life.

Miss Margland, equally void either of taste or of resources for the country, had languished and fretted away twelve years in its bosom, with no other opening to any satisfaction beyond a maintenance, except what she secretly nourished in her hopes, that, when her beautiful pupil was grown up, she should accompany her to the metropolis. Her former connections and acquaintance in high life still continued to be the stationary pride of her heart, the constant theme of her discourse, and the perpetual allusion of some lamentation and regret. This excursion, therefore, in prospect, had been her sole support during her retirement; nor had she failed to instruct her fair disciple to aid her scheme, though she had kept from her its private motive.

Most successfully, indeed, had she instilled into the youthful breast of Indiana, a wondering curiosity to see the place which she described as the sole residence of elegance and fashion, and an eager impatience to exhibit there a person which she was assured would meet with universal homage.

But neither the exhortations of the governess, nor the wishes of her pupil, could in this point move Sir Hugh. He had a fixt aversion to London, and to all public places, and had constantly some disaster to relate of every visit he had accidentally made to them. The amusements which had decided his partiality for the country were now, indeed, no longer within his reach; but his sanguine temper, which occasionally entertained him with hopes of a recovery, determined him always to keep upon the right spot, he said, for sport, in the case of any sudden and favourable change in his health.

Upon the visit of Camilla, Miss Margland grew yet more urgent, expecting through her powerful influence to gain her point. She strove, therefore, to engage her intercession, but Camilla, careless, easy, and gay, had no wish about the matter, and could not be brought into the cabal.

This disappointment so much soured and provoked Miss Margland, that she lost the usual discretion she had hitherto practised, of confining her remonstrances to those times when she saw Sir Hugh alone. Such opportunities, indeed, weary of the use she made of them, the baronet contrived daily to lessen; but every meeting now, whether public or private, was seized alike for the same purpose, and the necessity of *bringing the young ladies out*, and the duty of *thinking of their establishment*,[1] were the sentences with which he was so regularly assailed, that the moment he saw her he prepared to hear them, and commonly with a heavy sigh anticipated their fatigue to his spirits.

No arguments, however, relative to disposing of the young ladies, had any weight with him; he had long planned to give Eugenia to Clermont Lynmere, and he depended upon Edgar Mandlebert for Indiana, while with regard to Camilla, to keep her unmarried, that he might detain her under his own roof, was the favourite wish of his heart. Nevertheless, this perpetual persecution became by degrees insupportable, and, unused to be deaf to any claimant, he was upon the point of constrained compliance, when his passion for forming schemes came again to his aid, upon hearing that Edgar Mandlebert, after a twelve-month's absence, was just returned to Etherington.

This youth had been making the tour of England, Wales, and Scotland, with Dr. Marchmont, who had been induced by Mr. Tyrold to relinquish all other avocations, and devote to him his whole time.

Sir Hugh hastening, upon this news, to the parsonage-house, said: 'Don't imagine, brother, I am going to make any complaint against Mrs. Margland, for she is an excellent governess, and I have no fault to find with her, except her making too many objections, which I take to be her worst part; but as every body has something, it would be very unfair to quarrel with her for such a mere nothing, especially as she can't help it, after so many years going on the same way, without coming to a stop; but the thing I have thought of now may set it all to rights, which I hope you'll approve, and especially my sister.'

He then explained, that as he had fixt upon marrying Eugenia to Clermont Lynmere, she was put so completely under the care of Dr. Orkborne, in order to make her fit for the young scholar, that Miss Margland was of little or no use to her. He meant, therefore, to bring forward immediately the marriage of Indiana with young Mandlebert, and then to ask Miss Margland to go and live with them entirely, as he could very well spare her: 'This,' he continued, 'Indiana can't object to, from the point of having had her so long; and young Mr. Edgar's remarkably complaisant, for such a young youth, which I saw a great while ago. By this means, Mrs. Margland will get her main end of going to London, which she may show off to the young bride, without my budging from home, Lord help me! being a thing I don't much like, to be taken about to dances and shews, now that I am not a boy; so then Camilla will be left to stay with me, for my own companion; which I assure you I desire no better, though she knows no more, as the Doctor tells me, of the classics, than my old spaniel; which, to give every one his due, is much the same with myself.'

Mr. Tyrold, with a very unpleasant astonishment, enquired further into his meaning concerning Mandlebert; but his surprise ended in a smile, when he heard the juvenile circumstances upon which alone Sir Hugh built his expectations. To argue with him, however, was always fruitless; he had found out, he said, the intentions of Edgar from the first, and he came now to invite him to pass a month at Cleves, for the sake of cutting the courtship short, by letting him see Indiana every day, so that no time might be lost in coming to the conclusion.

The first wish of the secret heart of Mr. Tyrold was, that one of his own daughters should be the choice of his ward; he did not, therefore, totally unmoved, hear this project for Indiana, though its basis was so little alarming.

Edgar, who was now just of age, was receiving the last cares of his guardian, and taking into his own hands his fortune and affairs. He was at Etherington, at present, only for that purpose, Beech Park being already fitted up for his residence.

Sir Hugh, desiring to speak with him, most cordially made his invitation: 'Besides myself,' he cried, 'whom I only mention first, as being master of the house, which I hope is my excuse for it, you will meet three very good young girls, not to mention Dr. Orkborne and Miss Margland, who are rather not of the youngest at present, whatever they may have been in former times; and they will all, myself included, make you as welcome as themselves.'

Edgar accepted the proposal with pleasure, and agreed to wait upon him the next day, Mr. Tyrold consenting that they should transact their mutual business at Etherington, by morning rides.

At dinner Sir Hugh told the family at Cleves the new guest they were so soon to expect, assuring them he was become a very fine young gentleman, and bidding Indiana, with a significant nod, hold up her head.

Indiana wanted no charge upon this subject; she fully understood the views of her uncle, and it was now some years since she had heard the name of Beech Park without a smile or a blush.

Upon the arrival of the young man, Sir Hugh summoned his household to meet him in the hall, where he received him with an hearty welcome, and, in the flutter of his spirits, introduced him to them all, as if this had been his first appearance in the family; remarking, that a full week of shyness might be saved, by making acquaintance with the whole set in a clump.

From eagerness irrepressible, he began with Indiana, apologising when he had done, by saying it was only because she was oldest, having the advantage of three weeks over Camilla: 'For which, however,' he added, 'I must beg pardon of Mrs. Margland and Dr. Orkborne, who, to be sure, must be pretty much older.'

He next presented him to Camilla; and then, taking him apart, begged, in a whisper, that he would not seem to notice the ugliness of Eugenia, which, he said, was never mentioned in her hearing, by his particular order; 'though, to be sure,' he added, 'since that small-pox, she's grown plain enough, in point of beauty, considering how pretty she was before. However, she's a remarkable good girl, and with regard to Virgil and those others will pose you in a second, for aught I know to the contrary, being but an indifferent judge in things of that sort, from leaving off my own studies rather short, on account of the gout; besides some other reasons.'

Edgar assured him these introductions were by no means

necessary, a single twelvemonth's absence being very insufficient to obliterate from his memory his best and earliest friends.

Edgar Mandlebert was a young man who, if possessed neither of fortune nor its expectations, must from his person and his manners have been as attractive to the young, as from his morals and his conduct to those of riper years. His disposition was serious and meditative; but liberal, open, and candid. He was observant of the errors of others, and watched till he nearly eradicated his own. But though with difficulty he bestowed admiration, he diffused, both in words and deeds, such general amity and good will, that if the strictness of his character inspired general respect, its virtues could no less fail engaging the kinder mede of affection.[1] When to merit of a species so rare were added a fine estate and a large independent fortune, it is not easy to decide whether in prosperity or desert he was most distinguished.

The first week which he spent at Cleves, was passed with a gaiety as unremitting as it was innocent. All parties felt his arrival as an acquisition: Indiana thought the hour of public exhibition, long promised by Miss Margland, at length fast approaching; Camilla, who escaped all expectation for herself, from being informed of what was entertained by her cousin, enjoyed the tranquil pleasure of undesigning friendship, unchequered either by hope or fear; Eugenia met with a respect for her acquirements that redoubled her ambition to increase them; Sir Hugh looked forward with joy to the happy disposal of Indiana, and a blameless riddance of Miss Margland; who, on her part, with an almost boundless satisfaction, saw her near return to a town life, from the high favour in which she stood with the supposed bride elect; even Dr. Orkborne, though he disdained with so young a scholar to enter into much philological disquisition, was gratified by a presence which afforded a little relief to the stores of his burdened memory, from authorizing some occasional utterance of the learned recollections, which for many years had encumbered it without vent. Edgar, meanwhile, obliging and obliged, received pleasure from them all; for though not blind to any of their imperfections, they had not a merit which he failed to discern.

The second week opened with a plan which promised a scene more lively, though it broke into the calm retirement of this peaceful party. Lionel, who was now at Etherington, to spend his university vacation, rode over to Cleves, to inform Edgar, that there would be a ball the next evening at Northwick, at which the officers of the * * * regiment, which was quartered in the neighbourhood, and all the beaux and belles of the county, were expected to assemble.

Miss Margland, who was present, struck with a desire that Indiana might make her first public appearance in the county, at a ball where Edgar might be her partner, went instantly to Sir Hugh to impart the idea. Sir Hugh, though averse to all public places, consented to the plan, from the hope of accelerating the affair; but declared, that if there was any amusement, his little Camilla should not be left out. Eugenia, won by the novelty of a first expedition of this sort, made her own request to be included; Lionel undertook to procure tickets, and Miss Margland had the welcome labour of arranging their dress, for which Sir Hugh, to atone for the shortness of the time, gave her powers unlimited.

Indiana was almost distracted with joy at this event. Miss Margland assured her, that now was the moment for fixing her conquest of Mandlebert, by adroitly displaying to him the admiration she could not but excite, in the numerous strangers before whom she would appear; she gave her various instructions how to set off her person to most advantage, and she delighted Sir Hugh with assurances of what this evening would effect: 'There is nothing, Sir,' said she, 'so conducive towards a right understanding between persons of fashion, as a ball. A gentleman may spend months and months in this drowsy way in the country, and always think one day will do as well as another for his declaration; but when he sees a young lady admired and noticed by others, he falls naturally into making her the same compliments, and the affair goes into a regular train, without his almost thinking of it.'

Sir Hugh listened to this doctrine with every desire to give it credit; and though the occupations of the toilette left him alone the whole of the assembly day, he was as happy in the prospect of their diversion, as they were themselves in its preparation.

When the young ladies were ready, they repaired to the apartment of the baronet, to shew themselves, and to take leave. Edgar and Lionel were waiting to meet them upon the stairs. Indiana had never yet looked so lovely; Camilla, with all her attractions, was eclipsed; and Eugenia could only have served as a foil, even to those who had no pretensions to beauty.

Edgar, nevertheless, asked Camilla to dance with him; she

willingly, though not without wonder, consented. Lionel desired the hand of his fair cousin; but Indiana, self-destined to Edgar, whose address to Camilla, she had not heard, made him no answer, and ran on to present herself to her uncle; who, struck with admiration as he beheld her, cried, 'Indiana, my dear, you really look prettier than I could even have guessed; and yet I always knew there was no fault to be found with the outside; nor indeed with the inside neither, Mr. Mandlebert, so I don't mean anything by that; only, by use, one is apt to put the outside first.'

Lionel was now hurrying them away, when Sir Hugh calling to Edgar, said: 'Pray, young Mr. Mandlebert, take as much care of her as possible; which I am sure you will do of your own accord.'

Edgar, with some surprise, answered, he should be happy to take whatever care was in his power of all the ladies; 'but,' added he, 'for my own particular charge to-night, I have engaged Miss Camilla.'

'And how came you to do that? Don't you know I let them all go on purpose for the sake of your dancing with Indiana, which I mean as a particular favour?'

'Sir,' replied Edgar, a little embarrassed, "you are very good; but as Lionel cannot dance with his sisters, he has engaged Miss Lynmere himself.'

'Pho, pho, what do you mind Lionel for? not but what he's a very good lad; only I had rather have you and Indiana dance together, which I dare say so had she.'

Edgar, somewhat distressed, looked at Camilla: 'O, as to me,' cried she, gaily, 'pray let me take my chance; if I should not dance at all, the whole will be so new to me, that I am sure of entertainment.'

'You are the best good girl, without the smallest exception,' said Sir Hugh, 'that ever I have known in the world; and so you always were; by which I mean nothing as to Indiana, who is just such another, except in some points; and so here's her hand, young Mr. Mandlebert, and if you think you shall meet a prettier partner at the ball, I beg when you get her there, you will tell her so fairly, and give her up.'

Edgar, who had hardly yet looked at her, was now himself struck with the unusual resplendence of her beauty, and telling Camilla he saw she was glad to be at liberty, protested he could not but rejoice to be spared a decision for himself, where the choice would have been so difficult.

'Well then, now go,' cried the delighted baronet; 'Lionel will find himself a partner, I have no doubt, because he is nothing particular in point of shyness; and as to Camilla, she'll want nothing but to hear the fiddlers to be as merry as a grig,[1] which what it is I never knew: so I have no concern,' added he, in a low voice, to Edgar, 'except for little Eugenia, and poor Mrs. Margland; for Eugenia being so plain, which is no fault of her's, on account of the small-pox, many a person may overlook her from that objection; and as to Mrs. Margland, being with all these young chickens, I am afraid people will think her rather one of the oldest for a dancing match; which I say in no disrespect, for oldness gives one no choice.'

CHAPTER II

New Characters

THE dancing was not yet begun, but the company was met, and the sprightly violins were employed to quicken their motions, when the Cleves party entered the ball room. They were distinguished immediately by a large party of officers, who assured Lionel, with whom they were acquainted, that they had impatiently been expected.

'I shall recompense you for waiting,' answered he, in a whisper, 'by introducing you to the rich heiress of Cleves, who now makes her first appearance from the nursery; though no! upon farther thoughts, I will only tell you she is one of our set, and leave it to your own ingenuity to find her out.'

While this was passing, Indiana, fluttering with all the secret triumph of conscious beauty, attended by Edgar, and guarded by Miss Margland, walked up the room, through a crowd of admiring spectators; in whom a new figure, without half her loveliness, would have excited the same curiosity, that her extreme inexperience attributed solely to her peculiar charms. Camilla and Eugenia followed rather as if in her train, than of her party; but Lionel kept entirely with the officers, insisting upon their guessing which was the heiress; to whom, while he purposely misled their conjectures, he urged them to make their court, by enumerating the present possessions of Sir Hugh, and her future expectations.

Camilla, however, passed not long unnoticed, though the splendor of Indiana's appearance cast her at first on the back ground; a circumstance which, by impressing her with a sensation of inferiority, divested her mind of all personal considerations, and gave to her air and countenance a graceful simplicity, a disengaged openness, and a guileless freedom from affectation, that rendered her, to the observant eye, as captivating upon examination, as Indiana, from the first glance, was brilliant and alluring. And thus, as they patrolled the room, Indiana excited an unmixt admiration, Camilla awakened an endless variety of remark; while each being seen for the first time, and every one else of the company for at least the second, all attention was their own, whether for criticism or for praise. To Indiana this answered, in fulfilling her expectations; by Camilla, it was unheeded, for, not awaiting, she did not perceive it; yet both felt equal satisfaction. The eyes of Camilla sparkled with delight as she surveyed all around her the gay novelty of the scene; the heart of Indiana beat with a pleasure wholly new, as she discovered that all surrounding her regarded her as the principal object.

Eugenia, meanwhile, had not even the negative felicity to pass unobserved; impertinent witticisms upon her face, person, and walk, though not uttered so audibly as to be distinctly heard, ran round the room in a confused murmur, and produced a disposition for sneering in the satirical, and for tittering in the giddy, that made her as valuable an acquisition to the company at large, who collect for any amusement, indifferent to its nature, as her fair cousin proved to the admirers of beauty, and her sister to the developers of expression. She was shielded, however, herself, from all undeserved mortifications, by not suspecting any were meant for her, and by a mind delightedly pre-occupied with that sudden expansion of ideas, with which new scenery and new objects charm a youthful imagination.

When they had taken two or three turns up and down the room, the saunterers were called upon to give place to the dancers. Edgar then led out Indiana, and the master of the ceremonies brought Major Cerwood to Camilla.

Eugenia, wholly left out, became the exclusive charge of Miss Margland; she felt no resentment of neglect, for she had formed no species of expectation. She looked on with perfect contentment, and the motley and quick changing group afforded her ample entertainment.

Miss Margland was not so passive; she seized the opportunity of inveighing very angrily against the mismanagement of Sir Hugh: 'If you had all,' she cried, 'been taken to town, and properly brought out, according to my advice, such a disgrace as this could never have happened; everybody would have known who you were, and then, there is no doubt, you might have had partners enough; however, I heartily hope you won't be asked to dance all the evening, that he may be convinced who was in the right; besides, the more you are tired, the more you may see, against another time, Miss Eugenia, that it is better to listen a little to people's opinions, when they speak only for your own advantage, than to go on with just the same indifference, as if you had no proper person to consult with.'

Eugenia was too well amused to heed this remonstrance; and long accustomed to hear the voice of Miss Margland without profit or pleasure, her ear received its sound, but her attention included not its purpose.

Indiana and Camilla, in this public essay, acquitted themselves with all the merits, and all the faults common to a first exhibition. The spectators upon such occasions, though never equally observant, are never afterwards so lenient. Whatever fails is attributed to modesty, more winning than the utmost success of excellence. Timidity solicits that mercy which pride is most gratified to grant; the blushes of juvenile shame atone for the deficiencies which cause them; and aukwardness itself, in the un- founded terrors of youth, is perhaps more interesting than grace.

Indiana could with difficulty keep to the figure of the dance, from the exulting, yet unpractised certainty of attracting all eyes; and Camilla perpetually turned wrong, from the mere flutter of fear, which made her expect she should never turn right. Major Cerwood, her partner, with a view to encourage her, was profuse in his compliments; but, as new to what she heard as what she performed, she was only the more confused by the double claim to her attention.

Edgar, meanwhile, was most assiduous to aid his fair partner. Miss Margland, though scarcely even superficial in general knowledge, was conversant in the practical detail of the hackneyed mode of forming matrimonial engagements; she judged, therefore, rightly, that her pupil would be seen to most advantage, in the distinction of that adulation by which new beholders would stamp new value on her charms. From the time of his first boyish gallantry, on the ill-fated birth-day of Camilla, Indiana had never so much struck young Mandlebert, as while he attended her up the assembly-room.[1] Miss Margland observed this with triumph, and prophesied the speediest conclusion to her long and weary sojourn at Cleves, in the much wished-for journey to London, with a bride ready made, and an establishment ready formed.

When the two first dances were over, the gentlemen were desired to change partners.[2] Major Cerwood asked the hand of Indiana, and Edgar repaired to Camilla: 'Do you bear malice?' he cried, with a smile, 'or may I now make the claim that Sir Hugh relinquished for me?'

'O yes,' answered she, with alacrity, when informed of the plan of change; 'and I wish there was any body else, that would dance with me afterwards, instead of that Major.'

'I dare believe,' said he, laughing 'there are many bodies else, who would oblige you, if your declaration were heard. But what has the Major done to you? Has he admired you without knowing how to keep is own counsel?'

'No, no; only he has treated me like a country simpleton, and made me as many fine speeches, as if he had been talking to Indiana.'

'You think, then, Indiana would have swallowed flattery with less difficulty?'

'No, indeed! but I think the same things said to her would no longer have been so extravagant.'

Edgar, to whom the sun-beams of the mind gave a glow which not all the sparkling rays of the brightest eyes could emit, respected her modesty too highly to combat it, and, dropping the subject, enquired what was become of Eugenia.

'O poor Eugenia!' cried she, 'I see nothing of her, and I am very much afraid she has had no better partner all this time than Miss Margland.'

Edgar, turning round, presently discerned her; she was still looking on, with an air of the most perfect composure, examining the various parties, totally without suspicion of the examination she was herself sustaining; while Miss Margland was vainly pouring in her ears observations, or exhortations, evidently of a complaining nature.

'There is something truly respectable,' said Edgar, 'in the innate philosophy with which she bears such neglect.'

'Yet I wish it were put less to the proof;' said Camilla. 'I would give the world somebody would take her out!'

'You don't think she would dance?'

'O yes she would! her lameness is no impediment; for she never thinks of it. We all learnt together at Cleves. Dancing gives her a little more exertion, and therefore a little more fatigue than other people, but that is all.'

'After these two dances then—'

'Will you be her partner?' interrupted Camilla, 'O go to her at once! immediately! and you will give me twenty times more pleasure than I can have in dancing myself.'

She then flew to a form, and eagerly seated herself where she perceived the first vacancy, to stop any debate, and enforce his consent.

The dance, which had been delayed by a dispute about the tune, was now beginning. Edgar, looking after her with affected reproach, but real admiration, asked the hand of Eugenia; who gave it with readiness and pleasure; for, though contented as a spectatress, she experienced an agreeable surprise in becoming a party engaged.

Camilla, happy in her own good humour, now looked at her neighbours; one of which was an elderly lady, who, wholly employed in examining and admiring the performance of her own daughters, saw nothing else in the room. The other was a gentleman, much distinguished by his figure and appearance, and dressed so completely in the extreme of fashion, as more than to border upon foppery. The ease and negligence of his air denoted a self-settled superiority to all about him; yet, from time to time, there was an archness in the glance of his eye, that promised, under a deep and wilful veil of conceit and affectation, a secret disposition to deride the very follies he was practising. He was now lounging against the wainscoat; with one hand on his side, and the other upon his eye-lids, occupying the space, without using the seat, to the left of Camilla.

Miss Margland, perceiving what she regarded as a fair vacancy, made up to the spot, and saying, "Sir, by your leave,' was preparing to take possession of the place, when the gentleman, as if without seeing her, dropt suddenly into it himself, and, pouring a profusion of *eau suave*[1] upon his handkerchief, exclaimed: 'What a vastly bad room this is for dancing!'

Camilla, concluding herself addressed, turned round to him; but, seeing he was sniffing up the *eau suave*, without looking at her, imagined he meant to speak to Miss Margland.

Miss Margland was of the same opinion, and, with some pique at his seizing thus her intended seat, rather sharply answered: 'Yes, sir, and it's a vast bad room for *not* dancing; for if every body would dance that ought, there would be accommodation sufficient for other people.'

'Incomparably well observed!' cried he, collecting some bonbons from a bonboniere, and swallowing one after another with great rapidity: 'But won't you sit down? You must be enormously tired. Let me supplicate you to sit down.'

Miss Margland, supposing he meant to make amends for his inattention, by delivering up the place, civilly thanked him, and said she should not be sorry, for she had stood a good while.

'Have you, indeed?' cried he, sprinkling some jessamine drops upon his hands; 'how horribly abominable? Why don't some of those Mercuries, those Ganymedes, those waiters, I believe you call them, get you a chair?'

Miss Margland, excessively affronted, turned her back to him; and Camilla made an offer of her own seat; but, as she had been dancing, and would probably dance again, Miss Margland would not let her rise.

'Shall I call to one of those Barbarians, those Goths, those Vandals?' cried the same gentleman, who now was spirting lavender water all about him, with grimaces that proclaimed forcibly his opinion of the want of perfume in the room: 'Do pray let me harangue them a little for you upon their inordinate want of sensibility.'

Miss Margland deigned not any answer; but of that he took no notice, and presently called out, though without raising his voice, 'Here, Mr. Waiter! Purveyor, Surveyor, or whatsoever other title "*please thine ear*," art thou deaf?[2] why dost not bring this lady a chair? Those people are most amazing hard of hearing! Shall I call again? Waiter, I say!' still speaking rather lower than louder; 'Don't I stun you by this shocking vociferation?'

'Sir, you're vastly—obliging!' cried Miss Margland, unable longer to hold silence, yet with a look and manner that would much better have accorded with vastly—*impertinent*.

Shen then pursued a waiter herself, and procured a chair.

Casting his eyes next upon Camilla, he examined her with much attention. Abashed, she turned away her head; but not choosing to lose his object, he called it back again, by familiarly saying, 'How is Sir Hugh?'

A good deal surprised, she exclaimed, 'Do you know my uncle, sir?'

'Not in the least, ma'am,' he coolly answered.

Camilla, much wondering, was then forced into conversation with Miss Margland: but, without paying any regard to her surprise, he presently said, 'It's most extremely worth your while to take a glance at that inimitably good figure. Is it not exquisite? Can you suppose any thing beyond it?'

Camilla, looking at the person to whom he pointed, and who was sufficiently ludicrous, from an air of vulgar solemnity, and a dress stiffly new, though completely old-fashioned, felt disposed to join in his laugh, had she not been disconcerted by the mingled liberty and oddity of his attack.

'Sir,' said Miss Margland, winking at her to be silent, though eager to answer in her stead, 'the mixt company one always meets at these public balls, makes them very unfit for ladies of fashion, for there's no knowing who one may either dance with or speak to.'

'Vastly true, ma'am,' cried he, superciliously dropping his eyes, not to look at her.

Miss Margland, perceiving this, bridled resentfully, and again talked on with Camilla; till another exclamation interrupted them. 'O pray,' cried he, 'I do entreat you look at that group! Is it not past compare? If ever you held a pencil in your life, I beg and beseech you to take a memorandum of that tall may-pole. Have you ever seen any thing so excessively delectable?'

Camilla could not forbear smiling; but Miss Margland, taking all reply upon herself, said: 'Caricatures, sir, are by no means pleasing for young ladies to be taking, at their first coming out: one does not know who may be next, if once they get into that habit!'

'Immeasurably well spoken, ma'am,' returned he; and, rising with a look of disgust, he sauntered to another part of the room.

Miss Margland, extremely provoked, said she was sure he was some Irish fortune-hunter, dressed out in all he was worth; and charged Camilla to take no manner of notice of him.

When the two second dances were over, Edgar, conducting Eugenia to Miss Margland, said to Camilla: 'Now, at least, if there is not a spell against it, will you dance with me?'

'And if there is one, too,' cried she, gaily; 'for I am perfectly disposed to help breaking it.'

She rose, and they were again going to take their places, when Miss Margland, reproachfully calling after Edgar, demanded what he had done with Miss Lynmere?

At the same moment, led by Major Cerwood, who was paying her in full all the arrears of that gallantry Miss Margland had taught her to regret hitherto missing, Indiana joined them; the Major, in making his bow, lamenting the rules of the assembly, that compelled him to relinquish her hand.

'Mr. Mandlebert,' said Miss Margland, 'you see Miss Lynmere is again disengaged.'

'Yes, ma'am,' answered Edgar, drawing Camilla away; 'and every gentleman in the room will be happy to see it too.'

'Stop, Miss Camilla!' cried Miss Margland; 'I thought, Mr. Mandlebert, Sir Hugh had put Miss Lynmere under your protection?'

'O it does not signify!' said Indiana, colouring high with a new raised sense of importance; 'I don't at all doubt but one or other of the officers will take care of me.'

Edgar, though somewhat disconcerted, would still have proceeded; but Camilla, alarmed by the frowns of Miss Margland, begged him to lead out her cousin, and, promising to be in readiness for the next two dances, glided back to her seat. He upbraided her in vain; Miss Margland looked pleased, and Indiana was so much piqued, that he found it necessary to direct all his attention to appeasing her, as he led her to join the dance.

A gentleman now, eminently distinguished by personal beauty, approached the ladies that remained, and, in the most respectful manner, began conversing with Miss Margland; who received his attentions so gratefully, that, when he told her he only waited to see the master of the ceremonies at leisure, in order to have the honour of begging the hand of one of her young ladies, his civilities so conquered all her pride of etiquette, that she assured him there was no sort of occasion for such a formality, with a person of his appearance and manners; and was bidding Camilla rise, who was innocently preparing to obey, when, to the surprise of them all, he addressed himself to Eugenia.

'There!' cried Miss Margland, exultingly, when they were gone; 'that gentleman is completely a gentleman. I saw it from the beginning. How different to that impertinent fop that spoke to us just now! He has the politeness to take out Miss Eugenia, because he sees plainly nobody else will think of it, except just Mr. Mandlebert, or some such old acquaintance.'

Major Cerwood was now advancing towards Camilla, with that species of smiling and bowing manner, which is the usual precursor of an invitation to a fair partner; when the gentleman whom Miss Margland had just called an impertinent fop, with a sudden swing, not to be eluded, cast himself between the Major and Camilla, as if he had not observed his approach; and spoke to her in a voice so low, that, though she concluded he asked her to dance, she could not distinctly hear a word he said.

A good deal confused, she looked at him for an explanation; while the Major, from her air of attention, supposing himself too late, retreated.

Her new beau then, carelessly seating himself by her side, indolently said: 'What a heat! I have not the most distant idea how you can bear it!'

Camilla found it impossible to keep her countenance at such a result of a whisper, though she complied with the injunctions of Miss Margland, in avoiding mutual discourse with a stranger of so showy an appearance.

'Yet they are dancing on,' he continued, 'just as if the Greenland snows were inviting their exercise! I should really like to find out what those people are made of. Can you possibly imagine their composition?'

Heedless of receiving no answer, he soon after added: 'I am vastly glad you don't like dancing.'

'Me?' cried Camilla, surprised out of her caution.

'Yes; you hold it in antipathy, don't you?'

'No, indeed! far from it.'

'Don't you really?' cried he, starting back; 'that's amazingly extraordinary! surprising in the extreme! Will you have the goodness to tell me what you like in it?'

'Sir,' interfered Miss Margland, 'there's nothing but what's very natural in a young lady's taking pleasure in an elegant accomplishment; provided she is secure from any improper partner, or company.'

'Irrefragably just, ma'am!' answered he; affecting to take a pinch of snuff, and turning his head another way.

Here Lionel, hastily running up to Camilla, whispered, 'I have made a fine confusion among the red-coats about the heiress of Cleves! I have put them all upon different scents.'

He was then going back, when a faint laugh from the neighbour of Camilla detained him; 'Look, I adjure you,' cried he, addressing her, 'if there's not that delightful creature again, with his bran-new clothes? and they sit upon him so tight, he can't turn round his vastly droll figure, except like a puppet with one jerk for the whole body. He is really an immense treat: I should like of all things in nature, to know who he can be.'

A waiter then passing with a glass of water for a lady, he stopt him in his way, exclaiming: 'Pray, my extremely good friend, can you tell me who that agreeable person is, that stands there, with the air of a poker?'

'Yes, sir,' answered the man; 'I know him very well. His name is Dubster. He's quite a gentleman to my knowledge, and has very good fortunes.'

'Camilla,' cried Lionel, 'will you have him for a partner?' And, immediately hastening up to him, he said two or three words in a low voice, and skipped back to the dance.

Mr. Dubster then walked up to her, and, with an air conspicuously aukward, solemnly said, 'So you want to dance, ma'am?'

Convinced he had been sent to her by Lionel, but by no means chusing to display herself with a figure distinguished only as a mark for ridicule; she looked down to conceal her ever-ready smiles, and said she had been dancing some time.

'But if you like to dance again, ma'am,' said he, 'I am very ready to oblige you.'

She now saw that this offer had been requested as a favour; and, while half provoked, half diverted, grew embarrassed how to get rid of him, without involving a necessity to refuse afterwards Edgar, and every other; for Miss Margland had informed her of the general rules upon these occasions. She looked, therefore, at that lady for counsel; while her neighbour, sticking his hands in his sides, surveyed him from head to foot, with an expression of such undiguised amusement, that Mr. Dubster, who could not help observing it, cast towards him, from time to time, a look of the most angry surprise.

Miss Margland approving, as well understanding the appeal, now authoritatively interfered, saying: 'Sir, I suppose you know the etiquette in public places?'

'The what, ma'am?' cried he, staring.

'You know, I suppose, sir, that no young lady of any considera-tion dances with a gentleman that is a stranger to her, without he's brought to her by the master of the ceremonies?'

'O as to that, ma'am, I have no objection. I'll go see for him, if you've a mind. It makes no difference to me.'

And away he went.

'So you really intend dancing with him?' cried Camilla's neighbour. ''Twill be a vastly good sight. I have not the most remote conception how he will bear the pulling and jostling about. Bend he cannot; but I am immensely afraid he will break. I would give fifty guineas for his portrait. He is indubitably put together without joints.'

Mr. Dubster now returned, and, with a look of some disturb-ance, said to Miss Margland: 'Ma'am, I don't know which is the master of the ceremonies. I can't find him out; for I don't know as ever I see him.'

'O pray,' cried Camilla eagerly, 'do not take the trouble of looking for him; 'twill answer no purpose.'

'Why I think so too, ma'am,' said he, misunderstanding her; 'for as I don't know the gentleman myself, he could go no great way towards making us better acquainted with one another: so we may just as well take our skip at once.'

Camilla now looked extremely foolish; and Miss Margland was again preparing an obstacle, when Mr. Dubster started one himself. 'The worst is,' cried he, 'I have lost one of my gloves, and I am sure I had two when I came. I suppose I may have dropt it in the other room. If you shan't mind it, I'll dance without it; for I don't mind those things myself of a straw.'

'O! sir,' cried Miss Margland, 'that's such a thing as never was heard of. I can't possibly consent to let Miss Camilla dance in such a manner as that.'

'Why then, if you like it better, ma'am, I'll go back and look for it.'

Again Camilla would have declined giving him any trouble; but he seemed persuaded it was only from shyness, and would not listen. 'Though the worst is,' he said, 'you're losing so much time. However, I'll give a good hunt; unless, indeed, that gentleman, who is doing nothing himself, except looking on at us all, would be kind enough to lend me his.'

'I rather fancy, sir,' cried the gentleman, immediately recovering from a laughing fit, and surveying the requester with supercilious contempt; 'I rather suspect they would not perfectly fit you.'

'Why then,' cried he, 'I think I'll go and ask Tom Hicks to lend me a pair; for it's a pity to let the young lady lose her dance for such a small trifle as that.'

Camilla began remonstrating; but he tranquilly walked away.

'You are superlatively in the good graces of fortune to-night,' cried her new friend, 'superlatively to a degree: you may not meet with such an invaluably uncommon object in twenty lustres.'

'Certainly,' said Miss Margland, 'there's a great want of regulation at balls, to prevent low people from asking who they will to dance with them. It's bad enough one can't keep people one knows nothing of from speaking to one.'

'Admirably hit off! admirable in the extreme!' he answered; suddenly twisting himself round, and beginning a whispering conversation with a gentleman on his other side.

Mr. Dubster soon came again, saying, somewhat dolorously, 'I have looked high and low for my glove, but I am no nearer. I dare say somebody has picked it up, out of a joke, and put it in their pocket. And as to Tom Hicks, where he can be hid, I can't tell, unless he has hanged himself; for I can't find him no more than my glove. However, I've got a boy to go and get me a pair; if all the shops a'n't shut up.'

Camilla, fearing to be involved in a necessity of dancing with him, expressed herself very sorry for this step; but, again misconceiving her motive, he begged her not to mind it; saying, 'A pair of gloves here or there is no great matter. All I am concerned for is, putting you off so long from having a little pleasure, for I dare say the boy won't come till the next two batches; so if that gentleman that looks so particular at me, has a mind to jig it with you a bit himself, in the interim, I won't be his hindrance.'

Receiving no answer, he bent his head lower down, and said, in a louder voice, 'Pray, sir, did you hear me?'

'Sir, you are ineffably good!' was the reply; without a look, or any further notice.

Much affronted, he said no more, but stood pouting and stiff before Camilla, till the second dance was over, and another general separation of partners took place. 'I thought how it would be, ma'am,' he then cried; 'for I know it's no such easy matter to find shops open at this time of night; for if people's 'prentices can't take a little pleasure by now, they can't never.'

Tea being at this time ordered, the whole party collected to remove to the next room. Lionel, seeing Mr. Dubster standing by Camilla, with a rapturous laugh, cried, 'Well, sister, have you been dancing?'

Camilla, though laughing too, reproachfully shook her head at him; while Mr. Dubster gravely said, 'It's no fault of mine, sir, that the lady's sitting still; for I come and offered myself to her the moment you told me she wanted a partner; but I happened of the misfortune of losing one of my gloves, and not being able to find Tom Hicks, I've been waiting all this while for a boy as has promised to get me a pair; though, I suppose he's fell down in the dark and broke his skull, by his not coming. And, indeed, if that elderly lady had not been so particular, I might as well have done without; for, if I had one on, nobody would have been the wiser but that t'other might have been in my pocket.'

This speech, spoken without any ceremony in the hearing of Miss Margland, to the visible and undisguised delight of Lionel, so much enraged her, that, hastily calling him aside, she peremptorily demanded how he came to bring such a vulgar partner to his sister?

'Because you took no care to get her a better,' he answered, heedlessly.

Camilla also began to remonstrate; but, without hearing her, he courteously addressed himself to Mr. Dubster, and told him he was sure Miss Margland and his sister would expect the pleasure of his company to join their party at tea.

Miss Margland frowned in vain; Mr. Dubster[1] bowed, as at a compliment but his due; observing he should then be close at hand for his partner; and they were proceeding to the tea-room, when the finer new acquaintance of Camilla called after Mr. Dubster: 'Pray, my good sir, who may this Signor Thomaso be, that has the honour to stand so high in your good graces?'

'Mine, sir?' cried Mr. Dubster; 'I know no Signor Thomaso, nor Signor nothing else neither: so I don't know what you mean.'

'Did not I hear you dilating, my very good sir, upon a certain Mr. Tom somebody?'

'What, I suppose then, sir, if the truth be known, you would say Tom Hicks?'

'Very probably, sir: though I am not of the first accuracy as the gentleman's nomenclator.'

'What? don't you know him, sir? why he's the head waiter!'

Then, following the rest of the party, he was placed, by the assistance of Lionel, next to Camilla, in utter defiance of all the angry glances of Miss Margland, who herself invited the handsome partner of Eugenia to join their group, and reaped some consolation in his willing civilities; till the attention of the whole assembly was called, or rather commanded by a new object.

A lady, not young, but still handsome, with an air of fashion easy almost to insolence, with a complete but becoming undress, with a work-bag hanging on her arm, whence she was carelessly knotting, entered the ball-room alone, and, walking straight through it to the large folding glass doors of the tea-room, there stopt, and took a general survey of the company, with a look that announced a decided superiority to all she saw, and a perfect indifference to what opinion she incurred in return.

She was immediately joined by all the officers, and several other gentlemen, whose eagerness to shew themselves of her acquaintance marked her for a woman of some consequence; though she took little other notice of them, than that of giving to each some frivolous commission; telling one to hold her work-bag; bidding another fetch her a chair; a third, ask for a glass of water; and a fourth, take care of her cloak. She then planted herself just without the folding-doors, declaring there could be no breathing in the smaller apartment, and sent about the gentlemen for various refreshments; all which she rejected when they arrived, with extreme contempt, and a thousand fantastic grimaces.

The tea-table at which Miss Margland presided being nearest to these folding-doors, she and her party heard, from time to time, most of what was said, especially by the newly arrived lady; who, though she now and then spoke for several minutes in a laughing whisper, to some one she called to her side, uttered most of her remarks, and all her commands quite aloud, with that sort of deliberate ease which belongs to the most determined negligence of who heard, or who escaped hearing her, who were pleased, or who were offended.

Camilla and Eugenia were soon wholly engrossed by this new personage; and Lionel, seeing her surrounded by the most fashionable men of the assembly, forgot Mr. Dubster and his gloves, in an eagerness to be introduced to her.

Colonel Andover, to whom he applied, willingly gratified him: 'Give me leave, Mrs. Arlbery,' cried he, to the lady, who was then conversing with General Kinsale, 'to present to you Mr. Tyrold.'

'For Heaven's sake don't speak to me just now,' cried she; 'the General is telling me the most interesting thing in the world. Go on, dear General!'

Lionel, who, if guided by his own natural judgment, would have conceived this to be the height of ill-breeding or of ignorance, no sooner saw Colonel Andover bow in smiling submission to her orders, than he concluded himself all in the dark with respect to the last licences of fashion: and, while contentedly he waited her leisure for his reception, he ran over in his own mind the triumph with which he should carry to Oxford the newest flourish of the *bon ton*.

In a few minutes, after gaily laughing with the General, she turned suddenly to Colonel Andover, and, striking him on the arm with her fan, exclaimed: 'Well, now, Colonel, what is it you would say?'

'Mr. Tyrold,' he answered, 'is very ambitious of the honour of being introduced to you.'

'With all my heart. Which is he?' And then, nodding to Lionel's bow, 'You live, I think,' she added, 'in this neighbourhood? By the way, Colonel, how came you never to bring Mr. Tyrold to me before? Mr. Tyrold, I flatter myself you intend to take this very ill.'

Lionel was beginning to express his sense of the loss he had suffered by the delay, when, again, patting the Colonel, 'Only look, I beg you,' she cried, 'at that insupportable Sir Sedley Clarendel![1] how he sits at his ease there! amusing his ridiculous fancy with every creature he sees. Yet what an elegant posture the animal has found out! I make no doubt he would as soon forfeit his estate as give up that attitude. I must make him come to me immediately for that very reason;—do go to him, good Andover, and say I want him directly.'

The Colonel obeyed; but not so the gentleman he addressed, who was the new acquaintance of Camilla. He only bowed to the message, and, kissing his hand across the room to the lady, desired the Colonel to tell her he was ineffably tired; but would incontestably have the honour to throw himself at her feet the next morning.

'O, intolerable!' cried she, 'he grows more conceited every hour. Yet what an agreeable wretch it is! There's nothing like him. I cannot possibly do without him. Andover, tell him if he does not come this moment he kills me.'

'And is that a message,' said General Kinsale, 'to cure him of being conceited?'

'O, Heaven forbid, my good General, I should cure him! That would utterly spoil him. His conceit is precisely what enchants me. Rob him of that, and you lose all hold of him.'

'Is it then necessary to keep him a fop, in order to retain him in your chains?'

'O, he is not in my chains, I promise you. A fop, my dear General, wears no chains but his own. However, I like to have him, because he is so hard to be got; and I am fond of conversing with him, because he is so ridiculous. Fetch him, therefore, Colonel, without delay.'

This second embassy prevailed; he shrugged his shoulders, but arose to follow the Colonel.

'See, madam, your victory!' said the General. 'What would not a military man give for such talents of command?'

'Ay, but look with what magnificent tardiness he obeys orders! There is something quite irresistible in his impertinence; 'tis so conscious and so piquant. I think, General, 'tis a little like my own.'

Sir Sedley now advancing, seized the back of a chair, which he twirled round for a resting place to his elbow, and exclaimed, 'You know yourself invincible!' with an air that shewed him languidly prepared for her reproaches: but, to his own surprise, and that of all around him, she only, with a smile and a nod, cried,

'How do do?' and immediately turning wholly away from him, addressed herself to Colonel Andover, desiring him to give her the history of who was in the tea-room.

At this time a young Ensign, who had been engaged at a late dinner in the neighbourhood, stroamed into the ballroom, with the most visible marks of his unfitness for appearing in it; and, in total ignorance of his own condition, went up to Colonel Andover, and, clapping him upon the back, called out, with a loud oath, 'Colonel, I hope you have taken care to secure to me the prettiest little young angel in the room? You know with what sincerity I despise an old hag.'

The Colonel, with some concern, advised him to retire; but, insensible to his counsel, he uttered oath upon oath, and added, 'I'm not to be played upon, Colonel. Beauty in a pretty girl is as necessary an ingredient, as honour in a brave soldier; and I could find in my heart to sink down to the bottom of the Channel every fellow without one, and every dear creature without the other.'

Then, in defiance of all remonstrance, he staggered into the tea-room; and, after a short survey, stopt opposite to Indiana, and, swearing aloud she was the handsomest angel he had ever beheld, begged her hand without further ceremony; assuring her he had broken up the best party that had yet been made for him in the county, merely for the joy of dancing with her.

Indiana, to whom not the smallest doubt of the truth of this assertion occurred; and who, not suspecting he was intoxicated, thought his manner the most spirited and gallant she had ever seen, was readily accepting his offer; when Edgar, who faw her danger, started up, and exclaimed: 'This lady, sir, is engaged to dance the next two dances with me.'

'The lady did not tell me so, sir!' cried the Ensign, firing.

'Miss Lynmere,' replied Edgar, coolly, 'will pardon me, that on this occasion, my memory has an interest to be better than her's. I believe it is time for us to take our places.'

He then whispered a brief excuse to Camilla, and hurried Indiana to the ballroom.

The Ensign, who knew not that she had danced with him the last time, was obliged to submit; while Indiana, not conjecturing the motive that now impelled Edgar, was in a yet brighter blaze of beauty, from an exhilarating notion that there was a contest for the honour of her hand.

Camilla, once more disappointed of Edgar, had now no resource against Mr. Dubster, but the non-arrival of the gloves; for he had talked so publicly of waiting for them to dance with her, that every one regarded her as engaged.

No new proposition being made for Eugenia, Miss Margland permitted her again to be led out by the handsome stranger.

When she was gone, Mr. Dubster, who kept constantly close to Camilla, said: 'They tell me, ma'am, that ugly little body's a great fortune.'

Camilla very innocently asked who he meant.

'Why that little lame thing, that was here drinking tea with you. Tom Hicks says she'll have a power of money.'

Camilla, whose sister was deservedly dear to her, looked much displeased; but Mr. Dubster, not perceiving it, continued: 'He recommended it to me to dance with her myself, from the first, upon that account. But I says to him, says I, I had no notion that a person, who had such a hobble in their gait, would think of such a thing as going to dancing. But there I was out, for as to the women, asking your pardon, ma'am, there's nothing will put 'em off from their pleasure. But, however, for my part, I had no thought of dancing at all, if it had not been for that young gentleman's asking me; for I'm not over fond of such jiggets,[1] as they've no great use in 'em; only I happened to be this way, upon a little matter of business, so I thought I might as well come and see the hop, as Tom Hicks could contrive to get me a ticket.'

This was the sort of discourse with which Camilla was regaled till the two dances were over; and then, begging her to sit still till he came back, he quitted her, to see what he could do about his gloves.

Edgar, when he returned with Indiana, addressed himself privately to Miss Margland, whom he advised to take the young ladies immediately home; as it would not be possible for him, a second time, to break through the rules of the assembly, and Indiana must, therefore, inevitably accept the young Ensign, who already was following and claiming her, and whose condition was obviously improper for the society of ladies.

Miss Margland, extremely pleased with him, for thus protecting her pupil, instantly agreed; and, collecting her three young charges, hastened them down stairs; though the young Ensign, inflamed with angry disappointment, uttered the most bitter lamentations at their sudden departure; and though Mr. Dubster, pursuing them to the coach door, called out to Camilla, in a tone of pique and vexation, 'Why, what are you going for now, ma'am, when I have just got a new pair of gloves, that I have bought o' purpose?'

CHAPTER III

A Family Breakfast

IN their way home, Edgar apologised to Camilla for again fore-going the promised pleasure of dancing with her, by explaining the situation of the Ensign.

Camilla, internally persuaded that any reason would suffice for such an arrangement, where Indiana was its object, scarce listened to an excuse which she considered as unnecessary.

Indiana was eager to view in the glass how her dress and ornaments had borne the shaking of the dance, and curiously impatient to look anew at a face and a figure of which no self-vanity, nor even the adulation of Miss Margland, had taught her a consciousness, such as she had acquired from the adventures of this night. She hastened, therefore, to her apartment as soon as she arrived at Cleves, and there indulged in an examination which forbade all surprise, and commanded equal justice for the admirers and the admired.

Miss Margland, anxious to make her own report to Sir Hugh, accompanied Camilla and Eugenia to his room, where he was still sitting up for them.

She expatiated upon the behaviour of young Mandlebert, in terms that filled the baronet with satisfaction. She exulted in the success of her own measures; and, sinking the circumstance of the intended impartiality of Edgar, enlarged upon his dancing, out of his turn, with Indiana, as at an event which manifested his serious designs beyond all possibility of mistake.

Sir Hugh, in the fulness of his content, promised that when the wedding day arrived, they should all have as fine new gowns as the bride herself.

The next morning, not considering that every one else would

require unusual repose, he got up before his customary hour, from an involuntary hope of accelerating his favourite project; but he had long the breakfast parlour to himself, and became so fatigued and discomfited by fasting and waiting, that when Indiana, who appeared last, but for whom he insisted upon staying, entered the room, he said: 'My dear, I could really find a pleasure in giving you a little scold, if it were not for setting a bad example, which God forbid! And, indeed, it's not so much your fault as the ball's, to which I can never be a sincere friend, unless it be just to answer some particular purpose.'

Miss Margland defended her pupil, and called upon Mandlebert for assistance, which he readily gave. Sir Hugh then was not merely appeased but gratified, and declared, the next moment, with a marked smile at Indiana, that his breakfast [he] had not relished so well for a twelvemonth, owing to the advantage of not beginning till he had got an appetite.

Soon after, Lionel, galloping across the park, hastily dismounted, and scampered into the parlour.

The zealot for every species of sport, the candidate for every order of whim, was the light-hearted mirthful Lionel.[1] A stranger to reflection, and incapable of care, laughter seemed not merely the bent of his humour, but the necessity of his existence: he pursued it at all seasons, he indulged it upon all occasions. With excellent natural parts, he trifled away all improvement; without any ill temper, he spared no one's feelings. Yet, though not radically vicious, nor deliberately malevolent, the egotism which urged him to make his own amusement his first pursuit, sacrificed his best friends and first duties, if they stood in its way.

'Come, my little girls, come!' cried he, as he entered the room; 'get your hats and cloaks as fast as possible; there is a public breakfast[2] at Northwick, and you are all expected without delay.'

This sudden invitation occasioned a general commotion. Indiana gave an involuntary jump; Camilla and Eugenia looked delighted; and Miss Margland seemed ready to second the proposition; but Sir Hugh, with some surprise, exclaimed: 'A public breakfast, my dear boy! why where's the need of that, when we have got so good a private one?'

'O, let us go! let us go, uncle!' cried Indiana. 'Miss Margland, do pray speak to my uncle to let us go!'

'Indeed, sir,' said Miss Margland, 'it is time now, in all

conscience, for the young ladies to see a little more of the world, and that it should be known who they are. I am sure they have been immured long enough, and I only wish you had been at the ball last night, sir, yourself!'

'Me, Mrs. Margland! Lord help me! what should I do at such a thing as that, with all this gout in my hip?'

'You would have seen, sir, the fine effects of keeping the young ladies out of society in this manner. Miss Camilla, if I had not prevented it, would have danced with I don't know who; and as to Miss Eugenia, she was as near as possible to not dancing at all, owing to nobody's knowing who she was.'

Sir Hugh had no time to reply to this attack, from the urgency of Indiana, and the impetuosity of Lionel, who, applying to Camilla, said: 'Come, child, ask my uncle yourself, and then we shall go at once.'

Camilla readily made it her own request.

'My dear,' answered Sir Hugh, 'I can't be so unnatural to deny you a little pleasure, knowing you to be such a merry little whirligig; not but what you'd enjoy yourself just as much at home, if they'd let you alone. However, as Indiana's head is so much turned upon it, for which I beg you won't think the worse of her, Mr. Mandlebert, it being no more than the common fault of a young person no older than her; why, you must all go, I think, provided you are not satisfied already, which, by the breakfast you have made, I should think likely enough to be the case.'

They then eagerly arose, and the females hastened to make some change in their dress. Sir Hugh, calling Eugenia back, said: 'As to you, my little classic, I make but small doubt you will be half ready to break your heart at missing your lesson, knowing hic, haec, hoc, to be dearer to you, and for good reasons enough, too, in the end, than all the hopping and skipping in the world; so if you had rather stay away, don't mind all those dunces; for so I must needs call them, in comparison to you and Dr. Orkborne, though without the least meaning to undervalue them.'

Eugenia frankly acknowledged she had been much amused the preceding evening, and wished to be again of the party.

'Why then, if that's the case,' said the baronet, the best way will be for Dr. Orkborne to be your squire; by which means you may have a little study as you go along, to the end that the less time may be thrown away in doing nothing.'

Eugenia, who perceived no objection to this idea, assented, and went quietly up stairs, to prepare for setting out. Sir Hugh, by no means connecting the laughter of·Lionel, nor the smile of Edgar, with his proposal, gravely repeated it to Dr. Orkborne, adding: 'And if you want a nice pair of gloves, Doctor, not that I make the offer in any detriment to your own, but I had six new pair come home just before my gout, which, I can assure you, have never seen the light since, and are as much at your service as if I had bespoke them on purpose.'

The mirth of Lionel grew now so outrageous, that Dr. Orkborne, much offended, walked out of the room without making any answer.

'There is something,' cried Sir Hugh, after a pause, 'in these men of learning, prodigious nice to deal with; however, not understanding them, in point of their maxims, it's likely enough I may have done something wrong; for he could not have seemed much more affronted, if I had told him I had six new pair of gloves lying by me, which he should be never the better for.'

When they were all ready, Sir Hugh calling to Edgar, said: 'Now as I don't much chuse to have my girls go to these sort of places often, which is a prudence that I dare say you approve as much as myself, I would wish to have the most made of them at once; and, therefore, as I've no doubt but they'll strike up a dance, after having eat what they think proper, why I would advise you, Mr. Mandlebert, to let Indiana trip it away till she's heartily tired, for else she'll never give it up, with a good grace, of her own accord.'

'Certainly, sir,' answered Edgar, 'I shall not hurry the ladies.'

'O, as to any of the rest,' interrupted Sir Hugh, 'they'll be as soon satisfied as yourself, except,' lowering his voice, 'Mrs. Margland, who, between friends, seems to me as glad of one of those freaks, as when she was but sixteen; which how long it is since she was no more I can't pretend to say, being a point she never mentions.'

Then addressing them in general: 'I wish you a good breakfast,' he cried, 'with all my heart, which I think you pretty well deserve, considering you go so far for it, with one close at your elbow, but just swallowed. And so, my dear Indiana, I hope you won't tire Mr. Mandlebert more than can't be avoided.'

'How came you to engage Indiana again, Mandlebert?' cried Lionel, in their way to the carriage.

'Because,' said Miss Margland, finding he hesitated, 'there is no other partner so proper for Miss Lynmere.'

'And pray what's the matter with me? why am not I as proper as Mandlebert?'

'Because you are her relation, to be sure!'

'Well,' cried he, vaulting his horse, 'if I meet but the charming widow, I shall care for none of you.'

CHAPTER IV

A Public Breakfast

THE unfitting, however customary, occasion of this speedy repetition of public amusement in the town of Northwick, was, that the county assizes were now held there; and the arrival of the Judges of the land, to hear causes which kept life or death suspended, was the signal for entertainment to the surrounding neighbourhood: a hardening of human feelings against human crimes and human miseries, at which reflection revolts, however habit may persevere.

The young men, who rode on first, joined the ladies as they entered the town, and told them to drive straight to the ballroom, where the company had assembled, in consequence of a shower of rain which had forced them from the public garden intended for the breakfast.

Here, as they stopt, a poor woman, nearly in rags, with one child by her side, and another in her arms, approached the carriage, and presenting a petition, besought the ladies to read or hear her case. Eugenia, with the ready impulse of generous affluence, instantly felt for her purse; but Miss Margland, angrily holding her hand, said, with authority: "Miss Eugenia, never encourage beggars; you don't know the mischief you may do by it.' Eugenia reluctantly desisted, but made a sign to her footman to give something for her. Edgar then alighting, advanced to hand them from the coach, while Lionel ran forward to settle their tickets of admittance.

The woman now grew more urgent in her supplications, and Miss Margland in her remonstrances against attending to them.

Indiana, who was placed under the care of Edgar, enchanted to again display herself where sure of again being admired, neither heard nor saw the petitioner; but dimpling and smiling, quickened her motions towards the assembly room: while Camilla, who was last, stopping short, said: 'What is the matter, poor woman?' and took her paper to examine.

Miss Margland, snatching it from her, threw it on the ground, peremptorily saying: 'Miss Camilla, if once you begin such a thing as that, there will be no end to it; so come along with the rest of your company, like other people.'

She then haughtily proceeded; but Camilla, brought up by her admirable parents never to pass distress without inquiry, nor to refuse giving at all, because she could give but little, remained with the poor object, and repeated her question. The woman, shedding a torrent of tears, said she was wife to one of the prisoners who was to be tried the next day, and who expected to lose his life, or be transported, for only one bad action of stealing a leg of mutton; which, though she knew it to be a sin, was not without excuse, being a first offence, and committed in poverty and sickness. And this, she was told, the Judges would take into consideration; but her husband was now so ill, that he could not feed on the gaol allowance, and not having wherewithal to buy any other, would either die before his trial, or be too weak to make known his sad story in his own behalf, for want of some wine or some broth to support him in the meanwhile.

Camilla, hastily giving her a shilling, took one of her petitions, and promising to do all in her power to serve her, left the poor creature almost choked with sobbing joy. She was flying to join her party, when she perceived Edgar at her side. 'I came to see,' cried he, with glistening eyes, 'if you were running away from us; but you were doing far better in not thinking of us at all.'

Camilla, accustomed from her earliest childhood to attend to the indigent and unhappy, felt neither retreating shame, nor parading pride in the office; she gave him the petition of the poor woman, and begged he would consider if there was any thing that could be done for her husband.

'I have received a paper from herself,' he answered, 'before you alighted; and I hope I should not have neglected it: but I will now take yours, that my memory may run no risk.'

They then went on to the assembly room.

The company, which was numerous, was already seated at breakfast. Indiana and Camilla, now first surveyed by daylight, again attracted all eyes; but, in the simplicity of undress, the superiority of Indiana was no longer wholly unrivalled, though the general voice was still strongly in her favour.

Indiana was a beauty of so regular a cast, that her face had no feature, no look to which criticism could point as susceptible of improvement, or on which admiration could dwell with more delight than on the rest. No statuary could have modelled her form with more exquisite symmetry; no painter have harmonised her complexion with greater brilliancy of colouring. But here ended the liberality of nature, which, in not sullying this fair workmanship by inclosing in it what was bad, contentedly left it vacant of whatever was noble and desirable.

The beauty of Camilla, though neither perfect nor regular, had an influence so peculiar on the beholder, it was hard to catch its fault; and the cynic connoisseur, who might persevere in seeking it, would involuntarily surrender the strict rules of his art to the predominance of its loveliness. Even judgment itself, the coolest and last betrayed of our faculties, she took by surprise, though it was not till she was absent the seizure was detected. Her disposition was ardent in sincerity, her mind untainted with evil. The reigning and radical defect of her character—an imagination that submitted to no control—proved not any antidote against her attractions; it caught, by its force and fire, the quick-kindling admiration of the lively; it possessed, by magnetic pervasion, the witchery to create sympathy in the most serious.

In their march up the room, Camilla was spoken to by a person from the tea-table, who was distinct from every other, by being particularly ill dressed; and who, though she did not know him, asked her how she did, with a familiar look of intimacy. She slightly curtsied, and endeavoured to draw her party more nimbly on; when another person, equally conspicuous, though from being accoutred in the opposite extreme of full dress, quitting his seat, formally made up to her, and drawing on a stiff pair of new gloves as he spoke, said: 'So you are come at last, ma'am! I began to think you would not come at all, begging that gentleman's pardon, who told me to the contrary last night, when I thought, thinks I, here I've bought these new gloves, for no reason but to oblige the young lady, and now I might as well not have bought 'em at all.'

Camilla, ready to laugh, yet much provoked at this renewed claim from her old persecutor, Mr. Dubster, looked vainly for redress at the mischievous Lionel, who archly answered: 'O, ay, true, sister; I told the gentleman, last night, you would be sure to make him amends this morning for putting him to so much expence.'

'I'm sure, Sir,' said Mr. Dubster, 'I did not speak for that, expence being no great matter to me at this time; only nobody likes to fool away their money for nothing.'

Edgar having now, at the end of one of the tables, secured places for the ladies, Lionel again, in defiance of the frowns of Miss Margland, invited Mr. Dubster to join them: even the appealing looks of Camilla served but to increase her brother's ludicrous diversion, in coupling her with so ridiculous a companion; who, without seeming at all aware of the liberty he was taking, engrossed her wholly.

'So I see, ma'am,' he cried, pointing to Eugenia, 'you've brought that limping little body with you again? Tom Hicks had like to have took me in finely about her! He thought she was the great fortune of these here parts; and if it had not been for the young gentleman, I might have known no better neither, for there's half the room in the same scrape at this minute.'

Observing Camilla regard him with an unpleasant surprise, he more solemnly added: 'I ask pardon, ma'am, for mentioning the thing, which I only do in excuse for what I said last night, not knowing then you was the fortune yourself.'

An eager sign of silence from Lionel, forbade her explaining this mistake; Mr. Dubster, therefore, proceeded:

'When Tom Hicks told me about it, I said at the time, says I, she looks more like to some sort of a humble young person, just brought out of a little good-nature to see the company, and the like of that; for she's not a bit like a lady of fortunes, with that nudging[1] look; and I said to Tom Hicks, by way of joke, says I, if I was to think of her, which I don't think I shall, at least she would not be much in my way, for she could not follow a body much about, because of that hitch in her gait, for I'm a pretty good walker.'

Here the ill dressed man, who had already spoken to Camilla, quitting his seat, strolled up to her, and fastening his eyes upon her face, though without bowing, made some speech about the weather, with the lounging freedom of manner of a confirmed old acquaintance. His whole appearance had an air of even wilful slovenliness: His hair was uncombed; he was in boots,[1] which were covered with mud; his coat seemed to have been designedly [immersed] in powder, and his universal negligence was not only shabby but uncleanly. Astonished and offended by his forwardness, Camilla turned entirely away from him.

Not disconcerted by this distance, he procured a chair, upon which he cast himself, perfectly at his ease, immediately behind her.

Just as the general breakfast was over, and the waiters were summoned to clear away the tables, and prepare the room for dancing, the lady who had so strikingly made her appearance the preceding evening, again entered. She was alone, as before, and walked up the room with the same decided air of indifference to all opinion; sometimes knotting[2] with as much diligence and earnestness as if her subsistence depended upon the rapidity of her work; and at other times stopping short, she applied to her eye a nearsighted glass, which hung to her finger,[3] and intently examined some particular person or group; then, with a look of absence, as if she had not seen a creature, she hummed an opera song to herself, and proceeded. Her rouge was remarkably well put on, and her claim to being still a fine woman, though past her prime, was as obvious as it was conscious: Her dress was more fantastic and studied than the night before, in the same proportion as that of every other person present was more simple and quiet; and the commanding air of her countenance, and the easiness of her carriage, spoke a confirmed internal assurance, that her charms and her power were absolute, wherever she thought their exertion worth her trouble.

When she came to the head of the room, she turned about, and, with her glass, surveyed the whole company; then smilingly advancing to the sloven, whom Camilla was shunning, she called out: 'O! are you there? what rural deity could break your rest so early?'

'None!' answered he, rubbing his eyes; 'I am invulnerably asleep at this very moment! In the very centre of the morphetic dominions. But how barbarously late you are! I should never have

come to this vastly horrid place before my ride, if I had imagined
you could be so excruciating.'

Struck with a jargon of which she could not suspect two persons
to be capable, Camilla turned round to her slighted neighbour,
and with the greatest surprise recognised, upon examination, the
most brilliant beau of the preceding evening, in the worst dressed
man of the present morning.

The lady now, again holding her glass to her eye, which she
directed without scruple towards Camilla and her party, said:
'Who have you got there?'

Camilla looked hastily away, and her whole set, abashed by so
unseasoned an inquiry, cast down their eyes.

'Hey!' cried he, calmly viewing them, as if for the first time
himself: 'Why, I'll tell you!' Then making her bend to hear his
whisper, which, nevertheless, was by no means intended for her
own ear alone, he added: 'Two little things as pretty as angels,
and two others as ugly as—I say no more!'

'O, I take in the full force of your metaphor!' cried she,
laughing; 'and acknowledge the truth of its contrast.'

Camilla alone, as they meant, had heard them; and ashamed for
herself, and provoked to find Eugenia coupled with Miss
Margland, she endeavoured to converse with some of her own
society; but their attention was entirely engaged by the whispers;
nor could she, for more than a minute, deny her own curiosity
the pleasure of observing them.

They now spoke together for some time in low voices, laughing
immoderately at the occasional sallies of each other; Sir Sedley
Clarendel sitting at his ease, Mrs. Arlbery standing, and knotting
by his side.

The officers, and almost all the beaux, began to crowd to this
spot; but neither the gentleman nor the lady interrupted their
discourse to return or receive any salutations. Lionel, who with
much eagerness had quitted an inside seat at a long table, to pay
his court to Mrs. Arlbery, could catch neither her eye nor her ear
for his bow or his compliment.

Sir Sedley, at last, looking up in her face and smiling, said:
'A'n't you shockingly tired?'

'To death!' answered she, coolly.

'Why then, I am afraid, I must positively do the thing that's old
fashioned.'

And rising, and making her a very elegant bow, he presented her his seat, adding: 'There, ma'am! I have the honour to give you my chair—at the risk of my reputation.'

'I should have thought,' cried Lionel, now getting forward, 'that omitting to give it would rather have risked your reputation.'

'It is possible you could be born before all that was over?' said Mrs. Arlbery, dropping carelessly upon the chair as she perceived Lionel, whom she honoured with a nod: 'How do do, Mr. Tyrold? are you just come in?' But turning again to Sir Sedley, without waiting for his answer, 'I swear, you barbarian,' she cried, 'you have really almost killed me with fatigue.'

'Have I indeed?' said he, smiling.

Mr. Dubster now, leaning over the table, solemnly said: 'I am sure I should have offered the lady my own place, if I had not been so tired myself; but Tom Hicks over-persuaded me to dance a bit before you came in, ma'am,' addressing Camilla, 'for you have lost a deal of dancing by coming so late; for they all fell to as soon as ever they come; and, as I'm not over and above used to it, it soon makes one a little stiffish, as one may say; and indeed, the lady's much better off in getting a chair, for one sits mighty little at one's ease on these here benches, with nothing to lean one's back against.'

'And who's that?' cried Mrs. Arlbery to Sir Sedley, looking Mr. Dubster full in the face.

Sir Sedley made some answer in a whisper, which proved highly entertaining to them both. Mr. Dubster, with an air much offended, said to Camilla: 'People's laughing and whispering, which one don't know what it's about, is not one of the politest things, I know, for polite people to do; and, in my mind, they ought to be above it.'

This resentment excited Lionel to join in the laugh; and Mr. Dubster, with great gravity of manner, rose, and said to Camilla: 'When you are ready to dance, ma'am, I am willing to be your partner, and I shan't engage myself to nobody else; but I shall go to t'other end of the room till you choose to stand up; for I don't much care to stay here, only to be laughed at, when I don't know what it's for.'

They now all left the table; and Lionel eagerly begged permission to introduce his sisters and cousin to Mrs. Arlbery, who readily consented to the proposal.

Indiana advanced with pleasure into a circle of beaux, whose eyes were most assiduous to welcome her. Camilla, though a little alarmed in being presented to a lady of so singular a deportment, had yet a curiosity to see more of her, that willingly seconded her brother's motion. And Eugenia, to whose early reflecting mind every new character and new scene opened a fresh fund for thought, if not for knowledge, was charmed to take a nearer view of what promised such food for observation. But Miss Margland began an angry remonstrance against the proceedings of Lionel, in thus taking out of her hands the direction of her charges. What she urged, however, was vain: Lionel was only diverted by her wrath, and the three young ladies, as they had not requested the introduction, did not feel themselves responsible for its taking effect.

Lionel led them on: Mrs. Arlbery half rose to return their curtsies; and gave them a reception so full of vivacity and good humour, that they soon forgot the ill will with which Miss Margland had suffered them to quit her; and even lost all recollection that it belonged to them to return to her. The satisfaction of Indiana, indeed, flowed simply from the glances of admiration which every where met her eye; but Eugenia attended to every word, and every motion of Mrs. Arlbery, with that sort of earnestness which marks an intelligent child at a first play; and Camilla, still more struck by the novelty of this new acquaintance, scarce permitted herself to breathe, lest she should lose anything she said.

Mrs. Arlbery perceived their youthful wonder, and felt a propensity to increase it, which strengthened all her powers, and called forth all her faculties. Wit she possessed at will; and, with exertions which rendered it uncommonly brilliant, she displayed it, now to them, now to the gentlemen, with a gaiety so fantastic, a raillery so arch, a spirit of satire so seasoned with a delight in coquetry, and a certain negligence of air so enlivened by a whimsical pleasantry, that she could not have failed to strike with admiration even the most hackneyed seekers of character; much less the inexperienced young creatures now presented to her; who, with open eyes and ears, regarded her as a phenomenon, upon finding that the splendor of her talents equalled the singularity of her manners.

When the room was prepared for dancing, Major Cerwood brought to Indiana Mr. Macdersey, the young Ensign who had so improperly addressed her at the ball; and, after a formal apology, in his name, for what had passed, begged the honour of her hand for him this morning. Indiana, flattered and fluttered together by this ceremony, almost forgot Edgar, who stood quietly but watchfully aloof, and was actually giving her consent when, meeting his eye, she recollected she was already engaged. Mr. Macdersey hoped for more success another time, and Edgar advanced to lead his fair partner to her place.

Major Cerwood offered himself to Camilla; but Mr. Dubster coming forward, pulled him by the elbow, and making a stiff low bow, said: 'Sir, I ask your pardon for taking the liberty of giving you such a jog, but the young lady's been engaged to me ever so long.' The Major looked surprised; but, observing that Camilla coloured, he bowed respectfully and retreated.

Camilla, ashamed of her beau, determined not to dance at all: though she saw, with much vexation, upon the general dispersion, Miss Margland approach to claim her. Educated in all the harmony of contentment and benevolence, she had a horror of a temper so irascible, that made it a penance to remain a moment in its vicinity. Mr. Dubster, however, left her not alone to it: when she positively refused his hand, he said it was equal agreeable to him to have only a little dish of chat with her; and composedly stationed himself before her. Eugenia had already been taken out by the handsome stranger, with whom she had danced the evening before; and Lionel, bewitched with Mrs. Arlbery, enlisted himself entirely in her train; and with Sir Sedley Clarendel, and almost every man of any consequence in the room, declined all dancing for the pleasure of attending her.

Mr. Dubster, unacquainted with the natural high spirits of Camilla, inferred nothing to his own disadvantage from her silence, but talked incessantly himself with perfect complacency. 'Do you know, ma'am,' cried he, 'just as that elderly lady, that, I suppose, is your mamma, took you all away in that hurry last night, up comes the boy with my new pair of gloves! but, though I run down directly to tell you of it, there was no making the old lady stop; which I was fool to try at; for as to women, I know their obstinacy of old. But what I grudged the most was, as soon as I come up again, as ill luck would have it, Tom Hicks finds me my own t'other glove! So there I had two pair, when I might as well have had never a one!'

Observing that Eugenia was dancing, 'Lack a-day!' he exclaimed, 'I'll lay a wager that poor gentleman has been took in, just as I was yesterday! He thinks that young lady that's had the small-pox so bad, is you, ma'am!' 'Twould be a fine joke if such a mistake as that should get the little lame duck, as I call her, a husband! He'd be in a fine hobble when he found he'd got nothing but her ugly face for his bargain. Though, provided she'd had the rhino,[1] it would not much have signified: for, as to being pretty or not, it's not great matter in a wife. A man soon tires of seeing nothing but the same face, if it's one of the best.'

Camilla here, in the midst of her chagrin, could not forbear asking him if he was married? 'Yes, ma'am,' answered he calmly, 'I've had two wives to my share already; so I know what I'm speaking of; though I've buried them both. Why it was all along of my wives, what with the money I had with one, and what with the money I had with the other, that I got out of business so soon.'

'You were very much obliged to them, then?'

'Why, yes, ma'am, as to that, I can't say to the contrary, now that they're gone: but I can't say I had much comfort with 'em while they lived. They was always a thinking they had a right to what they had a mind, because of what they brought me; so that I had enough to do to scrape a little matter together, in case of outliving them. One of 'em has not been dead above a twelvemonth, or there about; these are the first clothes I've bought since I left off my blacks.'

When Indiana past them, he expressed his admiration of her beauty. 'That young lady, ma'am, he said, 'cuts you all up, sure enough. She's as fine a piece of red and white as ever I see. I could think of such a young lady as that myself, if I did not remember that I thought no more of my wife that was pretty, than of my wife that was ugly, after the first month or so. Beauty goes for a mere nothing in matrimony, when once one's used to it. Besides, I've no great thoughts at present of entering into the state again of one while, at any rate, being but just got to be a little comfortable.'

The second dance was now called, when Mrs. Arlbery, coming suddenly behind Camilla, said, in a low voice, 'Do you know who you are talking with?'

'No, ma'am!'

'A young tinker, my dear! that's all!' And, with a provoking nod, she retreated.

Camilla, half ready to laugh, half to cry, restrained herself with difficulty from running after her; and Mr. Dubster, observing that she abruptly turned away, and would listen no more, again claimed her for his partner; and, upon her absolute refusal, surprised and affronted, walked off in silence. She was then finally condemned to the morose society of Miss Margland: and invectives against Sir Hugh for mismanagement, and Lionel, with whom now that lady was at open war, for impertinence, filled up the rest of her time, till the company was informed that refreshments were served in the card-room.

Thither, immediately, every body flocked, with as much speed and avidity, as if they had learnt to appreciate the blessing of plenty, by the experience of want. Such is the vacancy of dissipated pleasure, that, never satisfied with what it possesses, an opening always remains for something yet to be tried, and, on that something still to come, all enjoyment seems to depend.[1]

The day beginning now to clear, the sashes of a large bow window were thrown up. Sir Sedley Clarendel sauntered thither, and instantly everybody followed, as if there were no breathing anywhere else; declaring, while they pressed upon one another almost to suffocation, that nothing was so reviving as the fresh air: and, in a minute, not a creature was to be seen in any other part of the room.

Here, in full view, stood sundry hapless relations of the poorer part of the prisoners to be tried the next morning, who, with supplicating hands and eyes, implored the compassion of the company, whom their very calamities assembled for amusement.

Nobody took any notice of them; nobody appeared even to see them: but, one by one, all glided gently away, and the bow-window was presently the only empty space in the apartment.

Camilla, contented with having already presented her mite, and Eugenia, with having given her's in commission, retired unaffectedly with the rest; while Miss Margland, shrugging up her shoulders, and declaring there was no end of beggars, pompously added, 'However, we gave before we came in.'

Presently, a paper was handed about, to collect half guineas for a raffle. A beautiful locket, set round with pearls, ornamented at the top with a little knot of small brilliants, and very elegantly shaped, with a space left for a braid of hair, or a cypher,[2] was produced; and, as if by magnetic power, attracted into almost every hand the capricious coin, which distress, but the moment before had repelled.

Miss Margland lamented she had only guineas or silver, but suffered Edgar to be her paymaster; privately resolving, that, if she won the locket, she would remember the debt: Eugenia, amused in seeing the humour of all that was going forward, readily put in; Indiana, satisfied her uncle would repay the expences of the day, with a heart panting from hope of the prize, did the same; but Camilla hung back, totally unused to hazard upon what was unnecessary the little allowance she had been taught to spend sparingly upon herself, that something might be always in her power to bestow upon others. The character of this raffle was not of that interesting nature which calls forth from the affluent and easy respect as well as aid: the prize belonged to no one whom adversity compelled to change what once was an innocent luxury, into the means of subsistence; it was the mere common mode of getting rid of a mere common bauble, which no one had thought worth the full price affixed to it by its toyman.[1] She knew not, however, till now, how hard to resist was the contagion of example, and felt a struggle in her self-denial, that made her, when she put the locket down, withdraw from the crowd, and resolve not to look at it again.

Edgar, who had observed her, read her secret conflict with an emotion which impelled him to follow her, that he might express his admiration; but he was stopt by Mrs. Arlbery, who just then hastily attacked her with, 'What have you done with your friend the tinker, my dear?'

Camilla, laughing, though extremely ashamed, said, she knew nothing at all about him.

'You talked with him, then, by way of experiment, to see how you might like him?'

'No, indeed! I merely answered him when I could not help it; but still I thought, at a ball, gentlemen only would present themselves.'

'And how many couple,' said Mrs. Arlbery, smiling, 'do you calculate would, in that case, stand up?'

She then ordered one of the beaux who attended her, to bring her a chair, and told another to fetch her the locket. Edgar was again advancing to Camilla, when Lionel, whose desire to obtain the good graces of Mrs. Arlbery, had suggested to him an anticipation of her commands, pushed forward with the locket.

'Well, really, it is not ugly,' cried she, taking it in her hand: 'Have you put in yet, Miss Tyrold?'

'No, ma'am.'

'O, I am vastly glad of that; for now we will try our fortune together.'

Camilla, though secretly blushing at what she felt was an extravagance, could not withstand this invitation: she gave her half guinea.

Edgar, disappointed, retreated in silence.

The money being collected, and the names of the rafflers taken down, information was given, that the prize was to be thrown for in three days time, at one o'clock at noon, in the shop of a book-seller at Northwick.

Some of the company now departed; others prepared for a last dance. Miss Margland desired Lionel to see for their carriage; but Lionel had no greater joy than to disregard her. Indiana asked earnestly to stay longer; Miss Margland said, she could only give way to her request, upon condition her partner should be Mr. Mandlebert. It was in vain she urged that she was already engaged to Colonel Andover; Miss Margland was inexorable, and Edgar, laughing, said, he should certainly have the whole corps upon his back; but the honour was sufficient to counterbalance the risk, and he would, therefore, beg the Colonel's patience.

'Mr. Mandlebert,' said Miss Margland, 'I know enough of quarrels at balls about partners, and ladies changing their minds, to know how to act pretty well in those cases: I shall desire, therefore, to speak to the Colonel myself, and not trust two gentlemen together upon such a nice matter.'

She then beckoned to the Colonel, who stood at a little distance, and, taking him apart, told him, she flattered herself he would not be offended, if Miss Lynmere should dance again with Mr. Mandlebert, though rather out of rule, as there were particular reasons for it.

The Colonel, with a smile, said he perceived Mr. Mandlebert was the happy man, and acquiesced.

A general murmur now ran buzzing round the room, that Mr. Mandlebert and Miss Lynmere were publicly contracted to each other; and, amongst many who heard with displeasure that the young beauty was betrothed before she was exhibited to view,

Mr. Macdersey appeared to suffer the most serious mortification.

As soon as this dance was over, Edgar conducted his ladies to an apartment below stairs, and went in search of the carriage.

He did not return for some time. Miss Margland, as usual, grumbled; but Camilla, perceiving Mrs. Arlbery, rejoiced in the delay; and stationed herself by her side, all alive in attending to the pleasantry with which she was amusing herself and those around her.

When Edgar, who seemed out of breath from running, came back, he made but short answers to the murmurs of Miss Margland; and, hastening to Camilla, said: 'I have been with your petitioner:—she has all that can comfort her for the present; and I have learnt the name of her husband's counsel. You will be so good as to excuse me at dinner to Sir Hugh. I shall remain here till I can judge what may be done.'

The attention of Camilla was now effectually withdrawn from Mrs. Arlbery, and the purest delight of which human feelings are susceptible, took sudden and sole possession of her youthful mind, in the idea of being instrumental to the preservation of a fellow-creature.

Edgar saw, in the change, yet brightness of her countenance, what passed within;—and his disappointment concerning the raffle was immediately forgotten.

A short consultation followed, in which both spoke with so much energy, as not only to overpower the remonstrances of Miss Margland for their departure, but to catch the notice of Mrs. Arlbery, who, coming forward, and leaning her hand on the shoulder of Camilla, said: 'Tell me what it is that has thus animated you? Have you heard any good tidings of your new friend?'

Camilla instantly and eagerly related the subject that occupied them, without observing that the whole company around were smiling, at her earnestness in a cause of such common distress.

'You are new, my dear,' said Mrs. Arlbery, patting her cheek, 'very new; but I take the whim sometimes of being charitable myself, for a little variety. It always looks pretty; and begging is no bad way of shewing off one's powers. So give me your documents, and I'll give you my eloquence.'

Camilla presented her the petition, and she invited Mandlebert to dine with her. Miss Margland then led the way, and the female party returned to Cleves.

CHAPTER V

A Raffle

IT was late when Edgar returned to Cleves. Camilla flew to meet him. He told her everything relative to her petitioner was in the most prosperous train; he had seen the prisoner, heard the particulars of his story, which all tended to his exculpation; and Mrs. Arlbery had contrived to make acquaintance with his counsel, whom she found perfectly well disposed to exert himself in the cause, and whom she had invited to a splendid supper. The trial was to take place the next morning.

Camilla, already powerfully struck with Mrs. Arlbery, was enchanted to find her thus active in benevolence.

Edgar was to dine with that lady the next day, and to learn the event of their joint exertions.

This proved all that could be wished. The prosecution had been mild: the judge and jury had been touched with compassion; and the venial offender had been released with a gentle reprimand.

Mandlebert returned to communicate these tidings to Camilla, with a pleasure exactly in unison with her own. Mrs. Arlbery, he avowed, had been as zealous as himself; and had manifested a charity of disposition which the flightiness of her manners had not let him to expect.

*   *   *   *

The next object of attention was the raffle, which was to take place the following morning.

Sir Hugh was averse to letting his nieces go abroad again so soon: but Miss Margland, extremely anxious about her own chance for the prize, solemnly asserted its necessity; inveighed against the mismanagement of everything at Cleves, stifled all her complaints of Lionel, and pronounced a positive decision, that, to carry Indiana to public places, was the sole method of promoting the match.

Sir Hugh then, willing to believe, and yet more willing to get rid of disputing with her, no longer withheld his consent.

They were advanced within half a mile of Northwick, when a sick man, painfully supported by a woman with a child in her arms, caught their eyes. The ready hand of Eugenia was immediately in her pocket; Camilla, looking more intently upon the group, perceived another child, and presently recognised the wife of the prisoner. She called to the coachman to stop, and Edgar, at the same moment, rode up to the carriage.

Miss Margland angrily ordered the man to drive on, saying, she was quite sick of being thus for ever infested with beggars; who really came so often, they were no better than pick-pockets.

'O, don't refuse to let me speak to them!' cried Camilla; 'it will be such a pleasure to see their joy!'

'O yes! they look in much joy indeed! they seem as if they had not eat a morsel these three weeks! Drive on, I say, coachman! I like no such melancholy sights, for my part. They always make me ill. I wonder how any body can bear them.'

'But we may help them; we may assist them!' said Camilla, with increasing earnestness.

'And pray, when they have got all our money, who is to help us?'

Eugenia, delighted to give, but unhabituated to any other exertion, flung half a crown to them; and Indiana, begging to look out, said, 'Dear! I never saw a prisoner before!'

Encouraged by an expressive look from Camilla, Edgar dismounted to hand her from the carriage, affecting not to hear the remonstrances of Miss Margland, though she scrupled not to deliver them very audibly. Eugenia languished to join them, but could not venture to disobey a direct command; and Indiana, observing the road to be very dusty, submitted, to save a pair of beautiful new shoes.

Camilla had all the gratification she promised herself, in witnessing the happiness of the poor petitioner. He was crawling to Cleves, with his family, to offer thanks. They were penniless, sick, and wretched; yet the preservation of the poor man seemed to make misery light to them all. Edgar desired to know what were their designs for the future. The man answered that he should not dare go back to his own country, because there his disgrace was known, and he should procure no work; nor, indeed, was he now able to do any. 'So we must make up our minds to beg from door to door, and in the streets, and on the high road,' he continued; 'till I get back a little strength; and can earn a living more creditably.'

'But as long as we have kept you alive, and saved you from being transported,' said his wife, 'for which all thanks be due to this good gentleman, we shall mind no hardships, and never go astray again, in wicked unthinkingness of this great mercy.'

Edgar inquired what had been their former occupations; they answered, they had both been day-workers in the field, till a fit of sickness had hindered the poor man from getting his livelihood: penury and hunger then pressing hard upon them all, he had been tempted to commit the offence for which he was taken, and brought to death's door. 'But as now,' he added, 'I have been saved, I shall make it a warning for the time to come, and never give myself up to so bad a course again.'

Edgar asked the woman what money she had left.

'Ah, sir, none! for we had things to pay, and people to satisfy, and so everything you and the good ladies gave us, is all gone; for, while anything was left us, they would not be easy. But this is no great mischief now, as my husband is not taken away from us, and is come to a right sense.'

'I believe,' said Edgar, 'you are very good sort of people, however distress had misguided you.'

He then put something into the man's hand, and Eugenia, who from the carriage window heard what passed, flung him another half crown; Camilla added a shilling, and turning suddenly away, walked a few paces from them all.

Edgar, gently following, inquired if anything was the matter; her eyes were full of tears: 'I was thinking,' she cried, 'what my dear father would have said, had he seen me giving half a guinea for a toy, and a shilling to such poor starving people as these!'

'Why, what would he have said?' cried Edgar, charmed with her penitence, though joining in the apprehended censure.

'He would more than ever have pitied those who want money, in seeing it so squandered by one who should better have remembered his lessons! O, if I could but recover that half guinea!'

'Will you give me leave to get it back for you?'

'Leave? you would lay me under the greatest obligation! How far half a guinea would go here, in poverty such as this!'

He assured her he could regain it without difficulty; and then, telling the poor people to postpone their walk to Cleves till the evening, when Camilla meant to prepare her uncle, also, to assist them, he handed her to the coach, with feelings yet more pleased than her own, and galloped forward to execute his commission.

He was ready at the door of the library[1] to receive them. As they alighted, Camilla eagerly cried: 'Well! have you succeeded?'

'Can you trust yourself to this spot, and to a review of the allurement,' answered he, smiling, and holding half a guinea between his fingers, 'yet be content to see your chance for the prize withdrawn?'

'O give it me! give it me!' cried she, almost seizing it from him, 'my dear father will be so glad to hear I have not spent it so foolishly.'

The rafflers were not yet assembled; no one was in the shop but a well dressed elegant young man, who was reading at a table, and who neither raised his eyes at their entrance, nor suffered their discourse to interrupt his attention; yet though abstracted from outward objects, his studiousness was not of a solemn cast; he seemed wrapt in what he was reading with a pleasure amounting to ecstasy. He started, acted, smiled, and looked pensive in turn, while his features were thrown into a thousand different expressions, and his person was almost writhed with perpetually varying gestures. From time to time his rapture broke forth into loud exclamations of 'Exquisite! exquisite!' while he beat the leaves of the book violently with his hands, in token of applause, or lifting them up to his lips, almost devoured with kisses the passages that charmed him. Sometimes he read a few words aloud, calling out 'Heavenly!' and vehemently stamping his approbation with his feet; then suddenly shutting up the book, folded his arms, and casting his eyes towards the ceiling, uttered: 'O too much! too much! there is no standing it!' yet again, the next minute, opened it and resumed the lecture.

The youthful group was much diverted with this unintended exhibition. To Eugenia alone it did not appear ridiculous; she simply envied his transports, and only wished to discover by what book they were excited. Edgar and Camilla amused themselves with conjecturing various authors; Indiana and Miss Margland required no such aid to pass their time, while, with at least equal delight, they contemplated the hoped-for prize.

Lionel now bounced in: 'Why what,' cried he, 'are you all

doing in this musty old shop, when Mrs. Arlbery and all the world
are enjoying the air on the public walks?'

Camilla was instantly for joining that lady; but Eugenia felt an
unconquerable curiosity to learn the running title of the book.
She stole softly round to look over the shoulder of the reader,
and her respect for his raptures increased, when she saw they were
raised by Thomson's Seasons.

Neither this approach, nor the loud call of Lionel, had interrupted the attention of the young student, who perceived and
regarded nothing but what he was about; and though occasionally
he ceased reading to indulge in passionate ejaculations, he seemed
to hold everything else beneath his consideration.

Lionel, drawn to observe him from the circuit made by Eugenia,
exclaimed: 'What, Melmond! why, how long have you been in
Hampshire?'

The youth, surprised from his absence of mind by the sound of
his own name, looked up and said: 'Who's that?'

'Why, when the deuce did you come into this part of the world?'
cried Lionel, approaching him to shake hands.

'O! for pity's sake,' answered he, with energy, 'don't interrupt
me!'

'Why not? have not you enough of that dry work at Oxford?
Come, come, have done with this boyish stuff, and behave like a
man.'

'You distract me,' answered Melmond, motioning him away;
'I am in a scene that entrances me to Elysium! I have never read
it since I could appreciate it.'

'What! old Thomson?' said Lionel, peeping over him; 'why, I
never read him at all. Come, man! (giving him a slap on the
shoulder) come along with me, and I'll shew you something more
worth looking at.'

'You will drive me mad, if you break in upon this episode! 'tis
a picture of all that is divine upon earth! hear it, only hear it!'

He then began the truly elegant and feeling description that
concludes Thomson's Spring; and though Lionel, with a loud
shout, cried: 'Do you think I come hither for such fogrum stuff
as that?' and ran out of the shop; the 'wrapt enthusiast' continued
reading aloud, too much delighted with the pathos of his own
voice in expressing the sentiments of the poet,[1] to deny himself a
regale so soothing to his ears.

Eugenia, enchanted, stood on tiptoe to hear him, her uplifted finger petitioning silence all around, and her heart fondly repeating, O just such a youth be Clermont! just such his passion for reading! just such his fervour for poetry! just such his exaltation of delight in literary yet domestic felicity!

Mandlebert, also, caught by the rehearsal of his favourite picture of a scheme of human happiness, which no time, no repetition can make vapid to a feeling heart, stood pleased and attentive to hear him; even Indiana, though she listened not to the matter, was struck by the manner in which it was delivered, which so resembled dramatic recitation, that she thought herself at a play, and full of wonder, advanced straight before him, to look full in his face, and watch the motions of his right arm, with which he acted incessantly, while the left held his book. Miss Margland concluded he was a strolling player, and did not suffer him to draw her eyes from the locket. But when, at the words

———content,
Retirement, rural quiet, friendship, books,
Ease and alternate labour, useful life,
Progressive virtue, and approving Heaven,[1]

Mandlebert turned softly round to read their impression on the countenance of Camilla—she was gone!

Attracted by her wish to see more of Mrs. Arlbery, she had run out of the shop after Lionel, before she either knew what was reading, or was missed by those the reader had engaged. Edgar, though disappointed, wondered he should have stayed himself to listen to what had long been familiar to him, and was quietly gliding away when he saw her returning. He then went back to his post, wondering, with still less satisfaction, how she could absent herself from hearing what so well was worth her studying.

The young man, when he came to the concluding line:

To scenes where love and bliss immortal reign! [2]

rose, let fall the book, clasped his hands with a theatrical air, and was casting his eyes upwards in a fervent and willing trance, when he perceived Indiana standing immediately before him.

Surprised and ashamed, his sublimity suddenly forsook him;

his arms dropt, and his hands were slipt into his waistcoat pockets.

But, the very next moment, the sensation of shame and of self was superseded by the fair object that had thus aroused him. Her beauty, her youth, her attitude of examination, struck him at first with an amazement that presently gave place to an admiration as violent as it was sudden. He started back, bowed profoundly, without any pretence for bowing at all, and then rivetting his eyes, in which his whole soul seemed centred, on her lovely face, stood viewing her with a look of homage, motionless, yet enraptured.

Indiana, still conceiving this to be some sort of acting, unabashed kept her post, expecting every moment he would begin spouting something more. But the enthusiasm of the young Oxonian had changed its object; the charms of poetry yielded to the superior charms of beauty, and while he gazed on the fair Indiana, his fervent mind fancied her some being of celestial order, wonderfully accorded to his view: How, or for what purpose, he as little knew as cared. The play of imagination, in the romance of early youth, is rarely interrupted with scruples of probability.

This scene of dumb transport and unfixed expectation, was broken up neither by the admirer nor the admired, but by the entrance of Mrs. Arlbery, Sir Sedley Clarendel, Lionel, the officers, and many of the rest of the company that had been present at the public breakfast: Nor would even this intrusion have disengaged the young Oxonian from his devout and ecstatic adoration, had it been equally indifferent to Indiana; but the appearance of a party of gay officers was not, to her, a matter of little moment. Eager for the notice in which she delighted, she looked round in full confidence of receiving it. The rapture of the Oxonian, as she had seen it kindled while he was reading, she attributed to something she did not understand, and took in it, therefore, no part; but the adulation of the officers was by no means ambiguous, and its acceptance was as obvious as its presentation.

Willingly, therefore, as well as immediately encompassed, she received a thousand compliments, and in the gratification of hearing them, completely forgot her late short surprise; but the Oxonian, more forcibly struck, ardently followed her with his eyes, started back theatrically at every change of attitude which displayed her fine figure, and at her smiles smiled again, from the uncontrollable sympathy of a fascinated imagination.

Miss Margland felt not small pride in seeing her pupil thus distinguished, since it marked the shrewdness of her capacity in foretelling the effect of bringing her forth. Anxious to share in a consequence to which she had industriously contributed, she paradingly forced her way through the group, and calling the attention of Indiana to herself, said: 'I am glad you came away, my dear; for I am sure that man is only a poor strolling player.'

'Dear! let me look at him again!' cried Indiana; 'for I never saw a player before; only at a play.'

Shen then turned back to examine him.

Enchanted to again meet her eyes, the youth bowed with intense respect, and advanced a few paces, as if with intention to speak to her, though immediately and with still more precipitance he retreated, from being ready with nothing to say.

Lionel, going up to him, and pulling him by the arm, cried: 'Why, man! what's come to you? These are worse heroics than I have seen you in yet.'

The bright eyes of Indiana being still fixed upon him, he disdained all notice of Lionel, beyond a silent repulse.

Indiana, having now satisfied her curiosity, restored her attention to the beaux that surrounded her. The Oxonian, half sighing, unfolded his clasped hands, one of which he reposed upon the shoulder of Lionel.

'Come, prithee, be a little less in alt,'[1] cried Lionel, 'and answer a man when he speaks to you. Where did you leave Smythson?'

'Who is that divinity; can you tell me?' said the Oxonian in a low and respectful tone of inquiry.

'What divinity?'

'What divinity? insensible Tyrold! tasteless! adamantine! Look, look yonder, and ask me again if you can!'

'O what; my cousin Indiana?'

'Your cousin? have you any affinity with such a creature as that? O Tyrold! I glory in your acquaintance! she is all I ever read of! all I ever conceived! she is beauty in its very essence! she is elegance, delicacy, and sensibility personified!'

'All very true,' said Lionel; 'but how should you know anything of her besides her beauty?'

'How? by looking at her! Can you view that countenance and

ask me how? Are not those eyes all soul? Does not that mouth promise every thing that is intelligent? Can those lips ever move but to diffuse sweetness and smiles? I must not look at her again! another glance may set me raving!'

'May?' cried Lionel, laughing; 'why what have you been doing all this time? However, be a little less in the sublime, and I'll introduce you to her.'

'Is it possible? shall I owe to you so celestial a happiness? O Tyrold! you bind me to you for life!'

Lionel, heartily hallowing, then brought him forward to Indiana: 'Miss Lynmere,' he cried, 'a fellow student of mine, though somewhat more given to study than your poor cousin, most humbly begs the honour of kissing your toe.'

The uncommon lowness of the bow which the Oxonian, ignorant of what Lionel would say, was making, led Miss Margland to imagine he was really going to perform that popish ceremony;[1] and hastily pulling Lionel by the sleeve, she angrily said: 'Mr. Lionel, I desire to know by whose authority you present such actor-men to a young lady under my care.'

Lionel, almost in convulsions, repeated this aloud; and the young student, who had just, in a voice of the deepest interest and respect, begun, 'The high honour, madam;' hearing an universal laugh from the company, stopt short, utterly disconcerted, and after a few vainly stammering attempts, bowed again, and was silent.

Edgar, who in this distress, read an ingenuousness of nature that counterpoised its romantic enthusiasm, felt for the young man, and taking Lionel by the arm, said: 'Will you not introduce me also to your friend?'

'Mr. Melmond of Brazen Nose! Mr. Mandlebert of Beech Park!' cried Lionel, flourishing, and bowing from one to the other.

Edgar shook hands with the youth, and hoped they should be better acquainted.

Camilla, gliding round, whispered him: 'How like my dear father was that! to give relief to embarrassment, instead of joining in the laugh which excites it!'

Edgar, touched by a comparison to the person he most honoured, gratefully looked his acknowledgment; and all displeasure at her flight, even from Thomson's scene of conjugal felicity, was erased from his mind.

The company grew impatient for the raffle, though some of the subscribers were not arrived. It was voted, at the proposition of Mrs. Arlbery, that the master of the shop should represent, as their turns came round, those who were absent.

While this was settling, Edgar, in some confusion, drew Camilla to the door, saying: 'To avoid any perplexity about your throwing, suppose you step into the haberdasher's shop that is over the way?'

Camilla, who already had felt very awkward with respect to her withdrawn subscription, gladly agreed to the proposal, and begging him to explain the matter to Miss Margland, tript across the street, while the rafflers were crowding to the point of action.

Here she sat, making some small purchases, till the business was over: The whole party then came forth into the street, and all in a body poured into the haberdasher's shop, smiling, bowing, and of one accord wishing her joy.

Concluding this to be in derision of her desertion, she rallied as well as she was able; but Mrs. Arlbery, who entered the last, and held the locket in her hand, said: 'Miss Tyrold, I heartily wish you equally brilliant success, in the next, and far more dangerous lottery, in which, I presume, you will try your fate.' And presented her the prize.

Camilla, colouring, laughing, and unwillingly taking it, said: 'I suppose, ma'am—I hope—it is yours?' And she looked about for Edgar to assist her; but, he was gone to hasten the carriage.

Every body crowded round her to take a last sight of the beautiful locket. Eager to get rid of it, she put it into the hands of Indiana, who regarded it with a partiality which her numerous admirers had courted, individually, in vain; though the young Oxonian, by his dramatic emotions, had engaged more of her attention than she had yet bestowed elsewhere. Eugenia too, caught by his eccentricity, was powerfully impelled to watch and admire him; and not the less, in the unenvying innocency of her heart, for his evident predilection in favour of her cousin. This youth was not, however, suffered to engross her; the stranger by whom she had already been distinguished at the ball and public breakfast, was one in the group, and resumed a claim upon her notice, too flattering in its manner to be repulsed, and too new to her extreme inexperience to be obtrusive.

Meanwhile, Camilla gathered from Major Cerwood, that the

prize had really fallen to her lot. Edgar had excused her not
staying to throw for herself, but the general proxy, the bookseller,
had been successful in her name.

In great perplexity how to account for this incident, she
apprehended Edgar had made some mistake, and determined,
through his means, to restore the locket to the subscription.

The carriage of Mrs. Arlbery was first ready; but, pushing
away the throng of beaux offering assistance, she went up to
Camilla, and said: 'Fair object of the spleen of all around, will you
bring a little of your influence with good fortune to my domain,
and come and dine with me?'

Delighted at the proposal, Camilla looked at Miss Margland;
but Miss Margland, not being included in the invitation, frowned
a refusal.

Edgar now entered and announced the coach of Sir Hugh.

'Make use of it as you can,' said Mrs. Arlbery; 'there is room
for one more to go back than it brought; so pray do the honours
prettily. Clarendel! take care of Miss Tyrold to my coach.'

Sir Sedley smiled, and played with his watch chain, but did not
move.

'O you laziest of all lazy wretches!' cried Mrs. Arlbery.

'I shall reverse the epithet, and be the alertest of the alert,' said
Major Cerwood; 'if the commission may be devolved to myself.'

'Positively not for the world! there is nothing so pleasant as
working the indolent; except, indeed, making the restless keep
quiet; so, come forth, Clarendel! be civil, and strike us all with
astonishment!'

'My adored Mrs. Arlbery!' cried he, (hoisting himself upon
the shop counter, and swinging a switch to and fro, with a languid
motion) your maxims are all of the first superlative, except this;
but nobody's civil now, you know; 'tis a fogramity quite out.'[1]

'So you absolutely won't stir, then?'

'O pray! pray!' answered he, putting on his hat and folding his
arms, 'a little mercy! 'tis so vastly insufferably hot! Calcutta
must be in the frigid zone to this shop! a very ice-house!'

Camilla, who never imagined rudeness could make a feature
of affectation, internally attributed this refusal to his pique that
she had disregarded him at the public breakfast, and would have
made him some apology, but knew not in what manner to word it.

The Major again came forward, but Miss Margland, advancing

also, said: 'Miss Camilla! you won't think of dining out unknown to Sir Hugh?'

'I am sure,' cried Mrs. Arlbery, 'you will have the goodness to speak for me to Sir Hugh.' Then, turning to Lionel, 'Mr. Tyrold,' she added, 'you must go with us, that you may conduct your sister safe home. Don't be affronted; I shall invite you for your own sake another time. Come, you abominable Clarendel! awake! and give a little spring to our motions.'

'You are most incommodiously cruel!' answered he; 'but I am bound to be your slave.' Then calling to one of the apprentices in the shop: 'My vastly good boy,' he cried, 'do you want to see me irrecoverably subdued by this immensely inhuman heat?'

The boy stared; and said, 'Sir.'

'If not, do get me a glass of water.'

'O worse and worse!' said Mrs. Arlbery; 'your whims are insupportable. I give you up! Major! advance.'

The Major, with alacrity, offered his hand; Camilla hesitated; she wished passionately to go, yet felt she had no authority for such a measure. The name, though not the person of Mrs. Arlbery, was known both at Cleves and at Etherington, as belonging to the owner of a capital house in the neighbourhood; and though the invitation was without form, Camilla was too young to be withheld by ceremony. Her uncle, she was sure, could refuse her nothing; and she thought, as she was only a visitor at Cleves, Miss Margland had no right to control her; the pleasure, therefore, of the scheme, soon conquered every smaller difficulty, and, looking away from her party, she suffered herself to be led to the coach.

Miss Margland as she passed, said aloud: 'Remember! I give no consent to this!'

But Eugenia, on the other side, whispered: 'Don't be uneasy; I will explain to my uncle how it all happened.'

Mrs. Arlbery was following, when Indiana exclaimed: 'Cousin Camilla, what am I to do with your locket?'

Camilla had wholly forgotten it; she called to Edgar, who slowly, and with a seriousness very unusual, obeyed her summons.

'There has been some great mistake,' said she, 'about the locket. I suppose they neglected to scratch out my name from the subscription; for Major Cerwood says it really came to me. Will you be so good as to return it to the bookseller?'

The gravity of Edgar immediately vanished: 'Are you so ready,' he said, 'even when it is in your possession, to part with so pretty a trinket?'

'You know it cannot be mine, for here is my half guinea.'

Mrs. Arlbery then got into the coach; but Camilla, still farther recollecting herself, again called to Edgar, and holding out the half guinea, said: 'How shall I get this to the poor people?'

'They were to come,' he answered, 'to Cleves this afternoon.'

'Will you, then, give it them for me?'

'No commission to Mr. Mandlebert!' interrupted Mrs. Arlbery; 'for he must positively dine with us.'

Mandlebert bowed a pleased assent, and Camilla applied to Eugenia; but Miss Margland, in deep wrath, refused to let her move a step.

Mrs. Arlbery then ordered the coach to drive home. Camilla, begging a moment's delay, desired Edgar to approach nearer, and said, in a low voice: 'I cannot bear to let those poor expectants toil so far for nothing. I will sooner go back to Cleves myself. I shall not sleep all night if I disappoint them. Pray, invent some excuse for me.'

'If you have set your heart upon this visit,' answered Mandlebert, with vivacity, though in a whisper, 'I will ride over myself to Cleves, and arrange all to your wishes; but if not, certainly there can need no invention, to decline an invitation of which Sir Hugh has no knowledge.'

Camilla, who at the beginning of this speech felt the highest glee, sunk involuntarily at its conclusion, and turning with a blank countenance to Mrs. Arlbery, stammeringly said: 'Can you, will you—be so very good, as not to take it ill if I don't go with you?'

Mrs. Arlbery, surprised, very coldly answered: 'Certainly not! I would be no restraint upon you. I hate restraint myself.' She then ordered the footman to open the door; and Camilla, too much abashed to offer any apology, was handed out by Edgar.

'Amiable Camilla!' said he, in conducting her back to Miss Margland, 'this is a self-conquest that I alone, perhaps, expected from you!'

Cheered by such approbation, she forgot her disappointment, and regardless of Miss Margland and her ill humour, jumped into her uncle's coach, and was the gayest of the party that returned to Cleves.

Edgar took the locket from Indiana, and promised to rectify the mistake; and then, lest Mrs. Arlbery should be offended with them all, rode to her house without any fresh invitation, accompanied by Lionel; whose anger against Camilla, for suffering Miss Margland to gain a victory, was his theme the whole ride.

CHAPTER VI

A Barn

THE first care of Camilla was to interest Sir Hugh in the misfortunes of the prisoner and his family; her next, to relate the invitation of Mrs. Arlbery, and to beg permission that she might wait upon the lady the next morning, with apologies for her abrupt retreat, and with acknowledgments for the services done to the poor woman; which first the Oxonian, and then the raffle, had driven from her mind. Sir Hugh readily consented, blaming her for supposing it possible he could ever hesitate in what could give her any pleasure.

Before the tea-party broke up, Edgar returned. He told Camilla he had stolen away the instant the dinner was over, to avoid any mistake about the poor people, whom he had just overtaken by the park-gate, and conducted to the great barn, where he had directed them to wait for orders.

'I'll run to them immediately,' cried she, 'for my half guinea is in an agony to be gone!'

'The barn! my dear young Mr. Mandlebert!' exclaimed Sir Hugh; 'and why did you not bring them to the servants' hall? My little girl has been telling me all their history; and, God forbid, I should turn hard-hearted, because of their wanting a leg of mutton, in preference to being starved; though they might have no great right to it, according to the forms of law; which, however, is not much impediment to the calls of nature, when a man sees a butcher's stall well covered, and has got nothing within him, except his own poor craving appetite; which is a thing I always take into consideration; though, God forbid, I should protect a thief, no man's property being another's, whether he's poor or rich.'

He then gave Camilla three guineas to deliver to them from himself, to set them a little a-going in an honest way, that they might not, he said, repent leaving off bad actions. Her joy was so excessive, that she passionately embraced his knees: and Edgar, while he looked on, could nearly have bent to her his own, with admiration of her generous nature. Eugenia desired to accompany her; and Indiana, rising also, said: 'Dear! I wonder how they will look in the barn! I should like to see them too.'

Miss Margland made no opposition, and they set out.

Camilla, leading the way, with a fleetness that mocked all equality, ran into the barn, and saw the whole party, according to their several powers, enjoying themselves. The poor man, stretched upon straw, was resting his aching limbs; his wife, by his side, was giving nourishment to her baby; and the other child, a little boy of three years old, was jumping and turning head over heels, with the true glee of unspoilt nature, superior to poverty and distress.

To the gay heart of Camilla whatever was sportive was attractive; she flew to the little fellow, whose skin was clean and bright, in the midst of his rags and wretchedness, and, making herself his play-mate, bid the woman finish feeding her child, told the man to repose himself undisturbed, and began dancing with the little boy, not less delighted than himself at the festive exercise.

Miss Margland cast up her hands and eyes as she entered, and poured forth a warm remonstrance against so demeaning a condescension: but Camilla, in whose composition pride had no share, though spirit was a principal ingredient, danced on unheeding, to the equal amaze and enchantment of the poor man and woman, at the honour done to their little son.

Edgar came in last; he had given his arm to Eugenia, who was always in the rear if unassisted. Miss Margland appealed to him upon the impropriety of the behaviour of Camilla, adding, 'If I had had the bringing up a young lady who could so degrade herself, I protest I should blush to shew my face: but you cannot, I am sure, fail remarking the difference of Miss Lynmere's conduct.'

Edgar attended with an air of complacency, which he thought due to the situation of Miss Margland in the family, yet kept his eyes fixt upon Camilla, with an expression that, to the least discernment, would have evinced his utmost approbation of her innocent gaiety: but Miss Margland was amongst that numerous tribe, who, content as well as occupied with making observations upon others, have neither the power, nor thought, of developing those that are returned upon themselves.

Camilla at length, wholly out of breath, gave over; but perceiving that the baby was no longer at its mother's breast, flew to the poor woman, and, taking the child in her arms, said: 'Come, I can nurse and rest at the same time; I assure you the baby will be safe with me, for I nurse all the children in our neighbourhood.' She then fondled the poor little half-starved child to her bosom, quieting, and kissing, and cooing over it.

Miss Margland was still more incensed; but Edgar could attend to her no longer. Charmed with the youthful nurse, and seeing in her unaffected attitudes, a thousand graces he had never before remarked, and reading in her fondness for children the genuine sweetness of her character, he could not bear to have the pleasing reflections revolving in his mind interrupted by the spleen of Miss Margland, and, slipping away, posted himself behind the baby's father, where he could look on undisturbed, certain it was a vicinity to which Miss Margland would not follow him.

Had this scene lasted till Camilla was tired, its period would not have been very short; but Miss Margland, finding her exhortations vain, suddenly called out: 'Miss Lynmere! Miss Eugenia! come away directly! It's ten to one but these people have all got the gaol distemper!'

Edgar, quick as lightning at this sound, flew to Camilla, and snatched the child from her arms. Indiana, with a scream, ran out of the barn; Miss Margland hurried after; and Eugenia, following, earnestly entreated Camilla not to stay another moment.

'And what is there to be alarmed at?' cried she; 'I always nurse poor children when I see them at home; and my father never prohibits me.'

'There may be some reason, however,' said Edgar, while still he tenderly held the baby himself, 'for the present apprehension: I beg you, therefore, to hasten away.'

'At least,' said she, 'before I depart, let me execute my commission.' And then, with the kindest good wishes for their better fortune, she put her uncle's three guineas into the hands of the poor man, and her own rescued half guinea into those of his wife; and, desiring Edgar not to remain himself where he would not

suffer her to stay, ran to give her arm to Eugenia; leaving it a
doubtful point, whether the good humour accompanying her
alms, made the most pleased impression upon their receivers, or
upon their observer.

CHAPTER VII

A Declaration

AT night, while they were enjoying the bright beams of the moon,
from an apartment in the front of the house, they observed a
strange footman, in a superb livery, ride towards the servants hall;
and presently a letter was delivered to Miss Margland.

She opened it with an air of exulting consequence; one which
was inclosed, she put into her pocket, and read the other three or
four times over, with looks of importance and complacency. She
then pompously demanded a private audience with Sir Hugh,
and the young party left the room.

'Well, sir!' she cried, proudly, 'you may now see if I judged
right as to taking the young ladies a little into the world. Please
to look at this letter, sir:'

To Miss Margland, *at Sir* Hugh Tyrold's, *Bart.* Cleves, Hampshire.

MADAM,

WITH the most profound respect I presume to address you,
though only upon the strength of that marked politeness which
shines forth in your deportment. I have the highest ambition to
offer a few lines to the perusal of Miss Eugenia Tyrold, previous to
presenting myself to Sir Hugh. My reasons will be contained in
the letter which I take the liberty to put into your hands. It is only
under your protection, madam, I can aim at approaching that
young lady, as all that I have either seen or heard convinces me of
her extraordinary happiness in being under your direction. Your
influence, madam, I should therefore esteem as an honour, and I
leave it wholly to your own choice, whether to read what I have
addressed to that young lady before or after she has deigned to cast

an eye upon it herself. I remain, with the most profound respect,
Madam,

> your most obedient,
>> and obliged servant,
>>> ALPHONSO BELLAMY.[1]

I shall take the liberty to send my servant for an answer to-morrow evening.

'This, sir,' continued Miss Margland, when Sir Hugh had read the letter; 'this is the exact conduct of a gentleman; all open, all respectful. No attempt at any clandestine intercourse. All is addressed where it ought to be, to the person most proper to superintend such an affair. This is that very same gentleman whose politeness I mentioned to you, and who danced with Miss Eugenia at Northwick, when nobody else took any notice of her. This is—'

'Why then this is one of the most untoward things,' cried Sir Hugh, who, vainly waiting for a pause, began to speak without one, 'that has ever come to bear; for where's the use of Eugenia's making poor young fellows fall in love with her for nothing? which I hold to be a pity, provided it's sincere, which I take for granted.'

'As to that, sir, I can't say I see the reason why Miss Eugenia should not be allowed to look about her, and have some choice; especially as the young gentleman abroad has no fortune; at least none answerable to her expectations.'

'But that's the very reason for my marrying them together. For as he has not had the small-pox himself, that is, not in the natural way;[2] which, Lord help me! I thought the best, owing to my want of knowledge; why he'll the more readily excuse her face not being one of the prettiest, for her kindness in putting up with his having so little money; being a thing some people think a good deal of.'

'But, sir, won't it be very hard upon poor Miss Eugenia, if a better offer should come, that she must not listen to it, only because of a person she has never seen, though he has no estate?'

'Mrs. Margland,' said Sir Hugh, (with some heat,) 'this is the very thing that I would sooner have given a crown than have had happen! Who knows but Eugenia may take a fancy to this young jackanapes? who, for aught I know, may be as good a man as another, for which I beg his pardon; but, as he is nothing to me, and my nephew's my nephew, why am I to have the best scheme

I ever made knocked on the head, for a person I had as lieve were twitched into the Red Sea? which, however, is a thing I should not say, being what I would not do.'

Miss Margland took from her pocket the letter designed for Eugenia, and was going to break the seal; but Sir Hugh, preventing her, said: 'No, Miss Margland; Eugenia shall read her own letters. I have not had her taught all this time, by one of the first scholars of the age, as far as I can tell, to put that affront upon her.'

He then rang the bell, and sent for Eugenia.

Miss Margland stated the utter impropriety of suffering any young lady to read a letter of that sort, till proposals had been laid before her parents and guardians. But Sir Hugh spoke no more till Eugenia appeared.

'My dear,' he then said, 'here is a letter just come to put your education to the trial; which, I make no doubt, will stand the test properly: therefore, in regard to the answer, you shall write it all yourself, being qualified in a manner to which I have no right to pretend; though I shall go to-morrow to my brother, which will give me a better insight; his head being one of the best.'

Eugenia, greatly surprised, opened the letter, and read it with visible emotion.

'Well, my dear, and what do you say to it?'

Without answering, she read it again.

Sir Hugh repeated the question.

'Indeed, sir,' said she, (in a tone of sadness,) 'it is something that afflicts me very much!'

'Lord help us!' cried Sir Hugh, 'this comes of going to a ball! which, begging Miss Margland's pardon, is the last time it shall be done.'

Miss Margland was beginning a vehement defence of herself; but Sir Hugh interrupted it, by desiring to see the letter.

Eugenia, with increased confusion, folded it up, and said: 'Indeed, sir—Indeed, uncle—it is a very improper letter for me to shew.'

'Well, that,' cried Miss Margland, 'is a thing I could never have imagined! that a gentleman, who is so much the gentleman, should write an improper letter!'

'No, no,' interrupted she, 'not improper—perhaps—for him to write,—but for me to exhibit.'

'O, if that's all, my dear,' said Sir Hugh, 'if it's only because of a few compliments, I beg you not to mind them, because of their having no meaning; which is a thing common enough in the way of making love, by what I hear; though such a young thing as you can know nothing of the matter, your learning not going in that line; nor Dr. Orkborne's neither, if one may judge; which, God forbid I should find fault with, being no business of mine.'

He then again asked to see the letter; and Eugenia, ashamed to refuse, gave it, and went out of the room.

To Miss Eugenia Tyrold, Cleves.

MADAM,

THE delicacy of your highly cultivated mind awes even the violent passion which you inspire. And to this I entreat you to attribute the trembling fear which deters me from the honour of waiting upon Sir Hugh, while uncertain, if my addressing him might not raise your displeasure. I forbear, therefore, to lay before him my pretensions for soliciting your favour, from the deepest apprehension you might think I presumed too far, upon an acquaintance, to my unhappiness, so short; yet, as I feel it to have excited in me the most lasting attachment, from my fixed admiration of your virtues and talents, I cannot endure to run the risk of incurring your aversion. Allow me then, once more, under the sanction of that excellent lady in whose care I have had the honour of seeing you, to entreat one moment's audience, that I may be graced with your own commands about waiting upon Sir Hugh, without which, I should hold myself ungenerous and unworthy to approach him; since I should blush to throw myself at your feet from an authority which you do not permit. I beseech you, madam, to remember, that I shall be miserable till I know my doom; but still, that the heart, not the hand, can alone bestow happiness on a disinterested mind.

I have the honour to be,
          Madam,
                    your most devoted and obedient humble servant,
                              ALPHONSO BELLAMY.

Sir Hugh, when he had finished the letter, heaved a sigh, and leant his head upon his hand, considering whether or not to let it be seen by Miss Margland; who, however, not feeling secure what his determination might be, had so contrived to sit at the table as to read it at the same time with himself. Nor had she weighed the interest of her curiosity amiss; Sir Hugh, dreading a debate with her, soon put the letter into his pocket-book, and again sent for Eugenia.

Eugenia excused herself from returning, pleaded a head-ache, and went to bed.

Sir Hugh was in the deepest alarm; though the evening was far advanced, he could scarce refrain from going to Etherington directly; he ordered his carriage to be at the door at eight o'clock the next morning; and sent a second order, a moment after, that it should not be later than half past seven.

He then summoned Camilla, and, giving her the letter, bid her run with it to her sister, for fear it was that she was fretting for. And soon after, he went to bed, that he might be ready in the morning.

Eugenia, meanwhile, felt the placid composure of her mind now for the first time shaken. The assiduities of this young man had already pleased and interested her; but, though gratified by them in his presence, they occurred to her no more in his absence. With the Oxonian she had been far more struck; his energy, his sentiments, his passion for literature, would instantly have riveted him in her fairest favour, had she not so completely regarded herself as the wife of Clermont Lynmere, that she denied her imagination any power over her reason.

This letter, however, filled her with sensations wholly new. She now first reflected seriously upon the nature of her situation with regard to Clermont, for whom she seemed bespoken by her uncle, without the smallest knowledge how they might approve or suit each other. Perhaps he might dislike her; she must then have the mortification of being refused: perhaps he might excite her own antipathy; she must then either disappoint her uncle, or become a miserable sacrifice.

Here, on the contrary, she conceived herself an elected object. The difference of being accepted, or being chosen, worked forcibly upon her mind; and, all that was delicate, feminine, or dignified in her notions, rose in favour of him who sought, when opposed to him who could only consent to receive her. Generous, too, he appeared to her, in forbearing to apply to Sir Hugh, without her permission; disinterested, in declaring he did not wish for her hand without her heart; and noble, in not seeking her in a clandestine manner, but referring every thing to Miss Margland.

The idea also of exciting an ardent passion, lost none of its force from its novelty to her expectations. It was not that she had hitherto supposed it impossible; she had done less; she had not thought of it all. Nor came it now with any triumph to her modest and unassuming mind; all it brought with it was gratitude towards Bellamy, and a something soothing towards herself, which, though inexplicable to her reason, was irresistible to her feelings.

When Camilla entered with the letter, she bashfully asked her, if she wished to read it? Camilla eagerly cried: 'O, yes.' But, having finished it, said: 'It is not such a letter as Edgar Mandlebert would have written.'

'I am sure, then,' said Eugenia, colouring, 'I am sorry to have received it.'

'Do you not observe every day,' said Camilla, 'the distance, the delicacy of his behaviour to Indiana, though Miss Margland says their marriage is fixed; how free from all distinction that might confuse her? This declaration, on the contrary, is so abrupt—and from so new an acquaintance—'

'Certainly, then, I won't answer it,' said Eugenia, much discomposed; 'it had not struck me thus at first reading; but I see now all its impropriety.'

She then bid good night to Camilla; who, concluding her the appropriated wife of Clermont, had uttered her opinion without scruple.

Eugenia now again read the letter; but not again with pleasure. She thought it forward and presumptuous; and the only gratification that remained upon her mind, was an half conscious scarce admitted, and, even to herself, unacknowledged charm, in a belief, that she possessed the power to inspire an animated regard.

CHAPTER VIII

An Answer

MR. and Mrs. Tyrold and Lavinia were at breakfast when Sir Hugh entered their parlour, the next morning. 'Brother,' he cried,

'I have something of great importance to tell you, which it is very
fit my sister should hear too; for which reason, I make no doubt
but my dear Lavinia's good sense will leave the room, without
waiting for a hint.'

Lavinia instantly retired.

'O, my dear brother,' continued the baronet; 'do you know
here's a young chap, who appears to be a rather good sort of man,
which is so much the worse, who has been falling in love with
Eugenia?'

He then delivered the two letters to Mr. Tyrold.

'Now the only thing that hurts me in this business is, that this
young man, who Miss Margland calls a person of fashion, writes
as well as Clermont would do himself; though that is what I shall
never own to Eugenia, which I hope is no sin being all for her own
sake; that is to say, for Clermont's.'

Mr. Tyrold, after attentively reading the letters, gave them to
his wife, and made many inquiries concerning their writer, and
his acquaintance with Eugenia and Miss Margland.

'Why it was all brought about,' said Sir Hugh, 'by their going
to a ball and a public breakfast; which is a thing my little Camilla
is not at all to blame for, because if nobody had put it in her head,
she would not have known there was a thing of the kind. And,
indeed, it was but natural in poor Lionel neither, to set her agog,
the chief fault lying in the assizes; to which my particular objection is against the lawyers, who come into a town to hang and
transport the poor, by way of keeping the peace, and then encourage the rich to make all the noise and riot they can, by their
own junkettings; for which, however, being generally, I believe,
pretty good scholars, I make no doubt but they have their own
reasons.'

'I flatter myself,' said Mrs. Tyrold, scarce deigning to finish the
letters, 'Eugenia, young as she is, will need no counsel how to
estimate a writer such as this. What must the man be, who,
presuming upon his personal influence, ventures to claim her
concurrence in an application to her friends, though he has seen
her but twice, and knows her to be destitute of the smallest
knowledge of his principles, his character, or his situation in life?'

'Good lack!' cried the baronet, 'what a prodigious poor head I
must have! here I could hardly sleep all night, for thinking what a
fine letter this jackanapes, which I shall make no more apology for

calling him, had been writing, fearing it would cut up poor Clermont in her opinion, for all his grand tour.'

Perfectly restored to ease, he now bad them good morning; but Mr. Tyrold entreated him to stay till they had settled how to get rid of the business.

'My dear brother,' he answered, 'I want no more help now, since I have got your opinion, that is, my sister's, which I take it for granted is the same. I make no doubt but Eugenia will pretty near have writ her foul copy by the time I get home, which Dr. Orkborne may overlook for her, to the end that this Mr. Upstart may have no more fault to find against it.'

They both desired to dine at Cleves, that they might speak themselves with Eugenia.

'And how,' said Mr. Tyrold, with a strong secret emotion, 'how goes on Edgar with Indiana?'

'Vastly well, vastly well indeed! not that I pretend to speak for myself, being rather too dull in these matters, owing to never entering upon them in the right season, as I intend to tell other young men doing the same.'

He then, in warm terms, narrated the accounts given him by Miss Margland of the security of the conquest of Indiana.

Mr. Tyrold fixed his hour for expecting the carriage, and the baronet desired that Lavinia should be of the party; 'because,' he said, 'I see she has the proper discretion, when she is wanted to go out of the way; which must be the same with Camilla and Indiana, too, to-day, as well as with young Mr. Edgar; for I don't think it prudent to trust such new beginners with every thing that goes on, till they get a little older.'

The anxiety of Mr. Tyrold, concerning Bellamy, was now mingled with a cruel regret in relation to Mandlebert. Even his own upright conduct could scarce console him for the loss of his favourite hope, and he almost repented that he had not been more active in endeavouring to preserve it.

All that passed in his mind was read and participated in by his partner, whose displeasure was greater, though her mortification could but be equal. 'That Edgar,' said she, 'should have kept his heart wholly untouched, would less have moved my wonder; he has a peculiar, though unconscious delicacy in his nature, which results not from insolence nor presumption, but from his own invariable and familiar exercise of every virtue and of every duty:

the smallest deviation is offensive, and even the least inaccuracy is painful to him. Was it possible, then, to be prepared for such an election as this? He has disgraced my expectations; he has played the common part of a mere common young man, whose eye is his sole governor.'

'My Georgiana,' said Mr. Tyrold, 'I am deeply disappointed. Our two eldest girls are but slightly provided for; and Eugenia is far more dangerously circumstanced, in standing so conspicuously apart, as a prize to some adventurer. One of these three precious cares I had fondly concluded certain of protection and happiness; for which ever I might have bestowed upon Edgar Mandlebert, I should have considered as the most fortunate of her sex. Let us, however, rejoice for Indiana; no one can more need a protector; and, next to my own three girls, there is no one for whom I am so much interested. I grieve, however, for Edgar himself, whose excellent judgment will, in time, assert its rights, though passion, at this period, has set it aside.'

'I am too angry with him for pity,' said Mrs. Tyrold; 'nor is his understanding of a class that has any claim to such lenity: I had often thought our gentle Lavinia almost born to be his wife, and no one could more truly have deserved him. But the soft perfection of her character relieves me from any apprehension for her conduct, and almost all my solicitude devolves upon Camilla. For our poor Eugenia I had never indulged a hope of his choice; though that valuable, unfortunate girl, with every unearned defect about her, intrinsically merits him, with all his advantages, his accomplishments, and his virtues: but to appreciate her, uninfluenced by pecuniary views, to which he is every way superior, was too much to expect from so young a man. My wishes, therefore, had guided him to our Camilla, that sweet, open, generous, inconsiderate girl, whose feelings are all virtues, but whose impulses have no restraints: I have not a fear for her, when she can act with deliberation; but fear is almost all I have left, when I consider her as led by the start of the moment. With him, however, she would have been the safest, and with him—next alone to her mother, the happiest of her sex.'

The kindest acknowledgments repaid this sympathy of sentiment, and they agreed that their felicity would have been almost too complete for this lower world, if such an event had come to pass. 'Nevertheless its failure,' added Mrs. Tyrold, 'is almost incredible, and wholly unpardonable. That Indiana should vanquish where Lavinia and Camilla have failed! I feel indignant at such a tiumph of mere external unintelligent beauty.'

Eugenia received her parents with the most bashful confusion; yet they found, upon conversing with her, it was merely from youthful shame, and not from any dangerous prepossession. The observations of Camilla had broken that spell with which a first declaration of regard is apt to entangle unreflecting inexperience; and by teaching her to less value the votary, had made the conquest less an object of satisfaction. She was gratified by the permission of her uncle to write her own answer, which was now produced.

To Alphonso Bellamy, *Esq.*

S IR ,

I AM highly sensible to the honour of your partiality, which I regret it is not possible for me to deserve. Be not, therefore, offended, and still less suffer yourself to be afflicted, when I confess I have only my poor thanks to offer, and poor esteem to return, for your unmerited goodness. Dwell not, sir, upon this disappointment, but receive my best wishes for your restored happiness; for never can I forget a distinction to which I have so little claim. Believe me,

Sir,
Your very much obliged,
and most grateful humble servant,
E UGENIA T YROLD .

Mr. Tyrold, who delighted to see how completely, in her studies with Dr. Orkborne, she had escaped any pedantry or affectation, and even preserved all the native humility of her artless character, returned her the letter with an affectionate embrace, and told her he could desire no alteration but that of omitting the word *grateful* at the conclusion.

Mrs. Tyrold was far less satisfied. She wished it to be completely re-written; protesting, that a man who, in all probability, was a mere fortune-hunter, would infer from so gentle a dismission encouragement rather than repulse.

Sir Hugh said there was one thing only he desired to have

added, which was a hint of a pre-engagement with a relation of her own.

Eugenia, at this, coloured and retreated; and Mrs. Tyrold reminded the baronet, with some displeasure, of his promise to guard the secret of his project. Sir Hugh, a little disturbed, said it never broke out from him but by accident, which he would take care should never get the upper hand again. He would not, however, consent to have the letter altered, which he said would be an affront to the learning of Eugenia, unless it were done by Dr. Orkborne himself, who, being her master, had a right to correct her first penmanship.

Dr. Orkborne, being called upon, slightly glanced his eye over the letter, but made no emendation, saying: 'I believe it will do very sufficiently; but I have only concerned myself with the progress of Miss Eugenia in the Greek and Latin languages; any body can teach her English.'

The fond parents finished their visit in full satisfaction with their irreproachable Eugenia, and with the joy of seeing their darling Camilla as happy and as disengaged as when she had left them; but Mandlebert had spent the day abroad, and escaped, therefore, the observations with which they had meant to have investigated his sentiments. Indiana, with whom they conversed more than usual, and with the most scrutinizing attention, offered nothing either in manner or matter to rescue his decision from their censure: Mrs. Tyrold, therefore, rejoiced at his absence, lest a coolness she knew not how to repress, should have led him to surmise her disappointment. Her husband besought her to be guarded: 'We had no right,' he said, 'to the disposal of his heart; and Indiana, however he may find her inadequate to his future expectations, will not disgrace his present choice. She is beautiful, she is young, and she is innocent; this in early life is sufficient for felicity; and Edgar is yet too new in the world to be aware how much of life remains when youth is gone, and too unpractised to foresee, that beauty loses its power even before it loses its charms, and that the season of declining nature sighs deeply for the support which sympathy and intelligence can alone bestow.'

CHAPTER IX

An Explication

THE visit which Camilla had designed this morning to Mrs. Arlbery, she had been induced to relinquish through a speech made to her by Lionel. 'You have done for yourself, now!' said he, exultingly; 'so you may be governed by that scare-crow, Miss Margland, at your leisure. Do you know you were not once mentioned again at the Grove, neither by Mrs. Arlbery nor any body else? and they all agreed Indiana was the finest girl in the world.'

Camilla, though of the same opinion with respect to Indiana, concluded Mrs. Arlbery was offended by her retreat, and lost all courage for offering any apology.

Edgar did not return to Cleves till some time after the departure of Mr. and Mrs. Tyrold, when he met Miss Margland and the young ladies strolling in the park.

Camilla, running to meet him, asked if he had restored the locket to the right owner.

'No,' answered he, smiling, 'not yet.'

'What can be done then? my half guinea is gone; and, to confess the truth, I have not another I can well spare!'

He made no immediate reply; but, after speaking to the rest of the party, walked on towards the house.

Camilla, in some perplexity, following him, exclaimed: 'Pray tell me what I must do? indeed I am quite uneasy.'

'You would really have me give the locket to its rightful proprietor?'

'To be sure I would!'

'My commission, then, is soon executed.' And taking a little shagreen case from his waistcoat pocket, he put it into her hand.

'What can you mean? is there still any mistake?'

'None but what you may immediately rectify, by simply retaining your own prize.'

Camilla, opening the case, saw the locket, and perceived under the crystal a light knot of braided hair. But while she looked at it, he hurried into the house.

She ran after him, and insisted upon an explanation, declaring it to be utterly impossible that the locket and the half guinea should belong to the same person.

'You must not then,' he said, 'be angry, if you find I have managed, at last, but aukwardly. When I came to the library, the master of the raffle told me it was against all rule to refund a subscription.' He stopt.

'The half guinea you put into my hand, then,' cried she, colouring, 'was your own?'

'My dear Miss Camilla, there is no other occasion upon which I would have hazarded such a liberty; but as the money was for a charity, and as I had undertaken what I could not perform, I rather ventured to replace it, than suffer the poor objects for whom it was destined, to miss your kind intention.'

'You have certainly done right,' said she (feeling for her purse); 'but you must not, for that reason, make me a second time do wrong.'

'You will not so much hurt me?' replied he, gravely; 'you will not reprove me as if I were a stranger, a mere common acquaintance? Where could the money have been so well bestowed? It is not you, but those poor people who are in my debt. So many were the chances against your gaining the prize, that it was an event I had not even taken into consideration: I had merely induced you to leave the shop, that you might not have the surprise of finding your name was not withdrawn; the rest was accident; and surely you will not punish me that I have paid to the poor the penalty of my own ill weighed officiousness?'

Camilla put up her purse, but, with some spirit, said: 'There is another way to settle the matter which cannot hurt you; if I do not pay you my half guinea, you must at least keep the fruits of your own.' And she returned him the locket.

'And what,' cried he, laughing 'must I do with it? would you have me wear it myself?'

'Give it,' answered she, innocently, 'to Indiana.'

'No;' replied he, (reddening and putting it down upon a table,) but *you* may, if you believe her value will be greater than your own for the hair of your two sisters.'

Camilla, surprised, again looked at it, and recognized the hair of Lavinia and Eugenia.

'And how in the world did you get this hair?'

'I told them both the accident that had happened, and begged them to contribute their assistance to obtain your pardon.'

'Is it possible,' cried she, with vivacity, 'you could add to all your trouble so kind a thought?' and, without a moment's further hesitation, she accepted the prize, returning him the most animated thanks, and flying to Eugenia to inquire further into the matter, and then to her uncle, to shew him her new acquisition.

Sir Hugh, like herself, immediately said: 'But why did he not give it to Indiana?'

'I suppose,' said Eugenia, 'because Camilla had herself drawn the prize, and he had only added our hair to it.'

This perfectly satisfied the baronet; but Indiana could by no means understand why it had not been managed better; and Miss Margland, with much ill will, nourished a private opinion that the prize might perhaps have been her own, had not Mandlebert interfered. However, as there seemed some collusion which she could not develope, her conscience wholly acquitted her of any necessity to refund her borrowed half guinea.

Camilla, meanwhile, decorated herself with the locket, and had nothing in her possession which gave her equal delight.

Miss Margland now became, internally, less sanguine, with regard to the preference of Edgar for Indiana; but she concealed from Sir Hugh a doubt so unpleasant, through an unconquerable repugnance to acknowledge it possible she could have formed a wrong judgment.

CHAPTER X

A Panic

UPON the ensuing Sunday, Edgar proposed that a party should be made to visit a new little cottage, which he had just fitted up. This was agreed to; and as it was not above a mile from the parish church, Sir Hugh ordered that his low garden phaeton[1] should be in readiness, after the service, to convey himself and Eugenia thither. The rest, as the weather was fine, desired to walk.

They went to the church, as usual, in a coach and a chaise, which were dismissed as soon as they alighted: but before that period, Eugenia, with a sigh, had observed, that Melmond, the young Oxonian, was strolling the same way, and had seen, with a blush, that Bellamy was by his side.

The two gentlemen recognised them as they were crossing the church-yard. The Oxonian bowed profoundly, but stood aloof: Bellamy bowed also, but immediately approached; and as Sir Hugh, at that moment, accidentally let fall his stick, darted forward to recover and present it him.

The baronet, from surprise at his quick motion, dropt his handkerchief in receiving his cane; this also Bellamy, attentively shaking, restored to him: and Sir Hugh, who could accept no civility unrequited, said: 'Sir, if you are a stranger, as I imagine, not knowing your face, you are welcome to a place in my pew, provided you don't get a seat in a better; which I'm pretty much afraid you can't, mine being the best.'

The invitation was promptly accepted.

Miss Margland, always happy to be of consequence, was hastening to Sir Hugh, to put him upon his guard; when a respectful offer from Bellamy to assist her down the steps, induced her to remit her design to a future opportunity. Any attentions from a young man were now so new to her as to seem a call upon her gratitude; nor had her charms ever been so attractive as to render them common.

Edgar and Indiana, knowing nothing of his late declaration, thought nothing of his present admission; to Dr. Orkborne he was an utter stranger; but Camilla had recourse to her fan to conceal a smile; and Eugenia was in the utmost confusion. She felt at a loss how to meet his eyes, and seated herself as much as possible out of his way.

A few minutes after, looking up towards the gallery, she perceived, in one of the furthest rows, young Melmond; his eyes fixt upon their pew, but withdrawn the instant he was observed, and his air the most melancholy and dejected.

Again a half sigh escaped the tender Eugenia. How delicate, how elegant, thought she, is this retired behaviour! what refinement results from a true literary taste! O such be Clermont! if he resemble not this Oxonian—I must be wretched for life!

These ideas, which unavoidably, though unwillingly, interrupted her devotion, were again broken in upon, when the service was nearly over, by the appearance of Lionel. He had ridden five miles to join them, merely not to be thought in leading-strings, by staying at Etherington to hear his father; though the name and the excellence of the preaching of Mr. Tyrold, attracted to his church all strangers who had power to reach it:—so vehement in early youth is the eagerness to appear independant, and so general is the belief that all merit must be sought from a distance.

The deeper understanding of Mandlebert rendered him superior to this common puerility: and, though the preacher at Cleves church was his own tutor, Dr. Marchmont, from whom he was scarce yet emancipated, he listened to him with reverence, and would have travelled any distance, and taken cheerfully any trouble, that would in the best and strongest manner have marked the respect with which he attended to his doctrine.

Dr. Marchmont was a man of the highest intellectual accomplishments, uniting deep learning with general knowledge, and the graceful exterior of a man of the world, with the erudition and science of a fellow of a college. He obtained the esteem of the scholar wherever he was known, and caught the approbation of the most uncultivated wherever he was seen.

When the service was over, Edgar proposed that Dr. Marchmont should join the party to the cottage. Sir Hugh was most willing, and they sauntered about the church, while the Doctor retired to the vestry to take off his gown.

During this interval, Eugenia, who had a passion for reading epitaphs and inscriptions, became so intently engaged in decyphering some old verses on an antique tablet, that she perceived not when Dr. Marchmont was ready, nor when the party was leaving the church: and before any of the rest missed her, Bellamy suddenly took the opportunity of her being out of sight of all others, to drop on one knee, and passionately seize her hand, exclaiming: 'O madam!—' When hearing an approaching step, he hastily arose; but parted not with her hand till he had pressed it to his lips.

The astonished Eugenia, though at first all emotion, was completely recovered by this action. His kneeling and his 'O madam!' had every chance to affect her; but his kissing her hand she thought a liberty the most unpardonable. She resented it as an injury to Clermont, that would risk his life should he ever know it, and a blot to her own delicacy, as irreparable as it was irremediable.

Bellamy, who, from her letter, had augured nothing of hardness of heart, tenderly solicited her forgiveness; but she made him no answer; silent and offended she walked away, and, losing her

timidity in her displeasure, went up to her uncle, and whispered:
'Sir, the gentleman you invited into your pew, is Mr. Bellamy!'

The consternation of Sir Hugh was extreme: he had concluded
him a stranger to the whole party because a stranger to himself;
and the discovery of his mistake made him next conclude, that
he had risked a breach of the marriage he so much desired by his
own indiscretion. He took Eugenia immediately under his arm, as
if fearful she might else be conveyed away for Scotland before his
eyes, and hurrying to the church porch, called aloud for his
phaeton.

The phaeton was not arrived.

Still more dismayed, he walked on with Eugenia to the railing
round the church-yard, motioning with his left hand that no one
should follow.

Edgar, Lionel, and Bellamy marched to the road, listening for
the sound of horses, but they heard none; and the carriages of
the neighbouring gentry, from which they might have hoped any
assistance, had been driven away while they had waited for Dr.
Marchmont.

Meanwhile, the eyes of Eugenia again caught the young
Oxonian, who was wandering around the church-yard: neither
was he unobserved by Indiana, who, though she participated not
in the turn of reasoning, or taste for the romantic, which awakened
in Eugenia so forcible a sympathy, was yet highly gratified by his
apparent devotion to her charms: and had not Miss Margland
narrowly watched and tutored her, would easily have been
attracted from the cold civilities of Edgar, to the magnetism of
animated admiration.

In these circumstances, a few minutes appeared many hours to
Sir Hugh, and he presently exclaimed: 'There's no possibility of
waiting here the whole day long, not knowing what may be the
end!' Then, calling to Dr. Orkborne, he said to him in a low
voice, 'My good friend, here's happened a sad thing; that young
man I asked into my pew, for which I take proper shame to
myself, is the same person that wanted to make Eugenia give up
Clermont Lynmere, her own natural relation, and mine into the
bargain, for the sake of a stranger to us all; which I hold to be
rather uncommendable, considering we know nothing about him;
though there's no denying his being handsome enough to look at;
which, however, is no certainty of his making a good husband; so

I'll tell you a mode I've thought of, which I think to be a pretty
good one, for parting them out of hand.'

Dr. Orkborne, who had just taken out his tablets,[1] in order to
enter some hints relative to his great work, begged him to say no
more till he had finished his sentence. The baronet looked much
distressed, but consented: and when he had done, went on:

'Why, if you will hold Eugenia, I'll go up to the rest, and send
them on to the cottage; and when they are gone, I shall get rid of
this young chap, by telling him Eugenia and I want to be alone.'

Dr. Orkborne assented; and Sir Hugh, advancing to the group,
made his proposition, adding: 'Eugenia and I will overtake you as
soon as the garden-chair comes, which, I dare say, won't be long,
Robert being so behind-hand already.' Then, turning to Bellamy,
'I am sorry, sir,' he said, 'I can't possibly ask you to stay with us,
because of something my little niece and I have got to talk about,
which we had rather nobody should hear, being an affair of our
own: but I thank you for your civility, sir, in picking up my stick
and my pocket handkerchief, and I wish you a very good morning
and a pleasant walk, which I hope you won't take ill.'

Bellamy bowed, and, saying he by no means intended to
intrude himself into the company, slowly drew back.

Edgar then pointed out a path through the fields that would
considerably abridge the walk, if the ladies could manage to cross
over a dirty lane on the other side of the church-yard.

The baronet, who was in high spirits at the success of his
scheme, declared that if there was a short cut, they should not part
company, for he could walk it himself. Edgar assured him it could
not be more than half a mile, and offered him the use of his arm.

'No, no, my good young friend,' answered he, smiling significantly; 'take care of Indiana! I have got a good stick, which I hold
to be worth any arm in Christendom, except for not being alive;
so take care of Indiana, I say.'

Edgar bowed, but with a silence and gravity not unmixt with
surprise; and Sir Hugh, a little struck, hastily added, 'Nay, nay, I
mean no harm!'

'No, sir,' said Edgar, recovering, 'you can mean nothing but
good, when you give me so fair a charge.' And he placed himself
at the side of Indiana.

'Well then, now,' cried Sir Hugh, I'll marshal you all; and,
first, for my little Camilla, who shall come to my proper share; for

she's certainly the best companion of the whole; which I hope nobody will take for a slight, all of us not being the same, without any fault of our own. Dr. Orkborne shall keep to Eugenia, because, if there should be a want of conversation, they can go over some of their lessons. Lionel shall take the care of Mrs. Margland, it being always right for the young to help people a little stricken; and as for the odd one, Dr. Marchmont, why he may join little Camilla and me; for as she's none of the steadiest, and I am none of the strongest, it is but fair the one over should be between us.'

Everybody professed obedience but Lionel; who, with a loud laugh, called to Edgar to change partners.

'We are all under orders,' answered he, quietly, 'and I must not be the first to mutiny.'

Indiana smiled with triumph; but Miss Margland, firing with anger, declared she wanted no help, and would accept none.

Sir Hugh was now beginning an expostulation with his nephew; but Lionel preferred compliance to hearing it; yet, to obviate the ridicule which he was persuaded would follow such an acquiescence, he strided up to Miss Margland with hasty steps, and dropping on one knee, in the dust, seized and kissed her hand; but precipitately rising, and shaking himself, called out: 'My dear ma'am, have you never a little cloaths-brush in your pocket? I can't kneel again else!'

Miss Margland wrathfully turned from him; and the party proceeded to a small gate, at the back of the church, that opened to the lane mentioned by Edgar, over which, when the rest of the company had passed, into a beautiful meadow, Lionel offered his hand for conducting Miss Margland, who rejected it disdainfully.

'Then, you will be sure to fall,' said he.

'Not unless you do something to make me.'

'You will be sure to fall,' he repeated coolly.

Much alarmed, she protested she would not get over before him.

He absolutely refused to go first.

The whole party stopt; and Bellamy, who had hitherto stood still and back, now ventured to approach, and in the most courteous manner, to offer his services to Miss Margland. She looked victoriously around her; but as he had spoken in a low voice, only said: 'Sir?' to make him repeat his proposal more audibly. He complied, and the impertinencies of Lionel rendered his civility irresistible: 'I am glad,' she cried, 'there is still one gentleman left in the world!' And accepted his assistance, though her persecutor whispered that her spark was a dead man! and strutted significantly away.

Half frightened, half suspecting she was laughed at, she repeated softly to Sir Hugh the menace of his nephew, begging that, to prevent mischief, she might still retain Bellamy.

'Lord be good unto me!' cried he, 'what amazing fools the boys of now a-days are grown! with all their learning, and teaching, and classics at their tongue's end for nothing! However, not to set them together by the ears, till they grow a little wiser, which, I take it, won't be of one while, why you must e'en let this strange gentleman walk with you till t'other boy's further off. However, this one thing pray mind! (lowering his voice,) keep him all to yourself! if he does but so much as look at Eugenia, give him to understand it's a thing I sha'n't take very kind of him.'

Beckoning then to Dr. Orkborne, he uneasily said: 'As I am now obliged to have that young fellow along with us, for the sake of preventing an affray, about nobody knows what, which is the common reason of quarrels among those raw young fry, I beg you to keep a particular sharp look out, that he does not take the opportunity to run off with Eugenia.'

The spirit of the baronet had over-rated his strength; and he was forced to sit upon the lower step of a broad stile at the other end of the meadow: while Miss Margland, who leant her tall thin figure against a five-barred gate, willingly obviated his solicitude about Eugenia, by keeping Bellamy in close and unabating conference with herself.

A circumstance in the scenery before him now struck Dr. Orkborne with some resemblance to a verse in one of Virgil's Eclogues, which he thought might be happily applied to illustrate a passage in his own work; taking out, therefore, his tablets, he begged Eugenia not to move, and wrote his quotation; which, leading him on to some reflections upon the subject, soon drove his charge from his thoughts, and consigned him solely to his pencil.

Eugenia willingly kept her place at his side: offended by Bellamy, she would give him no chance of speaking with her, and the protection under which her uncle had placed her she deemed sacred.

Here they remained but a short time, when their ears received the shock of a prodigious roar from a bull in the field adjoining. Miss Margland screamed, and hid her face with her hands. Indiana, taught by her lessons to nourish every fear as becoming, shriekt still louder, and ran swiftly away, deaf to all that Edgar, who attended her, could urge. Eugenia, to whom Bellamy instantly hastened, seeing the beast furiously make towards the gate, almost unconsciously accepted his assistance, to accelerate her flight from its vicinity; while Dr. Orkborne, intent upon his annotations, calmly wrote on, sensible there was some disturbance, but determining to evade inquiring whence it arose, till he had secured what he meant to transmit to posterity from the treachery of his memory.

Camilla, the least frightened, because the most enured to such sounds, from the habits and the instruction of her rural life and education, adhered firmly to Sir Hugh, who began blessing himself with some alarm; but whom Dr. Marchmont re-assured, by saying the gate was secured, and too high for the bull to leap, even supposing it a vicious animal.

The first panic was still in its meridian, when Lionel, rushing past the beast, which he had secretly been tormenting, skipt over the gate, with every appearance of terror, and called out: 'Save yourselves all! Miss Margland in particular; for here's a mad bull!'

A second astounding bellow put a stop to any question, and wholly checked the immediate impulse of Miss Margland to ask why she was thus selected; she snatched her hands from her face, not doubting she should see her esquire soothingly standing by her side; but, though internally surprised and shocked to find herself deserted, she gathered strength to run from the gate with the nimbleness of youth, and, flying to the stile, regardless of Sir Hugh, and forgetting all her charges, scrambled over it, and ran on from the noise, without looking to the right or the left.

Sir Hugh, whom Lionel's information, and Miss Margland's pushing past him, had extremely terrified, was now also getting over the stile, with the assistance of Dr. Marchmont, ejaculating: 'Lord help us! what a poor race we are! No safety for us! if we only come out once in a dozen years, we must meet with a mad bull!'

He had, however, insisted that Camilla should jump over first, saying, 'There's no need of all of us being tost, my dear girl, because, of my slowness, which is no fault of mine, but of Robert's not being in the way; which must needs make the poor fellow unhappy enough, when he hears of it: which, no doubt, I shall let him do, according to his deserts.'

The other side of the stile brought them to the high road. Lionel, who had only wished to torment Miss Margland, felt his heart smite him, when he saw the fright of his uncle, and flew to acquaint him that he had made a mistake, for the bull was only angry, not mad.

The unsuspicious baronet thanked him for his good news, and sat upon a bank till the party could be collected.

This, however, was not soon to be done; the dispersion from the meadow having been made in every possible direction.

CHAPTER XI

Two Lovers

INDIANA, intent but upon running on, had nearly reached the church-yard, without hearkening to one word of the expostulating Mandlebert; when, leaning over a tombstone, on which she had herself leant while waiting for the carriage, she perceived the young Oxonian. An instinctive spirit of coquetry made her now increase her pace; he heard the rustling of female approach, and looked up: her beauty, heightened by her flight, which animated her complexion, while it displayed her fine form, seemed more than ever celestial to the enamoured student; who darted forward from an impulse of irresistible surprise. 'O Heaven!' she cried, panting and stopping as he met her; 'I shall die! I shall die!—I am pursued by a mad bull!'

Edgar would have explained, that all was safe; but Melmond neither heard nor saw him.—'O, give me, then,' he cried, emphatically; 'give me the ecstasy to protect—to save you!'

His out-spread arms shewed his intention to bear her away; but Edgar, placing himself between them, said: 'Pardon me, sir! this lady is under my care!'

'O don't fight about me! don't quarrel!' cried Indiana, with an apprehension half simple, half affected.

'No, Madam!' answered Melmond, respectfully retreating; 'I know too—too well! my little claim in such a dispute!—Permit me, however, to assist you, Mr. Mandlebert, in your search of refuge; and deign, madam, to endure me in your sight, till this alarm passes away.'

Indiana, by no means insensible to this language, looked with some elation at Edgar, to see how he bore it.

Edgar was not surprised; he had already observed the potent impression made by the beauty of Indiana upon the Oxonian; and was struck, in defiance of its romance and suddenness, with its air of sincerity; he only, therefore, gently answered, that there was not the least cause of fear.

'O, how can you say so?' said Indiana; 'how can you take so little interest in me?'

'At least, at least,' cried Melmond, trembling with eagerness, 'condescend to accept a double guard!—Refuse not, Mr. Mandlebert, to suffer any attendance!'

Mandlebert, a little embarrassed, answered: 'I have no authority to decide for Miss Lynmere: but, certainly, I see no occasion for my assistance.'

Melmond fervently clasped his hands, and exclaimed: 'Do not, do not, madam, command me to leave you till all danger is over!'

The little heart of Indiana beat high with triumph; she thought Mandlebert jealous: Miss Margland had often told her there was no surer way to quicken him: and, even independently of this idea, the spirit, the ardour, the admiration of the Oxonian, had a power upon her mind that needed no auxiliary for delighting it.

She curtsied her consent; but declared she would never go back the same way. They proceeded, therefore, by a little round to the high road, which led to the field in which the party had been dispersed.

Indiana was full of starts, little shrieks, and palpitations; every one of which rendered her, in the eyes of the Oxonian, more and more captivating; and, while Edgar walked gravely on, reflecting, with some uneasiness, upon being thus drawn in to suffer the attendance of a youth so nearly a stranger, upon a young lady actually under his protection; Melmond was continually ejaculating in return to her perpetual apprehensions, 'What lovely timidity!—What bewitching softness!—What feminine, what beautiful delicacy!—How sweet in terror!—How soul-piercing in alarm!'

These exclamations were nearly enchanting to Indiana, whose only fear was, lest they should not be heard by Edgar; and, whenever they ceased, whenever a pause and respectful silence took their place, new starts, fresh palpitations, and designed false steps, again called them forth; while the smile with which she repaid their enthusiastic speaker, was fuel to his flame, but poison to his peace.

They had not proceeded far, when they were met by Miss Margland, who, in equal trepidation from anger and from fear, was still making the best of her way from the bellowing of the bull. Edgar inquired for Sir Hugh, and the rest of the party; but she could speak only of Lionel; his insolence and his ill usage; protesting nothing but her regard for Indiana, could induce her to live a moment longer under his uncle's roof.

'But where,' again cried Edgar, 'where is Sir Hugh? and where are the ladies?'

'Tossed by the bull,' answered she, pettishly, 'for aught I know; I did not choose to stay and be tossed myself; and a person like Mr. Lionel can soon make such a beast point at one, if he takes it into his humour.'

Edgar then begged they might hasten to their company; but Miss Margland positively refused to go back: and Indiana, always ready to second any alarm, declared, she should quite sink with fright, if they went within a hundred yards of that horrid field. Edgar still pleaded that the baronet would expect them; but Melmond, in softer tones, spoke of fears, sensibility, and dangers; and Edgar soon found he was talking to the winds.

All now that remained to prevent further separations was, that Edgar should run on to the party, and acquaint them that Miss Margland and Indiana would wait for them upon the high road.

Melmond, meanwhile, felt in paradise; even the presence of Miss Margland could not restrain his rapture, upon a casualty that gave him such a charge, though it forced him to forbear making the direct and open declaration of his passion, with which his heart was burning, and his tongue quivering. He attended them both with the most fervent respect, evidently very gratifying to the object of his adoration, though not noticed by Miss Margland, who was wholly absorbed by her own provocations.

Edgar soon reached the bank by the road's side, upon which the baronet, Dr. Marchmont, Lionel, and Camilla were seated. 'Lord help us!' exclaimed Sir Hugh, aghast at his approach, 'if here is not young Mr. Edgar without Indiana! This is a thing I could never have expected from you, young Mr. Edgar! that you should leave her, I don't know where, and come without her!'

Edgar assured him she was safe, and under the care of Miss Margland, but that neither of them could be prevailed with to come farther: he had, therefore, advanced to inquire after the rest of the party, and to arrange where they should all assemble.

'You have done very right, then, my dear Mr. Edgar, as you always do, as far as I can make out, when I come to the bottom. And now I am quite easy about Indiana. But as to Eugenia, what Dr. Orkborne has done with her is more than I can devise; unless, indeed, they are got to studying some of their Greek verbs, and so forgot us all, which is likely enough; only I had rather they had taken another time, not much caring to stay here longer than I can help.'

Edgar said, he would make a circuit in search of them; but, first, addressing Camilla, 'You alone,' he cried, with an approving smile, 'have remained thus quiet, while all else have been scampering apart, making *confusion worse confounded*.'[1]

'I have lived too completely in the country to be afraid of cattle,' she answered; 'and Dr. Marchmont assured me there was no danger.'

'You can listen, then, even when you are alarmed,' said he, expressively, 'to the voice of reason!'

Camilla raised her eyes, and looked at him, but dropt them again without making any answer: Can *you*, she thought, have been pleading it in vain? How I wonder at Indiana?

He then set out to seek Eugenia, recommending the same office to Lionel by another route; but Lionel no sooner gathered where Miss Margland might be met with, than his repentance was forgotten, and he quitted everything to encounter her.

Edgar spent near half an hour in his search, without the smallest success; he was then seriously uneasy, and returning to the party, when a countryman, to whom he was known, told him he had seen Miss Eugenia Tyrold, with a very handsome fine town gentleman, going into a farm house.

Edgar flew to the spot, and through a window, as he advanced, perceived Eugenia seated, and Bellamy kneeling before her.

Amazed and concerned, he abruptly made his way into the apartment. Bellamy rose in the utmost confusion, and Eugenia, starting and colouring, caught Edgar by the arm, but could not speak.

He told her that her uncle and the whole company were waiting for her in great anxiety.

'And where, where,' cried she, 'are they? I have been in agonies about them all! and I could not prevail—I could not—this gentleman said the risk was so great—he would not suffer me—but he has sent for a chaise, though I told him I had a thousand times rather hazard my life amongst them, and with them, than save it alone!'

'They are all perfectly safe, nor has there ever been any danger.'

'I was told—I was assured—' said Bellamy, 'that a mad bull was running wild about the country; and I thought it, therefore, advisable to send for a chaise from the nearest inn, that I might return this young lady to her friends.'

Edgar made no answer, but offered his arm to conduct Eugenia to her uncle. She accepted it, and Bellamy attended on her other side.

Edgar was silent the whole way. The attitude in which he had surprised Bellamy, by assuring him of the nature of his pretensions, had awakened doubts the most alarming of the destination in view for the chaise which he had ordered; and he believed that Eugenia was either to have been beguiled, or betrayed, into a journey the most remote from the home to which she belonged.

Eugenia increased his suspicions by the mere confusion which deterred her from removing them. Bellamy had assured her she was in the most eminent personal danger, and had hurried her from field to field, with an idea that the dreaded animal was in full pursuit. When carried, however, into the farm house, she lost all apprehension for herself in fears for her friends, and insisted upon sharing their fate. Bellamy, who immediately ordered a chaise, then cast himself at her feet, to entreat she would not throw away her life by so rash a measure.

Exhausted, from her lameness, she was forced to sit still, and such was their situation at the entrance of Edgar. She wished extremely to explain what had been the object of the solicitation

of Bellamy, and to clear him, as well as herself, from any further
surmises; but she was ashamed to begin the subject. Edgar had
seen a man at her feet, and she thought, herself, it was a cruel
injury to Clermont, though she knew not how to refuse it forgiveness, since it was merely to supplicate she would save her own
life.

Bellamy, therefore, was the only one who spoke; and his un-
answered observations contributed but little to enliven the
walk.

When they came within sight of the party, the baronet was
again seized with the extremest dismay. 'Why now, what's this?'
cried he; 'here's nothing but blunders. Pray, Sir, who gave you
authority to take my niece from her own tutor? for so I may call
him, though more properly speaking, he came amongst us to be
mine; which, however, is no affair but of our own.'

'Sir,' answered Bellamy, advancing and bowing; 'I hope I have
had the happiness of rather doing service than mischief; I saw
the young lady upon the point of destruction, and I hastened her
to a place of security, from whence I had ordered a post-chaise, to
convey her safe to your house.'

'Yes, my dear uncle,' said Eugenia, recovering from her
embarrassment; 'I have occasioned this gentleman infinite
trouble; and though Mr. Mandlebert assures us there was no real
danger, he thought there was, and therefore I must always hold
myself to be greatly obliged to him.'

'Well, if that's the case, I must be obliged to him too; which, to
tell you the truth, is not a thing I am remarkably fond of having
happened. But where's Dr. Orkborne? I hope he's come to no
harm, by his not shewing himself?'

'At the moment of terror,' said Eugenia, 'I accepted the first
offer of assistance, concluding we were all hurrying away at the
same time; but I saw Dr. Orkborne no more afterwards.'

'I can't say that was over and above kind of him, nor careful
neither,' cried Sir Hugh, 'considering some particular reasons;
however, where is he now?'

Nobody could say; no one had seen or observed him.

'Why then, ten to one, poor gentleman!' exclaimed the baronet,
'but he's the very person himself who's tossed, while we are all of
us running away for nothing!'

A suspicion now occurred to Dr. Marchmont, which led him to

return over the stile into the field where the confusion had begun; and there, on the exact spot where he had first taken out his tablets, calmly stood Dr. Orkborne; looking now upon his writing, now up to the sky, but seeing nothing any where, from intense absorption of thought upon the illustration he was framing.

Awakened from his reverie by the Doctor, his first recollection was of Eugenia; he had not doubted her remaining quietly by his side, and the moment he looked round and missed her, he felt considerable compunction. The good Doctor, however, assured him all were safe, and conducted him to the group.

'So here you are,' said the baronet, 'and no more tossed than myself, for which I am sincerely thankful, though I can't say I think you have taken much care of my niece, nobody knowing what might have become of her, if it had not been for that strange gentleman, that I never saw before.'

He then formally placed Eugenia under the care of Dr. Marchmont.

Dr. Orkborne, piqued by this transfer, sullenly followed, and now gave to her, pertinaciously, his undivided attention. Drawn by a total revulsion of ideas from the chain of thinking that had led him to composition, he relinquished his annotations in resentment of this dismission, when he might have pursued them uninterruptedly without neglect of other avocations.

CHAPTER XII

Two Doctors

A COUNCIL was now held upon what course must next be taken. Both Sir Hugh and Eugenia were too much fatigued to walk any further; yet it was concluded that the garden chair, by some mistake, was gone straight to the cottage. Edgar, therefore, proposed running thither to bring it round for them, while Dr. Orkborne should go forward for Miss Margland and Indiana, and conduct them by the high road to the same place; where the whole party might at length re-assemble. Sir Hugh approved the plan, and he set off instantly.

But not so Dr. Orkborne; he thought himself disgraced by being sent from one post to another; and though Eugenia was nothing to him, in competition with his tablets and his work, his own instructions had so raised her in his mind, that he thought her the only female worthy a moment of his time. Indiana he looked upon with ineffable contempt; the incapacity she had shewn during the short time she was under his pupillage, had convinced him of the futility of her whole sex, from which he held Eugenia to be a partial exception; and Miss Margland, who never spoke to him but in a voice of haughty superiority, and whom he never answered, but with an air of solemn superciliousness, was his rooted aversion. He could not brook being employed in the service of either; he stood, therefore, motionless, till Sir Hugh repeated the proposition.

Not caring to disoblige him, he then, without speaking, slowly and unwillingly moved forwards.

'I see,' said the baronet, softened rather than offended, 'he does not much like to leave his little scholar, which is but natural; though I took it rather unkind his letting the poor thing run against the very horns of the bull, as one may say, if it had not been for a mere accidental passenger. However, one must always make allowance for a man that takes much to his studies, those things generally turning the head pretty much into a narrow compass.'

He then called after him, and said if the walk would tire him, he would wait till they came of themselves, which no doubt they would soon do, as Lionel was gone for them.

Dr. Orkborne gladly stopt; but Dr. Marchmont, seeing little likelihood of a general meeting without some trouble, offered to take the commission upon himself, with a politeness that seemed to shew it to be a wish of his own.

Sir Hugh accepted his kindness with thanks; and Dr. Orkborne, though secretly disconcerted by such superior alacrity in so learned a man, was well content to reinstate himself by the side of his pupil.

Sir Hugh, who saw the eyes of Bellamy constantly turned towards Eugenia, thought his presence highly dangerous, and with much tribulation, said: 'As I find, sir, we may all have to stay here, I don't know how long, I hope you won't be affronted, after my best thanks for your keeping my niece from the bull, if I don't make any particular point of begging the favour of you to stay much longer with us.'

Bellamy, extremely chagrined, cast an appealing look at Eugenia, and expressing his regret that his services were inadmissible, made his retreat with undisguised reluctance.

Eugenia, persuaded she owed him a serious obligation for his care, as well as for his partiality, felt the sincerest concern at his apparent distress, and contributed far more than she intended to its removal, by the gentle countenance with which she received his sorrowful glance.

Bellamy, hastily overtaking Dr. Marchmont, darted on before him in search of Miss Margland and Indiana, who, far from advancing, were pacing their way back to the church-yard. Lionel had joined them, and the incensed Miss Margland had encouraged the glad attendance of the Oxonian, as a protection to herself.

The sight of Bellamy by no means tended to disperse the storm: She resented his deserting her while she was in danger, and desired to see no more of him. But when he had respectfully suffered her wrath to vent itself, he made apologies, with an obsequiousness so rare to her, and a deference so strikingly contrasted with the daring ridicule of Lionel, that she did not long oppose the potent charm of adulation—a charm which, however it may be sweetened by novelty, seldom loses its effect by any familiarity.

During these contests, Indiana was left wholly to young Melmond, and the temptation was too strong for his impassioned feelings to withstand: 'O fairest,' he cried, 'fairest and most beautiful of all created beings! Can I resist—no! this one, one effusion—the first and the last! The sensibility of your mind will plead for me—I read it in those heavenly eyes—they emit mercy in their beauty! they are as radiant with goodness as with loveliness! alas! I trespass—I blush and dare not hope your forgiveness.'

He stopt, terrified at his own presumption; but the looks of Indiana were never more beautiful, and never less formidable. A milder doom, therefore, seemed suddenly to burst upon his view. Elated and enraptured, he vehemently exclaimed: 'Oh, were my lot not irrevocably miserable! were the smallest ray of light to beam upon my despondence!'—

Indiana still spoke not a word, but she withdrew not her smiles; and the enraptured student, lifted into the highest bliss by the permission even of a doubt, walked on, transported, by her side, too happy in suspense to wish an explanation.

In this manner they proceeded, till they were joined by Dr. Marchmont. The task he had attempted was beyond his power of performance; Miss Margland was inexorable; she declared nothing should induce her to go a step towards the field inhabited by the bull, and every assurance of safety the Doctor could urge was ineffectual.

He next assailed Indiana; but her first terror, soothed by the compassion and admiration of Melmond, was now revived, and she protested, almost with tears, that to go within a hundred yards of that dreadful meadow would make her undoubtedly faint away. The tender commiseration of Melmond confirmed her apprehensions, and she soon looked upon Dr. Marchmont as a barbarian for making the proposal.

The Doctor then commended them to the care of Lionel, and returned with this repulse to Sir Hugh.

The baronet, incapable of being angry with any one he conceived to be frightened, said they should be pressed no more, for he would give up going to the cottage, and put his best foot forward to walk on to them himself; adding he was so overjoyed to have got rid of that young spark, that he had no fear but that he, and poor Eugenia, too, should both do as well as they could.

They proceeded very slowly, the baronet leaning upon Dr. Marchmont, and Eugenia upon Dr. Orkborne, who watchful, with no small alarm, of the behaviour of the only man he had yet seen with any internal respect, since he left the university, sacrificed completely his notes and his tablets to emulate his attentions.

When they approached the church-yard, in which Miss Margland and her party had halted, Sir Hugh perceived Bellamy. He stopt short, calling out, with extreme chagrin, 'Lord help us! what a thing it is to rejoice! which one never knows the right season to do, on the score of meeting with disappointments!'

Then, after a little meditation, 'There is but one thing,' he cried, 'to be done, which is to guard from the first against any more mischief, having already had enough of it for one morning, not to say more than I could have wished by half: So do you, good Dr. Marchmont, take Eugenia under your own care, and I'll make shift with Dr. Orkborne for myself; for, in the case he should take again to writing or thinking, it will be nothing to me to keep still

till he has done; provided it should happen at a place where I can sit down.'

Dr. Orkborne had never felt so deeply hurt; the same commission transferred to Edgar, or to Lionel, would have failed to affect him; he considered them as of an age fitted for such frivolous employment, which he thought as much below his dignity, as the young men themselves were beneath his competition; but the comfort of contempt, a species of consolation ever ready to offer itself to the impulsive pride of man, was here an alleviation he could not call to his aid; the character of Dr. Marchmont stood as high in erudition as his own; and, though his acquaintance with him was merely personal, the fame of his learning, the only attribute to which fame, in his conception, belonged, had reached him from authority too unquestionable for doubt. The urbanity, therefore, of his manners, his general diffusion of discourse, and his universal complaisance, filled him with astonishment, and raised an emotion of envy which no other person would have been deemed worthy of exciting.

But though his long and fixed residence at Cleves had now removed the timid circumspection with which he first sought to ensure his establishment, he yet would not venture any positive refusal to the baronet; he resigned, therefore, his young charge to his new and formidable opponent, and even exerted himself to mark some alacrity in assisting Sir Hugh. But his whole real attention was upon Dr. Marchmont, whom his eye followed in every motion, to discover, if possible, by what art unknown he had acquired such a command over his thoughts and understanding, as to bear patiently, nay pleasantly, with the idle and unequal companions of general society.

Dr. Marchmont, who was rector of Cleves, had been introduced to Sir Hugh upon the baronet's settling in the large mansion-house of that village; but he had not visited at the house, nor had his company been solicited. Sir Hugh, who could never separate understanding from learning, nor want of education from folly, concluded that such a man as Dr. Marchmont must necessarily despise him; and though the extreme sweetness of his temper made him draw the conclusion without resentment, it so effectually prevented all wish of any intercourse, that they had never conversed together till this morning; and his surprise, now, at such civilities and good humour in so great a scholar, differed only from that of Dr. Orkborne, in being accompanied with admiration instead of envy.

Eugenia thus disposed of, they were proceeding, when Sir Hugh next observed the young Oxonian: He was speaking with Indiana, to whom his passionate devotion was glaring from his looks, air, and whole manner.

'Lord held me!' exclaimed he; 'if there is not another of those new chaps, that nobody knows anything about, talking to Indiana! and, for aught I can tell to the contrary, making love to her! I think I never took such a bad walk as this before, since the hour I was born, in point of unluckiness. Robert will have enough to answer for, which he must expect to hear; and indeed I am not much obliged to Mrs. Margland herself, and so I must needs tell her, though it is not what I much like to do.'

He then made a sign to Miss Margland to approach him: 'Mrs. Margland,' he cried, 'I should not have taken the liberty to beckon you in this manner, but that I think it right to ask you what those two young gentlemen, that I never saw before, do in the church-yard; which is a thing I think rather odd.'

'As to that gentleman, sir,' she answered, bridling, 'who was standing by me, he is the only person I have found to protect me from Mr. Lionel, whose behaviour, sir, I must freely tell you—'

'Why certainly, Mrs. Margland, I can't deny but he's rather a little over and above giddy; but I am sure your understanding won't mind it, in consideration of his being young enough to be your son, in the case of your having been married time enough.'

He then desired Indiana would come to him.

The rapture of the Oxonian was converted into torture by this summons; and the suspence which the moment before he had gilded with the gay colours of hope, he felt would be no longer supportable when deprived of the sight of his divinity. Scarce could he refrain from casting himself publicly at her feet, and pouring forth the wishes of his heart. But when again the call was repeated, and he saw her look another way, as if desirous not to attend to it, the impulse of quick rising joy dispersed his small remains of forbearance, and precipitately clasping his hands, 'O go not!' he passionately exclaimed; 'leave me not in this abyss of suffering! Fairest and most beautiful! tell me at least, if my death is inevitable! if no time—no constancy—no adoration—may ever dare hope to penetrate that gentlest of bosoms!'

Indiana herself was now, for the first time, sensible of a little emotion; the animation of this address delighted her; it was new, and its effect was highly pleasing. How cold, she thought, is Edgar! She made not any answer, but permitted her eyes to meet his with the most languishing softness.

Melmond trembled through his whole frame; despair flew him, and expectation wore her brightest plumage: 'O pronounce but one word,' he cried, 'one single word!—are, are you—O say not yes!—irrevocably engaged?—lost to all hope—all possibility for ever?'

Indiana again licensed her fine eyes with their most melting powers, and all self-control was finally over with her impassioned lover; who, mingling prayers for her favour, with adoration of her beauty, heeded not who heard him, and forgot every presence but her own.

Miss Margland, who, engrossed by personal resentment and debates, had not remarked the rising courage and energy of Melmond, had just turned to Indiana, upon the second call of Sir Hugh, and became now utterly confounded by the sight of her willing attention: 'Miss Lynmere,' cried she, angrily, 'what are you thinking of? Suppose Mr. Mandlebert should come, what might be the consequence?'

'Mandlebert?' repeated Melmond, while the blood forsook his cheeks; 'is it then even so?—is all over?—all decided? is my destiny black and ireful for ever?'

Indiana still more and more struck with him, looked down, internally uttering: Ah! were this charming youth but master of Beech Park!

At this instant, the rapid approach of a carriage caught their ears; and eager to avoid making a decisive reply, she ran to the church-yard gate to look at it, exclaiming: 'Dear! what an elegant chariot.' When it came up to the party, it stopt, and, opening the door himself, Edgar jumped hastily out of it.

The Oxonian stood aghast: but Indiana, springing forward, and losing in curiosity every other sensation, cried: 'Dear! Mr. Mandlebert, whose beautiful new carriage is that?'

'Yours,' answered he, gallantly, 'if you will honour it with any commands.'

She then observed his crest and cypher were on the panels; and another entire new set of ideas took instant possession of her mind. She received literally an answer which he had made in gay courtesy, and held out her hand to be helped into the chariot.

Edgar, though surprised and even startled at this unexpected appropriation of his civility, could not recede; but the moment he had seated her, hastily turned round, to inquire who else was most fatigued.

The Oxonian now felt lost! suddenly, abruptly, but irretrievably lost! The cypher he saw—the question 'whose carriage is that?' he heard—the answer '*yours*' made him gasp for breath, and the instantaneous acceptance stung him to the soul. Wholly in desperation, he rushed to the opposite window of the chariot, and calling out, 'enough, cruel!—cruel!—enough—I will see you no more!' hurried out of sight.

Indiana, who, for the first time, thought herself mistress of a new and elegant equipage, was so busily employed in examining the trappings and the lining, that she bore his departure without a sigh; though but an instant before it might have cost her something near one.

Eugenia had been touched more deeply. She was ignorant of what had passed, but she had seen the agitation of Melmond, and the moment he disappeared, she ejaculated secretly: 'Ah! had he conceived the prepossession of Bellamy! where had been my steadiness? where, O Clermont! thy security!—'

The scrupulous delicacy of her mind was shocked at this suggestion, and she rejoiced she had not been put to such a trial.

Edgar now explained, that when he arrived at the cottage, he found, as he had foreseen, the garden chair waiting there, by mistake, and Robert in much distress, having just discovered that an accident had happened to one of the wheels. He had run on, therefore, himself, to Beech Park, for his own new chariot, which was lately arrived from town, making Robert follow with Sir Hugh's horses, as his own were out at grass.

It was dinner-time, and Sir Hugh, equally vexed and fatigued, resolved to return straight home. He accepted, therefore, a place in the chariot, bid Eugenia follow him, and Robert make haste; solemnly adding to the latter: 'I had fully intended making you the proper lecture upon your not coming in time; but as it has turned out not to be your fault, on account of an accident, I shall say no more; except to give you a hint not to do such a thing again, because we have all been upon the point of being tossed by a mad bull; which would certainly have happened, but for the lucky chance of its turning out a false alarm.'

The remainder of the party proceeded without further adventure. Edgar attended Camilla; Miss Margland adhered to Bellamy: Lionel, who durst not venture at any new frolic, but with whom time lingered when none was passing, retreated; Dr. Marchmont, who was near his home, soon also made his bow; and Dr. Orkborne, who was glad to be alone, ruminated with wonder upon what appeared to him a phenomenon, a man of learning who could deign to please and seem pleased where books were not the subject of discourse, and where scholastic attainments were not required to elucidate a single sentence.

CHAPTER XIII

Two Ways of looking at the same Thing

WHEN the party arrived at Cleves, Camilla, who had observed that Edgar seemed much disappointed by the breaking up of the cottage expedition, proposed that it should take place in the evening; and her uncle, though too much fatigued to venture out again himself, consented, or rather insisted, that the excursion should be made without him.

Before they set out, Edgar desired to speak with Sir Hugh in private.

Sir Hugh concluded it was to make his proposals of marriage for Indiana; and had not patience to step into his own apartment, but told them all to retire, with a nod at Indiana, which prepared not only herself but Miss Margland, Camilla, and Eugenia to join in his expectation.

Indiana, though a good deal fluttered, flew to a window, to see if the new chariot was in sight; and then, turning to Miss Margland, asked, 'Pray, should I refuse him at first?'

Miss Margland spared not for proper instructions; and immediately began a negociation with the fair questioner, for continuing to live with her.

Eugenia was occupied in reflecting with pity upon the idleness of Indiana, which so ill had fitted her for becoming the companion of Mandlebert.

Camilla, unusually thoughtful, walked alone into the garden, and sought a path least in sight.

Sir Hugh, meanwhile, was most unpleasantly undeceived. Edgar, without naming Indiana, informed him of the situation in which he had surprised Bellamy, and of his suspicions with regard to the destination of the chaise, but for his own timely arrival at the farm-house; adding, that his gratitude to Mr. Tyrold, his respect for himself, and his affection for all the family, made him think it is duty to reveal these circumstances without delay.

The baronet shuddered with horror; and declared he would instantly send an express to bring Clermont home, that Eugenia might be married out of hand; and, in the mean time, that he would have every window in the house barred, and keep her locked up in her room.

Edgar dissuaded him from so violent a measure; but advised him to speak with his niece upon the danger she had probably escaped, and of which she seemed wholly unconscious; to prevail with her not to go out again this evening, and to send for Mr. Tyrold, and acquaint him with the affair.

Sir Hugh thanked him for his counsel, and implicitly acted by his opinion.

He then ordered the coach for Miss Margland, Indiana, and Camilla.

Dr. Orkborne, finding neither Sir Hugh nor Eugenia of the party, declined joining it. Lionel was returned to Etherington; and Edgar rode on before, to invite Dr. Marchmont, with the consent of the Baronet, to take the fourth place in the carriage.

Arrived at the rectory, he went straight, by prescriptive privilege, into the study of Dr. Marchmont, whom he found immersed in books and papers, which, immediately, at the request of Edgar, he put aside; not without regret to quit them, though wholly without reluctance to oblige.

Edgar had ridden so hard, that they had some time to wait for the coach. But he did not appear anxious for its arrival; though he wore a look that was far from implying him to be free from anxiety.

He was silent,—he hemmed,—he was silent again,—and again he hemmed,—and then, gently laying his hand upon the shoulder of the Doctor, while his eyes, full of meaning, were fixed upon his face; 'Doctor,' he cried, 'you would hardly have known these young ladies?—they are all grown from children into women since you saw them last.'

'Yes,' answered the Doctor, 'and very charming women. Indiana has a beauty so exquisite, it is scarce possible to look away from it a moment: Eugenia joins so much innocence with information, that the mind must itself be deformed that could dwell upon her personal defects, after conversing with her: Camilla'—

He paused, and Edgar hastily turned another way, not to look at him, nor be looked at, while he proceeded:

'Camilla,' he presently continued, 'seems the most inartificially sweet, the most unobtrusively gay, and the most attractively lovely of almost any young creature I ever beheld.'

With a heart all expanded, and a face full of sensibility, Edgar now turned to him, and seizing, involuntarily, his hand, which he eagerly shook, 'You think her, then,'—he cried,—but suddenly stopt, dropt his hand, coughed two or three times; and, taking out his pocket handkerchief, seemed tormented with a violent cold.

Dr. Marchmont affectionately embraced him. 'My dear young young friend,' he cried, 'I see the situation of your mind—and think every possible happiness promises to be yours; yet, if you have taken no positive step, suffer me to speak with you before you proceed.'

'Far from having taken any positive step, I have not yet even formed any resolution.'

Here the carriage stopt for the Doctor, who repeated, 'Yes! I think every possible happiness promises to be yours!' before he went on to the ladies. Edgar, in a trepidation too great to be seen by them, kept behind till they drove off, though he then galloped so fast, that he arrived at the cottage before them: the words, 'I think every possible happiness promises to be yours,' vibrating the whole time in his ears.

When the coach arrived, Edgar handed out Miss Margland and Indiana; leaving Camilla to the Doctor; willing to let him see more of her, and by no means displeased to avoid his eyes at that moment himself.

Indiana was in the most sprightly spirits she had ever experienced; she concluded herself on the verge of becoming mistress of a fine place and a large fortune; she had received adulation all the morning that had raised her beauty higher than ever in her own estimation; and she secretly revolved, with delight, various articles of ornament and of luxury, which she had long wished to possess, and which now, for her wedding clothes, she should have riches sufficient to purchase.

Miss Margland, too, was all smoothness, complacency, and courtesy.

Camilla, alone, was grave; Camilla, who, by nature, was gay.

'Dear! is this the cottage we have been coming to all this time?' cried Indiana, upon entering; 'Lord! I thought it would have been something quite pretty.'

'And what sort of prettiness,' said Edgar, 'did you expect from a cottage?'

'Dear, I don't know—but I thought we were come on purpose to see something extraordinary?'

Camilla, who followed, made an exclamation far different; an exclamation of pleasure, surprise, and vivacity, that restored for an instant, all her native gaiety: for no sooner had she crossed the threshold, than she recognised, in a woman who was curtsying low to receive her, and whom Indiana had passed without observing, the wife of the poor prisoner for whom she had interceded with Mandlebert.

'How I rejoice to see you!' cried she, 'and to see you here! and how much better you look! and how comfortable you seem! I hope you are now all well?'

'Ah, madam,' answered the woman; 'we owe everything to that good young gentleman! he has put us in this nice new cottage, and employs us in his service. Blessings on his head! I am sure he will be paid for it!'

Edgar, somewhat agitated, occupied himself with jumping the little boy; Camilla looked round with rapture; Indiana seemed wonder-struck, without knowing why; Dr. Marchmont narrowly watched them all; and Miss Margland, expecting a new collection would be next proposed for setting them up, nimbly re-crossed the threshold, to examine the prospect without.

The husband, now in decent garb, and much recovered, though still weak and emaciated, advanced to Camilla, to make his humble acknowledgments, that she had recommended them to their kind benefactor.

'No!' cried Camilla; 'you owe me nothing! your own distress recommended you;—your own distress—and Mr. Mandlebert's generosity.'

Then, going up to Edgar, 'It is your happy fate,' she said, in an accent of admiration, 'to act all that my father so often plans and wishes, but which his income will not allow him to execute.'

'You see,' answered he, gratefully, 'how little suffices for content! I have scarce done anything—yet how relieved, how satisfied are these poor people! This hut was fortunately vacant'—

'O, madam!' interrupted the poor woman, 'if you knew but how that good gentleman has done it all! how kindly he has used us, and made everybody else use us! and let nobody taunt us with our bad faults!—and what good he has done to my poor sick husband! and how he has clothed my poor little half naked children! and, what is more than all, saved us from the shame of an ill life.'—

Camilla felt the tears start into her eyes;—she hastily snatched the little babe into her arms; and, while her kisses hid her face, Happy, and thrice happy Indiana! with a soft sigh, was the silent ejaculation of her heart.

She seated herself on a stool, and, without speaking or hearing any thing more, devoted herself to the baby.

Indiana, meanwhile, whose confidence in her own situation gave her courage to utter whatever first occurred to her, having made a general survey of the place and people, with an air of disappointment, now amused herself with an inspection more minute, taking up and casting down everything that was portable, without any regard either to deranging its neatness, or endangering its safety:—exclaiming, as she made her round of investigation, 'Dear! Crockery ware! how ugly!—Lord, what little mean chairs!—Is that your best gown, good woman?—Dear, what an ugly pattern!—Well, I would not wear such a thing to save my life!—Have you got nothing better than this for a floor-cloth?— Only look at those curtains! Did you ever see such frights?— Lord! do you eat off these platters? I am sure I could sooner die! I should not mind starving half as much!'

Miss Margland, hoping the collection was now either made or relinquished, ventured to re-enter, and inquire if they never meant to return home? Camilla unwillingly gave up the baby; but would not depart without looking over the cottage, where everything she saw excited a sensation of pleasure. 'How neat is this! How tidy that!' were her continual exclamations; 'How bright you have rubbed your saucepans! How clean every thing is all round! How soon you will all get well in this healthy and comfortable little dwelling!'

Edgar, in a low voice, then told Dr. Marchmont the history of his new cottagers, saying: 'You will not, I hope, disapprove what I have done? Their natures seemed so much disposed to good, I could not bear to let their wants turn them again to evil.'

'You have certainly done right,' answered the Doctor; 'to give money without inquiry, or further aid, to those who have adopted bad practices, is, to them, but temptation, and to society an injury; but to give them both the counsel and the means to pursue a right course, is, to them, perhaps, salvation, and to the community, the greatest service.'[1]

Indiana and Miss Margland, quite wearied, both got into the carriage; Edgar, having deposited them, returned to Camilla, who kissed both the children, poured forth good wishes upon the father and mother; and, then, gave him her hand. Enchanted, he took it, exclaiming; 'Ah! who is like you! so lively—yet so feeling!'

Struck and penetrated, she made no answer: Alas! she thought, I fear he is not quite satisfied with Indiana!

Dr. Marchmont was set down at his own house; where, he begged to have a conference with Edgar the next morning.

The whole way home, the benevolence of Edgar occupied the mind of Camilla; and, not in the present instance, the less, that its object had been originally of her own pointing out.

CHAPTER XIV

Two Retreats

MR. and Mrs. Tyrold had obeyed the summons of Sir Hugh, whom they found in extreme tribulation; persuaded by his fears not only of the design of Bellamy, but of its inevitable success. His brother, however, who knew his alarms to be generally as unfounded as his hopes; and Mrs. Tyrold, who almost undisguisedly despised both; no sooner heard his account, than, declining to discuss it, they sent for Eugenia. She related the transaction with a confusion so innocent, that it was easy to discern shame alone had hitherto caused her silence; and with a simplicity so unaffected, that not a doubt could rest upon their minds, but that her heart was as disengaged as her intentions had been irreproachable. Yet they were not the less struck with the danger she had incurred; and, while her father blessed Mandlebert for her preservation, her mother was so sensible to his care for the family welfare and honour, that the anger she had conceived against him subsided, though the regret to which it had owed its birth increased.

Mr. Tyrold gave his daughter some slight cautions and general advice; but thought it wisest, since he found her tranquil and unsuspicious, not to raise apprehensions that might disturb her composure, nor awaken ideas of which the termination must be doubtful.

Her mother deemed the matter to be undeserving the least serious alarm. The man had appeared to her from the beginning to be a despicable adventurer; and her lofty contempt of all low arts made her conclude her well-principled Eugenia as superior to their snares as to their practice.

This conference completely quieted the fears of Sir Hugh; who relinquished his design of sending for Clermont, and imagined Edgar to have been too severe in his judgment of Bellamy, who had only knelt in pure compassion, to prevail with Eugenia to take care of her life.

The rector and his lady were already gone before the cottage group came home. Edgar was anxious to inquire of Sir Hugh what had passed. The three females, concluding he had still something to say relative to his proposals, by tacit agreement, retired to their own rooms.

They were not, however, as concurrent in their eagerness to re-assemble. Miss Margland and Indiana watched the moment when they might appease their burning curiosity by descending: but Eugenia wished to prolong her absence, that she might recover from the embarrassment she had just suffered; and Camilla determined not to appear again till the next morning.

For the first time in her life after the shortest separation, she forbore to seek Eugenia, [who] she supposed would have gathered all the particular of the approaching nuptials. She felt no desire to hear them. It was a period to which, hitherto, she had looked

forward as to a thing of course; but this day it had struck her that
Edgar and Indiana could not be happy together.—She had even
surmised, from his last speech, that he lamented, in secret, the
connexion he had formed.

The gentlest pity took possession of her breast; an increasing
admiration succeeded to her pity. She could not bear to witness
so unequal a scene, as the full satisfaction of Sir Hugh contrasted
with the seriousness, perhaps repentance, of Edgar. She pleaded
an head-ache, and went to bed.

The morning did not find her less averse to hear the confirmation of the suspected news. On the contrary, her repugnance to
have it ascertained became stronger. She did not ask herself why;
she did not consider the uselessness of flying for one hour what
she must encounter the next. The present moment was all she
could weigh; and, to procrastinate any evil, seemed, to her ardent
and active imagination, to conquer it. Again, therefore, she
planned a visit to Mrs. Arlbery; though she had given it up so
long, from the discouragement of Lionel, that she felt more of
shame than of pleasure in the idea of making so tardy an apology;
but she could think of no other place to which the whole party
would not accompany her; and to avoid them and their communications, for however short a space of time, was now her sole aim.

Before breakfast, she repaired to the apartment of her uncle;
her request was granted, as soon as heard; and she ordered the
chaise.

Indiana and Miss Margland, meanwhile, had learnt from the
baronet, that the proposals were not yet made. Miss Margland
softened the disappointment of Indiana, by suggesting that her
admirer was probably waiting the arrival of some elegant trinket,
that he destined to present her upon his declaration: but she was by
no means free from doubt and suspicion herself. She languished
to quit Cleves, and Sir Hugh had almost thought her account-
able for the slowness of Mandlebert's proceedings. To keep up
her own consequence, she had again repeated her assurances,
that all was in a prosperous train; though she had frequently, with
strong private uneasiness, observed the eyes of Edgar fixed upon
Camilla, with an attention far more pointed than she had ever
remarked in them when their direction was towards her fair pupil.

Camilla hurried over her breakfast in expectation of the chaise,
and in dread continual, lest her cousin should call her aside, to

acquaint her that all was arranged. Edgar perceived, with surprise, that she was going out alone; and, no sooner gathered whither, than, drawing her to one of the windows, he earnestly said: 'Is it by appointment you wait upon Mrs. Arlbery?'

'No.'

'Does she at all expect you this morning?'

'No.'

'Would it, then, be asking too much, if I should entreat you to postpone your visit for a short time?'

The whole design of Camilla was to absent herself immediately; yet she hated to say no. She looked disturbed, and was silent.

'Have you made any further acquaintance with her since the morning of the raffle?'

'No, none; but I wish excessively to know more of her.'

'She is certainly, very—agreeable,' said he, with some hesitation; 'but, whether she is all Mrs. Tyrold would approve'—

'I hope you know no harm of her?—If you do, pray keep it to yourself!—for it would quite afflict me to hear anything to her disadvantage.'

'I should be grieved, indeed, to be the messenger of affliction to you; but I hope there may be no occasion; I only beg a day or two's patience; and, in the meanwhile, I can give you this assurance; she is undoubtedly a woman of character. I saw she had charmed you, and I made some immediate inquiries. Her reputation is without taint.'

'A thousand, thousand thanks,' cried Camilla, gaily, 'for taking so much trouble; and ten thousand more for finding it needless!'

Edgar could not forbear laughing, but answered, he was not yet so certain it was needless; since exemption from actual blemish could only be a negative recommendation: he should very soon, he added, see a lady upon whose judgment he could rely, and who would frankly satisfy him with respect to some other particulars, which, he owned, he considered as essential to be known, before any intimacy should be formed.

Wishing to comply with his request, yet impatient to leave the house, Camilla stood suspended till the chaise was announced.

'I think,' cried she, with a look and tone of irresolution, 'my going this once can draw on no ill consequence?'

Edgar only dropt his eyes.

'You are not of that opinion?'

'I have a very particular engagement this morning,' he replied; 'but I will readily give it up, and ride off instantly to make my application to this lady, if it is possible you can defer only till tomorrow your visit. Will you suffer me to ask such a delay? It will greatly oblige me.'

'Why, then,—I will defer it till to-morrow,—or till to-morrow week!' cried she, wholly vanquished; 'I insist, therefore, that you do not postpone your business.'

She then desired the servant, who was taking away the breakfast equipage, to order the chaise to be put up.

Edgar, subdued in his turn, caught her hand: but, instantly, recollecting himself, hastily let it go; and, throwing up the window sash, abruptly exclaimed: 'I never saw such fine weather: —I hope it will not rain!'

He then rapidly wished them all good morning, and mounted his horse.

Miss Margland, who, sideling towards the window, on pretence of examining a print, had heard and seen all that had passed, was almost overpowered with rage, by the conviction she received that her apprehensions were not groundless. She feared losing all weight both with the baronet and with Indiana, if she made this acknowledgment, and retreated, confounded, to her own room, to consider what path to pursue at so dangerous a crisis; wearing a scowl upon her face, that was always an indication she would not be followed.

Camilla also went to her chamber, in a perturbation at once pleasing and painful. She was sorry to have missed her excursion, but she was happy to have obliged Edgar; she was delighted he could take such interest in her conduct and affairs, yet dreaded, more than ever, a private conversation with Indiana;—Indiana, who, every moment, appeared to her less and less calculated to bestow felicity upon Edgar Mandlebert.

She seated herself at a window, and soon, through the trees, perceived him galloping away. 'Too—too amiable Edgar!' she cried, earnestly looking after him, with her hands clasped, and tears starting into her eyes.

Frightened at her own tenderness, she rose, shut the window, and walked to another end of the apartment.

She took up a book; but she could not read: 'Too—too amiable Edgar!' again escaped her. She went to her piano-forte; she could not play: 'Too—too amiable Edgar!' broke forth in defiance of all struggle.

Alarmed and ashamed, even to herself, she resolved to dissipate her ideas by a long walk; and not to come out of the park, till the first dinner-bell summoned her to dress.

CHAPTER XV

Two Sides of a Question

THE intention of Edgar had been to ride to Mrs. Needham, the lady of whom he meant to ask the information to which he had alluded; but a charm too potent for resistance demanded his immediate liberation from the promise to Dr. Marchmont, which bound him to proceed no further till they had again conversed together.

He galloped, therefore, to the parsonage-house of Cleves, and entering the study of the Doctor, and taking him by the hand, with the most animated gesture; 'My dear and honoured friend,' he cried, 'I come to you now without hesitation, and free from every painful embarrassment of lurking irresolution! I come to you decided, and upon grounds which cannot offend you, though the decision anticipates your counsel. I come to you, in fine, my dear Doctor, my good and kind friend, to confess that yesterday you saw right, with regard to the situation of my mind, and that, today, I have only your felicitations to beg, upon my confirmed, my irrevocable choice!'

Dr. Marchmont embraced him: 'May you then,' he cried, 'be as happy, my dear young friend, as you deserve! I can wish you nothing higher.'

'Last night,' continued Edgar, 'I felt all doubt die away: captivating as I have ever thought her, so soft, so gentle, so touchingly sweet, as last night, I had never yet beheld her; you witnessed it, my dear Doctor? you saw her with the baby in her arms? how beautiful, how endearing a sight!'

The Doctor looked assentingly, but did not speak.

'Yet even last night was short of the feelings she excited this morning. My dear friend! she was upon the point of making an excursion from which she had promised herself peculiar pleasure, and to see a lady for whom she had conceived the warmest admiration—I begged her to postpone—perhaps relinquish entirely the visit—she had obtained leave from Sir Hugh—the carriage was at the door—would you, could you believe such sweetness with such vivacity? she complied with my request, and complied with a grace that has rivetted her—I own it—that has rivetted her to my soul!'

Doctor Marchmont smiled, but rather pensively than rejoicingly; and Edgar, receiving no answer, walked for some time about the room, silently enjoying his own thoughts.

Returning then to the Doctor, 'My dear friend,' he cried, 'I understood you wished to speak with me?'

'Yes—but I thought you disengaged.'

'So, except mentally, I am still.'

'Does she not yet know her conquest?'

'She does not even guess it.'

Dr. Marchmont now rising, with much energy said: 'Hear me then, my dear and most valued young friend; forbear to declare yourself, make no overtures to her relations, raise no expectations even in her own breast, and let not rumour surmise your passion to the world, till her heart is better known to you.'

Edgar, starting and amazed, with great emotion exclaimed: 'What do you mean, my good Doctor? do you suspect any prior engagement? any fatal prepossession?'—

'I suspect nothing. I do not know her. I mean not, therefore, the propensities alone, but the worth, also, of her heart; deception is easy, and I must not see you thrown away.'

'Let me, then, be her guarantee!' cried Edgar, with firmness; 'for I know her well! I have known her from her childhood, and cannot be deceived. I fear nothing—except my own powers of engaging her regard. I can trace to a certainty, even from my boyish remarks, her fair, open, artless, and disinterested character.'

He then gave a recital of the nobleness of her sentiments and conduct when only nine years old; contrasting the relation with the sullen and ungenerous behaviour of Indiana at the same age.

Dr. Marchmont listened to the account with attention and pleasure, but not with an air of that full conviction which Edgar expected. 'All this,' he said, 'is highly prophetic of good, and confirms me in the opinion I expressed last night, that every possible happiness promises to be yours.'

'Yet, still,' said Edgar, a little chagrined, 'there seems some drawback to your entire approbation?'

'To your choice I have none.'

'You perplex me, Doctor! I know not to what you object, what you would intimate, nor what propose?'

'All I have to suggest may be comprised in two points: First, That you will refuse confirmation even to your own intentions, till you have positively ascertained her actual possession of those virtues with which she appears to be endowed: and secondly, That if you find her gifted with them all, you will not solicit her acceptance till you are satisfied of her affection.'

'My dear Doctor,' cried Edgar, half laughing, 'from what an alarm of wild conjecture has your explanation relieved me! Hear me, however, in return, and I think I can satisfy you, that, even upon your own conditions, not an obstacle stands in the way of my speaking to Mr. Tyrold this very evening.

'With regard to your first article, her virtues, I have told you the dawning superiority of her most juvenile ideas of right; and though I have latterly lost sight of her, by travelling during our vacations, I know her to have always been under the superintendence of one of the first of women; and for these last three weeks, which I have spent under the same roof with her, I have observed her to be all that is amiable, sweet, natural, and generous. What then on this point remains? Nothing. I am irrefragably convinced of her worth.

'With respect to your second condition, I own you a little embarrass me; yet how may I inquire into the state of her affections, without acknowledging her mistress of mine?'

'Hold! hold!' interrupted the Doctor, 'you proceed too rapidly. The first article is all unsettled, while you are flying to the last.

'It is true, and I again repeat it, every promise is in your favour; but do not mistake promise for performance. This young lady appears to be all excellence; for an acquaintance, for a friend, I doubt not you have already seen enough to establish her in your good opinion; but since it is only within a few hours you have taken the resolution which is to empower her to colour the rest of your life, you must study her, from this moment, with new eyes, new ears, and new thoughts. Whatever she does, you must ask

yourself this question: "Should I like such behaviour in my
wife?" Whatever she says, you must make yourself the same
demand. Nothing must escape you; you must view as if you had
never seen her before; the interrogatory, *Were she mine?* must
be present at every look, every word, every motion; you must
forget her wholly as Camilla Tyrold, you must think of her only as
Camilla Mandlebert; even justice is insufficient during this period of probation, and instead of inquiring, "Is this right in her?"
you must simply ask, "Would it be pleasing to me?" '

'You are apprehensive, then, of some dissimilitude of character
prejudicial to our future happiness?'

'Not of character; you have been very peculiarly situated for
obviating all risk upon that first and most important particular.
I have no doubt of her general worthiness; but though esteem
hangs wholly upon character, happiness always links itself with
disposition.'

'You gratify me, Doctor, by naming disposition, for I can give
you the most unequivocal assurance of her sweetness, her
innocence, her benevolence, joined to a spirit of never-dying
vivacity—an animation of never-ceasing good humour!'

'I know you, my dear Mandlebert, to be, by nature, penetrating
and minute in your observations; which, in your general commerce with the world, will protect both your understanding and
your affections from the usual snares of youth: But here—to be
even scrupulous is not enough; to avoid all danger of repentance,
you must become positively distrustful.'

'Never, Doctor, never! I would sooner renounce every prospect
of felicity, than act a part so ungenerous, where I am conscious of
such desert! Upon this article, therefore, we have done; I am
already and fully convinced of her excellence. But, with respect to
your second difficulty, that I will not seek her acceptance, till
satisfied of her regard—there—indeed, you start an idea that comes
home to my soul in its very inmost recesses! O Doctor!—could
I hope—however distantly—durst I hope—the independent,
unsolicited, involuntary possession of that most ingenuous,
most inartificial of human hearts!—'

'And why not? why, while so liberally you do justice to another,
should you not learn to appreciate yourself?'

A look of elation, delight, and happiness conveyed to Dr.
Marchmont his pupil's grateful sense of this question.

'I do not fear making you vain,' he continued; 'I know your understanding to be too solid, and your temperament too philosophic, to endanger your running into the common futility of priding yourself upon the gifts of nature, any more than upon those of fortune; 'tis in their uses only you can claim any applause. I will not, therefore, scruple to assert, you can hardly any where propose yourself with much danger of being rejected. You are amiable and accomplished; abounding in wealth, high in character; in person and appearance unexceptionable; you can have no doubt of the joyful approbation of her friends, nor can you entertain a reasonable fear of her concurrence; yet, with all this, pardon me, when I plainly, explicitly add, it is very possible you may be utterly indifferent to her.'

'If so, at least,' said Edgar, in a tone and with a countenance whence all elation was flown, 'she will leave me master of myself; she is too noble to suffer any sordid motives to unite us.'

'Do not depend upon that; the influence of friends, the prevalence of example, the early notion which every female imbibes, that a good establishment must be her first object in life—these are motives of marriage commonly sufficient for the whole sex.'

'Her choice, indeed,' said Edgar, thoughtfully, 'would not, perhaps, be wholly uninfluenced;—I pretend not to doubt that the voice of her friends would be all in my favour.'

'Yes,' interruped Dr. Marchmont, 'and, be she noble as she may, Beech Park will be also in your favour! your mansion, your equipage, your domestics, even your table, will be in your favour—'

'Doctor,' interrupted Edgar, in his turn, 'I know you think ill of women.—'

'Do not let that idea weaken what I urge; I have not had reason to think well of them; yet I believe there are individuals who merit every regard: your Camilla may be one of them. Take, however, this warning from my experience; whatever is her appearance of worth, try and prove its foundation, ere you conclude it invulnerable; and whatever are your pretensions to her hand, do not necessarily connect them with your chances for her heart.'

Mandlebert, filled now with a distrust of himself and of his powers, which he was incapable of harbouring of Camilla and her magnanimity, felt struck to the soul with the apprehension of failing to gain her affection, and wounded in every point both of honour and delicacy, from the bare suggestion of owing his wife to his situation in the world. He found no longer any difficulty in promising not to act with precipitance; his confidence was gone; his elevation of sentiment was depressed; a general mist clouded his prospects, and a suspensive discomfort inquieted his mind. He shook Dr. Marchmont by the hand, and assuring him he would weigh well all he had said, and take no measure till he had again consulted with him, remounted his horse, and slowly walked it back to Cleves.

END OF THE FIRST VOLUME.

VOLUME II

BOOK III

CHAPTER I

A few kind Offices

W ITH deep concern Edgar revolved in his mind the suggestions of Dr. Marchmont; and meditation, far from diminishing, added importance to the arguments of his friend. To obtain the hand of an object he so highly admired, though but lately his sole wish, appeared now an uncertain blessing, a suspicious good, since the possession of her heart was no longer to be considered as its inseparable appendage. His very security of the approbation of Mr. and Mrs. Tyrold became a source of solicitude; and, secret from them, from her, and from all, he determined to guard his views, till he could find some opportunity of investigating her own unbiassed sentiments.

Such were his ruminations, when, on re-entering the Park, he perceived her wandering alone amidst the trees. Her figure looked so interesting, her air so serious, her solitude so attractive, that every maxim of tardy prudence, every caution of timid foresight, would instantly have given way to the quick feelings of generous impulse, had he not been restrained by his promise to Dr. Marchmont. He dismounted, and giving his horse to his groom, re-traced her footsteps.

Camilla, almost without her own knowledge, had strolled towards the gate, whence she concluded Edgar to have ridden from the Park, and, almost without consciousness, had continued sauntering in its vicinity; yet she no sooner descried him, than, struck with a species of self-accusation for this appearance of awaiting him, she crossed over to the nearest path towards the house, and, for the first time, was aware of the approach of Edgar without hastening to meet him.

He slackened his pace, to quiet his spirits, and restore his manner to its customary serenity, before he permitted himself to overtake her. 'Can you,' he then cried, 'forgive me, when you hear

I have been fulfilling my own appointment, and have postponed my promised investigation?'

'Rather say,' she gently answered, 'could I have forgiven you, if you had shewn me you thought my impatience too ungovernable for any delay?'

To find her thus willing to oblige him, was a new delight, and he expressed his acknowledgments in terms the most flattering.

An unusual seriousness made her hear him almost without reply; yet peace and harmony revisited her mind, and, in listening to his valued praise, she forgot her late alarm at her own sensations, and without extending a thought beyond the present instant, again felt tranquil and happy: while to Edgar she appeared so completely all that was adorable, that he could only remember to repent his engagement with Dr. Marchmont.

Her secret opinion that he was dissatisfied with his lot, gave a softness to her accents that enchanted him; while the high esteem for his character, which mingled with her pity, joined to a lowered sense of her own, from a new-born terror lest that pity were too tender, spread a charm wholly new over her native fire and vivacity.

In a few minutes, they were overtaken by Mandlebert's gardener, who was bringing from Beech Park a basket of flowers for his master. They were selected from curious hot-house plants, and Camilla stopt to admire their beauty and fragrance.

Edgar presented her the basket; whence she simply took a sprig of myrtle and geranium, conceiving the present to be designed for Indiana. 'If you are fond of geraniums,' said he, 'there is an almost endless variety in my greenhouse, and I will bring you to-morrow some specimens.'

She thanked him, and while he gave orders to the gardener, Miss Margland and Indiana advanced from the house.

Miss Margland had seen them from her window, where, in vain deliberation, she had been considering what step to take. But, upon beholding them together, she thought deliberation and patience were hopeless, and determined, by a decisive stroke, to break in its bud the connection she supposed forming, or throw upon Camilla all censure, if she failed, as the sole means she could devise to exculpate her own sagacity from impeachment. She called upon Indiana, therefore, to accompany her into the Park, exclaiming, in an angry tone, 'Miss Lynmere, I will shew you the true cause why Mr. Mandlebert does not declare himself—your cousin, Miss Camilla, is wheedling him away from you.'

Indiana, whose belief in almost whatever was said, was undisturbed by any species of reflection, felt filled with resentment, and a sense of injury, and readily following, said—'I was sure there was something more in it than I saw, because Mr. Melmond behaved so differently. But I don't take it very kind of my cousin, I can tell her!'

They then hurried into the Park; but, as they came without any plan, they were no sooner within a few yards of the meeting, than they stopt short, at a loss what to say or do.

Edgar, vexed at their interruption, continued talking to the gardener, to avoid joining them; but seeing Camilla, who less than ever wished for their communications, walk instantly another way, he thought it would be improper to pursue her, and only bowing to Miss Margland and Indiana, went into the house.

'This is worse than ever,' cried Miss Margland, 'to stalk off without speaking, or even offering you any of his flowers, which, I dare say, are only to be put into the parlour flower-pots, for the whole house.'

'I'm sure I'm very glad of it,' said Indiana, for I hate flowers; but I'm sure Mr. Melmond would not have done so; nor colonel Andover; nor Mr. Macdersey more than all.'

'No, nor any body else, my dear, that had common sense, and their eyes open; nor Mr. Mandlebert neither, if it were not for Miss Camilla. However, we'll let her know we see what she is about; and let Sir Hugh know too: for as to the colonels, and the ensigns, and that young Oxford student, they won't at all do; officers are commonly worth nothing; and scholars, you may take my word for it, my dear, are the dullest men in the world. Besides, one would not give such a fine fortune as Mr. Mandlebert's without making a little struggle for it. You don't know how many pretty things you may do with it. So let us shew her we don't want for spirit, and speak to her at once.'

These words, reviving in the mind of Indiana her wedding clothes, the train of servants, and the new equipage, gave fresh pique to her provocation: but finding some difficulty to overtake the fleet Camilla, whose pace kept measure with her wish to avoid them, she called after her, to desire she would not walk so fast.

Camilla reluctantly loitered, but without stopping or turning to meet them, that she might still regale herself with the perfume of the geranium presented her by Edgar.

'You're in great haste, ma'am,' said Miss Margland, 'which I own I did not observe to be the case just now!'

Camilla, in much surprize, asked, what she meant.

'My meaning is pretty plain, I believe, to any body that chose to understand it. However, though Miss Lynmere scorns to be her own champion, I cannot, as a friend, be quite so passive, nor help hinting to you, how little you would like such a proceeding to yourself, from any other person.'

'What proceeding?' cried Camilla, blushing, from a dawning comprehension of the subject, though resenting the manner of the complaint.

'Nay, only ask yourself, ma'am, only ask yourself, Miss Camilla, how you should like to be so supplanted, if such an establishment were forming for yourself, and every thing were fixt, and every body else refused, and nobody to hinder its all taking place, but a near relation of your own, who ought to be the first to help it forward. I should like to know, I say, Miss Camilla, how you would feel, if it were your own case?'

Astonished and indignant at so sudden and violent an assault, Camilla stood suspended, whether to deign any vindication, or to walk silently away: yet its implications involuntarily filled her with a thousand other, and less offending emotions than those of anger, and a general confusion crimsoned her cheeks.

'You cannot but be sensible, ma'am,' resumed Miss Margland, 'for sense is not what you want, that you have seduced Mr. Mandlebert from your cousin; you cannot but see he takes hardly the smallest notice of her, from the pains you are at to make him admire nobody but yourself.'

The spirit of Camilla now rose high to her aid, at a charge thus impertinent and unjust. 'Miss Margland,' she cried, 'you shock and amaze me! I am at a loss for any motive to so cruel an accusation: but you, I hope at least, my dear Indiana, are convinced how much it injures me.' She would then have taken the hand of Indiana, but disdainfully drawing it back, 'I shan't break my heart about it, I assure you,' she cried, 'you are vastly welcome to him for me; I hope I am not quite so odious, but I may find other people in the world besides Mr. Mandlebert!'

'O, as to that,' said Miss Margland, 'I am sure you have only to look in order to chuse; but since this affair has been settled by your uncle, I can't say I think it very grateful in any person to try to overset his particular wishes. Poor old gentleman! I'm sure I pity him! It will go hard enough with him, when he comes to hear it! Such a requital!—and from his own niece!'

This was an attack the most offensive that Camilla could receive; nothing could so nearly touch her as an idea of ingratitude to her uncle, and resting upon that, the whole tide of those feelings which were, in fact, divided and subdivided into many crossing channels, she broke forth, with great eagerness, into exclaiming, 'Mis Margland, this is quite barbarous! You know, and you, Indiana, cannot but know, I would not give my uncle the smallest pain, to be mistress of a thousand universes!'

'Why, then,' said Miss Margland, 'should you break up a scheme which he has so much set his heart upon? Why are you always winning over Mr. Mandlebert to yourself, by all that flattery? Why are you always consulting him? always obliging him? always of his opinion? always ready to take his advice?'

'Miss Margland,' replied Camilla, with the extremest agitation, 'this is so unexpected—so undeserved an interpretation,—my consultation, or my acquiescence have been merely from respect; no other thought, no other motive—Good God! what is it you imagine?—what guilt would you impute to me?'

'O dear,' cried Indiana, 'pray don't suppose it signifies. If you like to make compliments in that manner to gentlemen, pray do it. I hope I shall always hold myself above it. I think it's their place to make compliments to me.'

A resentful answer was rising to the tongue of Camilla, when she perceived her two little sprigs, which in her recent disorder she had dropt, were demolishing under the feet of Indiana, who, with apparent unmeaningness, but internal suspicion of their giver, had trampled upon them both. Hastily stooping she picked them up, and, with evident vexation, was blowing from them the dust and dirt, when Indiana scoffingly said, 'I wonder where you got that geranium?'

'I don't wonder at all,' said Miss Margland, 'for Sir Hugh has none of that species; so one may easily guess.'

Camilla felt herself blush, and letting the flowers fall, turned to Indiana, and said, 'Cousin, if on my account, it is possible you

can suffer the smallest uneasiness, tell me but what I shall do—
you shall dictate to me—you shall command me.'

Indiana disclaimed all interest in her behaviour; but Miss
Margland cried, 'What you can do, ma'am, is this, and nothing
can be easier, nor fairer: leave off paying all that court to Mr.
Mandlebert, of asking his advice, and follow your own way,
whether he likes it or not, and go to see Mrs. Arlbery, and Mrs.
every body else, when you have a mind, without waiting for his
permission, or troubling yourself about what he thinks of it.'

Camilla now trembled in every joint, and with difficulty
restrained from tears, while, timidly, she said—'And do you, my
dear Indiana, demand of me this conduct? and will it, at least,
satisfy you?'

'Me? O dear no! I demand nothing, I assure you. The whole
matter is quite indifferent to me, and you may ask his leave for
every thing in the world, if you chuse it. There are people enough
ready to take my part, I hope, if you set him against me ever so
much.'

'Indeed, indeed, Indiana,' said Camilla, overpowered with
conflicting sensations, 'this is using me very unkindly!' And,
without waiting to hear another word, she hurried into the house,
and flew to hide herself in her own room.

This was the first bitter moment she had ever known. Peace,
gay though uniform, had been the constant inmate of her breast,
enjoyed without thought, possessed without struggle; not the
subdued gift of accommodating philosophy, but the inborn and
genial produce of youthful felicity's best aliment, the energy of its
own animal spirits.

She had, indeed, for some time past, thought Edgar, of too
refined and too susceptible a character for the unthinking and
undistinguishing Indiana; and for the last day or two, her regret at
his fate had strengthened itself into an averseness of his supposed
destination, that made the idea of it painful, and the subject
repugnant to her; but she had never, till this very morning,
distrusted the innoxiousness either of her pity or her regard; and,
startled at the first surmise of danger, she had wished to fly even
from herself, rather than venture to investigate feelings so unwelcome; yet still and invariably, she had concluded Edgar the
future husband of Indiana.

To hear there were any doubts of the intended marriage, filled

her with emotions indefinable; to hear herself named as the cause
of those doubts, was alarming both to her integrity and her
delicacy. She felt the extremest anger at the unprovoked and
unwarrantable harshness of Miss Margland, and a resentment
nearly equal at the determined petulance, and unjustifiable
aspersions of Indiana.

Satisfied of the innocence of her intentions, she knew, not what
alteration she could make in her behaviour; and, after various
plans, concluded, that to make none would best manifest her
freedom from self-reproach. At the summons therefore to dinner,
she was the first to appear, eager to shew herself unmoved by the
injustice of her accusers, and desirous to convince them she was
fearless of examination.

Yet, too much discomposed to talk in her usual manner, she
seized upon a book till the party was seated. Answering then to
the call of her uncle, with as easy an air as she could assume, she
took her accustomed place by his side, and began, for mere
employment, filling a plate from the dish that was nearest to her;
which she gave to the footman, without any direction whither to
carry, or enquiry if any body chose to eat it.

It was taken round the table, and, though refused by all, she
heaped up another plate, with the same diligence and speed as if it
had been accepted.

Edgar, who had been accidentally detained, only now entered,
apologizing for being so late.

Engrossed by the pride of self-defence, and the indignancy of
unmerited unkindness, the disturbed mind of Camilla had not yet
formed one separate reflexion, nor even admitted a distinct idea
of Edgar himself, disengaged from the accusation in which he
stood involved. But he had now amply his turn. The moment he
appeared, the deepest blushes covered her face; and an emotion so
powerful beat in her breast, that the immediate impulse of her impetuous feelings, was to declare herself ill, and run out of the room.

With this view she rose; but ashamed of her plan, seated herself
the next moment, though she had first overturned her plate and
a sauce-boat in the vehemence of her haste.

This accident rather recovered than disconcerted her, by
affording an unaffected occupation, in begging pardon of Sir
Hugh, who was the chief sufferer, changing the napkins, and
restoring the table to order.

'What upon earth can be the matter with Miss Camilla, I can't guess!' exclaimed Miss Margland, though with an expression of spite that fully contradicted her difficulty of conjecture.

'I hope,' said Edgar surprised, 'Miss Camilla is not ill?'

'I can't say I think my cousin looks very bad!' said Indiana.

Camilla, who was rubbing a part of her gown upon which nothing had fallen, affected to be too busy to hear them: which Sir Hugh, concluding her silent from shame, entreated her not to think of his cloaths, which were worth no great matter, not being his best by two or three suits. Her thoughts had not waited this injunction; yet it was in vain she strove to behave as if nothing had happened. Her spirit instigated, but it would not support her; her voice grew husky, she stammered, forgot, as she went on, what she designed to say when she began speaking, and frequently was forced to stop short, with a faint laugh at herself, and with a colour every moment encreasing. And the very instant the cloth was removed, she rose, unable to constrain herself any longer, and ran up stairs to her own room.

There all her efforts evaporated in tears. 'Cruel, cruel, Miss Margland,' she cried, 'unjust, unkind Indiana! how have I merited this treatment! What can Edgar think of my disturbance? What can I devise to keep from his knowledge the barbarous accusation which has caused it?'

In a few minutes she heard the step of Eugenia.

Ashamed, she hastily wiped her eyes; and before the door could be opened, was at the further end of the room, looking into one of her drawers.

'What is it that has vexed my dearest Camilla?' cried her kind sister, 'something I am sure has grieved her.'

'I cannot guess what I have done with—I can no where find—' stammered Camilla, engaged in some apparent search, but too much confused to name anything of which she might probably be in want.

Eugenia desired to assist her, but a servant came to the door, to tell them that the company was going to the summer-house, whither Sir Hugh begged they would follow.

Camilla besought Eugenia to join them, and make her excuses: but, fearing Miss Margland would attribute her absconding to guilt, or cowardice, she bathed her eyes in cold water, and overtook her sister at the stairs of the little building.

In ascending them, she heard Miss Margland say, 'I dare believe nothing's the matter but some whim; for to be sure as to whims, Miss Camilla has the most of any creature I ever saw, and Miss Lynmere the least; for you may imagine, Mr. Mandlebert, I have pretty good opportunity to see all these young people in their real colours.'

Overset by this malignancy, she was again flying to the refuge of her own room, and the relief of tears, when the conviction of such positive ill-will in Miss Margland, for which she could assign no reason, but her unjust and exclusive partiality to Indiana, checked her precipitancy. She feared she would construe to still another whim her non-appearance, and resuming a little fresh strength from fresh resentment, turned back; but the various keen sensations she experienced as she entered the summer-house, rendered this little action the most severe stretch of fortitude, her short and happy life had yet called upon her to make.

Sir Hugh addressed her some some kind enquiries, which she hastily answered, while she pretended to be busy in preparing to wind some sewing silk upon cards.

She could have chosen no employment less adapted to display the cool indifference she wished to manifest to Miss Margland and Indiana. She pulled the silk the wrong way, twisted, twirled, and entangled it continually; and while she talked volubly of what she was about, as if it were the sole subject of her thoughts, her shaking hands shewed her whole frame disordered, and her high colour betrayed her strong internal emotion.

Edgar looked at her with surprize and concern. What had dropt from Miss Margland of her whims, he had heard with disdain; for, without suspecting her of malice to Camilla, he concluded her warped by her prejudice in favour of Indiana. Dr. Marchmont, however, had bid him judge by proof, not appearance; and he resolved therefore to investigate the cause of this disquiet, before he acted upon his belief in its blamelessness.

Having completely spoilt one skein, she threw it aside, and saying 'the weather's so fine, I cannot bear to stay within,'—left her silk, her winders, and her work-bag, on the first chair, and skipt down the stairs.

Sir Hugh declined walking, but would let nobody remain with him. Edgar, as if studying the clouds, glided down first. Camilla, perceiving him, bent her head, and began gathering some flowers.

He stood by her a moment in silence, and then said: 'To-morrow morning, without fail, I will wait upon Mrs. Needham.'

'Pray take your own time. I am not in any haste.'

'You are very good, and I am more obliged to you than I can express, for suffering my officious interference with such patience.'

A rustling of silk made Camilla now look up, and she perceived Miss Margland leaning half out of the window of the summer-house, from earnestness to catch what she said.

Angry thus to be watched, and persuaded that both innocence and dignity called upon her to make no change in her open consideration for Edgar, she answered, in a voice that strove to be more audible, but that irresistibly trembled, 'I beg you will impartially consult your own judgment, and decide as you think right.'

Edgar, now, became as little composed as herself: the power with which she invested him, possessed a charm to dissolve every hesitating doubt; and when, upon her raising her head, he perceived the redness of her eyes, and found that the perturbation which had perplexed him was mingled with some affliction, the most tender anxiety filled his mind, and though somewhat checked by the vicinity of Miss Margland, his voice expressed the warmest solicitude, as he said, 'I know not how to thank you for this sweetness; but I fear something disturbs you?—I fear you are not well, or are not happy?'

Camilla again bent over the flowers; but it was not to scent their fragrance; she sought only a hiding place for her eyes, which were gushing with tears; and though she wished to fly a thousand miles off, she had not courage to take a single step, nor force to trust her voice with the shortest reply.

'You will not speak? yet you do not deny that you have some uneasiness?—Could I give it but the smallest relief, how fortunate I should think myself!—And is it quite impossible?—Do you forbid me to ask what it is?—forbid me the indulgence even to suggest——'

'Ask nothing! suggest nothing! and think of it no more!' interrupted Camilla, 'if you would not make me quite——'

She stopt suddenly, not to utter the word unhappy, of which she felt the improper strength at the moment it was quivering on her lips, and leaving her sentence unfinished, abruptly walked away.

Edgar could not presume to follow, yet felt her conquest irresistible. Her self-denial with regard to Mrs. Arlbery won his highest approbation; her compliance with his wishes convinced him of her esteem; and her distress, so new and so unaccountable, centered every wish of his heart in a desire to solace, and to revive her.

To obtain this privilege hastened at once and determined his measures; he excused himself, therefore, from walking, and went instantly to his chamber, to reclaim, by a hasty letter to Dr. Marchmont, his procrastinating promise.

CHAPTER II

A Pro and a Con

WITH a pen flowing quick from feelings of the most generous warmth, Edgar wrote the following letter:

To Dr. Marchmont.

Accuse me not of precipitance, my dear Doctor, nor believe me capable of forgetting the wisdom of your suggestions, nor of lightly weighing those evils with which your zeal has encompassed me, though I write at this instant to confess a total contrariety of sentiment, to call back every promise of delay, and to make an unqualified avowal, that the period of caution is past! Camilla is not happy—something, I know not what, has disturbed the gay serenity of her bosom: she has forbid me to enquire the cause; —one way only remains to give me a claim to her confidence.—O Doctor! wonder not if cold, tardy, suspicious—I had nearly said unfeeling, caution, shrinks at such a moment, from the rising influence of warmer sympathy, which bids me sooth her in distress, shield her from danger, strengthen all her virtues, and participate in their emanations!

You will not do me the injustice to think me either impelled or blinded by external enchantments; you know me to have withstood their yet fuller blaze in her cousin: O no! were she despoiled of all personal attraction by the same ravaging distemper that has been so fierce with her poor sister; were a similar cruel accident to rob her form of all symmetry, she would yet be more fascinating to my soul, by one single look, one single word, one sweet beaming smile, diffusing all the gaiety it displays, than all of beauty, all of elegance, all of rank, all of wealth, the whole kingdom, in some wonderful aggregate, could oppose to her.

Her face, her form, however penetrating in loveliness, aid, but do not constitute, her charms; no, 'tis the quick intelligence of soul that mounts to her eyes, 'tis the spirit checked by sweetness, the sweetness animated by spirit, the nature so nobly above all artifice, all study—O Doctor! restore to me immediately every vestige, every trait of any promise, any acquiescence, any idea the most distant, that can be construed into a compliance with one moment's requisition of delay!

EDGAR MANDLEBERT.

Cleves Park, Friday Evening.

*   *   *

Camilla, meanwhile, shut up in her room, wept almost without cessation, from a sense of general unhappiness, though fixed to no point, and from a disturbance of mind, a confusion of ideas and of feelings, that rendered her incapable of reflection. She was again followed by Eugenia, and could no longer refuse, to her tender anxiety, a short detail of the attack which occasioned her disorder; happy, at least, in reciting it, that by unfolding the cause, there no longer remained any necessity to repress the effects of her affliction.

To her great surprise, however, Eugenia only said: 'And is this all, my dear Camilla?'

'All!' exclaimed Camilla.

'Yes, is it all?—I was afraid some great misfortune had happened.'

'And what could happen more painful, more shocking, more cruel?'

'A thousand things! for this is nothing but a mere mistake; and you should not make yourself unhappy about it, because you are not to blame.'

'Is it then nothing to be accused of designs and intentions so criminal?'

'If the accusation were just, it might indeed make you wretched:

but it is Miss Margland only who has any reason to be afflicted; for it is she alone who has been in the wrong.'

Struck with this plain but uncontrovertible truth, Camilla wiped her eyes, and strove to recover some composure; but finding her tears still force their way, 'It is not,' she cried, with some hesitation, 'it is not the aspersions of Miss Margland alone that give me so much vexation—the unkindness of Indiana—'

'Indeed she is highly reprehensible; and so I will tell her;—but still, if she has any fears, however ill-founded, of losing Edgar, you cannot but pardon—you must even pity her.'

Struck again, and still more forcibly, by this second truth, Camilla, ashamed of her grief, made a stronger and more serious effort to repress it; and receiving soon afterwards a summons from her uncle, her spirit rose once more to the relief of her dejection, upon seeing him seated between Miss Margland and Indiana, and discerning that they had been making some successful complaint, by the air of triumph with which they waited her approach.

'My dear Camilla,' he cried, with a look of much disturbance, 'here's a sad ado, I find; though I don't mean to blame you, nor young Mr. Mandlebert neither, taste being a fault one can't avoid; not but what a person's changing their mind is what I can't commend in any one, which I shall certainly let him know, not doubting to bring him round by means of his own sense: only, my dear, in the meanwhile, I must beg you not to stand in your cousin's way.'

'Indeed, my dear uncle, I do not merit this imputation; I am not capable of such treachery!' indignantly answered Camilla.

'Treachery! Lord help us! treachery!' cried Sir Hugh, fondly embracing her, 'don't I know you are as innocent as the baby unborn? and more innocent too, from the advantage of having more sense to guide you by! treachery, my dear Camilla! why, I think there's nobody so good in the wide world!—by which I mean no reflections, never thinking it right to make any.'

Indiana, sullenly pouting, spoke not a word; but Miss Margland, with a tone of plausibility that was some covert to its malice, said 'Why then all may be well, and the young ladies as good friends as ever, and Mr. Mandlebert return to the conduct of a gentleman, only just by Miss Camilla's doing as she would be done by; for nothing that all of us can say will have any effect, if she does not discourage him from dangling about after her in the manner he does now, speaking to nobody else, and always asking her opinion about every trifle, which is certainly doing no great justice to Miss Lynmere.'

Indiana, with a toss of the head, protested his notice was the last thing she desired.

'My dear Indiana,' said Sir Hugh, 'don't mind all that outward shew. Mr. Mandlebert is a very good boy, and as to your cousin Camilla, I am sure I need not put you in mind how much she is the same; but I really think, whatever's the reason, the young youths of now-a-days grow backwarder and backwarder. Though I can't say but what in my time it was just the same; witness myself; which is what I have been sorry for often enough, though I have left off repenting it now, because it's of no use; age being a thing there's no getting ahead of.'

'Well, then, all that remains is this,' said Miss Margland, 'let Miss Camilla keep out of Mr. Mandlebert's way; and let her order the carriage, and go to Mrs. Arlbery's to-morrow, and take no notice of his likings and dislikings; and I'll be bound for it he will soon think no more of her, and then, of course, he will give the proper attention to Miss Lynmere.'

'O, if that's all,' cried Sir Hugh, 'my dear Camilla, I am sure, will do it, and as much again too, to make her cousin easy. And so now, I hope, all is settled, and my two good girls will kiss one another, and be friends; which I am sure I am myself, with all my heart.'

Camilla hung her head, in speechless perturbation, at a task which appeared to her equally hard and unjust; but while fear and shame kept her silent, Sir Hugh drew her to Indiana, and a cold, yet unavoidable salute, gave a species of tacit consent to a plan which she did not dare oppose, from the very strength of the desire that urged her opposition.

They then separated; Sir Hugh delighted, Miss Margland triumphant, Indiana half satisfied, half affronted, and Camilla with a mind so crowded, a heart so full, she scarcely breathed. Sensations the most contrary, of pain, pleasure, hope, and terror, at once assailed her. Edgar, of whom so long she had only thought as of the destined husband of Indiana, she now heard named with suspicions of another regard, to which she did not dare give full extension; yet of which the most distant surmise made her consider herself, for a moment, as the happiest of human beings, though she held herself the next as the most culpable for even wishing it.

She found Eugenia still in her room, who, perceiving her increased emotion, tenderly enquired, if there were any new cause.

'Alas! yes, my dearest Eugenia! they have been exacting from me the most cruel of sacrifices! They order me to fly from Edgar Mandlebert—to resist his advice—to take the very measures I have promised to forbear—to disoblige, to slight, to behave to him even offensively! my uncle himself, lenient, kind, indulgent as he is, my uncle himself has been prevailed with to inflict upon me this terrible injunction.'

'My uncle,' answered Eugenia, 'is incapable of giving pain to any body, and least of all to you, whom he loves with such fondness; he has not therefore comprehended the affair; he only considers, in general, that to please or to displease Edgar Mandlebert can be a matter of no moment to you, when compared with its importance to Indiana.'

'It is a thousand and a thousand, a million and a million times more important to me, than it can ever be to her!' exclaimed the ardent Camilla, 'for she values not his kindness, she knows not his worth, she is insensible to his virtues!'

'You judge too hastily, my dear Camilla; she has not indeed your warmth of heart; but if she did not wish the union to take place, why would she shew all this disquiet in the apprehension of its breach?'

Camilla, surprised into recollection, endeavoured to become calmer.

'You, indeed,' continued the temperate Eugenia, 'if so situated, would not so have behaved; you would not have been so unjust; and you could not have been so weak; but still, if you had received, however causelessly, any alarm for the affection of the man you meant to marry, and that man were as amiable as Edgar, you would have been equally disturbed.'

Camilla, convinced, yet shocked, felt the flutter of her heart give a thousand hues to her face, and walking to the window, leaned far out to gasp for breath.

'Weigh the request more coolly, and you cannot refuse a short compliance. I am sure you would not make Indiana unhappy.'

'O, no! not for the world!' cried she, struggling to seem more reasonable than she felt.

'Yet how can she be otherwise, if she imagines you have more of the notice and esteem of Edgar than herself?'

Camilla now had not a word to say; the subject dropt; she took up a book, and by earnest internal remonstrances, commanded herself to appear at tea-time with tolerable serenity.

The evening was passed in spiritless conversation, or in listening to the piano-forte, upon which Indiana, with the utmost difficulty, played some very easy lessons.

At night, the following answer arrived from Dr. Marchmont:

> *To* Edgar Mandlebert, *Esq.*
> *Parsonage House, Cleves,*
> MY DEAR FRIEND,   *Friday Night.*

I must be thankful, in a moment of such enthusiasm, that you can pay the attention of even recollecting those evils with which my zeal only has, you think, encompassed you. I cannot insist upon the practice of caution which you deem unfounded; but as you wait my answer, I will once more open upon my sentiments, and communicate my wishes. It is now only I can speak them; the instant you have informed the young lady of your own, silences them for ever. Your honour and her happiness become then entangled in each other, and I know not which I would least willingly assail. What in all men is base, would to you, I believe, be impossible—to trifle with such favour as may be the growth of your own undisguised partiality.

Your present vehemence to ascertain the permanent possession of one you conceive formed for your felicity, obscures, to your now absorbed faculties, the thousand nameless, but tenacious, delicacies annexed by your species of character to your powers of enjoyment. In two words, then, let me tell you, what, in a short time, you will daily tell yourself: you cannot be happy if not exclusively loved; for you cannot excite, you cannot bestow happiness.

By exclusively, I do not mean to the exclusion of other connections and regard; far from it; those who covet in a bride the oblivion of all former friendships, all early affections, weaken the finest ties of humanity, and dissolve the first compact of unregistered but genuine integrity. The husband, who would rather rationally than with romance be loved himself, should seek to cherish, not obliterate the kind feelings of nature in its first expansions. These, where properly bestowed, are the guarantees to that constant and respectable tenderness, which a narrow and selfish jealousy rarely fails to convert into distaste and disgust.

The partiality which I mean you to ascertain, injures not these prior claims; I mean but a partiality exclusive of your situation in life, and of all declaration of your passion: a partiality, in fine, that is appropriate to yourself, not to the rank in the world with which you may tempt her ambition, nor to the blandishments of flattery, which only soften the heart by intoxicating the understanding.

Observe, therefore, if your general character, and usual conduct, strike her mind; if her esteem is yours without the attraction of assiduity and adulation; if your natural disposition and manners make your society grateful to her, and your approbation desirable.

It is thus alone you can secure your own contentment; for it is thus alone your reflecting mind can snatch from the time to come the dangerous surmises of a dubious retrospection.

Remember, you can always advance; you can never, in honour, go back; and believe me when I tell you, that the mere simple avowal of preference, which only ultimately binds the man, is frequently what first captivates the woman. If her mind is not previously occupied, it operates with such seductive sway, it so soothes, so flatters, so bewitches her self-complacency, that while she listens, she imperceptibly fancies she participates in sentiments, which, but the minute before, occurred not even to her imagination; and while her hand is the recompence of her own eulogy, she is not herself aware if she has bestowed it where her esteem and regard, unbiassed by the eloquence of acknowledged admiration, would have wished it sought, or if it has simply been the boon of her own gratified vanity.

I now no longer urge your acquiescence, my dear friend; I merely entreat you twice to peruse what I have written, and then leave you to act by the result of such perusal.

I remain
Your truly faithful and obliged

Gabriel Marchmont.

Edgar ran through this letter with an impatience wholly foreign to his general character. 'Why,' cried he, 'will he thus obtrude upon me these fastidious doubts and causeless difficulties? I begged but the restitution of my promise, and he gives it me in words that nearly annihilate my power of using it.'

Disappointed and displeased, he hastily put it into his pocket-book, resolving to seek Camilla, and commit the consequences of an interview to the impulses it might awaken.

He was half way down stairs, when the sentence finishing with, 'you cannot excite, you cannot bestow happiness,' confusedly recurred to him: 'If in that,' thought he, 'I fail, I am a stranger to it myself, and a stranger for ever;' and, returning to his room, he re-opened the letter to look for the passage.

The sentence lost nothing by being read a second time; he paused upon it dejectedly, and presently re-read the whole epistle.

'He is not quite wrong!' cried he, pensively; 'there is nothing very unreasonable in what he urges: true, indeed, it is, that I can never be happy myself, if her happiness is not entwined around my own.'

The first blight thus borne to that ardent glee with which the imagination rewards its own elevated speculations, he yet a third time read the letter.

'He is right!' he then cried; 'I will investigate her sentiments, and know what are my chances for her regard; what I owe to real approbation; and what merely to intimacy of situation. I will postpone all explanation till my visit here expires, and devote the probationary interval, to an examination which shall obviate all danger of either deceiving my own reason, or of beguiling her inconsiderate acceptance.'

This settled, he rejoiced in a mastery over his eagerness, which he considered as complete, since it would defer for no less than a week the declaration of his passion.

CHAPTER III

An Author's Notion of Travelling

THE next morning Camilla, sad and unwilling to appear, was the last who entered the breakfast-parlour. Edgar instantly discerned the continued unhappiness, which an assumed smile concealed from the unsuspicious Sir Hugh, and the week of delay before him seemed an outrage to all his wishes.

While she was drinking her first cup of tea, a servant came in, and told her the carriage was ready.

She coloured, but nobody spoke, and the servant retired. Edgar was going to ask the design for the morning, when Miss Margland said—'Miss Camilla, as the horses have got to go and return, you had better not keep them waiting.'

Colouring still more deeply, she was going to disclaim having ordered them, though well aware for what purpose they were come, when Sir Hugh said—'I think, my dear, you had best take Eugenia with you, which may serve you as a companion to talk to, in case you want to say anything by the way, which I take for granted; young people not much liking to hold their tongues for a long while together, which is very natural, having so little to think of.'

'Miss Eugenia, then,' cried Miss Margland, before Camilla could reply, 'run for your cloak as soon as you have finished your breakfast.'

Eugenia, hoping to aid her sister in performing a task, which she considered as a peace-offering to Indiana, said, she had already done.

Camilla now lost all courage for resistance; but feeling her chagrin almost intolerable, quitted the room with her tea un-drunk, and without making known if she should return or not.

Eugenia followed, and Edgar, much amazed, said, he had forgotten to order his horse for his morning's ride, and hastily made off: determined to be ready to hand the sisters to the carriage, and learn whither it was to drive.

Camilla, who, in flying to her room, thought of nothing less than preparing for an excursion which she now detested, was again surprised in tears by Eugenia.

'What, my dearest Camilla,' she cried, 'can thus continually affect you? you cannot be so unhappy without some cause!—why will you not trust your Eugenia?'

'I cannot talk,' she answered, ashamed to repeat reasons which she knew Eugenia held to be inadequate to her concern—'If there is no resource against this persecution—if I must render myself hateful to give them satisfaction, let us, at least, be gone immediately, and let me be spared seeing the person I so ungratefully offend.'

She then hurried down stairs; but finding Edgar in waiting, still more quickly hurried back, and in an agony, for which she attempted not to account, cast herself into a chair, and told Eugenia, that if Miss Margland did not contrive to call Edgar away, the universe could not prevail with her to pass him in such defiance.

'My dear Camilla,' said Eugenia, surprized, yet compassionately, 'if this visit is become so painful to you, relinquish it at once.'

'Ah, no! for that cruel Miss Margland will then accuse me of staying away only to follow the counsel of Edgar.'

She stopt; for the countenance of Eugenia said—'*And is that not your motive?*' A sudden consciousness took place of her distress; she hid her face, in the hope of concealing her emotion, and with as calm a voice as she could attain, said, the moment they could pass unobserved she would set off.

Eugenia went downstairs.

'Alas! alas!' she then cried, 'into what misery has this barbarous Miss Margland thrown me! Eugenia herself seems now to suspect something wrong; and so, I suppose, will my uncle; and I can only convince them of my innocence by acting towards Edgar as a monster.—Ah! I would sooner a thousand times let them all think me guilty!'

Eugenia had met Miss Margland in the hall, who, impatient for their departure, passed her, and ascended the stairs.

At the sound of her footsteps, the horror of her reproaches and insinuations conquered every other feeling, and Camilla, starting up, rushed forward, and saying 'Good morning!' ran off.

Edgar was still at the door, and came forward to offer her his hand. 'Pray take care of Eugenia,' she cried, abruptly passing him, and darting, unaided, into the chaise. Edgar, atsonished, obeyed, and gave his more welcome assistance to Eugenia; but when both were seated, said—'Where shall I tell the postillion to drive?'

Camilla, who was pulling one of the green blinds up, and again letting it down, twenty times in a minute, affected not to hear him; but Eugenia answered, 'to the Grove, to Mrs. Arlbery's.'

The postillion had already received his orders from Miss Margland, and drove off; leaving Edgar mute with surprise, disappointment and mortification.

Miss Margland was just behind him, and conceived this the fortunate instant for eradicating from his mind every favourable pre-possession for Camilla; assuming, therefore, an air of concern, she said—'So, you have found Miss Camilla out, in spite of all her precautions! she would fain not have had you know her frolic.'

'Not know it! has there, then, been any plan? did Miss Camilla intend——'

'O, she intends nothing in the world for two minutes together! only she did not like you should find out her fickleness. You know, I told you, before, she was all whim; and so you will find. You may always take my opinion, be assured. Miss Lynmere is the only one among them that is always the same, always good, always amiable.'

'And is not Miss——' he was going to say Camilla, but checking himself, finished with—'Miss Eugenia, at least, always equal, always consistent?'

'Why, she is better than Miss Camilla; but not one among them has any steadiness, or real sweetness, but Miss Lynmere. As to Miss Camilla, if she has not her own way, there's no enduring her, she frets, and is so cross. When you put her off, in that friendly manner, from gadding after a new acquaintance so improper for her, you set her into such an ill humour, that she has done nothing but cry, as you may have seen by her eyes, and worry herself and all of us round, except you, ever since; but she was afraid of you, for fear you should take her to task, which she hates of all things.'

Half incredulous, yet half shocked, Edgar turned from this harangue in silent disgust. He knew the splenetic nature of Miss Margland, and trusted she might be wrong; but he knew, too, her opportunities for observation, and dreaded lest she might be right. Camilla had been certainly low spirited, weeping, and restless; was it possible it could be for so slight, so unmeaning a cause? His wish was to follow her on horseback; but this, un-authorized, might betray too much anxiety: he tried not to think of what had been said by Dr. Marchmont, while this cloud hung over her disposition and sincerity; for whatever might be the malignity of Miss Margland, the breach of a promise, of which the voluntary sweetness had so lately proved his final captivation, could not be doubted, and called aloud for explanation.

He mounted, however, his horse, to make his promised enquiries of Mrs. Needham; for though the time was already past for impeding the acquaintance from taking place, its progress might yet be stopt, should it be found incompatible with propriety.

The young ladies had scarce left the Park, when Sir Hugh, recollecting a promise he had made to Mr. and Mrs. Tyrold, of never suffering Eugenia to go abroad unattended by some gentleman, while Bellamy remained in the country, sent hastily to beg that Edgar would follow the carriage.

Edgar was out of sight, and there was no chance of overtaking him.

'Lack-a-day!' said Sir Hugh, 'those young folks can never walk a horse but full gallop!' He then resolved to ask Dr. Orkborne to go after his pupil, and ride by the side of the chaise. He ordered a horse to be saddled; and, to lose no time by messages, the tardiness of which he had already experienced with this gentleman, he went himself to his apartment, and after several vain rappings at his door, entered the room unbid, saying—'Good Dr. Orkborne, unless you are dead, which God forbid! I think it's something uncomfortable that you can't speak to a person waiting at your door; not that I pretend to doubt but you may have your proper reasons, being what I can't judge.'

He then begged he would get booted and spurred instantly, and follow his two nieces to Mrs. Arlbery's, in order to take care of Eugenia; adding, 'though I'm afraid, Doctor, by your look, you don't much listen to me, which I am sorry for; my not being able to speak like Horace and Virgil being no fault of mine, but of my poor capacity, which no man can be said to be answerable for.'

He then again entreated him to set off.

'Only a moment, sir! I only beg you'll accord me one moment!' cried the Doctor, with a fretful sigh; while, screening his eyes with his left hand, he endeavoured hastily to make a memorandum of his ideas, before he forced them to any other subject.

'Really, Dr. Orkborne,' said Sir Hugh, somewhat displeased, 'I must needs remark, for a friend, I think this rather slow: however, I can't say I am much disappointed, now, that I did not turn out a scholar myself, for I see, plain enough, you learned men think nothing of any consequence but Homer and such; which, however, I don't mean to take ill, knowing it was like enough to have been my own case.'

He then left the room, intending to send a man and horse after the chaise, to desire his two nieces to return immediately.

Dr. Orkborne, who, though copiously stored with the works of the ancients, had a sluggish understanding, and no imagination, was entirely overset by this intrusion. The chain of his observations was utterly broken; he strove vainly to rescue from oblivion the slow ripening fruits of his tardy conceptions, and, proportioning his estimation of their value by their labour, he not only considered his own loss as irreparable, but the whole world to be injured by so unfortunate an interruption.

The recollection, however, which refused to assist his fame, was importunate in reminding him that the present offender was his patron; and his total want of skill in character kept from him the just confidence he would otherwise have placed in the unalterable goodness of heart of Sir Hugh, whom, though he despised for his ignorance, he feared for his power.

Uneasy, therefore, at his exit, which he concluded to be made in wrath, he uttered a dolorous groan over his papers, and compelled himself to follow, with an apology, the innocent enemy of his glory.

Sir Hugh, who never harboured displeasure for two minutes in his life, was more inclined to offer an excuse himself for what he had dropt against learning, than to resist the slightest concession from the Doctor, whom he only begged to make haste, the horse being already at the door. But Dr. Orkborne, as soon as he comprehended what was desired, revived from the weight of sacrificing so much time; he had never been on horseback since he was fifteen years of age, and declared, to the wondering baronet, he could not risk his neck by undertaking such a journey.

In high satisfaction, he would then have returned to his room, persuaded that, when his mind was disembarrassed, a parallel between two ancient authors which, with much painful stretch of thought, he had suggested, and which, with the most elaborate difficulty, he was arranging and drawing up, would recur again to his memory: but Sir Hugh, always eager in expedients, said, he should follow in the coach, which might be ready time enough for him to arrive at Mrs. Arlbery's before the visit was over, and to bring Eugenia safe back; 'which,' cried he, 'is the main point, for the sake of seeing that she goes no where else.'

Dr. Orkborne, looking extremely blank at this unexpected proposition, stood still.

'Won't you go, then, my good friend?'

The Doctor, after a long pause, and in a most dejected tone, sighed out, 'Yes, sir, certainly, with the greatest—alacrity.'

Sir Hugh, who took everything literally that seemed right or good-natured, thanked him, and ordered the horses to be put to the coach with all possible expedition.

It was soon at the door, and Dr. Orkborne, who had spent in his room the intervening period, in moaning the loss of the time that was to succeed, and in an opinion that two hours of this morning would have been of more value to him than two years when it was gone, reluctantly obeyed the call that obliged him to descend: but he had no sooner entered the carriage, and found he was to have it to himself, than leaping suddenly from it, as the groom, who was to attend him, was preparing to shut the door, he hastened back to his chamber to collect a packet of books and papers, through the means of which he hoped to recall those flowers of rhetoric, upon which he was willing to risk his future reputation.

The astonished groom, concluding something had frightened him, jumped into the coach to find the cause of his flight; but Sir Hugh, who was advancing to give his final directions, called out, with some displeasure 'Hollo, there, you Jacob! if Dr. Orkborne thinks to get you to go for my nieces in place of himself, it's what I don't approve; which, however, you need not take amiss, one man being no more born with a livery upon his back than another; which God forbid I should think otherwise. Nevertheless, my little girls must have a proper respect shewn them; which, it's surprising Dr. Orkborne should not know as well as me.'

And, much disconcerted, he walked to the parlour, to ruminate upon some other measure.

'I am sure, your honour,' said Jacob, following him, 'I got in with no ill intention; but what it was as come across the Doctor I don't know; but just as I was a going to shut the door, without saying never a word, out he pops, and runs upstairs again; so I only got in to see if something had hurt him; but I can't find nothing of no sort.'

Then, putting to the door, and looking sagaciously, 'Please your honour,' he continued, 'I dare say it's only some maggot got into his brain from over reading and writing; for all the maids think he'll soon be cracked.'

'That's very wrong of them, Jacob; and I desire you'll tell them they must not think any such thing.'

'Why, your honour don't know half, or you'd be afraid too,' said Jacob, lowering his voice; 'he's like nothing you ever see. He won't let a chair nor a table be dusted in his room, though they are covered over with cobwebs, because he says, it takes him such a time to put his things to rights again; though all the while what he calls being to rights is just the contrary; for it's a mere higgledy piggledy, one thing heaped o'top of t'other, as if he did it for fun.'

The baronet gravely answered, that if there were not the proper shelves for his books he would order more.

'Why, your honour, that's not the quarter, as I tell you! why, when they're cleaning out his room, if they happen but to sweep away a bit of paper as big as my hand, he'll make believe they've done him as much mischief as if they'd stole a thousand pound. It would make your honour stare to hear him. Mary says, she's sure he has never been quite right ever since he come to the house.'

'But I desire you'll tell Mary I don't approve of that opinion. Dr. Orkborne is one of the first scholars in the world, as I am credibly informed; and I beg you'll all respect him accordingly.'

'Why, your honour, if it i'n't owing to something of that sort, why does he behave so unaccountable? I myself heard him making such a noise at the maids one day, that I spoke to Mary afterwards, and asked her what was the matter?—"Laws, nobody knows," says she, "but here's the Doctor been all in a huff again; I was just a dusting his desk (says she) and so I happened to wipe down a little bundle of papers, all nothing but mere scraps, and he took on as if they'd been so many guineas (says she) and he kept me there for an hour looking for them, and scolding, and telling such a heap of fibs, that if he was not out of his head, would be a shame for a gentleman to say" (says she).'

'Fie, fie, Jacob! and tell Mary fie, too. He is a very learned gentleman, and no more a story-teller than I am myself; which God forbid.'

'Why, your honour, how could this here be true? he told the maids how they had undone him, and the like, only because of their throwing down them few bits of papers; though they are ready to make oath they picked them up, almost every one; and that they were all of a crump, and of no manner of use.'

'Well, well, say no more about it, good Jacob, but go and give my compliments to Dr. Orkborne, and ask him, what's the reason of his changing his mind; I mean, provided it's no secret.'

Jacob returned in two minutes, with uplifted hands and eyes; 'your honour,' cried he, 'now you'll believe me another time! he is worse than ever, and I'll be bound he'll break out before another quarter.'

'Why, what's the matter?'

'Why, as sure as I'm here, he's getting together ever so many books, and stuffing his pockets, and cramming them under his arms, just as if he was a porter! and when I gave him your honour's message, I suppose it put him out, for he said, "Don't hurry me so, I'm a coming;" making believe as if he was only a preparing for going out, in the stead of making that fool of himself.'

Sir Hugh, now really alarmed, bid him not mention the matter to anyone; and was going upstairs himself, when he saw Dr. Orkborne, heavily laden with books in each hand, and bulging from both coat pockets, slowly and carefully coming down.

'Bless me,' cried he, rather fearfully, 'my dear sir, what are you going to do with all that library?'

Dr. Orkborne, wishing him good morning, without attending to his question, proceeding to the carriage, calling to Jacob, who stood aloof, to make haste and open the door.

Jacob obeyed, but with a significant look at his master, that said, 'you see how it is, sir!'

Sir Hugh following him, gently put his hand upon his shoulder, and mildly said, 'My dear friend, to be sure you know best, but I don't see the use of loading yourself in that manner for nothing.'

'It is a great loss of time, sir, to travel without books,' answered the Doctor, quietly arranging them in the coach.

'Travel, my good friend? Why, you don't call it travelling to go four or five miles? why, if you had known me before my fall—However, I don't mean to make any comparisons, you gentlemen scholars being no particular good horsemen. However, if you were to go one hundred miles instead of four or five, you could not get through more than one of those books, read as hard as you please; unless you skip half, which I suppose you solid heads leave to the lower ignoramusses.'

'It is not for reading, sir, that I take all these books, but merely to look into. There are many of them I shall never read in my life, but I shall want them all.'

Sir Hugh now stared with increased perplexity; but Dr. Orkborne, as eager to go, since his books were to accompany him, as before to stay, told Jacob to bid the coachman make haste. Jacob looked at his master, who ordered him to mount his mare, and the carriage drove off.

The baronet, in some uneasiness, seated himself in the hall, to ruminate upon what he had just heard. The quietness and usual manner of speaking and looking of Dr. Orkborne, which he had remarked, removed any immediate apprehensions from the assertions of Jacob and Mary; but still he did not like the suggestion; and the carrying off so many books, when he acknowledged he did not mean to read one of them, disturbed him.

In every shadow of perplexity, his first wish was to consult with his brother; and if he had not parted with both his carriages, he would instantly have set off for Etherington. He sent, however, an express[1] for Mr. Tyrold, begging to see him at Cleves with all speed.

CHAPTER IV

An internal Detection

WHEN the chaise drove from Cleves Park, all attempt at any disguise was over with Camilla, who alive only to the horror of appearing ungrateful to Edgar, wept without controul; and, leaning back in the carriage, entreated Eugenia to dispense with all conversation.

Eugenia, filled with pity, wondered, but complied, and they travelled near four miles in silence; when, perceiving, over the paling round a paddock, Mrs. Arlbery and a party of company, Camilla dried her eyes, and prepared for her visit, of which the impetuosity of her feelings had retarded all previous consideration.

Eugenia, with true concern, saw the unfitness of her sister to appear, and proposed walking the rest of the way, in the hope that a little air and exercise might compose her spirits.

She agreed; they alighted, and bidding the footman keep with the carriage, which they ordered should drive slowly behind, they proceeded gently, arm in arm, along a clean raised bank by the side of the road, with a pace suiting at once the infirmity of Eugenia, and the wish of delay in Camilla.

The sound of voices reached them from within the paddock, though a thick shrubbery prevented their seeing the interlocutors.

'Can you make out the arms?' said one.

'No,' answered another, 'but I can see the postillion's livery, and I am certain it is Sir Hugh Tyrold's.'

'Then it is not coming hither,' said a third voice, which they recollected for Mrs. Arlbery's; 'we don't visit: though I should not dislike to see the old baronet. They tell me [he] is a humorist; and I have a taste for all oddities: but then he has a house full of females, and females I never admit in a morning, except when I have secured some men to take the entertaining them off my hands.

'Whither is Bellamy running?' cried another voice, 'he's off without a word.'

'Gone in hopes of a rencounter, I doubt not,' answered Mrs. Arlbery; 'he made palpable aim at one of the divinities of Cleves at the ball.'

Eugenia now grew uneasy. 'Let us be quick,' she whispered 'and enter the house!'

'Divinities! Lord! are they divinities?' said a girlish female voice; 'pray how old are they?'

'I fancy about seventeen.'

'Seventeen! gracious! I thought they'd been quite young; I wonder they a'n't married!'

'I presume, then, you intend to be more expeditious?' said another, whose voice spoke him to be General Kinsale.

'Gracious! I hope so, for I hate an old bride. I'll never marry at all, if I stay till I am eighteen.'

'A story goes about,' said the General, 'that Sir Hugh Tyrold has selected one of his nieces for his sole heiress; but no two people agree which it is; they have asserted it of each.'

'I was mightily taken with one of the girls,' said Mrs. Arlbery; 'there was something so pleasant in her looks and manner, that I even felt inclined to forgive her being younger and prettier than myself; but she turned out also to be more whimsical—and that there was no enduring.'

Camilla, extremely ashamed, was now upon the point of begging Eugenia to return, when a new speech seized all her attention.

'Do you know, General, when that beautiful automaton, Miss Lynmere, is to marry young Mandlebert?'

'Immediately, I understand; I am told he has fitted up his house very elegantly for her reception.'

A deep sigh escaped Camilla at such publicity in the report and belief of the engagement of Edgar with her cousin, and brought with it a consciousness too strong for any further self-disguise, that her distress flowed not all from an unjust accusation: the sound alone of the union struck as a dagger at her heart, and told her, incontrovertibly, who was its master.

Her sensations were now most painful: she grew pale, she became sick, and was obliged, in her turn, to lean upon Eugenia, who, affrighed to see her thus strangely disordered, besought her to go back to the chaise.

She consented, and begged to pass a few minutes there alone. Eugenia therefore stayed without, walking slowly upon the bank.

Camilla, getting into the carriage, pulled up the blinds, and, no longer self-deceived, lamented in a new burst of sorrow, her unhappy fate, and unpropitious attachment.

This consciousness, however, became soon a call upon her integrity, and her regret was succeeded by a summons upon propriety. She gave herself up as lost to all personal felicity, but hoped she had discovered the tendency of her affliction, in time to avoid the dangers, and the errors to which it might lead. She determined to struggle without cessation for the conquest of a partiality she deemed it treachery to indulge; and to appease any pain she now blushed to have caused to Indiana, by strictly following the hard prescription of Miss Margland, and the obvious opinion of Eugenia, in shunning the society, and no longer coveting the approbation of Edgar. 'Such, my dear father,' she cried, 'would be your lesson, if I dared consult you! such, my most honoured mother, would be your conduct, if thus cruelly situated!'

This thought thrilled through every vein with pleasure, in a sense of filial desert, and her sole desire was to return immediately to those incomparable parents, under whose roof she had experienced nothing but happiness, and in whose bosoms she hoped to bury every tumultuous disturbance.

These ideas and resolutions, dejecting, yet solacing, occupied her to the forgetfulness of her intended visit, and even of Eugenia, till the words: 'Pray let me come to you, my dear Camilla!' made her let down the blinds.

She then perceived Mr. Bellamy earnestly addressing her sister.

He had advanced suddenly towards her, by a short cut from the paddock, of which she was not aware, when she was about twenty yards from the chaise.

She made an effort to avoid him; but he planted himself in the way of her retreat, though with an air of supplication, with which she strove in vain to be angry.

He warmly represented the cruelty of thus flying him, entreated but the privilege of addressing her as a common acquaintance; and promised, upon that condition, to submit unmurmuring to her rejection.

Eugenia, though in secret she thought this request but equitable, made him no answer.

'O madam,' he cried, 'what have I not suffered since your barbarous letter! why will you be so amiable, yet so inexorable?'

She attempted to quicken her pace; but again, in the same manner, stopping her, he exclaimed: 'Do not kill me by this disdain! I ask not now for favour or encouragement—I know my hard doom—I ask only to converse with you—though, alas! it was by conversing with you I lost my heart.'

Eugenia felt softened; and her countenance, which had forfeited nothing of expression, though every thing of beauty, soon shewed Bellamy his advantage. He pursued it eagerly; depicted his passion, deprecated her severity, extolled her virtues and accomplishments, and bewailed his unhappy, hopeless flame.

Eugenia, knowing that all she said, and believing that all she heard issued from the fountain of truth, became extremely distressed. 'Let me pass, I conjure[1] you, Sir,' she cried, 'and do not take it ill—but I cannot hear you any longer.'

The vivacity of bright hope flashed into the sparkling eyes of Bellamy, at so gentle a remonstrance; and entreaties for lenity, declarations of passion, professions of submission, and practice of resistance, assailed the young Eugenia with a rapidity that confounded her: she heard him with scarce any opposition, from a fear of irritating his feelings, joined to a juvenile embarrassment how to treat with more severity so sincere and so humble a suppliant.

From this situation, to the extreme provocation of Bellamy, she was relieved by the appearance of Major Cerwood, who having observed, from the paddock, the slow motion of the carriage, had come forth to find out the cause.

Eugenia seized the moment of interruption to press forward, and make the call to her sister already mentioned; Bellamy accompanying and pleading, but no longer venturing to stop her: he handed her, therefore, to the chaise, where Major Cerwood also paid his compliments to the two ladies; and hearing they were going to the seat of Mrs. Arlbery, whither Camilla now forced herself, though more unwillingly than ever, he ran on, with Bellamy, to be ready to hand them from the carriage.

They were shewn into a parlour, while a servant went into the garden to call his mistress.

This interval was not neglected by either of the gentlemen, for Bellamy was scarce more eager to engage the attention of Eugenia, than the Major to force that of Camilla. By Lionel he had been informed she was heiress of Cleves; he deemed, therefore, the opportunity by no means to be thrown away, of making, what he believed required opportunity alone, a conquest of her young heart. Accustomed to think compliments always welcome to the fair, he construed her sadness into softness, and imputed her silence to the confusing impression made upon an inexperienced rural beauty, by the first assiduities of a man of figure and gallantry.

In about a quarter of an hour the servant of Mrs. Arlbery slowly returned, and, with some hesitation, said his lady was not at home. The gentlemen looked provoked, and Camilla and Eugenia, much disconcerted at so evident a denial, left their names, and returned to their carriage.

The journey back to Cleves was mute and dejected: Camilla was shocked at the conscious state of her own mind, and Eugenia was equally pensive. She began to think with anxiety of a contract with a person wholly unknown, and to consider the passion and constancy of Bellamy as the emanations of a truly elevated mind, and meriting her most serious gratitude.

At the hall door they were eagerly met by Sir Hugh, who, with infinite surprise, enquired where they had left Dr. Orkborne.

'Dr. Orkborne?' they repeated, 'we have not even seen him.'

'Not seen him? did not he come to fetch you?'

'No, Sir.'

'Why, he went to Mrs. Arlbery's on purpose! And what he stays for at that lady's, now you are both come away, is a thing I can't pretend to judge of; unless he has stopt to read one of those books he took with him; which is what I dare say is the case.'

'He cannot be at Mrs. Arlbery's, Sir,' said Eugenia, 'for we have but this moment left her house.'

'He must be there, my dear girls, for he's no where else. I saw him set out myself, which, however, I shan't mention the particulars of, having sent for my brother, whom I expect every minute.'

They then concluded he had gone by another road, as there were two ways to the Grove.

Edgar did not return to Cleves till the family were assembling to dinner. His visit to Mrs. Needham had occasioned him a new disturbance. She had rallied him upon the general rumour of his approaching marriage; and his confusion, from believing his partiality for Camilla detected, was construed into a confirmation of the report concerning Indiana. His disavowal was rather serious than strong, and involuntarily mixt with such warm eulogiums of the object he imagined to be meant, that Mrs. Needham, who had only named *a certain fair one at Cleves*, laughed at his denial, and thought the engagement undoubted.

With respect to his enquiries relative to Mrs. Arlbery, Mrs. Needham said, that she was a woman far more agreeable to the men, than to her own sex; that she was full of caprice, coquetry, and singularity; yet, though she abused the gift, she possessed an excellent and uncommon understanding. She was guilty of no vices, but utterly careless of appearances, and though her character was wholly unimpeached, she had offended or frightened almost all the county around, by a wilful strangeness of behaviour, resulting from an undaunted determination to follow in every thing the bent of her own humour.

Edgar justly deemed this a dangerous acquaintance for Camilla, whose natural thoughtlessness and vivacity made him dread the least imprudence in the connexions she might form; yet, as the reputation of Mrs. Arlbery was unsullied, he felt how difficult would be the task of demonstrating the perils he feared.

Sir Hugh, during the dinner, was exceedingly disturbed. 'What Dr. Orkborne can be doing with himself,' said he, 'is more than any man can tell, for he certainly would not stay at the lady's, when he found you were both come away; so that I begin to think it's ten to one but he's gone nobody knows where! for why else should he take all those books? which is a thing I have been thinking of ever since; especially as he owned himself he should never read one half of them. If he has taken something amiss, I am very ready to ask his pardon; though what it can be I don't pretend to guess.'

Miss Margland said, he was so often doing something or other that was ill-bred, that she was not at all surprised he should stay out at dinner time. He had never yet fetched her a chair, nor opened the door for her, since he came to the house; so that she did not know what was too bad to expect.

As they were rising from the table, a note arrived from Mr. Tyrold, with an excuse, that important business would prevent his coming to Cleves till the next day. Camilla then begged permission to go in the chaise that was to fetch him, flattering herself something might occur to detain her, when at Etherington. Sir Hugh readily assented, and composing himself for his afternoon nap, desired to be awaked if Dr. Orkborne came back.

All now left the room except Camilla, who, taking up a book, stood still at a window, till she was aroused by the voice of Edgar, who, from the Park, asked her what she was reading.

She turned over the leaves, ashamed at the question, to look for the title; she had held the book mechanically, and knew not what it was.

He then produced the promised nosegay, which had been brought by his gardener during her excursion. She softly lifted up the sash, pointing to her sleeping uncle; he gave it her with a silent little bow, and walked away; much disappointed to miss an opportunity from which he had hoped for some explanation.

She held it in her hand some time, scarcely sensible she had taken it, till, presently, she saw its buds bedewed with her falling tears.

She shook them off, and pressed the nosegay to her bosom.

'This, at least,' she cried, 'I may accept, for it was offered me before that barbarous attack. Ah! they know not the innocence of my regard, or they would not so wrong it! The universe could not tempt me to injure my cousin, though it is true, I have valued the kindness of Edgar—and I must always value it!— These flowers are more precious to me, coming from his hands, and reared in his grounds, than all the gems of the East could be from any other possessor. But where is the guilt of such a prefer-ence? And who that knows him could help feeling it?'

Sir Hugh now awakening from a short slumber, exclaimed— 'I have just found out the reason why this poor gentleman has made off; I mean, provided he is really gone away, which, how-ever, I hope not: but I think, by his bringing down all those books, he meant to give me a broad hint, that he had got no proper book-case to keep them in; which the maids as good as think too.'

Then, calling upon Camilla, he asked if she was not of that opinion.

'Y--e--s, Sir,' she hesitatingly answered.

'Well, then, my dear, if we all think the same, I'll give orders immediately for getting the better of that fault.'

Miss Margland, curious to know how Camilla was detained, now re-entered the room. Struck with the fond and melancholy air with which she was bending over her nosegay, she abruptly demanded—'Pray, where might you get those flowers?'

Covered with shame, she could make no answer.

'O, Miss Camilla! Miss Camilla!—ought not those flowers to belong to Miss Lynmere?'

'Mr. Mandlebert had promised me them yesterday morning,' answered she, in a voice scarce audible.

'And is this fair, Ma'am?—can you reckon it honourable?—I'll be judged by Sir Hugh himself. Do you think it right, Sir, that Miss Camilla should accept nosegays every day from Mr. Mandlebert, when her cousin has had never a one at all?'

'Why, it's not her fault, you know, Miss Margland, if young Mr. Mandlebert chuses to give them to her. However, if that vexes Indiana, I'm sure my niece will make them over to her with the greatest pleasure; for I never knew the thing she would not part with, much more a mere little smell at the nose, which, whether one has it or not, can't much matter after it's over.'

Miss Margland now exultingly held out her hand: the decision was obliged to be prompt; Camilla delivered up the flowers, and ran into her own room.

The sacrifice, cried she, is now complete! Edgar will conclude I hate him, and believe Indiana loves him!—no matter!—it is fitting he should think both. I will be steady this last evening, and to-morrow I will quit this fatal roof!

CHAPTER V

An Author's Opinion of Visiting

WHEN summoned to tea, Camilla, upon entering the parlour, found Sir Hugh in mournful discourse with Edgar upon the non-appearance of Dr. Orkborne. Edgar felt a momentary disappointment that she did not honour his flowers with wearing them; but consoled himself with supposing she had preserved them in water. In a few minutes, however, Indiana appeared with them in her bosom.

Almost petrified, he turned towards Camilla, who, affecting an air of unconcern, amused herself with patting a favourite old terrier of her uncle's.

As soon as he could disengage himself from the Baronet, he leant also over the dog, and, in a low voice, said—'You have discarded, then, my poor flowers?'

'Have I not done right?' answered she, in the same tone; 'are they not where you must be far happier to see them?'

'Is it possible,' exclaimed he, 'Miss Camilla Tyrold can suppose——'. He stopt, for surprised off his guard, he was speaking loud, and he saw Miss Margland approaching.

'Don't you think, Mr. Mandlebert,' said she, 'that Miss Lynmere becomes a bouquet very much? she took a fancy to those flowers, and I think they are quite the thing for her.'

'She does them,' he coldly answered, 'too much honour.'

Ah, Heaven! he loves her not! thought Camilla, and, while trembling between hope and terror at the suggestion, determined to redouble her circumspection, not to confirm the suspicion that his indifference was produced by her efforts to attach him to herself.

She had soon what she conceived to be an occasion for its exertion. When he handed her some cakes, he said—'You would think it, I conclude, impertinent to hear anything more concerning Mrs. Arlbery, now you have positively opened an acquaintance with her?'

She felt the justice of this implied reproach of her broken promise; but she saw herself constantly watched by Miss Margland, and repressing the apology she was sighing to offer, only answered—'You have nothing, you own, to say against her reputation—and as to any thing else——'

'True,' interrupted he, 'my information on that point is all still in her favour: but can it be Miss Camilla Tyrold, who holds that to be the sole question upon which intimacy ought to depend? Does she account as nothing manners, disposition, way of life?'

'No, not absolutely as nothing,' said she, rising; 'but taste settles all those things, and mine is entirely in her favour.'

Edgar gravely begged her pardon, for so officiously resuming an irksome subject; and returning to Sir Hugh, endeavoured to listen to his lamentations and conjectures about Dr. Orkborne.

He felt, however, deeply hurt. In naming Mrs. Arlbery, he had flattered himself he had opened an opportunity for which she must herself be waiting, to explain the motives of her late visit; but her light answer put an end to that hope, and her quitting her seat shewed her impatient of further counsel.

Not a word that fell from Sir Hugh reached his ear: but he bowed from time to time, and the good Baronet had no doubt of his attention. His eyes were perpetually following Camilla, though they met not a glance from her in return. She played with the terrier, talked with Eugenia, looked out of the window, turned over some books, and did everything with an air of negligence, that while it covered absence and anxiety, displayed a studied avoidance of his notice.

The less he could account for this, the more it offended him. And dwells caprice, thought he, while his eye followed her, even there! in that fair composition!—where may I look for single-ness of mind, for nobleness of simplicity, if caprice, mere girlish, unmeaning caprice, dwell there!

The moment she had finished her tea, she left the room, to shorten her cruel task. Struck with the broken sentence of 'is it

possible Miss Camilla Tyrold can suppose——' the soft hope
that his heart was untouched by Indiana, seized her delighted
imagination; but the recollection of Miss Margland's assertions,
that it was the real right of her cousin, soon robbed the hope of all
happiness, and she could only repeat—To-morrow I will go!—I
ought not to think of him!—I had rather be away—to-morrow I
will go!

She had hardly quitted the parlour, when the distant sound of a
carriage roused Sir Hugh from his fears; and, followed by Edgar
and the ladies, he made what haste he could into the courtyard, where, to his infinite satisfaction, he saw his coach driving in.

He ordered it should stop immediately, and called out—'Pray,
Dr. Orkborne, are you there?'

Dr. Orkborne looked out of the window, and bowed
respectfully.

'Good lack, I could never have thought I should be so glad to
see you! which you must excuse, in point of being no relation.
You are heartily welcome, I assure you; I was afraid I should
never see you again; for, to tell you the honest truth, which I
would not say a word of before, I had got a notion you were going
out of your mind.'

The Doctor took not the smallest heed of his speech, and the
carriage drove up to the door. Sir Hugh then seating himself
under the portico, said—'Pray, Dr. Orkborne, before you go to
your studies, may I just ask you how you came to stay out all day?
and why you never fetched Eugenia? for I take it for granted it's
no secret, on the account Jacob was with you; besides the coachman and horses.'

Dr. Orkborne, though not at all discomposed by these
questions, nor by his reception, answered, that he must first collect
his books.

'The poor girls,' continued the Baronet, 'came home quite
blank; not that they knew a word of my asking you to go for them,
till I told them; which was lucky enough, for the sake of not
frightening them. However, where you can have been, particularly
with regard to your dinner, which, I suppose, you have gone
without, is what I can't guess; unless you'd be kind enough to tell
me.'

The Doctor, too busy to hear him, was packing up his books.

'Come, never mind your books,' said Sir Hugh; 'Jacob can

carry them for you, or Bob, or any body. Here, Bob, (calling to the postillion, who, with all the rest of the servants, had been drawn by curiosity into the courtyard) whisk me up those books, and take them into the Doctor's room; I mean, provided you can find a place for them, which I am sorry to say there is none; owing to my not knowing better in point of taking the proper care; which I shall be sure to do for the future.'

The boy obeyed, and mounting one step of the coach, took what were within his reach; which, when the Doctor observed, he snatched away with great displeasure, saying, very solemnly, he had rather at any time be knocked down, than see any body touch one of his books or papers.

Jacob, coming forward, whispered his master not to interfere; assuring him, he was but just got out of one of his tantarums.[1]

Sir Hugh, a little startled, rose to return to the parlour, begging Dr. Orkborne to take his own time, and not hurry himself.

He then beckoned Jacob to follow him.

'There is certainly something in all this,' said he to Edgar, 'beyond what my poor wit can comprehend: but I'll hear what Jacob has to say before I form a complete judgment; though, to be sure, his lugging out all those books to go but four or five miles, has but an odd look; which is what I don't like to say.'

Jacob now was called upon to give a narrative of the day's adventures. 'Why, you Honour,' said he, 'as soon as we come to the Grove, I goes up to the coach door, to ask the Doctor if he would get out, or only send in to let the young ladies know he was come for them; but he was got so deep into some of his larning, that, I dare say, I bawled it three good times in his ears, before he so much as lifted up his head; and then it was only to say, I put him out! and to it he went again, just as if I'd said never a word; till, at last, I was so plaguy mad, I gives the coach such a jog, to bring him to himself like, that it jerked the pencil and paper out of his hand. So then he went straight into one of his takings,[2] pretending I had made him forget all his thoughts, and such like out of the way talk, after his old way. So when I found he was going off in that manner, I thought it only time lost to say no more to him, and so I turned me about not to mind him; when I sees a whole heap of company at a parlour window, laughing so hearty, that I was sure they had heard us. And a fine comely lady, as clever as ever you see, that I found after was the lady of the house, bid me come to the window, and asked what I wanted. So I told her we was come for two of the Miss Tyrolds. Why, says she, they've been gone a quarter of an hour, by the opposite road. So then I was coming away, but she made me a sign to come into the parlour, for all it was brimful of fine company, dressed all like I don't know what. It was as pretty a sight as you'd wish to see. And then, your honour, they all begun upon me at once! there was such a clatter, I thought I'd been turned into a booth at a fair; and merry enough they all was sure!—'specially the lady, who never opened her lips, but what they all laughed: but as to all what they asked me, I could as soon conjure a ghost as call a quarter of it to mind.'

'Try, however,' said Edgar, curious for further information of whatever related to Mrs. Arlbery.

'Why as to that, 'squire,' answered Jacob, with an arch look, 'I am not so sure and certain you'd like to hear it all.'

'No? and why not?'

'O! pray tell, Jacob,' cried Miss Margland; 'did they say anything of Mr. Mandlebert?'

'Yes, and of more than Mr. Mandlebert,' said Jacob, grinning.

'Do tell, do tell,' cried Indiana, eagerly.

'I'm afeard, Miss!'

Every body assured him no offence should be taken.

'Well, then, if you must needs know, there was not one of you, but what they had a pluck at.—Pray, says one of them, what does the old gentleman do with all those books and papers in the coach?—That's what nobody knows, says I, unless his head's cracked, which is Mary's opinion.—Then they all laughed more and more, and the lady of the house said:—Pray can he really read?—Whoo! says I, why he does nothing else; he's at it from morning till night, and Mary says she's sure before long he'll give up his meat and drink for it.—I've always heard he was a quiz, says another, or a quoz,[1] or some such word; but I did not know he was such a book-worm.—The old quoz is generous, however, I hear, says another, pray do you find him so?—As to that, I can't say, says I, for I never see the colour of his money.—No! then, what are you such a fool as to serve him for?—So, then, your honour, I found, owing to the coach and the arms, and the like, they thought all the time it was your honour was in the coach. I hope your honour don't take it amiss of me?'

'Not at all Jacob; only I don't know why they call me an old quiz and quoz for; never having offended them; which I take rather unkind; especially not knowing what it means.'

'Why, your honour, they're such comical sort of folks; they don't mind what they say of nobody. Not but what the lady of the house is a rare gentlewoman. Your honour could not help liking her. I warrant she's made many a man's heart ache, and then jumped for joy when she'd done. And as to her eyes, I think in my born days I never see nothing like 'em: they shines like two candles on a dark night afar off on the common———.'

'Why Jacob,' said Sir Hugh, 'I see you have lost your heart. However, go on.'

'Why, as soon as I found out what they meant—That my master? says I, no, God be thanked! What should I have to live upon if a was? Not so much as a cobweb! for there would not be wherewithal for a spider to make it.'

Here Sir Hugh, with much displeasure, interrupted him; 'As to the poor gentleman's being poor,' said he, 'it's no fault of his own, for he'd be rich if he could, I make no doubt; never having heard he was a gambler. Besides which, I always respect a man the more for being poor, knowing how little a rich man may have in him; which I can judge by my own case.'

Jacob proceeded.

'Well, if it is not Sir Hugh, says one of them, who is it?—Why, it's only our Latin master, says I; upon which they all set up as jolly a laugh again as ever I heard in my days. Jobbins, they're pure merry!—And who learns Latin! says one, I hope they don't let him work at poor old Sir Hugh? No, says I, they tried their hands with him at first, but he thanked 'em for nothing. He soon grew tired on't.—So then they said, who learns now, says they, do you?—Me! says I, no, God be praised, I don't know *A* from *B*, which is the way my head's so clear, never having muddled it with what I don't understand.—And so then they all said I was a brave fellow; and they ordered me a glass of wine.'

What a set! thought Edgar, is this, idle, dissipated, curious— for Camilla to associate with!—the lively, the unthinking, the inexperienced Camilla!

'So then they asked me, says they, does Miss Lynmere learn, says they?—Not, as I know of, says I, she's no great turn for her book, as ever I heard of; which I hope Miss you won't take ill, for they all said, no, to be sure, she's too handsome for that.'

Indiana looked uncertain whether to be flattered or offended.

'But you have not told us what they said of Mr. Mandlebert yet?' cried Miss Margland.

'No, I must come to you first, Miss,' answered he, 'for that's what they come upon next. But mayhap I must not tell?'

'O yes, you may;' said she, growing a little apprehensive of some affront, but determined not to seem hurt by it; 'I am very indifferent to any thing they can say of me, assure yourself!'

'Why, I suppose, says they, this Latin master studies chiefly with the governess?—They'd study fisty-cuffs I believe, if they did, says I, for she hates him like poison; and there's no great love lost between them.'

'And what right had you to say that, Mr. Jacob? I did not ask what you said. Not that I care, I promise you!'

'Why, some how, they got it all out; they were so merry and so full of their fun, I could not be behind hand.[1] But I hope no offence?'

'O dear no! I'm sure it's not worth while.'

'They said worse than I did,' resumed Jacob, 'by a deal; they said, says they, she looks duced crabbed—she looks just as if she was always eating a sour apple, says the lady; she looks—'

'Well, well, I don't want to hear any more of their opinions. I may look as I please I hope. I hate such gossiping.'

'So then they said, pray does Miss Camilla learn? says they;— Lord love her, no! says I.'

'And what said they to that?' cried Edgar.

'Why, they said, they hoped not, and they were glad to hear it, for they liked her the best of all. And what does the ugly one do? says they.—'

'Come, we have heard enough now,' interrupted Edgar, greatly shocked for poor Eugenia, who fortunately, however, had retired with Camilla.

Sir Hugh too, angrily broke in upon him, saying: 'I won't have my niece called ugly, Jacob! you know it's against my commands such a thing's being mentioned.'

'Why, I told 'em so, sir,' said Jacob; 'ugly one, says I, she you call the ugly one, is one of the best ladies in the land. She's ready to lend a hand to every mortal soul; she's just like my master for that. And as to learning, I make no quæry she can talk you over the Latin grammar as fast as e'er a gentleman here. So then they laughed harder than ever, and said they should be afeard to speak to her, and a deal more I can't call to mind.—So then they come to Mr. Mandlebert. Pray, says they, what's he doing among you all this time?—Why, nothing particular, says I, he's only squiring about our young ladies.—But when is this wedding to be? says another. So then I said—'

'What did you say?' cried Edgar hastily.

'Why—nothing,' answered Jacob, drawing back.

'Tell us, however, what they said,' cried Miss Margland.

'Why, they said, says they, everything has been ready some time at Beech Park;—and they'll make as handsome a couple as ever was seen.'

'What stuff is this!' cried Edgar, 'do prithee have done.'—

'No, no,' said Miss Margland; 'go on, Jacob!'

Indiana, conscious and glowing at the words handsome couple, could not restrain a simper; but Edgar, thinking only of Camilla, did not understand it.

'He'll have trouble enough, says one of the gentlemen,' continued Jacob, 'to take care of so pretty a wife.—She'll be worth a little trouble, says another, for I think she is the most beautifullest girl I ever see—Take my word of it, says the lady of the house, young Mandlebert is a man who won't be made a fool of; he'll have his own way, for all her beauty.'

'What a character to give of me to young ladies!' cried Edgar, doubtful, in his turn, whether to be hurt or gratified.

'O she did not stop at that, sir,' resumed Jacob, 'for she said, I make no question, says she, but in half a year he'll lock her up.'

Indiana, surprized, gave an involuntary little shriek: but Edgar, not imputing it to any appropriate alarm, was filled with resentment against Mrs. Arlbery. What incomprehensible injustice! he said to himself: O Camilla! is it possible any event, any circumstance upon earth, could induce me to practise such an outrage? to degenerate into such a savage?

'Is this all?' asked Miss Margland.

'No, ma'am; but I don't know if Miss will like to hear the rest.'

'O yes,' said Indiana, 'if it's about me, I don't mind.'

'Why, they all said, Miss, you'd make the most finest bride that ever was seen, and they did not wonder at Mr. Mandlebert's chusing you; but for all that—.'

He stopt, and Edgar, who, following the bent of his own

thoughts, had till now concluded Camilla to be meant, was utterly confounded by discovering his mistake. The presence of Indiana redoubled the aukwardness of the situation, and her blushes, and the increased lustre of her eyes, did not make the report seem either unwelcome, or perfectly new to her.

Miss Margland raised her head triumphantly. This was precisely such a circumstance as she flattered herself would prove decisive.

The Baronet, equally pleased, returned her nod of congratulation, and nodding himself towards Edgar, said; 'you're blown,[1] you see! but what matters secrets about nothing? which, Lord help me, I never knew how to keep.'

Edgar was now still more disconcerted, and, from mere distress what to say or do, bid Jacob go on.

'Why then, they said a deal more, how pretty she was, he continued, but they did not know how it would turn out, for the young lady was so much admired, that her husband had need look sharp after her; and if—'

'What complete impertinence!' cried Edgar, walking about the room; 'I really can listen no longer.'

'If he had done wisely, says the lady of the house, he would have left the professed beauty, and taken that pretty Camilla.'

Edgar surprized, stopt short; this seemed to him less impertinent.

'Camilla is a charming creature, says she; though she may want a little watching too; but so does every thing that is worth having.'

That woman does not want discernment, thought Edgar, nor she does not want taste.—I can never totally dislike her, if she does such justice to Camilla.

He now again invited Jacob to proceed; but Indiana, with a pouting lip, walked out of the room, and Miss Margland said, there was not need to be hearing him all night.

Jacob, therefore, when no more either interrupted or encouraged, soon finished his narrative. Mrs. Arlbery, amused by watching Dr. Orkborne, had insisted, for an experiment, that Jacob should not return to the coach till he was missed and called for; and so intense was the application of the Doctor to what he was composing, that this did not happen till the whole family had dined; Jacob and the coachman, at the invitation of Mrs. Arlbery, having partaken of the servants' fare, equally pleased with the regale and the joke. Dr. Orkborne then, suddenly recollecting himself, demanded why the young ladies were so late, and was much discomposed and astonished when he heard they were gone. Mrs. Arlbery invited him into the house, and offered him refreshments, while she ordered water and a feed of corn for the horses; but he only fretted a little, and then went on again with his studies.

Sir Hugh now sent some cold dinner into the Doctor's room, and declared he should always approve his niece's acquaintance with Mrs. Arlbery, as she was so kind to his servants and his animals.

CHAPTER VI

An Author's Idea of Order

NOT a bosom of the Cleves party enjoyed much tranquillity this evening. Miss Margland, though to the Baronet she would not recede from her first assertions, strove vainly to palliate to herself the ill grace and evident dissatisfaction with which Edgar had met the report. To save her own credit, however, was always her primary consideration; she resolved, therefore, to cast upon unfair play in Camilla, or upon the instability of Edgar, all the blame really due to her own undiscerning self-sufficiency.

Indiana thought so little for herself, that she adopted, of course, every opinion of Miss Margland; yet the immoveable coldness of Edgar, contrasted frequently in her remembrance by the fervour of Melmond and of Macdersey, became more and more distasteful to her; and Mrs. Arlbery's idea, that she should be locked up in half a year, made her look upon him alternately as something to shun or to over-reach. She even wished to refuse him:—but Beech Park, the equipage, the servants, the bridal habiliment.—No! she could enjoy those, if not him. And neither her own feelings, nor the lessons of Miss Margland, had taught her to look upon marriage in any nobler point of view.

But the person most deeply dissatisfied this evening was Edgar. He now saw that, deceived by his own consciousness, he had misunderstood Mrs. Needham, who, as well as Mrs. Arlbery, he was convinced concluded him engaged to Indiana. He had observed with concern the approving credulity of Sir Hugh, and though glad to find his real plan, and all his wishes unsuspected, the false report excited his fears, lest Indiana should give it any credit, and secretly hurt his delicacy for the honour of his taste.

All the influence of pecuniary motives to which he deemed Camilla superior, occurred to him in the very words of Dr. Marchmont for Indiana; whose capacity he saw was as shallow as her person was beautiful. Yet the admiration with which she had already made her first appearance in the world, might naturally induce her belief of his reported devotion. If, therefore, his situation appeared to her to be eligible, she had probably settled to accept him.

The most timid female delicacy was not more scrupulous, than the manly honour of Edgar to avoid this species of misapprehension; and though perfectly confident his behaviour had been as irreproachable as it was undesigning, the least idea of any self-delusion on the part of Indiana, seemed a call upon his integrity for the most unequivocal manifestation of his intentions. Yet any declaration by words, with whatever care selected, might be construed into an implication that he concluded the decision in his own hands. And though he could scarcely doubt the fact, he justly held nothing so offensive as the palpable presumption. One only line of conduct appeared to him, therefore, unexceptionable; which was wholly to avoid her, till the rumour sunk into its own nothingness.

This demanded from him a sacrifice the most painful, that of retiring from Cleves in utter ignorance of the sentiments of Camilla; yet it seemed the more necessary, since he now, with much uneasiness, recollected many circumstances which his absorbed mind had hitherto suffered to pass unnoticed, that led him to fear Sir Hugh himself, and the whole party, entertained the same notion.

He was shocked to consider Camilla involved in such a deception, though delighted by the idea he might perhaps owe to an explanation, some marks of that preference for which Dr. Marchmont had taught him to wait, and which he now hoped might lie dormant from the persuasion of his engagement. To clear this mistake was, therefore, every way essential, as otherwise the very purity of her character must be in his disfavour.

Still, however, the visit to the Grove hung upon his mind, and he resolved to investigate its cause the following morning, before he made his retreat.

Early the next day, Camilla sent to hasten the chaise which was to fetch Mr. Tyrold, and begged leave of her uncle to breakfast at Etherington. His assent was always ready; and believing every evil would yield to absence, she eagerly, and even with happiness set off.

When the rest of the party assembled without her, Edgar, surprised, enquired if she were well? Miss Margland answered yes; but for the sake of what she loved best in the world, a frolic, she was gone in the chaise to Etherington. Edgar could not prevail with himself to depart till he had spoken with her, and privately deferred his purposed leave-taking till noon.

During this report, Sir Hugh was anxiously engaged in some business he seemed to wish to conceal. He spoke little, but nodded frequently to himself, with an air of approving his own ideas; he summoned Jacob to him repeatedly, with whom he held various whispering conferences; and desired Miss Margland, who made the tea, not to pour it out too fast, as he was in no hurry to have breakfast over.

When nothing he could urge succeeded, in making any of the company eat or drink any thing more, he pulled Edgar by the sleeve; and, in an eager but low voice, said, 'My dear Mr. Edgar, I have a great favour to beg of you, which is only that you will do something to divert Dr. Orkborne.'

'I should be very happy, Sir,' cried Edgar, smiling, 'but I much doubt my capability.'

'Why, my dear Mr. Edgar, it's only to keep him from finding out my new surprise till it's got ready. And if you will but just spout out to him a bit or two of Virgil and Horace, or some of those Greek and Latin language-masters, he'll be in no hurry to budge, I promise you.'

A request from Sir Hugh, who with the most prompt alacrity met the wishes of everyone, was by Edgar held to be indisputable. He advanced, therefore, to Dr. Orkborne, who was feeling for his tablets,[1] which he commonly examined in his way up the stairs, and started a doubt, of which he begged an exposition, upon a passage of Virgil.

Dr. Orkborne willingly stopt, and displayed, with no small satisfaction, an erudition, that did him nearly as much honour in the ears of the ignorant and admiring Sir Hugh, as in those of the cultivated and well-judging Edgar. 'Ah!' said the Baronet, sighing, though addressing himself to no one, 'if I had but addicted myself to these studies in due season, I might have understood all this too! though now I can't for my life make out much sense of what they're talking of; nor a little neither, indeed, as to that; thanks to my own idleness; to which, however, I am not much obliged.'

Unfortunately, the discussion soon led to some points of comparison, that demanded a review of various authors, and the doctor proposed adjourning to his own apartment. The Baronet winked at Edgar, who would have changed the discourse, or himself have sought the books, or have been satisfied without them; but Dr. Orkborne was as eager here, as in other matters he was slow and phlegmatic; and, regardless of all opposition, was making off, when Sir Hugh, catching him by the arm, exclaimed, 'My good friend, I beg it as a particular favour, you won't stir a step!'

'Not stir a step, Sir?' repeated the doctor, amazed.

'That is, not to your own room.'

'Not go to my own room, Sir?'

The Baronet gently begged him not to take it amiss, and presently, upon the appearance of Jacob, who entered with a significant smile, said, he would keep him no longer.

Dr. Orkborne, to whom nothing was so irksome as a moment's detention from his books and papers, instantly departed, inviting Edgar to accompany him; but without troubling himself to inquire for what end he had been held back.

When they were gone, Sir Hugh, rubbing his hands, said, 'Well, I think this good gentleman won't go about the country again, with all his books fastened about him, to shew he has nowhere to put them: for as to his telling me he only took them to look at, I am not quite such an ignoramus, with all my ignorance, as to believe such a thing as that, especially of a regular bred scholar.'

A loud and angry sound of voices from above here interrupted the pleased harangue of the Baronet; Miss Margland opened the door to listen, and, with no small delight, heard words, scarce intelligible for rage, breaking from Dr. Orkborne, whose anger, while Edgar was endeavouring to moderate, Jacob and Mary were vociferously resenting.

Sir Hugh, all astonished, feared there was some mistake. He had sent, the preceding day, as far as Winchester, for two book-cases, which he had ordered should arrive early, and be put up during the breakfast; and he had directed Mary to place upon the shelves, with great care, all the loose books and papers she found dispersed about the room, as neatly as possible: after which Jacob was to give notice when all was arranged.

The words now 'If I must have my manuscripts rummaged at pleasure, by every dunce in the house, I would rather lie in the street!' distinctly caught their ears. Sir Hugh was thunderstruck with amazement and disappointment, but said nothing. Miss Margland looked all spite and pleasure, and Eugenia all concern.

Louder yet, and with accents of encreasing asperity, the Doctor next exclaimed 'A twelvemonth's hard labour will not repair this mischief! I should have been much more obliged to you if you had blown out my brains!'

The Baronet, aghast, cried, 'Lord help us! I think I had best go and get the shelves pulled down again, what I have done not being meant to offend, being what will cost me ten pounds and up-wards.'

He then, though somewhat irresolute, whether or not to proceed, moved towards the foot of the stairs; but there a new storm of rage startled him. 'I wish you had been all of you annihilated ere ever you had entered my room! I had rather have lost my ears than that manuscript! I wish with all my heart you had been at the bottom of the sea, every one of you, before you had touched it!'

'If you won't believe me, it can't be helped,' said Mary; 'but if I was to tell it you over and over, I've done nothing to no mortal thing. I only just swept the room after the carpenter was gone, for it was all in such a pickle it was a shame to be seen.'

'You have ruined me!' cried he, 'you have swept it behind the fire, I make not a moment's doubt; and I had rather you had given me a bowl of poison! you can make me no reparation; it was a clue to a whole section.'

'Well, I won't make no more words about it,' said Mary, angrily; 'but I'm sure I never so much as touched it with a pair of tongs, for I never see it; nor I don't so much as know it if I do.'

'Why, it's a piece of paper written all over; look! just such another as this: I left it on the table, by this corner—'

'O! that?' cried Mary; 'yes, I remember that.'

'Well, where is it? What have you done with it?'

'Why, I happened of a little accident about that;—for as I was a sweeping under the table, the broom knocked the ink down; but, by good luck, it only fell upon that little morsel of paper.'

'Little morsel of paper? it's more precious than a whole library! But what did you do with it? what is become of it? whatever condition it is in, if you have but saved it—where is it, I say?'

'Why—it was all over ink, and good for nothing, so I did not think of your missing it—so I throwed it behind the fire.'

'I wish you had been thrown there yourself with all my heart! But if ever you bring a broom into my room again—'

'Why, I did nothing but what my master ordered—'

'Or if ever you touch a paper, or a book of mine, again—'

'My master said himself—'

'Your master's a blockhead! and you are another—go away, I say!'

Mary now hurried out of the room, enraged for her master, and frightened for herself; and Edgar, not aware Sir Hugh was within hearing, soon succeeded in calming the doctor, by mildly listening to his lamentations.

Sir Hugh, extremely shocked, sat upon the stairs to recover himself. Miss Margland, who never felt so virtuous, and never so elated, as when witnessing the imperfections or improprieties of others, descanted largely against ingratitude; treating an unmeaning sally of passion as a serious mark of turpitude: but Eugenia, ashamed for Dr. Orkborne, to whom, as her preceptor, she felt a constant disposition to be partial, determined to endeavour to induce him to make some apology. She glided, therefore, past her uncle, and tapped at the doctor's door.

Mary, seeing her master so invitingly in her way, could by no means resist her desire of appeal and complaint; and, descending the stairs, begged his honour to hear her.

'Mary,' said he, rising, and returning to the parlour, 'you need not tell me a word, for I have heard it all myself; by which it may be truly said, listeners never hear good of themselves; so I've got the proper punishment; for which reason, I hope you won't look upon it as an example.'

'I am sure, Sir,' said Mary, 'if your honour can excuse his speaking so disrespectful, it's what nobody else can; and if it was not for thinking as his head's got a crack in it, there is not a servant among us as would not affront him for it.'

The Baronet interrupted her with a serious lecture upon the civility he expected for all his guests; and she promised to restrain her wrath; 'But only, sir,' she continued, 'if your honour had seen the bit of paper as he made such a noise at me for, your honour would not have believed it. Not a soul could have read it. My Tom would ha' been well licked if he'd wrote no better at school. And as to his being a twelvemonth a scrawling such another, I'll no more believe it than I'll fly. It's as great a fib as ever was told.'

Sir Hugh begged her to be quiet, and to think no more of the matter.

'No, your honour, I hope I'm not a person as bears malice; only I could not but speak of it, because he behaves more comical every day. I thought he'd ha' beat me over and over. And as to the stories he tells about them little bits of paper, mortal patience can't bear it no longer.'

The remonstrance of Eugenia took immediate effect. Dr. Orkborne, shocked and alarmed at the expression which had escaped him, protested himself willing to make the humblest reparation, and truly declared, he had been so greatly disturbed by the loss he had just sustained, that he not merely did not mean, but did not know what he had said.

Edgar was the bearer of his apology, which Sir Hugh accepted with his usual good humour. 'His calling me a blockhead,' cried he, 'is a thing I have no right to resent, because I take it for granted, he would not have said it, if he had not thought it; and a man's thoughts are his castle, and ought to be free.'

Edgar repeated the protestation, that he had been hurried on by passion, and spoke without meaning.

'Why, then, my dear Mr. Edgar, I must fairly own I don't see the great superiorness of learning, if it can't keep a man's temper out of a passion. However, say nothing of the sort to poor Clermont, upon his coming over, who I expect won't speak one word in ten I shall understand; which, however, as it's all been done for the best, I would not have the poor boy discouraged in.'

He then sent a kind message by Edgar to Dr. Orkborne, desiring him not to mind such a trifle.

This conciliating office was congenial to the disposition of Edgar, and softened his impatience for the return of Camilla, but when, soon after, a note arrived from Mr. Tyrold, requesting Sir Hugh to dispense with seeing him till the next day, and apologising for keeping his daughter, he felt equally disappointed and provoked, though he determined not to delay any longer his departure. He gave orders, therefore, for his horses immediately, and with all the less regret, for knowing Camilla no longer in the circle he was to quit.

The ladies were in the parlour with Sir Hugh, who was sorrowfully brooding over his brother's note, when he entered it to take leave. Addressing himself somewhat rapidly to the Baronet, he told him he was under an unpleasant necessity, to relinquish some days of the month's sojourn intended for him. He made acknowledgments full of regard for his kindness and hospitality; and then, only bowing to the ladies, left the room, before the astonished Sir Hugh comprehended he was going.

'Well,' cried Miss Margland, 'this is curious indeed! He has flown off from everything, without even an apology!'

'I hope he is not really gone?' said Eugenia, walking to the window.

'I'm sure I don't care what he does,' cried Indiana, 'he's welcome to go or to stay. I'm grown quite sick of him, for my part.'

'Gone?' said Sir Hugh, recovering breath; 'it's impossible! Why, he never has said one word to me of the day, nor the settlements, nor all those things!'

He then rang the bell, and sent to desire Mr. Mandlebert might be called immediately.

Edgar, who was mounting his horse, obeyed with some chagrin. As soon as he re-entered the room, Sir Hugh cried; 'My dear Mr. young Edgar, it's something amazing to me you should think of going away without coming to an explanation?'

'An explanation, sir?'

'Yes, don't you know what I mean?'

'Not in the least, sir,' cried Edgar, staggered by a doubt whether he suspected what he felt for Camilla, or referred to what was reported of Indiana.

'Why, then, my pretty dear,' said Sir Hugh to Indiana, 'you won't object, I hope, to taking a little walk in the garden, provided it is not disagreeable to you; for you had better not hear what we are going to talk about before your face.'

Indiana, pouting her beautiful under lip, and scornfully passing Edgar, complied. Eugenia accompanied her; but Miss Margland kept her ground.

Sir Hugh, always unwilling to make any attack, and at a loss how to begin, simply said; 'Why, I thought Mr. Mandlebert, you would stay with us till next year?'

Edgar only bowed.

'Why, then, suppose you do?'

'Most probably, sir, I shall by that time be upon the Continent. If some particular circumstance does not occur, I purpose shortly making the tour of Europe.'

Sir Hugh now lost all guard and all restraint, and with un-disguised displeasure exclaimed; 'So here's just the second part of Clermont! at the moment I sent for him home, thinking he would come to put the finish to all my cares about Eugenia, he sends me word he must travel!—And though the poor girl took it very well, from knowing nothing of the matter, I can't say I take it very kind of you, Mr. young Edgar, to come and do just the same by Indiana!'

The surprize of Edgar was unspeakable: that Sir Hugh should wish the relation of Jacob, with respect to Indiana, confirmed, he could not wonder; but that his wishes should have amounted to expectations, and that he should deem his niece ill used by their failure, gave him the most poignant astonishment.

Miss Margland, taking advantage of his silent consternation, began now to pour forth very volubly, the most pointed reflections upon the injury done to young ladies by reports of this nature, which were always sure to keep off all other offers. There was no end, she said, to the admirers who had deserted Indiana in despair; and she questioned if she would ever have any more, from the general belief of her being actually pre-engaged.

Edgar, whose sense of honour was tenaciously delicate, heard her with a mixture of concern for Indiana, and indignation against herself, that kept him long uninterrupted; for though burning to assert the integrity of his conduct, the fear of uttering a word that might be offensive to Indiana, embarrassed and checked him.

Sir Hugh, who in seeing him overpowered, concluded he was relenting, now kindly took his hand, and said: 'My dear Mr. Mandlebert, if you are sorry for what you were intending, of going away, and leaving us all in the lurch, why, you shall never hear a word more about it, for I will make friends for you with Indiana, and beg of Miss Margland that she'll do us the favour to say no more.'

Edgar, affectionately pressing the hand of the Baronet, uttered the warmest expressions of personal regard, and protested he should always think it an honour to have been held worthy of pretending to any alliance in his family; but he knew not how the present mistake had been made, or report had arisen: he could boast of no partiality from Miss Lynmere, nor had he ever addressed her with any particular views: yet, as it was the opinion of Miss Margland, that the rumour, however false, might prevent the approach of some deserving object, he now finally determined to become, for awhile, a stranger at Cleves, however painful such self-denial must prove.

He then precipitately left the room, and, in five minutes, had galloped out of the Park.

The rest of the morning was spent by Sir Hugh in the utmost discomposure; and by Miss Margland in alternate abuse of Camilla and of Edgar; while Indiana passed from a piqued and short disappointment, to the consolatory idea that Melmond might now re-appear.

Edgar rode strait to Beech Park, where he busied himself the whole day in viewing alterations and improvements; but where nothing answered his expectations, since Camilla had disappointed them. That sun-beam, which had gilded the place to his eyes, was now over-clouded, and the first possession of his own domain, was his first day of discontent.

CHAPTER VII

A Maternal Eye

THE vivacity with which Camilla quitted Cleves, was sunk before she reached Etherington. She had quitted also Edgar, quitted him offended, and in doubt if it might ever be right she should vindicate herself in his opinion. Yet all seemed strange and unintelligible that regarded the asserted nuptials: his indifference was palpable; she believed him to have been unaccountably drawn in, and her heart softly whispered, it was herself he preferred.

From this soothing but dangerous idea, she struggled to turn her thoughts. She anticipated the remorse of holding the affections of the husband of her cousin, and determined to use every possible method to forget him—unless, which she strove vainly not to hope, the reported alliance should never take place.

These reflections so completely engrossed her the whole way, that she arrived at the Parsonage House, without the smallest mental preparation how to account for her return, or how to plead for remaining at Etherington. Foresight, the offspring of Judgment, or the disciple of Experience, made no part of the character of Camilla, whose impetuous disposition was open to every danger of indiscretion, though her genuine love of virtue glowed warm with juvenile ardour.

She entered, therefore, the breakfast parlour in a state of sudden perplexity what to say; Mr. Tyrold was alone and writing. He looked surprized, but embraced her with his accustomed affection, and enquired to what he owed her present sight.

She made no answer; but embraced him again, and enquired after her mother.

'She is well,' he replied: 'but, tell me, is your uncle impatient of my delay? It has been wholly unavoidable. I have been deeply engaged; and deeply chagrined. Your poor mother would be still more disturbed, if the nobleness of her mind did not support her.'

Camilla, extremely grieved, earnestly enquired what had happened.

He then informed her that Mrs. Tyrold, the very next morning, must abruptly quit them all and set out for Lisbon to her sick brother, Mr. Relvil.

'Is he so much worse?'

'No: I even hope he is better. An act of folly has brought this to bear. Do not now desire particulars. I will finish my letter, and then return with you for a few minutes to Cleves. The carriage must wait.'

'Suffer me first to ask, does Lavinia go with my mother?'

'No, she can only take old Ambrose. Lavinia must supply her place at home.'

'Ah! my dearest father, and may not I, too, stay with you and assist her?'

'If my brother will spare you, my dear child, there is nothing can so much contribute to wile away to me your mother's absence.'

Enchanted thus, without any explanation, to have gained her point, she completely revived; though when Mrs. Tyrold, whom she almost worshipped, entered the room, in all the hurry of preparing for her long journey, she shed a torrent of tears in her arms.

'This good girl,' said Mr. Tyrold, 'is herself desirous to quit the present gaieties of Cleves, to try to enliven my solitude till we all may meet again.'

The conscious and artless Camilla could not bear this undeserved praise. She quitted her mother, and returning to Mr. Tyrold, 'O my father!' she cried, 'if you will take me again under your beloved roof, it is for my sake—not your's—I beg to return!'

'She is right,' said Mrs. Tyrold; 'there is no merit in having an heart; she could have none, if to be with you were not her first gratification.'

'Yes, indeed, my dear mother, it would always be so, even if no other inducement—.' She stopt short, confused.

Mr. Tyrold, who continued writing, did not heed this little blunder; but his wife, whose quickness of apprehension and depth of observation, were always alive, even in the midst of business, cares, and other attentions, turned hastily to her daughter, and asked to what 'other inducement' she alluded.

Camilla, distressed, hung her head, and would have forborne making any answer.

Mrs. Tyrold, then, putting down various packets which she was sorting and selecting, came suddenly up to her, and taking both her hands, looked earnestly in her face, saying: 'My Camilla! something has disquieted you?—your countenance is not itself. Tell me, my dear girl, what brought you hither this morning? and what is it you mean by some other inducement?'

'Do not ask me now, my dearest mother,' answered she, in a faltering voice; 'when you come back again, no doubt all will be over; and then—'

'And is that the time, Camilla, to speak to your best friends? would it not be more judicious to be explicit with them, while what affects you is still depending?'

Camilla, hiding her face on her mother's bosom, burst afresh into tears.

'Alas!' cried Mrs. Tyrold, 'what new evil is hovering? If it must invade me again through one of my children, tell me, at least, Camilla, it is not wilfully that you, too, afflict me? and afflict the best of fathers?'

Mr. Tyrold, dropping his pen, looked at them both with the most apprehensive anxiety.

'No, my dearest mother,' said Camilla, endeavouring to meet her eyes; 'not wilfully,—but something has happened—I can hardly myself tell how or what—but indeed Cleves, now—' she hesitated.

'How is my brother?' demanded Mr. Tyrold.

'O! all that is good and kind! and I grieve to quit him—but, indeed, Cleves, now—' Again she hesitated.

'Ah, my dear child!' said Mrs. Tyrold, 'I always feared that residence!—you are too young, too inconsiderate, too innocent, indeed, to be left so utterly to yourself.—Forgive me, my dear Mr. Tyrold; I do not mean to reflect upon your brother, but he is not *you*!—and with you alone, this dear inexperienced girl can be secure from all harm. Tell me, however, what it is—?'

Camilla, in the extremest confusion changed colour, but tried vainly to speak. Mr. Tyrold, suspended from all employment, waited fearfully some explanation.

'We have no time,' said Mrs. Tyrold, 'for delay;—you know I am going abroad,—and cannot ascertain my return; though all my heart left behind me, with my children and their father, will urge every acceleration in my power.'

Camilla, wept again, fondly folding her arms round her mother; 'I had hoped,' she cried, 'that I should have come home to peace, comfort, tranquillity! to both of you, my dearest father and mother, and to all my unbroken happiness under your roof!— How little did I dream of so cruel a separation!'

'Console yourself, my Camilla, that you have not been its cause; may Heaven ever spare me evil in your shape at least!— you say it is nothing wilful? I can bear everything else.'

'We will not,' said Mr. Tyrold, 'press her; she will tell us all in

her own way, and at her own time. Forced confidence is neither
fair nor flattering. I will excuse her return to my brother, and she
will the sooner be able to give her account for finding herself not
hurried.'

'Calm yourself, then,' said Mrs. Tyrold, 'as your indulgent
father permits, and I will proceed with my preparations.'

Camilla now, somewhat recovering, declared she had almost
nothing to say; but her mother continued packing up, and her
father went on with his letter.

She had now time to consider that her own fears and emotion
were involving her in unnecessary confessions; she resolved,
therefore, to repress the fulness of her heart, and to acknowledge
only the accusation of Miss Margland. And in a few minutes,
without waiting for further enquiry, she gathered courage to open
upon the subject; and with as much ease and quietness as she
could command, related, in general terms, the charge brought
against her, and her consequent desire to quit Cleves, 'till,——
till——' Here she stopt for breath. Mr. Tyrold instantly finished
the sentence, 'till the marriage has taken place?'

She coloured, and faintly uttered, 'Yes.'

'You are right, my child,' said he, 'and you have acted with a
prudence which does you honour. Neither the ablest reasoning,
nor the most upright conduct, can so completely obliterate a
surmise of this nature, from a suspicious mind, as absence. You
shall remain, therefore, with me, till your cousin is settled in her
new habitation. Do you know if the day is fixed?'

'No, sir,' she answered, while the roses fled her cheeks at a
question which implied so firm a belief of the union.

'Do not suffer this affair to occasion you any further uneasiness,'
he continued; 'it is the inherent and unalienable compact of
Innocence with Truth, to hold themselves immovably superior to
the calumny of false imputations. But I will go myself to Cleves,
and set this whole matter right.'

'And will you, too, sir, have the goodness—' She was going to
say, *to make my peace with Edgar;* but the fear of misinterpretation
checked her, and she turned away.

He gently enquired what she meant; she avoided any explanation, and he resumed his writing.

Ah me! thought she, will the time ever come, when with openness, with propriety, I may clear myself of caprice to Edgar?

Less patient, because more alarmed than her husband, Mrs. Tyrold followed her to the window. She saw a tear in her eye, and again she took both her hands: 'Have you, my Camilla,' she cried, 'have you told us all? Can unjust impertinence so greatly have disturbed you? Is there no sting belonging to this wound that you are covering from our sight, though it may precisely be the spot that calls most for some healing balm?'

Again the cheeks of Camilla received their fugitive roses. 'My dearest mother,' she cried, 'is not this enough?—to be accused— suspected—and to fear—'

She stammered, and would have withdrawn her hands; but Mrs. Tyrold, still holding them, said, 'To fear what? speak out, my best child! open to us your whole heart!—Where else will you find repositories so tender?'

Tears again flowed down the burning cheeks of Camilla, and dropping her eyes, 'Ah, my mother!' she cried, 'you will think me so frivolous—you will blush so for your daugher—if I own—if I dare confess—'

Again she stopped, terrified at the conjectures to which this opening might give birth; but when further and fondly pressed by her mother, she added, 'It is not alone these unjust surmises,— nor even Indiana's unkind concurrence in them—but also—I have been afraid—I must have made a strange—a capricious—an ungrateful appearance in the eyes of Edgar Mandlebert.'

Here her voice dropt; but presently recovering, she rapidly continued, 'I know it is very immaterial—and I am sensible how foolish it may sound—but I shall also think of it no more now,—and therefore, as I have told the whole—'

She looked up, conscience struck at these last words, to see if they proved satisfactory; she caught, in the countenance of her mother, an expression of deep commiseration, which was followed by a thousand maternal caresses of unusual softness, though unaccompanied by any words.

Penetrated, yet distressed, she gratefully received them, but rejoiced when, at length, Mr. Tyrold, rising, said, 'Go, my love, upstairs to your sister; your mother, else, will never proceed with her business.'

She gladly ran off, and soon, by a concise narration, satisfied Lavinia, and then calmed her own troubled mind.

Mr. Tyrold now, though evidently much affected himself,

strove to compose his wife. 'Alas!' cried she, 'do you not see what thus has touched me? Do you not perceive that our lovely girl, more just to his worth than its possessor, has given her whole heart to Edgar Mandlebert?'

'I perceived it through your emotion, but I had not discovered it myself. I grieve, now, that the probability of such an event had not struck me in time to have kept them apart for its prevention.'

'I grieve for nothing,' cried she, warmly, 'but the infatuated blindness of that self-lost young man. What a wife would Camilla have made him in every stage of their united career! And how unfortunately has she sympathised in my sentiments, that he alone seemed worthy to replace the first and best protector she must relinquish when she quits this house! What will he find in Indiana but a beautiful doll, uninterested in his feelings, unmoved by his excellencies, and incapable of comprehending him if he speaks either of business or literature!'

'Yet many wives of this description,' replied Mr. Tyrold, 'are more pleasing in the eyes of their husbands than women who are either better informed in intellect, or more alive in sensation; and it is not an uncommon idea amongst men, that where, both in temper and affairs, there is least participation, there is most repose. But this is not the case with Edgar.'

'No! he has a nobler resemblance than this portrait would allow him; a resemblance which made me hope from him a far higher style of choice. He prepares himself, however, his own ample punishment; for he has too much understanding not to sicken of mere personal allurements, and too much generosity to be flattered, or satisfied, by mere passive intellectual inferiority. Neither a mistress nor a slave can make him happy; a companion is what he requires; and for that, in a very few months, how vainly his secret soul may sigh, and *think of our Camilla*!'

They then settled, that it would be now essential to the peace of their child to keep her as much as possible from his sight; and determined not to send her back to Cleves to apologize for the new plan, but to take upon themselves that whole charge. 'Her nature,' said Mrs. Tyrold, 'is so gay, so prompt for happiness, that I have little fear but in absence she will soon cease to dwell upon him. Fear, indeed, I have, but it is of a deeper evil than this early impression; I fear for her future lot! With whom can we trust her?—She will not endure negligence; and those she cannot respect she will soon despise. What a prospect for her, then, with our present race of young men! their frivolous fickleness nauseates whatever they can reach; they have a weak shame of asserting, or even listening to what is right, and a shallow pride in professing what is wrong. How must this ingenuous girl forget all she has yet seen, heard, or felt, ere she can encounter wickedness, or even weakness, and disguise her abhorrence or contempt?'

'My dear Georgiana, let us never look forward to evil.'

'Will it not be doubly hard to bear, if it come upon us without preparation?'

'I think not. Terror shakes, and apprehension depresses: hope nerves as well as gladdens us. Remember always, I do not by hope mean presumption; I mean simply a cheerful trust in heaven.'

'I must always yield,' cried Mrs. Tyrold, 'to your superior wisdom, and reflecting piety; and if I cannot conquer my fears, at least I will neither court nor indulge them.'

The thanks of a grateful husband repaid this compliance. They sent for Camilla, to acquaint her they would make her excuses at Cleves: she gave a ready though melancholy consent, and the virtue of her motives drew tears from her idolizing mother, as she clasped her to her heart.

They then set out together, that Mr. Tyrold might arrange this business with Sir Hugh, of whom and of Eugenia Mrs. Tyrold was to take leave.

CHAPTER VIII

Modern Ideas of Duty

CAMILLA now felt more permanently revived, because better satisfied with the rectitude of her conduct. She could no longer be accused of interfering between Edgar and Indiana; that affair would take its natural course, and, be it what it might, while absent from both parties, she concluded she should at least escape all censure.

Peaceably, therefore, she returned to take possession of her usual apartment, affectionately accompanied by her eldest sister.

The form and the mind of Lavinia were in the most perfect harmony. Her polished complexion was fair, clear, and transparent; her features were of the extremest delicacy, her eyes of the softest blue, and her smile displayed internal serenity. The unruffled sweetness of her disposition bore the same character of modest excellence. Joy, hope, and prosperity, sickness, sorrow, and disappointment, assailed alike in vain the uniform gentleness of her temper: yet though thus exempt from all natural turbulence, either of pleasure or of pain, the meekness of her composition degnerated not into insensibility; it was open to all the feminine feelings of pity, of sympathy, and of tenderness.

Thus copiously gifted with 'all her sex's softness,'[1] her society would have contributed to restore Camilla to repose, had they continued together without interruption; but, in a few minutes, the room door was opened, and Lionel, rushing into the apartment, called out, 'How do, do, my girls? how do, do?' and shook them each by the hand, with a swing that nearly brought them to the ground.

Camilla always rejoiced at his sight; but Lavinia gravely said, 'I thought, brother, you had been at Dr. Marchmont's?'

'All in good time, my dear! I shall certainly visit the old gentleman before long.'

'Did you not sleep there, then, last night?'

'No, child.'

'Good God, Lionel!—if my mother—'

'My dear little Lavinia,' cried he, chucking her under the chin, 'I have a vast notion of making visits at my own time, instead of my mamma's.'

'O Lionel! and can you, just now——'

'Come, come,' interrupted he, 'don't let us waste our precious minutes in old moralizing. If I had not luckily been hard by, I should not have known the coast was clear. Pray where are they gone, tantivying?'[2]

'To Cleves.'

'To Cleves! what a happy escape! I was upon the point of going thither myself. Camilla, what is the matter with thee?'

'Nothing—I am only thinking—pray when do you go to Oxford?'

'Pho, pho,—what do you talk of Oxford for? you are grown quite stupid, girl. I believe you have lived too long with Miss

Margland. Pray how does that dear creature do? I am afraid she
will grow melancholy from not seeing me so long. Is she as pretty
as she used to be? I have some notion of sending her a suitor.'

'O brother,' said Lavinia, 'is it possible you can have such
spirits?'

'O hang it, if one is not merry when one can, what is the world
good for? besides, I do assure you, I fretted so consumed hard at
first, that for the life of me I can fret no longer.'

'But why are you not at Dr. Marchmont's?'

'Because, my dear, you have no conception the pleasure those
old doctors take in lecturing a youngster who is in any disgrace.'

'Disgrace!' repeated Camilla.

'At all events,' said Lavinia, 'I beseech you to be a little careful;
I would not have my poor mother find you here for the world.'

'O, as to that, I defy her to desire the meeting less than I do.
But come, let's talk of something else. How go on the classics?
Is my old friend, Dr. Orkborne, as chatty and amusing as ever?'

'My dear Lionel,' said Camilla, 'I am filled with apprehension
and perplexity. Why should my mother wish not to see you? And
why—and how is it possible you can wish not to see her?'

'What, don't you know it all?'

'I know only that something must be wrong; but how, what, or
which way, I have not heard.'

'Has not Lavinia told you, then?

'No,' answered Lavinia; 'I could be in no haste to give her
pain.'

'You are a good girl enough. But how came you hither, Camilla?
and what is the reason you have not seen my mother yourself?'

'Not seen her! I have been with her this half hour.'

'What! and in all that time did not she tell you?'

'She did not name you.'

'Is it possible!—Well, she's a noble creature! I wonder how she
could ever have such a son as me. And I am still less like my father
than her. I suppose I was changed in the cradle. Will you countenance me, young ladies, if some villainous attorney or exciseman
should by and by come to own me?'

'Dear Lionel,' cried Camilla, 'do explain to me what has
happened. You make me think it important and trifling twenty
times in a minute.'

'O, a horrid business!—Lavinia must tell it you. I'll go away till she has done. Don't despise me, Camilla; I am confounded sorry, I promise you.'

He then hurried out of the room, evidently feeling more emotion than he cared to display.

Yet Lavinia had but just begun her relation, when he abruptly returned. 'Come, I had better tell it you myself,' cried he, 'for she'll make such a dismal ditty[1] of it, that it won't be over this half year; the sooner we have done with it the better; it will only put you out of spirits.'

Then, sitting down, and taking her hand, he began, 'You must know I was in rather a bad scrape at Oxford last year—'

'Last year! and you never told us of it before!'

'O, 'twas about something you would not understand, so I shall not mention particulars now. It is enough for you to know that two or three of us wanted a little cash!—well, so—in short, I sent a letter—somewhat of a threatening sort—to poor old uncle Relvil!'—

'O Lionel!'

'O, I did not sign it,—it was only begging a little money, which he can afford to spare very well; and just telling him, if he did not come to a place I mentioned, he would have his brains blown out.'—

'How horrible!'

'Pho, pho,—he had only to send the money, you know, and then his brains might keep their place; besides, you can't suppose there was gunpowder in the words. So I got this copied, and took the proper measures for concealment, and,—would you believe it! the poor old gull was fool enough actually to send the money where he was bid?'

'Fie, Lionel!' cried Lavinia; 'do you call him a fool because you terrified him?'

'Yes, to be sure, my dear; and you both think him so too, only you don't hold it pretty to say so. Do you suppose, if he had had half the wit of his sister, he would have done it? I believe, in my conscience, there was some odd mistake in their births, and that my mother took away the brains of the man, and left the woman's for the noddle[2] of my poor uncle.'

'Fie, fie, brother!' said Lavinia again; 'you know how sickly he has always been from his birth, and how soon therefore he might be alarmed.'

'Why, yes, Lavinia—I believe it was a very bad thing—and I

would give half my little finger I had not done it. But it's over, you know; so what signifies making the worst of it?'

'And did he not discover you?'

'No; I gave him particular orders, in my letter, not to attempt anything of that sort, assuring him there were spies about him to watch his proceedings. The good old ass took it all for gospel. So there the matter dropt. However, as ill luck would have it, about three months ago we wanted another sum—'

'And could you again—'

'Why, my dear, it was only taking a little of my own fortune beforehand, for I am his heir; so we all agreed it was merely robbing myself; for we had several consultations about it, and one of us is to be a lawyer.'

'But you give me some pleasure here,' said Camilla; 'for I had never heard that my uncle had made you his heir.'

'No more have I neither, my dear; but I take it for granted. Besides, our little lawyer put it into my head. Well, we wrote again, and told the poor old gentleman—for which I assure you I am heartily repentant—that if he did not send me double the sum, in the same manner, without delay, his house was to be burnt to the ground the first night that he and all his family were asleep in bed.—Now don't make faces and shruggings, for, I promise you, I think already I deserve to be hanged for giving him the fright; though I would not really have hurt him, all the time, for half his fortune. And who could have guessed he would have bit so easily? The money, however, came, and we thought it all secure, and agreed to get the same sum annually.'

'Annually!' repeated Camilla, with uplifted hands.

'Yes, my dear. You have no conception how convenient it would have been for our extra expenses. But, unluckily, uncle grew worse, and went abroad, and then consulted with some crab of a friend, and that friend with some demagogue of a magistrate, and so all is blown!—However, we had managed it so cleverly, it cost them near three months to find it out, owing, I must confess, to poor uncle's cowardice in not making his enquiries before the money was carried off, and he himself over the seas and far away. The other particulars Lavinia must give you; for I have talked of it now till I have made myself quite sick. Do tell me something diverting to drive it a little out of my head. Have you seen any thing of my enchanting widow lately?'

'No, she does not desire to be seen by me. She would not admit me.'

'She is frankness itself, and does not pretend to care a fig for any of her own sex.—O, but, Camilla, I have wanted to ask you this great while, if you think there is any truth in this rumour, that Mandlebert intends to propose to Indiana?'

'To propose! I thought it had all long since been settled.'

'Ay, so the world says; but I don't believe a word of it. Do you think, if that were the case, he would not have owned it to me? There's nothing fixed yet, depend upon it.'

Camilla, struck, amazed, and delighted, involuntarily embraced her brother; though, recollecting herself almost at the same moment, she endeavoured to turn off the resistless impulse into taking leave, and hurrying him away.

Lionel, who to want of solidity and penetration principally owed the errors of his conduct, was easily put upon a wrong scent, and assured her he would take care to be off in time. 'But what,' cried he, 'has carried them to Cleves? Are they gone to tell tales? Because I have lost one uncle by my own fault, must I lose another by their's?'

'No,' answered Lavinia, 'they have determined not to name you. They have settled that my uncle Hugh shall never be told of the affair, nor anybody else, if they can help it, except your sisters, and Dr. Marchmont.'

'Well, they are good souls,' cried he, attempting to laugh, though his eyes were glistening; 'I wish I deserved them better; I wish, too, it was not so dull to be good. I can be merry and harmless here at the same time,—and so I can at Cleves;—but at Oxford—or in London,—your merry blades there—I can't deny it, my dear sisters—your merry blades there are but sad fellows. Yet there is such fun, such spirit, such sport amongst them, I cannot for my life keep out of their way. Besides, you have no conception, young ladies, what a bye word you become among them if they catch you flinching.'[1]

'I would not for the world say anything to pain you, my dear brother,' cried Lavinia; 'but yet I must hope that, in future, your first study will be to resist such dangerous examples, and to drop such unworthy friends?'

'If it is not to tell tales, then, for what else are they gone to Cleves, just at this time?'

'For my mother to take leave of Eugenia and my uncle before her journey.'

'Journey! Why whither is she going?'

'Abroad.'

'The deuce she is!—And what for?'

'To try to make your peace with her brother; or at least to nurse him herself till he is tolerably recovered.'

Lionel slapped his hat over his eyes, and saying, 'This is too much!—if I were a man I should shoot myself!'—rushed out of the room.

The two sisters rapidly followed him, and caught his arm before he could quit the house. They earnestly besought him to return, to compose himself, and to promise he would commit no rash action.

'My dear sisters,' cried he, 'I am worked just now only as I ought to be; but I will give you any promise you please. However, though I have never listened to my father as I ought to have listened, he has implanted in my mind a horror of suicide, that will make me live my natural life, be it as good for nothing as it may.'

He then suffered his sisters to lead him back to their room, where he cast himself upon a chair, in painful rumination upon his own unworthiness, and his parents' excellence; but the tender soothings of Lavinia and Camilla, who trembled lest his remorse should urge him to some act of violence, soon drew him from reflections of which he hated the intrusion; and he attended, with complacency, to their youthful security of perfect reconciliations, and re-established happiness.

With reciprocal exultation, the eyes of the sisters congratulated each other on having saved him from despair: and seeing him now calm, and, they hoped, safe, they mutually, though tacitly, agreed to obtrude no further upon meditations that might be useful to him, and remained silently by his side.

For some minutes all were profoundly still; Lionel then suddenly started up; the sisters, affrighted, hastily arose at the same instant; when stretching himself and yawning, he called out, 'Pr'ythee, Camilla, what is become of that smug Mr. Dubster?'

Speechless with amazement, they looked earnestly in his face, and feared he was raving.

They were soon, however undeceived; the tide of penitence and sorrow was turned in his buoyant spirits, and he was only restored to his natural volatile self.

'You used him most shabbily,' he continued, 'and he was a very pretty fellow. The next time I have nothing better to do, I'll send him to you, that you may make it up.'

This quick return of gaiety caused a sigh to Lavinia, and much surprise to Camilla; but neither of them could prevail with him to depart, till Mr. and Mrs. Tyrold were every moment expected; they then, though with infinite difficulty, procured his promise that he would go straight to Dr. Marchmont, according to an arrangement made for that purpose by Mrs. Tyrold herself.

Lavinia, when he was gone, related some circumstances of this affair which he had omitted. Mr. Relvil, the elder brother of Mrs. Tyrold, was a country gentleman of some fortune, but of weak parts, and an invalid from his infancy. He had suffered these incendiary letters to prey upon his repose, without venturing to produce them to any one, from a terror of the menaces hurled against him by the writer, till at length he became so completely hypochondriac,[1] that his rest was utterly broken, and, to preserve his very existence, he resolved upon visiting another climate.

The day that he set out for Lisbon, his destined harbour, he delivered his anonymous letters to a friend, to whom he left in charge to discover, if possible, their author.

This discovery, by the usual means of enquiries and rewards, was soon made; but the moment Mr. Relvil learnt that the culprit was his nephew, he wrote over to Mrs. Tyrold a statement of the transaction, declaring he should disinherit Lionel from every shilling of his estate. His health was so much impaired, he said, by the disturbance this had given to his mind, that he should be obliged to spend the ensuing year in Portugal; and he even felt uncertain if he might ever return to his own country.

Mrs. Tyrold, astonished and indignant, severely questioned her son, who covered, with shame, surprise, and repentance, confessed his guilt. Shocked and grieved in the extreme, she ordered him from her sight, and wrote to Dr. Marchmont to receive him. She then settled with Mr. Tyrold the plan of her journey and voyage, hoping by so immediately following, and herself nursing her incensed brother, to soften his wrath, and avert its final ill consequences.

CHAPTER IX

A Few Embarrassments

Mr. and Mrs. Tyrold returned to Etherington somewhat relieved in their spirits, though perplexed in their opinions. They had heard from Sir Hugh, that Edgar had decidedly disavowed any pretensions to Indiana, and had voluntarily retreated from Cleves, that his disavowal might risk no misconstruction, either in the family or the neighbourhood.

This insensibility to beauty the most exquisite wanted no advocate with Mrs. Tyrold. Once more she conceived some hope of what she wished, and she determined upon seeing Edgar before her departure. The displeasure she had nourished against him vanished, and justice to his general worth, with an affection nearly maternal to his person, took again their wonted place in her bosom, and made her deem herself unkind in having purposed to quit the kingdom without bidding him farewell.

Mr. Tyrold, whom professional duty and native inclination alike made a man of peace, was ever happy to second all conciliatory measures, and the first to propose them, where his voice had any chance of being heard. He sent a note, therefore, to invite Edgar to call the next morning; and Mrs. Tyrold deferred her hour of setting off till noon.

Her own natural and immediate impulse, had been to carry Camilla with her abroad; but when she considered that her sole errand was to nurse and appease an offended sick man, whose chamber she meant not to quit till she returned to her family, she gave up the pleasure she would herself have found in the scheme, to her fears for the health and spirits of her darling child, joined to the superior joy of leaving such a solace with her husband.

Sir Hugh had heard the petition for postponing the further visit of Camilla almost with despondence; but Mr. Tyrold restored him completely to confidence, with respect to his doubts concerning Dr. Orkborne, with whom he held a long and satisfactory conversation; and his own benevolent heart received a sensible pleasure, when, upon examining Indiana with regard to Edgar, he found her, though piqued and pouting, untouched either in affection or happiness.

Early the next morning Edgar came. Mrs. Tyrold had taken

measures for employing Camilla upstairs, where she did not even hear that he entered the house.

He was received with kindness, and told of the sudden journey, though not of its motives. He heard of it with unfeigned concern, and earnestly solicited to be the companion of the voyage, if no better male protector were appointed.

Mr. Tyrold folded his arms around him at this grateful proposal, while his wife, animated off her guard, warmly exclaimed— 'My dear, excellent Edgar! you are indeed the model, the true son of your guardian!'

Sorry for what had escaped her, from her internal reference to Lionel, she looked anxiously to see if he comprehended her; but the mantling blood which mounted quick into his cheeks, while his eyes sought the ground, soon told her there was another mode of affinity, which at that moment had struck him.

Willing to establish whether this idea were right, she now considered how she might name Camilla; but her husband, who for no possible purpose could witness distress without seeking to alleviate it, declined his kind offer, and began a discourse upon the passage to Lisbon.

This gave Edgar time to recover, and, in a few seconds, something of moment seemed abruptly to occur to him, and scarcely saying adieu, he hurried to remount his horse.

Mrs. Tyrold was perplexed; but she could take not steps towards an explanation, without infringing the delicacy she felt due to her daughter: she suffered him, therefore, to depart.

She then proceeded with her preparations, which entirely occupied her till the chaise was at the gate; when, as the little party, their eyes and their hearts all full, were taking a last farewell, the parlour door was hastily opened, and Dr. Marchmont and Edgar entered the room.

All were surprised, but none so much as Camilla, who, forgetting, in sudden emotion, every thing but former kindness and intimacy, delightedly exclaimed—'Edgar! O how happy, my dearest mother!—I was afraid you would go without seeing him!'

Edgar turned to her wich a quickness that could only be exceeded by his pleasure; her voice, her manner, her unlooked-for interest in his appearance, penetrated to his very soul. 'Is it possible,' he cried, 'you could have the goodness to wish me this gratification? At a moment such as this, could you——?' think of me, he would have added; but Dr. Marchmont, coming forward, begged him to account for their intrusion.

Almost overpowered by his own sudden emotion, he could scarce recollect its motive himself; while Camilla, fearful and repentant that she had broken her deliberate and well-principled resolutions, retreated to the window.

Mr. and Mrs. Tyrold witnessed the involuntary movements which betrayed their mutual regard with the tenderest satisfaction; and the complacency of their attention, when Edgar advanced to them, soon removed his embarrassment.

He then briefly acquainted them, that finding Mrs. Tyrold would not accept him for her chevalier, he had ridden hard to the parsonage of Cleves, whence he hoped he had brought her one too unexceptionable for rejection.

Dr. Marchmont, with great warmth, then made a proffer of his services, declaring he had long desired an opportunity to visit Portugal; and protesting that, besides the pleasure of complying with any wish of Mr. Mandlebert's, it would give him the most serious happiness to shew his gratitude for the many kind offices he owed to Mr. Tyrold, and his high personal respect for his lady; he should require but one day for his preparations, and for securing the performance of the church duty at Cleves during his absence.

Mr. and Mrs. Tyrold were equally struck by the goodness of Dr. Marchmont, and the attentive kindness of Edgar. Mrs. Tyrold, nevertheless, would immediately have declined the scheme; but her husband interposed. Her travelling, he said, with such a guard, would be as conducive to his peace at home, as to her safety abroad. 'And with respect,' cried he, 'to obligation, I hold it as much a moral duty not to refuse receiving good offices, as not to avoid administering them. That species of independence, which proudly flies all ties of gratitude, is inimical to the social compact of civilized life, which subsists but by reciprocity of services.'

Mrs. Tyrold now opposed the scheme no longer, and the chaise was ordered for the next day.

Dr. Marchmont hurried home to settle his affairs; but Edgar begged a short conference with Mr. Tyrold.

Every maternal hope was now awake in Mrs. Tyrold, who concluded this request was to demand Camilla in marriage; and her husband himself, not without trepidation, took Edgar into his study.

But Edgar, though his heart was again wholly Camilla's, had received a look from Dr. Marchmont that guarded him from any immediate declaration. He simply opened upon the late misconception at Cleves; vindicated himself from any versatility of conduct, and affirmed, that both his attentions and his regard for Indiana had never been either more or less than they still continued. All this was spoken with a plainness to which the integrity of his character gave a weight superior to any protestations.

'My dear Edgar,' said Mr. Tyrold, 'I am convinced of your probity. The tenor of your life is its guarantee, and any other defence is a degradation. There is, indeed, no perfidy so unjustifiable, as that which wins but to desert the affections of an innocent female. It is still, if possible, more cowardly than it is cruel; for the greater her worth, and the more exquisite her feelings, the stronger will be the impulse of her delicacy to suffer uncomplaining; and the deluder of her esteem commonly confides, for averting her reproach, to the very sensibility through which he has ensnared her good opinion.'

'No one,' said Edgar, 'can more sincerely concur in this sentiment than myself; and, I trust, there is no situation, and no character, that could prompt me to deviate in this point. Here, in particular, my understanding must have been as defective as my morals, to have betrayed me into such an enterprise.'

'How do you mean?'

'I beg pardon, my dear sir; but, though I have a sort of family regard for Miss Lynmere, and though I think her beauty is transcendent, her heart, I believe——' he hesitated.

'Do you think her heart invulnerable?'——

'Why—no—not positively, perhaps,' answered he, embarrassed, 'not positively invulnerable; but certainly I do not think it composed of those finely subtle sensations which elude all vigilance, and become imperceptibly the prey of every assailing sympathy; for itself, therefore, I believe it not in much danger; and, for others—I see not in it that magnetic attraction which charms away all caution, beguiles all security, enwraps the imagination, and masters the reason!'——

The chain of thinking which, from painting what he thought insensible in Indiana, led him to describe what he felt to be resistless in Camilla, made him finish the last sentence with an energy that surprised Mr. Tyrold into a smile.

'You seem deeply,' he said, 'to have studied the subject.'

'But not under the guidance of Miss Lynmere,' he answered, rising, and colouring, the moment he had spoken, in the fear he had betrayed himself.

'I rejoice, then, the more,' replied Mr. Tyrold, calmly, 'in her own slackness of susceptibility.'

'Yes,' cried Edgar, recovering, and quietly re-placing himself; 'it is her own security, and it is the security of all who surround her; though to those, indeed, there was also another, a still greater, in the contrast which——' he stopt, confused at his own meaning; yet presently, almost irresistibly, added—'Not that I think the utmost vivacity of sentiment, nor all the charm of soul, though eternally beaming in the eyes, playing in every feature, glowing in the complection, and brightening every smile——' he stopt again, overpowered with the consciousness of the picture he was portraying; but Mr. Tyrold continuing silent, he was obliged, though he scarce knew what he said, to go on. 'Nothing, in short, so selfishly are we formed,—that nothing, not even the loveliest of the lovely, can be truly bewitching, in which we do not hope or expect some participation.—I believe I have not made myself very clear?—However, it is not material—I simply meant to explain my retreat from Cleves. And, indeed, it is barbarous, at a season such as this, to detain you a moment from your family.'

He then hastily took leave.

Mr. Tyrold was sensibly touched by this scene. He saw, through a discourse so perplexed, and a manner so confused, that his daughter had made a forcible impression upon the heart of Mandlebert, but could not comprehend why he seemed struggling to conceal it. What had dropt from him appeared to imply a distrust of exciting mutual regard; yet this, after his own observations upon Camilla, was inconceivable. He regretted, that at a period so critical, she must part with her mother, with whom again he now determined to consult.

Edgar, who hitherto had opened his whole heart upon every occasion to Mr. Tyrold, felt hurt and distressed at this first withholding of confidence. It was, however, unavoidable, in his present situation.

He went back to the parlour to take leave once more of Mrs.

Tyrold; but, opening the door, found Camilla there alone. She was looking out of the window, and had not heard his entrance.

This was not a sight to still his perturbed spirits; on the contrary, the moment seemed to him so favourable, that it irresistibly occurred to him to seize it for removing every doubt.

Camilla, who had not even missed her mother and sister from the room, was contemplating the horse of Edgar, and internally arraigning herself for the dangerous pleasure she had felt and manifested at the sight of his master.

He gently shut the door, and approaching her, said, 'Do I see again the same frank and amiable friend, who in earliest days, who always, indeed, till—'

Camilla, turning round, startled to behold him so near, and that no one else remained in the room, blushed excessively, and without hearing what he said, shut the window; yet opened it the same minute, stammering out something, but she herself knew not what, concerning the weather.

The gentlest thoughts crossed the mind of Edgar at this evident embarrassment, and the most generous alacrity prompted him to hasten his purpose. He drew a chair near her, and, in penetrating accents, said: 'Will you suffer me, will you, can you permit me, to take the privilege of our long friendship, and honestly to speak to you upon what has passed within these last few days at Cleves?'

She could not answer: surprise, doubt, fear of self-deception, and hope of some happy explanation, all suddenly conspired to confound and to silence her.

'You cannot, I think, forget,' he soon resumed, 'that you had condescended to put into my hands the management and decision of the new acquaintance you are anxious to form? My memory, at least, will never be unfaithful to a testimony so grateful to me, of your entire reliance upon the deep, the unspeakable interest I have ever taken, and ever must take, in my invaluable guardian, and in every branch of his respected and beloved family.'

Camilla now began to breathe. This last expression, though zealous in friendliness, had nothing of appropriate partiality; and in losing her hope she resumed her calmness.

Edgar observed, though he understood not, the change; but as he wished to satisfy his mind before he indulged his inclination, he endeavoured not to be sorry to see her mistress of herself during the discussion. He wished her but to answer him with openness:

she still, however, only listened, while she rose and looked about the room for some work. Edgar, somewhat disconcerted, waited for her again sitting down; and after a few minutes spent in a useless search, she drew a chair to a table at some distance.

Gravely then following, he stood opposite to her, and, after a little pause, said, 'I perceive you think I go too far? you think that the intimacy of childhood, and the attachment of adolescence, should expire with the juvenile sports and intercourse which nourished them, rather than ripen into solid friendship and permanent confidence?'

'Do not say so,' cried she, with emotion; 'believe me, unless you knew all that had passed, and all my motives, you should judge nothing of these last few days, but think of me only, whether well or ill, as you thought of me a week ago.'

The most laboured and explicit defence could not more immediately have satisfied his mind than this speech. Suspicion vanished, trust and admiration took its place, and once more drawing a chair by her side, 'My dear Miss Camilla,' he cried, 'forgive my having thus harped upon this subject; I here promise you I will name it no more.'

'And I,' cried she, delighted, 'promise you'—she was going to add, that she would give up Mrs. Arlbery, if he found reason to disapprove the acquaintance; but the parlour door opened, and Miss Margland stalked into the room.

Sir Hugh was going to send a messenger to enquire how and when Mrs. Tyrold had set out; but Miss Margland, from various motives of curiosity, offered her services, and came herself. So totally, however, had both Edgar and Camilla been engrossed by each other, that they had not heard the carriage drive up to the garden gate, which, with the door of the house, being always open, required neither knocker nor bell.

A spectre could not more have startled or shocked Camilla. She jumped up, with an exclamation nearly amounting to a scream, and involuntarily seated herself at the other end of the room.

Edgar, though not equally embarrassed, was still more provoked; but he rose, and got her a chair, and enquired after the health of Sir Hugh.

'He is very poorly, indeed,' answered she, with an austere air, 'and no wonder!'

'Is my uncle ill?' cried Camilla, alarmed.

Miss Margland deigned no reply.

The rest of the family, who had seen the carriage from the windows, now entered the room, and during the mutual enquiries and account which followed, Edgar, believing himself unobserved, glided round to Camilla, and in a low voice, said, 'The promise—I think I guess its gratifying import—I shall not, I hope, lose, through this cruel intrusion?'

Camilla, who saw no eyes but those of Miss Margland, which were severely fastened upon her, affected not to hear him, and planted herself in the group out of his way.

He anxiously waited for another opportunity to put in his claim; but he waited in vain; Camilla, who from the entrance of Miss Margland had had the depressing feel of self-accusation, sedulously avoided him; and though he loitered till he was ashamed of remaining in the house at a period so busy, Miss Margland, by indications not to be mistaken, shewed herself bent upon out-staying him; he was obliged, therefore, to depart; though, no sooner was he gone, than, having nothing more to scrutinize, she went also.

But little doubt now remained with the watchful parents of the mutual attachment of Edgar and Camilla, to which the only apparent obstacle seemed, a diffidence on the part of Edgar with respect to her internal sympathy. Pleased with the modesty of such a fear in so accomplished a young man, Mr. Tyrold protested that, if the superior fortune were on the side of Camilla, he would himself clear it up, and point out the mistake. His wife gloried in the virtuous delicacy of her daughter, that so properly, till it was called for, concealed her tenderness from the object who so deservingly inspired it; yet they agreed, that though she could not, at present, meet Edgar too often, she should be kept wholly ignorant of their wishes and expectations, lest they should still be crushed by any unforeseen casualty: and that, meanwhile, she should be allowed every safe and innocent recreation, that might lighten her mind from its depression, and restore her spirits to their native vivacity.

Early the next morning Dr. Marchmont came to Etherington, and brought with him Lionel, by the express direction of his father, who never objected to admit the faulty to his presence; his hopes of doing good were more potent from kindness than from severity, from example than from precept: yet he attempted not to conquer the averseness of Mrs. Tyrold to an interview; he knew it proceeded not from an inexorable nature, but from a repugnance insurmountable to the sight of a beloved object in disgrace.

Mrs. Tyrold quitted her husband with the most cruel regret, and her darling Camilla with the tenderest inquietude; she affectionately embraced the unexceptionable Lavinia, with whom she left a message for her brother, which she strictly charged her to deliver, without softening or omitting one word.

And then, attended by Dr. Marchmont, she set forward on her journey towards Falmouth: whence a packet, in a few days, she was informed, would sail for Lisbon.

CHAPTER X

Modern Ideas of Life

GRIEVED at this separation, Mr. Tyrold retired to his study; and his two daughters went to the apartment of Lionel, to comfort him under the weight of his misconduct.

They found him sincerely affected and repentant; yet eager to hear that his mother was actually gone. Ill as he felt himself to deserve such an exertion for his future welfare, and poignant as were his shame and sorrow to have parted her from his excellent father, he thought all evil preferable to encountering her eye, or listening to her admonitions.

Though unaffectedly beloved, Mrs. Tyrold was deeply feared by all her children, Camilla alone excepted; by Lionel, from his horror of reproof; by Lavinia, from the timidity of her humility; and by Eugenia, from her high sense of parental superiority. Camilla alone escaped the contagion; for while too innocent, too undesigning, wilfully to excite displeasure, she was too gay and too light-hearted to admit apprehension without cause.

The gentle Lavinia knew not how to perform her painful task of delivering the message with which she was commissioned. The sight of Lionel in dejection was as sad as it was new to her, and she resolved, in conjunction with Camilla, to spare him till the next day, when his feelings might be less acute. They each sat down, therefore, to work, silent and compassionate; while he, ejaculating blessings upon his parents, and calling for just vengeance upon himself, stroamed[1] up and down the room, biting his knuckles, and now and then striking his forehead.

This lasted about ten minutes: and then, suddenly advancing to his sisters, and snatching a hand of each: 'Come, girls,' he cried, 'now let's talk of other things.'

Too young to have developed the character of Lionel, they were again as much astonished as they had been the preceding day: but his defects, though not originally of the heart, were of a species that soon tend to harden it. They had their rise in a total aversion to reflection, a wish to distinguish himself from his retired, and, he thought, unfashionable relations, and an unfortunate coalition with some unprincipled young men, who, because flashy and gay, could lead him to whatever they proposed. Yet, when mischief or misfortune ensued from his wanton faults, he was always far more sorry than he thought it manly to own; but as his actions were without judgment, his repentance was without principle; and he was ready for some new enterprise the moment the difficulties of an old one subsided.

Camilla, who, from her affection to him, read his character through the innocence of her own, met his returning gaiety with a pleasure that was proportioned to her pain at his depression; but Lavinia saw it with discomfort, as the signal for executing her charge, and, with extreme reluctance, gave him to understand she had a command to fulfil to him from his mother.

The powers of conscience were again then instantly at work; he felt what he had deserved, he dreaded to hear what he had provoked; and trembling and drawing back, entreated her to wait one half hour before she entered upon the business.

She chearfully consented; and Camilla proposed extending the reprieve to the next day: but not two minutes elapsed, before Lionel protested he could not bear the suspense, and urged an immediate communication.

'She can have said nothing,' cried he, 'worse than I expect, or than I merit. Probe me then without delay. She is acting by me like an angel, and if she were to command me to turn anchoret, I know I ought to obey her.'

With much hesitation, Lavinia then began. 'My mother says, my dear Lionel, the fraud you have practised—'

'The fraud! what a horrid word! why it was a mere trick! a

joke! a frolic! just to make an old hunks[1] open his purse-strings
for his natural heir. I am astonished at my mother! I really don't
care if I don't hear another syllable.'

'Well, then, my dear Lionel, I will wait till you are calmer: my
mother, I am sure did not mean to irritate, but to convince.'

'My mother,' continued he, striding about the room, 'makes no
allowances. She has no faults herself, and for that reason she
thinks nobody else should have any. Besides, how should she
know what it is to be a young man? and to want a little cash, and
not know how to get it?'

'But I am sure,' said Lavinia, 'if you wanted it for any proper
purpose, my father would have denied himself everything, in
order to supply you.'

'Yes, yes; but suppose I want it for a purpose that is *not*
proper, how am I to get it then?'

'Why, then, my dear Lionel, surely you must be sensible you
ought to go without it,' cried the sisters, in a breath.

'Ay, that's as you girls say, that know nothing of the matter. If a
young man, when he goes into the world, was to make such a
speech as that, he would be pointed at. Besides, who must he live
with? You don't suppose he is to shut himself up, with a few
musty books, sleeping over the fire, under pretence of study, all
day long, do you? like young Melmond, who knows no more of the
world than one of you do?'

'Indeed,' said Camilla, 'he seemed to me an amiable and modest
young man, though very romantic.'

'O, I dare say he did! I could have laid any wager of that. He's
just a girl's man, just the very thing, all sentiment, and poetry
and heroics. But we, my little dear, we lads of spirit, hold all that
amazing cheap. I assure you, I would as soon be seen trying on a
lady's cap at a glass, as poring over a crazy old author when I
could help it. I warrant you think, because one is at the university,
one must all be book-worms?'

'Why, what else do you go there for but to study?'

'Every thing in the world, my dear.'

'But are there not sometimes young men who are scholars
without being book-worms?' cried Camilla, half colouring; 'is not
—is not Edgar Mandlebert—'

'O yes, yes; an odd thing of that sort happens now and then.
Mandlebert has spirit enough to carry it off pretty well, without

being ridiculous; though he is as deep, for his time, as e'er an old fellow of a college. But then this is no rule for others. You must not expect an Edgar Mandlebert at every turn.'

Ah no! thought Camilla.

'But, Edgar,' said Lavinia, 'has had an extraordinary education, as well as possessing extraordinary talents and goodness: and you, too, my dear Lionel, to fulfil what may be expected from you, should look back to your father, who was brought up at the same university, and is now considered as one of the first men it has produced. While he was respected by the learned for his application, he was loved even by the indolent for his candour and kindness of heart. And though his income, as you know, was so small, he never ran in debt, and by an exact but open œconomy, escaped all imputation of meanness: while by forbearing either to conceal, or repine at his limited fortune, he blunted even the raillery of the dissipated, by frankly and good humouredly meeting it half way. How often have I heard my dear mother tell you this!'

'Yes; but all this, child, is nothing to the purpose; my father is no more like other men than if he had been born in another planet, and my attempting to resemble him, is as great a joke, as if you were to dress up Miss Margland in Indiana's flowers and feathers, and then expect people to call her a beauty.'

'We do not say you resemble my father, now,' said Camilla, archly; 'but is there any reason why you should not try to do it by and by?'

'O yes! a little one! nature, nature, my dear, is in the way. I was born a bit of a buck. I have no manner of natural taste for study, and poring, and expounding, and black-letter work. I am a light, airy spark, at your service, not quite so wise as I am merry;—but let that pass. My father, you know, is firm as a rock. He minds neither wind nor weather, nor fleerer[1] nor sneerer: but this firmness, look ye, he has kept all to himself; not a whit of it do I inherit; every wind that blows veers me about, and makes me look some new way.'

Soon after, gathering courage from curiosity, he desired to hear the message at once.

Lavinia, unwillingly complying, then repeated: 'The fraud which you have practised, my mother says, whether from wanton folly to give pain, or from rapacious discontent to gain money, she will leave without comment, satisfied that if you have any heart at all, its effects must bring its remorse, since it has dangerously encreased the infirmities of your uncle, driven him to a foreign land, and forced your mother to forsake her home and family in his pursuit, unless she were willing to see you punished by the entire disinheritance with which you are threatened. But——'

'O, no more! no more! I am ready to shoot myself already! My dear, excellent mother! what do I not owe you! I had never seen, never thought of the business in this solemn way before. I meant nothing at first but a silly joke, and all this mischief has followed unaccountably. I assure you, I had no notion at the beginning he would have minded the letter; and afterwards, Jack Whiston persuaded me, the money was as good as my own, and that it was nothing but a little cribbing from myself. I will never trust him again; I see the whole now in its true and atrocious colours.—I will devote myself in future to make all the amends in my power to my dear incomparable mother.'

The sisters affectionately encouraged this idea, which produced near a quarter of an hour's serious thinking and penitence.

He then begged to hear the rest; and Lavinia continued.

'But since you are re-admitted, said my mother, to Etherington, by the clemency of your forbearing father, she charges you to remember, you can only repay his goodness by an application the most intense to those studies you have hitherto neglected, and of which your neglect has been the cause of all your errors; by committing to idle amusements the time that innocently, as well as profitably, ought to have been dedicated to the attainment of knowledge. She charges you also to ask yourself, since, during the vacation, your father himself is your tutor, upon what pretext you can justify wasting his valuable time, however little you may respect your own?—Finally—'

'I never wasted his time! I never desired to have any instruction in the vacations. 'Tis the most deuced thing in life to be studying so hard incessantly. The waste of time is all his own affair;—his own choice—not mine, I assure you! Go on, however.'

'Finally, she adjures you to consider, that if you still persevere to consume your time in wilful negligence, to bury all thought in idle gaiety, and to act without either reflection or principle, the career of faults which begins but in unthinking folly, will terminate in shame, in guilt, and in ruin! And though such a declension of all good, must involve your family in your affliction, your

disgrace, she bids me say, will ultimately fall but where it ought;
since your own want of personal sensibility to the horror of
your conduct, will neither harden nor blind any human being
besides yourself. This is all.'

'And enough too,' cried he, reddening: 'I am a very wretch!
—I believe that—though I am sure I can't tell how; for I never
intend any harm, never think, never dream of hurting any mortal!
But as to study—I must own to you, I hate it most deucedly.
Anything else—if my mother had but exacted any thing else—with
what joy I would have shewn my obedience!—If she had ordered
me to be horse-ponded,[1] I do protest to you, I would not have
demurred.'

'How always you run into the ridiculous!' cried Camilla.

'I was never so serious in my life; not that I should like to be
horse-ponded in the least, though I would submit to it for a
punishment, and out of duty: but then, when it was done, it
would be over: now the deuce of study is, there is no end of it!
And it does so little for one! one can go through life so well
without it! There is not above here and there an old codger that
asks one a question that can bring it into any play. And then, a
turn upon one's heel, or looking at one's watch, or wondering at
one's short memory, or happening to forget just that one single
passage, carries off the whole in two minutes, as completely as if
one had been working one's whole life to get ready for the assault.
And pray, now, tell me, how can it be worth one's best days, one's
gayest hours, the very flower of one's life—all to be sacrificed to
plodding over musty grammars and lexicons, merely to cut a
figure just for about two minutes once or twice in a year?'

The sisters, brought up with an early reverence for learning, as
forming a distinguished part of the accomplishments of their
father, could not subscribe to this argument. But they laughed;
and that was ever sufficient for Lionel, who, though sincerely, in
private, he loved and honoured his father, never bestowed upon
him one voluntary moment that frolic or folly invited elsewhere.

Lavinia and Camilla, perfectly relieved now from all fears for
their brother, repaired to the study of their father, anxious to
endeavour to chear him, and to accelerate a meeting and reconciliation for Lionel; but they found him desirous to be alone,
though kindly, and unsolicited, he promised to admit his son
before dinner.

Lionel heard this was a just awe; but gave it no time for deep impression. It was still very early, and he could settle himself to nothing during the hours yet to pass before the interview. He persuaded his sisters, therefore, to walk out with him, to while away at once expectation and retrospection.

CHAPTER XI

Modern Notions of Penitence

THEY set out with no other plan than to take a three hours' stroll. Lionel led the way, and they journeyed through various pleasant lanes and meadows, till, about three miles distance from Etherington, upon ascending a beautiful little hill, they espied, fifty yards off, the Grove, and a party of company sauntering round its grounds.

He immediately proposed making a visit to Mrs. Arlbery; but Lavinia declined presenting herself to a lady who was unknown to her mother; and Camilla, impressed with the promise she had intended for Edgar, which she was sure, though unpronounced, he had comprehended, dissented also from the motion.

He then said he would go alone; for his spirits were so low from vexation and regret, that they wanted recruit; and he would return to them by the time they would be sufficiently rested to walk home.

To this they agreed; and amused themselves with watching to see him join the group; in which, however, they were no sooner gratified, than, to their great confusion, they perceived that he pointed them out, and that all eyes were immediately directed towards the hill.

Vexed and astonished at his quick passing penitence, they hastened down the declivity, and ran on till a lane, with an high hedge on each side, sheltered them from view.

But Lionel, soon pursuing them, said he brought the indisputable orders of his invincible widow to convoy them to the mansion. She never, she had owned, admitted formal visitors, but whatever was abrupt and out of the way, won her heart.

To the prudent Lavinia, this invitation was by no means

alluring. Mrs. Tyrold, from keeping no carriage, visited but little, and the Grove was not included in her small circle; Lavinia, therefore, though she knew not how to be peremptory, was steady in refusal; and Camilla, who would naturally with pleasure have yielded, had a stronger motive for firmness, than any with which she was gifted by discretion, in her wish to oblige Mandlebert. But Lionel would listen to neither of them; and when he found his insistance insufficient, seized Lavinia by one arm, and Camilla by the other, and dragged them up the hill, in defiance of their entreaties, and in full view of the party. He then left the more pleading, though less resisting, Lavinia alone; but pulled Camilla down by the opposite side, with a velocity that, though meant but to bring her to the verge of a small rivulet, forced her into the midst of it so rapidly that he could not himself at last stop: and wetted her so completely, that she could with difficulty, when she got across it, walk on.

The violent spirits of Lionel always carried him beyond his own intentions; he was now really sorry for what he had done: and Lavinia, who had quietly followed, was uneasy from the fear of some ill consequence to her sister.

Mrs. Arlbery, who had seen the transaction, came forth now herself, to invite them all into her house, and offer a fire and dry clothing to Camilla; not sparing, however, her well-merited raillery at the awkward exploit of young Tyrold.

Camilla, ashamed to be thus seen, would have hidden herself behind her sister, and retreated; but even Lavinia now, fearing for her health, joined in the request, and she was obliged to enter the house.

Mrs. Arlbery took her upstairs, to her own apartment, and supplied her immediately with a complete change of apparel; protesting that Lionel should be punished for his frolic, by a solitary walk to Etherington, to announce that she would keep his two sisters for the day.

Opposition was vain; she was gay, good humoured, and pleasant, but she would not be denied. She meant not, however, to inflict the serious penalty which the face of Lionel proclaimed him to be suffering, when he prepared to depart; and the sisters, who read in it his dread of meeting Mr. Tyrold alone, in the present circumstances of his affairs, conferred together, and agreed that Lavinia should accompany him, both to intercede for returning favour from his father, and to explain the accident of Camilla's staying at the Grove. Mrs. Arlbery, meanwhile, promised to restore her young guest safe at night in her own carriage.

Notwithstanding the pleasure with which Camilla, in any other situation, would have renewed this acquaintance, was now changed into reluctance, she was far from insensible to the flattering kindness with which Mrs. Arlbery received and entertained her, nor to the frankness with which she confessed, that her invisibility the other morning, had resulted solely from pique that the visit had not been made sooner.

Camilla would have attempted some apology for the delay, but she assured her apologies were what she neither took nor gave; and then laughingly added—'We will try one another to day, and if we find it won't do—we will shake hands and part. That, you must know, is my mode; and is it not vastly better than keeping up an acquaintance that proves dull, merely because it has been begun?'

She then ordered away all her visitors, without the smallest ceremony; telling them, however, they might come back in the evening, only desiring they would not be early. Camilla stared; but they all submitted as to a thing of course.

'You are not used to my way, I perceive,' cried she, smiling; 'yet, I can nevertheless assure you, you can do nothing so much for your happiness as to adopt it. You are made a slave in a moment by the world, if you don't begin life by defying it. Take your own way, follow your own humour, and you and the world will both go on just as well, as if you ask its will and pleasure for everything you do, and want, and think.'

She then expressed herself delighted with Lionel, for bringing them together by this short cut, which abolished a world of formalities, not more customary than fatiguing. 'I pass, I know,' continued she, 'for a mere creature of whim; but, believe me, there is no small touch of philosophy in the composition of my vagaries. Extremes, you know, have a mighty knack of meeting. Thus I, like the sage, though not with sage-like motives, save time that must otherwise be wasted; brave rules that would murder common sense; and when I have made people stare, turn another way that I may laugh.'

She then, in a graver strain, and in a manner that proved the laws of politeness all her own, where she chose, for any particular purpose, or inclination, to exert them, hoped this profession of her faith would plead her excuse, that she had thus incongruously made her fair guest a second time enter her house, before her first visit was acknowledged; and enquired whether it were to be returned to Etherington or at Cleves.

Camilla answered, she was now at home, on account of her mother's being obliged to make a voyage to Lisbon.

Mrs. Arlbery said, she would certainly, then, wait upon her at Etherington; and very civilly regretted having no acquaintance with Mrs. Tyrold; archly, however, adding: 'As we have no where met, I could not seek her at her own house without running too great a risk; for then, whether I had liked her or not, I must have received her, you know, into mine. So, you see, I am not quite without prudence, whatever the dear world says to the contrary.'

She then spoke of the ball, public breakfast, and raffle; chatting both upon persons and things with an easy gaiety, and sprightly negligence, extremely amusing to Camilla, and which soon, in despite of the unwillingness with which she had entered her house, brought back her original propensity to make the acquaintance, and left no regret for what Lionel had done, except what rested upon the repugnance of Edgar to his intercourse. As he could not, however, reproach what was begun without her concurrence, he would see, she hoped, like herself, that common civility henceforward would exact its continuance.

In proportion as her pleasure from this accidental commerce was awakened, and her early partiality revived, her own spirits re-animated, and, in the course of the many hours they now spent completely together, she was set so entirely at her ease, by the good humour of Mrs. Arlbery, that she lost all fear of her wit. She found it rather playful than satirical; rather seeking to amuse than to disconcert; and though sometimes, from the resistless pleasure of uttering a *bon mot* she thought more of its brilliancy than of the pain it might inflict, this happened but rarely, and was more commonly succeeded by regret than by triumph.

Camilla soon observed she had, personally, nothing to apprehend, peculiar partiality supplying the place of general delicacy, in shielding her from every shaft that even pleasantry could render poignant. The embarrassment, therefore, which, in ingenuous youth, checks the attempt to please, by fear of failure, or shame of exertion, gave way to natural spirits, which gaily rising from entertainment received, restored her vivacity, and gradually, though unconsciously, enabled her to do justice to her own abilities, by unaffectedly calling forth the mingled sweetness and intelligence of her character; and Mrs. Arlbery, charmed with all she observed, and flattered by all she inspired, felt such satisfaction in her evident conquest, that before the *tête à tête* was closed, their admiration was become nearly mutual.

When the evening party was announced, they both heard with surprise that the day was so far advanced. 'They can wait, however,' said Mrs. Arlbery, 'for I know they have nothing to do.'

She then invited Camilla to return to her the next day for a week.

Camilla felt well disposed to comply, hoping soon to reason from Edgar his prejudice against a connection that afforded her such singular pleasure; but to leave her father at this period was far from every wish. She excused herself, therefore, saying, she had still six weeks due to her uncle at Cleves, before any other engagement could take place.

'Well, then, when you quit your home for Sir Hugh, will you beg off a few days from him, and set them down to my account?'

'If my uncle pleases—'

'If he pleases?' repeated she, laughing; 'pray never give that *If* into his decision; you only put contradiction into people's heads, by asking what pleases them. Say at once, My good uncle, Mrs. Arlbery has invited me to indulge her with a few days at the Grove; so to-morrow I shall go to her. Will you promise me this?'

'Dear madam, no! my uncle would think me mad.'

'And suppose he should! A little alarm now and then keeps life from stagnation. They call me mad, I know, sometimes; wild, flighty, and what not; yet you see how harmless I am, though I afford food for such notable commentary.'

'But can you really like such things should be said of you?'

'I adore the frankness of that question! why, n - - o,—I rather think I don't. But I'm not sure. However, to prevent their minding me, I must mind them. And it's vastly more irksome to give up one's own way, than to hear a few impertinent remarks. And as to the world, depend upon it, my dear Miss Tyrold, the more you see of it, the less you will care for it.'

She then said she would leave her to re-invest herself in her own attire, and go downstairs, to see what the poor simple souls, who had had no more wit than to come back thus at her call, had found to do with themselves.

Camilla, having only her common morning dress, and even that utterly spoilt, begged that her appearance might be dispensed with; but Mrs. Arlbery, exclaiming, 'Why, there are only men; you don't mind men, I hope!' ashamed, she promised to get ready; yet she had not sufficient courage to descend, till her gay hostess came back, and accompanied her to the drawing room.

CHAPTER XII

Airs and Graces

UPON entering the room, Camilla saw again the Officers who had been there in the morning, and who were now joined by Sir Sedley Clarendel. She was met at the door by Major Cerwood, who seemed waiting for her appearance, and who made her his compliments with an air that studiously proclaimed his devotion. She seated herself by the side of Mrs. Arlbery, to look on at a game of chess, played by Sir Sedley and General Kinsale.

'Clarendel,' said Mrs. Arlbery, 'you have not the least in the world the air of knowing what you are about.'

'Pardon me, ma'am,' said the General, 'he has been at least half an hour contemplating this very move,—for which, as you see, I now check-mate him. Pray, Sir Sedley, how came you, at last, to do no better?'

'Thinking of other things, my dear General. 'Tis impossible in the extreme to keep one's faculties pinioned down to the abstruse vagaries of this brain-besieging game. My head would be deranged past redress, if I did not allow it to visit the four quarters of the globe once, at least, between every move.'

'You do not play so slow, then, from deliberating upon your chances, but from forgetting them?'

'Defined, my dear General, to scrupulosity! Those exquisite little moments we steal from any given occupation, for the pleasure of speculating in secret upon something wholly foreign to it, are resistless to deliciousness.'

'I entreat, and command you then,' cried Mrs. Arlbery, 'to make your speculations public. Nothing will more amuse me, than to have the least intimation of the subjects of your reveries.'

'My dear Mrs. Arlbery! your demand is the very quintessence of impossibility! Tell the subject of a reverie! know you not it wafts one at once out of the world, and the world's powers of expression? while all it substitutes is as evanescent as it is delectable. To attempt the least description would be a presumption of the first monstrousness.'

'O never heed that! presumption will not precisely be a novelty to you; answer me, therefore, my dear Clarendel, without all this conceit. You know I hate procrastination; and procrastinators still worse.'

'Softly, dearest madam, softly! There is nothing in nature so horribly shocking to me as the least hurry. My poor nerves seek repose after any turbulent words, or jarring sounds, with the same craving for rest that my body experiences after the jolts, and concussions of a long winded chase. By the way, does anybody want a good hunter? I have the first, perhaps, in Europe; but I would sell it a surprising bargain, for I am excruciatingly tired of it.'

All the gentlemen grouped round him to hear further particulars, except Mr. Macdersey, the young Ensign, who had so unguardedly exposed himself at the Northwick ball, and who now, approaching Camilla, fervently exclaimed; 'How happy I should have been, madam, if I had had the good fortune to see you meet with that accident this morning, instead of being looking another way! I might then have had the pleasure to assist you. And O! how much more if it had been your divine cousin! I hope that fair angel is in perfect health! O what a beautiful creature she is! her outside is the completest diamond I ever saw! and if her inside is the same, which I dare say it is, by her smiles and delicate dimples, she must be a paragon upon earth!'

'There is at least something very inartificial in your praise,' said General Kinsale, 'when you make your panegyric of an absent lady to a present one.'

'O General, there is not a lady living can bear any comparison with her. I have never had her out of my thoughts from the first darling moment that ever I saw her, which has made me the most miserable of men ever since. Her eyes so beautiful, her mouth so divine, her nose so heavenly!—'

'And how,' cried Sir Sedley, 'is the tip of her chin?'

'No joking, sir!' said the Ensign, reddening; 'she is a piece of perfection not to be laughed at; she has never had her fellow upon the face of the earth; and she never will have it while the earth holds, upon account of there being no such person above ground.'

'And pray,' cried Sir Sedley, carelessly, 'how can you be sure of that?'

'How! why by being certain,' answered the inflamed admirer; 'for though I have been looking out for pretty women from morning to night, ever since I was conscious of the right use of my eyes, I never yet saw her parallel.'

A servant was now bringing in the tea; but his lady ordered him to set it down in the next room, whence the gentlemen should fetch it as it was wanted.

Major Cerwood took in charge all attendance upon Camilla; but he was not, therefore, exempt from the assiduities required by Mrs. Arlbery, for whom the homage of the General, the Colonel, and the Ensign, were insufficient; and who, had a score more been present, would have found occupation for them all. Sir Sedley alone was excepted from her commands; for knowing they would be issued to him in vain, she contented herself with only interchanging glances of triumph with him, at the submission of every vassal but himself.

'Heavens!' cried she, to Colonel Andover, who had hastened to present her the first cup, 'you surely think I have nerves for a public orator! If I should taste but one drop of this tea, I might envy the repose of the next man who robs on the highway. Major Cerwood, will you try if you can do any better for me?'

The Major obeyed, but not with more success. 'What in the world have you brought me?' cried she; 'Is it tea? It looks prodigiously as if just imported out of the slop bason. For pity sake, Macdersey, arise, and give me your help; you will at least never bring me such maudlin stuff[1] as this. Even your tea will have some character; it will be very good or very bad; very hot or very cold; very strong or very weak; for you are always in flames of fire, or flakes of snow.'

'You do me justice, ma'am; there is nothing upon the face of the earth so insipid as a medium. Give me love or hate! a friend that will go to jail for me, or an enemy that will run me through the body! Riches to chuck guineas about like halfpence, or poverty to beg in a ditch! Liberty wild as the four winds, or an oar to work in a galley! Misery to tear my heart into an hundred thousand millions of atoms, or joy to make my soul dance into my brain! Every thing has some gratification, except a medium. 'Tis a poor little soul that is satisfied between happiness and despair.'

He then flew to bring her a dish of tea.

'My dear Macdersey,' cried she, in receiving it, 'this is according to your system indeed; for 'tis a compound of strong, and rich, and sweet, to cloy an alderman,[1] making altogether so luscious a syrup, that our spring would be exhausted before I could slake my thirst, if I should taste it only a second time. Do, dear General, see if it is not possible to get me some beverage that I can swallow.'

The youngest man present was not more active than the General in this service; but Mrs. Arlbery, casting herself despondingly back the moment she had tasted what he brought her, exclaimed, 'Why this is worst of all! If you can do no better for me, General, than this, tell me, at least, for mercy's sake, when some other regiment will be quartered here?'

'What a cruelty,' said the Major, looking with a sigh towards Camilla, 'to remind your unhappy prey they are but birds of passage!'

'O, all the better, Major. If you understand your own interest you will be as eager to break up your quarters, as I can be to see your successors march into them. I have now heard all your compliments, and you have heard all my repartees; both sides, therefore, want new auditors. A great many things I have said to you will do vastly well again for a new corps; and, to do you justice, some few things you have said yourselves may do again in a new county.'

Then, addressing Camilla, she proposed, though without moving, that they should converse with one another, and leave the men to take care of themselves. 'And excessively they will be obliged to me,' she continued, without lowering her voice, 'for giving this little holiday to their poor brains; for, I assure you, they have not known what to say this half hour. Indeed, since the first fortnight they were quartered here, they have not, upon an average, said above one new thing in three days. But one's obliged to take up with Officers in the country, because there's almost nothing else. Can you recommend me any agreeable new people?'

'O no, ma'am! I have hardly any acquaintance, except immediately round the rectory; but, fortunately, my own family is so large, that I have never been distressed for society.'

'O, ay, true! your own family, begin with that; do, pray, give me a little history of your own family?'

'I have no history, ma'am, to give, for my father's retired life——'

'O, I have seen your father, and I have heard him preach, and I like him very much. There's something in him there's no turning into ridicule.'

Camilla, though surprised, was delighted by such a testimony to the respectability of her father; and, with more courage, said— 'And, I am sure, if you knew my mother, you would allow her the same exemption.'

'So I hear; therefore, we won't talk of them. It's a delightful thing to think of perfection; but it's vastly more amusing to talk of errors and absurdities. To begin with your eldest sister, then— but no; she seems in just the same predicament as your father and mother: so we'll let her rest, too.'

'Indeed she is; she is as faultless——'

'O, not a word more then; she won't do for me at all. But, pray, is there not a single soul in all the round of your large family, that can afford a body a little innocent diversion?'

'Ah, madam,' said Camilla, shaking her head; 'I fear, on the contrary, if they came under your examination, there is not one in whom you would not discern some foible!'

'I should not like them at all the worse for that; for, between ourselves, my dear Miss Tyrold, I am half afraid they might find a foible or two in return in me; so you must not be angry if I beg the favour of you to indulge me with a few of their defects.'

'Indulge you!'

'Yes, for when so many of a family are perfect, if you can't find me one or two that have a little speck of mortality, you must not wonder if I take flight at your very name. In charity, therefore, if you would not drop my acquaintance, tell me their vulnerable parts.'

Camilla laughed at this ridiculous reasoning, but would not enter into its consequences.

'Well, then, if you will not assist me, don't take it ill that I assist myself. In the first place, there's your brother; I don't ask you to tell me any thing of him; I have seen him! and I confess to you he does not put me into utter despair! he does not alarm me into flying all his race.'

Camilla tried vainly to look grave.

'I have seen another, too, your cousin, I think; Miss Lynmere, that's engaged to young Mandlebert.'

Camilla now tried as vainly to look gay.

'She's prodigiously pretty. Pray, is not she a great fool?'

'Ma'am?'

'I beg your pardon! but I don't suppose you are responsible for the intellects of all your generation. However, she'll do vastly well; you need not be uneasy for her. A face like that will take very good care of itself. I am glad she is engaged, for your sake, though I am sorry for Mandlebert; that is, if, as his class of countenance generally predicts, he marries with any notion of expecting to be happy.'

'But why, ma'am,' cried Camilla, checking a sigh, 'are you glad for my sake?'

'Because there are two reasons why she would be wonderfully in your way; she is not only prettier than you, but sillier.'

'And would both those reasons,' cried Camilla, again laughing, 'make against me?'

'O, intolerably, with the men! They are always enchanted with something that is both pretty and silly; because they can so easily please and so soon disconcert it; and when they have made the little blooming fools blush and look down, they feel nobly superior, and pride themselves in victory. Dear creatures! I delight in their taste; for it brings them a plentiful harvest of repentance, when it is their connubial criterion; the pretty flies off, and the silly remains, and a man then has a choice companion for life left on his hands!'

The young Ensign here could no longer be silent: 'I am sure and certain,' cried he, warmly, 'Miss Lynmere is incapable to be a fool! and when she marries, if her husband thinks her so, it's only a sign he's a blockhead himself.'

'He'll be exactly of your opinion for the first month or two,' answered Mrs. Arlbery, 'or even if he is not, he'll like her just as well. A man looks enchanted while his beautiful young bride talks nonsense; it comes so prettily from her ruby lips, and she blushes and dimples with such lovely attraction while she utters it; he casts his eyes around him with conscious elation to see her admirers, and his enviers; but he has amply his turn for looking like a fool himself, when youth and beauty take flight, and when his ugly old wife exposes her ignorance or folly at every word.'

'The contrast of beginning and end,' said the General, 'is almost always melancholy. But how rarely does any man,—nay, I had nearly said, or any woman—think a moment of the time to come, or of any time but the present day, in marrying?'

'Except with respect to fortune!' cried Mrs. Arlbery, 'and there, methinks, you men, at least, are commonly sufficiently provident. I don't think reflection is generally what you want in that point.'

'As to reflection,' exclaimed Mr. Macdersey, ''tis the thing in the world I look upon to be the meanest! a man capable of reflection, where a beautiful young creature is in question, can have no soul nor vitals. For my part, 'tis my only misfortune that I cannot get at that lovely girl, to ask her for her private opinion of me at once, that I might either get a licence tomorrow, or drive her out of my head before sleep overtakes me another night.'

'Your passions, my good Macdersey,' said Mrs. Arlbery, 'considering their violence, seem tolerably obedient. Can you really be so fond, or so forgetful at such short warning?'

'Yes, but it's with a pain that breaks my heart every time.'

'You contrive, however, to get it pretty soon mended!'

'That, madam, is a power that has come upon me by degrees; I have paid dear enough for it!—nobody ever found it harder than I did at the beginning; for the first two or three times I took my disappointments so to heart, that I should have been bound for ever to any friend that would have had the good nature to blow my brains out.'

'But now you are so much in the habit of experiencing these little failures, that they pass on as things of course?'

'No, madam, you injure me, and in the tenderest point; for, as long as I have the least hope, my passion's as violent as ever; but you would not be so unreasonable as to have a man love on, when it can answer no end? It's no better than making him unhappy for a joke. There's no sense in such a thing.'

'By the way, my dear Miss Tyrold, and *apropos* to this Miss Lynmere,' said Mrs. Arlbery, 'do tell me something about Mr. Mandlebert—what is he?—what does he do always amongst you?'

'He—he!—' cried Camilla, stammering, 'he was a ward of my father's—'

'O, I don't mean all that; but what is his style?—his class?—is he agreeable?'

'I believe—he is generally thought so.'

'If he is, do pray, then, draw him into my society, for I am terribly in want of recruits. These poor gentlemen you see here are very good sort of men; but they have a trick of sleeping with their eyes wide open, and fancy all the time they are awake; and, indeed, I find it hard to persuade them to the contrary, though I often ask them for their dreams. By the way, can't you contrive, some or other amongst you, to make the room a little cooler?'

'Shall I open this window?' said the Major.

'Nay, nay, don't ask me; I had rather bear six times the heat, than give my own directions: nothing in the world fatigues me so much as telling stupid people how to set about things. Colonel, don't you see I have no fan?'

'I'll fetch it directly—have you left it in the dining-parlour?'

'Do you really think I would not send a footman at once, if I must perplex myself with all that recollection? My dear Miss Tyrold, did you ever see any poor people, that pretended at all to walk about, and mingle with the rest of the world, like living creatures, so completely lethargic?—'tis really quite melancholy! I am sure you have good nature enough to pity them. It requires my utmost ingenuity to keep them in any employment; and if I left them to themselves, they would stand before the fire all the winter, and lounge upon sofas all the summer. And that indolence of body so entirely unnerves the mind, that they find as little to say as to do. Upon the whole, 'tis really a paltry race, the men of the present times. However, as we have got no better, and as the women are worse, I do all I can to make them less insufferable to me.'

'And do you really think the women are worse?' cried Camilla.

'Not in themselves, my dear; but worse to me, because I cannot possibly take the same liberties with them. Macdersey, I wish I had my salts.

'It shall be the happiness of my life to find them, be they hid where they may; only tell me where I may have the pleasure to go and look for them.'

'Nay, that's your affair.'

'Why, then, if they are to be found from the garret to the cellar, be sure I am a dead man, if I do not bring them you!

This mode of displaying airs and graces was so perfectly new to Camilla, that the commands issued, and the obedience paid, were equally amusing to her. Brought up herself to be contented with whatever came in her way, in preference either to giving trouble, or finding fault, the ridiculous, yet playful wilfulness with which she saw Mrs. Arlbery send every one upon her errands, yet object to what every one performed, presented to her a scene of such whimsical gaiety, that her concern at the accident which had made her innocently violate her intended engagement with Edgar, was completely changed into pleasure, that thus, without any possible self blame, an acquaintance she had so earnestly desired was even by necessity established: and she returned home at night with spirits all revived, and eloquent in praise of her new favourite.

CHAPTER XIII

Attic Adventures

MR. Tyrold, according to the system of recreation which he had settled with his wife, saw with satisfaction the pleasure with which Camilla began this new acquaintance, in the hope it would help to support her spirits during the interval of suspense with regard to the purposes of Mandlebert. Mrs. Arlbery was unknown to him, except by general fame; which told him she was a woman of reputation as well as fashion, and that though her manners were lively, her heart was friendly, and her hand ever open to charity.

Upon admitting Lionel again to his presence, he spoke forcibly, though with brevity, upon the culpability of his conduct. What he had done, he said, let him colour it to himself with what levity he might, was not only a robbery, but a robbery of the most atrocious and unjustifiable class; adding terror to violation of property, and playing upon the susceptibility of the weakness and infirmities, which he ought to have been the first to have sheltered and sheathed. Had the action contained no purpose but a frolic, even then the situation of the object on whom it fell, rendered it inhuman; but as its aim and end was to obtain money, it was dishonourable to his character, and criminal by the laws of his country. 'Yet shudder no more,' continued he, 'young man, at the justice to which they make you amenable, than at having deserved, though you escape it! From this day, however, I will name it no more. Feeble must be all I could utter, compared with what the least reflection must make you feel! Your uncle, in a broken state of health, is sent abroad; your mother, though too justly incensed to see you, sacrifices her happiness to serve you!'

Lionel, for a few hours, was in despair after this harangue; but as they passed away, he strove to drive it from his mind, persuading himself it was useless to dwell upon what was irretrievable.

Mrs. Arlbery, the following day, made her visit at Etherington, and invited the two sisters to a breakfast she was to give the next morning. Mr. Tyrold, who with surprize and concern at a coldness so dilatory, found a second day wearing away without a visit from Mandlebert, gladly consented to allow of an amusement, that might shake from Camilla the pensiveness into which, at times, he saw her falling.

Mrs. Arlbery had declared she hated ceremony in the summer; guarded, therefore, by Lionel, the sisters walked to the Grove. From the little hill they had again to pass, they observed a group of company upon the leads of her house, which were flat, and balustraded round; and when they presented themselves at the door, they were met by Major Cerwood, who conducted them to the scene of business.

It was the end of July, and the weather was sultry; but though the height of the place upon which the present party was collected, gave some freshness to the air, the heat reflected from the lead would have been nearly intolerable, had it not been obviated by an awning, and by matts, in the part where seats and refreshments were arranged. French horns and clarinets were played during the repast.

This little entertainment had for motive a young lady's quitting her boarding school. Miss Dennel, a niece, by marriage, of Mrs. Arlbery, who, at the age of fourteen, came to preside at the house and table of her father, had begged to be felicitated by her aunt, upon the joyful occasion, with a ball: but Mrs. Arlbery declared she never gave any entertainments in which she did not expect to play the principal part herself; and that balls and concerts were

therefore excluded from her list of home diversions. It was vastly
well to see others shine superior, she said, elsewhere, but she
could not be so accommodating as to perform Nobody under her
own roof.[1] She offered her, however, a breakfast, with full choice
of its cakes and refreshments; which, with leave to fix upon the
spot where it should be given, was all the youthful pleader could
obtain.

The Etherington trio met with a reception the most polite, and
Camilla was distinguished by marks of peculiar favour. Few
guests were added to the party she had met there before, except
the young lady who was its present foundress; and whose voice
she recollected to have heard, in the enquiries which had reached
her ear from within the paddock.

Miss Dennel was a pretty, blooming, tall girl, but as childish
in intellect as in experience; though self-persuaded she was a
woman in both, since she was called from school to sit at the head
of her father's table.

Camilla required nothing further for entertainment than to
listen to her new friend; Lavinia, though more amazed than
amused, always modestly hung back as a mere looker on; and the
company in general made their diversion from viewing, through
various glasses, the seats of the neighbouring gentlemen, and re-
viewing, with yet more scrutiny, their characters and circumstances. But Lionel, ever restless, seized the opportunity to patrol
the attic regions of the house, where, meeting with a capacious
lumber room, he returned to assure the whole party it would make
an admirable theatre, and to ask who would come forth to spout
with him.

Mr. Macdersey said, he did not know one word of any part, but
he could never refuse anything that might contribute to the
company's pleasure.

Away they sped together, and in a few minutes reversed the face
of everything. Old sofas, bedsteads, and trunks, large family
chests, deal boxes and hampers, carpets and curtains rolled up for
the summer, tables with two legs, and chairs without bottoms,
were truckled from the middle to one end of the room, and
arranged to form a semi-circle, with seats in front, for a pit.
Carpets were then uncovered and untied, to be spread for the
stage, and curtains, with as little mercy, were unfurled, and hung
up to make a scene.

They then applied to Miss Dennel, who had followed to peep at what they were about, and asked if she thought the audience might be admitted.

She declared she had never seen any place so neat and elegant in her life.

Such an opinion could not but be decisive; and they prepared to re-ascend; when the sight of a small door, near the entrance of the large apartment, excited the ever ready curiosity of Lionel, who, though the key was on the outside, contrived to turn it wrong; but while endeavouring to rectify by force what he had spoilt by aukwardness, a sudden noise from within startled them all, and occasioned quick and reiterated screams from Miss Dennel, who, with the utmost velocity burst back upon the company on the leads, calling out; 'O Lord! how glad I am I'm coming back alive! Mr. Macdersey and young Mr. Tyrold are very likely killed! for they've just found I don't know how many robbers shut up in a dark closet!'

The gentlemen waited for no explanation to this unintelligible story, but hastened to the spot; and Mrs. Arlbery ordered all the servants who were in waiting to follow and assist.

Miss Dennel then entreated to have the trap door through which they ascended, from a small staircase, to the leads, double locked till the gentlemen should declare upon their honours that the thieves were all dead.

Mrs. Arlbery would not listen to this, but waited with Lavinia and Camilla the event.

The gentlemen, meanwhile, reached the scene of action, at the moment when Macdersey, striking first his foot, and then his whole person against the door, had forced it open with such sudden violence, that he fell over a pail of water into the adjoining room.

The servants arriving at the same time, announced that this was merely a closet for mops, brooms, and pails, belonging to the housemaid: and it appeared, upon examination, that the noise from within, had simply been produced by the falling down of a broom, occasioned by their shaking the door in endeavouring to force the lock.

The Ensign, wetted or splashed all over, was in a fury; and, turning to Lionel, who laughed vociferously, whilst the rest of the gentlemen were scarce less moderate, and the servants joined in the chorus, peremptorily demanded to know if he had put the pail there on purpose; 'In which case, sir,' said he, 'you must never let me see you laugh again to the longest hour you have to live!'

'My good Macdersey,' said the General, 'go into another room, and have your cloaths wiped and dried; it will be time enough then to settle who shall laugh longest.'

'General,' said he, 'I scorn to mind being either wet or dry; a soldier ought to be above such delicate effeminacy: it is not, therefore, the sousing I regard, provided I can once be clear it was not done for a joke.'

Lionel, when he could speak, declared, that far from placing the pail there on purpose, he had not known there was such a closet in the house, nor had ever been up those stairs till they all mounted them together.

'I am perfectly satisfied, then, my good friend,' said the Ensign, shaking him by the hand with an heartiness that gave him no small share of the pail's contents; 'when a gentleman tells me a thing seriously, I make it a point to believe him; especially if he has a good honest countenance, that assures me he would not refuse me satisfaction, in the case he had meant to make game of me.'

'And do you always terminate your jests with the ceremony of a tilting match?' cried Sir Sedley.

'Yes, Sir! if I'm made a joke of by a man of any honour. For, to tell you a piece of my mind, there's no one thing upon earth I hate like a joke; unless it's against another person; and then it only gives me a little joy inwardly; for I make it a point of complaisance not to laugh out: except where I happen to wish for a little private conversation with the person that gives me the diversion.'

'Facetious in the extreme!' cried Sir Sedley, 'an infallibly excellent mode to make a man die of laughter? Droll to the utmost!'

'With regard to that, Sir, I have no objection to a little wit or humour, provided a person has the politeness to laugh only at himself, and his own particular friends and relations; but if once he takes the liberty to turn me into ridicule, I look upon it as an affront, and expect the proper reparation.'

'O, to refuse that would be without bowels[1] to a degree!'

Lionel now ran up stairs, to beg the ladies would come and see

the theatre; but suddenly exclaimed, as he looked around, 'Ah ha!'
and hastily galloped down, and to the bottom of the house. Mrs.
Arlbery descended with her young party, and the Ensign, in mock
heroics, solemnly prostrated himself to Miss Dennel, pouring into
her delighted ears, from various shreds and scraps of different
tragedies, the most high flown and egregiously ill-adapted com-
plements: while the Major, less absurdly, though scarce less
passionately, made Camilla his Juliet, and whispered the tenderest
lines of Romeo.

Lionel presently running, out of breath, up stairs again, cried:
'Mrs. Arlbery, I have drawn you in a new beau.'

'Have you?' cried she, coolly; 'why then I permit you to draw
him out again. Had you told me he had forced himself in, you
had made him welcome. But I foster only willing slaves. So off, if
you please, with your boast and your beau.'

'I can't, upon my word, ma'am, for he is at my heels.'

Mandlebert, at the same moment, not hearing what passed,
made his appearance.

The surprised and always unguarded Camilla, uttered an
involuntary exclamation, which instantly catching his ear, drew
his eye towards the exclaimer, and there fixed it; with an astonishment which suspended wholly his half made bow, and beginning
address to Mrs. Arlbery.

Lionel had descried him upon the little hill before the house;
where, as he was passing on, his own attention had been caught
by the sound of horns and clarinets, just as, without any explanation, Lionel flew to tell him he was wanted, and almost forced him
off his horse, and up the stairs.

Mrs. Arlbery, in common with those who dispense with all
forms for themselves, exacted them punctiliously from all others.
The visit therefore of Mandlebert not being designed for her,
afforded her at first no gratification, and produced rather a
contrary feeling, when she observed the total absence of all
pleasure in the surprise with which he met Camilla at her house.
She gave him a reception of cold civility, and then chatted almost
wholly with the General, or Sir Sedley.

Edgar scarce saw whether he was received or not; his bow was
mechanical, his apology for his intrusion was unintelligible.
Amazement at seeing Camilla under this roof, disappointment at
her breach of implied promise, and mortification at the air of

being at home, which he thought he remarked in her situation, though at an acquaintance he had taken so much pains to keep aloof from her, all conspired to displease and perplex him; and though his eyes could with difficulty look any other way, he neither spoke to nor approached her.

Nor was even thus meeting her all he had to give him disturbance; the palpable devoirs of Major Cerwood incensed as well astonished him; for, under pretext of only following the humour of the day, in affecting to act the hero in love, the Major assailed her, without reserve, with declarations of his passion, which though his words passed off as quotations, his looks and manner made appropriate. How, already, thought Edgar, has he obtained such a privilege? such confidence? To have uttered one such sentence, my tongue would have trembled, my lips would have quivered!

Camilla felt confounded by his presence, from the consciousness of the ill opinion she must excite by this second apparent disregard of a given engagement. She would fain have explained to him it's history; but she could not free herself from the Major, whose theatrical effusions were not now to be repressed, since, at first, she had unthinkingly attended to them.

Lionel joined with Macdersey in directing similar heroics to Miss Dennel, who, simply enchanted, called out: 'I'm determined when I've a house of my own, I'll have just such a room as this at the top of it, on purpose to act a play every night.'

'And when, my dear,' said Mrs. Arlbery, 'do you expect to have a house of your own?'

'O, as soon as I am married, you know.'

'Is your marrying, then, already decided?'

'Dear no, not that I know of, aunt. I'm sure I never trouble myself about it; only I suppose it will happen some day or other.'

'And when it does, you are very sure your husband will approve your acting plays every night?'

'O, as to that, I shan't ask him. Whenever I'm married I'll be my own mistress, that I'm resolved upon. But papa's so monstrous cross, he says he won't let me act plays now.'

'Papas and mamas,' cried Sir Sedley, 'are ever most egregiously in the way. 'Tis prodigiously surprising they have never yet been banished society. I know no mark more irrefragable of the supineness of mankind.'

Then rising, and exclaiming: 'What savage heat! I wish the

weather had a little feeling!' he broke up the party by ordering his curricle,[1] and being the first to depart.

'That creature,' cried Mrs. Arlbery, 'if one had the least care for him, is exactly an animal to drive one mad! He labours harder to be affected than any ploughman does for his dinner. And, completely as his conceit obscures it, he has every endowment nature can bestow, except common sense!'

They now all descended to take leave, except the Ensign and Lionel, who went, arm in arm, prowling about, to view all the garrets, followed on tip-toe by Miss Dennel. Lavinia called vainly after her brother; but Camilla, hoping every instant she might clear her conduct to Edgar, was not sorry to be detained.

They had not, however, been five minutes in the parlour, before a violent and angry noise from above, induced them all to remount to the top of the house; and there, upon entering a garret whence it issued, they saw Miss Dennel, decorated with the Ensign's cocked hat and feather, yet looking pale with fright; Lionel accoutred in the maid's cloaths, and almost in a convulsion of laughter; and Macdersey, in a rage utterly incomprehensible, with the coachman's large bob-wig hanging loose upon his head.

It was sometime before it was possible to gather, that having all paraded into various garrets, in search of adventures, Lionel, after attiring himself in the maid's gown, cap, and apron, had suddenly deposited upon Miss Dennel's head the Ensign's cocked hat, replacing it with the coachman's best wig upon the toupee of Macdersey; whose resentment was so violent at this liberty, that it was still some minutes before he could give it articulation.

The effect of this full buckled bob-jerom[2] which stuck hollow from the young face and powdered locks of the Ensign, was irresistibly ludicrous; yet he would have deemed it a greater indignity to take it quietly off, than to be viewed in it by thousands; though when he saw the disposition of the whole company to sympathise with Lionel, his wrath rose yet higher, and stamping with passion, he fiercely said to him—'Take it off, sir!—take it off my head!'

Lionel, holding this too imperious a command to be obeyed, only shouted louder. Macdersey then, incensed beyond endurance, lowered his voice with stifled choler, and putting his arms akimbo, said—'If you take me for a fool, sir, I shall demand satisfaction; for it's what I never put up with!'

Then, turning to the rest, he solemnly added—'I beg pardon of all the worthy company for speaking this little whisper, which certainly I should scorn to do before ladies, if it had not been a secret.'

Mrs. Arlbery, alarmed at the serious consequences now threatening this folly, said—'No, no; I allow of no secrets in my house, but what are entrusted to myself. I insist, therefore, upon being umpire in this cause.'

'Madam,' said Macdersey, 'I hope never to become such a debased brute of the creation, as to contradict the commands of a fair lady: except when it's upon a point of honour. But I can't consent to pass for a fool; and still more not for a poltroon— You'll excuse the little hint.'

Then, while making a profound and ceremonious bow, his wig fell over his head on the ground.

'This is very unlucky,' cried he, with a look of vexation; 'for certainly, and to be sure no human mortal should have made me take it off myself, before I was righted.'

Camilla, picking it up, to render the affair merely burlesque, pulled off the maid's cap from her brother's head, and put on the wig in its place, saying—'There, Lionel, you have played the part of *Lady Wrong Head* long enough; be so good now as to perform that of *Sir Francis*.'[1]

This ended the business, and the whole party, in curricles, on horseback, or on foot, departed from the Grove.

BOOK IV

CHAPTER I

A Few Explanations

THE last words of Dr. Marchmont, in taking leave of Edgar, were injunctions to circumspection, and representations of the difficulty of drawing back with honour, if once any incautious eagerness betrayed his partiality. To this counsel he was impelled to submit, lest he should risk for Camilla a report similar to that which for Indiana had given him so much disturbance. There, indeed, he felt himself wholly blameless. His admiration was but such as he always experienced at sight of a beautiful picture, nor had it ever been demonstrated in any more serious manner. He had distinguished her by no particular attention, singled her out by no pointed address, taken no pains to engage her good opinion, and manifested no flattering pleasure at her approach or presence.

His sense of right was too just to mislead him into giving himself similar absolution with respect to Camilla. He had never, indeed, indulged a voluntary vent to his preference; but the candour of his character convinced him that what so forcibly he had felt, he must occasionally have betrayed. Yet the idea excited regret without remorse; for though it had been his wish, as well as intention, to conceal his best hopes, till they were ratified by his judgment, he had the conscious integrity of knowing that, should her heart become his prize, his dearest view in life would be to solicit her hand.

To preserve, therefore, the appearance of an undesigning friend of the house, he had forced himself to refrain, for two days, from any visit to the rectory, whither he was repairing, when thus, unlooked and unwished for, he surprised Camilla at the Grove.

Disappointed and disapproving feelings kept him, while there, aloof from her; by continual suggestions, that her character was of no stability, that Dr. Marchmont was right in his doubts, and

Miss Margland herself not wrong in accusing her of caprice; and when he perceived, upon her preparing to walk home with her brother and sister, that Major Cerwood stept forward to attend her, he indignantly resolved to arrange without delay his continental excursion. But again, when, as she quitted the room, he saw her head half turned round, with an eye of enquiry if he followed, he determined frankly, and at once, in his capacity of a friend, to request some explanation of this meeting.

The assiduities of the Major made it difficult to speak to her; but the aid of her desire for a conversation, which was equally anxious, and less guarded then his own, anticipated his principal investigation, by urging her, voluntarily to seize an opportunity of relating to him the history of her first visit to Mrs. Arlbery; and of assuring him that the second was indispensably its consequence.

Softened by this apparent earnestness for his good opinion, all his interest and all his tenderness for her returned; and though much chagrined at the accident, or rather mischief, which had thus established the acquaintance, he had too little to say, whatever he had to feel, of positive weight against it, to propose its now being relinquished. He thanked her impressively for so ready an explanation; and then gently added; 'I know your predilection in favour of this lady, and I will say nothing to disturb it; but as she is yet new to you, and as all residence, all intercourse, from your own home or relations, is new to you also—tell me, candidly, sincerely tell me, can you condescend to suffer an old friend, though in the person of but a young man, to offer you, from time to time, a hint, a little counsel, a few brief words of occasional advice? and even, perhaps, now and then, to torment you into a little serious reflection?'

'If you,' cried she, gaily, 'will give me the reflection, I promise, to the best of my power, to give you in return, the seriousness; but I can by no means engage for both!'

'O, never, but from your own prudence,' he answered, gratefully, 'may your delightful vivacity know a curb! If now I seem myself to fear it, it is not from moroseness, it is not from insensibility to its charm——'

He was stopt here by Macdersey, who, suddenly overtaking him, entreated an immediate short conference upon a matter of moment.

Though cruelly vexed by the interruption, he could not refuse to turn back with him; and Camilla again was left wholly to the gallant Major; but her heart felt so light that she had thus cleared herself to Edgar, so gratified by his request to become himself her monitor, and so enchanted to find her acquintance with Mrs. Arlbery no longer disputed, that she was too happy to admit any vexation; and the Major had never thought her so charming, though of the Major she thought not one moment.

Macdersey, with a long, ceremonious, and not very clear apology, confessed he had called Mandlebert aside only to enquire into the certain truth, if it were not a positive secret, of his intended nuptials with the beautiful Miss Lynmere. Mandlebert, with surprize, but without any hesitation, declared himself wholly without any pretensions to that lady. Macdersey then embraced him, and they parted mutually satisfied.

It seemed now too late to Mandlebert to go to Etherington till the next day, whither, as soon as he had breakfasted, he then rode.

According to his general custom, he went immediately to the study, where he met with a calm, but kind reception from Mr. Tyrold; and after half an hour's conversation, upon Lisbon, Dr. Marchmont, and Mrs. Tyrold, he left him to seek his young friends.

In the parlour, he found Lavinia alone; but before he could enquire for her sister, who was accidentally up stairs, Lionel, just dismounted from his horse, appeared.

'O, ho, Edgar!' cried he, 'you are here, are you? this would make fine confusion, if that beauty of nature, Miss Margland, should happen to call. They've just sent for you to Beech Park. I don't know what's to be done to you; but if you have an inclination to save poor Camilla's eyes, or cap, at least, from that meek, tender creature, you'll set off for Cleves before they know you are in this house.'

Edgar amazed, desired an explanation; but he protested the wrath of Miss Margland had been so comical, and given him so much diversion, that he had not been able to get at any particulars; he only knew there was a great commotion, and that Edgar was declared in love with some of his sisters or cousins, and Miss Margland was in a rage that it was not with herself; and that, in short, because he only happened to drop a hint of the latter notion, that delectable paragon had given him so violent a blow with her fine eyes, that in order to vent an ungovernable fit of laughter, without the risk of having the house pulled about his ears, he had hastily mounted his horse, and galloped off.

The contempt of Edgar for Miss Margland would have made him disdain another question, if the name of Camilla had not been mingled in this relation; no question, however, could procure further information. Lionel, enchanted that he had tormented Miss Margland, understood nothing more of the matter, and could only repeat his own merry sayings, and their effect.

Lavinia expressed, most innocently, her curiosity to know what this meant; and was going for Camilla, to assist in some conjecture; but Edgar, who by this strange story had lost his composure, felt unequal to hearing it discussed in her presence, and, pleading sudden haste, rode away.

He did not, however, go to Cleves; he hardly knew if Lionel had not amused him with a feigned story; but he no sooner arrived at Beech Park, then he found a message from Sir Hugh, begging to see him with all speed.

The young Ensign was the cause of this present summons and disturbance. Elated by the declaration of Mandlebert, that the rumour of his contract was void of foundation, and buoyed up by Mrs. Arlbery, to whom he returned with the communication, he resolved to make his advances in form. He presented himself, therefore, at Cleves, where he asked an audience of Sir Hugh, and at once, with his accustomed vehemence, declared himself bound eternally, life and soul, to his fair niece, Miss Lynmere; and desired that, in order to pay his addresses to her, he might be permitted to see her at odd times, when he was off duty.

Sir Hugh was scarce able to understand him, from his volubility, and the extravagance of his phrases and gestures; but he imputed them to his violent passion, and therefore answered him with great gentleness, assuring him he did not mean to doubt his being a proper alliance for his niece, though he had never heard of him before; but begging he would not be affronted if he could not accept him, not knowing yet quite clearly if she were not engaged to a young gentleman in the neighbourhood.

The Ensign now loudly proclaimed his own news: Mandlebert had protested himself free, and the whole county already rang with the mistake.

Sir Hugh, who always at a loss how to say no, thought this

would have been a good answer, now sent for Miss Margland, and desired her to speak herself with the young gentleman.

Miss Margland, much gratified, asked Macdersey if she could look at his rent roll.

He had nothing of the kind at hand, he said, not being yet come to his estate, which was in Ireland, and was still the property of a first cousin, who was not yet dead.

Miss Margland, promising he should have an answer in a few days, then dismissed him; but more irritated than ever against Mandlebert, from the contrast of his power to make settlements, she burst forth into her old declarations of his ill usage of Miss Lynmere; attributing it wholly to the contrivances of Camilla, whom she had herself, she said, surprized wheedling Edgar into her snares, when she called last at Etherington; and who, she doubted not, they should soon hear was going to be married to him.

Sir Hugh always understood literally whatever was said; these assertions therefore of ill humour, merely made to vent black bile,[1] affected him deeply for the honour and welfare of Camilla, and he hastily sent a messenger for Edgar, determining to beg, if that were the case, he would openly own the whole, and not leave all the blame to fall all upon his poor niece.

At this period, Lionel had called, and, by inflaming Miss Margland, had aggravated the general disturbance.

When Edgar arrived, Sir Hugh told him of the affair, assuring him he should never have taken amiss his preferring Camilla, which he thought but natural, if he had only done it from the first.

Edgar, though easily through all this he saw the malignant yet shallow offices of Miss Margland, found himself, with infinite vexation, compelled to declare off[2] equally from both the charges; conscious, that till the very moment of his proposals, he must appear to have no preference nor designs. He spoke, therefore, with the utmost respect of the young ladies, but again said it was uncertain if he should not travel before he formed any establishment.

The business thus explicitly decided, nothing more could be done: but Miss Margland was somewhat appeased, when she heard that her pupil was not so disgracefully to be supplanted.

Indiana herself, to whom Edgar had never seemed agreeable, soon forget she had ever thought of him; and elated by the acquisition of a new lover, doubted not, but, in a short time, the publication of her liberty would prove slavery to all mankind.

Early the next morning, the carriage of Sir Hugh arrived at the rectory for Camilla. She never refused an invitation from her uncle, but she felt so little equal to passing a whole day in the presence of Miss Margland, after the unaccountable, yet alarming relation she had gathered from Lionel, that she entreated him to accompany her, and to manage that she should return with him as soon as the horses were fed and rested.

Lionel, ever good humoured, and ready to oblige, willingly complied; but demanded that she should go with him, in their way back, to see a new house which he wanted to examine.

Sir Hugh received her with his usual affection, Indiana with indifference, and Miss Margland with a malicious smile: but Eugenia, soon taking her aside, disclosed to her that Edgar, the day before, had publicly and openly disclaimed any views upon Indiana, and had declared himself without any passion whatever, and free from all inclination or intention but to travel.

The blush of pleasure, with which Camilla heard the first sentence of this speech, became the tingle of shame at the second, and whitened into surprise and sorrow at the last.

Eugenia, though she saw some disturbance, understood not these changes. Early absorbed in the study of literature and languages, under the direction of a preceptor who had never mingled with the world, her capacity had been occupied in constant work for her memory; but her judgment and penetration had been wholly unexercised. Like her uncle, she concluded every body, and every thing to be precisely what they appeared; and though, in that given point of view, she had keener intellects to discern, and more skill to appreciate persons and characters, she was as unpractised as himself in those discriminative powers, which dive into their own conceptions to discover the latent springs, the multifarious and contradictory sources of human actions and propensities.

Upon their return to the company, Miss Margland chose to relate the history herself. Mr. Mandlebert, she said, had not only thought proper to acknowledge his utter insensibility to Miss Lynmere, but had declared his indifference for every woman under the sun, and protested he held them all cheap alike. 'So I would advise nobody,' she continued, 'to flatter themselves with making a conquest of him, for they may take my word for it, he won't be caught very easily.'

Camilla disdained to understand this but in a general sense, and made no answer. Indiana, pouting her lip, said she was sure she did not want to catch him: she did not fear having offers enough without him, if she should happen to chuse to marry.

'Certainly,' said Miss Margland, 'there's no doubt of that; and this young officer's coming the very moment he heard of your being at liberty, is a proof that the only reason of your having had no more proposals, is owing to Mr. Mandlebert. So I don't speak for you, but for any body else, that may suppose they may please the difficult gentleman better.'

Camilla now breathed hard with resentment; but still was silent, and Indiana, answering only for herself, said: 'O, yes! I can't say I'm much frightened. I dare say if Mr. Melmond had known, . . . but he thought like everybody else . . . however, I'm sure, I'm very glad of it, only I wish he had spoke a little sooner, for I suppose Mr. Melmond thinks me as much out of his reach as if I was married. Not that I care about it; only it's provoking.'

'No, my dear,' said Miss Margland, 'it would be quite below your dignity to think about him, without knowing better who he is, or what are his expectations and connexions. As to this young officer, I shall take proper care to make enquiries, before he has his answer. He belongs to a very good family; for he's related to Lord O'Lerney, and I have friends in Ireland who can acquaint me with his situation and fortune. There's time enough to look about you; only as Mr. Mandlebert has behaved so unhandsomely, I hope none of the family will give him their countenance. I am sure it will be to no purpose, if any body should think of doing it by way of having any design upon him. It will be lost labour, I can tell them.'

'As to that, I am quite easy,' said Indiana, tossing her head, 'any body is welcome to him for me;—my cousin, or any body else.'

Camilla, now, absolutely called upon to speak, with all the spirit she could assume, said, 'With regard to me, there is no occasion to remind me how much I am out of the question; yet suffer me to say, respect for myself would secure me from forming such plans as you surmise, if no other sense of propriety could save me from such humiliation.'

'Now, my dear, you speak properly,' said Miss Margland, taking her hand; 'and I hope you will have the spirit to shew him you care no more for him than he cares for you.'

'I hope so too,' answered Camilla, turning pale; 'but I don't suppose—I can't imagine—that it is very likely he should have mentioned anything good or bad—with regard to his care for me?'

This was painfully uttered, but from a curiosity irrepressible.

'As to that, my dear, don't deceive yourself; for the question was put home to him very properly, that you might know what you had to expect, and not keep off other engagements from a false notion.'

'This indeed,' said Camilla, colouring with indignation, 'this has been a most useless, a most causeless enquiry!'

'I am very glad you treat the matter as it deserves, for I like to see young ladies behave with dignity.'

'And pray, then, what—was there any—did he make—was there any—any answer—to this—to—.'

'O, yes, he answered without any great ceremony, I can assure you! He said, in so many words, that he thought no more of you than of our cousin, and was going abroad to divert and amuse himself, better than by entering into marriage, with either one or other of you; or with any body else.'

Camilla felt half killed by this answer; and presently quitting the room, ran out into the garden, and to a walk far from the house, before she had power to breathe, or recollection to be aware of the sensibility she was betraying.

She then as hastily went back, secretly resolving never more to think of him, and to shew both to himself and to the world, by every means in her power, her perfect indifference.

She could not, however, endure to encounter Miss Margland again, but called for Lionel, and begged him to hurry the coachman.

Lionel complied—she took a hasty leave of her uncle, and only saying, 'Good by, good by!' to the rest, made her escape.

Sir Hugh, ever unsuspicious, thought her merely afraid to detain her brother; but Eugenia, calm, affectionate, and divested of cares for herself, saw evidently that something was wrong, though she divined not what, and entreated leave to go with her sister to Etherington, and thence return, without keeping out the horses.

Sir Hugh was well pleased, and the two sisters and Lionel set off together.

CHAPTER II

Specimens of Taste

THE presence of Lionel stifled the enquiries of Eugenia; and pride, all up in arms, absorbed every softer feeling in Camilla.

When they had driven half a mile, 'Now, young ladies,' said he, 'I shall treat you with a frolic.' He then stopt the carriage, and told the coachman to drive to Cornfield; saying, 'Tis but two miles about, and Coachy won't mind that; will you Coachy?'

The coachman, looking forward to half a crown, said his horses would be all the better for a little more exercise; and Jacob, familiarly fond of Lionel from a boy, made no difficulty.

Lionel desired his sisters to ask no questions, assuring them he had great designs, and a most agreeable surprise in view for them.

In pursuance of his directions, they drove on till they came before a small house, just new fronted with deep red bricks, containing, on the ground floor, two little bow windows, in a sharp triangular form, enclosing a door ornamented with small panes of glass, cut in various shapes; on the first story, a little balcony, decorated in the middle and at each corner with leaden images of Cupids; and, in the attic story, a very small venetian window,[1] partly formed with minute panes of glass, and partly with glazed tiles; representing, in blue and white, various devices of dogs and cats, mice and birds, rats and ferrets, as emblems of the conjugal state.

'Well, young ladies, what say you to this?' cried he, 'does it hit your fancy? If it does, 'tis your own!'

Eugenia asked what he meant.

'Mean? to make a present of it to which ever is the best girl, and can first cry bo! to a goose. Come, don't look disdainfully. Eugenia, what say you? won't it be better to be mistress of this little neat, tight, snug box, and a pretty little tidy husband, that belongs to it, than to pore all day long over a Latin theme with old Dr. Orkborne? I have often thought my poor uncle was certainly out of his wits, when he set us all, men, women, and children, to learn Latin, or else be whipt by the old doctor. But we all soon got our necks out of the collar, except poor Eugenia, and she's had to work for us all. However, here's an opportunity—see but what a pretty place—not quite finished, to be sure, but look at that lake? how cool, how rural, how refreshing!'

'Lake?' repeated Eugenia, 'I see nothing but a very dirty little pond, with a mass of rubbish in the middle. Indeed I see nothing else but rubbish all round, and every where.'

'That's the very beauty of the thing, my dear; it's all in the exact state for being finished under your own eye, and according to your own taste.'

'To whom does it belong?'

'It's uninhabited yet; but it's preparing for a very spruce young spark, that I advise you both to set your caps at. Hold! I see somebody peeping; I'll go and get some news for you.'

He then jumped from the coach, and ran up five deep narrow steps, formed of single large rough stones, which mounted so much above the threshold of the house, that upon opening the door, there appeared a stool to assist all comers to reach the floor of the passage.

Eugenia, with some curiosity, looked out, and saw her brother, after nearly forcing his entrance, speak to a very mean little man, dressed in old dirty cloaths, who seemed willing to hide himself behind the door, but whom he almost dragged forward, saying aloud, 'O, I can take no excuse, I insist upon your shewing the house. I have brought two young ladies on purpose to see it; and who knows but one of them may take a fancy to it, and make you a happy man for life.'

'As to that, sir,' said the man, still endeavouring to retreat, 'I can't say as I've quite made my mind up yet as to the marriage ceremony. I've known partly enough of the state already; but if ever I marry again, which is a moot point, I sha'n't do it hand over head,[1] like a boy, without knowing what I'm about. However, it's time enough o'conscience to think of that, when my house is done, and my workmen is off my hands.'

Camilla now, by the language and the voice, gathered that this was Mr. Dubster.

'Pho, pho,' answered Lionel, 'you must not be so hard-hearted when fair ladies are in the case. Besides, one of them is that pretty girl you flirted with at Northwick. She's a sister of mine, and I shall take it very ill if you don't hand her out of the coach, and do the honours of your place to her.'

Camilla, much provoked, earnestly called to her brother, but utterly in vain.

'Lauk-a-day! why it is not half finished,' said Mr. Dubster; 'nor a quarter neither: and as to that young lady, I can't say as it was much in my mind to be over civil to her any more, begging pardon, after her giving me the slip in that manner. I can't say as I think it was over and above handsome, letting me get my gloves. Not that I mind it in the least, as to that.'

'Pho, pho, man, you must never bear malice against a fair lady. Besides, she's come now on purpose to make her excuses.'

'O, that's another thing; if the young lady's sorry, I sha'n't think of holding out. Besides, I can't say but what I thought her agreeable enough, if it had not been for her behaving so comical just at the last. Not that I mean in the least to make any complaint, by way of getting of the young lady scolded.'

'You must make friends now, man, and think no more of it;' cried Lionel, who would have drawn him to the carriage; but he protested he was quite ashamed to be seen in such a dishabille, and should go first and dress himself. Lionel, on the contrary, declaring nothing so manly, nor so becoming, as a neglect of outward appearance, pulled him to the coach door, notwithstanding all his efforts to disengage himself, and the most bashful distortions with which he strove to sneak behind his conductor.

'Ladies,' said he, 'Mr. Dubster desires to have the honour of walking over his house and grounds with you.'

Camilla declared she had no time to alight; but Lionel insisted, and soon forced them both from the coach.

Mr. Dubster, no longer stiff, starched, and proud, as when full dressed, was sunk into the smallest insignificance; and when they were compelled to enter his grounds, through a small Chinese gate, painted of a deep blue, would entirely have kept out of sight; but for a whisper from Lionel, that the ladies had owned they thought he looked to particular advantage in that careless attire.

Encouraged by this, he came boldly forward, and suddenly facing them, made a low bow saying: 'Young ladies, your humble.'

They courtsied slightly, and Camilla said she was very sorry to break in upon him.

'O, it don't much matter,' cried he, extremely pleased by this civility, 'I only hope, young ladies, you won't take umbrage at my receiving you in this pickle; but you've popt upon me unawares, as one may say. And my best coat is at this very minute at Tom Hicks's, nicely packed and papered up, and tied all round, in a drawer of his, up stairs, in his room. And I'd have gone for it with the greatest pleasure in life, to shew my respect, if the young gentleman would have let me.'

And then, recollecting Eugenia, 'Good lauk, ma'am,' said he, in a low voice to Camilla, 'that's that same lame little lady as I saw at the ball?'

'That lady, sir,' answered she, provoked, 'is my sister.'

'Mercy's me!' exclaimed he, lifting up his hands, 'I wish I'd known as much at the time. I'm sure, ma'am, if I'd thought the young lady was any ways related to you, I would not have said a word disrespectful upon no account.'

Lionel asked how long he had had this place.

'Only a little while. I happened of it quite lucky. A friend of mine was just being turned out of it, in default of payment, and so I got it a bargain. I intend to fit it up a little in taste, and then, whether I like it or no, I can always let it.'

They were now, by Lionel, dragged into the house, which was yet unfurnished, half papered, and half white washed. The workmen, Mr. Dubster said, were just gone to dinner, and he rejoiced that they had happened to come so conveniently, when he should be no loser by leaving the men to themselves, in order to oblige the young ladies with his company.

He insisted upon shewing them not only every room, but every closet, every cupboard, every nook, corner, and hiding place; praising their utility, and enumerating all their possible appropriations, with the most minute encomiums.

'But I'm quite sorry,' cried he, 'young ladies, to think as I've nothing to offer you. I eats my dinner always at the Globe, having nobody here to cook. However I'd have had a morsel of cake or so, if the young gentleman had been so kind as to give me an item beforehand of your intending me the favour. But as to getting things into the house hap hazard, really everything is so dear—it's quite out of reason.'

The scampering of horses now carrying them to a window, they saw some hounds in full cry, followed by horse-men in full gallop. Lionel declared he would borrow Jacob's mare, and join them, while his sisters walked about the grounds: but Camilla, taking him aside, made a serious expostulation, protesting that her father, with all his indulgence, and even her uncle himself, would be certainly displeased, if he left them alone with this man; of whom they knew nothing but his very low trade.

'Why what is his trade?'

'A tinker's: Mrs. Arlbery told me so.'

He laughed violently at this information, protesting he was rejoiced to find so much money could be made by the tinkering business, which he was determined to follow in his next distress for cash: yet added, he feared this was only the malice of Mrs. Arlbery, for Dubster, he had been told, had kept a shop for ready made wigs.

He gave up, however, his project, forgetting the chace when he no longer heard the hounds, and desired Mr. Dubster to proceed in shewing his lions?

'Lauk a day! sir, I've got no lions, nor tygers neither. It's a deal of expence keeping them animals; and though I know they reckon me near, I sha'n't do no such thing; for if a man does not take a little care of his money when once he has got it, especially if it's honestly, I think he's a fool for his pains; begging pardon for speaking my mind so freely.'

He then led them again to the front of the house, where he desired they would look at his pond. 'This,' said he, 'is what I value the most of all, except my summer house and my labyrinth. I shall stock it well; and many a good dinner I hope to eat from it. It gets me an appetite, sometimes, I think, only to look at it.'

''Tis a beautiful piece of water,' said Lionel, 'and may be useful to the outside as well as the inside, for, if you go in head foremost, you may bathe as well as feed from it.'

'No, I sha'n't do that, sir, I'm not over and above fond of water at best. However, I shall have a swan.'

'A swan? why sure you won't be contented with only one?'

'O yes, I shall. It will only be made of wood, painted over in white. There's no end of feeding them things if one has 'em alive. Besides it will look just as pretty; and won't bite. And I know a friend of mine that one of them creatures flew at, and gave him such a bang as almost broke his leg, only for throwing a stone at it, out of mere play. They are mortal spiteful, if you happen to hurt them when you're in their reach.'

He then begged them to go over to his island, which proved to be what Eugenia had taken for a mass of rubbish. They would fain have been excused crossing a plank which he called a bridge, but Lionel would not be denied.

'Now here,' said he, 'when my island's finished, I shall have something these young ladies will like; and that's a lamb.'

'Alive, or dead?' cried Lionel.

'Alive,' he replied, 'for I shall have good pasture in a little bit of ground just by, where I shall keep me a cow; and here will be grass enough upon my island to keep it from starving on Sundays, and for now and then, when I've somebody come to see me. And when it's fit for killing, I can change it with the farmer down the lane, for another young one, by a bargain I've agreed with him for already; for I don't love to run no risks about a thing for mere pleasure.'

'Your place will be quite a paradise,' said Lionel.

'Why, indeed, sir, I think I've earned having a little recreeting, for I worked hard enough for it, before I happened of meeting with my first wife.'

'O, ho! so you began with marrying a fortune?'

'Yes, sir, and very pretty she was too, if she had not been so puny. But she was always ailing. She cost me a mort of money to the potecary[1] before she went off. And she was a tedious while a dying, poor soul!'

'Your first wife? surely you have not been twice married already?'

'Yes, I have. My second wife brought me a very pretty fortune too. I can't say but I've rather had the luck of it, as far as I've gone yet awhile.'

They now repassed the plank, and were conducted to an angle, in which a bench was placed close to the chinese rails, which was somewhat shaded by a willow, that grew in a little piece of stagnant water on the other side. A syringa was planted in front, and a broom-tree on the right united it with the willow; in the middle there was a deal table.

'Now, young ladies,' said Mr. Dubster, 'if you have a taste to breathe a little fresh country air, here's where I advise you to take your rest. When I come to this place first, my arbour, as I call this, had no look out, but just to the fields, so I cut away them lilacs, and now there's a good pretty look out. And it's a thing not to be believed what a sight of people and coaches, and gentlemen's whiskeys and stages, and flys,[1] and wagons, and all sorts of things as ever you can think of, goes by all day long. I often think people's got but little to do at home.'

Next, he desired to lead them to his grotto, which he said was but just begun. It was, indeed, as yet, nothing but a little square hole, dug into a chalky soil, down into which, no steps being yet made, he slid as well as he could, to the no small whitening of his old brown coat, which already was thread bare.

He begged the ladies to follow, that he might shew them the devices he had marked out with his own hand, and from his own head, for fitting up the inside. Lionel would not suffer his sisters to refuse compliance, though Mr. Dubster himself cautioned them to come carefully, 'in particular,' he said, 'the little lady, as she has happened of an ugly accident already, as I judge, in one of her hips, and 'twould be pity, at her time of life, if she should happen of another at t'other side.'

Eugenia, not aware this misfortune was so glaring, felt much hurt by this speech; and Camilla, very angry with its speaker, sought to silence him by a resentful look; but not observing it; 'Pray, ma'am,' he continued, 'was it a fall? or was you born so?'

Eugenia looked struck and surprized; and Camilla hastily whispered it was a fall, and bid him say no more about it; but, not understanding her, 'I take it, then,' he said, 'that was what stinted your growth so, Miss? for, I take it, you're not much above the dwarf as they shew at Exeter Change?[2] Much of a muchness, I guess. Did you ever see him, ma'am?'

'No, sir,'

'It would be a good sight enough to see you together. He'd think himself a man in a minute. You must have had the small pox mortal bad, ma'am. I suppose you'd the conflint sort?'[3]

Camilla here, without waiting for help, slid down into the intended grotto, and asked a thousand questions to change the subject; while Eugenia, much disconcerted, slowly followed, aided by Lionel.

Mr. Dubster then displayed the ingenious intermixture of circles and diamonds projected for the embellishment of his grotto; the first of which were to be formed with cockle-shells, which he meant to colour with blue paint; and the second he proposed shaping with bits of shining black coal. The spaces between would each have an oyster-shell in the middle, and here and there he designed to leave the chalk to itself, which would always, he observed, make the grotto light and cheary. Shells he said, unluckily, he did not happen to have; but as he had thoughts of taking a little pleasure some summer at Brighthelmstone or Margate, for he intended to see all those places, he should make a collection then; being told he might have as curious shells, and pebbles too, as a man could wish to look at, only for the trouble of picking them up off the shore.

They next went to what he called his labyrinth, which was a little walk he was cutting, zig-zag, through some brushwood, so low that no person above three foot height could be hid by it. Every step they took here, cost a rent to some lace or some muslin of one of the sisters; which Mr. Dubster observed with a delight he could not conceal; saying this was a true country walk, and would do them both a great deal of good; and adding: 'we that live in town, would give our ears for such a thing as this.' And though they could never proceed a yard at a time, from the continual necessity of disentangling their dress from thorns and briars, he exultingly boasted that he should give them a good appetite for their dinner; and asked if this rural ramble did not make them begin to feel hungry. 'For my part,' continued he, 'if once I get settled a bit, I shall take a turn in this zig-zag every day before dinner, which may save me my five grains of rhubarb, that the doctor ordered me for my stomach,[1] since my having my illness, which come upon me almost as soon as I was a gentleman; from change of life, I believe, for I never knew no other reason; and none of the doctors could tell me nothing about it. But a man that's had a deal to do, feels quite unked[2] at first, when he's only got to look and stare about him, and just walk from one room to another, without no employment.'

Lionel said he hoped, at least, he would not require his rhubarb to get down his dinner to day.

'I hope so too, 'squire,' answered he, licking his lips, 'for I've ordered a pretty good one, I can tell you; beef steaks and onions; and I don't know what's better. Tom Hicks is to dine with me at the Globe, as soon as I've give my workmen their tasks, and seen

after a young lad that's to do me a job there, by my grotto. Tom
Hicks is a very good fellow; I like him best of any acquaintance
I've made in these here parts. Indeed, I've made no other, on
account of the unconvenence of dressing, while I'm so much about
with my workmen. So I keep pretty incog from the genteel; and
Tom does well enough in the interim.'

He then requested them to make haste to his summer-house,
because his workmen would be soon returned, and he could not
then spare a moment longer, without spoiling his own dinner.

'My summer-house,' said he, 'is not above half complete yet;
but it will be very pretty when it's done. Only I've got no stairs
yet to it; but there's a very good ladder, if the ladies a'n't afraid.'

The ladies both desired to be excused mounting; but Lionel
protested he would not have his friend affronted; and as neither of
them were in the habit of resisting him, nor of investigating with
seriousness any thing that he proposed, they were soon teized into
acquiescence, and he assisted them to ascend.

Mr. Dubster followed.

The summer-house was, as yet, no more than a shell; without
windows, scarcely roofed, and composed of lath and plaister, not
half dry. It looked on to the high road, and Mr. Dubster assured
them, that, on market days, the people passed so thick, there was
no seeing them for the dust.

Here they had soon cause to repent their facility,—that dangerous, yet venial, because natural fault of youth;—for hardly had
they entered this place, ere a distant gimpse of a fleet stag, and
a party of sportsmen, incited Lionel to scamper down; and calling
out: 'I shall be back presently,' he made off towards the house,
dragging the ladder after him.

The sisters eagerly and almost angrily remonstrated; but to no
purpose; and while they were still entreating him to return
and supposing him, though out of sight, within hearing, they
suddenly perceived him passing the window by the high road, on
horse-back, switch in hand, and looking in the utmost glee. 'I have
borrowed Jacob's mare,' he cried, 'for just half an hour's sport,
and sent Jacob and Coachy to get a little refreshment at the next
public house; but don't be impatient; I shan't be long.'

Off then, he galloped, laughing; in defiance of the serious
entreaties of his sisters, and without staying to hear even one
sentence of the formal exhortations of Mr. Dubster.

CHAPTER III

A few Compliments

THE two young ladies and Mr. Dubster, left thus together, and so situated that separation without assistance was impossible, looked at one another for some time in nearly equal dismay; and then Mr. Dubster, with much displeasure, exclaimed—'Them young gentlemen are as full of mischief, as an egg's full of meat! Who'd have thought of a person's going to do such a thing as this?—it's mortal unconvenent, making me leave my workmen at this rate; for I dare say they're come, or coming, by this time. I wish I'd tied the ladder to this here rafter.'

The sisters, though equally provoked, thought it necessary to make some apology for the wild behaviour of their brother.

'O, young ladies,' said he, formally waving his hand by way of a bow, 'I don't in the least mean to blame you about it, for you're very welcome to stay as long as it's agreeable; only I hope he'll come back by my dinner time; for a cold beef-steak is one or other the worst morsel I know.'

He then kept an unremitting watch from one window to another, for some passenger from whom he could claim aid; but, much as he had boasted of the numbers perpetually in sight, he now dolorously confessed, that, sometimes, not a soul came near the place for half a day together: 'And, as to my workmen,' continued he, 'the deuce can't make 'em hear if once they begin their knocking and hammering.'

And then, with a smirk at the idea, he added—'I'll tell you what; I'd best give a good squall¹ at once, and then if they are come, I may catch 'em; in the proviso you won't mind it, young ladies.'

This scheme was put immediately into practice; but though the sisters were obliged to stop their ears from his vociferation, it answered no purpose.

'Well, I'll bet you what you will,' cried he, 'they are all deaf: however, it's as well as it is, for if they was to come, and see me hoisted up in this cage, like, they'd only make a joke of it; and then they'd mind me no more than a pin never again. It's surprising how them young gentlemen never think of nothing. If he'd served me so when I was a 'prentice, he'd have paid pretty dear for his frolic;

master would have charged him half a day's work, as sure as a gun.'

Soon after, while looking out of the window, 'I do think,' he exclaimed, 'I see somebody!—It shall go hard but what I'll make 'em come to us.'

He then shouted with great violence; but the person crossed a stile into a field, without seeing or hearing him.

This provoked him very seriously; and turning to Camilla, rather indignantly, he said—'Really, ma'am, I wish you'd tell your brother, I should take it as a favour he'd never serve me o' this manner no more!'

She hoped, she said, he would in future be more considerate.

'It's a great hindrance to business, ma'am, such things; and it's a sheer love of mischief, too, begging pardon, for it's of no manner of use to him, no more than it is to us.'

He then desired, that if any body should pass by again, they might all squall out at once; saying, it was odds, then, but they might be heard.

'Not that it's over agreeable, at the best,' added he; 'for if one was to stop any poor person, and make 'em come round, and look for the ladder, one could not be off giving them something: and as to any of the gentlefolks, one might beg and pray as long as one would before they'd stir a step for one: and as to any of one's acquaintance, if they was to go by, it's ten to one but they'd only fall a laughing. People's generally ill-natured when they sees one in jeopardy.'

Eugenia, already thoughtful and discomposed, now grew uneasy, lest her uncle should be surprised at her long absence; this a little appeased Mr. Dubster, who, with less resentment, said—'So I see, then, we're all in the same quandary! However, don't mind it, young ladies; you can have no great matters to do with your time, I take it; so it does not so much signify. But a man's quite different. He looks like a fool, as one may say, poked up in such a place as this, to be stared at by all comers and goers; only nobody happens to pass by.'

His lamentations now were happily interrupted by the appearance of three women and a boy, who, with baskets on their heads, were returning from the next market town. With infinite satisfaction, he prepared to assail them, saying, he should now have some chance to get a bit of dinner: and assuring the ladies, that if they should like a little scrap for a relish, he should be very willing to send 'em it by their footman; 'For it's a long while,' said he, 'young ladies, to be fasting, that's the truth of it.'

The market women now approached, and were most clamour-ously hailed, before their own loud discourse, and the singing and whistling of the boy, permitted their hearing the appeal.

'Pray, will you be so kind,' said Mr. Dubster, when he had made them stop, 'as to step round by the house, and see if you can see the workmen; and if you can, tell 'em a young gentleman, as come here while they was at dinner, has taken away the ladder, and left us stuck up here in the lurch.'

The women all laughed, and said it was a good merry trick; but were preparing to follow his directions, when Mr. Dubster called after the boy, who loitered behind, with an encouraging nod: 'If you'll bring the ladder with you upon your shoulders, my lad, I'll give you a half-penny!'

The boy was well contented; but the women, a little alarmed, turned back and said—'And what will you give to us, master?' 'Give?' repeated he, a little embarrassed; 'why, I'll give—why I'll thank you kindly; and it won't be much out of your way, for the house is only round there.'

'You'll thank us kindly, will you?' said one of the women; it's like you may! But what will you do over and above?'

'Do? why it's no great matter, just to stop at the house as you go by, and tell 'em——'

Here Eugenia whispered she would herself satisfy them, and begged he would let them make their own terms.

'No, Miss, no; I don't like to see nobody's money fooled away, no more than my own. However, as you are so generous, I'll agree with 'em to give 'em a pot of beer.'

He then, with some parade, made this concession; but said, he must see the ladder, before the money should be laid down.

'A pot of beer for four!—a pot of beer for four!' they all exclaimed in a breath; and down everyone put her basket, and set her arms a-kembo, unanimously declaring, they would shame him for such stinginess.

The most violent abuse now followed, the boy imitating them, and every other sentence concluding with—'A pot of beer for four!—ha!'

Camilla and Eugenia, both frightened, besought that they might have any thing, and every thing, that could appease them;

but Mr. Dubster was inflexible not to submit to imposition, because of a few foul words; 'For, dear heart,' said he, 'what harm will they do us!—they an't of no consequence.'

Then, addressing them again, 'As to four,' he cried, 'that's one over the bargain, for I did not reckon the boy for nothing.'

'You didn't, didn't you?' cried the boy; 'i'cod,[1] I hope I'm as good as you, any day in the year!'

'You'll thank us kindly, will you?' said one of the women; 'I'fackens,[2] and so you shall, when we're fools enough to sarve you!—A pot of beer for four!'

'We help you down!—we get you a ladder!' cried another; 'yes, forsooth, it's like we may!—no, stay where you are like a toad in a hole[3] as you be!'

Camilla and Eugenia now, tired of vain application to Mr. Dubster, who heard all this abuse with the most sedate unconcern, advanced themselves to the window; and Eugenia, ever foremost where money was to be given, began—'Good women——' when, with a violent loud shout, they called out—'What! are you all in Hob's pound?[4] Well, they as will may let you out for we; so I wish you a merry time of it!'

Eugenia began again her—'Good women——' when the boy exclaimed—'What were you put up there for, Miss? to frighten the crows?'

Eugenia, not understanding him, was once more re-commencing; but the first woman said—'I suppose you think we'll sarve you for looking at?—no need to be paid?'

'Yes, yes,' cried the second, 'Miss may go to market with her beauty; she'll not want for nothing if she'll shew her pretty face!'

'She need not be afeard of it, however,' said the third, 'for 'twill never be no worse. Only take care, Miss, you don't catch the small pox!'

'O fegs,[5] that would be pity!' cried the boy, 'for fear Miss should be marked.'

Eugenia, astonished and confounded, made no farther attempt; but Camilla, though at that moment she could have inflicted any punishment upon such unprovoked assailants, affected to give but little weight to what they said, and gently drew her away.

'Hoity, toity!' cried one of the women, as she moved off, 'why, Miss, do you walk upon your knees?'

'Why my Poll would make two of her,' said another, 'though she's only nine years old.'

'She won't take much for cloaths,' cried another, 'that's one good thing.'

'I'd answer to make her a gown out of my apron,' said the third.

'Your apron?' cried another, 'your pocket handkerchief you mean!—why she'd be lost in your apron, and you might look half an hour before you'd find her.'

Eugenia, to whom such language was utterly new, was now in such visible consternation, that Camilla, affrighted, earnestly charged Mr. Dubster to find any means, either of menace or of reward, to make them depart.

'Lauk, don't mind them, ma'am,' cried he, following Eugenia, 'they can't do you no hurt; though they are rather rude, I must needs confess the truth, to say such things to your face. But one must not expect people to be over polite, so far from London. However, I see the sporting gentry coming round, over that way, yonder; and I warrant they'll gallop 'em off. Hark'ee, Mistresses! them gentlemen that are coming here, shall take you before the justice, for affronting Sir Hugh's Tyrold's Heiresses to all his fortunes.

The women, to whom the name and generous deeds of Sir Hugh Tyrold were familiar, were now quieted and dismayed. They offered some aukward apologies, of not guessing such young ladies could be posted up in such a place; and hoped it would be no detriment to them at the ensuing Christmas, when the good Baronet gave away beef and beer; but Mr. Dubster pompously ordered them to make off, saying, he would not accept the ladder from them now, for the gentry that were coming would get it for nothing: 'So troop off,' cried he; 'and as for you,' to the boy, 'you shall have your jacket well trimmed,[1] I promise you: I know who you are, well enough; and I'll tell your master of you, as sure as you're alive.'

Away then, with complete, though not well-principled repentance, they all marched.

Mr. Dubster, turning round with exultation, cried—'I only said that to frighten them, for I never see 'em before, as I know of. But I don't mind 'em of a rush; and I hope you don't neither. Though I can't pretend it's over agreeable being made fun of. If I see anybody snigger at me, I always ask 'em what it's for; for I'd as lieve they'd let it alone.'

Eugenia, who, as there was no seat, had sunk upon the floor
for rest and for refuge, remained silent, and seemed almost
petrified; while Camilla, affectionately leaning over her, began
talking upon other subjects, in hopes to dissipate a shock she was
ashamed to console.

She made no reply, no comment; but, sighed deeply.

'Lauk!' cried Mr. Dubster, 'what's the matter with the young
lady! I hope she don't go for to take to heart what them old women
says? she'll be never the worse to look at, because of their impudence. Besides, fretting does no good to nothing. If you'll only
come and stand here, where I do, Miss, you may have a peep at
ever so many dogs, and all the gentlemen, riding helter skelter
round that hill. It's a pretty sight enough for them as has nothing
better to mind. I don't know but I might make one among them
myself, now and then, if it was not for the expensiveness of hiring
of a horse.'

Here some of the party came galloping towards them; and Mr.
Dubster made so loud an outcry, that two or three of the sportsmen
looked up, and one of them, riding close to the summer-house,
perceived the two young ladies, and, instantly dismounting,
fastened his horse to a tree, and contrived to scramble up into the
little unfinished building.

Camilla then saw it was Major Cerwood. She explained to him
the mischievous frolic of her brother, and accepted his offered
services to find the ladder and the carriage.

Eugenia meanwhile rose and courtsied in answer to his enquiries after her health, and then, gravely fixing her eyes upon the
ground, took no further notice of him.

The object of the Major was not Eugenia; her taciturnity
therefore did not affect him; but pleased to be shut up with
Camilla, he soon found out that though to mount had been easy,
to descend would be difficult; and, after various mock efforts,
pronounced it would be necessary to wait till some assistance
arrived from below: adding, young Mr. Tyrold would soon
return, as he had seen him in the hunt.

Camilla, whose concern now was all for her sister, heard this
with indifference; but Mr. Dubster lost all patience. 'So here,'
said he, 'I may stay, and let Tom Hicks eat up all my dinner! for I
can't expect him to fast, because of this young gentleman's
comical tricks. I've half a mind to give a jump down myself, and

go look for the ladder; only I'm not over light. Besides, if one should break one's leg, it's but a hard thing upon a man to be a cripple in the middle of life. It's no such great hindrance to a lady, so I don't say it out of disrespect; because ladies can't do much at the best.'

The Major, finding Dubster was his host, thought it necessary to take some notice of him, and ask him if he never rode out.

'Why no, not much of that, Sir,' he answered; 'for when a man's not over used to riding, one's apt to get a bad tumble sometimes. I believe it's as well let alone. I never see as there was much wit in breaking one's neck before one's time. Besides, half them gentlemen are no better than sharpers,[1] begging pardon, for all they look as if they could knock one down.'

'How do you mean sharpers, Sir?'

'Why they don't pay everyone his own, not one in ten of them. And they're as proud as Lucifer. If I was to go among them to-morrow, I'll lay a wager they'd take no notice of me: unless I was to ask them to dinner. And a man may soon eat up his substance, if he's so over complaisant.'

'Surely, Major,' cried Camilla, 'my brother cannot be much longer before he joins us?—remembers us rather.'

'Who else could desert or forget you?' cried the Major.

'It's a moot point whether he'll come or no, I see that,' said Mr. Dubster, quite enraged; 'them young 'squires never know what to do for their fun. I must needs say I think it's pity but what he'd been brought up to some calling. 'Twould have steadied him a little, I warrant. He don't seem to know much of the troubles of life.'

A shower of rain now revived his hopes that the fear of being wet might bring him back; not considering how little sportsmen regard wet jackets.

'However,' continued he, 'it's really a piece of good luck that he was not taken with a fancy to leave us upon my island; and then we might all have been soused by this here rain: and he could just as well have walked off with my bridge as with the ladder.'

Here, to his inexpressible relief, Lionel, from the road, hailed them; and Camilla, with emotion the most violent, perceived Edgar was by his side.

Mr. Dubster, however, angry as well as glad, very solemnly

said, 'I wonder, Sir, what you think my workmen has been doing
all this time, with nobody to look after them? Besides that I
promised a pot o'beer to a lad to wheel me away all that rubbish
that I'd cut out of my grotto; and it's a good half day's work,
do it who will; and ten to one if they've stirred a nail, all left to
themselves so.'

'Pho, pho, man, you've been too happy, I hope, to trouble your
mind about business. How do do my little girls? how you have
been entertained?'

'This is a better joke to you than to us 'squire; but pray, Sir,
begging pardon, how come you to forget what I told you about the
Globe? I know very well that they say it's quite alley-mode to
make fun, but I can't pretend as I'm over fond of the custom.'

He then desired that, at least, if he would not get the ladder
himself, he would tell' that other gentleman, that was with him,
what he had done with it.

Edgar, having met Lionel, and heard from him how and where
he had left his sisters, had impatiently ridden with him to their
relief; but when he saw that the Major made one in the little party,
and that he was standing by Camilla, he felt hurt and amazed, and
proceeded no farther.

Camilla believed herself careless of his opinion; what she had
heard from Miss Margland of his professed indifference, gave
her now as much resentment, as at first it had caused her grief.
She thought such a declaration an unprovoked indignity; she
deigned not even to look at him, resolved for ever to avoid him; yet
to prove herself, at the same time, unmortified and disengaged,
talked cheerfully with the Major.

Lionel now, producing the ladder, ran up it to help his sisters
to descend; and Edgar, dismounting, could not resist entering the
grounds, to offer them his hand as they came down.

Eugenia was first assisted; for Camilla talked on with the
Major, as if not hearing she was called: and Mr. Dubster, his
complaisance wholly worn out, next followed, bowing low to
everyone separately, and begging pardon, but saying he could
really afford to waste no more time, without going to give a little
look after his workmen, to see if they were alive or dead.

At this time the horse of the Major, by some accident, breaking
loose, his master was forced to run down, and Lionel scampered
after to assist him.

Camilla remained alone; Edgar, slowly mounting the ladder, gravely offered his services; but, hastily leaning out of the window, she pretended to be too much occupied in watching the motions of the Major and his horse, to hear or attend to any thing else.

A sigh now tore the heart of Edgar, from doubt if this were preference to the Major, or the first dawn of incipient coquetry; but he called not upon her again; he stood quietly behind, till the horse was seized, and the Major re-ascended the ladder. They then stood at each side of it, with offers of assistance.

This appeared to Camilla a fortunate moment for making a spirited display of her indifference: she gave her hand to the Major, and, slightly courtesying to Edgar as she passed, was conducted to the carriage of her uncle.

Lionel again was the only one who spoke in the short route to Etherington, whence Eugenia, without alighting, returned to Cleves.

CHAPTER IV

The Danger of Disguise

EDGAR remained behind, almost petrified: he stood in the little building, looking after them, yet neither descending nor stirring, till one of the workmen advanced to fetch the ladder. He then hastily quitted the spot, mounted his horse, and galloped after the carriage; though without any actual design to follow it, or any formed purpose whither to go.

The sight, however, of the Major, pursuing the same route, made him, with deep disgust, turn about, and take the shortest road to Beech Park.

He hardly breathed the whole way from indignation; yet his wrath was without definition, and nearly beyond comprehensibility even to himself, till suddenly recurring to the lovely smile with which Camilla had accepted the assistance of Major Cerwood, he involuntarily clasped his hands and called out: 'O happy Major!'

Awakened by his ejaculation to the true state of his feelings, he started as from a sword held at his breast. 'Jealousy!' he cried, 'am I reduced to so humiliating a passion? Am I capable of love without trust? Unhappy enough to cherish it with hope? No! I will not be such a slave to the delusions of inclination. I will abandon neither my honour nor my judgment to my wishes. It is not alone even her heart that can fully satisfy me; its delicacy must be mine as well as its preference. Jealousy is a passion for which my mind is not framed, and which I must not find a torment, but an impossibility!'

He now began to fear he had made a choice the most injudicious, and that coquetry and caprice had only waited opportunity, to take place of candour and frankness.

Yet, recollecting the disclaiming speeches he had been compelled to make at Cleves, he thought, if she had heard them, she might be actuated by resentment. Even then, however, her manner of shewing it was alarming, and fraught with mischief. He reflected with fresh repugnance upon the gay and dissipated society with which she was newly mixing, and which, from her extreme openness and facility, might so easily, yet so fatally, sully the fair artlessness of her mind.

He then felt tempted to hint to Mr. Tyrold, who, viewing all things, and all people in the best light, rarely foresaw danger, and never suspected deception, the expediency of her breaking off this intercourse, till she could pursue it under the security of her mother's penetrating protection. But it occurred to him next, it was possible the Major might have pleased her. Ardent as were his own views, they had never been declared, while those of the Major seemed proclaimed without reserve. He felt his face tingle at the idea, though it nearly made his heart cease to beat; and determined to satisfy his conjecture ere he took any measure for himself.

To speak to her openly, he thought the surest as well as fairest way, and resolved, with whatever anguish, should he find the Major favoured, to aid her choice in his fraternal character, and then travel till he should forget her in every other.

For this purpose, it was necessary to make immediate enquiry into the situation of the Major, and then, if she would hear him, relate to her the result; well assured to gather the state of her heart upon this subject, by her manner of attending to the least word by which it should be introduced.

Camilla, meanwhile, was somewhat comforted by the exertion

she had shewn, and by her hopes it had struck Edgar with
respect.

*   *   *   *

The next morning, Sir Hugh sent for her again, and begged she
would pass the whole day with her sister Eugenia, and use all her
pretty ways to amuse her; for she had returned home, the
preceding morning, quite moped with melancholy,[1] and had
continued pining ever since; refusing to leave her room, even for
meals, yet giving no reason for her behaviour. What had come to
her he could not tell; but to see her so, went to his heart; for she
had always, he said, till now, been chearful and even tempered,
though thinking over her learning made her not much of a young
person.

Camilla flew up stairs, and found her, with a look of despondence, seated in a corner of her room, which she had darkened by
nearly shutting all the shutters.

She knew but too well the rude shock she had received, and
sought to revive her with every expression of soothing kindness.
But she shook her head, and continued mute, melancholy, and
wrapt in meditation.

More than an hour was spent thus, the strict orders of Sir Hugh
forbidding them any intrusion: but when, at length, Camilla
ventured to say, 'Is it possible, my dearest Eugenia, the passing
insolence of two or three brutal wretches can affect you thus
deeply?' She awakened from her silent trance, and raising her
head, while something bordering upon resentment began to
kindle in her breast, cried, 'Spare me this question, Camilla, and
I will spare you all reproach.'

'What reproach, my dear sister,' cried Camilla, amazed, 'what
reproach have I merited?'

'The reproach,' answered she, solemnly; 'that, from me, all my
family merit! the reproach of representing to me, that thousands
resembled me! of assuring me I had nothing peculiar to myself,
though I was so unlike all my family—of deluding me into utter
ignorance of my unhappy defects, and then casting me, all
unconscious and unprepared, into the wide world to hear them!'

She would now have shut herself into her book-closet; but
Camilla, forcing her way, and almost kneeling to be heard,

conjured her to drive such cruel ideas from her mind, and to treat the barbarous insults that she had suffered with the contempt they deserved.

'Camilla,' said she, firmly; 'I am no longer to be deceived nor trifled with. I will no more expose to the light a form and face so hideous:—I will retire from all mankind, and end my destined course in a solitude that no one shall discover.'

Camilla, terrified, besought her to form no such plan, bewailed the unfortunate adventure of the preceding day, inveighed against the inhuman women, and pleaded the love of all her family with the most energetic affection.

'Those women,' said she, calmly, 'are not to blame; they have been untutored, but not false; and they have only uttered such truths as I ought to have learnt from my cradle. My own blindness has been infatuated; but it sprung from inattention and ignorance.—It is now removed!—Leave me, Camilla; give notice to my Uncle he must find me some retreat. Tell all that has passed to my father. I will myself write to my mother—and when my mind is more subdued, and when sincerely and unaffectedly I can forgive you all from my heart, I may consent to see you again.'

She then positively insisted upon being left.

Camilla, penetrated with her undeserved, yet irremediable distress, still continued at her door, supplicating for re-admittance in the softest terms; but without any success till the second dinner bell summoned her down stairs. She then fervently called upon her sister to speak once more, and tell her what she must do, and what say?

Eugenia steadily answered: 'You have already my commission: I have no change to make in it.'

Unable to obtain anything further, she painfully descended: but the voice of her Uncle no sooner reached her ears from the dining parlour, than, shocked to convey to him so terrible a message, she again ran up stairs, and casting herself against her sister's door, called out 'Eugenia, I dare not obey you! would you kill my poor Uncle? My Uncle, who loves us all so tenderly? Would you afflict—would you make him unhappy?'

'No, not for the universe!' she answered, opening the door; and then, more gently, yet not less steadfastly, looking at her, 'I know,' she continued, 'you are all very good; I know all was meant for the best; I know I must be a monster not to love you for the very error to which I am a victim.—I forgive you therefore all! and I blush to have felt angry.—But yet—at the age of fifteen—at the instant of entering into the world—at the approach of forming a connection which—O Camilla! what a time, what a period, to discover—to know—that I cannot even be seen without being derided and offended!'

Her voice here faltered, and, running to the window curtain, she entwined herself in its folds, and called out: 'O hide me! hide me! from every human eye, from every thing that lives and breathes! Pursue me, persecute me no longer, but suffer me to abide by myself, till my fortitude is better strengthened to meet my destiny!'

The least impatience from Eugenia was too rare to be opposed; and Camilla, who, in common with all her family, notwithstanding her extreme youth, respected as much as she loved her, sought only to appease her by promising compliance. She gave to her, therefore, an unresisted, though unreturned embrace, and went to the dining-parlour.

Sir Hugh was much disappointed to see her without her sister; but she evaded any account of her commission till the meal was over, and then begged to speak with him alone.

Gently and gradually she disclosed the source of the sadness of Eugenia: but Sir Hugh heard it with a dismay that almost overwhelmed him. All his contrition for the evils of which, unhappily, he had been the cause, returned with severest force, and far from opposing her scheme of retreat, he empowered Camilla to offer her any residence she chose; and to tell her he would keep out of her sight, as the cause of all her misfortunes; or give her the immediate possession and disposal of his whole estate, if that would make her better amends than to wait till his death.

This message was no sooner delivered to Eugenia, than losing at once every angry impression, she hastened down stairs, and casting herself at the knees of her Uncle, begged him to pardon her design, and promised never to leave him while she lived.

Sir Hugh, most affectionately embracing her, said—'You are too good, my dear, a great deal too good, to one who has used you so ill, at the very time when you were too young to help yourself. I have not a word to offer in my own behalf; except to hope you will forgive me, for the sake of its being all done out of pure ignorance.'

'Alas, my dearest Uncle! all I owe to your intentions, is the deepest gratitude; and it is your's from the bottom of my heart. Chance alone was my enemy; and all I have to regret is, that no one was sincere enough, kind enough, considerate enough, to instruct me of the extent of my misfortunes, and prepare me for the attacks to which I am liable.'

'My dear girl,' said he, while tears started into his eyes, 'what you say nobody can reply to; and I find I have been doing you one wrong after another, instead of the least good: for all this was by my own order; which it is but fair to your brothers and sisters, and father and mother, and the servants, to confess. God knows, I have faults enough of my own upon my head, without taking another of pretending to have none!'

Eugenia now sought to condole him in her turn, voluntarily promising to mix with the family as usual, and only desiring to be excused from going abroad, or seeing any strangers.

'My dear,' said he, 'you shall judge just what you think fit, which is the least thing I can do for you, after your being so kind as to forgive me; which I hope to do nothing in future not to deserve more; meaning always to ask my brother's advice; which might have saved me all my worst actions, if I had done it sooner: for I've used poor Camilla no better; except not giving her the small pox, and that bad fall. But don't hate me, my dears, if you can help it, for it was none of it done for want of love; only not knowing how to shew it in the proper manner; which I hope you'll excuse for the score of my bad education.'

'O, my Uncle!' cried Camilla, throwing her arms round his neck, while Eugenia embraced his knees, 'what language is this for nieces who owe so much to your goodness, and who, next to their parents, love you more than anything upon earth!'

'You are both the best little girls in the world, my dears, and I need have nothing upon my conscience if you two pass it over; which is a great relief to me; for there's nobody else I've used so bad as you two young girls; which, God knows, goes to my heart whenever I think of it.—Poor little innocents!—what had you ever done to provoke me?'

The two sisters, with the most virtuous emulation, vied with each other in demonstrative affection, till he was tolerably consoled.

The rest of the day was ruffled but for one moment; upon Sir

Hugh's answering, to a proposition of Miss Margland for a party to the next Middleton races,[1]—that there was no refusing to let Eugenia take that pleasure, after her behaving so nobly: her face was then again overcast with the deepest gloom; and she begged not to hear of the races, nor of any other place, public or private, for going abroad, as she meant during the rest of her life, immoveably to remain at home.

He looked much concerned, but assured her she should be mistress in every thing.

Camilla left them in the evening, with a promise to return the next day; and with every anxiety of her own, lost in pity for her innocent and unfortunate sister.

She was soon, however, called back to herself, when, with what light yet remained, she saw Edgar ride up to the coach door.

With indefatigable pains he had devoted the day to the search of information concerning the Major. Of Mrs. Arlbery he had learned, that he was a man of fashion, but small fortune; and from the Ensign he had gathered, that even that small fortune was gone, and that the estate in which it was vested, had been mortgaged for three thousand pounds, to pay certain debts of honour.

Edgar had already been to the Parsonage House, but hearing Camilla was at Cleves, had made a short visit, and determined to walk his horse upon the road till he met the carriage of Sir Hugh; believing he could have no better opportunity of seeing her alone.

Yet when the coach, upon his riding up to the door, stopt, he found himself in an embarrassment for which he was unprepared. He asked how she did; desired news of the health of all the family one by one; and then, struck by the coldness of her answers, suffered the carriage to drive on.

Confounded at so sudden a loss of all presence of mind, he continued, for a minute or two, just where she left him; and then galloped after the coach, and again presented himself at its window.

In a voice and manner the most hurried, he apologised for this second detention. 'But, I believe,' he said, 'some genius of officiousness has today taken possession of me, for I began it upon a Quixote sort of enterprise, and a spirit of knight-errantry seems willing to accompany me through it to the end.'

He stopt; but she did not speak. Her first sensation at his sight had been wholly indignant: but when she found he had something to say which he knew not how to pronounce, her curiosity was awakened, and she looked earnest for an explanation.

'I know,' he resumed, with considerable hesitation, 'that to give advice and to give pain is commonly the same thing:—I do not, therefore, mean—I have no intention—though so lately you allowed me a privilege never to be forgotten'—

He could not get on; and his embarrassment, and this recollection, soon robbed Camilla of every angry emotion. She looked down, but her countenance was full of sensibility, and Edgar, recovering his voice, proceeded—

'My Quixotism, I was going to say, of this morning, though for a person of whom I know almost nothing, would urge me to every possible effort—were I certain the result would give pleasure to the person for whom alone—since with regard to himself,—I—it is merely——'

Involved in expressions he knew not how to clear or to finish, he was again without breath: and Camilla, raising her eyes, looked at him with astonishment.

Endeavouring then to laugh, 'One would think,' cried he, 'this same Quixotism had taken possession of my intellects, and rendered them as confused as if, instead of an agent, I were a principal.'—

Still wholly in the dark as to his aim, yet, satisfied by these last words, it had no reference to himself, she now lost enough of the acuteness of her curiosity to dare avow what yet remained; and begged him, without further preface, to be more explicit.

Stammering, he then said, that the evident admiration with which a certain gentleman was seen to sigh in her train, had awakened for him an interest, which had induced some inquiries into the state of his prospects and expectations. 'These,' he continued, 'turn out to be, though not high, nor by any means adequate to—to——however they are such as some previous friendly exertions, with settled future œconomy, might render more propitious: and for those previous exertions—Mr. Tyrold has a claim which it would be the pride and happiness of my life to see him honour;—if—if—'

The if almost dropt inarticulated: but he added—'I shall make some further enquiries before I venture to say any more.'

'For yourself, then, be they made, Sir!' cried she, suddenly seizing the whole of the meaning—'not for me?—whoever this person may be to whom you allude—to me he is utterly indifferent.'

A flash of involuntary delight beamed in the eyes of Edgar at these words: he had almost thanked her, he had almost dropt the reins of his horse to clasp his hands: but filled only with her own emotions, without watching his, or waiting for any answer, she coldly bid him good night, and called to the coachman to drive fast home.

Edgar, however, was left with a sunbeam of the most lively delight. 'He is wholly indifferent to her,' he cried, 'she is angry at my interference; she has but acted a part in the apparent preference—and for *me*, perhaps, acted it!'

Momentary, however, was the pleasure such a thought could afford him;—'O, Camilla,' he cried, 'if, indeed, I might hope from you any partiality, why act any part at all?—how plain, how easy, how direct your road to my heart, if but straightly pursued!'

CHAPTER V

Strictures on Deformity

CAMILLA went on to Etherington in deep distress; every ray of hope was chaced from her prospects, with a certainty more cruel, though less offensive, to her feelings, than the crush given them by Miss Margland. He cares not for me! she cried; he even destines me for another! He is the willing agent of the Major; he would portion me, I suppose, for him, to accelerate the impossibility of ever thinking of me! And I imagined he loved me!—what a dream!—what a dream!—how has he deceived me!—or, alas! how have I deceived myself!

She rejoiced, however, that she had made so decided an answer with regard to Major Cerwood, whom she could not doubt to be the person meant, and who, presented in such a point of view, grew utterly odious to her.

The tale she had to relate to Mr. Tyrold, of the sufferings and sad resolution of Eugenia, obviated all comment upon her own disturbance. He was wounded to the heart by the recital. 'Alas!' he cried, 'your wise and excellent mother always foresaw some mischief would ensue, from the extreme caution used to keep this dear unfortunate child ignorant of her peculiar situation. This dreadful shake might have been palliated, at least, if not spared, by the lessons of fortitude that noble woman would have inculcated in her young and ductile mind. But I could not resist the painful entreaties of my poor brother, who, thinking himself the author of her calamities, believed he was responsible for saving her from feeling them; and, imagining all the world as soft-hearted as himself, concluded, that what her own family would not tell her, she could never hear elsewhere. But who should leave any events to the caprices of chance, which the precautions of foresight can determine?'

These reflections, and the thoughts of her sister, led at once and aided Camilla to stifle her own unhappiness; and for three days following, she devoted herself wholly to Eugenia.

On the morning of the fourth, instead of sending the carriage, Sir Hugh arrived himself to fetch Camilla, and to tell his brother, he must come also, to give comfort to Eugenia; for, though he had thought the worst was over, because she appeared quiet in his presence, he had just surprised her in tears, by coming upon her unawares. He had done all he could, he said, in vain; and nothing remained but for Mr. Tyrold to try his hand himself: 'For it is but justice,' he added, 'to Dr. Orkborne, to say she is wiser than all our poor heads put together; so that there is no answering her for want of sense.' He then told him to be sure to put one of his best sermons in his pocket to read to her.

Mr. Tyrold was extremely touched for his poor Eugenia, yet said he had half an hour's business to transact in the neighbourhood, before he could go to Cleves. Sir Hugh waited his time, and all three then proceeded together.

Eugenia received her Father with a deliberate coldness that shocked him. He saw how profound was the impression made upon her mind, not merely of her personal evils, but of what she conceived to be the misconduct of her friends.

After a little general discourse, in which she bore no share, he proposed walking in the park; meaning there to take her aside, with less formality than he could otherwise desire to speak with her alone.

The ladies and Sir Hugh immediately looked for their hats or gloves: but Eugenia, saying she had a slight head-ache, walked away to her room.

'This, my dear brother,' cried Sir Hugh, sorrowfully following her with his eyes, 'is the very thing I wanted you for; she says she'll never more stir out of these doors as long as she's alive; which is a sad thing to say, considering her young years; and nobody knowing how Clermont may approve it. However, it's well I've had him brought up from the beginning to the classics, which I rejoice at every day more and more, it being the only wise thing I ever did of my own head; for as to talking Latin and Greek, which I suppose is what they will chiefly be doing, there's no doubt but they may do it just as well in a room as in the fields, or the streets.'

Mr. Tyrold, after a little consideration, followed her. He tapped at her door; she asked, in a tone of displeasure, who was there?—'Your Father, my dear,' he answered; and then, hastily opening it, she proposed returning with him down stairs.

'No,' he said; 'I wish to converse with you alone. The opinion I have long cherished of your heart and your understanding, I come now to put to the proof.'

Eugenia, certain of the subject to which he would lead, and feeling she could not have more to hear than to say, gave him a chair, and composedly seated herself next to him.

'My dear Eugenia,' said he, taking her passive hand, 'this is the moment that more grievously than ever I lament the absence of your invaluable Mother. All I have to offer to your consideration she could much better have laid before you; and her dictates would have met with the attention they so completely deserve.

'Was my Mother, then, Sir,' said she, reproachfully, 'un-apprized of the worldly darkness in which I have been brought up? Is she unacquainted that a little knowledge of books and languages is what alone I have been taught?'

'We are all but too apt,' answered Mr. Tyrold, mildly, though surprised, 'to deem nothing worth attaining but what we have missed, nothing worth possessing but what we are denied. How many are there, amongst the untaught and unaccomplished, who would think an escape such as yours, of all intellectual darkness, a compensation for every other evil!'

'They could think so only, Sir, while, like me, they lived immured always in the same house, were seen always by the same people, and were total strangers to the sensations they might excite in any others.'

'My dear Eugenia, grieved as I am at the present subject of your ruminations, I rejoice to see in you a power of reflection, and of combination, so far above your years. And it is a soothing idea to me to dwell upon the ultimate benevolence of Providence, even in circumstances the most afflicting: for if chance has been unkind to you, Nature seems, with fostering foresight, to have endowed you with precisely those powers that may best set aside her malignity.'

'I see, Sir,' cried she, a little moved, 'the kindness of your intention; but pardon me if I anticipate to you its ill success. I have thought too much upon my situation and my destiny to admit any fallacious comfort. Can you, indeed, when once her eyes are opened, can you expect to reconcile to existence a poor young creature who sees herself an object of derision and disgust? Who, without committing any crime, without offending any human being, finds she cannot appear but to be pointed at, scoffed and insulted!'

'O my child! with what a picture do you wound my heart, and tear your own peace and happiness! Wretches who in such a light can view outward deficiencies cannot merit a thought, are below even contempt, and ought not to be disdained, but forgotten. Make a conquest, then, my Eugenia, of yourself; be as superior in your feelings as in your understanding, and remember what Addison admirably says in one of the Spectators: 'A too acute sensibility of personal defects, is one of the greatest weaknesses of self-love.'[1]

'I should be sorry, Sir, you should attribute to vanity what I now suffer. No! it is simply the effect of never hearing, never knowing, that so severe a call was to be made upon my fortitude, and therefore never arming myself to sustain it.'

Then, suddenly, and with great emotion clasping her hands: 'O if ever I have a family of my own,' she cried, 'my first care shall be to tell my daughters of all their infirmities! They shall be familiar, from their childhood, to their every defect—Ah! they must be odious indeed if they resemble their poor mother!'

'My dearest Eugenia! let them but resemble you mentally, and there is no person, whose approbation is worth deserving, that will not love and respect them. Good and evil are much more equally divided in this world than you are yet aware: none possess the first without alloy, nor the second without palliation. Indiana, for example, now in the full bloom of all that beauty can bestow, tell me, and ask yourself strictly, would you change with Indiana?'

'With Indiana?' she exclaimed; 'O! I would forfeit every other good to change with Indiana! Indiana, who never appears but to be admired, who never speaks but to be applauded.'

'Yet a little, yet a moment, question, and understand yourself before you settle you would change with her. Look forward, and look inward. Look forward, that you may view the short life of admiration and applause for such attractions from others, and their inutility to their possessor in every moment of solitude or repose; and look inward, that you may learn to value your own peculiar riches, for times of retirement, and for days of infirmity and age!'

'Indeed, Sir,—and pray believe me, I do not mean to repine I have not the beauty of Indiana; I know and have always heard her loveliness is beyond all comparison. I have no more, therefore, thought of envying it, than of envying the brightness of the sun. I knew, too, I bore no competition with my sisters; but I never dreamt of competition. I knew I was not handsome, but I supposed many people besides not handsome, and that I should pass with the rest; and I concluded the world to be full of people who had been sufferers as well as myself, by disease or accident. These have been occasionally my passing thoughts; but the subject never seized my mind; I never reflected upon it at all, till abuse, without provocation, all at once opened my eyes, and shewed me to myself! Bear with me, then, my father, in this first dawn of terrible conviction! Many have been unfortunate,—but none unfortunate like me! Many have met with evils—but who with an accumulation like mine!'

Mr. Tyrold, extremely affected, embraced her with the utmost tenderness: 'My dear, deserving, excellent child,' he cried, 'what would I not endure, what sacrifice not make, to soothe this cruel disturbance, till time and your own understanding can exert their powers?' Then, while straining her to his breast with the fondest parental commiseration, the tears, with which his eyes were overflowing, bedewed her cheeks.

Eugenia felt them, and, sinking to the ground, pressed his knees. 'O my father,' she cried, 'a tear from your revered eyes afflicts me more than all else! Let me not draw forth another, lest I should become not only unhappy, but guilty. Dry them up, my dearest father—let me kiss them away.'

'Tell me, then, my poor girl, you will struggle against this ineffectual sorrow! Tell me you will assert that fortitude which only waits for your exertion; and tell me you will forgive the misjudging compassion which feared to impress you earlier with pain!'

'I will do all, every thing you desire! my injustice is subdued! my complaints shall be hushed! you have conquered me, my beloved father! Your indulgence, your lenity shall take place of every hardship, and leave me nothing but filial affection!'

Seizing this grateful moment, he then required of her to relinquish her melancholy scheme of seclusion from the world: 'The shyness and the fears which gave birth to it,' said he, 'will but grow upon you if listened to; and they are not worthy the courage I would instil into your bosom—the courage, my Eugenia, of virtue—the courage to pass by, as if unheard, the insolence of the hard-hearted, and ignorance of the vulgar. Happiness is in your power, though beauty is not; and on that to set too high a value would be pardonable only in a weak and frivolous mind; since, whatever is the involuntary admiration with which it meets, every estimable quality and accomplishment is attainable without it: and though, which I cannot deny, its immediate influence is universal, yet in every competition and in every decision of esteem, the superior, the elegant, the better part of mankind give their suffrages[1] to merit alone. And you, in particular, will find yourself, through life, rather the more than the less valued, by every mind capable of justice and compassion, for misfortunes which no guilt has incurred.'

Observing her now to be softened, though not absolutely consoled, he rang the bell, and begged the servant, who answered it, to request his brother would order the coach immediately, as he was obliged to return home; 'And you, my love,' said he, 'shall accompany me; it will be the least exertion you can make in first breaking through your averseness to quit the house.'

Eugenia would not resist; but her compliance was evidently repugnant to her inclination; and in going to the glass to put on her hat, she turned aside from it in shuddering, and hid her face with both her hands.

'My dearest child,' cried Mr. Tyrold, wrapping her again in his arms, 'this strong susceptibility will soon wear away; but you cannot be too speedy nor too firm in resisting it. The omission of what never was in our power cannot cause remorse, and the bewailing what never can become in our power cannot afford comfort. Imagine but what would have been the fate of Indiana, had your situations been reversed, and had she, who can never acquire your capacity, and therefore never attain your knowledge, lost that beauty which is her all; but which to you, even if retained, could have been but a secondary gift. How short will be the reign of that all! how useless in sickness! how unavailing in solitude! how inadequate to long life! how forgotten, or repiningly remembered in old age! You will live to feel pity for all you now covet and admire; to grow sensible to a lot more lastingly happy in your own acquirements and powers; and to exclaim, with contrition and wonder, Time was when I would have changed with the poor mind-dependent Indiana!'

The carriage was now announced; Eugenia, with reluctant steps, descended; Camilla was called to join them, and Sir Hugh saw them set off with the utmost delight.

CHAPTER VI

Strictures on Beauty

To lengthen the airing, Mr. Tyrold ordered the carriage by a new road; and to induce Eugenia to break yet another spell, in walking as well as riding, he proposed their alighting, when they came to a lane, and leaving the coach in waiting while they took a short stroll.

He walked between his daughters a considerable way, passing, wherever it was possible, close to cottages, labourers, and children. Eugenia submitted with a sigh, but held down her head, affrighted at every fresh object they encountered, till, upon approaching a small miserable hut, at the door of which several children were playing, an unlucky boy called, out, 'O come! come! look!— here's the little hump-back gentlewoman!'

She then, clinging to her father, could not stir another step, and cast upon him a look of appeal and reproach that almost overset him; but, after speaking to her some words of kindness, he urged her to go on, and alone, saying, 'Throw only a shilling to the senseless little crew, and let Camilla follow and give nothing, and see which will become the most popular.'

They both obeyed, Eugenia fearfully and with quickness casting amongst them some silver, and Camilla quietly walking on.

'O, I have got a sixpence!' cried one; 'and I've got a shilling!' said another; while the mother of the little tribe came from her wash-tub, and called out, 'God bless your ladyship!' and the father quitted a little garden at the side of his cottage, to bow down to the ground, and cry, 'Heaven reward you, good madam! you'll have a blessing go with you, go where you will!'

The children then, dancing up to Camilla, begged her charity; but when, seconding the palpable intention of her father, she said she had nothing for them, they looked highly dissatisfied, while they redoubled their blessings to Eugenia.

'See, my child,' said Mr. Tyrold, now joining them, 'how cheaply preference, and even flattery, may be purchased!'

'Ah, Sir!' she answered, recovered from her terrour, yet deep in reflection, 'this is only by bribery, and gross bribery, too! And what pleasure, or what confidence can accrue from preference so earned!'

'The means, my dear Eugenia, are not beneath the objects: if it is only from those who unite native hardness with uncultured minds and manners, that civility is to be obtained by such sordid materials, remember, also, it is from such only it can ever fail you. In the lowest life, equally with the highest, wherever nature has been kind, sympathy springs spontaneously for whatever is unfortunate, and respect for whatever seems innocent. Steel yourself, then, firmly to withstand attacks from the cruel and unfeeling, and rest perfectly secure you will have none other to apprehend.'

The clear and excellent capacity of Eugenia, comprehended in this lesson, and its illustration, all the satisfaction Mr. Tyrold hoped to impart; and she was ruminating upon it with abated despondence, when, as they came to a small house, surrounded with a high wall, Mr. Tyrold, looking through an iron gate at a female figure who stood at one of the windows, exclaimed—'What a beautiful creature! I have rarely, I think seen a more perfect face.'

Eugenia felt so much hurt by this untimely sight, that, after a single glance, which confirmed the truth of what he said, she bent her eyes another way; while Camilla herself was astonished that her kind father should call their attention to beauty, at so sore and critical a juncture.

'The examination of a fine picture,' said he, fixing his eyes upon the window, and standing still at the iron gate, 'is a constant as well as exquisite pleasure; for we look at it with an internal security, that such as it appears to us today, it will appear again tomorrow, and tomorrow, and tomorrow; but in the pleasure given by the examination of a fine face, there is always, to a contemplative mind, some little mixture of pain; an idea of its fragility steals upon our admiration, and blends with it something like solicitude; the consciousness how short a time we can view it perfect, how quickly its brilliancy of bloom will be blown, and how ultimately it will be nothing.—'

'You would have me, Sir,' said Eugenia, now raising her eyes, 'learn to see beauty with unconcern, by depreciating its value? I feel your kind intention; but it does not come home to me; reasoning such as this may be equally applicable to any thing else, and degrade whatever is desirable into insignificance.'

'No, my dear child, there is nothing, either in its possession or its loss, that can be compared with beauty; nothing so evanescent, and nothing that leaves behind it a contrast which impresses such regret. It cannot be forgotten, since the same features still remain, though they are robbed of their effect upon the beholder; the same complexion is there, though faded into a tint bearing no resemblance with its original state; and the same eyes present themselves to the view, though bereft of all the lustre that had rendered them captivating.'

'Ah, Sir! this is an argument but formed for the moment. Is not the loss of youth the same to every body? and is not age equally unwelcome to the ugly and to the handsome?'

'For activity, for strength, and for purposes of use, certainly, my dear girl, there can be no difference; but for motives to mental regret, there can be no comparison. To those who are commonly moulded, the gradual growth of decay brings with it its gradual endurance, because little is missed from day to day; hope is not roughly chilled, nor expectation rudely blasted; they see their friends, their connections, their contemporaries, declining by the same laws, and they yield to the immutable and general lot rather imperceptibly than resignedly; but it is not so with the beauty; her loss is not only general, but peculiar; and it is the peculiar, not the general evil, that constitutes all hardship. Health, strength, agility, and animal spirits, she may sorrowing feel diminish; but she hears everyone complain of similar failures, and she misses them unmurmuring, though not unlamenting; but of beauty, every declension is marked with something painful to self-love. The change manifested by the mirror might patiently be borne; but the change manifested in the eyes of every beholder, gives a shock that does violence to every pristine feeling.'

'This may certainly, sir, be cruel; trying at least; but then,— what a youth has she first passed! Mortification comes upon her, at least, in succession; she does not begin the world with it, —a stranger at all periods to anything happier!'

'Ah, my child! the happiness caused by personal attractions pays a dear after-price! The soldier who enters the field of battle requires not more courage, though of a different nature, than the faded beauty who enters an assembly-room. To be wholly disregarded, after engaging every eye; to be unassisted, after being habituated to seeing crowds anxiously offer their services; to be unheard, after monopolising every ear—can you, indeed, persuade yourself a change such as this demands but ordinary firmness? Yet the altered female who calls for it, has the least chance to obtain it; for even where nature has endowed her with fortitude, the world and its flatteries have almost uniformly enervated it, before the season of its exertion.'

'All this may be true,' said Eugenia, with a sigh; 'and to me, however sad in itself, it may prove consolatory; and yet—forgive my sincerity, when I own—I would purchase a better appearance at any price, any expence, any payment, the world could impose!'

Mr. Tyrold was preparing an answer, when the door of the house, which he had still continued facing, was opened, and the beautiful figure, which had for some time retired from the window, rushed suddenly upon a lawn before the gate against which they were leaning.

Not seeing them, she sat down upon the grass, which she plucked up by hands full, and strewed over her fine flowing hair.

Camilla, fearing they should seem impertinent, would have retreated; but Eugenia, much struck, sadly, yet with earnestness, compelled herself to regard the object before her, who was young, fair, of a tall and striking figure, with features delicately regular.

A sigh, not to be checked, acknowledged how little either

reasoning or eloquence could subdue a wish to resemble such an appearance, when the young person, flinging herself suddenly upon her face, threw her white arms over her head, and sobbed aloud with violence.

Astonished, and deeply concerned, Eugenia internally said, alas! what a world is this! even beauty so exquisite, without waiting for age or change, may be thus miserable!

She feared to speak, lest she should be heard; but she looked up to her father, with an eye that spoke concession, and with an interest for the fair afflicted, which seemed to request his assistance.

He motioned to her to be quiet; when the young person, abruptly half rising, burst into a fit of loud, shrill, and discordant laughter.

Eugenia now, utterly confounded, would have drawn her father away; but he was intently engaged in his observations, and steadily kept his place.

In two minutes, the laugh ceased all at once, and the young creature, hastily rising, began turning round with a velocity that no machine could have exceeded.

The sisters now fearfully interchanged looks that shewed they thought her mad, and both endeavoured to draw Mr. Tyrold from the gate, but in vain; he made them hold by his arms, and stood still.

Without seeming giddy, she next began to jump; and he now could only detain his daughters, by shewing them the gate, at which they stood, was locked.

In another minute, she perceived them, and, coming eagerly forward, dropt several low courtesies, saying, at every fresh bend—'Good day!—Good day!—Good day!'

Equally trembling, they now both turned pale with fear; but Mr. Tyrold, who was still immovable, answered her by a bow, and asked if she were well.

'Give me a shilling!' was her reply, while the slaver drivelled unrestrained from her mouth, rendering utterly disgusting a chin that a statuary might have wished to model.

'Do you live at this house!' said Mr. Tyrold.

'Yes, please—yes, please—yes, please,' she answered, twenty times following, and almost black in the face before she would allow herself to take another breath.

A cat now appearing at the door, she seized it, and tried to twine it round her neck with great fondling, wholly unresisting the scratches which tore her fine skin.

Next, capering forward with it towards the gate, 'Look! look!' she cried, 'here's puss!—here's puss!—here's puss!'

Then, letting it fall, she tore her handkerchief off her neck, put it over her face, strained it as tight as she was able, and tied it under her chin; and then struck her head with both her hands, making a noise that resembled nothing human.

'Take, take me away, my father!' cried Eugenia, 'I see, I feel your awful lesson! but impress it no further, lest I die in receiving it!'

Mr. Tyrold immediately moved off without speaking; Camilla, penetrated for her sister, observed the same silence; and Eugenia, hanging upon her father, and absorbed in profound rumination, only by the depth of her sighs made her existence known; and thus, without the interchange of a word, slowly and pensively they walked back to the carriage.

Eugenia broke the silence as soon as they were seated: 'O, my father!' she exclaimed, 'what a sight have you made me witness! how dread a reproof have you given to my repining spirit! Did you know this unhappy beauty was at that house? Did you lead me thither purposely to display to me her shocking imbecility?'

'Relying upon the excellence of your understanding, I ventured upon an experiment more powerful, I well knew, than all that reason could urge; an experiment not only striking at the moment, but which, by playing upon the imagination, as well as convincing the judgment, must make an impression that can never be effaced. I have been informed for some time, that this poor girl was in our neighbourhood; she was born an idiot, and therefore, having never known brighter days, is insensible to her terrible state. Her friends are opulent, and that house is taken, and a woman is paid, to keep her in existence and in obscurity. I had heard of her uncommon beauty, and when the news reached me of my dear Eugenia's distress, the idea of this meeting occurred to me; I rode to the house, and engaged the woman to detain her unfortunate charge at the window till we appeared, and then to let her loose into the garden. Poor, ill fated young creature! it has been, indeed, a melancholy sight.'

'A sight,' cried Eugenia, 'to come home to me with shame!—O, my dear Father! your prescription strikes to the root of my disease!—shall I ever again dare murmur!—will any egotism ever again make me believe no lot so hapless as my own! I will think of her when I am discontented; I will call to my mind this spectacle of human degradation—and submit, at least with calmness, to my lighter evils and milder fate.'

'My excellent child! this is just what I expected from the candour of your temper, and the rectitude of your sentiments. You have seen, here, the value of intellects in viewing the horrour of their loss; and you have witnessed, that beauty, without mind, is more dreadful than any deformity. You have seized my application, and left me nothing to enforce; my dear, my excellent child! you have left for your fond Father nothing but tender approbation! With the utmost thankfulness to Providence, I have marked from your earliest childhood, the native justness of your understanding; which, with your studious inclination to sedentary accomplishments, has proved a reviving source of consolation to your mother and to me, for the cruel accidents we have incessantly lamented. How will that admirable mother rejoice in the recital I have to make to her! What pride will she take in a daughter so worthily her own, so resembling her in nobleness of nature, and a superior way of thinking! Her tears, my child, like mine, will thank you for your exertions! she will strain you to her fond bosom, as your father strains you at this moment!'

'Yes, Sir,' cried Eugenia, 'your kind task is now completed with your vanquished Eugenia! her thoughts, her occupations, her happiness, shall henceforth all be centred in filial gratitude and contentment.'

The affectionate Camilla, throwing her arms about them both, bathed each with the tears of joy and admiration, which this soothing conclusion to an adventure so severe excited.

CHAPTER VII

The Pleadings of Pity

To oblige Mr. Tyrold, who had made the arrangement with Sir Hugh, Eugenia consented to dine and spend the day at Etherington, which she quitted at night in a temper of mind perfectly composed.

Camilla was deeply penetrated[1] by the whole of this affair. The sufferings, so utterly unearned by fault or by folly, of a sister so dear to her, and the affecting fortitude which, so quickly upon her wounds, and at so early a period of life, she already began to display, made her blush at the dejection into which she was herself cast by every evil, and resolve to become in future more worthy of the father and the sister, who at this moment absorbed all her admiration.

Too reasonable, in such a frame of mind, to plan forgetting Mandlebert, she now only determined to think of him as she had thought before her affections became entangled; to think of him, in short, as he seemed himself to desire; to seek his friendly offices and advice, but to reject every offered establishment, and to live single for life.

Gratified by indulgent praise, and sustained by exerted virtue, the revived Eugenia had nearly reached Cleves, on her return, when the carriage was stopt by a gentleman on horseback, who, approaching the coach window, said, in a low voice, as if unwilling to be heard by the servants—'O, Madam! has Fate set aside her cruelty? and does Fortune permit me to live once more?'

She then recollected Mr. Bellamy. She had only her maid in the carriage, who was sent for her by Sir Hugh, Miss Margland being otherwise engaged.

All that had so lately passed upon her person and appearance being full upon her mind, she involuntarily shrunk back, hiding her face with her cloak.

Bellamy, by no means conceiving this mark of emotion to be unfavourable, steadied his horse, by leaning one hand on the coach-window, and said, in a yet lower voice—'O, Madam! is it possible you can hate me so barbarously?—will you not even deign to look at me, though I have so long been banished from your presence?'

Eugenia, during this speech, called to mind, that though new, in some measure, to herself, she was not so to this gentleman, and ventured to uncover her face; when the grief painted on the fine features of Bellamy, so forciby touched her, that she softly answered—'No, Sir, indeed I do not hate you; I am incapable of such ingratitude; but I conjure—I beseech you to forget me!'

'Forget you?—O, Madam! you command an impossibility!—No, I am constancy itself, and not all the world united shall tear you from my heart!'

Jacob, who caught a word or two, now rode up to the other window, and as Eugenia began—'Conquer, Sir, I entreat you, this ill-fated partiality!—' told her the horses had been hard-worked, and must go home.

As Jacob was the oracle of Sir Hugh about his horses, his will was prescriptive law: Eugenia never disputed it, and only saying—'Think of me, Sir, no more!' bid the coachman drive on.

Bellamy, respectfully submitting, continued, with his hat in his hand, as the maid informed her mistress, looking after the carriage till it was out of sight.

A tender sorrow now stole upon the just revived tranquillity of the gentle and generous Eugenia. 'Ah!' thought she, 'I have rendered, little as I seem worthy of such power, I have rendered this amiable man miserable, though possibly, and probably, he is the only man in existence whom I could render happy!—Ah! how may I dare expect from Clermont a similar passion?'

Molly Mill, a very young girl, and daughter of a poor tenant of Sir Hugh, interrupted these reflections from time to time, with remarks upon their object. 'Dearee me, Miss,' she cried, 'what a fine gentleman that was!—he sighed like to split his heart when you said, don't think about me no more. He's some loveyer,[1] like, I'm sure.'

Eugenia returned home so much moved by this incident, that Sir Hugh, believing his brother himself had failed to revived her, was disturbed all anew with acute contrition for her disasters, and feeling very unwell, went to bed before supper time.

Eugenia retired also; and after spending the evening in soft compassion for Bellamy, and unfixed apprehensions and distaste for young Lynmere, was preparing to go to bed, when Molly Mill, out of breath with haste, brought her a letter.

She eagerly opened it, whilst enquiring whence it came.

'O, Miss, the fine gentleman—that same fine gentleman—brought it himself: and he sent for me out, and I did not know who I was to go to, for Mary only said a boy wanted me; but the boy said, I must come with him to the stile; and when I come there, who should I see but the fine gentleman himself! And he gave me this letter, and he asked me to give it you—and see! look Miss! what I got for my trouble!'

She then exhibited a half-guinea.

'You have not done right, Molly, in accepting it. Money is bribery; and you should have known that the letter was improperly addressed, if bribery was requisite to make it delivered.'

'Dearee me, Miss, what's half-a-guinea to such a gentleman as that? I dare say he's got his pockets full of them!'

'I shall not read it, certainly,' cried Eugenia, 'now I know this circumstance. Give me the wax—I will seal it again.'

She then hesitated whether she ought to return it, or shew it to her uncle, or commit it to the flames.

That to which she was most unwilling, appeared, to the strictness of her principles, to be most proper: she therefore determined that the next morning she would relate her evening's adventure, and deliver the unread letter to Sir Hugh.

Had this epistle not perplexed her, she had meant never to name its writer. Persuaded her last words had finally dismissed him, she thought it a high point of female delicacy never to publish an unsuccessful conquest.

This resolution taken, she went to bed, satisfied with herself, but extremely grieved at the sufferings she was preparing for one who so singularly loved her.

The next morning, however, her uncle did not rise to breakfast, and was so low spirited, that fearing to disturb him, she deemed it most prudent to defer the communication.

But when, after she had taken her lesson from Dr. Orkborne, she returned to her room, she found Molly Mill impatiently waiting for her: 'O, Miss,' she cried, 'here's another letter for you! and you must read it directly, for the gentleman says if you don't it will be the death of him.'

'Why did you receive another letter?' said Eugenia, displeased.

'Dearee me, Miss, how could I help it? if you'd seen the taking he was in, you'd have took it yourself. He was all of a quake, and ready to go down of his two knees. Dearee me, if it did not make my heart go pit-pat to see him! He was like to go out of his mind, he said, and the tears, poor gentleman, were all in his eyes.'

Eugenia now turned away, strongly affected by this description.

'Do, Miss,' continued Molly, 'write him a little scrap, if it's never so scratched and bad. He'll take it kinder than nothing. Do, Miss, do. Don't be ill-natured. And just read this little letter, do,

Miss, do;—it won't take you much time, you reads so nice and fast.'

'Why,' cried Eugenia, 'did you go to him again? how could you so incautiously entrust yourself to the conduct of a strange boy?'

'A strange boy! dearee me, Miss, don't you know it was Tommy Hodd? I knows him well enough; I knows all the boys, I warrant me, round about here. Come, Miss, here's pen and ink; you'll run it off before one can count five, when you've a mind to it. He'll be in a sad taking till he sees me come back.'

'Come back? is it possible you have been so imprudent as to have promised to see him again?'

'Dearee me, yes, Miss! he'd have made away with himself if I had not. He'd been there ever since six in the morning, without nothing to eat or drink, a riding up and down the road, till he could see me coming to the stile. And he says he'll keep a riding there all day long, and all night too, till I goes to him.'

Eugenia conceived herself now in a situation of unexampled distress. She forced Molly Mill to leave her, that she might deliberate what course to pursue.

Having read no novels, her imagination had never been awakened to scenes of this kind; and what she had gathered upon such subjects in the poetry and history she had studied with Dr. Orkborne, had only impressed her fancy in proportion as love bore the character of heroism, and the lover that of an hero. Though highly therefore romantic, her romance was not the common adoption of a circulating library: it was simply that of elevated sentiments, formed by animated credulity playing upon youthful inexperience.

'Alas!' cried she, 'what a conflict is mine! I must refuse a man who adores me to distraction, in disregard of my unhappy defects, to cast myself under the guidance of one who, perhaps, may estimate beauty so highly as to despise me for its want!'

This idea pleaded so powerfully for Bellamy, that something like a wish to open his letters, obtained pardon to her little maid for having brought them. She suppressed, however, the desire, though she held them alternately to her eyes, conjecturing their contents, and bewailing for their impassioned writer the cruel answer they must receive.

Though checked by shame, she had some desire to consult Camilla; but she could not see her in time, Mrs. Arlbery having

insisted upon carrying her in the evening to a play, which was to
be performed, for one night only, by a company of passing
strollers at Northwick.

'My decision,' she cried, 'must be my own, and must be
immediate. Ah! how leave a man such as this, to wander night
and day neglected and uncertain of his fate! With tears he sent
me his letters!—what must not have been his despair when such
was his sensibility? tears in a man!—tears, too, that could not be
restrained even till his messenger was out of sight!—how
touching!—'

Her own then fell, in tender commiseration, and it was with
extreme repugnance she compelled herself to take such measures
as she thought her duty required. She sealed the two letters in an
empty cover,[1] and having directed them to Mr. Bellamy, summoned Molly Mill, and told her to convey them to the gentleman,
and positively acquaint him he must receive no more, and that
those which were returned had never been read. She bid her,
however, add, that she should always wish for his happiness, and
be grateful for his kind partiality; though she earnestly conjured
him to vanquish a regard which she did not deserve, and must
never return.

Molly Mill would fain have remonstrated; but Eugenia, with
that firmness which, even in the first youth, accompanies a
consciousness of preferring duty to inclination, silenced, and sent
her off.

Relieved for herself, now the struggle was over, she secretly
rejoiced that it was not for Melmond she had so hard a part to act:
and this idea, while it rendered Bellamy less an object of regret,
diminished also something of her pity for his conflict, by reminding her of the success which had attended her own similar
exertions.

But when Molly returned, her distress was renewed: she
brought her these words, written with a pencil upon the back of
her own cover:

'I do not dare, cruellest of your sex, to write you another letter;
but if you would save me from the abyss of destruction, you will
let me hear my final doom from your own mouth. I ask nothing
more! Ah! walk but one moment in the park, near the pales; deny
not your miserable adorer this last single request, and he will fly

this fatal climate which has swallowed up his repose for ever! But, till then, here he will stay, and never quit the spot whence he sends you these lines, till you have deigned to pronounce verbally his doom, though he should famish for want of food!

ALPHONSO BELLAMY.'

Eugenia read this with horrour and compassion. She imagined he perhaps thought her confined, and would therefore believe no answer that did not issue immediately from her own lips. She sent Molly to him again with the same message; but Molly returned with a yet worse account of his desperation, and a strong assurance, that if she would only utter to him a single word, he would obey, depart, and live upon it the rest of his life.

This completely softened her. Rather than imperiously suffer such a pattern of respectful constancy to perish, she consented to speak her own negative. But fearing she might be moved to some sympathy by his grief, she resolved to be accompanied by Camilla, and deferred, therefore, the interview till the next day.

Molly brought back his humble acknowledgments for this concession, and an account that, at last, slowly and sadly, he had ridden away.

Her feelings were now better satisfied than her understanding. She feared what she had granted was a favour; yet her heart was too tender to reproach a compliance made upon such conditions, and to prevent such evils.

CHAPTER VIII

The disastrous Buskins

CAMILLA, though her personal sorrows were blunted by the view of the calamities and resignation of her sister, was so little disposed for amusement, that she had accepted the invitation of Mrs. Arlbery, only from wanting spirit to resist its urgency. Mr. Tyrold was well pleased that such a recreation came in her way, but desired Lavinia might be of the party: not only that she might partake of the same pleasure, but from a greater security in her prudence, than in that of her naturally thoughtless sister.

The town of Etherington afforded no theatre; and the room fitted up for the night's performance could contain but two boxes, one of which was secured for Mrs. Arlbery and her friends.

The attentive Major was ready to offer his hand to Camilla upon her arrival. The rest of the officers were in the box.

The play was Othello; and so miserably represented, that Lavinia would willingly have retired after the first scene: but the native spirits of Camilla revisited her in the view of the ludicrous personages of the drama. And they were soon joined by Sir Sedley Clarendel, whose quaint conceits and remarks assisted the risibility of the scene. She thought him the least comprehensible person she had ever known; but as he was totally indifferent to her, his oddity entertained without tormenting her.

The actors were of the lowest strolling kind, and so utterly without merit, that they had never yet met with sufficient encouragement to remain one week in the same place. They had only a single scene for the whole performance, which depictured a camp, and which here served for a street, a senate, a city, a castle, and a bed-chamber.

The dresses were almost equally parsimonious, everyone being obliged to take what would fit him, from a wardrobe that did not allow quite two dresses a person for all the plays they had to enact. Othello, therefore, was equipped as king Richard the third, save that instead of a regal front he had a black wig, to imitate wool: while his face had been begrimed with a smoked cork.

Iago wore a suit of cloaths originally made for Lord Foppington:[1] Brabantio had borrowed the armour of Hamlet's Ghost: Cassio, the Lieutenant General in the christian army, had only been able to equip himself in Osmyn's Turkish vest;[2] and Roderigo, accoutred in the garment of Shylock, came forth a complete Jew.

Desdemona, attired more suitably to her fate than to her expectations, went through the whole of her part, except the last scene, in the sable weeds of Isabella.[3] And Amelia was fain to content herself with the habit of the first witch in Macbeth.

The gestures, both of the gentlemen and ladies, were as outrageous as if meant rather to intimidate the audience, than to shew their own animation; and the men approached each other so closely with arms a-kimbo, or double fists, that Sir Sedley, with pretended alarm, said they were giving challenges for a boxing match.

The ladies also, in the energy of their desire not to be eclipsed, took so much exercise in their action, that they tore out the sleeves of their gowns; which, though pinned up every time they left the stage, completely exposed their shoulders at the end of every act; and they raised their arms so high while facing each other, that Sir Sedley expressed frequent fears they meant to finish by pulling caps.[1]

So imperfect were they also in their parts, that the prompter was the only person from whom any single speech passed without a blunder.

Iago, who was the master of the troop, was the sole performer who spoke not with a provincial dialect; the rest all betrayed their birth and parentage the first line they uttered.[2]

Cassio proclaimed himself from Norfolk:

> The Deuk dew greet yew, General,
> - - - - - - - - - - -
> Being not at yew're lodging to be feund   -   -   -
> The senate sent above tree several quests, &c.[3]

Othello himself proved a true Londoner; and with his famed soldier-like eloquence in the senate-scene, thus began his celebrated defence.

> Most potent, grawe, and rewerend Seignors,
> My wery noble and approved good masters,
> That I have ta'en avay this old man's darter—
> I vill a round, unwarnish'd tale deliver
> Of my whole course of love; vhat drugs, vhat charms,
> Vhat conjuration, and vhat mighty magic
> I von his darter with — — —
> Her father lov'd me, oft invited me — —
> — — — My story being done,
> She gave me for my pains a vorld of sighs,
> She svore in faith 'tvas strange, 'tvas passing strange,
> 'Tvas pitiful, 't'vas vondrous pitiful;
> She vish'd she had not heard it; yet she vish'd
> That Heawen had made her such a man. — —
> This only is the vitchcraft I have us'd;
> Here comes the lady, let her vitness it.[4]

This happily making the gentle Desdemona recognised, notwithstanding her appearance was so little bridal, her Somersetshire father cried:

> I preay you hear 'ur zpeak.
> If a confez that a waz half the woer
> Deztruction on my head, if my bead bleame
> Light o' the mon![1]

His daughter, in the Worcestershire pronunciation, answered:

> Noble father,
> Hi do perceive ere a divided duty;
> To you hi howe my life hand heducation,
> My life hand heducation both do teach me
> Ow to respect you. You're the lord hof duty;
> Hi'm itherto your daughter: but ere's my usband!———[2]

The fond Othello then exclaimed:

> Your woices, lords! beseech you let her vill
> Have a free vay! — — —[3]

And Brabantio took leave with

> Look to'ur, Moor! if th' azt eyez to zee;
> A haz deceiv'd 'ur veather, and may thee.—[4]

They were detained so long between the first and second act, that Sir Sedley said he feared poor Desdemona had lost the thread-paper from which she was to mend her gown, and recommended to the two young ladies to have the charity to go and assist her. 'Consider,' he said, 'the trepidation of a fair bride but just entered into her shackles. Who knows but Othello may be giving her a strapping, in private, for wearing out her cloaths so fast! you young ladies think nothing of these little conjugal freedoms.'

Mrs. Arlbery, though for some time she had been as well diverted by the play as Camilla, less new to such exhibitions, was soon tired of the sameness of the blunders, and, at the end of the fourth act, proposed retiring. But Camilla, who had long not felt so much entertained, looked so disappointed, that her good humour overcame her fatigue, and she was insisting upon staying; when a gentleman, who visited them from the opposite box, proposed that the young ladies should be carried home by his mother, a lady who lived at Etherington, and was acquainted at the rectory, and who intended to stay out not only the play but the farce.[5] Lavinia consented; the son went with the proposition, and the business was soon arranged. Mrs. Arlbery, who had three miles to go beyond the parsonage-house, and who, though she delighted to oblige, was but little in the habit of practising self-denial, then consigned the young ladies to General Kinsale, to be conducted to the opposite box, and was handed by Colonel Andover to her coach.

The General guarded the eldest sister; the Major took care of Camilla: but they were all stopt in their passage by the sudden seizure of a pickpocket, and forced hastily back to the box they had quitted.

This commotion, though it had disturbed all the audience, had not stopt the performance; and Desdemona being just now discovered in bed, Camilla, not to lose the interesting scene, persuaded her sister to wait till the play was over, before they attempted again to cross to the opposite box; into which, in a few minutes after, she saw Mandlebert enter.

They had both already seated themselves as much out of sight as possible; and Camilla now began to regret she had not accompanied Mrs. Arlbery. She had thought only of the play and its entertainment, till the sight of Mandlebert told her that her situation was improper; and the idea only occurred to her by considering that it would occur to him.

Mandlebert had dined out with a party of men, and had stept in to see what was going forwards, without any knowledge whom he should meet: he instantly discerned Lavinia, and felt anxious to know why Camilla was not with her, and why she sat so much out of sight: but Camilla so completely hid herself, he could only see there was a female, whom he concluded to be some Etherington lady; and he determined to make further enquiry when the act should be over.

The performance now became so truly ludicrous, that Camilla, notwithstanding all her uneasiness, was excited to almost perpetual laughter.

Desdemona, either from the effect of a bad cold, or to give more of nature to her repose, breathed so hard, as to raise a general laugh in the audience; Sir Sedley, stopping his ears, exclaimed, 'O! if she snores I shall plead for her no more, if she tear her gown to tatters! Suffocation is much too lenient for her. She's an immense horrid personage! nasal to alarm!'

Othello then entered, with a tallow candle in his hand, staring and dropping grease at every step; and, having just declared he would not

Scar that vhiter skin of hers than snow,[1]

perceived a thief in the candle,[2] which made it run down so fast over his hand, and the sleeve of his coat, that, the moment not being yet arrived for extinguishing it, he was forced to lay down his sword, and, for want of better means, snuff it with his fingers.

Sir Sedley now protested himself completely disordered: 'I must be gone,' cried he, 'incontinently; this exceeds resistance: I shan't be alive in another minute. Are you able to form a notion of anything more annihilating? If I did not build upon the pleasure of seeing him stop up those distressing nostrils of the gentle Desdemona, I could not breathe here another instant.'

But just after, while Othello leant over the bed to say—

> Vhen I've pluck'd the rose
> I cannot give it wital growth again,
> It needs must vither - - -[3]

his black locks caught fire.

The candle now fell from his hand, and he attempted to pull off his wig; but it had been tied close on, to appear more natural, and his fright disabled him; he therefore flung himself upon the bed, and rolled the coverlid over his head.

Desdemona, excessively frightened, started up, and jumped out, shrieking aloud—'O, Lord! I shall be burnt!'

This noble Venetian Dame then exhibited, beneath an old white satin bedgown, made to cover her arms and breast, the dress in which she had equipped herself, between the acts, to be ready for trampling home; namely, a dirty red and white linen gown, an old blue stuff quilted coat, and black shoes and stockings.

In this pitiable condition, she was running, screaming, off the stage, when Othello, having quenched the fire, unconscious that half his curls had fallen a sacrifice to the flames, hastily pursued her, and, in a violent passion, called her a fool, and brought her back to the bed; in which he assisted her to compose herself, and then went behind the scenes to light his candle; which having done, he gravely returned, and, very carefully putting it down, renewed his part with the line.

> Be thus vhen thou art dead, and I vill kill thee
> And love thee after — [4]

Amidst roars of laughter from the whole audience, who, when he kissed her, almost with one voice called out—'Ay ay, that's right—kiss and friends!'

And when he said—

I must veep - - - [1]

'So must I too, my good friend,' cried Sir Sedley, wiping his eyes, 'for never yet did sorrow cost me more salt rheum! Poor Blacky! thou hast been most indissolubly comic, I confess. Thou hast unstrung me to a degree. A baby of half an hour might demolish me.'

And again, when Othello exclaimed—

She vakes! [2]

'The deuce she does?' cried Sir Sedley, 'what! has she been asleep again already? She's a very caricatura of Morpheus. Ay, do thy worst, honest Mungo. [3] I can't possibly beg her off. I would sooner snift thy farthing candle [4] once a day, than sustain that nasal cadence ever more.'

'He's the finest fellow upon the face of the earth,' cried Mr. Macdersey, who had listened to the whole play with the most serious interest; 'the instant he suspects his wife, he cuts her off without ceremony; though she's dearer to him than his eye sight, and beautiful as an angel. How I envy him!'

'Don't you think 'twould have been as well,' said General Kinsale, 'if he'd first made some little enquiry?'

'He can do that afterwards, General; and then nobody will dare surmise it's out of weakness. For to be sure and certain, he ought to right her fame; that's no more than his duty, after once he has satisfied his own. But a man's honour is dearest to him of all things. A wife's a bauble to it—not worth a thought.'

The suffocating was now beginning but just as Desdemona begged to be spared—

But alf han our — [5]

the door-keeper forced his way into the pit, and called out— 'Pray, is one Miss Tyrold here in the play-house?'

The sisters, in much amazement hung back, entreating the gentlemen to screen them; and the man, receiving no answer, went away.

While wondering what this could mean, the play was finished, when one of the comedians, a brother of the Worcestershire Desdemona, came to the pit door, calling out—'Hi'm desired to hask hif Miss Camilla Tyrold's hany way ere hin the ouse, for hi'm hordered to call er hout, for her Huncle's hill and dying.'

A piercing shriek from Camilla now completed the interruption of all attention to the performance, and betrayed her hiding place. Concealment, indeed, was banished her thoughts, and she would herself have opened the box door to rush out, had not the Major anticipated her, seizing, at the same time, her hand to conduct her through the crowd.

CHAPTER IX

Three Golden Maxims

LAVINIA, almost equally terrified, followed her sister; and Sir Sedley, burying all foppery in compassion and good nature, was foremost to accompany and assist. Camilla had no thought but to get instantly to Cleves; she considered not how; she only forced herself rapidly on, persuaded she could walk it in ten minutes, and ejaculating incessantly, 'My Uncle!—my dear Uncle!'—

They almost instantly encountered Edgar, who, upon the fatal call, had darted round to meet them, and finding each provided with an attendant, inquired whose carriage he should seek?

Camilla, in a broken voice, answered she had no carriage, and should walk.

'Walk?' he repeated; 'you are near five miles from Cleves!'

Scarce in her senses, she hurried on without reply.

'What carriage did you come in, Miss Tyrold?' said Edgar to Lavinia.

'We came with Mrs. Arlbery.'

'Mrs. Arlbery?—she has been gone this half hour; I met her as I entered.'

Camilla had now rushed out of doors, still handed by the Major.

'If you have no carriage in waiting,' said Edgar, 'make use, I beseech you, of mine!'

'O, gladly! O, thankfully!' cried Camilla, almost sobbing out her words.

He flew then to call for his chaise, and the door-keeper, for whom Sir Sedley had inquired, came to them, accompanied by Jacob.

'O, Jacob!' she cried, breaking violently from the Major, 'tell me!—tell me!—my Uncle!—my dearest Uncle!'

Jacob, in a tone of deep and unfeigned sorrow, said, his Master had been seized suddenly with the gout in his stomach,[1] and that the doctor, who had been instantly fetched, had owned there was little hope.

She could hear no more; the shock overpowered her, and she sunk nearly senseless into the arms of her sister.

She was recovered, however, almost in a minute, and carried by Edgar into his chaise, in which he placed her between himself and the weeping Lavinia; hastily telling the two gentlemen, that his intimate connection with the family authorized his assisting and attending them at such a period.

This was too well known to be disputed; and Sir Sedley and the Major, with great concern, uttered their good wishes and retreated.

Jacob had already been for Mr. Tyrold, who had set off instantaneously on horseback.

Camilla spoke not a word the first mile, which was spent in an hysteric sobbing: but, recovering a little afterwards, and sinking on the shoulder of her sister, 'O, Lavinia!' she cried, 'should we lose my Uncle——'

A shower of tears wetted the neck of Lavinia, who mingled with them her own, though less violently, from having less connection with Sir Hugh, and a sensibility less ungovernable.

She called herself upon the postillion to drive faster, and pressed Edgar continually to hurry him; but though he gave every charge she could desire, so much swifter were her wishes than any possible speed, that twenty times she entreated to get out, believing she could walk quicker than the horses galloped.

When they arrived at the park gate, she was with difficulty held back from opening the chaise door; and when, at length, they stopt at the house porch, she could not wait for the step, and before Edgar could either precede or prevent her, threw herself into the arms of Jacob, who, having just dismounted, was fortunately at hand to save her from falling.

She stopt not to ask any question; 'My Uncle!—my Uncle!' she cried, impetuously, and, rushing past all she met, was in his room in a moment.

Edgar, though he could not obstruct, followed her close, dreading lest Sir Hugh might already be no more, and determined, in that case, to force her from the fatal spot.

Eugenia, who heard her footstep, received her at the door, but took her immediately from the room, softly whispering, while her arms were thrown round her waist—'He will live! he will live, my sister! his agonies are over—he is fallen asleep, and he will live!'

This was too sudden a joy for the desponding Camilla, whose breath instantly stopt, and who must have fallen upon the floor, had she not been caught by Edgar; who, though his own eyes copiously overflowed with delight, at such unexpected good news of the universally beloved Baronet, had strength and exertion sufficient to carry her downstairs into the parlour, accompanied by Eugenia.

There, hartshorn[1] and water presently revived her, and then, regardless of the presence of Edgar, she cast herself upon her knees, to utter a fervent thanksgiving, in which Eugenia, with equal piety, though more composure, joined.

Edgar had never yet beheld her in a light so resplendent—What a heart, thought he, is here! what feelings, what tenderness, what animation!—O, what a heart!—were it possible to touch it!

The two sisters went both gently up stairs, encouraging and congratulating each other in soft whispers, and stationed themselves in an ante-room: Mr. Tyrold, by medical counsel, giving directions that no one but himself should enter the sick chamber.

Edgar, though he only saw the domestics, could not persuade himself to leave the house till near two o'clock in the morning: and by six, his anxiety brought him thither again. He then heard, that the Baronet had passed a night of more pain than danger, the gout having been expelled his stomach, though it had been threatening almost every other part.

Three days and nights passed in this manner; during which, Edgar saw so much of the tender affections, and softer character of Camilla, that nothing could have withheld him from manifesting his entire sympathy in her feelings, but the unaccountable circumstance of her starting forth from a back seat at the play, where she had sat concealed, attended by the Major, and without any matron protectress.

Miss Margland, meanwhile, scowled at him, and Indiana pouted in vain. His earnest solicitude for Sir Hugh surmounted every such obstacle to his present visits at Cleves; and he spent there almost the whole of his time.

On the fourth day of the attack, Sir Hugh had a sleep of five hours' continuance, from which he awoke so much revived, that he raised himself in his bed, and called out—'My dear Brother! you are still here?—you are very good to me, indeed; poor sinner that I am! to forgive me for all my bad behaviour to your Children.'

'My dearest Brother! my Children, like myself, owe you nothing but kindness and beneficence; and, like myself, feel for you nothing but gratitude and tenderness.'

'They are very good, very good indeed,' said Sir Hugh, with a deep sigh; 'but Eugenia!—poor little Eugenia has nearly been the death of me; though not meaning it in the least, being all her life as innocent as a lamb.'

Mr. Tyrold assured him, that Eugenia was attached to him with the most unalterable fondness. But Sir Hugh said, that the sight of her, returning from Etherington, with nearly the same sadness as ever, had wounded him to the heart, by shewing him she would never recover; which had brought back upon him all his first contrition, about the smallpox, and the fall from the plank, and had caused his conscience to give him so many twitches, that it never let him rest a moment, till the gout seized upon his stomach, and almost took him off at once.

Mr. Tyrold attributed solely to his own strong imagination the idea of the continuance of the dejection of Eugenia, as she had left Etherington calm, and almost chearful. He instantly, therefore, fetched her, intimating the species of consolation she could afford.

'Kindest of Uncles!' cried she, 'is it possible you can ever, for a moment, have doubted the grateful affection with which your goodness has impressed me from my childhood? Do me more justice, I beseech you, my dearest Uncle! recover from this terrible attack, and you shall soon see your Eugenia restored to all the happiness you can wish her.'

'Nobody has got such kind nieces as me!' cried Sir Hugh, again dissolving into tenderness; 'for all nobody has deserved so ill of them. My generous little Camilla, forgave me from the very first, before her young soul had any guile in it, which, God knows, it never has had to this hour, no more than your own. However, this I can tell you, which may serve to keep you from repenting being good, and that is, that your kindness to your poor Uncle may be the means of saving a christian's life; which, for a young person at your age, is as much as can be expected: for I think, I may yet get about again, if I could once be assured I should see you as happy as you used to be; and you've been the contentedest little thing, till those unlucky market-women, that ever was seen: always speaking up for the servants, and the poor, from the time you were eight years old. And never letting me be angry, but taking every body's part, and thinking them all as good as yourself, and only wanting to make them as happy.'

'Ah, my dear Uncle! how kind a memory is yours! retaining only what can give pleasure, and burying in oblivion whatever might cause pain!—'

'Is my Uncle well enough to speak?' cried Camilla, softly opening the door, 'and may I—for one single moment,—see him?'- - - -

'That's the voice of my dear Camilla!' said Sir Hugh; 'come in, my little love, for I shan't shock your tender heart now, for I'm going to get better.'

Camilla, in an ecstasy, was instantly at his bedside, passionately exclaiming, 'My dear, dear Uncle! will you indeed recover?—'

Sir Hugh, throwing his feeble arms round her neck, and leaning his head upon her shoulder, could only faintly articulate, 'If God pleases, I shall, my little darling, my heart's delight and joy! But don't vex, whether I do or not, for it is but in the course of nature for a man to die, even in his youth; but how much more when he comes to be old? Though I know you can't help missing me, in particular at the first, because of all your goodness to me.'

'Missing you? O my Uncle! we can never be happy again without you! never never!—when your loved countenance no longer smiles upon us,—when your kind voice no longer assembles us around you!- - - -'

'My dear child—my own little Camilla,' cried Sir Hugh, in a faint voice, 'I am ready to die!'

Mr. Tyrold here forced her away, and his brother grew so much worse, that a dangerous relapse took place, and for three days more, the physician, the nurse, and Mr. Tyrold, were alone allowed to enter his room.

During this time, the whole family suffered the truest grief, and Camilla was inconsolable.

When again he began to revive, he called Mr. Tyrold to him, and said that this second shake persuaded him he had but a short time more for this world; and begged therefore he would prepare him for his exit.

Mr. Tyrold complied, and found, with more happiness than surprise, his perfect and chearful resignation either to live or to die, rejoicing as much as himself, in the innocent benevolence of his past days.

Composed and strengthened by religious duties, he then desired to see Eugenia and Indiana, that he might give them his last exhortations and counsel, in case of a speedy end.

Mr. Tyrold would fain have spared him this touching exertion, but he declared he could not go off with a clear conscience, unless he told them the advice which he had been thinking of for them, between whiles, during all his illness.

Mr. Tyrold then feared that opposition might but discompose him, and summoned his youngest daughter and his niece, charging them both to repress their affliction, lest it should accelerate what they most dreaded.

Camilla, always upon the watch, glided in with them, supplicating her Father not to deny her admittance; though fearful of her impetuous sorrows, he wished her to retreat; but Sir Hugh no sooner heard her murmuring voice, than he declared he would have her refused nothing, though he had meant to take a particular leave of her alone, for the last thing of all.

Gratefully thanking him, she advanced trembling to his bed-side; solemnly promising her Father that no expression of her grief should again risk agitating a life and health so precious.

Sir Hugh then desired to have Lavinia called also, because, though he had thought of nothing to say to her, she might be hurt, after he was gone, in being left out.

He was then raised by pillows and sat upright, and they knelt round his bed. Mr. Tyrold entreated him to be concise, and insisted upon the extremest forbearance and fortitude in his little audience. He seated himself at some distance, and Sir Hugh, after swallowing a cordial medicine,[1] began:

'My dear Nieces, I have sent for you all upon a particular account, which I beg you to listen to, because, God only knows whether I may ever be able to give you so much advice again. I see you all look very melancholy, which I take very kind of you. However don't cry, my little dears, for we must all go off, so it matters but little the day or the hour; dying being, besides, the greatest comfort of us all, taking us off from our cares; as my Brother will explain to you better than me.

'The chief of what I have got to say, in regard to what I have been studying in my illness, is for you two, my dear Eugenia and Indiana; because, having brought you both up, I can't get it out of my head what you'll do, when I am no longer here to keep you out of the danger of bad designers.

'My hope had been to have seen you both married while I was alive and amongst you, and I made as many plans as my poor head knew how, to bring it about; but we've all been disappointed alike, for which reason we must put up with it properly.

'What I have now last of all, to say to you, my little dears, is three maxims, which may serve for you all four alike, though I thought of them, at first, only for you two.

'In the first place, *Never be proud:* if you are, your superiors will laugh at you, your equals won't love you, and your dependants will hate you. And what is there for poor mortal man to be proud of?—Riches! - - - why they are but a charge, and if we don't use them well, we may envy the poor beggar that has so much less to answer for.—Beauty! - - - why, we can neither get it when we haven't it; nor keep it when we have it.—Power!- - -why we scarce ever use it one way, but what we are sorry we did not use it another!

'In the second place, *Never trust a Flatterer*. If a man makes you a great many compliments, always suspect him of some bad design, and never believe him your friend, till he tells you of some of your faults. Poor little things! you little imagine how many you have, for all you're so good!

'In the third place, *Do no harm to others, for the sake of any good it may do to yourselves;* because the good will last you but a little while; and the repentance will stick by you as long as you live; and what is worse, a great while longer, and beyond any count the best Almanack-maker knows how to reckon.

'And now, my dear Nieces, this is all; except the recommending to my dear Eugenia to be kind to my poor servants, who have all used me so well, knowing I have nothing to leave them.'

Eugenia, suppressing her sobs, promised to retain them all, as long as they should desire to remain with her, and to provide for them afterwards.

'I know, you'll forget nobody, my dear little girl,' cried the Baronet, 'which makes me die contented; not even Mrs. Margland, a little particularity[1] not being to be considered at one's last end: and much less Dr. Orkborne, who has so much a better right from you. As to Indiana, she'll have her own little fortune when she comes of age; and I dare say her pretty face will marry her before long.—And as to Clermont, he'll come off rather short, finding I leave him nothing; but you'll make up for the deficiency, by giving him the whole, as well as a good wife. As to Lionel, I leave him my blessing; and as to any other legacy I never happened to promise him any; which is very good luck for me, as well as my best excuse; and I may say the same to my dear Lavinia, which is the reason I called her in, because she may not often have an opportunity to hear a man speak upon his death-bed. However all I wish for is, that I could leave you all equal shares, as well as give Eugenia the whole.'

'O my dear Uncle!' exclaimed Eugenia, 'make a new Will immediately! do everything your tenderness can dictate!—or tell me what I shall do in your name, and every word, every wish shall be sacredly obeyed!'

'Dear, generous, noble girl! no! I won't take from you a shilling! keep it all—nobody will spend it so well;—and I can't give you back your beauty; so keep it, my dear, all, for my oath's sake, when I am gone; and don't make me die under a prevaricating; which would be but a grievous thing for a person to do; unless he was but a bad believer: which, God help us! there are enough, without my helping to make more.'

Mr. Tyrold now again remonstrated, motioning to the weeping group to be gone.

'Ah! my dear Brother!' said Sir Hugh, 'you are the only right person that ought to have had it all, if it had not been for my poor weak brain, that made me always be looking askew, instead of strait forward. And indeed I always meant you to have had it for your life, till the smallpox put all things out of my head. However, I hope you won't object to preach my funeral sermon, for all my bad faults, for nobody else will speak of me so kindly; which may serve as a better lesson for those I leave behind.'

Tears flowed fast down the cheeks of Mr. Tyrold, as he uttered whatever he could suggest most tenderly soothing to his Brother: and the young mourners, not daring to resist, were all gliding away, except Camilla, whose hand was fast grasped in that of her Uncle.

'Ah, my Camilla,' cried he, as she would gently have withdrawn it, 'how shall I part with my little dear darling? this is the worst twitch to me of all, with all my contentedness! And the more because I know you love your poor old Uncle, just as well as if he had left you all he was worth, though you won't get one penny by his death!'

'O my dear, dearest Uncle—' exclaimed Camilla, in a passionate flood of tears; when Mr. Tyrold, assuring them both the consequences might be fatal, tore her away from the bed and the room.

END OF THE SECOND VOLUME.

VOLUME III

====

BOOK V

CHAPTER I

A Pursuer

NOTWITHSTANDING the fears so justly excited from the mixt emotions and exertions of Sir Hugh, Mr. Tyrold had the happiness to see him fall into a tranquil sleep, from which he awoke without any return of pain; his night was quiet; the next day was still better; and the day following he was pronounced out of danger.

The rapture which this declaration excited in the house, and diffused throughout the neighbourhood, when communicated to the worthy baronet, gave a gladness to his heart that recompensed all he had suffered.

The delight of Camilla exceeded whatever she had yet experienced: her life had lost half its value in her estimation, while she believed that of her uncle to be in danger.

No one single quality is perhaps so endearing, from man to man, as good-nature.[1] Talents excite more admiration; wisdom, more respect; and virtue, more esteem: but with admiration envy is apt to mingle, and fear with respect; while esteem, though always honourable, is often cold: but good-nature gives pleasure without any allay; ease, confidence, and happy carelessness, without the pain of obligation, without the exertion of gratitude.

If joy was in some more tumultuous, content was with none so penetrating as with Eugenia. Apprised now that she had been the immediate cause of the sufferings of her uncle, his loss would have given to her peace a blow irrecoverable; and she determined to bend the whole of her thoughts to his wishes, his comfort, his entire restoration.

To this end all her virtue was called in aid; a fear, next to aversion, having seized her of Clermont, from the apprehension she might never inspire in him such love as she had inspired in Bellamy, nor see in him, as in young Melmond, such merit as might raise similar sentiments for himself.

Molly Mill had not failed to paint to her the disappointment of Bellamy in not seeing her; but she was too much engrossed by the dangerous state of her uncle, to feel any compunction in her breach of promise; though touched with the account of his continual sufferings, she became very gentle in her reprimands to Molly for again meeting him; and, though Molly again disobeyed, she again was pardoned. He came daily to the lane behind the park pales, to hear news of the health of Sir Hugh, without pressing either for an interview or a letter; and Eugenia grew more and more moved by his respectful obsequiousness.[1] She had yet said nothing to Camilla upon the subject; not only because a dearer interest mutually occupied them, but from a secret shame of naming a lover at a period so ungenial.

But now that Sir Hugh was in a fair way of recovery, her situation became alarming to herself. Openly, and before the whole house, she had solemnly been assigned to Clermont Lynmere; and, little as she wished the connexion, she thought it, from circumstances, her duty not to refuse it. Yet this gentleman had attended her so long, had endured so many disappointments, and borne them so much to her satisfaction, that, though she lamented her concession as an injury to Clermont, and grew ashamed to name it even to Camilla, she believed it would be cruelty unheard of to break it. She determined, therefore, to see him, to pronounce a farewell, and then to bend all her thoughts to the partner destined her by her friends.

Molly Mill was alone to accompany her to give her negative, her good wishes, and her solemn declaration that she could never again see or hear of him more. He could deem it no indelicacy that she suffered Molly to be present, since she was the negociator of his own choice.

Molly carried him, therefore, this news, with a previous condition that he was not to detain her mistress one minute. He promised all submission; and the next morning, after breakfast, Eugenia, in extreme dejection at the ungrateful task she had to perform, called for Molly, and walked forth.

Camilla, who was then accidentally in her own room, was, soon after, summoned by three smart raps to her chamber door.

There, to her great surprise, she saw Edgar, who, after a hasty apology, begged to have a few minutes conference with her alone.

She descended with him into the parlour, which was vacant.

'You suspect, perhaps,' said he, in an hurried manner, though attempting to smile, 'that I mean to fatigue you with some troublesome advice; I must, therefore, by an abrupt question, explain myself. Does Mr. Bellamy still continue his pretensions to your sister Eugenia?'

Startled in a moment from all thoughts of self, that at first had been rushing with violence to her heart, Camilla answered, 'No! why do you ask?'

'I will tell you: In my regular visits here of late, I have almost constantly met him, either on foot or on horseback, in the vicinity of the park. I suspected he watched to see Eugenia; but I knew she now never left the house; and concluded he was ignorant of the late general confinement. This moment, however, upon my entrance, I saw him again; and, as he hastily turned away upon meeting my eye, I dismounted, gave my horse to my man, and determined to satisfy myself which way he was strolling. I then followed him to the little lane to the right of the park, where I perceived an empty post-chaise-and-four in waiting: he advanced, and spoke with the postillion—I came instantly into the house by the little gate. This may be accidental; yet it has alarmed me; and I ventured, therefore, thus suddenly to apply to you, in order to urge you to give a caution to Eugenia, not to walk out, just at present, unattended.'

Camilla thanked him, and ran eagerly to speak to her sister; but she was not in her room; nor was she with her uncle; nor yet with Dr. Orkborne. She returned uneasily to the parlour, and said she would seek her in the park.

Edgar followed; but they looked around for her in vain: he then, deeming the danger urgent, left her, to hasten to the spot where he had seen the post-chaise.

Camilla ran on alone; and, when she reached the park gate, perceived her sister, Molly Mill, and Bellamy, in the lane.

They heard her quick approach, and turned round.

The countenance of Bellamy exhibited the darkest disappointment, and that of Eugenia the most excessive confusion. 'Now then, Sir,' she cried, 'delay our separation no longer.'

'Ah, permit me,' said he, in a low voice, 'permit me to hope you will hear my last sad sentence, my final misery, another day!—I will defer my mournful departure for that melancholy joy, which is the last I shall feel in my wretched existence!'

He sighed so deeply, that Eugenia, who seemed already in much sorrow, could not utter an abrupt refusal; and, as Camilla now advanced, she turned from him, without attempting to say any thing further.

Camilla, in the delight of finding her sister safe, after the horrible apprehensions she had just experienced, could not speak to her for tears.

Abashed at once, and amazed, Eugenia faintly asked what so affected her? She gave no explanation, but begged her to turn immediately back.

Eugenia consented; and Bellamy, bowing to them both profoundly, with quick steps walked away.

Camilla asked a thousand questions; but Eugenia seemed unable to answer them.

In a few minutes they were joined by Edgar, who, walking hastily up to them, took Camilla apart.

He told her he firmly believed a villainous scheme to have been laid: he had found the chaise still in waiting, and asked the postillion to whom he belonged. The man said he was paid for what he did; and refused giving any account of himself. Bellamy then appeared: he seemed confounded at his sight; but neither of them spoke; and he left him and his chaise, and his postillion, to console one another. He doubted not, he said, but the design had been to carry Eugenia off, and he had probably only pretended to take leave, that the chaise might advance, and the postillion aid the elopement: though finding help at hand, he had been forced to give up his scheme.

Camilla even with rapture blest his fortunate presence; but was confounded with perplexity at the conduct of Eugenia. Edgar, who feared her heart was entangled by an object who sought only her wealth, proposed dismissing Molly Mill, that he might tell her himself the opinion he had conceived of Bellamy.

Camilla overtook her sister, who had walked on without listening to or regarding them; and, sending away Molly, told her Edgar wished immediately to converse with her, upon something of the utmost importance.

'You know my high esteem of him,' she answered; 'but my mind is now occupied upon a business of which he has no information, and I entreat that you will neither of you interrupt me.'

Camilla, utterly at a loss what to conjecture, joined Mandlebert alone, and told him her ill success. He thought every thing was to be feared from the present state of the affair, and proposed revealing at once all he knew of it to Mr. Tyrold: but Camilla desired him to take no step till she had again expostulated with her sister, who might else be seriously hurt or offended. He complied, and said he would continue in the house, park, or environs, incessantly upon the watch, till some decisive measure were adopted.

Joining Eugenia then again, she asked if she meant seriously to encourage the addresses of Bellamy.

'By no means,' she quietly answered.

'My dear Eugenia, I cannot at all understand you; but it seems clear to me that the arrival of Edgar has saved you from some dreadful violence.'

'You hurt me, Camilla, by this prejudice. From whom should I dread violence? from a man who—but too fatally for his peace— values me more than his life?'

'If I could be sure of his sincerity,' said Camilla, 'I should be the last to think ill of him: but reflect a little, at least, upon the risk that you have run; my dear Eugenia! there was a post-chaise in waiting, not twenty yards from where I stopt you!'

'Ah, you little know Bellamy! that chaise was only to convey him away; to convey him, Camilla, to an eternal banishment!'

'But why, then, had he prevailed with you to quit the park?'

'You will call me vain if I tell you.'

'No; I shall only think you kind and confidential.'

'Do me then the justice,' said Eugenia, blushing, 'to believe me as much surprised as yourself at his most unmerited passion: but he told me, that if I only cast my eyes upon the vehicle which was to part him from me for ever, it would not only make it less abhorrent to him, but probably prevent the loss of his senses.'

'My dear Eugenia,' said Camilla, half smiling, 'this is a violent passion, indeed, for so short an acquaintance!'

'I knew you would say that,' answered she, disconcerted; 'and it was just what I observed to him myself: but he satisfied me that the reason of his feelings being so impetuous was, that this was the first and only time he had ever been in love.—So handsome as he is!—what a choice for him to make!'

Camilla, tenderly embracing her, declared, 'the choice was all that did him honour in the affair.'

'He never,' said she, a little comforted, 'makes me any compliments; I should else disregard, if not disdain him: but indeed he seems, notwithstanding his own extraordinary manly beauty, to be wholly superior to external considerations.'

Camilla now forbore expressing farther doubt, from the fear of painful misapprehension; but earnestly entreated her to suffer Edgar to be entrusted and consulted: she decidedly, however, refused her consent. 'I require no advice,' cried she, 'for I am devoted to my uncle's will: to speak then of this affair would be the most cruel indelicacy, in publishing a conquest which, since it is rejected, I ought silently, though gratefully, to bury in my own heart.'

Shen then related the history of all that had passed to Camilla; but solemnly declared she would never, to any other human being, but him who should hereafter be entitled to her whole heart, betray the secret of the unhappy Bellamy.

CHAPTER II

An Adviser

THE wish of Camilla was to lay this whole affair before her father; but she checked it, from an apprehension she might seem displaying her duty and confidence at the expence of those of her sister; whose motives for concealment were intentionally the most pure, however, practically, they might be erroneous; and whom she both pitied and revered for her proposed submission to her uncle, in opposition to her palpable reluctance.

She saw not, however, any obstacle to consulting with Edgar, since he was already apprised of the business, and since his services might be essentially useful to her sister: while, with respect to herself, there seemed, at this time, more of dignity in meeting than shunning his friendly intercourse, since his regard for her seemed to have lost all its peculiarity. He has precisely, cried she, the same sentiments for my sisters as for me,—he is equally kind, disinterested, and indifferent to us all! anxious alike for Eugenia with Mr. Bellamy, and for me with the detestable Major! Be it so!—we can no where obtain a better friend; and I should blush, indeed, if I could not treat as a brother one who can treat me as a sister.

Tranquil, though not gay, she returned to converse with him; but when she had related what had passed, he confessed that his uneasiness upon the subject was increased. The heart of Eugenia appeared to him positively entangled; and he besought Camilla not to lose a moment in acquainting Mr. Tyrold with her situation.

She pleaded against giving this pain to her sister with energetic affection: her arguments failed to convince, but her eloquence powerfully touched him; and he contented himself with only entreating that she would again try to aid him with an opportunity of conversing with Eugenia.

This she could not refuse; nor could he then resist the opportunity to inquire why Mrs. Arlbery had left her and Lavinia at the play. She thanked him for remembering his character of her monitor, and acknowledged the fault to be her own, with a candour so unaffected, that, captivated by the soft seriousness of her manner, he flattered himself his fear of the Major was a chimæra, and hoped that, as soon as Sir Hugh was able to again join his family, no impediment would remain to his begging the united blessings of the two brothers to his views.

When Camilla told her sister the request of Edgar, she immediately suspected the attachment of Bellamy had been betrayed to him; and Camilla, incapable of any duplicity, related precisely how the matter had passed. Eugenia, always just, no sooner heard than she forgave it, and accompanied her sister immediately down stairs.

'I must rest all my hope of pardon,' cried Edgar, 'for the part I am taking, to your conviction of its motive; a filial love and gratitude to Mr. Tyrold, a fraternal affection and interest for all his family.'

'My own sisterly feelings,' she answered, 'make me both comprehend and thank your kind solicitude: but, believe me, it is now founded in error. I am shocked to find you informed of this unhappy transaction; and I charge and beseech that no interference may wound its ill-fated object, by suffering him to surmise your knowledge of his humiliating situation.'

'I would not for the world give you pain,' answered Edgar: 'but permit me to be faithful to the brotherly character in which I consider myself to stand with you . . . all.'

A blush had overspread his face at the word Brotherly; while at that of *all*, which recovered him, a still deeper stained the cheeks of Camilla: but neither of them looked at the other; and Eugenia was too self-absorbed to observe either.

'Your utter inexperience in life,' he continued, 'makes me, though but just giving up leading-strings myself, an adept in the comparison. Suffer me then, as such, to represent to you my fears, that your innocence and goodness may expose you to imposition. You must not judge all characters by the ingenuousness of your own; nor conclude, however rationally and worthily a mind such as yours might - - - may - - - - and will inspire a disinterested regard, that there is no danger of any other, and that mercenary views are out of the question, because mercenary principles are not declared.'

'I will not say your inference is severe,' replied Eugenia, 'because you know not the person of whom you speak: but permit me to make this irrefragable vindication of his freedom from all sordid motives; he has never once named the word fortune, neither to make any inquiries into mine, nor any professions concerning his own. Had he any inducement to duplicity, he might have asserted to me what he pleased, since I have no means of detection.'

'Your situation,' said Edgar, 'is pretty generally known; and for his . . . pardon me if I hint it may be possible that silence is no virtue. However, since I am unacquainted, you say, with his character, will you give me leave to make myself better informed?'

'There needs no investigation; to me it is perfectly known.'

'Forgive me if I ask how!'

'By his letters and by his conversation.'

A smile which stole upon the features of Edgar obliged him to turn his head another way; but presently recovering, 'My dear Miss Eugenia,' he cried, 'will it not be most consonant to your high principles, and scrupulous delicacy, to lay the whole of what has passed before Mr. Tyrold?'

'Undoubtedly, if my part were not strait forward. Had I the least hesitation, my father should be my immediate and decisive umpire. But . . . I am not at liberty even for deliberation!—I am not . . . I know . . . at my own disposal!'—

She blushed and looked down, confused; but presently, with firmness, added, 'It is not, indeed, fit that I should be; my uncle completely merits to be in all things my director. To know his wishes, therefore, is not only to know, but to be satisfied with my doom. Such being my situation, you cannot misunderstand my defence of this unhappy young man. It is but simple justice to rescue an amiable person from calumny.'

'Let us allow all this,' said Edgar; 'still I see no reason why Mr. Tyrold. . . .'

'Mr. Mandlebert,' interrupted she, 'you must do what you judge right. I can desire no one to abstain from pursuing the dictates of their own sense of honour. I leave you, therefore, unshackled: but there is no consideration which, in my opinion, can justify a female in spreading, even to her nearest connexions, an unrequited partiality. If, therefore, I am forced to inflict this undue mortification, upon a person to whom I hold myself so much obliged, an uneasiness will remain upon my mind, destructive of my forgetfulness of an event which I would fain banish from my memory.'

She then refused to be any longer detained.

'How I love the perfect innocence, and how I reverence the respectable singularity of that charming character!' cried Edgar; 'yet how vain are all arguments against such a combination of fearless credulity, and enthusiastic reasoning? What can we determine?'

'I am happy to retort upon you that question,' replied Camilla; 'for I am every way afraid to act myself, lest I should hurt this dear sister, or do wrong by my yet dearer father.'

'What a responsibility you cast upon me! I will not, however, shrink from it, for the path seems far plainer to me since I have had this conversation. Eugenia is at present safe; I see, now, distinctly, her heart is yet untouched. The readiness with which she met the subject, the openness with which she avows her esteem, the un-embarrassed, though modest simplicity with which she speaks of his passion and his distress, all shew that her pity results from generosity, not from love. Had it been otherwise, with all her steadiness, all her philosophy, some agitation and anxiety would have betrayed her secret soul. The internal workings of hopes and fears, the sensitive alarms of repressed consciousness. . . .' A deep glow, which heated his face, forced him here to break off; and, abruptly leaving his sentence unfinished, he hastily began another.

'We must not, nevertheless, regard this as security for the

future, though it is safety for the present; nor trust her unsuspicious generosity of mind to the dangerous assault of artful distress. I speak without reserve of this man; for though I know him not, as she remonstrated, I cannot, from the whole circumstances of his clandestine conduct, doubt his being an adventurer. . . . You say nothing? tell me, I beg, your opinion.'

Camilla had not heard one word of this last speech. Struck with his discrimination between the actual and the possible state of Eugenia's mind, and with the effect the definition had produced upon himself, her attention was irresistibly seized by a new train of ideas, till finding he waited for an answer, she mechanically repeated his last word 'opinion?'

He saw her absence of mind, and suspected his own too palpable disturbance had occasioned it: but in what degree, or from what sensations, he could not conjecture. They were both some time silent; and then, recollecting herself, she said it was earnestly her wish to avoid disobliging her sister, by a communication, which, made by any one but herself, must put her into a disgraceful point of view.

Edgar, after a pause, said, they must yield, then, to her present fervour, and hope her sounder judgment, when less played upon, would see clearer. It appeared to him, indeed, that she was so free, at this moment, from any dangerous impression, that it might, perhaps, be even safer to submit quietly to her request, than to urge the generous romance of her temper to new workings. He undertook, meantime, to keep a constant watch upon the motions of Bellamy, to make sedulous inquiries into his character and situation in life, and to find out for what ostensible purpose he was in Hampshire: entreating leave to communicate constantly to Camilla what he might gather, and to consult with her, from time to time, upon what measures should be pursued: yet ultimately confessing, that if Eugenia did not steadily persist in refusing any further rejections, he should hold himself bound in conscience to communicate the whole to Mr. Tyrold.

Camilla was pleased, and even thankful for the extreme friendliness and kind moderation of this arrangement; yet she left him mournfully, in a confirmed belief his regard for the whole family was equal.

Eugenia, much gratified, promised she would henceforth take no step with which Edgar should not first be acquainted.

CHAPTER III

Various Confabulations

MR. Tyrold saw, at first, the renewed visits of Edgar at Cleves with extreme satisfaction; but while all his hopes were alive from an intercourse almost perpetual, he perceived, with surprise and perplexity, that his daughter became more and more pensive after every interview: and as Edgar, this evening, quitted the house, he observed tears start into her eyes as she went up stairs to her own room.

Alarmed and disappointed, he thought it now high time to investigate the state of the affair, and to encourage or prevent future meetings, as it appeared to him to be propitious or hopeless.

Penetrated with the goodness, while lamenting the indifference of Edgar, Camilla had just reached her room; when, as she turned round to shut her door, Mr. Tyrold appeared before her.

Hastily, with the back of her hand, brushing off the tears from her eyes, she said, 'May I go to my uncle, Sir? . . . can my uncle admit me?'

'He can always admit you,' he answered; 'but, just now, you must forget him a moment, and consign yourself to your father.'

He then entered, shut the door, and making her sit down by him, said, 'What is this sorrow that assails my Camilla? Why is the light heart of my dear and happy child thus dejected?'

Speech and truth were always one with Camilla; who, as she could not in this instance declare what were her feelings, remained mute and confounded.

'Hesitate not, my dear girl,' cried he kindly, 'to unbosom your griefs or your apprehensions, where they will be received with all the tenderness due to such a confidence, and held sacred from every human inspection; unless you permit me yourself to entrust your best and wisest friend.'

Camilla now trembled, but could not even attempt to speak.

He saw her disorder, and presently added, 'I will forbear to probe your feelings, when you have satisfied me in one doubt; —Is the sadness I have of late remarked in you the effect of secret personal disturbance, or of disappointed expectation?'

Camilla could neither answer nor look up: she was convinced, by this question, that the subject of her melancholy was understood, and felt wholly overcome by the deeply distressing confusion, with which wounded pride and unaffected virgin modesty impress a youthful female, in the idea of being suspected of a misplaced, or an unrequited partiality.

Her silence, a suffocating sigh, and her earnest endeavour to hide her face, easily explained to Mr. Tyrold all that passed within; and respecting rather than wishing to conquer a shame flowing from fearful delicacy, 'I would spare you,' he said, 'all investigation whatever, could I be certain you are not called into any action; but, in that case, I know not that I can justify to myself so implicit a confidence, in youth and inexperience so untried in difficulties, so unused to evil or embarrassment as yours. Tell me then, my dear Camilla, do you sigh under the weight of any disingenuous conduct? or do you suffer from some suspence which you have no means of terminating?'

'My dearest father, no!' cried she, sinking upon his breast. 'I have no suspence!'

She gasped for breath.

'And how has it been removed, my child?' said Mr. Tyrold, in a mournful tone; 'has any deception, any ungenerous art . . . .'

'O no, no! . . . he is incapable . . . he is superior . . . he . . .' She stopt abruptly; shocked at the avowal these few words at once inferred of her partiality, of its hopelessness, and of its object.

She walked, confused, to a corner of the room, and, leaning against the wainscot, enveloped her face in her handkerchief, with the most painful sensations of shame.

Mr. Tyrold remained in deep meditation. Her regard for Edgar he had already considered as undoubted, and her undisguised acknowledgment excited his tenderest sympathy: but to find she thought it without return, and without hope, penetrated him with grief. Not only his own fond view of the attractions of his daughter, but all he had observed, even from his childhood, in Edgar, had induced him to believe she was irresistibly formed to captivate him; and what had lately passed had seemed a confirmation of all he had expected. Camilla, nevertheless, exculpated him from all blame; and, while touched by her artlessness, and honouring her truth, he felt, at least, some consolation to find that Edgar, whom he loved as a son, was untainted by deceit, unaccused of any evil. He concluded that some unfortunate secret entanglement, or some mystery not yet to be developed, directed compulsatorily his conduct, and checked the dictates of his taste and inclination.

Gently, at length, approaching her, 'My dearest child,' he said, 'I will ask you nothing further; all that is absolutely essential for me to know, I have gathered. You will never, I am certain, forget the noble mother whom you are bound to revere in imitating, nor the affectionate father whom your ingenuousness renders the most indulgent of your friends. Dry up your tears then, my Camilla, and command your best strength to conceal for ever their source, and, most especially . . . from its cause.'

He then embraced, and left her.

'Yes, my dearest father,' cried she, as she shut the door, 'most perfect and most lenient of human beings! yes, I will obey your dictates; I will hide till I can conquer this weak emotion, and no one shall ever know, and Edgar least of all, that a daughter of yours has a feeling she ought to disguise!'

Elevated by the kindness of a father so adored, to deserve his good opinion now included every wish. The least severity would have chilled her confidence, the least reproof would have discouraged all effort to self-conquest; but, while his softness had soothed, his approbation had invigorated her; and her feelings received additional energy from the conscious generosity with which she had represented Edgar as blameless. Blameless, however, in her own breast, she could not deem him: his looks, his voice, his manner, . . . words that occasionally dropt from him, and meanings yet more expressive which his eyes or his attentions had taken in charge, all, from time to time, had told a flattering tale, which, though timidity and anxious earnestness had obscured from her perfect comprehension, her hopes and her sympathy had prevented from wholly escaping her. Yet what, internally, she could not defend she forgave; and, acquitting him of all intentional deceit, concluded that what he had felt for her, he had thought too slight and immaterial to deserve repressing on his own part, or notice on her's. To continue with him her present sisterly conduct was all she had to study, not doubting but that what as yet was effort, would in time become natural.

Strengthened thus in fortitude, she descended chearfully to supper, where Mr. Tyrold, though he saw with pain that her spirits were constrained, felt the fondest satisfaction in the virtue of her exertion.

Her night passed in the consolation of self-applause. My dear father, thought she, will see I strive to merit his lenity, and that soothing consideration with the honourable friendship of Edgar, will be sufficient for the happiness of my future life, in the single and tranquil state in which it will be spent.

Thus comforted, she again met the eye of Mr. Tyrold the next day at breakfast; in the midst of which repast Edgar entered the parlour. The tea she was drinking was then rather gulped than sipped; yet she maintained an air of unconcern, and returned his salutation with apparent composure.

Edgar, while addressing to Mr. Tyrold his inquiries concerning Sir Hugh, saw, from the window, his servant, whom he had out-galloped, thrown with violence from his horse. He rushed out of the parlour; and the first person to rise, with involuntary intent to follow him, was Camilla. But, as she reached the hall-door, she saw that the man was safe, and perceived that her father was the only person who had left the room besides herself. Ashamed, she returned, and found the female party collected at the windows.

Hoping to retrieve the error of her eagerness, she seated herself at the table, and affected to finish her breakfast.

Eugenia told her they had discovered the cause of the accident, which had been owing to a sharp stone that had penetrated into the horse's hoof, and which Edgar was now endeavouring to extract.

A general scream, just then, from the window party, and a cry from Eugenia of 'O Edgar!' carried her again to the hall-door with the swiftness of lightning, calling out, 'Where? . . . What? . . . Good Heaven!' . . . .

Molly Mill, accidentally there before her, said, as she approached, that the horse had kicked Mr. Mandlebert upon the shoulder.

Every thing but tenderness and terror was now forgotten by Camilla; she darted forward with unrestrained velocity, and would have given, in a moment, the most transporting amazement to Edgar, and to herself the deepest shame, but that Mr. Tyrold, who alone had his face that way, stopt, and led her back to the house, saying, 'There is no mischief; a bee stung the poor animal at the instant the stone was extracted, and the surprise and pain made it kick; but, fortunately, without any bad effect. I wish to know how your uncle is; I should be glad you would go and sit with him till I can come.'

With these words he left her; and, though abashed and overset, she found no sensation so powerful as joy for the safety of Edgar.

Still, however, too little at ease for conversing with her uncle, she went straight to her own chamber, and flew involuntarily to a window, whence the first object that met her eyes was her father, who was anxiously looking up. She retreated, utterly confounded, and threw herself upon a chair at the other end of the room.

Shame now was her only sensation. The indiscretion of her first surprise, she knew, he must forgive, though she blushed at its recollection; but a solicitude so pertinacious, an indulgence so repeated of feelings he had enjoined her to combat . . . how could she hope for his pardon? or how obtain her own, to have forfeited an approbation so precious?

She could not go to her uncle; she would have remained where she was still summoned to dinner, if the house-maid, after finishing all her other work, had not a third time returned to inquire if she might clean her room.

She then determined to repair to the library, where she was certain only to encounter Eugenia, who would not torment, or Dr. Orkborne, who would not perceive her: but at the bottom of the stairs she was stopt by Miss Margland, who, with a malicious smile, asked if she was going to hold the bason?

'What bason?' cried she, surprised.

'The bason for the surgeon.'

'What surgeon?' repeated she, alarmed.

'Mr. Burton, who is come to bleed Mr. Mandlebert.'

She asked nothing more. She felt extremely faint, but made her way into the park, to avoid further conference.

Here, in the most painful suspense, dying for information, yet shirking whoever could give it her, she remained, till she saw the departure of the surgeon. She then went round by a back way to the apartment of Eugenia, who informed her that the contusion, though not dangerous, was violent, and that Mr. Tyrold had insisted upon immediate bleeding. The surgeon had assured them this precaution would prevent any ill consequence; but Sir Hugh, hearing from the servants what had happened, had desired that Edgar would not return home till the next day.

The joy of Camilla, that nothing was more serious, banished all that was disagreeable from her thoughts, till she was called back to reflections less consoling, by meeting Mr. Tyrold, as she was returning to her own room; who, with a gravity unusual, desired to speak with her, and preceded her into the chamber.

Trembling, and filled with shame, she followed, shut the door, and remained at it without daring to look up.

'My dear Camilla,' cried he with earnestness, 'let me not hope in vain for that exertion you have promised me, and to which I know you to be fully equal. Risk not, my dear girl, to others, those outward marks of sensibility which, to common or unfeeling observers, seem but the effect of an unbecoming remissness in the self-command which should dignify every female who would do herself honour. I had hoped, in this house at least, you would not have been misunderstood; but I have this moment been undeceived: Miss Margland has just expressed a species of compassion for what she presumes to be the present state of your mind, that has given me the severest pain.'

He stopt, for Camilla looked thunderstruck.

Approaching her, then, with a look of concern, and a voice of tenderness, he kindly took her hand, and added: 'I do not tell you this in displeasure, but to put you upon your guard. You will hear from Eugenia that we shall not dine alone; and from what I have dropt you will gather how little you can hope to escape scrutiny. Exert yourself to obviate all humiliating surmises, and you will amply be repaid by the balm of self-approbation.'

He then kissed her, and quitted the room.

She now remained in utter despair: the least idea of disgrace totally broke her spirit, and she sat upon the same spot on which Mr. Tyrold had left her, till the ringing of the second dinner bell.

She then gloomily resolved to plead an head-ache, and not to appear.

When a footman tapt at her door, to acquaint her every body was seated at the table, she sent down this excuse: forming to herself the further determination, that the same should suffice for the evening, and for the next morning, that she might avoid the sight of Edgar, in presence either of her father or Miss Margland.

Eugenia, with kind alarm, came to know what was the matter, and informed her, that Sir Hugh had been so much concerned at the accident of Edgar, that he had insisted upon seeing him, and, after heartily shaking hands, had promised to think no more of past mistakes and disappointments, as they had now been cleared up to the county, and desired him to take up his abode at Cleves for a week.

Camilla heard this with mixt pleasure and pain. She rejoiced that Edgar should be upon his former terms with her beloved uncle; but how preserve the caution demanded from her for so long a period, in the constant sight of her now watchful father, and the malicious Miss Margland?

She had added to her own difficulties by this present absconding, and, with severe self-blame, resolved to descend to tea. But, while settling how to act, after her sister had left her, she was struck with hearing the name of Mandlebert pronounced by Mary, the house-maid, who was talking with Molly Mill upon the landing place. Why it had been spoken she knew not; but Molly answered: 'Dearee me, never mind; I'll help you to do his room, if Nanny don't come in time. My little mistress would rather do it herself, than he should want for anything.'

'Why, it's natural enough,' said Mary, 'for young ladies to like young gentlemen; and there's none other comes a nigh 'em, which I often thinks dull enough for our young misses. And, to be certain, Mr. Mandlebert would be as pretty a match for one of 'em as a body could desire.'

'And his man,' said Molly, 'is as pretty a gentleman sort of person, to my mind, as his master. I'm sure I'm as glad as my young lady when they comes to the house.'

'O, as to Miss Eugeny,' said Mary, 'I believe, in my conscience, she likes our crack-headed old Doctor as well as e'er a young gentleman in Christendom; for there she'll sit with him, hour by hour, poring over such a heap of stuff as never was seed, reading, first one, then t'other, God knows what; for I believe never nobody heard the like of it before; and all the time never give the old Doctor a cross word.—'

'She never given nobody a cross word,' interrupted Molly; 'if I was Mr. Mandlebert, I'd sooner have her than any of 'em, for all she's such a nidging[1] little thing.'

'For certain,' said Mary, 'she's very good, and a deal of good she does, to all as asks her; but Miss Camilla for my money. She's all alive and merry, and makes poor master young again to look at her. I wish Mr. Mandlebert would have her, for I have overheard Miss Margland telling Miss Lynmere she was desperate fond of him, and did all she could to get him.'

Camilla felt flushed with the deepest resentment, and could scarcely command herself to forbear charging Miss Margland with this persecuting cruelty.

Nanny, the under house-maid, now joining them, said she had been detained to finish altering a curtain for Miss Margland. 'And the cross old Frump,' she added, 'is in a worse spite than ever, and she kept abusing that sweet Mr. Mandlebert to Miss Lynmere all the while, till she went down to dinner, and she said she was sure it was all Miss Camilla's doings his staying here again, for she could come over master for any thing: and she said she supposed it was to have another catch at the young 'Squire's heart, but she hoped he would not be such a fool.'

'I'm sure I wish he would,' cried Molly Mill, 'if it was only to spite her, she's such a nasty old viper. And Miss Camilla's always so good-natured, and so affable, she'd make him a very agreeable wife, I dare say.'

'And she's mortal fond of him, that's true,' said Mary, 'for when they was both here, I always see her a running to the window, to see who was a coming into the park, when he was rode out; and when he was in the house, she never so much as went to peep, if there come six horses, one after t'other. And she was always a saying, "Mary, who's in the parlour? Mary, who's below?" while he was here; but before he come, duce a bite[1] did she ask about nobody.'

'I like when I meets her,' said Molly Mill, 'to tell her Mr. Mandlebert's here, Miss; or Mr. Mandlebert's there, Miss;—Dearee me, one may almost see one self in her eyes, it makes them shine so.'

Camilla could endure no more; she arose, and walked about the room; and the maids, who had concluded her at dinner, hearing her step, hurried away, to finish their gossiping in the room of Mandlebert.

Camilly now felt wholly sunk; the persecutions of Miss Margland seemed nothing to this blow: they were cruel, she could therefore repine at them; they were unprovoked, she could therefore repel them: but to find her secret feelings, thus generally spread, and familiarity commented upon, from her own unguarded conduct, exhausted, at once, patience, fortitude, and hope, and left her no wish but to quit Cleves while Edgar should remain there.

Certain, however, that her father would not permit her to return to Etherington alone, a visit to Mrs. Arlbery was the sole refuge she could suggest; and she determined to solicit his permission to accept immediately the invitation of that lady.

CHAPTER IV

A Dodging

CAMILLA waited in the apartment of Mr. Tyrold till he came up stairs, and then begged his leave to spend a few days at the Grove; hinting, when he hesitated, though with a confusion that was hardly short of torture, at what had passed amongst the servants.

He heard her with the tenderest pity, and the kindest praise of her sincerity; and, deeply as he was shocked to find her thus generally betrayed, he was too compassionate to point out, at so suffering a moment, the indiscretions from which such observations must have originated. Yet he saw consequences the most unpleasant in this rumour of her attachment; and though he still privately hoped that the behaviour of Mandlebert was the effect of some transient embarrassment, he wished her removed from all intercourse with him that was not sought by himself, while the incertitude of his intentions militated against her struggles for indifference. The result, therefore, of a short deliberation was to accede to her request.

Camilla then wrote her proposition to Mrs. Arlbery, which Mr. Tyrold sent immediately by a stable-boy of the baronet's.

The answer was most obliging; Mrs. Arlbery said she would herself fetch her the next morning, and keep her till one of them should be tired.

The relief which this, at first, brought to Camilla, in the week's exertions it would spare, was soon succeeded by the most acute uneasiness for the critical situation of Eugenia, and the undoubted disapprobation of Edgar. To quit her sister at a period when she might serve her; . . . to forsake Cleves at the moment Edgar was restored to it, seemed selfish even to herself, and to him must appear unpardonable. 'Alas!' she cried, 'how for ever I repent my

hasty actions! Why have I not better struggled against my unfortunate feelings?'

She now almost hated her whole scheme, regretted its success,
wished herself suffering every uneasiness Miss Margland could
inflict, and all the shame of being watched and pitied by every
servant in the house, in preference to deserting Eugenia, and
making Mandlebert deem her unworthy. But self-upbraiding was
all that followed her contrition: Mrs. Arlbery was to fetch her by
appointment; and it was now too late to trifle with the conceding
goodness of her father.

She did not dare excuse herself from appearing at breakfast the
next morning, lest Mr. Tyrold should think her utterly incorrigible to his exhortations.

Edgar earnestly inquired after her health as she entered the
room; she slightly answered she was better; and began eating,
with an apparent eagerness of appetite: while he, who had
expected some kind words upon his own accident, surprised and
disappointed, could swallow nothing.

Mr. Tyrold, seeing and pitying what passed in her mind, gave
her a commission, that enabled her, soon, to leave the room
without affectation; and, happy to escape, she determined to go
down stairs no more till Mrs. Arlbery arrived. She wished to have
conversed first upon the affairs of Eugenia with Edgar: but to
name to him whither she was herself going, when she could not
possibly name why; to give to him a surprise that must recoil upon
herself in disapprobation, was more than she could endure. She
had invested him with full powers to counsel and to censure her;
he would naturally use them to dissuade her from a visit so ill-
timed; and what could she urge in opposition to his arguments
what would not seem trifling or wilful?

The present moment was all that occupied, the present evil all
that ever alarmed the breast of Camilla: to avoid him, therefore,
now, was the whole of her desire, unmolested with one anxiety
how she might better meet him hereafter.

She watched at her window till she saw the groom of Mrs.
Arlbery gallop into the Park. She hastened then to take leave of
Sir Hugh, whom Mr. Tyrold had prepared for her departure; but,
at the door of his apartment, she encountered Edgar.

'You are going out?' cried he, perceiving an alteration in her
dress.

'I am ... just going to ... to speak to my uncle,' cried she, stammering and entering the room at the same moment.

Sir Hugh kindly wished her much amusement, and hoped she would make him long amends when he was better. She took leave; but again, on the landing-place, met Edgar, who, anxious and perlexed, watched to speak to her before she descended the stairs. Eagerly advancing, 'Do you walk?' he cried; 'may I ask? or ... am I indiscreet?'

She answered she had something to say to Eugenia, but should be back in an instant. She then flew to the chamber of her sister, and conjured[1] her to consult Edgar in whatever should occur during her absence. Eugenia solemnly consented.

Jacob presently tapped at the door, to announce that Mrs. Arlbery was waiting below in her carriage.

How to pass or escape Edgar became now her greatest difficulty; she could suggest nothing to palliate to him the step she was taking, yet could still less bear to leave him to wild conjecture and certain blame: and she was standing irresolute and thoughtful, when Mr. Tyrold came to summon her.

After mildly representing the indecorum of detaining any one she was to receive by appointment, he took her apart, and putting a packet into her hand, 'I would not,' he said, 'agitate your spirits this morning, by entering upon any topic that might disturb you: I have therefore put upon paper what I most desire you to consider. You will find it a little sermon upon the difficulties and the conduct of the female heart. Read it alone, and with attention. And now, my dearest girl, go quietly into the parlour, and let one brief and cheerful good-morrow serve for every body alike.'

He then returned to his brother.

She made Eugenia accompany her down stairs, to avoid any solitary attack from Edgar; he suffered them to pass; but followed to the parlour, where she hastily bid adieu to Miss Margland and Indiana; but was stopt from running off by the former, who said, 'I wish I had known you intended going out, for I designed asking Sir Hugh for the chariot for myself this morning, to make a very particular visit.'

Camilla, in a hesitating voice, said she should not use her uncle's chariot.

'You walk then?'

'No, . . . ma'am . . . but—there is—there is a carriage—I believe, now at the door.'

'O dear, whose?' cried Indiana; 'do, pray, tell me where you are going?' while Edgar, still more curious than either, held out his hand to conduct her, that he might obtain better information.

'I am very glad your head-ache is so well,' said Miss Margland; 'but, pray—is Mr. Mandlebert to be your chaperon?'

They both blushed, though both affected not to hear her: but, before they could quit the room, Indiana, who had run to a bow-window, exclaimed, 'Dear! if there is not Mrs. Arlbery in a beautiful high phaeton!'[1]

Edgar, astonished, was now as involuntarily drawing back, as Camilla, involuntarily, was hurrying on: but Miss Margland, insisting upon an answer, desired to know if she should return to dinner?

She stammered out, No. Miss Margland pursued her to ask at what time the chariot was to fetch her; and forced from her a confession that she should be away for some days.

She was now permitted to proceed. Edgar, impressed with the deepest displeasure, leading her in silence across the hall: but, stopping an instant at the door, 'This excursion,' he gravely said, 'will rescue you from no little intended importunity: I had purposed tormenting you, from time to time, for your opinion and directions with respect to Miss Eugenia.'

And then, bowing coldly to Mrs. Arlbery, who eagerly called out to welcome her, he placed her in the phaeton, which instantly drove off.

He looked after them for some time, almost incredulous of her departure: but, as his amazement subsided into certainty, the most indignant disappointment succeeded. That she could leave Cleves at the very moment he was reinstated in its society, seemed conviction to him of her indifference; and that she could leave it in the present state of the affairs of Eugenia, made him conclude her so great a slave to the love of pleasure, that every duty and all propriety were to be sacrificed to its pursuit. 'I will think of her,' cried he, 'no more! She concealed from me her plan, lest I should torment her with admonitions: the glaring homage of the Major is better adapted to her taste,—She flies from my sincerity to receive his adulation,—I have been deceived in her disposition,—I will think of her no more!'

CHAPTER V

A Sermon[1]

THE kind reception of Mrs. Arlbery, and all the animation of her discourse, were thrown away upon Camilla. An absent smile, and a few faint acknowledgments of her goodness were all she could return: Eugenia abandoned when she might have been served, Edgar contemning when he might have been approving . . . these were the images of her mind, which resisted entrance to all other.

Tired of fruitless attempts to amuse her, Mrs. Arlbery, upon their arrival at the Grove, conducted her to an apartment prepared for her, and made use of no persuasion that she would leave it before dinner.

Camilla then, too unhappy to fear any injunction, and resigned to whatever she might receive, read the discourse of Mr. Tyrold.

For Miss Camilla Tyrold.

IT is not my intention to enumerate, my dear Camilla, the many blessings of your situation; your heart is just and affectionate, and will not forget them: I mean but to place before you your immediate duties, satisfied that the review will ensure their performance.

Unused to, because undeserving control, your days, to this period, have been as gay as your spirits. It is now first that your tranquillity is ruffled; it is now, therefore, that your fortitude has its first debt to pay for its hitherto happy exemption.

Those who weigh the calamities of life only by the positive, the substantial, or the irremediable mischiefs which they produce, regard the first sorrows of early youth as too trifling for compassion. They do not enough consider that it is the suffering, not its abstract cause, which demands human commiseration. The man who loses his whole fortune, yet possesses firmness, philosophy, a disdain of ambition, and an accommodation to circumstances, is less an object of contemplative pity, than the person who, without one real deprivation, one actual evil, is first, or is suddenly forced to recognise the fallacy of a cherished and darling hope.

That its foundation has always been shallow is no mitigation of disappointment to him who had only viewed it in its superstructure. Nor is its downfall less terrible to its visionary elevator, because others had seen it from the beginning as a folly or a chimæra; its dissolution should be estimated, not by its romance in the unimpassioned examination of a rational looker on, but by its believed promise of felicity to its credulous projector.

Is my Camilla in this predicament? had she wove her own destiny in the speculation of her wishes? Alas! to blame her, I must first forget, that delusion, while in force, has all the semblance of reality, and takes the same hold upon the faculties as truth. Nor is it till the spell is broken, till the perversion of reason and error of judgment become wilful, that Scorn ought to point 'its finger' or Censure its severity.

But of this I have no fear. The love of right is implanted indelibly in your nature, and your own peace is as dependant as mine and as your mother's upon its constant culture.

Your conduct hitherto has been committed to yourself. Satisfied with establishing your principles upon the adamantine pillars of religion and conscience, we have not feared leaving you the entire possession of general liberty. Nor do I mean to withdraw it, though the present state of your affairs, and what for some time past I have painfully observed of your precipitance, oblige me to add partial counsel to standing precept, and exhortation to advice. I shall give them, however, with diffidence, fairly acknowledging and blending my own perplexities with yours.

The temporal destiny of woman is enwrapt in still more impenetrable obscurity than that of man. She begins her career by being involved in all the worldly accidents of a parent; she continues it by being associated in all that may environ a husband: and the difficulties arising from this doubly appendant state, are augmented by the next to impossibility, that the first dependance should pave the way for the ultimate. What parent yet has been gifted with the foresight to say, 'I will educate my daugher for the station to which she shall belong?' Let us even suppose that station to be fixed by himself, rarely as the chances of life authorise such a presumption; his daughter all duty, and the partner of his own selection solicitous of the alliance: is he at all more secure he has provided even for her external welfare? What, in this sublunary existence, is the state from which she shall neither rise nor fall? Who shall say that in a few years, a few months, perhaps less, the situation in which the prosperity of his own views has placed her, may not change for one more humble than he has fitted her for enduring, or more exalted than he has accomplished her for sustaining? The conscience, indeed, of the father is not responsible for events, but the infelicity of the daughter is not less a subject of pity.

Again, if none of these outward and obvious vicissitudes occur, the proper education of a female, either for use or for happiness, is still to seek, still a problem beyond human solution; since its refinement, or its negligence, can only prove to her a good or an evil, according to the humour of the husband into whose hands she may fall. If fashioned to shine in the great world, he may deem the metropolis all turbulence; if endowed with every resource for retirement, he may think the country distasteful. And though her talents, her acquirements, may in either of these cases be set aside, with an only silent regret of wasted youth and application; the turn of mind which they have induced, the appreciation which they have taught of time, of pleasure, or of utility, will have nurtured inclinations and opinions not so ductile to new sentiments and employments, and either submission becomes a hardship, or resistance generates dissention.

If such are the parental embarrassments, against which neither wisdom nor experience can guard, who should view the filial without sympathy and tenderness?

You have been brought up, my dear child, without any specific expectation. Your mother and myself, mutually deliberating upon the uncertainty of the female fate, determined to educate our girls with as much simplicity as is compatible with instruction, as much docility for various life as may accord with invariable principles, and as much accommodation with the world at large, as may combine with a just distinction of selected society. We hoped, thus, should your lots be elevated, to secure you from either exulting arrogance, or bashful insignificance; or should they, as is more probable, be lowly, to instil into your understandings and characters such a portion of intellectual vigour as should make you enter into an humbler scene without debasement, helplessness, or repining.

It is now, Camilla, we must demand your exertions in return. Let not these cares, to fit you for the world as you may find it, be utterly annihilated from doing you good, by the uncombated sway of an unavailing, however well-placed attachment.

We will not here canvass the equity of that freedom by which women as well as men should be allowed to dispose of their own affections. There cannot, in nature, in theory, nor even in common sense, be a doubt of their equal right: but disquisitions on this point will remain rather curious than important, till the speculatist can superinduce to the abstract truth of the position some proof of its practicability.

Meanwhile, it is enough for every modest and reasonable young woman to consider, that where there are two parties, choice can belong only to one of them: and then let her call upon all her feelings of delicacy, all her notions of propriety, to decide: Since Man must choose Woman, or Woman Man, which should come forward to make the choice? Which should retire to be chosen?

A prepossession directed towards a virtuous and deserving object wears, in its first approach, the appearance of a mere tribute of justice to merit. It seems, therefore, too natural, perhaps too generous, to be considered either as a folly or a crime. It is only its encouragement where it is not reciprocal, that can make it incur the first epithet, or where it ought not to be reciprocal that can brand it with the second. With respect to this last, I know of nothing to apprehend:—with regard to the first—I grieve to wound my dearest Camilla, yet where there has been no subject for complaint, there can have been none for expectation.

Struggle then against yourself as you would struggle against an enemy. Refuse to listen to a wish, to dwell even upon a possibility, that opens to your present idea of happiness. All that in future may be realised probably hangs upon this conflict. I mean not to propose to you in the course of a few days to reinstate yourself in the perfect security of a disengaged mind. I know too much of the human heart to be ignorant that the acceleration, or delay, must depend upon circumstance: I can only require from you what depends upon yourself, a steady and courageous warfare against the two dangerous underminers of your peace and of your fame, imprudence and impatience. You have champions with which to encounter them that cannot fail of success, . . . good sense and delicacy.

Good sense will shew you the power of self-conquest, and point out its means. It will instruct you to curb those unguarded movements which lay you open to the strictures of others. It will talk to you of those boundaries which custom forbids your sex to pass, and the hazard of any individual attempt to transgress them.

It will tell you, that where allowed only a negative choice, it is your own best interest to combat against a positive wish. It will bid you, by constant occupation, vary those thoughts that now take but one direction, and multiply those interests which now recognise but one object: and it will soon convince you, that it is not strength of mind which you want, but reflection, to obtain a strict and unremitting control over your passions.

This last word will pain, but let it not shock you. You have no passions, my innocent girl, at which you need blush, though enough at which I must tremble!—For in what consists your constraint, your forbearance? your wish is your guide, your impulse is your action. Alas! never yet was mortal created so perfect, that every wish was virtuous, or every impulse wise!

Does a secret murmur here demand: if a discerning predilection is no crime, why, internally at least, may it not be cherished? whom can it injure or offend, that, in the hidden recesses of my own breast, I nourish superior preference of superior worth?

This is the question with which every young woman beguiles her fancy; this is the common but seductive opiate, with which inclination lulls reason.

The answer may be safely comprised in a brief appeal to her own breast.

I do not desire her to be insensible to merit; I do not even demand she should confine her social affections to her own sex, since the most innocent esteem is equally compatible, though not equally general with ours: I require of her simply, that, in her secret hours, when pride has no dominion, and disguise would answer no purpose, she will ask herself this question, 'Could I calmly hear that this elect of my heart was united to another? Were I to be informed that the indissoluble knot was tied, which annihilates all my own future possibilities, would the news occasion me no affliction?' This, and this alone, is the test by which she may judge the danger, or the harmlessness of her attachment.

I have now endeavoured to point out the obligations which you may owe to good sense. Your obligations to delicacy will be but their consequence.

Delicacy is an attribute so peculiarly feminine, that were your reflections less agitated by your feelings, you could delineate more distinctly than myself its appropriate laws, its minute exactions, its sensitive refinements. Here, therefore, I seek but to bring back to your memory what livelier sensations have inadvertently driven from it.

You may imagine, in the innocency of your heart, that what you would rather perish than utter can never, since untold, be suspected: and, at present, I am equally sanguine in believing no surmise to have been conceived where most it would shock you: yet credit me when I assure you, that you can make no greater mistake, than to suppose that you have any security beyond what sedulously you must earn by the most indefatigable vigilance. There are so many ways of communication independent of speech, that silence is but one point in the ordinances of discretion. You have nothing, in so modest a character, to apprehend from vanity or presumption; you may easily, therefore, continue the guardian of your own dignity: but you must keep in mind, that our perceptions want but little quickening to discern what may flatter them; and it is mutual to either sex to be to no gratification so alive, as to that of a conscious ascendance over the other.

Nevertheless, the female who, upon the softening blandishment of an undisguised prepossession, builds her expectation of its reciprocity, is, in common, most cruelly deceived. It is not that she has failed to awaken tenderness; but it has been tenderness without respect: nor yet that the person thus elated has been insensible to flattery; but it has been a flattery to raise himself, not its exciter in his esteem. The partiality which we feel inspires diffidence: that which we create has a contrary effect. A certainty of success in many destroys, in all weakens, its charm: the bashful excepted, to whom it gives courage; and the indolent, to whom it saves trouble.

Carefully, then, beyond all other care, shut up every avenue by which a secret which should die untold can further escape you. Avoid every species of particularity;[1] neither shun nor seek any intercourse apparently; and in such meetings as general prudence may render necessary, or as accident may make inevitable, endeavour to behave with the same open esteem as in your days of unconsciousness. The least unusual attention would not be more suspicious to the world, than the least undue reserve to the subject of our discussion. Coldness or distance could only be imputed to resentment; and resentment, since you have received no offence, how, should it be investigated, could you vindicate? or how, should it be passed in silence, secure from being attributed to pique and disappointment?

There is also another motive, important to us all, which calls for the most rigid circumspection. The person in question is not merely amiable; he is also rich: mankind at large, therefore, would not give merely to a sense of excellence any obvious predilection. This hint will, I know, powerfully operate upon your disinterested spirit.

Never from personal experience may you gather, how far from soothing, how wide from honourable, is the species of compassion ordinarily diffused by the discovery of an unreturned female regard. That it should be felt unsought may be considered as a mark of discerning sensibility; but that it should be betrayed uncalled for, is commonly, however ungenerously, imagined rather to indicate ungoverned passions, than refined selection. This is often both cruel and unjust; yet, let me ask—Is the world a proper confident for such a secret? Can the woman who has permitted it to go abroad, reasonably demand that consideration and respect from the community, in which she has been wanting to herself? To me it would be unnecessary to observe, that her indiscretion may have been the effect of an inadvertence which owes its origin to artlessness, not to forwardness: She is judged by those, who, hardened in the ways of men, accustom themselves to trace in evil every motive to action; or by those, who, preferring ridicule to humanity, seek rather to amuse themselves wittily with her susceptibility, than to feel for its innocence and simplicity.

In a state of utter constraint, to appear natural is, however, an effort too difficult to be long sustained; and neither precept, example, nor disposition, have enured my poor child to the performance of any studied part. Discriminate, nevertheless, between hypocrisy and discretion. The first is a vice; the second a conciliation to virtue. It is the bond that keeps society from disunion; the veil that shades our weakness from exposure, giving time for that interior correction, which the publication of our infirmities would else, with respect to mankind, make of no avail.

It were better no doubt, worthier, nobler, to meet the scrutiny of our fellow-creatures by consent, as we encounter, per force, the all-viewing eye of our Creator: but since for this we are not sufficiently without blemish, we must allow to our unstable virtues

all the encouragement that can prop them. The event of discovered faults is more frequently callousness than amendment;
and propriety of example is as much a duty to our fellow-creatures,
as purity of intention is a debt to ourselves.

To delicacy, in fine, your present exertions will owe their future
recompence, be your ultimate lot in life what it may. Should you,
in the course of time, belong to another, you will be shielded from
the regret that a former attachment had been published; or should
you continue mistress of yourself, from a blush that the world is
acquainted it was not by your choice.

I shall now conclude this little discourse by calling upon you to
annex to whatever I have offered you of precept, the constant
remembrance of your mother for example.

In our joint names, therefore, I adjure you, my dearest Camilla,
not to embitter the present innocence of your suffering by
imprudence that may attach to it censure, nor by indulgence that
may make it fasten upon your vitals! Imprudence cannot but end
in the demolition of that dignified equanimity, and modest
propriety, which we wish to be uniformly remarked as the
attributes of your character: and indulgence, by fixing, may
envenom a dart that as yet may be gently withdrawn, from a
wound which kindness may heal, and time may close; but which,
if neglected, may wear away, in corroding disturbance, all your
life's comfort to yourself, and all its social purposes to your friends
and to the world.

AUGUSTUS TYROLD.

CHAPTER VI

A Chat

THE calm sadness with which Camilla had opened her letter was
soon broken in upon by the interest of its contents, the view it
displayed of her duties, her shame at her recent failures, and her
fears for their future execution; and yet more than all, by the full
decision in which it seemed written, that the unhappy partiality
she had exposed, had been always, and would for ever remain
unreturned.

She started at the intimation how near she stood to detection even from Edgar himself, and pride, reason, modesty, all arose to strengthen her with resolution, to guard every future conflict from his observation.

The article concerning fortune touched her to the quick. Nothing appeared to her so degrading as the most distant idea that such a circumstance could have any force with her. But the justice done to Edgar she gloried in, as an apology for her feelings, and exculpatory of her weakness. Her tears flowed fast at every expression of kindness to herself, her burning blushes dried them up as they were falling, at every hint of her feebleness, and the hopelessness of its cause; but wholly subdued by the last paragraph, which with reverence she pressed to her lips, she offered up the most solemn vows of a strict and entire observance of every injunction which the letter contained.

She was thus employed, unnoticing the passage of time, when Mrs. Arlbery tapped at her door, and asked if she wished to dine in her own room.

Surprised at the question, and ashamed to be thus seen, she was beginning a thousand apologies for not being yet dressed: but Mrs. Arlbery, interrupting her, said, 'I never listen to excuses. 'Tis the only battery that overpowers me. If, by any mischance, and in an evil hour, some country cousin, not knowing my ways, or some antediluvian prig, not minding them, happen to fall upon me with formal speeches, where I can make no escape, a fit of yawning takes me immediately, and I am demolished for the rest of the day.'

Camilla, attempting to smile, promised to play the country cousin no more. Mrs. Arlbery then observed she had been weeping; and taking her hand, with an examining look, 'My lovely young friend,' she cried, 'this will never do!'

'What, ma'am? . . . how? . . . what? . . .'

'Nay, nay, don't be frightened. Come down to dinner, and we'll talk over the hows? and the whats? afterwards. Never mind your dress; we go no where this evening; and I make a point not to suffer any body to change their attire in my house, merely because the afternoon is taking place of the morning. It seems to me a miserable compliment to the mistress of a mansion, to see her guests only equip themselves for the table. For my part, I deem the garb that is good enough for me, good enough for my geese and turkies . . . apple and oyster-sauce included.'

Camilla then followed her down stairs, where she found no company but Sir Sedley Clarendel.

'Come, my dear Miss Tyrold,' said Mrs. Arlbery, 'you and I may now consider ourselves as *tête-à-tête;* Sir Sedley won't be much in our way. He hears and sees nothing but himself.'

'Ecstatically flattering that!' cried Sir Sedley; 'dulcet to every nerve!'

'O, I know you listen just now, because you are yourself my theme. But the moment I take another, you will forget we are either of us in the room.'

'Inhuman to the quick!' cried he; 'barbarous to a point!'

'This is a creature so strange, Miss Tyrold,' said Mrs. Arlbery, 'that I must positively initiate you a little into his character;—or, rather, into its own caricature; for as to character, he has had none intelligible these three years.—See but how he smiles at the very prospect of being portrayed, in defiance of all his efforts to look unconcerned! yet he knows I shall shew him no mercy. But, like all other egotists, the only thing to really disconcert him, would be to take no notice of him. Make him but the first subject of discourse, and praise or abuse are pretty much the same to him.'

'O shocking! shocking! killing past resuscitation! Abominably horrid, I protest!'

'O I have not begun yet. This is an observation to suit thousands. But do not fear; you shall have all your appropriations. Miss Tyrold, you are to be auditor and judge: and I will save you the time and the trouble which decyphering this animal, so truly a non-descript, might cost you.'

'What a tremendous exordium! distressing to a degree! I am agued with trepidation!'

'O you wretch! you know you are enchanted. But no further interruption! I send you to Coventry for the next ten minutes.

'This man, my dear Miss Tyrold, whom we are about to delineate, was meant by nature, and prepared by art, for something greatly superior to what he now appears: but, unhappily, he had neither solidity of judgment, nor humility of disposition, for bearing meekly the early advantages with which he set out in life; a fine person, fine parts, and a fine estate, all dashed into consciousness at the presuming age of one and twenty. By this aggregate of wealthy, of mental, and of personal prosperity, he has become at once self spoilt, and world spoilt. Had you known him, as I have done, before he was seized with this systematic affectation, which, I am satisfied, causes him more study than the united pedants of both universities could inflict upon him, you would have seen the most delightful creature breathing! a creature combining, in one animated composition, the very essences of spirit, of gaiety, and of intelligence. But now, with every thing within his reach, nothing seems worth his attainment. He has not sufficient energy to make use of his own powers. He has no one to command him, and he is too indolent to command himself. He has therefore turned fop from mere wantonness of time and of talents; from having nothing to do, no one to care for, and no one to please. Take from him half his wit, and by lessening his presumption, you will cure him of all his folly. Rob him of his fortune, and by forcing him into exertion, you will make him one of the first men of his day. Deface and maim his features and figure, and by letting him see that to appear and be admired is not the same thing, you will render him irresistible.'

'Have you done?' cried the baronet smiling.

'I protest,' said Mrs. Arlbery, 'I believe you are a little touched! And I don't at all want to reform you. A perfect character only lulls me to sleep.'

'Obliging in the superlative! I must then take as a consolation, that I have never given you a nap?'

'Never, Clarendel, I assure you; and yet I don't hate you! Vice is detestable; I banish all its appearances from my coteries; and I would banish its reality, too, were I sure I should then have any thing but empty chairs in my drawing-room—but foibles make all the charm of society. They are the only support of convivial raillery, and domestic wit. If formerly, therefore, you more excited my admiration, it is now, believe me, you contribute most to my entertainment.'

'Condoling to a phenomenon! I have really, then, the vastly prodigious honour to be exalted in your fair graces to the level of a mountebank? a quack doctor? his merry Andrew? or any other such respectable buffoon?'

'Piqued! piqued! I declare! this exceeds my highest ambition. But I must not weaken the impression by dwelling upon it.'

She then asked Camilla if she had any message for Cleves, as one of her servants was going close to the park gate.

Camilla, glad to withdraw, said she would write a few words to her father, and retired for that purpose.

*   *   *   *

'What in the world, my dear Clarendel,' said Mrs. Arlbery, 'can I do with this poor thing? She has lost all her sprightliness, and vapours[1] me but to look at her. She has all the symptoms upon her of being in the full meridian of that common girlish disease, an hopeless passion.'

'Poor little tender dove!' cried the baronet. ''Twould be odious to cure her. Unfeeling to excess. What in nature can be half so mellifluously interesting? I shall now look at her with most prodigious softness. Ought one not to sigh as she approaches?'

'The matter to be sure is silly enough,' answered Mrs. Arlbery; 'but, this nonsense apart, she is a charming girl. Besides, I perceive I am a violent favourite with her; and flattery, my dear Clarendel, will work its way, even with me! I really owe her a good turn: Else I should no longer endure her; for the tender passion has terribly flattened her. If we can't restore her spirits, she will be a mere dead weight to me.'

'O a very crush! a cannon ball would be a butterfly in the comparison! But who is the irresistible? What form has the little blind traitor assumed?'

'O, assure yourself, that of the first young man who has come in her sight. Every damsel, as she enters the world, has some picture ready painted upon her imagination, of an object worthy to enslave her: and before any experience forms her judgment, or any comparison her taste, she is the dupe of the first youth who presents himself to her, in the firm persuasion of her ductile fancy, that he is just the model it had previously created.'

She then added, she had little doubt but young Mandlebert was the hero, from their private conferences after the raffle, and from her blushes when forced to name him.

'Nay, nay, this is not the first incongruity!' said the young baronet, 'not romantic to outrage. Beech Park has nothing very horrific in it. Nothing invincibly beyond the standard of a young lady's philosophy.'

'Depend upon it, that's the very idea its master has conceived of the matter himself. You wealthy Cavaliers rarely want flappers[2]

to remind you of your advantages. That Mandlebert, you must
know, is my aversion. He has just that air and reputation of
faultlessness that gives me the spleen. I hope, for her sake, he won't
think of her; he will lead her a terrible life. A man who piques
himself upon his perfections, finds no mode so convenient and
ready for displaying them, as proving all about him to be constantly in the wrong. However, a character of that stamp rarely
marries; especially if he is rich, and has no obstacles in his way.
What can I do, then, for this poor thing? The very nature of her
malady is to make her entertain false hopes. I am quite bent upon
curing them. The only difficulty, according to custom, is how. I
wish you would take her in hand yourself.'

'I? . . . preposterous in the extreme! what particle of chance
should I have against Mandlebert?'

'O you vain wretch! to be sure you don't know, that though he
is rich, you are richer? and, doubtless, you never took notice,
that though he is handsome, you are handsomer? As to manners,
there is little to choose between you, for he is as much too correct,
as you are too fantastic. In conversation, too, you are nearly upon
a par, for he is as regularly too right, as you are ridiculously too
wrong,—but O the charm of dear amusing wrong, over dull
commanding right! you have but to address yourself to her with a
little flattering distinction, and Mandlebert ever after will
appear to her a pedant.'

'What a wicked sort of sprite is a female wit!' cried Sir Sedley,
'breathing only in mischief! a very will-o'-the-wisp, personified
and petticoated, shining but to lead astray. Dangerous past all
fathom! Have the goodness, however, my fair Jack-o'-lanthorn,
to intimate what you mean I should do with this languishing
dulcinea, should I deliver her from thraldom? You don't advise me,
I presume, to take unto myself a wife? I protest I am shivered to the
utmost point north at the bare suggestion! frozen to an icicle!'

'No, no; I know you far too confirmed an egotist for any thing
but an old bachelor. Nor is there the least necessity to yoke the
poor child to the conjugal plough so early. The only sacrifice I
demand from you is a little attention; the only good I aim at for
her, is to open her eyes, which have now a film before them, and
to let her see that Mandlebert has no other pre-eminence, than
that of having been the first young man with whom she became
acquainted. Never imagine I want her to fall in love with you.

Heaven help the poor victim to such a complication of caprice!'

'Nay, now I am full south again! burning with shame and choler! How you navigate my sensations from cold to heat at pleasure! Cooke[1] was a mere river water-man to you. My blood chills or boils at your command. Every sentence is a new climate. You waft me from extreme to extreme, with a rapidity absolutely dizzying. A balloon is a broad-wheeled wagon to you.'[2]

'Come, come, jargon apart,[3] will you make yourself of any use? The cure of a romantic first flame is a better surety to subsequent discretion, than all the exhortations of all the fathers, and mothers, and guardians, and maiden aunts in the universe. Save her now, and you serve her for life;—besides giving me a prodigious pleasure in robbing that frigid Mandlebert of such a conquest.'

'Unhappy young swain! I pity him to immensity. How has he fallen thus under the rigour of your wrath? Do you banish him your favour, like another Aristides, to relieve your ear from hearing him called the Just?'[4]

'Was ever allusion so impertinent? or, what is worse, for aught I can determine, so true? for, certainly, he has given me no offence; yet I feel I should be enchanted to humble him. Don't be concerned for him, however; you may assure yourself he hates me. There is a certain spring in our propensities to one another, that involuntarily opens and shuts in almost exact harmony, whether of approbation or antipathy. Except, indeed, in the one article of love, which, distinguishing nothing, is ready to grasp at any thing.'

'But why have you not recourse to the gallant cockade?'

'The Major? O, I have observed, already, she receives his devoirs without emotion; which, for a girl who has seen nothing of the world, is respectable enough, his red coat considered. Whether the man has any meaning himself, or whether he knows there is such a thing, I cannot tell: but as I do not wish to see her surrounded with brats, while a mere brat herself, it is not worth inquiry. You are the thing, Clarendel, the very thing! You are just agreeable enough to annul her puerile fascination, yet not interesting enough to involve her in any new danger.'

'Flattering past imitability! divine Arlberiana!'

'Girls, in general,' continued she, 'are insupportable nuisances to women. If you do not set them to prate about their admirers, or their admired, they die of weariness;—if you do, the weariness reverberates upon yourself.'

Camilla here returned. She had written a few lines to Eugenia, to enforce her reliance upon Edgar, with an earnest request to be sent for immediately, if any new difficulty occurred. And she had addressed a few warmly grateful words to her father, engaging to follow his every injunction with her best ability.

Sir Sedley now rung for his carriage; and Camilla, for the rest of the evening, exerted herself to receive more cheerfully the kind civilities of her lively hostess.

CHAPTER VII

A Recall

AFTER two days passed with tolerable, though not natural cheerfulness at the Grove, Camilla was surprised by the arrival of the carriage of Sir Hugh with a short note from Eugenia.

To Miss Camilla Tyrold.

AN incident has happened that overpowers me with sadness and horror. I cannot write. I send the chariot. O! come and pass an hour or two at Cleves with your distressed.

EUGENIA!

Camilla could scarcely stop to leave a message for Mrs. Arlbery, before she flew to the carriage; nor even inquire for her uncle at Cleves, before she ran to the apartment of Eugenia, and, with a thousand tender caresses, desired to know what had thus cruelly afflicted her.

'Alas!' she answered, 'my uncle has written to Clermont to come over,—and informed him with what view!'

She then related, that Indiana, the preceding day, had prevailed with Sir Hugh to let her go to the Middleton races;[1] and she found he would be quite unhappy if she refused to be also of the party. That they had been joined by Bellamy on the race ground, who only, however, spoke to Miss Margland, as Edgar, watchful and uneasy, scarce let him even see anyone else. But the horses having taken fright, while they were in a great crowd, Bellamy had

persuaded Miss Margland to alight, while the coach passed a
terrible concourse of carriages; and, in that interval, he had
contrived to whisper a claim upon her tacit promise of viewing the
chaise which was for ever to convey him away from her; and,
though her engagement to Edgar made her refuse, he had drawn
her, she knows not herself how, from her party, and, while she
was angrily remonstrating, and he seemed in the utmost despair
at her displeasure, Edgar, who had been at first eluded by being
on horseback, dismounted, forced his way to her, and almost
carried her back to the coach, leaving Bellamy, who she was sure
had no sinister design, nearly dead with grief at being unworthily
suspected. Edgar, she however added, was fixed in believing he
meant to convey her away; and Jacob, asserting he saw him
purposely frighten the horses, had told his surmises to Sir Hugh;
which he had corroborated by an account that the same gentleman
had stopt to converse with her in her last return from Etherington.
Sir Hugh, terrified, had declared he would no longer live without
Clermont upon the spot. She had felt too much for his disturbance to oppose him at the moment, but had not imagined his plan
would immediately be put into execution, till, early this morning,
he had sent for her, and produced his letter of recall, which had
taken him, he said, the whole night to compose and finish. Urged
by surprise and dissatisfaction, she was beginning a little remonstrance; but found it made him so extremely unhappy, that, in
the fear of a relapse, she desisted; and, with a shock she knew not
when she should overcome, saw the fatal letter delivered for the
post.

Camilla, with much commiseration, inquired if she had consulted with Edgar. Yes, she answered; and he had extorted her
permission to relate the whole transaction to her father, though in
a manner wide from justice to the ill-fated Bellamy; whose design
might be extraordinary, but whose character, she was convinced,
was honourable.

Camilla, whose education, though private, had not like that of
Eugenia, been secluded and studious, was far less credulous than
her sister, though equally artless. She knew, too, with regard to
this affair, the opinion of Edgar, and to know and be guided by
it was imperceptibly one. She declared herself, therefore, openly
against Bellamy, and made her motives consist in a commentary
upon his proceedings.

Eugenia warmly defended him, declaring the judgment of Camilla, and that of all her friends, to be formed in the dark; for that none of them could have doubted a moment his goodness or his honour, had they seen the distracted suffering that was marked in his countenance.

'And what,' cried Camilla, 'says my father to all this?'

'He says just what Edgar says:—he is all that is kind and good, but he has never beheld Bellamy—how, then, should he know him?'

A message came now from Sir Hugh to Camilla, that he would see her before she went, but that he was resting at present from the fatigue of writing a letter. He sent her, however, with his love, the foul copy, to amuse her till she could come to him.

To Clermont Lynmere *Esq.*

Dear Nephew,

I HAVE had a very dangerous illness, and the doctors themselves are all surprised that I recovered; but a greater doctor than them was pleased to save me, for which I thank God. But as this attack has made me think more than ever I thought before, I am willing to turn my thoughts to good account.

Now, as I have not the gift of writing, at which, thank God, I have left off repining, from the reason of its great troublesomeness in acquiring, I can't pretend to any thing of a fine letter, but shall proceed to business.

My dear Clermont, I write now to desire you would come over out of hand; which I hope you won't take unkind, foreign parts being no great pleasure to see, in comparison of old England; besides which, I have another apology to offer, which is, having a fine prize in view for you; which is the more essential, owing to some unlucky circumstances, in which I did not behave quite as well as I wish, though very unwillingly; which I mention to you as a warning. However, you have no need to be cast down, for this prize will set all right, and make you as rich as a lord, at the same time that you are as wise as a philosopher. And as learning, though I have the proper respect for it, won't serve to make the pot boil, you must needs be glad of more substantial fuel; for there's no living upon air, however you students may affect to think eating mere gluttony.

Now, this prize is no other than your cousin Eugenia Tyrold, whom I don't tell you is a beauty; but if you are the sensible lad I take you for, you won't think the worse of her for wanting such frail perfections. Besides, we should not be too nice amongst relations, for if we are, what can we expect from the wide world? So I beg you to come over with all convenient speed, for fear of her falling a prey to some sharper,[1] many such being to be found; especially at horse-races, and so forth. I remain,

> Dear nephew,
> Your affectionate uncle,
> HUGH TYROLD.

Eugenia, from motives of delicacy and of shame, declined reading the copy as she had declined reading the letter; but looked so extremely unhappy, that Camilla offered to plead with her uncle, and use her utmost influence that he would countermand the recall.

'No,' answered she, 'no! 'tis a point of duty and gratitude, and I must bear its consequences.'

She was now called down to Mr. Tyrold. Camilla accompanied her.

He told her he had gathered, from the kind zeal and inquiries of Edgar, that Bellamy had certainly laid a premeditated plan for carrying her off, if she went to the races; which, as the whole neighbourhood was there, might reasonably be expected.

Eugenia, with fervour, protested such wickedness was impossible.

'I am unwilling, my dear child,' he answered, 'to adulterate the purity of your thoughts and expectations, by inculcating suspicions; but, though nature has blessed you with an uncommon understanding, remember, in judgment you are still but fifteen, and in experience but a child. One thing, however, tell me candidly, is it from love of justice, or is it for your happiness you combat thus ardently for the integrity of this young man?'

'For my justice, Sir!' said she firmly.

'And no latent reason mingles with and enforces it?'

'None, believe me! save only what gratitude dictates.'

'If your heart, then, is your own, my dear girl, do not be uneasy at the letter to Clermont. Your uncle is the last man upon earth to put any constraint upon your inclinations; and need I add to my dearest Eugenia, I am the last father to thwart or distress them? Resume, therefore, your courage and composure; be just to your friends, and happy in yourself.'

Reason was never thrown away upon Eugenia. Her mind was a soil which received and naturalized all that was sown in it. She promised to look forward with more cheerfulness, and to dwell no longer upon this agitating transaction.

Edgar now came in. He was going to Beech Park to meet Bellamy. He was charged with a long message for him from Sir Hugh; and an order to inform him that his niece was engaged; which, however, he declined undertaking, without first consulting her.

This was almost too severe a trial of the duty and fortitude of Eugenia. She coloured, and was quitting the room in silence: but presently turning back, 'My uncle,' she cried, 'is too ill now for argument, and he is too dear to me for opposition:—Say, then, just what you think will most conduce to his tranquillity and recovery.'

Her father embraced her; Camilla shed tears; and Edgar, in earnest admiration, kissed her hand. She received their applause with sensibility, but looked down with a secret deduction from its force, as she internally uttered, 'My task is not so difficult as they believe! touched as I am with the constancy of Bellamy—It is not Melmond who loves me! it is not Melmond I reject!—'

Edgar was immediately setting off, but, stopping him—'One thing alone I beg,' she said; 'do not communicate your intelligence abruptly. Soften it by assurances of my kind wishes.—Yet, to prevent any deception, any future hope—say to him—if you think it right—that I shall regard myself, henceforward, as if already in that holy state so sacred to one only object.'

She blushed, and left them, followed by Camilla.

'If born but yesterday,' cried Mr. Tyrold, while his eyes glistened, 'she could not be more perfectly free from guile.'

'Yet that,' said Edgar, 'is but half her praise; she is perfectly free, also, from self! she is made up of disinterested qualities and liberal sensations. To the most genuine simplicity, she joins the most singular philosophy; and to knowedge and cultivation, the most uncommon, adds all the modesty as well as innocence of her extreme youth and inexperience.'

Mr. Tyrold subscribed with frankness to this just praise of his highly-valued daughter; and they then conferred upon the steps to be taken with Bellamy, whom neither of them scrupled to pronounce a mere fortune-hunter. All the inquiries of Edgar were ineffectual to learn any particulars of his situation. He said he was travelling for his amusement; but he had no recommendation to anyone; though, by being constantly well-dressed, and keeping a shewy footman, he had contrived to make acquaintance almost universally in the neighbourhood. Mr. Tyrold determined to accompany Edgar to Beech Park himself, and there, in the most peremptory terms, to assure him of the serious measures that would ensue, if he desisted not from his pursuit.

He then went to take leave of Camilla, who had been making a visit to her uncle, and was returning to the Grove.

He had seen with concern the frigid air with which Edgar had bowed to her upon his entrance, and with compassion the changed countenance with which she had received his formal salutation. His hope of the alliance now sunk; and so favourite a wish could not be relinquished without severe disappointment; yet his own was immaterial to him when he looked at Camilla, and saw in her expressive eyes the struggle of her soul to disguise her wounded feelings. He now regretted that she had not accompanied her mother abroad; and desired nothing so earnestly as any means to remove her from all intercourse with Mandlebert. He seconded, therefore, her speed to be gone, happy she would be placed where exertion would be indispensable; and gently, yet clearly, intimated his wish that she should remain at the Grove, till she could meet Edgar without raising pain in her own bosom, or exciting suspicions in his. Cruelly mortified, she silently acquiesced. He then said whatever was most kind to give her courage; but, dejected by her conscious failure, and afflicted by the change in Edgar, she returned to Mrs. Arlbery in a state of mind the most melancholy.

And here, nothing could be less exhilarating nor less seasonable than the first news she heard.

The regiment of General Kinsale was ordered into Kent, in the neighbourhood of Tunbridge: It was the season for drinking the water of that spring;[1] and Mr. Dennel was going thither with his daughter. Sir Sedley Clarendel conceived it would be serviceable also to his own health; and had suddenly proposed to Mrs. Arlbery forming a party to pass a few weeks there. With a vivacity always ready for any new project, she instantly agreed to it, and

the journey was settled to take place in three days. When Camilla
was informed of this intended excursion, the disappointment with
which it overpowered her was too potent for disguise: and Mrs.
Arlbery was so much struck with it, that, during coffee, she took
Sir Sedley apart, and said; 'I feel such concern for the dismal
alteration of that sweet girl, that I could prevail with myself, all
love-lorn as she is, to take her with me to Tunbridge, if you will
aid my hardy enterprise of driving that frozen composition of
premature wisdom from her mind. If you are not as invulnerable
as himself, you cannot refuse me this little sleight of gallantry.'[1]

Sir Sedley gave a laughing assent, declaring, at the same time,
with the strongest professed diffidence, his conscious inability.
Mrs. Arlbery, in high spirits, said she scarce knew which would
most delight her, to mortify Edgar, or restore Camilla to gaiety
and independance. Yet she would watch, she said, that matters
went no further than just to shake off a whining first love; for
the last thing upon earth she intended was to entangle her in a
second.

Camilla received the invitation with pleasure yet anxiety: for
though glad to be spared returning to Cleves in a state of disturbance so suspicious, she was bitterly agitated in reflecting upon the
dislike of Edgar to Mrs. Arlbery, the pains he had taken to
prevent her mingling with this society, and the probably final
period to his esteem and good-will, that would prove the result of
her accompanying such a party to a place of amusement.

CHAPTER VIII

A Youth of the Times

MRS. Arlbery accompanied Camilla the next day to Cleves, to ask
permission of Mr. Tyrold for the excursion. She would trust the
request to none but herself, conscious of powers of persuasion
unused to repulse.

Mr. Tyrold was distressed by the proposition: he was not
satisfied in trusting his unguarded Camilla to the dissipation of a
public place, except under the wing of her mother; though he felt
eager to remove her from Edgar, and rejoiced in any opportunity

to allow her a change of scene, that might revive her natural spirits, and unchain her heart from its unhappy subjection.

Perceiving him undetermined, Mrs. Arlbery called forth all her artillery of eloquence and grace, to forward her conquest. The licence she allowed herself in common of fantastic command, gave way to the more feminine attraction of soft pleading: her satire, which, though never malignant, was often alarming, was relinquished for a sportive gaiety that diffused general animation; and Mr. Tyrold soon, though not caught like his daughter, ceased to wonder that his daughter had been caught.

In this indecision he took Camilla apart, and bad her tell him, without fear or reserve, her own feelings, her own wishes, her own opinion upon this scheme. She held such a call too serious and too kind for disguise: she hid her face upon his shoulder and wept; he soothed and encouraged her to confidence; and, in broken accents, she then acknowledged herself unequal, as yet, to fulfilling his injunctions of appearing cheerful and easy, though sensible of their wisdom.

Mr. Tyrold, with a heavy heart, saw how much deeper was her wound, than the airiness of her nature had prepared him to expect, and could no longer hesitate in granting his consent. He saw it was her wish to go; but he saw that the pleasures of a public place had no share in exciting it. To avoid betraying her conscious mortification was her sole and innocent motive; and though he would rather have sent her to a more private spot, and have trusted her to a more retired character; he yet thought it possible, that what opportunity presented unsought, might, eventually, prove more beneficial than what his own choice would have dictated; for public amusements, to the young and unhackneyed, give entertainment without requiring exertion; and spirits lively as those of Mrs. Arlbery create nearly as much gaiety as they display.

Fixed, now, for the journey, he carried Camilla to her uncle to take leave. The prospect of not seeing her again for six weeks was gloomy to Sir Hugh; though he bore it better at this moment, when his fancy was occupied by arranging preparations for the return of Clermont, than he could have done at almost any other. He put into her hand a fifty pound Bank note for her expences, and when, with mingled modesty and dejection, she would have returned the whole, as unnecessary even to her wishes, Mr.

Tyrold, interfering, made her accept twenty pounds. Sir Hugh pressed forward the original sum in vain; his brother, though always averse to refuse his smallest desire, thought it here a duty to be firm, that the excursion, which he granted as a relief to her sadness, might not lead to pleasures ever after beyond her reach, nor to their concomitant extravagance. She could not, he knew, reside at Tunbridge with the œconomy and simplicity to which she was accustomed at Etherington; but he charged her to let no temptation make her forget the moderate income of which alone she was certain; assuring her, that where a young woman's expences exceeded her known expectations, those who were foremost to praise her elegance, would most fear to form any connection with her, and most despise or deride her in any calamity.

Camilla found no difficulty in promising the most exact observance of this instruction; her heart seemed in sackcloth and ashes, and she cared not in what manner her person should be arrayed.

Sir Hugh earnestly enjoined her not to fail to be at Cleves upon the arrival of Clermont, intimating that the nuptials would immediately take place.

She then sought Eugenia, whom she found with Dr. Orkborne, in a state of mind so perfectly calm and composed, as equally to surprise and rejoice her. She saw with pleasure that all Bellamy had inspired was the most artless compassion; for since his dismission had now positively been given, and Clermont was actually summoned, she devoted her thoughts solely to the approaching event, with the firm, though early wisdom which distinguished her character.

Indiana joined them; and, in a low voice, said to Camilla, 'Pray, cousin, do you know where Mr. Macdersey is? because I am sadly afraid he's dead.'

Camilla, surprised, desired to know why she had such an apprehension?

'Because he told me he'd shoot himself through the brains if I was cruel—and I am sure I had no great choice given me: for, between ourselves, Miss Margland gave all the answers for me, without once stopping to ask me what I should chuse. So if he has really done it, the fault is more her's than mine.'

She then said, that, just after Camilla's departure the preceding day, Mr. Macdersey arrived, and insisted upon seeing her, and speaking to Sir Hugh, as he was ordered into Kent, and could not go so far in suspence. Sir Hugh was not well enough to admit him; and Miss Margland, upon whom the office devolved, took upon her to give him a positive refusal; and though she went into the room while he was there, never once would let her make an answer for herself.

Miss Margland, she added, had frightened Sir Hugh into forbidding him the house, by comparing him with Mr. Bellamy; but Mr. Macdersey had frightened them all enough, in return, as he went away, by saying, that as soon as ever Sir Hugh was well, he would call him out, because of his sending him word down stairs not to come to Cleves any more, for he had been disturbed enough already by another Irish fortune-hunter, that came after another of his nieces; and he was the more sure Mr. Macdersey was one of them, because of his being a real Irishman, while Mr. Bellamy was only an Englishman. 'But don't you think now, cousin,' she continued, 'Miss Margland might as well have let me speak for myself?'

Camilla inquired if she was sorry for the rejection.

'N . . . o,' she answered, with some hesitation; 'for Miss Margland says he's got no rent-roll; besides, I don't think he's so agreeable as Mr. Melmond; only Mr. Melmond's worth little or no fortune they say: for Miss Margland inquired about it, after Mr. Mandlebert behaved so. Else I can't say I thought Mr. Melmond disagreeable.'

Mrs. Arlbery now sent to hasten Camilla, who, in returning to the parlour, met Edgar. He had just gathered her intended excursion, and, sick at heart, had left the room. Camilla felt the consciousness of a guilty person at his sight; but he only slightly bowed; and coldly saying, 'I hope you will have much pleasure at Tunbridge,' went on to his own room.

And there, replete with resentment for the whole of her late conduct, he again blessed Dr. Marchmont for his preservation from her toils; and, concluding the excursion was for the sake of the Major, whose regiment he knew to be just ordered into Kent, he centered every former hope in the one single wish that he might never see her more.

Camilla, shocked by such obvious displeasure, quitted Cleves with still increasing sadness; and Mrs. Arlbery would heartily have repented her invitation, but for her dependance upon Sir Sedley Clarendel.

At Etherington they stopt, that Camilla might prepare her package for Tunbridge. Mrs. Arlbery would not alight.

While Camilla, with a maid-servant, was examining her drawers, the chamber door was opened by Lionel, for whom she had just inquired, and who, telling her he wanted to speak to her in private, turned the maid out of the room.

Camilla begged him to be quick, as Mrs. Arlbery was waiting.

'Why then, my dear little girl,' cried he, 'the chief substance of the matter is neither more nor less than this: I want a little money.'

'My dear brother,' said Camilla, pleasure again kindling in her eyes as she opened her pocket-book, 'you could never have applied to me so opportunely. I have just got twenty pounds, and I do not want twenty shillings. Take it, I beseech you, any part, or all.'

Lionel paused and seemed half choaked. 'Camilla,' he cried presently, 'you are an excellent girl. If you were as old and ugly as Miss Margland, I really believe I should think you young and pretty. But this sum is nothing. A drop of water to the ocean.'

Camilla now, drawing back, disappointed and displeased, asked how it was possible he should want more.

'More, my dear child? why I want two or three cool hundred.'

'Two or three hundred?' repeated she, amazed.

'Nay, nay, don't be frightened. My uncle will give you two or three thousand, you know that. And I really want the money. It's no joke, I assure you. It's a case of real distress.'

'Distress? impossible! what distress can you have to so prodigious an amount?'

'Prodigious! poor little innocent! dost think two or three hundred prodigious?'

'And what is become of the large sums extorted from my uncle Relvil?'

'O that was for quite another thing. That was for debts. That's gone and over. This is for a perfectly different purpose.'

'And will nothing—O Lionel!—nothing touch you? My poor mother's quitting England . . . her separation from my father and her family . . . my uncle Relvil's severe attack . . . will nothing move you to more thoughtful, more praise-worthy conduct?'

'Camilla, no preaching! I might as well cast myself upon the old ones at once. I come to you in preference, on purpose to avoid sermonising. However, for your satisfaction, and to spur you to serve me, I can assure you I have avoided all new debts since the last little deposit of the poor sick hypochondriac miser, who is pining away at the loss of a few guineas, that he had neither spirit nor health to have spent for himself.'

'Is this your reasoning, your repentance, Lionel, upon such a catastrophe?'

'My dear girl, I am heartily concerned at the whole business, only, as it's over, I don't like talking of it. This is the last scrape I shall ever be in while I live. But if you won't help me, I am undone. You know your influence with my uncle. Do, there's a dear girl, use it for your brother! I have not a dependance in the world, now, but upon you!'

'Certainly I will do whatever I can for you,' said she, sighing; 'but indeed, my dear Lionel, your manner of going on makes my very heart ache! However, let this twenty pounds be in part, and tell me your very smallest calculation for what must be added?'

'Two hundred. A farthing less will be of no use; and three will be of thrice the service. But mind! . . . you must not say it's for me!'

'How, then, can I ask for it?'

'O, vamp up some dismal ditty.'[1]

'No, Lionel!' exclaimed she, turning away from him; 'you propose what you know to be impracticable.'

'Well, then, if you must needs say it's for me, tell him he must not for his life own it to the old ones.'

'In the same breath, must I beg and command?'

'O, I always make that my bargain. I should else be put into the lecture room, and not let loose again till I was made a milksop. They'd talk me so into the vapours, I should not be able to act like a man for a month to come.'

'A man, Lionel?'

'Yes, a man of the world, my dear; a knowing one.'

Mrs. Arlbery now sent to hasten her, and he extorted a promise that she would go to Cleves the next morning, and procure a draft for the money, if possible, to be ready for his calling at the Grove in the afternoon.

She felt this more deeply than she had time or courage to own to Lionel, but her increased melancholy was all imputed to reflections concerning Mandlebert by Mrs. Arlbery.

*   *   *   *

That lady lent her chaise the next morning, with her usual promptitude of good humour, and Camilla went to Cleves, with a reluctance that never before accompanied her desire to oblige.

Her visit was received most kindly by all the family, as merely an additional leave taking; in which light, though she was too sincere to place it, she suffered it to pass. Having no chance of being alone with her uncle by accident, she was forced to beg him, in a whisper, to request a *tête-à-tête* with her: and she then, covered with all the confusion of a partner in his extravagance, made the petition of Lionel.

Sir Hugh seemed much surprised, but protested he would rather part with his coat and waistcoat than refuse anything to Camilla. He gave her instantly a draft upon his banker for two hundred pounds; but added, he should take it very kind of her, if she would beg Lionel to ask him for no more this year, as he was really so hard run,[1] he should not else be able to make proper preparations for the wedding, till his next rents became due.

Camilla was now surprised in her turn; and Sir Hugh then confessed, that, between presents and petitions, his nephew had had no less than five hundred pounds from him the preceding year, unknown to his parents; and that for this year, the sum she requested made the seventh hundred; without the least account for what purpose it was given.

Camilla now heartily repented being a partner in a business so rapacious, so unjustifiable, and so mysterious; but, kindly interrupting her apology, 'Don't be concerned, my dear,' he cried, 'for there's no help for these things; though what the young boys do with all their money now-a-days, is odd enough, being what I can't make out. However, he'll soon be wiser, so we must not be too severe with him; though I told him, the last time, I had rather he would not ask me so often; which was being almost too sharp, I'm afraid, considering his youngness; for one can't expect him to be an old man at once.'

Camilla gave voluntarily her word no such application should find her its ambassadress again: and though he would have dispensed with the promise, she made it the more readily as a guard against her own facility.

'At least,' cried the baronet, 'say nothing to my poor brother, and more especially to your mother; it being but vexatious to such good parents to hear of such idleness, not knowing what to think of it; for it is a great secret, he says, what he does with it all; for which reason one can't expect him to tell it. My poor brother, to be sure, had rather he should be studying *hic, hæc, hoc;* but, Lord help him! I believe he knows no more of that than I do myself; and I never could make out much meaning of it, any further than it's being Latin; though I suppose, at the time, Dr. Orkborne might explain it to me, taking it for granted he did what was right.'

Camilla was most willing to agree to concealing from her parents what she knew must so painfully afflict them, though she determined to assume sufficient courage to expostulate most seriously with her brother, against whom she felt sensations of the most painful anger.

Again she now took leave; but upon re-entering the parlour, found Edgar there alone.

Involuntarily she was retiring; but the counsel of her father recurring to her, she compelled herself to advance, and say, 'How good you have been to Eugenia! how greatly are we all indebted for your kind vigilance and exertion!'

Edgar, who was reading, and knew not she was in the house, was surprised, both by her sight and her address, out of all his resolutions; and, with a softness of voice he meant evermore to deny himself, answered, 'To me? can any of the Tyrold family talk of being indebted to me?—my own obligations to all, to every individual of that name, have been the pride, have been—hitherto —the happiness of my life!—'

The word 'hitherto,' which had escaped, affected him: he stopt, recollected himself, and presently, more drily added, 'Those obligations would be still much increased, if I might flatter myself that one of that race, to whom I have ventured to play the officious part of a brother, could forget those lectures, she can else, I fear, with difficulty pardon.'

'You have found me unworthy your counsel,' answered Camilla, gravely, and looking down; 'you have therefore con-cluded I resent it: but we are not always completely wrong, even when wide from being right. I have not been culpable of quite so much folly as not to feel what I have owed to your good offices; nor am I now guilty of the injustice to blame their being withdrawn. You do surely what is wisest, though not—perhaps—what is kindest.'

To these last words she forced a smile; and, wishing him good morning, hurried away.

Amazed past expression, and touched to the soul, he remained, a few instants, immoveable; then, resolving to follow her, and almost resolving to throw himself at her feet, he opened the door she had shut after her: he saw her still in the hall, but she was in the arms of her father and sisters, who had all descended, upon hearing she had left Sir Hugh, and of whom she was now taking leave.

Upon his appearance, she said she could no longer keep the carriage; but, as she hastened from the hall, he saw that her eyes were swimming in tears.

Her father saw it too, with less surprise, but more pain. He knew her short and voluntary absence from her friends could not excite them: his heart ached with paternal concern for her; and, motioning everybody else to remain in the hall, he walked with her to the carriage himself, saying, in a low voice, as he put her in, 'Be of better courage, my dearest child. Endeavour to take pleasure where you are going—and to forget what you are leaving: and, if you wish to feel or to give contentment upon earth, remember always, you must seek to make circumstance contribute to happiness, not happiness subservient to circumstance.'

Camilla, bathing his hand with her tears, promised this maxim should never quit her mind till they met again.

She then drove off.

'Yes,' she cried, 'I must indeed study it; Edgar cares no more what becomes of me! resentment next to antipathy has taken place of his friendship and esteem!'

She wrote down in her pocket-book the last words of her father; she resolved to read them daily, and to make them the current lesson of her future and disappointed life.

*   *   *   *

Lionel, too impatient to wait for the afternoon, was already at the Grove, and handed her from the chaise. But, stopping her in the portico, 'Well,' he cried, 'where's my draft?'

'Before I give it you,' said she, seriously, and walking from the servants, 'I must entreat to speak a few words to you.'

'You have really got it, then?' cried he, in a rapture; 'you are a charming girl! the most charming girl I know in the world! I won't take your poor twenty pounds: I would not touch it for the world. But come, where's the draft? It it for the two or the three?'

'For the two; and surely, my dear Lionel—'

'For the two? O, plague take it!—only for the two?—And when will you get me the odd third?'

'O brother! O Lionel! what a question! Will you make me repent, instead of rejoice, in the pleasure I have to assist you?'

'Why, when he was about it, why could he not as well come down like a gentleman at once? I am sure I always behaved very handsomely to him.'

'How do you mean?'

'Why, I never frightened him; never put him beside his poor wits, like t'other poor nuncle. I don't remember I ever did him an ill turn in my life, except wanting Dr. Pothook,[1] there, to flog him a little for not learning his book. It would have been a rare sight if he had!—Don't you think so?'

'Rare, indeed, I hope!'

'Why, now, what could he have done, if the Doctor had really performed it? He could not in justice have found fault, when he put himself to school to him. But he'd have felt a little queer. Don't you think he would?'

'You only want to make me laugh, to prevent my speaking to the purpose; but I am not disposed to laugh; and therefore—'

'O, if you are not disposed to laugh, you are no company for me. Give me my draft, therefore.'

'If you will not hear, I hope, at least, Lionel, you will think; and that may be much more efficacious. Shall I put up the twenty? I really do not want it. And it is all, all, all I can ever procure you! Remember that!'

'What?—all?—this all?—what, not even the other little mean hundred?'

'No, my dear brother! I have promised my uncle no further application—'

'Why what a stingy, fusty old codger, to draw such a promise from you!'

'Hold, hold, Lionel! I cannot endure to hear you speak in such a manner of such an uncle! the best, the most benevolent, the most indulgent—'

'Lord, child, don't be so precise and old maidish. Don't you know it's a relief to a man's mind to swear, and say a few cutting things when he's in a passion? when all the time he would no more do harm to the people he swears at, than you would, that mince out all your words as if you were talking treason, and thought every man a spy that heard you. Besides, how is a man the worse for a little friendly curse or two, provided he does not hear it? It's a very innocent refreshment to a man's mind, my dear; only you know nothing of the world.'

Mrs. Arlbery now approaching, he hastily took the draft, and, after a little hesitation, the twenty pounds, telling her, if she would not ask for him, she must ask for herself, and that he felt no compunction, as he was certain she might draw upon her uncle for every guinea he was worth.

He then heartily embraced her; said she was the best girl in the world, when she did not mount the pulpit, and rode off.

Camilla felt no concern at the loss of her twenty pounds: lowered and unhappy, she was rather glad than sorry that her means for being abroad were diminished, and that to keep her own room would soon be most convenient.

The next day was fixed for the journey.

BOOK VI

CHAPTER I

A Walk by Moonlight

MRS. Arlbery and Camilla set off in the coach of Mr. Dennel, widower of a deceased sister of the husband of Mrs. Arlbery, whom she was induced to admit of the party that he might aid in bearing the expenses, as she could not, from some family considerations, refuse taking her niece into her coterie. Sir Sedley Clarendel drove his own phaeton; but instead of joining them, according to the condition which occasioned the treaty, cantered away his ponies from the very first stage, and left word, where he changed horses, that he should proceed to the hotel upon the Pantiles.[1]

Mrs. Arlbery was nearly provoked to return to the Grove. With Mr. Dennel she did not think it worth while to converse; her niece she regarded as almost an idiot; and Camilla was so spiritless, that, had not Sir Sedley acceded to her plan, this was the last period in which she would have chosen her for a companion.

They travelled very quietly to within a few miles of Tunbridge, when an accident happened to one of the wheels of the carriage, that the coachman said would take some hours to repair. They were drawn on, with difficulty, to a small inn upon the road, whence they were obliged to send a man and horse to Tunbridge for chaises.

As they were destined, now, to spend some time in this place, Mrs. Arlbery retired to write letters, and Mr. Dennel to read newspapers; and, invited by a bright moon, Camilla and Miss Dennel wandered from a little garden to an adjoining meadow, which conducted them to a lane, rendered so beautiful by the strong masses of shade with which the trees intercepted the resplendent whiteness of the moon, that they walked on, catching fresh openings with fresh pleasure, till the feet of Miss Dennel grew as weary with the length of the way, unbroken by any company, as the ears of Camilla with her incessant prattling, unaided by any idea. Miss Dennel proposed to sit down, and, while relieving herself by a fit of yawning and stretching, Camilla strolled a little further in search of a safe and dry spot.

Miss Dennel, following in a moment, on tiptoe, and trembling, whispered that she was sure she heard a voice. Camilla, with a smile, asked if only themselves were privileged to enjoy so sweet a night? 'Hush!' cried she, 'hush! I hear it again!' They listened; and, in a minute, a soft plaintive tone reached their ears, too distant to be articulate, but undoubtedly female.

'I dare say it's a robber!' exclaimed Miss Dennel shaking; 'If you don't run back, I shall die!'

Camilla assured her, from the gentleness of the sound, she must be mistaken; and pressed her to advance a few steps further, in case it should be anybody ill.

'But you know,' said Miss Dennel, speaking low, 'people say that sometimes there are noises in the air, without its being any-body? Suppose it should be that?'

Still, though almost imperceptibly, Camilla drew her on, till, again listening, they distinctly heard the words, 'My lovely friend.'

'La! how pretty!' said Miss Dennel; 'let's go a little nearer.'

They advanced, and presently, again stopping heard, 'Could pity pour balm into my woes, how sweetly would they be allevi-ated by your's, my lovely friend?'

Miss Dennel now looked enchanted, and eagerly led the way herself.

In a few minutes, arriving at the end of the lane, which opened upon a wild and romantic common, they caught a glimpse of a figure in white.

Miss Dennel turned pale. 'Dear!' cried she, in the lowest whisper, 'what is it?'

'A lady,' answered Camilla, equally cautious not to be heard, though totally without alarm.

'Are you sure of that?' said Miss Dennel, shrinking back, and pulling her companion to accompany her.

'Do you think it's a ghost?' cried Camilla, unresisting the retreat, yet walking backwards to keep the form in sight.

'Fie! how can you talk so shocking? all in the dark so, except only for the moon?'

'Your's, my lovely friend!' was now again pronounced in the tenderest accent.

'She's talking to herself!' exclaimed Miss Dennel; 'Lord, how frightful!' and she clung close to Camilla, who, mounting a little hillock of stones, presently perceived that the lady was reading a letter.

Miss Dennel, tranquillised by hearing this, was again content to stop, when their ears were suddenly struck by a piercing shriek.

'O Lord! we shall be murdered!' cried she, screaming still louder herself.

They both ran back some paces down the lane, Camilla determining to send somebody from the inn to inquire what all this meant: but presently, through an opening in the common, they perceived the form in white darting forwards, with an air wild and terrified. Camilla stopt, struck with compassion and curiosity at once; Miss Dennel could not quit her, but after the first glance, hid her face, faintly articulating, 'O, don't let it see us! don't let it see us! I am sure it's nothing natural! I dare say it's somebody walking!'

The next instant, they perceived a man, looking earnestly around, as if to discover who had echoed the scream; the place they occupied was in the shade, and he did not observe them. He soon rushed hastily on, and seized the white garment of the flying figure, which appeared, both by its dress and form, to be an elegant female. She clasped her hands in supplication, cast up her eyes towards heaven, and again shrieked aloud.

Camilla, who possessed that fine internal power of the thinking and feeling mind to adopt courage for terror, where any eminent service may be the result of immediate exertion, was preparing to spring to her relief; while Miss Dennel, in extreme agony holding her, murmured out, 'Let's run away! let's run away! she's going to be murdered!' when they saw the man prostrate himself at the lady's feet, in the humblest subjection.

Camilla stopt her flight; and Miss Dennel, appeased, called out; 'La! his kneeling! how pretty it looks! I dare say it's a lover. How I wish one could hear what he says!'

An exclamation, however, from the lady, uttered in a tone of mingled affright and disgust, of 'leave me! leave me!' was again the signal to Miss Dennel of retreat, but of Camilla to advance.

The rustling of the leaves, caused by her attempt to make way through the breach, caught the ears of the suppliant, who hastily arose; while the lady folded her arms across her breast, and seemed ejaculating the most fervent thanks for this relief.

Camilla now forced a passage through the hedge, and the lady, as she saw her approach, called out, in a voice the most touching, 'Surely 'tis some pitying Angel, mercifully come to my rescue!'

The pursuer drew back, and Camilla, in the gentlest words, besought the lady to accompany her to the friends she had just left, who would be happy to protect her.

She gratefully accepted the proposal, and Camilla then ventured to look round, to see if the object of this alarm had retreated: but, with an astonishment that almost confounded her, she perceived him, a few yards off, taking a pinch of snuff, and humming an opera air.

The lady, then, snatching up her letter, which had fallen to the ground, touched it with her lips, and carefully folding, put it into her bosom, tenderly ejaculating, 'I have preserved thee! . . . O from what danger! what violation!'

Then pressing the hand of Camilla, 'You have saved me,' she cried, 'from the calamity of losing what is more dear than I have words to express! Take me but where I may be shielded from that wretch, and what shall I not owe to you?'

The moon now shining full upon her face, Camilla saw seated on it youth, sensibility, and beauty. Her pleasure, involuntarily rather than rationally, was redoubled that she had proved serviceable to her, as, in equal proportion, was her abhorrence of the man who had caused the disturbance.

The three females were now proceeding, when the offender, with a careless air, and yet more careless bow, advancing towards them, negligently said, 'Shall I have the honour to see you safe home, ladies?'

Camilla felt indignant; Miss Dennel again screamed; and the stranger, with a look of horror and disgust, said; 'Persecute me no more!'

'O hang it! O curse it!' cried he, swinging his cane to and fro, 'don't be serious. I only meant to frighten you about the letter.'

The lady deigned no answer, but murmured to herself 'that letter is more precious to me than life or light!'

They now walked on; and, when they entered the lane, they had the pleasure to observe they were not pursued. She then said to

Camilla, 'You must be surprised to see any one out, and unprotected, at this late hour; but I had employed myself, unthinkingly, in reading some letters from a dear and absent friend, and forgot the quick passage of time.'

A man in a livery now appearing at some distance, she hastily summoned him, and demanded where was the carriage?

In the road, he answered, where she had left it, at the end of the lane.

She then took the hand of Camilla, and with a smile of the utmost softness said, 'When the shock I have suffered is a little over, I must surely cease to lament I have sustained it, since it has brought to me such sweet succour. Where may I find you tomorrow, to repeat my thanks?'

Camilla answered, 'she was going to Tunbridge immediately, but knew not yet where she should lodge.'

'Tunbridge!' she repeated; I am there myself; I shall easily find you out tomorrow morning, for I shall know no rest till I have seen you again.'

She then asked her name, and, with the most touching acknowledgments, took leave.

Camilla recounted her adventure to Mrs. Arlbery, with an animated description of the fair Incognita, and with the most heart-felt delight of having, though but accidentally, proved of service to her. Mrs. Arlbery laughed heartily at the recital, assuring her she doubted not but she had made acquaintance with some dangerous fair one, who was playing upon her inexperience, and utterly unfit to be known to her. Camilla warmly vindicated her innocence, from the whole of her appearance, as well as from the impossibility of her knowing that her scream could be heard: yet was perplexed how to account for her not naming herself, and for the mystery of the carriage and servant in waiting so far off. These latter she concluded to belong to her father, as she looked too young to have any sort of establishment of her own.

'What I don't understand in the matter is, that there reading of letters by the light of the moon;' said Mr. Dennel. 'Where's the necessity of doing that, for a person that can afford to keep her own coach and servants?'

Mr. Dennel was a man as unfavoured by nature as he was uncultivated by art. He had been accepted as a husband by the sister of Mr. Arlbery, merely on account of a large fortune, which he had acquired in business. The marriage, like most others made upon such terms, was as little happy in its progression as honourable in its commencement; and Miss Dennel, born and educated amidst domestic dissention, which robbed her of all will of her own, by the constant denial of one parent to what was accorded by the other, possessed too little reflexion to benefit by observing the misery of an alliance not mentally assorted; and grew up with no other desire but to enter the state herself, from an ardent impatience to shake off the slavery she experienced in singleness. The recent death of her mother had given her, indeed, somewhat more liberty; but she had not sufficient sense to endure any restraint, and languished for the complete power which she imagined a house and servants of her own would afford.

When they arrived at the hotel, in Tunbridge, Mrs. Arlbery heard, with some indignation, that Sir Sedley Clarendel was gone to the rooms, without demonstrating, by any sort of inquiry, the smallest solicitude at her non-appearance.

CHAPTER II

The Pantiles

A SERVANT tapt early at the door of Camilla, the next morning, to acquaint her that a lady, who called herself the person that had been so much obliged to her the preceding day, begged the honour of being admitted.

Camilla was sorry, after the suspicions of Mrs. Arlbery, that she did not send up her name; yet, already partially disposed, her prepossession was not likely to be destroyed by the figure that now appeared.

A beautiful young creature, with an air of the most attractive softness, eyes of the most expressive loveliness, and a manner which by every look and every motion announced a soul 'tremblingly alive,' glided gently into the room, and advancing, with a graceful confidence of kindness, took both her hands, and pressing them to her heart, said, 'What happiness so soon to have found you! to be able to pour forth all the gratitude I owe you, and the esteeem with which I am already inspired!'

Camilla was struck with admiration and pleasure; and gave way to the most lively delight at the fortunate accident which occasioned her walking out in a place entirely unknown to her; declaring she should ever look back to that event as to one of the marked blessings of her life.

'If you,' answered the fair stranger, 'have the benevolence thus to value our meeting, how should it be appreciated by one who is so eternally indebted to it? I had not perceived the approach of that person. He broke in upon me when least a creature so ungenial was present to my thoughts. I was reading a letter from the most amiable of friends, the most refined—perhaps—of human beings!'

Camilla, impatient for some explanation, answered, 'I hope, at least, that friend will be spared hearing of your alarm?'

'I hope so! for his own griefs already overwhelm him. Never may it be my sad lot to wound where I mean only to console.'

At the words *his own*, Camilla felt herself blush. She had imagined it was some female friend. She now found her mistake, and knew not what to imagine next.

'I had retired,' she continued, 'from the glare of company, and the weight of uninteresting conversation, to read, at leisure and in solitude, this dear letter—heart-breaking from its own woes, heart-soothing to mine! In a place such as this, seclusion is difficult. I drove some miles off, and ordered my carriage to wait in the high road, while I strolled alone upon the common. I delight in a solitary ramble by moonlight. I can then indulge in uninterrupted rumination, and solace my melancholy by pronouncing aloud such sentences, and such names, as in the world I cannot utter. How exquisitely sweet do they sound to ears unaccustomed to such vibrations!'

Camilla was all astonishment and perplexity. A male friend so beloved, who seemed to be neither father, brother, nor husband; a carriage at her command, though without naming one relation to whom either that or herself might belong; and sentiments so tender she was almost ashamed to listen to them; all conspired to excite a wonder that painfully prayed for relief: and in the hope to obtain it, with some hesitation, she said, 'I should have sought you myself this morning, for the pleasure of inquiring after your safety, but that I was ignorant by what name to make my search.'

The fair unknown looked down for a moment, with an air that

shewed a perfect consciousness of the inquiry meant by this speech; but turning aside the embarrassment it seemed to cause her, she presently raised her head, and said, 'I had no difficulty to find you, for my servant, happily, made his inquiry at once at this hotel.'

Disappointed and surprised by this evasion, Camilla saw now an evident mystery, but knew not how to press forward any investigation. She began, therefore, to speak of other things, and her fair guest, who had every mark of an education rather sedulously than naturally cultivated, joined readily in a conversation less personal.

They did not speak of Tunbridge, of public places, nor diversions; their themes, all chosen by the stranger, were friendship, confidence, and sensibility, which she illustrated and enlivened by quotations from favourite poets, aptly introduced and feelingly recited; yet always uttered with a sigh, and an air of tender melancholy. Camilla was now in a state so depressed, that, notwithstanding her native vivacity, she fell as imperceptibly into the plaintive style of her new acquaintance, who seemed habitually pensive, as if sympathy rather than accident had brought them together.

Yet when chance led to some mention of the adventure of the preceding evening, and the lady made again an animated eulogium of the friend whose letter she was perusing; she hazarded, with an half smile, saying: 'I hope—for his own sake, this friend is some sage and aged personage?'

'O no!' she answered; 'he is in the bloom of youth.'

Camilla, again a little disconcerted, paused; and the lady went on.

'It was in Wales I first met him; upon a spot so beautiful that painting can never do it justice. I have made, however, a little sketch of it, which, some day or other, I will shew you, if you will have the goodness to let me see more of you.'

Camilla could not refrain from an eager affirmative; and the conversation was then interrupted by a message from Mrs. Arlbery, who always breakfasted in her own room, to announce that she was going out lodging-hunting.

Camilla would rather have remained with her new acquaintance, better adapted to her present turn of mind than Mrs. Arlbery; but this was impossible, and the lovely stranger hastened away, saying she would call herself the next morning to shew the way to her house, where she hoped they might pass together many soothing and consolatory hours.

*   *   *   *

Camilla found Mrs. Arlbery by no means in her usual high spirits. The opening of her Tunbridge campaign had so far from answered its trouble and expence, that she heartily repented having quitted the Grove. The Officers either were not arrived in the neighbourhood, or were wholly engaged in military business; Camilla, instead of contributing to the life of the excursion, seemed to hang heavily both upon that, and upon herself; and Sir Sedley Clarendel, whose own proposition had brought it to bear, had not yet made his appearance, though lodging in the same hotel.

Thus vexatiously disappointed, she was ill-disposed to listen with pleasure to the history Camilla thought it indispensable to relate of her recent visit: and in answer to all praise of this fair Incognita, only replied by asking her name and connexions. Camilla felt extremely foolish in confessing she had not yet learnt them. Mrs. Arlbery then laughed unmercifully at her commendations, but concluded with saying: 'Follow, however, your own humour; I hate to torment or be tormented: only take care not to be seen with her.'

Camilla rejoiced she did not exact any further restriction, and hoped all raillery would soon be set aside, by an honourable explanation.

*   *   *   *

They now repaired to the Pantiles, where the gay company and gay shops afforded some amusement to Camilla, and to Miss Dennel a wonder and delight, that kept her mouth open, and her head jerking from object to object, so incessantly, that she saw nothing distinctly, from the eagerness of her fear lest anything should escape her.

Mrs. Arlbery, meeting with an old acquaintance in the book-seller's shop, there sat down with him, while the two young ladies loitered at the window of a toy-shop, struck with just admiration of the beauty and ingenuity of the Tunbridge ware it presented to their view; till Camilla, in a party of young men who were strolling down the Pantiles, and who went into the book-seller's shop,[1] distinguished the offender of the fair unknown.

To avoid following, or being recollected by a person so odious to her, she entered the toy-shop with Miss Dennel, where she amused herself, till Mrs. Arlbery came in search of her, in select-ing such various little articles for purchase as she imagined would amount to about half a crown; but which were put up for her at a guinea. This a little disconcerted her: though, as she was still unusually rich, from Mr. Tyrold's having advanced her next quarterly allowance, she consoled herself that they would serve for little keep-sakes for her sisters and her cousin: yet she determined, when next she entered a shop for convenience, to put nothing apart as a buyer, till she had inquired its price.

The assaulter, Lord Newford, a young nobleman of the *ton*,[2] after taking a staring survey of every thing and every body around, and seeing no one of more consequence, followed Mrs. Arlbery, with whom formerly he had been slightly acquainted, to the toy-shop. He asked her how she did, without touching his hat; and how long she had been at Tunbridge, without waiting for an answer; and said he was happy to have the pleasure of seeing her, without once looking at her.

To his first sentence, Mrs. Arlbery made a civil answer; but, repenting it upon the two sentences that succeeded, she heard them without seeming to listen, and fixing her eyes upon him, when he had done, coolly said, 'Pray have you seen any thing of my servant?'

Lord Newford, somewhat surprised, replied, 'No.'

'Do look for him, then,' cried she, negligently, 'there's a good man.'

Lord Newford, a little piqued, and a little confused at feeling so, said he should be proud to obey her; and turning short off to his companion, cried, 'Come, Offy, why dost loiter? where shall we ride this morning?' And, taking him by the arm, quitted the Pantiles.

Mrs. Arlbery, laughing heartily, now felt her spirits a little revive; 'I doat,' she cried, 'upon meeting, now and then, with insolence, for I have a little taste for it myself, which I make some conscience of not indulging unprovoked.'

They then proceeded to the milliner's, to equip themselves for going to the rooms at night. Mrs. Arlbery and Miss Dennel, who were both rich, gave large orders: Camilla, indifferent to every thing except to avoid appearing in a manner that might disgrace her party, told the milliner to choose for her what she thought fashionable that was most reasonable. She was soon fitted up with what was too pretty to disapprove, and desiring immediately to pay her bill, found it amounted to five guineas; though she had imagined she should have change out of two.

She had only six, and some silver; but was ashamed to dispute, or desire any alteration; she paid the money; and only determined to apply to another person than the seller, when next she wanted any thing reasonable.

Mrs. Arlbery now ordered the carriage, and they drove to Mount Pleasant,[1] where she hired a house for the season, to which they were to remove the next day.

* * * *

In the evening, they went to the Rooms, where the decidedly fashionable mien and manner of Mrs. Arlbery, attracted more general notice and admiration than the youthful captivation of Camilla, or the pretty face and expensive attire of Miss Dennel.

Dressed by the milliner of the day, Camilla could not fail to pass uncensured, at least, with respect to her appearance; but her eyes wanted their usual lustre, from the sadness of her heart, and she never looked less herself, nor to less advantage.

The master of the ceremonies brought to her Sir Theophilus Jarard; but as she had seen him the companion of Lord Newford, to whom she had conceived a strong aversion, she declined dancing. He looked surprised, but rather offended than disappointed, and with a little laugh, half contemptuous, as if ashamed of having offered himself, stalked away.

Sir Sedley Clarendel was now sauntering into the room. Mrs. Arlbery, willing to shew her young friend in a favourable point of view to him, though more from pique at his distance, than from any thought at that moment of Camilla, told her she must positively accept Sir Theophilus, whose asking her must be regarded as a particular distinction, for he was notoriously a man of the *ton*. And, heedless of her objections, told Mr. Dennel to call him back.

'How can I do that,' said Mr. Dennel, 'after seeing her refuse him with my own eyes?'

'O, nobody cares about a man's eyes,' said Mrs. Arlbery; 'go and tell him Miss Tyrold has changed her mind, and chooses to dance.'

'As to her changing her mind,' he answered, 'that's likely enough; but I don't see how it's any reason I should go of a fool's errand.'

'Pho, pho, go directly; or you sha'n't dine before eight o'clock for the whole Tunbridge season.'[1]

'Nay,' said Mr. Dennel, who had an horror of late hours, 'if you will promise we shall dine more in reason'—

'Yes, yes,' cried Mrs. Arlbery, hurrying him off, notwithstanding the reiterated remonstrances of Camilla.

'See, my dear,' she then added, laughing, 'how many weapons you must have in use, if you would govern that strange animal called man! yet never despair of victory; for, depend upon it, there is not one of the race that, with a little address, you may not bring to your feet.'

Camilla, who had no wish but for one single votary, and whose heart was sunk from her failure in obtaining that one, listened with so little interest or spirit, that Mrs. Arlbery, quite provoked, resolved not to throw away another idea upon her for the rest of the evening. And therefore, as her niece went completely and constantly for nothing with her, she spoke no more, till, to her great relief, she was joined by General Kinsale.

Mr. Dennel returned with an air not more pleased with his embassy, than her own appeared with her auditress. The gentleman, he said, had joined two others, and they were all laughing so violently together, that he could not find an opportunity to deliver his message, for they seemed as if they would only make a joke of it.

Mrs. Arlbery then saw that he had got between Lord Newford and Sir Sedley, and that they were all three amusing themselves, without ceremony or disguise, at the expense of every creature in the room; up and down which they strolled, arm in arm, looking familiarly at every body, but speaking to nobody; whispering one another in hoarse low voices, and then laughing immoderately loud: while nothing was distinctly heard, but from time to time, 'What in the world is become of Mrs. Berlinton to night?' or else, 'How stupid the Rooms are without Lady Alithea.'

Mrs. Arlbery, who, like the rest of the world, saw her own

defects in as glaring colours, and criticised them with as much animated ridicule as those of her neighbours, when exhibited by others, no sooner found she was neglected by this set, than she raved against the prevailing ill manners of the leaders in the *ton*, with as much asperity of censure, as if never for a moment betrayed herself, by fashion, by caprice, nor by vanity, to similar foibles. 'Yet, after all,' cried she presently, 'to see fools behave like fools, I am well content. I have no anger, therefore, against Lord Newford, nor Sir Theophilus Jarard; if they were not noticed for being impertinent, how could they expect to be noticed at all? When there is but one line that can bring them forward, I rather respect them that they have found it out. But what shall we say to Sir Sedley Clarendel? A man as much their superior in capacity as in powers of pleasing? 'Tis a miserable thing, my dear General, to see the dearth of character there is in the world. Pope has bewailed it in women;[1] believe me, he might have extended his lamentation. You may see, indeed, one man grave, and another gay; but with no more "mark or likelihood," no more distinction of colouring, than what simply belongs to a dismal face or a merry one: and with just as little light and shade, just as abrupt a skip from one to the other, as separates inevitably the old man from the young one. We are almost all, my good General, of a nature so pitifully plastic, that we act from circumstances, and are fashioned by situation.'

Then, laughing at her own pique, 'General,' she added, 'shall I make you a confession? I am not at all sure, if that wretched Sir Sedley had behaved as he ought to have done, and been at my feet all the evening, that I should not, at this very moment, be amused in the same manner that he is himself! yet it would be very abominable, I own.'

'This is candid, however.'

'O, we all acknowledge our faults, now; 'tis the mode of the day: but the acknowledgment passes for current payment; and therefore we never amend them. On the contrary, they take but deeper root, by losing all chance of concealment. Yet I am vexed to see that odious Sir Sedley shew so silly a passion for being a man of the *ton*, as to suffer himself to be led in a string by those two poor paltry creatures, who are not more troublesome as fops, than tiresome as fools, merely because they are better known than himself upon the turf and at the clubs.'

Here, she was joined by Lord O'Lerney and the honourable Mr. Ormsby. And, in the next saunter of the *tonnish* triumvirs, Lord Newford, suddenly seeing with whom she was associated, stopt, and looking at her with an air of surprise, exclaimed, 'God bless me! Mrs. Arlbery! I hope you are perfectly well?'

'Infinitely indebted to your lordship's solicitude!' she answered, rather sarcastically. But, without noticing her manner, he desired to be one in her tea-party, which she was then rising to form.

She accepted the offer, with a glance of consciousness at the General, who, as he conducted her, said: 'I did not expect so much grace would so immediately have been accorded.'

'Alas! my dear General, what can one do? These *tonnish* people, cordially as I despise them, lead the world; and if one has not a few of them in one's train, 'twere as well turn hermit. However, mark how he will fare with me! But don't judge from the opening.

She now made his lordship so many gay compliments, and mingled so much personal civility with the general entertainment of her discourse, that, as soon as they rose from tea, he professed his intention of sitting by her, for the rest of the evening.

She immediately declared herself tired to death of the Rooms, and calling upon Miss Dennel and Camilla, abruptly made her exit.

The General, again her conductor, asked how she could leave thus a conquest so newly made.

'I leave,' she answered, 'only to secure it. He will be piqued that I should go, and that pique will keep me in his head till to-morrow. 'Tis well, my dear General, to put any thing there! But if I had stayed a moment longer, my contempt might have broken forth into satire, or my weariness into yawning: and I should then inevitably have been cut by the *ton* party for the rest of the season.'

Miss Dennel, who had been dancing, and was again engaged to dance, remonstrated against retiring so soon; but Mrs. Arlbery had a regular system never to listen to her. Camilla, whom nothing had diverted, was content to retreat.

At the door stood Sir Sedley Clarendel, who, as if now first perceiving them, said to Mrs. Arlbery, 'Ah! my fair friend!— And how long have you been at the Wells?'

'Intolerable wretch!' cried she, taking him apart, 'is it thus you keep your conditions? did you draw me into bringing this poor love-sick thing with me, only to sigh me into the vapours?'

'My dear madam!' exclaimed he, in a tone of expostulation, 'who can think of the same scheme two days together? Could you possibly form a notion of anything so patriarchal?'

*   *   *   *

Before they retired to their chambers at the hotel, Camilla told Mrs. Arlbery how shocking to her was the sight, much more any acquaintance with Lord Newford, who was the person that had so much terrified the lady she had met on their journey. Mrs. Arlbery assured her he should be exiled her society, if, upon investigation, he was found the aggressor; but while there appeared so much mystery in the complaint and the conduct of this unknown lady, she should postpone his banishment.

Camilla was obliged to submit: but scarce rested till she saw again her new favourite the next morning.

CHAPTER III

Mount Ephraim

THIS expected guest arrived early. Camilla received her with the only sensation of pleasure she had experienced at Tunbridge. Yet what she excited seemed still stronger: the fair stranger besought her friendship as a solace to her existence, and hung upon her as upon a treasure long lost, and dearly recovered. Camilla soon caught the infection of her softness, and felt a similar desire to cultivate her regard. She found her beauty attractive, her voice melodious, and her manners bewitchingly caressing.

Fearing, nevertheless, while yet in ignorance of her connexions, to provoke further ridicule from Mrs. Arlbery by going abroad with her, she proposed deferring to return her visit till another day: the lady consented, and they spent together two hours, which each thought had been but two minutes, when Mrs. Arlbery summoned Camilla to a walk.

The fair unknown then took leave, saying her servant was in waiting; and Camilla and Mrs. Arlbery went to the bookseller's.

Here, that lady was soon joined by Lord O'Lerney and General

Kinsale, who were warm admirers of her vivacity and observations. Mr. Dennel took up the Daily Advertiser;[1] his daughter stationed herself at the door to see the walkers upon the Pantiles; Sir Theophilus Jarard, under colour of looking at a popular pamphlet, was indulging in a nap in a corner; Lord Newford, noticing nothing, except his own figure as he past a mirrour, was shuffling loud about the floor, which was not much embellished by the scraping of his boots; and Sir Sedley Clarendel, lounging upon a chair in the middle of the shop, sat eating *bon bons*.

Mrs. Arlbery, for some time, confined her talents to general remarks: but finding these failed to move a muscle in the face of Sir Sedley, at whom they were directed, she suddenly exclaimed: 'Pray, my Lord O'Lerney, do you know any thing of Sir Sedley Clarendel?'

'Not so much,' answered his Lordship, 'as I could wish; but I hope to improve my acquaintance with him.'

'Why then, my lord, I am much afraid you will conclude, when you see him in one of those reveries, from the total vacancy of his air, that he is thinking of nothing. But pray permit me to take his part. Those apparent cogitations, to which he is so much addicted, are moments only of pretended torpor, but of real torment, devoted, not as they appear, to supine insipidity, but to painful secret labour how next he may call himself into notice. Nevertheless, my lord, don't let what I have said hurt him in your opinion; he is quaint, to be sure, but there's no harm in him. He lives in my neighbourhood; and, I assure your lordship, he is, upon the whole, what may be called a very good sort of man.'

Here she yawned violently; and Sir Sedley, unable to maintain his position, twice crossed his legs, and then arose and took up a book: while Lord Newford burst into so loud a laugh, that he awakened Sir Theophilus Jarard, by echoing, 'A good sort of man! O poor Clary! . . . O hang it! . . . O curse it! . . . poor Clary!'

'What's the matter with Clary?' cried Sir Theophilus, rubbing his eyes; 'I have been boring myself with this pamphlet, till I hardly know whether I am awake or asleep.'

'Why, he's a good sort of man!' replied Lord Newford.

Sir Sedley, though he expected, and even hoped for some pointed strictures, and could have defied even abuse, could not stand this mortifying praise; and, asking for the subscription books, which, already, he had twice examined, said: 'Is there any body here one knows?'

'O, ay, have you any names?' cried Lord Newford, seizing them first; and with some right, as they were the only books in the shop he ever read.

'Come, I'll be generous,' said Mrs. Arlbery, 'and add another signature against your lordship's next lecture.'

She then wrote her name, and threw down half-a-guinea.[1] Camilla, to whom the book was next presented, concluded this the established custom, and, from mere timidity, did the same; though somewhat disturbed to leave herself no more gold than she gave. Miss Dennel followed; but her father, who said he did not come to Tunbridge to read, which he could do at home, positively refused to subscribe.

Sir Theophilus now, turning, or rather, tossing over the leaves, cried: 'I see no name here one knows any thing of, but Lady Alithea Selmore.'

'Why, there's nobody else here,' said Lord Newford, 'not a soul!'

Almost every body present bowed; but wholly indifferent to reproof, he again whistled, again stroamed[2] up and down the room, and again took a bold and full survey of himself in the looking-glass.

'On the contrary,' cried Sir Sedley, 'I hear there is a most extraordinary fine creature lately arrived, who is invincible to a degree.'

'O that's Mrs. Berlinton;' said Sir Theophilus; 'yes, she's a pretty little thing.'

'She's very beautiful indeed,' said Lord O'Lerney.

'Where can one see her?' cried Mrs. Arlbery.

'If she is not at the Rooms to-night,' said Sir Sedley, 'I shall be stupified to petrifaction. They tell me she is a marvel of the first water; turning all heads by her beauty, winning all hearts by her sweetness, fascinating all attention by her talents, and setting all fashions by her elegance.'

'This paragon,' cried Mrs. Arlbery, to Camilla, 'can be no other than your mysterious fair. The description just suits your own.'

'But my fair mysterious,' said Camilla, 'is of a disposition the most retired, and seems so young, I don't at all think her married.'

'This divinity,' said Sir Sedley, 'for the blessing of everyone, yet

Lord of Himself, uncumber'd by a Wife*,[3]

*Dryden

is safely noosed; and amongst her attributes are two others cruel to desperation; she excited every hope by a sposo properly detestable—yet gives birth to despair, by a coldness the most shivering.'

'And what,' said Mrs. Arlbery, 'is this Lady Alithea Selmore?'

'Lady Alithea Selmore,' drily, but with a smile, answered General Kinsale.

'Nay, nay, that's not to be mentioned irreverently,' returned Mrs. Arlbery; 'a title goes for a vast deal, where there is nothing else; and, where there is something, doubles its value.

Mr. Dennel, saying he found, by the newspaper, a house was to be sold upon Mount Ephraim, which promised to be a pretty good bargain, proposed walking thither, to examine what sort of condition it was in.

Lord O'Lerney inquired if Camilla had yet seen Mount Ephraim.[1] No, she answered; and a general party was made for an airing. Sir Sedley ordered his phaeton; Mrs. Arlbery drove Camilla in her's; Miss Dennel walked with her father; and the rest of the gentlemen went on horseback.

*   *   *   *

Arrived at Mount Ephraim, they all agreed to alight, and enjoy the view and pure air of the hill, while Mr. Dennel visited the house. But, just as Mrs. Arlbery had descended from the phaeton, her horses, taking fright at some object that suddenly struck them, reared up, in a manner alarming to the spectators, and still more terrific to Camilla, in whose hands Mrs. Arlbery had left the reins: and the servant, who stood at the horses' heads, received a kick that laid him flat on the ground.

'O, jump out! jump out!' cried Miss Dennel, 'or else you'll be murdered!'

'No! no! keep your seat, and hold the reins!' cried Mrs. Arlbery: 'For heaven's sake, don't jump out!'

Camilla, mentally giddy, but personally courageous, was sufficiently mistress of herself to obey the last injunction, though with infinite labour, difficulty, and terror, the horses plunging and flouncing incessantly.

'Don't you think she'll be killed?' cried Lord Newford, dismounting, lest his own horse should also take fright.

'Do you think one could help her?' said Sir Theophilus Jarard, steadily holding the bridle of his mare from the same apprehension.

Lord O'Lerney was already on foot to afford her assistance, when the horses, suddenly turning round, gave to the beholders the dreadful menace of going down the steep declivity of Mount Ephraim full gallop.

Camilla now, appalled, had no longer power to hold the reins; she let them go, with an idea of flinging herself out of the carriage, when Sir Sedley, who had darted like lightning from his phaeton, presented himself at the horses' heads, on the moment of their turning, and, at the visible and imminent hazard of his life, happily stopt them while she jumped to the ground. They then, with a fury that presently dashed the phaeton to pieces, plunged down the hill.

The fright of Camilla had not robbed her of her senses, and the exertion and humanity of Sir Sedley seemed to restore to him the full possession of his own: yet one of his knees was so much hurt, that he sunk upon the grass.

Penetrated with surprise, as well as gratitude, Camilla, notwithstanding her own tremor, was the first to make the most anxious inquiries: secretly, however, sighing to herself: Ah! had Edgar thus rescued me! yet struck equally with a sense of obligation and of danger, from the horrible, if not fatal mischief she had escaped, and from the extraordinary hazard and kindness by which she had been saved, she expressed her concern and acknowledgments with a softness, that even Sir Sedley himself could not listen to unmoved.

He received, indeed, from this adventure, almost every species of pleasure of which his mind was capable. His natural courage, which he had nearly annihilated, as well as forgotten, by the effeminate part he was systematically playing, seemed to rejoice in being again exercised; his good nature was delighted by the essential service he had performed; his vanity was gratified by the publicity of the praise it brought forth; and his heart itself experienced something like an original feeling, unspoilt by the apathy of satiety, from the sensibility he had awakened in the young and lovely Camilla.

The party immediately flocked around him, and he was conveyed to a house belonging to Lord O'Lerney, who resided upon

Mount Ephraim, and his lordship's carriage was ordered to take him to his apartment at the hotel.

Mrs. Arlbery, whose high spirits were totally subdued by the terror with which she had been seized at the danger of Camilla, was so delighted by her rescue, and the courage with which it was effected, that all her spleen against Sir Sedley was changed into the warmest approbation. When he was put into the coach, she insisted upon seeing him safe to the hotel; Camilla, with her usual inartificial quickness, seconding the motion, and Lord O'Lerney, a nobleman far more distinguished by benevolence and urbanity than by his rank, taking the fourth place himself. The servant, who was considerably hurt, he desired might remain at his house.

In descending Mount Ephraim, Camilla turned giddy with the view of what she had escaped, and cast her eyes with doubled thankfulness upon Sir Sedley as her preserver. Fragments of the phaeton were strewed upon the road; one of the horses [lay] dead at the bottom of the hill; and the other was so much injured as to be totally disabled for future service.

When they came to the hotel, they all alighted with the young baronet, Camilla with as little thought, as Mrs. Arlbery with little care for doing any thing that was unusual. They waited in an adjoining apartment till they were assured nothing of any consequence was the matter, and Lord O'Lerney then carried them to their new lodging upon Mount Pleasant.

Mrs. Arlbery bore her own share in this accident with perfect good-humour, saying it would do her infinite good, by making her a rigid œconomist; for she could neither live without a phaeton, nor yet build one, and buy ponies, but by parsimonious savings from all other expenses.

*   *   *   *

At night they went again to the Rooms. But Mrs. Arlbery found in them as little amusement as Camilla. Sir Sedley was not there, either to attack or to flatter; the celebrated Mrs. Berlinton still appeared not to undergo a scrutiny; and Lady Alithea Selmore sat at the upper end of the apartment, attended by all the beaux, except the General, now at Tunbridge.

This was not to be supported. She arose, and declaring she would take her tea with the invalid, bid the General escort her to his room.

In their way out, she perceived the assembly books. Recollecting she had not subscribed, she entered her name, but protested she could afford but half-a-guinea, upon her present new and avaricious plan.

Camilla, with much secret consternation, concluded it impossible to give less; and a few shillings were now all that remained in her purse. Her uneasiness, however, presently passed away, upon recollecting she should want no more money, as she was now free of the rooms, and of the library, and equipped in attire for the whole time she should stay.

Miss Dennel put down a guinea; but her father, telling her half-a-crown would have done, said, for that reason, he should himself pay nothing.

Sir Sedley received them with the most unaffected pleasure: forced upon solitude, and by no means free from pain, he had found no resource but in reading, which of late had been his least occupation, except the mere politics of the day. Even reflection had discovered its way to him, though a long banished guest, which had quitted her post, to make room for affectation, vanity, and every species of frivolity. Reduced, however, to be reasonable, even by this short confinement, he now felt the obligation of their charitable visit, and set his foppery and conceit apart, from a desire to entertain them. Camilla had not conceived he had the power of being so pleasantly natural; and the strong feeling of gratitude in her ever warm heart made her contribute what she was able to the cheerfulness of the evening.

Some time after, General Kinsale was called out, and presently returned with Major Cerwood, just arrived from the regiment; who, with some apology to Sir Sedley, hoped he might be pardoned for the liberty he took, upon hearing who was at the hotel, of preferring such society to the Rooms.

As the Major had nothing in him either brilliant or offensive, his sight, after the first salutations, was almost all of which the company was sensible.

Camilla, his sole object, he could not approach; she sat between the baronet and Mrs. Arlbery; and all her looks and all her attention were divided between them.

Mrs. Arlbery, emerging from the mortifications of neglect, which she had experienced, almost for the first time in her life, at the Rooms, was unusually alive and entertaining; Sir Sedley kept pace with her, and the discourse was so whimsical, that Camilla, amused, and willing to encourage a sensation so natural to her, after a sadness till now, for so long a time unremitting, once more heard and welcomed the sound of her own laughter.

It was instantly, however, and strangely checked; a sigh, so deep that it might rather be called a groan, made its way through the wainscot of the next apartment.

Much raillery followed the sight of her changed countenance; the hotel was pronounced to be haunted, and by a ghost reduced to that plight from her cruelty. But the good-humour and gaiety of the conversation soon brought her again to its tone; and time passed with general hilarity, till they observed that Miss Dennel, who, having no young female to talk with of her own views and affairs, was thoroughly tired, had fallen fast asleep upon her chair.

Her father was already gone home to a hot supper, which he had ordered in his own room, and meant to eat before their return; Mrs. Arlbery, to his great discomfort, allowing nothing to appear at night but fruit or oysters.

They now took leave, Mrs. Arlbery conducted by the General, and Camilla by the Major; while Miss Dennel, unassisted and half asleep, stumbled, screamed, and fell, just before she reached the staircase.

The General was first to aid her; the Major, not choosing to quit Camilla; who, looking round at a light which came from the room whence the sigh they had heard had issued, perceived, as it glared in her eyes, it was held by Edgar.

Astonishment, pleasure, hope, and shame, took alternate rapid possession of her mind; but the last sensation was the first that visibly operated, and she snatched her hand involuntarily from the Major.

Mrs. Arlbery exclaimed, 'Bless me, Mr. Mandlebert! are you the ghost we heard sighing in that room yonder?'

Mandlebert attempted to make some slight answer; but his voice refused all sound.

She went on, then, to the carriage of Mr. Dennel, followed by her young ladies, and drove off for Mount Pleasant.

CHAPTER IV

Knowle

THE last words of Camilla to Mandlebert, in quitting Cleves, and the tears with which he saw her eyes overflowing, had annihilated all his resentment, and left him no wish but to serve her. Her distinction between what was wisest and what was kindest, had penetrated him to the quick. To be thought capable of severity towards so sweet a young creature, the daughter of his guardian, his juvenile companion, and earliest favourite, made him detestable in his own eyes. He languished to follow her, to apologise for what had hurt her, and to vow to her a fair and disinterested friendship for the rest of his life: and he only forced himself, from decency, to stay out his promised week with the baronet, before he set out for Tunbridge.

Upon his arrival, which was late, he went immediately to the Rooms; but he only saw her name in the books, and learnt, upon inquiring for Mrs. Arlbery, that she and her party were already retired.

Glad to find her so sober in hours, he went to the hotel, meaning quietly to read till bed-time, and to call upon her the next morning.

In a few moments, a voice struck his ear that effectually interrupted his studies. It was the voice of Camilla. Camilla at an hotel at past eleven o'clock! He knew she did not lodge there; he had seen, in the books, the direction[1] of Mrs. Arlbery at Mount Pleasant. Mrs. Arlbery's voice he also distinguished, Sir Sedley Clarendel's, General Kinsale's, and, least of all welcome, . . . the Major's.

Perhaps, however, some lady, some intimate friend of Mrs. Arlbery, was just arrived, and had made them spend the evening there. He rang for his man, and bid him inquire who had taken the next room, . . . and learnt it was Sir Sedley Clarendel.

To visit a young man at an hotel; rich, handsome, and splendid; and with a *chaperon* so far from past her prime, so elegant, so coquetish, so alluring, and still so pretty; and to meet there a flashy Officer, her open pursuer and avowed admirer—'Tis true, he had concluded, Tunbridge and the Major were one; but not thus, not with such glaring impropriety; his love, he told himself, was past; but his esteem was still susceptible, and now grievously wounded.

To read was impossible. To hold his watch in his hand, and count the minutes she still stayed, was all to which his faculties were equal. No words distinctly reached him; that the conversation was lively, the tone of every voice announced, but when that of Camilla struck him by its laughter, the depth of his concern drew from him a sigh that was heard into the next apartment.

Of this, with infinite vexation, he was himself aware, from the sudden silence and pause of all discourse which ensued. Ashamed both of what he felt and what he betrayed, he grew more upon his guard, and hoped it might never be known to whom the room belonged.

When, however, as they were retiring, a scream reached his ear, though he knew it was not the voice of Camilla, he could not command himself, and rushed forth with a light; but the lady who screamed was as little noticed as thought of: the Major was holding the hand of Camilla, and his eye could take in no more: he saw not even that Mrs. Arlbery was there; and when roused by her question, all voice was denied him for answer; he stood motionless even after they had descended the stairs, till the steps of the General and the Major, retiring to their chambers, brought to him some recollection, and enabled him to retreat.

Fully now, as well as cruelly convinced, of the unabated force of his unhappy passion, he spent the night in extreme wretchedness; and all that was not swallowed up in repining and regret, was devoted to ruminate upon what possible means he could suggest, to restore to himself the tranquillity of indifference.

The confusion of Camilla persuaded him she thought she was acting wrong; but whether from disapprobation of the character of the Major, or from any pecuniary obstacles to their union, he could not devise. To assist the marriage according to his former plan, would best, he still believed, sooth his internal sufferings, if once he could fancy the Major at all worthy of such a wife. But Camilla, with all her inconsistencies, he thought a treasure unequalled: and to contribute to bestow her on a man who, probably, only prized her for her beauty, he now persuaded himself would rather be culpable than generous.

Upon the whole, therefore, he could resolve only upon a complete change of his last system; to seek, instead of avoiding her; to familiarise himself with her faults, till he ceased to doat upon her virtues; to discover if her difficulties were mental or worldly; to enforce them if the first, and . . . whatever it might cost him—to invalidate them if the last.

This plan, the only one he could form, abated his misery. It reconciled him to residing where Camilla resided, it was easy to him, therefore, to conclude it the least objectionable.

*   *   *   *

Camilla, meanwhile, in her way to Mount Pleasant, spoke not a syllable. Dismay that Edgar should have seen her so situated, while in ignorance how it had happened, made an uneasiness the most terrible combat the perplexed pleasure, that lightened, yet palpitated in her bosom, from the view of Edgar at Tunbridge, and from the sigh which had reached her ears. Yet, was it for her he sighed? was it not, rather, from some secret inquietude, in which she was wholly uninterested, and might never know? Still, however, he was at Tunbridge; still, therefore, she might hope something relative to herself induced his coming; and she determined, with respect to her own behaviour, to observe the injunctions of her father, whose letter she would regularly read every morning.

Mrs. Arlbery, also, spoke not; the unexpected sight of Mandlebert occupied all her thoughts; yet, though his confusion was suspicious, she could not, ultimately, believe he loved Camilla, as she could suggest no possible impediment to his proclaiming any regard he entertained. His sigh she imagined as likely to be mere lassitude as love; and supposed, that having long discovered the partiality of Camilla, his vanity had been confounded by the devoirs of the Major.

Miss Dennel, therefore, was the only one whose voice was heard during the ride; for now completely awaked, she talked without cessation of the fright she had endured. 'La, I thought,' cried she, 'when I tumbled down, somebody threw me down on purpose, and was going to kill me! dear me! I thought I should have died! And then I thought it was a robber; and then I thought that candle that come was a ghost! O la! I never was so frightened in my life!'

*   *   *   *

The next morning they went, as usual, to the Pantiles, and Mrs. Arlbery took her seat in the bookseller's shop, where the usual beaux were encountered; and where, presently, Edgar entering, addressed to her some discourse, and made some general inquiries after the health of Camilla.

It was a cruel drawback to her hopes to see him first thus in public: but the manner of Mrs. Arlbery at the hotel, he had thought repulsive; he had observed that she seemed offended with him since the rencounter at the breakfast given for Miss Dennel; and he now wished for some encouragement for renewing his rights to the acquaintance.

Sir Sedley, though with the assistance of a stick he had reached the library, was not sufficiently at his ease to again mount his horse; a carriage expedition was therefore agitating for the morning, and to see Knowle[1] being fixed upon, equipages and horses were ordered.

While they waited their arrival. Lady Alithea Selmore, and a very shewy train of ladies and gentlemen, came into the library. Sir Sedley, losing the easy, natural manner which had just so much pleased Camilla, resumed his affectation, indolence, and inattention, and flung himself back in his chair, without finishing a speech he had begun, or listening to an inquiry why he stopt short. His friends, Lord Newford and Sir Theophilus Jarard, shuffled up to her ladyship; and Sir Sedley, muttering to himself life would not be life without being introduced to her, got up, and seizing Lord Newford by the shoulder, whispered what he called the height of his ambition, and was presented without delay.

He then entered into a little abrupt, half articulated conversation with Lady Alithea, who, by a certain toss of the chin, a short and half scornful laugh, and a supercilious dropping of the eye, gave to every sentence she uttered the air of a *bon mot;* and after each, as regularly stopt for some testimony of admiration, as a favourite actress in some scene in which every speech is applauded. What she said, indeed, had no other mark than what this manner gave to it; for it was neither good nor bad, wise nor foolish, sprightly nor dull. It was what, if naturally spoken, would have passed, as it deserved, without censure or praise. This manner, however, prevailed not only upon her auditors, but herself, to believe that something of wit, of *finesse*, of peculiarity, accompanied her every phrase. Thought, properly speaking, there was none in any thing she pronounced: her speeches were all replies, which her admirers dignified by the name of repartees, and which mechanically and regularly flowed from some word, not idea, that preceded.

Mrs. Arlbery, having listened some time, turned entirely away, though with less contempt of her ladyship than of her hearers. Her own auditors, however, except the faithful General, had all deserted her. Even the Major, curious to attend to a lady of some celebrity, had quitted the chair of Camilla; and Edgar himself, imagining, from this universal devotion, there was something well worth an audience, had joined the group.

'We are terribly in the back ground, General!' cried Mrs. Arlbery, in a low voice. 'What must be done to save our reputations?'

The General, laughing, said, he feared they were lost irretrievably; but added that he preferred defeat with her, to victory without her.

'Your gallantry, my dear General,' cried she, with a sudden air of glee, 'shall be rewarded! Follow me close, and you shall see the fortune of the day reversed.'

Rising then, she advanced softly, and with an air of respect, towards the party, and fixing herself just opposite to Lady Alithea, with looks of the most profound attention, stood still, as if in admiring expectation.

Lady Alithea, who had regarded this approach as an intrusion that strongly manifested ignorance of high life, thought much better of it when she remarked the almost veneration of her air. She deemed it, however, wholly beneath her to speak when thus attended to; till, observing the patient admiration with which even a single word seemed to be hoped for, she began to pardon what appeared to be a mere tribute to her fame; and upon Sir Theophilus Jarard's saying, 'I don't think we have had such a bore of a season as this, these five years;' could not refuse herself the pleasure of replying: 'I did not imagine, Sir Theophilus, you were already able to count by lustres.'

Her own air of complacency announced the happiness of this answer. The company, as usual, took the hint, and approbation was buzzed around her. Lord Newford gave a loud laugh, without the least conception why; and Sir Theophilus, after paying the same compliment, wished, as it concerned himself, to know what had been said; and glided to the other end of the shop, to look for the word lustre in Entick's dictionary.[1]

But this triumph was even less than momentary; Mrs. Arlbery, gently raising her shoulders with her head, indulged herself in a smile that favoured yet more of pity than derision; and, with a hasty glance at the General, that spoke an eagerness to compare notes with him, hurried out of the shop; her eyes dropt, as if fearful to trust her countenance to an instant's investigation.

Lady Alithea felt herself blush. The confusion was painful and unusual to her. She drew her glove off and on; she dabbed a highly scented pocket handkerchief repeatedly to her nose; she wondered what it was o'clock; took her watch in her hand, without recollecting to examine it; and then wondered if it would rain, though not a cloud was to be discerned in the sky.

To see her thus completely disconcerted, gave a weight to the mischievous malice of Mrs. Arlbery, of which the smallest presence of mind would have robbed it. Her admirers, one by one, dwindled away, with lessened esteem for her talents; and, finding herself presently alone in the shop with Sir Theophilus Jarard, she said, 'Pray, Sir Theophilus, do you know anything of that queer woman?'

The words *queer woman* were guides sufficient to Sir Theophilus, who answered, 'No! I have seen her, somewhere, by accident, but—she is quite out of our line.'

This reply was a sensible gratification to Lady Alithea, who, having heard her warmly admired by Lord O'Lerney, had been the more susceptible to her ridicule. Rudeness she could have despised without emotion; but contempt had something in it of insolence; a commodity she held herself born to dispense, not receive.

*   *   *   *

When Mrs. Arlbery arrived, laughing, at the bottom of the Pantiles, she found Edgar making inquiries of the time and manner of drinking the mineral water.[1]

Camilla heard him, also, and with deep apprehensions for his health. He did not however look ill; and a second sadness, not less deep, ensued, that she could now retain no hope of being herself his inducement to this journey.

But egotism was no part of her composition; when she saw, therefore, the next minute, Sir Sedley Clarendel advance limping, and heard him ask if his phaeton were ready, she approached him, saying, 'Will you venture, Sir Sedley, in your phaeton?'

'There's no sort of reason why not,' answered he, sensibly flattered; 'yet I had certainly rather go as you go!'

'Then that,' said Mrs. Arlbery, 'must be in Dennel's coach, with him and my little niece here: and then I'll drive the General in your phaeton.'

'Agreed!' cried Sir Sedley, seating himself on one of the forms; and then, taking from a paper some tickets, added; 'I want a few guineas.'

'So do I!' exclaimed Mrs. Arlbery; 'do you know where such sort of things are to be met with?'

'Lady Alithea Selmore has promised to disperse some twenty tickets for the master of the ceremonies' ball,[1] and she commands me to help. How many shall I give you?'

'Ask Mr. Dennel,' answered she negligently; 'he's the only paymaster just now.'

Mr. Dennel turned round, and was going to walk away; but Mrs. Arlbery, taking him by the arm, said: 'My good friend, how many tickets shall Sir Sedley give you?'

'Me!—none at all.'

'O fie! every body goes to the master of the ceremonies' ball. Come, you shall have six. You can't possibly take less.'

'Six! What should I do with them?'

'Why, you and your daughter will use two, and four you must give away.'

'What for?'

'Was ever such a question? To do what's proper and right, and handsome and gallant.'

'O, as to all that, it's what I don't understand. It's out of my way.'

He would then have made off; but Mrs. Arlbery, piqued to succeed, held him fast, and said: 'Come, if you'll be good, I'll be good too, and you shall have a plain joint of meat at the bottom of the table every day for a fortnight.'

Mr. Dennel softened a little here into something like a smile; and drew two guineas from his purse; but more there was no obtaining.

'Come,' cried Sir Sedley, 'you have canvassed well so far. Now for your fair self.'

'You are a shocking creature!' cried she; 'don't you know I am turned miser?'

Yet she gave her guinea.

'But the fair Tyrolda does not also, I trust, assume that character?'

Camilla had felt very uneasy during this contest; and now, colouring, said she did not mean to go to the ball.

'Can you ever expect, then,' said Mrs. Arlbery, 'to have a partner at any other? You don't know the rules of these places. The master of the ceremonies is always a gentleman, and every body is eager to shew him every possible respect.'

Camilla was now still more distressed; and stammered out, that she believed the fewer balls she went to, the better her father would be pleased.

'Your father, my dear, is a very wise man, and a very good man, and a very excellent preacher: but what does he know of Tunbridge Wells? Certainly not so much as my dairy maid, for she has heard John talk of them; but as to your father, depend upon it, the sole knowledge he has ever obtained, is from some treatise upon its mineral waters; which, very possibly, he can analyse as well as a physician: but for the regulation of a country dance, be assured he will do much better to make you over to Sir Sedley, or to me.'

Camilla laughed faintly, and feeling in her pocket to take out her pocket handkerchief, by way of something to do, Mrs. Arlbery concluded she was seeking her purse, and suddenly putting her hand upon her arm to prevent her, said, 'No, no! if you don't wish to go, or choose to go, or approve of going, I cannot, in sober earnestness, see you compelled. Nothing is so detestable as forcing people to be amused. Come, now for Knowle.'

Sir Sedley was then putting up his tickets; but the Major, taking one of them out of his hand, presented it to Camilla, saying: 'Let the ladies take their tickets now, and settle with us afterwards.'

Camilla felt extremely provoked, yet not knowing how to resist, took the ticket; but, turning pointedly from the Major to Sir Sedley, said: 'I am your debtor, then, sir, a guinea—the smallest part, indeed, of what I owe you, though all I can pay!' And she then resolved to borrow that sum immediately of Mrs. Arlbery.

Sir Sedley began to think she grew handsomer every moment:

and, contrary to his established and systematic inattention, upon hearing the sound of the carriages, conducted her himself to Mr. Dennel's coach, which he ascended after her.

Edgar, unable to withstand joining the party, had ordered his horse during the debate about the tickets.

Lords O'Lerney and Newford, and Sir Theophilus Jarard, and Major Cerwood, went also on horseback.

Sir Sedley made it his study to procure amusement for Camilla during the ride; and while he humoured alternately the loquacious folly of Miss Dennel, and the under-bred positiveness of her father, intermingled with both comic sarcasms against himself, and pointed annotations upon the times, that somewhat diverted her solicitude and perplexity.

She forgot them however, more naturally, in examining the noble antique mansion, pictures, and curiosities of Knowle; and in paying the tribute that taste must ever pay to the works exhibited there of Sir Joshua Reynolds.[1]

The house viewed, they all proceeded to the park, where, enchanted with the noble old trees which venerably adorn it, they strolled delightedly, till they came within sight of an elegant white form, as far distant as their eyes could reach, reading under an oak.

Camilla instantly thought of her moonlight friend; but Sir Theophilus called out, 'Faith, there's the divine Berlinton!'

'Is there, faith?' exclaimed Lord Newford, suddenly rushing forward to satisfy himself if it were true.

Deeming this an ill-bred and unauthorised intrusion, they all stopt. The studious fair, profoundly absorbed by her book, did not hear his lordship's footsteps, till his coat rustled in her ears. Raising then her eyes, she screamed, dropt her book, and darting up, flew towards the wood, with a velocity far exceeding his own, though without seeming to know, or consider, whither her flight might lead her.

Camilla, certain now this was her new friend, felt an indignation the most lively against Lord Newford, and involuntarily sprung forward. It was evident the fair fugitive had perceived none of the party but him she sought to avoid; notwithstanding Lord Newford himself, when convinced who it was, ceased his pursuit, and seemed almost to find out there was such a sensation as shame; though by various antics, of swinging his cane, looking up in the air, shaking his pocket handkerchief, and sticking his arms a-kimbo, he thought it essential to his credit to disguise it.

Camilla had no chance to reach the flying beauty, but by calling to her to stop; which she did instantly at the sound of her voice, and, turning round with a look of rapture, ran into her arms.

The Major, whose devoirs to Camilla always sought, not avoided the public eye, eagerly pursued her. Edgar, cruelly envying a licence he concluded to result from his happy situation, looked on in silent amaze; but listened with no small attention to the remarks that now fell from Mrs. Arlbery, who said she was sure this must be the fair Incognita that Miss Tyrold had met with upon the road; and gave a lively relation of that adventure.

He could not hear without delight the benevolent courage thus manifested by Camilla, nor without terror the danger to which it might have exposed her. But Lord O'Lerney, with an air of extreme surprise, exclaimed: 'Is it possible Lord Newford could give any cause of alarm to Mrs. Berlinton?'

'Is she then, my lord, a woman of character?' cried Mrs. Arlbery.

'Untainted!' he answered solemnly; 'as spotless, I believe, as her beauty: and if you have seen her, you will allow that to be no small praise. She comes from a most respectable family in Wales, and has been married but a few months.'

'Married, my lord? my fair female Quixote[1] assured me she was single.'

'No, poor thing! she was carried from the nursery to the altar, and, I fear, not very judiciously nor happily.'

'Dear!' cried Miss Dennel, 'i'n't she happy?'

'I never presume to judge,' answered his lordship, smiling; 'but she has always something melancholy in her air.'

'Pray how old is she?' said Miss Dennel.

'Eighteen.'

'Dear! and married?—La! I wonder what makes her unhappy!'

'Not a husband, certainly!' said Mrs. Arlbery, laughing, 'that is against all chance and probability.'

'Well, I'm resolved when I'm married myself, I won't be unhappy.'

'And how will you help it?'

'O, because I'm determined I won't. I think it's very hard if I may'nt have my own way when I'm married.'

"Twill at least be very singular!' answered Mrs. Arlbery.

Camilla now returned to her party, having first conducted her new friend towards a door in the park where her carriage was waiting.

'At length, my dear,' said Mrs. Arlbery, 'your fair mysterious has, I suppose, avowed herself?'

'I made no inquiry,' answered she, painfully looking down.

'I can tell you who she is, then, myself,' said Miss Dennel; 'she is Mrs. Berlinton, and she's come out of Wales, and she's married, and she's eighteen.'

'Married!' repeated Camilla, blushing from internal surprise at the conversations she had held with her.

'Yes; your fair Incognita is neither more nor less,' said Mrs. Arlbery, 'than the honourable Mrs. Berlinton, wife to Lord Berlinton's brother, and, next only to Lady Alithea Selmore, the first toast, and the reigning cry of the Wells for this season.'

Camilla, who had seen and considered her in almost every other point of view, heard this with less of pleasure than astonishment. When a further investigation brought forth from Lord O'Lerney that her maiden name was Melmond, Mrs. Arlbery exclaimed: 'O, then, I cease to play the idiot, and wonder! I know the Melmonds well. They are all half crazy, romantic, love-lorn, studious, and sentimental. One of them was in Hampshire this summer, but so immensely "melancholy and gentleman-like*,"[1] that I never took him into my society.'

"Twas the brother of this young lady, I doubt not,' said Lord O'Lerney; 'he is a young man of very good parts, and of an exemplary character; but strong in his feelings, and wild in pursuit of whatever excites them.'

'When will you introduce me to your new friend, Miss Tyrold?' said Mrs. Arlbery; 'or, rather,' (turning to Lord Newford,) 'I hope your lordship will do me that honour; I hear you are very kind to her; and take much care to convince her of the ill effects and danger of the evening air.'

'O hang it! O curse it!' cried his lordship; 'why does a woman walk by moon-light?'

'Why, rather, should man,' said Lord O'Lerney, 'impede so natural a recreation?'

The age of Lord O'Lerney, which more than doubled that of Lord Newford, made this question supported, and even drew

*Ben Jonson

forth the condescension of an attempted exculpation. 'I vow, my lord,' he cried, 'I had no intention but to look at a letter; and that I thought, she only read in public to excite curiosity.'

'O but you knelt to her!' cried Miss Dennel, 'you knelt to her! I saw you! and why did you do that, when you knew she was married, and you could not be her lover?'

The party being now disposed to return to the Wells, Mrs. Arlbery called upon the General to attend her to the phaeton. Camilla, impatient to pay Sir Sedley, followed to speak to her; but, not aware of her wish, Mrs. Arlbery hurried laughingly on, saying, 'Come, General, let us be gone, that the coach may be last, and then Dennel must pay the fees! That will be a good guinea towards my ponies!'

CHAPTER V

Mount Pleasant

THE shame and distress natural to every unhackneyed mind, in any necessity of soliciting a pecuniary favour, had now, in that of Camilla, the additional difficulty of coping against the avowed desire of Mrs. Arlbery not to open her purse.

When they arrived at Mount Pleasant, she saw all the horsemen alighted, and in conversation with that lady; and Edgar move towards the carriage, palpably with a design to hand her out: but as the Major advanced, he retreated, and, finding himself unnoticed by Mrs. Arlbery, remounted his horse. Provoked and chagrined, she sprung forwards alone, and when pursued by the Major, with some of his usual compliments, turned from him impatiently and went up stairs.

Intent in thinking only of Edgar, she was not herself aware of this abruptness, till Mrs. Arlbery, following her to her chamber, said, 'Why were you so suddenly haughty to the Major, my dear Miss Tyrold? Has he offended you?'

Much surprised, she answered, no; but, forced by further questions, to be more explicit, confessed she wished to distance him,[1] as his behaviour had been remarked.

'Remarked! how? by whom?'

She coloured, and was again hardly pressed before she answered, 'Mr. Mandlebert—once—named it to me.'

'O, ho, did he?' said Mrs. Arlbery, surprised in her turn; 'why then, my dear, depend upon it, he loves you himself.'

'Me!—Mr. Mandlebert!—' exclaimed Camilla, doubting what she heard.

'Nay, why not?'

'Why not?' repeated she in an excess of perturbation; 'O, he is too good! too excelling! he sees all my faults—points them out himself—'

'Does he?' . . . said Mrs. Arlbery thoughtfully, and pausing: 'nay, then,—if so—he wishes to marry you!'

'Me, ma'am!' cried Camilla, blushing high with mingled delight at the idea, and displeasure at its free expression.

'Why, else, should he caution you against another?'

'From goodness, from kindness, from generosity!—'

'No, no; those are not the characteristics of young men who counsel young women! We all heard he was engaged to your beautiful vacant-looking cousin; but I suppose he grew sick of her. A very young man seldom likes a silly wife. It is generally when he is further advanced in life that he takes that depraved taste. He then flatters himself a fool will be easier to govern.'

She now went away to dress; leaving Camilla a new creature; changed in all her hopes, though overwhelmed with shame at the freedom of this attack, and determined to exert her utmost strength of mind, not to expose to view the secret pleasure with which it filled her.

She was, however, so absent when they met again, that Mrs. Arlbery, shaking her head, said: 'Ah, my fair friend! what have you been thinking of?'

Excessively ashamed, she endeavoured to brighten up. The General and Sir Sedley had been invited to dinner. The latter was engaged in the evening to Lady Alithea Selmore, who gave tea at her own lodgings. 'The Rooms, then, will be quite empty,' said Mrs. Arlbery; 'so we had better go to the play.'

Mr. Dennel had no objection, and Sir Sedley promised to attend them, as it would be time enough for her ladyship afterwards.

*   *   *   *

So completely was Camilla absorbed in her new ideas, that she forgot both her borrowed guinea, and the state of her purse, till she arrived at the theatre. The recollection was then too late; and she had no resource against completely emptying it.

She was too happy however, at this instant, to admit any regret. The sagacity of Mrs. Arlbery she thought infallible; and the sight of Edgar in a box just facing her, banished every other consideration.

The theatre was almost without company. The assembly at Lady Alithea Selmore's had made it unfashionable, and when the play was over, Edgar found easily a place in the box.

Lord Newford and Sir Theophilus Jarard looked in just after, and affected not to know the piece was begun. Sir Sedley retired to his toilette, and Mr. Dennel to seek his carriage.

Some bills now got into the box, and were read by Sir Theophilus, announcing a superb exhibition of wild beasts for the next day, consisting chiefly of monkies who could perform various feats, and a famous ourang outang, just landed from Africa.

Lord Newford said he would go if he had but two more days to live. Sir Theophilus echoed him. Mr. Dennel expressed some curiosity; Miss Dennel, though she protested she should be frightened out of her wits, said she would not stay at home; Mrs. Arlbery confessed it would be an amusing sight to see so many representations of the dear human race; but Camilla spoke not: and scarce heard even the subject of discourse.

'You,' cried the Major, addressing her, 'will be there?'

'Where?' demanded she.

'To see this curious collection of animals.'

'It will be curious, undoubtedly,' said Edgar, pleased that she made no answer; 'but 'tis a species of curiosity not likely to attract the most elegant spectators; and rather, perhaps, adapted to give pleasure to naturalists, than to young ladies.'

Softened, at this moment, in every feeling of her heart towards Edgar, she turned to him, and said, 'Do you think it would be wrong to go?'

'Wrong,' repeated he, surprised though gratified, 'is perhaps too hard a word; but, I fear, at an itinerant show, such as this, a young lady would run some chance of finding herself in a neighbourhood that might seem rather strange to her.'

'Most certainly then,' cried she, with quickness, 'I will not go!'

The astonished Edgar looked at her with earnestness, and saw the simplicity of sincerity on her countenance. He looked then at the Major; who, accustomed to frequent failures in his solicitations, exhibited no change of features. Again he looked at Camilla, and her eyes met his with a sweetness of expression that passed straight to his heart.

Mrs. Arlbery now led the way to the coach; the forwardness of the Major, though in her own despight,[1] procured him the hand of Camilla; but she had left upon Edgar an impression renovating to all his esteem. She is still, he thought, the same; candid, open, flexible; still, therefore, let me follow her, with such counsel as I am able to give. She has accused me of unkindness;—She was right! I retreated from her service at the moment when, in honour, I was bound to continue in it. How selfish was such conduct! how like such common love as seeks only its own gratification, not the happiness or welfare of its object! Could she, though but lately so dear to me, that all the felicity of my life seemed to hang upon her, become as nothing, because destined to another? No! Her father has been my father, and so long as she retains his respected name, I will watch by her unceasingly.

*   *   *   *

In their way home, one of the horses tired, and could not be made to drag the carriage up to Mount Pleasant. They were therefore obliged to alight and walk. Mrs. Arlbery took the arm of Mr. Dennel, which she did not spare, and his daughter, almost crying with sleep and fatigue, made the same use of Camilla's. She protested she had never been so long upon her feet in her life as that very morning in Knowle Park, and, though she leant upon her companion with as little scruple as upon a walking stick, she frequently stopt short, and declared she should stay upon the road all night, for she could not move another step: and they were still far from the summit, when she insisted upon sitting down, saying fretfully, 'I am sure I wish I was married! Nobody minds me. I am sure if I was, I would not be served so. I'm resolved I'll always have two coaches, one to come after me, and one to ride in; for I'm determined I won't marry a man that has not a great fortune. I'm sure papa could afford it too, if he'd a mind; only he won't. Every body vexes me. I'm sure I'm ready to cry!'

Mr. Dennel and Mrs. Arlbery, who neither of them, at any time, took the smallest notice of what she said, passed on, and left the whole weight both of her person and her complaints to Camilla. The latter, however, now reached the ears of a fat, tidy, neat looking elderly woman, who, in a large black bonnet, and a blue checked apron, was going their way; she approached them, and in a good-humoured voice, said: 'What! poor dear! why you seem tired to death? come, get up, my dear; be of good heart, and you shall hold by my arm; for that t'other poor thing's almost hauled to pieces.'

Miss Dennel accepted both the pity and the proposal; and the substantial arm of her new friend, gave her far superior aid to the slight one of Camilla.

'Well, and how did you like the play, my dears?' cried the woman.

'La!' said Miss Dennel, 'how should you know we were at the play?'

'O, I have a little bird,' answered she, sagaciously nodding, 'that tells me everything! you sat in the stage box?'

'Dear! so we did! How can you tell that? Was you in the gallery?'

'No, my dear, nor yet in the pit[1] neither. And you had three gentlemen behind you, besides that gentleman that's going up the Mount?'

'Dear! So we had! But how do you know? did you peep at us behind the scenes?'

'No, my dear; I never went behind the scenes. But come, I hope you'll do now, for you ha'n't much further to go.'

'Dear! how do you know that?'

'Because you live at that pretty house, there, up Mount Pleasant, that's got the little closet window.'

'La, yes! who told you so?'

'And there's a pretty cat belonging to the house, all streaked brown and black?'

'O, la!' exclaimed Miss Dennel, half screaming, and letting go her arm, 'I dare say you're a fortune-teller! Pray, don't speak to me till we get to the light!'

She now hung back, so terrified that neither Camilla could encourage, nor the woman appease her; and she was going to run down the hill, forgetting all her weariness, to seek refuge from the servants, when the woman said, 'Why what's here to do? Why see, my dear, if I must let you into the secret—you must know— but don't tell it to the world!—I'm a gentlewoman!' She then removed her checked apron, and shewed a white muslin one, embroidered and flounced.

Miss Dennel was now struck with a surprise, of which Camilla bore an equal share. Their new acquaintance appeared herself in some confusion, but having exacted a promise not to be discovered to *the world*, she told them, she lodged at a house upon Mount Pleasant, just by their's, whence she often saw them; that, having a ticket given her, by a friend, for the play, she dressed herself and went into a box, with some very genteel company, who kept their coach, and who sat her down afterwards at another friend's, where she pretended she should be fetched: 'But I do my own way,' continued she, 'and nobody knows a word of the matter: for I keep a large bonnet, and cloak, and a checked apron, and a pair of clogs, or pattens,[1] always at this friend's; and then when I have put them on, people take me for a mere common person, and I walk on, ever so late, and nobody speaks to me; and so by that means I get my pleasure, and save my money; and yet always appear like a gentlewoman when I'm known.'

She then again charged them to be discreet, saying that if this were spread to *the world*, she should be quite undone, for many ladies that took her about with them, would notice her no more. At the same time, as she wished to make acquaintance with such pretty young ladies, she proposed that they should all three meet in a walk before the house, the next morning, and talk together as if for the first time.

Camilla, who detested all tricks, declined entering into this engagement; but Miss Dennel, charmed with the ingenuity of her new acquaintance, accepted the appointment.

*   *   *   *

Camilla had, however, her own new friend for the opening of the next day. 'Ah! my sweet protectress!' cried she, throwing her arms about her neck, 'what am I not destined to owe you? The very sight of that man is horror to me. Amiable, generous creature! what a sight was yours, when turning round, I met your eyes, and beheld him no more!'

'Your alarm, at which I cannot wonder,' said Camilla, 'prevented your seeing your safety; for Lord Newford was with a large party.'

'O, he is obnoxious to my view! wherever I may see him, in public or in private, I shall fly him. He would have torn from me the loved characters of my heart's best correspondent!—'

Camilla now felt a little shocked, and colouring and interrupting her, said: 'Is it possible, Mrs. Berlinton—' and stopt not knowing how to go on.

'Ah! you know me, then! You know my connexions and my situation!' cried she, hiding her face on Camilla's bosom: 'tell me, at least, tell me, you do not therefore contemn and abhor me?'

'Heaven forbid!' said Camilla, terrified at such a preparation; 'what can I hear that can give you so cruel an idea?'

'Alas! know you not I have prophaned at the altar my plighted vows to the most odious of men? That I have formed an alliance I despise? and that I bear a name I think of with disgust, and hate ever to own?'

Camilla, thunderstruck, answered; 'No, indeed! I know nothing of all this!'

'Ah! guard yourself, then, well,' cried she, bursting into tears, 'from a similar fate! My friends are kind and good, but the temptation of seeing me rich beguiled them. I was disinterested and contented myself, but young and inexperienced; and I yielded to their pleadings, unaware of their consequences. Alas! I was utterly ignorant both of myself and the world! I knew not how essential to my own peace was an amiable companion; and I knew not, then,—that the world contained one just formed to make me happy!'

She now hung down her head, weeping and desponding. Camilla sought to sooth her, but was so amazed, so fearful, and so perplext, she scarce knew what either to say or to think.

The fair mourner, at length, a little recovering, added: 'Let me not agitate your gentle bosom with my sorrows. I regard you as an angel sent to console them; but it must be by mitigating, not partaking of them.'

Camilla was sensibly touched; and though strangely at a loss what to judge, felt her affections deeply interested.

'I dreaded,' she continued, 'to tell you my name, for I dreaded to sink myself into your contempt, by your knowledge of an

alliance you must deem so mercenary. 'Twas folly to hope you
would not hear it; yet I wished first to obtain, at least, your good
will. The dear lost name of Melmond is all I love to pronounce!
That name, I believe, is known to you; so may be, also, perhaps,
my brother's unhappy story?'

Melmond, she then said, believing Miss Lynmere betrothed to
Mr. Mandlebert, had quitted Hampshire in misery, to finish his
vacation in Wales, with their mutual friends. There he heard that
the rumour was false; and would instantly have returned and
thrown himself at the feet of the young lady, by whose cousin, Mr.
Lionel Tyrold, he had been told she was to inherit a large
fortune; when this second report, also, was contradicted, and he
learnt that Miss Lynmere had almost nothing; 'My brother,'
added she, 'with the true spirit of true sentiment, was but the
more urgent to pursue her; but our relations interfered—and he,
like me, is doomed to endless anguish!'

The accident, she said, of the preceding morning, was owing to
her being engaged in reading Rowe's letters from the dead to the
living;[1] which had so infinitely enchanted her, that, desiring to
peruse them without interruption, yet fearing to again wander in
search of a rural retreat, she had driven to Knowle; where,
hearing the noble family[2] was absent, she had asked leave to view
the park, and there had taken out her delicious book, which she was
enjoying in the highest luxury of solitude and sweet air, when
Lord Newford broke in upon her.

Camilla enquired if she feared any bad consequences, by telling
Mr. Berlinton of his impertinence.

'Heaven forbid,' she answered, 'that I should be condemned to
speak to Mr. Berlinton of anything that concerns or befalls me! I
see him as little as I am able, and speak to him as seldom.'

Camilla heard this with grief, but durst not further press a
subject so delicate. They continued together till noon, and then
reluctantly parted, upon a message from Mrs. Arlbery that the
carriages were waiting. Mrs. Berlinton declined being introduced
to that lady, which would only, she said, occasion interruptions to
their future *tête-à-têtes*.

Neither the thoughtlessness of the disposition, nor the gaiety of
the imagination of Camilla, could disguise from her understanding
the glaring eccentricity of this conduct and character: but she saw
them with more of interest than blame; the various attractions

with which they were mixed, blending in her opinion something between pity and admiration, more captivating, though more dangerous, to the fond fancy of youth, than the most solid respect, and best founded esteem.

CHAPTER VI

The accomplished Monkies

WHEN Camilla descended, she found Sir Sedley Clarendel and General Kinsale in attendance; and saw, from the parlour window, Miss Dennel sauntering before the house, with the newly made acquaintance of the preceding evening.

The Baronet, who was to drive Mrs. Arlbery, enquired if Camilla would not prefer, also, an open carriage. Mrs. Arlbery seconded the motion. Miss Dennel, then, running to her father, exclaimed, 'Pray, papa, let's take this lady I've been talking with in the coach with us. She's the good-naturedest creature I ever knew.'

'Who is she? what's her name?'

'O, I don't know that, papa; but I'll go and ask her.'

Flying then back, 'Pray, ma'am,' she cried, 'what's your name? because papa wants to know.'

'Why, my dear, my name's Mittin. So you may think of me when you put on your gloves.'

'Papa, her name's Mittin,' cried Miss Dennel, scampering again to her father.

'Well, and who is she?'

'O, la, I'm sure I can't tell, only she's a gentlewoman.'

'And how do you know that?'

'She told me so herself.'

'And where does she live?'

'Just by, papa, at that house you see there.'

'O, well, if she's a neighbour, that's enough. I've no more to say.'

'O, then, I'll ask her!' cried Miss Dennel, jumping, 'dear! I'm so glad! 'twould have been so dull, only papa and I. I'm resolved, when I've a house of my own, I'll never go alone any where with papa.'

This being muttered, the invitation was made and accepted, and the parties set forward.

The ride was perfectly pleasing to Camilla, now revived and chearful; Sir Sedley was free from airs; Mrs. Arlbery drew them into conversation with one another, and none of them were glad when Mr. Dennel, called 'stop! or you'll drive too far.'

Camilla, who, supposing she was going, as usual, to the Pantiles, had got into the phaeton without inquiry; and who, finding afterwards her mistake, concluded they were merely taking an airing, now observed she was advancing towards a crowd, and presently perceived a booth, and an immense sign hung out from it, exhibiting a man monkey, or ourang outang.

Though excessively fluttered, she courageously, and at once, told Mrs. Arlbery she begged to be excused proceeding.

Mrs. Arlbery, who had heard, at the play, the general objections of Mandlebert, though she had not attended to her answer, conjectured her reason for retreating, and laughed, but said she would not oppose her.

Camilla then begged to wait in Mr. Dennel's carriage, that she might keep no one else from the show. Sir Sedley, saying it would be an excruciatingly vulgar sight, proposed they should all return; but she pleaded strongly against breaking up the party, though, while she was handed out, to go back to the coach, the Dennels and Mrs. Mittin had alighted, and it had driven off.

The chagrin of Camilla was so palpable, that Mrs. Arlbery herself agreed to resign the scheme; and Sir Sedley, who drew up to them, said he should rejoice in being delivered from it: but Miss Dennel, who was waiting without the booth for her aunt, was ready to cry at the thought of losing the sight, which Mrs. Mittin had assured her was extremely pretty; and, after some discussion, Camilla was reduced to beg she might do no mischief, and consent to make one.

A more immediate distress now occurred to her; she heard Mr. Dennel call out to the man stationed at the entrance of the booth, 'What's to pay?' and recollected she had no money left.

'What your Honor pleases,' was the answer, 'but gentlefolks gives half-a-crown.'

'I'm sure it's well worth it,' said Mrs. Mittin, 'for it's one of the most curious things you ever saw. You can't give less, sir.' And she passed nimbly by, without paying at all: but added, 'I had a ticket the first day, and now I come every day for nothing, if it don't rain, for one only need to pay at first.'

Mr. Dennel and his daughter followed, and Camilla was beginning a hesitating speech to Mrs. Arlbery, as that lady, not attending to her, said to Mr. Dennel: 'Well, frank me also; but take care what you pay; I'm not at all sure I shall ever return it. All I save goes to my ponies.' And, handed by the General, she crossed the barrier; not hearing the voice of her young friend, which was timidly beseeching her to stop.

Camilla was now in extreme confusion. She put her hand into her pocket, took it out, felt again, and again brought forth the hand empty.

The Major, who was before her, and who watched her, begged leave to settle with the booth-keeper; but Camilla, to whom he grew daily more irksome, again preferred a short obligation to the Baronet, and blushingly asked if he would once more be her banker?

Sir Sedley, by no means suspecting the necessity that urged this condescension, was surprised and delighted, and almost without knowing it himself, became all that was attentive, obliging, and pleasing.

Before they were seated, the young Ensign, Mr. Macdersey, issuing from a group of gentlemen, addressed himself to Camilla, though with an air that spoke him much discomposed and out of spirits. 'I hope you are well, Miss Camilla Tyrold,' he cried; 'and have left all your family well? particularly the loveliest of your sex, that angel of beauty, the divine Miss Lynmere?'

'Except the company present!' said Mrs. Arlbery; 'always except the company present, when you talk of beauty to women.'

'I would not except even the company absent!' replied he, with warmth; but was interrupted from proceeding, by what the master of the booth called his *Consort of Musics:*[1] in which not less than twenty monkies contributed their part; one dreadfully scraping a bow across the strings of a vile kit,[2] another beating a drum, another with a fife, a fourth with a bagpipe, and the sixteen remainder striking together tongs, shovels, and pokers, by way of marrowbones and cleavers.[3] Every body stopt their ears, though no one could forbear laughing at their various contortions, and horrible grimaces, till the master of the booth, to keep them, he said, in tune, dealt about such fierce blows with a stick, that they set up a general howling, which he called the *Wocal* part of his *Consort*, not more stunning to the ear, than offensive to all humanity. The audience applauded by loud shouts, but Mrs. Arlbery, disgusted, rose to quit the booth. Camilla eagerly started up to second the motion, but her eyes still more expeditiously turned from the door, upon encountering those of Edgar; who, having met the empty coach of Mr. Dennel, had not been able to refrain from inquiring where its company had been deposited; nor, upon hearing it was at the *accomplished Monkies*, from hastening to the spot, to satisfy himself if or not Camilla had been steady to her declaration. But he witnessed at once the propriety of his advice, and its failure.

The master of the booth could not endure to see the departure of the most brilliant part of his spectators, and made an harangue, promising the company, at large, if they would submit to postponing the *Consort*, in order to oblige his friends the Quality, they should have it, with the newest squalls in taste, afterwards.

The people laughed and clapped, and Mrs. Arlbery sat down.

In a few minutes, the performers were ready for a new exhibition. They were dressed up as soldiers, who, headed by a corporal, came forward to do their exercises.

Mrs. Arlbery, laughing, told the General, as he was upon duty, he should himself take the command: the General, a pleasant, yet cool and sensible man, did not laugh less; but the Ensign, more warm tempered, and wrong headed, seeing a feather in a monkey's cap, of the same colour, by chance, as in his own, fired with hasty indignation, and rising, called out to the master of the booth: 'What do you mean by this, sir? do you mean to put an affront upon our corps?'

The man, startled, was going most humbly to protest his innocence of any such design; but the laugh raised against the Ensign amongst the audience gave him more courage, and he only simpered without speaking.

'What do you mean by grinning at me, sir?' said Macdersey; 'do you want me to cane you?'

'Cane me!' cried the man enraged, 'by what rights?'

Macdersey, easily put off all guard, was stepping over the benches, with his cane uplifted, when his next neighbour, tightly holding him, said, in a half whisper, 'If you'll take my advice, you'd a deal better provoke him to strike the first blow.'

Macdersey, far more irritated by this counsel than by the original offence, fiercely looked back, calling out 'The first blow! What do you mean by that, sir?'

'No offence, sir,' answered the person, who was no other than the slow and solemn Mr. Dubster; 'but only to give you a hint for your own good; for if you strike first, being in his own house, as one may say, he may take the law of you.'

'The law!' repeated the fiery Ensign; 'the law was made for poltroons: a man of honour does not know what it means.'

'If you talk at that rate, sir,' said Dubster, in a low voice, 'it may bring you into trouble.'

'And who are you, sir, that take upon you the presumption to give me your opinion?'

'Who am I, sir? I am a gentleman, if you must needs know.'

'A gentleman! who made you so?'

'Who made me so? why leaving off business! what would you have make me so? you may tell me if you are any better, if you come to that.'

Macdersey, of an ancient and respectable family, incensed past measure, was turning back upon Mr. Dubster; when the General, taking him gently by the hand, begged he would recollect himself.

'That's very true, sir, very true, General!' cried he, profoundly bowing; 'what you say is very true. I have no right to put myself into a passion before my superior officer, unless he puts me into it himself; in which case 'tis his own fault. So I beg your pardon, General, with all my heart. And I'll go out of the booth without another half syllable. But if ever I detect any of those monkies mocking us, and wearing our feathers, when you a'n't by, I sha'n't put up with it so mildly. I hope you'll excuse me, General.'

He then bowed to him again, and begged pardon of all the ladies; but, in quitting the booth, contemptuously said to Mr. Dubster: 'As to you, you little dirty fellow, you a'n't worth my notice.'

'Little dirty fellow!' repeated Mr. Dubster, when he was gone; 'How come you to think of that? why I'm as clean as hands can make me!'

'Come, sir, come,' said Mrs. Mittin, reaching over to him, and stroking his arm, 'don't be angry; these things will happen, sometimes, in public companies; but gentlemen should be above minding them. He meant no harm, I dare say.'

'O, as to that, ma'am,' answered Mr. Dubster proudly, 'I don't much care if he did or not: it's no odds to me. Only I don't know much what right he has to defame me. I wonder who he thinks he is that he may break the peace for nothing. I can't say I'm much a friend to such behaviour. Treating people with so little ceremony.'

'I protest,' cried Sir Sedley to Camilla, ''tis your favourite swain from the Northwick assembly! wafted on some zephyr of Hope, he has pursued you to Tunbridge. I flatter myself he has brought his last bran new cloaths to claim your fair hand at the master of the ceremonies' ball.'

'Hush! hush!' cried Camilla, in a low voice; 'he will take you literally should he hear you!'

Mr. Dubster, now perceiving her, bowed low from the place where he stood, and called out, 'How do you do, ma'am? I ask pardon for not speaking to you before; but I can't say as I see you.'

Camilla was forced to bow, though she made no answer. But he continued with his usual steadiness; 'Why, that was but a unked morning we was together so long, ma'am, in my new summer-house. We was in fine jeopardy, that's the truth of it. Pray, how does the young gentleman do as took away our ladder?'

'What a delectable acquaintance!' cried Sir Sedley; 'would you have the cruelty to keep such a treasure to yourself? present me, I supplicate!'

'O, I know you well enough, sir,' said Mr. Dubster, who over-heard him; 'I see you at the hop at the White Hart; and I believe you know me pretty well too, sir, if I may take account by your staring. Not that I mind it in the least.'

'Come, come, don't be touchy,' said Mrs. Mittin; 'can't you be good-natured, and hold your tongue? what signifies taking things amiss? It only breeds ill words.'

'That's very sensibly observed upon!' said Mr. Dennel; 'I don't know when I've heard any thing more sensibly said.'

'O, as to that, I don't take it amiss in the least,' cried Mr. Dubster; 'if the gentleman's a mind to stare, let him stare. Only I should like to know what it's for. It's no better than child's play, as one may say, making one look foolish for nothing.'

The ourang outang was now announced, and Mrs. Arlbery immediately left the booth, accompanied by her party, and speedily followed by Edgar.

Neither of the carriages were in waiting, but they would not return to the booth. Sir Sedley, to whom standing was still rather inconvenient, begged a cast[1] in the carriage of a friend, who was accidentally passing by.

Macdersey, who joined them, said he had been considering what that fellow had proposed to him, of taking the first blow, and found he could not put up with it: and upon the appearance of Mr. Dubster, who in quitting the booth was preparing, with his usual leisurely solemnity, to approach Camilla, darted forward and seizing him by the collar, exclaimed, 'Retract, sir! Retract!'

Mr. Dubster stared, at first, without speech or opposition; but being released by the Major, whom the General begged to interfere, he angrily said: 'Pray, sir, what business have you to take hold of a body in such a manner as that? It's an assault, sir, and so I can prove. And I'm glad of it; for now I can serve you as I did another gentleman once before, that I smarted out of a good ten pound out of his pocket, for a knock he gave me, for a mere nothing, just like this here pulling one by the collar, nobody knows why.'

The Major, endeavouring to quiet Macdersey, advised him to despise so low a person.

'So I will, my dear friend,' he returned, 'as soon as ever I have given him the proper chastisement for his ignorance. But I must do that first. You won't take it ill, Major.'

'I believe,' cried Mr. Dubster, holding up both his hands, 'the like of this was never heard of! Here's a gentleman, as he calls himself, ready to take away my life, with his own good will, for nothing but giving him a little bit of advice! However, it's all one to me. The law is open to all. And if any one plays their tricks upon me, they shall pay for their fun. I'm none of your tame ones to put up with such a thing for nothing. I'm above that, I promise you.'

'Don't talk, sir, don't talk!' cried Macdersey; 'it's a thing I can't bear from a mean person, to be talked to. I had a hundred thousand times rather stand to be shot at.'

'Not talk, sir? I should be glad to know what right you has to hinder me, provided I say nothing against the law? And as to being a mean person, it's more than you can prove, for I'm sure you don't know who I am, nor nothing about me. I may be a lord, for any thing you know, though I don't pretend to say I am. But as to what people take me for, that behave so out of character, it's what I sha'n't trouble my head about. They may take me for a chimney-sweeper, or they may take me for a duke; which they like. I sha'n't tell them whether I'm one or t'other, or whether I'm neither. And as to not talking, I shall hold my tongue when I think proper.'

'Ask my pardon this instant, fellow!' cried the Ensign, whom the Major, at the motion of the General, now caught by the arm, and hurried from the spot: Mrs. Mittin, at the same moment pulling away Mr. Dubster, and notably expounding to him the advantages of patience and good humour.

Mrs. Arlbery, wearied both of this squabble and of waiting, took the arm of the General, and said she would walk home; Miss Dennel lovingly held by Mrs. Mittin, with whom her father also assorted, and by whom Mr. Dubster was drawn on.

Camilla alone had no immediate companion, as the Major was occupied by the Ensign. Edgar saw her disengaged. He trembled, he wavered; he wished the Major back; he wished him still more at a distance too remote ever to return; he thought he would instantly mount his horse, and gallop towards Beech Park; but the horse was not ready, and Camilla was in sight;—and, in less than a minute, he found himself, scarce knowing how, at her side.

Camilla felt a pleasure that bounded to her heart, though the late assertions of Mrs. Arlbery prepared her to expect him. He knew not, however, what to say; he felt mortified and disappointed, and when he had uttered something scarce intelligible about the weather, he walked on in silence.

Camilla, whose present train of thoughts had no discordant tendency, broke through this strangeness herself, and said: 'How frivolous I must appear to you! but indeed I was at the very door of the booth, before I knew whither the party was going.'

'You did not, I hope, at least,' he cried, 'when you had entered it, deem me too rigid, too austere, that I thought the species, both of company and of entertainment, ill calculated for a young lady?'

'Rigid! austere!' repeated she; 'I never thought you either! never—and if once again—' she stopt; embarrassed, ashamed.

'If once again what?' cried he in a tremulous voice; 'what would Miss Camilla say?—would she again—Is there yet—What would Miss Camilla say?—'

Camilla felt confounded, both with ideas of what he meant to allude to, and what construction he had put upon her half finished sentence. Impatient, however, to clear that, 'If once more,' she cried, 'you could prevail with yourself—now and then—from time to time—to give me an hint, an idea—of what you think right—I will promise, if not a constant observance, at least a never-failing sense of your kindness.'

The revulsion in the heart, in the whole frame of Edgar, was almost too powerful for restraint: he panted for an immediate explanation of every past and every present difficulty, and a final avowal that she was either self-destined to the Major, or that he had no rival to fear: But before he could make any answer, a sudden and violent shower broke up the conference, and grouped the whole party under a large tree.

This interruption, however, had no power upon their thoughts; neither of them heard a word that was saying; each ruminated intently, though confusedly, upon what already was passed. Yet where the wind precipitated the rain, Edgar stationed himself, and held his hat to intercept its passage to Camilla; and as her eye involuntarily was caught by the shower that pattered upon his head and shoulders, she insensibly pressed nearer to the trunk of the tree, to afford more shelter to him from its branches.

The rest of the party partook not of this taciturnity: Mr. Dubster, staring Mrs. Mittin full in the face, exclaimed: 'I think I ought to know you, ma'am, asking your pardon?'

'No matter for that!' cried she, turning with quickness to Camilla; 'Lord, miss—I don't know your name,—how your poor hat is all I don't know how! as limp, and as flimzy, as if it had been in a wash-tub!'

'I've just bethought me,' continued he, 'where it was we used to see one another, and all the whole manner of it. I've got it as clear in my head as if it was but yesterday. Don't you remember—'

'Can't you stand a little out, there?' interrupted she; 'what signifies a man's old coat? don't you see how you let all the rain come upon this young lady? you should never think of yourself, but only of what you can do to be obliging.'

'A very good rule, that! a very good one indeed!' said Mr. Dennel; 'I wish everybody would mind it.'

'I'm as willing to mind it, I believe,' said Mr. Dubster, 'as my neighbours; but as to being wet through, for mere complaisance, I don't think it fair to expect such a thing of nobody. Besides, this is not such an old coat as you may think for. If you was to see what

I wear at home, I promise you would not think so bad of it. I don't say it's my best; who'd be fool then, to wear it every day? However, I believe it's pretty nigh as good as that I had on that night I saw you at Mrs. Purdle's, when, you know, one of your pattens—'

'Come, come, what's the man talking about? one person should not take all the conversation up so. Dear miss . . . do tell me your name? . . . I am so sorry for your hat, I can't but think of it; it looks as dingy! . . .'

'Why, now, you won't make me believe,' said Mr. Dubster, 'you've forgot how your patten broke; and how I squeezed my finger under the iron?[1] And how I'd like to have lost the use of it? There would have been a fine job! And how Mrs. Purdle . . . .'

'I'm sure the shower's over,' cried Mrs. Mittin, 'and if we stay here, we shall have all the droppings of the leaves upon us. Poor miss thing-o-me's[2] hat is spoilt already. There's no need to make it worse.'

'And how Mrs. Purdle,' he continued, 'was obliged to lend you a pair of shoes and stockings, because you was wet through your feet? And how they would not fit you, and kept tumbling off? And how, when somebody come to fetch you in their own coach, you made us say you was taken ill, because you was so daubed with mud and mire, you was ashamed to shew yourself? And how . . . .'

'I can't think what you are talking of,' said Mrs. Mittin; 'but come, let's you and I go a little way on, to see if the rain's over.' She then went some paces from the tree, and said: 'What signifies running on so, Mr. Dubster, about things nobody knows any thing of? It's tiring all the company to death. You should never talk about your own fingers, and hap-hazards, to genteel people. You should only talk about agreeable subjects as I do. See how they all like me! That gentleman brought me to the monkies in his own coach.'

'As to that,' answered he, gravely, 'I did not mean, in the least, to say anything disagreeable; only I thought it odd you should not seem to know me again, considering Mrs. Purdle used——'

'Why you've no nous, Mr. Dubster; Mrs. Purdle's a very good sort of woman and the best friend I have in the world, perhaps, at the bottom; but she i'n't a sort of person to talk of before gentlefolks. You should talk to great people about their own affairs, and what you can do to please them, and find out how you can serve them, if you'd be treated genteelly by them, as I am. Why, I go every where, and see every thing, and it costs me nothing. A friend, a lady of great fashion, took me one day to the monkies, and paid for me; and I've gone since, whenever I will, for nothing.'

'Nobody treats me to nothing,' answered he, in a melancholy voice, 'whatever's the reason: except when I make friends with somebody that can let me in free, sometimes. And I get a peep, now and then, at what goes forward, that way.'

'But you are rich enough to pay for yourself now, Mr. Dubster; good lack! if I had such a fortune as yours, I'd go all the world over, and thanks to nobody.'

'And how long would you be rich then, Mrs. Mittin? Who'd give you your money again when you'd spent it? I got mine hard enough. I sha'n't fool it away in a hurry, I promise you!'

'I can't say I see that, Mr. Dubster, when two of your wives died so soon, and left you so handsome.'

'Why, yes, I don't say to the contrary of that; but then, think of the time before, when I was 'prentice!—'

The shower was now over, and the party proceeded as before.

Edgar, uncertain, irresolute, walked on in silence: yet attentive, assiduous, even tenderly watchful to guide, guard, and assist his fair companion in her way. The name of the Major trembled perpetually upon his lips; but fear what might be the result of his inquiries stopt his speech till they approached the house; when he commanded voice to say: 'You permit, then, the renewal of my old privilege?—'

'Permit! I wish for it!'

They were now at the door. Edgar, not daring to speak again to Camilla, and not able to address any one else, took his leave; enchanted that he was authorized, once more, to inform himself with openness of the state of her affairs, and of her conduct. And Camilla, dwelling with delight upon the discernment of Mrs. Arlbery, blest the happy penetration that had endowed her with courage to speak again to Edgar in terms of friendship and confidence.

Mrs. Mittin, declaring she could not eat till she had seen what could be done for the hat of Miss Tyrold, accompanied her up-stairs, took it off herself, wiped it, smoothed, and tried to new arrange it; and, at last, failing to succeed, insisted upon taking it home, to put it in order, and promised to return it in the morning time enough for the Pantiles. Camilla was much ashamed; but she had no means to buy another, and she had now lost her indifference to going abroad. She thought, therefore, this new acquaintance at least as useful as she was officious, and accepted her civility with thanks.

CHAPTER VII

The Rooms

THE evening, as usual, was destined to the Rooms. The first object Camilla perceived upon her entrance was Edgar, and the smile with which she met his eye brought him instantly to her side. That smile was not less radiant for his nearer approach; nor was his pleasure in it less animated for observing that Major Cerwood was not of her party, nor as yet in the room. The opportunity seemed inviting to engage her himself; to suggest and to find it irresistible was the same thing, and he inquired if her whole evening were arranged, or she would go down two dances with an old friend.

The softness of her assent was even exquisite delight to him; and, as they all walked up and down the apartment, though he addressed her but little, and though she spoke but in answer, every word he uttered she received as couching some gentle meaning, and every syllable she replied, he thought conveyed something of flattering interest: and although all was upon open and unavoidable subjects, he had no eyes but for her, she had no attention but for him.

This quiet, yet heart-felt intercourse, was soon a little interrupted by the appearance of a large and striking party, led on by Lady Alithea Selmore; for which every body made way, to which every body turned, and which, passing by all the company without seeming conscious there was any to pass, formed a mass at the upper end of the room, with an air and manner of such exclusive attention to their chief, or to one another, that common observation would have concluded some film before their eyes obstructed their discerning that they were not the sole engrossers of the apartment.

But such was not the judgment formed of them by Mrs. Arlbery, who, forced by the stream to give them passage, paid herself for the condescension by a commentary upon the passengers. 'Those good people,' said she, 'strive to make us believe we are nothing to them. They strive even to believe it themselves. But this is the mere semblance worn by pride and affectation, to veil internal fatigue. They come hither to recruit their exhausted powers, not, indeed, by joining in our society, but by a view of new objects for their senses, and the flattering idea, for their minds, of the envy or admiration they excite. They are all people of some consequence, and many of them are people of title: but these are far the most supportable of the group; their privileged superiority over the rest is so marked and indisputable, that they are saved the trouble either of claiming or ascertaining it: but those who approach their rank without reaching it, live in a constant struggle to make known their importance. Indeed, I have often seen that people of title are less gratified with the sound of their own honours, than people of no title in pronouncing them.'

Sir Sedley Clarendel was of this set. Like the rest he passed Mrs. Arlbery without seeming to notice her, and was passing Camilla in the same manner; but not aware this was only to be fine, like the party to which he belonged, she very innocently spoke to him herself, to hope he got safe to his lodgings, without feeling any further ill effect from his accident.

Sir Sedley, though internally much gratified by this interest in his safety, which in Camilla was the result of having herself endangered it, looked as if he scarce recollected her, and making hastily a kind of half bow, walked on with his company.

Camilla, who had no view, nor one serious thought concerning him, was rather amused than displeased by his caprices; and was preparing to relate the history of his lameness to Edgar, who seemed surprised and even hurt by her addressing him, and by his so slightly passing her, when the entrance of another splendid party interrupted all discourse.

And here, to her utter amaze, she beheld, as chief of the group, her romantic new friend; not leading, indeed, like Lady Alithea Selmore, a train, but surrounded by admirers, who, seeking no eye but hers, seemed dim and humble planets, moving round a radiant sun.

Camilla now, forgetting Sir Sedley, would have taken this

moment to narrate her adventure with Mrs. Berlinton, had not her design been defeated by the approach of the Major. He belonged to this last group, but was the only one that separated from it. He spoke to Camilla with his usual air of devotion, told her he had dined with Mrs. Berlinton, to whose husband, whom he had taken for her grandfather, he had been just introduced; and begged to know of Mrs. Arlbery if he might have the pleasure of bringing them all acquainted; an offer which Camilla, unauthorised by Mrs. Berlinton, had not ventured to make. Mrs. Arlbery declined the proposal; not anxious to mix where she had small chance of presiding.

The party, after traversing the room, took full and exclusive possession of a considerable spot just below that occupied by Lady Alithea.

These two companies completely engrossed all attention, amply supplying the rest of the assembly with topics for discourse. The set with Lady Alithea Selmore was, in general, haughty, super-cilious, and taciturn; looking around with eyes determined to see neither any person nor any thing before them, and rarely speaking, except to applaud what fell from her ladyship; who far less proud, because a lover of popularity, deigned herself, from time to time, a slight glance at the company, to see if she was observed, and to enjoy its reverence.

The party to which Mrs. Berlinton was the loadstone, was far more attractive to the disciples of nature, though less sedulously sought by those whom the manners and maxims of the common world had sophisticated. They were gay, elegant, desirous to please, because pleased themselves; and though some of them harboured designs deeper and more dangerous than any formed by the votaries of rank, they appeared to have nothing more in view than to decorate with flowers the present moment. The magnetic influence of beauty was, however, more powerful than that of the *ton;* for though Mrs. Berlinton, from time to time, allured a beau from Lady Alithea Selmore, her ladyship, during the whole season, had not one retaliation to boast. But, on the other hand, the females, in general, strove to cluster about Lady Alithea; Mrs. Berlinton leaving them no greater chance of rival-ship in conversation than in charms.

Edgar had made way upon the approach of the Major, who wore an air of superior claim extremely unpleasant to him; but, since already engaged to Camilla, he meant to return to her when the dancing began.

She concluded he left her but to speak to some acquaintance, and was, herself, amply occupied in observing her new friend. The light in which she now beheld her, admired, pursued, and adulated, elegantly adorned in her person, and evidently with but one rival for fame and fashion in Tunbridge, filled her with astonishment. Nothing could less assort with her passion for solitude, her fondness for literary and sentimental discussions, and her enthusiasm in friendship. But her surprise was mixed with praise and admiration, when she reflected upon the soft humility, and caressing sweetness of her manners, yet found her, by general consent, holding this elevated rank in society.

The Major earnestly pressed to conduct Camilla to this coterie, assuring her Mrs. Berlinton would not have passed, had she seen her, for, during dinner, and at coffee, she had talked of nobody else. Camilla heard this with pleasure, but shrunk from all advances, and strove rather to hide than shew herself, that Mrs. Berlinton might have full liberty either to seek or avoid her. She wished to consult Edgar upon this acquaintance; though the present splendour of her appearance, and the number of her followers, made her fear she could never induce him to do justice to the sweetness and endearment of her social powers.

When the Major found he pleaded in vain, he said he would at least let Mrs. Berlinton know where to look for her; and went himself to that lady.

Edgar, who had felt sensibly mortified to observe, when he retreated, that the eyes and attention of Camilla had been wholly bestowed upon what he considered merely as a new scene, was now coming forward; when he saw Mrs. Berlinton hastily rise, suddenly break from all her adulators, and, with quick steps and animated gestures, traverse the apartment, to address Camilla, whom, taking by both her hands, which she pressed to her heart, she conjured, in the most flattering terms, to accompany her back.

Camilla was much gratified; yet, from delicacy to Mrs. Arlbery, stimulated by the fear of missing her expected partner in the country dances, declined the invitation: Mrs. Berlinton looked disappointed; but said she would not be importunate, and returned alone.

Camilla, a little disturbed, besought the Major to follow, with an offer of spending with her, if she pleased, the whole of the ensuing day.

'Charming!' cried the Major, 'for I am engaged to her myself already.'

To Camilla this hearing was distressing; to Edgar it was scarcely endurable. But she could not retract, and Edgar was stopt in the inquiries he meant to make concerning this striking new acquaintance, by an abrupt declaration from Mrs. Arlbery, that the Rooms were insufferable, and she would immediately go home. She then gave her hand to the General, and Miss Dennel took the arm of Camilla, murmuring, that she would never leave the Rooms at such an early hour again, when once she was married.

To quit Edgar thus, at the very moment of renewed intercourse and amity, seemed too cruel; and Camilla, though with blushes, and stammering, whispered Mrs. Arlbery, 'What can I do, ma'am? most unfortunately I have engaged myself to dance?'

'With whom?'

'With—Mr.—Mandlebert.'

'O, vastly well! Stay, then by all means: but, as he has not engaged me too, allow me, I beseech you, to escape. Mrs. Berlinton will, I am sure, be happy to take care of you.'

This scheme was, to Camilla, the most pleasant that could be proposed; and, at the same instant, the Major returned to her, with these words written with a pencil upon the back of a letter.

'To-morrow, and next day, and next day, come to me, my lovely friend; every thing, and every body fatigues me but yourself.'

Camilla, obliged again to have recourse to the Major, wrote, upon the same paper, 'Can you have the goodness to convey me to Mount Pleasant tonight, if I stay?' and begged him to bring her an answer. She entreated, also, Mrs. Arlbery to stop till it arrived, which was almost in the same minute; for the eye of Mrs. Berlinton had but glanced upon the words, ere her soft and lovely form was again with their fair writer, with whom, smiling and delighted, she walked back, arm in arm, to her place.

Mrs. Arlbery and the General, and Mr. and Miss Dennel, now left the room.

Edgar viewed all this with amazement. He found that the young lady she joined was sister-in-law to a peer, and as fashionable as she was beautiful; but could not fathom how so great an intimacy had so suddenly been formed.

Camilla, thus distinguished, became now herself an object of peculiar notice; her own personal claim to particular attention, her dejection had forfeited, for it had robbed her eyes of their animation, and her countenance of its play; but no contagion spreads with greater certainty nor greater speed than that of fashion; slander itself is not more sure of promulgation. She was now looked at by all present as if seen for the first time; every one discovered in her some charm, some grace, some excellence; those who, the minute before, had passed her with perfect indifference, said it was impossible to see and not be struck with her; and all agreed she could appear upon no spot under the sun, and not instinctively be singled out, as formed to shine in the highest sphere.

But he by whom this transaction was observed with most pleasure, was Sir Sedley Clarendel. The extraordinary service he had performed for Camilla, and the grateful interest she had shewn him in return, had led him to consider her with an attention so favourable, that, without half her merit, or half her beauty, she could not have failed rising in his estimation, and exciting his regard: and she had now a superior charm that distanced every other; she had been asked to dance, yet refused it, by a man of celebrity in the *ton;* and she was publicly sought and caressed by the only rival at Tunbridge, in that species of renown, to Lady Alithea Selmore.

He felt an increased desire to be presented to Mrs. Berlinton himself; and, gliding from his own circle as quietly as he could contrive, not to offend Lady Alithea, who, though she laughed at *the little Welsh rustic,* was watchful of her votaries, and jealous of her rising power, came gently behind Lord O'Lerney and whispered his request.

He was received by the young beauty with that grace, and that sweetness which rendered her so generally bewitching, yet with an air that proved her already accustomed to admiration, and untouched by its intoxicating qualities. All that was voluntary of her attention was bestowed exclusively upon Camilla, though, when addressed and called upon by others, she answered without impatience, and looked without displeasure.

This conduct, at the same time that it shewed her in a point of view the most amiable, raised Camilla higher and higher in the eyes of the by-standers: and, in a few minutes more, the general cry throughout the assembly was, to inquire who was the young lady thus brought forward by Mrs. Berlinton.

Edgar heard this with increased anxiety. Has she discretion, has she fortitude, thought he, to withstand public distinction? Will it not spoil her for private life; estrange her from family concerns? render tasteless and insipid the conjugal and maternal characters, meant by Nature to form not only the most sacred of duties, but the most delicious of enjoyments?

Very soon after, this anxiety was tinctured with a feeling more severe; he saw her spoken to negligently by Sir Sedley; he required, after what he had already himself deemed impertinence from the Baronet, that she should have assumed to him a distant dignity; but he perceived, on the contrary, that she answered him with pleasant alacrity, and, when not engaged by Mrs. Berlinton, attended to him, even with distinction.

Alas! thought he, the degradation from the true female character is already begun! already the lure of fashion draws her from what she owes to delicacy and propriety, to give a willing reception to insolence and foppery!

Camilla, meanwhile, unsuspicious of his remarks, and persuaded every civility in her power was due to Sir Sedley, was gay, pleased, and pleasing; happy to consider herself under the guidance, and restored to the amity of Edgar, and determined to acquaint him with all her affairs, and consult him upon all her proceedings.

The dancing, for which mutually they languished, as the mutual means of reunion, seemed not to be the humour of the evening, and those who were ready for it, were not of sufficient consequence to bring it forward. But when Mrs. Berlinton mentioned, that she had been taking some lessons in a cotillon,[1] a universal cry was raised by all her party, to try one immediately. She pleaded in vain her inexperience in such dances; they insisted there was nobody present that could criticise, that her form alone would compensate for every mistake of rule, and that the best lesson was easy practice.

She was soon gained, for she was not addicted to denials; but the application which ensued to Camilla was acceded to less promptly. As there were but two other ladies in the circle of Mrs. Berlinton, her assistance was declared to be indispensable. She pleaded inability of every sort, though to dance without Edgar was her only real objection; for she had no false shame in being ignorant of what she never had learnt. But Mrs. Berlinton protested she would not rise if she were the only novice to be exhibited; and the Major then prepared to prostrate himself at the feet of Camilla; who, hastily, and ashamed, stood up, to prevent an action that Edgar might misinterpret.

Hoping, however, now, to at least draw him into their set, she ventured to acknowledge to Mrs. Berlinton, that she was already engaged, in case she danced.

The Major, who heard her, and who knew it was not to himself, strenuously declared this could only be for country dances,[1] and therefore would not interfere with a cotillon.

'Will country dances, then,' said she, blushing, 'follow?'

'Certainly, if any one has spirit to begin them.'

The cotillon was now played, and the preceding bow from the opposite Major forced her courtsie in return.

The little skill in this dance of one of the performers, and the total want of it in another, made it a mere pleasantry to all, though the youth and beauty of the two who did the worst, rendered them objects of admiration, that left nearly unnoticed those who did best.

To Camilla what belonged to pleasantry in this business was of short duration. When the cotillon was over, she saw nothing of Edgar. She looked around, mortified, disappointed. No one called for a country dance; and the few who had wished for it, concluding all chance over when a cotillon was begun, had now retired, or given it up.

What was this disappointment, compared with the sufferings of Edgar? Something of a contest, and of entreaties, had reached his ears, while he had hovered near the party, or strolled up and down the room. He had gathered the subject was dancing, and he saw the Major most earnest with Camilla. He was sure it was for her hand, and concluded it was for a country dance; but could she forfeit her engagement? were matters so far advanced, as to make her so openly shew him all prevailing, all powerful, not only over all rivals, but, according to the world's established customs upon these occasions, over all decorum?

Presently, he saw the Major half kneel; he saw her rise to prevent the prostration; and he heard the dance called.

He could bear no more; pain intolerable seized, distracted him, and he abruptly quitted the ballroom, lest the Major should approach him with some happy apology, which he was unfitted to receive.

He could only settle his ideas by supposing she really loved Major Cerwood, and had suffered her character to be infected by the indelicacy that made a part of his own. Yet why had she so striven to deny all regard, all connection? what an unaccountable want of frankness! what a miserable dereliction of truth!

His first impulse was to set off instantly from Tunbridge; but his second thoughts represented the confession this would make. He was too proud to leave the Major, whom he despised, such a triumph, and too much hurt to permit Camilla herself to know him so poignantly wounded. She could not, indeed, but be struck by his retreat; he resolved, however, to try to meet with her the next day, and to speak to her with the amity they had so lately arranged, yet in a way that should manifest him wholly free from all other interest or view.

CHAPTER VIII

Ways to the Heart

ALL pleasure to Camilla was completely over from the moment that Edgar disappeared.

When she returned to Mount Pleasant, Mrs. Arlbery, whom she found alone, said, 'Did I not understand that you were going to dance with Mr. Mandlebert? How chanced he to leave you? We were kept ages waiting for the coach; and I saw him pass by, and walk off.'

Camilla, colouring, related the history of the cotillon; and said, she feared, not knowing how she had been circumstanced, he was displeased.

'Displeased!' cried Mrs. Arlbery, laughing; 'and do you, at seventeen, suffer a man to be displeased? How can you do worse when you are fifty? Know your own power more truly, and use it better. Men, my dear, are all spoilt by humility, and all conquered by gaiety. Amuse and defy them!—attend to that maxim, and you will have the world at your feet.'

'I have no such ambition: . . . but I should be sensibly hurt to make an old friend think ill of me.'

'When an old friend,' said Mrs. Arlbery, archly, 'happens to be a young man, you must conduct yourself with him a little like what you are; that is, a young woman. And a young woman is never in her proper place, if such sort of old friends are not taught to know their own. From the instant you permit them to think of being offended, they become your masters; and you will find it vastly more convenient to make them your slaves.'

Camilla pretended to understand this in a mere general sense, and wished her good night.

*   *   *   *

The next morning, at an early hour, her chamber door was opened with great suddenness, and no preparation, and Mrs. Mittin tript nimbly into the room, with a hat in her hand.

'Look here! my dear Miss Tyrold,' cried she, 'for now that other young lady has told me your name, and I writ it down upon paper, that I might not forget it again: look at your hat now! Did you ever see anything so much improved for the better? I declare nobody would know it! Miss Dennel says it's as pretty again as it was at first. I'll go and shew it to the other lady.'

Away she went, triumphant, with the trophy of her notability; but presently returned, saying, 'Do, pray, Miss Tyrold, write me down that other lady's name upon a scrap of paper. It always goes out of my head. And one looks as if one knew nobody, when, one forgets people's names.'

Camilla complied, and expressed her shame to have caused her so much trouble.

'O, my dear, it's none at all. I got all the things at Mrs. Tillden's.'

'Who is Mrs. Tillden?' cried Camilla, staring.

'Why the milliner. Don't you know that?'

'What things?' asked Camilla, alarmed.

'Why these, my dear; don't you see? Why it's all new, except just the hat itself, and the feathers.'

Camilla was now in extreme embarrassment. She had concluded Mrs. Mittin had only newly arranged the ornaments, and had not the smallest idea of incurring a debt which she had no means to discharge.

'It all comes to quite a trifle,' continued Mrs. Mittin, 'for all it's so pretty. Mrs. Tillden's things are all monstrous cheap. I get things for next to nothing from her, sometimes, when they are a little past the mode. But then I recommend her a heap of customers. I get all my friends, by hook or by crook, to go to her shop.'

'And what,' stammered out Camilla, 'besides my thanks, do I owe you?'

'Oh nothing. She would not be paid; she said, as you was her customer, and had all your things of her at first, she'd put it down in your bill for the season.'

This was, at least, some respite; though Camilla felt the disagreeable necessity of increasing her intended demand upon Mrs. Arlbery.

Miss Dennel came with a summons from that lady to the Pantiles, whither, as the day was fine, she proposed they should walk.

'O,' cried Mrs. Mittin, 'if you are going upon the Pantiles, you must go to that shop where there's the curious ear-rings that are be to raffled for. You'll put in to be sure.'

Camilla said no, with a sigh attributed to the ear-rings, but due to a tender recollection of the raffle in which Edgar had procured her the trinket she most valued. Mrs. Mittin proposed accompanying them, and asked Camilla to introduce her to Mrs. Arlbery. This was very disagreeable; but she knew not how, after the civility she owed her, to refuse.

Mrs. Arlbery received her with much surprize, but perfect unconcern; conscious of her own importance, she feared no disgrace from being seen with one in a lower station; and she conceived it no honour to appear with one in a higher.

When they came to the Pantiles, Mrs. Mittin begged to introduce them to a view of the ear-rings, which belonged, she said, to one of her particular friends; and as Mrs. Arlbery caught the eye of Sir Sedley Clarendel in passing the window, she entered the shop.

'Well,' cried Mrs. Mittin, to its master, 'don't say I bring you no company. I am sure you ought to let me throw for nothing, if it's only for good luck; for I am sure these three ladies will all put in. Come, Miss Dennel, do lead the way. 'Tis but half a guinea, and only look what a prize.'

'Ask papa to pay for me!' cried Miss Dennel.

'Come, good sir, come, put down the half guinea for the young lady. I'm sure you can't refuse her. Lord! what's half a guinea?'

'That's a very bad way of reasoning,' answered Mr. Dennel; 'and what I did not expect from a woman of your sense.'

'Why you don't think, sir, I meant that half a guinea's a trifle? No indeed! I know what money is better than that. I only mean half a guinea is nothing in comparison to ten guineas, which is the price of the ear-rings; and so that makes me think it's pity the young lady should lose an opportunity of getting them so cheap. I'm sure if they were dear, I should be the last to recommend them, for I think extravagance the greatest sin under the sun.'

'Well, now you speak like the sensible woman I took you for.'

A very little more eloquence of this sort was necessary, before Mr. Dennel put down half a guinea.

'Well, I declare,' cried Mrs. Mittin, 'there's only three more names wanted; and when these two ladies have put in, there will be only one! I'm sure if I was rich enough, that one would not be far off. But come, ma'am, where's your half guinea? Come, Miss Tyrold, don't hold back; who knows but you may win? there's only nineteen against you. Lord, what's that?'

Camilla turned away, and Mrs. Arlbery did not listen to a word; but when Sir Sedley said, 'They are really very pretty; won't you throw?' she answered, 'I must rather make a raffle with my own trinkets, than raffle for other people's. Think of my ponies! However, I'll put in, if Mr. Dennel will be my paymaster.'

Mr. Dennel, turning short off, walked out of the shop.

'This is a bad omen!' cried she, laughing; and then desired to look at the list of rafflers; when seeing amongst the names those of Lady Alithea Selmore and the Hon. Mrs. Berlinton, she exclaimed: ''Tis a coalition of all fashion and reputation! We shall be absolutely scouted,[1] my dear Miss Tyrold, if we shrink. My poor ponies must wait half a guinea longer! Let us put in together.'

Camilla answered, she had no intention to try for them.

'Well, then, lend me half a guinea; for I never trust myself, now, with my purse.'

'I have not a half guinea . . . I have . . . I have no . . . gold . . . in my purse,' answered Camilla, with a face deeply tinged with red.

Major Cerwood, who joined the party during this discussion, intreated to be banker for both the ladies. Camilla positively refused any share; but Mrs. Mittin said it would be a shame for such a young lady to go without her chance, and wrote down her name next to that of Mrs. Arlbery; while the Major, without further question, put down a guinea upon the counter.

Camilla could not endure this; yet, from a youthful shame of confessing poverty, forced herself to the ear of Mrs. Arlbery, and whispered an entreaty that she would pay the guinea herself.

Mrs. Arlbery, surprized, answered she had really come out without her purse; but seeing her seriously vexed, added, 'If you do not approve of the Major for a banker till we go home, what say you to Sir Sedley?'

'I shall prefer him a thousand times!'

Mrs. Arlbery, in a low voice, repeated this to the young Baronet, and receiving his guinea, threw it down; making the Major, without the smallest excuse or ceremony, take back his own.

This was by no means lost upon Sir Sedley; he felt flattered . . . . he felt softened; he thought Camilla looked unusually lovely; he began to wonder at the coldness of Mandlebert, and to lament that the first affections of so fair a creature should be cast away.

Mandlebert himself was an object of nothing less than envy. He had entered the shop during the contest about the raffle, and seen Major Cerwood pay for Camilla as well as for Mrs. Arlbery. Confirmed in his notions of her positive engagement, and sick at heart from the confirmation, he walked further into the shop, upon pretence of looking at some other articles, before he could assume sufficient composure to speak to her.

Mrs. Mittin now began woefully to repine that she could not take the last share for the ear-rings; and, addressing herself to Mr. Dennel, who re-entered as soon as he saw the money was paid for Mrs. Arlbery, she said, 'You see, sir, if there was somebody ready to take the last chance at once, this gentleman might fix a day for the throwing immediately; but else, it may be dawdled on, nobody knows how long; for one will be gone, and t'other will be gone, and there'll be no getting the people together; and all the pleasure of the thing is being here to throw for one's self: for I don't much like trusting money matters out of sight.'

'If I'd thought of all that,' said Mr. Dennel, 'I should not have put in.'

'True, sir. But here, if it was not that I don't happen to have half a guinea to spare just now, how nicely it might all be finished in a trice! For, as I have been saying to Miss Dennel, this may turn out a real bargain; for they'll fetch their full value at any time. And I tell Miss Dennel that's the only way to lay out money, upon things that will bring it back again if it's wanted; not upon frippery froppery,[1] that's spoilt in a minute, and then i'n't worth a farthing.'

'Very sensibly said,' cried Mr. Dennel; 'I'm sure she can't hear better advice; I'm much obliged to you for putting such sensible thoughts into her head.' And then, hoping she would continue her good lessons to his daughter, he drew out his purse, and begged her to accept a chance from it for the prize.

Mrs. Mittin was in raptures; and the following week was settled for the raffle.

Mrs. Arlbery, who had attended to this scene with much amusement, now said to General Kinsale, who had taken a seat by her: 'Did I not tell you well, General, that all men are at the disposition of women? If even the shrewd monied man cannot resist, what heart shall we find impenetrable? The connoisseur in human characters knows, that the pursuit of wealth is the petrifaction of tenderness: yet yonder is my good brother-in-law, who thinks cash and existence one, allured even to squander money, merely by the address of that woman, in allowing that money should be the first study of life! Let even Clarendel have a care of himself! or, when least he suspects any danger, some fair dairy-maid will praise his horsemanship, or take a fancy to his favourite spaniel, or any other favourite that happens to be the foible of the day, and his invulnerability will be at her feet, and Lady Clarendel be brought forward in a fortnight.'

Lord O'Lerney now entered the shop, accompanying a lady whose countenance and appearance were singularly pleasing, and who, having made some purchase, was quietly retiring, when the master of the shop inquired if she wished to look at the ear-rings; adding, that though the number was full, he knew of one person, who would give up her chance, in case it would oblige a customer.

She answered she had no present occasion for ear-rings, and would not therefore take up either his time or her own unnecessarily; and then walked gently away, still attended by Lord O'Lerney.

'Bless me,' cried Mrs. Arlbery, 'who is that? to hear a little plain common sense is so rare, it strikes one more than wit.'

'It's Lady Isabella Irby, madam,' answered the master of the shop.

Here Lord O'Lerney, who had only handed her to her carriage, returned.

'My Lord,' cried Mrs. Arlbery, 'do you know what a curiosity you brought in amongst us just now? A woman of rank who looks round upon other people just as if she thought they were her fellow creatures?'

'Fie, fie!' answered Lord O'Lerney, laughing, 'why will you suppose that so rare? If we have not as many women who are amiable with titles as without, it is only because we have not the same number from which to select them. They are spoilt or unspoilt, but in the same proportion as the rest of their sex. Their fall, or their escape, is less local than you imagine; it does not depend upon their titles, but upon their understandings.'

'Well, my lord, I believe you are right. I was adopting a narrow prejudice, merely from indolence of thought.'

'But why, my lord,' cried Sir Sedley, 'does this paragon of a divinity deny her example to the world? Is it in contempt of our incorrigibility? or in horror of our contagion?'

'My dear Sir Sedley,' said Mrs. Arlbery, 'don't flatter yourself with being so dangerous. Her ladyship does not fly you from fear, take my word for it. There is nothing in her air that looks as if she could only be good by being shut up. I dare believe she could meet you every day, yet be mistress of herself! Nevertheless, why, my lord, is she such a recluse? Why does one never see her at the Rooms?'

'Never see her there, my dear madam! she is there almost every night; only being unintruding, she is unnoticed.'

'The satire, then, my lord,' said Mrs. Arlbery, 'falls upon the company. Why is she not surrounded by volunteer admirers? Why, with a person and manner so formed to charm, joined to such a character, and such rank, has she not her train?'

'The reason, my dear madam, you could define with more sagacity than myself; she must be sought! And the world is so lazy, that the most easy of access, however valueless, is preferred to the most perfect, who must be pursued with any trouble.'

Admirable Lord O'Lerney! thought Edgar, what a lesson is this to youthful females against the glare of public homage, the false brilliancy of unfeminine popularity!

This conversation, however, which alone of any he had heard at Tunbridge promised him any pleasure, was interrupted by Mr.

Dennel, who said the dinner would be spoilt, if they did not all go home.

Camilla felt extremely vexed to quit the shop, without clearing up the history of the dance; and Edgar, seeing the persevering Major at her side as she departed, in urgency to put any species of period to his own sufferings, followed the party, and precipitately began a discourse with Lord O'Lerney upon making the tour of Europe. Camilla, for whom it was designed, intent upon planning her own defence, heard nothing that was said, till Lord O'Lerney asked him if his route would be through Switzerland, and he answered: 'My route is not quite fixed, my lord.'

Startled, she now listened, and Mrs. Arlbery, whom she held by the arm, was equally surprised, and looked to see how she bore this intimation.

'If you will walk with me to my lodgings,' replied Lord O'Lerney, 'I will shew you my own route, which may perhaps save you some difficulties. Shall you set out soon?'

'I fancy within a month,' answered Edgar; and, arm in arm, they walked away together, as Camilla and her party quitted the Pantiles for Mount Pleasant.

CHAPTER IX

Counsels for Conquest

FORTUNATELY for Camilla, no eye was upon her at this period but that of Mrs. Arlbery; her changed countenance, else, must have betrayed still more widely her emotion. Mrs. Arlbery saw it with real concern, and saying she had something to consult her about, hurried on with her alone.

Camilla scarce knew that she did, or what she suffered; the suddenness of surprise, which involved so severe a disappointment, almost stupified her faculites. Mrs. Arlbery did not utter one word by the way, and, when they arrived at home, saw her to her chamber, pressed her hand, and left her.

She now, from a sense of shame, came to her full recollection. She was convinced all her feelings were understood by Mrs. Arlbery; she thought over what her father had said upon such exposures, and hopeless of any honorable end to her suspences, earnestly wished herself back at Etherington, to hide in his revered breast her confusion and grief.

Even Mrs. Arlbery she now believed had been mistaken; Edgar appeared never to have loved her; his attentions, his kindness, had all flowed from friendship; his solicitude, his counsel had been the result of family regard.

When called to dinner, she descended with downcast eyes. She found no company invited; she felt thankful, yet abashed; and Mrs. Arlbery let her retire when the meal was over, but soon followed to beg she would prepare for the play.

She saw her hastily putting away her handkerchief, and dispersing her tears. 'Ah! my dear,' cried she, taking her hand, 'I am afraid this old friend of yours does not much contribute to make Tunbridge Wells salubrious to you!'

Camilla, affecting not to understand her, said she had never been in better health.

'Of mind, do you mean, or body?' cried Mrs. Arlbery, laughing; but seeing she only redoubled her distress, more seriously added, 'Will you suffer me, my dear Miss Tyrold, to play the old friend, also, and speak to you with openness?'

Camilla durst not say no, though she feared to say yes.

'I must content myself with a tacit compliance, if I can obtain no other. I am really uneasy to talk with you; not, believe me, from officiousness nor impertinence, but from a persuasion I may be able to promote your happiness. You won't speak, I see? And you judge perfectly right; for the less you disclaim, the less I shall torment you. Permit me, therefore, to take for granted that you are already aware I am acquainted with the state of your heart.'

Camilla, trembling, had now no wish but to fly; she fastened her eyes upon the door, and every thought was devoted to find the means of escape.

'Nay, nay, if you look frightened in sober sadness, I am gone. But shall I think less, or know less, for saying nothing? It is not speech, my dear Miss Tyrold, that makes detections: It only proclaims them.'

A sigh was all the answer of Camilla: though, assured, thus, she had nothing to gain by flight, she forced herself to stay.

'We understand one another, I see, perfectly. Let me now, then, as unaffectedly go on, as if the grand explanation had been verbally made. That your fancy, my fair young friend, has hit upon a tormentor, I will not deny; yet not upon an ingrate; for this person, little as you seem conscious of your power, certainly loves you.'

Surprised off all sort of guard, Camilla exclaimed, 'O no!—O no!'

Mrs. Arlbery smiled, but went on. 'Yes, my dear, he undoubtedly does you that little justice; yet, if you are not well advised, his passion will be unavailing; and your artlessness, your facility, and your innocence, with his knowledge, nay, his very admiration of them, will operate but to separate you.'

Glowing with opposing yet strong emotions at these words, the countenance of Camilla asked an explanation, in defiance of her earnest desire to look indifferent or angry.

'You will wonder, and very naturally, how such attractions should work as repulses; but I will be plain and clear, and you must be candid and rational, and forgive me. These attractions, my dear, will be the source of this mischief, because he sees, by their means, that you are undoubtedly at his command.'

'No, madam! no, Mrs. Arlbery!' cried Camilla, in whose pride now every other feeling was concentrated, 'he does not, cannot see it!—'

'I would not hurt you for the world, my very amiable young friend; but pardon me if I say, that not to see it—he must be blinder than I imagine him!—blinder than . . . to tell you the truth, I am much inclined to think any of his race.'

Confounded, irritated, and wounded, Camilla remained a moment silent, and then, though scarce articulately, answered: 'If such is your opinion . . . at least he shall see it . . . fancy it, I mean . . . no more! . . .'

'Keep to that resolution, and you will behold him . . . where he ought to be . . . at your feet.'

Irresistibly, though most unwillingly, appeased by this unexpected conclusion, she turned away to hide a blush in which anger had not solely a place, and suffered Mrs. Arlbery to go on.

'There is but one single method to make a man of his ruminating class know his own mind: give him cause to fear he will lose you. Animate, inspirit, inspire him with doubt.'

'But why, ma'am,' cried Camilla, in a faltering voice; 'why shall you suppose I will take any method at all?'

'The apprehension you will take none is the very motive that urges me to speak to you. You are young enough in the world to think men come of themselves. But you are mistaken, my dear. That happens rarely; except with inflamed and hot-headed boys, whose passions are in their first innocence as well as violence. Mandlebert has already given the dominion of his to other rulers, who will take more care of his pride, though not of his happiness. Attend to one who has travelled further into life than yourself, and believe me when I assert, that his bane, and yours alike, is his security.'

With a colour yet deeper than ever, Camilla resentfully repeated, 'Security!'

'Nay, how can he doubt? with a situation in life such as his . . .'

'Situation in life! Do you think he can ever suppose that would have the least, the most minute weight with me?'

'Why, it would be a very shocking supposition, I allow! but yet, somehow or other, that same sordid thing called money, does manage to produce such abundance of little comforts and pretty amusements, that one is apt . . . to half suspect . . . it may really not much add to any matrimonial aversion.'

The very idea of such a suspicion offended Camilla beyond all else that had passed; Mrs. Arlbery appeared to her indelicate, unkind, and ungenerous, and regretting she had ever seen, and repenting she had ever known her, she sunk upon a chair in a passionate burst of tears.

Mrs. Arlbery embraced her, begged her pardon a thousand times; assured her all she had uttered was the effect of esteem as well as of affection, since she saw her too delicate, and too inexperienced, to be aware either of the dangers or the advantages surrounding her; and that very far from meaning to hurt her, she had few things more at heart than the desire of proving the sincerity of her regard, and endeavouring to contribute to her happiness.

Camilla thanked her, dried her eyes, and strove to appear composed; but she was too deeply affected for internal consolation: she felt herself degraded in being openly addressed as a love-sick girl; and injured in being supposed, for a moment, capable of any mercenary view. She desired to be excused going out, and to have the evening to herself; not on account of the expence of the play; she had again wholly forgotten her poverty;

but to breathe a little alone, and indulge the sadness of her mind.

Mrs. Arlbery, unfeignedly sorry to have caused her any pain, would not oppose her inclination; she repeated her apologies, dragged from her an assurance of forgiveness, and went down stairs alone to a summons from Sir Sedley Clarendel.

The first moments of her departure were spent by Camilla in the deepest dejection; from which, however, the recollection of her father, and her solemn engagement to him, soon after awakened her. She read again his injunctions, and resolving not to add to her unhappiness by any failure in her duty, determined to make her appearance with some spirit before Mrs. Arlbery set out.

*   *   *   *

'My dear Clarendel,' cried that lady, as she entered the parlour, 'this poor little girl is in a more serious plight than I had conjectured. I have been giving her a few hints, from the stores of my worldly knowledge, and they appear to her so detestably mean and vulgar, that they have almost broken her heart. The arrival of this odious Mandlebert has overthrown all our schemes. We are cut up, Sir Sedley! completely cut up!'[1]

'O, indubitably to a degree!' cried the Baronet, with an air of mingled pique and conceit; 'how could it be otherwise? Exists the wight who could dream of competition with Mandlebert!'

'Nay, now, my dear Clarendel, you enchant me. If you view his power with resentment, you are the man in the world to crumble it to the dust. To work, therefore, dear creature, without delay.'

'But how must I go about it? a little instruction, for pity!'

'Charming innocent! So you don't know how to try to make yourself agreeable?'

'Not in the least! I am ignorant to a redundance.'

'And were you never more adroit?'

'Never. A goth in grain![2] Witless from the first *muling in my nurse's arms!*'[3]

'Come, come, a truce for a moment, with foppery, and answer me seriously; Were you ever in love, Clarendel? speak the truth. I am just seized with a passionate desire to know.'

'Why ... yes ...' answered he, pulling his lips with his fingers, 'I think—I rather think ... I was once.'

'O tell! tell! tell!'

'Nay, I am not very positive. One hears it is to happen; and one is put upon thinking of it, while so very young, that one soon takes it for granted. Define it a little, and I can answer you more accurately. Pray, is it any thing beyond being very fond, and very silly, with a little touch of melancholy?'

'Precise! precise! Tell me, therefore, what it was that caught you. Beauty? Fortune? Flattery? or Wit? Speak! speak! I die to know!'

'O, I have forgotten all that these hundred years! I have not the smallest trace left!'

'You are a terrible coxcomb, my dear Clarendel! and I am a worse myself for giving you so much encouragement. But, however, we must absolutely do something for this fair and drooping violet. She won't go even to the play tonight.'

'Lovely lily! how shall we rear it? Tell her I beg her to be of our party.'

'You beg her? My dear Sir Sedley! what do you talk of?'

'Tell her 'tis my entreaty, my supplication!'

'And you think that will make her comply?'

'You will see.'

'Bravo, my dear Clarendel, bravo! However, if you have the courage to send such a message, I have not to deliver it: but I will write it for you.'

She then wrote,

'Sir Sedley Clarendel asserts, that if you are not as inexorable as you are fair, you will not refuse to join our little party tonight at the theatre.'

Camilla, after a severe conflict from this note, which she concluded to be the mere work of Mrs. Arlbery to draw her from retirement, sent word she would wait upon her.

Sir Sedley heard the answer with exultation, and Mrs. Arlbery with surprise. She declared, however, that since he possessed this power, she should not suffer it to lie dormant, but make it work upon her fair friend, till it either excited jealousy in Mandlebert, or brought indifference to herself. 'My resolution,' cried she, 'is fixt; either to see him at her feet, or drive him from her heart.'

Camilla, presently descending, looked away from Mrs. Arlbery; but, unsuspicious as she was undesigning, thanked the Baronet for his message, and told him she had already repented her solitary plan. The Baronet felt but the more flattered, from supposing this was said from the fear of flattering him.

In the way to the theatre, Camilla, with much confusion, recollected her empty purse; but could not, before Mr. and Miss Dennel and Sir Sedley, prevail with herself to make it known; she could only determine to ask Mrs. Arlbery to pay for her at present, and defer the explanation till night.

But, just as she alighted from the coach, Mrs. Arlbery, in her usual manner, said: 'Do pay for me, good Dennel; you know how I hate money.'

Camilla, hurrying after her, whispered, 'May I beg you to lend me some silver?'

'Silver! I have not carried any about with me since I lost my dear ponies and my pet phaeton. I am as poor as Job; and therefore bent upon avoiding all temptation. Somebody or other always trusts me. If they get paid, they bless their stars. If not, —do you hear me, Mr. Dennel?—'twill be all the same an hundred years hence; so what man of any spirit will think of it? hey, Mr. Dennel?'

'But—dear madam!—pray—'

'O, they'll change for you, here, my dear, without diffi ulty.'

'But . . . but . . . pray stop! . . . I . . . I have no gold neither!'

'Have you done like me, then, come out without your purse?'

'No! . . .'

This single negative, and the fluttered manner, and low voice in which it was pronounced, gave Mrs. Arlbery the utmost astonishment. She said nothing, however, but called aloud to Mr. Dennel to settle for the whole party.

Mr. Dennel, during the dialogue, had paid for himself and his daughter, and walked on into the box.

'What a Hottentot!' exclaimed Mrs. Arlbery. 'Come, then, Clarendel, take pity on two poor distressed objects, and let us pass.'

Sir Sedley, little suspicious of the truth, yet flattered to be always called upon to be the banker of Camilla, obeyed with alacrity.

Mrs. Arlbery placed Camilla upon a seat before her, and motioned to the Baronet to remain in a row above; and then, in a low voice, said: 'My dear Clarendel, do you know they have let that poor girl come to Tunbridge without a sixpence in her pocket!'

'Is it possible?'

''Tis a fact. I never suspected it till suspicion was followed by confirmation. She had a guinea or two, I fancy, at first, just to equip her with one set of things to appear in; which, probably, the good Parson imagined would last as clean and as long at a public place as at his parsonage-house, where my best suit is worn about twice in a summer. But how that rich old uncle of hers could suffer her to come without a penny, I can neither account for nor forgive. I have seen her shyness about money-matters for some days past; but I so little conjectured the possibility of her distress, that I have always rather increased than spared it.'

'Sweet little angel!' exclaimed the Baronet, in a tone of tenderness; 'I had indeed no idea of her situation. Heavens! I could lay half my fortune at her feet to set her at ease!'

'Half, my dear Clarendel!' cried Mrs. Arlbery, laughing; 'nay, why not the whole? where will you find a more lovely companion?'

'Pho, pho!—but why should it be so vastly horrid an incongruity that a man who, by chance, is rich, should do something for a woman who, by chance, is poor? How immensely impertinent is the prejudice that forbids so natural a use of money! why should the better half of a man's actions be always under the dominion of some prescriptive slavery? 'Tis hideous to think of. And how could he more delectably spend, or more ecstatically enjoy his fortune, than by so equitable a participation?'

'True, Sir Sedley. And you men are all so disinterested, so pure in your benevolence, so free from any spirit of encroachment, that no possible ill consequence could ensue from such an arrangement. When once a fair lady had made you a civil courtesy, you would wholly forget you had ever obliged her. And you would let her walk her ways, and forget it also: especially if, by chance, she happened to be young and pretty.'

This raillery was interrupted by the appearance of Edgar in an opposite box. 'Ah!' cried Mrs. Arlbery, 'look but at that piece of congelation that nothing seems to thaw! Enter the lists against him, dear Clarendel! He has stationed himself there merely to watch and discountenance her. I hate him heartily; yet he rolls in wealth, and she has nothing. I must bring them, therefore, together, positively: for though a husband . . . such a fastidious one especially . . . is not what I would recommend to her for happiness, 'tis better than poverty. And, after his cold and selfish manner, I am convinced he loves her. He is evidently in pursuit of her, though he wants generosity to act openly. Work him but with a little jealousy, and you will find me right.'

'Me, my dear madam? me, my divine Mrs. Arlbery? Alas! with what chance? No! see where enters the gallant Major. Thence must issue those poignant darts that newly vivify the expiring embers of languishing love.'

'Now don't talk such nonsense when I am really serious. You are the very man for the purpose: because, though you have no feeling, Mandlebert does not know you are without it. But those Officers are too notoriously unmeaning to excite a moment's real apprehension. They have a new dulcinea wherever they newly quarter, and carry about the few ideas they possess from damsel to damsel, as regularly as from town to town.'

The Major was now in the box, and the conversation ended.

He endeavoured, as usual, to monopolize Camilla; but while her thoughts were all upon Edgar, the whole she could command of her attention was bestowed upon Sir Sedley.

This was not unobserved by Edgar, who now again wavered in believing she loved the Major: but the doubt brought with it no pleasure; it led him only the more to contemn her. Does she turn, thought he, thus, from one to the other, with no preference but of accident or caprice? Is her favour thus light of circulation? Is it now the mawkish Major, and now the coxcomb Clarendel? Already is she thus versed in the common dissipation of coquetry? ... O, if so, how blest has been my escape! A coquette wife! ...

His heart swelled, and his eye no longer sought her.

*　　*　　*　　*

At night, as soon as she went to her own room, Mrs. Arlbery followed her, and said: 'My dear Miss Tyrold, I know much better than you how many six-pences and three-pences are perpetually wanted at places such as these. Do suffer me to be your banker. What shall we begin our account with?'

Camilla felt really thankful for being spared an opening upon this subject. She consented to borrow two guineas; but Mrs. Arlbery would not leave her with less than five, adding, 'I insist upon doubling it in a day or two. Never mind what I say about my

distress, and my phaeton, and my ponies; 'tis only to torment
Dennel, who trembles at parting with half-a-crown for half an
hour; or else, now and then, to set other people a staring; which
is not unamusing, when nothing else is going forward. But
believe me, my dear young friend, were I really in distress, or
were I really not to discharge these petty debts I incur, you would
soon discover it by the thinness of our parties! These men that
now so flock around us; would find some other loadstone. I know
them pretty well, dear creatures! . . .'

Though shocked to appear thus destitute, Camilla was somewhat relieved to have no debt but with Mrs. Arlbery; for she
resolved to pay Sir Sedley and the milliner the next day, and to
settle with Mrs. Arlbery upon her return to Etherington.

CHAPTER X

Strictures upon the Ton

THE next day was appointed for the master of the ceremonies'
ball; which proved a general rendezvous of all parties, and almost
all classes of company.

Mrs. Mittin, in a morning visit to Camilla, found out that she
had only the same cap for this occasion that she had worn upon
every other; and, assuring her it was grown so old-fashioned, that
not a lady's maid in Tunbridge would now be seen in it, she
offered to pin her up a turban, which should come to next to
nothing, yet should be the prettiest, and simplest, and cheapest
thing that ever was seen.

Camilla, though a stranger to vanity, and without any natural
turn to extravagance, was neither of an age, nor a philosophy, to be
unmoved by the apprehension of being exposed to ridicule from
her dress: she thankfully, therefore, accepted the proposal; and
Mrs. Mittin, taking a guinea, said, she would pay Mrs. Tillden
for the hat, at the same time that she bought a new handkerchief
for the turban.

When she came back, however, she had only laid out a few
shillings at another shop, for some articles, so cheap, she said it
would have been a shame not to buy them; but without paying the

bill, Mrs. Tillden having desired it might not be discharged till the young lady was leaving the Wells.

As the turban was made up from a pattern of one prepared for Mrs. Berlinton, Camilla had every reason to be satisfied of its elegance. Nor did Mrs. Mittin involve her in much distress how her own trouble might be recompensed; the cap she found unfit for Camilla, she could contrive, she said, to alter for herself; and as a friend had given her a ticket for the ball, it would be mighty convenient to her, as she had nothing of the kind ready.

*   *   *   *

Far different were the sensations with which Edgar and Camilla saw each other this night, from those with which, so lately they had met in the same apartment. Edgar thought her degenerating into the character of a coquette, and Camilla, in his intended tour, anticipated a period to all their intercourse.

She was received, meanwhile, in general, with peculiar and flattering attention. Sir Sedley Clarendel made up to her, with public smiles and courtesy; even Lord Newford and Sir Theophilus Jarard, though they passed by Mrs. Arlbery without speaking to her, singled out Camilla for their devoirs. The distinction paid her by the admired Mrs. Berlinton had now not only marked her as an object whom it would not be derogatory to treat with civility, but as one who might, hence-forward, be regarded herself as admitted into *certain circles.*

Mrs. Arlbery, though every way a woman of fashion, they conceived to be somewhat wanting in *ton,* since she presided in no party, was unnoticed by Lady Alithea Selmore, and unknown to Mrs. Berlinton.

Ton, in the scale of connoisseurs in the *certain circles,* is as much above fashion, as fashion is above fortune: for though the latter is an ingredient that all alike covet to possess, it is courted without being respected, and desired without being honoured, except only by those who, from earliest life, have been taught to earn it as a business. *Ton,* meanwhile, is as attainable without birth as without understanding, though in all the *certain circles* it takes place of either. To define what it is, would be as difficult to the most renowned of its votaries, as to an utter stranger to its attributes. That those who call themselves of the *ton* either lead, or hold cheap all others, is obtrusively evident: but how and by what art they attain such pre-eminence, they would be perplexed to explain. That some whim has happily called forth imitators; that some strange phrase has been adopted; that something odd in dress has become popular; that some beauty, or some deformity, no matter which, has found annotators; may commonly be traced as the origin of their first public notice. But to whichever of these accidents their early fame may be attributed, its establishment and its glory is built upon vanity that knows no deficiency, or insolence that knows no blush.

Notwithstanding her high superiority both in capacity and knowledge, Mrs. Arlbery felt piqued by this behaviour, though she laughed at herself for heeding it. 'Nevertheless,' cried she, 'those who shew contempt, even though themselves are the most contemptible, always seem on the higher ground. Yet 'tis only, with regard to these animals of the *ton*, that nobody combats them. Their presumption is so notorious, that, either by disgust or alarm, it keeps off reprehension. Let anyone boldly, and face to face, venture to be more uncivil than themselves, and they would be overpowered at once. Their valour is no better than that of a barking cur, who affrights all that go on without looking at him, but who, the moment he is turned upon with a stamp and a fierce look, retreats himself, amazed, afraid, and ashamed.'

'If you, Mrs. Arlbery,' said the General, 'would undertake to tutor them, what good you might do!'

'O, Heavens, General, suspect me not of such reforming Quixotism! I have not the smallest desire to do them any good, believe me! If nature has given them no sense of propriety, why should I be more liberal? I only want to punish them; and that not, alas! from virtue, but from spite!'

The conversation of the two men of the *ton* with Camilla was soon over. It was made up of a few disjointed sentences, abusing Tunbridge, and praising the German Spa,[1] in cant words, emphatically and conceitedly pronounced, and brought round upon every occasion, and in every speech, with so precise an exclusion of all other terms, that their vocabulary scarce consisted of forty words in totality.

Edgar occupied the space they vacated the moment of their departure; but not alone; Mrs. Mittin came into it with him, eager to tell Camilla how everybody had admired her turban; how

sweetly she looked in it; how everybody said, they should not
have known her again, it became her so; and how they all agreed
her head had never been so well dressed before.

Edgar, when he could be heard, began speaking of Sir Sedley
Clarendel; he felt miserable in what he thought her inconsiderate
encouragement of such impertinence; and the delicacy which
restrained him from expressing his opinion of the Major, had no
weight with him here, as jealousy had no share in his dislike to the
acquaintance: he believed the young Baronet incapable of all love
but for himself, and a decidedly destined bachelor: without,
therefore, the smallest hesitation, he plainly avowed that he had
never met with a more thoroughly conceited fop, a more elaborate
and self-sufficient coxcomb.

'You see him only,' said Camilla, 'with the impression made by
his general appearance; and that is all against him: I always look
for his better qualities and rejoice in finding them. His very sight
fills me with grateful pleasure, by reminding me of the deliverance I owe to him.'

Edgar, amazed, intreated an explanation; and, when she had
given it, struck and affected, clasped his hands, and exclaimed:
'How providential such a rescue! and how differently shall I
henceforth behold him!' And, almost involuntarily turning to Mrs.
Arlbery, he intreated to be presented to the young Baronet.

Sir Sedley received his overtures with some surprise, but great
civility; and then went on with a ludicrous account he was giving
to Lord Newford and Sir Theophilus, of the quarrel of Macdersey
with Mr. Dubster.

'How awake thou art grown, Clary?' cried Sir. Theophilus;
'A little while ago thou wast all hip and vapour;[1] and now thou
dost nothing but patronise fun.'

'Why, yes,' answered the Baronet, 'I begin to tire of *ennui*. 'Tis
grown so common. I saw my footman beginning it but last week.'

'O, hang it! O, curse it!' cried Lord Newford, 'your footman!'

'Yes, the rogue is not without parts. I don't know if I shan't
give him some lessons, upon leaving it off myself. The only
difficulty is to find out what, in this nether world, to do without it.
How can one fill up one's time? Stretching, yawning, and all that,
are such delicious ingredients for coaxing on the lazy hours!'

'O, hang it, O, curse it,' cried Lord Newford; 'who can exist
without them? I would not be bound to pass half an hour without

yawning and stretching for the Mogul's empire. I'd rather snap short at once.'[1]

'No, no, don't snap short yet, little Newy,' cried Sir Sedley. 'As to me, I am never at a loss for an expedient. I am not without some thoughts of falling in love.'

He looked at Edgar; who, not aware this was designed to catch his attention, naturally exclaimed: 'Thoughts! can you choose, or avoid at pleasure?'

'Most certainly. After four-and-twenty a man is seldom taken by surprise; at least, not till he is past forty: and then, the fear of being too late, sometimes renovates the eagerness of the first youth. But, in general, your willing slaves are boys.'

Edgar, laughing, begged a little information, how he meant to put his thoughts in execution.

'Nothing so facile! 'Tis but to look at some fair object attentively, to follow her with your eyes when she quits the room; never to let them rest without watching for her return; filling up the interval with a few sighs; to which, in a short time, you grow so habituated, that they become natural; and then, before you are aware, a certain solicitude and restlessness arise, which the connoisseurs in natural history dub falling in love.'

'These would be good hints,' said Edgar, 'to urge on waverers, who wish to persuade themselves to marry.'

'O no, my dear sir! no! that's a mistake of the first magnitude; no man is in love when he marries. He may have loved before; I have even heard he has sometimes loved after: but at the time never. There is something in the formalities of the matrimonial preparations that drive away all the little cupidons. They rarely stand even a demand of consent—unless they doubt obtaining it; but a settlement! Parchments! Lawyers!—No! there is not a little Love in the Island of Cyprus,[2] that is not ready to lend a wing to set passion, inspiration, and tenderness to flight, from such excruciating legalities.'

'Don't prose,[3] Clary; don't prose,' cried Sir Theophilus, gaping till his mouth was almost distorted.

'O, killing! O, murder!' cried Lord Newford; 'what dost talk of marriage for?'

'It seems, then,' said Edgar, 'to be much the same thing what sort of wife falls to a man's lot; whether the woman of his choice, or a person he should blush to own?'

'Blush!' repeated Sir Sedley, smiling; 'no! no! A man of any fashion never blushes for his wife, whatever she may be. For his mistress, indeed, he may blush: for if there are any small failings there, his taste may be called in question.'

'Blush about a wife!' exclaimed Lord Newford; 'O, hang it! O, curse it! that's too bad!'

'Too bad, indeed,' cried Sir Theophilus; 'I can't possibly patronise[1] blushing for a wife.'

"'Tis the same, then, also,' said Edgar, 'how she turns out when the knot is tied, whether well or ill?'

'To exactitude! If he marry her for beauty, let her prove what she may, her face offers his apology. If for money, he needs none. But if, indeed, by some queer chance, he marries with a view of living with her, then, indeed, if his particularity gets wind, he may grow a little anxious for the acquittal of his oddity, in seeing her approved.'

'Approved! Ha! ha!' cried Lord Newford; 'a wife approved! That's too bad, Clary; that's too bad!'

'Poor Clary, what art prosing about?' cried Sir Theophilus. 'I can't possibly patronise this prosing.'

The entrance of the beautiful Mrs. Berlinton and her train now interrupted this conversation; the young Baronet immediately joined her; though not till he had given his hand to Edgar, in token of his willingness to cultivate his acquaintance.

Edgar, returning to Camilla, confessed he had too hastily judged Sir Sedley, when he concluded him a fool, as well as a fop; 'For,' added he, with a smile, 'I see, now, one of those epithets is all he merits. He is certainly far from deficient in parts, though he abuses the good gifts of nature with such pedantry of affectation and conceit.'

Camilla was now intent to clear the history of the cotillon; when Mrs. Berlinton approaching, and, with graceful fondness, taking her hand, entreated to be indulged with her society: and, since she meant not to dance, for Edgar had not asked her, and the Major she had refused, she could not resist her invitation. She had lost her fear of displeasing Mrs. Arlbery by quitting her, from conceiving a still greater, of wearying by remaining with her.

Edgar, anxious both to understand and to discuss this new connexion, hovered about the party with unremitting vigilance. But, though he could not either look at or listen to Mrs. Berlinton, without admiring her, his admiration was neither free from censure of herself, nor terrour for her companion: he saw her far more beautiful than prudent, more amiable than dignified. The females in her group were few, and little worthy notice; the males appeared, to a man, without disguise, though not without restraint, her lovers. And though no one seemed selected, no one seemed despised; she appeared to admit their devoirs with little consideration; neither modestly retiring from power, nor vainly displaying it.

Camilla quitted not this enchantress till summoned by Mrs. Arlbery; who, seeing herself again, from the arrival of Lady Alithea Selmore, without any distinguished party, that lady drawing into her circle all people of any consequence not already attracted by Mrs. Berlinton, grew sick of the ball and the rooms, and impatient to return home. Camilla, in retiring, presented, folded in a paper, the guinea, half-guinea, and silver, she had borrowed of Sir Sedley; who received it without presuming at any contest; though not, after what he had heard from Mrs. Arlbery, without reluctance.

Edgar watched the instant when Camilla moved from the gay group; but Mrs. Mittin watched it also; and, approaching her more speedily, because with less embarrassment, seized her arm before he could reach her: and before he could, with any discretion, glide to her other side, Miss Dennel was there.

'Well now, young ladies,' said Mrs. Mittin, 'I'm going to tell you a secret. Do you know, for all I call myself Mrs. I'm single?'

'Dear, la!' exclaimed Miss Dennel; 'and for all you're so old!'

'So old, Miss! Who told you I was so old? I'm not so very old as you may think me. I'm no particular age, I assure you. Why, what made you think of that?'

'La, I don't know; only you don't look very young.'

'I can't help that, Miss Dennel. Perhaps you mayn't look young yourself one of these days. People can't always stand still just at a particular minute. Why, how old, now, do you take me to be? Come, be sincere.'

'La! I'm sure I can't tell; only I thought you was an old woman.'

'An old woman! Lord, my dear, people would laugh to hear you. You don't know what an old woman is. Why it's being a cripple, and blind, and deaf, and dumb, and slavering, and without a tooth. Pray, how am I like all that?'

'Nay, I'm sure I don't know; only I thought, by the look of your face, you must be monstrous old.'

'Lord, I can't think what you've got in your head, Miss Dennel! I never heard as much before, since I was born. Why the reason I'm called Mrs. is not because of that, I assure you; but because I'd a mind to be taken for a young widow, on account everybody likes a young widow; and if one is called Miss, people being so soon to think one an old maid, that it's quite disagreeable.'

This discourse brought them to the carriage.

CHAPTER XI

Traits of Character

THE following morning, Mrs. Mittin came with eager intelligence, that the raffle was fixed for one o'clock; and, without any scruple, accompanied the party to the shop, addressing herself to every one of the set as to a confirmed and intimate friend. But her chief supporter was Mr. Dennel, whose praise of her was the vehicle to his censure of his sister-in-law. That lady was the person in the world whom he most feared and disliked. He had neither spirit for the splendid manner in which she lived, nor parts for the vivacity of her conversation. The first, his love of money made him condemn as extravagant, and the latter his self-love made him hate, because he could not understand. He persuaded himself, therefore, that she had more words than meaning; and extolled all the obvious truths uttered by Mrs. Mittin, to shew his superior admiration of what, being plain and incontrovertible, he dignified with the panegyric of being sensible.

When they came upon the Pantiles, they were accosted by Mr. Dubster; who having solemnly asked them, one by one, how they all did, joined Mrs. Mittin, saying: 'Well, I can't pretend as I'm over sorry you've got neither of those two comical gentlemen with you, that behaved so free to me for nothing. I don't think it's particular agreeable being treated so; though it's a thing I don't much mind. It's not worth fretting about.'

'Well, don't say any more about it,' cried Mrs. Mittin, endea-

vouring to shake him off; 'I dare say you did something to provoke
'em, or they're too genteel to have taken notice of you.'

'Me provoke them! why what did I do? I was just like a mere
lamb, as one may say, at the very time that young Captain fell
abusing me so, calling of me a little dirty fellow, without no
provocation. If I'm little, or big, I don't see that it's any business
of his. And as to dirty, I'd put on all clean linen but the very day
before, as the people can tell you at the inn; so the whole was a
mere piece of falsehood from one end to t'other.'

'Well, well, what do you talk about it for any more? You should
never take anything ill of a young gentleman. It's only aggravating
him so much the worse.'

'Aggravating him, Mrs. Mittin! why what need I mind that?
Do you think I'm to put up with his talking of caning me, and
such like, because of his being a young gentleman? Not I, I assure
you! I'm no such person. And if once I feel his switch across these
here shoulders, it won't be so well for him!'

The party now entered the shop where the raffle was to be
held.

Edgar was already there; he had no power to keep away from
any place where he was sure to behold Camilla; and a raffle
brought to his mind the most tender recollections. He was now
with Lord O'Lerney, in whose candour and benevolence of
character he took great delight, and with whom he had joined
Lady Isabella Irby, who had been drawn, as a quiet spectatress,
to the sight, by a friend, who, having never seen the humours of a
raffle, had entreated, through her means, to look on. He languished
to see Camilla presented to this lady, in whose manners and
conversation, dignity and simplicity were equally blended.

While he was yet, though absently, conversing with them, Lord
O'Lerney pointed out Camilla to Lady Isabella.

'I have taken notice of her already at the Rooms;' answered her
Ladyship; 'and I have seldom, I think, seen a more interesting
young creature.'

'The character of her countenance,' said Lord O'Lerney,
'strikes me very peculiarly. 'Tis so intelligent, yet so unhackneyed.
so full of meaning, yet so artless, that, while I look at her, I feel
myself involuntarily anxious for her welfare.'

'I don't think she seems happy,' said Lady Isabella; 'Do you
know who she is, my Lord?'

Edgar, here, with difficulty suppressed a sigh. Not happy! thought he; ah! wherefore? what can make Camilla unhappy?

'I understand she is a niece of Sir Hugh Tyrold,' answered his Lordship; 'a Yorkshire Baronet. She is here with an acquaintance of mine, Mrs. Arlbery, who is one of the first women I have ever known, for wit and capacity. She has an excellent heart, too; though her extraordinary talents, and her carelessness of opinion make it sometimes, but very unjustly, doubted.'

Edgar heard this with much pleasure. A good word from Lord O'Lerney quieted many fears; he hoped he had been unnecessarily alarmed; he determined, in future, to judge her more favourably.

'I should be glad,' continued his Lordship, 'to hear this young lady were either well established, or returned to her friends without becoming an object of public notice. A young woman is no where so rarely respectable, or respected, as at these water-drinking places, if seen at them either long or often. The search of pleasure and dissipation, at a spot consecrated for restoring health to the sick, the infirm, and the suffering, carries with it an air of egotism, that does not give the most pleasant idea of the feeling and disposition.'

'Yet, may not the sick, my Lord, be rather amended than hurt by the sight of gaiety around them?'

'Yes, my dear Lady Isabella; and the effect, therefore, I believe to be beneficial. But as this is not the motive why the young and the gay seek these spots, it is not here they will find themselves most honoured. And the mixture of pain and illness with splendor and festivity, is so unnatural, that probably it is to that we must attribute that a young woman is no where so hardly judged. If she is without fortune, she is thought a female adventurer, seeking to sell herself for its attainment; if she is rich, she is supposed a willing dupe, ready for a snare, and only looking about for an ensnarer.'

'And yet, young women seldom, I believe, my Lord, merit this severity of judgment. They come but hither in the summer, as they go to London in the winter, simply in search of amusement, without any particular purpose.'

'True; but they do not weigh what their observers weigh for them, that the search of public recreation in the winter is, from long habit, permitted without censure; but that the summer has not, as yet, prescription so positively in its favour; and those who, after meeting them all the winter at the opera, and all the spring at Ranelagh, hear of them all the summer at Cheltenham, Tunbridge, &c. and all the autumn at Bath,[1] are apt to inquire, when is the season for home.'

'Ah, my Lord! how wide are the poor inconsiderate little flutterers from being aware of such a question! How necessary to youth and thoughtlessness is the wisdom of experience!'

Why does she not come this way? thought Edgar; why does she not gather from these mild, yet understanding moralists, instruction that might benefit all her future life?

'There is nothing,' said Lord O'Lerney, 'I more sincerely pity than the delusions surrounding young females. The strongest admirers of their eyes are frequently the most austere satirists of their conduct.'

The entrance of Lord Newford, Sir Theophilus Jarard, and Sir Sedley Clarendel, all noisily talking and laughing together, interrupted any further conversation. The two former no sooner saw Camilla, and perceived neither Lady Alithea Selmore, nor Mrs. Berlinton, than they made up to her; and Sir Sedley, who now found she was completely established in the *bon ton*, felt something of pride mix with pleasure in publicly availing himself of his intimacy with her; and something like interest mix with curiosity, in examining if Edgar were struck with her ready attention to him.

Upon Edgar, however, it made not the slightest impression. While Sir Sedley had appeared to him a mere fop, he had thought it degraded her; but how he regarded him as her preserver, it seemed both natural and merited.

Sir Sedley, not aware of this reasoning, was somewhat piqued; and taking him to another part of the shop, whispered: 'I am horribly vapoured! Do you know I have some thoughts of trying that little girl? Do you think one could make anything of her?'

'How? what do you mean?' cried Edgar, with sudden alarm.

Sir Sedley, a little flattered, affectedly answered: 'O, if you have any serious designs that way, incontestably I won't interfere.'

'Me!' cried Edgar, surprised and offended; 'believe me, no! I have all my life considered her—as my sister.'

Sir Sedley saw this was spoken with effort; and negligently replied: 'Nay you are just at the first epocha for marrying from inclination; but you are in the right not to perform so soon the funeral honours of liberty. 'Tis what you may do at any time. So many girls want establishments, that a man of sixty can just as easily get a wife of eighteen, as a man of one-and-twenty. The only inconvenience in that sort of alliance is, that though she begins with submitting to her venerated husband as prettily as to her papa, she is terribly apt to have a knack of running away from him, afterwards, with equal facility.'

'That is rather a discouraging article, I confess,' cried Edgar, 'for the tardy votaries of Hymen!'

'O, no! 'tis no great matter!' answered he, patting his snuff-box; 'we are impenetrable in the extreme to those sort of griev-ances now-a-days. We are at such prodigious expence of sensibility in public, for tales of sorrow told about pathetically, at a full board, that if we suffered much for our private concerns to boot, we must always meet one another with tears in our eyes. We never weep now, but at dinner, or at some diversion.'

Lord Newford, pulling him by the arm, called out: 'Come, Clary, what art about, man? we want thee.'

'Come, Clary! don't shirk, Clary,' cried Sir Theophilus; 'I can't possibly patronise this shirking.' And they hauled him to a corner of the shop, where all three resumed their customary laughing whispers.

'You will not, perhaps, suspect, Lady Isabella,' said Lord O'Lerney, smiling, 'that one of that triumvirate is by no means deficient in parts, and can even, when he desires it, be extremely pleasing?'

'Your Lordship judges right, I confess! I had not, indeed, done him such justice!'

'See then,' said his Lordship, 'how futile an animal is man, without some decided character and principle!

He's every thing by turns, and nothing long*.[1]

Wise, foolish; virtuous, vicious; active, indolent; prodigal and avaricious! No contrast is too strong for him while guided but by accident or impulse. This gentleman also, in common with the rest of his *tonnish* brethren, is now daily, though unconsciously, hoarding up a world of unprepared-for mortification, by not foreseeing that the more he is celebrated in his youth, for being

*Dryden's Absalom and Achitophel.

the leader of the *ton*, and the man of the day, the earlier he will be regarded as a creature out of date, an old beau, and a fine gentleman of former times. But 'tis by reverses, such as these, that folly and impropriety pay their penalties. We might spare all our anger against the vanity of the beauty, or the conceit of the coxcomb. Are not wrinkles always in waiting to punish the one, and age, without honour, to chastise and degrade the other?'

All the rafflers were now arrived, except Mrs. Berlinton, who was impatiently expected. Lady Alithea Selmore had already sent a proxy to throw for her in her own woman; much to the dissatisfaction of most part of the company. A general rising and inquietude to look out for Mrs. Berlinton, gave Edgar, at length, an opportunity to stand next to Camilla. 'How I grieve,' he cried 'you should not know Lady Isabella Irby! she seems to me a model for a woman of rank in her manners, and a model for a woman of every station in her mind. The world, I believe, could scarce have tempted her to so offensive a mark of superiority as has just been exhibited by Lady Alithea Selmore, who has ingeniously discovered a method of being signalised as the most important person out of twenty, by making herself nineteen enemies.'

'I wonder,' said Camilla, 'she can think the chance of the earrings worth so high a price!'

A footman, in a splendid livery, now entering, inquired for Miss Tyrold. She was pointed out to him by Major Cerwood, and he delivered her a letter from Mrs. Berlinton.

The contents were to entreat she would throw for that lady, who was in the midst of Akenside's Pleasures of the Imagination,[1] and could not tear herself away from them.

Camilla blushed excessively in proclaiming she was chosen Mrs. Berlinton's proxy. Edgar saw with tenderness her modest confusion, and, with a pleasure the most touching, read the favourable impression it made upon Lord O'Lerney and Lady Isabella.

This seemed an opportunity irresistible for venting his fears and cautions about Mrs. Berlinton; and, taking the bustling period in which the rafflers were arranging the order and manner of throwing, he said, in a low, and diffident tone of voice, 'You have committed to me an important and, I fear, an importunate office; yet, while I hold, I cannot persuade myself not to fulfil it;

though I know that to give advice which opposes sentiment and feeling, is repugnant to independence and to delicacy. Such, therefore, I do not mean to enforce; but merely to offer hints—intimations—and observations—that without controlling, may put you upon your guard.'

Camilla, affected by this unexpected address, could only look her desire for an explanation.

'The lady,' he continued, 'whom you are presently to represent, appears to be uncommonly engaging?—'

'Indeed she is! She is attractive, gentle, amiable.'

'She seems, also, already to have caught your affection?'

'Who could have withheld it, that had seen her as I have seen her? She is as unhappy as she is lovely. . . .'

'I have heard of your first meeting, with as much pleasure in the presence of mind it called forth on one side, as with doubt and perplexity, upon every circumstance I can gather, of the other.—'

'If you knew her, you would find it impossible to hold any doubts; impossible to resist admiring, compassionating, and loving her!'

'If my knowledge of her bribed an interest in her favour, without convincing me she deserved it, I ought, rather, to regret that you have not escaped falling into such a snare, than that I could have escaped it myself.'

'I believe her free, nay incapable of all ill!' cried Camilla warmly; 'though I dare not assert she is always coolly upon her guard.'

'Do not let me hurt you,' said Edgar, gently; 'I have seen how lovely she is in person, and how pleasing in manners. And she is so young that, were she in a situation less exposed, want of steadiness or judgment might, by a little time, be set right. But here, there is surely much to fear from her early possession of power. . . . O, that some happier chance had brought about such a peculiar intercourse for you with Lady Isabella Irby! There, to the pleasure of friendship, might be added the modesty of retired elegance, and the security of established respectability.'

'And may not this yet happen, with Mrs. Berlinton? Lady Isabella, though still young, is not in the extreme youth of Mrs. Berlinton: a few more years, therefore, may bring equal discretion; and as she has already every other good quality, you may hereafter equally approve her.'

'Do you think, then,' said Edgar, half smiling, 'that the few years of difference in their age were spent by Lady Isabella in the manner they are now spent by Mrs. Berlinton? do you think she paved the way for her present dignified, though unassuming character, by permitting herself to be surrounded by professed admirers? by letting their sighs reach her ears? by suffering their eyes to fasten with open rapture on her face? and by holding it sufficient not to suppress such liberties, so long as she does not avowedly encourage them?'

Camilla was startled. She had not seen her conduct in this light: yet her understanding refused to deny it might bear this interpretation.

Charmed with the candour of her silence, Edgar continued, 'How wide from all that is open to similar comment, is the carriage and behaviour of Lady Isabella! how clear! how transparent, how free from all conjecture of blemish! They may each, indeed, essentially be equally innocent; and your opinion of Mrs. Berlinton corroborates the impression made by her beautiful countenance: yet how far more highly is the true feminine character preserved, where surmise is not raised, than where it can be parried! Think but of those two ladies, and mark the difference. Lady Isabella, addressed only where known, followed only because loved, sees no adulators encircling her, for adulation would alarm her; no admirers paying her homage, for such homage would offend her. She knows she has not only her own innocence to guard, but the honour of her husband. Whether she is happy with him or not, this deposit is equally sacred.—'

He stopt; for Camilla again started. The irrepressible frankness of her nature revolted against denying how much this last sentence struck her, and she ingenuously exclaimed: 'O that this most amiable young creature were but more aware of this duty!'

'Ah, my dear Miss Camilla,' cried Edgar, with energy, 'since you feel and own . . . and with you, that is always one . . . this baneful deficiency, drop, or at least suspend an intercourse too hazardous to be indulged with propriety! See what she may be sometime hence, ere you contract further intimacy. At present, unexperienced and unsuspicious, her dangers may be yours. You are too young for such a risk. Fly, fly from it, my dear Miss Camilla! . . . as if the voice of your mother were calling out to caution you!'

Camilla was deeply touched. An interest so warm in her welfare was soothing, and the name of her mother rendered it awful; yet, thus united, it appeared to her more strongly than ever to announce itself as merely fraternal. She could not suppress a sigh; but he attributed it to the request he had urged, and, with much concern, added: 'What I have asked of you, then, is too severe?'

Again irresistibly sighing, yet collecting all her force to conceal the secret cause, she answered, 'If she is thus exposed to danger . . . if her situation is so perilous, ought I not rather to stay by, and help to support her, than by abandoning, perhaps contribute to the evil you think awaiting her?'

'Generous Camilla!' cried he, melted into tender admiration, 'who can oppose so kind a design? So noble a nature! . . .'

No more could be said, for all preliminaries had been settled, and the throwing being arranged to take place alphabetically, she was soon summoned to represent Mrs. Berlinton.

From this time, Edgar could speak to her no more: even the Major could scarcely make way to her: the two men of the *ton* would not quit her, and Sir Sedley Clarendel appeared openly devoted to her.

Edgar looked on with the keenest emotion. The proof he had just received that her intrinsic worth was in its first state of excellence, had come home to his heart, and the fear of seeing her altered and spoilt, by the flatteries and dangers which environed her, with his wavering belief in her engagement with Major Cerwood, made him more wretched than ever. But when, some time after, she was called upon to throw for herself, the recollection that, from the former raffle, her half-guinea, even when the prize was in her hand, had been voluntarily withdrawn to be bestowed upon a poor family, so powerfully affected him, that he could not rest in the shop; he was obliged to breathe a freer air, and to hide his disturbance by a retreat.

Her throw was the highest the dice had yet afforded. A Miss Williams alone came after her, whose throw was the lowest; Miss Camilla Tyrold, therefore, was proclaimed to be the winner.

This second testimony of the favour of fortune was a most pleasant surprise to Camilla, and made the room resound with felicitations, till they were interrupted by a violent quarrel upon the Pantiles, whence the voice of Macdersey was heard, hollooing out: 'Don't talk, I say sir! don't presume to say a word!' and that of Mr. Dubster angrily answering, he would talk as long as he thought proper, whether it was agreeable or not.

Sir Sedley advanced to the combatants, in order to help on the dispute; but Edgar, returning at the sound of high words, took the Ensign by the arm, and prevailed with him to accompany him up and down the Pantiles; while Mrs. Mittin ran to Mr. Dubster, and pulling him into the shop, said: 'Mr. Dubster, if I'm not ashamed of you! how can you forget yourself so? talking to gentlemen at such a rate!'

'Why what should hinder me?' cried he; 'do you think I shall put up with every thing as I used to do when you first knew me, and we used to meet at Mr. Typton's, the tallow chandler's, in Shug-lane?[1] no, Mrs. Mittin, nor no such a thing; I'm turned gentleman myself, now, as much as the best of 'em; for I've nothing to do, but just what I choose.'

'I protest, Mr. Dubster,' cried Mrs. Mittin, taking him into a corner 'you're enough to put a saint into a pet![2] how come you to think of talking of Mr. Typton here? before such gentlefolks? and where's the use of telling every body he's a tallow chandler? and as to my meeting with you there once or so, in a way, I desire you'll mention it no more; for it's so long ago, I have no recollection of it.'

'No! why don't you remember—'

'Fiddle, faddle, what's the good of ripping up old stories about nothing? when you're with genteel people, you must do as I do; never talk about business at all.'

Macdersey now entered the shop, appeased by Edgar from shewing any further wrath, but wantonly inflamed by Sir Sedley, in a dispute upon the passion of love.

'Do you always, my dear friend,' said the Baronet, 'fall in love at first sight?'

'To be sure I do! If a man makes a scruple of that, it's ten to one but he's disappointed of doing it at all; because, after two or three second sights, the danger is you may spy out some little flaw in the dear angel, that takes off the zest, and hinders you to the longest day you have to live.'

'Profoundly cogitated that! you think then, my vast dear sir, the passion had more conveniently be kindled first, that the flaws may appear after, to cure it?'

'No, sir! no! when a man's once in love, those flaws don't signify, because he can't see them; or, if he could, at least he'd scorn to own them.'

'Live for ever brave Ireland!' exclaimed Mrs. Arlbery; 'what cold, phelgmatic Englishman would have made a speech of so much gallantry?'

'As to an Englishman,' said Macdersey, 'you must never mind what he says about the ladies, because he's too sheepish to speak out. He's just as often in love as his neighbours, only he's so shy he won't own it, till he sees if the young fair one is as much in love as himself; but a generous Irishman never scruples to proclaim the girl of his heart, though he should have twenty in a year.'

'But is that perfectly delicate, my dearest sir, to the several Dulcineas?'

'Perfectly! your Irishman is the delicatest man upon earth to the fair sex; for he always talks of their cruelty, if they are never so kind. He knows every honest heart will pity him, if it's true; and if it i'n't, he is too much a man of honour not to complain all one; he knows how agreeable it is to the dear creatures; they always take it for a compliment.'

'Whether avowedly or clandestinely,' said Mrs. Arlbery, 'still you are all in our chains. Even where you play the tyrant with us, we occupy all your thoughts; and if you have not the skill to make us happy, your next delight is to make us miserable; for though, now and then, you can contrive to hate, you can never arrive at forgetting us.'

'Contrive to hate you!' repeated Macdersey; 'I could as soon contrive to turn the world into a potato; there is nothing upon earth, nothing under the whole firmament I value but beauty!'

'A cheerful glass, then,' said Sir Sedley, 'you think horridly intolerable?'

'A cheerful glass, sir! do you take me for a milk-sop? do you think I don't know what it is to be a man? a chearful glass, sir, is the first pleasure in life; the most convivial, the most exhilarating, the most friendly joy of a true honest soul! what were existence without it? I should choose to be off in half an hour; which I should only make so long, not to shock my friends.'

'Well, the glass is not what I patronise,' said Sir Theophilus; 'it hips me so consumedly the next day; no, I can't patronise the glass.'

'Not patronise wine?' cried Lord Newford; 'O hang it! O curse it! that's too bad, Offy! but hunting! what dost think of that, little Offy?'

'Too obstreperous! It rouses one at such aukward hours; no, I can't patronise hunting.'

'Hunting!' cried Macdersey; 'O, it leaves everything behind it; 'tis the thing upon the earth for which I have the truest taste. I know nothing else that is not a bauble to it. A man is no more, in my estimation, than a child, or a woman, that don't enjoy it.'

'Cards, then,' said Sir Sedley, 'you reprobate?'

'And dice?'—cried Lord Newford—

'And betting?'—cried Sir Theophilus.

'Why what do you take me for, gentlemen?' replied Macdersey, hotly; 'Do you think I have no soul? no fire? no feeling? Do you suppose me a stone? a block? a lump of lead? I scorn such suspicions; I don't hold them worth answering. I am none of that torpid, morbid, drowsy tribe. I hold nobody to have an idea of life that has not rattled in his own hand the dear little box of promise. What ecstasy not to know if, in two seconds, one mayn't be worth ten thousand pounds! or else without a farthing! how it puts one on the rack! There's nothing to compare with it. I would not give up that moment to be sovereign of the East Indies! no, not if the West were to be put into the bargain.'

'All these things,' said Mr. Dennel, 'are fit for nothing but to bring a man to ruin. The main chance is all that is worth thinking of. 'Tis money makes the mare to go; and I don't know any thing that's to be done without it.'

'Money!' exclaimed Macdersey, 'tis the thing under heaven I hold in the most disdain. It won't give me a moment's concern never to see its colour again. I vow solemnly, if it were not just for the pleasures of the table, and a jolly glass with a friend, and a few horses in one's stable, and a little ready cash in one's purse, for odd uses, I should not care if the mint were sunk under ground to-morrow; money is what I most despise of all.'

'That's talking out of reason,' said Mr. Dennel, walking out of the shop with great disgust.

'Why, if I was to speak,' said Mr. Dubster, encouraged to come forward, by an observation so much to his own comprehension and taste as the last; 'I can't but say I think the same; for money—'

'Keep your distance, sir!' cried the fiery Ensign, 'keep your distance, I tell you! if you don't wish I should say something to you pretty cutting.'

This broke up the party, which else the lounging spirit of the place, and the general consent by which all descriptions of characters seem determined to occupy any spot whatever, to avoid a moment's abode in their lodgings, would still have detained till the dinner hour had forced to their respective homes. To suppress all possibility of further dissention, Mrs. Arlbery put Miss Dennel under the care of Macdersey, and bid him attend her towards Mount Pleasant.

Mr. Dubster, having stared after them some time in silence, called out: 'Keep my distance! I can't but say but what I think that young Captain the rudest young gentleman I ever happened to light upon! however, if he don't like me, I shan't take it much to heart; I can't pretend to say I like him any better; so he may choose; it's much the same to me; it breaks no squares.'

Edgar, almost without knowing it, followed Camilla, but he could displace neither the Baronet nor the Major, who, one with a look of open exultation, and the other with an air of determined perseverance, retained each his post at her side.

He saw that all her voluntary attention was to Sir Sedley, and that the Major had none but what was called for and inevitable. Was this indifference, or security? was she seeking to obtain in the Baronet a new adorer, or to excite jealousy, through his means, in an old one? Silent he walked on, perpetually exclaiming to himself: 'Can it be Camilla, the ingenuous, the artless Camilla, I find it so difficult to fathom, to comprehend, to trust?'

He had not spirits to join Mrs. Arlbery, though he lamented he had not, at once, visited her; since it was now awkward to take such a step without an invitation, which she seemed by no means disposed to offer him. She internally resented the little desire he had ever manifested for her acquaintance; and they had both too much penetration not to perceive how wide either was from being the favourite of the other.

CHAPTER XII

Traits of Eccentricity

THUS passed the first eight days of the Tunbridge excursion, and another week succeeded without any varying event.

Mrs. Arlbery now, impelled with concern for Camilla, and resentment against Edgar, renewed the subject of her opinion and advice upon his character and conduct. 'My dear young friend,' cried she, 'I cannot bear to see your days, your views, your feelings, thus fruitlessly consumed: I have observed this young man narrowly, and I am convinced he is not worth your consideration.'

Camilla, deeply colouring, was beginning to assure her she had no need of this counsel; but Mrs. Arlbery, not listening, continued.

'I know what you must say; yet, once more, I cannot refrain venturing at the liberty of lending you my experience. Turn your mind from him with all the expedition in your power, or its peace may be touched for the better half of your life. You do not see, he does not, perhaps, himself know, how exactly he is calculated to make you wretched. He is a watcher; and a watcher, restless and perturbed himself, infests all he pursues with uneasiness. He is without trust, and therefore without either courage or consistency. To-day he may be persuaded you will make all his happiness; to-morrow, he may fear you will give him nothing but misery. Yet it is not that he is jealous of any other; 'tis of the object of his choice he is jealous, lest she should not prove good enough to merit it. Such a man, after long wavering, and losing probable happiness in the terror of possible disappointment, will either die an old batchelor, with endless repinings at his own lingering fastidiousness, or else marry just at the eve of confinement for life, from a fit of the gout. He then makes, on a sudden, the first prudent choice in his way; a choice no longer difficult, but from the embarrassment of its ease; for she must have no beauty, lest she should be sought by others, no wit, lest others should be sought by herself; and no fortune, lest she should bring with it a taste of independence, that might curb his own will, when the strength and spirit are gone with which he might have curbed her's.'

Camilla attempted to laugh at this portait; but Mrs. Arlbery entreated her to consider it as faithful and exact. 'You have thought of him too much,' cried she, 'to do justice to any other, or you would not, with such perfect unconcern, pass by your daily increasing influence with Sir Sedley Clarendel.'

Excessively, and very seriously offended, Camilla earnestly besought to be spared any hints of such a nature.

'I know well,' cried she, 'how repugnant to seventeen is every idea of life that is rational. Let us, therefore, set aside, in our discussions, any thing so really beneficial, as a solid connection formed with a view to the worldly comforts of existence, and speak of Sir Sedley's devoirs merely as the instrument of teaching Mandlebert, that he is not the only rich, young, and handsome man in this lower sphere, who has viewed Miss Camilla Tyrold with complacency. Clarendel, it is true, would lose every charm in my estimation by losing his heart; for the earth holds nothing comparable for deadness of weight, with a poor soul really in love—except when it happens to be with oneself!—yet, to alarm the selfish irresolution of that impenetrable Mandlebert, I should really delight to behold him completely caught.'

Camilla, distressed and confused, sought to parry the whole as raillery: but Mrs. Arlbery would not be turned aside from her subject and purpose. 'I languish, I own,' cried she, 'to see that frozen youth worked up into a little sensibility. I have an instinctive aversion to those cold, haughty, drawing-back characters, who are made up of the egotism of looking out for something that is wholly devoted to them, and that has not a breath to breathe that is not a sigh for their perfections.'

'O! this is far . . .' Camilla began, meaning to say, far from the character of Mandlebert; but ashamed of undertaking his defence, she stopt short, and only mentally added, Even excellence such as his cannot, then, withstand prejudice!

'If there is any way,' continued Mrs. Arlbery, 'of animating him for a moment out of himself, it can only be by giving him a dread of some other. The poor Major does his best; but he is not rich enough to be feared, unless he were more attractive. Sir Sedley will seem more formidable. Countenance, therefore, his present propensity to wear your chains, till Mandlebert perceives that he is putting them on; and then . . . mount to the rising ground you ought to tread, and shew, at once, your power and

your disinterestedness, by turning from the handsome Baronet
and all his immense wealth, to mark . . . since you are determined
to indulge it . . . your unbiassed preference for Mandlebert.'

Camilla, irresistibly appeased by a picture so flattering to all
her best feelings, and dearest wishes, looked down; angry with
herself to find she felt no longer angry with Mrs. Arlbery.

Mrs. Arlbery, perceiving a point gained, determined to enforce
the blow, and then leave her to her reflections.

'Mandlebert is a creature whose whole composition is a pile of
accumulated punctilios. He will spend his life in refining away
his own happiness: but do not let him refine away yours. He is
just a man to bewitch an innocent and unguarded young woman
from forming any other connexion, and yet, when her youth and
expectations have been sacrificed to his hesitation, . . . to conceive
he does not use her ill in thinking of her no more, because he has
entered into no verbal engagement. If his honour cannot be
arraigned of breaking any bond, . . . What matters merely breaking her heart?'

She then left the room; but Camilla dwelt upon nothing she
had uttered except the one dear and inviting project of proving
disinterestedness to Edgar. 'O! if once,' she cried, 'I could
annihilate every mercenary suspicion! If once I could shew
Edgar that his situation has no charms for me . . . and it has
none! none! then, indeed, I am his equal, though I am nothing,
. . . . equal in what is highest, in mind, in spirit, in sentiment!

*   *   *   *

From this time the whole of her behaviour became coloured by
this fascinating idea; and a scheme which, if proposed to her
under its real name of coquetry, she would have fled and condemned with antipathy, when presented to her as a means to
mark her freedom from sordid motives, she adopted with inconsiderate fondness. The sight, therefore, of Edgar, wherever she
met him, became now the signal for adding spirit to the pleasure
with which, already, and without any design, she had attended to
the young Baronet. Exertion gave to her the gaiety of which
solicitude had deprived her, and she appeared, in the eyes of Sir
Sedley, every day more charming. She indulged him with the
history of her adventure at the house of Mr. Dubster, and his

prevalent taste for the ridiculous made the account enchant him. He cast off, in return, all airs of affectation, when he conversed with her separately; and though still, in all mixt companies, they were resumed, the real integrity, as well as indifference of her heart, made that a circumstance but to stimulate this new species of intercourse, by representing it to be equally void of future danger to them both.

All this, however, failed of its desired end. Edgar never saw her engaged by Sir Sedley, but he thought her youthfully grateful, and esteemed her the more, or beheld her as a mere coquette, and ceased to esteem her at all. But never for a moment was any personal uneasiness excited by their mutually increasing intimacy. The conversations he had held, both with the Baronet and herself, had satisfied him that neither entertained one serious thought of the other; and he took, therefore, no interest in their acquaintance, beyond that which was always alive,—a vigilant concern for the manner in which it might operate upon her disposition.

With respect to the Major, he was by no means so entirely at his ease. He saw him still the declared and undisguised pursuer of her favour; and though he perceived, at the same time, she rather avoided than sought him, he still imagined, in general, his acceptance was arranged, from the many preceding circumstances which had first given him that belief. The whole of her behaviour, nevertheless, perplexed as much as it grieved him, and frequently, in the same half hour, she seemed to him all that was most amiable for inspiring admiration, and all that was least to be depended upon, for retaining attachment.

Yet however, from time to time, he felt alarmed or offended, he never ceased to experience the fondest interest in her happiness, nor the most tender compassion for the dangers with which he saw her environed. He knew, that though her understanding was excellent, her temper was so inconsiderate, that she rarely consulted it; and that, though her mind was of the purest innocence, it was unguarded by caution, and unprotected by reflexion. He thought her placed where far higher discretion, far superior experience, might risk being shaken; and he did not more fervently wish, than internally tremble, for her safety. Wherever she appeared, she was sure of distinction: ''Tis Miss Tyrold, the friend of Mrs. Berlinton,' was buzzed round the moment she was seen; and the particular favour in which she stood with some

votaries of the *ton*, made even her artlessness, her retired education, and her ignorance of all that pertained to the *certain circles*,
past over and forgiven, in consideration of her personal attractions, her youth, and newness.

Still, however, even this celebrity was not what most he
dreaded: so sudden and unexpected an elevation upon the heights
of fashionable fame might make her head, indeed, giddy, but her
heart he thought formed of materials too pure and too good to be
endangered so lightly; and though frequently, when he saw her so
circumstanced, he feared she was undone for private life, he could
not reflect upon her principles and disposition, without soon
recovering the belief that a short time might restore her mind to
its native simplicity and worth. But another rock was in the way,
against which he apprehended she might be dashed, whilst least
suspicious of any peril.

This rock, indeed, exhibited nothing to the view that could
have affrighted any spectator less anxiously watchful, or less
personally interested in regarding it. But youth itself, in the
fervour of a strong attachment, is as open-eyed, as observant,
and as prophetic as age, with all its concomitants of practice,
time, and suspicion. This rock, indeed, far from giving notice
of danger by any sharp points or rough prominences, displayed
only the smoothest and most inviting surface: for it was Mrs.
Berlinton, the beautiful, the accomplished, the attractive Mrs.
Berlinton, whom he beheld as the object of the greatest risk she
had to encounter.

As he still preserved the character with which she had consented
to invest him of her monitor, he seized every opportunity of
communicating to her his doubts and apprehensions. But in
proportion as her connexion with that lady increased, use to her
manners and sentiments abated the wonderment they inspired,
and they soon began to communicate an unmixt charm, that
made all other society, that of Edgar alone excepted, heartless
and uninteresting. Yet, in the conversations she held with him
from time to time, she frankly related the extraordinary attachment of her new friend to some unknown correspondent, and
confessed her own surprise when it first came to her knowledge.

Edgar listened to the account with the most unaffected dismay,
and represented the probable danger, and actual impropriety of
such an intercourse, in the strongest and most eloquent terms;

but he could neither appal her confidence, nor subdue her esteem. The openness with which all had originally and voluntarily been avowed, convinced her of the innocence with which it was felt, and all that his exhortations could obtain, was a remonstrance on her own part to Mrs. Berlinton.

She found that lady, however, persuaded she indulged but an innocent friendship, which she assured her was bestowed upon a person of as much honour as merit, and which only with life she should relinquish, since it was the sole consolation of her fettered existence.

Edgar, to whom this was communicated, saw with terror the ascendance thus acquired over her judgment as well as her affections, and became more watchful and more uneasy in observing the progress of this friendship, than all the flattering devoirs of the gay Baronet, or the more serious assiduities of the Major.

Mrs. Berlinton, indeed, was no common object, either for fear or for hope, for admiration or for censure. She possessed all that was most softly attractive, most bewitchingly beautiful, and most irresistibly captivating, in mind, person, and manners. But to all that was thus most fascinating to others, she joined unhappily all that was most dangerous for herself; an heart the most susceptible, sentiments the most romantic, and an imagination the most exalted. She had been an orphan from earliest years, and left, with an only brother, to the care of a fanatical maiden aunt, who had taught her nothing but her faith and her prayers, without one single lesson upon good works, or the smallest instruction upon the practical use of her theoretical piety. All that ever varied these studies were some common and ill selected novels and romances, which a young lady in the neighbourhood privately lent her to read; till her brother, upon his first vacation from the University, brought her the works of the Poets.[1] These, also, it was only in secret she could enjoy; but, to her juvenile fancy, and irregularly principled mind, that did not render them more tasteless. Whatever was most beautifully picturesque in poetry, she saw verified in the charming landscapes presented to her view in the part of Wales she inhabited; whatever was most noble or tender in romance, she felt promptly in her heart, and conceived to be general; and whatever was enthusiastic in theology, formed the whole of her idea and her belief with respect to religion.[2]

Brought up thus, to think all things the most unusual and extraordinary, were merely common and of course; she was romantic without consciousness, and excentric without intention. Nothing steady or rational had been instilled into her mind by others; and she was too young, and too fanciful to have formed her own principles with any depth of reflection, or study of propriety. She had entered the world, by a sudden and most unequal marriage, in which her choice had no part, with only two self-formed maxims for the law of her conduct. The first of these was, that, from her early notions of religion, no vestal should be more personally chaste; the second, that, from her more recently imbibed ones of tenderness, her heart, since she was married without its concurrence, was still wholly at liberty to be disposed of by its own propensities, without reproach and without scruple.

With such a character, where virtue had so little guide even while innocence presided; where the person was so alluring, and the situation so open to temptation, Edgar saw with almost every species of concern the daily increasing friendship of Camilla. Yet while he feared for her firmness, he knew not how to blame her fondness; nor where so much was amiable in its object, could he cease to wish that more were right.

*   *   *   *

Thus again lived and died another week; and the fourth succeeded with no actual occurrence, but a new change of opinion in Mrs. Arlbery, that forcibly and cruelly affected the feelings of Camilla.

Uninformed of the motive that occasioned the indifference with which Edgar beheld the newly awakened gallantry of Sir Sedley, and the pleasure with which Camilla received it, Mrs. Arlbery observed his total unconcern, first with surprise, next with perplexity, and finally with a belief he was seriously resolved against forming any connection with her himself. This she took an early opportunity to intimate to Camilla, warmly exhorting her to drive him fast from her mind.

Camilla assured her that no task could be more easy; but the disappointment of the project with respect to Sir Sedley, which she blushed to have adopted, hurt her in every possible direction. Coquetry was as foreign to the ingenuousness of her nature, as to the dignity of all her early maternal precepts. She had hastily encouraged the devoirs of the Baronet, upon the recommendation of a woman she loved and admired; but now, that the failure of her aim brought her to reflexion, she felt penitent and ashamed to have heeded any advice so contrary to the singleness of the doctrines of her father, and so inferior to the elevation of every sentiment she had ever heard from her mother. If Edgar had seen her design, he had surely seen it with contempt: and though his manner was still the most gentle, and his advice ever ready and friendly, the opinion of Mrs. Arlbery was corroborated by all her own observations, that he was decidedly estranged from her.

What repentance ensued! what severity of regret! how did she canvass her conduct, how lament she had ever formed that fatal acquaintance with Mrs. Arlbery, which he had so early opposed, and which seemed eternally destined to lead her into measures and conduct most foreign to his approbation!

The melancholy that now again took possession of her spirits made her decline going abroad, from a renewed determination to avoid all meetings with Edgar. Mrs. Arlbery felt provoked to find his power thus unabated, and Sir Sedley was astonished. He still saw her perpetually, from his visits at Mount Pleasant; but his vanity, that weakest yet most predominant feature of his character, received a shock for which no modesty of apprehension or fore-thought had prepared him, in finding that, when he saw her no more in the presence of Mandlebert, he saw her no more the same. She was ready still to converse with him; but no peculiar attention was flattering, no desire to oblige was pointed. He found he had been merely a passive instrument, in her estimation, to excite jealousy; and even as such had been powerless to produce that effect. The raillery which Mrs. Arlbery spared not upon the occasion added greatly to his pique, and his mortification was so visible, that Camilla perceived it, and perceived it with pain, with shame, and with surprise. She thought now, for the first time, that the public homage he had paid her had private and serious motives, and that what she imagined mere sportive gallantry, arose from a growing attachment.

This idea had no gratifying power; believing Edgar without care for her, she could not hope it would stimulate his regard; and conceiving she had herself excited the partiality by wilful civilities, she could feel only reproach from a conquest, unduly, unfairly, uningenuously obtained.

In proportion as these self-upbraidings made her less deserving in her own eyes, the merits of the young Baronet seemed to augment; and in considering herself as culpable for having raised his regard, she appeared before him with a humility that gave a softness to her look and manners, which soon proved as interesting to Sir Sedley as her marked gaiety had been flattering.

When she perceived this, she felt distressed anew. To shun him was impossible, as Mrs. Arlbery not only gave him completely the freedom of her house, but assiduously promoted their belonging always to the same group, and being seated next to each other. There was nothing she would not have done to extenuate her error, and to obviate its ill effect upon Sir Sedley; but as she always thought herself in the wrong, and regarded him as injured, every effort was accompanied with a timidity that gave to every change a new charm, rather than any repulsive quality.

In this state of total self-disapprobation, to return to Etherington was her only wish, and to pass the intermediate time with Mrs. Berlinton became her sole pleasure. But she was forced again into public to avoid an almost single intercourse with Sir Sedley.

In meeting again with Edgar she saw him openly delighted at her sight, but without the least apparent solicitude, or notice, that the young Baronet had passed almost the whole of the interval upon Mount Pleasant.

This was instantly noticed, and instantly commented upon by Mrs. Arlbery, who again, and strongly pointed out to Camilla, that to save her youth from being wasted by fruitless expectation, she must forget young Mandlebert, and study only her own amusement.

Camilla dissented not from the opinion; but the doctrine to which it was easy to agree, it was difficult to put in practice; and her ardent mind believed itself fettered for ever, and for ever unhappy.

CHAPTER XIII

Traits of Instruction

THE sixth and last week destined for the Tunbridge sojourn was begun, when Mrs. Arlbery once more took her fair young guest apart, and intreated her attention for one final half hour. The time, she said, was fast advancing in which they must return to their respective homes; but she wished to make a full and clear representation of the advantages that might be reaped from this excursion, before the period for gathering them should be past.

She would forbear, she said, entering again upon the irksome subject of the insensibility of Mandlebert, which was, at least, sufficiently glaring to prevent any delusion. But she begged leave to speak of what she believed had less obviously struck her, the apparent promise of a serious attachment from Sir Sedley Clarendel.

Camilla would here instantly have broken up the conversation, but Mrs. Arlbery insisted upon being heard.

Why, she asked, should she wilfully destine her youth to a hopeless waste of affection, and dearth of all permanent comfort? To sacrifice every consideration to the honours of constancy, might be soothing, and even glorious in this first season of romance; but a very short time would render it vapid; and the epoch of repentance was always at hand to succeed. With the least address, or the least genuine encouragement, it was now palpable she might see Sir Sedley, and his title and fortune at her feet.

Camilla resentfully interrupted her, disclaiming with Sir Sedley, as with everyone else, all possibility of alliance from motives so degrading; and persisted, in declaring, that the most moderate subsistence with freedom, would be preferable to the most affluent obtained by any mercenary engagement.

Mrs. Arlbery desired her to recollect that Sir Sedley, though rich even to splendour, was so young, so gay, so handsome, and so pleasant, that she might safely honour him with her hand, yet run no risk of being supposed to have made a merely interested alliance. 'I throw out this,' she cried, 'in conclusion, for your deepest consideration, but I must press it no further. Sir Sedley is evidently charmed with you at present; and his vanity is so potent, and, like all vanity, so easily assailable, that the smallest food to it, adroitly administered, would secure him your slave for life, and rescue you from the antediluvian courtship of a man, who, if he marries at all, is so deliberate in his progress, that he must reach his grand climacteric before he can reach the altar.'

*   *   *   *

Far from meditating upon this discourse with any view to following its precepts, Camilla found it necessary to call all her original fondness for Mrs. Arlbery to her aid, to forgive the plainness of her attack, or the worldiness of her notions: and all that rested upon her mind for consideration was, her belief in the serious regard of Sir Sedley, which, as she apprehended it to be the work of her own designed exertions, she could only think of with contrition.

These ruminations were interrupted by a call down stairs to see a learned bullfinch. The Dennels and Sir Sedley were present; she met the eyes of the latter with a sensation of shame that quickly deepened her whole face with crimson. He did not behold it without emotion, and experienced a strong curiosity to define its exact cause.

He addressed himself to her with the most marked distinction; she could scarcely answer him; but her manner was even touchingly gentle. Sir Sedley could not restrain himself from following her in every motion by his eyes; he felt an interest concerning her that surprised him; he began to doubt if it had been indifference which caused her late change; her softness helped his vanity to recover its tone, and her confusion almost confirmed him that Mrs. Arlbery had been mistaken in rallying his failure of rivalry with Mandlebert.

The bird sung various little airs, upon certain words of command, and mounted his highest, and descended to his lowest perch; and made whatever evolutions were within the circumference of his limited habitation, with wonderful precision.

Camilla, however, was not more pleased by his adroitness, than pained to observe the severe aspect with which his keeper issued his orders. She inquired by what means he had obtained such authority.

The man, with a significant wag of the head, brutally answered, 'By the true old way, Miss; I licks him.'

'Lick him!' repeated she, with disgust; 'how is it possible you can beat such a poor delicate little creature?'

'O, easy enough, Miss,' replied the man, grinning; 'everything's the better for a little beating, as I tells my wife. There's nothing so fine set, Miss, but what will bear it, more or less.'

Sir Sedley asked with what he could strike it, that would not endanger its life.

'That's telling, sir!' cried the man, with a sneer; 'howbeit, we've plenty of ill luck in the trade. No want of that. For one that I rears, I loses six or seven. And sometimes they be so plaguy sulky, they tempt me to give 'em a knock a little matter too hard, and then they'll fall you into a fit, like, and go off in a twinkle.'

'And how can you have the cruelty,' cried Camilla, indignantly, 'to treat in such a manner a poor little inoffensive animal who does not understand what you require?'

'O, yes, a does, miss, they knows what I wants as well as I do myself; only they're so dead tiresome at being shy. Why now this one here, as does all his larning to satisfaction just now, mayhap won't do nothing at all by an hour or two. Why sometimes you may pinch 'em to a mummy[1] before you can make 'em budge.'

'Pinch them!' exclaimed she; 'do you ever pinch them?'

'Do I? Ay, miss. Why how do you think one larns them dumb creturs? It don't come to 'em natural. They are main dull of themselves. This one as you see here would do nothing at all, if he was not afraid of a tweak.'

'Poor unhappy little thing!' cried she! 'I hope, at least, now it has learnt so much, its sufferings are over!'

'Yes, yes, he's pretty well off. I always gives him his fill when he's done his day's work. But a little squeak now and then in the intrum does 'em no harm. They're mortal cunning. One's forced to be pretty tough with 'em.'

'How should I rejoice,' cried Camilla, 'to rescue this one poor unoffending and oppressed little animal from such tyranny!' Then, taking out her purse, she desired to know what he would have for it.

The man, as a very great favour, said he would take ten guineas; though it would be his ruin to part with it, as it was all his livelihood; but he was willing to oblige the young lady.

Camilla, with a constrained laugh, but a very natural blush, put up her purse, and said: 'Thou must linger on, then, in captivity, thou poor little undeserving sufferer, for I cannot help thee!'

Every body protested that ten guineas was an imposition; and the man offered to part with it for five.

Camilla, who had imagined it would have cost half a guinea, was now more ashamed, because equally incapable to answer such a demand; she declined, therefore, the composition, and the man was dismissed.

*   *   *   *

At night, when she returned to her own room from the play, she saw the little bullfinch, reposing in a superb cage, upon her table.

Delighted first, and next perplexed, she flew to Mrs. Arlbery, and inquired whence it came.

Mrs. Arlbery was as much amazed as herself.

Questions were then asked of the servants; but none knew, or none would own, how the bird became thus situated.

Camilla could not now doubt but Sir Sedley had given this commission to his servant, who could easily place the cage in her room, from his constant access to the house. She was enchanted to see the little animal relieved from so painful a life, but hesitated not a moment in resolving to refuse its acceptance.

When Sir Sedley came the next day, she carried it down, and, with a smile of open pleasure, thanked him for giving her so much share in his generous liberality; and asked if he could take it home with him in his carriage, or, if she should send it to his hotel.

Sir Sedley was disappointed, yet felt the propriety of her delicacy and her spirit. He did not deny the step he had taken, but told her that having hastily, from the truth of reflection her compassion had awakened, ordered his servant to follow the man, and buy the bird, he had forgotten, till it arrived, his incapability of taking care of it. His valet was as little at home as himself, and there was small chance, at an inn, that any maid would so carefully watch, as to prevent its falling a prey to the many cats with which it was swarming. He hoped, therefore, till their return to Hampshire, she would take charge of a little animal that owed its deliverance from slavery to her pitying comments.

Camilla, instinctively, would with unfeigned joy, have accepted such a trust: but she thought she saw something archly significant in the eye of Mrs. Arlbery, and therefore stammered out, she was afraid she should herself be too little at home to secure its safety.

Sir Sedley, looking extremely blank, said, it would be better to re-deliver it to the man, brute as he was, than to let it be unprotected; but, where generosity touched Camilla, reflection ever flew her; and off all guard at such an idea, she exclaimed she would rather relinquish going out again while at Tunbridge, than render his humanity abortive; and ran off precipitately with the bird to her chamber.

Mrs. Arlbery, soon following, praised her behaviour; and said, she had sent the Baronet away perfectly happy.

Camilla, much provoked, would now have had the bird conveyed after him; but Mrs. Arlbery assured her, inconsistency in a woman was as flattering, as in a man it was tedious and alarming; and persuaded her to let the matter rest.

Her mind, however, did not rest at the same time: in the evening, when the Baronet met them at the Rooms, he was not only unusually gay, but looked at her with an air and manner that seemed palpably to mark her as the cause of his satisfaction.

In the deepest disturbance, she considered herself now to be in a difficulty the most delicate; she could not come forward to clear it up, without announcing expectations from his partiality which he had never authorised by any declaration; nor yet suffer such symptoms of his believing it welcome to pass unnoticed, without risking the reproach of using him ill, when she made known, at a later period, her indifference.

Mrs. Arlbery would not aid her, for she thought the embarrassment might lead to a termination the most fortunate. To consult with Edgar was her first wish; but how open such a subject? The very thought, however, gave her an air of solicitude when he spoke to her, that struck him, and he watched for an opportunity to say, 'You have not, I hope, forgotten my province? .... May I, in my permitted office, ask a few questions?'

'O, yes!' cried she, with alacrity; 'And, when they are asked, and when I have answered them, if you should not be too much tired, may I ask some in my turn?'

'Of me!' cried he, with the most gratified surprise.

'Not concerning yourself!' answered she, blushing; 'but upon something which a little distresses me.'

'When, and where may it be?' cried he, while a thousand conjectures rapidly succeeded to each other; 'may I call upon Mrs. Arlbery to-morrow morning?'

'O, no! we shall be, I suppose, here again at night,' she answered; dreading arranging a visit Mrs. Arlbery would treat, she knew, with raillery the most unmerciful.

There was time for no more, as that lady, suddenly tired, led the way to the carriage. Edgar followed her to the door, hoping and fearing, at once, every thing that was most interesting from a confidence so voluntary and so unexpected.

Camilla was still more agitated; for though uncertain if she were right or wrong in the appeal she meant to make, to converse with him openly, to be guided by his counsel, and to convince him of her superiority to all mercenary allurements were pleasures to make her look forward to the approaching conference with almost trembling delight.

CHAPTER XIV

A Demander

THE next night, as the carriage was at the door, and the party preparing for the Rooms, the name of Mr. Tyrold was announced, and Lionel entered the parlour.

His manner was hurried, though he appeared gay and frisky as usual; Camilla felt a little alarmed; but Mrs. Arlbery asked if he would accompany them.

With all his heart, he answered, only he must first have a moment's chat with his sister. Then, saying they should have a letter to write together, he called for a pen and ink, and was taking her into another apartment, when Mr. Dennel objected to letting his horses wait.

'Send them back for us, then,' cried Lionel, with his customary ease, 'and we will follow you.'

Mr. Dennel again objected to making his horses so often mount the hill; but Lionel assuring him nothing was so good for them, ran on with so many farrier words and phrases of the benefit they would reap from such light evening exercise, that, persuaded he was master of the subject, Mr. Dennel submitted, and the brother and sister were left *tête-à-tête*.

At any other time, Camilla would have proposed giving up the Rooms entirely: but her desire to see Edgar, and the species of engagement she had made with him, counterbalanced every inconvenience.

'My dear girl,' said Lionel, 'I am come to beg a favour. You see this pen and ink. Give me a sheet of paper.'

She fetched him one.

'That's a good child,' cried he, patting her cheek; 'so now

sit down, and write a short letter for me. Come begin. Dear Sir.'

She wrote—Dear Sir.

'An unforeseen accident,—write on,—an unforeseen accident has reduced me to immediate distress for two hundred pounds . . . .'

Camilla let her pen drop, and rising said, 'Lionel! is this possible?'

'Very possible, my dear. You know I told you I wanted another hundred before you left Cleves. So you must account it only as one hundred, in fact, at present.'

'O Lionel, Lionel!' cried Camilla, clasping her hands, with a look of more remonstrance than any words she durst utter.

'Won't you write the letter?' said he, pretending not to observe her emotion.

'To whom is it to be addressed?'

'My uncle, to be sure, my dear! What can you be thinking of? Are you in love, Camilla?'

'My uncle again? no Lionel, no!—I have solemnly engaged myself to apply to him no more.'

'That was, for me, my dear; but where can your thoughts be wandering? Why you must ask for this, as if it were for yourself.'

'For myself!'

'Yes, certainly. You know he won't give it else.'

'Impossible! what should I want two hundred pounds for?'

'O, a thousand things; say you must have some new gowns and caps, and hats and petticoats, and all those kind of gear. There is not the least difficulty; you can easily persuade him they are all worn out at such a place as this. Besides, I'll tell you what is still better; say you've been robbed; he'll soon believe it, for he thinks all public places filled with sharpers.'

'Now you relieve me,' said she, with a sort of fearful smile, 'for I am sure you cannot be serious. You must be very certain I would not deceive or delude my uncle for a million of worlds.'

'You know nothing of life, child, nothing at all. However, if you won't say that, tell him it's for a secret purpose. At least you can do that. And then, you can make him understand he must ask no questions about the matter. The money is all we want from him.'

'This is so idle, Lionel, that I hope you speak it for mere nonsense. Who could demand such a sum, and refuse to account for its purpose?'

'Account, my dear? Does being an uncle give a man a right to be impertinent? If it does, marry out of hand yourself, there's a good girl, and have a family at once, that I may share the same privilege. I shall like it of all things; who will you have?'

'Pho, pho!'

'Major Cerwood?'

'No, never!'

'I once thought Edgar Mandlebert had a sneaking kindness for you. But I believe it is gone off. Or else I was out.'[1]

This was not an observation to exhilarate her spirits. She sighed: but Lionel, concluding himself the cause, begged her not to be low-spirited, but to write the letter at once.

She assured him she could never again consent to interfere in his unreasonable requests.

He was undone, then, he said; for he could not live without the money.

'Rather say, not with it,' cried she; 'for you keep nothing!'

'Nobody does, my dear; we all go on the same way now-a-days.'

'And what do you mean to be the end of it all, Lionel? How do you purpose living when all these resources are completely exhausted?'

'When I am ruined, you mean? why how do other people live when they're ruined? I can but do the same; though I have not much considered the matter.'

'Do consider it, then, dear Lionel! for all our sakes, do consider it!'

'Well,—let us see.'

'O, I don't mean so; I don't mean just now; in this mere idle manner.—'

'O, yes, I'll do it at once, and then it will be over. Faith I don't well know. I have no great *gusta* for blowing out my brains. I like the little dears mighty well where they are. And I can't say I shall much relish to consume my life and prime and vigour in the king's bench prison.[2] 'Tis horribly tiresome to reside always on the same spot. Nor I have no great disposition to whisk off to another country. Old England's a pretty place enough. I like it very well; ... with a little rhino understood! But it's the very deuce, with an empty purse. So write the letter, my dear girl.'

'And is this your consideration, Lionel? And is this its conclusion?'

'Why what signifies dwelling upon such dismalties? If I think upon my ruin beforehand, I am no nearer to enjoyment now than then. Live while we live, my dear girl! I hate prophesying horrors. Write, I say, write!'

Again she absolutely refused, pleading her promise to her uncle, and declaring she would keep her word.

'Keep a fiddlestick!' cried he, impatiently; 'you don't know what mischief you may have to answer for! you may bring misery upon all our heads! you may make my father banish me his sight, you may make my mother execrate me!—'

'Good Heaven!' cried Camilla interrupting him, 'what is it you talk of? what is it you mean?'

'Just what I say; and to make you understand me better, I'll give you a hint of the truth; but you must lose your life twenty times before you reveal it—There's—there's—do you hear me?— there's a pretty girl in the case!'

'A pretty girl!—And what has that to do with this rapacity for money?'

'What an innocent question! why what a baby thou art, my dear Camilla!'

'I hope you are not forming any connexion unknown to my father?'

'Ha, ha, ha!' cried Lionel laughing loud: 'Why thou hast lived in that old parsonage-house till thou art almost too young to be rocked in a cradle.'[1]

'If you are entering into any engagement,' said she, still more gravely, 'that my father must not know, and that my mother would so bitterly condemn,—why am I to be trusted with it?'

'You understand nothing of these things, child. 'Tis the very nature of a father to be an hunks, and of a mother to be a bore.'[2]

'O Lionel! such a father!—such a mother!—'

'As to their being perfectly good, and all that, I know it very well. And I am very sorry for it. A good father is a very serious misfortune to a poor lad like me, as the world runs; it causes one such confounded gripes of the conscience for every little awkward thing one does! A bad father would be the joy of my life; 'twould be all fair play there; the more he was choused[3] the better.'

'But this pretty girl, Lionel!—Are you serious? Are you really engaging yourself? And is she so poor? Is she so much distressed, that you require these immense and frequent sums for her?'

Lionel laughed again, and rubbed his hands; but after a short silence assumed a more steady countenance, and said, 'Don't ask me any thing about her. It is not fit you should be so curious. And don't give a hint of the matter to a soul. Mind that! But as to the money, I must have it. And directly: I shall be blown to the deuce else.'

'Lionel!' cried Camilla, shrinking, 'you make me tremble! you cannot surely be so wicked . . . so unprincipled . . . No! your connexions are never worse than imprudent!—you would not else be so unkind, so injurious as to place in me such a confidence!'

The whole face of Lionel now flashed with shame, and he walked about the room, muttering: ''Tis true, I ought not to have done it.' And soon after, with still greater concern, he exclaimed: 'If this appears to you in such a heinous light, what will my father think of it? And how can I bear to let it be known to my mother?'

'O never, never!' cried she emphatically; 'never let it reach the knowledge of either! If indeed you have been so inconsiderate, and so wrong—break up, at least, any such intercourse before it offends their ears.'

'But how, my dear, can I do that, if it gets blazed abroad?'

'Blazed abroad!'

'Yes; and for want, only, of a few pitiful guineas.'

'What can you mean? How can it depend upon a few guineas?'

'Get me the guineas;—and leave the how to me.'

'My dear Lionel,' cried she, affectionately, 'I would do any thing that is not absolutely improper to serve you; but my uncle has now nothing more to spare; he has told me so himself; and with what courage, then, in this dark, mysterious, and, I fear, worse than mysterious business, can I apply to him?'

'My dear child, he only wants to hoard up his money to shew off poor Eugenia at her marriage; and you know as well as I do what a ninny he is for his pains; for what a poor little dowdy thing will she look, dizened out in jewels and laces?'

'Can you speak so of Eugenia? the most amiable, the most deserving, the most excellent creature breathing!'

'I speak it in pure friendship. I would not have her exposed. I love dear little Greek and Latin as well as you do. Only the difference is I don't talk so like an old woman; and really when you do it yourself, you can't think the ridiculous effect it has, when one looks at your young face. However, only write the request as if from yourself, and tell him you'll acquaint him with the reason next letter; but that the post is just going out now, and you have time for no more. And then, just coax him over a little, with, how you long to be back, and how you hate Tunbridge, and how you adore Cleves, and how tired you are for want of his bright conversation,—and you may command half his fortune.—My dear Camilla, you don't know from what destruction you will rescue me! Think too of my father, and what a shock you will save him: And think of my mother, whom I can never see again if you won't help me!'

Camilla sighed, but let him put the pen into her hand, whence, however, the very next moment's reflection was urging her to cast it down, when he caught her in his arms in a transport of joy, called her his protectress from dishonour and despair, and said he would run to the Rooms while she wrote, just to take the opportunity of seeing them, and to un-order the carriage, that she might have no interruption to her composition, which he would come back to claim before the party returned, as he must set off for Cleves, and gallop all night, to procure the money, which the loss of a single day would render useless.

All this he uttered with a rapidity that mocked every attempt at expostulation or answer; and then ran out of the room and out of the house.

*   *   *   *

Horrour at such perpetual and increasing ill conduct, grief at the compulsive failure of meeting Edgar, and perplexity how to extricate herself from her half given, but wholly seized upon engagement to write, took for a while nearly equally shares in tormenting Camilla. But all presently concentred in one domineering sentiment of sharp repentance for what she had apparently undertaken.

To claim two hundred pounds of her uncle, in her own name, was out of all question. She could not, even a moment, dwell upon such a project; but how represent what she herself so little understood as the necessity of Lionel? or how ask for so large a sum, and postpone, as he desired, all explanation? She was incapable of any species of fraud, she detested even the most distant disguise. Simple supplication seemed, therefore, her only method;

but so difficult was even this, in an affair so dark and unconscionable, that she began twenty letters without proceeding in any one
of them beyond two lines.

Thus far, however, her task was light to what it appeared to her
upon a little further deliberation. That her brother had formed
some unworthy engagement or attachment, he had not, indeed,
avowed clearly, but he had by no means denied, and she had even
omitted, in her surprise and consternation, exacting his promise
that it should immediately be concluded. What, then, might she
be doing by endeavouring to procure this money? Aiding perhaps
vice and immorality, and assisting her misguided, if not guilty
brother, to persevere in the most dangerous errors, if not crimes?

She shuddered, she pushed away her paper, she rose from the
table, she determined not to write another word.

Yet, to permit parents she justly revered to suffer any evil she
had the smallest chance to spare them, was dreadful to her;
and what evil could be inflicted upon them, so deeply, so lastingly
severe, as the conviction of any serious vices in any of their
children?

This, for one minute, brought her again to the table; but the
next, her better judgment pointed out the shallowness and fallacy
of such reasoning. To save them present pain at the risk of future
anguish, to consult the feelings of her brother, in preference to his
morality, would be forgetting every lesson of her life, which, from
its earliest dawn, had imbibed a love of virtue, that made her
consider whatever was offensive to it as equally disgusting and
unhappy.

To disappoint Lionel was, however, terrible. She knew well
he would be deaf to remonstrance, ridicule all argument, and
laugh off whatever she could urge by persuasion. She feared he
would be quite outrageous to find his expectations thus thwarted;
and the lateness of the hour when he would hear it, and the weight
he annexed, to obtaining the money expeditiously, redoubled at
once her regret for her momentary compliance, and her pity for
what he would undergo through its failure.

After considering in a thousand ways how to soften to him her
recantation, she found herself so entirely without courage to
encounter his opposition, that she resolved to write him a short
letter, and then retire to her room, to avoid an interview.

In this, she besought him to forgive her error in not sooner being sensible of her duty, which had taught her, upon her first reflexion, the impossibility of demanding two hundred pounds for herself, who wanted nothing, and the impracticability of demanding it for him, in so unintelligible a manner.

Thus far only she had proceeded, from the length of time consumed in regret and rumination, when a violent ringing at the door, without the sound of any carriage, made her start up, and fly to her chamber; leaving her unfinished letter, with the beginnings of her several essays to address Sir Hugh, upon the table, to shew her various efforts, and to explain that they were relinquished.

CHAPTER XV

An Accorder

THUS, self-confined and almost in an agony, Camilla remained for a quarter of an hour, without any species of interruption, and in the greatest amazement that Lionel forbore pursuing her, either with letter or message.

Another violent ringing at the bell, but still without any carriage, then excited her attention, and presently the voice and steps of Lionel resounded upon the stairs, whence her name was with violence vociferated.

She did not move; and in another minute, he was rapping at her chamber door, demanding admittance, or that she would instantly descend.

Alarmed for her open letter and papers, she inquired who was in the parlour.

'Not a soul,' he answered; 'I have left them all at the Rooms.'

'Have you returned, then, twice?'

'No. I should have been here sooner, but I met two or three old cronies, that would not part with me. Come, where's your letter?'

'Have you not seen what I have written?'

Down upon this intimation he flew, without any reply; but was presently back, saying he found nothing in the parlour, except a letter to herself.

Affrighted, she followed him; but not one of her papers

remained. The table was cleared, and nothing was to be seen but a large packet, addressed to her in a hand she did not know.

She rang to inquire who had been in the house before her brother.

The servant answered, only Sir Sedley Clarendel, who he thought had been there still, as he had said he should wait till Mrs. Arlbery came home.

'Is it possible,' cried she, 'that a gentleman such as Sir Sedley Clarendel, can have permitted himself to touch my papers?'

Lionel agreed that it was shocking; but said the loss of time to himself was still worse; without suffering her, therefore, to open her packet, he insisted that she should write another letter directly; adding, he had met the Baronet in his way from the Rooms, but had little suspected whence he came, or how he had been amusing himself.

Camilla now hung about her brother in the greatest tribulation, but refused to take the pen he would have put into her hands, and, at last, not without tears, said: 'Forgive me, Lionel! but the papers you ought to have found would have explained—that I cannot write for you to my uncle.'

Lionel heard this with the indignation of an injured man. He was utterly, he said, lost; and his family would be utterly disgraced, for ruin must be the lot of his father, or exile or imprisonment must be his own, if she persisted in such unkind and unnatural conduct.

Terrour now bereft her of all speech or motion, till the letter, which Lionel had been beating about in his agitation, without knowing or caring what he was doing, burst open, and some written papers fell to the floor, which she recognised for her own.

Much amazed, she seized the cover,[1] which had only been fastened by a wafer that was still wet, and saw a letter within it to herself, which she hastily read, while a paper that was enclosed dropt down, and was caught by Lionel.

To Miss Camilla Tyrold.

F ORGIVE, fairest Camilla, the work of the Destinies. I came hither to see if illness detained you; the papers which I enclose from other curious eyes caught mine by accident. The pathetic sisterly address has touched me. I have not the honour to know

Mr. Lionel Tyrold; let our acquaintance begin with an act of confidence on his part, that must bind to him for ever his lovely sister's.

Most obedient and devoted
SEDLEY CLARENDEL.

The loose paper, picked up by Lionel, was a draft, upon a banker, for two hundred pounds.

While this, with speechless emotion, was perused by Camilla, Lionel, with unbounded joy, began jumping, skipping, leaping over every chair, and capering round and round the room in an ecstasy.

'My dearest Lionel,' cried she, when a little recovered, 'why such joy? you cannot suppose it possible this can be accepted.'

'Not accepted, child? do you think me out of my senses? Don't you see me freed from all my misfortunes at once? and neither my father grieved, nor my mother offended, nor poor numps[1] fleeced?'

'And when can you pay it? And what do you mean to do? And to whom will be the obligation? Weigh, weigh a little all this.'

Lionel heard her not; his rapture was too buoyant for attention, and he whisked every thing out of its place, from frantic merriment, till he put the apartment into so much disorder, that it was scarce practicable to stir a step in it; now and then interrupting himself to make her low bows, scraping his feet all over the room, and obsequiously saying: 'My sister Clarendel! How does your La'ship do? my dear Lady Clarendel, pray afford me your La'ship's countenance.'

Nothing could be less pleasant to Camilla than raillery which pointed out, that, even by the unreflecting Lionel, this action could be ascribed to but one motive. The draft, however, had fallen into his hands, and neither remonstrance nor petition, neither representation of impropriety nor persuasion, could induce him to relinquish it; he would only dance, sing, and pay her grotesque homage, till the coach stopt at the door; and then, ludicrously hoping her Ladyship would excuse his leaving her, for once, to play the part of the house-maid, in setting the room to rights, he sprang past them all, and bounded down the hill.

Mrs. Arlbery was much diverted by the confusion in the parlour, and Miss Dennel asked a thousand questions why the chairs and tables were all thrown down, the china jars removed from the chimney-piece into the middle of the room, and the side-board apparatus put on the chimney-piece in their stead.

Camilla was too much confounded either to laugh or explain, and hastily wishing them good-night, retired to her chamber.

Here, in the extremest perturbation, she saw the full extent of her difficulties, without perceiving any means of extrication. She had no hope of recovering the draft from Lionel, whom she had every reason to conclude already journeying from Tunbridge. What could she say the next day to Sir Sedley? How account for so sudden, so gross an acceptance of pecuniary obligation? What inference might he not draw? And how could she undeceive him, while retaining so improper a mark of his dependence upon her favour? The displeasure she felt that he should venture to suppose she would owe to him such a debt, rendered but still more palpable the species of expectation it might authorise.

To destroy this illusion occupied all her attention, except what was imperiously seized upon by regret of missing Edgar, with whom to consult was more than ever her wish.

In this disturbed state, when she saw Mrs. Arlbery the next morning, her whole care was to avoid being questioned: and that lady, who quickly perceived her fears by her avoidance, took the first opportunity to say to her, with a laugh, 'I see I must make no inquiries into the gambols of your brother last night: but I may put together, perhaps, certain circumstances that may give me a little light to the business: and if, as I conjecture, Clarendel spoke out to him, his wildest rioting is more rational than his sister's gravity.'

Camilla protested they had not conversed together at all.

'Nay, then, I own myself still in the dark. But I observed that Clarendel left the Rooms at a very early hour, and that your brother almost immediately followed.'

Camilla ventured not any reply; and soon after retreated.

Mrs. Arlbery, in a few minutes, pursuing her, laughingly, and with sportive reproach, accused her of intending to steal a march to the altar of Hymen; as she had just been informed, by her maid, that Sir Sedley had actually been at the house last night, during her absence.

Camilla seriously assured her, that she was in her chamber when he arrived, and had not seen him.

'For what in the world, then, could he come? He was sure I was not at home, for he had left me at the Rooms?'

Camilla again was silent; but her tingling cheeks proclaimed it was not for want of something to say. Mrs. Arlbery forbore to press the matter further; but forbore with a nod that implied *I see how it is!* and a smile that published the pleasure and approbation which accompanied her self-conviction.

The vexation of Camilla would have prompted an immediate confession of the whole mortifying transaction, had she not been endued with a sense of honour, where the interests of others were concerned, that repressed her natural precipitance, and was more powerful even than her imprudence.

She waited the greatest part of the morning in some little faint hope of seeing Lionel: but he came not, and she spent the rest of it with Mrs. Berlinton. She anxiously wished to meet Edgar in the way, to apologise for her non-appearance the preceding evening; but this did not happen; and her concern was not lessened by reflecting upon the superior interest in her health and welfare, marked by Sir Sedley, who had taken the trouble to walk from the Rooms to Mount Pleasant to see what was become of her.

She returned home but barely in time to dress for dinner, and was not yet ready, when she saw the carriage of the Baronet drive up to the door.

In the most terrible confusion how to meet him, what to say about the draft, how to mention her brother, whether to seem resentful of the liberty he had so unceremoniously taken, or thankful for its kindness, she had scarce the force to attire herself, nor, when summoned down stairs, to descend.

This distress was but increased upon her entrance, by the sight and the behaviour of the Baronet; whose address to her was so marked, that it covered her with blushes, and whose air had an assurance that spoke a species of secret triumph. Offended as well as frightened, she looked every way to avoid him, or assumed a look of haughtiness, when forced by any direct speech to answer him. She soon, however, saw, by his continued self-complacency, and even an increase of gaiety, that he only regarded this as coquetry, or bashful embarrassment, since every time she attempted thus to rebuff him, an arch smile stole over his features, that displayed his different conception of her meaning.

She now wished nothing so much as a prompt and positive declaration, that she might convince him of his mistake and her rejection. For this purpose, she subdued her desire of retreat, and spent the whole afternoon with Mrs. Arlbery and the Dennels in his company.

Nevertheless, when Mrs. Arlbery, who had the same object in view, though with a different conclusion, contrived to draw her other guests out of the apartment and to leave her alone with Sir Sedley, modesty and shame both interfered with her desire of an explanation, and she was hastily retiring; but the Baronet, in a gentle voice, called after her, 'Are you going?'

'Yes, I have forgotten something. . . .'

He rose to follow her, with a motion that seemed purporting to take her hand; but, gliding quickly on, she prevented him, and was almost at the same moment in her own chamber.

With augmented severity, she now felt the impropriety of an apparent acceptance of so singular and unpleasant an obligation, which obviously misled Sir Sedley to believe her at his command.

Shocked in her delicacy, and stung in her best notions of laudable pride, she could not rest without destroying this humiliating idea; and resolved to apply to Edgar for the money, and to pay the Baronet the next day. Her objections to betraying the extravagance of Lionel, though great and sincere, yielded to the still more dangerous evil of letting Sir Sedley continue in an errour, that might terminate in branding her in his opinion, with a character of inconsistency or duplicity.

Edgar, too, so nearly a brother to them both, would guard the secret of Lionel better, in all probability, than he would guard it himself; and could draw no personal inferences from the trust and obligation when he found its sole incitement was sooner to owe an obligation to a ward of her father, than to a new acquaintance of her own.

Pleased at the seeming necessity of an application that would lead so naturally to a demand of the counsel she languished to claim, she determined not to suffer Sir Sedley to wait even another minute under his mistake; but, since she now could speak of returning the money, to take courage for meeting what might either precede or ensue in a conference.

Down, therefore, she went; but as she opened the parlour door, she heard Sir Sedley say to Mrs. Arlbery, who had just entered before her: 'O, fie! fie! you know she will be cruel to excruciation! you know me destined to despair to the last degree.'

Camilla, whose so speedy re-appearance was the last sight he expected, was too far advanced to retreat; and the resentment that tinged her whole complexion shewed she had heard what he said, and had heard it with an application the most offensive.

An immediate sensibility to his own impertinence now succeeded in its vain display; he looked not merely concerned, but contrite; and, in a voice softened nearly to timidity, attempted a general conversation, but kept his eyes, with an anxious expression, almost continually fixed upon her's.

Anger with Camilla was a quick, but short-lived sensation; and this sudden change in the Baronet from conceit to respect, produced a change equally sudden in herself from disdain to inquietude. Though mortified in the first moment by his vanity, it was less seriously painful to her than any belief that under it was couched a disposition towards a really steady regard. With Mrs. Arlbery she was but slightly offended, though certain she had been assuring him of all the success he could demand: her way of thinking upon the subject had been openly avowed, and she did justice to the kindness of her motives.

No opportunity, however, arose to mention the return of the draft; Mrs. Arlbery saw displeasure in her air, and not doubting she had heard what had dropt from Sir Sedley, thought the moment unfavorable for a *tête-à-tête*, and resolutely kept her place, till Camilla herself, weary of useless waiting, left the room.

Following her then to her chamber, 'My dear Miss Tyrold,' she cried, 'do not let your extreme youth stand in the way of all your future life. A Baronet, rich, young, and amiable, is upon the very point of becoming your slave for ever; yet, because you discover him to be a little restive in the last agonies of his liberty, you are eager, in the high-flown disdain of juvenile susceptibility, to cast him and his fortune away; as if both were such every-day baubles, that you might command or reject them without thought of future consequence.'

'Indeed no, dear madam; I am not actuated by pride or anger; I owe too much to Sir Sedley to feel either above a moment, even where I think them ... pardon me! ... justly excited. But I should ill pay my debt, by accepting a lasting attachment, where certain I can return nothing but lasting, eternal, unchangeable indifference.'

'You sacrifice, then, both him and yourself, to the fanciful delicacy of a first love?'

'No, indeed!' cried she blushing. 'I have no thought at all but of the single life. And I sincerely hope Sir Sedley has no serious intentions towards me; for my obligations to him are so infinite, I should be cruelly hurt to appear to him ungrateful.'

'You would appear to him, I confess, a little surprising,' said Mrs. Arlbery, laughing; 'for diffidence certainly is not his weak part. However, with all his foibles, he is a charming creature, and prepossession only can blind you to his merit.'

Camilla again denied the charge, and strove to prevail with her to undeceive the Baronet from any false expectations. But she protested she would not be accessary to so much after-repentance; and left her.

The business now wore a very serious aspect to Camilla. Mrs. Arlbery avowed she thought Sir Sedley in earnest, and he knew she had herself heard him speak with security of his success. The bullfinch had gone far, but the draft seemed to have riveted the persuasion. The bird it was now impossible to return till her departure from Tunbridge; but she resolved not to defer another moment putting upon her brother alone the obligation of the draft, to stop the further progress of such dangerous inference.

Hastily, therefore, she wrote to him the following note:

To Sir Sedley Clarendel, *Bart.*

Sir,

Some particular business compelled my brother so abruptly to quit Tunbridge, that he could not have the honour to first wait upon you with his thanks for the loan you so unexpectedly put into his hands; by mine, however, all will be restored to-morrow morning, except his gratitude for your kindness.

I am, sir, in both our names,
your obliged humble servant,
CAMILLA TYROLD.

Mount Pleasant,
   Thursday Evening.

She now waited till she was summoned down stairs to the

carriage, and then gave her little letter to a servant, whom she desired to deliver it to Sir Sedley's man.

Sir Sedley did not accompany them to the Rooms, but promised to follow.

Camilla, on her arrival, with palpitating pleasure, looked round for Edgar. She did not, however, see him. She was accosted directly by the Major; who, as usual, never left her, and whose assiduity to seek her favour seemed increased.

She next joined Mrs. Berlinton; but still she saw nothing of Edgar. Her eyes incessantly looked towards the door, but the object they sought never met them.

When Sir Sedley entered, he joined the group of Mrs. Berlinton.

Camilla tried to look at him and to speak to him with her customary civility and chearfulness, and nearly succeeded; while in him she observed only an expressive attention, without any marks of presumption.

Thus began and thus ended the evening. Edgar never appeared.

Camilla was in the utmost amaze and deepest vexation. Why did he stay away? was his wrath so great at her own failure the preceding night, that he purposely avoided her? what, also, could she do with Sir Sedley? how meet him the next morning without the draft she had now promised?'

In this state of extreme chagrin, when she retired to her chamber, she found the following letter upon her table:

To Miss Camilla Tyrold.

CAN you think of such a trifle? or deem wealth so truly contemptible, as to deny it all honourable employment? Ah, rather, enchanting Camilla! deign further to aid me in dispensing it worthily!

SEDLEY CLARENDEL.

Camilla now was touched, penetrated, and distressed beyond what she had been in any former time. She looked upon this letter as a positive intimation of the most serious designs; and all his good qualities, as painted by Mrs. Arlbery, with the very singular obligation she owed to him, rose up formidably to support the arguments and remonstrances of that lady; though every feeling of her heart, every sentiment of her mind, and every wish of her soul, opposed their smallest weight.

CHAPTER XVI

An Helper

THE next morning, as Camilla had accompanied Mrs. Arlbery, in earnest discourse, from her chamber to the hall, she heard the postman say Miss Tyrold as he gave in a letter. She seized it, saw the hand-writing of Lionel, and ran eagerly into the parlour, which was empty, to read it, in some hopes it would at least contain an acknowledgment of the draft, that might be shewn to Sir Sedley, and relieve her from the pain of continuing the principal in such an affair.

The letter, however, was merely a sportive rhapsody, beginning; *My dear Lady Clarendel;* desiring her favour and protection, and telling her he had done what he could for her honour, by adding two trophies to the victorious car of Hymen, driven by the happy Baronet.

Wholly at a loss how to act, she sat ruminating over this letter, till Mrs. Arlbery opened the door. Having no time to fold it, and dreading her seeing the first words, she threw her handkerchief, which was then in her hand, over it, upon the table, hoping presently to draw it away unperceived.

'My dear friend,' said Mrs. Arlbery, 'I am glad to see you a moment alone. Do you know any thing of Mandlebert?'

'No!' answered she affrighted, lest any evil had happened.

'Did he not take leave of you at the Rooms the other night?'

'Leave of me? is he gone any where?'

'He has left Tunbridge.'

Camilla remained stupified.

'Left it,' she continued, 'without the poor civility of a call, to ask if you had any letters or messages for Hampshire.'

Camilla coloured high; she felt to her heart this evident coldness, and she knew it to be still more marked than Mrs. Arlbery could divine; for he was aware she wished particularly to speak with him; and though she had failed in her appointment, he had not inquired why.

'And this is the man for whom you would relinquish all mankind? this is the grateful character who is to render you insensible to every body?'

The disturbed mind of Camilla needed not this speech; her debt to Sir Sedley, cast wholly upon herself by the thoughtless Lionel; her inability to pay it, the impressive lines the Baronet had addressed to her, and the cruel and pointed indifference of Edgar, all forcibly united to make her wish, at this moment, her heart at her own disposal.

In a few minutes, the voice of Sir Sedley, gaily singing, caught her ear. He was entering the hall, the street door being open. She started up; Mrs. Arlbery would have detained her, but she could not endure to encounter him, and without returning his   ion, or listening to his address, crossed him in the hall, and flew up stairs.

There, however, she had scarcely taken breath, when she recollected the letter which she had left upon the table, and which the afflicting intelligence that Edgar had quitted Tunbridge, had made her forget she had received. In a terror immeasurable, lest her handkerchief should be drawn aside, and betray the first line, she re-descended the stairs, and hastily entered the room. Her shock was then inexpressible. The handkerchief, which her own quick motion in retiring had displaced, was upon the floor, the letter was in full view; the eyes of Sir Sedley were fixed upon his own name, with a look indefinable between pleasure and impertinence, and Mrs. Arlbery was laughing with all her might.

She seized the letter, and was running away with it, when Mrs. Arlbery slipt out of the room, and Sir Sedley, shutting the door, half archly, half tenderly repeated, from the letter, 'My dear Lady Clarendel!'

In a perfect agony, she hid her face, exclaiming: 'O Lionel! my foolish . . . cruel brother!' . . .

'Not foolish, not cruel, I think him,' cried Sir Sedley, taking her hand, 'but amiable . . . he has done honour to my name, and he will use it, I hope, henceforth, as his own.'

'Forget, forget his flippancy,' cried she, withdrawing impatiently her hand; 'and pardon his sister's breach of engagement for this morning. I hope soon, very soon, to repair it, and I hope. . . .'

She did not know what to add; she stopt, stammered, and then endeavoured to make her retreat.

'Do not go,' cried he, gently detaining her; 'incomparable Camilla! I have a thousand things to say to you. Will you not hear them?'

'No!' cried she, disengaging herself; 'no, no, no! I can hear nothing! . . .'

'Do you fascinate then,' said he, half reproachfully, 'like the rattlesnake, only to destroy?'

Camilla conceived this as alluding to her recent encouragement, and stood trembling with expectation it would be followed by a claim upon her justice.

But Sir Sedley, who was far from any meaning so pointed, lightly added; 'What thus agitates the fairest of creatures? can she fear a poor captive entangled in the witchery of her loveliness, and only the more enslaved the more he struggles to get free?'

'Let me go,' cried she, eager to stop him; 'I beseech you, Sir Sedley!'

'All beauteous Camilla!' said he, retreating yet still so as to intercept her passage; 'I am bound to submit; but when may I see you again?'

'At any time,' replied she hastily; 'only let me pass now!'

'At any time! adorable Camilla! be it then to-night! be it this evening! . . . be it at noon! . . . be it. . . .'

'No, no, no, no!' cried she, panting with shame and alarm; 'I do not mean at any time! I spoke without thought . . . I mean. . . .'

'Speak so ever and anon,' cried he, 'if thought is my enemy! This evening then. . . .'

He stopt, as if irresolute how to finish his phrase, but soon added: 'Adieu, till this evening, adieu!' and opened the door for her to pass.

Triumph sat in his eye; exultation spoke in every feature; yet his voice betrayed constraint, and seemed checked, as if from fear of entrusting it with his sentiments. The fear, however, was palpably not of diffidence with respect to Camilla, but of indecision with regard to himself.

Camilla, almost sinking with shame now hung back, from a dread of leaving him in this dangerous delusion. She sat down, and in a faltering voice, said: 'Sir Sedley! hear me, I beg! . . . .'

'Hear you?' cried he, gallantly casting himself at her feet; 'yes! from the fervid rays of the sun, to the mild lustre of the moon! . . . from. . . .'

A loud knock at the street door, and a ringing at the same time at the bell, made him rise, meaning to shut again the door of the parlour, but he was prevented by the entrance of a man into the hall, calling out, in a voice that reached to every part of the house, 'An express for Miss Camilla Tyrold.'

Camilla started up, concluding it some strange intelligence concerning Edgar. But a letter was put into her hand, and she saw it was the writing of Lavinia.

It was short, but most affectionate. It told her that news was just arrived from the Continent, which gave reason for hourly expectation of their cousin Lynmere at Cleves, in consequence of which Sir Hugh was assembling all the family to receive him. She was then, with her father, going thither from Etherington, where the restored health of her uncle had, for a week past, enabled them to reside, and she was ordered to send off an express to Tunbridge, to beg Camilla would prepare immediately for the post-chaise of Sir Hugh, which would be sent for her, with the Cleves housekeeper, and reach Mount Pleasant within a few hours after this notice.

A hundred questions assailed Camilla when she had run over this letter, the noise of the express having brought Mrs. Arlbery and the Dennels into the parlour.

She produced the letter, and putting it in the hands of Mrs. Arlbery, relieved her painful confusion, by quitting the room without again meeting the eyes of Sir Sedley.

She could make no preparation, however, for her journey, from mingled desire and fear of an explanation with the Baronet before her departure.

Again, therefore, in a few minutes she went down; gathering courage from the horror of a mistake that might lead to so much mischief.

She found only Mrs. Arlbery in the parlour.

Involuntarily staring, 'Where,' she cried, 'is Sir Sedley?'

'He is gone,' answered Mrs. Arlbery, laughing at her earnestness; 'but no doubt you will soon see him at Cleves.'

'Then I am undone!' cried she, bursting into tears, and running back to her chamber.

Mrs. Arlbery instantly followed, and kindly inquired what disturbed her.

'O, Mrs. Arlbery!' she cried, 'lend me, I beseech you, some aid, and spare me, in pity, your raillery! Sir Sedley, I fear, greatly mistakes me; set him right, I conjure you. . . .'

'Me, my dear? and do you think if some happy fatality is at work at this moment to force you to your good, I will come forth, like your evil genius, to counteract its operations?'

'I must write, then . . . yet, in this haste, this confusion, I fear
to involve rather than extricate myself!'

'Ay, write by all means; there is nothing so prettily forwards
these affairs, as a correspondence between the parties undertaken
to put an end to them.'

She went, laughing, out of the chamber, and Camilla, who had
seized a pen, distressfully flung it from her.

What indeed could she say? he had made no direct declaration;
she could give, therefore, no direct repulse; and though, through
her brother's cruel want of all consideration, she was so deeply in
his debt, she durst no longer promise its discharge; for the strange
departure of Edgar robbed her of all courage to make to him her
meditated application.

Yet to leave Sir Sedley in this errour was every way terrible. If,
which still seemed very possible, from his manner and behaviour,
he should check his partiality, and make the whole of what had
passed end in mere public-place gallantry, she must always have
the mortification to know he had considered her as ready to accept
him: If, on the contrary, encouraging what he felt for her, from
the belief she returned his best opinion, he should seriously
demand her hand . . . how could she justify the apparent attention
she once paid him? and how assert, while so hopelessly his debtor,
the independence to reject one who so many ways seemed to hold
himself secure?

*   *   *   *

She was broken in upon by Mrs. Mittin, who entered full of
lamentation at the intelligence she had just heard from Miss
Dennel of her sudden departure; which she ended with, 'But as
you are going in such haste, my dear, you must have fifty things
to do, so pray now, let me help you, Come, what shall I pack up
for you? Where's all your things?'

Camilla, incapable of doing any business for herself, accepted
the offer.

'Well then, now where's your gowns? Bless me! what a one is
here? why it's been in the dew, and then in the dust, and then
in the dew again, till all the bottom must be cut off; why you can
never shew it amongst your friends; it will quite bring a disgrace
upon poor Tunbridge; come, I think you must give it to me; I've

got a piece of muslin just like it, and I can piece it so that it won't appear; but it will never do for you again.'

Camilla was surprised; but her mind was filled with other matters, and the gown was put apart.

'What! are those all your neck handkerchiefs? why, my dear Miss Tyrold, that's a thing you want very bad indeed; why here's one you can never wear again; it wants more darning than it's worth.'

Camilla said she should have very good time to mend it at home.

'But then, my dear, you don't consider what a bad look that will have amongst your friends; what will they think of poor Tunbridge, that you should have let it go so far? why, may be they'll never let you come again; the best way will be not to let them see it; suppose I take it off your hands? I dare say they don't know your count.'

At any other time, Camilla would either have resisted these seizures, or have been diverted by the pretence that they were made only for her own benefit; but she was now glad at any rate to get rid of the care of the package.

When this was over, and Mrs. Mittin had pretty well paid herself for her trouble: 'Well, my dear,' she cried, 'and what can I do for you next? Have you paid Mrs. Tilldin, and Mr. Doust, and Mr. Tent?'

These were questions that indeed roused Camilla from her reverie; she had not once thought of what she owed to the milliner, to her shoemaker, nor to her haberdasher; from all of whom she had now, through the hands of Mrs. Mittin, had various articles. She thanked her for reminding her of so necessary an attention, and said she would immediately send for the bills.

'I'll run and pay 'em for you myself,' said Mrs. Mittin; 'for they always take that kind; and as I recommended them all to you, I have a right they should know how I stand their friend; for there's many an odd service they may do me in return; so I'll go for you with all my heart; only give me the money.'

Camilla took out her purse, in which, from her debt to Sir Sedley, and perpetually current expences, there now remained but fifteen shillings of her borrowed five guineas; though latterly, she had wholly denied herself whatever did not seem an expence unavoidable. What to do she now knew not; for though all she had ordered had been trifling, she was sure it must amount to four or five guineas. She had repeatedly refused to borrow anything more of Mrs. Arlbery, always hoping every call for money would be the last; but she was too inexperienced to know, That in gay circles, and public places, the demands for wealth are endless and countless; and that œconomy itself, which is always local, is there lavish and extravagant, compared with its character, in private scenes and retired life.

Yet was this the last moment to apply to Mrs. Arlbery upon such a subject, since it would be endowing her with fresh arms to fight the cause of Sir Sedley. She sat still, and ruminating, till Mrs. Mittin, who without scruple had taken a full inventory of the contents of the purse, exclaimed: 'La! my dear, why sure I hope that i'n't all you've got left?'

Camilla was fain to confess she had nothing more at Tunbridge.

'Well, don't be uneasy, my dear,' cried she, 'and I'll go to 'em all, and be caution[1] for you, till you get the money.'

Camilla thanked her very sincerely, and again resumed her first opinion of her real good nature, and kindness of heart. She took her direction in London, whither she was soon to return, and promised, in a short time, to transmit the money for her to distribute, as every one of the shopkeepers went to the metropolis in the winter.

Delighted both with the praise and the commission, Mrs. Mittin took leave; and Camilla determined to employ her next quarter's allowance in paying these debts, and frankly to beg from her uncle the five guineas that were due to Mrs. Arlbery.

She then wrote an affectionate adieu to Mrs. Berlinton, intreating to hear from her at Etherington; and, while she was sealing it, Mrs. Arlbery came to embrace her, as the carriage was at the door.

Camilla, in making her acknowledgments for the kindness she had received, intermingled a petition, that at least, she would not augment, if she refused to clear the mistake of Sir Sedley.

'I believe he may safely,' she answered, 'be left to himself; though it is plain that, at this moment, he is in a difficulty as great as your own; for marriage he still resists, though he finds you resistless. I wish you mutually to be parted till . . . pardon me, my fair friend . . . your understandings are mutually cleared, and he is divested of what is too factitious, and you of what is too artless. Your situation is, indeed, rather whimsical; for the two mortals with whom you have to deal require treatment diametrically opposite; yet, humour them a little adroitly, and you presently gain them both. He that is proud, must be distanced; he that is vain, must be flattered. This is paying them with their own coin; but they hold no other to be current. Pride, if not humbled, degenerates into contempt; vanity, if not indulged, dissolves into indifference.'

Camilla disclaimed taking any measures with respect to either; but Mrs. Arlbery insisted the field would be won by Sir Sedley, 'who is already,' she cried, 'persuaded you have for some time encouraged him, and that now you are fully propitious. . . .'

Camilla hastily interrupted her: 'O, Mrs. Arlbery!' she cried, 'I cannot endure this! add not to my disturbance by making it my own work!'

She then embraced her; took leave of the Dennels, and with the housekeeper of Sir Hugh set out from Tunbridge for Cleves.

END OF THE THIRD VOLUME.

VOLUME IV

BOOK VII

CHAPTER I

The right Style of Arguing

CAMILLA was received with the most tender joy by all her family, again re-assembled at Cleves to welcome the return of young Lynmere, who was expected every hour. Sir Hugh, perfectly recovered from his late illness, and busy, notwithstanding all remonstrance, in preparation for the approaching nuptials, was in spirits that exhilarated whoever saw him. Eugenia awaited that event with gentleness, though with varying sensations; from fears, lest her personal misfortunes should prove repulsive to Clermont, and from wishes to find him resembling Melmond in talents, and Bellamy in passion and constancy.

Dr. Orkborne gave now his lessons with redoubled assiduity, from an ambition to produce to the scholastic traveller, a phenomenon of his own workmanship in a learned young female: nor were his toils less ready, nor less pleasant, for a secret surmise they would shortly end; though not till honour should be united with independence, for his recompence. But Miss Margland fretted, that this wedding would advance no London journey; and Indiana could not for a moment recover from her indignation, that the deformed and ugly Eugenia, though two years younger than herself, should be married before her. Lavinia had no thought but for the happiness of her sister; and Mr. Tyrold lamented the absence of his wife, who, alike from understanding and affection, was the only person to properly superintend this affair, but from whom Dr. Marchmont, just arrived, brought very faint hopes of a speedy return.

Eugenia, however, was not the sole care of her father, at this period. The countenance of Camilla soon betrayed, to his inquiring eyes, the inefficacy of the Tunbridge journey. But he forbore all question; and left to time or her choice to unravel, if new incidents kept alive her inquietude, or, if no incident at all had been equally prejudicial to her repose.

*   *   *   *

Two days after, while Camilla, still astonished by no news, nor sight of Edgar, was sitting with her sisters, and recounting to them her late adventures, and present difficulties, with Sir Sedley Clarendel, Jacob brought her, in its own superb bird-cage, the learned little bullfinch; telling her, it had been delivered to him without any message, by a man who said she had left it, by mistake, at Tunbridge; whence he had had orders to follow her with it to Cleves park.

She was much provoked thus to receive it. Mrs. Arlbery had pressed her to take it in her uncle's chaise, which she had firmly refused; and she now concluded this method was adopted, that Sir Sedley might imagine she detained it as his gift.

In drawing out, soon after, the receptacle for the bird's nourishment, she perceived, written with a pencil upon the wood, these words: 'Thou art gone then, fair fugitive! Ah! at least, fly only where thou mayst be pursued!'

This writing had not been visible till the machine was taken out to be replenished. She recollected the hand of Sir Sedley, and was now sure it was sent by himself, and could no longer, therefore, doubt his intentions being serious.

With infinite perplexity she consulted with her sisters; but, when candidly she had related, that once, to her never-ending regret, she had apparently welcomed his civilities, Eugenia pronounced her rectitude to be engaged by that error, as strongly as her gratitude by the preservation of her life, and the extraordinary service done to Lionel, not to reject the young baronet, should he make his proposals.

She heard this opinion with horror. Timid shame, and the counsel of her father, united to impede her naming the internal obstacle which she felt to be insurmountable; and, while casting up, in silence, her appealing eyes to Heaven for relief, from the intricacy in which she found herself involved, she saw Lionel galloping into the park.

She flew to meet him, and he dismounted, and led his horse, to walk with her.

She flattered herself, she might now represent the mischief he was doing, and obtain from him some redress. But he was more wild and impracticable than ever. 'Well, my dear girl,' he cried, 'when are all these betterings and worsings to take place? Numps has sent for me to see poor little Greek and Latin hobble to the altar; but, 'tis a million to one, if our noble baronet does not whisk you there before her. He's a charming fellow, faith. I had a good long confab with him this morning.'

'This morning? I hope, then, you were so good, so just, as to tell him when you mean to pay the money you have borrowed?'

'My dear child, I often think you were born but yesterday, only, by some accident, you came into the world, like Minerva, grown up and ready dressed. What makes you think I mean to pay him? Have I given him any bond?'

'A bond? Is that necessary to justice and honour?'

'If I had asked the money, you are right, my dear; I ought, then, certainly, to refund. But, as it now stands, 'tis his own affair. I have nothing to do with it: except, indeed, receiving the dear little golden boys, and making merry with them.'

'O fie, Lionel, fie!'

'Why, what had I to do with it? Do you think he would care one fig if he saw me sunk to the bottom of the Red Sea? No, my dear, no; you are the little debtor; so balance your accounts for yourself, and don't cast them upon your poor neighbours, who have full enough to settle of their own.'

Camilla was thunderstruck; 'And have you been so cruel,' she cried, 'seeing the matter in such a light, to place me in such a predicament?'

'Cruel, my dear girl? why, what will it cost you, except a dimple or two the more? And don't you know you always look best when you smile? I assure you, it's a mercy he don't see you when you are giving me one of my lectures. It disfigures you so horribly, that he'd take fright and never speak to you again.'

'What can I ever say, to make you hear me, or feel for me? Tell me, at least, what has passed this morning; and assure me that nothing new, nothing yet worse, has occurred.'

'O no, nothing at all. All is in the fairest train possible.[1] I dare say, he'll come hither, upon the grand question, before sun-set.'

Camilla gasped for breath, and was some time before she could ask whence he drew such a conclusion.

'O, because I see he's in for it. I have a pretty good eye, my dear! He said, too, he had such a prodigious ... friendship, I think he called it, for you, that he was immeasurably happy, and all that, to be of the least service to your brother. A fine fellow, upon my word! a fine generous spark as ever I saw. He charged me to call upon him freely when I had any little embarrassment, or difficulty, or was hard run,¹ or things of that sort. He's a fine buck, I tell you, and knows the world perfectly, that I promise you. He's none of your drivellers, none of your ignoramuses. He has the true notion of things. He's just a right friend for me. You could not have made a better match.'

Camilla, in the most solemn manner, protested herself disengaged in thought, word, and deed; and declared her fixed intention so to continue. But he only laughed at her declarations, calling them maidenly fibs; and, assuring her, the young baronet was so much in earnest, she might as well be sincere as not. 'Besides,' he added, ''tis not fair to trifle where a man behaves so handsomely and honourably. Consider the £.200!'

'I shall quite lose my senses, Lionel!' cried she, in an agony; 'I shall quite lose my senses if you speak in this manner!'

Lionel shouted aloud; 'Why, my dear girl, what is £.200 to Sir Sedley Clarendel? You talk as if he had twenty pound a-year for pin-money, like you and Lavinia, that might go with half a gown a-year, if good old Numps did not help you. Why, he's as rich as Crœsus, child. Besides, he would have been quite affronted if I had talked of paying him such a trifle, for he offered me any thing I pleased. O, he knows the world, I promise you! He's none of your starched prigs. He knows life, my dear! He said, he could perfectly conceive how hard it must be to a lad of spirit, like me, to be always exact. I don't know that I ever made a more agreeable acquaintance in my life.'

Camilla was in an agitation that made him regard her, for a moment, with a serious surprise; but his natural levity soon resumed its post, and, laughing at himself for being nearly, he said, taken in, by her childish freaks, he protested he would bite no more: 'For, after all, you must not think to make a fool of me, my dear. It won't do. I'm too knowing. Do you suppose, if he had not already made up his mind to the noose, and was not sure you had made up yours to letting it be tied, he would have cared for poor me, and my scrapes? No, no; whatever he does for me,

before you are married, you may set down in your own memorandum book: whatever he may please to do afterwards, I am
content should be charged to poor Pillgarlic.'[1]

He then bid her good-morrow, by the name of Lady Clarendel;
and said, he would go and see if little Greek and Latin were as
preposterous a prude about young Lynmere.

Camilla remained almost petrified with amazement at her own
situation; and only was deterred from immediately opening her
whole heart and affairs to her father, with the confidence to which
his indulgence entitled him, by the impossibility of explaining her
full distress without betraying her brother.

CHAPTER II

A Council

THE next morning, Camilla, eager to try once more her influence
with her brother, accompanied him into the park, and renewed
her remonstrances, but with no better success; and while they
were passing by a private gate, that opened to the high road, they
saw Sir Sedley Clarendel driving by in his phaeton.

Lionel, bursting from his sister, opened the gate, called to Sir
Sedley to give his reins to one of his servants, and brought him,
not unwilling, though much surprised, into the park.

Camilla, in dismay unspeakable at this conduct, and the idea
of such a meeting, had run forward instantly to hide herself in the
summer-house, to avoid re-passing the gate in her way to the
mansion; but her scheme was more precipitate than wise; Lionel
caught a glimpse of her gown as she went into the little building,
and shouted aloud: 'Look! look! Sir Sedley! there's Camilla
making believe to run away from you!'

'Ah, fair fugitive!' cried the baronet, springing forward, and
entering the summer-house almost as soon as herself, 'fly only
thus, where you may be pursued!'

Camilla, utterly confounded, knew not where to cast her eyes,
where to hide her face; and her quick-changing colour, and short-
heaved breath, manifested an excess of confusion, that touched,
flattered, and penetrated the baronet so deeply and so suddenly,

as to put him off from all guard of consequences, and all recollection of matrimonial distaste: 'Beautiful, resistless Camilla!' he
cried; 'how vain is it to struggle against your witchery! Assure
me but of your clemency, and I will adore the chains that shackle
me!'

Camilla, wholly overcome, by sorrow, gratitude, repentance,
and shame, sunk upon a chair, and shed a torrent of tears that
she even sought not to restrain. The shock of refusing one, to
whose error in believing himself acceptable she had largely
contributed, or the horror of yielding to him her hand, while her
heart was in the possession of another, made her almost wish, at
this moment, he should divine her distress, that his own pride
might conclude it.

But far different from what would produce such an effect,
were the feelings of pride now working in his bosom. He imagined
her emotion had its source in causes the softest and most flattering.
Every personal obstacle sunk before this idea, and with a seriousness in his manner he had not yet used: 'This evening, lovely
Camilla,' he cried, 'let me beg, for this evening, the audience
accorded me upon that which I lost at Tunbridge.'

He was then going; but Camilla, hastily rising, cried, 'Sir
Sedley, I beseech . . .' when Lionel capering into the little
apartment, danced round it in mad ecstasy, chanting 'Lady
Clarendel, Lady Clarendel, my dear Lady Clarendel!'

Camilla now was not confused alone. Sir Sedley himself could
gladly have pushed him out of the building; but neither the looks
of surprise and provocation of the baronet, nor the prayers nor
reprimands of Camilla, could tame his wild transport. He shook
hands, whether he would or not, with the one; he bowed most
obsequiously, whether she would regard him or not, to the other;
and still chanting the same burden, made a clamour that shook the
little edifice to its foundation.

The strong taste for ridicule, that was a prominent part of the
character of Sir Sedley, was soon conquered by this ludicrous
behaviour, and both his amazement and displeasure ended in a
hearty fit of laughter. But Camilla suffered too severely to join in
the mirth; she blushed for her brother, she blushed for herself, she
hung her head in speechless shame, and covered her eyes with
her hand.

The noisy merriment of Lionel preventing any explanation,

though rendering it every moment more necessary, Sir Sedley, repeating his request for the evening, took leave.

Camilla looked upon his departing in this manner as her sentence ot misery, and was pursuing him, to decline the visit; but Lionel, seizing her two hands, swung her round the room, in defiance of her even angry expostulations and sufferings, which he neither credited nor conceived, and then skipt after the baronet himself, who was already out of the park.

She became now nearly frantic. She thought herself irretrievably in the power of Sir Sedley, and by means so forced and indelicate, that she was scarcely more afflicted at the event, than shocked by its circumstances; and though incapable to really harbour rancour against a brother she sincerely loved, she yet believed at this moment she never should forgive, nor willingly see him more.

In this state she was found by Lavinia. The history was inarticulately told, but Lavinia could give only her pity; she saw not any avenue to an honourable retreat, and thought, like Eugenia, she could now only free herself by the breach of what should be dearer to her even than happiness, her probity and honour.

Utterly inconsolable she remained, till again she heard the voice of Lionel, loudly singing in the park.

'Go to him! go to him! my dearest Lavinia,' she cried, 'and, if my peace is dear to you, prevail with him to clear up the mistakes of Sir Sedley, and to prevent his dreaded, killing visit this evening!'

Lavinia only answered by compliance; but, after an half hour's useless contest with her riotous brother, returned to her weeping sister, not merely successless with regard to her petition, but loaded with fresh ill tidings that she knew not how to impart. Lionel had only laughed at the repugnance of Camilla, which he regarded as something between childishness and affectation, and begged Lavinia to be wiser than to heed to it: 'Brother Sedley has desired me, however,' he added, 'not to speak of the matter to Numps nor my father, till he has had a little more conversation with his charmer; and he intends to call to-night as if only upon a visit to me.'

When Camilla learnt, at length, this painful end of her embassy, she gave herself up so completely to despair, that Lavinia, affrighted, ran to the house for Eugenia, whose extreme youth was no impediment, in the minds of her liberal sisters,[1] to their belief nor reverence of her superior wisdom. Her species of education had early prepossessed them with respect for her knowledge, and her unaffected fondness for study, had fixed their opinion of her extraordinary understanding. The goodness of her heart, the evenness of her temper, and her natural turn to contemplation, had established her character alike for sanctity and for philosophy throughout the family.

She listened with the sincerest commiseration to the present state of the case: 'Certainly,' she cried, 'you cannot, in honour, now refuse him; but deal with him sincerely, and he may generously himself relinquish his claims. Write to him, my dear Camilla; tell him you grieve to afflict, yet disdain to deceive him; assure him of your perfect esteem and eternal gratitude; but confess, at once, your heart refuses to return his tenderness. Entreat him to forgive whatever he may have mistaken, and nobly to restore to you the liberty of which your obligations, without his consent, must rob you.'

To Lavinia this advice appeared infallible; but Camilla, though she felt an entanglement which fettered herself, thought it by no means sufficiently direct or clear to authorise a rejection of Sir Sedley; since, strangely as she seemed in his power, circumstances had placed her there, and not his own solicitation.

Yet to prevent a visit of which her knowledge seemed consent, and which her consent must be most seriously to authorise, she deemed as indispensable to her character, as to her fears. She hesitated, therefore, not a moment in preferring writing to a meeting; and after various conversations, and various essays, the following billet was dispatched to Clarendel Place, through the means of Molly Mill, and by her friend Tommy Hodd.

To Sir Sedley Clarendel.

I SHOULD ill return what I owe to Sir Sedley Clarendel by causing him any useless trouble I can spare him. He spoke of a visit hither this evening, when I was too much hurried to represent that it could not be received, as my brother's residence is at Etherington, and my father and my uncle have not the honour to be known to Sir Sedley. For me, my gratitude must ever be unalterable; and where accident occasions a meeting, I shall be most happy to express it; but I have nothing to say, nothing to offer, that could recompense one moment of Sir Sedley's time given voluntarily to such a visit.

CAMILLA TYROLD.

Ill as this letter satisfied her, she could devise nothing better; but though her sisters had both thought it too rigorous, she would not risk anything gentler.

During the dinner, they all appeared absent and dejected; but Sir Hugh attributed it to the non-arrival of Clermont, in watching for whom his own time was completely occupied, by examining two weather-cocks, and walking from one to the other, to see if they agreed, or how they changed; Indiana was wholly engrossed in consultations with Miss Margland, upon the most becoming dress for a bride's maid; and Mr. Tyrold, having observed that his three girls had spent the morning together, concluded Camilla had divulged to them her unhappy perplexity, and felt soothed himself in considering she had soothers so affectionate and faithful.

Early in the evening Tommy Hodd arrived, and Molly Mill brought Camilla the following answer of Sir Sedley.

Miss Camilla Tyrold.

AH! what in this lower sphere can be unchequered, when even a correspondence with the most lovely of her sex, brings alarm with its felicity? Must I come, then, to Cleves, fair Insensible, but as a visitor to Mr. Lionel? Have you taken a captive only to see him in fetters? Allured a victim merely to behold him bleed? Ah! tomorrow, at least, permit the audience that today is denied, and at your feet, let your slave receive his doom.

SEDLEY CLARENDEL.

Camilla turned cold. She shrunk from a remonstrance she conceived she had merited, and regarded herself to be henceforth either culpable or unhappy. Unacquainted with the feminine indulgence which the world, by long prescription, grants to coquetry, its name was scarcely known to her; and she saw in its own native egotism the ungenerous desire to please, where she herself was indifferent, and anticipated from Sir Sedley reproach, if not contempt. No sophistications of custom had warped the first innocence of her innate sense of right, and to trifle with the feelings of another for any gratification of her own, made success bring a blush to her integrity, not exultation to her vanity.

The words *victim* and *bleeding*, much affected the tender Lavinia, while those of *fetters*, *captive*, and *insensible*, satisfied the heroic Eugenia that Sir Sedley deserved the hand of her sister; but neither of them spoke.

'You say nothing?' cried Camilla, turning paler and paler, and sitting down lest she should fall.

They both wept and embraced her, and Eugenia said, if, indeed, she could not conquer her aversion, she saw no way to elude the baronet, but by openly confessing her repugnance, in the conversation he demanded.

Camilla saw not less strongly the necessity of being both prompt and explicit; but how receive Sir Sedley at Cleves? and upon what pretence converse with him privately? Even Lionel the next day was to return to the university, though his presence, if he staid, would, in all probability, but add to every difficulty.

At length, they decided, that the conference should take place at the Grove; and to prevent the threatened visit of the next day, Camilla wrote the following answer:

To Sir Sedley Clarendel.

I SHOULD be grieved, indeed, to return my obligations to Sir Sedley Clarendel by meriting his serious reproach; yet I cannot have the honour of seeing him at Cleves, since my brother is immediately quitting it for Oxford. As soon as I hear Mrs. Arlbery is again at the Grove, I shall wait upon her, and always be most happy to assure Sir Sedley of my gratitude, which will be as lasting as it is sincere.

CAMILLA TYROLD.

Though wretched in this strange state of things, she knew not how to word her letter more positively, since his own, notwith-

standing its inferences, had so much more the style of florid
gallantry than plain truth. Molly Mill undertook that Tommy
Hodd should carry it early the next morning.

*　　*　　*　　*

Lionel was so enraged at the non-appearance of the young
baronet at night, that Camilla was compelled to confess she had
promised to see him, and to give him his answer at Mrs. Arlbery's.
He was out of humour, nevertheless, lest Sir Sedley should be
affronted by the delay, and feared that the best match in the whole
county would prove abortive, from his sister's foolish trimmings,[1]
and silly ignorance of life.

CHAPTER III

A Proposal of Marriage

THE increasing depression of Camilla, and the melancholy of
her sympathising sisters, though still attributed to the adverse
wind by the compass-watching baronet, escaped not the notice of
Mr. Tyrold; who, alarmed for the peace of his daughter, determined to watch for the first quiet opportunity of investigating her
actual situation.

Lionel, after breakfast, the next morning, was obliged to
relinquish waiting for Clermont, and to set off for Oxford. He
contrived to whisper to Camilla, that he hoped she would be a
good girl at last, and not play the fool; but, finding she only
sighed, he laughed at her calamitious state, in becoming mistress
of fifteen thousand per annum, only by the small trouble of
running over a short ceremony; and, assuring her he would assist
her off with part of the charge, if it were too heavy for her, bid her
inform him in time of the propitious day.

Camilla, shortly after, saw from her window, galloping full
speed across the park to the house, Major Cerwood. She suspected
her tormenting brother to have been again at work; nor was she
mistaken. He had met with the Major at the hotel at Tunbridge,
while his spirits, always violent, were in a state of almost intoxica-

tion of delight, at the first idea of such an accession to his powers of amusement, as a new brother rolling in immense wealth, which he already considered as nearly at his own disposal. High wrought, therefore, for what he deemed good sport, he confirmed what he had asserted at the ball at Northwick, of the expectations of Camilla from Sir Hugh, by relating the public fact, of her having been announced, to the family and neighbourhood, for his uncle's heiress, at ten years of age; and only sinking, in his account, the revocation made so soon after in favour of Eugenia. To this, he added his advice, that no time was to be lost, as numberless new suitors were likely to pursue her from Tunbridge.

The Major, upon alighting, inquired for Sir Hugh, deeming Mr. Tyrold of little consequence, since it was not from him Camilla was to inherit her fortune.

The baronet, as usual, was watching the winds and the clouds; but, concluding whoever came would bring some news from Clermont, received the Major with the utmost cordiality, saying: 'I see, sir, you are a stranger; by which I suppose you to be just come from abroad; where, I hope, you left all well?'

'I am just come, sir,' answered the Major, 'from Tunbridge, where I had the honour, through my acquaintance with Mrs. Arlbery, of meeting daily with your charming niece; an honour, sir, which must cause all the future happiness or misery of my life.'

He then made a declaration, in form, of the most ardent passion for Camilla; mentioned his family, which was an honourable one; talked of his expectations with confidence, though vaguely; and desired to leave the disposition of the settlement wholly to the baronet; who, he hoped, would not refuse to see his elder brother, a gentleman of fortune in Lincolnshire, who would have the honour to wait upon him, at any time he would be so good as to appoint, upon this momentous affair.

Sir Hugh heard this harangue with consternation. The Major was in the prime of life, his person was good, his speech was florid, his air was assured, and his regimentals were gay. Not a doubt of his success occurred to the baronet; who saw, in one blow, the darling scheme of his old age demolished, in the deprivation of Camilla.

The Major impatiently waited for an answer; but Sir Hugh was too much disordered to frame one; he walked up and down the room, muttering in a desponding manner, to himself, 'Lord, help us! what a set of poor weak mortals we are, we poor men! The best schemes and plans in the world always coming to nothing before we can bring them about! I'll never form another while I live, for the sake of this one warning. Nobody knows, next, but what Clermont will be carrying off Eugenia to see foreign parts! and then comes some other of these red-coats to take away Indiana; and, after doing all for the best so long, I may be left all alone, except just for Mrs. Margland and the Doctor! that I don't take much pleasure in, Lord help me! except as a Christian, which I hope is no sin.'

At length, endeavouring to compose himself, he sat down, and said, 'So you are come, sir, to take away from me my own particular little niece? which is a hard thing upon an uncle, intending her to live with him. However, I don't mean to find fault; but I can tell you this one thing, sir, which I beg you to remember; which is, if you don't make her happy, you'll break my heart! For she's what I love the best in the world, little as I've made it appear, by not leaving her a shilling. For which sake, however, I can't but respect you the more for coming after her, instead of Eugenia.'

'Sir?' cried the Major, amazed.

'The other two chaps,' continued he, 'that came about us not long ago, wanted to make their court to Eugenia and Indiana; as well as another that came to the house when I was ill, in the same coat as yourself, by what I can gather from the description; but never a one has come to Camilla yet, except yourself, because my brother can spare her but a trifle, having another young girl to provide for, besides Lionel; which is the most expensive of them all, poor boy! never having enough, by the reason Oxford is so dear, as I suppose.'

The Major now wore an air of surprise and uneasiness that Sir Hugh began to observe, but attributed to his unpleasant reception of his proposals. He begged his pardon, therefore, and again assured him of his respect for a choice so little mercenary, which he looked upon as a mark of a good heart.

The Major, completely staggered, and suspecting the information of Lionel to be ill grounded, if not purposely deluding, entreated his permission to wait upon him again; and offered for the present to take leave.

Sir Hugh, in a melancholy voice, said, he would first summon his niece, as he could not answer it to his conscience preventing the meeting, unless she gave him leave.

He then rang the bell, and told Jacob to call Camilla.

Major Cerwood was excessively distressed. To retreat seemed impossible; yet to connect himself without fortune, when he thought he was addressing a rich heiress, was a turn of fate he scarcely knew how either to support or to parry. All that, in this haste, he could resolve, was, to let the matter pass for the moment, and then insist upon satisfaction from Lionel, either in clearing up the mistake, or taking upon himself its blame.

When Camilla appeared, the disturbance of Sir Hugh still augmented; and he could hardly articulate, 'My dear, in the case you are willing to leave your family, here's a gentleman come to make his addresses to you; which I think it right you should know, though how I shall struggle through it, if I lose you, is more than my poor weak head can tell; for what shall I do without my dear little girl, that I thought to make the best comfort of my old age? which, however, I beg you not to think of, in case this young Captain's more agreeable.'

'Ah! my dear uncle!' cried she, 'your Camilla can never return half the comfort she receives from you! keep me with you still, and ever! I am much obliged to Major Cerwood. I beg him to accept my sincerest thanks; but to pardon me, when I assure him, they are all I have to offer him.'

Repulse was not new to the Major; who, in various country towns, had sought to retrieve his affairs by some prudent connection; his pride, however, had never so little suffered as on the present occasion, for his apprehension of error or imposition had removed from him all thought of even the possibility of a refusal; which, now, therefore, unexpectedly and joyfully obviated his embarrassment, and enabled him to quit the field by an honourable retreat. He bowed profoundly, called himself, without knowing what he said, the most unhappy of men; and, without risking one solicitation, or a moment for repentance, hastily took leave, with intention, immediately, to demand an explanation of Lionel.

But he had not escaped a mile from the house, ere he gave up that design, from anticipating the ridicule that might follow it. To require satisfaction for a young lady's want of fortune, however reasonable, would always be derided as ludicrous. He resolved, therefore, quietly to put up with the rejection; and to gather his next documents concerning the portion of a fair damsel, from authority better to be relied upon than that of a brother.

Sir Hugh, for some time, discovered not that he had retired. Enchanted by so unexpected a dismission, his favourite scheme of life seemed accorded to him, and he pressed Camilla to his bosom, in a transport of joy. 'We shall live together, now, I hope,' he cried, 'without any of these young chaps coming in again to part us. Not that I would object to your marrying, my dear girl, if it was with a relation, like Eugenia, or, with a neighbour, like Indiana, if it had not been for its going off; but to see you taken away from me by a mere stranger, coming from distant parts, and knowing nothing of any of us, is a thing that makes my heart ache but to think of; so I hope it will happen no more; for these trials do no good to my recovery.'

Turning round, then, with a view to say something consolatory to the Major, he was seriously concerned to find him departed. 'I can't say,' he cried, 'I had any intention to send him off so short, his meaning not being bad, considering him in the light of a person in love; which is a time when a man has not much thought, except for himself, by what I can gather.'

He then proposed a walk, to watch if Clermont were coming. The wind, he acknowledged, was indeed contrary; but, he did not doubt, upon such a particular occasion, his good lad would not mind such difficulties.

CHAPTER IV

A Bull-Dog

SIR HUGH called upon his other nieces to join him; purposing to stroll to the end of a lane which led to the London road.

Camilla accompanied the party in the most mournful silence. The assuming letter she had received; the interview she should have to sustain; and her apparent dependance upon Sir Sedley, sinking her into complete despondence.

When they came to the high road, Sir Hugh made a stop, and bid every body look sharp.

A horseman was seen advancing full gallop. By his figure he appeared to be young; by his pace, in uncommon speed.

'That's him,' cried Sir Hugh, striking his stick upon the ground, and smiling most complacently; 'I said he would not mind the wind, my dear Eugenia! what's the wind, or the waves either, to a lover? which is a thing, however, that I won't talk about; so don't be ashamed, my dear girl, nobody knowing what we mean.'

Eugenia looked down, deeply colouring, and much regretting the lameness that prevented her running back, to avoid so public and discountenancing a meeting.

The horseman now came up to them, and was preparing to turn down the lane; when, all at once, they perceived him to be Edgar Mandlebert.

He had left Tunbridge in a manner not more abrupt than comfortless. His disappointment in the failure of Camilla at the Rooms had been as bitter, as his expectations from the promised conference had been animated. When Lionel appeared, he inquired if his sister were absent from illness. . . . No; she was only writing a letter. To take this moment for such a purpose, be the letter what it might, seemed sporting with his curiosity and warm interest in her affairs: and he went back, mortified and dejected, to his lodgings; where, just arrived by the stage, he found a letter from Dr. Marchmont, acquainting him with his return to his rectory. In this suspensive state of mind, to cast himself upon his sagacious friend seemed a relief the most desirable: but, while considering whether first to claim from Camilla her promised communication, the voice of Lionel issuing from the room of Major Cerwood, struck his ears. He darted forth, and accompanied the youth to his horse, who was setting out upon some expedition, in the dark; and then received information, under the pretence of great secrecy, that Major Cerwood was going immediately to ask leave of absence, and proceed straight to Hampshire, with his final proposals of marriage with Camilla. He now concluded this was the subject upon which she had meant to consult with him; but delicacy, pride, and hope all combated his interference. He determined even to avoid her, till the answer should be given. 'I must owe her hand,' cried he, 'to her heart, not to a contest such as this: and, if impartially and unbiassed, the Major is refused, no farther cruel doubt, no torturing hesitation, shall keep me another minute from her feet!' With the dawn, therefore, he set out for Hampshire; but, fixed to avoid Cleves, till he could learn that the Major's visit were over, he devoted his mornings to rides, and his evenings to Dr. Marchmont, till now, a mile or two from the Park, he had met the Major himself, and concluded the acceptance or the rejection decided. They merely touched their hats as they passed each other; and he instantly took the route which the Major was quitting.

In the excess of his tribulation, he was galloping past the whole group, without discerning one of its figures; when Sir Hugh called out, 'Why it's young Mr. Edgar! So now we've walked all this way for nothing! and Clermont may be still at Jericho, or at Rome, for anything we know to the contrary!'

Edgar stopt short. He felt himself shiver at sight of Camilla, but dismounted, gave his horse to his groom, and joined the party.

Eugenia recovering, now fearlessly looked up; but Camilla, struck and affected, shook in every limb, and was forced to hold by Lavinia.

Edgar called upon his utmost presence of mind to carry him through what he conceived to be a final trial. He spoke to Sir Hugh, and compelled himself to speak separately to every one else; but, when he addressed Camilla, to whom he said something not very distinctly, about Tunbridge, she curtsied to him slightly, and turned away, without making any answer. Her mind, taking suddenly a quick retrospection of all that had passed between them, presented him to her view as uncertain and delusive; and, casting upon him, internally, the whole odium of her present distress, and her feelings were so indignant, that, in her present desperate state, she deemed it beneath her to disguise them, either from himself or the world.

Edgar, to whose troubled imagination everything painted his rival, concluded the Major had been heard with favour; and his own adverse counsel was now recollected with resentment.

Sir Hugh, far more fatigued by his disappointment than by his walk, said he should go no further, as he found it in vain to expect Clermont; and accepted the arm of Edgar to aid his stick in helping him home.

Camilla, still leaning upon Lavinia, mounted a little bank, which she knew Sir Hugh could not ascend, that she might walk on where Edgar could not join her; involuntarily ejaculating,

'Lavinia! if you would avoid deceit and treachery, look at a man as at a picture, which tells you only the present moment! Rely upon nothing of time to come! They are not like us, Lavinia. They think themselves free, if they have made no verbal profession; though they may have pledged themselves by looks, by actions, by attentions, and by manners, a thousand, and a thousand times!'

Edgar observed her avoidance with the keenest apprehension; and, connecting it with her failure at the Rooms, imagined the Major had now influenced her to an utter aversion of him.

Sir Hugh meanwhile, though wholly unheard, related, in a low voice, to Edgar, the history of his preparations for Clermont; begging him, however, to take no notice of them to Eugenia: and, then, adding, 'Very likely, Mr. Edgar, you are just come from Tunbridge? and, if so, you may have met with that young Captain that has been with us this morning; who, I understand to be a Major?'

Edgar was thrown into the utmost trepidation; the artless openness of Sir Hugh gave him every reason to suppose he should immediately gather full intelligence, and all his peace and all his hopes might hang upon another word. He could only bow to the question; but before Sir Hugh could go on, a butcher's boy, who was riding by, from a wanton love of mischief, gave a signal to his attending bull-dog, to attack the old spaniel that accompanied Sir Hugh.

Sustained by his master many a year, the proud old favourite, though unequal to the combat, disdained to fly; and the fierce bull-dog would presently have demolished him, had not Edgar, recovering all his vigour from his earnest desire to rescue an animal so dear to Sir Hugh, armed himself with the baronet's stick, and thrust it dexterously across the jaws of this intended antagonist.

Nothing, however, could withstand the fangs of the bull-dog; they soon severed it, and, again, he made at the spaniel; but Edgar rushed between them, with no other weapons than the broken fragments of the stick: and, while the baronet and Eugenia screamed out to old Rover to return to them, and Lavinia, with more readiness of common sense, exerted the fullest powers of which her gentle voice was capable, to conjure the wicked boy to call off his dog, Camilla, who was the last to look round at this scene, only turned about as the incensed and disappointed bull-dog, missing his object, aimed at Edgar himself. Roused at once from her sullen calm to the most agonising sensibility, every thing and every body, herself most of all, were forgotten in the sight of his danger; and, with a piercing shriek, she darted down the bank, and arrived at the tremendous[1] spot, at the same instant that the more useful exhortations of Lavinia, had induced the boy to withdraw the fierce animal; who, with all his might, and all his fury, obeyed the weak whistle of a little urchin he had been bred to love and respect, for bringing him his daily food.

Camilla perceived not if the danger were impending, or over; gasping, pale, and agitated, she caught Mandlebert by the arm, and, in broken accents, half pronounced, 'O Edgar! . . . are you hurt?'

The revulsion that had operated in her mind took now its ample turn in that of Mandlebert; he could hardly trust his senses, hardly believe he existed; yet he felt the pressure of her hand upon his arm, and saw in her countenance terror the most undisguised, and tenderness that went straight to his soul. 'Is it Camilla,' he cried, 'who thus speaks to me? . . . Is not my safety or my destruction alike indifferent to Camilla?'

'O no! O no!' cried she, scarce conscious she answered at all, till called to recollection by his own changed looks; changed from incredulity and amazement to animation that lightened up every feature, to eyes that shot fire. Abashed, astonished, ashamed, she precipitately drew away her hand, and sought quietly to retire.

But Edgar was no longer master of himself; he conceived he was on a pinnacle, whence he could only, and without any gradation, turn to happiness or despair. He followed her, trembling and uncertain, his joy fading into alarm at her retreat, his hope transforming into apprehension at her resumed coldness of demeanor. 'Do you repent,' he cried, 'that you have shewn me a little humanity? . . . will the Major . . . the happy Major! . . . be offended you do less than detest me?'

'The Major!' repeated she, looking back, surprised, 'can you think the Major has any influence with me?'

'Ah, Heaven!' he cried, 'what do you say!' . . .

Enchanted, affrighted, bewildered, yet silent, she hurried on; Edgar could not forget himself more than a moment; he forbore, therefore, to follow, and, though with a self-denial next to torture, returned to Sir Hugh, to whom his arm was doubly necessary, from the scene he had just witnessed, and the loss of his stick.

The butcher's boy and his bull-dog were decamped; and the baronet and Eugenia were rivalling each other in fondling the rescued spaniel, and in pouring thanks and praise unlimited upon Edgar.

They then walked back as before; and, as soon as they re-entered the mansion, the female party went upstairs, and Sir Hugh, warmly shaking Edgar by the hand, said: 'My dear Mr. Edgar, this is one of the happiest days of my life, except just that of my nephew's coming over, which it is but right to put before it. But here, first, my dear Camilla's refused that young Captain, who would have carried her the Lord knows where, immediately, as I make no doubt; and next, I've saved the life of my poor old Rover, by the means of your good-nature.'

'Refused?' cried Edgar; 'my dear Sir Hugh!—did you say refused?'

Sir Hugh innocently gratified him with the repetition of the word, but begged him not to mention it, 'For fear,' he said, 'it should hurt the young man when he falls in love somewhere else; which I heartily hope he will do soon, poor gentleman! for the sake of its not fretting him.'

'Miss Camilla, then, has refused him?' again repeated Edgar, with a countenance that, to any man but the baronet, must have betrayed his whole soul.

'Yes, poor gentleman! this very morning; for which I am thankful enough: for what do we know of those young officers, who may all be sent to the East Indies, or Jamaica, every day of their lives? Not but what I have the proper pity for him, which, I hope, is all that can be expected.'

Edgar walked about the room, in a perturbation of hope, fear, and joy, that disabled him from all further appearance of attention. He wished to relate this transaction to Dr. Marchmont, yet dreaded any retarding advice; he languished to make Camilla herself the sole mistress of his destiny: the interest she had shewn for his safety seemed to admit but one interpretation; and, finally, he resolved to stay at Cleves till he could meet with her alone.

Camilla had not uttered a word after the adventure of the bull-dog. The smallest idea that she could excite the least emotion in Edgar, brought a secret rapture to her heart, that, at any former period, would alone have sufficed to render her happy: but, at this instant of entanglement with another, she revolted from the indulgence of such pleasure; and instead of dwelling, as she would have done before, on the look, the accent, the manner, that were susceptible, by any construction, of partiality, she checked every idea that did not represent Edgar as unstable and consistent; and sought, with all her power, to regard him as Mrs. Arlbery had painted him, and to believe him, except in a few casual moments of caprice, insensible and hard of heart.

Yet this entanglement, in which, scarce knowing how, she now seemed to be entwined with Sir Sedley, grew more and more terrific; and when she considered that her sisters themselves thought her independence gone, and her honour engaged, she was seized with so much wonderment, how it had all been brought about, that her understanding seemed to play her false, and she believed the whole a dream.

CHAPTER V

An Oak Tree

WHEN the sisters were summoned down stairs to dinner, planted at the door, ready to receive them at their entrance, stood Edgar. Lavinia and Eugenia addressed him as usual; but Camilla could not speak, could not return his salutation, could not look at him. She sat hastily down in her accustomed place by her uncle, and even the presence of her father scarcely restrained her tears, as she contrasted the hopeless uncertainties of Edgar, with the perilous pursuit of Sir Sedley.

Edgar, for the first time, saw her avoidance without suspecting that it flowed from repugnance. The interest she had shewn for his safety was still bounding in his breast, and as, from time to time, he stole a glance at her, and observed her emotion, his heart whispered him the softest hopes, that soon the most perfect confidence would make every feeling reciprocal.

But these hopes were not long without alloy; he soon discerned something that far exceeded what could give him pleasure in her perturbation; he read in it not merely hurry and alarm, but suffering and distress.

He now ventured to look at her no more; his confidence gave place to pity; he saw she was unhappy, and breathed no present wish but to relieve and console her.

When the dessert was served, she was preparing to retire; but she caught the eye of her father, and saw she should not long be alone; she re-seated herself, therefore, in haste, to postpone, at least, his scrutiny.

Every body, at length, arose, and Sir Hugh proposed that they should all walk in the park, during his nap, but keep close to the pales, that they might listen for all passengers, in case of Clermont's coming.

To this, also, Camilla could make no objection, and they set out. She took an arm of each sister, and indulged the heaviness of her heart in not uttering a word.

They had not gone far, when a servant ran after Mr. Tyrold with a pacquet, just arrived, by a private hand, from Lisbon. He returned to read it in his own room; Lavinia and Eugenia accompanied him to hear its contents, and Camilla, for the first time, seemed the least affectionate of his daughters; she durst not encounter him but in the mixt company of all the house; she told Lavinia to make haste back with the news, and took the arm of Indiana.

The compulsion of uninteresting discourse soon became intolerable; and no longer chained to the party by the awe of her father, she presently left Indiana to Miss Margland, and perceiving that Edgar was conversing with Dr. Orkborne, said she would wait for her sisters; and, turning a little aside, sat down upon a bench under a large oak.

Here her painful struggle and unwilling forbearance ended; she gave free vent to her tears, and thought herself the most wretched of human beings; she found her heart, her aching heart, more than ever devoted to Mandlebert, filled with his image, revering his virtues, honouring even his coldness, from a persuasion she deserved not his affection, and sighing solely for the privilege to consign herself to his remembrance for life, though unknown to himself, and unsuspected by the world. The very idea of Sir Sedley was horror to her; she felt guilty to have involved herself in an intercourse so fertile of danger; she thought over, with severest repentance, her short, but unjustifiable deviation from that transparent openness, and undesigning plainness of conduct, which her

disposition as much as her education ought to have rendered unchangeable. To that, alone, was owing all her actual difficulty, for
to that alone was owing her own opinion of any claim upon her
justice. How dearly, she cried, do I now pay for the unthinking plan
with which I risked the peace of another, for the re-establishment
of my own! She languished to throw herself into the arms of her
father, to unbosom to him all her errors and distresses, and owe their
extrication to his wisdom and kindness. She was sure he would be
unmoved by the glare of a brilliant establishment, and that far
from desiring her to sacrifice her feelings to wealth and shew, he
would himself plead against the alliance when he knew the state
of her mind, and recommend to her, so circumstanced, the single
life, in the true spirit of Christian philosophy and moderation: but
all was so closely interwoven in the affairs and ill conduct of her
brother, that she believed herself engaged in honour to guard the
fatal secret, though hazarding by its concealment impropriety and
misery.

These afflicting ruminations were at length interrupted by the
sound of feet; she took her handkerchief from her eyes, expecting
to see her sisters; she was mistaken, and beheld Mandlebert.

She started and rose; she strove to chace the tears from her eyes
without wiping them, and asked what he had done with Dr.
Orkborne?

'You are in grief!' cried he in a tone of sympathy; 'some evil has
befallen you! . . . let me ask. . . .'

'No; I am only waiting for my sisters. They have just received
letters from Lisbon.'

'You have been weeping! you are weeping now! why do you
turn away from me? I will not obtrusively demand your confidence . . . yet, could I give you the most distant idea what a weight
it might remove from my mind, . . . you would find it difficult to
deny yourself the pleasure of doing so much good!'

The tears of Camilla now streamed afresh. Words so kind from
Edgar, the cold, the hard-hearted Edgar, surprised and overset
her; yet she endeavoured to hide her face, and made an effort to
pass him.

'Is not this a little unkind?' cried he, gravely; 'however, I have
no claim to oppose you.'

'Unkind!' she repeated, and involuntarily turning to him,
shewed a countenance so disconsolate, that he lost his self-

control, and taking her reluctant hand, said: 'O Camilla! torture me no longer!'

Almost transfixed with astonishment, she looked at him for a moment in a speechless wonder; but the interval of doubt was short; the character of Edgar, for unalienable steadiness, unalterable honour, was fixed in her mind, like 'truths from holy writ,' and she knew, with certainty incontrovertible, that his fate was at her disposal, from the instant he acknowledged openly her power over his feelings.

Every opposite sensation, that with violence the most ungovernable could encounter but to combat, now met in her bosom, elevating her to rapture, harrowing her with terror, menacing even her understanding. The most exquisite wish of her heart seemed accorded at a period so nearly too late for its acceptance, that her faculties, bewildered, confused, deranged, lost the capacity of clearly conceiving if still she were a free agent or not.

He saw her excess of disorder with alarm; he sought to draw her again to her seat; but she put her hand upon her forehead, and leant it against the bark of the tree.

'You will not speak to me!' cried he; 'you will not trust me! shall I call you cruel? No! for you are not aware of the pain you inflict, the anguish you make me suffer! the generosity of your nature would else, unbidden, impulsively interfere.'

'*You* suffer! *you!*' cried she, again distressfully, almost incredulously, looking at him, while her hands were uplifted with amazement: 'I thought you above any suffering! superior to all calamity! . . . almost to all feeling! . . .'

'Ah, Camilla! what thus estranges you from candor? from justice? what is it can prompt you to goad thus a heart which almost from its first beating. . . .'

He stopt, desirous to check himself; while penetrated by his softness, and ashamed of what, in the bitterness of her spirit, she had pronounced, she again melted into tears, and sunk down upon the bench; yet holding out to him one hand, while with the other she covered her face: 'Forgive me,' she cried, 'I entreat . . . for I scarce know what I say.'

Such a speech, and so accompanied, might have demolished the stoicism of an older philosopher than Edgar; he fervently kissed her proferred hand, exclaiming: 'Forgive you! can Camilla use such a word? has she the slightest care for my opinion? the most remote concern for me, or for my happiness?'

'Farewell! farewell!' cried she, hastily drawing away her hand, 'go now, I beseech you!'

'What a moment to expect me to depart! O Camilla! my soul sickens of this suspence! End it, generous Camilla! beloved as lovely! my heart is all your own! use it gently, and accept it nobly!'

Every other emotion, now, in the vanquished Camilla, every retrospective fear, every actual regret, yielded to the conquering charm of grateful tenderness; and restoring the hand she had withdrawn: 'O Edgar,' she cried, 'how little can I merit such a gift! yet I prize it . . . far, far beyond all words!'

The agitation of Edgar was, at first, too mighty and too delicious for speech; but his eyes, now cast up to heaven, now fixed upon her own, spoke the most ardent, yet purest felicity; while her hand, now held to his heart, now pressed to his lips, strove vainly to recover its liberty. 'Blest moment!' he at length uttered, 'that finishes for every such misery of uncertainty! that gives my life to happiness . . . my existence to Camilla!'

Again speech seemed too poor for him. Perfect satisfaction is seldom loquacious; its character is rather tender than gay; and where happiness succeeds abruptly to long solicitude and sorrow, its enjoyment is fearful; it softens rather than exhilarates. Sudden joy is sportive, but sudden happiness is awful.

The pause, however, that on his side was ecstatic thankfulness, soon became mixt, on that of Camilla, with confusion and remorse: Sir Sedley returned to her memory, and with him every reflection, and every apprehension, that most cruelly could sully each trembling, though nearly gratified hope.

The cloud that so soon dimmed the transient radiance of her countenance, was instantly perceived by Edgar; but as he was beginning the most anxious inquiries, the two sisters approached, and Camilla, whose hand he then relinquished, rushed forward, and throwing her arms around their necks, wept upon their bosoms.

'Sweet sisters!' cried Edgar, embracing them all three in one; 'long may ye thus endearingly entwine each other, in the sacred links of affectionate affinity! Where shall I find our common father? . . . where is Mr. Tyrold?'

The amazed sisters could with difficulty answer that he was with their uncle, to whom he was communicating news from their mother.

Edgar looked tenderly at Camilla, but, perceiving her emotion, forbore to speak to her, though he could not deny himself the pleasure of snatching one kiss of the hand which hung down upon the shoulder of Eugenia; he then whispered to both the sisters: 'You will not, I trust, be my enemies?' and hurried to the house.

'What can this mean?' cried Eugenia and Lavinia in a breath.

'It means,' said Camilla, 'that I am the most distressed . . . yet the happiest of human beings!'

This little speech, began with the deepest sigh, but finished with the most refulgent smile, only added to their wonder.

'I hope you have been consulting with Edgar,' said the innocent Eugenia; 'nobody can more ably advise you, since, in generosity to Lionel, you are prohibited from counselling with my father.'

Again the most expressive smiles played in every feature through the tears of Camilla, as she turned, with involuntary archness, to Eugenia, and answered: 'And shall I follow his counsel, my dear sister, if he gives me any?'

'Why not? he is wise, prudent, and much attached to us all. How he can have supposed it possible we could be his enemies, is past all divination!'

Gaiety was so truly the native growth of the mind of Camilla, that neither care nor affliction could chace it long from its home. The speeches of the unsuspicious Eugenia, that a moment before would have past unheeded, now regaled her renovated fancy with a thousand amusing images, which so vigorously struggled against her sadness and her terrors, that they were soon nearly driven from the field by their sportive assailants; and, by the time she reached her chamber, whither, lost in amaze, her sisters followed her, the surprise she had in store for them, the pleasure with which she knew they would sympathise in her happiness, and the security of Edgar's decided regard, had liberated her mind from the shackles of reminiscence, and restored her vivacity to its original spirit.

Fastening, then, her door, she turned to them with a countenance of the brightest animation; alternately and almost wildly embraced them, and related the explicit declaration of Edgar; now hiding in their bosoms the blushes of her modest joy, now offering up to Heaven the thanksgiving of her artless rapture, now dissolving in the soft tears of the tenderest sensibility, according to the quick changing impulses of her natural and lively, yet feeling and susceptible character. Nor once did she look at the reverse of this darling portrait of chosen felicity, till Eugenia, with a gentle sigh, uttered: 'Unhappy Sir Sedley Clarendel! how may this stroke be softened to him?'

'Ah Eugenia!' she cried; 'that alone is my impediment to the most perfect, the most unmixt content! why have you made me think of him?'

'My dear Camilla,' said Eugenia, with a look of curious earnestness, and taking both her hands, while she seemed examining her face, 'you are then, it seems, in love? and with Edgar Mandlebert?'

Camilla, blushing, yet laughing, broke away from her, denying the charge.

A consultation succeeded upon the method of proceeding with the young baronet. Tommy Hodd was not yet returned with the answer; it was five miles to Clarendel Place, which made going and returning his day's work. She resolved to wait but this one reply, and then to acknowledge to Edgar the whole of her situation. The delicacy of Lavinia, and the high honour of Eugenia, concurred in the propriety of this confession; and they all saw the urgent necessity of an immediate explanation with Sir Sedley, whose disappointment might every hour receive added weight from delay. Painful, therefore, confusing and distasteful, as was the task, Camilla determined upon the avowal, and as completely to be guided by Edgar in this difficult conjuncture, as if his advice were already sanctioned by conjugal authority.

CHAPTER VI

A Call of the House

EDGAR returned to the parlour with a countenance so much brightened, a joy so open, a confidence so manly, and an air so strongly announcing some interesting intelligence, that his history required no prelude. 'Edgar,' said Mr. Tyrold, 'you have a look to disarm care of its corrosion. You could not take a better time to wear so cheering an aspect; I have just learnt that my wife can fix no sort of date for her return; I must borrow, therefore, some reflected happiness; and none, after my children, can bring its sunshine so home to my bosom as yourself.'

'What a fortunate moment have you chosen,' cried Edgar, affectionately taking him by the hand, 'to express this generous pleasure in seeing me happy! will you repent, will you retract, when you hear in what it may involve you? . . . Dearest sir! my honoured, my parental friend! to what a test shall I put your kindness! . . . Will you give me in charge one of the dearest ties of your existence? will you repose in my care so large a portion of your peace? will you trust to me your Camilla?' . . .

With all the ardour of her character, all the keen and quick feelings of her sensitive mind, scarce had Camilla herself been more struck, more penetrated with sudden joy, sudden wonder, sudden gratification of every kind, than Mr. Tyrold felt at this moment. He more than returned the pressure with which Edgar held his hand, and instantly answered, 'Yes, my excellent young friend, without hesitation, without a shadow of apprehension for her happiness! though she is all the fondest father can wish; . . . and though she only who gave her to me is dearer!'

Felicity and tenderness were now the sole guests in the breast of Edgar. He kissed with reverence the hand of Mr. Tyrold, called him by the honoured and endearing title of father; acknowledged that, from the earliest period of observation, Camilla had seemed to him the most amiable of human creatures; spoke with the warm devotion he sincerely felt for her of Mrs. Tyrold; and was breathing forth his very soul in tender rapture upon his happy prospects, when something between a sigh and a groan from the baronet, made him hastily turn round, apologise for not sooner addressing him, and respectfully solicit his consent.

Sir Hugh was in an agitation of delight and surprise almost too potent for his strength. 'The Lord be good unto me,' he cried; 'have I lived to see such a day as this!' Then, throwing his arms about Edgar's neck, while his eyes were fast filling with tears, which soon ran plentifully down his cheeks, 'Good young Mr. Edgar!' he cried; 'good young man! and do you really love my poor Camilla, for all her not being worth a penny? And will my dear little darling come to so good an end at last, after being disinherited for doing nothing? And will you never vex her, nor speak an unkind word to her? Indeed, young Mr. Edgar, you are a noble boy! you are indeed; and I love you to the bottom of my old heart for this true good naturedness!'

Then, again and again embracing him, 'This is all of a piece,' he continued, 'with your saving my poor old Rover, which is a thing I shall never forget to my longest day, being a remarkable sign of a good heart; the poor dog having done nothing to offend, as we can all testify. So that it's a surprising thing what that mastiff owed him such a grudge for.'

Then quitting him abruptly to embrace Mr. Tyrold, 'My dear brother,' he cried, 'I hope your judgment approves this thing, as well as my sister's, when she comes to hear it, which I shall send off express, before I sleep another wink, for fear of accidents.'

'Approve,' answered Mr. Tyrold, with a look of the most expressive kindness at Edgar, 'is too cold a word; I rejoice, even thankfully rejoice, to place my dear child in such worthy and beloved hands.'

'Well, then,' cried the enchanted baronet, 'if that's the case, that we are all of one mind, we had better settle the business at once, all of us being subject to die by delay.'

He then rang the bell, and ordered Jacob to summon Camilla to the parlour, adding, 'And all the rest too, Jacob, for I have something to tell them every one, which, I make no doubt, they will be very glad to hear, yourself included, as well as your fellow-servants, who have no right to be left out; only let my niece come first, being her own affair.'

Camilla obeyed not the call without many secret sensations of distress and difficulty, but which, mingled with the more obvious ones of modesty and embarrassment, all passed for a flutter of spirits that appeared natural to the occasion.

Mr. Tyrold could only silently embrace her: knowing what she had suffered, and judging thence the excess of her present satisfaction, he would not add to her confusion by any information of his consciousness; but the softness with which he held her to his bosom spoke, beyond all words, his heartfelt sympathy in her happiness.

Camilla had no power to draw herself from his arms; but Edgar hovered round her, and Sir Hugh repeatedly and impatiently demanded to have his turn. Mr. Tyrold, gently disengaging himself from her embraces, gave one of her hands to Edgar, who, with grateful joy, pressed it to his lips. 'My children!' he then said, laying a hand upon the shoulder of each, 'what a sight is this to me! how precious a union! what will it be to your excellent mother! So long and so decidedly it has been our favourite earthly wish, that, were she but restored to me . . . to her country and to her family . . . I might, perhaps, require some new evil to prevent my forgetting where . . . and what I am!'

'My dear brother, I say! my dear niece! My dear Mr. young Edgar!' cried Sir Hugh, in the highest good humour, though with nearly exhausted patience, 'won't you let me put in a word? nor so much as give you my blessing? though I can hardly hold life and soul together for the sake of my joy!'

Camilla cast herself into his arms, he kissed her most fondly, saying: 'Don't forget your poor old uncle, my dear little girl, for the account of this young Mr. Edgar, because, good as he is, he has taken to you but a short time in comparison with me.'

'No,' said Edgar, still tenaciously retaining the hand parentally bestowed upon him; 'no, dear Sir Hugh, I wish not to rob you of your darling. I wish but to be admitted myself into this dear and respected family, and to have Etherington, Cleves, and Beech Park, considered as our alternate and common habitations.'

'You are the very best young man in the whole wide world!' cried Sir Hugh, almost sobbing with ecstasy; 'for you have hit upon just the very thing I was thinking of in my own private mind! What a mercy it is our not accepting that young Captain, who would have run away with her to I don't know where, instead of being married to the very nearest estate in the county, that will always be living with us!'

The rest of the family now, obedient to the direction of Jacob, who had intimated that something extraordinary was going forward, entered the room.

'Come in, come in,' cried Sir Hugh, 'and hear the good news; for we have just been upon the very point of losing the best opportunity that ever we had in our lives of all living together; which, I hope, we shall now do, without any more strangers coming upon us with their company, being a thing we don't desire.'

'But what's the good news, uncle?' said Indiana; 'is it only about our living together?'

'Why, yes, my dear, that's the first principle, and the other is, that young Mr. Edgar's going to marry Camilla; which I hope you won't take ill, liking being all fancy.'

'Me?' cried she, with a disdainful toss of the head, though severely mortified; 'it's nothing to me, I'm sure!'

Camilla ashamed, and Edgar embarrassed, strove now mutually to shew Sir Hugh they wished no more might be said: but he only embraced them again, and declared he had never been so full of joy before in his whole life, and would not be cut short.

Miss Margland, extremely piqued, vented her spleen in oblique sarcasms, and sought to heal her offended pride by appeals for justice to her sagacity and foresight in the whole business.

Jacob, now opening the door, said all the servants were come.

Camilla tried to escape; but Sir Hugh would not permit her, and the house-keeper and butler led the way, followed by every other domestic of the house.

'Well, my friends,' he cried, 'wish her joy, which I am sure you will do of your own accord, for she's going to be mistress of Beech Park; which I thought would have been the case with my other niece, till I found out my mistakes; which is of no consequence now, all having ended for the best; though unknown to us poor mortals.'

The servants obeyed with alacrity, and offered their hearty congratulations to the blushing Camilla and happy Edgar, Molly Mill excepted; who, having concluded Sir Sedley Clarendel the man, doubted her own senses, and, instead of open felicitations, whispered Camilla, 'Dear Miss, I've got another letter for you! It's here in my bosom.'

Camilla, frightened, said: 'Hush! hush!' while Edgar, imagining the girl, whose simplicity and talkativeness were familiar to him, had said something ridiculous, entreated to be indulged with hearing her remark: but seeing Camilla look grave, forbore to press his request.

The baronet now began an harangue upon the happiness that would accrue from these double unions, for which he assured them they should have double remembrances, though the same preparations would do for both, as he meant they should take place at the same time, provided Mr. Edgar would have the obligingness to wait for a fair wind, which he was expecting every hour.

Camilla could now stay no longer; nor could Edgar, though adoring the hearty joy of Sir Hugh, refuse to aid her in absconding.

He begged her permission to follow, as soon as it might be possible, which she tacitly accorded. She was impatient herself for the important conference she was planning, and felt, with increasing solicitude, that all her life's happiness hung upon her power to extricate herself honourably from the terrible embarrassment in which she was involved.

She sauntered about the hall till the servants came out, anxious to receive the letter which Molly Mill had announced. They all sought to surround her with fresh good wishes; but she singled out Molly, and begged the rest to leave her for the present. The letter, however, was not unpinned from the inside of Molly's neck handkerchief, before Edgar, eager and gay, joined her.

Trembling then, she entreated her to make haste.

'La, Miss,' answered the girl, 'if you hurry me so, I shall tear it as sure as can be; and what will you say then, Miss?'

'Well . . . then . . . another time will do . . . take it to my room.'

'No, no, Miss; the gentleman told Tommy Hodd he wanted an answer as quick as can be; he said, if Tommy'd come a-horseback, he'd pay for the horse, to make him quicker; and Tommy says he always behaves very handsome.'

She then gave her the squeezed billet. Camilla, in great confusion, put it into her pocket. Edgar, who even unavoidably heard what passed, held back till Molly retired; and then, with an air of undisguised surprise and curiosity, though in a laughing tone, said, 'Must not the letter be read till I make my bow?'

'O yes,' . . . cried she, stammering, 'it may be read . . . at any time.' And she put her hand in her pocket to reproduce it. But the idea of making known the strange and unexpected history she had to relate, by shewing so strange a correspondence, without one leading and softening previous circumstance, required a force and confidence of which she was not mistress. She twisted it, therefore, hastily round, to hide the hand-writing of the direction, and, then, with the same care, rolled it up, and encircled it with her fingers.

'Shall I be jealous?' said he, gently, though disappointed.

'You have much reason!' she answered, with a smile so soft, it dispersed every fear, yet with an attention so careful to conceal the address, that it kept alive every wonder. He took her other hand, and kissing it, cried: 'No, sweetest Camilla, such unworthy distrust shall make no part of our compact. Yet I own myself a little interested to know what gentleman has obtained a privilege I should myself prize above almost any other. I will leave you, however, to read the letter, and, perhaps, before you answer it . . . but no . . . I will ask nothing; I shall lose all pleasure in your confidence, if it is not spontaneous. I will go and find your sisters.'

The first impulse of Camilla was, to commit to him immediately the unopened letter: but the fear of its contents, its style, its requisitions, made her terror overpower her generosity; and, though she looked after him with regret, she stood still to break the seal of her letter.

Miss Camilla Tyrold.

Is it thus, O far too fair tormenter! thou delightest to torture? Dost thou give wings but to clip them? raise expectation but to bid it linger? fan bright the flame of hope, but to see it consume in its own ashes? Another delay? . . . Ah! tell me how I may exist till it terminates! Name to me, O fair tyrant! some period, . . . or build not upon longer forbearance, but expect me at your feet. You talk of the Grove: its fair owner is just returned, and calls herself impatient to see you. Tomorrow, then, . . . you will not, I trust, kill me again tomorrow? With the sun, the renovating sun, I will visit those precincts, nor quit them till warned away by the pale light of Diana: tell me, then, to what century of that period your ingenious cruelty condemns me to this expiring state, ere a vivifying smile recalls me back to life?

SEDLEY CLARENDEL.

The immediate presence of Edgar himself could not have made this letter dye the cheeks of Camilla of a deeper red. She saw that Sir Sedley thought her only coquettishly trifling, and she looked forward with nearly equal horror to clearing up a mistake that might embitter his future life, and to acknowledging to Edgar . . . the scrupulous, the scrutinising, the delicate Edgar . . . that such a mistake could have been formed.

She was ruminating upon this formidable, this terrible task, when Edgar again appeared, accompanied by her sisters. She hurried the letter into her pocket. Edgar saw the action with a concern that dampt his spirits; he wished to obtain from her immediately the unlimited trust, which immediately, and for ever, he meant to repose in her. They all strolled together for a short time in the park; but she was anxious to retreat to her room, and her sisters were dying with impatience to read Sir Sedley's letter. Edgar, disturbed to see how little any of their countenances accorded with the happy feelings he had so recently experienced, proposed not to lengthen the walk, but flattered himself, upon re-entering the house, Camilla would afford him a few minutes of explanation. But she only, with a faint smile, said she should soon return to the parlour; and he saw Molly Mill eagerly waiting for her upon the stairs, and heard her, in reply to some question concerning Tommy Hodd, desire the girl to be quiet till she got to her room.

Edgar could form no idea of what all this meant, yet, that some secret disturbance preyed upon Camilla, that some gentleman wrote to her, and expected impatiently an answer; and that the correspondence passed neither through her friends, nor by the post, but by the medium of Molly Mill, were circumstances not less unaccountable than unpleasant.

Camilla, meanwhile, produced the letter to her sisters, beseeching their ablest counsel. 'See but,' she cried, 'how dreadfully unprepared is Sir Sedley for the event of the day! And oh! . . . how yet more unprepared must be Edgar for seeing that such a letter could ever be addressed to me! How shall I shew it him, my dear sisters? how help his believing I must have given every possible encouragement, ere Sir Sedley could have written to me in so assured a style?'

Much deliberation ensued; but they were all so perplexed, that they were summoned to tea before they had come to any resolution.

The counsel of Eugenia, then, prevailed; and it was settled, that Camilla should avoid, for the present, any communication to Edgar, lest it should lead to mischief between him and the young baronet, who could not but be mutually displeased with each other; and that the next morning, before she saw Edgar again, she should set out for the Grove, and there cast herself wholly upon the generosity of Sir Sedley; and, when freed from all engagement, return, and relate, without reserve, the whole history to Edgar; who would so soon be brother of her brother, that he would pardon the faults of Lionel, and who would then be in no danger himself from personal contest or discussion with Sir Sedley. She wrote, therefore, one line, to say she would see Mrs. Arlbery early the next day, and delivered it to Molly Mill; who promised to borrow a horse of the under-groom, that Tommy Hodd might be back before bed-time, without any obligation to Sir Sedley.

She, then, went down stairs; when Edgar, disappointed by her long absence, sought vainly to recompense it by conversing with her. She was gentle, but seated herself aloof, and avoided his eyes.

His desire to unravel so much mystery he thought now so legitimated by his peculiar situation, that he was frequently upon the point of soliciting for information: but, to know himself privileged, upon further reflexion, was sufficient to insure his forbearance. Even when that knot was tied which would give to him all power, he sincerely meant to owe all her trust to willing communication. Should he now, then, make her deem him exacting, and tenacious of prerogative? no; it might shackle the freedom of her mind in their future intercourse. He would quietly, therefore, wait her own time, and submit to her own inclination. She could not doubt his impatience; he would not compel her generosity.

CHAPTER VII

The Triumph of Pride

THE three sisters were retired, at night, to another council in the room of Camilla, when Molly Mill, with a look of dismay, burst in upon them, bringing, with the answer of Sir Sedley, news that Tommy Hodd, by an accident he could not help, had rode the horse she had borrowed for him of the under-groom to death.

The dismay, now, spread equally to them all. What a tale would this misfortune unfold to Sir Hugh, to Edgar, to the whole house! The debt of Lionel, the correspondence with Sir Sedley, the expectations of the young baronet. . . . Camilla could not support it; she sent for Jacob to own to him the affair, and beg his assistance.

Jacob, though getting into bed, obeyed the call. He was, however, so much irritated at the loss of the horse, and the boldness of the under-groom, in lending him without leave, that, at first, he would listen to no entreaties, and protested that both the boy and Molly Mill should be complained of to his master. The eloquence, however, of his three young mistresses, for so all the nieces of Sir Hugh were called by the servants at Cleves, soon softened his ire; he almost adored his master, and was affectionately attached to the young family. They begged him, therefore, to buy another horse, as like it as possible, and to contrive not to employ it when Sir Hugh was in sight, till they were able to clear up the history[1] to their uncle themselves: this would not be difficult, as the baronet rarely visited his stables since his fall, from the melancholy with which he was filled by the sight of his horses.

There was to be a fair for cattle in the neighbourhood the next day, and Jacob promised to ride over to see what bargain he could make for them.

They then inquired about what money would be necessary for the purchase.

The cost, he said, of poor Tom Jones was 40 l.

Camilla held up her hands, almost screaming. Eugenia, with more presence of mind, said they would see him again in the morning before he went, and then told Molly Mill to wait for her in her own room.

'What can I now do?' cried Camilla; 'I would not add the history of this dreadful expence to the sad tale I have already to relate to Edgar for the universe! To begin my career by such a string of humiliations would be insupportable. Already I owe five guineas to Mrs. Arlbery, which the tumult of my mind since my return has prevented me from naming to my uncle; and I have left debts at Tunbridge that will probably take up all my next quarter's allowance!'

'As far as these three guineas will go,' said Lavinia, taking out her purse, 'here, my dearest Camilla, they are; . . . but how little that is! I never before thought my pittance too small! yet how well we all know my dear father cannot augment it.'

Eugenia, who, in haste, had stept to her own room, now came back, and putting twenty guineas into the hand of Camilla, said: 'This, my beloved sister, is all I now have by me; but Jacob is rich and good, and will rejoice to pay the rest for us at present; and I shall very soon reimburse him, for my uncle has insisted upon making me a very considerable present, which I shall, now, no longer refuse.'

Camilla burst into tears, and, hanging about their necks: 'O my sisters,' she cried, 'what goodness is yours! but how can I avail myself of it with any justice? Your three guineas, my Lavinia, your little all . . . how can I bear to take?'

'Do not teach me to repine, my dear Camilla, that I have no more! I am sure of being remembered by my uncle on the approaching occasions, and I can never, therefore, better spare my little store.'

'You are all kindness! and you my dear Eugenia, though you have more, have claims upon that more, and are both expected and used to answer them. . . .'

'Yes, I have indeed more!' interrupted Eugenia, 'which only sisters good as mine could pardon; but because my uncle has made me his heiress, has he made me a brute? No! whatever I have, must be amongst us all in common, not only now, but. . . .' She stopt, affrighted at the idea she was presenting to herself, and fervently clasping her hands, exclaimed: 'O long . . . long may it be ere I can shew my sisters all I feel for them! they will believe it, I am sure . . . and that is far happier!'

The idea this raised struck them all, at the same moment, to the heart. Not one of them had dry eyes, and with a sadness overpowering every other consideration, they sighed as heavily, and with looks as disconsolate, as if the uncle so dear to them were already no more.

The influence of parts, the predominance of knowledge, the honour of learning, the captivation of talents, and even the charm of fame itself, all shrink in their effects before the superior force of goodness, even where most simple and uncultivated, for power over the social affections.

*   *   *   *

At an early hour, the next morning the commission, with the

twenty guineas in hand, and the promise of the rest in a short time, were given to Jacob; and Camilla, then, begged permission of her father, and the carriage of her uncle, to visit Mrs. Arlbery, who, she had heard, was just returned to the Grove.

Concluding she wished to be the messenger of her own affairs to that lady, they made no opposition, and she set off before eight o'clock, without entering the parlour, where Edgar, she was informed, was already arrived for breakfast.

The little journey was terrible to her; scenes of disappointment and despair on the part of Sir Sedley, were anticipated by her alarmed imagination, and she reproached herself for every word she had ever spoken, every look she had ever given, that could have raised any presumption of her regard.

The last note was written in the style of all the others, and not one ever expressed the smallest doubt of success; how dreadful then to break to him such news, at the very moment he might imagine she came to meet him with partial pleasure!

Mrs. Arlbery was not yet risen. Camilla inquired, stammering, if any company were at the house. None, was the answer. She then begged leave to walk in the garden till Mrs. Arlbery came down stairs.

She was not sorry to miss her; she dreaded her yet more than Sir Sedley himself, and hoped to see him alone.

Nevertheless, she remained a full hour in waiting, ruminating upon the wonder her disappearance would give to Edgar, and nearly persuaded some chance had anticipated her account to Sir Sedley, whose rage and grief were too violent to suffer him to keep his appointment.

This idea served but to add to her perturbation, when, at last, she saw him enter the garden.

All presence of mind then forsook her; she looked around to see if she could escape, but his approach was too quick for avoidance. Her eyes, unable to encounter his, were bent upon the ground, and she stood still, and even trembling, till he reached her.

To the prepossessed notions and vain character of Sir Sedley, these were symptoms by no means discouraging; with a confidence almost amounting to arrogance he advanced, pitying her distress, yet pitying himself still more for the snare in which it was involving him. He permitted his eyes for a moment to fasten upon her, to admire her, and to enjoy triumphantly her confusion in silence: 'Ah, beauteous tyrant!' he then cried; 'if this instant were less inappreciable, in what language could I upbraid thy unexampled abuse of power? thy lacerating barbarity?'

He then, almost by force, took her hand; she struggled eagerly to recover it, but 'No,' he cried, 'fair torturer! it is now my prisoner, and must be punished for its inhuman sins, in the congealing and unmerciful lines it has portrayed for me.'

And then, regardless of her resistance, which he attributed to mere bashfulness, he obstinately and incessantly devoured it with kisses, in defiance of opposition, supplication, or anger, till, suddenly and piercingly, she startled him with a scream, and snatched it away with a force irresistible.

Amazed, he stared at her. Her face was almost convulsed with emotion; but her eyes, which appeared to be fixed, directed him to the cause. At the bottom of the walk, which was only a few yards distant, stood Mandlebert.

Pale and motionless, he looked as if bereft of strength and faculties. Camilla had seen him the moment she raised her eyes, and her horror was uncontrollable. Sir Sedley, astonished at what he beheld, astonished what to think, drew back, with a supercilious kind of bow. Edgar, recalled by what he thought insolence to his recollection, advanced a few steps, and addressing himself to Camilla, said: 'I had the commands of Sir Hugh to pursue you, Miss Tyrold, to give you immediate notice that Mr. Lynmere is arrived.' He added no more, deigned not a look at Sir Sedley, but rapidly retreated, remounted his horse, and galloped off.

Camilla looked after him till he was out of sight, with uplifted hands and eyes, deploring his departure, his mistake, and his resentment, without courage to attempt stopping him.

Sir Sedley stood suspended, how to act, what to judge. If Edgar's was the displeasure of a discarded lover, why should it so affect Camilla? if of a successful one, why came she to meet him? why had she received and answered his notes?

Finding she attempted neither to speak nor move, he again approached her, and saying, 'Fair Incomprehensible!...' would again have taken her hand; but rousing to a sense of her situation, she drew back, and with some dignity, but more agitation, cried: 'Sir Sedley, I blush if I am culpable of any part of your mistake;

but suffer me now to be explicit, and let me be fully, finally, and not too late understood. You must write to me no more; I cannot answer nor read your letters. You must speak to me no more, except in public society; you must go further, Sir Sedley . . . you must think of me no more.'

'Horrible!' cried he, starting back; 'you distress me past measure!'

'No, no, you will soon . . . easily . . . readily forget me.'

'Inhuman! you make me unhappy past thought!'

'Indeed I am inexpressibly concerned; but the whole affair. . . .'

'You shock, you annihilate me, you injure me in the tenderest point!'

Camilla now, amazed, cried 'what is it you mean, sir?'

'By investing me, fair barbarian, with the temerity of forming any claim that can call for repulse!'

Utterly confounded by so unexpected a disclaiming of all design, she again, though from far different sensations, cast up her eyes and hands. And is it, she thought, for a trifler such as this, so unmeaning, so unfeeling, I have risked my whole of hope and happiness?

She said, however, no more; for what more could be said? She coloured, past him, and hastily quitting the garden, told the footman to apologise to Mrs. Arlbery for her sudden departure, by informing her that a near relation was just arrived from abroad; and then got into the carriage and drove back to Cleves.

Sir Sedley followed carelessly, yet without aiming at overtaking her, and intreated, negligently, to be heard, yet said nothing which required the smallest answer.

Piqued completely, and mortified to the quick, by the conviction which now broke in upon him of the superior ascendance of Mandlebert, he could not brook to have been thought in earnest when he saw he should not have been accepted, nor pardon his own vanity the affront it had brought upon his pride. He sung aloud an opera air till the carriage of Sir Hugh was out of sight, and then drove his phaeton to Clarendel-Place, where he instantly ordered his post-chaise, and in less than an hour, set off on a tour to the Hebrides.

CHAPTER VIII

A Summons to Happiness

CAMILLA had but just set out from Cleves, when Sir Hugh, consulting his weather-cocks, which a new chain of ideas had made him forget to examine, saw that the wind was fair for the voyage of his nephew; and heard, upon inquiry, that the favourable change had taken place the preceding day, though the general confusion of the house had prevented it from being heeded by any of the family.

With eagerness the most excessive, he went to the room of Eugenia, and bid her put on a smart hat to walk out with him, as there was no knowing how soon a certain person might arrive.

Eugenia, colouring, said she would rather stay within.

'Well,' cried he, 'you'll be neater, to be sure, for not blowing about in the wind; so I'll go take t'other girls.'

Eugenia, left alone, became exceedingly fluttered. She could not bear to remain in the house under the notion of so degrading a consideration as owing any advantage to outward appearance; and fearing her uncle, in his extreme openness, should give that reason for her not walking, she determined to take a stroll by herself in the park.

She bent her steps towards a small wood at some distance from the house, where she meant to rest herself and read; for she had learnt of Dr. Orkborne never to be unprovided with a book. But she had not yet reached her place of intended repose, when the sound of feet made her turn round, and, to her utter consternation, she saw a young man, whose boots, whip, and foreign air, announced instantly to be Clermont Lynmere.

She doubted not but he was sent in pursuit of her; and though youthful timidity prompted her to shun him, she retained sufficient command over herself to check it, and to stop till he came up to her; while he, neither quickening nor slackening his pace as he approached, passed her with so little attention, that she was presently convinced he had scarce even perceived her.

Disconcerted by a meeting so strange and so ill timed, she involuntarily stood still, without any other power than that of looking after him.

In a few minutes Molly Mill, running up to her, cried: 'Dear Miss, have not you seen young Mr. Lynmere? He come by t'other way just as master, and Miss Margland, and Miss Lynmere, and Miss Tyrold, was gone to meet him by the great gate; and so he said he'd come and look who he could find himself.'

Eugenia had merely voice to order her back. The notion of having a figure so insignificant as to be passed, without even exciting a doubt [who] she might be, was cruelly mortifying. She knew not how to return to the house, and relate such an incident. She sat down under a tree to recollect herself.

Presently, however, she saw the stranger turn quick about, and before she could rise, slightly touching his hat, without looking at her: 'Pray, ma'am,' he said, 'do you belong to that house?' pointing to the mansion of Sir Hugh.

Faintly she answered, 'Yes, sir;' and he then added: 'I am just arrived, and in search of Sir Hugh and the young ladies; one of them, they told me, was this way; but I can trace nobody. Have you seen any of them?'

More and more confounded, she could make no reply. Inattentive to her embarrassment, and still looking every way around, he repeated his question. She then pointed towards the great gate, stammering she believed they went that way. 'Thank you;' he answered, with a nod, and then hurried off.

She now thought no more of moving nor of rising; she felt a kind of stupor, in which, fixed, and without reflection, she remained, till, startled by the sound of her uncle's voice, she got up, made what haste she was able to the house by a private path, and ascended to her own room by a back stair case.

That an interview to which she had so long looked forward, for which, with unwearied assiduity, she had so many years laboured to prepare herself, and which was the declared precursor of the most important æra of her life, should pass over so abruptly, and be circumstanced so aukwardly, equally dispirited and confused her.

In a few minutes, Molly Mill, entering, said: 'They're all come back, and Sir Hugh's fit to eat the young squire up; and no wonder, for he's a sweet proper gentleman, as ever I see. Come, miss, I hope you'll put on something else, for that hat makes you look worse than any thing. I would not have the young squire see you such a figure for never so much.'

The artlessness of unadorned truth, however sure in theory of extorting administration, rarely, in practice, fails inflicting pain or mortification. The simple honesty of Molly redoubled the chagrin of her young mistress, who, sending her away, went anxiously to the looking-glass, whence, in a few moments, she perceived her uncle, from the window, laughing, and making significant signs to some one out of her sight. Extremely ashamed to be so surprised, she retreated to the other end of the room, though not till she had heard Sir Hugh say: 'Ay, ay, she's getting ready for you; I told you why she would not walk out with us, so don't let's hurry her, though I can't but commend your being a little impatient, which I dare say so is she, only young girls can't so well talk about it.'

Eugenia now found that Clermont had no suspicion he had seen her. Sir Hugh concluded she had not left her room, and asked no questions that could lead to the discovery.

Presently the baronet came up stairs himself, and tapping at her door, said: 'Come, my dear, don't be too curious,[1] the breakfast having been spoilt this hour already; besides your cousin's having nothing on himself but his riding dress.'

Happy she could at least clear herself from so derogatory a design, she opened her door. Sir Hugh, surveying her with a look of surprise and vexation, exclaimed: 'What my dear! an't you dizen'd yet? why I thought to have seen you in all your best things!'

'No, sir,' answered she calmly; 'I shall not dress till dinner-time.'

'My dear girl,' cried he, kindly, though a little distressed how to explain himself; 'there's no need you should look worse than you can help; though you can do better things, I know, than looking well at any time; only what I mean is, you should let him see you to the best advantage at the first, for fear of his taking any dislike before he knows about Dr. Orkborne, and that.'

'Dislike, sir!' repeated she, extremely hurt; 'if you think he will take any dislike . . . I had better not see him at all!'

'My dear girl, you quite mistake me, owing to my poor head's always using the wrong word; which is a remarkable thing that I can't help. But I don't mean in the least to doubt his being pleased with you, except only at the beginning, from not being used to you; for as to all your studies, there's no more Greek and

Latin in one body's face than in another's; but, however, if you won't dress, there's no need to keep the poor boy in hot water for nothing.'

He then took her hand, and rather dragged than drew her down stairs, saying as they went: 'I must wish you joy, though, for I assure you he's a very fine lad, and hardly a bit of a coxcomb.'

The family was all assembled in the parlour, except Camilla, for whom the baronet had instantly dispatched Edgar, and Mr. Tyrold, who was not yet returned from a morning ride, but for whom Sir Hugh had ordered the great dinner bell to be rung, as a signal of something extraordinary.

Young Lynmere was waiting the arrival of Eugenia with avowed and unbridled impatience. Far from surmising it was her he had met in the park, he had concluded it was one of the maids, and thought of her no more. He asked a thousand questions in a breath when his uncle was gone. Was she tall? was she short? was she plump? was she lean? was she fair? was she brown? was she florid? was she pale? But as he asked them of every body, nobody answered; yet all were in some dismay at a curiosity implying such entire ignorance, except Indiana, who could not, without simpering, foresee the amazement of her brother at her cousin's person and appearance.

'Here's a noble girl for you!' cried Sir Hugh, opening the door with a flourish; 'for all she's got so many best things, she's come down in her worst, for the sake of looking ill at the beginning, to the end that there may be no fault to be found afterwards; which is the wiseness that does honour to her education.'

This was, perhaps, the first time an harangue from the baronet had been thought too short; but the surprise of young Lynmere, at the view of his destined bride, made him wish he would speak on, merely to annul any necessity for speaking himself. Eugenia aimed in vain to recover the calmness of her nature, or to borrow what might resemble it from her notions of female dignity. The injudicious speech of Sir Hugh, but publicly forcing upon the whole party the settled purpose of the interview, covered her with blushes, and gave a tremor to her frame that obliged her precipitately to seat herself, while her joined hands supplicated his silence.

'Well, my dear, well!' said he, kissing her, 'don't let me vex you; what I said having no meaning, except for the best; though your cousin might as well have saluted you before you sat down, I think; which, however, I suppose may be out of fashion now, every thing changing since my time; which, Lord help me! it will take me long enough to learn.'

Lynmere noticed not this hint, and they all seated themselves round the breakfast table; Sir Hugh scarce able to refrain from crying for joy, and continually exclaiming: 'This is the happiest day of all my life, for all I've lived so long! To see us all together, at last, and my dear boy come home to his native old England!'

Miss Margland made the tea, and young Lynmere instantly and almost voraciously began eating of every thing that was upon the table. Indiana, when she saw her brother as handsome as her cousin was deformed, thought the contrast so droll, she could look at neither without tittering; Lavinia observed, with extreme concern, the visible distress of her sister; Dr. Orkborne forbore to ruminate upon his work, in expectation, every moment, of being called upon to converse with the learned young traveller; but Sir Hugh alone spoke, though his delight and his loquacity joined to his pleasure in remarking the good old English appetite which his nephew had brought with him from foreign parts, prevented his being struck with the general taciturnity.

The entrance of Mr. Tyrold proved a relief to all the party, though a pain to himself. He suffered in seeing the distressed confusion of Eugenia, and felt something little short of indignation at the supercilious air with which Clermont seemed to examine her; holding his head high and back, as if measuring his superior height, while every line round his mouth marked that ridicule was but suppressed by contempt.

When Sir Hugh, at length, observed that the young traveller uttered not a syllable, he exclaimed: 'Lord help us! what fools it makes of us, being overjoyed! here am I talking all the talk to myself, while my young scholar says nothing! which I take to be owing to my speaking only English; which, however, I should not do, if it was not for the misfortune of knowing no other, which I can't properly call a fault, being out of no idleness, as that gentleman can witness for me; for I'll warrant nobody's taken more pains; but our heads won't always do what we want.'

He then gave a long and melancholy detail of his studies and their failure.

When the carriage arrived with Camilla, young Lynmere

loitered to a window, to look at it; Eugenia arose, meaning to seize the opportunity to escape to her room; but seeing him turn round upon her moving, she again sat down, experiencing, for the first time, a sensation of shame for her lameness, which, hitherto, she had regularly borne with fortitude, when she had not forgotten from indifference: neither did she feel spirits to exhibit, again, before his tall and strikingly elegant figure, her diminutive little person.

Camilla entered with traces of a disordered mind too strongly marked in her countenance to have escaped observation, had she been looked at with any attention. But Eugenia and Lynmere ingrossed all eyes and all thoughts. Even herself, at first sight of the husband elect of her sister, lost, for a moment, all personal consideration, and looked at him only with the interesting idea of the future fate of Eugenia. But it was only for a moment; when she turned round, and saw nothing of Edgar, when her uncle's inquiry what had become of him convinced her he was gone elsewhere, her heart sunk, she felt sick, and would have glided out of the room, had not Sir Hugh, thinking her faint for want of her breakfast, begged Miss Margland to make her some fresh tea; adding, 'As this is a day in which I intend us all to be happy alike, I beg nobody will go out of the room, for the sake of our enjoying it all together.'

This summons to happiness produced the usual effect of such calls; a general silence, succeeded by a general yawning, and a universal secret wish of separation, to the single exception of Sir Hugh, who, after a pause, said, 'Why nobody speaks but me! which I really think odd enough. However, my dear nephew, if you don't care for our plain English conversation, which, indeed, after all your studies, one can't much wonder at, nobody can be against you and the Doctor jabbering together a little of your Greek and Latin.'

Lynmere, letting fall his bread upon the table, leaned back in his chair, and, sticking his hands in his side, looked at his uncle with an air of astonishment.

'Nay,' continued the baronet, 'I don't pretend I should be much the wiser for it; however, it's what I've no objection to hear: so come, Doctor! you're the oldest; break the ice!'

A verse of Horace with which Dr. Orkborne was opening his answer, was stopt short, by the eager manner in which Lynmere re-seized his bread with one hand, while, with the other, to the great discomposure of the exact Miss Margland, he stretched forth for the tea-pot, to pour out a bason of tea; not ceasing the libation till the saucer itself, overcharged, sent his beverage in trickling rills from the tablecloth to the floor.

The ladies all moved some paces from the table, to save their clothes; and Miss Margland reproachfully inquired if she had not made his tea to his liking.

'Don't mind it, I beg, my dear boy,' cried Sir Hugh; 'a little slop's soon wiped up; and we're all friends: so don't let that stop your Latin.'

Lynmere, noticing neither the Latin, the mischief, nor the consolation, finished his tea in one draught, and then said: 'Pray, sir, where do you keep all your newspapers?'

'Newspapers, my dear nephew? I've got no newspapers: what would you have us do with a mere set of politics, that not one of us understand, in point of what may be their true drift; now we're all met together o'purpose to be comfortable?'

'No newspapers, sir?' cried Lynmere, rising, and vehemently ringing the bell; and, with a scornful laugh, adding, half between his teeth, 'Ha! ha! live in the country without newspapers! a good joke, faith!'

A servant appearing, he gave orders for all the morning papers that could be procured.

Sir Hugh looked much amazed; but presently, starting up, said, 'My dear nephew, I believe I've caught your meaning, at last; for if you mean, as I take for granted, that we're all rather dull company, why I'll take your hint, and leave you and a certain person together, to make a better acquaintance; which you can't do so well while we're all by, on account of modesty.'

Eugenia, frightened almost to sickness, [was] caught by her two sisters; and Mr. Tyrold, tenderly compassionating her apprehensions, whispered to Sir Hugh to dispense with a *tête-à-tête* so early: and, taking her hand, accompanied her himself to her room, composing, and re-assuring her by the way.

Sir Hugh, though vexed, then followed, to issue some particular orders; the rest of the party dispersed, and young Lynmere remained with his sister.

Walking on tiptoe to the door, he shut it, and put his ear to the key-hole, till he no longer heard any footstep. Turning then hastily round, he flung himself, full length, upon a sofa, and burst into so violent a fit of laughter, he was forced to hold his sides.

Indiana, tittering, said, 'Well, brother, how do you like her?'

'Like her!' he repeated, when able to speak; 'why the old gentleman doats! He can never, else, seriously suppose I'll marry her.'

'He! he! he! yes, but he does, indeed, brother. He's got every thing ready.'

'Has he, faith?' cried Lynmere, again rolling on the sofa, almost suffocated with violent laughter: from which, suddenly recovering, he started up to stroam[1] to a large looking-glass, and, standing before it, in an easy and most assured attitude, 'Much obliged to him, 'pon honour!' he exclaimed: 'Don't you think,' turning carelessly, yet in an elegant position, round to his sister, 'don't you think I am, Indiana?'

'Me, brother? la! I'm sure I think she's the ugliest little fright, poor thing! I ever saw in the world, poor thing! such a little, short, dumpty, hump backed, crooked, limping figure of a fright . . . poor thing!'

'Yes, yes,' cried he, changing his posture, but still undauntedly examining himself before the glass, 'he has taken amazing care of me, I confess; matched me most exactly!'

Then sitting down, as if to consider the matter more seriously, he took Indiana by the arm, and, with some displeasure, said, 'Why, what does the old quoz[2] mean? Does he want me to toss him in a blanket?'[3]

Indiana tittered more than ever at this idea, till her brother angrily demanded of her, why she had not written herself some description of this young Hecate, to prepare him for her sight? Sir Hugh having merely given him to understand that she was not quite beautiful.

Indiana had no excuse to plead, but that she did not think of it. She had, indeed, grown up with an aversion to writing, in common with whatever else gave trouble, or required attention; and her correspondence with her brother rarely produced more than two letters in a year, which were briefly upon general topics, and read by the whole family.

She now related to him the history of the will, and the vow, which only in an imperfect, and but half-credited manner had reached him.

His laughter than gave place to a storm of rage. He called himself ruined, blasted, undone; and abused Sir Hugh as a good-for-nothing dotard, defrauding him of his just rights and expectations.

'Why, that's the reason,' said Indiana, 'he wants to marry you to cousin Eugenia; because, he says, it's to make you amends.'

This led him to a rather more serious consideration of the affair; for, he protested, the money was what he could not do without. Yet, again parading to the glass, 'What a shame, Indiana,' he cried, 'what a shame would it be to make such a sacrifice? If he'll only pay a trifle of money for me, and give me a few odd hundreds to begin with, I'll hold him quit of all else, so he'll but quit me of that wizen little stump.'

A newspaper, procured from the nearest public house, being now brought, he pinched Indiana by the chin, said she was the finest girl he had seen in England, and whistled off to his appointed chamber.

Clermont Lynmere so entirely resembled his sister in person, that now, in his first youth, he might almost have been taken for her, even without change of dress: but the effect produced upon the beholders bore not the same parallel: what in her was beauty in its highest delicacy, in him seemed effeminacy in its lowest degradation. The brilliant fairness of his forehead, the transparent pink of his cheeks, the pouting vermillion of his lips, the liquid lustre of his languishing blue eyes, the minute form of his almost infantine mouth, and the snowy whiteness of his small hands and taper fingers, far from bearing the attraction which, in his sister, rendered them so lovely, made him considered by his own sex as an unmanly fop, and by the women, as too conceited to admire any thing but himself.

With respect to his understanding, his superiority over his sister was rather in education than in parts, and in practical intercourse with the world, than in any higher reasoning faculties. His character, like his person, wanted maturing, the one being as distinct from intellectual decision, as the other from masculine dignity. He had youth without diffidence, sprightliness without wit, opinion without judgment, and learning without knowledge. Yet, as he contemplated his fine person in the glass, he thought himself without one external fault; and, early cast upon his own responsibility, was not conscious of one mental deficiency.

CHAPTER IX

Offs and Ons

MR. TYROLD left Eugenia to her sisters, unwilling to speak of Lynmere till he had seen something more of him. Sir Hugh, also, was going, for he had no time, he said, to lose in his preparations: but Eugenia, taking his arm, besought that nothing of that kind might, at present, be mentioned.

'Don't trouble yourself about that, my dear,' he answered; 'for it's what I take all into my own hands; your cousin being a person that don't talk much; by which, how can any thing be brought forward, if nobody interferes? A girl, you know, my dear, can't speak for herself, let her wish it never so much.'

'Alas!' said Eugenia, when he was gone, 'how painfully am I situated! Clermont will surely suppose this precipitance all mine; and already, possibly, concludes it is upon my suggestion he has thus prematurely been called from his travels, and impeded in his praise-worthy ambition of studying the laws, manners, and customs of the different nations of Europe!'

The wan countenance of Camilla soon, however, drew all observation upon herself, and obliged her to narrate the cruel adventure of the morning.

The sisters were both petrified by the account of Sir Sedley; and their compassion for his expected despair was changed into disgust at his insulting impertinence. They were of opinion that his bird and his letters should immediately be returned; and their horror of any debt with a character mingling such presumption with such levity, made Eugenia promise that, as soon as she was mistress of so much money, she would send him, in the name of Lionel, his two hundred pounds.

The bird, therefore, by Tom Hodd, was instantly conveyed to Clarendel-Place; but the letters Camilla retained, till she could first shew them to Edgar, . . . if this event had not lost him to her for ever, and if he manifested any desire of an explanation.

*   *   *   *

Edgar himself, meanwhile, in a paroxysm of sudden misery, and torturing jealousy, had galloped furiously to the rector of Cleves.

'O, Doctor Marchmont!' he cried, 'what a tale have I now to unfold! Within these last twenty-four hours I have been the most wretched . . . the happiest . . . and again the most agonized of human beings! I have thought Camilla bestowed upon another, . . . I have believed her, . . . oh, Doctor! . . . my own! . . . I have conceived myself at the summit of all earthly felicity! . . . I find myself, at this moment deluded and undone!'

He then detailed the account, calling upon the Doctor to unravel to him the insupportable ænigma of his destiny; to tell him for what purpose Camilla had shewn him a tenderness so bewitching, at the very time she was carrying on a clandestine intercourse with another? with a man, who, though destitute neither of wit nor good qualities, it was impossible she should love, since she was as incapable of admiring as of participating in his defects? To what incomprehensible motives attribute such incongruities? Why accept and suffer her friends to accept him, if engaged to Sir Sedley? why, if seriously meaning to be his, this secret correspondence? Why so early, so private, so strange a meeting? 'Whence, Doctor Marchmont, the daring boldness of his seizing her hand? whence the never-to-be-forgotten licence with which he presumed to lift it to his lips, . . . and there hardily to detain it, so as never man durst do, whose hopes were not all alive, from his own belief in their encouragement! explain, expound to me this work of darkness and amazement; tell me why, with every appearance of the most artless openness, I find her thus eternally disingenuous and unintelligible? why, though I have cast myself wholly into her power, she retains all her mystery . . . she heightens it into deceit next perjury?'

'Ask me, my dear young friend, why the sun does not give night, and the moon day; then why women practise coquetry. Alas! my season for surprise has long been passed! They will rather trifle, even with those they despise, than be candid even with those they respect. The young baronet, probably, has been making his court to her, or she has believed such was his design; but as you first came to the point, she would not hazard rejecting you, while uncertain if he were serious. She was, possibly, putting him to the test, by the account of your declaration, at the moment of your unseasonable intrusion.'

'If this, Doctor, is your statement, and if your statement is just, in how despicable a lottery have I risked the peace of my life! You suppose then . . . that, if sure of Sir Sedley . . . I am discarded?'

'You know what I think of your situation: can I, when to yet more riches I add a title, suppose that of Sir Sedley less secure?'

The shuddering start, the distracted look of Edgar, with his hand clapped to his burning forehead, now alarmed the Doctor; who endeavoured to somewhat soften his sentence, dissuading him against any immediate measures, and advising him to pass over these first moments of emotion, and then coolly to suffer inquiry to take place of decision. But Edgar could not hear him; he shook hands with him, faintly smiled, as an apology for not speaking; and, hurrying off, without waiting for his servant, galloped towards the New Forest: leaving his absence from Cleves to declare his defection, and bent only to fly from Camilla, and all that belonged to her.

All, however, that belonged to Camilla was precisely what followed him; pursued him in every possible form, clung to his heart-strings, almost maddened his senses. He could not bear to reflect; retrospection was torture, anticipation was horror. To lose thus, without necessity, without calamity, the object of his dearest wishes, . . . to lose her from mere declension of esteem. . . .

'Any inevitable evil,' he cried, 'I could have sustained; any blow of fortune, however severe; any stroke of adversity, how-ever terrible; . . . but this . . . this error of all my senses . . . this deception of all my hopes . . . this extinction of every feeling I have cherished'—

He rode on yet harder, leaping over every thing, thoughtless rather than fearless of every danger he could encounter, and galloping with the speed and violence of some pursuit, though wholly without view, and almost without consciousness; as if, hoping by flight, to escape from the degenerate portrait of Camilla: but its painter was his own imagination, and mocked the attempt.

From the other side of a five-barred gate, which, with almost frantic speed, he was approaching with a view to clear, a voice halloo'd to stop him; and, at the same time, a man who was leading one horse, and riding another, dismounted, and called out, 'Why, as sure as I'm alive, it's 'Squire Mandlebert!'

Edgar now, perceiving Jacob, was going to turn back to avoid him; but, restraining this first movement, faintly desired him to stand by, as he had not a moment to lose.

'Good lack!' cried Jacob, with the freedom of an old servant, who had known him from a boy; 'why, I would not but have happened to come this way for never so much! why you might have broke your neck, else! Leap such a gate as this here? why, I can't let you do no such a thing! Miss Camilla's like a child of my own, as one may say; and she'll never hold up her head again, I'll be bound for it, if you should come to any harm; and, as to poor old master! 'twould go nigh to break his heart.'

Struck with words which, from so faithful an old servant, could not but be touching, Edgar was brought suddenly to himself, and felt the claim of the Tyrold family for a conduct more guarded. He endeavoured to put his own feelings apart, and consider how best he might spare those of the friends of Camilla; those of Camilla herself he concluded to be out of his reach, except as they might simply relate to the female pride and vanity of refusing rather than being given up.

He paused, now, to weigh how he might obviate any offence; and, after first resolving to write a sort of general leave-taking, and, next, seeing the almost insuperable objections to whatever he could state, determined upon gaining time for deliberation, by merely commissioning Jacob to carry a message to Cleves, that some sudden affairs called him, for the present, to a distant part of the country. This, at such a period, would create a surprise that might lead the way to what would follow: and Camilla, who could not, he thought, be much astonished, might then take her own measures for the defection she would see reason to expect.

But Jacob resisted bearing the intelligence: 'Good lack, sir,' he cried, 'what have you got in your head? something that will do you no good, I'll be bound, by the look of your eyes, which look as big as if they was both going to drop out; you'd better come yourself and tell 'em what's the matter, and speak a word to poor Miss Camilla, or she'll never believe but what some ill has betided you. Why we all knew about it, fast enough, before our master told us; servants have eyes as well as their masters; only Mary will have it she found it out at the first, which an't true, for I saw it by the time you'd been a week in the house; and if you'll take my word, squire, I don't think there's such another heart in the world as Miss Camilla's, except just my own old master's.'

Edgar leant against his horse, neither speaking nor moving, yet involuntarily listening, while deeply sighing.

'What a power of good she'll do,' continued Jacob, 'when she's mistress of Beech Park! I warrant she'll go about, visiting the poor, and making them clothes, and broths, and wine possets, and baby-linen, all day long. She has done it at Etherington quite from a child; and when she had nothing to give 'em, she used to take her thread papers and needle books, and sit down and work for them, and carry them bits and scraps of things to help 'em to patch their gowns. Why when she's got your fine fortunes, she'll bring a blessing upon the whole county.'

Edgar felt touched; his wrath was softened into tenderness, and he ejaculated to himself: 'Such, indeed, I thought Camilla! active in charity, gentle in good works! . . . I thought that in putting my fortune into her hands, I was serving the unhappy, . . . feeding the indigent, . . . reviving the sick!'

'Master,' continued Jacob, 'took a fancy to her from the very first, as well as I; and when master said she was coming to live with us, I asked to make it a holiday for all our folks, and master was as pleased as I. But nobody'd think what a tender heart she's got of her own, without knowing her, because of her singing, and laughing, and dancing so, except when old Miss Margland's in the way, who's what Mr. Lionel calls a kill-joy at any time. Howbeit, I'll take special care she shan't be by when I tell her of my stopping you from breaking your neck here; but I wish you could be in a corner yourself, to peep at her, without her knowing it; I'll warrant you she'll give me such a smile, you'd be fit to eat her!'

Shaken once more in every resolution, because uncertain in every opinion, Edgar found the indignant desperation which had seized him begin to subside, and his mind again become assailable by something resembling hope. Almost instinctively he remounted his horse, and almost involuntarily . . . drawn on by hearkening to the praise of Camilla, and fascinated by the details made by Jacob of her regard, accompanied him back to Cleves.

As they rode into the park, and while he was earnestly endeavouring to form some palliation, by which he might exculpate what seemed to him so guilty in the strange meeting and its strange circumstances, he perceived Camilla herself, walking upon the lawn. He saw she had observed him, and saw, from her air, she seemed irresolute if to re-enter the house, or await him.

Jacob, significantly pointing her out, offered to shew the effect he could produce by what he could relate; but Edgar, giving him the charge of his horse, earnestly besought him to retire in quiet, and to keep his opinions and experiments to himself.

Each now, separately, and with nearly equal difficulty, strove to attain fortitude to seek an explanation. They approached each other; Camilla with her eyes fixed upon the ground, her air embarrassed, and her cheeks covered with blushes; Edgar with quick, but almost tottering steps, his eyes wildly avoiding hers, and his complexion pale even to indisposition.

When they were met within a few yards, they stopt; Camilla still without courage to look up, and Edgar striving to speak, but finding no passage for his voice. Camilla, then, ashamed of her situation, raised her eyes, and forced herself to say, 'Have you been into the house? Have you seen my cousin Lynmere?'

'No . . . madam.'

Struck with a cold formality that never before, from Edgar, had reached her ears, and shocked by the sight of his estranged and altered countenance, with the cruel consciousness that appearances authorised the most depreciating suspicions, she advanced, and holding out her hand, 'Edgar,' she gently cried, 'are you ill? or only angry?'

'O Camilla!' he answered, 'can you deign to use to me such a word? can you distort my dearest affections, convulse my fairest hopes, eradicate every power of happiness . . . yet speak with so much sweetness . . . yet look at me with such mildness? such softness . . . I had almost said . . . such kindness?'

Deeply affected, she could hardly stand. He had taken her offered hand, but in a manner so changed from the same action the preceding day, that she scarce knew if he touched while he held it, scarce felt that he relinquished, as almost immediately she withdrew it.

But her condescension[1] at this moment was rather a new torment than any solace to him. The hand which she proffered, and which the day before he had received as the token of permanent felicity, he had now seen in the possession of another, with every licence, every apparent mark of permitted rapture in which he had been indulged himself. He knew not to whom it of right belonged; and the doubt not merely banished happiness, but mingled resentment with misery.

'I see,' cried she, after a mortified pause; 'you have lost your good opinion of me . . . I can only, therefore. . . .' She stopt, but his melancholy silence was a confirmation of her suggestion that offended her into more exertion, and, with sensibility raised into dignity, she added, 'only hope your intended tour to the Continent may take place without delay!'

She would then have walked on to the house; but following her, 'Is all over?' he cried, 'and is it thus, Camilla, we part?'

'Why not?' said she, suppressing a sigh, yet turning back.

'What a question! cruel Camilla! Is this all the explanation you allow me?'

'What other do you wish?'

'All! . . . every other! . . . that meeting . . . those letters. . . .'

'If you have any curiosity yet remaining . . . only name what your desire.'

'Are you indeed so good?' cried he, in a voice that shewed his soul again melting; 'those letters, then. . . .'

'You shall have them . . . every one!' she cried, with alacrity; and instantly taking out her pocket-book, presented him with the prepared packet.

Penetrated by this unexpected openness and compliance, he snatched her hand, with intent to press it to his lips; but again the recollection he had seen that liberty accorded to Sir Sedley, joined to the sight of his writing, checked him; he let it go; bowed his thanks with a look of grateful respect, and attempting no more to stop her, walked towards the summer-house, to peruse the letters.

CHAPTER X

Resolutions

THE sound of the dinner-bell, which rang in the ears of Edgar before he reached his intended reatreat, would have been un-noticed, if not seconded by a message from Sir Hugh, who had seen him from his window.

Compelled to obey, though in a state of suspense almost in-tolerable, he put up the important little packet, and repaired to the dining parlour; where, though none were equally disturbed with himself, no one was at ease. Young Lynmere, under an appearance of mingled assurance and apathy, the effect of acquired conceit, playing upon natural insipidity, was secretly tormented with the rueful necessity of sacrificing either a noble fortune, or his own fine person; Sir Hugh felt a strange disappointment from the whole behaviour of his nephew, though it was what he would not acknowledge, and could not define; Mr. Tyrold saw with much uneasiness the glaringly apparent unsuitableness of the intended alliance; Eugenia had never yet thought herself so plain and insignificant, and felt as if, even since the morning, the small-pox had renewed its ravages, and she had sunk into being shorter; Indiana and Miss Margland were both acutely incensed with Mandlebert; Dr. Orkborne saw but small reason to expect gratitude for his labours from the supercilious negligence of the boasted young student; Lavinia was disturbed for both her sisters; and Camilla felt that all she valued in life depended upon the next critical hour or two.

In this state of general discomfort, Sir Hugh, who could never be silent, alone talked. Having long prepared himself to look upon this meeting as a day of happiness, he strove to believe, for a while, the whole family were peculiarly enjoying themselves; but, upon a dead silence, which ensued upon his taking a copious draught of Madeira and water, 'Why, my dear nephew,' he cried, putting down his goblet, 'you don't tell us any thing? which I've no doubt but you know why yourself. However, as we're all met o' purpose to see you, I can't say I should be sorry to hear the sound of your voice, provided it won't be disagreeable.'

'We are not much—conversant, sir, in each other's connexions, I believe,' answered Lynmere, without ceasing a moment to eat, and to help himself, and ordering a fresh plate at every second mouthful; 'I have seen nothing, yet, of your folks hereabouts; and, I fancy, sir, you don't know a great deal of the people I have been used to.'

Sir Hugh, having good humouredly acknowledged this to be truth, was at a loss what further to purpose; and, imagining the taciturnity of the rest of the party to proceed from an awe of the knowledge and abilities of his nephew, soon became himself so infected with fear and reverence, that, though he could not be silent, he spoke only to those who were next him, and in a whisper.

When the dessert was served, something like a general relief was effected by the unexpected entrance of Dr. Marchmont. Alarmed by the ungoverned, and, in him, unprecedented, emotions of Edgar, he had been to Beech Park; and, finding he had not returned there, had ridden on, in the most uneasy uncertainty, to inquire for him at Cleves.

Happy to see him safe, though almost smiling to see with whom, he was beginning some excuse for his intrusion, when the baronet saved his proceeding, by calling out, 'Well, this is as good a piece of good luck as any we've met with yet! Here's Dr. Marchmont come to wish us joy; and as he's as good a scholar as yourself, nephew, for any thing I know to the contrary, why you need not be so afraid of speaking, for the sake of our not understanding you; which here's five of us can do now, as well as yourself.'

Lynmere, readily concluding Mr. Tyrold and Edgar, with the two Doctors, made four, glanced round the table to see who might be the fifth; when, supposing it Miss Margland, he withdrew his eyes with a look of derision, and, turning to the butler, asked what wines he might call for.

Sir Hugh then proposed that they should all pair off; the ignorant ones going one way, and the learned ones staying another.

It would be difficult to say which looked most averse to this proposition, Eugenia, or the young traveller; who hastily said, 'I always ride after dinner, sir. Is your groom at hand? Can he shew me your horses?'

'My nephew little suspects,' cried Sir Hugh, winking, 'Eugenia belongs to the scholars! Ten to one but he thinks he's got Homer and Horace to himself! But here, my dear boy, as you're so fond of the classics'—

Clermont, nimbly rising, and knocking down a decanter of water in his haste, but not turning back to look at it, nor staying to offer any apology, affected not to hear his uncle, and flung hastily out of the room, calling upon Indiana to follow him.

'In the name of all the *Diavoli*,' cried he, pulling her into the park with him, 'what does all this mean? Is the old gentleman *non compos?* what's all this stuff he descants upon so freely, of scholars, and classics, and Homer, and Horace?'

'O you must ask Eugenia, not me!' answered Indiana, scornfully.

'Why, what does Eugenia know of the matter?'

'Know? why every thing. She's a great scholar, and has been brought up by Dr. Orkborne; and she talks Greek and Latin.'

'Does she so? then, by the Lord! she's no wife of mine! I'd as soon marry the old Doctor himself! and I'm sure he'd make me as pretty a wife. Greek and Latin! why I'd as soon tie myself to a rod.[1] Pretty sort of dinners she'll give!'

'O dear, yes, brother; she don't care what she eats; she cares for nothing but books, and such kind of things.'

'Books! ha! ha! Books, and Latin and Greek! upon my faith, a pretty wife the old gentleman has been so good as to find me! why he must be a downright driveller!'

'Ah, brother, if we had all that fortune, what a different figure we should cut with it!'

'Why, yes, I rather flatter myself we should. No great need of five thousand a year to pore over books! Ha! ha! faith, this is a good hum enough![2] So he thinks to take me in, does he?'

'Why, you know, she is so rich, brother.' . . .

'Rich? well, and what am I? do you see such a figure as this,' (suddenly skipping before her,) 'every day? Am I reduced to my last legs, think you? Do you suppose I can't meet with some kind old dowager any time these twenty years?'

'La, brother, won't you have her then?'

'No, faith, won't I! It's not come to that, neither. This learning is worse than her ugliness; 'twould make me look like a dunce in my own house.'

He then protested he had rather lose forty estates, than so be sacrificed, and vowed, without venturing a direct refusal, he would soon sicken the old gentleman of his scheme.

*   *   *   *

Eugenia, in retreating to her room, was again accompanied by her father and her uncle, whom she conjured now, to name her to Clermont no more.

'I can't say I admire these puttings off, my dear,' said the baronet, 'in this our mortal state, which is always liable to end in our dying. Not that I pretend to tell you I think him over much alert; but there's no knowing but what he may have some meaning in it that we can't understand; a person having studied all his life, has a right to a little particularity.'

Mr. Tyrold himself now seriously interfered, and desired that, henceforth, Clermont might be treated as if his visit to Cleves was merely to congratulate his uncle upon his recovery; and that all schemes, preparations, and allusions, might be put aside, unless the youth himself, and with a good grace, brought them forward; meanwhile, he and Lavinia would return without delay to Etherington, to obviate all appearance of waiting the decision of any plan.

Sir Hugh was much discomfited by the exaction of such forbearance, yet could the less oppose it, from his own internal discontent with his nephew, which he inadvertently betrayed, by murmuring, in his way to his chamber, 'There's no denying but what they've got some odd-fangled new ways of their own, in those foreign parts; meeting a set of old relations for the first time, and saying nothing to them, but asking for the newspapers! Lord help us! caring about the wide world, so, when we know nothing of it, instead of one's own uncles and nephews, and kinspeople!'

*   *   *   *

During this time, Edgar, almost agonised by suspence and doubt, had escaped to the summer-house, whither he was followed by Dr. Marchmont, greatly to the wonder, almost with the contempt of Dr. Orkborne; whom he quitted, in anxiety for his young friend, just as he had intimated a design to consult him upon a difficult passage in an ancient author, which had a place in his work, that was now nearly ready for the press.

'I know well, Doctor,' said Edgar, 'that to find me here, after all that has passed, will make you conclude me the weakest of men . . . but I cannot now explain how it has been brought about . . . these letters must first tell me if Camilla and I meet more than once again.'

He then hastily ran over the letters; but by no means hastily could he digest, nor even comprehend their contents. He thought them florid, affected, and presuming; yet vague, studied, with little appearance of sincerity, and less of explicit decision. What related to Lionel, and to aiding him in the disposal of his wealth, seemed least intelligible, yet most like serious meaning; but when he found that the interview at the Grove was by positive appointment, and granted to a request made with a forwardness and assurance so wide from all delicacy and propriety, the blood mounted high into his cheeks, and, precipitately putting up the packet, he exclaimed: 'Here, then, it ends! the last little ray of hesitation is extinct . . . extinct to be kindled never more!'

The sound of these last words caused him an emotion of sorrow he was unable to resist, though unwilling to betray, and he hurried out of the summer-house to the wood, where he strove to compose his mind to the last leave-taking upon which he was now determined; but so dreadful was the resolution which exacted from his own mouth the resignation of all that, till now, had been dearest to his views and hopes, that the afternoon was far advanced, before he could assume sufficient courage to direct his steps to the spot where the sacrifice was to be made.

Accusing, himself, then, of weakness unpardonable, he returned to the summer-house, to apologise to Dr. Marchmont for his abrupt retreat; but the Doctor had already re-entered the mansion. Thither, therefore, he proceeded, purposing to seek Camilla, to return her the letters of Sir Sedley, and to desire her commands in what manner to conduct himself with her father and her uncle, in acknowledging his fears that the projected union would fail of affording, to either party, the happiness which, at first, it seemed to promise.

The carriage of Sir Hugh was in waiting at the door, and Mr. Tyrold and Lavinia were in the hall. Edgar, in no condition for such an encounter, would have avoided them; but Mr. Tyrold, little suspecting his desire, rejoiced at the meeting, saying he had had the house searched for him in vain, that he might shake hands with him before his return to Etherington.

Then, taking him apart, 'My dear Edgar,' he cried, 'I have long loved you as tenderly, and I may now confide in you as completely, as if you were my son. I go hence in some inquietude; I fear my brother has been too hasty in making known his views with regard to Clermont; who does not seem equal to appreciating the worth of Eugenia, though it is evident he has not been slack in noticing her misfortunes. I entreat you, during my absence, to examine him as if you were already the brother of that dear child, who merits, you well know, the best and tenderest of husbands.'

He then followed Lavinia into the carriage, prevented by his own occupied mind from observing the fallen countenance of Edgar, who, more wretched than ever, bemoaned now the kindness of which he had hitherto been proud, and lamented the paternal trust which he would have purchased the day before almost with life.

* * * *

Camilla, during this period, had gone through conflicts no less severe.

Jacob, who had bought a horse, for which he had cheerfully advanced 2ol. had informed her of the gate adventure of Edgar, and told her that, but for his stopping him, he was riding like mad from Cleves, and only sending them all a message that he could not come back.

Grieved, surprised, and offended, she instantly determined she would not risk such another mark of his cold superiority, but restore to him his liberty, and leave him master of himself. 'If the severity of his judgment,' cried she, 'is so much more potent than the warmth of his affection, it shall not be his delicacy, nor his compassion, that shall make me his. I will neither be the wife of his repentance nor of his pity. I must be convinced of his unaltered love, his esteem, his trust . . . or I shall descend to humiliation, not rise to happiness, in becoming his. Softness here would be meanness; submission degrading . . . if he hesitates . . . let him go!'

She then, without weighing, or even seeing one objection, precipitately resolved to beg permission of her friends, to accept an invitation she had received, without as yet answering, to meet Mrs. Berlinton at Southampton, where that lady was going to pass some weeks. She could there, she thought, give the rejection which here its inviolable circumstances made her, for Lionel's sake, afraid to risk; or she could there, if a full explanation should appease him, find opportunity to make it with equal safety; his dislike to that acquaintance rather urged than impeded her plan, for her wounded spirit panted to prove its independence and dignity.

Eugenia approved this elevation of sentiment, and doubted not it would shew her again in her true light to Edgar, and bring him, with added esteem, to her feet.

Camilla wept with joy at the idea: 'Ah!' she cried, 'if such should be my happy fate; if, after hearing all my imprudence, my precipitance, and want of judgment, he should voluntarily, when wholly set free, return to me ... I will confess to him every feeling ... and every failing of my heart! I will open to him my whole soul, and cast myself ever after upon his generosity and his goodness. ... O, my Eugenia! almost on my knees could I receive ... a second time ... the vows of Edgar Mandlebert!'

CHAPTER XI

Ease and Freedom

LYNMERE, at tea-time, returned from his ride, with a fixed plan of frightening or disgusting the baronet from the alliance; with Eugenia, herself, he imagined the attempt would be vain, for he did not conceive it possible any woman who had eyes could be induced to reject him.

Determined, therefore, to indulge, in full, both the natural presumption and acquired luxuriance of his character, he conducted himself in a manner that, to any thing short of the partiality of Sir Hugh, would have rendered him insupportably offensive: but Sir Hugh had so long cherished a reverence for what he had himself ordered with regard to his studies, and what he implicitly credited of his attainments, that it was more easy to him to doubt his senses, than to suppose so accomplished a scholar could do any thing but what was right.

'Your horses are worth nothing, sir,' cried he, in entering; 'I never rode so unpleasant a beast. I don't know who has the care of your stud; but whoever it is, he deserves to be hanged.'

Sir Hugh could not refuse, either to his justice or his kindness, to vindicate his faithful Jacob; and for his horses he made as many excuses, as if every one had been a human creature, whom he was recommending to his mercy, with a fear they were unworthy of his favour.

Not a word was said more, except what Miss Margland, from time to time, extorted, by begging questions, in praise of her tea, till Lynmere, violently ringing the bell, called out to order a fire.

Every body was surprised at this liberty, without any previous demand of permission from the baronet, or any inquiry into the feelings of the rest of the company; and Sir Hugh, in a low voice, said to Eugenia, 'I am a little afraid poor Mary will be rather out of humour to have the grate to polish again tomorrow morning, in the case my nephew should not like to have another fire then; which, I suppose, if the weather continues so hot, may very likely not be agreeable to him.'

Another pause now ensued; Dr. Marchmont, who, of the whole party, was alone, at this time, capable of leading to a general conversation, was separately occupied by watching Camilla; while himself, as usual, was curiously and unremittingly examined by Dr. Orkborne, in whom so much attention to a young lady raised many private doubts of the justice of his scholastic fame; which soon, by what he observed of his civility even to Miss Margland, were confirmed nearly to scepticism.

Mary, now, entering with a coal scuttle and a candle, Lynmere, with much displeasure, called out, 'Bring wood; I hate coals.'

Mary, as much displeased, and nearly as much humoured[1] as himself, answered that nothing but coals were ever burnt in that grate.

'Take it all away, then, and bid my man send me my pelisse.[2] That I made to cross the Alps in.'

'I am very sorry, indeed, nephew,' said Sir Hugh, 'that we were not better prepared for your being so chilly, owing to the weather being set in so sultry, that we none of us much thought of having a fire; and, indeed, in my young time, we were never allowed thinking of such things before Michaelmas-day; which I suppose is quite behind-hand now. Pray, nephew, if it is not too much trouble to you, what's the day for lighting fires in foreign parts?'

'There's no rule of that sort, now, sir, in modern philosophy; that kind of thing's completely out; entirely exploded, I give you my word.'

'Well, every thing's new, Lord help me, since I was born! But pray, nephew, if I may ask, without tiring you too much, on account of my ignorance, have they fires in summer as well as winter there?'

'Do you imagine there are grates and fires on the Continent, sir, the same as in England? ha! ha!'

Sir Hugh was discountenanced from any further inquiry.

Another silence ensued, broken again by a vehement ringing of the bell.

When the servant appeared, 'What have you got,' cried Lynmere, 'that you can bring me to eat?'

'Eat, nephew! why you would not eat before supper, when here's nobody done tea? not that I'd have you baulk your appetite, which, to be sure, ought to be the best judge.'

The youth ordered some oysters.

There were none in the house.

He desired a barrel might immediately be procured; he could eat nothing else.

Still Edgar, though frequent opportunities occurred, had no fortitude to address Camilla, and no spirits to speak. To her, however, his dejection was a revival; she read in it her power, and hoped her present plan would finally confirm it.

A servant now came in, announcing a person who had brought two letters, one for Sir Hugh, the other for Miss Camilla, but who said he would deliver them himself. The baronet desired he might be admitted.

Several minutes passed, and he did not appear. The wonder of Sir Hugh was awakened for his letter; but Camilla, dreading a billet from Sir Sedley, was in no haste.

Lynmere, however, glad of an opportunity to issue orders, or make disturbance, furiously rang the bell, saying: 'Where are these letters?'

'Jacob,' said the baronet, 'my nephew don't mean the slowness to be any fault of yours, it being what you can't help; only tell the person that brought us our letters, we should be glad to look at them, not knowing who they may be from.'

'Why he seems but an odd sort of fish, sir; I can't much make him out; he's been begging some flour to put in his hair; he'll make himself so spruce, he says, we sha'n't know him again; I can't much think he's a gentleman.'

He then, however, added he had made a mistake, as there was no letter for his master, but one for Miss Camilla, and the other for Miss Margland.

'For me?' exclaimed Miss Margland, breaking forth from a scornful silence, during which her under lip had been busy to express her contempt of the curiosity excited upon this subject. 'Why how dare they not tell me it was for me? it may be from somebody of consequence, about something of importance, and here's half a day lost before I can see it!'

She then rose to go in search of it herself, but opened the door upon Mr. Dubster.

A ghost, could she have persuaded herself she had seen one, could not more have astonished, though it would more have dismayed her. She drew haughtily back, saying: 'Is there nobody else come?'

The servant answered in the negative, and she retreated to her chair.

Camilla alone was not perplext by this sight; she had, already, from the description, suggested whom she might expect, according to the intimation given by the ever mischievous Lionel.

Miss Margland, concluding he would turn out to be some broken tradesman, prepared herself to expect that the letter was a petition, and watched for an opportunity to steal out of the room.

Mr. Dubster made two or three low bows, while he had his hand upon the door, and two or three more when he had shut it. He then cast his eyes round the room, and espying Camilla, with a leering sort of smile, said: 'O, you're there, ma'am! I should find you out in a hundred. I've got a letter for you, ma'am, and another for the gentlewoman I took for your mamma; and I was not much out in my guess, for there's no great difference, as one may say, between a mamma and a governess; only the mother's the more natural, like.'

He then presented her a letter, which she hastily put up, not daring to venture at a public perusal, lest it might contain not merely something ludicrous concerning Mr. Dubster, to which she was wholly indifferent, but allusions to Sir Sedley Clarendel, which, in the actual situation of things, might be fatally unseasonable.

'And now,' said Mr. Dubster, 'I must give up my t'other letter, asking the gentlewoman's pardon for not giving it before; only I was willing to give the young lady her's first, young ladies being apt to be more in a hurry than people a little in years.'

This address did not much add to the benevolent eagerness of Miss Margland to read the epistle, and endeavouring to decline accepting it: 'Really,' she said, 'unless I know what it's about, I'm not much used to receiving letters in that manner.'

'As to what it's about,' cried he, with a half suppressed simper, and nodding his head on one side; 'that's a bit of a secret, as you'll see when you've read it.'

'Indeed, good man, I wish you very well; but as to reading all the letters that every body brings one, it requires more time than I can pretend to have to spare, upon every trifling occasion.'

She would then have retired; but Mr. Dubster, stopping her, said: 'Why, if you don't read it, ma'am, nobody'll be never the wiser for what I come about, for it's ungain-like[1] to speak for one's self; and the young gentleman said he'd write to you, because, he said, you'd like it the best.'

'The young gentleman? what young gentleman?'

'Young squire Tyrold; he said you'd be as pleased as any thing to tell it to the old gentleman yourself; for you was vast fond, he said, of matrimony.'

'Matrimony? what have I to do with matrimony?' cried Miss Margland, reddening and bridling; 'if it's any vulgar trick of that kind, that Mr. Lionel is amusing himself with, I'm not quite the right sort of person to be so played upon; and I desire, mister, you'll take care how you come to me any more upon such errands, lest you meet with your proper deserts.'

'Dear heart! I'm not going to offer anything uncivil. As to matrimony, it's no great joke to a man, when once he's made his way in the world; it's more an affair of you ladies by half.'

'Of us? upon my word! this is a compliment rather higher than I expected. Mr. Lionel may find, however, I have friends who will resent such impertinence, if he imagines he may send who he will to me with proposals of this sort.'

'Lauk, ma'am, you need not be in such a fright for nothing! however, there's your letter, ma'am,' putting it upon the table; 'and when you are in better cue,[2] I suppose you'll read it.'

Then, advancing to Camilla: 'Now, ma'am, let's you and I have a little talk together; but first, by good rights, I ought to speak to your uncle; only I don't know which he is; 'twill be mortal kind if you'll help a body out.'

Sir Hugh was going to answer for himself, when Lynmere, fatigued with so long a scene in which he had no share, had recourse to his friend the bell, calling out, at the same time, in a voice of impatience, 'No oysters yet!'

Sir Hugh now began to grow unhappy for his servants; for himself he not only could bear any thing, but still concluded he had nothing to bear; but his domestics began all to wear long faces, and, accustomed to see them happy, he was hurt to observe the change. No partiality to his nephew could disguise to him, that, long used to every possible indulgence, it was vain to hope they would submit, without murmuring, to so new a bondage of continual and peremptory commands. Instead of attending, therefore, to Mr. Dubster, he considered what apology to offer to Jacob; who suspecting by whom he was summoned, did not make his appearance till Lynmere rung again.

'Where are these oysters?' he then demanded; 'have you been eating them?'

'No, sir,' answered he surlily; 'we're not so sharp set;[1] we live in Old England; we don't come from outlandish countries.'

This true John Bullism, Lynmere had neither sense to despise, nor humour to laugh at; and, seriously in a rage, called out, 'Sirrah, I'll break your bones!' and lifted up his riding switch, with which, as well as his boots, he had re-entered the parlour.

'The Lord be good unto me!' cried Sir Hugh, 'what new ways are got into the world! but don't take it to heart, Jacob, for as to breaking your bones, after all your long services, it's a thing I sha'n't consent to; which I hope my nephew won't take ill.'

Affronted with the master, and enraged with the man, Lynmere stroamed petulantly up and down the room, with loud and marked steps, that called, or at least disturbed the attention of every one, exclaiming, at every turning, 'A confounded country this! a villainous country! nothing to be had in it! I don't know what in the world to think of that there's any chance I can get!'

Sir Hugh, recovering, said he was sorry he was so badly off; and desired Jacob not to fail procuring oysters if they were to be had within a mile.

'A mile? . . . ten miles! say ten miles round,' cried Lynmere, 'or you do nothing; what's ten miles for a thing of that sort?'

'Ten miles, nephew? what? at this time of night! why you don't think, with all your travelling, that when they've got ten miles there, they'll have ten miles to come back, and that makes count twenty.'

'Well, sir, and suppose it was forty; what have such fellows to do better?'

Sir Hugh blessed himself, and Mr. Dubster said to Camilla: 'So, ma'am, why you don't read your letter, neither, no more than the gentlewoman; however, I think you may as well see a little what's in it; though I suppose no great matters, being from a lady.'

'A lady! what lady?' cried she, and eagerly taking it from her pocket, saw the hand-writing of Mrs. Berlinton, and inquired how it came into his possession.

He answered, that happening to meet the lady's footman, whom he had known something of while in business, as he was going to put it to the post, he told him he was coming to the very house, and so took it to bring himself, the man being rather in a hurry to go another way; 'so I thought 'twas as well, ma'am,' he added, 'to save you the postage; for as to a day or so sooner or later, I suppose it can break no great squares, in you ladies letter-writing.'

Camilla, hastily running it over, found it contained a most pressing repetition of invitation from Mrs. Berlinton for the Southampton plan, and information that she should make a little circuit, to call and take her up at Cleves, if not immediately forbidden; the time she named for her arrival, though four days distant from the date of her letter, would be now the following morning.

This seemed, to the agitated spirits of Camilla, an inviting opening to her scheme. She gave the letter to her uncle, saying, in a fluttered manner, she should be happy to accompany Mrs. Berlinton, for a few days, if her father should not disapprove the excursion, and if he could himself have the goodness to spare one of the carriages to fetch her home, as Southampton was but sixteen miles off.

While Sir Hugh, amazed at this request, yet always unable to pronounce a negative to what she desired, stammered, Edgar abruptly took leave.

Thunderstruck by his departure, she looked affrighted, after him, with a sigh impossible to repress; she now first weighed the hazard of what she was doing, the deep game she was inconsiderately playing. Would it sunder . . . would it unite them? . . . Tears started into her eyes at the doubt; she did not hear her uncle's answer; she rose to hurry out of the room; but before she could escape, the big drops rolled fast down her cheeks; and, when arrived at her chamber, 'I have lost him!' she cried, 'by my own unreflecting precipitance; I have lost him, perhaps, for ever!'

Dr. Marchmont now also took leave; Mr. Dubster desired he might speak with the baronet the next morning; and the family remained alone.

CHAPTER XII

Dilemmas

WHILE the baronet was pondering, in the most melancholy manner, upon this sudden and unexpected demand of absence in Camilla, the grim goddess of Envy took possession of the fine features of Indiana; who declared she was immured alive, while her cousin went everywhere. The curiosity of Lynmere being excited, to inquire what was to be had or done at Southampton, he heard it abounded in good company, and good fish, and protested he must undoubtedly set out for it the next morning.

Indiana then wept with vexation and anger, and Miss Margland affirmed, she was the only young lady in Hampshire, who had never been at Southampton. Sir Hugh, concluding Edgar would attend Camilla, feared it might hurt the other match to part Eugenia from Clermont; and, after a little pause, though deeply sighing at such a dispersion from Cleves, consented that they should all go together. Camilla, therefore, was commissioned to ask leave of Mr. Tyrold for Eugenia, as well as for herself, and to add a petition from Sir Hugh, that he and Lavinia would spend the time of their absence at Cleves. The baronet then, of his own accord, asked Dr. Orkborne to be of the party, that Eugenia, he said, might run over her lessons with him in a morning, for fear of forgetting them.

A breach, however, such as this, of plans so long formed, and a desertion so voluntary of his house, at the very epoch he had settled for rendering its residence the most desirable, sent him in complete discomfiture to his bed. But there, in a few hours, his sanguine temper, and the kindness of his heart new modelled and new coloured the circumstances of his chagrin. He considered he should have full time to prepare for the double marriages; and that, with the aid of Lavinia, he might delight and amaze them all, with new dresses and new trinkets, which he could now choose

without the torment of continual opposition from the document-
ising Miss Margland. Thus he restored his plastic mind to its
usual satisfaction, and arose the next morning without a cloud
upon his brow. The pure design of benevolence is to bestow
happiness upon others, but its intrinsic reward is bringing
happiness home!

But this sweetness of nature, so aptly supplying the first calls,
and the first virtues of philosophy, was yet more severely again
tried the next morning: for when, forgetting the caution he had
solemnly promised, but vainly endeavoured to observe, he
intimated to Lynmere these purposes, the youth, blushing at the
idea of being taken for the destined husband of Eugenia in public,
preferred all risks to being followed by such a rumour to Southampton; and, when he found she was to be of the party, positively
declared the match to be out of all question.

Sir Hugh now stood aghast. Many had been his disappointments; his rage for forming schemes, and his credulity in persuading himself they would be successful, were sources not more
fertile of amusement in their projection, than of mortification in
their event: but here, the length of time since his plan had been
arranged, joined to the very superficial view he had taken of any
chance of its failure, had made him, by degrees, regard it as so
fixed and settled, that it rather demanded congratulation than
concurrence, rather waited to be enjoyed than executed.

Lynmere took not the smallest interest in the dismay of his
uncle, but, turning upon his heel, said he would go to the stables,
to see if he could find something that would carry him any better
than the miserable jade he had mounted the preceding evening.

Sir Hugh remained in a kind of stupefaction. He seemed to
himself to be bereft of every purpose of life; and robbed at once, of
all view for his actions, all subject for his thoughts. The wide
world, he believed, had never, hitherto, given birth to a plan so
sagaciously conceived, so rationally combined, so infallibly secure:
yet it was fallen, crushed, rejected!

A gleam of sunshine, however, ere long, [burst] upon his
despondence; it occurred to him, that the learned education of
Eugenia was still a secret to her cousin; his whole scheme, therefore, might perhaps yet be retrieved, when Lynmere should be
informed of the peculiar preparations made for his conjugal
happiness.

Fetching now a long breath, to aid the revival of his faculties and his spirits, he considered how to open his discourse so as to render it most impressive, and then sent for Clermont to attend him in his chamber.

'Nephew,' cried he, upon his entrance, 'I am now going to talk to you a little in your own way, having something to tell you of, that, I believe, you won't know how to hold cheap, being a thing that belongs to your studies; that is to say, to your cousin's; which, I hope, is pretty much the same thing, at least as to the end. Now the case of what I have to say is this; you must know, nephew, I had always set my heart upon having a rich heir; but it's what did not turn out, which I am sorry enough for; but where's the man that's so wise as to know his own doom? that is, the doom of his fortune. However, that's what I should not talk of to you, having so little; which, I hope, you won't take to heart. And, indeed, it in't much worth a wise man's thinking of, when he han't got it, for what's a fortune, at bottom, but mere metal? And so having, as I said before, no heir, I'm forced, in default of it, to take up with an heiress. But, to the end of making all parties happy, I've had her brought up in the style of a boy, for the sake of your marrying her. For which reason, I believe, in point of the classics" . . . .

'Me, sir!' cried Lynmere, recovering from a long yawning fit, 'and what have I to do with marrying a girl like a boy? That's not my taste, my dear sir, I assure you. Besides, what has a wife to do with the classics? will they shew her how to order her table? I suppose when I want to eat, I may go to a cook's shop!'[1]

Here subsided, at once, every particle of that reverence Sir Hugh had so long nourished for Clermont Lynmere. To hear the classics spoken of with disrespect, after all the pains he had taken, all the orders he had given for their exclusive study and veneration, and to find the common calls of life, which he had believed every scholar regarded but as means of existence, not auxiliaries of happiness, named with preference, distanced, at a stroke, all high opinion of his nephew, and made way, in its stead, for a displeasure not wholly free from disdain.

'Well, Clermont,' said he, after a pause, 'I won't keep you any longer, now I know your mind, which I wish I had known before, for the account of your cousin, who has had plague enough about it in her bringing up; which, however, I shall put an end to now, not seeing that any good has come from it.'

Lynmere joyfully accepted the permission to retire, enchanted that the rejection was thus completely off his mind, and had incurred only so slight a reproof, unaccompanied with one menace, or even remonstrance.

The first consternation of Sir Hugh, at the fall of this favourite project, was, indeed, somewhat lessened, at this moment, by the fall of his respectful opinion of its principal object. He sent therefore, hastily, for Eugenia, to whom he abruptly exclaimed, 'My dear girl, who'd have thought it? here's your cousin Clermont, with all his Greek and Latin, which I begin to bless God I don't know a word of, turning out a mere common nothing, thinking about his dinners and suppers! for which reason I beg you'll think of him no more, it not being worth your while; in particular, as he don't desire it.'

Eugenia, at this intimation, felt nearly as much relieved as disturbed. To be refused was, indeed, shocking; not to her pride, she was a stranger to that passion; but to her delicacy, which pointed out to her, in strong colours, the impropriety of having been exposed to such a decision: nevertheless, to find herself unshackled from an alliance to which she looked forward with dread, without offending her uncle, to whom so many reasons made it dear, or militating against her own heroic sentiments of generosity, which revolted against wilfully depriving her cousin of an inheritance already offered to him, removed a weight from her mind, which his every word, look, and gesture, had contributed to increase since their first meeting.

*   *   *   *

Dr. Marchmont had ridden to Beech Park, where he had spent the night, though uninvited by its agitated owner, whom the very name of Mrs. Berlinton, annexed to an accepted party of pleasure, had driven, in speechless agony, from Cleves.

'I wonder not,' cried he, 'at your disturbance; I feel for it, on the contrary, more than ever, from my observations of this evening; for I now see the charm, the potent charm, as well as the difficulties of your situation. This strange affair with Sir Sedley Clarendel cannot, in common foresight of what may ensue from it, be passed over without the most rigid scrutiny, and severest deliberation; yet, I sincerely hope, inquiry may produce some palliation: this young lady, I see, will not easily, for sweetness, for countenance, for every apparent attraction, be replaced: and, the first of all requisites is certainly in your favour; it is evident she loves you.'

'Loves me?' cried Edgar, his arms involuntarily encircling him as he repeated the magnetising words: 'Ah! Dr. Marchmont, could she then thus grieve and defy me?—And yet, so too said Jacob,—that good, faithful, excellent old servant'. . . .

'Yes; I watched her unremittingly; and saw her so much hurt by your abrupt retreat, that her eyes filled with tears the moment you left the room.'

'O, Dr. Marchmont!—and for me were they shed?—my dear— dear friend! withhold from me such a picture—or reconcile me completely to viewing no other!'

'Once more, let me warn you to circumspection. The stake for which you are playing is life in its best part, 'tis peace of mind. That her manners are engaging, that her looks are captivating, and even that her heart is yours, admit no doubt: but the solidity or the lightness of that heart are yet to be proved.'

'Still, Doctor, though nearly in defiance of all my senses, still I can doubt anything rather than the heart of Camilla! Precipitate, I know, she has always been reckoned; but her precipitance is of kin to her noblest virtues; it springs but from the unsuspicious frankness of an unguarded, because innocent nature. And this, in a short time, her understanding will correct.'

'Are you sure it is adequate to the task? There is often, in early youth, a quickness of parts which raises expectations that are never realised. Their origin is but in the animal spirits, which, instead of ripening into judgment and sense by added years, dwindle into nothingness, or harden into flippancy. The character, at this period, is often so unstable, as to be completely new moulded by every new accident, or new associate. How innumerable are the lurking ill qualities that may lie dormant beneath the smiles of youth and beauty, in the season of their untried serenity! The contemporaries of half our fiercest viragos of fifty, may assure you that, at fifteen, they were all softness and sweetness. The present æra, however, my dear young friend, is highly favourable to all you can judiciously wish; namely, the entire re-establishment, or total destruction of all confidence. . . . To a man of your nice feelings, there is no medium. Your love demands respect, or your tranquillity exacts flight from its object. Set apart your offence at the cultivation of an acquaintance you disapprove; be yourself of the party to Southampton, and there, a very little observation will enable you to dive into the most secret recesses of her character.'

'Steadiness, Doctor, I do not want, nor yet, however I suffer from its exertion, fortitude: but a plan such as this, requires something more; it calls for an equivocal conduct, which, to me, would be impracticable, and to her, might prove delusive. No! . . . the openness I so much pine to meet with, I must, at least, not forfeit myself.'

'The fervour of your integrity, my dear Mandlebert, mistakes caution for deceit. If, indeed, this plan had any other view than your union, it would not merely be cruel, but infamous: the truth, however, is you must either pursue her upon proof, or abandon her at once, with every chance of repenting such a measure.'

'Alas! how torturing is hesitation! to believe myself the object of her regard . . . to think that first of all human felicities mine, yet to find it so pliant . . . so precarious . . . to see her, with such thoughtless readiness, upon the point of falling into the hands of another! . . . receiving . . . answering . . . his letters! . . . letters too so confident, so daring! made up of insolent demands and imperious reproaches . . . to meet him by his own appointment. . . . O, Dr. Marchmont! all delicious as is the idea of her preference . . . all entwined as she is around my soul, how, now, how ever again, can I be happy, either to quit . . . or to claim her? . . .'

'This division of sentiment is what gives rise to my plan. At Southampton, you will see if Sir Sedley pursues her; and, as she will be uncertain of your intentions, you will be enabled to judge the singleness of her mind, and the stability of her affection, by the reception she gives him.'

'But if . . . as I think I can gather from her delivering me his letters, the affair, whatever it has been, with Sir Sedley, is over. . . . What then?'

'You will have leisure to discuss it; and opportunity, also, to see her with other Sir Sedleys. Public places abound with those flutterers after youth and beauty; unmeaning admirers, who sigh

at every new face; or black traitors to society, who seek but to try,
and try but to publish their own power of conquest.'

'Will you, then, my dear Doctor, be also of the party? for my
sake, will you, once more, quit your studies and repose, to give me,
upon the spot, your counsel, according to the varying exigence of
varying circumstances? to aid me to prepare and compose my
mind for whatever may be the event, and to guide even, if possible,
my wavering and distracted thoughts?'

To the importance of the period, and to a plea so serious, every
obstacle yielded, and Dr. Marchmont agreed to accompany him to
Southampton.

CHAPTER XIII

Live and Learn

BEFORE the Cleves party assembled to breakfast, after the various
arrangements made for Southampton, Mr. Dubster arrived, and
demanded an interview with Sir Hugh, who, attending him to the
drawing-room, asked his pleasure.

'Why, have not you read the young gentleman's letter, sir?'
cried he, surprised, 'because, he said, he'd put it all down, clear
as a pike staff, to save time.'

Sir Hugh had not heard of it.

'Why, then, if you please, sir, we'll go and ask that elderly
gentlewoman, what she's done with it. She might as well have
shewed it, after the young gentleman's taking the trouble to write
it to her. But she is none of the good naturedest, I take it.'

Repairing, then, to Miss Margland, after his usual bows to all
the company, 'I ask pardon, ma'am,' he cried; 'but pray, what's
the reason of your keeping the young gentleman's letter to yourself, which was writ o'purpose to let the old gentleman know what
I come for?'

'Because I never trouble myself with any thing that's impertinent,' she haughtily answered: though, in fact, when the family
had retired, she had stolen downstairs, and read the letter; which
contained a warm recommendation of Mr. Dubster to her favour,
with abundant flippant offers to promote her own interest for so

desirable a match, should Camilla prove blind to its advantages. This she had then burnt, with a determination never to acknowledge her condescension in opening it.

The repeated calls of Mr. Dubster procuring no further satisfaction; 'Why, then, I don't see,' he said, 'but what I'm as bad off, as if the young gentleman had not writ the letter, for I've got to speak for myself at last.'

Taking Sir Hugh, then, by a button of his coat, he desired he would go back with him to the other parlour: and there, with much circumlocution, and unqualified declarations of his having given over all thoughts of further marrying, till the young gentleman over persuaded him of his being particular agreeable to the young lady, he solemnly proposed himself for Miss Camilla Tyrold.

Sir Hugh, who perceived in this address nothing that was ridiculous, was somewhat drawn from reflecting on his own disappointment, by the pity he conceived for this hopeless suitor, to whom, with equal circumlocution of concern, he communicated, that his niece was on the point of marriage with a neighbour.

'I know that,' replied Mr. Dubster, nodding sagaciously, 'the young gentleman having told me of the young baronight; but he said, it was all against her will, being only your over teasing, and the like.'

'The Lord be good unto me!' exclaimed the baronet, holding up his hands; 'if I don't think all the young boys have a mind to drive me out of my wits, one after t'other!'

Hurrying, then, back to the breakfast parlour, and to Camilla, 'Come hither, my dear,' he cried, 'for here's a gentleman come to make his addresses to you, that won't take an answer.'

Every serious thought, and every melancholy apprehension in Camilla gave place, at this speech, to the ludicrous image of such an admirer as Mr. Dubster, foisted upon her by the ridiculous machinations of Lionel. She took Sir Hugh by the hand, and, drawing him away to the most distant window, said, in a low voice, 'My dear uncle, this is a mere trick of Lionel; the person you see here is, I believe, a tinker.'

'A tinker!' repeated Sir Hugh, quite loud, in defiance of the signs and hists! hists! of Camilla, 'good lack! that's a person I should never have thought of!' Then, walking up to Mr. Dubster, who was taking into his hands all the ornaments from the chimney-piece, one by one, to examine, 'Sir,' he said, 'you may be a very good sort of man, and I don't doubt but you are, for I've a proper respect for every trade in its way; but in point of marrying my niece, it's a thing I must beg you to put out of your head; it not being a proper subject to talk of to a young lady, from a person in that line.'

'Very well, sir,' answered Mr. Dubster, stiffly, and pouting, 'it's not of much consequence; don't make yourself uneasy. There's nothing in what I was going to propose but what was quite genteel. I'd scorn to address a lady else. She'd have a good five hundred a-year, in case of outliving me.'

'Good lack! five hundred a-year! who'd have thought of such a thing by the tinkering business?'

'The what business, did you say, sir?' cried Mr. Dubster, strutting up to the baronet, with a solemn frown.

'The tinkering business, my good friend. An't you a tinker?'

'Sir!' cried Mr. Dubster, swelling, 'I did not think, when I was coming to make such a handsome offer, of being affronted at such a rate as this. Not that I mind it. It's not worth fretting about. However, as to a tinker, I'm no more a tinker than yourself, whatever put it in you head.'

'Good lack, my dear,' cried the baronet, to Camilla, 'the gentleman quite denies it.'

Camilla, though unable to refrain from laughing, confessed she had received the information from Mrs. Arlbery at the Northwick breakfast, who, she now supposed, had said it in random sport.

Sir Hugh cordially begged his pardon, and asked him to take a seat at the breakfast table, to soften the undesigned offence.

A note now arrived from Mr. Tyrold to the baronet. It contained his consent to return, with Lavinia, to Cleves, and his ready acquiescence in the little excursion to Southampton, since Miss Margland would be superintendant of the party; 'and since,' he added, 'they will have another guardian, to whom already I consign my Camilla, and, upon her account, my dear Eugenia also, with the same fearless confidence I should feel in seeing them again under the maternal wing.'

Sir Hugh, who always read his letters aloud, said, when he had done: 'See what it is to be a good boy! my brother looks upon young Mr. Edgar as these young girls' husband already; that is, of one of them; by which means the other becomes his sister;

which, I'm sure, is a trouble he won't mind, except as a pleasure.'

Camilla's distress at this speech past unnoticed, from the abrupt entrance of Lynmere, giving orders aloud to his servant to get ready for Southampton.

Inflamed with triumph in his recent success in baffling his uncle, that youth was in the most turbulent spirits, and fixed a resolution either to lord it over the whole house, or regain at once his liberty for returning to the Continent.

Forcing a chair between Sir Hugh and Camilla, he seized rapidly whatever looked most inviting from every plate on the table, to place upon his own, murmuring the whole time against the horses, declaring the stud the most wretched he had ever seen, and protesting the old groom must be turned away without loss of time.

'What, Jacob?' cried the baronet; 'why, nephew, he has lived with me from a boy; and now he's grown old, I'd sooner rub down every horse with my own hand, than part with him.'

'He must certainly go, sir. There's no keeping him. I may be tempted else to knock his brains out some day. Besides, I have a very good fellow I can recommend to you of my own.'

'Clermont, I've no doubt of his being a good fellow, which I'm very glad of; but as to your always knocking out the brains of my servants, it's a thing I must beg you not to talk of any more, being against the law. Besides which, it don't sound very kind of you, considering their having done you no harm; never having seen your face, as one may say, except just to wait upon you; which can hardly be reckoned a bad office; besides a servant's being a man, as well as you; whether Homer and Horace tell you so or no.'

To see Sir Hugh displeased, was a sight new to the whole house. Camilla and Eugenia, mutually pained for him, endeavoured, by various little kind offices, to divert his attention; but Indiana thought his displeasure proved her brother to be a wit; and Clermont rose in spirits and in insolence upon the same idea: too shallow to know, that of all the qualities with which the perversity of human nature is gifted, and power which is the most common to attain, and the most easy to practise, is the art of provoking.

Jacob now appearing, Lynmere ordered some shrimps.

There were none.

'No shrimps? There's nothing to be had! 'Tis a wretched county this!'

'You'll get nice shrimps at Southampton, sir, by what I can hear,' said Mr. Dubster. 'Tom Hicks says he has been sick with 'em many a day, he's eat such a heap. They gets 'em by hundreds, and hundreds, and hundreds at a time.'

'Pray, nephew, how long shall you stay? because of my nieces coming back at the same time.'

'A fortnight's enough to tire me anywhere, sir. Pray what do you all do with yourselves here after breakfast? What's your mode?'

'Mode, nephew? we've got no particular mode that ever I heard of. However, among so many of us, I think it's a little hard, if you can find nothing to say to us; all, in a manner, your relations too.'

'We take no notice of relations now, sir; that's out.'

'I'm sorry for it, nephew, for a relation's a relation, whether you take notice of him or not. And there's ne'er an ode in Virgil will tell you to the contrary, as I believe.'

A short silence now ensued, which was broken by a sigh from Sir Hugh, who ejaculated to himself, though aloud, 'I can't but think what my poor friend Westwyn will do, if his son's come home in this manner! caring for nobody, but an oyster, or a shrimp; . . . unless it's a newspaper!'

'And what should a man care for else, my good old friend, in a desart place such as this?'

'Good old friend!' repeated the baronet; 'to be sure, I'm not very young. . . . However, as to that . . . but you mean no harm, I know, for which reason I can't be so ill-natured as to take it ill. However, if poor Westwyn is served in this . . . way. . . . He's my dearest friend that I've got, out of us all here, of my own kin, and he's got only one son, and he sent him to foreign parts only for cheapness; and if he should happen to like nothing he can get at home, it won't answer much in saving, to send out for things all day long.'

'O don't be troubled, sir; Westwyn's but a poor creature. He'll take up with anything. He lived within his allowance the whole time. A mighty poor creature.'

'I'm glad of it! glad of it, indeed!' cried Sir Hugh, with involuntary eagerness; 'I should have been sorry if my poor good old friend had had such disappointment.'

'Upon my honour,' cried Lynmere, piqued, 'the quoz of the present season are beyond what a man could have hoped to see!'

'Quoz! what's quoz, nephew?'

'Why, it's a thing there's no explaining to you sort of gentlemen; and sometimes we say quiz, my good old sir.'

Sir Hugh, now, for almost the first time in his life, felt seriously affronted. His utmost lenity could not palliate the wilful disrespect of his language; and, with a look of grave displeasure, he answered, 'Really, nephew, I can't but say, I think you've got rather a particular odd way of speaking to persons. As to talking so much about people's being old, you'd do well to consider that's no fault in anybody; except one's years, which is what we can't be said to help.'

'You descant too much upon words, sir; we have left off, now, using them with such prodigious precision. It's quite over, sir.'

'O, my dear Clermont!' cried Sir Hugh, losing his short movement of anger in a more tender sensation of concern, 'how it goes to my heart to see you turn out such a jackanapes!'

Lynmere, resentfully hanging back, said no more: and Mr. Dubster, having drunk seven dishes of tea, with a long apology between each for the trouble, gladly seized the moment of pause, to ask Camilla when she had heard from *their friend Mrs. Mittin*, adding, 'I should have brought you a letter from her, ma'am, myself, but that I was rather out of sorts with her; for happening to meet her, the day as you went, walking on them Pantiles, with some of her quality binding, when I was not dressed out quite in my best becomes,[1] she made as if she did not know me. Not as it signifies. It's pretty much of a muchness to me. I remember her another sort of person to what she looks now, before I was a gentleman myself.'

'Why, pray, what was you then, sir?' cried Sir Hugh, with great simplicity.

'As to that, sir, there's no need to say whether I was one thing or another, as I know of; I'm not in the least ashamed of what I was.'

Sir Hugh seeing him offended, was beginning an apology; but, interrupting him, 'No, sir,' he said, 'there's no need to say nothing about it. It's not a thing to take much to heart. I've been defamed often enough, I hope, to be above minding it. Only just this one thing, sir; I beg I may have the favour to be introduced to that lady as had the obligingness to call me a tinker, when I never was no such thing.'

Breakfast now being done, the ladies retired to prepare for their journey.

'Well,' cried Mr. Dubster, looking after Eugenia, 'that little lady will make no great figure at such a place as Southton. I would not have her look out for a husband there.'

'She'd have been just the thing for me!' cried Lynmere, haughtily rising, and conceitedly parading his fine form up and down the room; his eyes catching it from looking-glass to looking-glass, by every possible contrivance; 'just the thing! matched to perfection!'

'Lord help me! if I don't find myself in the dark about every thing!' cried Sir Hugh; 'who'd have thought of you scholars thinking so much of beauty; I should be glad to know what your classics say to that point?'

'Faith, my good sir, I never trouble myself to ask. From the time we begin our tours, we wipe away all that stuff as fast as possible from our thoughts.'

'Why, pray, nephew, what harm could it do to your tours?'

'We want room, sir, room in the pericranium! As soon as we begin to travel, we give up everything to taste. And then we want clear heads. Clear heads, sir, for pictures, statues, busts, alto relievos, basso relievos, tablets, monuments, mausoleums.' . . .

'If you go on at that rate, nephew,' interrupted Sir Hugh, holding his ears, 'you'll put my poor head quite into a whirligig. And it's none of the deepest already, Lord help me!'

Lynmere now, without ceremony, made off; and Mr. Dubster, left alone with the baronet, said they might as well proceed to business. 'So pray, sir, if I may make bold, in the case we come to a right understanding about the young lady, what do you propose to give her down?'

Sir Hugh, staring, inquired what he meant.

'Why, I mean, sir, what shall you give her at the first? I know she's to have it all at your demise; but that i'n't the bird in the hand. Now, when once I know that, I can make my offers, which shall be handsome or not, according. And that's but fair. So how much can you part with, sir?'

'Not a guinea!' cried Sir Hugh, with some emotion; 'I can't give her anything! Mr. Edgar knows that.'

'That's hard, indeed, sir. What nothing for a setting out? And, pray, sir, what may the sum total be upon your demise?'

'Not a penny!' cried Sir Hugh, with still more agitation: 'Don't you know I've disinherited her?'

'Disinherited her? why this is bad news enough! And pray, sir, what for?'

'Nothing! She never offended me in thought, word, nor deed!'

'Well, that's odd enough. And when did you do it, sir?'

'The very week she was nine years old, poor thing! which I shall never forget as long as I live, being my worst action.'

'Well, this is particular enough! And young squire Tyrold's never heard a word of it: which is somewhat of a wonder too.'

'Not heard of it? why the whole family know it! I've settled everything I was worth in the world upon her younger sister, that you saw sitting by her.'

'Well, if Tom Hicks did not as good as tell me so ever so long ago, though the young squire said it was all to the contrary: what for, I don't know; unless to take me in. But he won't find that quite so easy, asking his pardon. Matrimony's a good thing enough, when it's to help a man forward: but a person must be a fool indeed, to put himself out of his way for nothing.'

He then formally wished the baronet a good day, and hastened from the house, puffed up with vain glory, at his own sagacious precautions, which had thus happily saved him from being tricked into unprofitable wedlock.

Mrs. Berlinton now arrived, and, as Camilla was ready, though trembling, doubtful, apprehensive of the step she was taking, declined alighting. A general meeting was to take place at the inn: and the baronet, putting a twenty pound note into her hand, with the most tender blessings parted with his darling niece. And then, surprised at not seeing Edgar to breakfast, sent his butler to tell him the history of the excursion.

Lynmere was already set off on horseback: and the party, consisting of Dr. Orkborne, Miss Margland, Indiana, and Eugenia, followed two hours after, in the coach of the baronet, which drove from the park as the chaise entered it with Mr. Tyrold and Lavinia, to supply their places.

BOOK VIII

CHAPTER I

A Way to make Friends

WHEN Camilla appeared at the hall-door, a gentleman descended from the carriage of Mrs. Berlinton, with an air the most melancholy, and eyes bent to the earth, in the mournful bow with which he offered her his hand: though, when he had assisted her into the coach, he raised them, and, turning round, cast upon the mansion a look of desponding fondness, that immediately brought to her recollection young Melmond, the Oxford student, and the brother of her new friend.

Mrs. Berlinton received her with tenderness, folding her to her breast, and declaring life to be now insupportable without her.

The affection of Camilla was nearly reciprocal, but her pleasure had no chance of equal participation; nor was the suspensive state of her mind the only impediment; opposite to her in the carriage, and immediately claiming her attention, was Mrs. Mittin.

The agitating events which had filled up the short interval of her residence at Cleves, had so completely occupied every faculty, that, till the affair of the horse involved her in new difficulties, her debts had entirely flown her remembrance; and the distressing scenes which immediately succeeded to that forced recollection, made its duration as short as it was irksome; but the sight of Mrs. Mittin brought it back with violence to her memory, and flashed it, with shame, upon her conscience.

The twenty pounds, however, just given her by Sir Hugh, occurred at the same moment to her thoughts; and she determined to repair her negligence, by appropriating it into parcels for the payment of all she owed, before she suffered sleep again to [close] her eyes.

Mrs. Berlinton informed her, that both herself and her brother had been summoned to Southampton to meet Mrs. Ecton, the aunt by whom she had been educated, who had just arrived there from Wales, upon some secret business, necessary for her to hear, but which could not be revealed by letters.

The journey, though in itself short and pleasant, proved to Camilla long and wearisome; the beauties of the prospect were acknowledged by her eye, but her mind, dead to pleasure, refused to give them their merited effect. To the charms of nature she could not be blind; her fervent imagination, and the lessons of her youth, combined to do them justice; but she thought not of them at this moment; hill, vale, or plain, were uninteresting, however beautiful; it was Edgar she looked for; Edgar, who thus coldly had suffered her to depart, but who still, it was possible, might pursue; and hope, ever active, painted him, as she proceeded, in every distant object that caught her eye, whether living or in-animate, brightening, from time to time, the roses of her cheeks with the felicity of a speedy reconciliation; but upon every near approach, the flattering error was detected, and neither hill, vale, nor plain, could dispel the disappointment. A fine country, and diversified views, may soften even the keenest affliction of decided misfortune, and tranquillise the most gloomy sadness into resignation and composure; but suspense rejects the gentle palliative; 'tis an absorbent of the faculties that suffers them to see, hear, and feel only its own perplexity; and the finer the fibres of the sensibility on which it seizes, the more exclusive is its despotism; doubt, in a fervent mind, from the rapidity of its evolutions between fear in its utmost despondence, and hope in its fullest rapture, is little short of torture.

They drove immediately to an elegant house, situated upon a small eminence, half a mile without the town of Southampton, which had already been secured; and Mrs. Berlinton, as soon as she had chosen the pleasantest apartment it afforded for Camilla, and suffered Mrs. Mittin to choose the next pleasant for herself, went, accompanied by her brother, to the lodging of Mrs. Ecton.

Left alone, Camilla stationed herself at a window, believing she meant to look at the prospect; but her eye, faithful to her heart, roved up and down the high road, and took in only chaises or horsemen, till Mrs. Mittin, with her customary familiarity, came into the room. 'Well, my dear miss,' she cried, 'you're welcome to Southampton, and welcome to Mrs. Berlinton; she's a nice lady as ever I knew; I suppose you're surprised to see us so great to-gether? but I'll tell you how it came about. You must know, just

as you was gone, I happened to be in the book shop[1] when she
came in, and asked for a book; the Peruvan Letters[2] she called it;
and it was not at home, and she looked quite vexed, for she said
she had looked the catalogue up and down, and saw nothing else
she'd a mind to; so I thought it would be a good opportunity to
oblige her, and be a way to make a prodigious genteel acquaintance besides; so I took down the name, and I found out the lady
that had got the book, and I made her a visit, and I told her it was
particular wanted by a lady that had a reason; so she let me have it,
and I took it to my pretty lady, who was so pleased, she did not
know how to thank me: So this got me footing in the house; and
there I heard, amongst her people she was coming to Southampton, and was to call for you, my dear miss; so when I found she
had not her coach full, I ask'd her to give me a cast;[3] for I told
her you'd be particular glad to see me, as we'd some business to
settle together, that was a secret between only us two; so she said
she would do anything to give you pleasure; so then I made free
to ask her to give me a night's lodging, till I could find out some
friend to be at; for I'd a vast mind to come to Southampton, as I
could do it so reasonable, for I like to go every where. And I dare
say, my dear miss, if you'll tell her 'twill oblige you, she'll make
me the compliment to let me stay all the time, for I know nobody
here; though I don't fear making friends, go where I will. And you
know, my dear miss, you can do no less by me, considering what
I've done for you; for I've kept all the good people quiet about
your debts; and they say you may pay them when you will, as I
told them you was such a rich heiress; which Mr. Dubster let me
into the secret of, for he had had it from your brother.'

Camilla now experienced the extremest repentance and shame,
to find herself involved in any obligation with a character so
forward, vulgar, and encroaching, and to impose such a person,
through the abuse of her name and influence, upon the time and
patience of Mrs. Berlinton.

The report spread by Lionel she immediately disavowed, and,
producing her twenty pound bank note, begged Mrs. Mittin
would have the goodness to get it changed for her, and to discharge her accounts without delay.

Surprised by this readiness, and struck by the view of the note,
Mrs. Mittin imputed to mere reserve the denial of her expected
wealth, but readily promised to get in the bills, and see her clear.

Camilla would now have been left alone; but Mrs. Mittin thought of nothing less than quitting her, and she knew not how to bid her depart. It was uncertain when Mrs. Berlinton could return; to obviate, therefore, in some measure, the fatigue of such conversation, Camilla proposed walking.

It was still but two o'clock, and the weather was delicious; every place that opened to any view, presented some prospect that was alluring; Camilla, notwithstanding her anxiety, was caught, and at intervals, at least, forgot all within, from admiration of all without.

Mrs. Mittin led immediately to the town, and Camilla was struck with its neatness, and surprised by its populousness. Mrs. Mittin assured her it was nothing to London, and only wished she could walk her from Charing-cross to Temple-bar,[1] just to shew her what it was to see a little of the world.

'But now, my dear,' she cried, 'the thing is to find out what we've got to look at; so don't let's go on without knowing what we're about; however, these shops are all so monstrous smart, 'twill be a pleasure to go into them, and ask the good people what there's to see in the town.'

This pretext proved so fertile to her of entertainment, in the opportunity it afforded of taking a near view of the various commodities exposed to sale, that while she entered almost every shop, with inquiries of what was worth seeing, she attended to no answer nor information, but having examined and admired all the goods within sight or reach, walked off, to obtain, by similar means, a similar privilege further on; boasting to Camilla, that, by this clever device they might see all that was smartest, without the expence of buying any thing.

It is possible that this might safely have been repeated, from one end of the town to the other, had Mrs. Mittin been alone; and she seemed well disposed to make the experiment; but Camilla, who, absent and absorbed, accompanied without heeding her, was of a figure and appearance not quite so well adapted for indulging with impunity such unbridled curiosity. The shop-keepers, who, according to their several tastes or opinions, gave their directions to the churches, the quays, the market-place, the antique gates, the town-hall, &c.[2] involuntarily looked at her as they answered the questioner, and not satisfied with the short view, followed to the door, to look again; this presently produced an effect that, for the whole length of the High-street,[1] was amply ridiculous; every one perceiving that, whatsoever had been his recommendation, whether to the right, to the left, or straight forward, the two inquirers went no further than into the next shop, whence they regularly drew forth either the master or the man to make another starer at their singular proceeding.

Some supposed they were only seeking to attract notice; others thought they were deranged in mind; and others, again, imagined they were shoplifters, and hastened back to their counters, to examine what was missing of their goods.

Two men of the two last persuasions communicated to one another their opinions, each sustaining his own with a positiveness that would have ended in a quarrel, had it not been accommodated by a wager. To settle this became now so important, that business gave way to speculation, and the contending parties, accompanied by a young perfumer as arbitrator, leaving their affairs in the hands of their wives, or their domestics, issued forth from their repositories, to pursue and watch the curious travellers; laying bets by the way at almost every shop as they proceeded, till they reached the quay, where the ladies made a full stand, and their followers opened a consultation how best to decide the contest.

Mr. Firl, a sagacious old linen-draper, who concluded them to be shoplifters, declared he would keep aloof, for he should detect them best when they least suspected they were observed.

Mr. Drim, a gentle and simple haberdasher, who believed their senses disordered, made a circuit to face and examine them, frequently, however, looking back, to see that no absconding trick was played him by his friends. When he came up to them, the pensive and absorbed look of Camilla struck him as too particular to be natural; and in Mrs. Mittin he immediately fancied he perceived something wild, if not insane. In truth, an opinion preconceived of her derangement might easily authorise strong suspicions of confirmation, from the contented volubility with which she incessantly ran on, without waiting for answerers, or even listeners; and his observation had not taught him, that the loquacious desire only to speak. They exact time, not attention.

Mrs. Mittin, soon observing the curiosity with which he examined them, looked at him so hard in return, talking the whole time, in a quick low voice, to Camilla, upon his oddity, that, struck with a direful panic, in the persuasion she was marking him for some mischief, he turned short about to get back to his companions; leaving Mrs. Mittin with precisely the same opinion of himself which he had imbibed of her.

'Well, my dear,' cried she, 'this is one of the most miraclous adventures I've met with yet; as sure as you're alive that man that stares so is not right in the head! for else what should he run away for, all in such a hurry, after looking at us so particular for nothing? I'll assure you, I think the best thing we can do, is to get off as fast as we can, for fear of the worst.'

They then sped their way from the quay; but, in turning down the first passage to get out of sight, they were led into one of the little rooms prepared for the accommodation of bathers.[1]

This seemed so secure, as well as pleasant, that Camilla, soothed by the tranquillity with which she could contemplate the noble Southampton water and its fine banks, sat down at the window, and desired not to walk any further.

The fright with which Mr. Drim had retreated, gained no proselyte to his opinion; Mr. Girt, the perfumer, asserted, significantly, they were only idle travellers, of light character; and Mr. Firl, when in dodging them, he saw they went into a bathing room, offered to double his wager that it was to make some assortment of their spoil.

This was accepted, and it was agreed that one should saunter in the adjoining passages to see which way they turned upon coming out, while the two others should patrol the beach,[2] to watch their disappearance from the windows.

Mrs. Mittin, meanwhile, was as much amused, though with different objects, as Camilla. A large mixt party of ladies and gentlemen, who had ordered a vessel for sailing down the water, which was not yet ready, now made their appearance; and their dress, their air of enjoyment, their outcries of impatience, the frisky gaiety of some, the noisy merriment of others, seemed to Mrs. Mittin marks of so much grandeur and happiness, that all her thoughts were at work to devise some contrivance for becoming of their acquaintance.

Camilla also surveyed, but almost without seeing them; for the only image of her mind now unexpectedly met her view; Dr. Marchmont and Edgar, just arrived, had patrolled to the beach, where Edgar, whose eye, from his eagerness, appeared to be every where in a moment, immediately perceived her; they both bowed, and Dr. Marchmont, amazed by the air and figure of her companion, inquired if Mrs. Berlinton had any particularly vulgar relation to whom she was likely to commit her fair guest.

Edgar, who had seen only herself, could not now forbear another glance; but the aspect of Mrs. Mittin, without Mrs. Berlinton, or any other more dignified or fitting protectress, was both unaccountable and unpleasant to him; he recollected having seen her at Tunbridge, where the careless temper, and negligent manners of Mrs. Arlbery, made all approaches easy, that answered any purpose of amusement or ridicule; but he could not conceive how Mrs. Berlinton, or Camilla herself, could be joined by such a companion.

Mr. Firl, having remarked these two gentlemen's bows, began to fear for his wager; yet, thinking it authorised him to seek some information, approached them, and taking off his hat, said: 'You seem to be noticing those two ladies up there; pray, gentlemen, if you've no objection, who may they be?'

'Why do you ask, sir?' cried Edgar, sternly.

'Why, we've a wager depending upon them, sir, and I believe there's no gentleman will refuse to help another about a wager.'

'A wager?' repeated Edgar, wishing, but vainly, to manifest no curiosity; 'what inducement could you have to lay a wager about them?'

'Why, I believe, sir, there's nobody's a better judge than me what I've laid about; though I may be out, to be sure, if you know the ladies; but I've seen so much of their tricks, in my time, that they must be pretty sharp before they'll over-reach me.'

'What tricks? who must be sharp? who are you talking of?'

'Shoplifters, sir.'

'Shoplifters! what do you mean?'

'No harm, sir; I may be out, to be sure, as I say; and if so, I ask pardon; only, as we've laid the wager, I think I may speak before I pay.'

The curiosity of Edgar would have been converted into ridicule, had he been less uneasy at seeing with whom Camilla was thus associated; Mrs. Mittin might certainly be a worthy woman, and, if so, must merit every kindness that could be shewn her; but her air and manner so strongly displayed the low bred society to which she had been accustomed, that he foresaw nothing but improper acquaintance, or demeaning adventures, that could ensue from such a connection at a public place.

Dr. Marchmont demanded what had given rise to this suspicion.

Mr. Firl answered, that they had been into every shop in the town, routing over every body's best goods, yet not laying out a penny.

Nothing of this could Edgar comprehend, except that Camilla had suffered herself to be led about by Mrs. Mittin, entirely at her pleasure; but all further inquiry was stopt, by the voluntary and pert junction of Girt, the young perfumer, who, during this period, had by no means been idle; for perceiving, in the group waiting for a vessel, a certain customer by whom he knew such a subject would be well received, he contrived to excite his curiosity to ask some questions, which could only be satisfied by the history of the wager, and his own opinion that both parties were out.

This drew all eyes to the bathing room; and new bets soon were circulated, consisting of every description of conjecture, or even possibility, except that the two objects in question were innocent: and for that, in a set of fourteen, only one was found who defended Camilla, though her face seemed the very index of purity, which still more strongly was painted upon it than beauty, or even than youth. Such is the prevalent disposition to believe in general depravity, that while those who are debased themselves find a consolation in thinking others equally worthless, those even, who are of a better sort, nourish a secret vanity in supposing few as good as themselves; and fully, without reflection, the fair candour of their minds, by aiding that insidious degeneracy, which robs the community of all confidence in virtue.

The approach of the perfumer to Edgar had all the hardiness of vulgar elation, bestowed, at this moment, by the recent encouragement of having been permitted to propagate his facetious opinions in a society of gentlefolks; for though to one only amongst them, a young man of large fortune, by whom he was particularly patronised, he had presumed verbally to address himself, he had yet the pleasure to hear his account repeated from one to another, till not a person of the company escaped hearing it.

'My friend Firl's been telling you, I suppose, sir,' said he, to Edgar, 'of his foolish wager? but, take my word for it. . . .'

Here Edgar, who again had irresistibly looked up at the room, saw that the three gentlemen had entered it; alarmed lest these surmises should be productive of impert nence to Camilla, he darted quickly from the beach to her immediate protection.

But the rapidity of his wishes were ill seconded by the uncertainty of his footsteps; and while, with eyes eagerly wandering all around, he hastily pushed forward, he was stopt by Mr. Drim, who told him to take care how he went on, for, in one of those bathing houses, to the best of his belief, there were two crazy women, one melancholy, and one stark wild, that had just, as he supposed, escaped from their keepers.

'How shall I find my way, then, to another of the bathing houses?' cried Edgar.

Mr. Drim undertook to shew him where he might turn, but said he must not lose sight of the door, because he had a bottle of port depending upon it; his neighbour, Mr. Firl, insisting they were only shoplifters.

Edgar here stopt short and stared.

Drim then assured him it was what he could not believe, as nothing was missing; though Mr. Firl would have it that it was days and days, sometimes, before people found out what was gone; but he was sure, himself, they were touched in the head, by their going about so wild, asking everybody the same questions, and minding nobody's answers.

Edgar, convinced now Camilla was here again implicated, broke with disgust from the man, and rushed to the door he charged him to avoid.

CHAPTER II

A Rage of Obliging

CAMILLA, from the instant she had perceived Edgar, had been in the utmost emotion, from doubt if his journey were to seek a reconciliation, or only to return her letters, and take a lasting farewell. Her first feeling at his sight urged her to retire: but something of a softer nature speedily interfered, representing, if now he should join her, what suffering might mutually be saved by an immediate conference. She kept, therefore, her seat, looking steadily straight down the water, and denying herself one moment's glance at anything, or person, upon the beach: little imagining she ingrossed, herself, the attention of all who paraded it. But, when the insinuations of the flippant perfumer had once made her looked at, her beauty, her apparently unprotected situation, and the account of the wager, seemed to render her an object to be stared at without scruple.

Mrs. Mittin saw how much they were observed, but Camilla, unheeding her remarks, listened only to hear if any footsteps approached; but when, at last, some struck her ears, they were accompanied by an unknown voice, so loud and clamorously jovial, that, disturbed, she looked round ... and saw the door violently flung open, and three persons, dressed like gentlemen, force their way into the small dwelling place.

Mr. Halder, the leader of this triumvirate, was the particular patron of Girt, the young perfumer; and, though his superior in birth and riches, was scarcely upon a par with him, from wilful neglect, in education; and undoubtedly beneath him in decency and conduct, notwithstanding young Girt piqued himself far less upon such sentimental qualifications, than upon his skill in cosmetics, and had less respect for unadulterated morals, than unadulterated powder.

The second who entered, was, in every particular, still less defensible: he was a peer of the realm; he had a daughter married, and his age entitled him to be the grandfather of young Halder. In point of fortune, speculatists deemed them equal; for though the estate of Halder was as yet unincumbered with the mortgages that hung upon that of Lord Valhurst, they computed, with great exactness, the term of its superiority, since already he had inlisted in the jockey meetings, and belonged to the gaming clubs.

The third, a young man of a serious, but pleasing demeanour, was rather an attendant than a partner in this intrusion. He was the only one of the whole party to whom the countenance of Camilla had announced innocence; and when Halder, instigated by the assertions of the facetious Girt, proposed the present measure, and Lord Valhurst, caught by the youthful beauty of the fair subject of discussion, acceded, this single champion stood forth, and modestly, yet firmly, declaring his opinion they were mistaken, accompanied them with a view to protect her, if he himself were right.

Boisterously entering, Halder addressed at once to Camilla, such unceremonious praise of her beauty, that, affrighted and offended, she hastily seized the arm of Mrs. Mittin, and, in a voice of alarm, though with an air of command that admitted no doubt of her seriousness, and no appeal from her resolution, said, 'Let us go home, Mrs. Mittin, immediately.'

Simple as were these words, their manner had an effect upon Halder to awe and distance him. Beauty, in the garb of virtue, is rather formidable than attractive to those who are natively un-enlightened, as well as habitually degenerate: though, over such as have ever known better sentiments, it frequently retains its primeval power, even in their darkest declension of depravity.

But while Halder, repulsed, stood back, and the young champion, with an air the most respectful, made way for her to pass; Lord Valhurst, shutting the door, planted himself against it.

Seeing terror now take possession of every feature of her face, her determined protector called out: 'Make way, my Lord, I beg!' and offered her his hand. But Camilla, equally frightened at them all, shrunk appalled from his assistance, and turned towards the window, with an intention of demanding help from Edgar, whom she supposed still on the beach; but the peer, slowly moving from the door, said he was the last to mean to disconcert the young lady, and only wished to stop her till he could call for his carriage, that he might see her safe wherever she wished to go.

Camilla had no doubt of the sincerity of this proposal, but would accept no aid from a stranger, even though an old man, while she hoped to obtain that of Edgar. Edgar, however, she saw not, and fear is generally precipitate: she concluded him gone; concluded herself deserted, and, from knowing neither, equally fearing both the young men, inclined towards Lord Valhurst; who, with delighted surprise, was going to take her under his care, when Edgar rushed forward.

The pleasure that darted into her eyes announced his welcome. Halder, from his reception, thought the enigma of his own ill success solved; the other youth, supposing him her brother, no longer sought to interfere; but Lord Valhurst exhibited signs of such irrepressible mortification, that inexperience itself could not mistake the dishonourable views of his offered services, since, to see her in safety, was so evidently not their purpose. Camilla, looking at him with the horror he so justly excited, gave her hand to Edgar, who had instantly claimed it, and, without one word being uttered by either, hastily walked away with him, nimbly accompanied by Mrs. Mittin.

The young man, whose own mind was sufficiently pure to make him give easy credit to the purity of another, was shocked at his undeserved implication in so gross an attack, and at his failure of manifesting the laudable motive which had made him one of the triumvirate; and, looking after her with mingled admiration and concern, 'Indeed, gentlemen,' he cried, 'you have been much to blame. You have affronted a young lady who carries in the whole of her appearance the marks of meriting respect.'

The sensibility of Lord Valhurst was not of sufficient magnitude to separate into two courses: the little he possessed was already occupied by his disappointment, in losing the beautiful prey he believed just falling into his hands, and he had no emotion, therefore, to bestow upon his young reprover. But Halder, who, to want of feeling, added want of sense, roared out, with rude raillery, a gross, which he thought witty attack, both of the defender and the defended.

The young man, with the proud probity of unhackneyed sentiment, made a vindication of his uncorrupt intentions; which produced but louder mirth, and coarser incredulity. The contest, however, was wholly unequal; one had nerves of the most irritable delicacy; the other had never yet, by any sensation, nor any accident, been admonished that nerves made any part of the human composition: in proportion, therefore, as one became more offended, the other grew more callous, till the chivalry of indignant honour, casting prudence, safety, and forbearance away, dictated a hasty challenge, which was accepted with a horse laugh of brutal senselessness of danger. Courage is of another description. It risks life with heroism; but it is only to preserve or pursue something, without which the charm of life were dissolved: it meets death with steadiness; but it prepares for immortality with reverence and emotion.

*   *   *   *

Edgar and Camilla continued their walk in a silence painful to both, but which neither knew how first to break; each wished with earnestness an opening to communication and confidence; but, mutually shocked by the recent adventure, Edgar waited the absence of Mrs. Mittin, to point out the impropriety and insufficiency of such a guard; and Camilla, still aghast with terror, had no power of any sort to begin a discourse.

Their taciturnity, if not well supplied, was, at least, well contrasted by the volubility of Mrs. Mittin, which, as in the bathing house it had been incessant, in declaring, to the three intruders, that both she and the other young lady were persons of honour, was now no less unremitting in boasting how well she had checked and kept them in order.

The horror of the attack she had just escaped became soon but a secondary suffering to Camilla, though, at the moment, it had impressed her more terribly than any actual event of her life, or any scene her creative imagination had ever painted; yet, however dreadful, it was now past; but who could tell the end of what remained? the mute distance of Edgar, her uncertainty of his intentions, her suspicions of his wished secession, the severe task she thought necessary to perform of giving him his liberty, with the anguish of a total inability to judge whether such a step would recall his tenderness, or precipitate his retreat, were suggestions which quickly succeeded, and, in a very short time, wholly domineered over every other.

When they arrived at the house, Edgar demanded if he might hope for the honour of being presented, as a friend of the family, to Mrs. Berlinton.

Reviving, though embarrassed, she looked assent, and went forward to inquire if Mrs. Berlinton were come home.

The servant answered no; but delivered her a letter from that lady; she took it with a look of distress whether or not to invite Edgar to enter, which the, at this period, welcome officiousness of Mrs. Mittin relieved, by saying, 'Come, let us all come in, and make the parlour a little comfortable against Mrs. Berlinton comes home; for, I dare say, there's nothing as it should be. These lodging-houses always want a heap of things one never thinks of before hand.'

They then all three entered, and Mrs. Mittin, who saw, she said, a thousand ways by which she might serve and oblige Mrs.

Berlinton, by various suggestions, and even directions, which she hazarded against her return, busied herself to arrange the two parlours to her satisfaction; and, then, went up stairs, to settle, also, all there; making abundant apologies for leaving them, and assuring them she would be back again as soon as she possibly could get all in order.

Her departure was a moment of extreme confusion to Camilla, who considered it as an invitation to her great scheme of rejection, but who stammered something upon every other subject, to keep that off. She looked at her letter, wondered what it could contain, could not imagine why Mrs. Berlinton should write when they must so soon meet; and spent in conjectures upon its contents the time which Edgar besought her to bestow upon their perusal.

Nothing gives so much strength to an adversary as the view of timidity in his opponent. Edgar grew presently composed, and felt equal to his purposed expostulation.

'You decline reading your letter till I am gone?' cried he; 'I must, therefore, hasten away. Yet, before I go, I earnestly wish once more to take upon me the office formerly allowed me, and to represent, with simple sincerity, my apprehensions upon what I have observed this morning.'

The beginning of this speech had made Camilla break the seal of her letter; but its conclusion agitated her too much for reading it.

'Is this silence,' said he, trying to smile, 'to repress me as arrogant, . . . or to disregard me as impertinent?'

'Neither!' she answered, forcing herself to look towards him with cheerfulness; 'it is merely . . . attention.'

'You are very good, and I will try to be brief, that I may put your patience to no longer proof than I can avoid. You know, already, all I can urge concerning Mrs. Berlinton; how little I wonder at the promptness of your admiration; yet how greatly I fear for the permanence of your esteem. In putting yourself under her immediate and sole protection, you have shewn me the complete dissonance of our judgments upon this subject; but I do not forget that, though you had the goodness to hear me, you had the right to decide for yourself. Trust indeed, even against warning, is so far more amiable than suspicion, that it must always, even though it prove unfortunate, call for praise rather than censure.'

The confusion of Camilla was now converted into self-reproach. What she thought coldness, she had resented; what

appeared to her to be haughtiness, she had resisted; but truth, in
the form of gentleness, brought her instantly to reason, and
reason could only resume its empire, to represent as rash and
imprudent an expedition so repugnant, in its circumstances, to
the wishes and opinions of the person whose approbation was
most essential to her happiness. Edgar had paused; and her every
impulse led to a candid recognition of what she felt to be wrong;
but her precarious situation with him, the report of his intended
flight by Jacob, the letters still detained of Sir Sedley Clarendel,
and no explanation demanded, by which she could gather if his
plighted honour were not now his only tie with her, curbed her
design, depressed her courage, and, silently, she let him proceed.

'Upon this subject, therefore, I must say no more, except to hint
a wish, that the apprehensions which first induced me to name it
may, unbidden, occur as timely heralds to exertion, should any
untoward circumstances point to danger, alarm, or impropriety.'

The new, but strong friendship of Camilla was alarmed for its
its delicacy by these words. The diffidence she felt, from conscious
error, for herself, extended not to Mrs. Berlinton, whom, since
she found guiltless, she believed to be blameless. She broke forth,
therefore, into a warm eulogy, which her agitation rendered
eloquent, while her own mind and spirits were relieved and
revived, by this flight from her mortified self, to the friend she
thought deserving her most fervent justification.

Edgar listened attentively, and his eyes, though they expressed
much of serious concern, shewed also an irrepressible admiration
of an enthusiasm so ardent for a female friend of so much beauty.

'May she always merit this generous warmth!' cried he; 'which
must have excited my best wishes for her welfare, even if I had
been insensible to her own claims upon every man of feeling. But
I had meant, at this time, to confine my ungrateful annotations to
another . . . to the person who had just quitted the room.'

'You do not mean to name her with Mrs. Berlinton? to imagine
it possible I can have for her any similar regard? or any, indeed, at
all, but such common good-will as all sorts and classes of people are
entitled to, who are well meaning?'

'Here, at least, then,' said Edgar, with a sigh half suppressed,
'our opinions may be consonant. No; I designed no such disgraceful parallel for your elegant favourite. My whole intention
is to remonstrate . . . can you pardon so plain a word? . . .

against your appearing in public with a person so ill adapted to insure you the respect that is so every way your due.'

'I had not the smallest idea, believe me, of appearing in public. I merely walked out to see the town, and to beguile, in a stroll, time, which, in this person's society, hung heavy upon me at home, in the absence of Mrs. Berlinton.'

The concise simplicity of this innocent account, banished, in a moment, all severity of judgment; and Edgar, expressively thanking her, rose, and was approaching her, though scarcely knowing with what purpose, when Mrs. Mittin burst into the room, exclaiming: 'Well, my dear, you'll never guess how many things I have done since I left you. In the first place, there was never a wash-ball;[1] in the next place, not a napkin nor a towel was in its proper place; then the tea-things were forgot; and as to spoons, not one could I find. And now, I've a mind to go myself to a shop I took good notice of, and get her a little almond powder for her nice white hands; which, I dare say, will please her. I've thought of a hundred things at least. I dare say I shall quite win her heart. And I'm sure of my money again, if I lay out never so much. And I don't know what I would not do for such a good lady.'

During this harangue, Camilla, ashamed of her want of resolution, secretly vowed, that, if again left alone with him, she would not lose a moment in restoring him his liberty, that with dignity she might once more receive, or with fortitude for ever resign it. She thought herself, at this moment, capable of either; but she had only thought it, since his softened look and air had made her believe she had nothing to fear from the alternative.

Mrs. Mittin soon went, though her continued and unmeaning chattery[2] made the short term of her stay appear long.

Each eager upon their own plan, both then involuntarily arose.

Camilla spoke first. 'I have something,' she cried, 'to say, . . .' but her voice became so husky, the inarticulate sounds died away unheard, and blushing at so feeble an opening, she strove, under the auspices of a cough, to disguise that she had spoken at all, for the purpose of beginning, in a more striking manner, again.

This succeeded with Edgar at this moment, for he had heard her voice, not her words: he began, therefore, himself. 'This good lady,' he said, 'seems bit with the rage of obliging, though not, I think, so heroically, as much to injure her interest. But surely she flatters herself with somewhat too high a recompence? The heart of Mrs. Berlinton is not, I fancy, framed for such a conquerer. But how, at the same time, is it possible conversation such as this should be heard under her roof? And how can it have come to pass that such a person. . . .'

'Talk of her,' interrupted Camilla, recovering her breath, 'some other time. Let me now inquire . . . have you burnt . . . I hope so! . . . those foolish . . . letters . . . . I put into your hands? . . .'

The countenance of Edgar was instantly overclouded. The mention of those letters brought fresh to his heart the bitterest, the most excruciating and intolerable pang it had ever experienced; it brought Camilla to his view no longer artless, pure, and single-minded, but engaged to, or trifling with, one man, while seriously accepting another. 'No, madam,' he solemnly said, 'I have not presumed so far. Their answers are not likely to meet with so violent a death, and it seemed to me that one part of the correspondence should be preserved for the elucidation of the other.'

Camilla felt stung by this reply, and tremulously answered, 'Give me them back, then, if you please, and I will take care to see them all demolished together, in the same flames. Meanwhile . . . .'

'Are you sure,' interrupted Edgar, 'such a conflagration will be permitted? Does the man live who would have the philosophy . . . the insensibility I must rather style it—ever to resign, after once possessing, marks so distinguishing of esteem? O, Camilla! I, at least, could not be that man!'

Cut to the soul by this question, which, though softened by the last phrase, she deemed severely cruel, she hastily exclaimed: 'Philosophy I have no right to speak of . . . but as to insensibility . . . who is the man that ever more can surprise me by its display? Let me take, however, this opportunity. . . .'

A footman, opening the door, said, his lady had sent to beg an answer to her letter.

Camilla, in whom anger was momentary, but the love of justice permanent, rejoiced at an interruption which prevented her from speaking, with pique and displeasure, a sentence that must lose all its purpose if not uttered with mildness. She would write, she said, immediately; and, bidding the man get her pen and ink, went to the window to read her letter; with a formal bow of apology to Edgar as she passed him.

'I have made you angry?' cried he, when the man was gone; 'and I hate myself to have caused you a moment's pain. But you must feel for me, Camilla, in the wound you have inflicted! you know not the disorder of mind produced by a sudden, unlooked-for transition from felicity to perplexity, ... from serenity to misery! ...'

Camilla felt touched, yet continued reading, or rather rapidly repeating to herself the words of her letter, without comprehending, or even seeking to comprehend, the meaning of one sentence.

He found himself quite unequal to enduring her displeasure; his own, all his cautions, all Dr. Marchmont's advice, were forgotten; and tenderly following her, 'Have I offended,' he cried, 'past forgiveness?' Is Camilla immoveable? and is the journey from which I fondly hoped to date the renewal of every hope, the termination of every doubt, the period of all suffering and sorrow ....'

He stopt abruptly, from the entrance of the servant with pen and ink, and the interruption was critical: it called him to his self-command: he stammered out that he would not impede her writing; and, though in palpable confusion, took his leave: yet, at the street-door, he gave a ticket with his name, to the servant who attended him, for Mrs. Berlinton; and, with his best respects, desired she might be told he should do himself the honour to endeavour to see her in the evening.

The recollection of Edgar came too late to his aid to answer its intended purpose. The tender avowal which had escaped him to Camilla, of the view of his journey, had first with astonishment struck her ear, and next with quick enchantment vibrated to her heart, which again it speedily taught to beat with its pristine vivacity; and joy, spirit, and confidence expelled in a breath all guests but themselves.

CHAPTER III

A Pleasant Adventure

CAMILLA was again called upon for her note, before she had read the letter it was to answer; but relieved now from the

pressure of her own terrifying apprehensions, she gave it complete
and willing attention.

It contained four sides of paper, closely yet elegantly written
in the language of romantic sentiment. Mrs. Berlinton said she
had spent, as yet, only a few minutes with her aunt; but they had
been awfully important; and since she had exacted from her a
promise to stay the whole day, she could not deny her disappointed friendship the transient solace of a paper conversation,
to sooth the lingering interval of this unexpected absence. 'My
soul pines to unburden the weight of its sorrows into thy sympathising bosom, my gentlest friend; but oh! there let them not
sojourn! receive but to lighten, listen but to commiserate, and
then, far, far thence dismiss them, retaining but the remembrance
thou hast dismissed them with consolation.' She then bewailed
the time lost to soft communication and confidence, in their
journey, from the presence of others; for though one was a
brother she so truly loved, she found, notwithstanding the
tenderness of his nature, he had the prejudices of a man upon
man's prerogatives, and her woes called for soothing not arguments; and the other, she briefly added, was but an accidental
passenger. ''Tis in thee only, O my beauteous friend! I would trust
the sad murmurs of my irreversible and miserable destiny, of
which I have learnt but this moment the cruel and desperate
secret cause.' She reserved, however, the discovery for their
meeting, and called upon her pity for her unfortunate brother, as
deeply involved in his future views, as she in her past, by this
mystery: 'And have I written this much,' she burst forth,
'without speaking of the cherished correspondent whom so often I
have described to thee? Ah! believe me not faithless to that
partner of my chosen esteem, that noble, that resistless possessor
of my purest friendship! No, charming Camilla, think not so
degradingly of her whom fate, in its sole pitying interval, has cast
into thy arms.' Two pages then ensued with this exclusive
encomium, painting him chief in every virtue, and master of every
grace. She next expressed her earnestness to see Indiana, [who]
Camilla had told her would be at Southampton. 'Present me, I
conjure thee, to the fair and amiable enslaver of my unhappy
brother! I die to see, to converse with her, to catch from her
lovely lips the modest wisdom with which he tells me they teem;
to read in her speaking eyes the intelligence which he assures me

illumines them.' She concluded with desiring her to give what orders she pleased for the coach, and the servants, and to pass the day with her friends.

Camilla, whose own sensations were now revived to happiness, read the letter with all the sympathy it claimed, and felt her eyes fill with generous tears at the contrast of their situations; yet she highly blamed the tenderness expressed for the unknown correspondent, though its innocence she was sure must vanquish even Edgar, since its so constant avowal proved it might be published to all mankind. She answered her in language nearly as affectionate, though less inflated than her own, and resolved to support her with Edgar, till her sweetness and purity should need no champions but themselves. She was ashamed of the species of expectation raised for Indiana, yet knew not how to interfere in Melmond's idea of her capacity, lest it might seem unkind to represent its fallaciousness; but she was glad to find her soft friend seemed to have a strict guardian in her brother; and wished eagerly to communicate to Edgar a circumstance which she was sure would be so welcome to him.

Impatient to see Eugenia, she accepted the offer of the carriage, and desirous to escape Mrs. Mittin, begged to have it immediately; but that notable person came to the door at the same time as the coach, and, without the smallest ceremony, said she would accompany her to the hotel,[1] in order to take the opportunity of making acquaintance with her friends.

Courage frequently, at least in females, becomes potent as an agent, where it has been feeble as a principal. Camilla, though she had wished, upon her own account, to repress Mrs. Mittin in the morning, had been too timid for such an undertaking; but now, in her anxiety to oblige Edgar, she gathered resolution for declining her company. She then found, as is generally the case with the fearful, the task less difficult than she had expected; for Mrs. Mittin, content with a promise self-made, that the introduction should take place the next day, said she would go and help Mrs. Berlinton's woman to unpack her lady's things, which would make a useful friend for her in the house, for a thousand odd matters.

*   *   *   *

The carriage of Sir Hugh was just driving off as Camilla arrived at the hotel.

She hurried from Mrs. Berlinton's coach, demanding which way the company was gone; and being answered, by a passing waiter, up stairs, ran on at once, without patience or thought for asking if she should turn to the right or left; till seeing a gentleman standing still upon the landing place, and leaning upon the bannisters, she was retreating, to desire a conductor, when she perceived it was Dr. Orkborne; who, while the ladies were looking at accommodations, and inquiring about lodgings, in profound cogitation, and with his tablets in his hands, undisturbed by the various noises around him, and unmoved by the various spectators continually passing and repassing, was finishing a period which he had begun in the coach for his great work.

Camilla, cheerfully greeting him, begged to know which way she should find Eugenia; but, making her a sign not to speak to him, he wrote on. Accustomed to his manner, and brought up to respect whatever belonged to study, from the studious life and turn of her father, she obeyed the mute injunction, and waited quietly by his side; till, tired of the delay, though unwilling to interrupt him, she glided softly about the passage, watching and examining if she could see any of the party, yet fearing to offend or mortify him if she called for a waiter.

While straying about thus, as far off as she could go without losing sight of Dr. Orkborne, a door she had just passed was flung open, and she saw young Halder, whose licentious insolence had so much alarmed her in the bathing-house, stroam out, yawning, stretching, and swearing unmeaningly, but most disgustingly, at every step.

Terrified at his sight, she went on, as she could not get to the Doctor without passing him; but the youth, recollecting her immediately, called out: 'Ah, ha! are you there again, you little vixen?' and pursued her.

'Dr. Orkborne! Dr. Orkborne!' she rather screamed than said, 'pray come this way! I conjure—I beseech—I entreat—Dr. Orkborne!—'

The Doctor, catching nothing of this but his name, querulously exclaimed: 'You molest me much!' but without raising his eyes from his tablets; while Halder, at the appeal, cried: 'Ay, ay,

Doctor! keep your distance, Doctor! you are best where you are, Doctor, I can tell you, Doctor!'

Camilla, then, too much scared to be aware she ran a far greater risk than she escaped, desperately sought refuge by opening the nearest door; though by the sudden noises upon the stairs, and in all the adjoining passages, it seemed as if Dr. Orkborne were the only one not alarmed by her cries.

No one, however, could approach so soon as the person of whose chamber she had burst the door; who was an old gentleman, of a good and lively countenance, who promptly presenting himself, looked at her with some surprise, but good humouredly asked her what she was pleased to want in his room.

'That gentleman,' she cried, panting and meaning to point to Dr. Orkborne; 'that gentleman I want, sir!' but such a medley of waiters, company, and servants, had in a moment assembled in the space between them, that the Doctor was no longer to be discerned.

'Do you only open my door, then,' said he, drily, 'to tell me you want somebody else?'

Yet when Halder, vowing he owed her an ill turn for which she should pay, would have seized her by the hand, he protected with his own arm, saying: 'Fie, boy, fie! let the girl alone! I don't like violence.'

A gentleman now, forcing himself through the crowd, exclaimed: 'Miss Camilla Tyrold! Is it possible! what can you do here, madam?'

It was Dr. Marchmont, whom the affrighted Camilla, springing forward, could only answer in catching by the arm.

'Tyrold!' repeated the old gentleman; 'Is her name Tyrold?'

Sorry now to have pronounced it in this mixt company, Dr. Marchmont evaded any answer; and, begging her to be composed, asked whither, or to whom, he might have the honour of conducting her.

'Almost all my family are here,' cried she, 'but I could not make Dr. Orkborne shew me the way to them.'

The old gentleman then, repeating 'Tyrold! why if her name is Tyrold, I'll take care of her myself;' invited her into his apartment.

Dr. Marchmont, thanking him, said: 'This young lady has friends, who in all probability are now uneasily seeking her; we must lose no time in joining them.'

'Well, but, well,' cried the old stranger, 'let her come into my room till the coast is clear, and then take her away in peace. Come, there's a good girl, come in, do! you're heartily welcome; for there's a person of your name that's the best friend I ever had in the world. He's gone from our parts, now; but he's left nothing so good behind. Pray, my dear, did you ever hear of a gentleman, an old Yorkshire Baronet, of your name?'

'What! my uncle?'

'Your uncle! why are you niece to Sir Hugh Tyrold?'

Upon her answering yes, he clapped his hands with delight, and saying: 'Why then I'll take care of you myself, if it's at the risk of my life!' carried, rather than drew her into his room, the Doctor following. Then, loudly shutting his door in the face of Halder, he called out: 'Enter my castle who dare! I shall turn a young man myself, at the age of seventy, to drub the first varlet that would attack the niece of my dear old friend!'

They soon heard the passage clear, and, without deigning to listen to the petulant revilings with which young Halder solaced his foolish rage, 'Why, my dear,' he continued, 'why did not you tell me your name was Tyrold at once? I promise you, you need carry nothing else with you into our parts, to see all the doors fly open to you. You make much of him, I hope, where he is? for he left not a dry eye for twenty miles round when he quitted us. I don't know how many such men you may have in Hampshire; but Yorkshire's a large county, yet the best man in it would find it hard to get a seat in Parliament, where Sir Hugh Tyrold would offer himself to be a candidate. We all say, in Yorkshire, he's so stuffed full of goodness and kindness, that there's no room left in him for anything else; that's our way of talking of him in Yorkshire; if you have a better way in Hampshire, I shall be glad to learn it; never too late for that; I hate pride.'

No possible disturbance could make Camilla insensible to pleasure in the praise of her uncle, or depress her spirits from joining in his eulogy; and her attention, and brightening looks, drew a narrative from the old gentleman of the baronet's good actions and former kindnesses, so pleasant both to the speaker and the hearer, that the one forgot he had never seen her before, and the other, the frightful adventure which occasioned their meeting now.

Dr. Marchmont at length, looking at his watch, inquired what she meant to do; to seek her sister and party, she answered; and, returning her host the warmest acknowledgments for his assistance and goodness, she was going; but, stopping her: 'How now?' he cried, 'don't you want to know who I am? Now I have told you I am a friend of your uncle, don't you suppose he'll ask you my name?'

Camilla, smiling, assured him she wished much to be informed, but knew not how to trouble him with the question.

'Why my name, my dear, is Westwyn, and when you say that to your uncle, he won't give you a sour look for your pains; take my word for that beforehand. I carried over his nephew and heir, a cousin, I suppose, of yours, to Leipsic with me, about eight years ago, along with a boy of my own, Hal Westwyn; a very good lad, I assure you, though I never tell him so to his face, for fear of puffing him up; I hate a boy puffed up; he commonly comes to no good; that's the only fault of my honoured friend; he spoils all young people—witness that same cousin of yours, that I can't say I much like; no more does he me; but tell your good uncle you have met me; and tell him I love and honour him as I ought to do; I don't know how to do more, or else I would; tell him this, my dear. And I have not forgot what he did for me once, when I was hard run; and I don't intend it; I'm no friend to short memories.'

Camilla said, his name, and her uncle's regard for him, had long been familiar to her; and told him Clermont Lynmere was of the party to Southampton, though she knew not how to enter abruptly into an explanation of his mistake concerning the inheritance. Mr. Westwyn answered he was in no hurry to see Clermont, who was not at all to his taste; but would not quit Hampshire without visiting Cleves: and when he gathered that two more nieces of Sir Hugh were in the house, he desired to be presented to them.

Upon re-entering the passage, to the great amusement of Dr. Marchmont, and serious provocation of Camilla, they perceived Dr. Orkborne, standing precisely where he had first stationed himself; attending no more to the general hubbub than to her particular entreaty, and as regardless of the various jolts he had received during the tumult, as of the obstruction he caused, by his inconvenient position, to the haste of the passers by. Still steadily reposing against the bannisters, he worked hard at refining his paragraph, persuaded, since not summoned by Miss Margland, he had bestowed upon it but a few minutes, though he had been fixed to that spot near an hour.

Miss Margland received Camilla with a civility which, since her positive and public affiance to Edgar, she thought necessary to the mistress of Beech Park; but she looked upon Dr. Marchmont, whom she concluded to have been her advocate, with a cold ill-will, which, for Mr. Westwyn, she seasoned still more strongly by a portion of contemptuous haughtiness; from a ready disposition to believe every stranger, not formally announced, beneath her notice.

The Doctor soon retired, and found Edgar in his apartment, just returned from a long stroll. He recounted to him the late transaction, with reiterated exhortations to circumspection, from added doubts of the solidity, though with new praise of the attractions of Camilla. 'She seems a character,' he said, 'difficult to resist, and yet more difficult to attach. Nothing serious appears to impress her for two minutes together. Let us see if the thoughtlessness and inadvertence thus perpetually fertile of danger, result from youthful inexperience, or have their source in innate levity. Time and reason will rectify the first; but time, and even reason, will but harden and embolden the latter. Prudence, therefore, must now interfere; or passion may fly, when the union it has formed most requires its continuance.'

CHAPTER IV

An Author's Time-keeper

MR. WESTWYN, charmed to meet so many near relations of a long-valued friend, struck by the extraordinary beauty of Indiana, and by the sensible answers of the child, as he called Eugenia; as well as caught by the united loveliness of person and of mind which he observed in Camilla, could not bring himself to retire till the dinner was upon the table: pleading, in excuse for his stay, his former intimacy with Sir Hugh. Miss Margland, seeing in him nothing that marked fashion, strove to distance him by a high demeanour: but though not wanting in shrewdness, Mr.

Westwyn was a perfectly natural man, and only thinking her manners disagreeable, without suspecting her intention, took but little notice of her, from the time he saw she could give him no pleasure: while with the young party, he was so much delighted, that he seriously regretted he had only one son to offer amongst them.

When the dinner was served, Eugenia grew uneasy that Dr. Orkborne should be summoned, whose non-appearance she had not ventured to mention, from the professed hatred of his very sight avowed by Miss Margland. But Camilla, brought up to exert constantly her courage for the absent, told the waiter to call the gentleman from the head of the stairs.

'My master himself, ma'am,' he answered, 'as well as me, both told the gentleman the company he came with were served; but he as good as bid us both hold our tongues. He seems to have taken a great liking to that place upon the stairs; though there's nothing I know of particular in it.'

'But, if you tell him we wait dinner—' cried Eugenia; when Miss Margland, interrupting her said, 'I'm sure, then, you won't tell him true: for I beg we may all begin. I think it would be rather more decorous he should wait for us!'

The waiter, nevertheless, went; but presently returned, somewhat ruffled; saying, 'The gentleman does not choose to hear me, ma'am. He says, if he mayn't be let alone one single minute, it will be throwing away all his morning. I can't say I know what he means; but he speaks rather froppish. I'd as lieve not go to him again, if you please.'

Miss Margland declared, she wished him no better dinner than his pot-hooks; but did not doubt he would come just before they had done, as usual; and he was no more mentioned: though she never in her life eat so fast; and the table was ordered to be cleared of its covers, with a speed exactly the reverse of the patience with which the Doctor was indulged on similar occasions by the baronet.

Miss Margland, when the cloth was removed, proposed a sally in search of lodgings. Camilla and Eugenia, desirous of a private conference, begged to remain within; though the latter sought to take care of her absent preceptor, before she could enjoy the conversation of her sister; and when Miss Margland and Indiana, in secret exultation at his dinnerless state, had glided, with silent simpering, past him, flew to beseech his consent to take some nourishment.

Such, however, was his present absorption in what he was writing, that the voluntary kindness of his pupil was as unwelcome as the forced intrusion of the waiter; and he conjured her to grant him a little respite from such eternal tormenting, with the plaintive impatience of deprecating some injury.

The sisters, now, equally eager to relate and to listen to their mutual affairs, shut themselves up in the apartment of Eugenia; who, with the greatest simplicity, began the discourse, by saying, 'Have you heard, my dear sister, that Clermont has refused me?'

Camilla was severely shocked. Accustomed herself to the face and form of Eugenia, which, to her innocent affection, presented always the image of her virtuous mind and cultivated understanding, she had not presaged even the possibility of such an event; and, though she had seen with concern the inequality of their outward appearance, Clermont had seemed to her, in all else, so inferior to her sister, that she had repined at his unworthiness, but never doubted the alliance.

She was distressed how to offer any consolation; but soon found none was required. Eugenia was composed and contented, though pensive, and not without some feeling of mortification. Yet anger and resentment had found no place in the transaction. Her equity acknowledged that Clermont had every right of choice: but while her candour induced her to even applaud his disinterestedness in relinquishing the Cleves estate, her capacity pointed out how terrible must be the personal defects, that so speedily, without one word of conversation, one trial of any sort how their tastes, tempers, or characters might accord, stimulated him to so decisive a rejection. This view of her unfortunate appearance cast her, at first, into a train of melancholy ideas, that would fast have led her to unhappiness, though wholly unmixed with any regret of Clermont, had not the natural philosophy of her mind come to her aid; or had her education been of a more worldly sort.

When Camilla related her own history, her plan of making Edgar again completely master of his own proceedings met the entire approbation of Eugenia, who, with a serious smile, said, 'Take warning by me, my dear sister! and, little as you have reason to be brought into any comparison with such a one as me, anticipate the disgrace of defection!'

Camilla, much touched, embraced her, sincerely wishing she were half as faultless as her excellent self.

The return of Miss Margland and Indiana obliged them to quit their retreat; and they now found Dr. Orkborne in the dining-room. Having finished his paragraph, he had sought his party of his own accord; but, meeting with no one, had taken a book from his pocket, with which he meant to beguile the appetite he felt rising, till the hour of dinner, which he had not the smallest suspicion was over; for of the progress of time he had no knowledge but by its palpable passage from the sun to the moon; his watch was never wound up, and the morning and the evening were but announced to him by a summons to breakfast and to supper.

The ladies seated themselves at the window. Indiana was enchanted by the concourse of gay and well-dressed people passing by, and far from insensible to the visible surprise and pleasure she excited in those who cast up their eyes at the hotel. Eugenia, to whom a great and populous town was entirely new, found also, in the diversity as well as novelty of its objects, much matter for remark and contemplation; Miss Margland experi-enced the utmost satisfaction in seeing, at last, some faces and some things less rustic than had been presented to her in York-shire or at Cleves; and Camilla had every hope that this place, in Edgar's own expression, would terminate every perplexity, and give local date to her life's permanent felicity.

In a few minutes, a youth appeared on the opposite pavement, whose air was new to none of the party, yet not immediately recollected by any. It was striking, however, in elegance and in melancholy. Eugenia recollected him first, and starting back, gasped for breath; Indiana the next moment called out, 'Ah! . . . it's Mr. Melmond!' and blushing high, her whole face was bright and dimpled with unexpected delight.

He walked on, without looking up, and Indiana, simply piqued as well as chagrined, said she was glad he was gone.

But Eugenia looked after him with a gentle sigh, which now first she thought blameless, and a pleasure, which, though half mournful, she now suffered herself to encourage. Free from all ties that made her shun this partiality as culpable, she secretly told herself she might now, without injury to any one, indulge it for an object [whom,] little as he was known to her, she internally painted with all the faultless qualities of ideal excellence.

From these meditations she was roused by Dr. Orkborne's looking rather wishfully round him, and exclaiming, 'Pray . . . don't we dine rather late?'

The mistake being cleared up, by Miss Margland's assuring him it was impossible to keep dinner waiting all day, for people who chose to stand whole hours upon a staircase, he felt rather discomforted: but when Eugenia privately ordered him a repast in his own chamber, he was amply consoled, by the unconstrained freedom with which he was empowered to have more books upon the table than plates; and to make more ink spots than he eat mouthfuls.

*   *   *   *

Camilla had the mortification to find, upon her return home, that Edgar had made his promised visit, not only in her absence, but while Mrs. Berlinton was still with her aunt.

The lady then communicated to Camilla the secret to which, while yet in ignorance of its existence, she now found she had been sacrificed. Mrs. Ecton, two years ago, had given her hand, in the most solemn privacy, to her butler, who now attended her to Southampton. To avoid disobliging a sick old relation, from whom she expected a considerable legacy, she had prevailed with her husband to consent that the marriage should not be divulged: but certain that whatever now might be her fortune, she had no power to bequeath it from her new connexion, the terror of leaving utterly destitute a beautiful young creature, who believed herself well provided for, had induced her to nearly force her acceptance of an almost superannuated old man of family; who, merely coveting her beauty, inquired not into her inclination. The same latent cause had made her inexorable to the pleadings of young Melmond; who, conceiving his fortune dependent upon the pleasure of his aunt, his certain income being trifling, thought it his duty to fly the fair object of his adoration, when he discovered the deceit of Lionel with regard to the inheritance of Sir Hugh. This sick old relation was now just dead, and had left to her sole disposal a considerable estate. The husband naturally refused to be kept any longer from his just rights; but the shame she felt of making the discovery of a marriage contracted clandestinely, after she was sixty years of age, with a man under thirty,

threw her into a nervous fever. And, in this state, unable to reveal
to her nephew an event which now affected him alone, she
prevailed with Mr. Ulst, who was willing to revisit his original
home, Southampton, to accompany her thither in his usual
capacity, till she had summoned her nephew and niece, and
acquainted them with the affair.

To herself, Mrs. Berlinton said, the evil of this transaction had
been over, while yet it was unknown; she had heard it, therefore, in
silence, and forborne unavailing reproach. But her brother, to
whom the blow was new, and the consequences were still impending, was struck with extreme anguish, that while thus every
possible hope was extinguished with regard to his love, he must
suddenly apply himself to some business, or be reduced to the
most obscure poverty.

Camilla heard the account with sincere concern for them both,
much heightened for young Melmond, upon finding that, by his
express desire, his sister now relinquished her design of cultivat-
ing an acquaintance with Indiana, whom he had the virtue to
determine to avoid, since his fortune, and even his hopes, were
thus irretrievably ruined.

They conversed together to a late hour; and Camilla, before
they parted, made the most earnest apologies for the liberty taken
with her house by Mrs. Mittin: but Mrs. Berlinton, with the
utmost sweetness, begged she might stay till all her business with
her was settled; smilingly adding, business alone, she was sure
could bring them together.

Much relieved, she then determined to press Mrs. Mittin to
collect and pay her accounts immediately; and to avoid with her,
in the meanwhile, any further transactions.

CHAPTER V

An agreeable Hearing

EARLY the next morning, Camilla went to the hotel, in the
carriage of Mrs. Berlinton; eluding, though not without difficulty,
the company of Mrs. Mittin. She found the party all in good
spirits; Indiana, in particular, was completely elated; joined to the

admiration she believed awaiting her in this large and fashionable town,[1] she now knew she might meet there the only person who had ever excited in her youthful, and nearly vacant breast, any appropriate pleasure, super-added to the general zest of being adored. She did not, indeed, think of marrying any one who could not offer her a coach and four; but so little was she disturbed by thinking at all, that the delight of being adulated by the man she preferred, carried with it no idea of danger. Eugenia too, soothed with the delusions of her romantic but innocent fancy, flattered herself she might now see continually the object she conceived formed for meriting her ever reverential regard; and Miss Margland was importantly occupied upon affairs best suited to her taste and ancient habits, in deliberating how first to bring forth her fair charge with the most brilliant effect.

Camilla was much embarrassed how to parry an introduction to Mrs. Berlinton, upon which all the females built as the foundation of their Southampton prosperity; the young ones, already informed she was the sister of Melmond, languishing to know her for his sake; and Miss Margland, formerly acquainted with the noble family of her husband, being impatient to resume her claims in similar circles; but an awkward beginning apology was set aside by the entrance of Edgar and Dr. Marchmont.

Indiana now poured forth innumerable questions upon what she might look forward to with respect to balls and public places; Eugenia asked nearly as many concerning the buildings, antiquities, and prospects; and Miss Margland more than either, relative to the company, their genealogies and connexions.[2] The two Doctors soon sat aloof, conferring upon less familiar matters; but Edgar only spoke in reply, and Camilla uttered not a word.

Soon after, a voice on the stairs called out, 'O never mind shewing me the way; if I come to a wrong room, I'll go on till I come to a right;' and the next minute young Lynmere sallied into the apartment.

'I could not get to you last night,' cried he; 'and I can only stay a moment now. I have a pretty serious business upon my hands; so if you can give me any breakfast, don't lose time.'

Miss Margland, willing to please the brother of Indiana, readily ordered for him whatever the inn would afford, of which he failed not heartily to partake, saying, 'I have met with a good comic sort of adventure here already. Guess what it is?'

Indiana complied; but his own wish to communicate was so much stronger than that of anyone to hear, that, before she could pronounce three words, he cried: 'Well, if you're so excessive curious, I'll tell it you. I'm engaged in a duel.'

Indiana screamed; Miss Margland echoed her cry; Eugenia, who had looked down from his entrance, raised her eyes with an air of interest; Camìlla was surprised out of her own concerns; and Edgar surveyed him with an astonishment not wholly unmixt with contempt; but the two Doctors went on with their own discourse.

'Nay, nay, Dye, don't be frightened; 'tis not a duel in which I am to fight myself; I am only to be second. But suppose I were first? what signifies? these are things we have in hand so often, we don't think of them.'

'La! brother! you don't say so?' cried Indiana: 'La! how droll!' He then pretended that he would tell nothing more.

Camilla inquired if he had seen Mr. Westwyn, whom she had met with the preceding day.

'Not I, faith! but that's a-propos enough; for it's his son that has asked me to be his second.'

'O, poor good old Mr. Westwyn!' cried Camilla, now much interested in this history; 'and can you not save him such a shock? can you not be mediator instead of second? he seems so fond of his son. . . .'

'O, as to him, it's no matter; he's such a harsh old hunks,[1] I shall be glad to have him worked a little; I've often wanted to pull him by the nose, myself, he takes such liberties with me. But did you ever hear of such a fool as his son? he deserves to be badgered as bad as his father; he's going to fight with as fine an honest fellow as ever I met with, for nothing at all! absolutely nothing!'

'Dear! how droll!' said Indiana.

'But why can you not interfere?' cried Camilla: 'poor Mr. Westwyn will be made so unhappy if any evil befalls his son!'

'O, faith, as to him, he may take it as he will; I shan't trouble my head about him; he has made free enough with me, I can assure you; it's only to have him out of the way, that the business is put off till noon; it was to have been in the morning, but the old tyrant took it into his pate to make poor Henry, who is one of your good ones, and does nothing to vex him on purpose, ride out with him; he has promised, however, to get off by twelve o'clock, when four of us are to be at a certain spot that I shan't name.'

Camilla again began to plead the merits of the father; but Indiana more urgently demanded the reason of the combat. 'I dare say, brother, they fight about being in love with somebody? don't they, brother? now do tell me?'

'Not a whit! it's for a girl he don't care a straw for, and never saw but once in his life, and don't care a farthing if he never sees again.'

'Dear, how droll, brother! I thought people always fought about being in love with somebody they wanted to marry; and never but when she was excessive pretty.'

'O, faith, marriage seldom deserves a fighting match; but as to being pretty, that's all Harry has in his excuse, so he pretends she's as divine as an angel.'

'Dear! well, and don't you know anything more than that about it?'

'No, nor he neither; he only saw her at a bathing house, where a fine jolly young buck was paying her a few compliments, that she affected not to like; and presently, in a silly dispute whether she was a girl of character, they had a violent quarrel, and Harry was such a fool as to end it with a challenge.'

At the words *a bathing house*, the blood forsook the cheeks of Camilla with sudden personal alarm; but it mounted high into them again, upon hearing the nature of the dispute; though yet again it sunk, and left them wholly pallid, at the brief and final conviction she was the sole cause of this duel, and upon so disgraceful a dispute.

The emotions of Edgar, though less fearful, were not less violent nor painful. That Camilla should be the subject of any challenge was shocking, but of such a one he thought a dishonour; yet to prevent, and with the least publicity, its effect, was the immediate occupation of his mind.

A short pause ensued, broken presently by Clermont, who, looking at his watch, suddenly jumped up, and calling out, 'Faith, I shall be too late!' was capering out of the room; but the shame of Camilla in the disgrace, was overpowered by her terror of its consequences, and starting up, and clasping her hands, 'O cousin! O Clermont!' she cried, 'for Heaven's sake stop this affair!'

Clermont, satisfied that a sufficient alarm was raised to impede the transaction, without any concession on his part, declared himself bound in honour to attend the appointment, and, in extreme seeming haste and earnestness, walked off: stopping, however, when he came to the door, not to listen to the supplications of his cousin, but to toss off a fresh cup of chocolate, which a waiter was just carrying to the next room.

Camilla now, her face varying in colour twenty times in a minute, and her whole frame shaking, while her eyes were cast, conscious and timid, on the floor, approached Edgar, and saying, 'This young man's father is my dear uncle's friend! . . .' burst into tears.

Edgar, wholly dissolved, took her hand, pressed it to his lips, besought her, in a low voice, to dismiss her apprehensions, in the confidence of his most ardent exertions, and again kissing her hand, with the words, 'Too . . . O, far too dear Camilla!' hastened after Lynmere.

Affected in a thousand ways, she dropt, weeping, upon a chair. Should the duel take place, and any fatal consequences follow, she felt she should never be happy again; and even, should it be prevented, its very suggestion, from so horrible a doubt of her character, seemed a stain from which it could never recover. The inconsiderate facility with which she had wandered about with a person so little known to her, so underbred, and so forward, appeared now to herself inexcusable; and she determined, if but spared this dreadful punishment, to pass the whole of her future life in unremitting caution.

Eugenia, with the kindest sympathy, and Indiana and Miss Margland, with extreme curiosity, sought to discover the reason of her emotion; but while begging them to dispense with an explanation, old Mr. Westwyn was announced and appeared.

The horrors of a culprit, the most cruel as well as criminal, seemed instantly the portion of the self-condemned Camilla; and, as he advanced with cheerful kindness, to inquire after her health, his ignorance that all his happiness, through her means, was that moment at stake, pierced her with a suffering so exquisite, that she uttered a deep groan, and sunk back upon her chair.

An instant's recollection brought her more of fortitude, though not of comfort; and springing up and addressing, though not looking at Mr. Westwyn, who was staring at her with astonishment and concern: 'Where, sir,' she cried, 'is your son? If you have the least knowledge which way he is gone . . . which way he may be traced . . . pursue and force him back this moment! . . . Immediately! . . .'

'My son!' repeated the good old gentleman, wanting no other word to participate in any alarm; 'what, Hal Westwyn?—'

'Follow him . . . seek him . . . send for him . . . and do not, a single instant, lose sight of him all day!'

'My dear young lady, what do you mean? I'll send for him, to be sure, if you desire it; but what makes you so good as to think about my son? did you ever see my son? do you know my son? do you know Hal Westwyn?'

'Don't ask now, dear sir! secure him first, and make what inquiries you please afterwards.'

Mr. Westwyn, in evident consternation, walked out, Camilla herself opening the door; but turning back in the passage, strongly said: 'If the boy has been guilty of any misbehaviour, I won't support him; I don't like misbehaviour; it's a bad thing; I can't take to it.'

'O no! no! quite the contrary!' exclaimed the agitated Camilla, 'he is good, kind, generous! I owe him the greatest obligation! and I desire nothing upon earth so much, at this moment, as to see him, and to thank him!'

The old gentleman's eyes now filled with tears, and coming back, and most affectionately shaking hands with her, 'I was afraid he had misbehaved,' he cried; 'but he was always a good lad; and if he has done any thing for the niece of my dear Sir Hugh Tyrold, I shall hug him to my heart!' and then, in great, but pleased perturbation, he hurried away, saying to himself, as he went: 'I'll take him to her, to be sure; I desire nothing better! God bless her! If she can speak so well of my poor Hal, she must be the best girl living! and she shall have him . . . yes, she shall have him, if she's a mind to him; and I don't care if she i'n't worth a groat; she's niece to my old friend; that's better.'

Camilla speeding, but not hearing him, returned to her seat; yet could not answer one question, from the horrors of her fears, and her shame of the detail of the business.

When the breakfast was over Miss Margland desired everyone would get ready to go to the lodgings; and, with Indiana, repaired herself to visit them, and give general orders. Dr. Marchmont had

glided out of the room, in anxiety for Edgar; to the great dissatisfaction, and almost contempt of Dr. Orkborne, with whom he
was just discussing some controverted points upon the shield of
Achilles;[1] which, that he could quit for the light concerns of a
young man, added again to his surmises that, though he had run
creditably the usual scholastic race, his reputation was more the
effect of general ability and address, than of such sound and
consummate learning as he himself possessed. Ruminating upon
the ignorant injustice of mankind, in suffering such quacks in
literature and philology to carry the palm of fame, he went to his
chamber, to collect, from his bolster and bedside, the hoard of
books and papers, from which, the preceding night, he had dis-
encumbered his coat, waistcoat, and great coat pockets, inside and
out, to review before he could sleep; and which now were again to
encircle him, to facilitate their change of abode.

But Eugenia would not quit her afflicted sister, who soon, in her
gentle breast, deposited the whole of her grief, her apprehensions,
and her plans; charging her instantly to retire, if Edgar should
return, that whatever might be the event he should unfold, she
might release him immediately from an engagement that his last
words seemed to avow did not make him happy, and that probably
he now repented. The design was so consonant to the native
heroism of Eugenia, that she consented, with applause, to aid its
execution.

About half an hour, which seemed to be prolonged to twenty
times the duration of the whole day, passed in terrible expectation;
Edgar then appeared, and Eugenia, suspending her earnest
curiosity, to comply with the acute feelings of her sister, retreated.

Camilla could scarce breathe; she stood up, her eyes and mouth
open, her face pale, her hands uplifted, waiting, but not daring to
demand intelligence.

Edgar, entering into her distress with a tenderness that drove
from him his own, eagerly satisfied her: 'All,' he cried, 'is safe;
the affair has been compromised; no duel has taken place; and
the parties have mutually pledged themselves to forget the
dispute.'

Tears again, but no longer bitter, flowed copiously down her
cheeks, while her raised eyes and clasped hands expressed the
fervency of her thankfulness.

Edgar, extremely touched, took her hand; he wished to seize a moment so nearly awful, to enforce upon her mind every serious subject with which he most desired it to be impressed; but sorrow was ever sacred to him; and desiring only, at this period, to console her: 'This adventure,' he cried, 'has now terminated so well, you must not suffer it to wound you. Dismiss it, sweet Camilla, from your memory! . . . at least till you are more composed.'

'No, sir!' cried Camilla, to whom his softness, by restoring her hope of an ultimately happy conclusion, restored strength; 'it ought never to be dismissed from my memory; and what I am now going to say will fix it there indelibly.'

Edgar was surprised, but pleased; his most anxious wishes seemed on the point of being fulfilled; he expected a voluntary explanation of every perplexity, a clearance of all mystery.

'I am sensible that I have appeared to you,' she resumed, 'in many points reprehensible; in some, perhaps, inexcusable. . . .'

'Inexcusable? O no! never! never!'

'The letters of Sir Sedley Clarendel I know you think I ought not to have received. . . .'

Edgar, biting his nails, looked down.

'And, indeed, I acknowledge myself, in that affair, a most egregious dupe! . . .'

She blushed; but her blush was colourless to that of Edgar. Resentment against Sir Sedley beat high in every vein; while disappointment to his delicacy, in the idea of Camilla duped by any man, seemed, in one blow, to detach him from her person, by a sudden dissolution of all charm to his mind in the connection.

Camilla saw, too late, she had been too hasty in a confession which some apologising account should have preceded; but what her courage had begun, pride now aided her to support, and she continued.

'For what belongs to that correspondence, and even for its being unknown to my friends, I may offer, perhaps, hereafter, something in exculpation; . . . hereafter, I say, building upon your long family regard; for though we part . . . it will be, I trust, in amity.'

'Part!' repeated Edgar, recovering from his displeasure by amazement.

'Yes, part,' said she, with assumed firmness; 'it would be vain to palliate what I cannot disguise from myself . . . I am lessened in

your esteem.' She could not go on; imperious shame took possession of her voice, crimsoned her very forehead, blushed even in
her eyes, demolished her strained energy, and enfeebled her
genuine spirit.

But the conscious taciturnity of Edgar recalled her exertions;
struck and afflicted by the truth she had pronounced, he could not
controvert it; he was mute; but his look spoke keen disturbance
and bitter regret.

'Not so low, however, am I yet, I trust, fallen in your opinion,
that you can wonder at the step I now take. I am aware of many
errours; I know, too, that appearances have often cruelly mis-
represented me; my errours you might have the candour to forget,
and false appearances I could easily clear in my own favour—but
where, and what is the talisman which can erase from my own
remembrance that you have thought me unworthy?'

Edgar started; but she would not give him time to speak; what
she had last uttered was too painful to her to dwell upon, or hear
answered, and rapidly, and in an elevated manner, she went on.

'I here, therefore, solemnly release you from all tie, all engagement whatever with Camilla Tyrold! I shall immediately acquaint my friends that henceforth . . . we Both are Free!'

She was then retiring. Edgar, confounded by a stroke so utterly
and every way unexpected, neither answering nor interposing, till
he saw her hand upon the lock of the door. In a voice then, that
spoke him cut to the soul, though without attempting to stop her,
'This then,' he cried, 'Camilla, is your final adieu.'

She turned round, and with a face glowing, and eyes glistening,
held out to him her hand: 'I knew not if you would accept,' she
said, 'a kinder word, or I should have assured you of my unaltered
regard . . . and have claimed the continuance of your friendship,
and even . . . if your patience is not utterly exhausted, of your
watchful counsel. . . . Farewell! remember me without severity!
my own esteem must be permanent as my existence!'

The door, here, was opened by Miss Margland and Indiana,
and Camilla hastily snatched away the hand which Edgar,
grasping with the fondness of renovated passion, secretly meant to
part with no more, till a final reconciliation once again made it his
own; but compelled to yield to circumstance, he suffered it to be
withdrawn; and while she darted into the chamber of Eugenia, to
hide her deep emotion from Indiana, who was tittering, and Miss

Margland, who was sneering, at the situation in which she was surprised, he abruptly took leave himself, too much impressed by this critical scene, to labour for uninteresting discourse.

CHAPTER VI

Ideas upon Marriage

WHILE, in the bosom of her faithful sister, Camilla reposed her feelings and her fears, alternately rejoicing and trembling in the temerity of the resolution she had exerted; Edgar sought his not less faithful, nor honourable, but far more worldly friend, Dr. Marchmont.

He narrated, with extreme emotion, the scene he had just had with Camilla; asserting her possession of every species of excellence from the nobleness of her rejection, and abhorring himself for having given her a moment's doubt of his fullest esteem. Not a solicitude, he declared, now remained with him, but how to appease her displeasure, satisfy her dignity, and recover her favour.

'Softly, softly!' said the Doctor; 'measure your steps more temperately, ere you run with such velocity. If this refusal is the result of an offended sensibility, you cannot exert yourself too warmly in its consolation; even if it is from pride, it has a just claim to your concessions, since she thinks you have injured it; yet pause before you act, may it not be merely from a confidence of power that loves to tyrannize over its slaves, by playing with their chains? or a lurking spirit of coquetry, that desires to regain the liberty of trifling with some new Sir Sedley Clarendel? or, perhaps, with Sir Sedley himself?'

'Dr. Marchmont! how wretchedly ill you think of women!'

'I think of them as they are! I think of them as I have found them. They are artful, though feeble; they are shallow, yet subtle.'

'You have been unfortunate in your connexions?'

'Yet who had better prospects? with energies as warm, with hopes as alive as your own, twice have I conducted to the altar two beings I thought framed for my peculiar felicity; but my peace, my happiness, and my honour, have been torn up by the root, exactly where I thought I had planted them for my whole temporal existence. This heart, which to you appears hard and suspicious, has been the dupe of its susceptibilities; first, in a creature of its own choice, next, where it believed itself chosen. That first, Mandlebert, had you seen her, you would have thought, as I thought her myself . . . an angel! She was another Camilla.'

'Another Camilla!'

'Grace, sweetness, and beauty vied in her for pre-eminence. Yes, another Camilla! though I see your incredulity; I see you think my comparison almost profane; and that grace, sweetness, and beauty, waited the birth of Camilla to be made known to the world. Such, however, she was, and I saw and loved at once. I knew her character fair, I precipitately made my addresses, and concluded myself beloved in return . . . because I was accepted!'

Edgar shrunk back, and cast down his eyes.

'Nor was it till the moment . . . heart-breaking yet to my recollection! . . . of her sudden death, that I knew the lifeless, soulless, inanimate frame was all she had bestowed upon me. In the private drawer of her bureau, I then found a pocketbook. In the first leaf, I saw a gentleman's name; . . . I turned over, and saw it again; I looked further, and still it met my view; I opened by chance, . . . but nothing else appeared: . . . there it was still, traced in every hand, charactered in every form, shape, and manner, the wayward, wistful eye could delight to fashion, for varying, yet beholding it without end: while, over the inter- mediate spaces, verses, quotations, short but affecting sentences, were every where scattered, bewailing the misery of disappointed hope, and unrequited love; of a heartless hand devoted at the altar; of vows enchaining liberty, not sanctifying affection! I then . . . alas, too late! dived deeper, with, then, useless investigation, . . . and discovered an early passion, never erased from her mind; . . . discovered . . . that I had never made her happy! that she was merely enduring, suffering me . . . while my whole confiding soul was undividedly hers!' . . .

Edgar shuddered at this picture; 'But why, then,' he cried, 'since she seemed amiable as well as fair, why did she accept you?'

'Ask half the married women in the nation how they became wives: they will tell you their friends urged them; . . . that they had no other establishment in view; . . . that nothing is so un- certain as the repetition of matrimonial powers in women; . . . and that those who cannot solicit what they wish, must accommodate themselves to what offers. This first adventure, however, is now no longer useful to you, though upon its hard remembrance was founded my former caution: but I am even myself satisfied, at present, that the earliest partiality of Camilla has been yours; what now you have to weigh, is the strength or inadequacy of her character, for guiding that partiality to your mutual happiness. My second melancholy history will best illustrate this difficulty. You may easily believe, the last of my intentions was any further essay in a lottery I had found so inauspicious; but, while cold even to apathy, it was my inevitable chance to fall in the way of a pleasing and innocent young creature, who gave me, unsought and unwished-for, her heart. The boon, nevertheless, soon caught my own: for what is so alluring as the voluntary affection of a virtuous woman?'

'Well,' cried Edgar, 'and what now could disturb your tranquillity?'

'The insufficiency of that heart to its own decision. I soon found her apparent predilection was simply the result of the casualty which brought me almost exclusively into her society, but unmarked by any consonance of taste, feeling, or understanding. Her inexperience had made her believe, since she preferred me to the few who surrounded her, I was the man of her choice: with equal facility I concurred in the same mistake; . . . for what is so credulous as self-love? But such a regard, the child of accident, not selection, was unequal, upon the discovery of the dissimilarity of our dispositions, to the smallest sacrifice. My melancholy returned with the view of our mutual delusion; lassitude of pleasing was the precursor of discontent. Dissipation then, in the form of amusement, presented itself to her aid: retirement and books came to mine. My resource was safe, though solitary; her's was gay, but perilous. Dissipation, with its usual Proteus powers, from amusement changed its form to temptation, allured her into dangers, impeached her honour, and blighted her with disgrace. I just discerned the precipice whence she was falling, in time to avert the dreadful necessity of casting her off for ever: . . . but what was our life thence forward? Cares unparticipated, griefs uncommunicated, stifled resentments, and unremitting weariness! She is now no more; and I am a lonely individual for the rest of my pilgrimage.

'Take warning, my dear young friend, by my experience. The entire possession of the heart of the woman you marry is not more essential to your first happiness, than the complete knowledge of her disposition is to your ultimate peace.'

Edgar thanked him, in deep concern to have awakened emotions which the absorption of study, and influence of literature, held generally dormant. The lesson, however, which they inculcated, he engaged to keep always present to his consideration; though, but for the strange affair of Sir Sedley Clarendel, he should feel confident that, in Camilla, there was not more of exterior attraction, than of solid excellence: and, with regard to their concordance of taste and humour, he had never seen her so gay, nor so lovely, as in scenes of active benevolence, or domestic life. She had promised to clear, hereafter, the transaction with Sir Sedley; but he could not hold back for that explanation: hurt, already, by his apparent scruples, she had openly named them as the motives of her rejection: could he, then, shew her he yet demurred, without forfeiting all hope of a future accommodation?

'Delicacy,' said Dr. Marchmont, 'though the quality the most amiable we can practise in the service of others, must not take place of common sense, and sound judgment, for ourselves. Her dismission does not discard you from her society; on the contrary, it invites your friendship. . . .'

'Ah, Doctor! what innocence, what sweetness does that very circumstance display!'

'Learn, however, their concomitants, ere you yield to their charms: learn if their source is from a present, yet accidental preference, or from the nobler spring of elevated sentiment. The meeting you surprised with Sir Sedley, the presumption you acknowledge of his letters, and the confession made by herself that she had submitted to be duped by him.'

'O, Dr. Marchmont! what harrowing drawbacks to felicity! And how much must we rather pity than wonder at the errors of common young women, when a creature such as this is so easy to be misled!'

'You must not imagine I mean a censure upon the excellent Mr. Tyrold, when I say she is left too much to herself: the purity of his principles, and the virtue of his character, must exempt him from blame; but his life has been both too private and too tranquil, to be aware of the dangers run by Female Youth, when straying from the mother's careful wing. All that belongs to religion, and to principle, he feels, and he has taught; but the impediments they have to encounter in a commerce with mankind, he could not point out, for he does not know. Yet there is nothing more certain, than that seventeen weeks is not less able to go alone in a nursery, than seventeen years in the world.'

This suggestion but added to the bias of Edgar to take her, if possible, under his own immediate guidance.

'Know, first,' cried the Doctor, 'if to your guidance she will give way; know if the affair with Sir Sedley has exculpations which render it single and adventitious, or if there hang upon it a lightness of character that may invest caprice, chance, or fickleness, with powers of involving such another entanglement.'

CHAPTER VII

How to treat a Defamer

As the lodgings taken by Miss Margland could not be ready till the afternoon, Camilla remained with her sister; a sojourn which, while it consoled her with the society, and gratified her by the approbation of Eugenia, had yet another allurement; it detained her under the same roof with Edgar; and his manner of listening to her rejection, and his undisguised suffering before they were parted, led her to expect he might yet demand a conference before she quitted the hotel.

In about an hour, as unpleasantly as unceremoniously, they were broken in upon by Mrs. Mittin.

'How monstrous lucky, my dear,' cried she, to Camilla, 'that I should find you, and your little sister, for I suppose this is she, together! I went into your dining-room to ask for you, and there I met those other two ladies; and I've made acquaintance with 'em, I assure you, already; for I told them I was on a visit at the Honourable Mrs. Berlinton's. So I've had the opportunity to recommend some shops to 'em, and I've been to tell some of the good folks to send them some of their nicest goods for 'em to look at; for, really, since I've been bustling a little about here, I've found some of the good people so vastly obliging, I can't but take a pleasure in serving 'em, and getting 'em a few customers, especially as I know a little civility of that sort makes one friends surprisingly. Often and often have I got things under prime cost myself, only by helping a person on in his trade. So one can't say good nature's always thrown away. However, I come now on purpose to put a note into your own hands, from Mrs. Berlinton; for all the servants were out of the way, except one, and he wanted to be about something else, so I offered to bring it, and she was very much pleased; so I fancy it's about some secret, for she never offered to shew it me; but as to the poor man I saved from the walk, I've won his heart downright; I dare say he'll go of any odd errand for me, now, without vails.[1] That's the best of good nature, it always comes home to one.'

The note from Mrs. Berlinton contained a tender supplication for the return of Camilla, and a pressing and flattering invitation that her sister should join their little party, as the motives of honour and discretion which made her, at the request and for the sake of her brother, sacrifice her eagerness to be presented to Miss Lynmere, operated not to impede her acquaintance with Miss Eugenia.

This proposition had exquisite charms for Eugenia. To become acquainted with the sister of him to whom, henceforward, she meant to devote her secret thoughts, enchanted her imagination. Camilla, therefore, negotiated the visit with Miss Margland, who, though little pleased by this separate invitation, knew not how to refuse her concurrence; but Indiana, indignant that the sister of Melmond should not, first, have waited upon her, and solicited her friendship, privately resolved, in pique of this disrespect, to punish the brother with every rigour she could invent.

Camilla, upon her return, found Mrs. Mittin already deeply engaged in proposing an alteration in the dress of Eugenia, which she was aiding Molly Mill to accomplish; and so much she found to say and to do, to propose and to object to, to contrive and to alter, that, from the simplicity of the mistress, and the ignorance of the maid, the one was soon led to conclude she should have appeared improperly before Mrs. Berlinton, without such useful advice; and the other to believe she must shortly have lost her place, now her young lady was come forth into the world, if she had not thus miraculously met with so good a friend.

During these preparations, Camilla was summoned back to the dining-room to receive Mr. Westwyn.

She did not hear this call with serenity. The danger which, however unwittingly, she had caused his son, and the shocking circumstances which were its foundation, tingled her cheeks, and confounded her wish of making acknowledgments, with an horror that such an obligation could be possible.

The door of the dining-room was open, and as soon as her steps were heard, Mr. Westwyn came smiling forth to receive her. She hung back involuntarily; but, pacing up to her, and taking her hand, 'Well, my good young lady,' he cried, 'I have brought you my son; but he's no boaster, that I can assure you, for though I told him how you wanted him to come to you, and was so good as to say you were so much obliged to him, I can't make him own he has ever seen you in his life; which I tell him is carrying his modesty over far; I don't like affectation . . . I have no taste for it.'

Camilla, discovering by this speech, as well as by his pleased and tranquil manner, that he had escaped hearing of the intended duel, and that his son was still ignorant whose cause he had espoused, ardently wished to avert farther shame by concealing herself; and, step by step, kept retreating back towards the room of Eugenia; though she could not disengage her hand from the old gentleman, who, trying to draw her on, said: 'Come, my dear! don't go away. Though my son won't confess what he has done for you, he can't make me forget that you were such a dear soul as to tell me yourself, of his good behaviour, and of your having such a kind opinion of him. And I have been telling him, and I can assure you I'll keep my word, that if he has done a service to the niece of my dear old friend, Sir Hugh Tyrold, it shall value him fifty pound a-year more to his income, if I straighten myself never so much. For a lad, that knows how to behave in that manner, will never spend his money so as to make his old father ashamed of him. And that's a good thing for a man to know.'

'Indeed, sir, this is some mistake,' said the young man himself, now advancing into the passage, while Camilla was stammering out an excuse from entering; 'it's some great mistake; I have not the honour to know. . . .'

He was going to add Miss Tyrold, but he saw her at the same moment, and instantly recollecting her face, stopt, blushed, and looked amazed.

The retreating effort of Camilla, her shame and her pride,

all subsided by his view, and gave place to the more generous feelings of gratitude for his intuitive good opinion, and emotion for the risk he had run in her defence: and with an expression of captivating sweetness in her eyes and manner, 'That you did not know me,' she cried, 'makes the peculiarity of your goodness, which, indeed, I am more sensible to than I can express.'

'Why, there! there, now! there!' cried Mr. Westwyn, while his son, enchanted to find whose character he had sustained, bowed almost to the ground with respectful gratitude for such thanks; 'only but listen! she says the very same things to your face, that she said behind your back! though I am afraid, it's only to please an old father; for if not, I can't for my life find out any reason why you should deny it. Come, Hal, speak out, Hal!'

Equally at a loss how either to avow or evade what had passed in the presence of Camilla, young Westwyn began a stammering and awkward apology; but Camilla, feeling doubly his forbearance, said: 'Silence may in you be delicate . . . but in me it would be graceless.' Then, turning from him to old Mr. Westwyn, 'you may be proud, sir,' she cried, 'of your son! It was the honour of an utter stranger he was protecting, as helpless as she was unknown at the time she excited his interest; nor had he even in view this poor mede he now receives of her thanks!'

'My dearest Hal!' cried Mr. Westwyn, wringing him by the hand; 'if you have but one small grain of regard for me, don't persist in denying this! I'd give the last hundred pounds I had in the world to be sure it was true!'

'That to hear the name of this lady,' said the young man, 'should not be necessary to inspire me with respect for her, who can wonder? that any opportunity could arise in which she should want defence, is all that can give any surprise.'

'You own it, then, my dear Hal? you own you've done her a kindness? why then, my dear Hal, you've done one to me! and I can't help giving you a hug for it, let who will think me an old fool.'

He then fervently embraced his son, who confused, though gratified, strove vainly to make disclaiming speeches. 'No, no, my dear Hal,' he cried, 'you sha'n't let yourself down with me again, I promise you, though you've two or three times tried to make me think nothing of you; but this young lady here, dear soul, speaks another language; she says I may be proud of my son! and I dare say she knows why, for she's a charming girl, as ever I saw; so I will be proud of my son! Poor dear Hal! thou hast got a good friend, I can tell thee, in that young lady! and she's niece to the best man I ever knew; and I value her good opinion more than anybody's.'

'You are much too good,' cried Camilla, in an accent of tender pleasure, the result of grateful joy, that she had not been the means of destroying the paternal happiness of so fond a father, joined to the dreadful certainty how narrowly she had escaped that misery; 'you are much too good, and I blush even to thank you, when I think—'

What she meant to add was in a moment forgotten, and that she blushed ceased to be metaphorical, when now, as they all three entered the dining-room together, the first object that met her eyes was Edgar.

Their eyes met not again; delighted and conscious, she turned hers hastily away. He comes, thought she, to [claim] me! he will not submit to the separation; he comes to re-assure me of his esteem, and to receive once more my faithful heart!

Edgar had seen, by chance, the Westwyns pass to the room of the Cleves party, and felt the most ardent desire to know if they would meet with Camilla, and what would be her reception of her young champion, whose sword, with extreme trouble, he had himself that morning sheathed, and whose gallantry he attributed to a vehement, however, sudden passion. Dr. Marchmont acknowledged the epoch to be highly interesting for observation, and, presuming upon their old right of intimacy with all the party, they abruptly made a second visit.

Miss Margland and Indiana, who were examining some goods sent by Mrs. Mittin, had received them all four without much mark of civility; and Mr. Westwyn immediately desired Camilla to be sent for, and kept upon the watch, till her step made him hasten out to meet her.

Edgar could not hear unmoved the dialogue which ensued; he imagined an amiable rival was suddenly springing up in young Westwyn, at the very moment of his own dismission, which he now even thought possible this incipient conquest had urged; and when Camilla, walking between the father and the son, with looks of softest sensibility, came into the room, he thought he had never seen her so lovely, and that her most bewitching smiles were purposely lavished for their captivation.

With this idea, he found it impossible to speak to her; their situation, indeed, was too critical for any common address, and when he saw that she turned from him, he attempted to converse with the other ladies upon their purchases; and Camilla, left to her two new beaux, had the unavoidable appearance of being engrossed by them, though the sight of Edgar instantly robbed them of all her real attention.

Soon after, the door was again opened, and Mr. Girt, the young perfumer, came, smirking and scraping, into the room, with a box of various toys, essences, and cosmetics, recommended by Mrs. Mittin.

Ignorant of the mischief he had done her, and not even recollecting to have seen him, Camilla made on to look at his goods; but Edgar, to whom his audacious assertions were immediately brought back by his sight, would have made him feel the effects of his resentment, had not his passion for Camilla been of so solid, as well as warm a texture, as to induce him to prefer guarding her delicacy, to any possible display he could make of his feelings to others, or even to herself.

Mr. Girt, in the midst of his exhibition of memorandum books, smelling bottles, tooth-pick cases, and pocket mirrors; with washes to immortalize the skin, powders becoming to all countenances, and pomatums to give natural tresses to old age, suddenly recollected Camilla. The gross mistake he had made he had already discovered, by having dodged[1] her to the house of Mrs. Berlinton; but all alarm at it had ceased, by finding, through a visit made to his shop by Mrs. Mittin, that she was uninformed he had propagated it. Not gifted with the discernment to see in the air and manner of Camilla her entire, though unassuming superiority to her accidental associate, he concluded them both to be relations of some of the upper domestics; and with a look and tone descending from the most profound adulation, with which he was presenting his various articles to Miss Margland and Indiana, into a familiarity the most facetious, 'O dear, ma'am,' he cried, 'I did not see you at first; I hope t'other lady's well that's been so kind as to recommend me? Indeed I saw her just now.'

Young Westwyn, to whom, as to Edgar, the bold defamation

of Girt occurred with his presence, but whom none of the nameless delicacies of the peculiar situation, and peculiar character of
Edgar, restrained into silence, felt such a disgust at the presumption of effrontery that gave him courage for this facetious address,
to a young lady whose innocence of his ill usage made him think
its injury double, that, unable to repress his indignation, he
abruptly whispered in his ear, 'Walk out of the room, sir!'

The amazed perfumer, at this haughty and unexpected order,
stared, and cried aloud, 'No offence, I hope, sir?'

Mr. Westwyn asked what was the matter? while Camilla,
crimsoned by the familiar assurance with which she had been
addressed, retired to a window.

'Nothing of any moment, sir,' answered Henry; and again, in a
low but still more positive voice, he repeated his command to
Girt.

'Sir, I'm not used to be used in this manner!' answered he,
hardily, and hoping, by raising his tone, for the favourable
intervention of the company.

Indiana, now, was preparing to scream, and Miss Margland
was looking round to see whom she should reprehend; but young
Westwyn, coolly opening the door, with a strong arm, and an able
jerk, twisted the perfumer into the passage, saying, 'You may send
somebody for your goods.'

Girt, who equally strong, but not equally adroit as Henry,
strove in vain to resist, vowed vengeance for this assault. Henry,
without seeming to hear him, occupied himself with looking at
what he had left. Camilla felt her eyes suffuse with tears; and
Edgar, for the first time in his life, found himself visited by the
baleful passion of envy.

Miss Margland could not comprehend what this meant;
Indiana comprehended but too much in finding there was some
disturbance of which she was not the object; but Mr. Westwyn,
losing his look of delight, said, with something of severity, 'Ha!
what did you turn that man out of the room for?'

'He is perfectly aware of my reason, sir,' said Henry; and
then added it was a long story, which he begged to relate another
time.

The blank face of Mr. Westwyn shewed displeasure and
mortification. He lifted the head of his cane to his mouth, and
after biting it for some time, with a frowning countenance,

muttered, 'I don't like to see a man turned out of a room. If he's done any harm, tell him so; and if it's worse than harm, souse him in a horsepond;[1] I've no objection: But I don't like to see a man turned out of a room; it's very unmannerly; and I did not think Hal would do such a thing.' Then suddenly, and with a succinct bow, bidding them all good bye, he took a hasty leave; still, however, muttering, all the way along the passage, and down the stairs, loud enough to be heard: 'Kicking and jerking a man about does not prove him to be in the wrong. I thought Hal had been more of a gentleman. If I don't find the man turns out to be a rascal, Hall shall beg his pardon; for I don't like to see a man turned out of a room.'

Henry, whose spirit was as irritable as it was generous, felt acutely this public censure, which, though satisfied he did not deserve, every species of propriety prohibited his explaining away. With a forced smile, therefore, and a silent bow, he followed his father.

Miss Margland and Indiana now burst forth with a torrent of wonders, conjectures, and questions; but the full heart of Camilla denied her speech, and the carriage of Mrs. Berlinton being already at the door, she called upon Eugenia, and followed, perforce, by Mrs. Mittin, left the hotel.

Edgar and Dr. Marchmont gave neither surprise nor concern by retiring instantly to their own apartment.

'Dr. Marchmont,' said the former, in a tone of assumed moderation, 'I have lost Camilla! I see it plainly. This young man steps forward so gallantly, so ingenuously, nay so amiably, that the contrast . . . chill, severe, and repulsive . . . must render me . . . in this detestable state . . . insupportable to all her feelings. Dr. Marchmont! I have not a doubt of the event!'

'The juncture is, indeed, perilous, and the trial of extremest hazard; but it is such as draws all uncertainty to a crisis, and, therefore, is not much to be lamented. You may safely, I think, rest upon it your destiny. To a general female heart a duel is the most dangerous of all assaults, and the most fascinating of all charms; and a duellist, though precisely what a woman most should dread, as most exposing her to public notice, is the person of all others she can, commonly, least resist. By this test, then, prove your Camilla. Her champion seems evidently her admirer, and his father her adorer. Her late engagement with you may possibly not reach them; or reaching but with its dissolution, serve only to render them more eager.'

'Do you suppose him,' cried Edgar, after a pause of strong disturbance; 'do you suppose him rich?'

'Certainly not. That the addition of fifty pounds a-year to his income should be any object, proves his fortune to be very moderate.'

'Clear her, then, at least,' said he, with a solemnity almost reproachful; 'clear her, at least, of every mercenary charge! If I lose her . . .' he gasped for breath . . . 'she will not, you find, be bought from me! and pique, anger, injustice, nay inconstancy, all are less debasing than the sordid corruption of which you suspected her.'

'This does not, necessarily, prove her disinterested; she is too young, yet, to know herself the value she may hereafter set upon wealth. And, independent of that inexperience, there is commonly so little stability, so little internal hold, in the female character, that any sudden glare of adventitious lure, will draw them, for the moment, from any and every regular plan of substantial benefit. It remains, therefore, now to be tried, if Beech Park, and its master united, can vie with the bright and intoxicating incense of a life voluntarily risked, in support . . . not of her fair fame, that was unknown to its defender . . . but simply of the fair countenance which seemed its pledge.'

Edgar, heartless and sad, attempted no further argument; he thought the Doctor prejudiced against the merits of Camilla; yet it appeared, even to himself, that her whole conduct, from the short period of his open avowal, had seemed a wilful series of opposition to his requests and opinions. And while terror for surrounding dangers gave weight to his disapprobation of her visiting Southampton, with a lady she knew him to think more attractive than safe or respectable, her sufferance of the vulgar and forward Mrs. Mittin, with whom again he saw her quit the hotel, was yet more offensive, since he could conceive for it no other inducement than a careless, if not determined humour, to indulge every impulse, in equal contempt of his counsel, and her own reflection.

All blame, however, of Camilla, was short of his self-dissatisfaction, in the distance imposed upon him by uncertainty, and the coldness dictated by discretion. At a period so sensitive, when her spirit was alarmed, and her delicacy was wounded, that a stranger should start forward, to vindicate her innocence, and chastise its detractors, was singular, was unfortunate, was nearly intolerable; and he thought he could with thankfulness, have renounced half his fortune, to have been himself the sole protector of Camilla.

CHAPTER VIII

The Power of Prepossession

THE two sisters were silent from the hotel to the house of Mrs. Berlinton. . . . From the height of happiest expectation, raised by the quick return of Edgar, Camilla was sunk into the lowest despondence, by the abortive conclusion of the meeting: while Eugenia was absorbed in mute joy, and wrapt expectation. But Mrs. Mittin, undisturbed by the pangs of uncertainty, and unoccupied by any romantic persuasion of bliss, spoke amply, with respect to quantity, for all three.

Mrs. Berlinton, though somewhat struck at first sight of Eugenia, with her strange contrast to Camilla, received her with all the distinguishing kindness due to the sister of her friend.

She had the poems of Collins in her hand; and, at their joint desire, instead of putting the book aside, read aloud, and with tenderest accent, one of his most plaintive odes.

Eugenia was enraptured. Ah! thought she, this is indeed the true sister of the accomplished Melmond! . . . She shall share with him my adoration. My heart shall be devoted . . . after my own dear family . . . to the homage of their perfections!

The ode, to her great delight, lasted till the dinner was announced, when Melmond appeared: but her prepossession could alone give any charm to his sight: he could barely recollect that he had seen her, or even Camilla before; he had conversed with neither; his eyes had been devoted to Indiana, and the despondence which had become his portion since the news of the marriage of his aunt, seemed but rendered the more peculiarly bitter, by this intimate connection with the family of an object so adored.

Yet, though nothing could be more spiritless than the hour of dinner, Eugenia discovered in it no deficiency; she had previously settled, that the presence of Melmond could only breathe sweets and perfection, and the magic of prejudice works every event into its own circle of expectation.

Melmond did not even accompany them back to the drawing-room. Eugenia sighed; but nobody heard her. Mrs. Mittin said, she had something of great consequence to do in her own room, and Mrs. Berlinton, to divert the languor she found creeping upon them all, had recourse to Hammond's elegies.[1]

These were still reading, when a servant brought in the name of Lord Valhurst. 'O, deny me to him! deny me to him!' cried Mrs. Berlinton; ''tis a relation of Mr. Berlinton's, and I hate him.'

The order was given, however, too late; he entered the room.

The name, as Camilla knew it not, she had heard unmoved; but the sight of a person who had so largely contributed to shock and terrify her in the bathing-house, struck her with horror. Brought up with the respect of other times, she had risen at his entrance; but she turned suddenly round upon recollecting him, and instead of the courtsie she intended making, involuntarily moved away her chair from the part of the room to which he was advancing.

This was unnoticed by Mrs. Berlinton, whose chagrin at his intrusion made her wish to walk away also; while with Lord Valhurst it only passed, joined to her rising, for a mark of her being but little accustomed to company. That Eugenia rose too was not perceived, as she rather lost than gained in height by standing.

Most obsequiously, but most unsuccessfully, the peer made his court to Mrs. Berlinton; inquiring after her health, with fulsome tenderness, and extolling her good looks with nearly gross admiration. Mrs. Berlinton listened, for she was incapable of incivility; though, weary and disgusted, she seldom made the smallest answer.

The two sisters might, with ease, equally have escaped notice, since, though Mrs. Berlinton occasionally addressed them the peer never turned from herself, had not Mrs. Mittin, abruptly entering in search of a pair of scissors, perceived him, and hastily called out, 'O lauk, sir, if it is not you! I know you again well enough! But I hope, now you see us in such good company as this good lady's, you'll believe me another time, when I tell you we're not the sort of persons you took us for! Miss Tyrold, my dear, I hope you've spoke to the gentleman?'

Lord Valhurst with difficulty recollected Mrs. Mittin, from the very cursory view his otherwise occupied eyes had taken of her; but when the concluding words made him look at Camilla, whose youth and beauty were not so liable to be forgotten, he knew at once her associate, and was aware of the meaning of her harangue.

Sorry to appear before his fair kinswoman to any disadvantage, though by no means displeased at an opportunity of again seeing a young creature he had thought so charming, he began an apology to Mrs. Mittin, while his eyes were fixed upon Camilla, vindicating himself from every intention that was not respectful, and hoping she did not so much injure as to mistake him.

Mrs. Mittin was just beginning to answer that she knew better, when the words, 'Why, my Lord, how have you offended Mrs. Mittin?' dropping from Mrs. Berlinton, instantly new strung all her notions. To find him a nobleman was to find him innocent; for, though she did not quite suppose that a peer was not a mortal, she had never spoken to one before; and the power of title upon the ear, like that of beauty upon the eye, is, in its first novelty, all-commanding; manifold as are the drawbacks to the influence of either, when awe is lost by familiarity, and habitual reflection takes place of casual and momentary admiration. Title then, as well as beauty, demands mental auxiliaries; and those who possess either, more watched than the common race, seem of higher responsibility; but proportioned to the censure they draw where they err, is the veneration they inspire where their eminence is complete. Nor is this the tribute of prejudice, as those who look up to all superiority with envy love to aver; the impartial and candid reflectors upon human frailty, who, in viewing it, see with its elevation its surrounding temptations, will call it but the tribute of justice.

To Mrs. Mittin, however, the mere sound of a title was enough; she felt its ascendance without examining its claims, and, dropping the lowest courtsie her knees could support, confusedly said, she hoped his lordship would excuse her speaking so quick and improperly, which she only did from not knowing who he was; for, if she had known him better, she should have been sure he was too much the gentleman to do anything with an ill design.

His lordship courteously accepted the apology; and advanced

to Camilla, to express his hopes she had not participated in such injurious suspicions.

She made no answer, and Mrs. Berlinton inquired what all this meant.

'I protest, my dear madam,' said the peer, 'I do not well comprehend myself. I only see there has been some misunderstanding; but I hope this young lady will believe me, when I declare, upon my honour, that I had no view but to offer my protection, at the time I saw her under alarm.'

This was a declaration Camilla could not dispute, and even felt inclined to credit, from the solemnity with which it was uttered; but to discuss it was every way impossible, and therefore, coldly bowing her head, she seemed acquiescent.

Lord Valhurst now pretty equally divided his attention between these two beautiful young women; looking at and complimenting them alternately, till a servant came in and said, 'The two Mr. Westwyns desire to see Miss Tyrold.'

Camilla did not wish to avoid persons to whom she was so much obliged, but begged she might receive them in the next apartment, that Mrs. Berlinton might not be disturbed.

The eager old gentleman stood with the door in one hand, and his son in the other, awaiting her. 'My dear young lady,' he cried, 'I have been hunting you out for hours. Your good governess had not a mind to give me your direction, thinking me, I suppose, but a troublesome old fellow; and I did not know which way to turn, till Hal found it out. Hal's pretty quick. So now, my dear young lady, let me tell you my errand; which I won't be tedious in, for fear, another time, you may rather not see me. And the more I see you, the less I like to think such a thing. However, with all my good will to make haste, I must premise one thing, as it is but fair. Hal was quite against my coming upon this business. But I don't think it the less right for that; and so I come. I never yet saw any good of a man's being ruled by his children. It only serves to make them think their old fathers superannuated. And if once I find Hal taking such a thing as that into his head, I'll cut him off with a shilling, well as I love him.'

'Your menace, sir,' said Henry, colouring, though smiling, 'gives me no alarm, for I see no danger. But . . . shall we not detain Miss Tyrold too long from her friends?'

'Ay now, there comes in what I take notice to be the taste of the present day! a lad can hardly enter his teens, before he thinks himself wiser than his father, and gives him his counsel, and tells him what he thinks best. And, if a man i'n't upon his guard, he may be run down for an old dotard, before he knows where he is, and see his son setting up for a member of parliament, making laws for him. Now this is what I don't like; so I keep a tight hand upon Hal, that he mayn't do it. For Hal's but a boy, ma'am, though he's so clever. Not that I pretend I'd change him neither, for e'er an old fellow in the three kingdoms. Well, but, now I'll tell you what I come for. You know how angry I was about Hal's turning that man out of the room? well, I took all the pains I could to come at the bottom of the fray, intending, all the time, to make Hal ask the man's pardon; and now what do you think is the end? Why, I've found out Hal to be in the right! The man proves to be a worthless fellow, that has defamed the niece of my dear Sir Hugh Tyrold; and if Hal had lashed him with a cat-o'nine-tails, I should have been glad of it. I can't say I should have found fault. So you see, my dear young lady, I was but a cross old fellow, to be so out of sorts with poor Hal.'

Camilla, with mingled gratitude and shame, offered her acknowledgments; though what she heard astonished, if possible, even more than it mortified her. How in the world, thought she, can I have provoked this slander?

She knew not how little provocation is necessary for calumny; nor how regularly the common herd, where appearances admit two interpretations, decide for the worst. Girt designed her neither evil nor good; but not knowing who nor what she was, simply filled up the doubts in his own mind, by the bias of his own character.

Confused as much as herself, Henry proposed immediately to retire; and, as Camilla did not invite them to stay, Mr. Westwyn could not refuse his consent: though, sending his son out first, he stopt to say, in a low voice, 'What do you think of Hal, my dear young lady? I'n't he a brave rogue? And did not you tell me I might be proud of my son? And so I am, I promise you! How do you think my old friend will like Hal? I shall take him to Cleves. He's another sort of lad to Master Clermont! I hope, my dear young lady, you don't like your cousin? He's but a sad spark,[1] I give you my word. Not a bit like Hal.'

*   *   *   *

When the carriage came for Eugenia, who was self-persuaded this day was the most felicitous of her life, she went so reluctantly, that Mrs. Berlinton, caught by her delight in the visit, though unsuspicious of its motive, invited her to renew it the next morning.

At night, Mrs. Mittin, following Camilla to her chamber, said, 'See here, my dear! what do you say to this? Did you ever see a prettier cloak? look at the cut of it, look at the capes! look at the mode! And as for the lace, I don't think all Southampton can produce its fellow; what do you say to it, my dear?'

'What every body must say to it, Mrs. Mittin; that it's remarkably pretty.'

'Well, now try it on. There's a set! there's a fall off the shoulders! do but look at it in the glass. I'd really give something you could but see how it becomes you. Now, do pray, only tell me what you think of it?'

'Always the same, Mrs. Mittin; that it's extremely pretty.'

'Well, my dear, then, now comes out the secret! It's your own! you may well stare; but it's true; it's your own, my dear!'

She demanded an explanation; and Mrs. Mittin said, that, having taken notice that her cloak looked very mean by the side of Mrs. Berlinton's, when she compared them together, she resolved upon surprising her with a new one as quick as possible. She had, therefore, got the pattern of Mrs. Berlinton's and cut it out, and then got the mode at an haberdasher's, and then the lace at a milliner's, and then set to work so hard, that she had got it done already.

Camilla, seeing the materials were all infinitely richer than any she had been accustomed to wear, was extremely chagrined by such officiousness, and gravely inquired how much this would add to her debts.

'I don't know yet, my dear; but I had all the things as cheap as possible; but as it was not all at one shop, I can't be clear as to the exact sum.'

Camilla, who had determined to avoid even the shadow of a debt, and to forbear every possible expence till she had not one remaining, was now not merely vexed, but angry. Mrs. Mittin, however, upon whose feelings that most troublesome of all qualities to its possessors, delicacy, never obtruded, went on, extolling her own performance, and praising her own good nature, without discovering that either were impertinent; and, so far from conceiving it possible they could be unwelcome, that she attributed the concern of Camilla to modesty, on account of her trouble; and mistook her displeasure for distress, what she could do for her in return. And, indeed, when she finished her double panegyric upon the cloak and its maker, with confessing she had sat up the whole night, in order to get it done, Camilla considered herself as too much obliged to her intention to reproach any further its want of judgment; and concluded by merely entreating she would change her note, pay for it immediately, discharge her other accounts with all speed, and make no future purchase for her whatsoever.

CHAPTER IX

A Scuffle

EUGENIA failed not to observe her appointment the next morning, which was devoted to elegiac poetry. A taste so similar operated imperceptibly upon Mrs. Berlinton, who detained her till she was compelled to return to prepare for a great ball at the public rooms;[1] the profound deliberations of Miss Margland, how to exhibit her fair pupil, having finished, like most deliberations upon such subjects, by doing that which is done by every body else upon the same occasion.

Sir Hugh had given directions to Miss Margland to clear his three nieces equally of all expenses relative to public places. Camilla, therefore, being entitled to a ticket, and having brought with her whatever was unspoilt of her Tunbridge apparel, thought this the most seasonable opportunity she could take for again seeing Edgar, who, in their present delicate situation, would no longer, probably, think it right to inquire for her at a stranger's.

Mrs. Berlinton had not purposed appearing in public, till she had formed her own party; but an irrepressible curiosity to see Indiana induced her to accompany Camilla, with no other attendant than Lord Valhurst.

Mrs. Mittin sought vainly to be of the party; Mrs. Berlinton, though permitting her stay in her house, and treating her with constant civility, had no idea of including her in her own society, which she aimed to have always distinguished by either rank, talents, or admirers: and Camilla, who now felt her integrity involved in her economy, was firm against every hint for assisting her with a ticket.

Lord Valhurst, who alone, of the fashionable sojourners, had yet discovered the arrival of Mrs. Berlinton, was highly gratified by this opportunity of attending two such fair creatures in public.

Mrs. Berlinton, as usual, was the last to enter the room; for she never began the duties of the toilette till after tea-time. Two such youthful beauties were not likely to pass without observation.

Mrs. Berlinton, already no longer new to it, had alternately the air of receiving it with the most winning modesty, or of not noticing she received it at all: for though, but a few months since, she had scarcely been even seen by twenty persons, and even of those had never met a fixed eye without a blush, the feelings are so often the mere concomitants of the habits, that she could now already know herself the principal object of a whole assembly, without any sensation of timidity, or appearance of confusion. To be bold was not in her nature, which was soft and amiable; but admiration is a dangerous assaulter of diffidence, and familiarity makes almost any distinction met unmoved.

Camilla was too completely engrossed by her heart, to think of her appearance.

Lord Valhurst, from his time of life, seemed to be their father, though his adulating air as little suited that character as his inclination. He scarce knew upon which most to lavish his compliments, or to regale his eyes, and turned, half expiring with ecstasy, from the soft charms of his kinswoman, with something, he thought, resembling animation, to the more quickening influence of her bright-eyed companion.

But the effect produced upon the company at large by the radiant beauty of Indiana, who had entered some time, was still more striking than any immediate powers from all the bewitching graces of Mrs. Berlinton, and all the intelligent loveliness of Camilla. Her faultless face, her perfect form, raised wonder in one sex, and overpowered envy in the other. The men looked at her, as at something almost too celestial for their devoirs; the women, even the most charming amongst them, saw themselves distanced from all pretensions to rivalry. She was followed, but not approached; gazed at, as if a statue, and inquired after, rather as a prodigy than a mortal.

This awful homage spread not, however, to her party; the watchful but disdainful eyes of Miss Margland obtained for herself, even with usury, all the haughty contempt they bestowed upon others: Eugenia was pronounced to be a foil, brought merely in ridicule: and Dr. Orkborne, whom Miss Margland, though detesting, forced into the set, in preference to being without a man, to hand them from the carriage, and to call it for them at night, had a look so forlorn and distressed, while obliged to parade with them up and down the room, that he seemed rather a prisoner than an esquire, and more to require a guardian to prevent his escaping himself, than to serve for one in securing his young charges from any attack.

Miss Margland augured nothing short of half a score proposals of marriage the next day, from the evident brilliancy of this first opening into life of her beautiful pupil; whose own eyes, while they dazzled all others, sought eagerly those of Melmond, which they meant to vanquish, if not annihilate.

The first care of Miss Margland was to make herself and her young ladies known to the master of the ceremonies.[1] Indiana needed not that precaution to be immediately the choice of the most elegant man in the room; yet she was piqued, not delighted, and Miss Margland felt still more irritated, that he proved to be only a baronet, though a nobleman, at the same time, had presented himself to Eugenia. It is true the peer was ruined; but his title was unimpaired; and though the fortune of the baronet, like his person, was in its prime, Indiana thought herself degraded by his hand, since the partner of her cousin was of superior rank.

Eugenia, insensible to this honour, looked only for Melmond; not like Indiana, splendidly to see and kill, but silently to view and venerate. Melmond, however, was not there; he knew his little command over his passion, in presence of its object; he knew, too, that the expence of public places was not beyond the propriety of his income, and virtuously devoted his evening to his sick aunt.

Edgar had waited impatiently the entrance of Camilla. His momentary sight of Lord Valhurst, at the bathing-room, did not bring him to his remembrance in his present more shewy apparel, and he was gratified to see only an old beau in her immediate suite.

He did not deem it proper, as they were now circumstanced, to ask her to dance; but he quietly approached and bowed to her, and addressed some civil inquiries to Mrs. Berlinton. The Westwyns had waited for her at the door; and the father had immediately made her give her hand to Henry to join the dancers.

'That's a charming girl,' cried old Mr. Westwyn, when she was gone; 'a very charming girl, I promise you. I have taken a prodigious liking to her; and so has Hal.'

Revived by this open speech, which made him hope there was no serious design, Edgar smiled upon the old gentleman, who had addressed it to the whole remaining party; and said, 'You have not known that young lady long, I believe, sir?'

'No, sir; but a little while; but that I don't mind. A long while and a short while is all one, when I like a person: for I don't think how many years they've got over their heads since first I saw them, but how many good things they've got on the inside their hearts to make me want to see them again. Her uncle's the dearest friend I have in the world; and when I go from this place, I shall make him a visit; for I'm sure of a welcome. But he has never seen my Hal. However, that good girl will be sure to speak a kind word for him, I know; for she thinks very well of him; she told me herself, I might be proud of my son. I can't say but I've loved the girl ever since for it.'

Edgar was so much pleased with the perfectly natural character of this old gentleman, that, though alarmed at his intended call upon the favour of Sir Hugh, through the influence of Camilla, for Henry, he would yet have remained in his society, had he not been driven from it by the junction of young Lynmere, whose shallow insolence he thought insupportable.

Mrs. Berlinton, who declined dancing, had arrived so late, that when Henry led back Camilla, the company was summoned to the tea-table. She was languishing for an introduction to Indiana, the absence of Melmond obviating all present objection to their meeting; she therefore gave Camilla the welcome task to propose that the two parties should unite.

Many years had elapsed since Miss Margland had received so sensible a gratification; and, in the coalition which took place, she displayed more of civility in a few minutes, than she had exerted during the whole period of her Yorkshire and Cleves residence.

Notwithstanding all she had heard of her charms, Mrs.

Berlinton still saw with surprise and admiration the exquisite face and form of the chosen of her brother, whom she now so sincerely bewailed, that, had her own wealth been personal or transferrable, she would not have hesitated in sharing it with him, to aid his better success.

Lord Valhurst adhered tenaciously to his kinswoman; and the three gentlemen who had danced the last dances with Indiana, Eugenia, and Camilla, asserted the privilege of attending their partners at the tea-table.

In a few minutes, Lynmere, coming up to them, with 'Well, have you got any thing here one can touch?' leant his hand on the edge, and his whole body over the table, to take a view at his ease of its contents.

'Suppose there were nothing, sir?' said old Westwyn; 'look round, and see what you could want.'

'Really, sir,' said Miss Margland, between whom and Camilla Lynmere had squeezed himself a place, 'you don't use much ceremony!'

Having taken some tea, he found it intolerable, and said he must have a glass of Champagne.

'La, brother!' cried Indiana, 'if you bring any wine, I can't bear to stay.'

Miss Margland said the same; but he whistled, and looked round him without answering.

Mrs. Berlinton, who, though she had thought his uncommonly fine person an excuse for his intrusion, thought nothing could excuse this ill-breeding, proposed they should leave the tea-table, and walk.

'Sit still, ladies,' said Mr. Westwyn, 'and drink your tea in peace.' Then, turning to Lynmere, 'I wonder,' he cried, 'you a'n't ashamed of yourself! If you were a son of mine, I'll tell you what; I'd lock you up! I'd serve you as I did when I carried you over to Leipsic, eight years ago. I always hated pert boys. I can't fancy 'em.'

Lynmere, affecting not to hear him, though inwardly firing, called violently after a waiter; and, in mere futile vengeance, not only gave an order for Champagne, but demanded some Stilton cheese.

'Cheese!' exclaimed Miss Margland, 'if you order any cheese, I can't so much as stay in the room. Think what a nauseous smell it will make!'

The man answered, they had no Stilton cheese in the house, but the very best of every other sort.

Lynmere, who had only given this command to shew his defiance of control, seized, with equal avidity, the opportunity to abuse the waiter; affirming he belonged to the worst served hotel in Christendom.

The man walked off in dudgeon, and Mr. Westwyn, losing his anger in his astonishment at this effrontery, said, 'And pray, Mr. Lynmere, what do you pretend to know of Stilton cheese?[1] do they make it at Leipsic? did you ever so much as taste it in your life?'

'O, yes! excellent! excellentissimo! I can eat no other.'

'Eat no other! it's well my Hal don't say the same! I'd churn him to a cheese himself if he did! And pray, Mr. Lynmere, be so good as to let me know how you got it there?'

'Ways and means, sir; ways and means!'

'Why you did not send across the sea for it?'

'A travelled man, sir, thinks no more of what you call across the sea, than you, that live always over your own fire-side, think of stepping across a kennel.'[2]

'Well, sir, well,' said the old gentleman, now very much piqued, 'I can't but say I feel some concern for my old friend, to have his money doused about at such a rantipole rate.[3] A boy to be sending over out of Germany into England for Stilton cheese! I wish it had been Hal with all my heart! I promise you I'd have given him enough of it. If the least little thought of the kind was but once to have got in his head, I'd have taken my best oaken stick, and have done him the good office to have helped it out for him: and have made him thank me after too! I hate daintiness;[4] especially in boys. I have no great patience with it.'

Only more incensed, Lynmere called aloud for his Champagne. The waiter civilly told him, it was not usual to bring wine during tea: but he persisted; and Mr. Westwyn, who saw the ladies all rising, authoritatively, told the waiter to mind no such directions. Lynmere, who had entered the ball-room in his riding-dress,[5] raised a switch at the man, which he durst not raise at Mr. Westwyn, and protested, in a threatening attitude, he would lay it across his shoulders, if he obeyed not. The man, justly provoked, thought himself authorised to snatch if from him: Clermont resisted; a fierce scuffle ensued; and though Henry, by immediate intervention, could have parted them, Mr. Westwyn insisted there should be no interference, saying, 'If any body's helped, let it be the waiter; for he's here to do his duty: he don't come only to behave unmannerly, for his own pleasure. And if I see him hard run, it's odds but I lend him my own fist to right him.—I like fair play.'

The female party, in very serious alarm at this unpleasant scene, rose to hurry away. Lord Valhurst was ambitious to suffice as guardian to both his fair charges; but Henry, when prohibited from stopping the affray, offered his services to Camilla, who could not refuse them; and Mrs. Berlinton, active and impatient, flew on foremost; with more speed than his lordship could follow, or even keep in sight. Indiana was handed out by her new adorer, the young baronet; and Eugenia was assisted by her new assailer, the young nobleman.

Edgar, who had hurried to Camilla at the first tumult, was stung to the heart to see who handed her away; and, forcing a passage, followed, till Henry, the envied Henry, deposited her in the carriage of Mrs. Berlinton.

The confusion in the room, meanwhile, was not likely soon to decrease, for old Mr. Westwyn, delighted by this mortifying chastisement to Clermont, would permit neither mediation nor assistance on his side; saying, with great glee, 'It will do him a great deal of good! My poor old friend will bless me for it. This is a better lesson than he got in all Leipsic. Let him feel that a Man's a Man; and not take it into his head a person's to stand still to be switched, when he's doing his duty, according to his calling. Switching a man is a bad thing. I can't say I like it. A gentleman should always use good words; and then a poor man's proud to serve him; or, if he's insolent for nothing, he may trounce him and welcome. I've no objection.'

Miss Margland, meanwhile, had not been remiss in what she esteemed a most capital feminine accomplishment, screaming; though, in its exercise, she had failed of any success; since, while her voice called remark, her countenance repelled its effect. Yet as she saw that not one lady of the group retreated unattended, she thought it a disgrace to seem the only female, who, from internal courage, or external neglect, should retire alone; she therefore called upon Dr. Orkborne, conjuring, in a shrill and pathetic voice, meant more for all who surrounded than for himself, that he would protect her.

The Doctor, who had kept his place in defiance of all sort of inconvenience, either to himself or to others; and who, with some curiosity, was viewing the combat, which he was mentally comparing with certain pugilistic games of old, was now, for the first time in the evening, receiving some little entertainment, and therefore composedly answered, 'I have a very good place here, ma'am; and I would rather not quit it till this scene is over.'

'So you won't come, then, Doctor?' cried she, modulating into a soft whine the voice which rage, not terror, rendered tremulous.

Dr. Orkborne, who was any thing rather than loquacious, having given one answer, said no more.

Miss Margland appealed to all present upon the indecorum of a lady's being kept to witness such unbecoming violence, and upon the unheard-of inattention of the Doctor: but a short, 'Certainly!—' 'To be sure, ma'am!—' or, 'It's very shocking indeed!' with a hasty decampment from her neighbourhood, was all of sympathy she procured.

The entrance, at length, of the master of the house, stopt the affray, by calling off the waiter. Clermont, then, though wishing to extirpate old Westwyn from the earth, and ready to eat his own flesh with fury at the double digrace he had endured, affected a loud halloo, as if he had been contending for his amusement; and protesting Bob, the waiter, was a fine fellow, went off with great apparent satisfaction.

'Now, then, at least, sir,' cried Miss Margland, imperiously to the Doctor, who, still ruminating upon the late contest, kept his seat, 'I suppose you'll condescend to take care of me to the coach?'

'These modern clothes are very much in the way,' said the Doctor, gravely; 'and give a bad effect to attitudes.' He rose, however, but not knowing what *to take care of a lady to a coach* meant, stood resolutely still, till she was forced, in desperation, to walk on alone. He then slowly followed, keeping many paces behind, notwithstanding her continually looking back; and when, with a heavy sigh at her hard fate, she got, unassisted, into the carriage, where her young ladies were waiting, he tranquilly mounted after her, tolerably reconciled to the loss of his evening, by some new annotations it had suggested for his work, relative to the games of antiquity.

CHAPTER X

A Youthful Effusion

CAMILLA now thought herself safe in harbour; the storms all over, the dangers all past, and but a light gale or two wanting to make good her landing on the bosom of permanent repose. This gale, this propitious gale, she thought ready to blow at her call; for she deemed it no other than the breath of jealousy. She had seen Edgar, though he knew her to be protected, follow her to the coach, and she had seen, by the light afforded from the lamps of the carriage, that her safety from the crowd and tumult was not the sole object of his watchfulness, since though that, at the instant she turned round, was obviously secure, his countenance exhibited the strongest marks of disturbance. The secret spring, therefore, she now thought, that was to re-unite them, was in her own possession.

All the counsels of Mrs. Arlbery upon this subject occurred to her; and imagining she had hitherto erred from a simple facility, she rejoiced in the accident which had pointed her to a safer path, and shewn her that, in the present disordered state of the opinions of Edgar, the only way to a lasting accommodation was to alarm his security, by asserting her own independence.

Her difficulty, however, was still considerable as to the means. The severe punishment she had received, and the self blame and penitence she had incurred, from her experiment with Sir Sedley Clarendel, all rendered, too, abortive, by Edgar's contempt of the object, determined her to suffer no hopes, no feelings of her own, to engross her ever more from weighing those of another. The end, therefore, of her deliberation was to shew general gaiety, without appropriate favour, and to renew solicitude on his part by a displayed ease of mind on her own.

Elated with this idea, she determined upon every possible public exhibition by which she could execute it to the best advantage. Mrs. Berlinton had but to appear, to secure the most fashionable persons at Southampton for her parties, and soon renewed the same course of life she had lived at Tunbridge, of seeing company either at home or abroad every day, except when some accidental plan offered a scheme of more novelty.

Upon all these occasions, young Westwyn, though wholly

unsought, and even unthought of by Camilla, was instinctively and incautiously the most alert to second her plan; he was her first partner when she danced, her constant attendant when she walked, and always in wait to converse with her when she was seated; while, not purposing to engage him, she perceived not his fast growing regard, and intending to be open to all alike, observed not the thwarting effect to her design of this peculiar assiduity.

By old Mr. Westwyn this intercourse was yet more urgently forwarded. Bewitched with Camilla, he carried his son to her wherever she appeared, and said aloud to every body but herself: 'If the boy and girl like one another, they shall have one another; and I won't inquire what she's worth; for she thinks so well of my son, that I'd rather he'd have her than an empress. Money goes but a little way to make people happy; and true love's not a thing to be got every day; so if she has a mind to my Hal, and Hal has a mind to her, why, if they have not enough, he must work hard and get more. I don't like to cross young people. Better let a man labour with his hands, than fret away his spirit. Neither a boy nor a girl are good for much when they've got their hearts broke.'

This new experiment of Camilla, like every other deduced from false reasoning, and formed upon false principles, was flattering in its promise, pernicious in its progress, and abortive in its performance. Edgar saw with agony what he conceived the ascendance of a new attachment built upon the declension of all regard for himself; and in the first horror of his apprehensions, would have resisted the supplanter by enforcing his own final claim; but Dr. Marchmont represented that, since he had heard in silence his right to that claim solemnly withdrawn, he had better first ascertain if this apparent connection with young Westwyn were the motive, or only the consequence of that resumption: 'If the first be the case,' he added, 'you must trust her no more; a heart so inflammable as to be kindled into passion by a mere accidental blaze of gallantry and valour, can have nothing in consonance with the chaste purity and fidelity your character requires and merits: If the last, investigate whether the net in which she is entangling herself is that of levity, delighting in change, or of pique, disguising its own agitation in efforts to agitate others.'

'Alas!' cried the melancholy Edgar, 'in either case, she is no more the artless Camilla I first adored! that fatal connection at the

Grove, formed while her character, pure, white, and spotless, was in its enchanting, but dangerous state of first ductility, has already broken into that clear transparent singleness of mind, so beautiful in its total ignorance of every species of scheme, every sort of double measure, every idea of secret view and latent expedient!'

'Repine not, however, at the connection till you know whether she owe to it her defects, or only their manifestation. A man should see the woman he would marry in many situations, ere he can judge what chance he may have of happiness with her in any. Though now and then 'tis a blessed, 'tis always a perilous state; but the man who has to weather its storms, should not be remiss in studying the clouds which precede them.'

'Ah, Doctor! by this delay . . . by these experiments . . . should I lose her! . . . .'

'If by finding her unworthy, where is the loss?'

Edgar sighed, but acknowledged this question to be un-answerable.

'Think, my dear young friend, what would be your sufferings to discover any radical, inherent failing, when irremediably her's! run not into the very common error of depending upon the gratitude of your wife after marriage, for the inequality of her fortune before your union. She who has no fortune at all, owes you no more for your alliance, than she who has thousands; for you do not marry her because she has no fortune! you marry her because you think she has some endowment, mental or personal, which you conclude will conduce to your happiness; and she, on her part, accepts you, because she supposes you or your situation will contribute to her's. The object may be differ-ent, but neither side is indebted to the other, since each has self, only, in contemplation; and thus, in fact, rich or poor, high or low, whatever be the previous distinction between the parties, on the hour of marriage they begin as equals. The obligation and the debt of gratitude can only commence when the knot is tied: self, then, may give way to sympathy; and whichever, from that moment, most considers the other, becomes immediately the creditor in the great account of life and happiness.'

*   *   *   *

While Camilla, in gay ignorance of danger, and awake only to hope, pursued her new course, Eugenia had the infinite delight of improving daily and even hourly in the good graces of Mrs. Berlinton; who soon discovered how wide from justice to that excellent young creature was all judgment that could be formed from her appearance. She found that she was as elegant in her taste for letters as herself, and far more deeply cultivated in their knowledge; that her manners were gentle, her sentiments were elevated, yet that her mind was humble; the same authors delighted and the same passages struck them; they met every morning; they thought every morning too short, and their friendship, in a very few days, knit by so many bands of sympathy, was as fully established as that which already Mrs. Berlinton had formed with Camilla.

To Eugenia this treaty of amity was a delicious poison, which, while it enchanted her faculties by day, preyed upon her vitals by night. She frequently saw Melmond, and though a melancholy bow was almost all the notice she ever obtained from him, the countenance with which he made it, his air, his figure, his face, nay his very dress, for the half instant he bestowed upon her, occupied all her thoughts till she saw him again, and had another to con over and dwell upon.

Melmond, inexpressibly wretched at the deprivation of all hope of Indiana, at the very period when fortune seemed to favour his again pursuing her, dreamt not of this partiality. His time was devoted to deliberating upon some lucrative scheme of future life, which his literary turn of mind rendered difficult of selection, and which his refined love of study and retirement made hateful to him to undertake.

He was kind, however, and even consoling to his aunt, who saw his nearly desolate state with a compunction bitterly increased by finding she had thrown their joint properties, with her own person, into the hands of a rapacious tyrant. To soften her repentance, and allow her the soothing of all she could spare of her own time, Mrs. Berlinton invited her to her own house. Mr. Ulst, of course included in the invitation, made the removal with alacrity, not for the pleasure it procured his wife, but for the money it saved himself; and Mrs. Mittin voluntarily resigned to them the apartment she had chosen for her own, by way of a little peace-offering for her undesired length of stay; for still, though incessantly Camilla inquired for her account, she had received no answer from the creditors, and was obliged to wait for another and another post.

Mrs. Ulst, though not well enough, at present, to see company, and at all times, fanatically averse to every species of recreation, could not entirely avoid Eugenia, whose visits were constant every morning, and whose expected inheritance made a similar wish occur for her nephew, with that which had disposed of her niece; for she flattered herself that if once she could see them both in possession of greath wealth, her mind would be more at ease.

She communicated this idea to Mr. Ulst, who, most willing, also, to get rid of the reproach of the poverty and ruin of Melmond, imparted it, with strong exhortation for its promotion, to the young man; but he heard with disdain the mercenary project, and protested he would daily labour for his bread, in preference to prostituting his probity, by soliciting a regard he could never return, for the acquirement of a fortune which he never could merit.

Mr. Ulst, much too hard to feel this as any reflection upon himself, applied for the interest of Mrs. Berlinton; but she so completely thought with her brother, that she would not interfere, till Mr. Ulst made some observations upon Eugenia herself, that inclined her to waver.

He soon remarked, in that young and artless character, the symptoms of the partiality she had conceived in favour of Melmond, which, when once pointed out, could not be mistaken by Mrs Berlinton, who, though more than equally susceptible with Eugenia, was self-occupied, and saw neither her emotion at his name, nor her timid air at his approach, till Mr. Ulst, whose discernment had been quickened by his wishes, told her when, and for what, to look.

Touched now, herself, by the double happiness that might ensue, from a gratified choice to Eugenia, and a noble fortune to her brother, she took up the cause, with delicacy, yet with pity; representing all the charming mental and intellectual accomplishments of Eugenia, and beseeching him not to sacrifice both his interest and his peace, in submitting to a hopeless passion for one object, while he inflicted all its horrors upon another.

Melmond, amazed and softened, listened and sighed; but protested such a change, from all of beauty to all of deformity, was

impracticable; and that though he revered the character she
painted, and was sensible to the honour of such a preference, he
must be base, double, and perjured, to take advantage of her
great, yet unaccountable goodness, by heartless professions of
feigned participation.

Mrs. Berlinton, to whom sentiment was irresistible, urged the
matter no longer, but wept over her brother, with compassionate
admiration.

Another day only passed, when Mrs. Mittin picked up a paper
upon the stairs, which she saw fall from the pocket of Eugenia, in
drawing out her handkerchief, but which, determining to read ere
she returned, she found contained these lines.

'O Reason! friend of the troubled breast, guide of the wayward
fancy, moderator of the flights of hope, and sinkings of despair,
Eugenia calls thee!'

> O! to a feeble, suppliant Maid,
> Light of Reason, lend thy aid!
> And with thy mild, thy lucid ray,
>> Point her the way
> To genial calm and mental joy!
> From Passion far! whose flashes bright
>> Startle—affright—
>> Yet ah! invite!
> With varying powers attract, repel,
>> Now fiercely beam,
>> Now softly gleam,
>> With magic spell
> Charm to consume, win to destroy!
> Ah! lead her from the chequer'd glare
>> So false, so fair!—
> Ah, quick from Passion bid her fly,
> Its sway repulse, its wiles defy;
> And to a feeble, suppliant heart
> Thy aid, O Reason's light, impart!

> Next, Eugenia, point thy prayer
>> That He whom all thy wishes bless,
>> Whom all thy tenderest thoughts confess,
> Thy calm may prove, thy peace may share.
> O, if the griefs to him assign'd,

To thee might pass—thy strengthened mind
Would meet all woe, support all pain,
Suffering despise, complaint disdain,
Brac'd with new nerves each ill would brave,
From Melmond but one pang to save!'

Overjoyed by the possession of the important secret this little juvenile effusion of tenderness betrayed, Mrs. Mittin ran with it to Mrs. Berlinton, and without mentioning she had seen whence the paper came, said she had found it upon the stairs: for even those who have too little delicacy to attribute to treachery a clandestine indulgence of curiosity, have a certain instinctive sense of its unfairness, which they evince without avowing, by the care with which they soften their motives, or their manner, of according themselves this species of gratification.

Mrs. Berlinton, who scrupulously would have withheld from looking into a letter, could not see a copy of verses, and recognise the hand of Eugenia, already known to her by frequent notes, and refrain reading. That she should find any thing personal, did not occur to her; to peruse, therefore, a manuscript ode or sonnet, which the humility of Eugenia might never voluntarily reveal, caused her no hesitation; and she ran through the lines with the warmest delight, till, coming suddenly upon the end, she burst into tears, and flew to the apartment of her brother.

She put the paper into his hand without a word. He read it hastily. Surprised, confounded, disordered, he looked at his sister for some explanation or comment; she was still silently in tears; he read it again, and with yet greater emotion; when, holding it back to her, 'Why, my sister,' he cried, 'why would she give you this? why would you deliver it? Ah! leave me, in pity, firm in integrity, though fallen in fortune!'

'My brother, my dear brother, this matchless creature merits not so degrading an idea; she gave me not the precious paper . . . she knows not I possess it; it was found upon the stairs: Ah! far from thus openly confessing her unhappy prepossession, she conceals it from every human being; even her beloved sister, I am convinced, is untrusted; upon paper only she has breathed it, and breathed it as you see . . . with a generosity of soul that is equal to the delicacy of her conduct.'

Melmond now felt subdued. To have excited such a regard in a mind that seemed so highly cultivated, and so naturally elegant, could not fail to touch him; and the concluding line deeply penetrated him with tender though melancholy gratitude. He took the hand of his sister, returned her the paper, and was going to say: 'Do whatever you think proper;' but the idea of losing all right to adore Indiana checked and silenced him; and mournfully telling her he required a little time for reflection, he entreated to be left to himself.

He was not suffered to ruminate in quiet; Mrs. Mittin, proud of having any thing to communicate to a relation of Mrs. Berlinton's, made an opportunity to sit with Mrs. Ulst, purposely to communicate to her the discovery that Miss Eugenia Tyrold was in love with, and wrote verses upon, her nephew. Melmond was instantly sent for; the important secret was enlarged upon with remonstrances so pathetic, not to throw away such an invitation to the most brilliant good fortune, in order to cast himself, with his vainly nourished passion, upon immediate hardships, or lasting penury; that reason as well as interest, compelled him to listen; and, after a severe conflict, he gave his reluctant promise to see Eugenia upon her next visit, and endeavour to bias his mind to the connexion that seemed likely to ensue.

Camilla, who was in total ignorance of the whole of this business, received, during the dinner, an incoherent note from her sister, conjuring that she would search immediately, but privately, in her own chamber, in the dressing-room of Mrs. Berlinton, in the hall, and upon the stairs, for a paper in her handwriting, which she had somewhere lost, but which she besought her, by all that she held dear, not to read when she found; protesting she should shut herself up for ever from the whole world, if a syllable of what she had written on that paper were read by a human being.

Camilla could not endure to keep her sister a moment in this suspensive state, and made an excuse for quitting the table that she might instantly seek the manuscript. Melmond and Mrs. Berlinton both conjectured the contents of the billet, and felt much for the modest and timid Eugenia; but Mrs. Mittin could not confine herself to silent suggestion; she rose also, and running after Camilla, said: 'My dear Miss, has your sister sent to you to look for any thing?'

Camilla asked the meaning of her inquiry; and she then owned she had picked up, from the stairs, a sort of love letter, in which Miss Eugenia had wrote couplets upon Mr. Melmond.

Inexpressibly astonished, Camilla demanded their restoration: this soon produced a complete explanation, and while, with equal surprise and concern, she learnt the secret of Eugenia, and its discovery to its object, she could not but respect and honour all she gathered from Mrs. Berlinton of the behaviour of her brother upon the detection; and his equal freedom from presumptuous vanity, or mercenary projects, induced her to believe her sister's choice, though wholly new to her, was well founded; and that if he could conquer his early propensity for Indiana, he seemed, of all the characters she knew, Edgar alone and always excepted, the most peculiarly formed for the happiness of Eugenia.

She begged to have the paper, and entreated her sister might never know into whose hands it had fallen. This was cheerfully agreed to; but Mrs. Mittin, during the conference, had already flown to Eugenia, and amidst a torrent of offers of service, and professions of power to do any thing she pleased for her, suffered her to see that her attachment was betrayed to the whole house.

The agony of Eugenia was excessive; and she resolved to keep her chamber till she returned to Cleves, that she might neither see nor be seen any more by Melmond nor his family. Scarce could she bear to be broken in upon even by Camilla, who tenderly hastened to console her. She hid her blushing conscious face, and protested she would inhabit only her own apartment for the rest of her life.

The active Mrs. Mittin failed not to carry back the history of this resolution; and Melmond, to his unspeakable regret in being thus precipitated, thought himself called upon in all decency and propriety to an immediate declaration. He could not, however, assume fortitude to make it in person; nor yet was his mind sufficiently composed for writing; he commissioned, therefore, his sister to be the bearer of his overtures.

He charged her to make no mention of the verses, which it was fitting should, on his part, pass unnoticed, though she could not but be sensible his present address was their consequence; he desired her simply to state his high reverence for her virtues and talents, and his consciousness of the inadequacy of his pretensions to any claim upon them, except what arose from the grateful integrity of esteem with which her happiness should become the first object of his future life, if she forbade not his application for the consent of Sir Hugh and Mr. Tyrold to solicit her favour.

With respect to Indiana, he begged her, unless questioned, to be wholly silent. To say his flame for that adorable creature was extinguished would be utterly false; but his peace, as much as his honour, would lead him to combat, henceforth, by all the means in his power, his ill-fated and woe-teeming passion.

This commission was in perfect consonance with the feelings of Mrs. Berlinton, who, though with difficulty she gained admission, executed it with the most tender delicacy to the terrified Eugenia, who, amazed and trembling, pale and incredulous, so little understood what she heard, so little was able to believe what she wished, that, when Mrs. Berlinton, with an affectionate embrace, begged her answer, she asked if it was not Indiana of whom she was speaking!

Mrs. Berlinton then thought it right to be explicit: she acknowledged the early passion of her brother for that young lady, but stated that, long before he had ventured to think of herself, he had determined its conquest; and that what originally was the prudence of compulsion, was now, from his altered prospects in life, become choice: 'And believe me,' added she, 'from my long and complete knowledge of the honour and the delicacy of his opinion, as well as of the tenderness and gratitude of his nature, the woman who shall once receive his vows, will find his life devoted to the study of her happiness.'

Eugenia flew into her arms, hung upon her bosom, wept, blushed, smiled, and sighed, alternately; one moment wished Indiana in possession of her fortune, the next thought she herself, in all but beauty, more formed for his felicity, and ultimately gave her tacit but transported consent to the application.

Melmond, upon receiving it, heaved what he fondly hoped would be his last sigh for Indiana; and ordering his horse, set off immediately for Cleves and Etherington; determined frankly to state his small income and crushed expectations; and feeling almost equally indifferent to acceptance or rejection.

Camilla devoted the afternoon to her agitated but enraptured sister, who desired her secret might spread no further, till the will of her father and uncle should decide its fate; but the loquacious Mrs. Mittin, having some cheap ribands and fine edgings to recommend to Miss Margland and Indiana, could by no means refrain from informing them, at the same time, of the discovered manuscript.

'Poor thing!' cried Indiana, 'I really pity her. I don't think,' imperceptibly gliding towards the glass; 'I don't think, by what I have seen of Mr. Melmond, she has much chance; I've a notion he's rather more difficult.'

'Really this is what I always expected!' said Miss Margland; 'It's just exactly what one might look for from one of your learned educations, which I always despised with all my heart. Writing love verses at fifteen! Dr. Orkborne's made a fine hand of her! I always hated him, from the very first. However, I've had nothing to do with the bringing her up, that's my consolation! I thank Heaven I never made a verse in my life! and I never intend it.'

CHAPTER XI

The Computations of Self-Love

CAMILLA left her sister to accompany Mrs. Berlinton to the Rooms; no other mode remaining for seeing Edgar, who, since her rejection, had held back from repeating his attempt of visiting Mrs. Berlinton.

In mutual solicitude, mutual watchfulness, and mutual trials of each other's hearts and esteem, a week had already passed, without one hope being extirpated, or one doubt allayed. This evening was somewhat more, though less pleasantly decisive.

Accident, want of due consideration, and sudden recollection, in an agitated moment, of the worldly doctrine of Mrs. Arlbery, had led Camilla, once more, into the semblance of a character, which, without thinking of, she was acting. Born simple and ingenuous, and bred to hold in horror every species of art, all idea of coquetry was foreign to her meaning, though an untoward contrariety of circumstances, playing upon feelings too potent for deliberations, had eluded her into a conduct as mischievous in its effects and as wide from artlessness in its appearance, as if she had been brought up and nourished in fashionable egotism.

Such, however, was not Camilla: her every propensity was pure, and, when reflection came to her aid, her conduct was as exemplary as her wishes. But the ardour of her imagination, acted upon by every passing idea, shook her Judgment from its yet unsteady seat, and left her at the mercy of wayward Sensibility—that delicate, but irregular power, which now impels to all that is most disinterested for others, now forgets all mankind, to watch the pulsations of its own fancies.

This evening brought her back to recollection.—Young Westwyn, urged by what he deemed encouragement, and prompted by his impatient father, spoke of his intended visit to Cleves, and introduction to Sir Hugh, in terms of such animated pleasure, and with a manner of such open admiration, that she could not mistake the serious purposes which he meant to imply.

Alarmed, she looked at him; but the expression of his eyes was not such as to still her suspicions. Frightened at what now she first observed, she turned from him, gravely, meaning to avoid conversing with him the rest of the evening; but her caution came too late; her first civilities had flattered both him and his father into a belief of her favour, and this sudden drawback he imputed only to virgin modesty, which but added to the fervour of his devoirs.

Camilla now perceived her own error: the perseverance of young Westwyn not merely startled, but appalled her. His character, unassuming, though spirited, was marked by a general decency and propriety of demeanour, that would not presumptuously brave distancing; and awakened her, therefore, to a review of her own conduct, as it related or as it might seem, to himself.

And here, not all the guiltlessness of her intentions could exonerate her from blame with that finely scrutinizing monitor to which Heaven, in pity to those evil propensities that law cannot touch, nor society reclaim, has devolved its earthly jurisdiction in the human breast. With her hopes she could play, with her wishes she could trifle, her intentions she could defend, her designs she could relinquish—but with her conscience she could not combat. It pointed beyond the present moment; it took her back to her imprudence with Sir Sedley Clarendel, which should have taught her more circumspection; and it carried her on to the disappointment of Henry and his father, whom while heedlessly she had won, though without the most remote view to beguile, she might seem artfully to have caught, for the wanton vanity of rejecting.

While advice and retrospection were thus alike oppressive in accusation, her pensive air and withdrawn smiles proved but more endearing to young Westwyn, whose internal interpretation was so little adapted to render them formidable, that his assiduities were but more tender, and allowed her no repose.

Edgar, who with the most suffering suspense, observed her unusual seriousness, and its effect upon Henry, drew from it, with the customary ingenuity of sensitive minds to torment themselves, the same inference for his causeless torture, as proved to his rival a delusive blessing. But while thus he contemplated Henry as the most to be envied of mortals, a new scene called forth new surprise, and gave birth to yet new doubts in his mind. He saw Camilla not merely turn wholly away from his rival, but enter into conversation, and give, apparently, her whole attention to Lord Valhurst, who, it was palpable, only spoke to her of her charms, which, alternately with those of Mrs. Berlinton, he devoted his whole time to worshipping.

Camilla by this action, meant simply to take the quickest road she saw in her power to shew young Westwyn his mistake. Lord Valhurst she held nearly in aversion; for, though his vindication of his upright motives at the bathing-house, joined to her indifference in considering him either guilty or innocent, made her conclude he might be blameless in that transaction, his perpetual compliments, enforced by staring eyes and tender glances, wearied and disgusted her. But he was always by her side, when not in the same position with Mrs. Berlinton; and while his readiness to engage her made this her easiest expedient, his time of life persuaded her it was the safest. Little aware of the effect this produced upon Edgar, she imagined he would not more notice her in any conversation with Lord Valhurst, than if she were discoursing with her uncle.

But while she judged from the sincerity of reality, she thought not of the mischief of appearance. What in her was designed with innocence, was rendered suspicious to the observers by the looks and manner of her companion. The pleasure with which he found, at last, that incense received, which hitherto had been slighted, gave new zest to an adulation which, while Camilla endured merely to shew her coldness to young Westwyn, seemed to Edgar to be offered with a gross presumption of welcome, that must result from an opinion it was addressed to a confirmed coquette.

Offended in his inmost soul by this idea, he scarce desired to know if she were now stimulated most by a wish to torment Henry, or himself, or only by the general pleasure she found in this new mode of amusement. 'Be it,' cried he, to Dr. Marchmont, 'as it may, with me all is equally over! I seek not to recall an attachment liable to such intermissions, such commotions. What would be my peace, my tranquillity, with a companion so un-stable? A mind all at large in its pursuits?—a dissipated wife!—No!—I will remain here but to let her know I acquiesce in her dismission, and to learn in what form she has communicated our breach to her friends.'

Dr. Marchmont was silent, and they walked out of the room together; leaving the deceived Camilla persuaded he was so indifferent with regard to the old peer, that all her influence was lost, and all her late exertions were thrown away, by one evening's remissness in exciting his fears of a young rival.

*   *   *   *

Melmond returned to Southampton the next morning with an air of deep and settled melancholy. He had found the two brothers together, and the candour of his appearance, the plainness of his declaration, the openness with which he stated his situation, and his near relationship to Mrs. Berlinton, procured him a courteous hearing; and he soon saw that both the father and the uncle, though they desired time for consideration and inquiry, were disposed to favour him. Mr. Tyrold, though, to his acknow-ledged recent disappointment of fortune, he attributed his address, had so little hope that any man at once amiable and rich would present himself to his unfortunate Eugenia, that, when he saw a gentleman well educated, well allied, of pleasing manners, and with every external promise of a good and feeling character, modestly, and with no professions but of esteem and respect, seek her of her friends, he thought himself not even entitled to refuse him. He told him, however, that he could conclude upon nothing in a matter of such equal interest to himself and his wife, without her knowledge and concurrence; and that during the time he demanded before he gave a final answer, he required a forbear-ance of all intercourse, beyond that of a common acquaintance. His first design was immediately to send for Eugenia home; but the young man appeared so reasonable, so mild, so unlike a fortune-hunter, that, constitutionally indulgent where he apprehended nothing criminal, he contented himself with writing to the same effect to Eugenia, fully satisfied of her scrupulous punctuality, when once his will was known.

Melmond, though thus well received, returned back to Southampton with any air rather than that of a bridegroom. The order, not to wait upon Eugenia in private, was the only part of his task he performed with satisfaction; for though a mind really virtuous made him wish to conquer his repugnance to his future partner, he felt it could not be by comparing her with Indiana.

Eugenia received the letter of her father, written in his own and her uncle's name, with transport; and, to testify her grateful obedience, resolved to name the impending transaction to no one, and even to relinquish her visits to Mrs. Berlinton, and only to see Melmond when accident brought him before her in public.

But Mrs. Mittin, through words casually dropt, or conversations not very delicately overheard, soon gathered the particulars of her situation, which happily furnished her with a new subject for a gossiping visit to Miss Margland and Indiana. The first of these ladies received the news with unconcern, rather pleased than otherwise, that the temptation of an heiress should be removed from any rivalry with the charms of her fair pupil; who, by no means, however, listened to the account with equal indifference. The sight of Melmond at Southampton, with the circumstance of his being brother to the Honourable Mrs. Berlinton, had awakened all the pleasure with which she had first met his impassioned admiration; and while she haughtily expected from every public exhibition, 'to bring home hearts by dozens,' the secret point she had in view, was shewing Melmond that her power over others was as mighty as it had been over himself. She had not taken the trouble to ask with what end: what was passed never afforded her an observation; what was to come never called forth an idea. Occupied only by the present moment, things gone remained upon her memory but as matters of fact, and all her expectations she looked forward to but as matters of course. To lose, therefore, a conquest she had thought the victim of her beauty for life, was a surprise nearly incredible; to lose him to Eugenia an affront scarcely supportable; and she waited but an opportunity to kill him with her disdain. But Melmond, who dreaded nothing so much as an interview, availed himself of the commands of Mr. Tyrold, in not going to the lodgings of Eugenia, and lived absorbed in a melancholy retirement, which books alone could a little alleviate.

The conclusion of the letter of Mr. Tyrold gave to Camilla as much pain as every other part of it gave to Eugenia pleasure: it was an earnest and parentally tender prayer, that the alliance with Melmond, should his worth appear such as to authorise its taking place, might prove the counterpart to the happiness so sweetly promised from that of her sister with Edgar.

While Camilla sighed to consider how wide from the certainty with which he mentioned it was such an event, she blushed that he should thus be uninformed of her insecurity: but while a reconciliation was not more her hope than her expectation with every rising sun, she could not endure to break his repose with the knowledge of a suspense she thought as disgraceful as it was unhappy. Yet her present scheme to accelerate its termination, became difficult even of trial.

The obviously serious regard of Henry was a continual reproach to her; and the undisguised approbation of his father was equally painful. Yet she could now only escape them by turning to some other, and that other was necessarily Lord Valhurst, whose close siege to her notice forced off every assailant but himself. This the deluded Camilla thought an expedient the most innoxious; and gave to him so much of her time, that his susceptibility to the charms of youth and beauty was put to a trial beyond his fortitude; and, in a very few days, notwithstanding their disproportion in age, his embarrassed though large estates, and the little or no fortune which she had in view, he determined to marry her: for when a man of rank and riches resolves to propose himself to a woman who has neither, he conceives his acceptance not a matter of doubt.

In any other society, his admiration of Camilla might easily, like what he had already experienced and forgotten for thousands of her sex, have escaped so grave or decided a tendency; but in Mrs. Berlinton he saw so much of youth and beauty bestowed upon a man whom he knew to be his own senior in age, that the idea of a handsome young wife was perpetually present to him. He weighed, like all people who seek to entice themselves to their own wishes, but one side of the question; and risked, like all who succeed in such self-seduction, the inconvenience of finding out the other side too late. He saw the attractions of his fair kinswoman; but neglected to consider of how little avail they were to her husband; he thought, with exultation of that husband's age, and almost childishness; but forgot to take into the scales, that they had obtained from his youthful choice only disgust and avoidance.

While he waited for some trinkets, which he had ordered from town, to have ready for presenting with his proposals, Edgar only sought an opportunity and courage to take his last farewell. Whenever Camilla was so much engaged with others that it was impossible to approach her, he thought himself capable of uttering an eternal adieu; but when, by any opening, he saw where and how he might address her, his feet refused to move, his tongue became parched, and his pleading heart seemed exclaiming: O, not to-night! yet, yet, another day, ere Camilla is parted with for ever!

But suddenly, soon after, Camilla ceased to appear. At the rooms, at the plays, at the balls, and at the private assemblies, Edgar looked for her in vain. Her old adulator, also, vanished from public places, while her young admirer and his father hovered about in them as usual, but spiritless, comfortless, and as if in the same search as himself.

CHAPTER XII

Juvenile Calculations

MRS. NORFIELD, a lady whom circumstances had brought into some intimacy with Mrs. Berlinton upon her marriage, had endeavoured, from the first of her entrance into high life, to draw her into a love of play; not with an idea of doing her any mischief, for she was no more her enemy than her friend; but to answer her own purposes of having a Faro[1] table under her own direction. She was a woman of fashion, and as such every-where received; but her fortune was small, and her passion for gaming inordinate; and as there was not, at this time, one Faro table at Southampton, whither she was ordered for her health,[1] she was almost wearied into a lethargy, till her reiterated intreaties prevailed, at length, with Mrs. Berlinton to hold one at her own house.

The fatigue of life without view, the peril of talents without prudence, and the satiety of pleasure without intermission, were already dangerously assaulting the early independence and the moment of vacancy and weariness was seized by Mrs. Norfield, to press the essay of a new mode of amusement.

Mrs. Berlinton's house opened, failed not to be filled; and opened for a Faro table, to be filled with a peculiar set. To game has, unfortunately, always its attractions; to game with a perfect novice is not what will render it less alluring; and to see that novice rich and beautiful is still less likely to be repelling.

Mr. Berlinton, when he made this marriage, supposed he had engaged for life a fair nurse to his infirmities; but when he saw her fixed aversion, he had not spirit to cope with it; and when she had always an excuse for a separation, he had not the sense to acquaint himself how she passed her time in his absence. A natural imbecility of mind was now nearly verging upon dotage, and as he rarely quitted his room but at meal times, she made a point never to see him in any other part of the day. Her antipathy rendered her obdurate, though her disposition was gentle, and she had now left him at Tunbridge, to meet her aunt at Southampton, with a knowledge he was too ill to follow her, and a determination, upon various pretences, to stay away from him for some months. The ill fate of such unequal alliances is almost daily exemplified in life; and though few young brides of old bridegrooms fly their mates thus openly and decidedly, their retainers have seldom much cause to rejoice in superior happiness, since they are generally regarded but as the gaolers of their young prey.

Moderation was the last praise to which Mrs. Berlinton had any claim; what she entered upon through persecution, in an interval of mental supineness, she was soon awake to as a pleasure, and next pursued as a passion. Her beloved correspondent was neglected; her favourite authors were set aside; her country rambles were given up; balls and the rooms were forgotten; and Faro alone engrossed her faculties by day, and her dreams during the short epoch she reserved for sleep at night. She lost, as might be expected, as constantly as she played; but as money was not what she naturally valued, she disdained to weigh that circumstance; and so long as she had any to pay, resigned it with more grace than by others it was won.

That Camilla was not caught by this ruinous fascination, was not simply the effect of necessity. Had the state of her finances been as flourishing as it was decayed, she would have been equally steady in this forbearance: her reason was fair, though her feelings frequently chaced it from the field. She looked on, therefore, with safety, though not wholly with indifference; she had too much fancy not to be amused by the spirit of the business, and was too animated not to take part in the successive hopes and fears of the several competitors; but though her quick sensations prompted a readiness, like that of Mrs. Berlinton, to enter warmly into all that was presented to her, the resemblance went no further; what she was once convinced was wrong she was incapable of practising.

Upon Gaming, the first feeling and the latest reflection are commonly one; both point its hazards to be unnecessary, its purposes rapacious, and its end desperate loss, or destructive gain; she not only, therefore, held back; she took the liberty, upon the privilege of their avowed friendship, to remonstrate against this dangerous pastime with Mrs. Berlinton. But that lady, though eminently designed to be amiable, had now contracted the fearful habit of giving way to every propensity; and finding her native notions of happiness were blighted in the bud, concluded that all which now remained for her was the indulgence of every luxury. She heard with sweetness the expostulation of her young friend; but she pursued her own course.

In a very few days, however, while the blush of shame dyed her beautiful cheeks, she inquired if Camilla could lend her a little ready money.

A blush of no less unpleasant feelings overspread the face of her fair guest, in being compelled to own she had none to lend; but she eagerly promised to procure some from Mrs. Mittin, who had a note in her hand to exchange for the payment of some small debts contracted at Tunbridge. Mrs. Berlinton, gathering, from her confusion, how ill she was stored, would not hear of applying to this resource, 'though I hate,' she cried, 'to be indebted to that odious old cousin, of whom I was obliged to borrow last night.'

Glaring imprudence in others is a lesson even to the most unthinking; Camilla, when she found that Mrs. Berlinton had lost every guinea she could command, ventured to renew still more forcibly her exhortations against the Faro table; but Mrs. Berlinton, notwithstanding she possessed an excellent capacity, was so little fortified with any practical tenets either of religion or morality, that where sentiment did not take the part of what was right, she had no preservative against what was wrong. The Faro table, therefore, was still opened; and Lord Valhurst, by the sums he lent, obtained every privilege of intimacy in the family, except that of being welcome.

Against this perilous mode of proceeding Camilla was not the only warner. Mrs. Ulst saw with extreme repugnance the mode of life her niece was pursuing, and reprimanded her with severe reproach; but her influence was now lost; and Mrs. Berlinton, though she kindly attended her, and sought to alleviate her sufferings, acted as if she were not in existence.

It was now Mrs. Mittin gained the highest point of her ambition; Mrs. Berlinton, tired of remonstrances she could not controvert, and would not observe, was extremely relieved by finding a person who would sit with her aunt, comply with her humours, hear her lamentations, subscribe to her opinions, and beguile her of her rigid fretfulness by the amusement of gossiping anecdotes.

Mrs. Mittin had begun life as the apprentice to a small country milliner; but had rendered herself so useful to a sick elderly gentlewoman, who lodged in the house, that she left her a legacy, which, by sinking into an annuity, enabled her to quit her business, and set up, in her own conception, for a gentlewoman herself; though with so very small an income, that to sustain her new post, she was frequently reduced to far greater dependence and hardships than she experienced in her old one. She was good-humoured, yet laborious; gay, yet subservient; poor, yet dissipated. To be useful, she would submit to any drudgery; to become agreeable, devoted herself to any flattery. To please was her incessant desire, and her rage for popularity included every rank and class of society. The more eminent, of course, were her first objects, but the same aim descended to the lowest. She would work, read, go of errands, or cook a dinner; be a parasite, a spy, an attendant, a drudge; keep a secret, or spread a report; incite a quarrel, or coax contending parties into peace; invent any expedient, and execute any scheme . . . all with the pretext to oblige others, but all, in fact, for simple egotism; as prevalent in her mind as in that of the more highly ambitious, though meaner and less dangerous.

Camilla was much relieved when she found this officious person was no longer retained solely upon her account; but still she could neither obtain her bills, no answers ever arriving, nor the money for her twenty pound note, Mrs. Mittin always evading to deliver it, and asserting she was sure somebody would come in the stage the next day for the payment she had promised; and when Camilla wanted cash for any of the very few articles she now allowed herself to think indispensable, instead of restoring it into her hands, she flew out herself to purchase the goods that were required, and always brought them home with assurances they were cheaper than the shopkeepers would let her have them for herself.

Camilla resisted all incitements to new dress and new ornaments, with a fortitude which must not be judged by the aged, nor the retired, who weighing only the frivolity of what she withstood, are not qualified to appreciate the merit of this sort of resignation; the young, the gay, the new in life, who know that, amongst minor calamities, none are more alarming to the juvenile breast than the fear of not appearing initiated in the reigning modes, can alone do justice to the present philosophy of Camilla, in seeing that all she wore, by the quick changes of fashion, seemed already out of date; in refusing to look at the perpetual diversity of apparel daily brought, by various dress modellers, for the approbation of Mrs. Berlinton, and in seeing that lady always newly, brightly, and in a distinguished manner attired, yet appearing by her side in exactly the same array that she had constantly worn at Tunbridge. Nor was Camilla indifferent to this contrast; but she submitted to it as the duty of her present involved situation, which exacted from her every privation, in preference to bestowing upon any new expence the only sum she could command towards clearing what was past.

But, after a very short time, the little wardrobe exhibited a worse quality than that of not keeping pace with the last devices of the *ton;* it lost not merely its newness, but its delicacy. Alas! thought she, how long, in the careful and rare wear of Etherington and Cleves, all this would have served me; while here, in this daily use, a fortnight is scarce passed, yet all is spoilt and destroyed. Ah! public places are only for the rich!

Now, therefore, Mrs. Mittin was of serious utility; she failed
not to observe the declining state of her attire; and though she
wondered at the parsimony which so resolutely prohibited all
orders for its renewal, in a young lady she considered as so great
an heiress, she was yet proud to display her various powers of
proving serviceable. She turned, changed, rubbed, cleaned, and
new made up all the several articles of which her dress was composed, to so much advantage, and with such striking effect, that
for yet a few days more all seemed renewed, and by the arts of
some few alterations, her appearance was rather more than less
fashionable than upon her first arrival.

But this could not last long; and when all, again, was fading
into a state of decay, Mrs. Berlinton received an invitation for
herself and her fair guest, to a great ball and supper, given upon
the occasion of a young nobleman's coming of age, in which all the
dancers, by agreement, were to be habited in uniform.

This uniform was to be clear fine lawn, with lilac plumes and
ornaments.

Camilla had now, with consuming regret, passed several days
without one sight of Edgar. This invitation, therefore, which was
general to all the company at Southampton, was, in its first sound,
delicious; but became, upon consideration, the reverse. Clear
lawn and lilac plumes and ornaments she had none; how to go she
knew not; yet Edgar she was sure would be there; how to stay
away she knew less.

This was a severe moment to her courage; she felt it faltering,
and putting down the card of invitation, without the force of
desiring Mrs. Berlinton to make her excuse, repaired to her own
room, terrified by the preponderance of her wishes to a consent
which she knew her situation rendered unwarrantable.

There, however, though she gained time for reflection, she
gathered not the resolution she sought. The stay at Southampton,
by the desire of Lynmere, had been lengthened; yet only a week
now remained, before she must return to her father and her
uncle . . . but how return? separated from Edgar? Edgar whom
she still believed she had only to see again in some more auspicious moment, to re-conquer and fix for life! But when and where
might that auspicious moment be looked for? not at Mrs.
Berlinton's; there he no more attempted to visit: not at the Rooms;
those now were decidedly relinquished, and all general invitations

were inadequate to draw Mrs. Berlinton from her new pursuit: where, then, was this happy explanation to pass?

When our wishes can only be gratified with difficulty, we conclude, in the ardour of combating their obstacle, that to lose them, is to lose everything, to obtain them is to ensure all good. At this ball, and this supper, Camilla painted Edgar completely restored to her; she was certain he would dance with her; she was sure he would sit by no one else during the repast; the many days since they had met would endear to him every moment they could now spend together, and her active imagination soon worked up scenes so important from this evening, that she next persuaded her belief that all chance of reconciliation hung wholly upon the meeting it offered.

Impelled by this notion, yet wavering, dissatisfied, and uncomfortable, she summoned Mrs. Mittin, and entreated she would make such inquiries concerning the value of the ball-dress uniform, as would enable her to estimate its entire expence.

Her hours passed now in extreme disquietude; for while all her hopes centred in the approaching festival, the estimate which was to determine her power of enjoying it was by no means easy to procure. Mrs. Mittin, though an adept in such matters, took more pleasure in the parade than in the performance of her task; and always answered to her inquiries, that it was impossible to speak so soon; that she must go to such another shop first; that she must consult with such and such a person; and that she must consider over more closely the orders given by Mrs. Berlinton, which were to be her direction, though with the stipulation of having materials much cheaper and more common.

At length, however, she burst into her room, one morning, before she was dressed, saying: 'Now, my dear miss, I hope I shall make you happy;' and displayed, upon the bed, a beautiful piece of fine lawn.

Camilla examined and admired it, asked what it was a yard, and how much would suffice for the dress.

'Why, my dear, I'll answer for it there's enough for three whole dresses; why it's a whole piece; and I dare say I can get a handkerchief and an apron out of it into the bargain.'

'But I want neither handkerchief, nor apron, nor three dresses, Mrs. Mittin; I shall take the smallest quantity that is possible, if I take any at all.'

Mrs. Mittin said that the man would not cut it, and she must take the whole, or none.

Camilla was amazed she could so far have misunderstood her as to bring it upon such terms, and begged she would carry it back.

'Nay, if you don't take this, my dear, there's nothing in the shops that comes near it for less than fifteen shillings a-yard; Mrs. Berlinton gives eighteen for her's, and it don't look one bit to choose; and this, if you take it all together, you may have for ten, for all its width, for there's 30 yards, and the piece comes to but fifteen pound.'

Camilla protested she would not, at this time, pay ten shillings a-yard for any gown in the world.

Mrs. Mittin, who had flattered herself that the handkerchief and apron, at least, if not one of the gowns, would have fallen to her share, was much discomposed by this unexpected declaration; and disappointed, murmuring, and conceiving her the most avaricious of mortals, was forced away; leaving Camilla in complete despondence of any power to effect her wish with propriety.

Mrs. Mittin came back late, and with a look of dismay; the man of whom she had had the muslin, who was a traveller, whom she had met at a friend's, had not waited her return; and, as she had left the fifteen pounds with him, for a pledge of the security of his goods, she supposed he had made off, to get rid of the whole piece at once.

Camilla felt petrified. No possible pleasure or desire could urge her, deliberately, to what she deemed an extravagance; yet here, in one moment, she was despoiled of three parts of all she possessed, either for her own use, or towards the restitution of her just debts with others.

Observing her distress, though with more displeasure than pity, from believing it founded in the most extraordinary covetousness, Mrs. Mittin proposed measuring the piece in three, and disposing of the two gowns she did not want to Mrs. Berlinton, or her sister and Miss Lynmere.

Camilla was a little revived; but the respite of difficulty was short; upon opening the piece, it was found damaged; and after the first few yards, which Mrs. Mittin had sedulously examined, not a breadth had escaped some rent, fray, or mischief.

The ill being now irremediable, to make up the dress in the cheapest manner possible was the only consolation that remained.

Mrs. Mittin knew a mantua-maker[1] who, to oblige her, would undertake this for a very small payment; and she promised to procure everything else that was necessary for the merest trifle.

Determined, however, to risk nothing more in such hands, she now positively demanded that the residue of the note should be restored to her own keeping. Mrs. Mittin, though much affronted, honestly refunded the five pounds. The little articles she had occasionally brought were still unpaid for; but her passion for detaining the money was merely with a view to give herself consequence, in boasting how and by whom she was trusted, and now and then drawing out her purse, before those who had less to produce; but wholly without any design of imposition or fraud; all she could obtain by hints and address she conceived to be fair booty; but further she went not even in thought.

Three days now only remained before this event-promising ball was to take place, and within three after it, the Southampton expedition was to close. Camilla scarce breathed from impatience for the important moment, which was preceded by an invitation to all the company, to take a sail on the Southampton water on the morning of the entertainment.

END OF THE FOURTH VOLUME.

VOLUME V

BOOK IX

CHAPTER I

A Water Party

THE ball dress of Camilla was not yet ready, when she set out for the amusement of the morning. Melmond, upon this occasion, was forced into the excursion; his sister represented, so pathetically, the ungrateful ill-breeding of sequestering himself from a company of which it must so publicly be judged Eugenia would make one, with the impossibility of for ever escaping the sight of Indiana, that he could not, in common decency, any longer postpone the double meeting he almost equally dreaded.

And this, with all that could aggravate its misery, from seeing the two objects together, immediately occurred. Sir Hugh Tyrold's coach, containing Miss Margland, Indiana, Eugenia, and Dr. Orkborne, was arrived just before that of Mrs. Berlinton; and, the morning being very fine, they had just alighted, to join the company assembling upon the beach for the expedition. Miss Margland still continued to exact the attendance of the Doctor, though his wry looks and sluggish pace always proclaimed his ill will to the task. But Clermont, the only proper beau for her parties, was completely unattainable. He had connected himself with young Halder, and his associates, from whom, while he received instructions relative to the stables and the dog-kennels, he returned, with suitable edification, lessons on the culinary art.

Melmond, deeply distressed, besought his sister not to alight till the last moment. She pitied him too sincerely not to comply; and, in a very short time, she had herself an aggregate of almost all the gentlemen on the beach before the coach.

Among these, the first to press forward were the two Westwyns, each enraptured to again see Camilla; and the most successful in obtaining notice was Lord Valhurst, with whom Camilla still thought it prudent, however irksome, to discourse, rather than receive again the assiduities of Henry: but her mind, far from them all, was hovering on the edge of the shore, where Edgar was walking.

Edgar, for some time past, had joined the utmost uneasiness what conduct to pursue with regard to the friends of Camilla, to the heart-rending decision of parting from her for ever. He soon learnt the new and dangerous manner in which Mrs. Berlinton spent her evenings, and the idea that most naturally occurred to him, was imparting it to Mr. Tyrold. But in what way could he address that gentleman, without first knowing if Camilla had acquainted him with the step she had taken? He felt too strongly the severe blow it would prove, not to wish softening it with every palliation; and while these still lingering feelings awed his proceedings, his servant learnt, from Molly Mill, that Melmond had been favourably received at Cleves, as a suitor to Eugenia. Finding so near an alliance likely to take place with the brother, he gave up his plan of remonstrating against the sister, except in private counsel to Camilla; for which, and for uttering his fearful adieu, he was now waiting but to speak to her unobserved.

Still, however, with pain unabating he saw the eager approach to her of Henry, with disgust that of Lord Valhurst, and with alarm the general herd.

Lord Pervil, the young nobleman who deemed it worth while to be at the expence of several hundred pounds, in order to let the world know how old he was, now, with his mother, a widow lady, and some other relations, came down in a superb new equipage, to the water-side. Mrs. Berlinton could not be so singular, as not to join in the general crowd, that flocked around them with congratulations; and all parties, in a few minutes, were assembled on one spot.

Edgar, when he had spoken to the group to which the honours of the day belonged, made up to Camilla, gravely enquired after her health; and then placed himself as near to her as he was able, in the hope of conferring with her when the company began to move.

Her spirits now rose, and her prospects re-opened to their wished termination. All her regret was for Henry, who saw her present avoidance, and bemoaned her long absence, with a sadness that reproached and afflicted her.

A very fine yacht, and three large pleasure-boats, were in readiness for this company, surrounded by various other vessels of all sorts and conditions, which were filled with miscellaneous parties, who meant to partake the same gales for their own diversion or curiosity. The invited set was now summoned to the water, Lord Pervil and his relations leading the way by a small boat to the yacht, to which Mrs. Berlinton and the Cleves party were particularly selected guests.

Camilla, depending upon the assistance of Edgar, in passing through the boat to the yacht, so obviously turned from Henry, that he lost all courage for persevering in addressing her, and was even, though most unwillingly, retiring from a vicinity in which he seemed palpably obtrusive, had not his father insisted upon detaining him, whispering, 'Be of good heart, Hal! the girl will come round yet.'

Edgar kept equally near her, with a design that was the counterpart of her own wish, of offering her his hand when it was her turn to enter the boat; but they were both disappointed, the Peer, not waiting that rotation, presented her his arm as soon as Lady Pervil had led the way. There was no redress, though Camilla was as much provoked as either of the young rivals.

Lord Valhurst did not long exult in his victory; the unsteadiness of the boat made him rather want help for himself, than find force to bestow it upon another, and, upon mounting at the helm to pass her on to the yacht, he tottered, his foot slipt, and he must have sunk between the two vessels, had not a waterman caught him up, and dragged him into the yacht, with no further misfortune than a bruised shin, wet legs and feet, and a deplorably rueful countenance, from mingled fright and mortification.

Edgar, not wholly unsuspicious such an accident might happen, was darting into the boat to snatch Camilla from its participation, when he felt himself forcibly pulled back, and saw, at the same moment, Henry, who had also started forward, but whom nothing had retarded, anticipate his purpose, and aid her into the yacht.

Looking round to see by what, or by whom, he had so unaccountably been stopt, he perceived old Mr. Westwyn, his forefinger upon his nose in sign of silence and secrecy, grasping him by the coat.

'What is the humour of this, Sir?' cried he, indignantly.

Mr. Westwyn, still making his token for discretion, and bending forward to speak in his ear, said, 'Do, there's a good soul,

let my boy help that young lady. Hal will be much obliged to you,
I can tell you; and he's a very good lad.'

The nature of Edgar was too candid to suffer his wrath to
resist a request so simple in sincerity; but deeply he sighed to
find, by its implication, that the passion of Henry was thus still
fed with hopes.

The passing of other ladies, with their esquires, prevented him,
who had no lady he wished to conduct, from making his way yet
into the yacht; and the honest old gentleman, detained by the
same reason, entered promptly into the history of the present
situation of his son with regard to Camilla; relating, frankly, that
he thought her the sweetest girl in the world, except that she did
not know her own mind; for she had been so pleased with his son
first of all, that he really thought he should oblige her by making it
a match: 'which I could not,' added he, 'have the heart to refuse to
a girl that gave the boy such a good character. You'd be surprised
to know how she took to him! you may be proud, says she to me,
you may be proud of your son! which is what I shall never forget;
for though I loved Hal just the same before, I never could tell but
what it was only because he was my own. And I'm so afraid of
behaving like a blind old goose, that I often snub Hal, when he's
no more to blame than I am myself, for fear of his getting out of
my hands, and behaving like a certain young man he has been
brought up with, and who, I assure you, deserves to have his ears
cropt ten times a day, for one piece of impudence or other. I
should not have been sorry if he'd fallen into the water along with
that old lord, whom I don't wish much good to neither; for,
between friends, it seems to me that it's he that has put her out of
conceit with my poor Hal: for all of a sudden, nobody can tell
why nor wherefore, she takes it into her head there's nothing else
worth listening to, but just his old compliments. And my poor
Hal, after thinking she had such a kindness for him, that he had
nothing to do but put on his best coat—for I told him I'd have
none of his new-fangled modes of affronting my worthy old
friend, by doing to him like a postillion, with a cropt head, and
half a coat—after thinking he'd only to ask his consent, for he'd
got mine without ever a word, all at once, without the least
quarrel, or either I or Hal giving her the least offence, she won't so
much as let him speak to her; but turns off to that old fellow that
tumbled into the water there, and had near made her slip in after,

if it had not been for my son's stopping her, which I sha'n't forget
your kindness in letting him do; but what's more, she won't
speak to me neither! though all I want is to ask her the reason of
her behaviour! which I shall certainly do, if I can catch her any
five minutes away from that lord; for you'll never believe what
good friends we were, before she took so to him. We three, that is,
she and I, and Hal, used to speak to nobody else, scarce. Poor Hal
thought he'd got it all his own way. And I can't but own I thought
as much myself; for there was no knowing she'd hold herself so
above us, all at once. I assure you, if we don't bring her to, it will
go pretty hard with us; for I like her just as well as Hal does. I'd
have made over to them the best half of my income immediately.'

Edgar had never yet felt such serious displeasure against
Camilla, as seized him upon this artless narrative. To have
trifled thus, and, as he believed, most wantonly, with the feelings
and peace of two amiable persons, whether from the vanity of
making a new conquest, or the tyranny of persecuting an old one,
shewed a love of power the most unjustifiable, and a levity the
most unpardonable. And when he considered himself as exactly
in the same suspensive embarrassment, as a young man of little
more than a fortnight's acquaintance, he felt indignantly ashamed
of so humiliating a rivalry, and a strong diminution of regret at his
present purpose.

Melmond, meanwhile, pressed by his sister, seconded by his
own sense of propriety, had forced himself to the Cleves' party;
and, after bowing civilly to Miss Margland, who courteously
smiled upon one who she imagined would become master of
Cleves, and most profoundly to Indiana, who coloured, but
deigned not the smallest salutation in return, offered his hand to
Eugenia; but with a mind so absorbed, and steps so uncertain,
that he was unable to afford her any assistance; and her lameness
and helplessness made her so much require it, that she was in
danger of falling every moment; yet she felt in Paradise; she
thought him but enfeebled, as she was enfeebled herself, by a
tender sensibility; and danger, therefore, was not merely braved,
it was dear, it was precious to her.

Indiana now consoled her mortification, with the solace of
believing a retaliation at hand, that would overcome the otherwise
indelible disgrace of being superseded by Eugenia in a conquest.
Full of her own little scheme, she imperiously refused all offers of

aid, and walked on alone, till crossing the boat, she gave a shriek
at every step, made hazardous by her wilful rejection of assistance,
and acted over again the charm of terror, of which she well
recollected the power upon a former occasion.

These were sounds to vibrate but too surely to the heart of
Melmond; he turned involuntarily to look at her; her beauty had
all its original enchantment; and he snatched away his eyes. He led
on her whom still less he durst view; but another glance, thus
surprised from him, shewed Indiana unguarded, unprotected;
his imagination painted her immediately in a watery grave; and,
seeing Eugenia safe, though not accommodated, he rushed back
to the boat, and with trembling respect implored her to accept
his aid.

Triumphant, now, she conceived herself in her turn, and
looking at him with haughty disdain, said, she chose to go alone;
and when again he conjured her not to risk her precious safety,
added, 'You know you don't care about it; so pray go to your Miss
Eugenia Tyrold.'

Young Melmond, delicate, refined, and well bred, was precisely
amongst the first to feel, that a reply such as this must be classed
amongst the reverse of those three epithets—had it come from
any mouth but that of Indiana!—but love is deaf, as well as
blind, to every defect of its chosen object, during the season of
passion: from her, therefore, this answer, leaving unobserved the
littleness and spleen which composed it, retained but so much of
meaning as belongs to announcing jealousy, and in giving him
that idea, filled him with sensations that almost tore him
asunder.

Urged by her pique, she contrived, and with real risk, to jump
into the yacht alone; though, if swayed by any less potent motive,
she would sooner have remained in the boat the whole day. But
what is the strength which may be put upon a par with inclination? and what the general courage that partial enterprise will not
exceed?

Melmond, who only to some amiable cause could attribute
whatever flowed from so beautiful an object, having once started
the idea of jealousy, could give its source only to love: the impure
spring of envy entered not into his suggestions. What, then, was
his distraction, to think himself so greatly miserable! to believe
he was secretly favoured by Indiana, at the instant of his first

devoirs to another! Duty and desire were equally urgent to be heard; he shrunk in utter despondence from the two objects that seemed to personify both, and retreated, to the utmost of his power, from the sight of either.

Miss Margland had more than echoed every scream of Indiana, though nobody had seemed to hear her. Dr. Orkborne, the only beau she could compel into her service, was missing; her eye and voice alike every where demanded him in vain; he neither appeared to her view, nor answered her indignant calls.—Nor, indeed, though she forced his attendance, had she the most remote hope of inspiriting him to any gallantry: but still he was a man, and she thought it a mark of consequence to have one in her train; nor was it by any means nothing to her to torment Dr. Orkborne with her reproaches. To dispositions highly irascible, it is frequently more gratifying to have a subject of complaint than of acknowledgment.

The ladies being now all accommodated upon the deck, sailing orders were given, when an 'holla! holla!' making the company look round, Lynmere desired to be admitted. All the party intended for the yacht were already on board, and Lord Pervil told Mr. Lynmere he would find a very good place in one of the pleasure boats: but he answered he was just come from them, and preferred going in the yacht. Lord Pervil then only hoped the ladies would excuse being a little crowded. Edgar had already glided in, and Mr. Westwyn had openly declared, when asked to go to one of the boats, that he always went where Hal went, be it where it might.

Clermont, now, elbowing his way into a group of gentlemen, and addressing himself to young Halder, who was amongst them, said: 'Do you know what they've got to eat here?'

'No.'

'What the deuce! have not you examined the larder? I have been looking over the three boats,—there's nothing upon earth!—so I came to see if I could do any better here.'

Halder vowed if there were nothing to eat, he would sooner jump over board, and swim to shore, than go starving on.

'Starving?' said Mr. Westwyn, 'why I saw, myself, several baskets of provisions taken into each of the boats.'

'Only ham and fowls,' answered Clermont, contemptuously.

'Only ham and fowls? why what would you have?'

'O the d——l,' answered he, making faces, 'not that ante-diluvian stuff! any thing's better than ham and fowls.'

'Stilton cheese, for instance?' cried Mr. Westwyn, with a wrathful sneer, that made Clermont, who could not endure, yet, for many reasons, could not resent it, hastily decamp from his vicinity.

Mr. Westwyn, looking after the young epicure with an expression of angry scorn, now took the arm of Edgar, whose evident interest in his first communication encouraged further confidence, and said: 'That person that you see walk that way just now, is a fellow that I have a prodigious longing to give a good caning to. I can't say I like him; yet he's nephew and heir to the very best man in the three kingdoms. However, I heartily hope his uncle will disinherit him, for he's a poor fool as well as a sorry fellow. I love to speak my mind plainly.'

Edgar was ill-disposed to conversation, and intent only upon Camilla, who was now seated between Mrs. Berlinton and Eugenia, and occupied by the fine prospects every where open to her; yet he explained the error of Clermont's being heir, as well as nephew, to Sir Hugh; at which the old gentleman, almost jumping with surprise and joy, said: 'Why, then who's to pay all his debts at Leipsic? I can't say but what I'm glad to hear this. I hope he'll be sent to prison, with all my heart, to teach him a little better manners. For my old friend will never cure him; he spoils young people prodigiously. I don't believe he'd so much as give 'em a horse-whipping, let 'em do what they would. That i'n't my way. Ask Hal!'

Here he stopt, disturbed by a new sight, which displaced Clermont from his thoughts.

Camilla, to whom the beauties of nature had mental, as well as visual charms, from the blessings, as well as pleasure, she had from childhood been instructed to consider as surrounding them, was so enchanted by the delicious scenery every way courting her eyes, the transparent brightness of the noble piece of water upon which she was sailing, the richness and verdure of its banks, the still and gently gliding motion of the vessel, the clearness of the heavens, and the serenity of the air, that all her cares, for a while, would have been lost in admiring contemplation, had she not painfully seen the eternal watching of Henry for her notice, and gathered from the expression of his eyes, his intended expostulation. The self-reproach with which she felt how ill she could make her defence, joined to a sincere and generous wish to spare him the humiliation of a rejection, made her seek so to engage herself, as to prevent the possibility of his uttering two sentences following. But as this was difficult with Eugenia, who was lost in silent meditation upon her own happiness, or Mrs. Berlinton, who was occupied in examining the beauty so fatal to the repose of her brother, she had found such trouble in eluding him, that, when she saw Lord Valhurst advance from the cabin, where he had been drying and refreshing himself, she welcomed him as a resource, and, taking advantage of the civility she owed him for what he had suffered in esquiring her, gave him her sole attention; always persuaded his admiration was but a sort of old fashioned politeness, equally without design in itself, or subject for comment in others.

But what is so hard to judge as the human heart? The fairest observers misconstrue all motives to action, where any received prepossession has found an hypothesis. To Edgar this conduct appeared the most degrading fondness for adulation, and to Mr. Westwyn a tyrannical caprice, meant to mortify his son. 'I hope you saw that! I hope you saw that!' cried he, 'for now I don't care a pin for her any longer! and if Hal is such a mere fool as ever to think of her any more, I'll never see his face again as long as I live. After looking askew at the poor boy all this time, to turn about and make way for that nasty old fellow; as who should say, I'll speak to nothing but a lord! is what I shall never forgive; and I wish I had never seen the girl, nor Hal neither. I can't say I like such ways. I can't abide 'em.'

A sigh that then escaped Edgar, would have told a more discerning person, that he came in for his ample share in the same wish.

'And, after all,' continued he, 'being a lord is no such great feat that ever I could learn. Hal might be a lord too, if he could get a title. There is nothing required for it but what any man may have; nobody asks after what he can do, or what he can say. If he's got a good head, it's well; and if he has not, it's all one. And that's what you can't say of such a likely young fellow as my son. You may see twenty for one that's as well looking. Indeed, to my mind, I don't know that ever I saw a prettier lad in my life. So she might do worse, I promise her, though she has used my son so

shabbily. I don't like her the better for it, I assure her; and so you
may tell her, if you please. I'm no great friend to not speaking my
mind.'

The fear of being too late for the evening's arrangements, made
Lord Pervil, after a two hours sail, give orders for veering about:
the ladies were advised to go into the cabin during this evolution,
and Camilla was amongst those who most readily complied, for
the novelty of viewing what she had not yet seen. But when, with
the rest, she was returning to the deck, Lord Valhurst, who had
just descended, entreated her to stop one moment.

Not at all conjecturing his reason, she knew not how to refuse,
but innocently begged him to speak quick, as she was in haste, not
to lose any of the beautiful landscapes they were passing.

'Ah what,' cried the enamoured peer, 'what in the world is
beautiful in any comparison with yourself? To me no possible
object can have such charms; and I have now no wish remaining
but never to lose sight of it.'

Amazed beyond all measure, she stared at him a moment in
silence, and then, confirmed by his looks that he was serious,
would have left the cabin with precipitance: but, preventing her
from passing; 'Charming Miss Tyrold!' he cried, 'let the confession of my flame meet your favour, and I will instantly make my
proposals to your friends.'

To Camilla this offer appeared as little delicate, as its maker
was attractive; yet she thought herself indebted for its general
purport, and, as soon as her astonishment allowed her, gracefully
thanked him for the honour of his good opinion, but entreated
him to make no application to her friends, as it would not be in
her power to concur in their consent.

Concluding this to be modest shyness, he was beginning a
passionate protestation of the warmth of his regard, when the
effusion was stopt by the appearance of Edgar.

Little imagining so serious a scene to be passing as the few
words he now gathered gave him to understand, his perplexity at
her not returning with the other ladies, made him suggest this to be
a favourable moment to seize for following her himself, and
demanding the sought, though dreaded conference. But when he
found that his lordship, instead of making, as he had supposed,
his usual fond, yet unmeaning compliments, was pompously
offering his hand, he precipitately retired.

No liveliness of temper had injured in Camilla the real modesty of her character. A sense, therefore, of obligation for this partiality accompanied its surprise, and was preparing her for repeating the rejection with acknowledgments though with firmness, when the sight of Edgar brought an entirely new train of feelings and ideas into her mind. O! happy moment! thought she; he must have heard enough of what was passed to know me, at least, to be dis-interested! he must see, now, it was himself, not his situation in life, I was so prompt in accepting—and if again he manifests the same preference, I may receive it with more frankness than ever, for he will see my whole heart, sincerely, singly, inviolably his own!

Bewitched with this notion, she escaped from the peer, and ran up to the deck, with a renovation of animal spirits, so high, so lively, and so buoyant, that she scarce knew what she said or did, from the uncontroulable gaiety, which made every idea dance to a happiness new even to her happy mind. Whoever she looked at, she smiled upon; to whatever was proposed, she assented: scarce could she restrain her voice from involuntarily singing, or her feet from instinctively dancing.

Edgar, compared with what he now felt, believed that hitherto he had been a stranger to what wonder meant. Is this, thought he, Camilla? Has she wilfully fascinated this old man seriously to win him, and has she won him but to triumph in the vanity of her conquest? How is her delicacy perverted! what is become of her sensibility? Is this the artless Camilla? modest as she was gay, docile as she was spirited, gentle as she was intelligent? O how spoilt! how altered! how gone!

Camilla, little suspicious of this construction, thought it would be now equally wrong to speak any more with either Henry or Lord Valhurst, and talked with all others indiscriminately, chang-ing her object with almost every speech.

A moment's reflection would have told her, that quietness alone, in her present situation, could do justice to the purity of her intentions: but reflection is rarely the partner of happiness in the youthful breast; it is commonly brought by sorrow, and flies at the first dawn of returning joy.

Thus, while she dispensed to all around, with views the most innocent, her gay and almost wild felicity, the very delight to which she owed her animation, of believing she was evincing to Edgar with what singleness she was his own, gave her the appearance, in his judgment, of a finished, a vain, an all-accomplished coquette. The exaltation of her ideas brightened her eyes into a vivacity almost dazzling, gave an attraction to her smiles that was irresistible, the charm of fascination to the sound of her voice, to her air a thousand nameless graces, and to her manner and expression an enchantment.

Powers so captivating, now for the first time united with a facility of intercourse, soon drew around her all the attendant admiring beaux.

No animal is more gregarious than a fashionable young man, who, whatever may be his abilities to think, rarely decides, and still less frequently acts for himself. He may wish, he may appreciate, internally with justice and wisdom; but he only says, and only does, what some other man of fashion, higher in vogue, or older in courage, has said or has done before him.

The young Lord Pervil, the star of the present day, was now drawn into the magic circle of Camilla; this was full sufficient to bring into it every minor luminary of his constellation; and even the resplendent and incomparable beauty of Indiana, even the soft and melting influence of the expressively lovely Mrs. Berlinton, gave way to the superior ascendance of that varied grace, and winning vivacity, which seemed instinctively sharing with the beholders its own pleasure and animation.

To Edgar alone this gave her not new charms: he saw in her more of beauty, but less of interest; the sentence dictated by Dr. Marchmont, as the watch-word to his feelings, *were she mine*, recurred to him incessantly; alas! he thought, with this dissipated delight in admiration, what individual can make her happy? to the rational serenity of domestic life, she is lost!

Again, as he viewed the thickening group before her, offering fresh and fresh incense, which her occupied mind scarce perceived, though her elevated spirits unconsciously encouraged, he internally exclaimed: 'O, if her trusting father saw her thus! her father who, with all his tender lenity, has not the blind indulgence of her uncle, how would he start! how would his sense of fair propriety be revolted!—or if her mother—her respectable mother, beheld thus changed, thus undignified, thus open to all flattery and all flatterers, her no longer peerless daughter—how would she blush! how would the tint of shame rob her impressive countenance of its noble confidence!'

These thoughts were too agitating for observation; his eyes moistened with sadness in associating to his disappointment that of her revered and exemplary parents, and he retreated from her sight till the moment of landing; when with sudden desperation, melancholy yet determined, he told himself he would no longer be withheld from fulfilling his purpose.

He made way, then, to the group, though with unsteady steps; his eye pierced through to Camilla; she caught and fixt it. He felt cold; but still advanced. She saw the change, but did not understand it. He offered her his hand before Lady Pervil arose to lead the way, lest some competitor should seize it; she accepted it, rather surprized by such sudden promptness, though encouraged by it to a still further dependance upon her revived and sanguine expectations.

Yet deeper sunk this flattering illusion, when she found his whole frame was shaking, and saw his complexion every moment varying. She continued, though in a less disengaged manner, her sprightly discourse with the group; for he uttered not a word. Content that he had secured her hand, he waited an opportunity less public.

Lady Pervil, who possessed that true politeness of a well-bred woman of rank, who knows herself never so much respected as when she lays aside mere heraldic claims to superiority, would not quit the yacht of which she did the honours, till every other lady was conducted to the shore. Edgar had else purposed to have detained Camilla in the vessel a moment later than her party, to hear the very few words it was his intention to speak. Frustrated of this design, he led her away with the rest, still totally silent, till her feet touched the beach: she was then, with seeming carelessness, withdrawing her hand, to trip off to Mrs. Berlinton; but Edgar, suddenly grasping it, tremulously said: 'Will it be too much presumption—in a rejected man—to beg the honour of three minutes conference with Miss Tyrold, before she joins her party?'

A voice piercing from the deep could not have caused in Camilla a more immediate revulsion of ideas; but she was silent, in her turn, and he led her along the beach, while Mrs. Berlinton, attended by a train of beaux, went to her carriage, where, thus engaged, she contentedly waited.

'Do not fear,' he resumed, when they had passed the crowd, 'do not fear to listen to me, though, once more, I venture to obtrude upon you some advice; let it not displease you; it is in the spirit of the purest good will; it is singly, solely, and disinterestedly as a friend.'

Camilla was now all emotion; pale she turned, but Edgar did not look at her; and she strove to thank him in a common manner, and to appear cool and unmoved.

'My opinion, my fears rather, concerning Mrs. Berlinton, as I find she hopes soon for a near connexion with your family, will henceforth remain buried in my own breast: yet, should you, to any use hereafter remember them, I shall rejoice: though should nothing ever recur to remind you of them, I shall rejoice still more. Nor will I again torment you about that very underbred woman who inhabits the same house, and who every where boasts an intimacy with its two ladies, that is heard with general astonishment: nor yet upon another, and far more important topic, will I now touch,—the present evening recreation at Mrs. Berlinton's. I know you are merely a spectatress, and I will not alarm your friends, nor dwell myself, upon collateral mischiefs, or eventual dangers, from a business that in three days will end, by your restoration to the most respectable of all protections. All that, now, I mean to enter upon, all that, now, I wish to enforce, a few words will comprise, and those words will be my—'

He would have said *my last* but his breath failed him; he stopt; he wanted her to seize his meaning unpronounced; and, though it came to her as a thunderbolt from heaven, its very horror helped her; she divined what he could not utter, by feeling what she could not hear.

'Few, indeed,' cried he, in broken accents, 'must be these final words! but how can I set out upon my so long procrastinated tour, with an idea that you are not in perfect safety, yet without attempting to point out to you your danger? And yet,—that you should be surrounded by admirers can create no wonder;—that you should feel your power without displeasure, is equally natural;—I scarcely know, therefore, what I would urge—yet perhaps, untold, you may conceive what struggles in my breast, and do justice to the conflict between friendship and respect, where one prompts a freedom, which the other [trembles] to execute. I need not, I think, say, that to offend you is nearly the only thing that could aggravate the affliction of this parting.'—

Camilla turned aside from him; but not to weep; her spirit was now re-wakened by resentment, that he could thus propose a separation, without enquiring if she persisted to desire it.

'I tire you?' resumed he, mournfully; 'yet can you be angry that a little I linger? Farewell, however—the grave, when it closes in upon me can alone end my prayers for your felicity! I commit wholly to you my character and my conduct, with regard to your most honoured father, whom I beseech and conjure you to assure of my eternal gratitude and affection. But I am uncertain of your wishes; I will, therefore, depart without seeing him. When I return to this country, all will be forgotten—or remembered only—' *by me,* he meant to say, but he checked himself, and, with forced composure, went on:

'That I travel not with any view of pleasure, you, who know what I leave—how I prize what I lose,—and how lately I thought all I most coveted mine for ever, will easily believe. But if earthly bliss is the lot of few, what right had I to expect being so selected? Severe as is this moment, with blessings, not with murmurs, I quit you! blessings which my life, could it be useful to you, should consecrate. If you were persuaded our dispositions would not assimilate; if mine appeared to you too rigorous, too ungenial, your timely precaution has spared more misery than it has inflicted. How could I have borne the light, when it had shewn me Camilla unhappy—yet Camilla my own—?'

His struggle here grew vain, his voice faltered; the resentment of Camilla forsook her; she raised her head, and was turning to him her softened countenance, and filling eyes, when she saw Melmond, and a party of gentlemen, fast approaching her from Mrs. Berlinton. Edgar saw them too, and cutting short all he meant to have added, kissed, without knowing what he did, the lace of her cloak, and ejaculating, 'Be Heaven your guard, and happiness your portion!' left her hand to that of Melmond, which was held out to her, and slightly bowing to the whole party, walked slowly, and frequently looking back, away: while Camilla, nearly blinded now by tears that would no longer be restrained, kept her eyes fixedly upon the earth, and was drawn, more dead than alive, by Melmond to the coach.

CHAPTER II

Touches of Wit and Humour

THE suddenness of this blow to Camilla, at the moment when her expectations from Edgar were wound up to the summit of all she desired, would have stupefied her into a consternation beyond even affliction, had not the mildness of his farewell, the kindness of his prayers, and the friendship of his counsels, joined to the generosity of leaving wholly to herself the account of their separation, subdued all the pride that sought to stifle her tenderness, and penetrated her with an admiration which left not one particle of censure to diminish her regret.

Melmond and his sister, always open to distress, and susceptible to pity, saw with true concern this melancholy change, and concluded that Mandlebert had communicated some painful intelligence.

She went straight to her own room, with a sign of supplication that Mrs. Berlinton would not follow; and turning quick from Mrs. Mittin, who met her at the street door.

Mrs. Berlinton yielded; but Mrs. Mittin was not easily rebuffed. She was loaded with lilac plumes, ribbands, and gauzes, and Camilla saw her bed completely covered with her new ball dress.

This sight was, at first, an aggravation of her agony, by appearing to her as superfluous as it was expensive: but wherever hope could find an aperture to creep in at, it was sure of a welcome from Camilla. Edgar was undoubtedly invited to the ball; why should he not be there? he had taken leave of her, indeed, and he certainly proposed going abroad; but could a mere meeting once more, be so repugnant as not to be endured.

The answer to this question was favourable to her wishes, for by her wishes it was framed: and the next play of her fertile and quick reviving imagination, described the meeting that would ensue, the accidents that would bring them into the same set, the circumstances that would draw them again into conversation, and the sincerity with which she would do justice to her unalterable esteem, by assuring him how injurious to it were his surmises that she thought him rigorous, austere, or in any single instance to blame.

These hopes somewhat appeased, though their uncertainty could not banish her terrors, and she was able to appear at dinner tolerably composed.

Another affair, immediately after, superseded them, for the present, by more urgent difficulties.

Soon after her arrival at Southampton, a poor woman, who washed for her, made a petition in behalf of her brother, a petty shop-keeper, who, by various common, yet pitiable circumstances of unmerited ill success in business, was unable to give either money or security to the wholesale dealers, for the renewal of his exhausted stock in trade; though the present full season, made it rational to suppose, that, if he had his usual commodities, he might retrieve his credit, save himself from bankruptcy, and his children from beggary. These last, which were five in number, were all, upon various pretences, brought to Camilla, whose pity they excited by the innocence with which they seemed ignorant of requiring it; and who received them with smiles and encouragement, however frivolous their errands, and frequent their interruptions. But the goods which their father wanted to lay in, to revive his trade, demanded full thirty pounds, which, Camilla declared, were as absolutely out of her power to give as thirty thousand, though she promised to plead to Sir Hugh for the sum, upon her return to Cleves, and was prevailed with to grant her name to this promise for the wholesale dealers. These would trust, however, to no verbal security; and Mrs. Mittin, who from collateral reasons was completely a friend of the poor man, offered to be bound for him herself, though thirty pounds were nearly her year's income, provided Camilla would sign a paper, by which she would engage *upon her honour*, to indemnify her of any loss she might eventually sustain by this agreement, as soon as she was of age, or should find it in her power before that time.

The seriousness of this clause, made Camilla refuse the responsibility, protesting she should have no added means in consequence of being of age. But Mrs. Mittin assured Higden, the poor man, as she assured all others, that she was heiress to immense wealth, for she had had it from one that had it from her own brother's own mouth; and that though she could not find out why she was so shy of owning it, she supposed it was only from the fear of being imposed upon.

The steadiness of Camilla, however, could not withstand her

compassion, when the washerwoman brought the poor children to beg for their father; and, certain of her uncle's bounty, she would have run a far more palpable risk, sooner than have assumed the force to send them weeping away.

The stores were then delivered; and all the family poured forth their thanks.

But this day, in quitting the dining parlour, she was stopt in the hall by Higden, who, in unfeigned agonies, related, that some flasks of oil, in a small hamper, which were amongst the miscellaneous articles of his just collected stores, had, by some cruel accident, been crushed, and their contents, finding their way into all the other packages, had stained or destroyed them.

Camilla, to whose foresight misfortune never presented itself, heard this with nearly equal terror for herself, and sorrow for the poor man: yet her own part, in a second minute, appeared that of mere inconvenience, compared with his, which seemed ruin irretrievable; she sought, therefore, to comfort him; but could afford no further help, since she had painfully to beg from her uncle the sum already so uselessly incurred. He ventured still to press, that, if again he could obtain a supply, every evil chance should be guarded against; but Camilla had now learned that accidents were possible; and the fear which arises from disappointed trust, made her think of probable mischiefs with too acute a discernment, to deem it right to run again any hazard, where, if there were a failure, another, not herself, would be the sufferer. Yet the despair of the poor man induced her to promise she would write in his favour, though not act in it again unauthorised.

With feelings of still augmented discomfort, from her denial, she repaired to her toilette; but attired herself without seeing what she put on, or knowing, but by Mrs. Mittin's descriptions and boastings, that her dress was new, of the Pervil uniform, and made precisely like that of Mrs. Berlinton. Her agitated spirits, suspended, not between hope and fear, but hope and despair, permitted no examination of its elegance: the recollection of its expence, and the knowledge that Edgar thought her degenerating into coquetry, left nothing but regret for its wear.

Mrs. Berlinton, who never before, since her marriage, had been of any party where her attractions had not been unrivalled, had believed herself superior to pleasure from personal homage, and

knew not, till she missed it, that it made any part of her amusement in public. But the Beauty, when first she perceives a
competitor for the adulation she has enjoyed exclusively, and the
Statesman, at the first turn of popular applause to an antagonist,
are the two beings who, perhaps, for the moment, require the
most severe display of self-command, to disguise, under the
semblance of good humour or indifference, the disappointment
they experience in themselves, or the contempt with which they
are seized for the changing multitude.

Mrs. Berlinton, though she felt no resentment against Camilla
for the desertion she had occasioned her, felt much surprize; not
to be first was new to her: and whoever, in any station of life, any
class of society, has had regular and acknowledged precedency,
must own a sudden descent to be rather aukward. Where resignation is voluntary, to give up the higher place may denote more
greatness of mind than to retain it; but where imposed by others,
few things are less exhilarating to the principal, or impress less
respect upon the by-stander.

Mrs. Berlinton had never been vain; but she could not be
ignorant of her beauty; and that the world's admiration should be
so wondrously fickle, or so curiously short-lived, as to make even
the bloom of youth fade before the higher zest of novelty, was an
earlier lesson than her mind was prepared to receive. She thought
she had dressed herself that morning with too much carelessness
of what was becoming, and devoted to this evening a greater
portion of labour and study.

While Camilla was impatiently waiting, Mrs. Pollard, the
washerwoman, gained admittance to her, and bringing two
interesting little children of from four to five years old, and an
elder girl of eleven, made them join with herself to implore their
benefactress to save them all from destruction.

Higden having had the imprudence, in his grief, to make known
his recent misfortune, it had reached the ears of his landlord,
who already was watchful and suspicious, from a year and half
arrears of his rent; and steps were immediately preparing to seize
whatever was upon the premises the next morning; which, by
bringing upon him all his other creditors, would infallibly im-
mure him in the lingering hopelessness of a prison.

Camilla now wavered; the debt was but eighteen pounds; the
noble largesses of her uncle in charity, till, of late, that he had been

somewhat drained by Lionel, were nearly unlimited.—She paused—looked now at the pleading group, now at her expensive dress; asked how, for her own hopes, she could risk so much, yet for their deliverance from ruin so little; and with a blush turning from the mirrour, and to the children with a tear, finally consented that the landlord should apply to her the next morning.

*   *   *   *

Lord Pervil had some time opened the ball before Mrs. Berlinton's arrival; but he looked every where for Camilla, to succeed to a young lady of quality with whom he had danced the first two dances. He could not, however, believe he had found, though he now soon saw and made up to her. The brilliancy of her eyes was dimmed by weeping, her vivacity was changed into dejection, sighs and looks of absence took place of smiles and sallies of gaiety, and her whole character seemed to have lost its spring and elasticity. She gave him her hand, to preserve her power of giving it if claimed by Edgar, and though he had thought of her without ceasing since she had charmed him in the yacht, till he had obtained it, not a lady appeared in the room, by the time these two dances were over, that he would not more chearfully have chosen for two more: her gravity every minute encreased, her eye rolled, with restless anxiety, every where, except to meet his, and so little were her thoughts, looks, or conversation bestowed upon her partner, that instead of finding the animated beauty who had nearly captivated him on board the yacht, he seemed coupled with a fair lifeless machine, whom the music, perforce, put in motion; and relinquished her hand with as little reluctance as she withdrew it.

Melmond had again, by his sister, been forced into the party, thought with added unwillingness, from his new idea of Indiana. Now, however, to avoid that fair bane was impossible: Indiana was the first object to meet every eye, from the lustre of her beauty, and the fineness of her figure, each more than ever transcendently conspicuous, from the uniform which had obliged every other female in the room to appear in exactly the same attire. Yet great and unrivalled as was the admiration which she met, what came simply and naturally was insufficient for the thirst with which she now quaffed this intoxicating beverage; and to render its draughts still more delicious, she made Eugenia always hold by her arm. The contrast here to the spectators was diverting as well as striking, and renewed attention to her own charms, when the eye began to grow nearly sated with gazing. The ingenuous Eugenia, incapable of suspecting such a design, was always the dupe to the request, from the opinion it was made in kindness, to save her from fatigue in the eternal sauntering of a public place; and, lost to all fear, in being lost to all hope, as to her own appearance, chearfully accompanied her beautiful kinswoman, without conjecturing that, in a company whence the illiterate and vulgar were excluded, personal imperfections could excite pleasantry, or be a subject of satire.

Camilla, who still saw nothing of Edgar, yet still thought it possible he might come, joined them as soon as she was able. Miss Margland was full of complaints about Dr. Orkborne, for his affording them no assistance in the yacht, and not coming home even to dinner, nor to attend them to Lord Pervil's; and Eugenia, who was sincerely attached to the Doctor, from the many years he had been her preceptor, was beginning to express her serious uneasiness at his thus strangely vanishing; when Clermont, with the most obstreperous laughter, made up to them, and said: 'I'll tell you a monstrous good joke! the best thing you ever heard in your life! the old Doctor's been upon the very point of being drowned!—and he has not had a morsel to eat all day!'

He then related that his man, having seen him composedly seated, and musing upon a pile of planks which were seasoning upon the beach, with his face turned away from the company to avoid its interruptions, had enquired if he had any commands at home, whither he was going: 'Not for meaning to do them,' continued Lynmere; 'No, no! catch Bob at that! but only to break in upon him; for Bob's a rare hand at a joke. He says he's ready to die with laughing, when he speaks to the old Doctor while he's studying, because he looks so much as if he wished we were all hanged. However, he answered tolerably civilly, and only desired that nobody might go into his room till he came home from the sail, for he'd forgot to lock it. So Bob, who smoked how the matter was,[1] says: 'The sail, Sir, what are you going alone, then? for all the company's been gone these two hours.' So this put him in such a taking, Bob says he never laughed so much in his life. He jumped up as if he'd been bit: 'Gone?' says he, 'why where's Miss

Eugenia, I promised Sir Hugh not to lose sight of her.' So he said he'd go after her that very moment. 'Call me a boat,' said he: just as if he'd ordered a hackney coach; for he knows about as much of winds and tides as my little bay Filly, that I bought of Halder yesterday for fifty pounds, but that I shall make worth seventy in less than a month. Well, there was nothing to be had but a small fishing boat, so Bob winks at the man to take in a friend; for he has all those fellows in a string.[1] So in went his Latinship, and off they put. Bob fell into such a fit of laughter, he says I might have heard him a mile off. I don't think Bob has his fellow upon earth for fun.'

Eugenia now interrupted the narration, with a serious enquiry where Dr. Orkborne was at present.

Lynmere, shouting at what he thought the ridicule of this concern, answered, that Bob had told the fisherman to go about his own business, unless the Doctor offered to pay him handsomely for taking him on board the yacht; but thinking it would be a good joke to know what was become of him, he had gone himself, with Halder, and some more choice blades, to the beach, about half an hour ago, to make Bob see if the fishing boat was come in; and, by good luck, they arrived at the very nick of time, and saw the Doctor, the fish, and the fishing-tackle, all hauled out together. 'And a better sight was never seen before, I promise you!' continued Lynmere; 'I thought I should quite have burst my sides with looking at him, he was so wet and so cold, and so miserable; and when I thought of his having had no dinner, I shouted till I was ready to roll on the beach—and he smelt so of the fish, that I could have hugged Bob, 'twas such monstrous good sport. He got three half crowns in a minute for his ingenuity. Halder began;—and two others of us gave two more.'

'Poor Dr. Orkborne! and where is he now?' said Eugenia.

'Why we got about the fisherman, and then we had all the same fun over again: He says, that, at first, the poor gentleman was in a great taking, fretting and fuming, and looking out for the yacht, and seeming almost beside himself for hurry to get to it; but after that, he takes out a little red book and a pencil, and falls to writing, just as hard as if he'd come into the boat for nothing else; insomuch, that when they were just coming along-side the yacht, he never lifted up his head, nor listened to one word, but kept making a motion with his hand to be let alone: and when the man said the yacht would be passed, he bid him hold his peace, and not interrupt him so, in such a pettish manner, that the man resolved to take honest Bob's advice, and go on about his own business. And so he did, and the Doctor was as content as a lord, till he had scribbled all he could scratch out of his noddle: but then came the best sport of all; for when he had nothing more to write, and looked up, and saw the boat stock still, and the man fishing at his leisure, and heard the yacht had been bound homeward of a good hour, he was in such a perilous passion, the man says, that he actually thought he'd have jumped overboard. I'll bet what you will he won't ask Bob to call him a boat again in a hurry.'

'As to his behaviour,' said Miss Margland, 'it's the last thing in the world to surprise me, after what I have seen myself; nor any body else, I believe, neither. Who is Dr. Orkborne? I doubt much if any body ever heard his name before. I should like to know if any body can tell who was his grandfather!'

She then declared, if she could get any soul to fetch him, he should still come, if it were only that he might not pass the evening all in his own way, which would be just the thing to encourage him to hide himself out of sight, on purpose not to help them another time.

Eugenia was going to beg he might not be disturbed, when Melmond, all alacrity to seize any means of absenting himself from the two cousins, who produced in him so severe a conflict, offered his services to carry a message to the Doctor; which, being readily accepted, he set off.

Indiana and Eugenia, not wholly without similarity of sensation, looked after him. Indiana had now caught his eye; and though quickness was no part of her character, the tale it told had convinced her that her power, though no longer acknowledged was not extinguished; it required neither elemental precepts, nor sagacious perceptions, to make this discovery, and she exultingly determined to appease her late mortification, by reducing him to her feet. She stopt not to enquire what such a step might be to Eugenia, nor what was likely, or even desirable to be its event. Where narrow minds imagine they have received injury, they seek revenge rather than redress, from an opinion that such a conduct asserts their own importance.

Still vainly, and wretchedly, the eyes of Camilla sought Edgar: the evening advanced, but he came not; yet, catching at every possible chance for hope, she thought some other room that they had not visited, might be open for company, where, finally, they might meet.

Dr. Orkborne accompanied Melmond back. Miss Margland was preparing him a reproachful reception, but was so much offended by the fishy smell which he brought into the room, that she had immediate recourse to her salts, and besought him to stand out of her way. He complied without reluctance, though with high disdain.

The young ladies were all dancing. Indiana had no sooner perceived Melmond, than she determined to engage his attention: the arts of coquetry require but slender parts, where the love of admiration is potent; she pretended, therefore, to feel extremely ill, put her hand to her forehead, and telling her partner, Mr. Halder, she could not stand another minute, hastened to Miss Margland, and cast herself, as if fainting, upon her neck.

This had all the success with Melmond that his own lively imagination could give it. He flew to a side-table to get her a glass of water, which his trembling hand could scarce hold, but which she received from him with a languishing sweetness, that dissolved every tie but of love, and he '*hung over her enamoured**;'[1] while Miss Margland related that she could hardly keep from fainting herself, so much she had been shocked and disordered by the horrid smell of Dr. Orkborne.

Indiana now caught the infection, and protested she was so much worse, that if she had not a little air she should die. Melmond was flying to open a window, but a lady who sat close to it, objected; and he had then recourse to two folding doors, leading to a portico open to a large garden.

Hither Indiana permitted herself to be led, and led by the thrice happy, yet thrice miserable Melmond. Miss Margland was accompanying them, but Lady Pervil, advancing to enquire what went wrong, gave her an opportunity irresistible to inveigh against Dr. Orkborne; and as her well-bred hearer, though little interested in such a detail, would not interrupt it, Indiana arrived alone in the portico with Melmond. Halder, who had danced with her, followed, but supposing Melmond the favoured man, walked singing off, and made the tour of the garden.

This situation was to Melmond as dangerous, as to Indiana it

*Milton

was exulting. She now suddenly withdrew her hand, with an air of poignant disdain, which the illuminated portico and house made amply visible; and when, surprised and much moved, he tremblingly enquired if she were worse, she answered, 'Why do you ask? I am sure you do not care.'

Easily deprived of all forbearance, 'Heavens!' he exclaimed, 'do I live, yet suffer this imputation! O divine Indiana! load me with every other reproach, rather than this dreadful charge of insensibility to all that is most lovely, most perfect upon earth!'

'I thought,' said Indiana, again softening her fine eyes, 'you had quite forgot me, and all the vows you made to me.'

'Wretch that I am,' cried Melmond nearly distracted by this charge, and by the regret at losing him, which seemed its purpose, 'condemned to every species of woe! O fair, angelic Indiana! in a cottage with you would I have dwelt, more delightedly, and more proudly, than any potentate in the most gorgeous palace:[1] but, alas! from you—formed to enchant all mankind, and add grace to every dignity—from you could I dare ask such a sacrifice?'

Indiana now listened with an attentive softness no longer factitious; though all her views wafted her to splendour and high life, her ear could not withstand the romantic sound of love and a cottage; and though no character was ever less formed to know and taste the blessings such a spot may bestow and reciprocate, she imagined she might there be happy, for she considered such a habitation but as a bower of eglantine and roses, in which she might repose and be adored all day long.

Melmond saw but too quickly the relenting cast of her countenance; and ecstasy and despair combated which should bear sway in his breast. 'Ah, madam,' he cried, 'most adorable and most adored of women! you know my terrible situation, but you know not the sufferings, nor the constancy of my heart!—the persecution of friends, the pressure of distress, the hopelessness of my idolized Indiana—'

A deep sigh interrupted him—it came not from Indiana—startled, he looked round—and beheld Eugenia, leaning against the door by which she seemed to have intended entering, pale, petrified, aghast.

Shame now tied his tongue, and tingled, with quick reproach, through his whole frame. He looked at Indiana with despair, at Eugenia with remorse; injured rectitude and blushing honour urged him to the swiftest termination of so every way terrible a scene, and bowing low to Eugenia, 'I durst not, madam,' he cried, 'ever hope for your pardon! yet I rather deluded myself than deceived you when I ventured to solicit your acceptance. Alas! I am a bankrupt both in fortune and in heart, and can only pray you will hasten to forget—that you may forbear to execrate me!'

He then disappeared, finding a way out by the garden, to avoid re-entering the ball-room.

Eugenia, who, in this speech, comprehended an eternal adieu, sunk upon the seat of the portico, cold, shivering, almost lifeless. Little prepared for such an event, she had followed Indiana the moment she was disengaged from the dance, not suspicious of any *tête-à-tête*, from believing Halder of the party. The energy of Melmond made her approach unheard; and the words she unavoidably caught, nearly turned her to marble.

Indiana was sorry for her distress, yet felt a triumph in its cause; and wondered how so plain a little creature could take it into her head to think of marrying.

Camilla now joined them, affrighted at the evident anguish of Eugenia, who, leaning upon her affectionate bosom, had the relief excited by pity, of bursting into tears, while despondingly she uttered: 'All is over, my sister, and over for life with Eugenia! Melmond flies and detests me! I am odious in his sight! I am horror to this thoughts!'

Camilla wept over her in silent, but heart-breaking sympathy. Indiana returned to the dance: but the two suffering sisters remained in the portico till summoned to depart. They were insensible to the night air, from the fever of their minds. They spoke no more; they felt the insufficiency of words to express their griefs, and their mutual compassion was all that softened their mutual sorrows.

CHAPTER III

An Adieu

LOST to all happiness, and for the first time in her life, divested of hope, Camilla at a late hour returned to Mrs. Berlinton's. And here, her heart-breaking disappointment received the cruel aggravation of the most severe self-reproach, when, in facing the mirror to deposit her ornaments upon the toilette table, she considered the expensive elegance of her whole dress, now, even in her own estimation, by its abortive purpose, rendered glaringly extravagant. Since her project had failed, she saw the impropriety of having risked so much in its attempt; and a train of just reflections ensued, to which her understanding was always equal, though her gaiety was seldom disposed. 'Would Edgar,' thought she, 'wait the event of a meeting at a ball to decide his conduct? Had he not every title to claim a conference with me, if he had the smallest inclination? Rejected as he calls himself, I had not pretended to demand our separation from any doubts, any displeasure of my own. From the moment he suffered me to quit, without reclamation, the roof under which I had proposed our parting, I ought to have seen it was but his own desire, perhaps design, I was executing. And all the reluctance he seemed to feel, which so weakly I attributed to regard, was but the expiring sensibility of the last moment of intercourse. Not with murmurs, he says, he will quit me—nor with murmurs will I now resign him! —with blessings, he says, he leaves me—O Edgar! mayest thou too be blest! The erring and unequal Camilla[1] deserved thee not!'

A more minute examination of her attire was not calculated to improve her serenity. Her robe was everywhere edged with the finest Valencienne lace; her lilac shoes, sash, and gloves, were richly spangled with silver, and finished with a silver fringe; her ear-rings and necklace were of lilac and gold beads; her fan and shoe roses were brilliant with lilac foil, and her bouquet of artificial lilac flowers, and her plumes of lilac feathers, were here and there tipt with the most tiny transparent white beads, to give them the effect of being glittering with the dew.

Of the cost of all this she was no judge, but, certain its amount must be high, a warm displeasure arose against the incorrigible Mrs. Mittin, who had not only taken the pattern, but the value of Mrs. Berlinton's dress for her guide: and a yet greater dissatisfaction ensued with herself, for trusting the smallest commission to so vain and ungovernable an agent. She could only hope to hoard the payment from the whole of her next year's allowance, by living in so forbearing and retired a manner, as to require nothing for herself.

The new, but all powerful guest which now assailed her, unhappiness, had still kept her eyes from closing, when she was called up to Mr. Tennet, the landlord of Higden. Her fuller knowledge of her own hopeless debts, could not make her faithless to her engagement; for her acquaintance with misery awakened but more pity for the misery of others. She admitted him, therefore, without demur; and found he was a land surveyor, who had often been employed by Sir Hugh at Cleves. He accepted her verbal promise to be answerable for the rent now due, declining her note of hand, which her minority made illegal, and engaging not to hurry her for the money; well satisfied, by the Tyrold character in the whole county, he might abide by her word of honour, founded upon the known munificence of her uncle.

This delay was a relief, as it saved a partial demand, that must have forced an abrupt confession of her own debts, or have deceived the baronet into a belief she had nothing to solicit.

When this business was transacted, she hastened to Eugenia, to console whose sufferings was all that could mitigate her own.

One of the maids then came to say she had forgotten to inform her, that, some time after she had set out for Lord Pervil's a stranger, much muffled up, and with a hat flapped over his face so as wholly to hide it, had enquired for her, and seemed much disturbed when he heard she was at the ball, but said he would call again the next day at noon.

No conjecture occurred to Camilla but that this must be Edgar; it was contrary to all probability; but no other image could find way to her mind. She hastened, inexpressibly perturbed, to her sister, determining to be at home before twelve o'clock, and fashioning to herself all the varieties such a meeting could afford; every one of which, however they began, ended regularly with a reconciliation.

She found Eugenia weeping in bed. She embraced her with the extremest tenderness: 'Ah my sister!' said the unhappy mourner, 'I weep not for my disappointment, great as it may be—and I do not attempt describing it!—it is but my secondary sorrow. I weep, Camilla, for my own infatuation! for the folly, the blindness of which I find myself culpable. O Camilla! is it possible I could ever—for a moment, a single moment, suppose Melmond could willingly be mine! could see his exquisite susceptibility of every thing that is most perfect, yet persuade myself, he could take, by

choice, the poor Eugenia for his wife! the mangled, deformed,—
unfortunate Eugenia!'

Camilla, touched to the heart, wept now more than her sister.
'That Eugenia,' she cried, 'has but to be known, to leave all
beauty, all figure, every exterior advantage aloof, by the nobler,
the more just superiority of intrinsic worth. Let our estimates but
be mental, and who will not be proud to be placed in parallel with
Eugenia?'

She was then beginning her own sad relation, when an unopened letter upon the toilette table caught her eye. It had been
placed there by Molly Mill, who thought her mistress asleep.
Struck by the shape of the seal, Camilla rose to examine it: what
was her palpitation, then, to see the cypher E M, and, turning
to the other side, to perceive the hand writing of Edgar!

She put it into her sister's hand, with expectation too big for
speech. Eugenia opened it, and they read it silently together.

To Miss EUGENIA TYROLD.

Southampton.

'Tis yet but a short time—in every account but my own—
since I thought myself forming a legal claim to address Miss
Eugenia Tyrold as my sister. Every other claim to that affectionate
and endearing title has been hers beyond her own memory; hers
by the filial love I bear her venerated parents; hers, by the tender
esteem due to the union of almost every virtue. These first and
early ties must remain for ever. Disappointment here cannot
pierce her barbarous shafts, fortune cannot wanton in reversing,
nor can time dissolve them.——

'O Edgar!' exclaimed Camilla, stopping the reading, and
putting her hand, as in benediction, upon the paper, 'do you deign
to talk of disappointment? do you condescend to intimate you are
unhappy? Ah, my Eugenia, you shall clear this dreadful error!—
'tis to you he applies—you shall be peace-maker; restorer!'

Eugenia dried her tears at the thought of so sweet an office, and
they read on.

Of the other—yet nearer claim, I will not speak. You have
probably known longer than myself, its annihilation, and I will

not pain your generous heart with any view of my sufferings in such a deprivation. I write but to take with my pen the leave I dare not trust myself to take by word of mouth; to wish to your opening prospects all the happiness that has flown mine, and to entreat you to answer for me to the whole of your loved family, that its name is what, through life, my ear with most reverence will hear, my heart with most devotion will love.

EDGAR MANDLEBERT.

At the kind wish upon her own opening prospects, Eugenia wept afresh; but when Camilla took the letter to press to her lips and her heart what he said of his sufferings, she perceived at the doubling down, two lines more:—

I am this moment leaving Southampton for the Isle of Wight, whence I shall sail to the first port, that the first vessel with which I may meet shall be bound.

'No, my dear Eugenia,' cried she, then colouring, and putting down the letter, 'your mediation will be spared. He acquaints us he is quitting England. He can only mention it to avoid the persecution of an answer. Certainly none shall be obtruded upon him.'

Eugenia pleaded that still a letter might overtake him at the Isle of Wight, and all misunderstanding might be rectified. 'And then, my sister, all may be well, and your happiness renewed.—It has not flown you—like that of Eugenia—from any radical cause. Her's is not only gone, past all resource, but has left behind it disgrace with sorrow, derision with disappointment!'

Camilla strove to soothe her, but would no longer listen to any mediation; she resolved, at once, to write of the separation to her father, and beseech him to send for her to Etherington, and never again suffer her to quit that roof, where alone her peace was without disturbance, her conduct without reproach. Even her debts, now, she felt equal to avowing, for as, far from contracting new ones, she meant in future to reside in complete obscurity, she hoped the feelings of this moment would procure pardon for her indiscretions, which her own sedulous future œconomy should be indefatigable to repair.

Eugenia would not strive longer against a procedure which she deemed dignified, and the departure of Camilla was hurried by a messenger, who brought word that the strange man, with the flapped hat, was returned, and entreated her, for Heaven's sake, to let him speak with her one moment.

Dead, now, to the hope she had entertained of this enquirer, she merely from his own urgency complied with his call; for her curiosity was gone since she now knew it could not be Edgar.

*   *   *   *

Edgar, indeed, was actually departed. His heart was loaded with sorrow, his prospect seemed black with despondence; but Camilla was lost to that perfect confidence, and unbounded esteem, he required to feel for his wife, and no tenderness without them, no partial good opinion, nor general admiration, could make him wish to lead her to the altar. 'No!' cried he, 'Dr. Marchmont; you judged me better than my first passion, and her untried steadiness enabled me to judge myself. Misery only could have followed my view of her in the mixt society in which the thousand accidents of life might occasionally have placed us. I can only be happy with a character as simple in the world, as in retirement; as artless at an assembly, as in a cottage. Without that heavenly simplicity, the union of all else that renders life desirable, were vain! without that—all her enchanting qualities, with which nothing can vie, and which are entwined around my heart-strings, were ineffectual to my peace.'

'You are right,' said the Doctor, 'and your timely caution, and early wisdom, will protect you from the bitterness of a personal experience like mine. With all the charms she assembles, her character seems too unstable for private domestic life. When a few years more have blunted the wild vivacity, the floating ambition, the changing propensities which now render her inconsistent to others, and fluctuating even to herself, she may yet become as respectable, as she must always be amiable. But now, . . . who-ever takes her from the circle in which she is playing, will see her lost to all gaiety, though without daring to complain, from the restraint of bidden duties, which make the bidder a tyrant.'

Edgar shrunk from such a part, and immediately prepared for his long projected tour.

He had, originally, purposed visiting Mr. Tyrold before he set out, and conversing with him upon the state of danger in which he thought his daughter; but his tenderness for her feelings, during his last adieu, had beguiled him of this plan, lest it should prove painful, injurious, or inauspicious to her own views or designs in breaking to her friends their breach. He now addressed a few lines to his revered guardian, to be delivered by Dr. Marchmont; to whom he gave discretionary powers, if any explanation should be demanded; though clogged with an earnest clause, that he would neither advance, nor confess any thing that could hurt Camilla, even a moment, unless to avert from her some danger, or substantiate some good.

Dr. Marchmont determined to accompany him to the Isle of Wight, whither he resolved to go, and wait for his baggage; and undertook the superintendance of his estate and affairs in his absence.

When they were summoned to the little vessel, Edgar changed colour, his heart beat quick, and he sighed rather than breathed. He held his hand upon his eyes and forehead for a few minutes, in agony inexpressible, then silently gave his servant the letter he had written for Eugenia, took the Doctor by the arm, walked to the beach, and got aboard; his head still turned wholly towards the town, his eyes looking above it, as if seeking to fix the habitation of Camilla. Dr. Marchmont sought to draw his attention another way, but it was rivetted to the spot they were quitting.

'I feel truly your unhappiness, my dear Mandlebert,' said he, 'that this young creature, with defects of so cruel a tendency, mingles qualities of so endearing a nature. Judge, however, the predominance of what is faulty, since parents so exemplary have not been able to make the scales weigh down on the side of right. Alas! Mr. Tyrold has himself erred, in committing, at so early a period, her conduct into her own reins. The very virtues, in the first youth, are so little regulated by reflection, that, were [they] not watched nor aided, they run into extremes nearly as pernicious, though not so unamiable as the vices. What instance more than this now before us can shew the futility of education, and the precariousness of innate worth, when the contaminating world is allowed to seize its inexperienced prey, before the character is fixed as well as formed?'

A deeply assenting sigh broke from the bosom of Edgar, whose strained eyes held their purpose, till neither beach, nor town, nor even a spire of Southampton, were discernible. Again, then, for a moment, he covered them with his hand, and exclaimed: 'Farewell! Camilla, farewell!'

CHAPTER IV

A modest Request

QUICK, though without a wish of speed, was the return home of Camilla; she felt at this moment in that crushed and desolate state, where the sudden extinction of hope leaves the mind without energy to form even a wish. She was quick only because too nervous to be slow, and hurried on, so little knowing why, that when she came to Mrs. Berlinton's, she was running to her own room, wholly forgetting what had called her from Eugenia, till the servant said, 'this is the man, ma'am.'

She then saw, parading up and down the hall, a figure wrapt round in a dark blue roquelo,[1] with no part of his face visible, from the flaps of his hat.

At another time she might have been startled: but she was now indifferent to everything, and only enquired what was his business.

He made no answer but by a low bow, pointing, at the same time to the door of one of the parlours, and then, in a supplicating manner, putting together his hands, as if begging to speak to her in private.

Careless, rather than courageous, she was going into an empty room with him, when the servant whispered her to be upon her guard, as the man had a very suspicious look.

Stopping short, then, she again repeated her question, adding, 'I can hear anything you have to say where we now are.'

The stranger shook his head, with a motion towards the servant, that seemed to demand his absence.

Alas! thought she, it is some gentleman in distress, who wants to beg and is ashamed. I have nothing to give him! I will, at least, therefore, not insist upon his exposing himself. She then whispered the footman to keep in the hall, and near the parlour, which she entered, telling the incognito he might follow.

But she was seriously alarmed out of her apathy, upon seeing him cautiously shut the door, and sedulously examine the apartment.

She wanted not presence of mind, when not robbed of it by some peculiar and poignant feelings. She turned immediately to the bell, certain its first touch would bring in the footman: but, perceiving her purpose, the stranger seized her by the arm, and in a hoarse low voice said: 'Are you mad, Camilla? don't you know me?' and she recognized her brother.

She expostulated upon his having so causelessly terrified her, and enquired why he came so disguised.

He laughed heartily at her affright, and extolled his own skill in personating a subtle ruffian; declaring he liked to have a touch at all trades, in case of accidents.

'And have you come hither, Lionel, only for this foolish and very unpleasant trick?'

'O no, my dear! this was only for my opening. I have an hundred smart freaks in my head, any one of them worth a little trip to Southampton. Besides, I wanted to know what you were about. How does a certain master Edgar Mandlebert do? Don't blush, child. What a little sly rogue you have been! hey ho? Tears?—My dear Camilla! what's all this?'

She entreated him to make his enquiries of Eugenia.

'Well, you took me in, I promise you. I fully thought the young Baronet had been the man. And, really he's as fine a fellow as I ever saw.'

'Do not speak of him, I beg! O Lionel!—if you knew—' She was going to say, how through your means, that affair has injured me—but she checked complaints which she now regarded as useless, and therefore degrading; and, wiping her eyes, asked if he had yet considered the large sum, for the obligation of which he had made her seem responsible to Sir Sedley, whom she should not know how ever to meet, nor consequently, how ever to visit in the county, till some payment, if not made, were at least arranged.

'Pho, pho, my dear child, don't be so Vellum-like;[1] you'll be fit for nothing, soon, but to file bills and score accounts. What's two hundred to him? Hang him! I wish 'twere as much again—I hate making a fuss about nothing. But come, tell me something to raise my spirits—I am horribly melancholy. I've some notion of making a little sport here with Miss Scare-crow. How does she go on? Waspish as ever?'

'Do tell me, seriously, Lionel, what it is has brought you hither?'

'Two things, my dear. The first of which is the pleasure of seeing you; and the second, is a little amusement I propose myself with old Dr. Hic, Hæc, Hoc. I find Clermont's had rare sport with him already. It's deuced unlucky I did not come sooner.'

'Clermont? When did you see Clermont?'

'Don't be curious, child. I never encourage curiosity. It always leads to disagreeable questions. You may tell me any thing you please, but ask nothing. That's my manner of dealing with little girls. How did you like my sending the Major to you? Was not that good fudge?[1] What do you look so grave for, my dear? You're enough to give one the vapours.'

Camilla attempted not to rally; she felt pierced as by a poniard at the very sight of Lionel. The debt he had made her contract with Sir Sedley, the secrecy it exacted, the correspondence it had drawn on, the cruel circumstances it had produced, and the heart-breaking event to which it had, ultimately, led, made his view excite sensations too corrosive, and reflections too bitter, for any enjoyment of a gaiety, which her utmost partiality could not dis-entangle from levity the most unfeeling.

'Come, come, for pity's sake, be a little less stupid, I conjure you. How terribly you want a good shaking! shall I give you one? By the way, you have never thanked me for sending you that smart young tinker. You are horribly ungrateful to all my tender care to provide you a good spouse. What! not a smile? Not one dear little dimple for all my rattle? Nay, then, if that's the case, let's to business at once. Anything is better than mawkishness. I always preferred being flogged for a frolic, to being told I was a good boy, at the expence of sitting still, and learning my lesson.'

'And what business, my dear Lionel? Have you really any?'

'O yes, always; nobody has more; only I do it so briskly, people always suppose it nothing but pleasure. However, just at this minute, I am really in rather an ugly dilemma. You know, my dear girl, there is a certain little rather awkward affair of mine, which I once hinted to you.'——

'Lionel, I hope, at least,'——

'O, none of your hopes with that grave face! Hope, with a grave face, always means fear. Now, as I am already half shoes over in the slough of despond,[1] 'twill be horrid ungenerous to poke me still lower.'

Camilla now began to tremble, and would ask no questions— Lionel, when he had silenced her, seemed at a loss how to proceed; he walked about the room with quick jerks, opened and shut the window, seated himself upon every chair, and every table; and then, in a half passion, said: 'so you don't want to hear any more? and you don't care a fig if I'm hanged or drowned?'

'My spirits are not high, my dear Lionel; and my head is full, and my heart is oppressed: if you have any thing, therefore, important to say, speak, I beg without trifling.'

'Nay, there's nothing new; so don't look frightened; it's all the same old story.'

'You continue, then, that dark, mysterious connexion? O brother!'

'Why she's so pretty! so monstrous pretty! besides, she doats upon me. You don't half conceive what a pretty fellow I am, Camilla. A sister never knows how to judge a man. All the women like me prodigiously.'

'Indeed, Lionel, you take an undue advantage of my affection. I must seriously insist that you mention this subject to me no more.'

'I don't intend it. I intend to finish with this once—provided you do me one last good turn. Will you, now? Come, don't be queer.'[2]

'I will do nothing, absolutely nothing in so improper—so shocking a business. Indeed, I know not how to forgive you for naming it again.'

'Well, then, I'll pledge you my word and honour you shall never hear of it more, if you'll only grant me this one favour.'

Displeased at the past, and frightened for what might be to come, she protested she would immediately leave the room, if he continued this persecution: adding, 'how affectionately I love you, I need not, I am sure, say; but a confidence such as this, from a brother to a sister, disgraces us both: and let me penetrate, but not irritate you, if I own, that I much doubt whether I ought not from the beginning, to have revealed this transaction at Etherington. Do not be angry Lionel: has not every consideration been surmounted by the fear of giving you pain?'

Finding he still would be heard, she was peremptorily quitting the room; but when she had her hand upon the door, he effectually stopt her, by saying, 'Nay, then, if nothing will content you but getting the whole out at once, you may make yourself easy, the business is at end, for——we're blown!'[1]

'I must certainly be glad if such a business is at an end, Lionel; but how do you mean blown? to whom? in what manner?'

'To every body, I'm afraid; for the husband's upon the point of getting at it.'

'Husband?'

'O, the deuce! I did not mean to say that: however, it's out! and as it must have been known sooner or later'——

Camilla now had an air the nearest to severity she had ever worn: 'Adieu, Lionel!' she cried, 'I am sorry for you, indeed; but you must find another hearer for this guilty history.—I will listen no more!'

Lionel now detained her by force. 'How can you take up the thing so wrong,' said he; 'when I tell you it's over, isn't that enough? Besides, I promise you I have not wanted for my punishment: when you hear all, you'll find that.'

Too sick for speech, yet too weak for resistance, she was constrained to return to her seat, and hear what he pleased to relate.

'My adventure, my dear, was discovered entirely by the want of a little hush money. 'Tis the very deuce and all for a man to be in love when he is poor. If I had only had a little hush-money— yes, yes, I understand that eye! but as to those paltry sums I have had, from time to time, since this affair, why they could not be expected to last for ever: And the first went to a housemaid,—and the second to the groom,—and the third'——

'Lionel! Lionel! is this a communication—are these particulars for me?'

'Nay, I only mention it to let you know it's all gone fairly. Besides, as to her being a married woman, which, I see, is what you think so much the worst of all, I assure you, if you knew her husband, you would not wonder; he deserves every thing. Such a tiresome quiz! It was often hours before we could get rid of him. You never knew such a blockhead. The poor thing can't bear him. But she's fond of me to distraction. Nay, nay, don't frown so! If you'll believe me, Camilla, you'll quite spoil your face. Well, the fellow that threatens to betray us, won't keep our secret under three hundred pounds! There's an unconscionable knave! However, I thought that better than a trial too; not that she would have broken her heart at a separation, you'll believe; but then . . . there's a certain horrid thing called damages! And then my father's particularities,—and my mother's seeing things in such strong lights—and a parson's son,—and all that.'—

Camilla, shaking and pale, now entreated him to get her a glass of water, and, for a while, at least, to forbear continuing this terrible story.

He consented to ring for the water, and then, more briefly, went on.

'Finding it vain to hope any longer for entire concealment, I thought a private discovery less shocking than a public one; and therefore, telling my story as well as I could, I stated that three hundred pounds would save both the expences and publicity of a trial; and, with every possible profession of contrition and reformation, I humbly petitioned for that sum from my uncle.'

'My poor uncle! alas! what unreasonable—unmerciful claims every way surround him!'

'He's well revenged for mine, I promise you! There's no plague lost between us,[1] as you'll own, when you've heard the end of my poor petition. I followed up my letter, according to my usual custom, the next day, in order to receive my money, knowing poor uncle hates writing worse than giving: well, and when I arrived, my mind just made up to a few gentle reprimands against naughtiness, and as many gentle promises to do so no more; out pops me the old butler, and says his master can't see me! Not see me? Why, who's with him? Your father, Sir! O,— then for your life, cries I, don't say I have been here—but now— Camilla will you think me punished or not?—My uncle had a little gout in his right-hand, and had made my father open and read—that very day,—all his letters! If ever you knew old Nick serve a poor young fellow a worse turn than that, tell me so! I owe him such a grudge for it, I could almost find [it] in my heart to turn parson myself.'

Camilla could not utter a word. She dropt her head over her folded arms upon the table, to hide her offending brother from her sight, whom now, placed in opposition to her all-excellent father, she blamed beyond her powers, beyond what she conceived even her rights of expression.

'Why now, my dear Camilla, what do you hide your face for? Do you think I'm not as sorry for this thing as you can be for the life of you? However, now comes the worst; and if you don't pity me when you hear this, you may depend upon it you have no bowels.[1] I was making off as fast as I could, mum the word to the servants, when in comes old Jacob with a letter. I snatched it from him, hoping my uncle had privately sent me a draft—but the direction[2] was written by my father! Don't you begin to feel a little for me now?'

She could only raise her head to ejaculate, 'My poor—poor father!' and then, nearly in an agony, drop it again.

'Hey-day, Camilla? how's this? what! not one word of poor, poor brother, too? why you are harder than flint. However, read that letter. And then, if you don't think me the most unhappy young fellow in existence, you are fit to devise tortures for the inquisition.'

She took the letter eagerly, yet awfully, kissed in weeping the hand-writing, and read what follows:

To LIONEL TYROLD, *Esq.*

To have brought up my family with the purity of principle which the holy profession of their father ought to inspire him to teach, has been, from the hour that my paternal solicitudes commenced, the most fervent of my prayers. How my hopes have been deluded you have but too long known; how grossly they have failed has reached my own knowledge but this moment. I here resign the vain expectation, that through my son the community might bless me: may a forfeiture so dread not extend to me, also, through my daughters!—

Camilla stopt, sunk upon her knees, and devoutly repeated the last sentence, with her own ardent supplications joined to it before she could proceed.

A few words more must, for the present, suffice between us. Accident, by throwing into my hands this last letter to the uncle whose goodness you have most unwarrantably and unfeelingly abused, has given birth to an investigation, by which I have arrived at the discovery of the long course of rapacity by which you have pillaged from the same source. Henceforth, you will find it dry. I have stated to my brother the mistake of his compliance, and obtained his solemn word, that all intercourse between you, that has not my previous approbation, shall here finally cease. You will now, therefore, empty no more those coffers which, but for you, have only been opened to the just claims of benevolence.

You will regard this detection as the wrath of ill-fortune; I view it, on the contrary, as the mercy of Providence. What were further pecuniary exonerations, but deeper plunges into vilifying dissoluteness? If, as you intimate, the refusal of your present demands will expose you to public shame, may its shock awaken feelings that may restore you to private virtue! I cannot spare you from disgrace, by aiding you in corruption; I cannot rescue you from worldly dishonour, by hiding and abetting crimes that may unfold to eternal misery. To errour I would be lenient; to penitence I would be consoling; to reformation I would open my arms: but to him who confesses his guilt only to save himself from punishment, to him who would elude the incurred penalties of his wickedness, by shamelessly soliciting a respectable old relation to use bribery for its concealment,—to him, I can only say, since all precepts of virtue have failed to shew thee its excellence, go! learn of misfortune the evils, at least of vice! Pay to the laws of society what retribution they require for their violation—and if suffering should lead to contrition, and seclusion from the world bring thee back to rectitude, then thou may'st find again thy father

AUGUSTUS TYROLD.

Another name I mention not. I present not to this sullied page an image of such purity: yet, if thy own thoughts dare paint it to thy view, will not thy heart, O Lionel! smite thee and say,—From her native land, from her sorrowing husband, from daughters just opening into life, by my follies and indiscretions I have driven my mother—by my guilt I shall make her blush to return to them?—

Camilla wept over this letter till its characters were almost effaced by her tears. To withhold from her father the knowledge of the misconduct of Lionel, what had she not suffered? what not sacrificed? yet to find it all unavailing, to find him thus informed of his son's wanton calls for money, his culpable connection, and his just fears of seeing it published and punished,—and to consider with all this, that Edgar, through these unpardonable deviations from right, was irretrievably lost to her, excited sorrow the most depressing for her father, and regrets scarce supportable for herself.

'Well,' cried Lionel, 'what do you think of my case now? Don't you allow I pay pretty handsomely for a mere young man's gambol? I assure you I don't know what might have been the consequence, if Jacob had not afforded me a little comfort. He told me you were going to be married to 'squire Mandlebert, and that you were all at Southton, and that he was sure you would do any thing in the world to get me out of jeopardy; and so, thinking pretty much the same myself, here I am! Well, what say you, Camilla? Will you speak a little word for me to Edgar?'

Shame, now taking place of affliction, stopt her tears, which dried upon her burning cheeks, as she answered, 'He is well known to you, Lionel:—you can address him yourself!'

'No; that's your mistake, my dear. I have a little odd money matter to settle with him already; and besides, we have had a sort of a falling out upon the subject; for when I spoke to him about it last, he gave himself the airs of an old justice of the peace, and said if he did not find the affair given up, nothing should induce him ever to help me again. What a mere codger that lad has turned out!'

'Ah, noble Edgar! just, high-principled, and firm!' half pronounced Camilla, while again the icicles dissolved, and trickled down her face.

'See but the different way in which things strike people! however, it is not very pretty in you, Camilla, to praise him for treating me so scurvily. But come, dost think he'll lend me the money?'

'Lend,' repeated she, significantly.

'Ay lend; for I shall pay it every farthing; and every thing else.'

'And how? And when?'

'Why,—with old unky Relvil's fortune.'

'For shame, brother!'

'Nay, nay, you know as well as I do, I must have it at last. Who else has he to leave it to? Come, will you beg the three hundred for me? He dare not refuse you, you know, in your day of power.'

'Lionel,' cried she, with extreme emotion, 'I shall see him no more! nor, perhaps may you!—He has left England.'

'Impossible! why Jacob told me unky was working night and day at preparations for your keeping the wedding at Cleves.'

'I cannot talk upon this subject. I must beseech you to reserve your enquiries for Eugenia.'

'I must go to her then, directly. I have not a moment to lose. If you won't make Edgar help me in this business—and I know he won't do it of his own accord, I am utterly done up. There will remain but one single thing for me. So now for my roquelo. But do only tell me, Camilla, if you ever knew such a poor unlucky wight? for before I came to you, certain it would not be easy to make that young prig do any thing he had already declared against, I found out cousin Clermont. What a handsome coxcomb that is! Well, I told him my case, for one young fellow soon comprehends the difficulties of another, and begged him to ask for the money of uncle Hugh, as if for himself, telling him, that as he was a new-comer, and a new beginner, he could not so readily be refused; and promising to serve him as good a turn myself, when he had got a little into our ways, and wanted it, with my good uncle Relvil. Well! what do you think was the next news? It's enough to make a man's hair stand on end, to see what a spite fortune has taken to me! Do you know he has got debts of his own, of one sort or another, that poor unky has never heard of, to the amount of upwards of a thousand pounds?'

He then muffled himself up and departed.

CHAPTER V

A Self-dissection

CAMILLA remained in a state of accumulated distress, that knew not upon what object most to dwell: her father, shocked and irritated beyond the mild endurance of his character; her brother, wantonly sporting with his family's honour, and his own morals and reputation; her uncle, preparing for nuptials broken off without his knowledge; Edgar, by a thousand perversities of accident, of indiscretion, of misunderstanding, for ever parted from her;—rushed all together upon her mind, each combating for precedence, each individually foiled, yet all collectively triumphant. Nor were even these her sole subjects of affliction: yet another cause was added, in debts contracted from mingled thoughtlessness, inexperience, and generosity, augmented to she knew not what sum, and to be paid by she knew not what means. And this topic, which in itself seemed to her the least interesting, soon, by the circumstances with which it was connected, grew the most pressing of any. How, at a moment like this, could she make her purposed confession to her father, whose wounded mind demanded all she could offer of condolement? How call upon her uncle to be responsible for what she owed, when she now knew the enormous accounts preparing for him from Clermont, of which he was himself yet uninformed?

*　　*　　*　　*

Lionel soon returned. 'So it's really all off?' he cried; 'dame Fortune, methinks, has a mind to give me a taste of her art that I shan't easily forget. Eugenia would tell me no particulars. But, since things are thus, there is only one step left for poor Pillgarlick.[1] I must whisk over to the Continent.'

'To the Continent? without consulting my father? without—'

'My father?—Why, you see he gives me up. He thinks—I thank him!—a little wholesome discipline will do me good. Don't you understand what he means by *seclusion from the world?* A prison, my dear! a gaol! However, I'm not quite of that opinion. I really think a man's as well off in a little open air. So fare thee well, child. As soon as ever my dear uncle Relvil says good night, I'll come home again, and wish you all good morning.'

'Lionel! Lionel!—'

'Well, well! I know it's very wrong, and all that; so say nothing. Don't distress me, I beg, for I hate to be hipped.[2] Besides, old Relvil don't deserve much better; why can't he behave like a man, and settle an annuity upon himself, and an old servant, and a dog, and a cat, and a parrot, and then let an honest young fellow see a little of the world handsomely, and like a gentleman? But your bachelor uncles, and maiden aunts, are the most tantalizing fellows and fellowesses in the creation.'

He then kissed her, and was going; but, earnestly detaining

him, she conjured that he would let her first hint his design to their father, that at least it might be set aside, if it would still more deeply disturb him.

'No, child, no; I know his way of reasoning already. He thinks every man should pay for what he owes, either with money or stripes. Now my poor dear little body is not of that opinion. And what would they get by having me shut up in prison? And I'll defy 'em to cast me in any other damages. I've a few debts, too, of my own, that make me a little uneasy. I don't mean to trades people; they can wait well enough; our credit is good: but a man looks horrid small, walking about, when he can't pay his debts of honour. However, when I disappear, perhaps my father will take compassion upon my character. If not, the Relvil estate shall wipe off all in the long run.'

'And is it possible, Lionel, thus lightly, thus negligently, thus unmoved, you can plan such a journey? such an exile?'

'Why what can I do? what can I possibly do? I am obliged to be off in my own defence. Unless, indeed, I marry little Miss Dennel, which I have once or twice thought of; for she's a monstrous fool. But then she is very rich. How should you like her for a sister? Nay, nay, I'm serious. Don't shake your head as if I was joking. What do you think of her for my spouse?'

'She is a good girl, I believe, Lionel, though a simple one; and I should be sorry to see her unhappy; and how could either of you be otherwise, with contempt such as this?'

'Bless thy heart, my little dear, what have husbands and wives to do with making one another unhappy? Prithee don't set about forming thy notions of married people from the parsonage-house, and conclude a wife no better than a real rib, sticking always close to a man's side. You grow so horrid sententious, I really begin to believe you intend to take out your diploma soon, and put on the surplice my father meant for his poor son.'

'Alas, Lionel!—how changed, how hard—forgive me if I say how hard must you be grown, to be capable of gaiety and rattle at this period!'

'You'll die an old maid, Camilla, take my word for it. And I'm really sorry, for you're not an ugly girl. You might have been got off. But come, don't look so melancholy at a little silly sport. The world is so full of sorrow, my dear girl, so little visited by happiness, that chearfulness is almost as necessary as existence, in such a vale of tears.'

'What can induce you to laugh, Lionel, at such words?'

'I can't help it, faith! I was thinking I spoke so like a parson's son!'

Camilla cast up her eyes and hands: 'Lionel,' she cried, 'what have you done with your heart? has it banished every natural feeling? has the affecting letter of the best of fathers, his cruel separation from the most excellent of mothers, and even your own dreadfully censurable conduct, served but to amuse you with ridicule and derision?'

'Camilla,' cried he, taking her hands, 'you wrong me! you think I have no feeling, because I am not always crying. However, shall I tell you the truth? I hate myself! and so completely hate myself at this moment, that I dare not be grave! dare not suffer reflection to take hold of me, lest it should make life too odious for me to bear it. I have run on from folly to wickedness for want of thought; and now thought is ready to come back, I must run from that, for want of fortitude. What has bewitched me, I know no more than you; but I never meant to play this abominable part. And now, if I did not flog up my spirits to prevent their flagging, I suppose I should hang or drown. And, believe me, if I were condemned to the galleys, I should think it less than I deserve; for I hate myself, I repeat—I honour my father, though I have used him so ill; I love my mother,—for all her deuced severity,—to the bottom of my soul; I would cut off my left arm for Lavinia and Eugenia; and for thee, Camilla, I would lop off my right!—But yet, when some frolic or gambol comes into my way, I forget you all! clear out of my memory you all walk, as if I had never beheld you!'

Camilla now embraced him with a deluge of tears, entreated him to forgive the asperity his seeming want of all feeling had drawn from her, and frequently to write to her, and acquaint her how he went on, and send his direction for her answers; that so, at least, their father might know how he employed himself, and have the power to give him counsel.

'But how, my poor Lionel,' she added, 'how will you live abroad? How will you even travel?'

'Why as to how I shall live there, I don't know; but as well as I deserve easily: however, as to how I shall get there, look here,' taking from his pocket a handful of guineas, 'that good little

Eugenia has given me every thing, even to the last half crown, that she had at Southampton, to help me forward.'

'Dear excellent, ever generous Eugenia! O that I could follow her example! but alas! I have nothing!—and worse than nothing!'

They then affectionately embraced each other, and parted.

CHAPTER VI

A Reckoning

WHAT Camilla experienced at this juncture she believed inadmissible of aggravation. Even the breaking off with Edgar seemed as a new misfortune from the new force which circumstances gave to its affliction. With his sympathising aid, how might she have softened the sorrows of her father! how have broken the shock of the blow Clermont was preparing for her uncle? But now, instead of lessening their griefs, she must herself inflict upon them a heavier evil than any they had yet suffered. And how could she reveal tidings for which they were so wholly unprepared? how be even intelligible in the history, without exposing the guilty Lionel beyond all chance of pardon?

Again she went to counsel with Eugenia, who, with her usual disinterested affection, proposed taking the painful business upon herself at their return home. Camilla with tears of gratitude accepted the sisterly office, and resolved to devote the rest of her short time for Southampton to Mrs. Berlinton; who, shocked to see her evident unhappiness, hung over her with the most melting tenderness: bewailing alike the disappointment of Eugenia, and the conduct of her brother; who now, with exquisite misery, shut himself wholly up in his room.

This compassionate kindness somewhat softened her anguish; but when the engagements of Mrs. Berlinton called her away, Mrs. Mittin burst briskly into her chamber.

'Well, my dear,' cried she, 'I come with better news now than ever! only guess what it is!'

Nothing could less conduce to the tranquillity of Camilla than such a desire; her conjectures always flowed into the channels of her wishes; and she thought immediately that Mrs. Mittin had been informed of her situation, and came to her with some intelligence of Edgar.

Mrs. Mittin, after keeping her a full quarter of an hour in suspense, at last said: 'Do you know Miss Dennel's going to be married?—though she was fifteen only yesterday!—and I am invited to the wedding?'

No surprise had ever yet produced less pleasure to Camilla, who now ceased to listen, though Mrs. Mittin by no means ceased to speak, till her attention was awakened by the following sentence: 'So, as I am to go to town, to shop with her, at her own papa's desire, you can give me the money, you know, my dear, and I can pay off your Tunbridge bills for you.'

Shen then took out of her pockets some accounts, which, she said, she had just received; though, in fact, they had been in her possession more than a week: but till the invitation of Miss Dennel called her so pleasantly away, she had thought it prudent to keep every motive in reserve, that added importance to her stay.

Camilla, with the utmost apprehension, took the papers into her hands; they were the bills from Tunbridge, of the milliner, the shoe-maker, the haberdasher, and the glover, and amounted altogether to sixteen pounds.

The chief articles had been nearly forced upon her by Mrs. Mittin, with assurances of their cheapness, and representations of their necessity, that, joined to her entire ignorance of the enormous charges of fashion, had led her to imagine four or five guineas the utmost sum at which they could be estimated.

What now, then, was her horror! if to sixteen pounds amounted the trifles she had had at Tunbridge, what calculation must she make of articles, so infinitely more valuable, that belonged to her debts at Southampton? And to whom now could she apply? The unhappy situation of her father was no longer an only reason to forbear such a call upon him: Lionel, still under age, was flying the kingdom with debts, which, be they small as they might, would, to Mr. Tyrold's limited income, be as heavy as the more considerable ones of her cousin upon Sir Hugh; yet who besides could give her aid? Eugenia, whose yearly allowance, according to her settled future fortune, was five times that of her sisters, had given what help she had in her power, before she quitted Cleves, upon the affair of the horse; and all that remained of a considerable present made for her Southampton expedition by her uncle, who in every thing distinguished her as his successor and heiress, she had just bestowed upon Lionel, even, as he had declared, to her last half crown. Mrs. Berlinton, whose tender friendship might, in this emergence, have encouraged solicitation, was involved in debts of honour, and wanted money for herself; and to Mrs. Arlbery, her only other acquaintance rich enough to give assistance, and with whom she was intimate enough to ask it, she already owed five guineas; and how, in conscience or decency, could she address her for so much more, when she saw before her no time, no term, upon which she could fix for restitution?

In this terrible state, with no one to counsel her, and no powers of self-judgment, she felt a dread of going home, that rendered the coming day a day of horror, though to a home to which, hitherto, she had turned as the first joy of her happiness, or softest solace of any disturbance. Her filial affections were in their pristine force; her short commerce with the world had robbed them of none of their vivacity; her regard for Edgar, whom she delighted to consider as a younger Mr. Tyrold, had rather enlarged than divided them; but to return a burthen to an already burthened house, an affliction to an already afflicted parent—'No!' she broke out, aloud, 'I cannot go home!—I cannot carry calamity to my father!—He will be mild—but he will look unhappy; and I would not see his face in sorrow—sorrow of my own creating—for years of after joy!'

She threw herself down upon the bed, hid her face with the counterpane, and wept, in desperate carelessness of the presence of Mrs. Mittin, and answering nothing that she said.

In affairs of this sort, Mrs. Mittin had a quickness of apprehension, which, though but the attribute of ready cunning, was not inferior to the keenest penetration, possessed, for deeper investigations, by characters of more solid sagacity. From the fear which Camilla, in her anguish, had uttered of seeing her father, she gathered, there must be some severe restriction in money concerns; and, without troubling herself to consider what they might be, saw that to aid her at this moment would be the highest obligation; and immediately set at work a brain as fertile in worldly expedients, as it was barren of intellectual endowments, in forming a plan of present relief, which she concluded would gain her a rich and powerful friend for life.

She was not long in suggesting a proposition, which Camilla

started up eagerly to hear, almost breathless with the hope of any reprieve to her terrors.

Mrs. Mittin, amongst her numerous friends, counted a Mr. Clykes, a money-lender, a man, she said, of the first credit for such matters with people of fashion in any difficulty. If Camilla, therefore, would collect her debts, this gentleman would pay them, for a handsome premium, and handsome interest, till she was able, at her own full leisure, to return the principal, with a proper present.

Camilla nearly embraced her with rapture for this scheme. The premium she would collect as she could, and the interest she would pay from her allowance, certain that when her uncle was cleared from his embarrassments, her own might be revealed without any serious distress. She put, therefore, the affair wholly into the hands of Mrs. Mittin, besought her, the next morning, to demand all her Southampton bills, to add to them those for the rent and the stores of Higden, and then to transact the business with Mr. Clykes; promising to agree to whatever premium, interest, and present, he should demand, with endless acknowledgments to herself for so great a service.

She grieved to employ a person so utterly disagreeable to Edgar; but to avert immediate evil was ever resistless to her ardent mind.

The whole of the Southampton accounts were brought her early the next morning by the active Mrs. Mittin, who now concluded, that what she had conceived to be covetousness in Camilla, was only the fear of a hard tyrant of a father, who kept her so parsimoniously, that she could allow herself no indulgence, till the death of her uncle should endow her with her own rich inheritance.

Had this arrangement not taken place before the arrival of the bills, Camilla, upon beholding them, thought she should have been driven to complete distraction. The ear-rings and necklace, silver fringes and spangles, feathers, nosegay, and shoe-roses, with the other parts of the dress, and the fine Valencienne edging, came to thirty-three pounds. The cloak also, that cheapest thing in the world, was nine guineas; and various small articles, which Mrs. Mittin had occasionally brought in, and others with which Camilla could not dispense, came to another five pounds. To this, the rent for Higden added eighteen; and the bill of stores, which had been calculated at thirty, was sent in at thirty-seven.

The whole, therefore, with the sixteen pounds from Tunbridge, amounted to one hundred and eighteen pounds nine shillings.

Struck to the very soul with the idea of what she must have endured to have presented, at such a period, so large an account, either at Cleves or at Etherington, she felt lifted into paradise by the escape of this expedient, and lost sight of every possible future difficulty, in the relief of avoiding so severe a present penalty.

By this means, also, the tradesmen would not wait; and she had been educated with so just an abhorrence of receiving the goods, and benefiting from the labours of others, without speeding them their rights and their rewards, that she felt despicable as well as miserable, when she possessed what she had not repaid.

Mrs. Mittin was now invested with full powers for the agency, which her journey to London would give her immediate means to execute. She was to meet Miss Dennel there in two days, to assist in the wedding purchases, and then to accompany that young lady to her father's house in Hampshire, whence she could visit Etherington, and finally arrange the transaction.

Camilla, again thanking, took leave of her, to consign her few remaining hours to Mrs. Berlinton, who was impatient at losing one moment of the society she began sincerely to regret she had not more uniformly preferred to all other. As sad now with cares as Camilla was with afflictions, she had robbed her situation of nearly the only good which belonged to it—an affluent power to gratify every luxury, whether of generosity or personal indulgence. Her gaming, to want of happiness, added now want of money; and Camilla, with a sigh, saw something more wretched, because far deeper and more wilful in error than herself.

They mingled their tears for their separate personal evils, with the kindest consolation that either could suggest for the other, till Camilla was told that Eugenia desired to see her in the parlour.

Mrs. Berlinton, ashamed, yet delighted to meet her again, went down at the same time. She embraced her with fondness, but ventured not to utter either apology or concern. Eugenia was serious but composed, sighed often, yet both accepted and returned her caresses.

Camilla enquired if Miss Margland expected them immediately.

'Yes,' she answered; 'but I have first a little business of my own to transact.' Then, turning to Mrs. Berlinton, and forcing a smile, 'You will be surprised,' she said, 'to hear me ask for . . . your brother! . . . but I must see him before I can leave Southampton.'

Mrs. Berlinton hung her head: 'There is certainly,' she cried, 'no reproach he does not merit . . . yet, if you knew . . . the respect . . . the . . . the. . . .'

Eugenia rang the bell, making a slight apology, but not listening to what Mrs. Berlinton strove to say; who, colouring and uneasy, still attempted to utter something softening to what had passed.

'Be so good,' said Eugenia, when the footman appeared, 'to tell Mr. Melmond I beg to speak with him.'

Camilla astonished, and Mrs. Berlinton silenced, waited, in an unpleasant pause, the event.

Eugenia, absorbed in thought, neither spoke to, nor looked at them, nor moved, till the door opened, and Melmond, who durst not refuse so direct a summons, though he would have preferred any punishment to obeying it, blushing, bowing, and trembling, entered the room.

She then started, half heaved, and half checked a sigh, took a folded note out of her pocket-book, and with a faint smile, said, 'I fear my desire must have been painful to you; but you see me now for the last time—I hope!—with any ill-will.'

She stopt for breath to go on; Melmond, amazed, striving vainly to articulate one word of excuse, one profession even of respect.

'Believe me, Sir,' she then continued, 'surprise was the last sensation I experienced upon a late . . . transaction. My extraordinary personal defects and deformity have been some time known to me, though—I cannot tell how—I had the weakness or vanity not to think of them as I ought to have done!——But I see I give you uneasiness, and therefore I will be more concise.'

Melmond, confounded, had bowed down his head not to look at her, while Camilla and Mrs. Berlinton both wept.

'The sentiments, Sir,' she then went on, 'of my cousin have never been declared to me; but it is not very difficult to me to divine what they may be. All that is certain, is the unkindness of Fortune, which forbids her to listen, or you to plead to them. This, Sir, shall be my care'—she stopt a moment, looking paler, and wanting voice; but presently recovering, proceeded—'my happiness, let me say, to endeavour to rectify. I have much influence with my kind uncle; can I doubt, when I represent to him that I have just escaped making two worthy people wretched, he will deny aiding me to make them happy? No! the residence already intended at Cleves will still be open, though one of its parties will be changed. But as my uncle, in a manner un-exampled, has bound himself, in my favour, from any future disposition of what he possesses, I have ventured, Sir, upon this paper, to obviate any apprehensions of your friends, for the unhappy time when that generous uncle can no longer act for himself.'

She then unfolded, and gave him the paper, which contained these words:

'I here solemnly engage myself, if Miss Indiana Lynmere accepts, with the consent of Sir Hugh Tyrold, the hand of Frederic Melmond, to share with them, so united, whatever fortune or estate I may be endowed with, to the end of my life, and to bequeath them the same equal portion by will after my death.

Signed.   EUGENIA TYROLD.'

Unable to read, yet conceiving the purport of the writing, Melmond was at her feet. She endeavoured to raise him, and though extremely affected, said, with an air of some pleasantry, 'Shew less surprise, Sir, or I shall conclude you thought me as frightful within as without! But no! Providence is too good to make the mind necessarily deformed with the body.'

'Ah, Madam!' exclaimed Melmond, wholly overcome, 'the noblest as well as softest of human hearts I perceive to be yours ——and were mine at my own disposal—it must find you resistless!'—

'No more, no more!' interrupted she, penetrated with a pleasure in these words which she durst not indulge, 'you shall hear from me soon.—Meanwhile, be Hope your motto, Friendship shall be mine.'

She was then going to hold out her hand to him; but her courage failed; she hastily embraced Mrs. Berlinton, took the arm of Camilla, and hurried out of the house, followed by the footman who had attended her.

Melmond, who had seen the motion of her hand now advancing,

now withdrawn, would have given the universe to have stamped upon it his grateful reverence; but his courage was still less than her own; she seemed to him, on the sudden, transformed to a deity, benignly employed to rescue and bless him, but whose transcendent goodness he could only, at a distance, and in all humility, adore.

Mrs. Berlinton was left penetrated nearly as much as her brother, and doubtful if even the divine Indiana could render him as happy as the exalted, the incomparable Eugenia.

*   *   *   *

The two sisters found Miss Margland in extreme ill-humour waiting their arrival, and the whole party immediately quitted Southampton.

It not seldom occurred to Miss Margland to be cross merely as a mark of consequence; but here the displeasure was as deep with herself as with others. She had entered Southampton with a persuasion her fair pupil would make there the establishment so long the promised mede of her confinement; and Indiana herself, not knowing where to stop her sanguine and inflated hopes, imagined that the fame of her beauty would make the place where it first was exhibited the resort of all of fashion in the nation. And the opening of the scene had answered to their fullest expectations: no other name was heard but Indiana Lynmere, no other figure was admired, no other face could bear examination.

But her triumph, though splendid, was short; she soon found that the overtures of eyes were more ready than those of speech; and though one young baronet, enchanted with her beauty, immediately professed himself her lover, when he was disdained, in the full assurance of higher offers, and because a peer had addressed himself to Eugenia, she saw not that he was succeeded by any other, nor yet that he broke his own heart. Men of taste, after the first conversation, found her more admirable to look at than speak with; adventurers soon discovered that her personal charms were her only dower; the common herd were repulsed from approaching her by the repulsive manners of Miss Margland; and all evinced, that though a passion for beauty was still as fashionable as it was natural, the time was past when the altar of Hymen required no other incense to blaze upon it.

The governess, therefore, and the pupil, quitted Southampton with equal disappointment and indignation; the first foreseeing another long and yawning sojourn at Cleves; the second firmly believing herself the most unaccountably ill-used person in the creation, that one offer only had reached her, and that without repetition, though admired nearly to adoration, she literally rather than metaphorically conceived herself a demi-goddess.

One solitary offer to Eugenia, of an every way ruined young nobleman, though a blast both to the settlement and the peace of Indiana, was to herself wholly nugatory. Intent, at that period, upon dedicating for ever to Melmond her virgin heart, she was sorry, upon his account, for the application, but gave it not, upon her own, a moment's consideration. This proposition was made upon her first arrival, and was followed by no other. She was then, by the account given to the master of the ceremonies by Miss Margland, regarded as the heiress of Cleves: but, almost immediately after, the report spread by Mrs. Mittin, that Camilla was the true heiress, gained such ground amongst the shop-keepers, and thence travelled so rapidly from gossip to gossip, and house to house, that Eugenia was soon no more thought of; though a species of doubt was cast upon the whole party, from the double assertion, that kept off from Camilla, also, the fortune seekers of the place.

But another rumour got abroad, that soon entirely cleared Eugenia, not merely of lovers but acquaintances; namely, her studies with Dr. Orkborne. This was a prevailing theme of spite with Miss Margland, when the Doctor had neglected and dis-pleased her; and a topic always at hand for her spleen, when it was angered by other circumstances not so easy of blame or of mention.

This, shortly, made Eugenia stared at still more than her peculiar appearance. The misses, in tittering, ran away from the learned lady; the beaux contemptuously sneering, rejoiced she was too ugly to take in any poor fellow to marry her. Some imagined her studies had stinted her growth; and all were con-vinced her education had made her such a fright.

Of the whole party, the only one who quitted Southampton in spirits was Dr. Orkborne. He was delighted to be no longer under the dominion of Miss Margland, who, though she never left him tranquil in the possession of all he valued, his leisure, and his books and papers, eternally annoyed him with reproaches upon his absence, non-attendance, and ignorance of high life; asking always, when angry, 'If any one had ever heard who was his grandfather?'

The doctor, in return, despising, like most who have it not, whatever belonged to noble birth, regarded her and her progenitors as the pest of the human race; frequently, when incensed by interruption, exclaiming, 'Where intellect is uncultivated, what is man better than a brute, or woman than an idiot?'

Nor was his return to his own room, books, and hours, under the roof of the indulgent Sir Hugh, the only relief of this removal: he knew not of the previous departure of Dr. Marchmont, and he was glad to quit a spot where he was open to a comparison which he felt to be always to his disadvantage.

So much more powerful and more prominent is character than education, that no two men could be more different than Dr. Marchmont and Dr. Orkborne, though the same university had finished their studies, and the same passion, pursuit, and success in respect to learning, had raised and had spread their names and celebrity. The first, with all his scholastic endowments, was a man of the world, and a grace to society; the second, though in erudition equally respectable, was wholly lost to the general community, and alive only with his pen and his books. They enjoyed, indeed, in common, that happy and often sole reward of learned labours, the privilege of snatching some care from time, some repining from misfortune, by seizing for themselves, and their own exclusive use, the whole monopoly of mind; but they employed it not to the same extension. The things and people of this lower sphere were studiously, by Dr. Orkborne, sunk in oblivion by the domineering prevalence of the alternate transport and toil of intellectual occupation; Dr. Marchmont, on the contrary, though his education led to the same propensities, still held his fellow creatures to be of higher consideration than their productions. Without such extravagance in the pursuit of his studies, he knew it the happy province of literary occupations, where voluntary, to absorb worldly solicitudes, and banish for a while even mental anxieties; and though the charm may be broken by every fresh intrusion of calamity, it unites again with the first retirement, and, without diminishing the feelings of social life, has a power, from time to time, to set aside their sufferings.

CHAPTER VII

Brides and no Brides

IN the hall of the Cleves mansion the party from Southampton were received by Sir Hugh, Mr. Tyrold, and Lavinia. The baronet greeted in particular the two nieces he regarded as brides elect, with an elation that prevented him from observing their sadness; while their confusion at his mistake he attributed to the mere bashfulness of their situation. He enquired, nevertheless, with some surprise, why the two bridegrooms did not attend them? which, he owned, he thought rather odd; though he supposed it might be only the new way.

The changing colour and starting tears of the two sisters still escaped his kindly occupied but undiscerning eyes: while Mr. Tyrold, having tenderly embraced, avoided looking at them from the fear of adding to their blushes, and sat quiet and grave, striving to alleviate his present new and deep sorrow, by participating in the revived happiness of his brother. But Lavinia soon saw their mutual distress, and with apprehensive affection watched an opportunity to investigate its cause.

'But come,' cried Sir Hugh, 'I sha'n't wait for those gentlemen to shew you what I've done for you, seeing they don't wait for me, by their following their own way, which, however, I suppose they may be with their lawyers, none of those gentleman having been here, which I think rather slow, considering the rooms are almost ready.'

He would now have taken them round the house; but, nearly expiring with shame, they entreated to be excused; and, insupportably oppressed by the cruel discovery they had to divulge, stole apart to consult upon what measures they should take. They then settled that Camilla should accompany Mr. Tyrold to Etherington, but keep off all disclosure till the next morning, when Eugenia would arrive, and unfold the sad tidings.

When they returned to the parlour, they found Sir Hugh, in the innocency of his heart, had forced Indiana, Miss Margland, and even Dr. Orkborne, to view his improvements for the expected nuptials, judging the disinterestedness of their pleasure by his own; though to the two ladies, nothing could be less gratifying than preparations for a scene in which they were to bear no part, and the Doctor thought every evil genius at work to detain him from his study and his manuscripts.

'But what's the oddest' cried the Baronet, 'of all, is nobody's coming for poor Indiana; which I could never have expected, especially in the point of taking off little Eugenia first, whom her own cousin did not think pretty enough; which I can never think over and above good natured in him, being so difficult. However, I hope we shall soon forget that, now for which reason, I forgive him.'

Indiana was so much piqued, she could scarce refrain from relating the portico history at Lord Pervil's; but the Baronet, not remarking her discomposure, turned to Camilla and Eugenia, smilingly exclaiming: 'Well, my dear girls, I sha'n't mention what we have been looking at in your absence, because of your blushes, which I hope you approve. But we shall soon, I hope, see it all together, without any of your modesty's minding it. I shall have to pinch a little for it the rest of the year, which, God knows, will be a pleasure to me, for the sake of my two dear girls, as well as of Mr. Edgar; not to mention the new young gentleman; who seems a pretty kind of person too, though he is not one of our own relations.'

He was rather disappointed when he found Camilla was to go to Etherington, but desired there might be a general meeting the next day, when he should also invite Dr. Marchmont. 'For I think' said he, 'he's as little proud as the best dunce amongst us; which makes me like him as well. And I can't say but I was as much obliged to him that day about the mad bull, as if he had been one of my nephews or nieces himself: which is what I sha'n't forget.'

In the way back to Etherington, Camilla could scarce utter a word; and Lavinia, who had just gathered from her, in a whisper 'All is over with Edgar!' with divided, but silent pity, looked from her father to her sister, thought of her brother, and wept for all three. Mr. Tyrold alone was capable of any exertion. Unwilling to give Camilla, whom he concluded impressed with the thousand solicitudes of her impending change of situation, any abrupt account of her brother's cruel conduct, he spoke with composure though not with chearfulness, and hoped, by a general gravity, to prepare, without alarming her, for the ill news he must inevitably relate. But he soon, however, observed an excess of sadness upon her countenance, far deeper than what he could attribute to the thoughts he had first suggested, and wholly different from an agitation in which though fear bears a part, hope preponderates.

It now struck him that probably Lionel had been at South-ampton: for so wide was every idea from supposing any mischief with Edgar, that, like Sir Hugh, upon his non-appearance, he had concluded him engaged with his lawyer. But of Melmond, less sure, he had been more open in enquiry, and with inexpressible concern, for his beloved and unfortunate Eugenia, gathered that the affair was ended: though her succeeding plan, by her own desire, Camilla left for her own explanation.

When they arrived at Etherington, taking her into his study, 'Camilla,' he said, 'tell me, I beg . . . do you know anything of Lionel?'

An unrestrained burst of tears convinced him his conjecture was right, and he soon obtained all the particulars of the meeting, except its levity and flightiness. Where directly questioned, no sisterly tenderness could induce her to filial prevarication; but she rejoiced to spare her brother all exposure that mere silence could spare; and as Mr. Tyrold suspected not her former knowledge of his extravagance and ill conduct, he neither asked, nor heard, any thing beyond the last interview.

At the plan of going abroad, he sighed heavily, but would take no measures to prevent it. Lionel, he saw was certain of being cast in any trial;[1] and though he would not stretch out his arm to avert the punishment he thought deserved, he was not sorry to change the languid waste of imprisonment at home, for the hardships with which he might live upon little abroad.

A calamity such as this seemed cause full sufficient for the distress of Camilla; Mr. Tyrold sought no other; but though she wept, now, at liberty, his very freedom from suspicion and enquiry increased her anguish. 'Your happy fate,' cried he, 'is what most, at this moment supports me; and to that I shall chiefly owe the support of your mother; whom a blow such as this will more bitterly try than the loss of our whole income, or even than the life itself of your brother. Her virtue is above misfortune, but her soul will shudder at guilt.'

The horror of Camilla was nearly intolerable at this speech, and the dreadful disappointment which she knew yet to be awaiting her loved parents. 'Take comfort, my dearest girl,' said Mr. Tyrold, who saw her suffering, 'it is yours, for all our sakes to be chearful, for to you we shall owe the worthiest of sons, at the piercing juncture when the weakest and most faulty fails us.'

'O my father!' she cried, 'speak not such words! Lionel himself . . .' she was going to say: has made you less unhappy than you will be made by me: but she durst not finish her phrase; she turned away from him her streaming eyes, and stopt.

'My dearest child,' he cried, 'let not your rising prospects be thus dampt by this cruel event. The connection you have formed will be a consolation to us all. It binds to us for life a character already so dear to us; it will afford to our Lavinia, should we leave her single, a certain asylum; it will give to our Eugenia a counsellor that may save her hereafter from fraud and ruin; it may aid poor Lionel, when, some time hence, he returns to his country, to return to the right path, whence so widely he has strayed; and it will heal with lenient balm the wounded, bleeding bosom of a meritorious but deeply afflicted mother! While to your father, my Camilla. . . .'

These last words were not heard; such a mention of her mother had already overpowered her, and unable to let him keep up his delusion, she supported her shaking frame against his shoulder, and exclaimed in a tone of agony: 'O my father! you harrow me to the soul!—Edgar has left me!—has left England!— left us all!'——

Shocked, yet nearly incredulous, he insisted upon looking at her: her countenance impelled belief. The woe it expressed could be excited by nothing less than the deprivation of every worldly expectation, and a single glance was an answer to a thousand interrogatories.

Mr. Tyrold now sat down, with an air between calmness and despondence, saying, 'And how has this come to pass?'

Again she got behind him, and in a voice scarce audible, said, Eugenia would, the next morning, explain all.

'Very well, I will wait;' he quietly, but with palpably stifled emotions, answered: 'Go, my love, go to Lavinia; open to her your heart; you will find consolation in her kindness. My own, I confess, is now weighed down with sorrow! this last and unexpected stroke will demand some time, some solitude, to be yielded to as it ought.' He then held out to her his hand, which she could scarcely approach from trembling, and scarcely kiss for weeping, and added: 'I know what you feel for me—and know, too, that my loss to yours is nothing,—for yours is not to be estimated! you are young, however, and, with yourself, it may pass away . . . but your mother—my heart, Camilla, is rent for your unfortunate mother!'

He then embraced her, called Lavinia, and retired for the night.

Terribly it passed with them all.

The next morning, before they assembled to breakfast, Eugenia was in the chamber of Camilla.

She entered with a bright beam upon her countenance, which, in defiance of the ravaging distemper that had altered her, gave it an expression almost celestial. It was the pure emanation of virtue, of disinterested, of even heroic virtue. 'Camilla!' she cried, 'all is settled with my uncle! Indiana . . . you will not wonder—consents; and already this morning I have written to Mr. Mel. . . .'

With all her exaltation, her voice faltered at the name, and, with a faint smile, but deep blush, she called for the congratulations of her sister upon her speedy success.

'Ah, far more than my congratulations, my esteem, my veneration is yours, dear and generous Eugenia! true daughter of my mother! and proudest recompence of my father!'

She was not sufficiently serene to give any particulars of the transaction; and Mr. Tyrold soon sent for her to his room.

Camilla, trembling and hanging over her, said: 'You will do for me, I know better than I could do for myself:—but spare poor Lionel—and be just to Edgar!'—

Eugenia strictly obeyed: in sparing Lionel she spared also her father, whom his highly unfeeling behaviour with regard to Sir Sedley would yet further have incensed and grieved; and, in doing justice to Edgar, she flattered herself she prevented an alienation from one yet destined to be nearly allied to him, since time, she still hoped, would effect the reconciliation of Camilla with the youth whom—next to Melmond—she thought the most amiable upon earth.

Mr. Tyrold, by this means, gathered no further intelligence than that they had parted upon some mutual, though slight dissatisfaction. He hoped, therefore, with Eugenia, they might soon meet again; and resolved, till he could better judge what might prove the event, to keep this distress from Sir Hugh.

He then met Camilla with the most consolatory kindness; yet would not trust her ardent mind with the hopes he cherished himself, dreading infinitely more to give than to receive disappointment. He blamed her for admitting any doubts of the true regard of Edgar, in whom promise was always short of performance, and whom he conceived displeased by unjust suspicions, or offended by undue expectations of professions, which the very sincerity of his rational and manly character prevented him from making.

Camilla heard in silence suggestions she could not answer, without relating the history of Sir Sedley: 'No, Lionel, no!' she said to herself, 'I will not now betray you! I have lost all!—and now the loss to me is irreparable, shall I blast you yet further to my poor father, whose deepest sigh is already for your misconduct?'

The story of Eugenia herself he learnt with true admiration, and gave to her magnanimity its dearest mede, in her mother's promised, and his own immediate approbation.

But Sir Hugh, notwithstanding all Eugenia could urge in favour of Melmond, had heard her account with grief and resentment. All, however, being actually ready for the double wedding, he could not, he said, answer to his conscience doing so much for the rest, and refusing the same for Indiana, whom he called upon to accept or reject the preparations made for her cousin.

Indiana stood fluttering for a few minutes between the exultation of being the first bride, and the mortification of marrying a man without fortune or title. But the observation of Sir Hugh, upon the oddity of her marrying the last, she was piqued with a most earnest ambition to reverse. Nor did Melmond himself go for nothing in this affair, as all she had of heart he had been the first to touch.

She retired for a short conference with Miss Margland, who was nearly in an equal dilemma, from unwillingness to dispose of her beautiful pupil without a title, and from eagerness to quit Cleves, which she thought a convent for dullness, and a prison for confinement. Melmond had strongly in his favour the received maxim amongst match-makers, that a young lady without fortune has a less and less chance of getting off upon every public appearance, which they call a public failure: their joint deliberations were, however, interrupted by an abrupt intrusion of Molly Mill, who announced she had just heard that Miss Dennel was going to be married.

This information ended the discussion. The disgrace of a bridal appearance anticipated in the neighbourhood by such a chit, made Indiana hastily run down stairs, and tell her uncle that the merit of Melmond determined her to refuse every body for his sake.

A man and horse, therefore, at break of day the next morning, was sent off by Eugenia to Southampton with these words:

To FREDERIC MELMOND, *Esq*;

You will be welcome, Sir, at Cleves, where you will forget, I hope, every painful sensation, in the happiness which awaits you, and dismiss all retrospection, to return with sincerity the serene friendship of

EUGENIA TYROLD.

Mr. Tyrold now visited Cleves with only his younger daughter, and excused the non-appearance there, for the present, of Camilla; acknowledging that some peculiar incidents, which he could not yet explain, kept Mandlebert away, and must postpone the celebration of the marriage.

The vexation this gave Sir Hugh, redoubled his anxiety to break to him the evil by degrees, if to break it to him at all should become indispensable.

CHAPTER VIII

A Hint for Debtors

MR. Tyrold was well aware that to keep from Sir Hugh the affliction of Camilla, he must keep from him Camilla herself: for though her sighs she could suppress, and her tears disperse, her voice had lost its tone, her countenance its gaiety; her eyes no longer sparkled, her very smiles betrayed anguish. He was the last to wonder at her sufferings, for Edgar was nearly as dear to him as herself; but he knew not, that, added to this annihilation of happiness, her peace was consumed by her secret knowledge of the blows yet impending for himself and for her uncle. Concealment, always abhorrent to her nature, had, till now, been unknown even to her thoughts; and its weight, from a species of culpability that seemed attached to its practice, was, at times, more dreadful to bear than the loss even of Edgar himself. The latter blackened every prospect of felicity; but the former, still more tremendous to the pure principles in which she had been educated, seemed to strike even at her innocence. The first wish of an ingenuous mind is to anticipate even enquiry; the feeling, therefore, that most heavily weighs it down, is any fear of detection.

While they were at breakfast the following morning, the servant brought in the name of Dr. Marchmont.

Camilla felt nearly fainting. Why he was come—whence—whether Edgar accompanied him—or sent by him any message—whether he were returned to Beech Park—or sailed for the Continent——were doubts that pressed so fast, and so vehemently upon her mind, that she feared to quit the room lest she should meet Edgar in the passage, and feared still more to continue in it, lest Dr. Marchmont should enter without him. Mr. Tyrold, who participated in all her feelings, and shared the same ideas, gently committed her to Lavinia, and went into his study to the doctor.

His own illusion was there quickly destroyed. The looks of Dr. Marchmont boded nothing that was happy. They wore not their customary expression. The gravity of Mr. Tyrold shewed a mind prepared for ill news, if not already oppressed with it, and the doctor, after a few general speeches, delivered the letter from Edgar.

Mr. Tyrold received it with a secret shuddering: 'Where,' he said, 'is Mandlebert at present?'

'I believe, by this time—at the Hague.'

This sentence, with the grieved, yet still air and tone of voice which accompanied it, was death at once to every flattering hope: he immediately read the letter, which, conceived in the tenderest terms of reverence and affection, took a short and simple, though touchingly respectful leave of the purposed connection, and demolished at once every distant view of future conciliation.

He hung his head a moment, and sighed from the bottom of his heart; but the resignation which he summoned upon every sorrow was never deaf to his call, and when he had secretly ejaculated a short and silent prayer for fortitude to his beloved wife, he turned calmly to the doctor, and began conversing upon other affairs.

Dr. Marchmont presumed not to manifest the commiseration with which he was filled. He saw the true Christian, enduring with humility misfortune, and the respectable parent supporting the dignity of his daughter by his own. To the first character, complaint was forbidden; to the second, it would have been degrading. He looked at him with veneration, but to spare further useless and painful efforts, soon took leave.

Mr. Tyrold, shaking hands with him, said, as they were parting, 'when you write to Mandlebert, assure him of my constant affection. The world, Dr. Marchmont is too full of real evil, for me at least, to cause one moment of unnecessary uneasiness to any of its poor pilgrims. 'Tis strange, my dear doctor, this is not more generally considered, since the advantage would be so reciprocal from man to man. But wrapt up in our own short moment, we forget our neighbour's long hour! and existence is ultimately embittered to all, by the refined susceptibility for ourselves that monopolizes our feelings.'

Doctor Marchmont, who in this last sentence construed a slight reflection upon Edgar, expressively answered, 'Our sensibility for others is not always dormant, because not apparent.—How much of worth and excellence may two characters separately possess, where yet there are disuniting particles which impede their harmonizing with each other!'

Mr. Tyrold, powerfully struck, saw now the general nature of the conceptions which had caused this lamented breach. He could not concur, but he would not attempt to controvert: opinion in this case must have even the precedence of justice. If Edgar thought his daughter of a disposition with which his own could not sympathise, it were vain to expatiate upon her virtues or her sweetness; that one doubt previously taken might mar their assimilating efficacy. Comprehending, therefore, the cause at large, he desired no detail; the words of Dr. Marchmont, though decisive, were not offensive, and they parted perfect friends, each perceiving, yet forgiving, that each cast upon the other the error of false reasoning; Edgar to the one, and Camilla to the other, appearing faultless in the separation.

But not in the tasks which succeeded were their offices as easily to be compared. Dr. Marchmont wrote to Edgar that all was quietly relinquished, and his measures were honourably acquitted; while Mr. Tyrold, shut up in his study, spent there some of the severest minutes of his life, in struggling for the equanimity he coveted to pronounce to his daughter this last doom. Pity for her suspence accelerated his efforts, and he then sent for her down stairs.

His utmost composure, in such an interview, was highly necessary for both. The pale and trembling Camilla advanced with downcast eyes; but when he took her in his arms, and kissed her, a sudden ray of hope shot across her quick imagination, and she looked up: an instant was now sufficient to rectify her mistake. The tenderness of her father wore no air of congratulation, it was the mere offspring of compassion, and the woe with which it was mixt, though mild, though patient, was too potent to require words for explanation.

The glance sufficed; her head dropt, her tears in torrents bathed his bosom; and she retired to Lavinia while yet neither of them had spoken.

Mr. Tyrold, contented with virtuous exertions, demanded not impossibilities; he left to nature that first grief which too early exhortation or controul rather inflames than appeases. He then brought her back to his apartment.

He conjured her, there, to remember that she grieved not alone; that where the tears flowed not so fast from the eyes, the sources were not dry whence they sprung, and that bridled sorrow was sometimes the most suffering.

'Alas, my dearest father, to think you mourn too—and for me!—will that lessen what I feel?'

'Yes, my dear child, by a generous duty it will point out to watch that the excess of one affliction involve you not in another.'

'What a motive,' she answered, 'for exertion! If the smallest part of your happiness—of my honoured mother's—depends upon mine, I shall be unhappy, I think, no more!'

A gush of tears ill accorded with this fond declaration; but Mr. Tyrold, without noticing them, kindly replied, 'Let your filial affection, my child, check the inordinacy of your affliction, and I will accept with pleasure for your virtuous mother, and with thanks for myself, the exertion which, beginning for our sakes, may lead you to that self denial which is the parent of our best human actions, and approximates us the most to what is divine.'[1]

Broken-hearted as was Camilla, her sorrows would, at least apparently, have abated from consolation so tender, if all she felt had been known; if no latent and lurking evil had hung upon her spirits, defeating all argument, and blighting all comfort, by the cruel consciousness of concealed mischief, which while incessantly she studied the best moment for revealing, accident might prematurely betray.

Upon this subject her thoughts were unremittingly bent, till, in a few days time, she received a letter from Mrs. Mittin, informing her she had just seen the money-lender, Mr. Clykes, who, finding her so much under age, would not undertake the business for less than ten per cent. nor without a free premium of at least twenty pounds.[2]

The latter demand, so entirely out of her power to grant, gave to her the mental strength she had yet sought in vain; and determining to end this baneful secret, she seized her own first moment of emotion to relate to her father the whole of her distresses, and cast herself upon his mercy.

I shall be happier, she cried, much happier, as, with tottering steps, she hurried to the study; he will be lenient, I know;—and even if not, what displeasure can I incur so severe as the eternal apprehension of doing wrong?

But her plan, though well formed, had fixed upon an ill-timed moment for its execution. She entered the room with an agitation which rather sought than shunned remark, that some enquiry might make an opening for her confession: but Mr. Tyrold was intently reading a letter, and examining some papers, from which he raised not his eyes at her approach. She stood fearfully before him till he had done; but then, still not looking up, he leant his head upon his hand, with a countenance so disturbed, that, alarmed from her design, by the apprehension he had received some ill tidings from Lisbon, she asked, in a faint voice, if the foreign post were come in?

'I hope not!' he answered: 'I should look with pain, at this moment, upon the hand of your unhappy mother!'

Camilla, affrighted, knew not now what to conjecture; but gliding into her pocket the letter of Mrs. Mittin, stood suspended from her purpose.

'What a reception,' he presently added, 'is preparing for that noblest of women when her exile may end! That epoch, to which I have looked forward as the brightener of my every view upon earth—how is it now clouded!'

Giving her, then, the letter and papers; 'The son,' he said, 'who once I had hoped would prove the guardian of his sisters, the honour of his mother's days, the future prop of my own— See, Camilla, on how sandy a foundation mortal man builds mortal hopes!'

The letter was from a very respectable tradesman, containing a complaint that, for the three years Lionel had been at the University, he had never paid one bill, though he continually ordered new articles: and begging Mr. Tyrold would have the goodness to settle the accounts he enclosed; the young gentleman, after fixing a day for payment, having suddenly absconded without notice to any one.

'The sum, you see,' continued Mr. Tyrold, 'amounts to one hundred and seventy-one pounds; a sum, for my income, enormous. The allowance I made this cruel boy, was not only adequate to all his proper wants, and reasonable desires, but all I could afford without distressing myself, or injuring my other children: yet it has served him, I imagine, but for pocket money! The immense sums he has extorted from both his uncles, must have been swallowed up at a gaming table. Into what wretched courses has he run! These bills, large as they are, I regard but as forerunners of others; all he has received he has squandered upon his vices, and to-morrow, and the next day, and the next, I may expect an encreasing list of his debts, from his hatter, his hosier, his shoe-maker, his taylor,—and whoever he has employed.'

Camilla, overwhelmed with internal shame, yet more powerful

than grief itself, stood motionless. These expences appeared but like a second part of her own, with her milliner, her jeweller, and her haberdasher; which now seemed to herself not less wanton in extravagance.

Surprised by her entire silence, Mr. Tyrold looked up. Her cheeks, rather livid than pale, and the deep dismay of her countenance, extremely affected him. The kindness of his embraces relieved her by melting her into tears, though the speech which accompanied them was, to her consciousness, but reproach: 'Let not your sisterly feelings thus subdue you, my dearest Camilla. Be comforted that you have given us no affliction yourself, save what we must feel for your own undeservedly altered prospects. No unthinking imprudence, no unfeeling selfishness, has ever, for an instant, driven from your thoughts what you owe to your duty, or weakened your pleasure in every endearing filial tie. Let this cheer you, my child; and let us all try to submit calmly to our general disappointment.'

Praise thus ill-timed, rather probed than healed her wounds. Am I punished? am I punished? She internally exclaimed; but could not bear to meet the eyes of her father, whose indulgence she felt as if abusing, and whose good opinion seemed now but a delusion. Again, he made her over to the gentle Lavinia for comfort, and fearing serious ill effects from added misery, exerted himself, from this time, to appear chearful when she was present.

His predictions failed not to be fulfilled: the application made by one creditor, soon reached every other, and urged similar measures. Bills, therefore, came in daily, with petitions for payment; and as Lionel still wanted a month or two of being of age, his creditors depended with confidence upon the responsibility of his father.

Nor here closed the claims springing from general ill conduct. Two young men of fashion, hard pressed for their own failures, stated to Mr. Tyrold the debts of honour owing them from Lionel: and three notorious gamesters, who had drawn in the unthinking youth to his ruin, enforced the same information, with a hint that, if they were left unsatisfied, the credit of the young man would fall the sacrifice of their ill treatment.

The absence of Mrs. Tyrold at this period, by sparing her daily difficulty as well as pain, was rejoiced in by her husband;

though never so strongly had he wanted her aiding counsel, her equal interest, and her consoling participation. Obliged to act without them, his deliberation was short and decisive for his measures, but long and painful for their means of execution. He at once determined to pay, though for the last time, all the trades people; but the manner of obtaining the money required more consideration.

The bills, when all collected, amounted to something above five hundred pounds, which was but one hundred short of his full yearly income.

Of this, he had always contrived to lay by an hundred pounds annually, which sum, with its accumulating interest, was destined to be divided between Lavinia and Camilla. Eugenia required nothing; and Lionel was to inherit the paternal little fortune. The portion of Mrs. Tyrold, which was small, the estate of her father having been almost all entailed upon Mr. Relvil, was to be divided equally amongst her children.

To take from the little hoard which, with so tender a care, he had heaped for the daughters, so large a share for the son, and to answer demands so unduly raised, and ill deserved, was repulsive to his inclination, and shocked his strong sense of equal justice. To apply to Mr. Relvil would be preposterous; for though upon him dwelt all his ultimate hopes for Lionel, he knew him, at this moment, to be so suffering and so irritated by his means, that to hear of any new misdemeanours might incense him to an irrevocable disinheritance.

With regard to Sir Hugh, nothing was too much to expect from his generous kindness; yet he knew that his bountiful heart had always kept his income from overflowing; and that, for three years past, Lionel had drained it without mercy. His preparations, also, for the double marriages had, of late, much straitened him. To take up even the smallest part of what, in less expensive times, he had laid by, he would regard as a breach of his solemn vow, by which he imagined himself bound to leave Eugenia the full property she would have possessed, had he died instantly upon making it. Reason might have shewn this a tie of supererogation; but where any man conceived himself obeying the dictates of his conscience, Mr. Tyrold held his motives too sacred for dispute.

The painful result of this afflicting meditation, was laying before his daughters the whole of his difficulties, and demanding if they would willingly concur in paying their brother's bills from their appropriate little store, by adopting an altered plan of life, and severe self-denial of their present ease and elegance, to aid its speedy replacement.

Their satisfaction in any expedient to serve their brother that seemed to fall upon themselves, was sincere, was even joyful: but they jointly besought that the sum might be freely taken up, and deducted for ever more from the hoard; since no earthly gratification could be so great to them, as contributing their mite to prevent any deprivation of domestic enjoyment to their beloved parents.

His eyes glistened, but not from grief; it was the pleasure of virtuous happiness in their purity of filial affection. But though he knew their sincerity, he would not listen to their petition. 'You are not yet,' said he, 'aware what your future calls may be for money. What I have yet been able to save, without this unexpected seizure, would be inadequate to your even decent maintenance, should any accident stop short its encrease. Weep not, my dear children! my health is still good, and my prospect of lengthened life seems fair. It would be, however, a temporal folly as well as a spiritual presumption, to forget the precarious tenure of human existence. My life, my dear girls, will be happier, without being shorter, for making provisions for its worldly cessation.'

'But, Sir! but my father!' cried Camilla, hanging over him, and losing in filial tenderness her personal distresses; 'if your manner of living is altered, and my dear mother returns home and sees you relinquishing any of your small, your temperate indulgencies, may it not yet more embitter her sufferings and her displeasure for the unhappy cause? For her sake then, if not for ours'——

'Do not turn away, dearest Sir!' cried Lavinia; 'what mother ever merited to have her peace the first study of her children, if it is not ours?'

'O Providence benign!' said Mr. Tyrold, folding them to his heart, 'how am I yet blessed in my children!—True and excellent daughters of my invaluable wife—this little narration is the solace I shall have to offer for the grief I must communicate.'

He would not, however, hearken to their proposition; his peace, he said, required not only immediate measures for replacing what he must borrow, but also that no chasm should have lieu in funding his usual annual sum for them. All he would accept was the same severe forbearance he should instantly practice himself, and which their mother, when restored to them, would be the first to adopt and improve. And this, till its end was answered, they would all steadily continue, and then, with chearful self-approvance, resume their wonted comforts.

Mr. Tyrold had too frequent views of the brevity of human life to postpone, even from one sun to another, any action he deemed essential. A new general system, therefore, immediately pervaded his house. Two of the servants, with whom he best could dispense, were discharged; which hurt him more than any other privation, for he loved, and was loved by every domestic who lived with him. His table, always simple though elegant, was now reduced to plain necessaries; he parted with every horse, but one to whose long services he held himself a debtor; and whatever, throughout the whole economy of his small establishment, admitted simplifying, deducting, or abolishment, received, without delay, its requisite alteration or dismission.

These new regulations were quietly, but completely, put in practice, before he would discharge one bill for his son; to whom, nevertheless, though his conduct was strict, his feelings were still lenient. He attributed not to moral turpitude his errours nor his crimes, but to the prevalence of ill example, and to an unjustifiable and dangerous levity, which irresistibly led him to treat with mockery and trifling the most serious subjects. The punishment, however, which he had now drawn upon himself, would yet, he hoped, touch his heart.

But the debts called debts of honour, met not with similar treatment. He answered with spirited resentment demands he deemed highly flagitious, counselling those who sent them, when next they applied to an unhappy family to whose calamities they had contributed, to enquire first if its principles, as well as its fortune, made the hazards of gaming amongst its domestic responsibilities.

CHAPTER IX

A Lover's Eye

THE serenity of virtue would now again have made its abode the breast of Mr. Tyrold, but for the constant wretchedness to which he saw his daughter a prey. With the benignest pity he strove to revive her; a pity unabated by any wonder, unalloyed with any blame. His wonder fell all upon Edgar, whom he considered as refining away mortal happiness, by dissatisfaction that it was not divine; but his censure, which he reserved wholly for vice, exonerated them both. Still, however, he flattered himself that ere long, to her youthful mind and native chearfulness, tranquillity, if not felicity, would imperceptibly return, from such a union for exertion of filial and sisterly duties: that industry would sweeten rest, virtue gild privation, and self-approvance convert every sacrifice into enjoyment.

But peace such as this was far from her bosom. While the desertion of Edgar had tolled the death bell to all her hopes, an unremitting contention disturbed her mind, whether to avow or conceal her situation with regard to the money-lender. The reflections of every night brought a dissatisfaction in her conduct, which determined her upon an openness the most undisguised for the following morning: but timidity, and the desire of reprieve from the fearful task, again, the following morning, regularly postponed her purpose.

In the first horror occasioned by her father's distress from the bills of her brother, she wrote a supplicating letter to Mrs. Mittin, to intreat she would endeavour to quiet her creditors till she could arrange something for their payment. And while this produced a correspondence replete with danger, difficulty, and impropriety, a new circumstance occurred, which yet more cruelly embittered her conflicting emotions. Lavinia, in the virtuous eagerness of her heart to forward the general œconomy, insisted wholly to relinquish, for this year, her appropriate allowance; declaring that, by careful management, she could dispense with anything new, and that the very few expences she might find utterly unavoidable, she would demand from time to time as they occurred. Camilla, at this proposition, retreated, in agony, to her chamber. To make the same was impossible; for how, then, find interest for the money-lender? yet to withstand so just an example, seemed a disgrace to every duty and every feeling.

Lavinia, who, in her countenance and abrupt departure, read the new distress she had incautiously excited, with a thousand self-reproaches followed her. She had considered but the common cause when she spoke, without weighing the strange appearance of not being seconded by her sister: But her mind was amongst the last to covet the narrow praise of insidious comparison; and her concern for the proposal she had made, when she saw its effect, was as deep as that of Camilla in hearing it, though not attended with the same aggravations.

Mr. Tyrold remained utterly surprised. The generous and disinterested nature of Camilla, made it impossible to suspect her restrained by a greater love of money than Lavinia; and he could not endure to suppose her late visits to public places, had rendered personal œconomy more painful. But he would make no enquiry that might seem a reproach; nor suffer any privation or contribution that was not chearful and voluntary.

*   *   *   *

The purchases for the wedding of Miss Dennel being now made, that young lady came down to the country to solemnize her nuptials, accompanied by Mrs. Mittin, who instantly visited Camilla. She could settle nothing, she said, with the money-lender, without the premium; but she had coaxed all the creditors, by assuring them, that, as the debtor was a great heiress, they were certain of their money when she came to her estate. Camilla could not endure to owe their forbearance to a falsehood; though to convince Mrs. Mittin of her errour, in contradiction to the assertion of Lionel, was a vain attempt. The business, however, pressed; and to keep back these but too just claimants was her present most fervent desire. Mrs. Mittin was amongst the most expert of expedient-mongers,[1] and soon started a method for raising the premium. She asked to look at what Camilla possessed of trinkets: and the prize ear-rings of Tunbridge, the ear-rings and necklace of Southampton, and several small toys occasionally given her, were collected. The locket she also demanded, to make weight; but neither that, nor the peculiar gifts, as keep-sakes, of her father, mother, or uncle, consisting of a seal, a ring, and a watch, would she part with. What she would relinquish, however, Mrs. Mittin disposed of to one of her numerous friends; but they raised only, when intrinsically valued, sixteen pounds. Lavinia then insisted upon coming forward with a contribution of every trinket she was worth, save what had the same sacred motives of detention: and the twenty pounds, without any ceremony of acknowledgment, were delivered to Mr. Clykes; who then took into his own hands the payment of the hundred and eighteen pounds; for which he received a bond, signed by Camilla, and witnessed by Mrs. Mittin; and another note of hand, promising ten per cent. interest for the sum, till the principal were repaid. These two notes, he acknowledged, were mere pledges of honour, as the law would treat her as an infant: but he never acted without them, as they prevented mistakes in private dealings.

This important affair arranged, Camilla felt somewhat more at ease; she was relieved from hourly alarms, and left the mistress to make her confession as circumstances directed. But she obtained not for nothing the agency of Mrs. Mittin, who was not a character to leave self out of consideration in her transactions for others; and at every visit made at Etherington from this time, she observed something in the apparel of Camilla that was utterly old fashioned, or too mean for her to wear; but which would do well enough for herself, when vamped up, as she knew how. Her obligations and inexperience made it impossible to her to resist, though, at this season of saving care, she gave up nothing which she could not have rendered useful, by industry and contrivance.

*   *   *   *

During this unhappy period at Etherington, a brighter, though not unclouded scene, was exhibited at Cleves. Melmond arrived; he was permitted to pay his addresses to the fair Indiana, and believed felicity celestial accorded to him even upon earth.

But this adored object herself suffered some severe repining at her fate, when she saw, from her window, her lover gallop into the park without equipage, without domestics, and mounted on a hired horse. The grimacing shrugs of Miss Margland shewed she entered into this mortification; and they were nearly conspiring to dismiss the ignoble pretender, when a letter, which he modestly sent up, from his sister, inviting Indiana to pass a few weeks in Grosvenor Square, once again secured the interest of the brother. She suffered, therefore, Sir Hugh to hand her down stairs, and the enamoured Melmond thought himself the most blest of men.

The sight of such eager enjoyment, and the really amiable qualities of this youth, soon completely reconciled the Baronet to this new business; for he saw no reason, he said, in fact, why one niece had not as good a right to be married first as another. The generous and sentimental Eugenia never ceased her kind offices, and steadily wore an air of tolerable chearfulness all day, though her pillow was nightly wetted with tears for her unfortunate lot.

Nor, with all her native equanimity and acquired philosophy, was this a situation to bring back serenity. The enthusiastic raptures of Melmond elevated him, in her eyes, to something above human; and while his adoration of Indiana presented to her a picture of all she thought most fascinating, his grateful softness of respect to herself, was penetratingly touching to her already conquered heart.

Indiana, meanwhile, began ere long, to catch some of the pleasure she inspired. The passionate animation of Melmond, soon not only resumed its first power, but became even essential to her. No one else had yet seemed to think her so completely a goddess, except Mr. Macdersey, whom she scarce expected ever to see again. With Melmond she could do nothing that did not make her appear to him still more lovely: and though her whims, thus indulged, became almost endless, they but kindled with fresh flame his admiration. If she fretted, he thought her all sensibility; if she pouted, all dignity; if her laughter was unmeaning, she was made up of innocent gaiety; if what she said was shallow, he called her the child of pure nature; if she were angry, how becoming was her spirit! if illiberal, how noble was her frankness! Her person charmed his eye, but his own imagination framed her mind, and while his enchanted faculties were the mere slaves of her beauty, they persuaded themselves they were vanquished by every other perfection.

*   *   *   *

Mr. Tyrold had not yet related Edgar's defection to Sir Hugh; though from the moment the time of hope was past, he wished to end that of expectation. But the pressure of the affairs of Lionel detained him at Etherington, and he could not bear to give grief to his brother, till he could soften its effect by the consolation of some residence at Cleves. This time now arrived; and the next day was fixed for his painful task, in which he meant to spare Camilla any share, when Jacob begged immediate admittance into the study, where Mr. Tyrold and his daughters were drinking tea.

His scared look instantly announced ill news. Mr. Tyrold was alarmed, Lavinia was frightened, and Camilla exclaimed, 'Jacob, speak at once!'

He begged to sit down.

Camilla ran to get him a chair.

'Is my brother well, Jacob?' cried Mr. Tyrold.

'Why, pretty well, considering, Sir,—but these are vast bad times for us!'

'O! if my uncle is but well,' cried Camilla, relieved from her first dreadful doubt, 'all, I hope, will do right!'

'Why, ay, Miss,' said Jacob, smiling, 'I knew you'd be master's best comfort; and so I told him, and so he says, for that matter himself, as I've got to tell you from him. But, for all that, he takes on prodigious bad. I never saw him in the like way, except just that time when Miss Geny had the small pox.'

They all supplicated him to forbear further comments, and then gathered, that a money-agent, employed by young Lynmere, had just arrived at Cleves; where, with bitter complaints, he related that, having been duped into believing him heir to Sir Hugh Tyrold, he had been prevailed with to grant him money, from time to time, to pay certain bills, contracted not only there, but in London, for goods sent thence by his order, to the amount of near thirteen hundred pounds, without the interest, of which he should give a separate account; that he had vainly applied to the young gentleman for re-imbursement, who finally assured him he was just disinherited by his uncle. No hope, therefore, remained to save him from the ruin of this affair, but in the compassion of the Baronet, which he now came to most humbly solicit.

While Mr. Tyrold, in silent surprise and concern, listened to an account that placed his brother in difficulties so similar to his own, Camilla, sinking back in her chair, looked pale, looked almost lifeless. The history of the debts she already knew, and had daily expected to hear; but the circumstance of the money-lender, and the delusion concerning the inheritance, so resembled her own terrible, and yet unknown story, that she felt personally involved in all the shame and horror of the relation.

Mr. Tyrold, who believed her suffering all for her uncle, made further enquiries, while Lavinia tenderly sustained her. 'Don't take on so, dear Miss,' said Jacob, 'for all our hope is in you, as Master and I both said; and he bid me tell your papa, that if he'd only give young 'Squire Mandlebert a jog, to egg him on, that he might not be so shilly shally, as soon as ever the wedding's over, he'd accept his kind invitation to Beech Park, and bide there till he got clear, as one may say.'

Mr. Tyrold now required no assigned motive for the excessive distress of his daughter, and hastened to turn Jacob from this too terribly trying subject, by saying, 'My brother then means to pay these demands?'

'Lauk, yes, Sir! his honour pays every thing as any body asks him; only he says he don't know how, because of having no more money, being so hard run with all our preparations we have been making this last fortnight.'

Camilla, with every moment encreasing agitation, hid her face against Lavinia; but Mr. Tyrold, with some energy, said: 'The interest, at least, I hope he will not discharge; for those dangerous vultures, who lie in wait for the weak or erring, to encourage their frailties or vices, by affording them means to pursue them, deserve much severer punishment, than merely losing a recompense for their iniquitous snares.'

This was quite too much for the already disordered Camilla; she quitted her sister, glided out of the room, and delivered herself over as a prey no longer to sorrow but remorse. Her conduct seemed to have been precisely the conduct of Clermont, and she felt herself dreadfully implicated as one of the *weak or erring*, guilty of *frailties or vices*.

That an uncle so dearly loved should believe she was forming an establishment which would afford him an asylum during his difficulties, now every prospect of that establishment was over, was so heart-piercing a circumstance, that to her father it seemed sufficient for the whole of what she endured. He made her over, therefore, to Lavinia, while he hastened to Cleves; for Jacob, when he had said all he was ordered to say, all he had gathered himself, and all he was able to suggest, finished with letting him know that his master begged he would set out that very moment.

The time of his absence was spent by Camilla in an anguish that, at his return, seemed quite to have changed her. He was alarmed, and redoubled his tenderness; but his tenderness was no longer her joy. He knows not, she thought, whom he caresses; knows not that the wounds just beginning to heal for the son, are soon to be again opened for the daughter!

Yet her affections were all awake to enquire after her uncle; and when she heard that nothing could so much sooth him as her sight, all fear of his comments, all terror of exertion, subsided in the possible chance of consoling him: and Mr. Tyrold, who thought every act of duty led to chearfulness, sent ₁o desire the carriage might fetch her the next morning.

He passed slightly over to Camilla the scene he had himself gone through; but he confessed to Lavinia its difficulty and pain. Sir Hugh had acknowledged he had drawn his bankers dry, yet had merely current cash to go on till the next quarter, whence he intended to deduct the further expences of the weddings. Nevertheless, he was determined upon paying every shilling of the demand, not only for the debts, but for all the complicate interest.[1] He would not listen to any reasoning upon this subject, because, he said, he had it upon his conscience that the first fault was his own, in letting poor Clermont leave the kingdom, without clearing up to him that he had made Eugenia his exclusive heiress. It was in vain Mr. Tyrold pointed out, that no future hopes of wealth could exculpate this unauthorized extravagance in Clermont, and no dissipation in Clermont could apologize for the clandestine loan, and its illegal interest: 'The poor boy,' said he, 'did it all, knowing no better, which how can I expect, when I did wrong myself, being his uncle? Though, if I were to have twenty more nephews and nieces in future, the first word I should say to them would be to tell them I should give them nothing; to the end that having no hope, they might all be happy one as another.' All, therefore, that was left for Mr. ↖yrold, was to counsel him upon the best and shortest means of raising the sum; and for this purpose, he meant to be with him again the next day.

This affair, however, with all its reproach for the past, and all its sacrifices for the time to come, by no means so deeply affected Sir Hugh as the blow Mr. Tyrold could no longer spare concerning Edgar. It sunk to his heart, dispirited him to tears, and sent him, extremely ill, to bed.

The chaise came early the next morning, and Mr. Tyrold had the pleasure to see Camilla exert herself to appear less sad. Lavinia was also of the party, as he meant to stay the whole day.

Eugenia met them in the hall, with the welcome intelligence that Sir Hugh, though he had passed a wretched night, was now somewhat better, and considerably cheared, by a visit from his old Yorkshire friend, Mr. Westwyn.

Nevertheless, Sir Hugh dismissed him, and everybody else, to receive Camilla alone.

She endeavoured to approach him calmly, but his own unchecked emotions soon overset her borrowed fortitude, and the interview proved equally afflicting to both. The cruel mischiefs brought upon him by Clermont, were as nothing in the balance of his misfortunes, when opposed to the sight of sorrow upon that face which, hitherto, had so constantly enlivened him as an image of joy: and with her, every self-disappointment yielded, for the moment, to the regret of losing so precious a blessing, as offering a refuge, in a time of difficulty, to an uncle so dear to her.

Mr. Tyrold would not suffer this scene to be long uninterrupted; he entered, with a chearing countenance, that compelled them to dry their tears, and told them the Westwyns could not much longer be left out, though they remained, well contented, for the present, with Miss Margland and his other daughters. 'Melmond and Indiana,' added he, smiling, 'seem at present not beings of this lower sphere, nor to have a moment to spare for those who are.'

'That, my dear brother,' answered the Baronet, 'is all my comfort; for as to all the rest of my marrying, you see what it's come to! who could have thought of young Mr. Edgar's turning out in the same way? I can't say but what I take it pretty unkind of him, letting me prepare at this rate for nothing; besides Beech Park's being within but a stone's throw, as one may say, as well as his own agreeableness. However, now I've seen a little more of the world, I can't say I find much difference between the good and the bad, with respect to their all doing alike. The young boys now-a-days, whatever's come to 'em, don't know what they'd be at. They think nothing of disappointing a person if once they've a mind to change their minds. All one's preparations go for nothing; which they never think of.'

Mr. Tyrold now prevailed for the re-admission of Mr. Westwyn, who was accompanied by his son, and followed by the Cleves family.

The cheeks of Camilla recovered their usual hue at the sight of Henry, from the various interesting recollections which occurred with it. She was seen herself with their original admiration, both by the father and the son, though with the former it was now mingled with anger, and with the latter no longer gilded with hope. Yet the complaints against her, which, upon his arrival, Mr. Westwyn meant to make, were soon not merely relinquished, but transformed into pity, upon the view of her dejected countenance, and silent melancholy.

The Baronet, however, revived again, by seeing his old friend, whose humour so much resembled his own, that, in Yorkshire, he had been always his first favourite. Each the children of untutored nature, honest and open alike in their words and their dealings, their characters and their propensities were nearly the same, though Sir Hugh, more self-formed, had a language and manner of his own; and Mr. Westwyn, of a temper less equal and less gentle, gave way, as they arose, to such angry passions as the indulgent Baronet never felt.

'My dear friend,' said Mr. Westwyn, 'you don't take much notice of my Hal, though, I'll give you my word, you won't see such another young fellow every day. However, it's as well not, before his face, for it might only make him think himself somebody: and that, while I am alive, I don't intend he should do. I can't bear a young fellow not dutiful. I've always a bad opinion of him. I can't say he pleases me.'

'My dear Westwyn,' answered the Baronet, 'I've no doubt but what master Hal is very good, for which I am truly glad. But as to much over-rejoicing, now, upon the score of young boys, it's what I can't do, seeing they've turned out so ill, one after another, as far as I have had to do with them; for which, however, I hope

I bear 'em no malice. They've enough to answer for without that, which, I hope, they'll think of in time.'

'Why to be sure, Sir Hugh, if you set about thinking of a young fellow by the pattern of my friend Clermont, I can't say I'm much surprised you don't care to give him a good word; I can't say I am. I am pretty much of the same way of thinking. I love to speak the truth.' He then took Mr. Tyrold apart, and ran on with a history of all he had gathered, while at Leipsic, of the conduct and way of life of Clermont Lynmere. 'He was a disgrace,' said he, 'even to the English name, as a Professor told me, that I can't remember the name of, it's so prodigious long; but, if it had not been for my son, he told me, they'd have thought all the English young fellows good for nothing, except extravagance, and eating and drinking! "They'd all round have got an ill name," says he, "if it had not been for your son," were his words which I shall never forget. I sent him over a noble pipe of Madeira, which I'd just got for myself, as soon as I came home. I took to him very much, I can't say but I did; he was a very good man; he had prodigiously the look of an Englishman. He said Hal was an ornament to the university. I took it very well of him. I wish he had not such a hard name. I can never call it to mind. I hate a hard name. I can never speak it without a blunder.'

Sir Hugh now, who had been talking with Henry, called upon Mr. Westwyn, to beg his pardon for not speaking of him more respectfully, saying: 'I see he's quite agreeable, which I should have noticed from the first, only being what I did not know; which I hope is my excuse; my head, my dear friend, not getting on much, in point of quickness: though I can't say it's for want of pains, since you and I used to live so much together; but to no great end, for I always find myself in the back, however it happens: which your son, Master Hal, is, I see, quite the contrary.'

Mr. Westwyn was so much gratified by this praise, that he immediately confessed the scheme and wish he had formed of marrying Hal to Camilla, only for her not approving it. Sir Hugh protested nothing could give him more pleasure than such a connexion, and significantly added, he had other nieces, besides Camilla.

'Why, yes,' said Mr. Westwyn, 'and I can't keep from looking at 'em; I like 'em all mightily. I'm a great friend to taking from a good stock. I chuse to know what I'm about. That girl at

Southampton hit my fancy prodigiously. But I'm not for the beauty. A beauty won't make a good wife. It takes her too much time to put her cap on.[1] That little one, there, with the hump, which I don't mind, nor the limp, neither, I like vastly. But I'm afraid Hal won't take to her. A young man don't much fancy an ugly girl. He's always hankering after something pretty. There's that other indeed, Miss Lavinia, is as handsome a girl as I'd wish to see. And she seems as good, too. However, I'm not for judging all by the eye. I'm past that. An old man should not play the fool. Which I wish somebody would whisper to a certain Lord that I know of, that don't behave quite to my mind. I'm not fond of an old fool: nor a young one neither. They make me sick.'

Sir Hugh heard and agreed to all this, with the same simplicity with which it was spoken; and, soon after, Yorkshire becoming their theme, Mr. Tyrold had the pleasure of seeing his brother so much re-animated by the revival of old scenes, ideas, and connexions, that he heartily joined in pressing the Mr. Westwyns to spend a fortnight at Cleves, to which they consented with pleasure.

CHAPTER X

A Bride's Resolves

WITH every allowance for a grief in which so deeply he shared, Mr. Tyrold felt nearly bowed down with sorrow, when he observed his own tenderness abate of its power to console, and his exhortations of their influence with his miserable daughter, whose complicated afflictions seemed desperate to herself, and to him nearly hopeless.

He now began to fear the rigid œconomy and retirement of their present lives might add secret disgust or fatigue to the disappointment of her heart. He sighed at an idea so little in unison with all that had hitherto appeared of her disposition; yet remembered she was very young and very lively, and thought that, if caught by a love of gayer scenes than Etherington afforded, she was at a season of life which brings its own excuse for such venial ambition.

He mentioned, therefore, with great kindness, their exclusion from all society, and proposed making an application to Mrs. Needham, a lady high in the esteem of Mrs. Tyrold, to have the goodness to take the charge of carrying them a little into the world, during the absence of their mother. 'I can neither exact nor desire,' he said, 'to sequester you from all amusement for a term so utterly indefinite as that of her restoration; since it is now more than ever desirable to regain the favour of your uncle Relvil for Lionel, who has resisted every profession for which I have sought to prepare him; though his idle and licentious courses so little fit him for contentment with the small patrimony he will one day inherit.'

The sisters mutually and sincerely declined this proposition; Lavinia had too much employment to find time ever slow of passage; and Camilla, joined to the want of all spirit for recreation, had a dread of appearing in the county, lest she should meet with Sir Sedley Clarendel, whose two hundred pounds were amongst the evils ever present to her. The money which Eugenia meant to save for this account had all been given to Lionel; and now her marriage was at an end, and no particular sum expected, she must be very long in replacing it; especially as Jacob was first to be considered; though he had kindly protested he was in no haste to be paid.

Mr. Tyrold was not sorry to have his proposition declined; yet saw the sadness of Camilla unabated, and suggested, for a transient diversity, a visit to the Grove; enquiring why an acquaintance begun with so much warmth and pleasure, seemed thus utterly relinquished. Camilla had herself thought with shame of her apparently ungrateful neglect of Mrs. Arlbery; but the five guineas she had borrowed, and forgotten to pay, while she might yet have asked them of Sir Hugh, and which now she had no ability any where to raise, made the idea of meeting with her painful. And thus, overwhelmed with regret and repentance for all around, her spirits gone, and her heart sunk, she desired never more, except for Cleves, to stir from Etherington.

Had he seen the least symptom of her revival, Mr. Tyrold would have been gratified by her strengthened love of home; but this was far from being the case; and, upon the marriage of Miss Dennel, which was now celebrated, he was glad of an opportunity to force her abroad, from the necessity of making a congratulatory visit to the bride's aunt, Mrs. Arlbery.

The chariot, therefore, of Sir Hugh being borrowed, she was compelled into this exertion; which was ill repaid by her reception from Mrs. Arlbery, who, hurt as well as offended by her long absence and total silence, wore an air of the most chilling coldness. Camilla felt sorry and ashamed; but too much disturbed to attempt any palliation for her non-appearance, and remissness of even a note or message.

The room was full of morning visitors, all collected for the same complimentary purpose; but she was relieved with respect to her fears of Sir Sedley Clarendel, in hearing of his tour to the Hebrides.

Her mournful countenance soon, however, dispersed the anger of Mrs. Arlbery. 'What,' cried she, 'has befallen you, my fair friend? if you are not immeasurably unhappy, you are very seriously ill.'

'Yes,—no,—my spirits—have not been good—' answered she, stammering;—'but yours may, perhaps, assist to restore them.'

The composition of Mrs. Arlbery had no particle of either malice or vengeance; she now threw off, therefore, all reserve, and taking her by the hand, said: 'shall I keep you to spend the day with me? Yes, or no? Peace or war?'

And without waiting for an answer, she sent back the chariot, and a message to Mr. Tyrold, that she would carry home his daughter in the evening.

'And now, my faithless Fair,' cried she, as soon as they were alone, 'tell me what has led you to this abominable fickleness? with me, I mean! If you had grown tired of any body else, I should have thought nothing so natural. But you know, I suppose, that the same thing we philosophise into an admirable good joke for our neighbours, we moralise into a crime against ourselves.'

'I thought,' said Camilla, attempting to smile, 'none but country cousins ever made apologies?'

'Nay, now, I must forgive you without one word more!' answered Mrs. Arlbery, laughing, and shaking hands with her; 'a happy citation of one *bon mot*, is worth any ten offences. So, you see, you have nine to commit, in store, clear of all damages. But the pleasure of finding one has not said a good thing only for once, thence to be forgotten and die away in the winds, is far greater than you can yet awhile conceive. In the first pride of youth and beauty, our attention is all upon how we are looked at. But when those begin to be somewhat on the wane—when that barbarous time comes into play, which revenges upon poor miserable woman all the airs she has been playing upon silly man —our ambition, then, is how we are listened to. So now, cutting short reproach and excuse, and all the wearying round of explanation, tell me a little of your history since we last met.'

This was the last thing Camilla meant to undertake: but she began, in a hesitating manner, to speak of her little debt. Mrs. Arlbery, eagerly interrupting her, insisted it should not be mentioned; adding: 'I go on vastly well again; I am breaking in two ponies, and building a new phaeton; and I shall soon pay for both, without the smallest inconvenience,—except just pinching my servants, and starving my visitors. But tell me something of your adventures. You are not half so communicative as Rumour, which has given me a thousand details of you, and married you and your whole set to at least half a dozen men a piece, since you were last at the Grove. Amongst others, it asserts, that my old Lord Valhurst was seriously at your feet? That prating Mrs. Mittin, who fastened upon my poor little niece at Tunbridge, and who is now her factotum, pretends that my lord's own servants spoke of it publicly at Mrs. Berlinton's.'

This was a fact that, being thus divulged, a very few questions made impossible to deny; though Camilla was highly superior to the indelicacy and ingratitude of repaying the preference of any gentleman by publishing his rejection.

'And what in the world, my dear child,' said Mrs. Arlbery, 'could provoke you to so wild an action as refusing him?'

'Good Heaven, Mrs. Arlbery!'

'O, what—you were not in love with him? I believe not!—but if he was in love with you, take my word for it, that would have done quite as well. 'Tis such a little while that same love lasts, even when it is begun with, that you have but a few months to lose, to be exactly upon a par with those who set out with all the quivers of Cupid, darting from heart to heart. He has still fortune enough left for a handsome settlement;[1] you can't help outliving him, and then, think but how delectable would be your situation! Freedom, money at will, the choice of your own friends, and the enjoyment of your own humour!'

'You would but try me, my dear Mrs. Arlbery; for you cannot, I'm sure, believe me capable of making so solemn an engagement for such mercenary hopes, and selfish purposes.'

'This is all the romance of false reasoning. You have not sought the man, but the man you. You would not have solicited his acceptance, but yielded to his solicitation of yours. The balance is always just, where force is not used. The man has his reasons for chusing you; you have your reasons for suffering yourself to be chosen. What his are, you have no business to enquire; nor has he the smallest right to investigate yours.'

This was by no means the style in which Camilla had been brought up to think of marriage; and Mrs. Arlbery presently added: 'You are grave? yet I speak but as a being of the world I live in: though I address one that knows nothing about it. Tell me, however, a little more of your affairs. What are all these marriages and no marriages, our neighbourhood is so busy in making and unmaking?'

Camilla returned the most brief and quiet answers in her power; but was too late to save the delicacy of Eugenia in concealing her late double disappointments, the abortive preparations of Sir Hugh having travelled through all the adjoining country. 'Poor little dear ugly thing!' cried Mrs. Arlbery, 'she must certainly go off with her footman;—unless, indeed, that good old pedant, who teaches her that vast quantity of stuff she will have to unlearn, when once she goes a little about, will take compassion upon her and her thousands, and put them both into his own pockets.'

This raillery was painful nearly to disgust to Camilla; who frankly declared she saw her sister with no eyes but those of respect and affection, and could not endure to hear her mentioned in so ridiculous a manner.

'Never judge the heart of a wit,' answered she, laughing, 'by the tongue! We have often as good hearts, ay, and as much good nature, too, as the careful prosers[1] who utter nothing but what is right, or the heavy thinkers who have too little fancy to say anything that is wrong. But we have a pleasure in our own rattle that cruelly runs away with our discretion.'

She then more seriously apologized for what she had said, and declared herself an unaffected admirer of all she had heard of the good qualities of Eugenia.

Other subjects were then taken up, till they were interrupted by a visit from the young bride, Mrs. Lissin.

Jumping into the room, 'I'm just run away,' she cried, 'without saying a word to any body! I ordered my coach myself, and told my own footman to whisper me when it came, that I might get off, without saying a word of the matter. Dear! how they'll all stare when they miss me! I hope they'll be frightened!'

'And why so, you little chit? why do you want to make them uneasy?'

'O! I don't mind! I'm so glad to have my own way, I don't care for anything else. Dear, how do you do, Miss Camilla Tyrold? I wonder you have not been to see me! I had a great mind to have invited you to have been one of my bride's maids. But papa was so monstrous cross, he would not let me do hardly any thing I liked. I was never so glad in my life as when I went out of the house to be married! I'll never ask him about any one thing as long as I live again. I'll always do just what I chuse.'

'And you are quite sure Mr. Lissin will never interfere with that resolution?'

'O, I sha'n't let him! I dare say he would else. That's one reason I came out so, just now, on purpose to let him see I was my own mistress. And I told my coachman, and my own footman, and my maid, all three, that if they said one word, I'd turn 'em all away. For I intend always to turn 'em away when I don't like 'em. I shall never say anything to Mr. Lissin first, for fear of his meddling. I'm quite determined I won't be crossed any more, now I've servants of my own. I'm sure I've been crossed long enough.'

Then, turning to Camilla, 'Dear,' she cried, 'how grave you look! Dear, I wonder you don't marry too! When I ordered my coach, just now, I was ready to cry for joy, to think of not having to ask papa about it. And to-day, at breakfast, I dare say I rung twenty times, for one thing or another. As fast as ever I could think of any thing, I went to ringing again. For when I was at papa's, every time I rang the bell, he always asked me what I wanted. Only think of keeping one under so!'

'And what in the world said Mr. Lissin to so prodigious an uproar?'

'O, he stared like any thing. But he could not say much: I intend to use him to it from the first, that he may never plague me, like papa, with asking me what's the reason for every thing. If I don't like the dinner to-day, I'll order a new one, to be dressed for me on purpose. And Mr. Lissin, and papa, and Mrs. Mittin, and the rest of 'em, may eat the old one. Papa never let me order the dinner at home; he always would know what there was himself, and have what he chose. I'm resolved I'll have every thing I like best, now, every day. I could not get at the cook alone this morning, because so many of 'em were in the way; though I rung for her a dozen times. But to-morrow, I'll tell her of some things I intend to have the whole year through; in particular, currant tarts, and minced veal, and mashed potatoes. I've been determined upon that these three years, for against I was married.'

Then, taking Camilla by the hand, she begged she would accompany her to next room, saying, 'Pray excuse me, Aunt Arlbery, because I want to talk to Miss Tyrold about a secret.'

When they came to another apartment, after carefully shutting the door, 'Only think,' she cried, 'Miss Camilla Tyrold, of my marrying Mr. Lissin at last! Pray did you ever suspect it? I'm sure I did not. When papa told me of it, you can't think how I was surprised. I always thought it would have been Colonel Andover, or Mr. Macdersey, or else Mr. Summers; unless it had been Mr. Wiggan; or else your brother; but Mr. Lissin never once came into my head, because of his being so old. I dare say he's seven and twenty! only think!—But I believe he and papa had settled it all along, only papa never told it me, till just before hand. I don't like him much; do you?'

'I have not the pleasure to know him: but I hope you will endeavour to like him better, now.'

'I don't much care whether I do or not, for I shall never mind him. I always determined never to mind a husband. One minds one's papa because one can't help it: But only think of my being married before you! though you're seventeen years old—almost eighteen, I dare say—and I'm only just fifteen. I could not help thinking of it all the time I was dressing for a bride. You can't think how pretty my dress was. Papa made Mrs. Mittin buy it, because, he said, she could get every thing so cheap: but I made her ˙get it the dearest she could, for all that. Papa's monstrous stingy.'

This secret conference was broken up by a violent ringing at the gate, succeeded by the appearance of Mr. Lissin, who, without any ceremony, opened the door of the chamber into which the ladies had retired.

'So, ma'am!' said he, visibly very angry, 'I have the pleasure at last to find you! dinner has waited till it is spoilt, and I hope, therefore, now, you will do us the favour to come and sit at the head of your table.'

She looked frightened, and he took her hand, which she had not courage to draw back, though in a voice that spoke a sob near at hand, 'I'm sure,' she cried, 'this is not being treated like a married woman! and I'm sure if I'd known I might not do as I like, and come out when I'd a mind, I would not have married at all!'

Mr. Lissin, with little or no apology to Mrs. Arlbery, then conveyed his fair bride to her coach.

'Poor simple girl!' exclaimed Mrs. Arlbery. 'Mr. Lissin, who is a country squire of Northwick, will soon teach her another lesson, than that of ordering her carriage just at dinner time! The poor child took it into her head that, because, upon marrying, she might say, "my house," "my coach," and "my servants," instead of "my papa's;" and ring her bell for [whom] she pleased, and give her own orders, that she was to arrive at complete liberty and independence, and that her husband had merely to give her his name, and lodge in the same dwelling: and she will regard him soon, as a tyrant and a brute, for not letting her play all day long the part of a wild school girl, just come home for the holidays.'

The rest of the visit passed without further investigation on the part of Mrs. Arlbery, or embarrassment on that of Camilla; who found again some little pleasure in the conversation which, at first, had so much charmed, and the kindness which even her apparent neglect had not extinguished.

* * * *

Mrs. Arlbery, in two days, claimed her again. Mr. Tyrold would not permit her to send an excuse, and she found that lady more kindly disposed to her than ever; but with an undisguised compassion and concern in her countenance and manner. She had now learnt that Edgar was gone abroad; and she had learnt that

Camilla had private debts, to the amount of one hundred and eighteen pounds.

The shock of Camilla, when spoken to upon this subject, was terrible. She soon gathered, she had been betrayed by Mrs. Mittin, who, though she had made the communication as a profound secret to Mrs. Arlbery, with whom she had met at Mrs. Lissin's, there was every reason to suppose would whisper it, in the same manner, to an hundred persons besides.

Mrs. Arlbery, seeing her just uneasiness, promised, in this particular, to obviate it herself, by a conference with Mrs. Mittin, in which she would represent, that her own ruin would be the consequence of divulging this affair, from the general opinion which would prevail, that she had seduced a young lady under age, to having dealings with a usurer.

Camilla, deeply colouring, accepted her kind offer; but was forced upon a confession of the transaction; though with a shame for her trust in such a character as Mrs. Mittin, that made her deem the relation a penance almost adequate to its wrong.

CHAPTER XI

The Workings of Sorrow

THE visit of the Westwyns to Sir Hugh shewed Lavinia in so favourable a light, that nothing less than the strong prepossession already conceived for Camilla could have guarded the heart of the son, or the wishes of the father, from the complete captivation of her modest beauty, her intrinsic worth, and the chearful alacrity, and virtuous self-denial, with which she presided in the new œconomy of the rectory. But though the utter demolition of hope played with Henry its usual part of demolishing, also, half the fervour of admiration, he still felt, in consequence of his late failure, a distaste of any similar attempt: and Mr. Westwyn, unbribed by the high praise of his son, which had won him in Camilla, left him master of his choice. Each, however, found a delight in the Tyrold society, that seconded the wishes of the Baronet to make them lengthen their visit.

The retrenchments, by which the debts of Clermont were to

be paid, could no longer, nevertheless, be deferred; and Mr. Tyrold was just setting out for Cleves, to give his counsel for their arrangement, when his daughters were broken in upon by Mrs. Mittin.

Camilla could scarcely look at her, for displeasure at her conduct; but soon observed she seemed herself full of resentment and ill humour. She desired a private interview; and Camilla then found, that Mrs. Arlbery had not only represented her fault, and frightened her with its consequences, but occasioned, though most undesignedly, new disturbances and new dangers to herself: for Mrs. Mittin at length learnt, in this conference, with equal certainty, surprise, and provocation, that the inheritance of Sir Hugh was positively and entirely settled upon his youngest niece; and that the denials of all expectation on the part of Camilla, which she had always taken for closeness, conveyed but the simple truth. Alarmed lest she should incur the anger of Mr. Clykes, who was amongst her most useful friends, she had written him word of the discovery, with her concern at the mistake: and Mr. Clykes, judging now he had no chance of the gratuity finally promised for *honour* and *secrecy*, and even that his principal was in danger, had sent an enraged answer, with an imperious declaration, that he must either immediately be repaid all he had laid out, or receive some security for its being refunded, of higher value than the note of a minor of no fortune nor expectations.

Mrs. Mittin protested she did not know which way to turn, she was so sorry to have disobliged so good a friend; and broke forth into a vehement invective against Mr. Dubster, for pretending he knew the truth from young Squire Tyrold himself.

Long as was her lamentation, and satisfied as she always felt to hear her own voice, her pause still came too soon for any reply from Camilla, who now felt the discovery of her situation to be inevitable, compulsatory and disgraceful. Self-upbraidings that she had ever listened to such an expedient, assailed her with the cruellest poignancy, mingling almost self-detestation with utter despair.

In vain Mrs. Mittin pressed for some satisfaction; she was mute from inability to devise any; till the coachman of Mr. Lissin sent word he could wait no longer. She then, in a broken voice, said, 'Be so good as to write to Mr. Clykes, that if he will have the patience to wait a few days, I will prepare my friends to settle my accounts with him.'

Mrs. Mittin then, recovering from her own fright in this business, answered, 'O, if that's the case, my dear young lady, pray don't be uneasy, for it grieves me to vex you; and I'll promise you I'll coax my good friend to wait such a matter as that; for he's a vast regard for me; he'll do any thing I ask him, I know.'

She now went away; and Lavinia, who ran to her sister, found her in a state of distress, that melted her gentle heart to behold: but when she gathered what had passed, 'This disclosure, my dearest Camilla,' she cried, 'can never be so tremendous as the incessant fear of its discovery. Think of that, I conjure you! and endeavour to bear the one great shock, that will lead to after peace and ease.'

'No, my dear sister, peace and ease are no more for me!—My happiness was already buried;—and now, all that remained of consolation will be cut off also, in the lost good opinion of my father and mother!—that destroyed—and Edgar gone—what is life to me?—I barely exist!'

'And is it possible you can even a moment doubt their forgiveness? dear as you are to them, cherished, beloved!—'

'No—not their forgiveness—but their esteem, their confidence, their pleasure in their daughter will all end!—think, Lavinia, of my mother!—when she finds I, too, have contributed to the distress and disturbance of my father—that on my account, too, his small income is again straitened, his few gratifications are diminished—O Lavinia! how has she strove to guard her poor tottering girl from evil! And how has her fondness been always the pride of my life! What a conclusion is this to her cares! what a reward to all the goodness of my father!'

In this state of desperate wretchedness, she was still incapable to make the avowal which was now become indispensable, and which must require another loan from the store her father held so sacred. Lavinia had even less courage; and they determined to apply to Eugenia, who, though as softly feeling as either, mingled in her character a sort of heroic philosophy, that enabled her to execute and to endure the hardest tasks, where she thought them the demand of virtue. They resolved, therefore, the next morning, to send a note to Cleves for the carriage, and to commit the affair to this inexperienced and youthful female sage.

Far from running, as she was wont, to meet her father upon his entrance, Camilla was twice sent for before she could gain strength to appear in his presence; nor could his utmost kindness enable her to look up.

The heart of Mr. Tyrold was penetrated by her avoidance, and yet more sunk by her sight. His best hopes were all defeated of affording her parental comfort, and he was still to seek for her revival or support.

He related what had passed at Cleves, with the accustomed openness with which he conversed with his children as his friends. Clermont, he said, was arrived, and had authenticated all the accounts, with so little of either shame or sense, that a character less determined upon indulgence than that of Sir Hugh, must have revolted from affording him succour, if merely to mortify him into repentance. The manner of making payment, however, had been the difficult discussion of the whole day. Sir Hugh was unequal to performing any thing, though ready to consent to every thing. When he proposed the sale of several of his numerous horses, he objected, that what remained would be hard worked: when he mentioned diminishing his table, he was afraid the poor would take it ill, as they were used to have his orts: and when he talked of discharging some of his servants, he was sure they would think it very unkind. 'His heart,' continued Mr. Tyrold, 'is so bountiful, and so full of kindness, that he pleads his tender feelings, and regretting wishes, against the sound reason of hard necessity. What is right, however, must only in itself seek what is pleasant; and there, when it ceases to look more abroad, it is sure to find it.'

He stopt, hearing a deep sigh from Camilla, who secretly ejaculated a prayer that this sentence might live, henceforward, in her memory. He divined the wish, which devoutly he echoed, and continued:

'There is so little, in fine, that he could bear to relinquish, that, with my utmost efforts, I could not calculate any retrenchment, to which he will agree, at more than an hundred a year. Yet his scruples concerning his vow resist all the entreaties of our disinterested Eugenia, to either sell out for the sum, or cut down any trees in Yorkshire. These difficulties, too potent for his weak frame, were again sinking him into that despondence which we should all sedulously guard against, as the most prevailing of foes

to active virtue, when, to relieve him, I made a proposal which
my dear girls will both, I trust, find peculiar pleasure in seconding.'

Camilla had already [attempted] to raise her drooping head, conscience struck at what was said of despondence; and now
endeavoured to join in the chearful confidence expressed by
Lavinia, that he could not be mistaken.

'The little hoard, into which already we have broken for
Lionel,' he went on, 'I have offered to lend him for present
payment, as far as it will go, and to receive it again at stated
periods. In the mean while, I shall accept from him the same
interest as from the bank. For this I am to have also security. I
run no risk of the little all I have to leave to my two girls.'

He now looked at them both, expecting to see pleasure even in
Camilla, that what was destined, hereafter, for herself, could
prove of the smallest utility to Sir Hugh; but his disappointment,
and her shock were equal. Too true for the most transitory
disguise, the keenest anguish shot from her eye; and Mr. Tyrold,
amazed, said: 'Is it Camilla who would draw back from any
service to her uncle?'

'Ah no!' cried she, with clasped hands, 'I would die to do him
any good! and O!—that my death at this moment'——

She stopt, affrighted, for Mr. Tyrold frowned. A frown upon
a face so constantly benign, was new, was awful to her; but she
instantly recollected his condemnation of wishes so desperate,
and fearfully taking his hand, besought his forgiveness.

His brow instantly resumed its serenity. 'I have nothing,' said
he, 'my dearest child, to forgive, from the moment you recollect
yourself. But try, for your own sake, to keep in mind, that the
current sorrows, however acute, of current life, are but uselessly
aggravated by vain wishes for death. The smallest kind office
better proves affection than any words, however elevated.'

The conference here broke up; something incomprehensible
seemed to Mr. Tyrold to be blended with the grief of Camilla;
and though from her birth she had manifested, by every opportunity, the most liberal disregard of wealth, the something not to
be understood seemed always to have money for its object. What
this might be, he now fervently wished to explore; yet still hoped,
by patient kindness, to receive her confidence voluntarily.

Camilla now was half dead; Lavinia could with difficulty
sustain, but by no possible means revive her. What a period was

this to disclose to her Father that she must deprive him, in part, even of his promised solace in his intended assistance to his brother, to satisfy debts of which he suspected not the existence!

When forced down stairs, by a summons to supper, Mr. Tyrold, to console her for his momentary displeasure, redoubled his caresses; but his tenderness only made her weep yet more bitterly, and he looked at her with a heart rent with anguish. For Lavinia, for Eugenia, he would have felt similar grief; but their far less gay, though equally innocent natures, would have made the view of their affliction less strikingly oppressive. Camilla had, hitherto, seemed in the spring of joy yet more than of life. Anxiety flew at her approach, and animation took its place. Nothing could shake his resignation; yet to behold her constant sadness, severely tried his fortitude. To see tears trickling incessantly down the pale cheeks so lately blooming; to see her youthful countenance wear the haggard expression of care; to see life, in its wish and purposes seem at an end, 'ere, in its ordinary calculation, it was reckoned to have begun, drew him from every other consideration, and filled his whole mind with monopolizing apprehension.

He now himself pressed her, for change of scene, to accept an invitation she had received from Mrs. Berlinton to Grosvenor Square, whither Indiana was going in a few days, to spend a fortnight or three weeks before her marriage. But she declined the excursion, as not more unseasonable in its expence, than ungenial to her feelings.

*   *   *   *

The following morning, while they were at their melancholy breakfast, a letter arrived from Lisbon, which Mr. Tyrold read with visible disturbance, exclaiming, from time to time, 'Lionel, thou art indeed punished!'

The sisters were equally alarmed, but Lavinia alone could make any enquiry.

Mr. Tyrold then informed them, their uncle Relvil had just acknowledged to their Mother, that he could no longer, in justice, conceal that, previously to his quitting England, he had privately married his house-keeper, to induce her to accompany him in his voyage: and that, during his first wrath upon the detection of Lionel, he had disinherited him in favour of a little boy of her own, by a former marriage, whom they had brought with them to Lisbon.

Mr. Tyrold, though it had been his constant study to bring up his children without any reference to their rich uncles, had never internally doubted, but that the bachelor brother of Mrs. Tyrold would leave his fortune to the son of his only sister, who was his sole near relation. And Lionel, he knew, in defiance of his admonitions, had built upon it himself, rather as a certainty than a hope. 'He will now see,' said Mr. Tyrold, 'his presumption, and feel, by what he suffers, what he has earned. Yet culpable as he has been, he is now, also, unfortunate; and where crimes are followed by punishment, it is not for mortal man to harbour unabating resentment. I will write a few lines of comfort to him.'

Camilla, in this concession, experienced all she could feel of satisfaction; but the short sensation died away at the last words of the letter of her Mother, which Mr. Tyrold read aloud.

'You, I well know, will immediately in this evil, find for yourself, and impart to our children, something of instruction, if not of comfort. Shall I recollect this without emulation? No, I will bear up from this stroke, which, at least, permits my return to Etherington; where, in the bosom of my dear family, and supported by its honoured chief, I will forget my voyage, my painful absence, and my disappointment, in exertions of practical œconomy, strict, but not rigid, which our good children will vie with each other to adopt: sedulous, all around, to shew in what we can most forbear. I hope almost immediately to claim my share in these labours, which such motives will make light, and such companions render precious.'

In agony past repression at these words, Camilla glided out of the room. The return of her Mother was now horrour to her, not joy; her shattered nerves could not bear the interview, while under a cloud threatening to burst in such a storm; and she entreated Lavinia to tell her Father that she accepted his proposal for going to Mrs. Berlinton's; 'and there,' she cried, 'Lavinia, I will wait, till Eugenia has told the dreadful history that thus humbles me to the dust!'

Lavinia was too timid to oppose reason to this suffering; and Mr. Tyrold, already cruelly apprehensive the obscurity of their recluse lives contributed to her depression, and believing she compared her present privations to the lost elegancies of Beech

Park, sighed heavily, yet said he was glad she would remove from a spot in which reminiscence was so painful. This was not, indeed, he added, the period he should have selected for her visiting the capital, or residing at Mrs. Berlinton's; but she was too much touched by the state of her family, not to be guarded in her expences; and the pressure of her even augmenting sadness, was heavier upon his mind than any other alarm.

The conscience-struck Camilla could make no profession, no promise; nor yet, though ardently wishing it, refuse his offered advance of her next quarter's allowance, lest she should be reduced again to the necessity of borrowing.

This step once decided, brought with it something like a gloomy composure. 'I shall avoid,' she cried, 'at least, with my Mother, these killing caresses of deluded kindness that break my heart with my Father. She, too, would soon discover there was something darker in my sadness than even grief! She would be sure that even my exquisite loss could not render me ungrateful to all condolement; she would know that a daughter whom she had herself reared and instructed, would blush so unceasingly to publish any personal disappointment, let her feel it how she might. O my loved Mother! how did the delight of knowing your kind expectations keep me, while under your guidance in the way I ought to go! O Mother of my heart! what a grievous disappointment awaits your sad return! To find, at the first opening of your virtuous schemes of general saving—that I, as well as Lionel, have involved my family in debts—that I, as well as Clermont, have committed them clandestinely to a usurer!'

Lavinia undertook to give Eugenia proper instructions for her commission; but news arrived, the next day, that Sir Hugh would take no denial to Eugenia's being herself of the party. This added not, however, to the courage of Camilla for staying, and her next determination was to reveal the whole by letter.

Mr. Tyrold would not send her to Cleves to take leave, that her uncle might not be tempted to exercise his wonted, but now no longer convenient generosity, nor yet be exposed to the pain of withholding it. 'You will go, now, my dear girl,' he said, 'in your pristine simplicity, and what can so every way become you? It is not for a scheme of pleasure, but for a stimulus to mental exertion, I part with you. When you return, your excellent Mother will aid your task, and reward its labour. Remember but, while in your own hands, that open œconomy, springing from discretion, is always respected. It is false shame alone that begets ridicule.'

Weeping and silent she heard him, and his fears gained ground that her disappointment, joined to a view of gayer life, had robbed Etherington of all charms to her. Bitterly he regretted he had ever suffered her to leave his roof, though he would not now force her stay. Compulsion could only detain her person; and might heighten the disgust of her mind.

The little time which remained was given wholly to packing and preparing; and continued employment hid from Mr. Tyrold her emotion, which encreased every moment, till the carriage of Sir Hugh stopt at the gate. Lost, then, to all sensation, but the horrour of the avowal that must intervene 'ere they met again, with incertitude if again he would see her with the same kindness, she flew into his arms, rather agonised than affectionate; kissed his hands with fervour, kissed every separate finger, rested upon his shoulder, hid her face in his bosom, caught and pressed to her lips even the flaps of his coat, and scarce restrained herself from bending to kiss his feet; yet without uttering a word, without even shedding a tear.

Strangely surprised, and deeply affected, Mr. Tyrold, straining her to his breast, said: 'Why, my dear child, why, my dearest Camilla, if thus agitated by our parting, do you leave me?'

This question brought her to recollection, by the impossibility she found to answer it; she tore herself, therefore, away from him, embraced Lavinia, and hurried into the coach.

BOOK X

CHAPTER I

A Surprise

CAMILLA strove to check her grief upon entering the carriage, in which Miss Margland had again the charge of the young party; but the interrogatory of her Father, *Why will you leave me?* was mentally repeated without ceasing. Ah! why, indeed! thought she, at a moment when every filial duty called more than ever for my stay!—Well, might he not divine the unnatural reason! can I believe it myself?—Believe such an hour arrived?—when my Mother—the best of Mothers!—is expected—when she returns to her family, Camilla seeks another abode! is not this a dream? and may I not one day awake from it?

Miss Margland was in the highest good humour at this expedition: and Indiana was still enraptured to visit London, from old expectations which she knew not how to relinquish; though they were fixed to no point, and as fantastic as vague. Eugenia, whose dejection had made Sir Hugh press her into the party, found nothing in it to revive her; and Camilla entered Grosvenor-square with keen dissatisfaction of every sort. The cautions of Edgar against Mrs. Berlinton broke into all the little relief she might have experienced upon again seeing her. She had meant to keep his final exhortations constantly in her mind, and to make all his opinions and counsels the rule and measure of her conduct: but a cruel perversity of events seemed to cast her every action into an apparent defiance of his wishes.

Mrs. Berlinton, who, in a mansion the most splendid, received her with the same gentle sweetness she had first sought her regard, was delighted by the unexpected sight of Eugenia, whose visit had been settled too late to be announced by letter; and caressed Indiana immediately as a sister. Miss Margland, who came but for two days, sought with much adulation to obtain an invitation for a longer stay; but Mrs. Berlinton, though all courtesy and grace, incommoded herself with no society that she did not find pleasing.

Melmond, who had accompanied them on horseback, was eager to engage the kindness of his sister for Indiana; and Mrs. Berlinton, in compliment to her arrival, refused all parties for the evening, and bestowed upon her an almost undivided attention.

This was not quite so pleasant to him in proof as in hope. Passionless, in this case, herself, the delusions of beauty deceived not her understanding; and half an hour sufficed to shew Indiana to be frivolous, uncultivated, and unmeaning. The perfection, nevertheless, of her face and person, obviated either wonder or censure of the choice of her brother; though she could not but regret that he had not seen with mental eyes the truly superior Eugenia.

The wretched Camilla quitted them all as soon as possible, to retire to her chamber, and ruminate upon her purposed letter. She meant, at first, to write in detail; but her difficulties accumulated as she weighed them. 'What a season,' cried she, 'to sink Lionel still deeper in disgrace! What a treachery, after voluntarily assisting him, to complain of, and betray him! ah! let my own faults teach me mercy for the faults of others!' yet, without this acknowledgment, what exculpation could she offer for the origin of her debts? and all she had incurred at Tunbridge? those of Southampton she now thought every way unpardonable. Even were she to relate the vain hopes which had led to the expence of the ball dress, could she plead, to an understanding like that of her Mother, that she had been deceived and played upon by such a woman as Mrs. Mittin? 'I am astonished now myself,' she cried, 'at that passive facility!—but to me, alas, thought comes only with repentance!' The Higden debt, both for the rent and the stores, was the only one at which she did not blush, since, great as was her indiscretion, in not enquiring into her powers before she plighted her services, it would be palliated by her motive.

Vainly she took up her pen; not even a line could she write. 'How enervating,' she cried, 'is all wrong! I have been, till now, a happy stranger to fear! Partially favoured, and fondly confiding, I have looked at my dear Father, I have met my beloved Mother, with the same courage, and the same pleasure that I looked at and met my brother and my sisters, and only with more reverence. How miserable a change! I shudder now at the presence of the most indulgent of Fathers! I fly with guilty cowardice from the fondest of Mothers!'

Eugenia, when able, followed her; and had no sooner heard the whole history, than, tenderly embracing her, she said, 'Let not this distress seem so desperate to you, my dearest sister! your own account points out to me how to relieve it, without either betraying our poor Lionel, or further weighing down our already heavily burthened friends.'

'And how, my dear Eugenia?' cried Camilla, with fearful gratitude, and involuntarily reviving by the most distant idea of such a project.

By adopting, she said, the same means that had been invented by Mrs. Mittin. She had many valuable trinkets, the annual offerings of her munificent uncle, the sale of which would go far enough, she could not doubt, towards the payment of the principal, to induce the money-lender to accept interest for the rest, till the general affairs of their house were re-established; when what remained of the sum could be discharged, without difficulty, by herself; now no longer wanting money, nor capable of receiving any pleasure from it, but by the pleasure she might give.

Camilla pressed her in her arms, almost kneeling with fond acknowledgments, and accepted, without hesitation, her generous offer.

'All, then, is arranged,' said Eugenia, with a smile so benign it seemed nearly beautiful; 'and to friendship, and each other, we will devote our future days. My spirits will revive in the revival of Camilla. To see her again gay will be renovation to my uncle; and who knows, my dear sister, but our whole family may again be blest, 'ere long, with peace?'

*   *   *   *

The next morning they sent off a note to the money-lender, whose direction Camilla had received from Mrs. Mittin, entreating his patience for a fortnight, or three weeks, when he would receive the greatest part of his money, with every species of acknowledgment.

Camilla, much relieved, went to sit with Mrs. Berlinton, but on entering the dressing room, was struck by the sight of Bellamy, just quitting it.

Mrs. Berlinton, upon her appearance, with a look of soft rapture approaching her, said: 'Felicitate me, loveliest Camilla!—my friend, my chosen friend is restored to me, and the society for which so long I have sighed in vain, may be once more mine!'

Camilla, startled, exclaimed with earnestness, 'My dearest Mrs. Berlinton, pardon me, I entreat—but is Mr. Bellamy known to Mr. Berlinton?'

'No!' answered she, disdainfully; 'but he has been seen by him. Mr. Berlinton is a stranger to merit or taste; and Alphonso, to him, is but as any other man.'

'They are, however, acquainted with each other?' said Camilla.

Mrs. Berlinton answered, that, after her marriage, she remained three months in Wales with her aunt, where Bellamy was travelling to view the country, and where, almost immediately after that unhappy enthralment, she first knew him, and first learnt the soothing charms of friendship; but from that period they had met no more, though they had constantly corresponded.

Camilla was now first sensible to all the alarm with which Edgar had hitherto striven to impress her in vain. The impropriety of such a connexion, the danger of such a partiality, filled her with wonder and disturbance. She hesitated whether to relate or not the adventure of Bellamy with her sister; but the strong repugnance of Eugenia to having it named, and the impossibility of proving the truth of the general opinion of his base scheme, decided her to silence. Upon the plans and the sentiments, however, of Mrs. Berlinton herself, she spared not the extremest sincerity; but she gained no ground by the contest, though she lost not any kindness by the attempt.

At dinner, she felt extremely disturbed by the re-appearance of Bellamy, [who] alone, she found, had been excepted by Mrs. Berlinton, in the orders of general denial to company. He seemed, himself, much struck at the sight of Eugenia, who blushed and looked embarrassed by his presence. He did not, however, address her; he confined his attentions to Mrs. Berlinton, or Miss Margland.

The former received them with distinguishing softness; the latter, at first, disdainfully repelled them, from the general belief at Cleves of his attempted elopement with Eugenia; but afterwards, finding she was left wholly to a person who had no resources for entertaining her, namely, herself,—and knowing

Eugenia safe while immediately under her eye, she deigned to treat him with more consideration.

The opera was proposed for the evening, Mrs. Berlinton, having both tickets and her box at the service of her fair friends, as the lady with whom she had subscribed was out of town. Indiana was enchanted, Miss Margland was elevated, and Eugenia not unwilling to seek some recreation, though hopeless of finding it. But Camilla, notwithstanding she was lightened, at this moment, from one of her most corrosive cares, was too entirely miserable for any species of amusement. The same strong feelings that gave to pleasure, when she was happy, so high a zest, rendered it nearly abhorrent to her, when grief had possession of her mind.

After dinner, when the ladies retired to dress, Camilla, with some uneasiness, conjured Eugenia to avoid renewing any acquaintance with Bellamy.

Eugenia blushing, while a tear started into either eye, said she was but too well guarded from Bellamy, through a late transaction; which had exalted her to a summit of happiness, from which she could never now descend to any new plan of life, beyond the single state and retirement.

*   *   *   *

At night, the whole party went to the Opera, except Camilla, who, in spending the evening alone, meant to ruminate upon her affairs, and arrange her future conduct: but Edgar, his virtues, and his loss, took imperious possession of all her thoughts; and while she dwelt upon his honour, his sincerity, and his goodness, and traced, with cherished recollection, every scene in which she had been engaged with him, he and they recurred to her as visions of all earthly felicity.

Awakened from these reveries, by the sound of the carriage, and the rapping at the street door, she was hastening down stairs to meet her sister, when she heard Melmond call out from the coach: 'Is Miss Eugenia Tyrold come home?'

'No;' the man answered; and Melmond exclaimed; 'Good Heaven!—I must run then back to the theatre. Do not be alarmed, my Indiana, and do not alarm Miss Camilla, for I will not return without her.'

They all entered but himself; while Camilla, fixed to the stair upon which she had heard these words, remained some minutes motionless. Then, tottering down to the parlour, with a voice hollow from affright, and a face pale as death, she tremulously articulated, 'where is my sister?'

They looked all aghast, and not one of them, for some time, was capable to give any account that was intelligible. She then gathered that, in coming out of the theatre, to get to the coach, they had missed her. None of them knew how, which way, in what manner.

'And where's Mr. Bellamy?' cried she, in an agony of apprehension; 'was he at the Opera? where—where is he?'

Miss Margland looked dismayed, and Mrs. Berlinton amazed, at this interrogatory; but they both said he had only been in the box at the beginning of the Opera, and afterwards to help them out of the crowd.

'And who did he help? who? who?' exclaimed Camilla.

'Me,—first—' answered Miss Margland,—'and, when we got into a great crowd, he took care of Miss Eugenia too.' She then added, that in this crowd, both she and Eugenia had been separated from Mrs. Berlinton and Indiana, who by Melmond and another gentleman had been handed straight to the carriage, without difficulty; that soon after, she had lost the arm of Bellamy, who, by some mistake, had turned a wrong way; but she got to the coach by herself; where they had waited full half an hour, Melmond running to and fro and searching in every direction, but in vain, to find Eugenia. Nor had Bellamy again appeared. They then came home, hoping he had put her into a chair, and that she might be arrived before them.

'Dreadful! dreadful!' cried Camilla, sinking on the floor, 'she is forced away! she is lost!'

When again her strength returned, she desired that some one might go immediately to the house or lodgings of Bellamy, to enquire if he were come home.

This was done by a footman, who brought word he had not been seen there since six o'clock in the evening, when he dressed, and went out.

Camilla now, confirmed in her horrible surmise, was nearly frantic. She bewailed her sister, her father, her uncle; she wanted herself to rush forth, to search Eugenia in the streets; she could scarce be detained within, scarce kept off from entire delirium.

CHAPTER II

A Narrative

IT was four o'clock in the morning when Melmond returned. Camilla rushed to the street-door to meet him. His silence and his mournful air announced his ill success. She wrung her hands in anguish, and besought him to send instantly an express to Etherington, with the fatal tidings.

He went himself to the nearest stables, desiring she would prepare a letter while he got a man and horse for the journey.

In scrawling and indistinct characters she then wrote:

'O my Father—our Eugenia has disappeared! she was lost last night at the Opera—Mr. Bellamy was conducting her to Mrs. Berlinton's coach—but we have seen neither of them since!—what—what must we do?'

Melmond wrote the address, which her hand could not make legible; and Miss Margland prepared for the post a laboured vindication to Sir Hugh of her own conduct upon this occasion.

Indiana was long gone to bed. She was really very sorry; but she was really much tired; and she could do, as she said, no good.

But Mrs. Berlinton felt an alarm for Eugenia, and an astonishment concerning Bellamy, that would fully have wakened her faculties, had she been wholly unmoved by the misery of Camilla. Far other was, however, her nature, gentle, compassionate, and sympathising; and her own internal disturbance, though great even beyond her own conception why, sunk at sight of the excess of wretchedness which disordered her poor friend.

There could be but one possible opinion of this disastrous adventure, which was, that Bellamy had spirited this young creature away, to secure her fortune, by her hand. Melmond again went forth, to make enquiry at all the stables in London, for any carriage that might have been hired for a late hour. And at six o'clock, in great perturbation, he came back, saying, he had just traced that she was put into a chaise and four from a hackney coach; that the chaise was hired in Piccadilly, and engaged for a week. He was now determined to ride post himself in the pursuit, that, if any accidental delay retarded them, he might recover her before she arrived at Gretna Green,[1] whither he could not doubt she was to be conveyed: but as she could not be married by force, his presence might yet be in time to prevent persecution, or foul play.

Camilla nearly embraced him with transport at this ray of hope, and, leaving his tenderest condolements for Indiana, whom he implored his sister to watch sedulously, he galloped northwards.

His heart was most sincerely in the business; what he owed to the noble conduct which the high sentiments and pure regard of Eugenia had dictated, had excited a tender veneration, which made him hold his life as too small an offering to be refused for her service, if its sacrifice could essentially shew his gratitude. And often his secret mind had breathed a wish, that her love of literature had been instilled into her cousin; though he studiously checked, as profane, all that was not admiration of that most exquisite workmanship of nature.

Mrs. Berlinton wanted not to be told this proceeding was wrong, yet still found it impossible to persuade herself Eugenia would not soon think it right; though Eugenia was the creature that she most revered in the whole world, and though, with Bellamy himself she felt irritated and disappointed.

Camilla in every evil reverted to the loss of Edgar, whose guardian care, had she preserved him, would have preserved, she thought, her loved Eugenia.

The express from Etherington brought back only a few lines written by Lavinia, with an account that Mr. Tyrold, in deep misery, was setting out post for Scotland.

A week past thus in suspence, nearly intolerable to Camilla, before Melmond returned.

Always upon the watch, she heard his voice, and flew to meet him in the dressing room. He was at the feet of Indiana, to whom he was pouring forth his ardent lamentations at this long deprivation of her sight.

But joy had evidently no part in his tenderness; Camilla saw at once depression and evil tidings, and, sinking upon a chair, could scarcely pronounce, 'Have you not then found her?'

'I have left her but this minute,' he answered, in a tone the most melancholy.

'Ah! you have then seen her! you have seen my dearest Eugenia?—O, Mr. Melmond, why have you left her at all?'

It was long before he could answer; he besought her to compose herself; he expressed the extremest solicitude for the uneasiness of Indiana, whose eternal interruptions of 'Dear! where is she?—Dear! why did not she come back?—Dear! who took her away?' he attributed to the agitation of the fondest friendship, and conjured, while tears of terror started into his eyes, that she would moderate the excess of her sensibility. It seems the peculiar province of the lover, to transfuse all that he himself most prizes, and thinks praise-worthy, into the breast of his chosen object; nor is he more blind to the defects with which she may abound, than prodigal in gifts of virtues which exist but in his own admiration.

'And my Father? my poor Father!' cried Camilla, 'you have seen nothing of my Father?'

'Pardon me; I have just left him also.'

'And not with Eugenia?'

'Yes; they are together.'

Rapture now defied all apprehension with Camilla; the idea of Eugenia restored to her Father, was an idea of entire happiness; but her joy affected Melmond yet more than her alarm: he could not let her fasten upon any false expectations; he bid his sister aid him to support Indiana, and then, with all the gentleness of the sincerest concern, confessed that Eugenia was married before she was overtaken.

This was a blow for which Camilla was still unprepared. She concluded it a forced marriage; horror froze her veins, her blood no longer flowed, her heart ceased to beat, she fell lifeless on the ground.

Her recovery was more speedy than it was happy, and she was assisted to her chamber, no longer asking any questions, no longer desiring further information. All was over of hope: and the particulars seemed immaterial, since the catastrophe was as irreversible as it was afflicting.

Mrs. Berlinton still attended her, grieved for her suffering, yet believing that Eugenia would be the happiest of women; though an indignation the most forcible mingled with her surprise at the conduct of Bellamy.

This dread sort of chasm in the acuteness of the feelings of Camilla lasted not long; and Mrs. Berlinton then brought from Melmond the following account.

With the utmost speed he could use, he could not, though a

single horseman, overtake them. They never, as he learnt by the way, remitted their journey, nor stopt for the smallest refreshment but at some cottage. At length, in the last stage to Gretna Green, he met them upon their return. It was easy to him to see that his errand was vain, and the knot indissolubly tied, by the blinds being down, and the easy air with which Bellamy was look ng around him.

Eugenia sat back in the chaise with a handkerchief to her eyes. He stopt the vehicle, and told Bellamy he must speak with that lady. 'That lady, Sir,' he proudly answered, 'is my wife; speak to her, therefore; . . . but in my hearing.' Eugenia at this dropt her handkerchief, and looked up. Her eyes were sunk into her head by weeping, and her face was a living picture of grief. Melmond loudly exclaimed: 'I come by the authority of her friends, and I demand her own account of this transaction.' 'We are now going to our friends,' replied he, 'ourselves, and we shall send them no messages.' He then ordered the postillion to drive on, telling him at his peril to stop no more; Eugenia, in a tone but just audible, saying: 'Adieu, Mr. Melmond! Adieu!'

To have risked his life in her rescue, at such a moment, seemed to him nothing, could he but more certainly have ascertained her own wishes, and real situation: but as she attempted neither resistance nor remonstrance, he concluded Bellamy spoke truth; and if they were married, he could not unmarry them; and if they were going to her friends, they were doing all he could now exact. He resolved, however, to follow, and if they should turn any other road, to call for assistance till he could investigate the truth.

They stopt occasionally for refreshments at the usual inns, and travelled no more in the dark; but Bellamy never lost sight of her; and Melmond, in watching, observed that she returned to the chaise with as little opposition as she quitted it, though weeping always, and never, for a voluntary moment, uncovering her face. Bellamy seemed always most assiduous in his attentions: she never appeared to repulse him, nor to receive from him any comfort.

On the second day's journey, just as Bellamy had handed her from the chaise, at the inn where they meant to dine, and which Melmond, as usual, entered at the same time, he saw Mr. Tyrold —hurrying, but so shaking he could scarcely support himself, from a parlour, whence he had seen them alight, into the passage.

The eyes, ever downcast, of Eugenia, perceived him not, till she was clasped, in mute agony, in his arms. She then looked up, saw who it was, and fainted away. Bellamy, though he knew him not, supposed who he might be, and his reverend appearance seemed to impress him with awe. Nevertheless, he was himself seizing the now senseless Eugenia, to convey her to some room; when Mr. Tyrold, reviving from indignation, fixed his eyes upon his face, and said: 'By what authority, Sir, do you presume to take charge of my daughter?'—'By the authority,' he answered, 'of a husband.' Mr. Tyrold said no more; he caught at the arm of Melmond, though he had not yet seen who he was, and Bellamy carried Eugenia into the first vacant parlour, followed only by the woman of the house.

Melmond then, respectfully, and filled with the deepest commiseration, sought to make himself known to Mr. Tyrold; but he heard him not, he heeded no one; he sat down upon a trunk, accidentally in the passage where all this had passed, saying, but almost without seeming conscious that he spoke aloud: 'This, indeed, is a blow to break both our hearts!' Melmond then stood silently by, for he saw, by his folded hands and uplighted eyes, he was ejaculating some prayer: after which, with a countenance more firm, and limbs better able to sustain him, he rose, and moved towards the parlour into which the fainting Eugenia had been carried.

Melmond then again spoke to him by his name. He recollected the voice, turned to him, and gave him his hand, which was of an icy coldness. 'You are very kind, Mr. Melmond,' he said; 'my poor girl'—but stopt, checking what he meant to add, and went to the parlour-door.

It was locked. The woman of the house had left it, and said, the lady was recovered from her fit. Mr. Tyrold, from a thousand feelings, seemed unable to demand admission for himself: he desired Melmond to speak, and claim an audience alone for him with his daughter.

Bellamy opened the door with a look evidently humbled and frightened, yet affecting perfect ease. When Melmond made known his commission, Eugenia, starting up, exclaimed: 'Yes, yes! I will see my dear Father alone!—and O! that this poor frame might sink to rest on his loved bosom!'

'In a moment! in a moment!' cried Bellamy, motioning

Melmond to withdraw; 'tell Mr. Tyrold he shall come in a moment.'

Melmond was forced to retreat; but heard him hastily say, as again he fastened the door, 'My life, O Eugenia! is in your hands —and is it thus you requite my ardent love and constancy?'

Mr. Tyrold now would wait but a few minutes: it was palpable Bellamy feared the interview; and he could fear it but from one motive: he sent him, therefore, word by Melmond, that if he did not immediately retire, and leave him to a conference alone with his daughter, he would apply no more for a meeting till he claimed it in a court of justice.

Bellamy soon came out, bowed obsequiously to Mr. Tyrold, who passed him without notice, and who was then for half an hour shut up with Eugenia. Longer Bellamy could not endure; he broke in upon them, and left the room no more.

Soon after, Mr. Tyrold came out, his own eyes now as red as those of the weeping bride. He took Melmond apart, thanked him for his kindness, but said nothing could be done. He entreated him therefore to return to his own happier affairs; adding, 'I cannot talk upon this miserable event. Tell Camilla, her sister is, for the present, going home with me—though not, alas! alone! Tell her, too, I will write to her upon my arrival at Etherington.'

'This,' concluded Mrs. Berlinton, 'is all my brother has to relate; all that for himself he adds, is, that if ever, to something human, the mind of an angel was accorded—that mind seems enshrined in the heart of Eugenia!'

Nothing that Camilla had yet experienced of unhappiness, had penetrated her with feelings of such deadly woe as this event. Eugenia, from her childhood, had seemed marked by calamity: her ill health, even from infancy, and her subsequent misfortunes, had excited in her whole house the tenderest pity, to which the uncommon character with which she grew up, had added respect and admiration. And the strange, and almost continual trials she had had to encounter, from the period of her attaining her fifteenth year, which, far from souring her mind, had seemed to render it more perfect, had now nearly sanctified her in the estimation of them all. To see her, therefore, fall, at last, a sacrifice to deceit or violence,—for one, if not both, had palpably put her into the possession of Bellamy, was a grief more piercingly wounding than all she had yet suffered. Whatever she had personally to bear, she constantly imagined some imprudence or impropriety had provoked; but Eugenia, while she appeared to her so blameless, that she could merit no evil, was so amiable, that willingly she would have borne for her their united portions.

How it had been effected, since force would be illegal, still kept amazement joined to sorrow, till the promised letter arrived from Mr. Tyrold, with an account of the transaction.

Eugenia, parted from Miss Margland by Bellamy, in the crowd, was obliged to accept his protection, which, till then, she had refused, to restore her to her company. The coach, he said, he knew, had orders to wait in Pall Mall, whither the other ladies would be conveyed in chairs, to avoid danger from the surrounding carriages. She desired to go, also, in a chair: but he hurried her by quick surprize into a hackney-coach,[1] which, he said, would be more speedy, and bidding the man drive to Pall Mall, seated himself opposite to her. She had not the most remote suspicion of his design, as his behaviour was even coldly distant, though she wondered Pall Mall was so far off, and that the coachman drove so fast, till they stopt at a turnpike——and then, in one quick and decided moment, she comprehended her situation, and made an attempt for her own deliverance—but he prevented her from being heard.—And the scenes that followed she declined relating. Yet, what she would not recount, she could not, to the questions of her Father, deny, that force, from that moment, was used, to repel all her efforts for obtaining help, and to remove her into a chaise.

Mr. Tyrold required to hear nothing more, to establish a prosecution, and to seize her, publickly, from Bellamy. But from this she recoiled. 'No, my dear Father,' she continued, 'the die is cast! and I am his! Solemn has been my vow! sacred I must hold it!'

She then briefly narrated, that though violence was used to silence her at every place where she sought to be rescued, every interval was employed, by Bellamy, in the humblest supplications for her pardon, and most passionate protestations of regard, all beginning and all ending in declaring, that to live longer without her was impossible, and pledging his ardent attachment for obtaining her future favour; spending the period from stage to stage, or turnpike to turnpike, in kneeling to beseech forgiveness for the desperation to which he was driven, by the most cruel and hopeless passion that ever seized the heart of man. When they were near their journey's end, he owned that his life was in her hands, but he was indifferent whether he lost it from the misery of living without her, or from her vengeance of this last struggle of his despair. She assured him his life was safe, and offered him pardon upon condition of immediate restoration to her friends; but, suddenly producing a pistol, 'Now then,' he said, 'O! amiable object of my constant love! bless me with your hand, or prepare to see me die at your feet!' And, with a terrifying oath, he bound himself not to lose her and outlive her loss. She besought him to be more reasonable, with the gentlest prayers; but his vehemence only encreased; she offered him every other promise he could name; but he preferred death to every other she should grant. She then pronounced, though in trembling, a positive refusal. Instantly he lifted up his pistol, and calling out; 'Forgive, then, O hard-hearted Eugenia, my uncontroulable passion, and shed a tear over the corpse I am going to prostrate at your feet!' was pointing it to his temple, when, overcome with horror, she caught his arm, exclaiming; 'Ah! stop! I consent to what you please!' It was in vain she strove afterwards to retract; one scene followed another, till he had bound her by all she herself held sacred, to rescue him from suicide, by consenting to the union. He found a person who performed the marriage ceremony on the minute of her quitting the chaise. She uttered not one word; she was passive, scared, and scarce alive; but resisted not the eventful ring, with which he encircled her finger, and seemed rousing as from a dream, upon hearing him call her his wife. He professed eternal gratitude, and eternal devotion; but no sooner was all conflict at an end, than, consigning herself wholly to grief, she wept without intermission.

When Mr. Tyrold had heard her history, abhorrence of such barbarous force, and detestation of such foul play upon the ingenuous credulity of her nature, made him insist, yet more strongly, upon taking legal measures for procuring an immediate separation, and subsequent punishment; but the reiterated vows with which, since the ceremony, he had bound her to himself, so forcibly awed the strict conscientiousness of her principles, that no representations could absolve her opinion of what she now held her duty; and while she confessed her unhappiness at a connection formed by such cruel means, she conjured him not to encrease it, by rendering her, in her own estimation, perjured.

'Patiently, therefore,' continued Mr. Tyrold, 'we must bear, what vainly we should combat, and bow down to those calamities of which the purpose is hidden, nor fancy no good is answered, because none is obvious. Man develops but little, though he experiences much. The time will come for his greater diffusion of knowledge; let him meet it without dread, by using worthily his actual portion. I resign myself, therefore, with reverence to this blow; though none yet has struck so hardly at my heart. We must now do what we can for this victim to her own purity, by seeking means to secure her future independence, and by bettering—if possible!—her betrayer. What a daughter, what a sister, what a friend, has her family thus lost! How will your poor Mother receive such killing tidings! Misfortune, sickness, and poverty, she has heroism to endure; but innocence oppressed through its own artlessness, and inexperience duped by villainy, will shake her utmost firmness, and harass into disorder her, as yet, unbroken powers of encountering adversity. Alas!—no evils that visited the early years of this loved child, have proved to her so grievous as the large fortune with which they were followed! We repined, my Camilla, at the deprivation you sustained at that period.—We owe to it, perhaps, that you have not as treacherously been betrayed!

'How has the opening promise of our Eugenia more than answered our fondest expectations! Her knowledge is still less uncommon than her simplicity, her philosophy for herself than her zeal in the service of others. She is singular with sweetness, peculiar, yet not impracticable; generous without parade, and wise without consciousness. Yet now, so sacrificed seems all,—that I dwell upon her excellencies as if enumerating them over her tomb!'

A letter from Lavinia contained some further particulars. Their Father, she said, finding the poor victim resolute, meant to spare Sir Hugh all that was possible of the detestable craft of Bellamy; and Eugenia was already struggling to recover her natural serenity, that she might appear before him without endangering his own. Bellamy talked of nothing but love and rapture; yet the unsuspicious Eugenia was the only person he deceived; for so little from the heart seemed either his looks or his expressions, that it was palpable he was acting a part, to all who believed it possible words and thoughts could be divided.

A postscript to this letter was added by Eugenia herself.

'Ah, my Camilla! . . . where now are all our sweet promised participations?—But let me not talk of myself; nor do you, my affectionate sister, dwell upon me at this period. One thing I undertook shall yet be performed; the moment I am able to go to Cleves, I will deliver, through Lavinia, what I mentioned. Does anything else remain that is yet in my power? Tell me, my Camilla, and think but with what joy you will give joy again to your

EUGENIA.'

Broken hearted over these letters, Camilla spent her time in their perpetual perusal, in wiping from them her tears, and pressing with fond anguish to her lips the signature of her hapless sister, self-beguiled by her own credulous goodness, and self-devoted by her conscientious scruples.

CHAPTER III

The Progress of Dissipation

MR. Clykes, by the promised payment and reward, being for the present appeased, Camilla still admitted some hope of waiting a more favourable moment for her cruel confession. She received, also, a little, though mournful, reprieve from terror, by a letter from Lisbon, written to again postpone the return of Mrs. Tyrold, at the earnest request of Mr. Relvil; and she flattered herself that, before her arrival, she should be enabled to resume those only duties which could draw her from despondence. She lived, meanwhile, wholly shut up from all company, consigned to penitence for her indiscretions, to grief for the fate of her sister, and to wasting regret of her own causelessly lost felicity.

Indiana smiled not more sweetly upon Melmond, for Miss Margland's advising her to consider in time, whether the promises made by Miss Eugenia Tyrold would be binding to Mrs. Bellamy. She saw, nevertheless, no good, she said, it could do her cousin, that she should neglect such an opportunity of seeing London: and Miss Margland, in aid of this desire, spared so much trouble to Mrs. Berlinton, who soon wearied of Indiana, that she had the satisfaction of being invited to remain in Grosvenor-square till the two young ladies returned into the country.

Mrs. Berlinton, who indulged, in full extent, every feeling, but investigated none, had been piqued and hurt to extreme un-happiness at the late conduct of Bellamy. Attracted by his fine person, and caught by the first flattery which had talked to her of her own, she had easily been captivated by his description of the sympathy which united, and penetrated by his lamentations at the destiny which parted them. His request for her friendship had been the first circumstance, after her marriage, which had given her any interest in life; and soon, with the common effect of such dangerous expedients to while away chagrin, had occupied all her thoughts, and made the rest of the universe seem to her as a blank. But their continued separation from each other, made the day soon too long for mere regret; and her pliant mind, in this state of vacancy, had readily been bent to the new pursuit pressed upon her by Mrs. Norfield; which, however, upon the re-appearance of Bellamy, would speedily have given way to the resumption of his influence, had not his elopement with Eugenia left her again all at large. It destroyed an illusion strong though not definable; demolished a friendship ill conceived, and worse understood; and brought with it a disappointment which confused all her ideas. To be inactive was, however, impossible; simplicity, once given up, returned to the dissipated no more; or returns but when experience brings conviction, That all is hollow where the heart bears no part; all is peril where principle is not the guide.

The Faro Table was now re-opened, and again but too powerfully sharpened the faculties which mortification had blunted. A company the most miscellaneous composed her evening assem-blies, which were soon, nevertheless, amongst the most fashion-able, as well as crowded of the metropolis. Whatever there, is new and splendid, is sure of a run for at least a season. Enquiries into what is right, or strictures upon what is wrong, rarely molest popularity, till the rise of some fresher luminary gives fashion another abode.

Calamity requires not more fortitude than pleasure. What she began but to divert disappointment and lassitude, she continued to attain celebrity; and the company which Faro and Fashion brought together, she soon grew ambitious to collect by motives of more appropriate flattery. All her aim, now, was to be universally alluring; and she looked from object to object, in smiling discourse, till one by one, every object could look only at her: and grace and softness which had been secretly bewitching while she had the dignity to keep admiration aloof, were boldly declared to be invincible, since she permitted such professions to reach her ear.

Long surrounded by gazing admirers, she became now encircled by avowed adorers; and what for victory she had essayed, she pursued ardently for pleasure. Coquetry is as fascinating to those who practise it, as to those whom it seduces; and she found herself, shortly, more happy by a conquest effected by wiles and by art, than by any devotion paid straight forward, and uncourted. The generality of her new ambition protected it from permanent ill consequences; aiming at everyone, she cared for no one; mortified by Bellamy, she resolved to mortify others, and in proportion as her smiles grew softer her heart became harder.

Indiana, at this period, immersed at once from the most private retreat into the gayest vortex of pleasure, thought herself in the upper regions, where happiness, composed by her own ideas, consisted of perpetual admiration to unfading beauty: but though the high qualities with which the devotion of Melmond had gifted her, had enslaved his reason and understanding from suspecting that so fair a form could enclose aught short of its own perfection, his heart was struck, and all his feelings were offended, when he saw her capable of dissipation upon a season of calamity to Eugenia; Eugenia, whom though he could not love, he venerated; Eugenia, whose nature he thought divine, though her person, unhappily, was but too human; Eugenia, to whom he owed the union upon which hung all his wishes . . . to seek pleasure while Eugenia suffered, was astonishing, was incomprehensible. He felt as if every principle of his love were violated; he looked another way, to disguise his shock;—but when he looked at her again, it was forgotten.

*   *   *   *

Camilla soon after learnt, from Lavinia, that Sir Hugh had been deeply affected by the history of the elopement, though it had been softened to him by all possible means, at the desire of the heroic Eugenia herself; who would now own to no one the force with which she had been carried off. Bellamy continued the most unremitting demonstrations of affection, which she received with gentleness, and appeared entirely to credit as sincere; but he had already absolutely refused a residence offered for them both at Cleves, and made Eugenia herself ask a separate provision of her uncle, though she could not even a moment pretend that the desire was her own. Sir Hugh, nevertheless, had yielded; and notwithstanding his present embarrassments from Clermont, had insisted upon settling a thousand pounds a year upon her immediately; in consequence of which, Bellamy had instantly taken a house at Belfont, to which they were already removing. Eugenia had recovered her gentle fortitude, seemed to submit to her destiny, and repined solely she could not, yet, keep her engagement with respect to the trinkets, which though she had openly told Bellamy were promised to a friend, he had seized to pack up, and said, 'he could not re-deliver till they were arranged in their new dwelling.' But she charged Lavinia to express her hopes that the detention would not last long.

*   *   *   *

When the given three weeks expired, Indiana, infatuated with London, begged and obtained leave to stretch her residence there to a month.

Eugenia was now settled at Belfont; but still Camilla received no intelligence of the promised boon, and spent her lingering hours in her chamber, no longer even invited thence, except at meals, by Mrs. Berlinton; whose extreme and encreasing dissipation, from first allowing no time, took off, next, all desire for social life. Surprised and hurt, Camilla was called off a little from herself, through concern. She sincerely loved Mrs. Berlinton, whom it was difficult to see and know with indifference, and she softly represented to her how ill she felt at ease in the falling off she experienced in her partiality.

Mrs. Berlinton tenderly embraced her, protesting she was dear to her as ever; and feeling, while she spoke, her first affection return; but not a moment had she to bestow from her new mode of life: some party was always formed which she had not force of mind to break; an internal restlessness, from the want of some right pursuit, joined to a disappointment she could not own, made that party induce another; and though none gave her real pleasure, which her strong, however undisciplined and unguided feelings, shut out from such a species of vague life, all gave employment to expectation, and were preferable to a regret at once consuming and mortifying.

Her gentleness, however, and her returned personal kindness, encouraged Camilla to repeat her admonitions, and engage assistance from Melmond; who, at any other period, would, uncalled, have given his whole attention to a sister dear at once to his honour and his heart; but Indiana more than occupied, she engrossed him. She now expected an adoration so unremitting, that if she surprised his eyes turned any other way even a moment, she reproached him with abated love, and it was the business of a day to obtain a reconciliation.

Gratefully, however, at the instigation of Camilla, he resumed the vigilance with which, upon her first entering London the preceding year, he had attended to all the actions of his sister. But the difference already produced by the effect of flattery, the hardening of example, and the sway of uncontrolled early power, astonished and alarmed him. At her first setting out, she had hearkened to all counsel, frightened by every representation of danger, and humbled by every remonstrance against impropriety. But she now heard him with little or no emotion; and from beginning to listen unmoved, soon proceeded to reply and resist. A search, rather than a love, of pleasure had seized her young mind, which had now gained an ascendant that rendered contest less shocking, than yielding would have been painful.

The tribulation of Melmond at this ill success, rested not solely upon his sister; he saw yet more danger for Indiana, who now seemed scarce to live but while arraying, or displaying herself. His passion had lost its novelty, and her eyes lost their beaming pleasure in listening to it; and the regard he had fondly expected to take place of first ecstacy, he now found unattainable, from want of all materials for its structure. His discourse, when not of her beauty, but strained her faculties; his reading, when compelled to hear it, but wearied her intellects. She had no genius to catch his meaning, and no attention to supply its place.

Deeply he now thought of Eugenia, with that regret ever

attached to frail humanity, for what is removed from possible possession. The purity of her love, the cultivation of her mind, and the nobleness of her sentiments, now bore forth a contrast to the general mental and intellectual littleness of Indiana, which made him blame the fastidious eyes,[1] that could dwell upon her face and form; and feel that, even with the matchless Indiana, he must sigh at their mutual perversity of fate.

Nor missed he more in soul, than Indiana in adoration, who turned from what she now resented as coldness, to the violent praises of Macdersey, who became, at this period, a frequenter of Mrs. Berlinton's assemblies. She understood not the inevitable difference of the altered situation; that he who was accepted might be grateful, but could not be anxious; and that Melmond, while in suspense, wore the same impassioned air, and spoke the same impassioned feelings as Macdersey. To her, all seemed the change not from doubt to security, but from love to insensibility.

To live always at her feet, while he thought her all-divine, was his own first joy and greatest pride: but when once he found his goddess had every mortal imperfection, his homage ceased, with amazement that ever it could have been excited. Those eyes, thought he, which I have gazed at whole days with such un-reflecting admiration; and whose shape, colour, size, and sweet proportion still hold their pre-eminence, now, while retaining their first lustre, have lost all their illusory charm! I meet them—but to deplore their vacancy of the soul's intelligence—I fondly—vainly seek!

*   *   *   *

Even when again the time arrived for returning to Cleves, Indiana, hanging languidly upon every minute she could steal from it, petitioned for a few days more from the ever-granting Baronet, which, while by her devoted to coquetry, admiration, and dress, were consumed by Camilla in almost every species of wretchedness. Mrs. Mittin wrote her word that Mr. Clykes was become more uneasy than ever for his money, as she had thought it indispensable to acquaint him of the reports in the neighbour-hood, that Mr. Tyrold had met with misfortunes, and was retrenching: if he could not, therefore, be paid quickly, he must put in his claims elsewhere.

The same post brought from Lavinia an account so afflicting of Eugenia, as nearly to annihilate even this deep personal distress. It was known, through Molly Mill, who, by the express insistance of Sir Hugh, continued to live with her young Mistress, that Bellamy had already, at Belfont, cast off the mask of pretended passion, and grossly demanded of her Mistress to beg money for him of Sir Hugh; acknowledging, without scruple, large debts, that demanded speedy payment, and pressing her to ask for the immediate possession of the Yorkshire estate. Her Mistress, though mildly, always steadily refused; which occasioned reproaches so rude and violent as almost to frighten her into fits; and so loud, that they were often heard by every servant in the house.

Camilla, at this dreadful history, grew nearly indifferent to all else, and would have relinquished, almost unrepining, her expectations of personal relief, but that Lavinia, in the name of their unhappy sister, bid her still cherish them; assuring her she hoped yet to perform her engagement, as Mr. Bellamy never disputed her already given promise, though he had mislaid the key of the box in which the trinkets were deposited.

Nor even here rested the misery of Camilla: another alarm stole upon her mind, of a nature the most dreadful.

Upon the first evening of this newly-granted stay, while she was conversing alone with Mrs. Berlinton before the nocturnal *toilette* of that lady, a servant announced Mr. Bellamy. Mrs. Berlinton blushed high, evidently with as much of anger as surprise; Camilla hastily withdrawing, to avoid an object abhorrent to her, wondered she would admit him: yet, anxious for any intelligence that could relate to her sister, enquired when he was gone, and ran towards the dressing-room to ask what had passed: but before she reached the door, the sound of his voice re-entering the hall, and of his step re-ascending the stairs, made her fly into the adjoining apartment, not to encounter him; where the instant he had shut the door, and before she could move, she heard him exclaim, 'You weep still, my lovely friend? Ah! can one doubt so injurious remain upon your mind as to suppose any thing but the cruel necessity of my misfortunes could have made me tarnish our celestial friendship with any other engagement? Ah! look at her . . . and look at yourself!'

Camilla, who, at first, had been immoveable from consternation, now recovered sufficiently to get back to her room. But she returned no more to Mrs. Berlinton, though Bellamy soon departed; her eagerness for information subsided in indignant sorrow. That Eugenia, the injured, the inestimable Eugenia, should be spoken of, by the very violator who had torn her from her friends, as a mere burthen attached to the wealth she procured him, struck at her heart as a poniard. And the impropriety to herself, and the wrong to Eugenia, of Mrs. Berlinton, in listening to such a discourse, totally sunk that lady in her esteem; though it determined her, as a duty due to them all around, to represent what she felt upon this subject; and the next day, the instant she was visible, she begged an audience.

Mrs. Berlinton was pensive and dejected, but, as usual, open and unguarded; she began herself to speak of the visit of Bellamy, and to ask why she ran away.

Camilla, without answer or hesitation, related what she had overheard; adding: 'O, Mrs. Berlinton! can you suffer him to talk thus? Can you think of my injured Eugenia—lately your own favourite friend—and bear to hear him?'

'How injured, my ever-dear Camilla? Does she know what he says? Can it hurt her unheard? Can it affect her unimagined? He but solaces his sadness by a confidence he holds sacred; 'tis the type of our friendship, now dearer, he says, than ever, since reciprocated by such sympathy.'

'You affright me, Mrs. Berlinton! what a perversion of reason to talk of sympathy in your situations? Did Eugenia press him to the altar? Did any friends solicit the alliance? Oh, Mrs. Berlinton! think but a moment, and your own feeling mind will paint his conduct in colours I have not the skill to attain!'

'You are right!' cried she, blushing in her unwilling conviction: 'I know not how he could delude me to believe our fates resembled. Certainly nothing can be less similar.'

Camilla was happy in this victory; but the following day, Bellamy, at the same hour was announced, and in the same manner was admitted; Camilla flying, and Mrs. Berlinton protesting she should attack his mistaken comparison with severity.

Severity, however, was a quality with which she was unacquainted; Camilla, anxious in every way, hastened to her when he was gone, but found her dissolved in tender tears, shed, she declared, in regret of the uneasiness she had given him, for he had now made her fully sensible his destiny alone was to blame.

The understanding of Camilla was highly superior to being duped by such flimsy sophistry, which she heard with added detestation of the character of Bellamy; yet perceived that no remonstrance could prevent his admittance, and that every interview regularly destroyed the effect of every exhortation.

In this melancholy period, the sole satisfaction she received was through a letter written by Lionel from Ostend, in which he told her that the dread of imprisonment, or want, in a foreign country, made him lead a life so parsimonious, so totally deprived of all pleasure and all comfort, that he was almost consumed with regret for the wilfulness with which he had thrown away his innumerable advantages; and so much struck with the retrospection of the wanton follies and vices which had involved him in such dishonour and ruin, that he began now to think he had rather been mad than wicked;—so unmeaning, unreflecting, and unprovoked, as well as worthless, had been the course he had pursued.

Camilla sent this letter immediately to her Father, who remitted to Lionel such a sum as must obviate distress, with such intimation for the future as he hoped would best encourage more solid reformation.

Thus passed the time, improperly, or unhappily to all, till the third period fixed for the return to the country elapsed: and Camilla, finding the whole view of her journey abortive, saw the accumulated yet useless suffering involved through her ill-judged procrastination. Yet, as Eugenia still did not despair, even her confession was unwritten; and as Miss Margland and Indiana granted her request of going round by Belfont, which she had previously arranged from an ardent desire to embrace her loved sister, she still dwelt on a last hope from that interview.

CHAPTER IV

Hints upon National Prejudice

WITH mingled disquietude and distaste, Melmond saw the reluctance of Indiana to quit town, and that he was less than a cypher with her upon the last evening's assembly, where, without deigning to bestow one look upon him, she chatted, smiled, and fluttered with every one else; undisguisedly betraying that [he] whom she should soon have alone, and have always, should not rob of even one precious moment this last splendid blaze of general admiration. He sighed; and in common with the hapless perverseness of mortals, thought he had *thrown away*, in Eugenia, *a gem richer than all her tribe!*[*][1]

Camilla, whose heart, however dead to joy, was invariably open to tenderness, was melted with fond emotions in the idea of again meeting her beloved Eugenia, and ready for her journey nearly with the light.

Soon after she was dressed, a house maid, tapping at her door, said, 'Pray, Ma'am, is Miss Lynmere with you?'

'No.'

Presently Miss Margland came herself.

'Pray, Miss Camilla, do you know any thing of Miss Lynmere? It's the oddest thing in the world where she can be!'

Camilla, now, went forth to aid the search; Melmond, who was waiting to hand her into the carriage, looked amazed at the enquiry. It soon, however, was clear, that she was no where in the house; and, after sundry examinations and researches, one of the maids was brought to confess having aided her, in the middle of the night, to go into the street, where she was handed into a post chaise by Mr. Macdersey.

Melmond appeared thunder struck. An action so unexpected at the period of a solemn engagement which waited but the journey to Cleves for being compleated, seemed to him, at first, incredible. But, when Miss Margland exclaimed 'O pursue her; Mr. Melmond! order your horse, and gallop to Scotland immediately!' he gravely, and rather drily answered: 'By no means, Ma'am! The man who has the honour of her preference, is the only one who can have any hope to make her happy. I have no ambition for a hand that has been voluntarily held out to another.'

He then returned, quietly, to his own lodgings; far more indignant than hurt at this abrupt conclusion of a connexion which, though it had opened to him as a promise of Elysium, was closing with every menace of mutual discontent.

Camilla was truly concerned; and not merely for the future risk

* Shakespeare

run by her Cousin, in this rash flight, but for the new disappointment to her Uncle. She was obliged, however, to bestow
her whole attention upon Miss Margland, whose tribulation was
yet greater, and who, in losing thus her pupil, lost the expected
reward of near thirteen years of unwilling attendance. She had,
by no means, indeed, merited this treachery from Indiana, whom
though incapable to instruct in much good, she had sedulously
guarded from all evil.

To return to Sir Hugh without her charge, without indeed
either of the young ladies who were put under her care, she had
not courage. Nor could Camilla so little feel for her distress as to
request it. An express, therefore, was ordered to Cleves, for
informing him of these ill tidings, with a very elaborate panegyric
from Miss Margland of her own conduct; and a desire to know if
she should remain in town till something transpired concerning
Indiana.

The express was but just gone, when a packet, which ought to
have arrived two days before, by the stage, was delivered to
Camilla. Its intention was merely to convey more speedily a letter
from Lavinia, containing the terrible information that Mr. Clykes
had just been at Etherington himself, to deliver in his accounts,
and press immediate payment! Their Father, Lavinia said,
conceived the whole some imposition, till the man produced the
paper signed by his daughter. She had then been called in, and
obliged to confess her knowledge of the transaction. She would
avoid, she said, particulars that could be only uselessly afflicting;
but the interview had ended in their Father's agreeing to pay,
when it should be possible, the sums actually delivered to the
creditors, and for which Mr. Clykes could produce their own
receipts; but refusing, positively and absolutely, any gratuity
whatsoever, from detestation of so dangerous and seductive a
species of trade, as clandestine and illegal money-lending to
minors: The man, much provoked, said a friend of his had been
used far more handsomely by Sir Hugh Tyrold; but finding his
remonstrances vain, acknowledged the law against him for the
interest; but threatened to send in an account for his own trouble,
in collecting and paying the bills, that he would dispute, for
validity, in any court of justice to which he could be summoned:
and, in leaving the house, he menaced an immediate writ, if all he
could legally claim were not paid the next day; unless a new bond

were properly signed, with a promise to abide by that already drawn up. Their Father, she was forced to confess, had now lent his every guinea, for the debts of Clermont, to Sir Hugh; and was at this instant, deliberating to whom he should apply; but desired, meanwhile, an exact statement of the debts which this man had in commission to discharge. The letter concluded with Lavinia's unfeigned grief in the task of writing it.

Camilla read it with a distraction that made it wholly unintelligible to her; yet could not read it a second time; her eyes became dim, her faculties confused, and she rather felt deprived of the power of thinking, than filled with any new and dreadful subjects for rumination.

In this state, the letter on the floor, her eyes staring around, yet looking vacant, and searching nothing she was called to Lord O'Lerney, who begged the honour of a conference with her upon business.

She shook her head, in token of denial, but could not speak. The servant looked amazed; yet brought her a second message, that his Lordship was extremely sorry to torment her, but wished to communicate something concerning Mr. Macdersey.

She then faintly articulated, 'I can see nobody.'

Still the same dreadful vacuity superseded her sensibility, till, soon after, she received a note from Lady Isabella Irby, desiring to be admitted to a short conversation with her upon the part of Lord O'Lerney.

With the name of Lady Isabella Irby recurred the remembrance that she was a favourite of Edgar—and bursting into tears, she consented to the interview; which took place immediately.

The terrible state in which she appeared was naturally, though not justly, attributed by her ladyship to the elopement of her Cousin: while Camilla, called by her sight to softer regrets, beheld again, in mental view, the loved and gentle image of Edgar.

Lady Isabella apologised politely, but briefly, for her intrusion, saying: 'My Lord O'Lerney, whose judgment is never in any danger, but where warped by his wish of giving pleasure, insists upon it that you will be less incommoded by a quick forced admission of me than of himself. Nobody else will think so: but it is not easy to refuse him: so here I am. The motive of this intrusion you can but too readily divine. Lord O'Lerney is truly concerned at this rash action in his kinsman, which he learnt by an accidental call at his lodgings, where various circumstances had just made it known. He could not rest without desiring to see some part of the young lady's family, and making an offer of his own best services with respect to some arrangement for her future establishment. It is for this purpose, you have been so importunately hurried; Lord O'Lerney wishing to make the first news that is sent to Sir Hugh Tyrold less alarming, by stating, at once, what he can communicate concerning Mr. Macdersey.'

Camilla, who only now recollected that Mr. Macdersey was related to Lord O'Lerney, was softened into some attention, and much gratitude for his goodness, and for her Ladyship's benevolence in being its messenger.

'Will you, then,' said Lady Isabella, 'now you understand the purport of his visit, see Lord O'Lerney himself? He can give you much better and clearer documents than I can; and it is always the best and shortest mode to deal with principals.'

Camilla mechanically complied, and Lady Isabella sent her footman with a note to his Lordship, who was waiting at her house in Park-lane.

The discourse still fell wholly upon Lady Isabella; Camilla, lost alternately in misery and absence, spoke not, heard not; yet former scenes, though not present circumstances, were brought to her mind by the object before her, and almost with reverence, she looked at the favourite of Edgar, in whose sweetness of countenance, good sense, delicacy, and propriety, she conceived herself reading every moment the causes of his approbation. Ah, why, thought she, while unable to reply, or to listen to what was said, why knew I not this charming woman, while yet he took an interest in my conduct and connexions! Perhaps her gentle wisdom might have drawn me into its own path! how would he have delighted to have seen me under such influence! how now, even now,—lost to him as I am!—would he generously rejoice, could he view the condescending partiality of looks and manner that seem to denote her disposition to kindness!

Lord O'Lerney soon joined them; and after thanking Camilla for granting, and his Ambassadress for obtaining him an audience, said; 'I have been eager for the honour of a conference with Miss Tyrold, in the hope of somewhat alleviating the fears for the future, that may naturally join with displeasure for the present, from the very unadvised step of this morning. But, however wrong the manner in which this marriage may be effected, the alliance in itself will not, I hope, be so disadvantageous, as matches of this expeditious character prove in general. The actual possessions of Macdersey are, indeed, far beneath what Miss Lynmere, with her uncommon claims, might demand; but his expectations are considerable, and well founded; and his family will all come forward to meet her, with every mark of respect, for which, as its head, I shall lead the way. He is honest, honourable, and good natured; not particularly endowed, with judgment or discretion, but by no means wanting in parts, though they are rather wild and eccentric.'

His Lordship then gave a full and satisfactory detail of the present state, and future hopes of his kinsman; and added, that it should be his own immediate care to endeavour to secure for the fair bride a fixed settlement, from the rich old cousin who had long promised to make Macdersey his heir. He told Camilla to write this, without delay, to the young lady's Uncle, with full leave to use his name and authority.

'At all times,' he continued, 'it is necessary to be quick, and as explicit as possible, in representing what can conciliate an adventure of this sort, of which the clandestine measure implies on one side, if not on both, something wrong; but most especially it is necessary to use speed where the flight is made with an Hibernian; for with the English in general, it is nearly enough that a man should be born in Ireland, to decide him for a fortune-hunter. If you lived, however, in that country, you would see the matter pretty equally arranged; and that there are not more of our pennyless beaux who return laden with the commodity of rich wives, than of those better circumstanced who bring home wives with more estimable dowries.'

He then added, that it was from Miss Lynmere herself he had learnt the residence of Camilla in Grosvenor Square; for, having made some acquaintance with her at one of Mrs. Berlinton's evening parties, he had heard she was a niece of Sir Hugh Tyrold, and immediately enquired after her fair kinswoman, whom he had seen at Tunbridge.

Camilla thanked him for remembering her; and Lady Isabella, with a countenance that implied approbation in the remark, said; 'I have never once heard of Miss Tyrold at the assemblies of this house.'

She quietly replied she had never been present at them; but a look of sensibility with which her eyes dropt, spoke more than she intended, of concern at their existence, or at least frequency.

'Your lovely young Hostess,' said Lord O'Lerney, 'has entered the world at too early an hour to be aware of the surfeit she is preparing herself, by this unremitting luxury of pleasure; but I know so well her innocence and good qualities, that I doubt not but the error will bring its own cure, and she will gladly return to the literary and elegant intercourse, which she has just now given up for one so much more tumultuous.'

'I am glad you still think so, my Lord;' said Lady Isabella, also looking down; 'she is a very sweet creature, and the little I have seen of her, made me, while in her sight, warmly her well-wisher. Nevertheless I should rather see any young person, for whom I was much interested,—unless endowed with the very remarkable forbearance of Miss Tyrold,—under her influence after the period your Lordship expects to return, than during its *interregnum!*'

Camilla disavowed all claim to such praise, blushing both for her friend and herself at what was said. Lord O'Lerney, looking concerned, paused, and then answered, 'You know my partiality for Mrs. Berlinton: yet I always see with fresh respect the courage with which my dear Lady Isabella casts aside her native reserve and timidity, where she thinks a hint—an intimation—may do good, or avert dangers.'

His eye was then fixed upon Camilla, who surprized, turned hastily to Lady Isabella, and saw a tender compassion in her countenance, that confirmed the interpretation of Lord O'Lerney; joined with a modest confusion that seemed afraid, or ashamed, of what had escaped her.

Grateful for herself, but extremely grieved for the idea that seemed to have gone forth of Mrs. Berlinton, she felt a tear start into her eye. She chaced it, with as little emotion as she could shew; and Lord O'Lerney, with an air of gayer kindness, said; 'As we must now, Miss Tyrold, account ourselves to be somewhat allied, you permit me, I hope, to recommend my gallant Cousin to your protection with Sir Hugh? That he has his share of the wildness, the blunders, the eccentricities, and the rhodomontade, which form, with you English, our stationary national character, must not be denied; but he has also, what may equally, I hope, be given us in the lump, generosity, spirit, and good intentions. With all this. . . .'

He was here interrupted; the door being suddenly burst open by Mrs. Mittin, who entered, exclaiming, 'Lord, Miss, what a sad thing this is! I declare it's put me quite into a quiver! And all Winchester's quite in an uproar, as one may say. You never see how every body's in a turmoil!'

Here ended the little interval of horrour in Camilla. Mrs. Mittin and Mr. Clykes seemed to her as one; yet that, already, her Cousin's elopement should have spread so near home, seemed impossible. 'When,' she cried, 'were you in Winchester? And how came this affair known to you?'

'Known? why, my dear Miss, it was there it all happened. I come through it with Mr. Dennel, who was so obliging as to bring me to town, for a little business I've got to do; and next week he'll take me back again; for as to poor little Mrs. Lissin, she'll be quite lost without me. She don't know her right hand from her left, as one may say. But how should she, poor child? Why she is but a baby. What's fifteen? And she's no more.'

'We'll talk of that,' said Camilla, colouring at her loquacious familiarity, 'some other time.' And attempted to beg Lord O'Lerney would finish what he was saying. But Mrs. Mittin, somewhat affronted, cried; 'Lord, only think of your sitting here, talking, and making yourself so comfortable, just as if nothing was the matter! when every body else is in such a taking as never was the like! I must say, as to that, a gentleman more liked, and in more respect never was, I believe; and I can't say but what I'm very sorry myself for what Mr. Clykes has done; however, I told you, you know, you'd best not provoke him; for though there can't be a better sort of man, he'll leave no stone unturned to get his money.'

'For Heaven's sake,' cried Camilla, startled, 'what. . . .'

'What? . . . Why, Lord, Miss! don't you know your Papa's took up? He's put in Winchester Prison, for that debt, you know.'

The breath of Camilla instantly stopt, and senseless, lifeless, she sunk upon the floor.

Lord O'Lerney quitted the room in great concern, to call some female assistants; but Lady Isabella remained, contributing with equal tenderness and judgment to her aid, though much personally affected by the incident.

Her recovery was quick, but it was only to despair; to screams rather than lamentations, to cries rather than tears. Her reason felt the shock as forcibly as her heart; the one seemed tottering on its seat, the other bursting its abode. Words of alarming incoherency proclaimed the danger menacing her intellects, while agonies nearly convulsive distorted her features, and writhed her form.

Unaffectedly shocked, yet not venturing, upon so slight an acquaintance, to interfere, Lady Isabella uttered gently but impressively her good wishes and concern, and glided away.

The nearly distracted Camilla saw not that she went; and knew no longer that she had been in the room. She held her forehead one moment; called for death the next; and the next wildly deprecated eternal punishment. But as the horrour nearly intolerable of this first abrupt blow gave way, the desire of flying instantly to her Father was the symptom of restored recollection.

Hastening then to Miss Margland, she conjured her, by all that was most affecting, to set off immediately for Winchester. But Miss Margland, though she spared not the most severe attacks upon the already self-condemned and nearly demolished Camilla, always found something relative to herself that was more pressing than what could regard any other, and declared she could not stir from town till she received an answer from Sir Hugh.

Camilla besought at least to have the carriage; but of this she asserted herself at present the indisputable mistress, and as the express might come back in a few hours, with directions that she should set off immediately, she would not listen to parting with it. Camilla, frantic to be gone, flew then down stairs, and called to the porter in the hall, that some one should instantly seek her a chaise, coach, or any conveyance whatever, that could carry her to Winchester.

She perceived not that Lady Isabella, waiting for her footman, who had, accidentally, gone on further, upon some message, now opened the door of the parlour, where Lord O'Lerney was conversing with her upon what had happened; she was flying back, though not knowing whither nor which way she turned, when Lord O'Lerney, gently stopping her, asked, why she would not, on such an emergence, apply for the carriage of Mrs. Berlinton? Lady Isabella seconded the motion, by a soft, but just hint, of the danger of her taking such a journey, in a hired carriage, entirely unprotected.

She had scarce consideration enough left to either thank or understand them, yet mechanically followed their counsel, and went to Mrs. Berlinton; Lord O'Lerney, deeply touched by her distress, sending in a servant at the same time with his name, and following: while Lady Isabella, too much interested to go till something was decided, quietly shut herself into the parlour, there to wait his Lordship's information.

The request for the carriage was, indeed, rather made by him than by Camilla, who, when she entered the room, and would have spoken, found herself deprived of the power of utterance, and looked a picture of speechless dismay.

The tender feelings of Mrs. Berlinton were all immediately awakened by this sight, and she eagerly answered Lord O'Lerney, that both her carriage and herself should be devoted to her distressed friend: yet, the first emotion over, she recollected an engagement she could not break, though one she hesitated to mention, and at last only alluded to unexplained, though making known it was insurmountable; while the colour, of which her late hours had robbed her lovely cheeks, returned to them as she stammered her retractation.

The next day, however, she was beginning to promise,—but Camilla, to whom the next minute seemed endless, flew down again to the hall, to supplicate the first footman she could meet, to run and order any sort of carriage he could find; with but barely sufficient recollection to refrain running out with that view herself.

Lady Isabella, again coming forth, entreated to know if there were any commission, any possible service she could herself perform. Camilla thanked her, without knowing what she said; and Lord O'Lerney, who was descending the stairs, repeated similar offers. But wild with affright, or shuddering with horrour, she passed without hearing or observing him.

To see a young creature in a state so deplorable, and to consider her as travelling without any friend or support, in so shaken a condition, to visit an imprisoned Father, touched these benign observers with the sincerest commiseration; and the connexion of a part of his family forming at this moment with a branch of her own, induced Lord O'Lerney to believe he was almost bound to take care of her himself. 'And yet,' said he to Lady Isabella, 'though I am old enough to be her grandfather, the world, should

I travel with her, might impute my assistance to a species of admiration which I hope to experience no more—as witness my trusting myself so much with Lady Isabella Irby!'

Lady Isabella, from the quick coincidence of similar feelings, instantly conceived his wishes, and paused to weigh their possibility. A short consideration was sufficient for this purpose. It brought to her memory her various engagements; but it represented at the same time to her benevolence that they would be all, by the performance of one good action,

More honour'd in the breach than the observance :[1]

She sent, therefore, a message after Camilla, entreating a short conference.

Camilla, who was trying to comprehend some further account from Mrs. Mittin, silently, but hastily obeyed the call; and her look of wild anguish would have fixed the benign intention of Lady Isabella, had it been wavering. In a simple phrase, but with a manner the most delicate, her Ladyship then offered to conduct her to Winchester. A service so unexpected, a goodness so consoling, instantly brought Camilla to the use of her frightened away faculties, but with sensations of gratitude so forcible, that Lord O'Lerney with difficulty saved her from falling at the feet of his amiable friend, and with yet more difficulty restrained his own knees from doing her that homage. And still the more strongly he felt this active exertion, from the disappointment he had just endured through the failure of his favourite Mrs. Berlinton.

No time was to be lost; Lady Isabella determined to do well what she once undertook to do at all; she went to Park-lane, to make known her excursion, and arrange some affairs, and then instantly returned, in her own post-chaise, and four horses, for Camilla; who was driven from the metropolis.

CHAPTER V

The Operation of Terror

LADY Isabella, for the first two or three miles, left Camilla uninterruptedly to her own thoughts; she then endeavoured to engage her in some discourse, but was soon forced to desist. Her misery exceeded all measure of restraint, all power of effort. Her Father in prison! and for her own debts! The picture was too horrible for her view, yet too adhesive to all her thoughts, all her feelings, all her faculties, to be removed from them a moment. Penetrated by what she owed to Lady Isabella, she frequently took her hand, pressed it between her own, pressed it to her lips; but could shew her no other gratitude, and force herself to no other exertion.

It was still early, they travelled post, and with four horses, and arrived at Winchester before eight o'clock.

Shaking, she entered the town, half fainting, half dead. Lady Isabella would have driven straight on to Etherington, which was but a stage further; but to enter the rectory, whence the Rector himself was torn—'No!' cried she, 'no! there where abides my Father, there alone will I abide! No roof shall cover my head, but that which covers his! I have no wish but to sink at his feet—to crawl in the dust—to confine myself to the hardest labour for the remnant of my miserable existence, so it might expiate but this guilty outrage!'

Lady Isabella took not any advantage of the anguish that was thus bursting forth with secret history; she was too delicate and too good to seize such a moment for surprising confidence, and only enquired if she had any friend in the town, who could direct her whither to go, and accompany as well as direct.

She knew no one with sufficient intimacy to endure presenting herself to them upon such an occasion; and preferred proceeding alone to the sad and cruel interview. Lady Isabella ordered the chaise to an hotel, where she was shewn into a room upstairs, whence she sent one of her own servants to enquire out where debtors were confined, and if Mr. Tyrold were in custody: charging him not to name, from whom or why he came, and begging Camilla to get ready a note to prepare her Father for the meeting, and prevent any affecting surprise. She then went to chuse herself a chamber, determined not to quit her voluntary charge, till she saw her in the hands of her own friends.

Camilla could not write: to kneel, to weep, to sue, was all she could bear to plan; to present to him the sight of her hand writing she had not courage.

Presently she heard a chaise drive rapidly through the inn gate: it might be him, perhaps released; she flew down the stairs with that wild hope; but no sooner had descended them, than a dread of his view took its place, and she ran back: she stopt, however, in the landing place, to hear who entered.

Suddenly a voice struck her ear that made her start; that vibrated quick to her heart, and there seemed to arrest the springs of life; she thought it the voice of her Mother——

It ceased to speak; and she dropt on one knee, inwardly, but fervently praying her senses might deceive her.

Again, however, and more distinctly, it reached her; doubt then ceased, and terrour next to horrour took its place. What was said she knew not, her trepidation was too great to take in more than the sound.

Prostrate she fell on the floor; but hearing a waiter say, 'Up stairs, madam, you may have a room to yourself.' She started, rose, and rushing violently back to the apartment she had quitted, bolted herself in; exclaiming, 'I am not worthy to see you, my Mother! I have cast my Father into prison—and I know you will abhor me!'

She then sat down against the door, to listen if she were pursued; she heard a footstep, a female step; she concluded it that of her Mother; 'She can come,' cried she, 'but to give me her malediction!' And flew frantic about the room, looking for any means of escape, yet perceiving only the window, whence she must be dashed to destruction.

She now heard a hand upon the lock of the door. 'O that I could die! that I could die!' she cried, madly advancing to the window, and throwing up the sash, yet with quick instinctive repentance pulling it down, shuddering and exclaiming: 'Is there no death for me but murder—no murder but suicide?'

A voice now found its way through her cries to her ear, that said, 'It is me, my dear Miss Tyrold; will you not admit me?'

It was Lady Isabella; but her Mother might be with her: she could not, however, refuse to open the door, though desperately she said to herself: If she is there, I will pass her, and rush into the streets!

Seeing, however, Lady Isabella alone, she dropt on her knees, ejaculating 'Thank Heaven! thank Heaven! one moment yet I am spared!'

'What is it, my dear Miss Tyrold,' said Lady Isabella, 'that causes you this sudden agony? what can it be that thus dreadfully disorders you?'

'Is she with you?' cried she, in a voice scarce audible, 'does she follow me? does she demand my Father?'

'Rise, dear madam, and compose yourself. If you mean a Lady whom this minute I have passed, and whose countenance so much resembles yours, that I thought her at once some near relation, she is just gone from this house.'

'Thank Heaven! thank Heaven!' again ejaculated the prostrate Camilla; 'My Mother is spared a little longer the dreadful sight of all she must now most abominate upon earth!'

She then begged Lady Isabella instantly to order the chaise, and return to town.

'On the contrary,' answered her Ladyship, extremely surprised at so wild a request, 'Let me rather, myself, carry you to your family.'

'O no, Lady Isabella, no!' cried Camilla, speaking with frightful rapidity, and shaking in every limb, 'all now is changed. I came to wait upon my Father—to humble myself at his feet—not to obtrude myself upon my Mother!—O Lady Isabella!—I shall have broken her heart—and I dare not offend her with my sight!

Lady Isabella, with the most judicious gentleness, endeavoured to render her more reasonable. 'I pretend not,' she said, 'to decide upon your situation, though I comprehend its general affliction: yet still, and at all events, its termination must be a meeting. Suffer me, therefore, rather to hasten than retard so right a measure. Allow of my mediation, and give me the infinite pleasure of leaving you in the hands of your friends.'

Camilla, though scarcely able to articulate her words, declared again the motive to her journey was at an end; that her Father had now one to watch, soothe, and attend him, who had none of her dreadful drawbacks to consoling powers; and that she would remain at Mrs. Berlinton's till summoned home by their immediate commands.

Lady Isabella began pleading their own rights to decide if or not the meeting should be deferred: but wildly interrupting her, 'You know not,' she cried, 'what it is you ask. I have not nerves, I have not hardiness to force myself into such a presence. An injured Father . . . an offended Mother . . . O Lady Isabella! if you knew how I adore—and how I have ruined them! . . . .'

'Let me go to them from you, myself; let me represent your situation. They are now probably together. That Lady whom I saw but from the stairs, though her countenance so much struck me, and whom I now conclude to be Mrs. Tyrold, said, as she passed, I shall walk; I only want a guide;'—

'They had not, then, even met!' cried Camilla, starting up with fresh horrour; 'she is but just arrived—has but just been at Etherington—and there heard—that her husband was in prison—and in prison for the debts of her daughter! her guilty . . . perhaps reprobated daughter!'—

Again, wringing her hands, half distracted, 'O, that the earth,' she cried, 'had received me, ere I quitted the parental roof! Innocent I had then died, beloved, regretted,—no shame would have embittered my Father's sorrow—no wrath my Mother's—no culpable misconduct would have blighted with disgrace their so long—long wished-for meeting!'

The compassionating, yet judicious Lady Isabella, willing to shorten the sufferings she pitied, made yet another effort to prevent this unadvised return, by proposing they should both sleep this night at Winchester, that Camilla might gather some particulars of her family, and some composure for herself, to better judge what step to pursue. But all desire of meeting was now converted into horrour; she was too much known in the neighbourhood to escape being recognized if she stayed till the morning, and her shattered intellects, she declared, could not bear passing a whole night in expectation of a discovery through some accident. 'Have I not already,' cried she, 'heard her voice and fled its sound? Judge then, Lady Isabella, if I can present myself before her! No, I must write, first. I have a long and dreadful history to relate—and then, when she has heard it—and when the rectory has again its reverend master—and when they find some little palliation, where now they can see only guilt—and when all is committed without disguise to their goodness—their mercy—they may say to me perhaps themselves: Unhappy

Camilla! thou hast paid thy just penalty; come home, then, to thy parents' roof, thou penitent child!'

Lady Isabella knew too little of the characters with which she had to deal, to judge if it would be right to insist any further: she ordered, therefore, fresh horses to her chaise, and as soon as her footman came back, who brought the now useless direction where Mr. Tyrold was to be found, they galloped out of Winchester.

At Alton[1] they stopt to sleep; and, her immediate terrour removed, she became more sensible of what she owed to Lady Isabella, to whom, in the course of the evening, she recounted frankly the whole history of her debts, except what related to Lionel.

'Your Ladyship hears me,' said she, in conclusion, 'with the patience of benevolence, though I fear, with the censure of all judgment. What evils have accrued from want of consideration and foresight! My errours have all been doubled by concealment—every mischief has been augmented by delay. O, Lady Isabella! how sad an example shall I add to your powers of benign instruction!—From day to day, from hour to hour, I planned expedients, where I ought to have made confessions! To avoid one dreadful—but direct evil, what I have suffered has been nearly intolerable—what I have inflicted, unpardonable!'

Lady Isabella, much touched by her openness and confidence, repaid them by all that compassion could suggest, or that a sincere disposition towards esteem could anticipate of kindness. She gathered the amount of the sum for which Mr. Tyrold was confined, and besought Camilla to let it less weigh upon her spirits, as she could herself undertake that Lord O'Lerney would accommodate him with it immediately, and wait his perfect leisure for re-payment. 'I have known him,' said she, 'from a child, and have always seen, with respect and admiration, the prompt pleasure with which he rather seizes than accepts every opportunity to do good.'

Camilla returned the most grateful thanks; but acknowledged she had no apprehension but that the writ would immediately be withdrawn, as the county was almost filled with friends to her Father, who would come forward upon such an occasion. 'What rests thus upon my mind,' said she, 'and what upon his—and upon my Mother's will rest—is the disgrace—and the cause! the one so public, the other so clandestine! And besides, though this debt will be easily discharged, its payment by a loan is but incurring another: and how that is to be paid, I know not indeed. Alas! Lady Isabella!—the Father I have thus dreadfully involved, has hitherto, throughout his exemplary life, held it a sacred duty to adapt his expences to his income!'

Again Lady Isabella gave what consolation she could bestow; and in return for her trust, said she would speak to her with sincerity upon a point of much delicacy. It was of her friend, Mrs. Berlinton; 'who now,' said she, 'you are not, perhaps, aware, is become a general topic of discourse. To the platonics, with which she set out in life, she has, of late, joined coquetry; nor even there stops the ardour with which she seeks to animate her existence; to two characters, hitherto thought the most contradictory, the sentimental and the flirting, she unites yet a third, till now believed incompatible with the pleasures and pursuits of either; this, I need not tell you, is that of a gamestress. And when to three such attributes is added an open aversion to her husband, a professed, an even boasted hatred of his person, his name, his very being—what hope can be entertained, be her heart, her intentions what they may, that the various dangers she sets at defiance, will not ultimately take their revenge, and surprise her in their trammels?'

Edgar himself seemed, to Camilla, to be speaking in this representation; and that idea made it catch her attention, in the midst of her utmost misery. She urged, however, all she knew, and could suggest, in favour of Mrs. Berlinton; and Lady Isabella expressed much concern in occasioning her any painful sensations. 'But who,' said she, 'can see you thus nearly, and not be interested in your happiness? And I have known, alas!—though I am still under thirty, instances innumerable of self-deluded young women, who trusting to their own pure intentions, have neither feared nor heeded the dangers which encircled them, till imperceptibly, from the insidious influence of levity, they have pursued the very course they began with disclaiming, and followed the very steps from which at first they unaffectedly recoiled.'

Instructed and grateful, though incapable of being tranquillised, Camilla the next day reached Grosvenor Square long before her fair friend had left her downy pillow. Lady Isabella exacted a promise to be informed of her proceedings, and, loaded with merited acknowledgments, returned to her own mansion.

Camilla took possession of the first room in which she found a pen and ink, and wrote instantly to Lavinia a short, rapid, and incoherent letter, upon the distraction of her mind at the dreadful calamity she had occasioned her Father, and the accumulated horrours to which her Mother had returned. She durst not present herself before them uncalled, not even by letter; but she would live in the strictest retirement and penance till they ordered her home, for which epoch, not more longed [for] than dreaded, she besought her sister's mediation.

This sent off, she forced herself to wait upon Miss Margland, who had received an answer from Cleves to continue in town till Indiana wrote or re-appeared. She was put immediately into uncommon good-humour, by the ill success at the journey of Camilla, which she protested was exactly what she expected.

Camilla then strove to recollect all she had been told by Lord O'Lerney of Mr. Macdersey, and to relate it to Miss Margland, who, pleased and surprised, undertook to write it to Sir Hugh.

To three days of dreadful suspense she now saw herself inevitably condemned, in waiting an answer from Lavinia: but as her eyes were opened to remark, by the admonitions of Lady Isabella, and her attention was called back to the earlier cautions of Edgar, her time, though spent with misery, hung not upon her unoccupied. She thought herself called upon by every tie of friendship, faithfully and courageously to represent to Mrs. Berlinton her impropriety of conduct with regard to Bellamy, and the reports that were spread abroad to her more general disadvantage.

Her reception from that Lady, she had thought, for the first time, cold. She had welcomed her, indeed, with an accustomed embrace, but her kindness seemed strained, her smile was faint, and the eyes which so softly used to second it, were averted.

As soon as they were alone together, Camilla took her hand; but, without returning its pressure, Mrs. Berlinton presented her with a new poem for her evening's amusement.

Camilla put it down, but while hesitating how to begin, Bellamy was announced. She started, and flew away, but returned when he was gone, and begged a conference.

Mrs. Berlinton answered certainly; though she looked embarrassed, and added not immediately, as she was obliged to dress for the evening.

Camilla entreated she might speak with her before dinner the next day.

To this she received a gentle assent: but no interview at the time appointed took place; and when at dinner they met, no notice was taken of the neglect.

She now saw she was pointedly avoided. Her courage, however, was called upon, her gratitude was indebted for past kindnesses, and her honour felt a double engagement. The opportunity therefore she could not obtain by request, she resolved to seize by surprise.

Bellamy was again, however, announced; but the moment that, from her own chamber, she heard him descend the stairs, she flew to the dressing-room, and abruptly entered it.

The surprise she gave was not greater than that she received. Mrs. Berlinton, her fine eyes streaming with tears, and her white hands uplifted with an air of supplication, was evidently in an act of devotion. Camilla drew back, and would have retired, but she hastily dried her eyes, and said: 'Miss Tyrold? Do you want me? where's Miss—Miss Margland?'

'Ah! my dearest Mrs. Berlinton! my friend, as I had hoped, and by me, surely I trust loved for ever,' cried Camilla, throwing her arms round her neck, 'why this sorrow? why this distance? why this unkind avoidance?'

Mrs. Berlinton, who, at first, had shrunk from her embrace, now fell, in trembling agitation, upon her breast. Camilla hoped this was the instant to improve; when she appeared to be, herself, calling religion to her aid, and when the tenderness of her appeal seemed to bring back a movement of her first partiality. 'Suffer, suffer me,' she therefore cried, 'to speak to you now! hear me, my dear and amiable friend, with the sweetness that first won my affection!'

Mrs. Berlinton, affrighted, drew back, acknowledging herself unhappy; but shrinking from all discourse, and starting when Camilla named Bellamy, with a confusion she vainly strove to repress.

Unhackneyed in the world as was Camilla, her understanding and sense of right stood here in the place of experience, to point out the danger and impropriety surrounding her friend; and catching her by the gown, as she would have quitted the room, 'Mrs. Berlinton,' she emphatically cried, 'if you persist in this unhappy, this perilous intercourse, you risk your reputation, you risk my sister's peace, you risk even your own future condemnation!—O forgive me, forgive me! I see how I have affected you—but you would listen to no milder words!'

Mrs. Berlinton had sunk upon a chair, her hands clasped upon for forehead, and tears running rapidly down her cheeks. Brought up with religious terrours, yet ill instructed in religious principles, the dread of future punishment nearly demolished her, though no regular creed of right kept her consistently or systematically in any uniform exercise of good. But thus forcibly surprised into sudden conscientious recollections, she betrayed, rather than opened her heart, and acknowledged that she was weeping at a denial she had given to Bellamy; who, molested by the impossibility of ever conversing with her undisturbed, had entreated her to grant him, from time to time, a few hours society, in a peaceful retirement. 'Nor should I—nor could I—' she cried, 'refuse him—for I have every reliance in his honour—but that the guilty world, ignorant of the purity of our friendship, might causelessly alarm my brother for my fame. And this, and the fear of any—though so groundless—uneasiness to your sister, makes me resist his powerful eloquence, and even my own notions of what is due to our exalted league of friendship.'

Camilla listened with horrour to this avowal, yet saw, with compassion, that her friend endeavoured to persuade herself she was free from wrong; though with censure that she sought to gloss over, rather than investigate, every doubt to the contrary: but while fear was predominant for the event of such a situation to herself, abhorrence filled her whole mind against Bellamy, in every part, every plan, and every probability of the business.

'O Mrs. Berlinton!' she cried, 'conquer this terrible infatuation, which obscures danger from your sight, and right from your discernment! Mr. Bellamy is married; and if you think, yourself, my sister would be hurt to know of these unhallowed leagues and bonds, you must be sure, with the least reflection, that they are wrong; you too, are married; and if Mr. Melmond would join with the world in contemning the extraordinary project you mention, you must feel, with the least reflexion, it ought not to be granted. Even were you both single, it would be equally improper, though not so wide spreading in its mischief. I have committed many errours; yet not one of them wilfully, or against conviction:

nevertheless, the ill consequences that have ensued, tear me at this
moment with repentant sorrow:—Ah! think then, what you—so
tender, so susceptible, so feeling, will suffer, if with your apprehensions all awake, you listen to any request that may make my
sister unhappy, or involve your deserving brother in any difficulty
or hazard!'

Mrs. Berlinton was now subdued. Touched, terrified, and
convinced, she embraced Camilla, wept in her arms, and promised to see Bellamy no more.

The next day arrived an answer from Lavinia, long,
minute, and melancholy, but tenderly affectionate and replete with
pity.

'Ah, my sister,' she began, 'we cannot yet meet! Our Mother is
in no state to bear any added emotion. The firmness of her whole
character, the fortitude of her whole life, hitherto unbroken by
any passion, and superior to any misfortune, have both given way,
suddenly and dreadfully, to the scene following her arrival.'

She then went back to particulars.

Mr. Clykes, she had heard, finding his bill for his own trouble
positively refused, had conceived the Tyrold family in danger of
bankruptcy, by the general rumours of the joint claimants of
Lionel and Clermont; and imagining he had no time to lose,
hoped by an arrest to frighten their Father to terms, in order to
obviate the disgrace of such a measure. Their Father would,
however, hear of none, nor pay any thing above the exact amount
of the signed receipts of the various creditors; and submitted to
the confinement, in preference to applying to any friend to be his
bail, till he could consult with a lawyer. He was already at
Winchester, where he had given Clykes a meeting, when the
writ was served against him. He sent a dispatch to Etherington,
to prevent any surprise at his not returning, and to desire the
affair might not travel to Cleves, where Lavinia was then with
Sir Hugh. This note, addressed to the upper servant, fell into the
hands of Mrs. Tyrold herself, the next evening, upon her sudden
arrival. She had been thus unexpectedly brought back by the news
of the flight of Bellamy with Eugenia: her brother was still ill;
but every consideration gave way to the maternal; and in the hope
to yet rescue her daughter from this violator, she set off in a
packet which was just sailing. But what, upon descending from
the chaise, was the horrour of her first news! She went on instantly

to Winchester, and alighting at an hotel, took a guide and went to the place of confinement.

'The meeting that ensued,' continued Lavinia, 'no one witnessed, but everyone may imagine. I will not therefore, wound your feelings, my dearest Camilla, with even touching upon my own. The impression, however, left upon the mind of our poor Mother, I should try vainly to disguise, since it has given her a shock that has forced from me the opening of this letter.'

She then besought her to take, nevertheless, some comfort, since she had the unspeakable satisfaction to inform her that their Father was returned to the rectory. He had been liberated, from the writ's being withdrawn; though without his consent, without even his knowledge, and contrary to his wishes. Nor was it yet ascertained by whom this was done, though circumstances allowed no division to their conjectures.

Harry Westwyn had learnt the terrible event in a ride he had accidentally taken to Winchester; and, upon returning to Cleves, had communicated it, with the most feeling circumspection, to herself. The excess of grief with which she had heard him, had seemed to penetrate to his quickly sensitive soul, 'for he is yet more amiable,' she added, 'than his Father's partiality paints him;' they agreed not to name it to Sir Hugh; though Harry assured her that no less than five gentlemen in the vicinity had already flown to Mr. Tyrold, to conjure to be accepted as his bail: but he chose first to consult his lawyer upon the validity of the claim made against him. All their care, however, was ineffectual; through some of the servants, Sir Hugh was informed of the affair, and his affliction was despair. He accused himself as being the cause of this evil, from the money he had borrowed for Clermont, which might wholly have been avoided, had he followed his brother's advice in immediate and severe retrenchments. These, however, he now began, in a manner that threatened to rob him of every comfort; and Mr. Westwyn was so much affected by his distress, that, to relieve him, at least, from the expence of two guests and their servants, he instantly took leave, promising nevertheless, to yet see him again, before he returned for the rest of his days to his native home. In a few hours after the departure of these gentlemen, news arrived that Mr. Tyrold was again at the rectory. Mr. Clykes had suddenly sent his receipt, in full of all demands, and then set off for London.

'There cannot be a doubt this was the deed of the generous Mr. Westwyn, in compact with his deserving Son,' continued Lavinia; 'they have been traced to Winchester; but we none of us know where, at present, to direct to them. The delight of my Uncle at this act of his worthy old friend, has extremely revived him. My Father is much dissatisfied the wretched Clykes should thus be paid all his fraudulent claims; but my Mother and my Uncle would, I believe, scarce have supported life under his longer confinement.'

The letter thus concluded.

'My Mother, when first she heard you were in town, was herself going to send for you; but when she understood that Miss Margland was with you, and you lived in utter seclusion from company, she said; "Since she is safe, I had rather not yet see her." Our beloved Father acquiesces, for he thinks you, at present, too much shaken, as well as herself, for so agitating an interview, till her mind is restored to its usual firmness. Judge then, my sister, since even he is for the delay, if your Lavinia can gather courage to plead against it?

'You know, my dearest Camilla, her extreme and tender fondness; you cannot, therefore, doubt, but her displeasure will soon pass away. But when, to the dreadful pangs of finding the hapless fate of Eugenia irremediable, was added the baneful sight of an adored Husband in custody, you cannot wonder such complicate shocks should have disordered her frame, and taught her,—even her, as my imcomparable Father has just said to me, "that always to be superior to calamity, demands a mental strength beyond the frail texture of the human composition; though to wish, and to try for it, shews we have *that within*, which aspires at a higher state, and prepares us for fuller perfection".'

'Can I better finish my letter than with words such as these? Adieu, then, my dear sister, I hope soon to write more chearful tidings.

'Our poor Mother is gone to Belfont. What a meeting again there!
                                        LAVINIA TYROLD.'

A wish for death, immediate death, in common with every youthful mourner, in the first paroxysm of violent sorrow, was the sole sensation which accompanied the reading, or remained after the finishing of this letter, with Camilla. 'Here,' she cried, falling prostrate, 'here might I but at once expire! close these unworthy eyes, forbidden to raise themselves to the authors of my existence! finish my short and culpable career, forgotten—since no longer cherished—by the parents I have offended—by the Mother who no longer wishes to see me!'

She laid down her head, and her sight became dim; a convulsive shivering, from feelings over-strained, and nerves dreadfully shattered, seized her; she sighed short and quick, and thought her prayer already accomplishing; but the delusion soon ceased; she found life still in its vigour, though bereft of its joy; and death no nearer to her frame, for being called upon by her wishes.

In the heaviness of disappointment, 'I have lived,' she cried, 'too long, and yet I cannot die! I am become an alien to my family, and a burthen to myself! ordered from my home by my Father, lest my sight should be destructive to my Mother—while my sister durst not even plead for me. . . . O happy Edgar! how great has been thy escape not to have taken for thy wife this excommunicated wretch!'—

To live thus, seemed to her impossible; to pass even the day in such wretchedness she believed impracticable. Any, every period appeared to her preferable, and in the desperation of her heart, she determined instantly to pursue her Mother to Belfont; and there, by the gentle intercession of Eugenia, to obtain her pardon, or, which she thought immediately would follow its refusal, to sink to death at her feet.

Relieved from the intenseness of her agony by this plan, and ever eager to pursue the first idea that arose, she flew to borrow from Mrs. Berlinton her post-chaise for the next morning, and to supplicate that Miss Margland would accompany her to Belfont; whence, if she missed Mrs. Tyrold, they could easily return the same day, as the distance was not more than thirteen miles.

The chaise was accorded promptly by Mrs. Berlinton, and no regret expressed at the uncertainty of Camilla whether or not she should return; but Miss Margland, though burning with curiosity to see Eugenia as Mrs. Bellamy, would not quit town, from continual expectation of some news of Indiana.

At an early hour the following morning, and feeling as if suspended but by a thread between life and death, Camilla set off for Belfont.

CHAPTER VI

The Reverse of a Mask

THE plan of Camilla was to stop within twenty yards of the house of Bellamy, and then send for Molly Mill. But till she gave this direction to the driver, she was not aware of the inconvenience of being without a servant, which had not previously occurred either to Mrs. Berlinton or herself. The man could not leave his horses, and she was compelled to let him draw up to the gate. There, when he rang at a bell, her terrour, lest she should suddenly encounter Mrs. Tyrold, made her bid him open the chaise door, that she might get out and walk on, before he enquired for Molly. But, in stepping from the carriage, she discerned, over a paling at some distance, Eugenia herself, alone, slowly walking, and her head turned another way.

Every personal, and even every filial idea, was buried instantly in this sight. The disastrous state of this beloved and unhappy sister, and her own peculiar knowledge of the worthless character of the wretch who had betrayed her into his snares, penetrated her with an anguish that took thought from all else; and darting through the great gate, and thence through a smaller one, which opened to the spot where she saw her walking, she flew to her in a speechless transport of sorrow, folded her in her arms, and sobbed upon her shoulder.

Starting, shaking, amazed, Eugenia looked at her; 'Good Heaven!' she exclaimed, 'is it my Sister?—Is it Camilla?—Do I, indeed, see one so dear to me?' And, too weak to sustain herself, she sunk, though not fainting, upon the turf.

Camilla could not articulate a syllable. The horrour she had conceived against Bellamy chilled all attempt at consolation, and her own misery which, the preceding moment, seemed to be crushing the springs of life, vanished in the agonized affection with which she felt the misfortunes of her sister.

Eugenia soon recovered, and rising, and holding her by the hand, yet seeming to refuse herself the emotion of returning her embraces, said, with a faint effort to smile; 'You have surprised me, indeed, my dear Camilla, and convicted me to myself of my vain philosophy.[1] I had thought I should never more be moved thus again. But I see now, the affections are not so speedily to be all vanquished.'

The melancholy conveyed by this idea of believed apathy, in a young creature so innocent, and but just dawning into life, still beyond speech, and nearly beyond sufferance, affected Camilla, who hanging over her, sighed out: 'My dearest! . . . dearest Eugenia!'

'And what is it has brought to me this unexpected, but loved sight? Does Mr. Bellamy know you are here?'

'No,' she answered, shuddering at his name.

Eugenia looked pensive, looked distressed; and casting down her eyes and hesitating, with a deep sigh said: 'I, . . . I have not the trinkets for my dear Sister . . . Mr. Bellamy . . .' she stopt.

Called to her sad self by this shock, of which she strove to repress the emotion, Camilla recollected her own 'almost blunted purpose*,'[1] and fearfully asked if their Mother were yet at Belfont.

'Ah, no!' she answered, clasping her hands, and leaning her head upon her sister's neck: 'She is gone!—The day before yesterday she was with me,—with me only for one hour!—yet to pass with her such another, I think, my dear Camilla, would soon lead me where I might learn a better philosophy than that I so vainly thought I had already acquired here!'

Camilla, struck with awe, ventured not even at an enquiry; and they both, for some little time, walked on in silence.

'Did she name to you,' at length, in broken accents, she asked, 'did she name to you, my Eugenia, . . . the poor, banished . . . Camilla?'——

'Banished? No. How banished?'

'She did not mention me?'

'No. She came to me but upon one subject. She failed in her purpose, . . . and left me.'

A sigh that was nearly a groan finished this short little speech.

'Ah, Heaven! my Eugenia,' cried Camilla, now in agony unresisted, 'tell me, then, what passed! what new disappointment had my unhappy Mother to sustain? And how, and by what cruel fatality, has it fallen to your lot . . . even to yours . . . to suffer her wishes to fail?'

'You know nothing, then,' said Eugenia, after a pause, 'of her view—her errand hither?'

'Nothing; but that to see you brought her not only hither, but to England.'

* Hamlet

'Blessed may she be!' cried Eugenia, fervently, 'and rewarded where rewards are just, and are permanent!'

Camilla zealously joined in the prayer, yet besought to know if she might not be informed of the view to which she alluded?

'We must go, then,' said Eugenia, 'into the house; my poor frame is yet feebler than my mind, and I cannot support it unaided while I make such a relation.'

Camilla, affrighted, now gave up her request; but the generous Eugenia would not leave her in suspense. They went, therefore, to a parlour, where, shutting the doors and windows, she said, 'I must be concise, for both our sakes; and when you understand me, we must talk instantly of other things.'

Camilla could give only a tacit promise; but her air shewed she would hold it sacred as any bond.

'The idea which brought over this inestimable Parent, and which brought her, at a moment when she knew me to be alone, to this sad house, these sad arms . . . Camilla! how shall I speak it? It was to exonerate me from my vows, as forced! to annul all my engagements, as compulsatory! and to restore me again . . . O, Camilla! Camilla! to my Parents, my Sisters, my Uncle, my dearly-loved Cleves!'

She gasped almost convulsively; yet though Camilla now even conjured her to say no more, went on: 'A proposal such as this, pressed upon me by one whose probity and honour hold all calamity at nought, if opposed to the most minute deviation from right—a proposal such as this . . . ah! let me not go back to the one terrible half instant of demur! It was heart-rending, it was killing! I thought myself again in the bosom of my loved family!'—

'And is it so utterly impossible? And can it not yet be effected?'—

'No, my dear Sister, no! The horrible scenes I must go through in a public trial for such a purpose[1]—the solemn vows I must set aside, the re-iterated promises I must break,——no, my dear Sister, no! . . . And now, we will speak of this no more.'

Camilla knew too well her firmness, her enthusiasm to perform whatever she conceived to be her duty, to enter into any contest. Yet to see her thus self devoted, where even her upright Mother, and pious Father, those patterns of resignation to every heaven-inflicted sorrow, thought her ties were repealed by the very villainy which had formed them, seemed more melancholy, and yet harder for submission, than her first seizure by the worthless Bellamy.

'And how bore my poor Mother . . . my poor unfortunate Mother! destined thus to woes of every sort, though from children who adore her!—how bore she the deprivation of a hope that had brought her so far?'

'Like herself! nobly! when once it was decided, and she saw that though, upon certain avowals, the law might revoke my plighted faith, it could not abrogate the scruples of my conscience. She thinks them overstrained, but she knows them to be sincere, and permitted them, therefore, to silence her. Unfit to be seen by any others, she hurried then away. And then, Camilla, began my trial! Indeed I thought, when she had left me, . . . when my arms no more embraced her honoured knees, and neither her blessings, nor her sorrows soothed or wounded my ears, I thought I might defy all evil to assault, all woe to afflict me ever again! that my eyes were exhausted of every tear, and my heart was emptied of all power of future feeling. I seemed suddenly quite hardened;— transformed I thought to stone, as senseless, as immovable, and as cold!'

The sensations of Camilla were all such as she durst not utter; but Eugenia, assuming some composure; added, 'Of this and of me now enough—speak, my dear Sister, of yourself. How have you been enabled to come hither? And what could you mean by saying you were banished?'

'Alas! my dearest Eugenia, if my unhappy situation is unknown to you, why should I agitate you with new pain? my Mother, I find, spared you; and not only you, but me—though I have wrung her heart, tortured it by a sight never to be obliterated from her memory—she would not rob me of my beloved sister's regard; nor even name me, lest the altered tone of her voice should make you say, Of what Camilla does my Mother speak?'

Eugenia, with earnest wonder, begged an explanation; but when Camilla found her wholly uninformed of the history of their Father's confinement, she recoiled from giving her such a shock: yet having gone too far entirely to recede, she rested the displeasure of their Mother upon the debts, and the dealings with a usurer; both sufficiently repugnant to the strictness and nobleness of Mrs. Tyrold, to seem ample justification of her displeasure.

Eugenia entered into the distresses of her sister, as if exempt herself from all suffering: and Camilla, thus commiserating and commiserated, knew now how to tear herself away; for though Eugenia pressed not her stay, she turned pale, when a door opened, a clock struck, or any thing seemed to prognosticate a separation; and looked as if to part with her were death.

At length, however, the lateness of the day forced more of resolution. But when Camilla then rang to give orders for the carriage, the footman said it had been gone more than two hours. The postillion, being left without any directions, thought it convenient to suppose he was done with; and knowing Camilla had no authority, and his lady no inclination to chide him, had given in her little packet, and driven off, without enquiry.

Far from repining at this mixture of impertinence and careless-ness, Camilla would have rejoiced in an accident that seemed to invite her stay, had not her sister seemed more startled than pleased by it. She begged, therefore, that a post chaise might be ordered; and Molly Mill, the only servant to whom the mistress of the house appeared willing to speak, received the commission. At sight of Camilla, Molly had cried bitterly, and beginning 'O Miss!—' seemed entering into some lamentation and detail; but Eugenia, checking her, half whispered: 'Good Molly, remember what you promised!'

When Molly came back, she said that there were no horses at Belfont, and would be none till the next morning.

The sisters involuntarily congratulated one another upon this accident, though they reciprocated a sigh, that to necessity alone they should owe their lengthened intercourse.

'But, my dear mistress,' cried Molly, 'there's a lad that I know very well, for I always see him when I go of an errand, that's going to Salisbury; and he says he must go through Etherington, and if you've any thing you want to send he'll take it for you; and he can bring any thing back, for he shall be here again to morrow, for he goes post.'

Eugenia, sending away Molly, said, 'Why should you not seize such an opportunity to address a few lines to our dear Mother? I may then have the satisfaction to see her answer: and if, . . . as I cannot doubt, she tells you to return home with Miss Margland;— for she will not, I am sure, let you travel about alone;—what a relief will it be to me to know the distresses of my beloved sister are terminated! I shall paint your meeting in my "mind's eye,"[1] see you again restored to the sunshine of her fondness, and while away my solitary languor with reveries far more soothing than any that I have yet experienced at Belfont.'

Camilla embraced her generous Sister; and always readiest for what was speediest, wrote these lines, directed

To Miss TYROLD.

I cannot continue silent, yet to whom may I address myself? I dare not apply to my Father—I scarce dare even think of my Mother—Encompassed with all of guilt with which imprudence could ensnare me, my courage is gone with my happiness! which way may I then turn? In pity to a wretched sister, drop, O Lavinia, at the feet of her I durst not name, but whom I revere, if possible, even more than I have offended, this small and humble memorial of my unhappy existence—my penitence, my supplication, my indescribable, though merited anguish!

CAMILLA.

Could the two sisters, even in this melancholy state, have continued together, they felt that yet from tender sympathy, consolation might revisit their bosoms. The day closed in; but they could not bear to part; and though, from hour to hour, they pronounced an adieu, they still sat on, talked on, and found a balm in their restored intercourse, so healing and so sweet, that the sun, though they hailed not its beams, rose while they were yet repeating Good Night!

They then thought it too late to retire, mutually agreeing with how much greater facility they might recover their lost rest, than an opportunity such as this for undisturbed conversation.

Every minute of this endearing commerce made separation seem harder; and the answer for which they waited from Etherington, anxiously and fearfully as it was expected, so whiled away the minutes, that it was noon, and no chaise had been ordered, when they heard one driving up to the house.

Alarmed, they listened to know what it portended. 'Mr. Bellamy,' said Eugenia, in a low voice, 'scarce ever comes home at this hour.'

'Can it be my Mother herself?' cried Camilla.

In a few minutes, however, Eugenia looked pale, "Tis his step!' she whispered; and presently Bellamy opened the door.

Obliged to acknowledge his entrance, Camilla arose; but her parched lips and clammy mouth made her feel as if his sight had given her a fever, and she attempted not to force any speech.

He did not seem surprized at seeing her, asked how she did, rather cavalierly than civilly: rang the bell, and gave various orders; addressed scarce a word to his wife, and walked whistling about the room.

A change so gross and quick from the obsequious Bellamy Camilla had hitherto seen, was beyond even her worst expectations, and she conceived as low an opinion of his understanding and his manners, as of his morals.

Eugenia kept her eyes rivetted to the ground; and though she tried, from time to time, to say something to them both, evidently required her utmost fortitude to remain in the room.

At length; 'Miss Camilla,' he said, 'I suppose you know Miss Margland is gone?'

'Gone? whither?—how gone?'

'Why home. That is to her home, as she thinks it, Cleves. She set off this morning with the light.'

Camilla, astonished, was now called forth from her taciturnity; 'What possibly,' she cried, 'can have induced this sudden journey? Has my uncle sent for her?'

'No; your uncle has nothing to do with it. She had a letter last night from Mrs. Macdersey, with one enclosed for Sir Hugh, to beg pardon and so forth; and this morning she set off to carry it.'

Camilla was confounded. Why Miss Margland had not, at least, called at Belfont to enquire if she would proceed with her, was beyond all her conjecture.

Soon after, Bellamy's servant came in with a letter for Camilla, which had arrived after she left town, and was given to him by Mrs. Berlinton's butler. She retired into the next room to read it, where, to her great consternation, she found it was from Jacob, and had been written the day of Mr. Tyrold's arrest, though, as it was sent by a private hand, it had only now arrived. 'Things going,' he said, 'so bad at Cleves, on account of so many misfortunes, his master was denying himself all his natural comforts, and in particular he had sent to un-order a new pipe of Madeira, saying he would go without; though, as Miss might remember, it was the very wine the doctors had ordered for his stomach. This all the servants had taken so to heart, that they had resolved to buy it among 'em, and get it privately laid in, and not let his honour know but what it was always the same, till he had drunk so much he could not help himself. For this, they were to join, according to their wages or savings; Now I' says Jacob, 'being, by his gud honnur's genrosty, the ritchist ammung us, fur my kalling, wants to do the most, after nixt to the buttlur and huskippir, so, der Miss, awl I've gut beng in the funs, witch I cant sil out withowt los, if you can lit me have the munny fur the hurs, without ullconvenince, til Miss Geny that was can pay it, I shul be mutch obbleggd, poor Miss Geny nut havving of a fardin, witch wil be a gret fevur to, Madm,

Yur humbbel survent til deth

Jaccub Mord.'

So touching a mark of the fond gratitude of the Cleves' servants to their kind master, mingled tenderness, in defiance of all horrour, in the tears of Camilla; but her total inability to satisfy the just claims of Jacob, since now her resource even in Eugenia failed, with the grief of either defeating his worthy project, or making it lastingly hurtful to him, was amongst the severest strokes which had followed her ill advised schemes. To proclaim such an additional debt, was a shame from which she shrunk; yet to fly immediately to Cleves, and try to soothe her oppressed uncle, was an idea that still seemed gifted with some power to soothe herself. Whither indeed else could she now go? she had no longer either carriage or protectress in town; and what she gathered of the re-admission of Bellamy to Grosvenor-square, made the cautions and opinions of Edgar burst forcibly upon her mind, to impede, though most mournfully, all future return to Mrs. Berlinton.

A pliancy so weak, or so wilful, seemed to announce in that lady an almost determined incorrigibility in wrong, however it might be checked, in its progress, by a mingled love of right, and a fear of ill consequences.

'Ah Edgar!' she cried, 'had I trusted you as I ought, from the moment of your generous declaration—had my confidence been as firm in your kindness as in your honour, what misery had I been saved!—from this connexion—from my debts—from every wide-spreading mischief!—I could then have erred no more, for I should have thought but of your approvance!'

These regrets were, as usual, resuming their absorbing powers; —for all other evils seemed fluctuating, but here misery was stationary; when the voice of Bellamy, speaking harshly to his unhappy wife, and some words she unavoidably caught, by which she found he was requesting that she would demand money of Sir Hugh, made her conclude him not aware he was overheard, and force herself back to the parlour. But his inattention upon her return was so near rudeness, that she soon felt convinced Mrs. Berlinton had acquainted him with her remonstrances and ill opinion: he seemed in guilty fear of letting her converse even a moment with Eugenia; and presently, though with an air of pretended unconcern, said: 'You have no commands for the chaise I came in, Miss Camilla?'

'No, Sir, . . . What chaise? . . . Why? . . .' she stammered.

'It's difficult sometimes to get one at this place; and these horses are very fresh. I bid them stay till they asked you.'

This was so palpable a hint for her to depart, that she could not but answer she would make use of it, when she had taken leave of her sister; whom she now looked at with emotions near despair at her fate, and with difficulty restrained even its most unbridled expressions. But Bellamy kept close, and no private conference could take place. Eugenia merely said: 'Which way, my dear sister, shall you go?'

'I . . . I am not, fixed—to . . . to Cleves, I believe,' answered she, scarce knowing herself what she said.

'I am very glad of it,' she replied, 'for the sake of my poor—' she found her voice falter, and did not pronounce 'uncle;' but added, 'as Miss Margland has already left London, I think you right to go thither at once; it may abridge many difficulties; and with post-horses, you may be there before it is dark.'

They then embraced tenderly, but parted without any further speech, and she set off rather mechanically than designedly for Cleves.

CHAPTER VII

A New View of an old Mansion

CAMILLA, for some time, bestowed no thought upon what she was doing, nor whither she was going. A scene so dreadful as that she now quitted, and a character of such utter unworthiness as that with which her sister for life was tied, absorbed her faculties, and nearly broke her heart.

When she stopt, however, at Bagshot,[1] for fresh horses, the obligation of giving directions to others, made her think of herself; and, bewildered with uncertainty whether the step she took were right or wrong, she regretted she had not, at least, desired to stay till the answer arrived from Etherington. Yet her journey had the sanction of Eugenia's concurrence; and Eugenia seemed to her oracular.

When she came upon the cross road leading from Winchester to Cleves, and felt her quick approach to the spot so loved yet dreaded, the horses seemed to her to fly. Twenty times she called out to the driver not to hurry; who as often assured her the bad roads prevented any haste; she wanted to form some appropriate plan and speech for every emergence; but she could suggest none for any. She was now at the feet of her Mother, now kissing the hands of her Father, now embraced again by her fond uncle;— and now rejected by them all. But while her fancy was at work alternately to soothe and to torture her, the park lodge met her eyes, with still no resolution taken.

Vehemently she stopt the chaise. To drive in through the park would call a general attention, and she wished, ere her arrival were announced, to consult alone with Lavinia. She resolved, therefore, to get out of the carriage, and run by a private path, to a small door at the back of the house, whence she could glide to the chamber commonly appropriated to her sister.

She told the postillion to wait, and alighting, walked quick and fearfully towards the lodge.

She passed through the park-gate for foot passengers without notice from the porter. It was twilight. She saw no one; and rejoiced in the general vacancy. Trembling, but with celerity, she '*skimmed*,' like her celebrated name-sake,[2] the turf; and annoyed only by the shadows of the trees, which all, as first they caught her eye, seemed the precursors of the approach of Mrs. Tyrold, speedily reached the mansion: but when she came to the little door by which she meant to enter, she found it fastened.

To the front door she durst not go, from the numerous chances by which she might surprise some of the family in the hall: and to present herself at the servant's gate would have an appearance degrading and clandestine.

She recollected, at last, the sash-door of a bow-window belonging to a room that was never occupied but in summer. Thither she went, and knowing the spring by which it could be opened on the outside, let herself into the house.

With steps not to be heard, and scarce breathing, she got thence into a long stone passage, whence she meant to mount the back stairs.

She was relieved by not meeting anyone in the way, though surprised to hear no foot-steps about the house, and no voices from any of the apartments.

Cautiously she went on, looking round at every step, to avoid any sudden encounter; but when she came to the bed-chamber gallery, she saw that the door of the room of Sir Hugh, by which she must necessarily pass, was wide open.

It was possible he might be in it: she had not courage to pass; her sight, thus unprepared, after so many heavy evils, might be too affecting for his weak frame. She turned short round, and entered a large apartment at the head of the stairs, called the billiard-room, where she resolved to wait and watch ere she ventured any further.

Its aspect was to the front of the house; she stole gently to a window, whence she thought the melancholy of her own mind pervaded the park. None of her uncle's horses were in sight; no one was passing to and fro; and she looked vainly even for the house-dog who ordinarily patrolled before the mansion.

She ventured to bend forwarder, to take a view of the side wings; these, however, presented not any sight more exhilarating nor more animated. Nothing was in motion, no one was visible, not even a fire blazed chearfulness.

She next strove to catch a glance of the windows belonging to the chamber of Eugenia; but her sigh, though sad, was without surprise to see their shutters shut. Those of Indiana were closed also. 'How mournfully,' cried she, 'is all changed! what of virtues are gone with Eugenia! what of beauty with Indiana! the one so constantly interesting! the other looking always so lovely!'—

But deeper still was her sigh, since mingled with self-reproach, to perceive her own chamber also shut up. 'Alas!' she cried, 'my poor uncle considers us all as dead to him!' She durst not lean sufficiently forward to examine the drawing-room, in which she concluded the family assembled; but she observed, with wonder, that even the library was not open, though it was still too light for candles; and Dr. Orkborne, who usually sat there, from the forget-fulness of application, was the last to demand them.

The fear of discovery was now combated by an anxiety to see some one,—any one, . . . and she returned to the passage. All there was still quiet, and she hazarded gliding past the open door, though without daring to look into the room; but when she came to the chamber of Lavinia, which she softly entered, all was dark, and it was evidently not in present use.

This was truly distressful. She concluded her sister was returned to Etherington, and knew not to whom to apply for counsel or mediation. She no longer, however, feared meeting her parents, who certainly had not made her sister quit Cleves without themselves; and, after a little hesitation, relying upon the ever sure lenity of her uncle, she determined to cast herself upon his kindness: but first to send in a short note, to avoid giving him any surprise.

She returned down the gallery, meaning to apply for pen and ink to the first person she could find: she could only, she knew, meet with a friend; unless, by ill fortune, she should encounter Miss Margland, the way to whose apartment she sedulously shunned.

No longer, however, quite so cautious, she stopt near the chamber of Sir Hugh, and convinced by the stillness it was empty, could not resist stepping into the apartment.

It looked despoiled and forsaken. Nothing was in its wonted order; his favourite guns hung not over the chimney-piece; the corners of the room were emptied of his sticks; his great chair was in a new place; no cushions for his dogs were near the fire; the bedstead was naked.

She now felt petrified; she sunk on the floor, to ejaculate a prayer for his safety, but knew not how to rise again, for terrour; nor which way next to turn, nor what even to conjecture.

Thus she remained, till suspense grew worse than certainty, and she forced herself from the room to seek some explanation. It was possible the whole family residence might be changed to the back front of the house. She descended the stairs with almost equal apprehension of meeting any one or seeing no one. The stone passage was now nearly dark. It was always the first part of the house that was lighted, as its windows were small and high: but no preparations were now making for that purpose. She went to the house-keeper's room, which was at the foot of the stairs she had descended. The door was shut, and she could not open it. She tried repeatedly, but vainly, to be heard by soft taps and whisperings; no one answered.

Amazed, confounded, she turned slowly another away; not a soul was in sight, not a sound within hearing. Every thing looked desolate, all the family seemed to be vanished.

Insensibly, yet irresistibly, she now moved on towards the drawing-room. The door was shut. She hesitated whether or not to attempt it. She listened. She hoped to catch the voice of her uncle: but all was inviolably still.

This was the only place of assembling in the evening; but her uncle might have dropt asleep, and she would not hazard startling him with her presence. She would sooner go to the hall at once, and be announced in the common way by a servant.

But what was her astonishment in coming to the hall, to find neither servant, light nor fire? and the marble pavement covered with trunks, packing mats, straw, ropes, and boxes? Terrified and astonished, she thought herself walking in her sleep. She could combine no ideas, either good or bad, to account for such a scene, and she looked at it bewildered and incredulous.

After a long hesitation, spent in wonder rather than thought, she at length determined to enter the breakfast parlour, and ring the bell: when the distant sound of a carriage, that was just entering the park, made her shut herself into the room, hastily, but silently.

It advanced rapidly; she trembled; it was surely, she thought, her Mother.

When it drove up to the portico, and she heard the house-bell ring, she instinctively barred her door; but finding no one approach to the call, while the bell was impatiently re-rung, her strong emotions of expectation were taking her again into the hall: but as her hand was upon the lock of the door, a light glimmered through the key hole. She heard some step advancing, and precipitately drew back.

The hall-door was now opened, and a man enquired for a young lady just come from Alresford.[1]

'There's no young lady here at all,' was the answer, in the voice of Jacob.

Finding it only her own driver, she ventured out; crying 'O Jacob! where is my dear uncle?'

Jacob was, at first, incapable of all answer, through surprise at her strange appearance; but then said, 'O Miss Camilla! you'll go nigh to break your good heart when you knows it all! But how, you've got into the house is what I can't guess; but I wish, for my poor master's sake, it had been before now!'

Horrour crept through every vein of Camilla, in the explanation she awaited of this fearful mystery. She motioned to the driver to stay, returned back to the parlour, and beckoned, for she could not speak, to Jacob to follow her.

When he came, and, shutting the door, was beginning a diffuse lamentation, eagerness to avert lengthened suspense recovered her voice, and she passionately exclaimed: 'Jacob! in two words, where is my uncle?—Is he well?'

'Why, yes, Miss Camilla, considering—' he began; but Camilla, whose fears had been fatal, interrupted him with fervent thanksgiving, till she was called back from joy by the following words:

'He's gone away Miss Camilla! gone Lord knows where! given up all his grand house-keeping, turned off almost all his poor servants, left this fine place, to have it let to whoever will hire it, and is going to live, he says, in some poor little lodging, till he can scrape together wherewithal to pay off every thing for your papa.'

A thunder-bolt that had instantly destroyed her, would gratefully have been received, in preference to this speech, by Camilla, who, casting up her hands and eyes, exclaimed: 'Then am I the most detestable, as well as the most wretched of human beings! My Father I have imprisoned!—my Uncle I have turned from his house and home! and for thee, O my Mother!—this is the reception I have prepared!'

Jacob tried to console her; but his account was only added torture.

The very instant he told her, that his master had received the

news of the arrest of Mr. Tyrold, he determined upon this
violent plan; and though the so speedy release, through the
generosity of Mr. Westwyn, had exceedingly calmed his first
emotions, he would not change his purpose, and protested he
would never indulge himself in peace nor comfort more, till he
had cleared off their joint debts; of which he attributed the whole
fault to himself, from having lived up to the very verge of his
yearly income, when he ought, he said, considering there were so
many young people, to have always kept a few odd sums at hand
for accidents. 'We all did what we could,' continued Jacob, 'to
put him off from such a thing, but all to no purpose; but if you'd
been here, Miss Camilla, you'd have done more with him than
all of us put together: but he called Miss Lavinia and all of us up
to him, and said to us, I won't have nobody tell this to my poor
little girl, meaning you, Miss Camilla, till I've got somewhere
settled and comfortable; because of her kind heart, says he.'

Tenderness so partial, at so suffering an instant, almost killed
Camilla. 'O Jacob,' she cried, 'where is now my dear generous
uncle? I will follow him in this chaise (rushing out as she spoke)
I will be his servant, his nurse, and attend him from morning to
night!'

She hurried into the carriage as she spoke, and bade him give
directions to the postillion. But when she heard he was, at present,
only at Etherington, whence he was seeking a new abode, her
head drooped, and she burst into tears.

Jacob remained, he said, alone, to take care of all the things,
and to shew the place to such as might come.

Miss Margland had been at the house about three hours ago;
and had met Sir Hugh, who had come over, to give directions
about what he would have packed up; and he had read a letter
from Miss Indy that was, and had forgiven her; but he was sore
vexed Miss Margland had come without Miss Camilla; only she
said Miss Camilla was at Mrs. Bellamy's, and she did not call,
because she thought it would be better to go back again, and see
more about Miss Indy, and so bring Miss Camilla next time; so
she wheedled his master to spare the chaise again, and let her go
off directly to settle every thing to Miss Indy's mind.

Camilla now repented she had not returned to Mrs. Berlinton's,
there, notwithstanding all objections, to have waited her recall;
since there her parents still believed her, and thence, under the

protection of Miss Margland, would in all probability summon her. To present herself, after this barbarous aggravation of the calamities she had caused, undemanded and unforgiven at Etherington, she thought impossible. She enquired if, by passing the night at Cleves, she might have any chance of seeing her uncle the next day. Jacob answered, no; but that Mr. Tyrold himself, with a gentleman from Winchester, who thought of hiring the house, were to be there early in the morning to take a survey of the premises.

A meeting, thus circumstanced, with her Father, at a moment when he came upon so direful a business, as parting with a place of which she had herself occasioned the desertion, seemed to her insupportable: and she resolved to return immediately to Belfont, to see there if her answer from Lavinia contained any new directions; and if not, to again go to London, and await final commands; without listening ever more to any hopes, projects, or judgments of her own.

Beseeching the worthy Jacob to pardon her non-payment, with every kind assurance that her uncle should know all his goodness, she told the postillion to take her to Belfont.

He could go no further, he said, and that but a foot pace, than to Alresford. Jacob marvelled, but blessed her, and Camilla, ejaculating, 'Adieu, dear happy Cleves!' was driven out of the park.

CHAPTER VIII

A Last Resource

To leave thus a spot where she had experienced such felicity; to see it naked and forlorn, despoiled of its hospitality, bereft of its master,—all its faithful old servants unrewarded dismissed; in disgrace to have re-entered its pales, and in terrour to quit them; —to fly even the indulgent Father, whose tenderness had withstood every evil with which errour and imprudence could assail him, set her now all at war with herself, and gave her sensations almost maddening. She reviewed her own conduct without mercy; and though misery after misery had followed every failing, all her sufferings appeared light to her repentant sense of her criminality; for as criminal alone, she could consider what had inflicted misfortunes upon persons so exemplary.

She arrived at Alresford so late, with the return horses, that she was forced to order a room there for the night.

Though too much occupied to weigh well her lonely and improper situation, at an inn, and at such hours, she was too uneasy to go to bed, and too miserable for sleep. She sat up, without attempting to read, write, or employ herself, patrolling her chamber in mournful rumination.

Nearly as soon as it was light, she proceeded, and arrived at the house of Bellamy as the servants were opening the window-shutters.

Fearfully she asked who was at home; and hearing only their mistress, sent for Molly Mill, and enquired for the answer from Etherington; but the lad had not yet brought any. She begged her to run to the inn, to know what had detained him; and then, ordering the chaise to wait, went to her sister.

Eugenia was gently rejoiced to see her, though evidently with encreased personal unhappiness. Camilla would fain have spared her the history of the desertion of Cleves; but it was an act that in its own nature must be public; and she had no other way to account for her so speedy return.

Eugenia heard it with the most piercing affliction; and, in the fulness of her heart, from this new blow, acknowledged the rapacity of Bellamy, and the barbarity with which he now scrupled not to avow the sordid motives of his marriage; cruelly lamenting the extreme simplicity with which she had been beguiled into a belief of the sincerity and violence of his attachment. 'For myself, however,' she continued, 'I now cease to murmur. How can misfortune, personally, cut me deeper? But with pity, indeed, I think of a new victim!'

She then put into her sister's hand a written paper she had picked up the preceding evening in her room, and which, having no direction, and being in the handwriting of Mrs. Berlinton, she had thought was a former note to herself, accidentally dropt: but the first line undeceived her.

'I yield, at length, O Bellamy, to the eloquence of your friendship! on Friday,—at one o'clock, I will be there—as you appoint.'

Camilla, almost petrified, read the lines. She knew better than her sister the plan to which this was the consent; which to have been given after her representations and urgency, appeared so utterly unjustifiable, that, with equal grief and indignation, she gave up this unhappy friend as wilfully lost; and her whole heart recoiled from ever again entering her doors.

Retracing, nevertheless, her many amiable qualities, she knew not how, without further effort, to leave her to her threatening fate; and determined, at all risks, to put her into the hands of her brother, whose timely knowledge of her danger might rescue her from public exposure. She wrote therefore the following note:

'*To* FREDERIC MELMOND, *Esq.*

'Watch and save,—or you will lose your sister.

C.T.'

His address, from frequently hearing it, was familiar to her; she went herself into the hall, to give the billet to a footman for the post-office. She would not let her sister have any share in the transaction, lest it should afterwards, by any accident, be known; though, to give force to her warning, she risked without hesitation the initials of her own name.

The repugnance, nevertheless, to going again to Mrs. Berlinton, pointed out no new refuge; and she waited, with added impatience, for the answer from Etherington, in hopes some positive direction might relieve her cruel perplexity.

The answer, however, came not, and yet greater grew her distress. Molly Mill brought word that when the messenger, who was a post-boy, returned, he was immediately employed to drive a chaise to London. The people at the inn heard him say something of wanting to go to 'Squire Bellamy's with a letter; but he had not time. He was to come back however at night.

To wait till he arrived seemed now to them both indispensable; but while considering at what hour to order the chaise, they heard a horseman gallop up to the house-door. 'Is it possible it should already be Mr. Bellamy?' cried Eugenia, changing colour.

His voice, loud and angry, presently confirmed the suggestion. Eugenia, trembling, said she would let him know whom he would find; and went into the next room, where, as he entered, he roughly exclaimed, 'What have you done with what I dropt out of my pocket-book?'

'There, Sir,' she answered, in the tone of firmness given by the ascendance of innocence over guilt, 'There it is: but how you can reconcile to yourself the delusions by which you must have obtained it I know not. I hope only, for her sake, and for yours, such words will never more meet my eyes.'

He was beginning a violent answer in a raised voice, when Eugenia told him her sister was in the next room.

He then, in a lowered tone, said, 'I warrant, you have shewn her my letter?'

The veracious Eugenia was incapable of saying no; and Bellamy, unable to restrain his rage, though smothering his voice, through his shut teeth, said, 'I shall remember this, I promise you! However, if she dare ever speak of it, you may tell her, from me, I shall lock you up upon bread and water for the rest of your life, and lay it at her door. I have no great terms to keep with her now. What does she say about Cleves? and that fool your uncle, who is giving up his house to pay your father's debts? What has brought her back again?'

'She is returning to Grosvenor-square, to Miss Margland.'

'Miss Margland? There's no Miss Margland in Grosvenor-square; nor any body else, that desires her company I can tell her. However, go, and get her off, for I have other business for you.'

Eugenia, then, opening the door, found her sister almost demolished with terrour and dismay. Silently, for some seconds, they sunk on the breast of each other; horrour closing all speech, drying up even their tears.

'You have no message to give me!' Camilla at length whispered; 'I have, perforce, heard all! and I will go;—though whither—'

She stopt, with a look of distress so poignant, that Eugenia, bursting into tears, while tenderly she clung around her, said, 'My sister! my Camilla! from me—from my house must you wander in search of an asylum!'

Bellamy here called her back. Camilla entreated she would inquire if he knew whither Miss Margland was gone.

He now came in himself, bowing civilly, though with constraint, and told her that Miss Margland was with Mrs. Macdersey, at Macdersey's own lodgings; but that neither of them would any

more be invited to Grosvenor-square, after such ill-treatment of
Mrs. Berlinton's brother.

Can you, thought Camilla, talk of ill-treatment? while, turning
to her sister, she said, 'Which way shall I now travel?'

Bellamy abruptly asked, if she was forced to go before dinner;
but not with an air of inviting any answer.

None could she make; she looked down, to save her eyes the
sight of an object they abhorred, embraced Eugenia, who seemed
a picture of death; and after saying adieu, added, 'If I knew
whither you thought I should go—that should be my guide?'

'Home, my dearest sister!'

'Drive then,' she cried, hurrying to the chaise, 'to Etherington.'

Bellamy advancing, said, with a smile, 'I see you are not much
used to travelling, Miss Camilla!' and gave the man a direction
to Bagshot.

She began, now, to feel nearly careless what became of her;
her situation seemed equally desolate and disgraceful, and in
gloomy despondence, when she turned from the high road, and
stopt at a small inn, called the half-way-house, about nine miles
from Etherington, she resolved to remain there till she received
her expected answer; ardently hoping, if it were not yielding and
favourable, the spot upon which she should read it, would be
that upon which her existence would close.

Alighting at the inn, which, from being upon a cross road, had
little custom, and was scarce more than a large cottage, she
entered a small parlour, discharged her chaise, and ordered a man
and horse to go immediately to Belfont.

Presently two or three gentle tappings at the door made her,
though fearfully, say, 'Come in!' A little girl then, with incessant
low courtesies, appeared, and looking smilingly in her face, said,
'Pray, ma'am, a'n't you the Lady that was so good to us?'

'When? my dear? what do you mean?'

'Why, that used to give us cakes and nice things, and gave 'em
to Jen, and Bet, and Jack? and that would not let my dad be
took up?'

Camilla now recollected the eldest little Higden, the washerwoman's niece, and kindly enquired after her father, her aunt,
and family.

'O, they all does pure now. My dad's had no more mishaps,
and he hopes, please God, to get on pretty well.'

'Sweet hearing!' cried Camilla, 'all my purposes have not, then, been frustrated!'

With added satisfaction she learnt also that the little girl had a good place, and a kind mistress. She begged her to hasten the Belfont messenger, giving her in charge a short note for Eugenia, with a request for the Etherington letter. She had spent nothing in London, save in some small remembrances to one or two of Mrs. Berlinton's servants; and though her chaise-hire had now almost emptied her purse, she thought every expence preferable to either lengthening her suspense, or her residence on the road.

In answer to the demand of what she would be pleased to have, she then ordered tea. She had taken no regular meal for two days; and for two nights had not even been in bed. But the wretchedness of her mind seemed to render her invulnerable to fatigue.

The shaken state of her nerves warped all just consideration of the impropriety of her present sojourn. Her judgment had no chance, where it had her feelings to combat, and in the despondence of believing herself parentally rejected, she was indifferent to appearances, and desperate upon all other events: nor was she brought to any recollection, till she was informed that the messenger, [who] she had concluded was half way to Belfont, could not set out till the next morning: this small and private inn not being able to furnish a man and horse at shorter warning.

To pass a second night at an inn, seemed, even in the calculations of her own harassed faculties, utterly improper; and thus, driven to extremity, she forced herself to order a chaise for home; though with a repugnance to so compulsatory a meeting, that made her wish to be carried in it a corpse.

The tardy prudence of the character naturally rash, commonly arrives but to point repentance that it came not before. The only pair of horses the little inn afforded, were now out upon other duty, and would not return till the next day.

Almost to herself incredible seemed now her situation. She was compelled to order a bed, and to go up stairs to a small chamber: but she could not even wish to take any rest. 'I am an outcast,' she cried, 'to my family; my Mother would *rather not see me*; my Father forbears to demand me; and he—dearer to me than life!— by whom I was once chosen, has forgotten me!—How may I support my heavy existence? and when will it end?

Overpowered, nevertheless, by fatigue, in the middle of the

night, she [lay] down in her cloaths: but her slumbers were so broken by visions of reproach, conveyed through hideous forms, and in menaces the most terrific, that she gladly got up; preferring certain affliction to wild and fantastic horrours.

Nearly as soon as it was light, she rang for little Peggy, whose Southampton anecdotes had secured her the utmost respect from the mistress of the inn, and heard that the express was set off.

Dreadful and dreary, in slow and lingering misery, passed the long interval of his absence, though his rapid manner of travelling made it short for the ground he traversed. She had now, however, bought sufficient experience to bespeak a chaise against his return. The only employment in which she could engage herself, was conversing with Peggy Higden, who, she was glad to find, could not remember her name well enough to make it known, through her pronunciation.

From the window, at length, she perceived a man and horse gallop up to the house. She darted forth, exclaiming: 'Have you brought me any answer?' And seizing the letter he held out, saw the hand-writing of Lavinia, and shut herself into her room.

She opened it upon her knees, expecting to find within some lines from her Mother; none, however, appeared, and sad and mortified, she laid down the letter, and wept. 'So utterly, then,' she cried, 'have I lost her? Even with her pen will she not speak to me? How early is my life too long!'

Taking up again, then, the letter, she read what follows.

'*To Miss* CAMILLA TYROLD.

'Alas, my dear sister, why can I not answer you according to our mutual wishes? My Father is at Winchester, with a lawyer, upon the affairs of Indiana; and my Mother is abroad with my uncle, upon business which he has asked her to transact; but even were she here . . . could I, while the man awaits, intercede? have you forgotten your ever fearful Lavinia? All that she dares, shall be done,—but that you may neither think she has been hitherto neglected, nor let your hopes expect too much speed from her future efforts, I am painfully reduced to own to you, what already has passed. But let it not depress you; you know when she is hurt, it is not lightly; but you know, also, where she loves, her displeasure, once passed, is never allowed to rise again.

'Yesterday I saw her looking at your picture; the moment seemed to be happy, and I ventured to say; "Ah, poor Camilla!" but she turned to me with quickness, and cried; "Lament rather, Lavinia, your Father! Did he merit so little trust from his child, that her affairs should be withheld from him till they cast him . . . where I found him! . . . Dread, memorable sight—when may I forget it!"

'Even after this, my dear Camilla, I hazarded another word, "she will be miserable," I said, "my dear Mother, till she returns." "She will return," she answered, "with Miss Margland. This is no season for any expence that may be avoided; and Camilla, most of all, must now see the duties of œconomy. Were her understanding less good, I should less heavily weigh her errours; but she sets it apart, to abandon herself to her feelings. Alas! poor thing! they will now themselves be her punishers! Let her not however despond; tell her, when you write, her angelic Father forgives her; and tell her she has always had my prayers, and will ever have my blessing;—though I am not eager, as yet, to add to her own reproaches, those she may experience from my presence."

'I knew not how to introduce this to my dearest Camilla, but your messenger, and his haste, now forces me to say all, and say it quick. He brings, I find, the letter from Belfont, where already we had heard you were removed through Miss Margland, much to the approbation of my Father and my Mother, who hope your sojourn there is a solace to you both. Adieu, my dearest sister— your messenger cannot wait.

'LAVINIA TYROLD.'

'She will not see me then!' cried Camilla, 'she cannot bear my sight! O Death! let me not pray to thee also in vain!'

Weak from inanition, confused from want of sleep, harassed with fatigue, and exhausted by perturbation, she felt now so ill, that she solemnly believed her fatal wish quick approaching.

The landlord of the inn entered to say that the chaise she had ordered was at the door; and put down upon the table the bill of what she had to pay.

Whither to turn, what course to take, she knew not; though to remain longer at an inn, while persuaded life was on its wane, was dreadful; yet how present herself at home, after the letter she had received? what asylum was any where open to her?

She begged the landlord to wait, and again read the letter of Lavinia, when, startled by what was said of abandoning herself to her feelings, she saw that her immediate duty was to state her situation to her parents. She desired, therefore, the chaise might be put up, and wrote these lines:

'I could not, unhappily, stay at Eugenia's; nor can I return to Mrs. Berlinton; I am now at the half-way-house where I shall wait for commands. My Lavinia will tell me what I may be ordered to do. I am ill,—and earnestly I pray with an illness from which I may rise no more. When my Father—my Mother, hear this, they will perhaps accord me to be blest again with their sight; the brevity of my career may, to their kindness, expiate its faults; they may pray for me where my own prayers may be too unsanctified to be heard; they may forgive me . . . though my own forgiveness never more will quiet this breast! Heaven bless and preserve them; their unoffending daughters; and my ever loved uncle!

'CAMILLA TYROLD.'

She then rang the bell, and desired this note might go by express to Etherington.

But this, the waiter answered, was impossible; the horse on which the messenger had set out to Belfont, though it had only carried him the first stage, and brought him back the last, had galloped so hard, that his master would not send it out again the same day; and they had but that one.

She begged he would see instantly for some other conveyance.

The man who was come back from Belfont, he answered, would be glad to be discharged, as he wanted to go to rest.

She then took up the bill, and upon examining the sum total, found, with the express, the chaise in which she came the last stage, that which she ordered to take her to Etherington, and the expence of her residence, it amounted to half a crown beyond what she possessed.

She had only, she knew, to make herself known as the niece of Sir Hugh Tyrold, to be trusted by all the environs; but to expose herself in this helpless, and even pennyless state, appeared to her to be a degradation to every part of her family.

To enclose the bill to Etherington was to secure its being paid; but the sentence, *Camilla most of all must now see the duties of œconomy*, made her revolt from such a step.

All she still possessed of pecuniary value she had in her pocket: the seal of her Father, the ring of her Mother, the watch of her Uncle, and the locket of Edgar Mandlebert. With one of these she now determined to part, in preference to any new exposure at Etherington, or to incurring the smallest debt. She desired to be left alone, and took them from her pocket, one by one, painfully ruminating upon which she could bear to lose. 'It may not, she thought, be for long; for quick, I hope, my course will end!—yet even for an hour,—even for the last final moment—to give up such dear symbols of all that has made my happiness in life!——'

She looked at them, kissed and pressed them to her heart; spoke to them as if living and understanding representatives of their donors, and bestowed so much time in lamenting caresses and hesitation, that the waiter came again, while yet she was undetermined.

She desired to speak with the mistress of the house.

Instinctively she now put away the gifts of her parents; but between her uncle and Edgar she wavered. She blushed, however, at her demur, and the modesty of duty made her put up the watch. Taking, then, an agitating last view of a locket which circumstances had rendered inappreciable to her, 'Ah! not in vain,' she cried, 'even now shall I lose what once was a token so bewitching . . . Dear precious locket! Edgar even yet would be happy you should do me one last kind office! generously, benevolently, he would rejoice you should spare me still one last menacing shame!'—

When Mrs. Marl, the landlady, came in, deeply colouring, she put it into her hand, turning her eyes another way, while she said; 'Mrs. Marl, I have not quite money enough to pay the bill; but if you will keep this locket for a security, you will be sure to be paid by and by.'

Mrs. Marl looked at it with great admiration, and then, with yet greater wonder, at Camilla. ''Tis pretty, indeed, ma'am,' she said; ''twould be pity to sell it. However, I'll shew it my husband.'

Mr. Marl soon came himself, with looks somewhat less satisfied,

'Tis a fine bauble, ma'am,' cried he, 'but I don't much understand those things; and there's nobody here can tell me what it's worth. I'd rather have my money, if you please.'

Weakened now in body, as well as spirits, she burst into tears. Alas! she thought, how little do my friends conjecture to what I am reduced! She offered, however, the watch, and the countenance of Mr. Marl lost its gloom.

'This,' said he, 'is something like! A gold watch one may be sure to get one's own for; but such a thing as that may'n't fetch six-pence, fine as it looks.'

Mrs. Marl objected to keeping both; but her husband said he saw no harm in it; and Camilla begged her note might be sent without delay.

A labourer, after some search, was found, who undertook, for handsome pay, to carry it on foot to the rectory.

CHAPTER IX

A Spectacle

THE messenger returned not till midnight; what, then, was the consternation of Camilla that he brought no answer! She suspected he had not found the house; she doubted if the letter had been delivered; but he affirmed he had put it into the hands of a maid-servant, though, as it was late, he had come away directly, and not thought of waiting for any answer.

It is not very early in life we learn how little is performed, for which no precaution is taken. Care is the offspring of disappointment; and sorrow and repentance commonly hang upon its first lessons. Unused to transact any sort of business for herself, she had expected, in sending a letter, an answer as a thing of course, and had now only herself to blame for not having ordered him to stay. She consoled herself, however, that she was known to be but nine miles distant from the rectory, and that any commands could be conveyed to her nearly in an hour.

What they might be, became now, therefore, her sole anxiety. Would not her Mother write? After an avowal such as she had made of her desolate, if not dying condition, would she not pardon and embrace her? Was it not even possible she might come herself?

This idea mingled emotions of a contrariety scarcely supportable. 'O how,' she cried, 'shall I see her? Can joy blend with such terrour? Can I wish her approach, yet not dare to meet her eye? —that eye which never yet has looked at me, but to beam with bright kindness!—though a kindness that, even from my childhood, seemed to say, Camilla, be blameless—or you break your Mother's heart! . . . my poor unhappy Mother! she has always seemed to have a presentiment, I was born to bring her to sorrow!'

Expectation being now, for this night, wholly dead, the excess of her bodily fatigue urged her to take some repose: but her ever eager imagination made her apprehensive her friends might find her too well, and suspect her representation was but to alarm them into returning kindness. A fourth night, therefore, passed without sleep, or the refreshment of taking off her cloaths; and by the time the morning sun shone in upon her apartment, she was too seriously disordered to make her illness require the aid of fancy. She was full of fever, faint, pallid, weak, and shaken by nervous tremors. 'I think,' she cried, 'I am now certainly going; and never was death so welcomed by one so young. It will end in soft peace my brief, but stormy passage, and I shall owe to its solemn call the sacred blessing of my offended Mother!'

Tranquillised by this hope, and this idea, she now lost all sufferings but those of disease: her mind grew calm, her spirits serene: all fears gave way to the certainty of soothing kindness, all grief was buried in the solemnity of expected dissolution.

But this composure outlived not the first hours of the morning; as they vainly advanced, producing no loved presence, no letter, no summons; solicitude revived, disappointment sunk her heart, and dread preyed again upon her nerves. She started at every sound; every breath of wind seemed portentous; she listened upon the stairs; she dragged her feeble limbs to the parlour, to be nearer at hand; she forced them back again to her bed-room, to strain her aching eyes out of the window; but still no voice demanded her, and no person approached.

Peggy, who repeatedly came to tell her the hour, now assured her it was dinner time: unable to eat, she was heedless of the hint this conveyed, and it obtained from her no orders, till Peggy gave her innocently to understand the expectations of her host and hostess; but when, at five o'clock, the table was served, all force and courage forsook her. To be left thus to herself, when her situation was known; to be abandoned at an inn where she had confessed she thought herself dying; 'My Mother,' she cried, 'cannot forgive me! my Father himself deserts me! O Edgar! you did well to fly so unhallowed a connexion!'

She left her dinner for Peggy, and crawling up stairs, cast herself upon the bed, with a desperate supplication she might rise from it no more. 'The time,' cried she, 'is past for consolation, and dead for hope! my parents' own prayers have been averted, and their prognostics fulfilled. *May the dread forfeiture*, said my dearest Father, *not extend through my daughters!*—Alas! Lionel himself has not brought upon him a disgrace such as I have done! —*May Heaven*, said my honoured Mother, *spare me evil under your shape at least!*—but under that it has come to her the most heavily!'

Dissolving, then, in sorrowing regret, recollections of maternal tenderness bathed her pillow with her tears, and reversing all the inducements to her sad resignation, abolished every wish but to fall again at the parental feet. 'To see,' cried she, 'once more, the dear authors of my being! to receive their forgiveness, their blessing . . . to view again their honoured countenances!—to hear once more their loved speech . . . Alas! was it I that fled the voice of my Mother? That voice which, till that moment, had been music to my mind! and never reached my ear, but as the precursor of all kindness! why did I not sooner at once kneel at her feet, and seek my lost path under my first and best guide?'

Shocked and contrite in this tardy view of the step she ought to have taken, she now languished to petition for pardon even for an offence unknown; and rising, took up a pen to relate the whole transaction. But her head was confused, and the attempt shewed her she was more ill than she had even herself suspected. She thought all rapidly advancing, and enthusiastically rejoiced.

Yet a second time she took the pen; but it had not touched the paper, when a buzzing, confused, stifled sort of noise from without drew her to the window.

She then perceived an immense crowd of people approaching slowly, and from a distance, towards the inn.

As they advanced, she was struck to hear no encrease of noise, save from the nearer trampling of feet. No voice was distinguishable; no one spoke louder than the rest; they seemed even to tread the ground with caution. They consisted of labourers, workmen, beggars, women, and children, joined by some accidental passengers: yet the general 'hum of many'[1] was all that was heard; they were silent though numerous, solemn though mixt.

As they came near, she thought she perceived something in the midst of them like a bier, and caught a glimpse of a gentleman's habit. Startled, she drew in; but soon, upon another view, discerned clearly a well-dressed man, stretched out his full length, and apparently dead.

Recoiling, shuddering, she hastily shut the window, 'Yet why,' she cried, the next moment, 'and whence this emotion? Is not death what I am meeting?—seeking?—desiring?—what I court? what I pray for?'

She sighed, walked feebly up and down the room, breathed hard and with effort, and then forced herself again to open the window, determined to contemplate steadily the anticipating object of her fervent demand.

Yet not without severe self-compulsion she flung up again the sash; but when she looked out, the crowd alone remained; the bier was gone.

Whether carried on, or brought into the house, she now wished to know, with some particulars, of whom it might be, and what belonged to so strange and horrible an appearance.

She rang for little Peggy; but Peggy came not. She rang again, but no one answered the bell. She opened her door, meaning to descend to her little parlour for information; but the murmuring buzz she had before heard upon the road, was now within the house, which seemed filled with people, all busy and occupied, yet speaking low, and appearing to partake of a general awe.

She could not venture to encounter so many spectators; she shut her door, to wait quietly till this first commotion should be passed.

This was not for more than an hour; when observing, from her window, that the crowd was dispersed, she again listened at the door, and found that the general disturbance was succeeded by a stillness the most profound.

She then rang again, and little Peggy appeared, but looking pale and much frightened.

Camilla asked what had been the matter.

'O ma'am,' she answered, crying, 'here's been murder! A gentleman has been murdered—and nobody knows who he is, nor who has done it!'

She then related that he had been found dead in a wood hard by, and one person calling another, and another, he had been brought to the inn to be owned.

'And is he here now?' with an involuntary shudder asked Camilla.

Yes, she answered, but her mistress had ordered her not to own it, for fear of frightening the young lady; and said he would soon be carried away.

The tale was shocking, and, though scarce conscious why, Camilla desired Peggy to stay with her.

The little girl was most willing; but she was presently called down stairs; and Camilla, with strong shame of nameless fears and weak horrour, strove to meditate to some use upon this scene.

But her mind was disturbed, her composure was gone; her thoughts were broken, abrupt, unfixed, and all upon which she could dwell with any steadiness, was the desire of one more appeal to her family, that yet they would consent to see her, if they received it in time; or that they should know in what frame of mind she expired, should it bring them too late.

With infinite difficulty, she then wrote the following lines; every bending down of her head making it ache nearly to distraction.

'Adieu, my dearest parents, if again it is denied me to see you! Adieu, my darling sisters! my tender uncle! I ask not now your forgiveness; I know I shall possess it fully; my Father never withheld it,—and my Mother, if against herself alone I had sinned, would have been equally lenient; would have probed but to heal, have corrected, but to pardon. O tenderest of united partners! bless, then, the early ashes of your erring, but adoring daughter, who, from the moment she inflicted one wound upon your bosoms, has found existence intolerable, and prays now but for her earthly release!

'CAMILLA TYROLD.'

This she gave to Peggy, with a charge that, at any expence, it might be conveyed to the rectory at Etherington immediately.

'And shall I not,' thought she, when she had rested from this exertion, 'and may I not at such a period, with innocence, with propriety, write one poor word to him who was so near becoming first to me in all things?'

She again took her pen, but had only written 'O Edgar! in this last farewell be all displeasure forgotten!—from the first to the final moment of my short life, dear and sole possessor of my heart!'—when the shooting anguish of her head stopt her hand, and hastily writing the direction, lest she could write no more, she, with difficulty added, '*Not to be delivered till I am dead;*' and was forced to lie down, and shut all light from her strained and aching eyes.

Peggy presently brought her word that all the horses were out, and every body was engaged, and that the note could not possibly go till the next day.

Extremely disappointed, she begged to speak with Mrs. Marl; who sent her word she was much engaged, but would wait upon her as soon as she was able.

Vainly, however, she expected her; it grew dusk; she felt herself worse every moment; flushed with fever, or shivering with cold, and her head nearly split asunder with agony. She determined to go once more down stairs, and offer to her host himself any reward he could claim, so he would undertake the immediate delivery of the letter.

With difficulty she arose; with slow steps, and tottering, she descended; but as she approached her little parlour, she heard voices in it, and stopt. They spoke low, and she could not distinguish them. The door of an adjoining room was open, and by its stillness empty; she resolved to ring there, to demand to speak with Mr. Marl. But as she dragged her weak limbs into the apartment, she saw, stretched out upon a large table, the same form, dress, and figure she had seen upon the bier.

Starting, almost fainting, but too much awed to call out, she held trembling by the door.

The bodily feebleness which impeded her immediate retreat, gave force to a little mental reflexion: Do I shrink thus, thought she, from what so earnestly I have prayed to become . . . and so soon I must represent . . . a picture of death?

She now impelled herself towards the table. A cloth covered the face; she stood still, hesitating if she had power to remove it: but she thought it a call to her own self-examination; and though mentally recoiling, advanced. When close to the table, she stood still, violently trembling. Yet she would not allow herself to retreat. She now put forth her hand; but it shook suspended over the linen, without courage to draw it aside. At length, however, with enthusiastic self-compulsion, slightly and fearfully, she lifted it up . . . but instantly, and with instinctive horrour, snatched her hand away, and placed it before her shut eyes.

She felt, now, she had tried herself beyond her courage, and, deeply moved, was fain to retreat; but in letting down her hand, to see her way, she found she had already removed the linen from a part of the face, and the view she unintentionally caught almost petrified her.

For some instants she stood motionless, from want of strength to stir, but with closed eyes, that feared to confirm their first surmise; but when, turning from the ghastly visage, she attempted, without another glance, to glide away, an unavoidable view of the coat, which suddenly she recognized, put her conjecture beyond all doubt, that she now saw dead before her the husband of her sister.

Resentment, in gentle minds, however merited and provoked, survives not the breath of the offender. With the certainty no further evil can be practised, perishes vengeance against the culprit, though not hatred of the guilt: and though, with the first movement of sisterly feelings, she would have said, Is Eugenia then released? the awe was too great, his own change was too solemn. He was now where no human eye could follow, no human judgment overtake him.

Again she endeavoured to escape the dreadful scene, but her shaking limbs were refractory, and would not support her. The mortal being requires use to be reconciled to its own visible mortality; dismal is its view; grim, repulsive, terrific its aspect.

But no sooner was her head turned from the dire object, than alarm for her sister took possession of her soul; and with what recollection she possessed, she determined to go to Belfont.

An idea of any active service invigorates the body as well as the mind. She made another effort to depart, but a glance she knew not how to avoid shewed her, upon the coat of the right arm and right side of this ghastly figure, large splashes of blood.

With horrour thus accumulate, she now sunk upon the floor,

inwardly exclaiming: He is murdered indeed! . . . and where may be Eugenia?

A woman who had in charge to watch by the corpse, but who had privately stolen out for some refreshment, now returning, saw with affright the new person in the room, and ran to call Mrs. Marl; who, alarmed also at the sight of the young lady, and at her deplorable condition, assisted the woman to remove her from the apartment, and convey her to the chamber, where she was laid down upon the bed, though she resisted being undressed, and was seized with an aguish shivering fit, while her eyes seemed emitting sparks of fire.

'It is certainly now,' cried she, 'over, and hence I move no more!'

The joy with which, a few minutes before, she would have welcomed such a belief, was now converted into an awe unspeakable, undefinable. The wish of death is commonly but disgust of life, and looks forward to nothing further than release from worldly care:—but the something yet beyond . . . the something unknown, untried, yet to come, the *bourne whence no traveller returns*[1] to prepare succeeding passengers for what they may expect, now abruptly presented itself to her consideration, . . . but came to scare, not to soothe.

All here, she cried, I have wished to leave . . . but . . . have I fitted myself for what I am to meet?

Conscience now suddenly took the reins from the hands of imagination, and a mist was cleared away that hitherto, obscuring every duty by despondence, had hidden from her own perceptions the faulty basis of her desire. Conscience took the reins—and a mist was cleared away that had concealed from her view the cruelty of this egotism.

Those friends, it cried, which thus impatiently thou seekest to quit, have they not loved, cherished, reared thee with the most exquisite care and kindness? If they are offended, who has offended them? If thou art now abandoned, may it not be from necessity, or from accident? When thou hast inflicted upon them the severe pain of harbouring anger against what is so dear to them, wouldst thou load them with regret that they manifested any sensibility of thy errours? Hast thou plunged thy house in calamity, and will no worthier wish occur to thee, than to leave it to its sorrows and distress, with the aggravating pangs of causing thy afflicting, however blamable self-desertion? of coming to thee ... perhaps even now! ... with mild forgiveness, and finding thee a self-devoted corpse?—not fallen, indeed, by the profane hand of daring suicide, but equally self-murdered through wilful self-neglect.

Had the voice been allowed sound which spoke this dire admonition, it could scarcely with more horrour, or keener repentance have struck her. 'That poor man,' she cried, 'now delivering up his account, by whatever hand he perished, since less principled, less instructed than myself, may be criminal, perhaps, with less guilt!'

The thought now of her Father,—the piety he had striven to inculcate into her mind; his resignation to misfortune, and his trust through every suffering, all came home to her heart, with religious veneration; and making prayer succeed to remorse, guided her to what she knew would be his guidance if present, and she desired to hear the service for the sick.

Peggy could not read; Mrs. Marl was too much engaged; the whole house had ample employment, and her request was unattainable.

She then begged they would procure her a prayer-book, that she might try to read herself; but her eyes, heavy, aching, and dim, glared upon the paper, without distinguishing the print from the margin.

'I am worse!' she cried faintly, 'my wish comes fast upon me! Ah! not for my punishment let it finally arrive!'

With terror, however, even more than with malady, she now trembled. The horrible sight she had witnessed, brought death before her in a new view. She feared she had been presumptuous; she felt that her preparations had all been worldly, her impatience wholly selfish. She called back her wish, with penitence and affright: her agitation became torture, her regret was aggravated to remorse, her grief to despair.

CHAPTER X

A Vision

WHEN the first violence of this paroxysm of sorrow abated, Camilla again strove to pray, and found that nothing so much stilled her. Yet, her faculties confused, hurried, and in anguish, permitted little more than incoherent ejaculations. Again she sighed for her Father; again the spirit of his instructions recurred, and she enquired who was the clergyman of the parish, and if he would be humane enough to come and pray by one who had no claim upon him as a parishioner.

Peggy said he was a very good gentleman, and never refused even the poorest person, that begged his attendance.

'O go to him, then,' cried she, 'directly! Tell him a sick and helpless stranger implores that he will read to her the prayers for the dying! . . . Should I yet live . . . they will compose and make me better;—if not . . . they will give me courage for my quick exit.'

Peggy went forth, and she lay her beating head upon the pillow, and endeavoured to quiet her nerves for the sacred ceremony she demanded.

It was dark, and she was alone; the corpse she had just quitted seemed still bleeding in full view. She closed her eyes, but still saw it; she opened them, but it was always there. She felt nearly stiff with horrour, chilled, frozen, with speechless apprehension.

A slumber, feverish nearly to delirium, at length surprised her harassed faculties; but not to afford them rest. Death, in a visible figure, ghastly, pallid, severe, appeared before her, and with its hand, sharp and forked, struck abruptly upon her breast. She screamed—but it was heavy as cold, and she could not remove it. She trembled; she shrunk from its touch; but it had iced her heart-strings. Every vein was congealed; every stiffened limb stretched to its full length, was hard as marble: and when again she made a feeble effort to rid her oppressed lungs of the dire weight that had fallen upon them, a voice hollow, deep, and distant, dreadfully pierced her ear, calling out: 'Thou hast but thy own wish! Rejoice, thou murmurer, for thou diest!' Clearer, shriller, another voice quick vibrated in the air: 'Whither goest thou,' it cried, 'and whence comest thou?'

A voice from within, over which she thought she had no

controul, though it seemed issuing from her vitals, low, hoarse, and tremulous, answered, 'Whither I go, let me rest! Whence I come from let me not look back! Those who gave me birth, I have deserted; my life, my vital powers I have rejected.' Quick then another voice assailed her, so near, so loud, so terrible . . . she shrieked at its horrible sound. 'Prematurely,' it cried, 'thou art come, uncalled, unbidden; thy task unfulfilled, thy peace unearned. Follow, follow me! the Records of Eternity are opened. Come! write with thy own hand thy claims, thy merits to mercy!' A repelling self-accusation instantaneously overwhelmed her. 'O, no! no! no!' she exclaimed, 'let me not sign my own miserable insufficiency!' In vain was her appeal. A force unseen, yet irresistible, impelled her forward. She saw the immense volumes of Eternity, and her own hand involuntarily grasped a pen of iron, and with a velocity uncontroulable wrote these words: 'Without resignation, I have prayed for death: from impatience of displeasure, I have desired annihilation: to dry my own eyes, I have left . . . pitiless, selfish, unnatural! . . . a Father the most indulgent, a Mother almost idolizing, to weep out their's!' Her head would have sunk upon the guilty characters; but her eyelids refused to close, and kept them glaring before her. They became, then, illuminated with burning sulphur. She looked another way; but they partook of the same motion; she cast her eyes upwards, but she saw the characters still; she turned from side to side; but they were always her object. Loud again sounded the same direful voice: 'These are thy deserts; write now thy claims:—and next,—and quick,—turn over the immortal leaves, and read thy doom.' . . . 'Oh, no!' she cried, 'Oh, no!' . . . 'O, let me yet return! O, Earth, with all thy sorrows, take, take me once again, that better I may learn to work my way to that last harbour, which rejecting the criminal repiner, opens its soft bosom to the firm, though supplicating sufferer!' In vain again she called;—pleaded, knelt, wept in vain. The time, she found, was past; she had slighted it while in her power; it would return to her no more; and a thousand voices at once, with awful vibration, answered aloud to every prayer, 'Death was thy own desire!' Again, un-licensed by her will, her hand seized the iron instrument. The book was open that demanded her claims. She wrote with difficulty . . . but saw that her pen made no mark! She looked upon the page, when she thought she had finished, . . . but the paper was blank! ... Voices then, by hundreds, by thousands, by millions, from side to side, above, below, around, called out, echoed and re-echoed, 'Turn over, turn over ... and read thy eternal doom!' In the same instant, the leaf, untouched, burst open ... and ... she awoke. But in a trepidation so violent, the bed shook under her, the cold sweat, in large drops, fell from her forehead, and her heart still seemed labouring under the adamantine pressure of the inflexibly cold grasp of death. So exalted was her imagination, so confused were all her thinking faculties, that she stared with wild doubt whether then, or whether now, what she experienced were a dream.

In this suspensive state, fearing to call, to move, or almost to breathe, she remained, in perfect stillness, and in the dark, till little Peggy crept softly into the chamber.

Certain then of her situation, 'This has been,' she cried, 'only a vision—but my conscience has abetted it, and I cannot shake it off.'

When she became calmer, and further recollected herself, she anxiously enquired if the clergyman would not come.

Peggy, hesitatingly, acknowledged he had not been sent for; her mistress had imagined the request proceeded from a disturbance of mind, owing to the sight of the corpse, and said she was sure, after a little sleep, it would be forgotten.

'Alas!' said Camilla, disappointed, 'it is more necessary than ever! my senses are wandering; I seem hovering between life and death—Ah! let not my own fearful fancies absorb this hour of change, which religious rites should consecrate!'

She then told Peggy to plead for her to her mistress, and assure her that nothing else, after the dreadful shock she had received, could still her mind.

Mrs. Marl, not long after came into the room herself; and enquiring how she did, said, if she was really bent upon such a melancholy thing, the clergyman had luckily just called, and would read the service to her directly, if it would give her any comfort.

'O, great and infinite comfort!' she cried, and begged he might come immediately, and read to her the prayer for those of whom there is but small hope of recovery. She would have risen, that she might kneel; but her limbs would not second her desire, and she was obliged to lie still upon the outside of the bed. Peggy drew the curtains, to shade her eyes, as a candle was brought into the room; but when she heard Mrs. Marl say: 'Come in, Sir,'—and 'here's the prayer-book;' overpowered with tender recollection of her Father, to whom such offices were frequent, she burst into an agony of tears, and hid her face upon the pillow.

She soon, however, recovered, and the solemnity of the preparation overawed her sorrow. Mrs. Marl placed the light as far as possible from the bed, and when Camilla waved her hand in token of being ready, said, 'Now, Sir, if you please.'

He complied, though not immediately; but no sooner had he begun, no sooner devoutly, yet tremblingly, pronounced, *O Father of Mercies!* than a faint scream issued from the bed.—

He stopt; but she did not speak; and after a short pause, he resumed: but not a second sentence was pronounced when she feebly ejaculated, 'Ah heaven!' and the book fell from his hands.

She strove to raise her head; but could not; she opened, however, the side curtain, to look out; he advanced, at the same moment, to the foot of the bed . . . fixed his eyes upon her face, and in a voice that seemed to come from his soul, exclaimed, 'Camilla!'

With a mental emotion that, for an instant, restored her strength, she drew again the curtain, covered up her face, and sobbed even audibly, while the words, 'O Edgar!' vainly sought vent.

He attempted not to unclose the curtain she had drawn, but with a deep groan, dropping upon his knees on the outside, cried, 'Great God!' but checking himself, hastily arose, and motioning to Mrs. Marl and to Peggy, to move out of hearing, said, through the curtain; 'O Camilla! what dire calamity has brought this about?—speak, I implore!—why are you here?—why alone? speak! speak!'

He heard she was weeping, but received no answer, and with energy next to torture exclaimed; 'Refuse not to trust me!—recollect our long friendship—forgive—forget its alienation!—By all you have ever valued—by all your wonted generosity—I call—I appeal . . . Camilla! Camilla!—your silence rends my soul!'

Camilla had no utterance, yet could not resist this urgency, and gently through the opening of the curtain, put forth her feeble hand.

He seemed affected to agony; he held it between each of his
own, and while softly he uttered, 'O ever—unchangeably generous
Camilla!' she felt it moistened with his tears.

Too weak for the new sensation this excited, she drew it away,
and the violence of her emotion menacing an hysteric fit, Mrs.
Marl came back to her, and wringing his hands as he looked
around the room, he tore himself away.

CHAPTER XI

Means to still Agitation

DECLINING all aid, Camilla continued in the same position,
wrapt up, coveting the dark, and stifling sighs that were rising into
sobs, till she heard a gentle tap at her door.

She started, but still hid herself: Mrs. Marl was already gone;
Peggy answered the summons, and returned to the bedside, with
a note in her hand, begging Camilla to take it, as it came from the
gentleman who was to have read the prayers.

'Is he then gone?' cried she, in a voice announcing deep
disappointment.

'Yes, he went directly, my dear Lady.'

She threw the covering from her face, and with uplifted hands,
exclaimed; 'O Edgar! could you see me thus . . . and leave me?'—
Yet eagerly seizing the letter, called for a candle, and strove to
read it. But the characters seemed double to her weak and dazzled
eyes, and she was forced to relinquish the attempt. She pressed it
to her bosom, and again covered herself up.

Something, nevertheless, like internal revival, once more, to her
own unspeakable amazement, began fluttering at her breast. She
had seen the beloved of her heart—dearer to her far than the life
she thought herself resigning; seen him penetrated to anguish by
her situation, awakened to the tenderest recollections, and upon
her hand had dropt a testimony of his sensibility, that, dead as she
had thought herself to the world, its views, its hopes, its cares,
passed straight to her heart—that wonderful repository of
successive emotions, whence the expulsion of one species of
interest but makes way for the entrance of another; and which

vainly, while yet in mortal life, builds, even from hour to hour, upon any chasm of mortal solicitude.

While wrapt up in this reverie, poignantly agitating, yet undefinably soothing, upon the return of Edgar to England, and his astonishing appearance in her room, her attention was again aroused by another gentle tap at the door.

Peggy opened it, and left the room; but soon came back, to beg an answer to the note, for which the gentleman was waiting upon the stairs.

'Waiting?' she repeated, in extreme trepidation, 'is he not then gone?'

'No ma'am, only out of the room; he can't go away without the answer, he says.'

A sensation of pleasure was now so new to Camilla, as almost to be too potent either for her strength or her intellects. She doubted all around her, doubted what she heard, doubted even her existence. Edgar, could it be Edgar who was waiting for an answer? . . . who was under the same roof—who had been in the same room—who was now separated from her but by a thin wainscot?—'O no, no, no!' she cried, 'my senses all delude me! one vision after another beguiles my deranged imagination!' Yet she called Peggy to her again, again asked her if it were indeed true; and, bidding her once more bring the candle, the new spirit with which she was invigorated, enabled her to persevere in her efforts, till she made out the following lines; which were sealed, but not directed.

'The sorrow, the tumult of my soul, I attempt not to paint.— Forgive, O Camilla! an intrusion which circumstances made resistless. Deign to bury in kind oblivion all remembrance but of our early friendship—our intuitive attachment, our confidence, esteem, and happy juvenile intercourse; and under such auspices —animated as they are innocent—permit me to hasten Mrs. Tyrold to this spot, or trust me—I conjure—with the mystery of this dreadful desolation—O Camilla!—by all the scenes that have passed between us—by the impression indelible they have engraved upon my heart, wound not the most faithful of your friends by rejecting his services!

E. M.'

Dissolved in tears of tenderness, relieving, nay delightful, she immediately sent him word that she accepted his kind office, and should feel eternal gratitude if he would acquaint her friends with her situation.

Peggy soon informed her the gentleman was gone; and she then inquired why he had been brought to her as a clergyman.

The little girl gave the account with the utmost simplicity. Her mistress, she said, knew the gentleman very well, who was 'Squire Mandlebert, and lived at a great house not many miles off; and had just alighted to bait his horses, as she went to ask about sending for the clergyman. He inquired who was ill; and her Mistress said it was a Lady who had gone out of her mind, by seeing a dead body, and raved of nothing but having prayers read to her; which her husband would do, when his house was clear, if the humour lasted: for they had nobody to send three miles off; and by drawing the curtains, she would not know if it was a clergyman or not. The young 'Squire then asked if she was a lodger or a traveller, and her mistress answered: 'She's a traveller, Sir; and if it had not been for Peggy's knowing her, we should have been afraid who she might be; for she stays here, and never pays us; only she has given us a watch and a locket for pledges.' Then he asked on some more questions, continued Peggy, and presently desired to see the locket; and when he had looked at it, he turned as white as a sheet, and said he must see the lady. Her mistress said she was laid down upon the bed, and she could not send in a gentleman; unless it was her husband, just to quiet her poor head by reading her a prayer or too. So then the 'Squire said he'd take the prayer book and read to her himself, if she'd spare time to go in the room first, and shut up the curtains. So her mistress said no, at first; but Peggy said the poor lady fretted on so badly, that presently up they came together.

Ah! dear darling locket! internally cried Camilla, how from the first have I loved—how to the last will I prize it! Ah dear darling locket! how for ever—while I live—will I wear it in my bosom!

A calm now took place of her agonies that made her seem in a renovated existence, till sleep, by gentle approaches, stole upon her again: not to bring to her the dread vision which accompanied its first return; nor yet to allow her tranquil repose. A softer form appeared before her; more afflictive, though not so horrible; it was the form of her Mother; all displeasure removed from her penetrating countenance; no longer in her dying child viewing the child that had offended her; yet while forgiving and embracing, seeing her expire in her arms.

She awakened, affrighted,—she started, she sat upright; she called aloud upon her mother, and wildly looking round, thought she saw her at the foot of the bed.

She crossed her eyes with her hands, to endeavour to clear her sight: but the object only seemed more distinct. She bent forward, seeking conviction, yet incredulous, though still meeting the same form.

Sighing, at last, from fruitless fatigue; ''Tis wondrous odd,' she cried, 'but I now never know when I wake or when I sleep!'

The form glided away; but with motion so palpable, she could no longer believe herself played upon by imagination. Awe-imprest, and wonder-struck, she softly opened her side curtain to look after it. It had stopt by a high chest of drawers, against which, leaning its head upon its arm, it stood erect, but seemed weeping. She could not discern the face; but the whole figure had the same sacred resemblance.

The pulses of her head beat now with so much violence, she was forced to hold her temples. Doubt, dread, and hope seized every faculty at once; till, at length, the upraised arm of the form before her dropt, and she distinctly saw the profile: 'It is herself! it is my Mother!' she screamed, rather than pronounced, and threw herself from the bed to the floor.

'Yes! it is your Mother!' was repeated, in a tone solemn and penetrating;—'to what a scene, O Camilla, returned! her house abandoned ... her son in exile ... her Eugenia lost ... her husband, the prop of all! ... where she dare not name! ... and thou, the child of her bosom! ... the constant terrour, yet constant darling of her soul ... where, and how, does she see, does she meet thee, again—O Camilla!'

Then tenderly, though with anguish, bending over her, she would have raised, and helped her to return to the bed: but Camilla would not be aided; she would not lift up her eyes; her face sought the ground, where leaning it upon her hands, without desiring to speak, without wishing to stir, torn by self-reproaches that made her deem herself unworthy to live, she remained speechless, immoveable.

'Repress, repress,' said Mrs. Tyrold, gently, yet firmly, 'these strong feelings, uselessly torturing to us both. Raise your head, my poor girl . . . raise . . . and repose it upon the breast of your Mother.'

'Of my Mother?' repeated Camilla, in a voice hardly audible; 'have I a Mother—who again will own the blast of her hopes and happiness?—the disgrace, the shame of the best and most injured of Fathers!'

'Let us pray,' said Mrs. Tyrold, with a sigh, 'that these evils may pass away, and by salutary exertions, not desponding repinings, earn back our fugitive peace.'

Again she then would have raised her; but Camilla sunk from all assistance: 'No,' she cried, 'I am unworthy your lenity—I am unable even to bear it, . . .'

'Camilla,' said Mrs. Tyrold, steadily, 'it is time to conquer this impetuous sensibility, which already, in its effects, has nearly broken all our hearts. With what horrour have we missed—with what agony sought you! Now then, that at length, we find you, excite not new terrour, by consigning yourself to willing despair.'

Struck with extreme dread of committing yet further wrong, she lifted up her head, with intention to have risen; but the weak state of her body, forgotten by herself, and by Mrs. Tyrold unsuspected, took its turn for demanding attention.

'Alas! my poor Child,' cried she, 'what horrible havock has this short absence produced! O Camilla! . . . with a soul of feeling like yours,—strong, tender, generous, and but too much alive, how is it you can thus have forgotten the first ties of your duty, and your heart, and have been wrought upon by your own sorrows to forget the sorrows you inflict? Why have you thus fled us? thus abandoned yourself to destruction? Was our anger to be set in competition with our misery? Was the fear of displeasure, from parents who so tenderly love you, to be indulged at the risk of never ending regret to the most lenient of Fathers? and nearly the loss of senses to a Mother who, from your birth, has idolized you in her inmost soul?'

Bending then over her, she folded her in her arms; where Camilla, overpowered with the struggles of joy and contrition, sunk nearly lifeless.

Mrs. Tyrold, seeing now her bodily feebleness, put her to bed, with words of soothing tenderness, no longer blended with retrospective investigation; conjuring her to be calm, to remember whose peace and happiness were encircled in her life and health, and to remit to her fuller strength all further interesting discourse.

'Ah, my Mother!' cried Camilla, 'tell me first—if the time may ever come when with truth you can forgive me?'

'Alas, my darling Child!' answered the generous Mother, 'I have myself now to pardon that I forgave thee not at first!'

Camilla seemed transported to another region; with difficulty Mrs. Tyrold could hold her in her bed, though hovering over her pillow with incessant caresses: but to raise her eye only to meet that of her Mother—not as her fertile terrour had prophesied, darting unrelenting ire, but softly solicitous, and exquisitely kind; to feel one loved hand anxiously upon her forehead, and to glue her own lips upon the other; to find fears that had made existence insupportable, transformed into security that rendered it delicious; —with a floating, uncertain, yet irrepressible hope, that to Edgar she owed this restoration, caused a revulsion in all her feelings, that soon operated upon her frame—not, indeed, with tranquillity, but with rapture approaching to delirium:—when suddenly, a heavy, lumbering noise, appalled her. 'Ah, my Mother!' she faintly cried, 'our beloved Eugenia! . . . that noise . . . where— and how—is Eugenia?—The wretched Mr. Bellamy is no more!'

Mrs. Tyrold answered, she was acquainted with the whole dreadful business, and would relate it in a season of more serenity; but meanwhile, as repose, she well knew, never associated with suspence, she satisfied immediate anxiety, by assurances that Eugenia was safe, and at Etherington.

This was a joy scarce inferior to that which so recently had transported her: but Mrs. Tyrold, gathering from the good Peggy, that she had not been in bed, nor scarce tasted food, since she had been at the half-way-house, refused all particulars, till she had been refreshed with nourishment and rest. The first immediately was ordered, and immediately taken; and Mrs. Tyrold, to propitiate the second, insisted upon total silence, and prepared to sit up with her all night.

Long as the extreme agitation of her spirits distanced

Tir'd Nature's sweet restorer, balmy sleep,[*1]

the change from so much misery to heart-felt peace and joy, with the judicious nursing and restoratives devised by Mrs. Tyrold,

* Young

for her weak and half famished frame, made her slumber, when at length, it arrived, last so long that, though broken by frequent starts, she awoke not till late the next morning.

Her eyes then opened upon a felicity that again made her think herself in a new world. Her Mother, leaning over her, was watching her breathe, with hands uplifted for her preservation, and looks of fondness which seemed to mark that her happiness depended upon its being granted; but as she raised herself, to throw her arms around the loved maternal neck, the shadow of another form, quickly, yet gently receding, struck her sight; . . . 'Ah, Heaven!' she exclaimed, 'who is that?'

'Will you be good,' said Mrs. Tyrold, gently, 'be tranquil, be composed, and earn that I should tell you who has been watching by you this hour?'

Camilla could not answer; certain, now, who it must be, her emotions became again uncontrollable; her horrour, her remorse, her self-abhorrence revived, and agonizingly exclaiming, ''Tis my Father!—O, where can I hide my head?' She strove again to envelop herself with the bed-curtain from all view.

'Here—in his own arms—upon his own breast you shall hide it,' said Mr. Tyrold, returning to the bed-side, 'and all now shall be forgotten, but thankfulness that our afflictions seem finding their period.'

'O my Father! my Father!' cried Camilla, forgetting her situation, in her desire to throw herself at his feet, 'can you speak to me thus, after the woe—the disgrace I have brought upon you?—I deserve your malediction! . . . I expected to be shut out from your heart,—I thought myself abandoned—I looked forward only in death to receiving your forgiveness!—'

Mrs. Tyrold held her still, while her Father now blessed and embraced her, each uttering, in the same moment, whatever was softest to console her: but all her quick feelings were re-awakened beyond their power to appease them; her penitence tortured, her very gratitude tore her to pieces: 'O my Mother,' she cried, 'how do you forbear to spurn me? Can you think of what is passed, and still pronounce your pardon? Will you not draw it back at the sight of my injured Father? Are you not tempted to think I deserve eternal banishment from you both?—and to repent that you have not ordered it?'

'No, my dearest Child, no! I lament only that I took you not at once to your proper security—to these arms, my Camilla, that now so fondly infold you! to this bosom—my darling girl!—where my heart beats your welcome!'

'You make me too—too happy! the change is almost killing! my Mother—my dearest Mother!—I did not think you would permit me to ever call you so again! My Father I knew would pardon me, for the chief suffering was his own; but even he, I never expected could look at me thus benignly again! and hardly—hardly would he have been tried, if the evil had been reversed!'

Mr. Tyrold exhorted her to silent composure; but finding her agitation over-power even her own efforts, he summoned her to join him in solemn thanks for her restoration.

Awfully, though most gratefully, impressed by such a call, she checked her emotion, and devoutly obeyed: and the short but pious ceremony quieted her nerves, and calmed her mind.

The gentlest tranquillity then took place in her breast, of the tumultuous joy which had first chaced her deadly affliction. The soothing, however serious turn, given by devotion to her changed sensations, softened the acute excess of rapture which mounted felicity nearly to agony. More eloquent, as well as safer than any speech, was the pause of deep gratitude, the silence of humble praise, which ensued. Camilla, in each hand held one of each beloved Parent; alternately she pressed them with grateful reverence to her lips, alternately her eye sought each revered countenance, and received, in the beaming fondness they emitted, a benediction that was balm to every woe.

CHAPTER XII

Means to obtain a Boon

MR. Tyrold was soon, by urgent claims, forced to leave them; and Camilla, with strong secret anxiety to know if Edgar had caused this blest meeting, led to a general explanation upon past events.

And now, to her utter amazement, she found that her letter sent by the labourer had never been received.

Mrs. Tyrold related, that she had no sooner read the first letter addressed to her through Lavinia, than, softened and affected, she wrote an answer of the utmost kindness to Belfont; desiring Camilla to continue with her sister till called for by Miss Margland, in her return home from Mrs. Macdersey. The visit, meanwhile to Cleves, had transpired through Jacob, and, much touched by, yet much blaming her travelling thus alone, she wrote to her a second time, charging her to remove no more from Belfont without Miss Margland. But, on the preceding morning, the first letter had been returned with a note from Eugenia, that her sister had set out two days before for Etherington.

The moment of this intelligence, was the most dreadful to Mr. Tyrold and herself of their lives. Every species of conjecture was horrible. He set out instantly for Belfont, determining to make enquiries at every inn, house, and cottage, by the way; but by taking, unfortunately, the road through Alton, he had missed the half-way-house. In the evening, while, with apprehensions surpassing all description, she was waiting some news, a chaise drove up to the door. She flew out, but saw in it . . . alone, cold, trembling, and scarce in her senses, Eugenia. Instantly imagining she came with tidings of fatal tendency concerning Camilla, she started back, exclaiming, 'All, then, is over?' The chaise-door had been opened; but Eugenia, shaking too violently to get out; only, and faintly, answered, 'Yes! my Mother . . . all is over!—' The mistake was almost instantaneous death to her—though the next words of Eugenia cleared it up, and led to her own dreadful narrative.

Bellamy, as soon as Camilla had left Belfont, had made a peremptory demand that his wife should claim, as if for some purpose of her own, a large sum of Sir Hugh. Her steady resistance sent him from the house in a rage; and she saw no more of him till that day at noon, when he returned in deeper, blacker wrath than she had ever yet seen; and vowed that nothing less than her going in person to her uncle with his request, should induce him ever to forgive her. When he found her resolute in refusal, he ordered a chaise, and made her get into it, without saying for what purpose. She saw they were travelling towards Cleves, but he did not once speak, except where they changed horses, till they came upon the cross-road, leading to the half-way-house. Suddenly then, bidding the postillion stop at the end of a lane, he told him he was going to look at a little farm, and, ordering him to wait,

made her alight and walk down it till they were out of sight of the
man and the carriage. Fiercely, then stopping short, 'Will you
give me,' he cried, 'your promise, upon oath, that you will ask
your Uncle for the money?' 'Indeed, Mr. Bellamy, I cannot!' she
answered. 'Enough!' he cried, and took from his pocket a pistol.
'Good Heaven,' she said, 'you will not murder me?'—'I cannot
live without the money myself,' he answered, 'and why should I
let you?' He then felt in his waistcoat pocket, whence he took two
bullets, telling her, she should have the pleasure of seeing him
load the pistol; and that when one bullet had dispatched her, the
other should disappoint the executioner. Horrour now conquered
her, and she solemnly promised to ask whatever he dictated. 'I
must hold the pistol to your ear,' cried he, 'while you take your
oath. See! 'tis loaded—This is no child's play.' He then lifted it
up; but, at the same moment, a distant voice exclaimed, 'Hold,
villain! or you are a dead man!' Starting, and meaning to hide it
within his waistcoat, his hand shook—the pistol went off—it shot
him through the body, and he dropt down dead. Without sense
or motion, she fell by his side; and, upon recovering, found
herself again in the chaise. The postillion, who knew her, had
carried her thither, and brought her on to Etherington. She then
conjured that proper persons might go back with the driver, and
that her Father would have the benevolence to superintend all
that could be done that would be most respectfully decent.

The postillion acknowledged that it was himself who had cried,
Hold, villain! A suspicion of some mischief had occurred to him,
from seeing the end of a pistol jerk from the pocket of the gentleman, as he got out of the chaise; and begging a man, who
accidentally passed while he waited, to watch his horses, he ran
down a field by the side of the lane, whence he heard the words:
'The pistol is loaded, and for no child's play!' upon which, seeing
it raised, and the young Lady shrink, he called out. Yet Eugenia
protested herself convinced that Bellamy had no real design
against either his own life or her's, though terrour, at the moment,
had conquered her: he had meant but to affright her into consent,
knowing well her word once given, with whatever violence torn
from her, would be held sacred. The rest was dreadful accident,
or Providence in that form playing upon himself his own toils.
The pious young Widow was so miserable at this shocking exit,
and the shocking manner in which the remains were left exposed,

that her Mother had set out herself to give orders in person, from
the half-way-house, for bringing thither the body, till Mr. Tyrold
could give his own directions. She found, however, that business
already done. The man called by the postillion had been joined by a
party of labourers, just leaving off work; those had gathered
others; they had procured some broad planks which served for a
bier, and had humanely conveyed the body to the inn, where the
landlord was assured the postillion would come back with some
account of him, though little Peggy had only learnt in general
that he had been found murdered near a wood.

'Eugenia is just now,' said Mrs. Tyrold, in conclusion, 'plunged
into an abyss of ideas, frightful to her humanity, and oppressive
to the tenderness of her heart. Her nature is too noble to rejoice
in a release to herself, worked by means so horrible, and big with
notions of retribution for the wretched culprit, at which even
vengeance the most implacable might shudder. Nevertheless, all
will imperceptibly pass away, save the pity inherent in all good
minds for vice and its penalties. To know his abrupt punishment,
and not to be shocked, would be inhuman; but to grieve with any
regard for a man of such principles and conduct, would be an
outrage to all that they have injured and offended.'

This view of the transaction, by better reconciling Camilla to
the ultimate lot of her sister, brought her back to reflect upon her
own. Still she had not gathered with precision how she had been
discovered. To pronounce the name of Edgar was impossible;
but after a long pause, which Mrs. Tyrold had hoped was given
again to repose, she ventured to say, 'I have not yet heard, my
dearest Mother, to what benign chance I immediately owe my
present unspeakable, unmerited happiness?'

Mrs. Tyrold looked at her a moment in silence, as if to read
what her question offered beyond its mere words: but she saw
her eye hastily withdrawn from the examination, and her cheeks
suddenly enveloped with the bed cloaths.

Quietly, and without turning towards her again, she resumed
her narrative.

'I engaged the worthy postillion of my poor Eugenia to drive
me, purposing to send Ambrose on with him, while I waited at
the half-way-house: but, about two miles off, Ambrose, who rode
before, was stopt by a gentleman, whom he met in a post chaise;
when I came up to him, I stopt also. It was Mr. Mandlebert.'

Camilla, who had looked up, now again hastily drew back, and Mrs. Tyrold, after a short pause, went on.

'His intelligence, of course, finished my search. My first idea was to convey you instantly home; but the particulars I gathered made me fear removing you. When I entered your room, you were asleep;—I dreaded to surprise yet could not refrain taking a view of you, and while I looked, you suddenly awoke.'

Ah! thought Camilla, 'tis to Edgar, then, that ultimately I owe this blest moment!

'But my Father,' she cried, 'my dearest Mother,—how came my dear Father to know where you had found me?'

'At Belfont he learnt the way you had set out, and that Eugenia and Bellamy were from home; and, without loss of time . . . regardless of the night and of fasting, . . . he returned by a route through which he traced you at every inn where you had changed horses. He, also, entered as you were sleeping—and we watched together by your side.'

Again filial gratitude silenced all but itself, and sleep, the softest she had known for many months, soon gave to oblivion every care in Camilla.

The changeful tide of mental spirits from misery to enjoyment, is not more rapid than the transition from personal danger to safety, in the elastic period of youth. 'Tis the epoch of extremes; and moderation, by which alone we learn the true use of our blessings, is a wisdom we are frequently only taught to appreciate when redundance no longer requires its practice.

Camilla, from sorrow the most desolate, bounded to joy that refused a solicitude; and from an illness that held her suspended between delirium and dissolution, to ease that had no complaint. The sufferings which had deprived her of the benefit of rest and nourishment were no sooner removed, than she appeared to be at once restored to health; though to repair the wastes of strength some time yet was necessary.

Mrs. Tyrold determined to carry her this afternoon to Etherington. The remains of the wretched Bellamy, in a coffin and hearse brought from Winchester, had been sent to Belfont in the morning: and Mr. Tyrold had followed, to give every direction that he should be buried as the master of the house; without reference to the conduct which had forfeited all such respect.

Though the evil committed by the non-deliverance of Camilla's letter was now past all remedy, Mrs. Tyrold thought it every way right to endeavour to discover where [lay] the blame: and by the two usual modes of menace and promises, she learnt that the countryman, when he stopt to drink by the way, had, in lighting his pipe, let the letter take fire; and fearing to lose the recompense he had expected, had set his conscience apart for a crown, and returned with the eventful falsehood, which had made Camilla think herself abandoned, and her friends deplore her as lost.

For the benefit of those with whom, in future, he might have to deal, Mrs. Tyrold took some pains to represent to him the cruel evils his dishonesty had produced; but, stupid rather than wicked, what he had done had been without weighing right from wrong, and what he heard was without understanding it.

Camilla found, with extreme satisfaction, that Mrs. Tyrold, notwithstanding the strictness of the present family œconomy, meant liberally to recompense Mrs. Marl, for the trouble and patience with which she had attended to a guest so little profitable: while Peggy, to whose grateful remembrance she owed the consideration she had met with in her deserted condition, was rewarded by a much larger sum than she had ever before possessed. Camilla was obliged to confess she had parted with two pledges for future payment: the watch was reclaimed without difficulty; but she shewed so much distress in naming the locket, that Mrs. Tyrold, though she looked anxiously surprised, demanded it without enquiring into its history.

The excess of delight to Camilla in preparing to return to Etherington, rendered her insensible to all fatigue, till she was descending the stairs; when the recollection of the shock she had received from the corpse of Bellamy, made her tremble so exceedingly, that she could scarce walk past the door of the room in which it had been laid. 'Ah, my dearest Mother,' she cried, 'this house must give me always the most penetrating sensations: I have experienced in it the deepest grief, and the most heart-soothing enjoyment that ever, perhaps, gave place one to the other in so short a time!'

                    *   *   *   *

Ambrose had announced their intended arrival, and at the door of the house, the timid, but affectionate Lavinia was waiting to receive them; and as Camilla, in alighting, met her tender embraces, a well-known voice reached her ears, calling out in hurried accents, 'Where is she? Is she come indeed? Are you quite sure?' And Sir Hugh, hobbling rather than walking into the hall, folded her in his feeble arms, sobbing over her: 'I can't believe it for joy! Poor sinner that I am, and the cause of all our bad doings! how can I have deserved such a thing as this, to have my own little Girl come back to me? which could not have made my heart gladder, if I had had no share in all this bad mischief! which, God knows I've had enough, owing to my poor head doing always for the worst, for all my being the oldest of us all; which is a thing I've often thought remarkable enough, in the point of my knowing no better; which however, I hope my dear little Darling will excuse for the sake of my love, which is never happy but in seeing her.'

The heart of Camilla bounded with grateful joy at sight of this dear Uncle, and at so tender a reception: and while with equal emotion, and equal weakness, they were unable to support either each other or themselves, the worthy old Jacob, his eyes running over, came to help his Master back to the parlour, and Mrs. Tyrold and Lavinia conveyed thither Camilla: who was but just placed upon a sofa, by the side of her fond Uncle, when the door of an inner apartment was softly opened, and pale, wan, and meagre, Eugenia appeared at it, saying, as faintly, yet with open arms, she advanced to Camilla: 'Let me too—your poor harassed, and but half-alive Eugenia, make one in this precious scene! Let me see the joy of my kind Uncle—the revival of my honoured Mother, the happiness of my dear Lavinia—and feel even my own heart beat once more with delight in the bosom of its darling Sister! ... my so mourned—but now for ever, I trust, restored to me, most dear Camilla!'

Camilla, thus encircled in her Mother's, Uncle's, Sister's, arms at once, gasped, sighed, smiled, and shed tears in the same grateful minute, while fondly she strove to articulate, 'Am I again at Etherington and at Cleves in one? And thus indulgently received? thus more than forgiven? My heart wants room for its joy! my Mother! my Sisters! if you knew what despair has been my portion! I feared even the sight of my dear Uncle himself, lest the sorrows and the errours of a creature he so kindly loved, should have demolished his generous heart!'

'Mine, my dearest little Girl?' cried the Baronet, 'why what would that have signified, in comparison to such a young one as yours, that ought to know no sorrow yet a while? God knows, it being time enough to begin: for it is but melancholy at best, the cares of the world; which if you can't keep off now, will be overtaking you at every turn.'

Mrs. Tyrold entreated Camilla might be spared further conversation. Eugenia had already glided back to her chamber, and begged, this one solacing interview over, to be dispensed with from joining the family at present; Camilla was removed also to her chamber; and the tender Mother divided her time and her cares between these two recovered treasures of her fondest affection.

CHAPTER XIII

Questions and Answers

MR. Tyrold did not return till the next day from Belfont, where, through the account he gave from his Daughter, the violent exit of the miserable Bellamy was brought in accidental death. Various circumstances had now acquainted him with the history of that wretched man, who was the younger son of the master of a great gaming-house. In his first youth, he had been utterly neglected, and left to run wild whither he chose; but his father afterwards becoming very rich, had bestowed upon him as good an education as the late period at which it was begun could allow. He was intended for a lucrative business; but he had no application, and could retain no post: he went into the army; but he had no courage, and was speedily cashiered. Inheriting a passion for the means by which the parental fortune had been raised, he devoted himself next to its pursuit, and won very largely. But as extravagance and good luck, by long custom, go hand in hand, he spent as fast as he acquired; and upon a tide of fortune in his disfavour, was tempted to reverse the chances by unfair play, was found out, and as ignominiously chaced from the field of hazard as from that of patriotism. His father was no more; his eldest brother would not assist him; he sold therefore his house, and all he possessed but his wardrobe, and, relying upon a very uncommonly handsome face and person, determined to seek a fairer lot, by eloping, if possible, with some heiress. He thought it, however, prudent not only to retire from London, but to make a little change in his name, which from Nicholas Gwigg he refined into Alphonso Bellamy. He began his career by a tour into Wales; where he insinuated himself into the acquaintance of Mrs. Ecton, just after she had married Miss Melmond to Mr. Berlinton: and though this was not an intercourse that could travel to Gretna Green, the beauty and romantic turn of the bride of so disproportioned a marriage, opened to his unprincipled mind a scheme yet more flagitious. Fortunately, however, for his fair destined prey, soon after the connexion was formed, she left Wales; and the search of new adventures carried him, by various chances, into Hampshire. But he had established with her, a correspondence, and when he had caught, or rather forced, an heiress into legal snares, the discovery of who and what he was, became less important, and he ventured again to town, and renewed his heinous plan, as well as his inveterate early habits; till surprised by some unpleasant recollectors, debts of honour, which he had found it convenient to elude upon leaving the Capital, were claimed, and he found it impossible to appear without satisfying such demands. Thence his cruel and inordinate persecution of his unhappy wife for money; and thence, ultimately, the brief vengeance which had reverberated upon his own head.

*　　*　　*　　*

Camilla, whose danger was the result of self-neglect, as her sufferings had all flowed from mental anguish, was already able to go down to the study upon the arrival of Mr. Tyrold: where she received, with grateful rapture, the tender blessings which welcomed her to the paternal arms—to her home—to peace—to safety—and primæval joy.

Mr. Tyrold, sparing to her yet weak nerves any immediate explanations upon the past, called upon his wife to aid him to communicate, in the quietest manner, what had been done at

Belfont to Eugenia; charging Camilla to take no part in a scene inevitably shocking.

Once more in the appropriate apartment of her Father, where all her earliest scenes of gayest felicity had passed, but which, of late, she had only approached with terrour, only entered to weep, she experienced a delight almost awful in the renovation of her pristine confidence, and fearless ease. She took from her pocket—where alone she could ever bear to keep it—her loved locket, delighting to attribute to it this restoration to domestic enjoyment; though feeling at the same time, a renewal of suspence from the return of its donor, and from the affecting interview into which she had been surprised, that broke in upon even her filial happiness, with bitter, tyrannical regret. Yet she pressed to her bosom the cherished symbol of first regard, and was holding it to her lips, when Mrs. Tyrold, unexpectedly, re-entered the room.

In extreme confusion, she shut it into its shagreen case, and was going to restore it to her pocket; but infolding it, with her daughter's hand, between each of her own, Mrs. Tyrold said, 'Shall I ever, my dear girl, learn the history of this locket?'

'O yes, my dearest Mother,' said the blushing Camilla, 'of that—and of every—and of all things—you have only—you have merely—'

'If it distresses you, my dear child, we will leave it to another day,' said Mrs. Tyrold, whose eyes Camilla saw, as she now raised her own, were swimming in tears.

'My Mother! my dearest Mother!' cried she, with the tenderest alarm, 'has any thing new happened?—Is Eugenia greatly affected?'

'She is all, every way, and in every respect,' said Mrs. Tyrold, 'whatever the fondest, or even the proudest Mother could wish. But I do not at this instant most think of her. I am not without some fears for my Camilla's strength, in the immediate demand that may be made upon her fortitude. Tell me, my child, with that sincerity which so long has been mutually endearing between us, tell me if you think you can see here, again, and as usual, without any risk to your health, one long admitted and welcomed as a part of the family?'

She started, changed colour, looked up, cast her eyes on the floor; but soon seeing Mrs. Tyrold hold an handkerchief bathed in tears to her face, lost all dread, and even all consciousness in tender gratitude, and throwing her arms round her neck, 'O my

Mother,' she cried, 'you who weep not for yourself—scarcely even in the most poignant sorrow—can you weep for me?—I will see—or I will avoid whoever you please—I shall want no fortitude, I shall fear nothing—no one—not even myself—now again under your protection! I will scarcely even think, my beloved Mother, but by your guidance!'

'Compose yourself, then, my dearest girl: and, if you believe you are equal to behaving with firmness, I will not refuse his request of re-admission.'

'His request?' repeated Camilla, with involuntary quickness; but finding Mrs. Tyrold did not notice it, gently adding, 'That person that—I believe—you mean—has done nothing, my dear Mother, to merit expulsion!—'

'I am happy to hear you say so: I have been fearfully, I must own, and even piercingly displeased with him.'

'Ah, my dear Mother! how kind was the partiality that turned your displeasure so wrong a way! that made you,—even you, my dear Mother, listen to your fondness rather than to your justice!—'

She trembled at the temerity of this vindication the moment it had escaped her, and looking another way, spoke again of Eugenia: but Mrs. Tyrold now, taking both her hands, and seeking, though vainly, to meet her eyes, said, 'My dearest child, I grow painfully anxious to end a thousand doubts; to speak and to hear with no further ambiguity, nor reserve. If Edgar—'

Camilla again changed colour, and strove to withdraw her hands.

'Take courage, my dear love, and let one final explanation relieve us both at once. If Edgar has merited well of you, why are you parted?—If ill—why this solicitude my opinion of him should be unshaken?'

Her head now dropt upon Mrs. Tyrold's shoulder, as she faintly answered, 'He deserves your good opinion, my dearest Mother—for he adores you—I cannot be unjust to him,—though he has made me—I own—not very happy!'

'Designedly, my Camilla?'

'O, no, my dearest Mother!—he would not do that to an enemy!'

'Speak out, then, and speak clearer, my dearest Camilla. If you think of him so well, and are so sure of his good intentions, what —in two words,—what is it that has parted you?'

'Accident, my dearest Mother,—deluding appearances, . . . and false internal reasoning on my part,—and on his, continual misconstruction! O my dearest Mother! how have I missed your guiding care! I had ever the semblance, by some cruel circumstance, some inexplicable fatality of incident, to neglect his counsel, oppose his judgment, deceive his expectations, and trifle with his regard!—Yet, with a heart faithful, grateful, devoted,—O my dearest Mother!—with an esteem that defies all comparison, . . . a respect closely meliorating even to veneration! . . . Never was heart . . . my dearest Mother, so truly impressed with the worth of another . . . with the nobleness. . . .'

A buzzing noise from the adjoining parlour, sounding something between a struggle and a dispute, suddenly stopt her, . . . and as she raised her head from the bosom of her Mother, in which she had seemed seeking shelter from the very confidence she was pouring forth, she saw the door opened, and the object of whom she was speaking appear at it. . . . Fluttered, colouring, trembling, . . . yet with eyes refulgent with joy, and every feature speaking ecstasy.

Almost fainting with shame and surprise, she gave herself up as disgraced, if not dishonoured evermore, for a short, but bitter half moment. It was not longer. Edgar, rushing forward, and seizing the hands of Mrs Tyrold, even while they were encircling her drooping, shrinking, half expiring Camilla, pressed them with ardent respect to his lips, rapidly exclaiming, 'My more than Mother! my dear, kind, excellent, inestimable friend!—Forgive this blest intrusion—plead for me where I dare not now speak— and raise your indeed maternal eyes upon the happiest—the most devoted of your family!'

'What is it overpowers me thus this morning?' cried Mrs. Tyrold, leaning her head upon her clinging Camilla, while large drops fell from her eyes; 'Misfortune, I see, is not the greatest test of our philosophy! . . . Joy, twice today, has completely demolished mine!'

'What goodness is this! what encouragement to hope some indulgent intercession here—where the sense that now breaks in upon me of ungenerous . . . ever to be lamented—and I had nearly said, execrated doubt, fills me with shame and regret— and makes me—even at this soft reviving, heart-restoring moment, feel undeserving my own hopes!'—

'Shall I . . . may I leave him to make his peace?' whispered Mrs. Tyrold to her daughter, whose head sought concealment even to annihilation; but whose arms, with what force they possessed, detained her, uttering faintly but rapidly, 'O no, no, no!'

'My more than Mother!' again cried Edgar, 'I will wait till that felicity may be accorded me, and put myself wholly under your kind and powerful influence. One thing alone I must say;—I have too much to answer for, to take any share of the misdemeanors of another!—I have not been a treacherous listener, though a wilful obtruder. . . . See, Mrs. Tyrold! who placed me in that room—who is the accomplice of my happiness!'

With a smile that seemed to beam but the more brightly for her glistening eyes, Mrs. Tyrold looked to the door, and saw there, leaning against it, the form she most revered; surveying them all with an expression of satisfaction so perfect, contentment so benign, and pleasure mingled with so much thankfulness, that her tears now flowed fast from unrestrained delight; and Mr. Tyrold, approaching to press at once the two objects of his most exquisite tenderness to his breast, said, 'This surprise was not planned, but circumstances made it more than irresistible. It was not, however, quite fair to my Camilla, and if she is angry, we will be self-exiled till she can pardon us.'

'This is such a dream,'—cried Camilla, as now, first, from the voice of her Father she believed it reality; 'so incredible . . . so unintelligible . . . I find it entirely . . . impossible . . . impossible to comprehend any thing I see or hear!'—

'Let the past, . . . not the present,' cried Edgar, 'be regarded as the dream! and generously drive it from your mind as a fever of the brain, with which reason had no share, and for which memory must find no place.'

'If I could understand in the least,' said Camilla, 'what this all means . . . what——'

Mr. Tyrold now insisted that Edgar should retreat, while he made some explanation; and then related to his trembling, doubting, wondering daughter, the following circumstances.

In returning from Belfont, he had stopt at the half-way-house, where he had received from Mrs. Marl, a letter that, had it reached him as it was intended, at Etherington, would have quickened the general meeting, yet nearly have broken his heart. It was that

which, for want of a messenger, had never been sent, and which
Peggy, in cleaning the bed room, had found under a table, where
it had fallen, she supposes, when the candle was put upon it for
reading prayers.

'There was another letter, too!' interrupted Camilla, with
quick blushing recollection;—'but my illness . . . and all that has
followed, made me forget them both till this very moment . . .
Did she say anything of any . . . other?'

'Yes; . . . the other had been delivered according to its address.'

'Good Heaven!'

'Be not frightened, my Camilla, . . . all has been beautifully
directed for the best. My accomplice had received his early in the
morning; he was at the house, by some fortunate hazard, when it
was found, and, being well known there, Mrs. Marl gave it to him
immediately.'

'How terrible! . . . It was meant only in case . . . I had seen no
one any more!' . . .

'The intent, and the event, have been happily, my child, at war.
He came instantly hither, and enquired for me; I was not
returned; he asked my route, and rode to follow or meet me.
About an hour ago, we encountered upon the road: he gave his
horse to his groom, and came into the chaise to me.'

Camilla now could with difficulty listen; but her Father
hastened to acquaint her, that Edgar, with the most generous
apologies, the most liberal self-blame, had re-demanded his
consent for a union, from which every doubt was wholly, and
even miraculously removed, by learning thus the true feelings of
her heart, as depicted at the awful crisis of expected dissolution.
The returning smiles which forced their way now through the
tears and blushes of Camilla, shewed how vainly she strove to
mingle the regret of shame with the felicity of fond security,
produced by this eventful accident. But when she further heard
that Edgar, in Flanders, had met with Lionel, who, in frankly
recounting his difficulties and adventures, had named some
circumstances which had so shaken every opinion that had urged
him to quit England, as to induce him instantly, from the conference, to seek a passage for his return, she felt all but happiness
retire from her heart;—vanish even from her ideas.

'You are not angry, then,' said Mr. Tyrold, as smilingly he
read her delighted sensations, 'that I waited not to consult you?

That I gave back at once my consent? That I folded him again in my arms? . . . again . . . called him my son?'

She could but seek the same pressure; and he continued, 'I would not bring him in with me; I was not aware my dear girl was so rapidly recovered, and I had a task to fulfil to my poor Eugenia that was still my first claim. But I promised within an hour, your Mother, at least, should welcome him. He would walk, he said, for that period. When I met her, I hinted at what was passing, and she followed me to our Eugenia; I then briefly communicated my adventure; and your Mother, my Camilla, lost herself in hearing it! Will you not, . . . like me! . . . withdraw from her all reverence? Her eyes gushed with tears, . . . she wept, as you weep at this moment; she was sure Edgar Mandlebert could alone preserve you from danger, yet make you happy— Was she wrong, my dear child? Shall we attack now her judgment, as well as her fortitude?'

Only at her feet could Camilla shew her gratitude; to action she had recourse, for words were inadequate, and the tenderest caresses now spoke best for them all.

Respect for the situation of Eugenia, who had desired, for this week, to live wholly up stairs and alone, determined Mr. and Mrs. Tyrold to keep back for some time the knowledge of this event from the family. Camilla was most happy to pay such an attention to her sister; but when Mr. Tyrold was leaving her, to consult upon it with Edgar, the ingenuousness of her nature urged her irresistibly to say, 'Since all this has passed, my dearest Father—my dearest Mother—does it not seem as if I should now myself— —'

She stopt; but she was understood; they both smiled, and Mr. Tyrold immediately bringing in Edgar, said, 'I find my pardon, my dear fellow-culprit, is already accorded; if you have doubts of your own, try your eloquence for yourself.'

He left the room, and Mrs. Tyrold was gently rising to quietly follow, but Camilla, with a look of entreaty of which she knew the sincerity, and would not resist the earnestness, detained her.

'Ah yes, stay, dearest Madam!' cried Edgar, again respectfully taking her hand, 'and through your unalterable goodness, let me hope to procure pardon for a distrust which I here for ever renounce; but which had its origin in my never daring to hope what, at this moment, I have the felicity to believe. Yet now, even now, without your kind mediation, this dear convalescent may plan some probationary trial at which my whole mind, after this long suffering, revolts. Will you be my caution,[1] my dearest Mrs. Tyrold? Will you venture—and will you deign to promise, that if a full and generous forgiveness may be pronounced. . . .'

'Forgiveness?' in a soft voice interrupted Camilla: 'Have I any thing to forgive? I thought all apology—all explanation, rested on my part? and that my imprudencies—my rashness—my so often-erring judgment . . . and so apparently, almost even culpable conduct.' . . .

'O, my Camilla! my now own Camilla!' cried Edgar, venturing to change the hand of the Mother for that of the daughter; 'what too, too touching words and concessions are these! Suffer me, then, to hope a kind amnesty may take place of retrospection, a clear, liberal, open forgiveness anticipate explanation and enquiry?'

'Are you sure,' said Camilla, smiling, 'this is your interest, and not mine? . . . Does he not make a mistake, my dearest Mother, and turn my advocate, instead of his own? And can I fairly take advantage of such an errour.'

The sun-shine of her returning smiles went warm to her Mother's heart, and gave a glow to the cheeks of Edgar, and a brightness to his eyes that irradiated his whole countenance. 'Your penetrating judgment,' said he, to Mrs. Tyrold, 'will take in at once more than any professions, any protestations can urge for me: . . . you see the peace, the pardon which those eyes do not seek to withhold . . . will you then venture, my more than maternal friend! my Mother, in every meaning which affection and reverence can give to that revered appellation—will you venture at once—now—upon this dear and ever after hallowed minute—to seal the kind consent of my truly paternal guardian, and to give me an example of that trust and confidence which my whole future life shall look upon as its lesson?'

'Yes!' answered Mrs. Tyrold, instantly joining their hands, 'and with every security that the happiness of all our lives—my child's, my husband's, your's, my valued Edgar's, and my own, will all owe their felicity to the blessing with which I now lay my hands upon my two precious children!'

Tears were the only language that could express the fulness of joy which succeeded to so much sorrow; and when Mr. Tyrold

returned, and had united his tenderest benediction with that of
his beloved wife, Edgar was permitted to remain alone with
Camilla; and the close of his long doubts, and her own long
perplexities, was a reciprocal confidence that left nothing untold,
not an action unrelated, not even a thought unacknowledged.

Edgar confessed that he no sooner had quitted her, than he
suspected the justice of his decision; the turn which of late, he
had taken, doubtfully to watch her every action, and suspiciously
to judge her every motive, though it had impelled him in her
presence, ceased to operate in her absence.—He was too noble to
betray the well meant, though not well applied warnings of Dr.
Marchmont, yet he acknowledged, that when left to cool reflection,
a thousand palliations arose for every step he could not positively
vindicate: and when, afterwards, from the frank communication
of Lionel, he learnt what belonged to the mysterious offer of Sir
Sedley Clarendel, that she would superintend the disposal of his
fortune, and the deep obligation in which she had been innocently
involved, his heart smote him for having judged ere he had
investigated that transaction; and in a perturbation unspeakable
of quick repentance, and tenderness, he set out for England. But
when, at the half-way-house, he stopt as usual to rest his horses
in his way to Beech Park,—what were his emotions at the sight of
the locket, which the landlady told him had been pledged by a
lady in distress! He besought her pardon for the manner in which
he had made way to her; but the almost frantic anxiety which
seized him to know if or not it was [she], and to save her, if so,
from the intended intrusion of the landlord, made him irresistibly
prefer it to the plainer mode which he should have adopted with
any one else, of sending in his name, and some message. His
shock at her view in such a state, he would not now revive; but
the impropriety of bidding the landlady quit the chamber, and the
impossibility of entering into an explanation in her hearing, alone
repressed, at that agitated moment, the avowal of every sensation
with which his heart was labouring. 'But when,' he added, 'shall I
cease to rejoice that I had listened to the good landlady's history
of a sick guest, while all conjecture was so remote from whom it
might be! when I am tempted to turn aside from a tale of distress,
I will recollect what I owe to having given [ear to one]!' Lost in
wonder at what could have brought her to such a situation, and
disturbed how to present himself at the rectory, till fixed in his

plans, he had ridden to the half-way-house that morning, to enquire concerning the corpse that Mrs. Marl had mentioned—and there—while he was speaking with her, the little maid brought down two letters—one of them directed to himself.—

'What a rapid transition,' cried he, 'was then mine, from regrets that robbed life of all charms, to prospects which paint it in its most vivid colours of happiness! from wavering the most deplorable, to resolutions of expiating by a whole life of devoted fondness, the barbarous waywardness that could deprive me, for one wilful moment, of the exquisite felicity of my lot! . . .'

'But still,' said Camilla, 'I do not quite understand how you came in that room this morning? and how you authorized yourself to overhear my confessions to my Mother?'

'Recollect my acknowledged accomplice before you hazard any blame! When I came hither . . . somewhat, I confess, within my given hour, Mr. Tyrold received me himself at the door. He told me I was too soon, and took me into the front parlour. The partition is thin. I heard my name spoken by Mrs. Tyrold, and the gentle voice of my Camilla, in accents yet more gentle than even that voice ever spoke before, answering some question; I was not myself, at first, aware of its tenour . . . but when, unavoidably, I gathered it . . . when I heard words so beautifully harmonizing with what I had so lately perused—I would instantly have ventured into the room; but Mr. Tyrold feared surprising you—you went on—my fascinated soul divested me of obedience—of caution—of all but joy and gratitude . . . and he could no longer restrain me. And now with which of her offenders will my Camilla quarrel?'

'With neither, I believe, just at present. The conspiracy is so complex, and even my Mother so nearly a party concerned, that I dare not risk the unequal contest. I must only, in future,' added she smiling, 'speak ill of you . . . and then you will find less pleasure in the thinness of a partition!'

Faithfully she returned his communication, by the fullest, most candid, and unsparing account of every transaction of her short life, from the still shorter period of its being put into voluntary motion. With nearly breathless interest, he listened to the detail of her transactions with Sir Sedley Clarendel, with pity to her debts, and with horrour to her difficulties. But when, through the whole ingenuous narration, he found himself the constant object of every view, the ultimate motive to every action, even where least it appeared, his happiness, and his gratitude, made Camilla soon forget that sorrow had ever been known to her.

They then spoke of her two favourites, Mrs. Arlbery, and Mrs. Berlinton; and though she was animated in her praise of the good qualities of the first, and the sweet attraction of the last, she confessed the danger, for one so new in the world, of chusing friends distinct from those of her family; and voluntarily promised, during her present season of inexperience, to repose the future choice of her connections, where she could never be happy without their approvance.

The two hundred pounds to Sir Sedley Clarendel, he determined, on the very day that Camilla should be his, to return to the Baronet, under the privilege, and in the name of paying it for a brother.

In conference thus softly balsamic to every past wound, and thus deliciously opening to that summit of earthly felicity . . . confidence unlimited entwined around affection unbounded . . . hours might have passed, unnumbered and unawares, had not prudence forced a separation, for the repose of Camilla.

CHAPTER XIV

The last Touches of the Picture

LATE as Edgar quitted the rectory, he went not straight to Beech Park; every tie both of friendship and propriety carried him first to Dr. Marchmont; who had too much feeling to wonder at the power of his late incitements, and too much goodness of heart not to felicitate him upon their issue, though he sighed at the recollection of the disappointments whence his own doubting counsel originated. Twice betrayed in his dearest expectations, he had formed two criterions from his peculiar experience, by which he had settled his opinion of the whole female sex; and where opinion may humour systematic prepossession, who shall build upon his virtue or wisdom to guard the transparency of his impartiality?

The following day, the Westwyns presented themselves at

Etherington; hurried from a tour they were taking through Devonshire and Cornwall, by intelligence which had reached them that Sir Hugh Tyrold was ruined, and Cleves was to be let. They met, by chance, with Edgar alone in the parlour; and the joy of the old gentleman in hearing how small a part of the rumour was founded in fact, made him shake hands with him as cordially for setting him right, as Edgar welcomed his kindness, from the pleasure afforded by the sight of such primitive regard. But when, presuming upon his peculiar intimacy in the family, as ward of Mr. Tyrold, though without yet daring to avow his approaching nearer affinity, Edgar insisted upon his superior claim for supplanting them in taking charge of the debt of his guardian; Mr. Westwyn, almost angrily, protested he would let no man upon earth, let him be whose ward he pleased, shew more respect than himself for the brother of Sir Hugh Tyrold; 'And Hal thinks the same too,' he added, 'or he's no son of mine. And so he'll soon shew you, in a way you can't guess, I give you my word. At least that's my opinion.'

He then took his son apart, and abruptly whispered to him, 'As that pretty girl you and I took such a fancy to, at Southton, served us in that shabby manner, because of meeting with that old Lord, it's my opinion you'd do the right thing to take her sister; who's pretty near as pretty, and gives herself no airs; and that will be shewing respect for my worthy old friend, now he's down in the world; which is exactly that he did for me when I was down myself. For if he had not lent me that thousand pounds I told you of, when not a relation I had would lend me a hundred, I might have been ruined before ever you were born. Come, tell me your mind Hal! off or on? don't stand shilly shally; it's what I can't bear; speak honestly; I won't have your choice controlled; only this one thing I must tell you without ceremony, I shall never think well of you again as long as ever I live, if you demur so much as a moment. It's what I can't bear; it i'n't doing a thing handsomely. I can't say I like it.'

The appearance of Lavinia relieved the immediate embarrassment of Henry, while the modest pleasure with which she received them confirmed the partiality of both. The eagerness, however, of the father, admitted of no delay, and when Sir Hugh entered the room, the son's assent being obtained, he warmly demanded the fair Lavinia for his daughter-in-law.

Sir Hugh received the proposition with the most copious satisfaction; Mr. and Mrs. Tyrold with equal, though more anxious delight; and Lavinia herself with blushing but unaffected hopes of happiness.

Whatever was known to Sir Hugh, no cautions, nor even his own best designs, could save from being known to the whole house. Eugenia, therefore, was unavoidably informed of this transaction; and the generous pleasure with which she revived from the almost settled melancholy left upon her, by continual misfortunes, justified the impatience of Edgar to accelerate the allowed period for publishing his own happy history.

Eugenia wept with joy at tidings so precious of her beloved sister, through whom, and her other dear friends, she was alone, she said, susceptible of joy, though to all sorrow she henceforth bid adieu, 'For henceforth,' she cried, 'I mean to regard myself as if already I had passed the busy period of youth and of life, and were only a spectatress of others. For this purpose, I have begun writing my memoirs, which will amuse my solitude, and confirm my—I hope, philosophical idea.'

She then produced the opening of her intended book.

SECTION I.

'No blooming coquette, elated with adulation and triumphant with conquest, here counts the glories of her eyes, or enumerates the train of her adorers: no beauteous prude, repines at the fatigue of admiration, nor bewails the necessity of tyranny: O gentle reader! you have the story of one from whom fate has withheld all the delicacy of vanity, all the regale of cruelty—!'[1]

'Here,' interrupted the young biographer, 'will follow my portrait, and then this further address to my readers.'

'O ye, who, young and fair, revel in the attractions of beauty, and exult in the pride of admiration, say, where is your envy of the heiress to whom fortune comes with such alloys? And which, however distressed or impoverished, would accept my income with my personal defects?

'Ye, too, O lords of the creation, mighty men! impute not to native vanity the repining spirit with which I lament the loss of beauty; attribute not to the innate weakness of my sex, the concern I confess for my deformity; nor to feminine littleness of soul, a regret of which the true source is to be traced to your own bosoms, and springs from your own tastes: for the value you yourselves set upon external attractions, your own neglect has taught me to know; and the indifferency with which you consider all else, your own duplicity has instructed me to feel.'

Camilla sought to dissuade her from reflexions so afflictive, and retrospections so poignant; but they aided her, she said, in her task of acquiring composure for the regulation of her future life.

Edgar now received permission to make his communication to the Baronet.

The joy with which Sir Hugh heard it, was for some time over-clouded by doubt. 'My dear Mr. young Edgar,' he said, 'in case you don't know your own mind yet, in the point of its not changing again, as it did before, I'd as leave you would not tell me of it till you've taken the proper time to be at a certainty; frettings about these ups and downs, being what do no good to me, in point of the gout.'

But when thoroughly re-assured, 'Well,' he cried, 'this is just the thing I should have chose out of all our misfortunes, being what makes me happier than ever I was in my life; except once before on the very same account, which all turned out to end in nothing: which, I hope, won't happen any more: for now I've only to pay off all our debts, and then I may go back again to Cleves, which I shall be glad enough to do, it being but an awkward thing to a man, after he's past boyhood, having no home of his own.'

A sigh at the recollection of the change in his situation, since his plan was last agitated, checked his felicity, and depressed even that of Edgar, who, with the most tender earnestness, besought his leave to advance the sum requisite to return him tranquilly to his mansion; but who could not prevail, till Camilla joined in the petition, and permitted Edgar, in both their names to entreat, as their dearest wish, that they might be united, according to the first arrangement, from Cleves.

This the Baronet could not resist, and preparations were rapidly made for re-instating him in his dwelling, and for the double marriages destined to take place upon his return.

'Well, then, this,' cried he, as he poured upon them his tenderest blessings and caresses, 'is the oddest of all! My dear little Camilla, that I took all my fortune from, is the very person to give me her's as soon as ever she gets it! as well as my own house over my old head again, after my turning her, as one may say, out of it! which is a thing as curious, in point of us poor ignorant mortals, as if my brother had put it in a sermon.'

'Such turns in the tide of fortune,' said Mr. Tyrold, 'are amongst the happiest lessons of humanity, where those who have served the humble and helpless from motives of pure disinterestedness, find they have made useful friends for themselves, in the perpetual vicissitudes of our unstable condition.'

'Why, then, there's but one thing more, by what I can make out,' said the Baronet, 'that need be much upon my mind, and that I've been thinking some time about, in point of forming a scheme to get rid of, which I think I've got a pretty good one: for here's Lavinia going to be married to the very oldest friend I have in the world; that is, to his son, which is the same thing in point of bringing us all together; and my own dear little girl, to the best gentleman in the county, except for that one thing of going off at the first, which I dare say he did not mean, for which reason I shall mention it no more: and Indiana, to one of those young captains, that I can't pretend I know much of; but that's very excusable in so young a person, not having had much head from the beginning; which I always make allowance for; my own not being over extraordinary: and Eugenia, poor thing, being a widow already; for which God be praised; which I hope is no sin, in point of the poor lad that's gone not belonging to any of us, by what I can make out, except by his own doing whether we would or not; which, however, is neither here nor there, now he's gone; for Eugenia being no beauty, and Clermont having as good as said so, I suppose she thought she must not be too difficult; which is a thing young girls are apt to fall into; and boys too, for the matter of that; for, by what I can make out of life, I don't see but what a scholar thinks a girl had better be pretty than not, as much as another man.'

'But what, my dear brother,' said Mr. Tyrold, 'is your new distress and new scheme?'

'Why I can't say but what I'm a little put out, that Indiana should forget poor Mrs. Margland, in the particular of asking her to go to live with her; which, however, I dare say she can't help, those young captains commonly not over liking having elderly persons about them; not that I mean to guess her age, which I take to be fifty, and upwards; which is no point of ours. But the thing I'm thinking of is Dr. Orkborne, in the case of their marrying one another.'

'My dear brother! . . . has any such idea occurred to them?'

'Not as I know of; but Indiana having done with one, and Eugenia with the other, and me, Lord help me! not wanting either of them, why what can I do if they won't? the Doctor's asked to go to town, for the sake of printing his papers, which I begged him not to hurry, for I'm but little fit for learned conversation just now; though when he's here, he commonly says nothing; only taking out his tablets to write down something that comes into his head, as I suppose: which I can't say is very entertaining in the light of a companion. However, as to his having called me a blockhead, it's not what I take umbrage at, not being a wit being a fault of no man's, except of nature, which nobody has a right to be angry at. Besides, as to his having a little pride, it's what I owe him no ill-will for; a scholar having nothing else but his learning, is excusable for making the most of it. However, if they would marry one another, I can't but say I should take it very well of them. The only thing I know against it, is the mortal dislike they have to one another: and that, my dear brother, is the point I want to consult you about; for then we shall be got off all round: which would be a great thing off my mind.'

When the happy day arrived for returning to Cleves, Sir Hugh re-took possession of his hospitable mansion, amidst the tenderest felicitations of his fond family, and the almost clamorous rejoicings of the assembled poor of the neighbourhood: and the following morning, Mr. Tyrold gave the hand of Lavinia to Harry Westwyn, and Dr. Marchmont united them; and Edgar, glowing with happiness, now purified from any alloy, received from the same revered hand, and owed to the same honoured voice, the final and lasting possession of the tearful, but happy Camilla.

*   *   *   *

What further remains to finish this small sketch of a Picture of Youth, may be comprised in a few pages.

Indiana was more fortunate in her northern expedition, than experiments of that nature commonly prove. Macdersey was a man of honour, and possessed better claims to her than he had either language or skill to explain: but the good Lord O'Lerney. who, to benevolence the most chearful, and keenness the least severe, joined judgment and generosity, acted as the guardian of his kinsman, and placed the young couple in competence and comfort.

The profession of Macdersey obliging him to sojourn frequently in country quarters, Indiana, when the first novelty of *tête-à-têtes* was over, wished again for the constant adulatress of her charms and endowments, and, to the inexpressible rapture of Sir Hugh, solicited Miss Margland to be her companion: and the influence of constant flattery was so seductive to her weak mind, that, though insensible to the higher motive of cherishing her in remembrance of her long cares, she was so spoilt by her blandishments, and so accustomed to her management, that she parted from her no more.

Lavinia, with her deserving partner, spent a month between Cleves and Etherington, and then accompanied him and his fond father to their Yorkshire estate and residence. Like all characters of radical worth,[1] she grew daily upon the esteem and affection of her new family, and found in her husband as marked a contrast with Clermont Lynmere, to annul all Hypothesis of Education, as Lord O'Lerney, cool, rational, and penetrating, opposed to Macdersey, wild, eccentric, and vehement, offered against all that is National. Brought up under the same tutor, the same masters, and at the same university, with equal care, equal expence, equal opportunities of every kind, Clermont turned out conceited, voluptuous, and shallow; Henry modest, full of feeling, and stored with intelligence.

Lionel, first enraged, but next tamed, by the disinheritance which he had drawn upon himself, had ample subject in his disappointment to keep alive his repentance. And though enabled to return from banishment, by the ignominious condemnation, with another culprit, of the late partner in his guilt, he felt so lowered from his fallen prospects, and so gloomy from his altered spirits, that when his parents, satisfied with his punishment, held out the olive-branch to invite him home, he came forth again rather as if condemned, than forgiven; and, wholly wanting fortitude either to see or to avoid his former associates, he procured an appointment that carried him abroad, where his friends induced him to remain, till his bad habits, as well as bad connections, were forgotten, and time aided adversity in forming him a new character.

Clermont, for whom his uncle bought a commission, fixed himself in the army; though with no greater love of his country, than was appendant to the opportunity it afforded of shewing his fine person to regimental advantage.

Mrs. Arlbery was amongst the first to hasten with congratulations to Camilla. With too much understanding to betray her pique upon the errour of her judgment, as to the means of attaching Mandlebert, she had too much goodness of heart not to rejoice in the happiness of her young friend.

Mrs. Lissin, who accompanied her in the wedding visit, confessed herself the most disappointed and distressed of human beings. She had not, she said, half so much liberty as when she lived with her Papa, and heartily repented marrying, and wished she had never thought of it. The servants were always teazing her for orders and directions; every thing that went wrong, it was always she who was asked why it was not right; when she wanted to be driving about all day, the coachman always said it was too much for the horses; when she travelled, the maids always asked her what must be packed up; if she happened to be out at dinner time, Mr. Lissin found fault with every thing's being cold: if she wanted to do something she liked, he said she had better let it alone; and, in fine, her violent desire for this state of freedom, ended in conceiving it a state of bondage; she found *her own house* the house of which she must take the charge; being *her own mistress*, having the burthen of superintending a whole family, and being *married*, becoming the property of another, to whom she made over a legal right to treat her just as he pleased. And as she had chosen neither for character, nor for disposition, neither from sympathy nor respect, she found it hard to submit where she meant to become independent, and difficult to take the cares where she had made no provision for the solaces of domestic life.

The notable Mrs. Mittin contrived soon to so usefully ingratiate herself in the favour of Mr. Dennel, that, in the full persuasion she would save him half his annual expences, he married her: but her friend, Mr. Clykes, was robbed in his journey home of the cash which he had so dishonourably gained.

The first care of Edgar was to clear every debt in which Camilla had borne any share, and then to make over to Lavinia the little portion intended to be parted between the sisters.

Henry would have resisted; but Mr. Tyrold knew the fortune of Edgar to be fully adequate to his generosity, and sustained the proposition. Sir Sedley Clarendel received his two hundred pounds without opposition, though with surprise; and was dubious whether to rejoice in the shackles he had escaped, or to lament the charmer he had lost.

Sir Hugh would suffer no one but himself to clear the debts of his two nephews, or refund what had been advanced by his excellent old friend Mr. Westwyn. He called back all his servants, liberally recompensed their marked attachment, provided particularly for good old Jacob; and took upon himself the most ample reward for the postillion who meant to rescue Eugenia.

The prisoner and his wife, now worthy established cottagers, were the first, at the entrance of Beech Park, to welcome the bride and bridegroom; and little Peggy Higden was sent for immediately, and placed, with extremest kindness, where she might rise in use and in profit.

Lord O'Lerney was sedulously sought by Edgar, who had the infinite happiness to see Camilla a selected friend of Lady Isabella Irby, whose benevolent care of her in the season of her utter distress, had softly enchained her tenderest gratitude, and had excited in himself an almost adoring respect.

Melmond had received in time the caution of Camilla, to prevent the meeting to which the baseness of Bellamy was deluding his misguided sister, through her own wild theories. He forbore to blast her fame by calling him publicly to account; and ere further arts could be practised, Bellamy was no more.

Mrs. Berlinton, in the shock of sudden sorrow, shut herself up from the world. Claims of debts of honour, which she had no means to answer, pursued her in her retreat; she became at once the prey of grief, repentance, and shame; and her mind was yet young enough in wrong, to be penetrated by the early chastisement of calamity. Removed from the whirl of pleasure, which takes reflexion from action, and feeling from thought, she reviewed, with poignant contrition, her graceless misconduct with regard to Eugenia, detested her infatuation, and humbled herself to implore forgiveness. Her aunt seized the agitating moment of self-upbraiding and worldly disgust, to impress upon her fears the lessons of her opening life: and thus, repulsed from passion, and sickened of dissipation, though too illiberally instructed for chearful and rational piety, she was happily snatched from utter ruin by protecting, though eccentric enthusiasm.

Eugenia, for some time, continued in voluntary seclusion, happily reaping from the fruits of her education and her virtues, resources and reflexions for retirement, that robbed it of weariness. The name, the recollection of Bellamy, always made her shudder, but the peace of perfect innocence was soon restored to her mind. The sufferings of Mrs. Berlinton from self-reproach, taught her yet more fully to value the felicity of blamelessness; and the generous liberality of her character, made the first inducement she felt for exertion, the benevolence of giving solace to a penitent who had injured her.

Melmond, long conscious of her worth, and disgusted with all that had rivalled it in his mind, with the fervour of sincerity, yet diffidence of shame and regret, now fearfully sought the favour he before had reluctantly received. But Eugenia retreated. She had no courage for a new engagement, no faith for new vows, no hope for new happiness: till his really exemplary character, with the sympathy of his feelings, and the similarity of his taste and turn of mind with her own, made the Tyrolds, when they perceived his ascendance, second his wishes. Approbation so sacred, joined to a prepossession so tender, soon conquered every timid difficulty in the ingenuous Eugenia; who in his well-earnt esteem, and grateful affection, received, at length, the recompence of every exerted virtue, and the solace of every past suffering. Melmond, in a companion delighting in all his favourite pursuits, and capable of joining even in his severer studies, found a charm to beguile from him all former regret, while reason and experience endeared his ultimate choice. Eugenia once loved, was loved for ever. Where her countenance was looked at, her complexion was forgotten; while her voice was heard, her figure was unobserved; where her virtues were known, they seemed but to be enhanced by her personal misfortunes.

The Baronet was enchanted to see her thus unexpectedly happy, and soon transferred to Melmond the classical respect which Clermont had forfeited, when he concurred with Eugenia in a petition, that Dr. Orkborne, without further delay, might be enabled to retire to his own plans and pursuits, with such just and honourable consideration for labours he well knew how to appreciate, as his friend Mr. Tyrold should judge to be worthy of his acceptance.

With joy expanding to that thankfulness which may be called the *beauty of piety*, the virtuous Tyrolds, as their first blessings, received these blessings of their children: and the beneficent Sir Hugh felt every wish so satisfied, he could scarcely occupy himself again with a project ... save a maxim of prudence, drawn from his own experience, which he daily planned teaching to the little generation rising around him; To avoid, from the disasters of their Uncle, the Dangers and Temptations, to their Descendants, of Unsettled Collateral Expectations.

Thus ended the long conflicts, doubts, suspences, and sufferings of Edgar and Camilla; who, without one inevitable calamity, one unavoidable distress, so nearly fell the sacrifice to the two extremes of Imprudence, and Suspicion, to the natural heedlessness of youth unguided, or to the acquired distrust of experience that had been wounded. Edgar, by generous confidence, became the repository of her every thought; and her friends read her exquisite lot in a gaiety no longer to be feared: while, faithful to his word, making Etherington, Cleves, and Beech Park, his alternate dwellings, he rarely parted her from her fond Parents and enraptured Uncle. And Dr. Marchmont, as he saw the pure innocence, open frankness, and spotless honour of her heart, found her virtues, her errours, her facility, or her desperation, but A PICTURE OF YOUTH; and regretting the false light given by the spirit of comparison, in the hypothesis which he had formed from individual experience, acknowledged its injustice, its narrowness, and its arrogance. What, at last, so diversified as man? what so little to be judged by his fellow?

FINIS

FANNY BURNEY'S REVISIONS
OF *CAMILLA*

Space does not allow more than a sampling of the numerous, frequently radical changes that distinguish the 1802 from the 1796 edition of *Camilla*. Similarly, the editors can merely offer random exhibits from the drafts FB compiled for the projected third or manuscript edition. The 1802 edition is over 500 pages shorter than the original. The differences between the two derive from the novelist's wish to satisfy the complaints of her critics, both public and private: to shorten her over-long novel, to 'ameliorate' its didacticism, and to purify her prose style by removing the grammatical errors and verbal infelicities itemized by William Enfield in the October (1796) number of the *Monthly Review* and by Thomas Twining in July 1797. (The changes suggested by either of these two men are designated in the sample collations by the symbols *MR* and *T*.) In the many years after 1802 FB apparently developed misgivings about the nature of the revisions made for the 'new edition'. For in working on the third edition, she amended her over-all technique of alteration. That is, she probably added more to the novel than she subtracted from it and took a scrupulous delight in the expansion of dialogue, description, and even scenes. References to the 1802 edition are to volume, page, and line numbers.

Present Text: 1796	*1802*
Page 8, line 21 expansive [*T*]	i. 2. 19 liberal
Page 8, line 26 scarce the gradation (The misuse of 'scarce' for 'scarcely', 'hardly', or 'almost' appears often in this edition. It was one of the grammatical 'inaccuracies' pointed out by *MR* that FB consistently corrected for the 1802 *Camilla*.)	i. 2. 26–7 scarcely the gradation
Page 29, line 13 aera [*T*]	i. 43. 4 time

Present Text: 1796　　　　　　　*1802*

Page 47, line 36–Page 48, line 3
thoughts.

'Why then we are all at a stand again! This is worse than I thought for! So the poor girl has really no head?—Hay, Doctor?—Do speak, pray?—Don't mind vexing me. Say so at once, if you can't help thinking it.'

Another extorted, 'Yes, sir,' completely overset Sir Hugh; who, imputing the absent and perplexed air with which it was pronounced to an unwillingness to give pain, shook him

i. 81. 5–9
thoughts.

Sir Hugh now, imputing the absent and perplexed air with which he spoke to an unwillingness to give pain, was completely overset; yet shook him

Page 72, lines 21–4
gloves, and not being able to find Tom Hicks, I've been waiting all this while for a boy as has promised to get me a pair; though, I suppose he's fell down in the dark and broke his skull, by his not coming. And indeed

i. 128. 28–30
gloves, and I've been waiting all this while for a boy as has promised to get me a pair; though indeed

Page 76, lines 4–5
Ensign, who ... stroamed [*T*; *MR*] into

i. 135. 1–3
Ensign, who ... staggered into

Page 84, line 32
distinct

i. 153. 1
distinguished

Page 99, lines 19–32
in what he was reading with a pleasure amounting to ecstasy. He started, acted, smiled, and looked pensive in turn, while his features were thrown into a thousand different expressions, and his person was almost writhed with perpetually varying gestures. From time to time his rapture broke forth into loud exclamations of 'Exquisite! exquisite!' while he beat

i. 181. 27–182.4
in what he was studying with a pleasure amounting to extacy. Sometimes he read a few words aloud, calling out "Exquisite! Heavenly!" then suddenly shutting up the book, he folded his arms, and casting his eyes towards the ceiling uttered: "O too much! too much! there is no standing it!" yet again, the next minute, he opened it and read on

Present Text: 1796	*1802*

the leaves of the book violently
with his hands, in token of applause, or lifting them up to his
lips, almost devoured with kisses
the passages that charmed him.
Sometimes he read a few words
aloud, calling out 'Heavenly!' and
vehemently stamping his approbation with his feet; then suddenly shutting up the book, folded
his arms, and casting his eyes to-
ward the ceiling, uttered: 'O too
much! too much! there is no
standing it!' yet again, the next
minute, opened it and resumed
the lecture [*T*]

| *Page* 168, *line* 32 | i. 316.28 |
| averseness of [*T*] | averseness to |

| *Page* 224, *line* 33 | ii. 70. 3 |
| such a son as me | such a son |

Page 239, *lines* 19–25
subsided.

    Camilla, who, from her af-
fection to him, read his character
through the innocence of her own,
met his returning gaiety with a
pleasure that was proportioned to
her pain at his depression; but
Lavinia saw it with discomfort, as
the signal for executing her
charge, and, with extreme reluctance, gave him to understand
she had

ii. 100. 7–10
subsided.

    Lavinia now, though with ex-
treme reluctance, thought it right to
acquaint him she had

| *Page* 242, *line* 27 | ii. 105. 24 |
| to ask yourself | to reflect |

Page 342, *lines* 35–40

    Camilla was pleased, and even
thankful for the extreme friendliness and kind moderation of this

Omitted

Present Text: 1796   *1802*

arrangement; yet she left him mournfully, in a confirmed belief his regard for the whole family was equal.

Eugenia, much gratified, promised she would henceforth take no step with which Edgar should not first be acquainted

Page 345, line 8
indulgent

Page 346, lines 12–13
out-galloped [*MR*]

Page 406, lines 31–8
rooms.

As the Major had nothing in him either brilliant or offensive, his sight, after the first salutations, was almost all of which the company was sensible.

Camilla, his sole object, he could not approach; she sat between the baronet and Mrs. Arlbery; and all her looks and all her attention were divided between them.

Mrs. Arlbery, emerging

Page 508, lines 29–30
the trust and obligation

Page 511, lines 31–2
distressed beyond what she had been in any former time

Page 522, lines 18–22
be pursued!'

This writing had not been visible till the machine was taken out to be replenished. She recollected the hand of Sir Sedley, and was now sure it was sent by himself, and could no longer, there-

ii. 300. 13
sympathizing

ii. 302. 20
out-ridden

iii. 60. 4–5
rooms.

Mrs. Arlbery, emerging

iii. 254. 11
the trust

iii. 259. 22
and distressed

iii. 278. 18–21
be pursued!" She recollected the hand of Sir Sedley, and in being now sure it was sent by himself, could no longer doubt that his intentions were serious

Present Text: 1796	*1802*
fore, doubt his intentions being serious	
Page 523, *line* 3 impracticable [*MR*]	iii. 279. 14 intractable
Page 528, *lines* 15–17 gratitude; but confess, at once, your heart refuses to return his tenderness. Entreat him to forgive whatever he may have mistaken, and nobly	iii. 289. 29 gratitude; but entreat him nobly
Page 530, *line* 2 egotism [*T*]	iii. 292. 24–5 selfishness
Page 541, *lines* 13–14 with so much wonderment [*T*; *MR*], how it had all been brought about	iii. 315. 13–14 astonishment at her own situation
Page 555, *lines* 2–5 Edgar; who would so soon be brother of her brother, that he would pardon the faults of Lionel, and who would then be in no danger himself from personal contest or discussion with Sir Sedley. She wrote	iii. 341. 29–30 Edgar. She wrote
Page 562, *lines* 36–40 squire up; and no wonder, for he's a sweet proper gentleman, as ever I see. Come, miss, I hope you'll put on something else, for that hat makes you look worse than any thing. I would not have the young squire see you such a figure for never so much	iv. 14. 20–3 squire up. Come, miss, I hope you'll put on something else, for that hat makes you look worse than any thing
Page 628, *lines* 32–3 table: pleading, in excuse for his stay, his former intimacy with Sir Hugh. Miss Margland, seeing	iv. 135. 9–10 table. Miss Margland, seeing
Page 629, *line* 13 as well as me	iv. 136. 4 as well as I

Present Text: 1796	*1802*
Page 630, *lines* 26–30	iv. 138. 21–2
the Cleves estate, her capacity pointed out how terrible must be the personal defects, that so speedily, without one word of conversation, one trial of any sort how their tastes, tempers, or characters might accord, stimulated him to so decisive a rejection. This view of her unfortunate	the Cleves estate, the view it forced upon her of her own unfortunate
Page 631, *lines* 15–16	iv. 139. 31
visible surprise and pleasure	visible pleasure
Page 631, *lines* 39–40	iv. 141. 5–6
who . . . she painted [*T*]	whom . . . she painted
Page 684, *lines* 5–24	iv. 231. 15–19
alleviate.	alleviate.

The conclusion of the letter of Mr. Tyrold gave to Camilla as much pain as every other part of it gave to Eugenia pleasure: . . .
 	
   While Camilla sighed to consider how wide from the certainty with which he mentioned it was such an event, she blushed that he should thus be uninformed of her insecurity: . . . Yet her present scheme to accelerate its termination, became difficult even of trial.
 	
   The obviously serious regard of Henry was a continual reproach to her; . . . Yet she could now only escape them by turning to some other, and that other was necessarily Lord Valhurst, whose close siege to her notice forced
	Mean time while, to shun the serious assiduities of Henry, Camilla attended to Lord Valhurst, the close siege to her notice of that noble man forced

Page 702, *lines* 12–13	iv. 266. 27–9
nephew and heir to the very best man in the three kingdoms. However, I heartily hope his uncle will disinherit him, for he's	nephew to the very best man in the three kingdoms; but he's

Present Text: 1796	1802
Page 732, lines 14–15	iv. 324. 1–2

Page 732, lines 14–15
stated that three hundred pounds

iv. 324. 1–2
stated, in a letter to my uncle, that three hundred pounds

Page 753, lines 10–17
The connection you have formed will be a consolation to us all. It binds to us for life a character already so dear to us; it will afford to our Lavinia, should we leave her single, a certain asylum; it will give to our Eugenia a counsellor that may save her hereafter from fraud and ruin; it may aid poor Lionel, when, some time hence, he returns to his country, to return to the right path, whence so widely he has strayed; and it will heal

v. 31. 15–17
The connection you have formed will be a consolation to us all; and may heal

Page 825, line 25
recollection

v. 158. 5
self-command

Page 830, lines 26–31
at Winchester, that Camilla might gather some particulars of her family, and some composure for herself, to better judge what step to pursue. But all desire of meeting was now converted into horrour; she was too much known in the neighbourhood to escape being recognized if she stayed till the morning, and her shattered intellects, she declared, could

v. 167. 26–30
at Winchester, that Camilla might better judge what step to pursue. But all desire of meeting was now converted into horrour; and her shattered intellects could

Page 833, lines 12–17
re-appeared. She was put immediately into uncommon good-humour, by the ill success at [T] the journey of Camilla, which she protested was exactly what she expected.
    Camilla then strove to recollect all she had been told by Lord O'Lerney of Mr. Macdersey, and to relate it to Miss Margland, who, pleased

v. 172. 27–30
re-appeared. She then strove to recollect all she had been told by Lord O'Lerney of Mr. Macdersey, and Miss Margland, pleased

Present Text : 1796	*1802*

Page 839, lines 23–5
and there, by the gentle intercession of Eugenia, to obtain her
pardon, or, which she thought
immediately would follow its refusal, to sink

v. 184. 16–17
and there obtain her pardon, or sink

Page 853, line 16
She motioned to [MR]

v. 211. 13
She made a motion

Page 869, lines 7–11
   'And is he here now?' with an
involuntary   shudder   asked
Camilla.
   Yes, she answered, but her
mistress had ordered her not to
own it, . . . and said he would soon
be carried away

Omitted

Present Text : 1796	*Manuscript Edition*

Page 741, lines 23–4
cheapness, and representations of
their necessity, that, joined to her
entire ignorance

cheapness that, from entire ignorance

Page 742, lines 35–6
at this moment would be the
highest obligation; and immediately set

at such a moment would be the
highest obligation. She immediately thereafter set

Page 743, line 40
dispense, came to

dispense, made the sum total amount

Page 750, lines 1–2
   In the hall of the Cleves mansion the party from Southampton
were received

   In the Portico of the Cleves mansion they were all received

Page 751, line 21
relations

relations which however not being
his fault we must make shift with as
well as we can

Present Text: 1796   *Manuscript Edition*

Page 756, lines 20–7

Mr. Tyrold now visited Cleves with only his younger daughter, and excused the non-appearance there, for the present, of Camilla; acknowledging that some peculiar incidents, which he could not yet explain, kept Mandlebert away, and must postpone the celebration of the marriage.

The vexation this gave Sir Hugh, redoubled his anxiety to break to him the evil by degrees, if to break it to him at all should become indispensable

Mr. Tyrold was now obliged to acknowledge to Sir H. that some peculiar incidents, which he could not yet explain, kept Mandlebert away and must postpone the celebration of the marriage and that during the interval, he thought it would be most proper to detain Camilla at Etherington.

Sir H. was [made] nearly pitiful by this intelligence. He sent for all his workmen in great dismay, & gave them a melancholy disquisition, but made a present nevertheless, to each of them, & as it was not, he said, their fault, which he hoped they would excuse: but he warned them never to build upon any job from people's marrying, for if they did, 'twas 10 to one but they'd be disappointed, as he was a remarkable instance of himself, having 2 of the best matches he ever made in his life broke all in a jerk, nobody knew why, nor for what: unless it might be the young gentlemen changing their minds who might have very good reasons, which he c^d not pretend to judge: only he sh^d have taken [it] rather kinder if they had [done it] before he had got all his rooms ready

Page 770, lines 35–6

finally assured him he was just   assured him that he had just been

Page 772, lines 4–5

letting him know that his master begged he would set out that very moment

making known that his master had begged his Brother to set out to him that very moment

Page 773, line 7

to bed   to his chamber

| *Present Text: 1796* | *Manuscript Edition* |

Page 791, *line* 30
of the party

of the party to Grosvenor Square

Page 798, *lines* 5–8
them, for some time, was capable to give any account that was intelligible. She then gathered that, in coming out of the theatre, to get to the coach, they had missed her. None

them was capable to give any answer that was intelligible: she c^d only learn that, in coming out of the theatre to get to the coach, Eugenia had been injured. None

Page 798, *line* 15
crowd

great mob

Page 798, *line* 40
kept off from entire delirium

kept off from entire delirium.

Mrs. Berlinton, during this scene, in a consternation indefinable from feelings of the same description, stood like a statue, transfixed between nameless sensations of astonishment & indignation which held her nearly motionless & utterly mute

Page 801, *lines* 37–40
chasm in the acuteness of the feelings of Camilla lasted not long; and Mrs. Berlinton then brought from Melmond the following account.

With the utmost speed he could use, he could not, though

chasm in the emotions of Camilla lasted not long; & as she awoke from it, Miss Margland brought her the following account from Melmond.

With the utmost speed he c^d use, he was unable, though

Page 804, *lines* 23–6
'This,' concluded Mrs. Berlinton, 'is all my brother has to relate; all that for himself he adds, is, that if ever, to something human, the mind of an angel was accorded—that mind seems enshrined in the heart of Eugenia

"This," concluded Miss Margland, "is all that Mr. Melmond can tell us of what has happened: & all he begged me to add to it from himself, is that if ever the mind of an angel was accorded to something human, that mind was enshrined in the frame of Eugenia

| *Present Text: 1796* | *Manuscript Edition* |

Page 804, line 40

wounding than all she had yet suffered

wounding to Camilla than any, even the bitterest misfortune that had assailed her own happiness

Page 806, line 31

had heard her

had listened to her

Page 808, line 32–Page 809, line 3

She saw, nevertheless, no good, she said, it would do her cousin, that she should neglect such an opportunity of seeing London: and Miss Margland, in aid of this desire, spared so much trouble to Mrs. Berlinton, who soon wearied of Indiana, that she had the satisfaction of being invited to remain in Grosvenor-square till the two young ladies returned into the country

And she further counselled her not to lose this opportunity of seeing London, as it c$^{\underline{d}}$ be of no service to her cousin Eugenia that she sh$^{\underline{d}}$ live moped up like Miss Camilla. Indiana listened with eagerness to this advice, & as Mrs. Berlinton was thoroughly wearied of Indiana, Miss Margland rose to the height of her own ambition in being initiated in the reigning fashionable circles of exhibition of the day as the appointed chaperone of the new Beauty, Miss Lynmere

Page 813, lines 17–20

all divine, was his own first joy and greatest pride ... his homage ceased, with amazement that ever it could have

all divine had been the first joy of Melmond & his greatest pride ... his homage involuntarily ceased, with amazement that it c$^{\underline{d}}$ ever have

Page 819, line 24

upon the part

at the request

Page 824, lines 33–5

where Lord O'Lerney was conversing with her upon what had happened; she was flying back, though not knowing whither nor which

where she was conversing with L$^{\underline{d}}$ O'Lerney upon what had happened; Camilla was flying back, though not knowing whither to go, nor which

Page 825, line 16

engagement she

engagement for the morning which she

Present Text: 1796	*Manuscript Edition*
Page 825, line 18	
colour	roseate colour
Page 827, line 5	
and for her own debts	and for debts of her own contracting
Page 828, line 40–*Page 829, line* 3	
however, refuse to open the door, though desperately she said to herself: If she is there, I will pass her, and rush into the streets!	however, but open the door, when, seeing L.ᵞ Isabella alone, she rapturously fell
Seeing, however, Lady Isabella alone, she dropt	
Page 830, line 25	
this unadvised return	this ill-advised return to town
Page 830, line 38	
guilt	wilful evil
Page 833, line 8	
epoch, not more longed [for] than dreaded [*T*]	epoch, not more longed for than dreaded
Page 836, line 10	
The next day arrived an answer	The next day an answer arrived
Page 840, lines 14–21	
this beloved and unhappy sister, and her own peculiar knowledge of the worthless character . . . and darting through the great gate, and thence through a smaller one, which opened to the spot where she saw her walking, she flew to her in a speechless transport of sorrow, folded her in her arms, and sobbed upon her shoulder	this dear, unhappy sister, & her own recent discovery of the worthless character . . . & dashing through the great gate, & thence thro[ugh] a smaller one which opened to the path upon which Eugenia was strolling. She flew on, & in a speechless transport of sorrow folded in her arms, her loved, ill fated sister, upon whose shoulder she sobbed, rather than wept convulsively
Page 852, line 13	
Amazed, confounded, she	Affrighted, vanquished, confounded, she
Page 853, line 32–*Page 854, line* 10	
Camilla, who, casting up her hands and eyes, exclaimed: 'Then	Camilla, whose grief, mixt with personal remorse, became almost in-

Present Text: 1796	*Manuscript Edition*
am I the most detestable, as well as the most wretched of human beings!' . . .	tolerable. And Jacob, while he sought to console her, but added to her suffering.
Jacob tried to console her; but his account was only added torture.	"The very instant," he said, "when he's reading of the news of Mr. Tyrold's being took up, he went to work about [xxx 2 words] for us all round till he c^d scrape out enough, he said, for wiping off all the debts saying the chief fault all laid at his own door, for living up to the very verge of his income when he ought, says he, to have considered how many giddy heads he had about him, to have always kept some odd sums in hand to be ready for the unthinkingness of such poor young boys, who had no right to be wise before their time. Them were Master's own words
The very instant he told her, that his master had received the news of the arrest of Mr. Tyrold, he determined upon this violent plan; . . . when he ought, he said, considering there were so many young people, to have always kept a few odd sums at hand for accidents	

Page 862, line 36

wish quick approaching	wish was quickly accomplishing

Page 863, line 39

She had only, she knew, to make herself known as	She was now much disturbed. She had but, she was well aware, to name herself as

Page 872, lines 29–30

the cruelty of this egotism	the selfishness of this wish

Page 883, lines 27–8

joy scarce inferior to that which so recently had transported her: but Mrs.	joy to Camilla scarcely inferior to that which so recently had revived her: but here stopt verbal intercourse: Mrs.

Page 887, lines 25–6

The postillion acknowledged that it was himself who had cried, Hold, villain! A suspicion of some mischief had	The worthy postillion acknowledged to Mrs. Tyrold that it was himself who had called out Hold villain. A suspicion of some foul play had

EXPLANATORY NOTES

ABBREVIATIONS

E.D.D.   *The English Dialect Dictionary*, ed. Joseph Wright (London, 1898–1905).

Grose   [Francis Grose], *A Classical Dictionary of the Vulgar Tongue*, 3rd. edn. (London, 1796).

Johnson   Samuel Johnson, *A Dictionary of the English Language* (London, 1755).

O.E.D.   *A New English Dictionary on Historical Principles*, ed. James A. H. Murray (Oxford, 1888–1933).

Partridge   *A Dictionary of Slang and Unconventional English* (London, 1961).

VOLUME I

Page 3. (1) *To The Queen*: Charlotte Sophia (1744–1818), Queen of George III. For FB's service in the royal household, see the *Introduction*, pp. ix–x.

(2) *the inhabitant of a retired cottage*: In 1796 Fanny Burney d'Arblay, with her husband and child, lived in a small house located in Bookham, Surrey. Renting it from the widowed Catherine Bailey in November 1793, they remained there until 1797 when nearby Camilla Cottage was ready for occupancy. (See p. xxi.)

(3) *while 'memory holds its seat'*: misquoting *Hamlet*, I. v. 96.

(4) *patronage*: In 1796, FB—now Madame d'Arblay—was eager to dedicate her third novel to the queen. The dedication would express loyalty to Her Majesty and gratitude for continuing royal patronage. But more importantly, the dedication would indicate the queen's acceptance of the novelist despite her marriage in 1793 to a *Constitutionnel* who was also Catholic. The following note from Madame Schwellenberg was received in Great Bookham with relief: 'I do assure you I never took my pen in hand with more pleasure to informe you I have her Majestys Commands to say she gives leave for you, to Dedicate youre Books to her' (Berg [26 February 1796]).

Page 5. (1) *her TWO former attempts*: *Evelina* (1778) and *Cecilia* (1782).

(2) *The Hon. Mrs. BOSCAWEN, Mrs. CREWE, and Mrs. LOCKE*: Frances (Glanville) Boscawen (d. 1805), whose husband was an admiral of the blue, became known to FB in 1778 with other members of the Streatham group. Frances Ann (Greville) Crewe (d. 1818) was the daughter of Fulke Greville, Charles Burney's patron in 1748–9. All the Burney children grew

up regarding her as a family friend. Frederica Augusta (Schaub) Locke (1750–1832) of Norbury Park, meeting FB and her sister Susan in the winter of 1784, became their steadfast ally.

Mrs. Boscawen, Mrs. Crewe, and Mrs. Locke were active in securing subscriptions for *Camilla*. In a letter to her friend Georgiana Mary Ann Waddington, FB wrote on 8 July 1795: 'The *booksellers* you will see in some news-paper: but my own best & favourite Bookkeepers are 3 ladies,— Mrs. Boscawen, Mrs. Crewe, & Mrs. Lock. And it is my own particular wish that those friends who chuse to *enter the lists* will subscribe to one of them. It is at once their gratification & my pride to have my business go through their hands' (*JL*, iii. L. 177).

Page 7. (1) *we must be born again*: See 3 John iii. 7.

(2) This preface, deleted from the 1802 edition, is a philosophical synthesis of the novel. Substantively and verbally it reflects the *Rambler*, particularly 4 on the nature of fictional portraiture and 17 on the perversion of the human spirit. FB was sensitive to the moral principles of the *Rambler* from the time she began to write *Camilla*. In the Egerton draft of the novel she began a scene (not in the printed edition) wherein a character reads appreciatively from the *Rambler*.

Page 8. (1) *Camilla*: name given to the heroine shortly before the novel's publication. At one time she was called Clarinda, but most frequently Ariella. As late as 15 July 1795, FB wrote to her brother Charles to say 'The name of my Heroine is ARIELLA' (*JL*, iii. L. 178). This name persisted in a near final manuscript (Berg). Dr. Burney, however, objected to the name Ariella, and the novelist capitulated to parental objection. In that same draft she struck out Ariella and wrote in Camilla. For the source of the substitution, see Pope's *Essay on Criticism*, ll. 372–3 and Dryden's translation of the *Aeneid*, vii. 1100–1103. See this edition, p. 849 *n*. 2.

(2) *Fortune, with a moderation yet kinder*: This concept of moderation, traceable to Proverbs 30:8, is a commonplace of Protestant thinking which pervades much of the moralistic literature of the eighteenth century, particularly its first half. See Joseph Addison, *Spectator* 464; Daniel Defoe, *Robinson Crusoe*, ed. George A. Aitken (1895), i. 2–4; and *The Complete English Tradesman* (1726–7), Pt. I. ii. 106–7; Sir Richard Steele, *The Conscious Lovers* (1722), I. i.

(3) *the varied landscapes of the New Forest*: Except for interludes in Tunbridge Wells and London, the main characters play out their roles in Hampshire, moving within a circumscribed area from the New Forest over to Southampton and northeast to Winchester. Prior to the writing of *Camilla*, FB had at least three times 'travelled through a most delicious country in parts of the New Forest, to Southampton' (*Diary and Letters*, v. 12). Creating an overall realistic locale for the novel, she associates her

characters with fictitiously named villages and estates: Cleves, Etherington, and Beech Park.

(4) *the house of Tyrold*: The family originated in Yorkshire. The name, however, is not distinctly English and appears to be a coinage. *Tyrold*, for example, is unlisted in P. H. Reaney, *A Dictionary of British Surnames* (1958). It reflects FB's technique of creating atypical or unusual names for characters drawn from the gentry. The first element, derived from Old French *tirer*, connotes one who is 'obstinate' or 'stubborn' (Reaney, p. 323), like the Tyrold brothers. The second element is characteristic of Old Norse influence on Yorkshire place names (see A. Goodall, *Place-Names of South-West Yorkshire* [Cambridge, 1914], p. 289). The name suggests a Yorkshireman of ancient lineage, one who is 'in obstinate virtue clad like a coat of mail'. (See *The Works of Charles and Mary Lamb*, ed. E. V. Lucas [1903], v. 82.) Relevant too are the Christian names given to the brothers. Sir Hugh's was common in northern England as early as the twelfth century. His brother Augustus is what his latinate name connotes: 'venerable' in wisdom, 'consecrated' in piety, and 'classical' in learning.

Page 9. Sir Hugh Tyrold was a baronet: he resembles the *Spectator*'s Sir Roger de Coverley. That FB modelled him after the spectatorial character is uncertain but her friends readily made the identification. In 1797 Mrs. Crewe, in four undated letters (Berg) written to Dr. Burney, hoped that Sir Hugh, like Sir Roger, might become a pivotal character in a periodical devoted to a commentary on the times.

Page 10. (1) *his niece Indiana*: name probably derived from Steele, *The Conscious Lovers*.

(2) *Clermont*: For FB 'the Names of all the personages annexed with me all the ideas I put in motion with them' ([21 July 1795], *JL*, iii. L. 180). Even the Christian names chosen for the young men in the novel are significant. *Edgar* was Old English in origin but infrequently used until its revival by romantic writers. *Lionel*, long associated with English tradition, was popular in Yorkshire. *Melmond* is identified by his surname (only once is his Christian name *Frederic* given), a hybrid that is probably modelled on Smollett's romantic Oxonian Melford in *Humphry Clinker*. *Clermont*, while long anglicized, stems from a common French place name and so makes ironical his airs and affectations.

(3) *complacency*: obsolete for 'a disposition to please, oblige, or comply with the wishes of others' (*O.E.D.*).

Page 11. Eugenia ... Lavinia: The name *Eugenia* ('nobility' or 'excellence') is suited to the character. Although it was the name of a third-century Roman martyr, it may have occurred to FB also because it was the title of a play by Beaumarchais in 1767. *Eugénie* dramatizes the plight of a young innocent girl lured into a mock marriage, a situation reminiscent of the Eugenia-Bellamy relationship. *Lavinia* had become a favourite name, perhaps because James Thomson had substituted it for *Ruth* in his romanticised version of the Book of Ruth. But see also the character of that name in Nicholas Rowe's *The Fair Penitent* where she speaks for 'Trust, Security, and mutual Tenderness' (iv. 1).

Page 13. The tide of youthful glee flowed jocund from her heart: sense is obscure. Whether *jocund* is used in its literary sense of 'mirthful, light-hearted' or in its obsolete sense of 'joyful, glad, well-pleased', it is redundant. This is a locution to which the *Monthly Review* took exception and to which FB clung in the 1802 edition.

Page 16. in reversion: rare or obsolete usage for 'the return of a courtesy' (*Johnson*).

Page 17. cards, trinkets, and blind fidlers: There were several games children could play with cards: Commerce, Speculation, The Recruiting Officer, Old Maid, or Old Bachelor (*The Book of Games* [*c.* 1844]). *Trinkets* is a generic term for 'toys'. *Blind fidler* is probably a pseudo- or quasi-instrument suitable for children's pastime. It suggests the humstrum: 'a musical instrument made of a mopstick, a bladder, and some packthreads, thence also called bladder and string, and hurdy gurdy; it is played on like a violin' (*Grose*). The term *blind fidler* appears to be an innocent extension of cant allusions to beggary; hence, pretended or make-believe musical play.

Page 18. She made him whiskers of cork, powdered his brown bob, and covered a thread paper with black ribbon ... for a queue: Whiskers of cork are a beard drawn on the cheeks and chin with blackened cork. A *brown bob* is a 'wig having the bottom locks turned up into "bobs" or short curls, as opposed to a "full-bottomed wig"'. *Thread paper* is 'a strip of thin soft paper folded in creases so as to form separate divisions for different skeins of thread; the paper so folded forming a long and narrow strip' (*O.E.D.*).

Page 19. garden chair: a wheel or bath chair.

Page 21. She charged me not to let Eugenia stir out from Cleves, because of the small pox: According to an article in the *Gentleman's Magazine* for November 1802, 'the whole number of deaths every year in Britain by the Smallpox is about 36,000; in London alone about 3,000; and in all Europe, in the same ratio of population, about 470,000'.

Page 22. The extreme delicacy ... from innoculating her: FB studied medical texts in which were described the physical deformities resulting from small pox and the difficulties attendant upon inoculation. In a letter to Dr.

Burney, dated 16 March 1797 (*JL*, iii. L. 229), she remarked: 'I had studied that misfortune [the ravages of the disease] so thoroughly under Eugenia, that I was prepared to meet . . . with philosophy' the disfigurement of Alex. Inoculation, as FB vividly described Alex's to Susan (*JL*, iii. L. 227 [27 February–15 March 1797]), was an often risky operation. Profuse bleeding from repeated incisions by an infected lancet was succeeded by a painful rash, lassitude, fever, shortness of breath, and violent muscular spasms. The danger period, after inoculation, could last as long as a fortnight.

Page 23. (1) *whether she is moped up or no*: Sir Hugh's meaning is ambiguous. Perhaps he wished to suggest a state of inactivity (see *Johnson*) or in a figurative sense a state of over-protection (see *E.D.D.*).

   (2) *and how did people do before these new modes of making themselves sick of their own accord*: Sir Hugh thinks of inoculation in its literal or physical sense; 'the transportation of distempers from one subject to another, particularly for the engraftment of the small-pox'. Not only a literalist, Sir Hugh is also anachronistic, for inoculation was a standard medical procedure in England and western Europe throughout most of the eighteenth century. See *The Encyclopedia Britannica* (1797), ix. 245.

Pages 24–5. chaise ... coach: A *chaise* is 'a light open carriage for one or two persons, often having a top or calash; those with four wheels resembling the phaeton, those with two the curricle' (*O.E.D.*). A *coach* is usually a large four-wheeled closed carriage, with facing seats.

Page 36. (1) *Dr. Orkborne*: For this name, FB may have had in mind the *ork*, a vaguely identified sea monster whose sounds were like so many snorts. Indeed, Dr. Orkborne was monstrous in his indifference to others; his pedantry expressed itself in seemingly unintelligible noises which (like the second syllable of his name) placed limitations on his ability to communicate to others.

   (2) *A scholastic education*: FB used *scholastic* in the two senses listed in *Johnson*—'1. Pertaining to the school; practised in schools. 2. . . . pedantick, needlessly subtle'.

Page 38. difficult work in philology: Among FB's scraps of paper (Berg) one contains a discarded bit of dialogue, probably between Sir Hugh and Dr. Orkborne. The dialogue deals with the latter's philological scholarship:
   Can you tell me what's its root?
   Root?
   Ay.
   I never knew it had any.
   No? how so?
   Root of a word! I believe never nobody heard of such an out of the way thing before. You may dig in my garden half a day long & I'll be bound

for it you'll find no such thing. If you do, I'll eat it! root of a word!

(Berg) *Scraps*, 51b.

Page 41. *Inaction bodily and intellectual*: FB's discourse on the evils of in-action are indebted to Johnson's *Idler* 1 and *Rasselas*, chs. 2–4.

Page 42. *I shall make no hand of it*: a colloquialism *to make a hand of it* means 'to turn something to account; to profit by it' (*Partridge*).

Page 46. *fogrum*: 'An antiquated or old-fashioned person, a fogy' (*O.E.D.*). FB had heard this word from her father and her friend Samuel Crisp, for both of whom it was a favourite pejorative. See *The Early Diary of Frances Burney*, ed. Annie Raine Ellis (1907), i. xxvi, xxxvii; ii. 135.

Page 48. *tight task in hand*: *tight* is a colloquialism from the mid-eighteenth to the mid-nineteenth centuries for 'difficult, hard, severe' (*Partridge*).

Page 51. *a practical philosopher*: Eugenia illustrates Locke's educational ideal that runs throughout the eighteenth century. Eschewing pedantry, the well-tutored individual was 'a practical philsopher', one who acknow-ledged that 'all virtue and excellency lie in the power of denying ourselves the satisfaction of our own desires, where reason does not authorize them' (*Some Thoughts concerning Education* [1693], sects, 38, 54, 56). Eugenia demonstrates this truism on pp. 340–2, 372–3.

Page 54. *their establishment*: 'Settlement in life; formerly often (now rarely) in the sense of marriage' (*O.E.D.*).

Page 57. *mede*: obsolete or rare usage for 'middle, mean' (*O.E.D.*).

Page 60. *merry as a grig*: 'Very active and lively'; archaic (*O.E.D.*).

Page 63. (1) *the assembly-room*: a room available for 'a stated and general meeting of the polite persons of both sexes, for the sake of conversation, gallantry, news, and play' (*Chambers' Encyclopedia* [1751]).

(2) *When the two first dances were over, the gentlemen were desired to change partners*: see pp. 414 *n.*, 714.

Page 65. (1) *eau suave*: scented water, like eau-de-cologne.

(2) *please thine ear*: a play on i. 19–20 of Pope's *Dunciad* ('O Thou! whatever title please thine ear,/Dean, Drapier, Bickerstaff, or Gulliver!'). Cf. also by Pope, *An Essay on Criticism*, l. 341 ('Who haunt Parnassus but to please their Ear'); trans. of *Odyssey*, xiii. 1–2 ('He ceased; but left so pleasing on their ear/His voice, . . .').

Page 72. *Mr. Dubster*: in his vulgarity modelled on the shopkeeper Mr. Branghton of *Evelina*, and in his stinginess on Mr. Briggs of *Cecilia*.

Page 74. Sir Sedley Clarendel: the fop is a favourite Burneyan character resembling Mr. Lovell of *Evelina* and Mr. Meadows of *Cecilia*. They are all men 'of the ton' who, to be 'conspicuous in the gay world, must invariably be insipid, negligent, and selfish' (*Cecilia*, i. 271). Yet Sir Sedley is more intelligent than his caricatured predecessors. To imply this intelligence, FB probably drew his name from that of Sir Charles Sedley (1639?–1701), the Restoration dramatist and song writer, whose work she knew. Like his fictional counterpart, Sir Charles Sedley was famous for his urbane wit and notorious for his fashionable profligacy.

Page 77. jiggets: a colloquialism derived from 'to jig, fidget, hop about, shake up and dance' (*Partridge*). It is one of Mr. Dubster's synonyms for *dance*, the others being 'skip' (p. 70) and 'hop' (p. 77).

Page 79. (1) *Lionel*: his portrait is a composite of three personalities significant in FB's life: her half-brother Richard Thomas; her brother Charles, Jr.; and her friend Charles Locke.

(2) *public breakfast*: 'People of fashion make public breakfasts at the assembly-houses, to which they invite their acquaintants, and they sometimes order private concerts' (Goldsmith, 'The Life of Richard Nash' [1762], in *Collected Works*, ed. Friedman, 1966, iii. 309).

Page 85. nudging: obsolete dialect word for 'cheerless, solitary, living in obscurity from penurious habits' (*E.D.D.*).

Page 86. (1) *he was in boots*: see p. 666 *n.* 5.

(2) *knotting*: the process by which one knits for fringes (*Johnson*). By the middle of the eighteenth century *knotting* became a synonym for making fringes.

(3) *a near-sighted glass*: probably a quizzing glass, i.e., a framed eye glass provided with a loop-like handle through which a finger may be inserted. For an illustration, see Isaac Cruikshank's 'A Box-Lobby Challenge' (Plate 30) *et passim*, in *Drawings for Drolls*, ed. Wark (San Marino, Calif., 1968). Just before her presentation to Louis XVIII, FB was able to peer at the monarch—and as she said—'my Eye Glass in my hand' (Berg: Journal for 22 April 1814, written in 1825).

Page 91. the rhino: cant expression until *c.* 1820 and then low slang until *c.* 1870, meaning 'large sums of money or wealth' (*Partridge*). Shortly before publication of *Camilla*, FB playfully told her brother Charles, if the booksellers 'proffer the Rhino thence due—you won't refuse it' (*JL* [17 June 1796], iii. L. 193).

Page 92. (1) *the vacancy of dissipated pleasure*: cf. Johnson on novelty and pleasure in *Rambler* 80.

(2) *cypher*: i.e., cipher. Rare or obsolete, 'an intermixture of letters,

especially the initials of a name, engraved or stamped on plate, linen; monogram' (*O.E.D.*).

Page 93. *toyman*: one who sold 'fans, silks, ribbands, laces, and gewgaws' (*Johnson*). Among the 'gewgaws', according to Fielding, was paste jewellery 'which Derdaeus Magnus, an ingenious Toyman, doth at a very moderate Price dispose of to the second Rate Beaus of the Metropolis' (*The Life of Jonathan Wild*, bk. ii, ch. 3).

Page 99. *the library*: At most resort areas the library became a gathering place for elegant holiday-makers. When FB was at Sandgate in 1813, she wrote to her father that she had 'avoided going to the Library, the general rendezvous of the Social' (Berg, *c.* 23 September–6 October). About a quarter of a century earlier Charles Rivington at the seaside sought out company who 'at Margate amuse themselves in the morning with riding and walking, and going to the circulating libraries. ... The two libraries are much frequented, and are both very convenient lounging places, and a person who has any acquaintances is sure to meet with some of them at these shops. Here you may sit and chat, or read the newspapers, or if you have a few shillings to sport away, try your luck in the raffles. The rooms are open from eleven to one for the company to walk, and there is music' (from Charles Rivington's Journal, in *The Publishing House of Rivington* [1894], pp. 60–1).

Page 100. *wrapt enthusiast*: refers to the idealized portraits of the poet (ll. 556 ff.) and the lover (ll. 820 ff., 983 ff.) in *Spring*.

Page 101. (1) *content . . . Heaven*: *Spring*, ll. 1161–4.

(2) *To scenes . . . reign*: *Spring*, l. 1176, the last line of the poem.

Page 103. *in alt*: colloquialism, now obsolete, for 'haughty' (*Partridge*).

Page 104. *kissing your toe ... that popish ceremony*: Lionel's irreverent allusion to that part of the ritual for the Pope's induction when members of the College of Cardinals kiss his toe as a symbol of 'humble obedience'.

Page 106. *fogramity*: rare, for 'an old-fashioned way or custom'; i.e., an eccentricity (*E.D.D.*).

Page 113. (1) *Alphonso Bellamy*: his surname is derived from the French *bel ami*. Since the name is only an alias, it indicates his personality by ironic reversal. He is the opposite of a 'fair friend' to anyone with whom he is associated.

(2) *he has not had the small-pox himself, that is, not in the natural way*: Clermont has had a mild and artificially induced case of small pox as the result of being inoculated. See p. 23 *n.* 2.

Page 125. *low garden phaeton*: four-wheeled open carriage of light construction, with two seats facing forward, and probably drawn by a pony.

Page 129. *tablets*: erasable notebooks made of thin sheets of ivory, bound
in cases of silver, ivory, etc. Widely used throughout the eighteenth
century; see Walter Harte, *An Essay on Satire* (1730), p. 34.

> Some more refin'd transcribe their Opera-loves
> On Iv'ry Tablets, or in clean white Gloves.

Page 136. *confusion worse confounded*: Milton, *Paradise Lost*, ii. 996.

Page 152. *to give money without inquiry ... but to give them both the counsel
and the means to pursue a right course, is, to them, perhaps, salvation, and to
the community, the greatest service*: this view of charity characterizes almost
the whole of the eighteenth century, not lacking in pity but tending to
subordinate the needs of the individual to the good of society. It spurns the
so-called idler, as a monster, a drone, a cipher, and a parasite. At the same
time it looks upon the honest but poor man as redeemable, as one who—
obedient and submissive—performs for the benefit of the community and
so achieves salvation in eternal life. In short, charity became a 'moral
virtue' rather than an 'amiable instinct'—to use Addison's distinction in
Spectator 177.

VOLUME II

Page 189. *an express*: 'A message sent on purpose' (*Johnson*); now historical
or archaic.

Page 192. *conjure*: obsolete for 'implore'.

Page 200. (1) *tantarums*: Devonshire variant of 'tantrums' and used to
suggest 'high or affected airs' (*E.D.D.*).
    (2) *takings*: 'A state of excitement, grief, or perplexity; a fit of petulance
or temper; a dilemma; a sorry plight or condition'; in general colloquial
use (*E.D.D.*).

Page 201. *quiz ... quoz*: eighteenth-century Oxford slang for 'a strange
fellow; an odd dog' (*Grose*). See pp. 568 *n*. 2, 600–1.

Page 203. *behind hand*: 'In secret or in an underhanded way' (*E.D.D.*).

Page 205. *you're blown*: you are discovered, or your secrets are disclosed
(*Grose*).

Page 208. *tablets*: see p. 129 *n*.

Page 223. (1) '*all her sex's softness*': recurrent metaphor in Nicholas Rowe's plays. See especially *Tamerlane* (v. 1) 'softness of thy Sex'. Cf. *The Fair Penitent*, ii. 1; *Jane Shore*, i. 2, iii. 1.

(2) *ṭantivying*: archaic or rare for 'riding full tilt, to hurry away' (*O.E.D.*).

Page 225. (1) *a dismal ditty*: colloquialism for 'a psalm sung by a criminal just before his death at the gallows' (*Grose*).

(2) *noddle*: 'The head' (*Grose*).

Page 227. *flinching*: obsolete for 'slinking or sneaking off' (*O.E.D.*).

Page 229. *hypochondriac*: 'Melancholy; disordered in the imagination' (*Johnson*).

Page 239. *stroamed*: obsolete word meaning 'to walk with long strides' (*O.E.D.*). Used often in the 1796 *Camilla*, the word was consistently altered for the second edition upon the advice of Thomas Twining and the *Monthly Review*. See the alteration of an earlier use (p. 76) in 'Fanny Burney's Revisions of *Camilla*' (p. 916).

Page 240. *hunks*: 'A covetous miserable fellow, a miser' (*Grose*).

Page 241. *fleerer*: 'A mocker; a fawner' (*Johnson*).

Page 243. *horse-ponded*: a horse-pond in proverbial usage connotes a ducking-place for obnoxious persons.

Page 251. *maudlin* [*tea*]: a strange use of *maudlin*, documented by no dictionary; apparently 'watery' tea.

Page 252. [*Tea*] *to cloy an alderman*: tea so rich and sweet it would have surfeited even one associated with gastronomic greed. Thus Samuel Butler described an alderman as one who 'does no public Business without eating and drinking, and never meets about Matters of Importance, but the Cramming his Inside is the most weighty Part of the Work of the Day. . . . He is so careful of the Interest of his Belly, and manages it so industriously, that in a little Space it grows great and takes Place of all the rest of his Members. . . .' (*Characters and Passages from Note-Books* [published posthumously in 1759], ed. A. R. Waller, 1908, p. 109).

Page 259. *to perform Nobody under her own roof*: reminiscent of FB's reference to herself, 'addressed to a Certain Miss Nobody'. As she explains: 'To Nobody, then, will I write my Journal! since to Nobody can I be wholly unreserved—to Nobody can I reveal every thought, every wish of my heart. . . . For what chance, what accident can end my connections with Nobody? No secret *can* I conceal from Nobody, and to Nobody can I be ever unreserved' (*Early Diary*, i. 5).

Page 261. without bowels: without 'tenderness, compassion' (*Johnson*).

Page 264. (1) *curricle*: a light two-wheeled carriage, usually drawn by two horses abreast.

(2) *full buckled bob-jerom*: a crisp and curled bobwig.

Page 265. Lady Wrong Head ... Sir Francis: two characters in Colley Cibber's *The Provok'd Husband; or, A Journey to London*, first produced in 1727/8. The amateur performance of this play becomes part of the pivotal action of volume one of FB's last novel, *The Wanderer*.

Page 270. (1) *black bile*: the fourth of the 'humours' of early physiology, its presence caused melancholy or spleen.

(2) *to declare off*: colloquialism, 'to withdraw arbitrarily' and in this case impartially (*Grose*).

Page 274. venetian window: obsolete phrase for an architectural unit consisting of a central window with an arched head and on each side a usually narrower window with a square head.

Page 275. hand over head: obsolete colloquialism for 'thoughtlessly'.

Page 279. She cost me a mort of money to the potecary: *Mort* is a dialect word for 'a great deal, an abundance'; *potecary* is an obsolete dialect word for 'apothecary' (*E.D.D.*).

Page 280. (1) *whiskeys ... stages ... flys*: A *whisky* or *whiskey* or *timwhisky* is a light two-wheeled one-horse carriage of the late eighteenth and early nineteenth centuries. A *stage* is a shortened version of *stage-coach* (see pp. 24-5 *n.*). A *fly* is 'a stage-coach distinguished by this name in order to impress a belief of its extraordinary quickness in traveling' (*Johnson*).

(2) *Exeter Change*: a market place adjacent to the Strand. One of the features of the Change was a freak show and menagerie (H. B. Wheatley, *London Past and Present* [1891], ii. 26). Despite the visits of celebrities—like Lord Byron—'to see the tigers sup', the area had long had a reputation for squalor. See Hawkins's account of Johnson's residence in Exeter Street, adjacent to the Change (*The Life of Samuel Johnson, LL. D.*, 1787, p. 57).

(3) *the conflint sort*: Dubster's rendition of 'confluent', as contrasted with 'distinct', two forms of small pox identified in the eighteenth century. The 'confluent sort' (*variola major*) is more violent and dangerous than the latter. (See the article on 'Medicine', No. 224, in *The Encyclopedia Britannica* [1797], xi. 193.)

Page 281. (1) *rhubarb*: 'A medicinal root slightly purgative, referred by botanists to the dock' (*Johnson*).

(2) *unked*: variant of the dialect *unco*, i.e., 'strange, alien, altered so as to be scarcely recognizable' (*E.D.D.*).

Page 283. *squall*: slang for 'voice' (*A New Canting Dictionary*, 1725). As Dubster uses *squall*, it means a shout or penetrating yell or whistle.

Page 286. (1) *i'cod*: mild oath (now obsolete), which is perhaps suggestive of the more emphatic 'by God!' It is a variant of *Ecod, Egad, Agad*, etc.

(2) *I'fackens*: Norfolk variant of 'in fact' (*E.D.D.*).

(3) *toad in a hole*: *toad-holes* are 'a poor class of dwelling, or houses in a low, unpleasant locality' (*E.D.D.*). A *toad in a hole* is therefore one who lives in a slum or hovel.

(4) *Hob's pound*: variant of *Lob's pound*, i.e., 'a prison, lock-up; also figuratively, an entanglement, difficulty'.

(5) *O fegs*: dialectal variant of 'O faith' (*E.D.D.*).

Page 287. *your jacket well trimmed*: i.e., you shall be thrashed (*Grose*).

Page 289. *sharpers*: a sharper is 'a cheat, one that lives by his wits' (*Grose*).

Page 293. *quite moped with melancholy*: see p. 23 n. 1.

Page 297. *Middleton races*: see p. 369.

Page 302. *Addison ... one of the Spectators*: Mr. Tyrold has selected an appropriate *Spectator* (17) to bolster Eugenia's spirit. But it is Steele, not Addison, discoursing on physical deformity or unattractiveness. 'Great tenderness and sensibility in this point is one of the greatest weaknesses of self-love.'

Page 304. *suffrages*: obsolete for 'expressions or tokens of approval' (*O.E.D.*).

Page 312. *penetrated*: Addicted to this word, FB used *to penetrate* as a synonym for 'to affect the mind' (*Johnson*).

Page 313. *loveyer*: variant of *lovier*, 'a lover' (*E.D.D.*).

Page 316. *cover*: sheet of paper folded over a letter and sealed.

Page 318. (1) *Lord Foppington*: a character in Vanbrugh's *The Relapse*, Sheridan's *Trip to Scarborough*, and Colley Cibber's *The Careless Husband*.

(2) *Osmyn's Turkish vest*: FB probably had in mind the lead in *Ozmyn and Daraxia*, an afterpiece by James Boaden (first performed 7 March 1793) with music by Thomas Attwood and with airs from the works of Giornovichi and Mozart.

(3) *Isabella*: a character in Thomas Kyd's *The Spanish Tragedy* and Shakespeare's *Measure for Measure*.

Page 319. (1) *pulling caps*: obsolete expression, used only of women who 'wrangle in unseemly fashion' (*Partridge*).

(2) *The description of the performance of Othello*: However good her ear

for dialect, FB was unskilled in the art of reporting sounds and her spellings do not always indicate her intention, particularly when she tries to reproduce vowel sounds. She has partial success with consonants. She is correct when she has Desdemona's father, played by an actor from Somerset, substitute a *z* for *s* both in the initial and final position. On the other hand, when she characterises Worcestershire speech by the dropping of *h* where it is pronounced in standard English and the voicing of it where it is silent or non-existent in standard English, she fails to recognize that this practise is typical of many other dialects. FB was especially familiar with the dialect of her native Norfolk. She catches many of its speech patterns: the pronunciation of *do* like *dew*; the use of a short vowel before *nd* in words like *find* and *pound* where standard English has diphthongs descended from Middle English long vowels. A Londoner by adoption, she also knew Cockney well. She identifies it here by having Othello, 'a true Londoner', widen his diphthongs as in *daughter* and confuse *v* and *w*, a stereotype of Cockney speech. What is remarkable about FB's reproduction of *Othello* in dialect is its bold originality. For unlike many of her predecessors and contemporaries, she avoided stock Welshmen, Scotsmen, and Irishmen to carry the wit of a scene.

(3) *The Deuk dew . . . tree several quests*: I. ii. 36, 45–7.

(4) *Most potent, . . . let her vitness it*: I. iii. 76 ff.

Page 320. (1) *I preay . . . light o' the mon*: I. iii. 175–8.

(2) *Noble father . . . but ere's my usband*: I. iii. 180–5.

(3) *Your woices . . . have a free vay*: I. iii. 260–1.

(4) *Look to 'ur, Moor . . . and may thee*: I. iii. 292–3.

(5) *who intended to stay out not only the play but the farce*: The entertainment provided by a theatre on any single evening included a full-length drama and also a one-act sketch, usually a farce, which followed the major attraction.

Page 322. (1) *Scar that vhiter skin of hers than snow*: V. ii. 4.

(2) *a thief in the candle*: 'An excrescence in the snuff of a candle' (*Johnson*).

(3) *Vhen I've pluck'd the rose . . . It needs must vither*: V. ii. 13–15.

(4) *Be thus vhen thow . . . love thee after*: V. ii. 18–19.

Page 323. (1) *I must veep*: V. ii. 20.

(2) *She vakes*: V. ii. 22.

(3) *Mungo*: obsolete for a Negro.

(4) *farthing candle*: the cheapest of candles; its scent was unpleasant.

(5) *But alf han our*: V. ii. 83.

Page 325. *gout in his stomach*: FB refers to what was medically called at the end of the eighteenth century *atonic gout*. 'In this case, the morbid symptoms which appear, are chiefly affectations of the stomach, such as loss of appetite;

indigestion, and its various attendants of sickness, nausea, flatulency, and eructations, and pains in the region of the stomach. ... These affections of the [stomach and the alimentary canal] are often attended with all the symptoms of hypochondriasis, such as dejection of the mind, a constant anxious attention to the slightest feelings, an imaginary aggravation of these, and an apprehension from them. ... In the same atonic gout, the viscera of the thorax also are sometimes affected, and palpitations, faintings, and asthma occur' (See the article on 'Medicine', No. 213, in *The Encyclopedia Britannica* [1797], xi. 213.)

Page 326. *hartshorn*: shortened version of spirit of hartshorn; i.e., an aqueous solution of ammonia. 'It is used to bring people out of faintings by its pungency, holding it under the nose, and pouring down some drops of it in water' (*Johnson*).

Page 330. *a cordial medicine*: 'A medicine that increases the force of the heart, or quickens the circulation; any medicine that increases strength' (*Johnson*).

Page 331. *particularity*: 'Singleness, individuality' (*Johnson*).

VOLUME III

Page 333. *No one single quality is perhaps so endearing ... as good nature*: For this description of good-nature, FB is primarily indebted to Addison's *Spectator* 169.

Page 334. *obsequiousness*: 'Obedience; compliance' (*Johnson*); obsolete as used here.

Page 349. *nidging*: 'Restless; troublesome.' FB's is the only usage recorded by *O.E.D.*, but it is not a word descriptive of Eugenia. Perhaps FB had in mind another rare word *nidgetty*, i.e., 'trifling' in the sense of small and confused it with *nidging*.

Page 350. *duce a bite*: variant of *deuce a bit*, an emphatic negative (*Partridge*).

Page 353. *conjured*: see p. 192 n. 1.

Page 354. *phaeton*: see p. 125 n. 1.

Pages 355–62. This is the moralistic essence of the novel, setting forth an ideal of ethical conduct. So well known did this section become that in slightly abridged form it was reprinted in *A Father's Legacy to his Daughter* [by John Gregory] ... *To which is added, Mr. Tyrold's Advice to his Daughter ... from 'Camilla', by Mrs. d'Arblay. Also a Picture of the Female Form* by G. Horne ... [Poughmill, 1809]. Between 1809 and 1816 this anthology underwent five printings.

Page 360. *particularity*: see p. 331 *n*. 1.

Page 366. (1) *vapours*: archaic verb form, meaning 'to depress' (*O.E.D.*).

(2) *flappers*: 'One who flaps or strikes another. Hence (after Swift): a person who arouses the attention or jogs the memory; a remembrancer' (*O.E.D.*).

Page 368. (1) *Cooke*: James Cook (1728–79), English naval captain and explorer, made three voyages to Australia, New Zealand, and other areas of the South Pacific. He was killed by natives in Hawaii on the morning of 14 February 1779. FB's brother James sailed with Cook's second expedition, July 1772.

(2) *A balloon is a broad-wheeled wagon to you*: a *balloon* is 'a Siamese state-barge, upwards of a hundred feet long and richly decorated'; a *broad-wheeled wagon* is an open four-wheeled vehicle built for carrying hay, corn, etc., consisting of a long body furnished with 'shelboards' (*O.E.D.*).

(3) *jargon apart*: rare usage for 'any mixture of heterogeneous elements' (*O.E.D.*).

(4) *Aristides ... called the Just*: He 'flourished at Athens at the same time with Themistocles, who triumphed over him by his boisterous eloquence, and got him banished, 483 years before Christ: ... But Aristides being recalled a short time after, would never join with the enemies of Themistocles to get him banished; for nothing could make him deviate from the strictest rules of moderation and justice' (*The Encyclopedia Britannica* [1797], ii. 282).

Page 369. *Middleton races*: FB either gave a fictitious name to these races or confused Middleton with the well-known Maddington Stakes, the race run on the Stockbridge course in Hampshire. Of the alternatives the latter seems the reasonable one.

Page 372. *sharper*: see p. 289 *n*. 1.

Page 374. *It was the season for drinking the water of that spring*: 'Tunbridge Wells ... has ... become the general rendezvous of gaiety and politeness during the summer' (J. Sprange, *The Tunbridge Wells Guide* [1797], p. 115).

Page 375. *sleight*: 'Trick, artifice' (*Johnson*).

Page 380. *dismal ditty*: see p. 225 *n*. 1.

Page 381. *hard run*: colloquialism for 'hard-up; very short of money' (*Partridge*). See also pp. 667, 771.

Page 384. *Dr. Pothook*: a pothook is 'ill formed or scrawling letters or characters' (*Johnson*).

Page 386. *he should proceed to a hotel upon the Pantiles*: 'The Wells, properly so called, is the centre of business and pleasure, because there the markets, the medicinal water, the chapel, the assembly rooms, and the public parades are situated. These parades are usually called the Upper and Lower Walk, the first which was formerly paved with a square brick called a pantile, raised about four steps above the other, ...' (*The Tunbridge Wells Guide*, pp. 104–5). FB visited Tunbridge in 1779 and found the Pantiles so drab that she wondered how it could be considered 'a fashionable pleasure-walk' (*Diary and Letters*, i. 274–5).

Page 395. (1) *in the bookseller's shop*: see p. 99 *n.* 1.
  (2) *the ton*: colloquialism for 'the fashion, fashionable society' (*Partridge*).

Page 396. *Mount Pleasant*: 'Mount-Pleasant gives site to a noble modern brick house, built in a genteel taste, upon the brow of this delightful hill, which commands an extensive prospect of the place. The situation of this house is extremely happy, the grounds and gardens belonging to it are well disposed, ... His Grace the Duke of Leeds, has honored it with his residence for several seasons past, ... There are two other houses on this hill, one late belonging to the Rev. Mr. Brett; the other, called little Mount-Pleasant, was purchased by Lady Peachey, who has made great additions to it, and laid out a neat garden, parterres, walks, &c.' (*Tunbridge Wells Guide*, pp. 107–8).

Page 397. *you sha'n't dine before eight o'clock*: in *The Early Diary* (i. 15), FB says, 'We breakfast always at ten, and rise as much before as we please,—we dine precisely at two, drink tea about six—and sup exactly at nine.' For the more fashionable Mrs. Arlbery and others in her set, each meal was later by an hour or two.

Page 398. *Pope has bewailed it in women*: *Epistle II, To a Lady: Of the Characters of Women*, ll. 1–2.

Page 401. *the Daily Advertiser*: London newspaper published from 3 February 1731 to 8 June 1809.

Pages 401–2. (1) *the subscription books. ... She then wrote her name and threw down half-a-guinea*: Mrs. Arlbery paid too much. According to *The Tunbridge Wells Guide* (p. 120), 'The renters of the public rooms, to pay *six-pence* out of the money they receive for the admission of every person at the balls, and a general subscription of the company,—every gentleman 10s. 6d. and every lady 5s. A book for which purpose is open in the rooms.'
  (2) *stroamed*: see p. 239 *n.*

(3) *Lord of Himself, uncumber'd by a Wife*: misquoting *To my Honour'd Kinsman, John Driden, of Chesterton, in the County of Huntingdon, Esquire,* l. 18.

Page 403. Mount Ephraim: 'Mount-Ephraim is about half a mile from the water, and on account of which distance hath lost much of its former regard. . . . The houses on this hill are all very good buildings, have the advantage of being surrounded with capacious gardens, groves, and pleasant fields; and of commanding diversified extensive prospects on every side; and the hill itself is situated in so exceeding fine an air, as may well compensate for all its disadvantages . . .' (*The Tunbridge Wells Guide*, pp. 109–10).

Page 408. direction: address.

Page 411. Knowle: 'Knowle stands at a small distance from Sevenoaks; a pleasant road leads to it through the park, from Sevenoaks-common, a mile from that town, on the road leading to Tunbridge; and has been a remarkable seat from the days of William the Conqueror' (*The Tunbridge Wells Guide*, pp. 207 ff.). See p. 416.

Page 412. to count by lustres. . . . in Entick's dictionary: The definition of *lustre* that Sir Theophilus would have found is 'a period of 5 years'. In John Entick's *New Spelling Dictionary . . . for those who read . . . English Authors of Repute in Prose or Verse, and in particular to assist Young People, Artificers, Tradesmen and Foreigners. . . . A New Edition. . . . By* William Crakett, Dublin 1790. FB is presenting a double-edged joke here: first in having Lady Alithea utter a high-flown phrase; and second in exposing to the reader Sir Theophilus's ignorance by having him use an elementary dictionary largely designed for individuals of inferior social station.

Page 413. she found Edgar making inquiries of the time and manner of drinking the mineral water: 'But, as the summer is the only season at present employed in drinking this water, we will return to that happy period; and then it is said, that the best time of day for this purpose is soon in the morning, before the sun has reached any great height, or at least before it has attained force enough to raise the mineral spirit, and so that the quantity prescribed may be drank, and tolerable well digested before breakfast. . . . begin cautiously with a small quantity, to rise by degrees to the proper pitch, and having continued there as long as it is expedient, then to decline and decrease by the same slow degrees and leave off at the quantity begun with' (*Tunbridge Wells Guide*, pp. 68–71).

Page 414. tickets for the master of the ceremonies' ball: The first of the 'Rules and Regulations Humbly recommended by the Master of Ceremonies to the Company Resorting to Tunbridge-Wells' maintains 'that there be two balls every week during the season, on Tuesdays at the Upper Rooms; on Fridays at the Lower Rooms; each to begin at seven, and end at eleven. Admission to the balls.—Subscribers—Gentlemen, 3s. 6d. Ladies 2s. Children half price. Non Subscribers, whether Ladies or Gentlemen, 5s.—Gentlemen change their partners every two dances' (*Tunbridge Wells Guide*, p. 119).

Page 416. the noble antique mansion, pictures, and curiosities of Knowle; and in paying the tribute that taste must ever pay to the works exhibited there of Sir Joshua Reynolds: Knowle was a major attraction for FB when in 1779 she accompanied Mr. and Mrs. Thrale to Tunbridge Wells. She was awed by the 'monastic and gloomy' grandeur of a house begun in the reign of Henry II and which was often the dwelling of monarchs. Most splendid of all for FB were the house's 'pictures, of which there is, indeed a delicious collection': in addition to numerous portraits by Reynolds, she admired works by Guido, Raphael, Dolci, Poussin, Lorraine (*Diary and Letters*, ii. 270–2).

Page 417. fair female Quixote: a play on Charlotte Lennox's novel *The Female Quixote* (1752).

Page 418. melancholy and gentleman-like: Ben Jonson, *Every Man in his Humour*, I. ii. 113–15.

Page 419. to distance him: obsolete; 'to keep at a distance from' (*O.E.D.*).

Page 422. though in her own despight: archaic construction for 'regardless of her own indignation'.

Page 423. stage box ... pit: In the eighteenth-century theatre the pit was the entire floor before the stage. Two boxes were on either side of the stage in front of the curtain. A seat in a stage box was the most expensive in the house; for example, 5s. at the Drury Lane.

Page 424. pattens: see p. 436 n. 1.

Page 426. (1) *Rowe's letters from the dead*: Elizabeth Rowe (1674–1737) wrote a didactic romance *Friendship in Death: In Twenty Letters from the Dead to the Living*, published in 1728 with Part I of *Letters Moral and Entertaining*, which were continued with Part II in 1731 and Part III in 1732. New editions appeared throughout the century and as late as 1818. In each of Mrs. Rowe's intense novellas death must capitulate to those achieving a true, pure, and matrimonial-minded love.

(2) *the noble family*: the family of John Sackville, 3rd duke of Dorset.

Page 429. (1) *Consort of Musics*: a term in the sixteenth and seventeenth centuries for a group of instruments playing concerted music. In a 'whole' consort all the instruments (most commonly viols) belong to the same family. A 'broken' consort consists of instruments of different kinds using different methods of producing sounds.

(2) *the strings of a vile kit*: the strings of a small fiddle, obviously very cheap (*E.D.D.*).

(3) *marrow-bones and cleavers*: FB suggests a sense of the cacophony raised by marrow bones and cleavers, instruments traditionally responsible for 'music' produced by English and Scottish butchers on festive occasions. See Bonnell Thornton, *An Ode on St. Caecilia's Day, Adapted to Ancient British Musick* (1749); William Hogarth, *The Industrious 'Prentice ... Married to his Master's Daughter* (1747); Percy A. Scholes, *The Oxford Companion to Music* (1950), p. 540.

Page 433. A cast: 'A chance lift, ride, help forward on a journey' (*E.D.D.*).

Page 436. (1) *patten ... under the iron*: 'A kind of overshoe or sandal worn to raise the ordinary shoe out of the mud or wet; consisting, since the seventeenth century, of a wooden sole passing over the instep, and mounted on an iron oval ring, or similar device, by which the wearer is raised an inch or two from ground' (*O.E.D.*).

(2) *thing-o-me*: rare form (popular in the late 1790's) of *thingumay*, i.e., 'a thing or a person one does not wish to, or cannot specify, or the name of which one has forgotten' (*E.D.D.*).

(3) *nous*: slang or colloquial expression for 'intelligence, common sense' (*Partridge*).

Page 444. cotillon: After French for 'petticoat', this elaborate, popular dance originated in a simple form during the reign of Louis XIV. Mrs. Berlinton's lessons would have been adapted to the complex and varied figures of the late eighteenth-century cotillon that was often used to close a ball.

Page 445. country dances: 'The most fashionable and proper dance to open a Ball with is a Minuet' (T. Wilson, *Etiquette of the Ball-Room in Analysis of Country Dancing* [1811]). Thereafter the country dances began. (Cf. *Horace Walpole's Correspondence with Sir Horace Mann*, ed. W. S. Lewis, W. H. Smith, and George L. Lam, 1955, xvii. 184.)

Page 449. scouted: flouted, scorned.

Page 451. frippery froppery: Mrs. Mittin's coinage to emphasise *frippery*, i.e., 'articles of small worth' (*E.D.D.*).

Page 457. (1) *cut up*: 'ruined' (*E.D.D.*).

(2) *A goth in grain*: 'a downright barbarian' (*Partridge*).

(3) *muling in my nurse's arms*: misquoting *As You Like It*, II. vii. 143.

Page 464. German Spa: Baden, 'a town of Germany, in the arch-duchy of Austria, seated on the Little Suechat, is a neat little walled town, standing in a plain not far from a ridge of hills which run out from the mountain Cetius. It is much frequented by the people of Vienna, and the neighbouring parts, on account of its baths. The springs supply two convenient baths within the town, five without the walls, and one beyond the river. They are good for distempers of the head, the gout, dropsy, and most chronic diseases' (*The Encyclopedia Britannica* [1797], ii. 729).

Page 465. hip and vapour: colloquial for 'the hypochondriac; low spirits' (*Grose*).

Page 466. (1) *I'd rather snap short at once*: apparently FB's figurative improvisation of the expression 'to break straight across', i.e., decisively and beyond repair. Like an anticipation of an Oscar Wilde character, Lord Newford expresses the ultimate satisfaction with being idle: he would rather have his existence terminated at once than live without ennui.

(2) *Island of Cyprus*: Venus and her inseparable companion were associated with and worshipped principally at Cyprus.

(3) *prose*: colloquialism for 'chat, gossip' (*Partridge*). Cf. p. 780.

Page 467. patronize: obsolete; to 'advocate, justify, countenance' (*O.E.D.*).

Page 472. winter at the opera ... Ranelagh ... Cheltenham, Tunbridge ... Bath: The London season began in November and ended with the birthday of George III on 4 June. Operatic performances were given all through the winter and well into the spring. But it was in the winter that the fashionable went to the opera, not to hear the music but to be present in the coffee room where, for example, 'Cecilia found rather the appearance of a brilliant assembly of ladies and gentlemen, collected merely to see and entertain one another, than of distinct and casual parties, mixing solely from necessity, and waiting only for room to enter a theatre' (i. 127). Attendance at the opera fell off when the public resort Ranelagh in Chelsea was opened for the evening on Easter Monday and then on every Monday, Wednesday, and Friday evening until mid-July. Here one could listen to concerts, attend ridottos and masquerades, walk through the gardens, and enjoy light refreshments. The summer, as FB indicates (p. 413 *n.* 1), was the proper season to visit Tunbridge, and presumably Cheltenham. And while it is true that the autumn constituted one six weeks' period for bathing and drinking the waters at Bath, so the spring offered comparable opportunities.

Page 473. He's every thing by turns, and nothing long: misquoting Dryden, *Absalom and Achitophel*, l. 548.

Page 474. Akenside's Pleasures of the Imagination: a popular poem by Mark Akenside (1721–1770), published in January 1744.

Page 478. (1) *Shug-lane*: an alley of small shops near Piccadilly.
(2) *into a pet*: 'In a passion or miff' (*Grose*).

Page 487. (1) *the Poets*: probably the poetic works for which Johnson had written the prefatory *Lives of the English Poets* (1779–81).
(2) *whatever was enthusiastic ... with respect to religion*: Mrs. Berlinton spurned the rational bases of belief. Her piety was emotional, erratic, and self-delusory.

Page 493. pinch 'em to a mummy: 'Squeeze them to a pulp' (*Grose*).

Page 498. (1) *Or else I was out*: colloquialism for 'astray from what is right or correct; in the wrong, in error, mistaken' (*Partridge*). See *Evelina*, iii. L. xxi.
(2) *king's bench prison*: a jail formerly appropriated to debtors and criminals confined by authority of the supreme courts at Westminster.

Page 499. (1) *thou art almost too young to be rocked in a cradle*: i.e., you are even more naive than an infant in a cradle.
(2) *father to be an hunks, ... mother to be a bore*: hunks (see p. 240 n.) and *bore* represent popular university slang in the last two decades of the eighteenth century.
(3) *choused*: cant for 'cheat, trick, impose upon' (*Johnson*).

Page 504. cover: see p. 316 n.

Page 505. numps: obsolete for 'a silly or stupid person' (*O.E.D.*).

Page 518. caution: 'One who is surety for another' (*E.D.D.*).

VOLUME IV

Page 523. All is in the fairest train possible: i.e., 'all is in good order.'

Page 524. hard run: see p. 381.

Page 525. Pillgarlic: 'Said originally to mean one whose skin or hair had fallen off from some disease, chiefly the venereal one; but now commonly used by persons speaking of themselves: as, "There stood some poor pill garlic; i.e. there stood I"' (*Grose*).

Page 528. liberal: 'generous, not low in mind' (*Johnson*).

Page 531. his sister's foolish trimmings: ambiguous. *Trimmings* could refer to a woman's dressing up, her 'self-adornment'; it could also refer to her indecisiveness.

Page 539. *tremendous*: 'dreadful, horrible' (*Johnson*).

Page 556. *history*: throughout the novel in its obsolete sense, 'a narrative, tale, story' (*O.E.D.*).

Page 563. *curious*: archaic or obsolete for 'fastidious, careful, anxious, cautious' (*O.E.D.*).

Page 568. (1) *stroam*: see p. 239 *n*.
   (2) *quoz*: see p. 201 *n*.
   (3) *Does he want me to toss him in a blanket*: a rough, irregular mode of punishment.

Page 575. *condescension*: obsolete for 'the action or fact of acceding or consenting' (*O.E.D.*).

Page 579. (1) *I'd as soon tie myself to a rod*: perhaps a play on the school-master's *rod*; i.e., he would just as soon be whipped.
   (2) *this is a good hum enough*: a deception or imposition on one by some story or device (*Grose*).

Page 584. (1) *humoured*: 'Ill humoured, bad tempered'; 'petulant' (*Johnson*).
   (2) *pelisse*: 'A long mantle or cloak lined with fur' (*O.E.D.*).

Page 587. (1) *ungain-like*: 'Awkward, unsuitable' (*E.D.D.*).
   (2) *cue*: 'Humour, disposition, mood, frame of mind' (*O.E.D.*).

Page 588. *not so sharp set*: probably, 'not as hungry as that, not so eager or keen for food' (suggested by *E.D.D.*).

Page 592. *a cook's shop*: 'An eating-house, a shop where cooked food is sold' (*O.E.D.*).

Page 601. *with some of her quality binding, when I was not dressed out quite in my best becomes*: FB's knowledge of dialect here is uncertain. She misuses *quality binding*, which is Sussex for 'a kind of worsted tape commonly used for binding the borders of carpets' (*E.D.D.*). The word *becomes* is Norfolk, meaning 'one's best clothes' (*E.D.D.*).

Page 606. (1) *book shop*: obviously a circulating library. In *The South-ampton Guide* (6th ed., *c.* 1801, pp. 74–5), there is a description of such a library. 'T. Baker's Library, in the High-street, contains a well chosen selection of nearly seven thousand volumes, forming a more general col-lection of useful and polite literature than is usually found in circulating libraries. The books are lent to read, at 15s. the year, 4s. 6d. the quarter, and 5s. for the season.'
   (2) *Peruvan Letters*: Mrs. Mittin meant either Charles de Secondat

Montesquieu's *Persian Letters* (tr., 1722) or George Lyttleton's *Letters from a Persian in England to his Friend in Ispahan* (1735). In her ignorance she failed to distinguish between Persia and Peru.

(3) *cast*: see p. 433 *n*.

Page 607. (1) *Charing-cross to Temple-bar*: the Strand.

(2) *The shopkeepers ... gave their directions to the churches, the quays, the market-place, the antique gates, the town-hall, &c.*: Southampton boasted of its six parish churches. The landmarks of the city also included the Great or East Quay and the smaller West Quay. Of additional interest were the Audit House and the adjoining market place on the High Street, four gates in the ancient walls which once guarded the approaches to the town, and—over the arches of Bar-Gate—the large town hall. See *The Southampton Guide* (4th ed., 1787), and H. C. Englefield, *A Walk through Southampton* (1801).

Page 608. *for the whole length of the High-street*: 'The High-street, in *Leland*'s time was supposed to be the *finest street of any town in all England*, and even at present, few towns can boast of one equal, it is three quarters of a mile in length' (*1787 Guide*, p. 32).

Page 609. (1) *little rooms prepared for the accommodation of bathers*: 'Near the west quay is a range of convenient Baths, for ladies and gentlemen to bathe in at all times, and in any depth of water, by means of artificial bottoms which are raised up and let down at pleasure. There is also a hot bath for those to whom this mode of bathing may be recommended' (*1787 Guide*, p. 50).

(2) *the beach*: 'From this point [the Itchen ferry], a caussey of near half a mile long, planted with trees, leads to the platform and south gate. This walk, which is called the Beach, commands in its whole length a view of the Southampton water, closed by the Isle of Wight' (Englefield, p. 79).

Page 619. (1) *a wash-ball*: 'Ball made of soap' (*Johnson*).

(2) *chattery*: FB's coinage for 'a chat, a gossip'.

Page 623. *the hotel*: either the well-established 'Mitre inn in the High-street' (*The Southampton Guide* [*c*. 1801], p. 74), or 'Harland's Hotel' on the east side of the same street (Englefield, p. 35). The latter had ceased to function as a hotel shortly before 1801.

Page 634. (1) *this large and fashionable town*: 'The great resort of nobility and gentry in the summer season to this natural seat of pleasure and entertainment, serves to increase that politeness and good breeding so generally found amongst the inhabitants. Every gentleman of fortune, who has once been acquainted with this beautiful situation, is desirous and ambitious of acquiring even a cottage in this region of politeness and elegance, whereon to display his taste and genius. The royal family have at various times visited this town; to which they have shewn an evident partiality' (*1787 Guide*, p. 29). The population of Southampton at the end of the eighteenth century was 'about, 12,000 persons' (*1801 Guide*, p. 47).

(2) *Indiana ... and public places; Eugenia ... the buildings, antiquities, and prospects; and Miss Margland ... the company, their genealogies and connexions*: Each looked to Southampton for the satisfaction of her dominant interest. Indiana wanted from the town a maximum of pleasure that she would find in the public rooms near the West Quay, especially in the ball room decorated with pier glasses. Miss Margland sought in Southampton a snobbish fulfilment (see p. 663), and Eugenia an increase in antiquarian knowledge (see p. 607 *n.* 2).

Page 635. *hunks*: see p. 240 *n.*

Page 639. *some controverted points upon the shield of Achilles*: the allusion is to Homer's description of Achilles' shield in *The Iliad*, Bk. xviii. Orkborne was joining scholars, critics, and philosophers who since distant times had been debating the allegorical meanings of this complex passage. Although it has long been acknowledged that Homer was setting forth a cosmic interpretation, there has been less agreement about particulars: e.g., the size and shape of the shield in relation to the multiple figures on it, questions about the arts, Greek justice, the poet's knowledge of astronomy, etc. Further, there are philosophical mysteries, suggested thus by Pope:

> Then first he form'd the immense and solid *Shield*
> Rich, various Artifice emblaz'd the Field; (ll. 551–2)

> There shone the Image of the Master Mind:
> There Earth, there Heav'n, there Ocean
>   he design'd. (ll. 557–8)

Page 647. *vails*: 'Money given to servants' (*Johnson*).

Page 651. *dodged*: followed in someone's track (*E.D.D.*).

Page 653. *souse him in a horse-pond*: see p. 243 *n.*

Page 656. *Hammond's elegies*: James Hammond wrote the *Love Elegies* to celebrate his own unrequited love. He died in 1743 and his *Elegies* were published by the Earl of Chesterfield in that same year.

Page 659. *He's but a sad spark*: this seems to be a paradox, for a spark is 'a spruce, trim, or smart fellow' (*Grose*).

Page 661. *a great ball at the public rooms*: 'That the balls shall begin as soon as possible after seven o'clock, and finish precisely at eleven, even in the middle of a dance. That ladies and gentlemen who dance down a country dance, shall not quit their places till the dance is finished, unless they mean to dance no more that night. That after a lady has called a dance and danced it down, her place in the next, is at the bottom. That gentlemen are not to appear in the rooms in boots on [ball nights]' (*1787 Guide*, pp. 52–3).

Page 663. The first care of Miss Margland was to make herself and her young ladies known to the master of ceremonies: 'That as it is the wish of the master of ceremonies that all improper company should be kept from these rooms, he respectfully requests that all strangers, as well as ladies and gentlemen, to whom he has not the honour to be personally known will offer him some occasion of being presented to them, to enable him to shew that attention and respect to every individual resorting to this place, which he will be ever studious to observe' (*1787 Guide*, p. 53).

Page 666. (1) *Stilton cheese*: Called English Parmesan, this was an expensive delicacy in the eighteenth century requiring several months of care and fermentation before it became edible. At this time it was distrusted by many Englishmen because it was a relatively new cheese and because it was 'brought to the table full of mites or maggots' (*The Encyclopedia Britannica* [1797], xvii. 800). See also Pope, *Imitations of Horace*, Bk. II, Satire vi. 165–8.

(2) *kennel*: an open drain that ran down the centre of the road with the surface sloping towards it from either side. See Swift, *A Description of a City Shower*, ll. 53–4; and Gay, *Trivia*, Bk. i, ll. 159–60.

(3) *to have his money doused about at such a rantipole rate*: To *douse* is 'to throw about'; *rantipole* is a low word for 'wild, roving, rakish' (*Johnson*).

(4) *daintiness*: 'Squeamishness; fastidiousness' (*Johnson*).

(5) *Lynmere, who had entered the ball-room in his riding dress*: see p. 86 *n.* 1. The gaucherie of wearing boots either at a public breakfast or at assembly balls became a special target of Richard Nash, for example, when he was master of ceremonies at Bath. See Goldsmith, *Works*, iii. 506.

Page 685. Faro: a gambling game in which the players bet on the order in which certain cards will appear when taken singly from the top of the pack.

Page 686. whither she was ordered for her health: Southampton advertised its mineral waters as comparable to Tunbridge water, its air 'so essential both to the preservation and recovery of health', and its bathing that 'greatly braces the solids and accelerates the blood's motion' (*1787 Guide*, pp. 47–9).

Page 693. a mantua-maker: a dress-maker (*O.E.D.*).

Page 715. *smoked how the matter was*: To smoke is 'to observe, to suspect' (*Grose*).

Page 716. *fellows in a string*: colloquialism for 'to have completely under control' (*Partridge*).

Page 718. *'hung over her enamoured'*: Milton, *Paradise Lost*, v. 13.

Page 719. *cottage ... palace*: Melmond's poetic version of the proverb 'Love lives in cottages as well as in courts'. See John Ray, *A Collection of English Proverbs* (1670).

Page 721. *unequal Camilla*: capricious, unreliable Camilla.

Page 727. *roquelo*: from *roquelaure*, a knee-length cloak for men in the eighteenth century and early part of the nineteenth. In this description of Lionel, FB may have remembered the garb of her brother Charles when he peddled *Evelina*. 'The young agent [Charles] was muffled up now by the laughing committee, in an old great coat and a large old hat, to give him a somewhat antique as well as vulgar disguise; and was sent forth in the dark of the evening with the two first volumes to Fleet-street, where he left them to their fate' (Mme. D'Arblay, *The Memoirs of Dr. Burney* [1832], ii. 128-9). Cf. *Trivia*, Bk, i. l. 51.

Page 728. *don't be so Vellum-like*: figurative extension of vellum-binding, 'the process or trade of binding account books'. Lionel accuses Camilla of being mercenary, a mere bookkeeper.

Page 729. *fudge*: 'A made-up story, a deception' (*Partridge*).

Page 730. (1) *half shoes over in the slough of despond*: probably 'almost or nearly depressed'.
   (2) *queer*: cant for 'base, roguish, bad, naughty, or worthless' (*Grose*).

Page 731. *we're blown*: see p. 205 *n.*

Page 732. *There's no plague lost between us*: They have been equally troublesome to each other.

Page 733. (1) *no bowels*: see p. 261 *n.*
   (2) *direction*: see p. 408 *n.*

Page 737. (1) *Pillgarlic*: see p. 525 *n.*
   (2) *hipped*: in low spirits (*Grose*).

Page 752. *of being cast in any trial*: to *cast*, in its obsolete sense, 'to find or declare guilty' (*O.E.D.*).

Page 760. (1) *and I will accept ... to what is divine*: see p. 51 *n*.

(2) *the money-lender ... twenty pounds*: Mr. Clykes is a usurer. The rate of interest upon the lending of money was legally five per cent as fixed by the statute 12 Annae, st. 2. c. 16. Moreover, 'if any scrivener or broker takes more than 5*s*. per cent procuration-money, or more than 12*d*. for making a bond, he shall forfeit 20 *l*. with costs, and shall suffer imprisonment for half a year' (*The Encyclopedia Britannica* [1797], xviii. 694). The contract that Mr. Clykes made with Camilla is in fact 'null' for two reasons: first, because it is usurious and two, because it was made with a person incapable of contracting, i.e., a minor.

Page 767. expedient-mongers: FB's coinage. A monger usually implies one who carries on a contemptible or discreditable 'trade' or 'traffic'. Johnson defines *expedient* as 'a shift, means to an end which are contrived in an exigence'. Mrs. Mittin virtually plies a trade in craft and trickery for those hard pressed for money.

Page 772. the complicate interest: archaism for 'compound interest'.

Page 776. A beauty won't make a good wife. It takes her too much time to put her cap on: Throughout most of the eighteenth century women of fashion had elaborately dressed hair, i.e., teased or 'frizzled' hair covering a concealed structure of wire and cushions. On top of this 'head' a cap frequently rested. What took time was not putting on the cap but preparing the hair for it.

Page 779. He has still fortune enough left for a handsome settlement, etc.: This ironical view of courtship, stated in financial terms, anticipates that of Jane Austen, particularly in *Pride and Prejudice*.

Page 780. prosers: those who express themselves in dull, commonplace ways.

Page 800. Gretna Green: a village between Carlisle and Edinburgh. As early as 1753, largely through the activities of Joseph Paisley, one of the 'Gretna Priests', the village was recognised as a place of escape from the rigorous English marriage laws. The marriages performed at Gretna Green required neither the publishing of banns nor a church setting. Nevertheless, they were legally binding.

Page 805. hackney-coach: a hired four-wheeled coach, drawn by two horses and seating six persons.

Page 813. the fastidious eyes: obsolete for 'disdainful, scornful' (*O.E.D.*).

Page 817. thrown away, ... a gem richer than all her tribe: misquoting *Othello*, V. ii. 347–8.

Page 826. More honour'd in the breach than the observance: *Hamlet*, I. iv. 16.

Page 831. Alton: 'A town in Hampshire, seated on the river Wey. .... It is governed by a constable; and consists of about 300 houses, indifferently built, chiefly laid out in one pretty broad street. It has one church, a Presbyterian and a Quaker's meeting, a famous free school, a large manufacture of plain and figured baragons, ribbed druggets, and serges de Nismes: and round the town is a large plantation of hops' (*The Encyclopedia Britannica* [1797], i. 508).

Page 840. my vain philosophy: a typical eighteenth-century attitude, indicating mistrust of Stoicism's excision of the passions. See e.g., *Spectator* 408; Pope's *Essay on Man*, epistle ii, ll. 101 ff.; Fielding's *Joseph Andrews*, bk. iv, ch. 8.

Page 841. almost blunted purpose: *Hamlet*, III. iv. 111.

Page 842. The horrible scenes I must go through in a public trial for such a purpose: In forcing Eugenia to marry him, Bellamy is guilty of a felony by the statute 3 H. 7. c. 2. Forcible marriage, when proved in a court of law, is void, and the perpetrator is made to suffer both fine and imprisonment. What is abhorrent to Eugenia is the need to make her experience public, to take an oath saying that hers was a forcible marriage.

Page 845. in my "mind's eye": *Hamlet*, I. ii. 185.

Page 849. (1) *Bagshot*: in Surrey, a post stage for mail coaches travelling from London through Winchester to Exeter. In August 1791, FB spent a dull day in Bagshot and stayed the night at its coaching inn The White Hart. She remembered the town only for its dreariness (*JL*, i. L. 3).
   (2) *she* 'skimmed', *like her celebrated name-sake*: Pope, *An Essay on Criticism*, ll. 370–3.

Page 853. Alresford: 'A town of Hampshire, seated on the road from London to Southampton, close by the river Itchen, which feeds a great pond to the left of the town. Part of the Roman highway runs from hence to Alton. ... It consists of about 200 houses; has one church; two principle streets, which are large and broad; and a small manufacture of linseys' (*The Encyclopedia Britannica* [1797], i. 502).

Page 868. 'hum of many': probably misquoting 'And the busy hum of men'. Milton, *L'Allegro*, l. 118.

Page 872. bourne whence no traveller returns: misquoting *Hamlet*, III. i. 79–80.

Page 883. *Tir'd Nature's sweet restorer, balmy sleep*: Edward Young, *Night Thoughts* ('Night 1'), l. 1.

Page 900. *caution*: see p. 518 *n*.

Page 905. *regale*: obsolete for 'the principle or prerogative of royalty' (*O.E.D.*). Eugenia lacked the privilege or prerogative of cruelty that belonged to beautiful or vain women.

Page 909. *Like all characters of radical worth*: those who have never lost their natural or original goodness.